Mermaid and Other Water Spirit Tales From Around the World

SurLaLune Fairy Tale Series

Mermaid and Other Water Spirit Tales From Around the World

Folklore About Mermaids and Other Merfolk

Collected and edited with an introduction by
by Heidi Anne Heiner

SurLaLune Press

Copyright 2011 by Heidi Anne Heiner.

Published by SurLaLune Press
All Rights Reserved.

1. Mermaids.
2. Folklore.
3. Women—Folklore.

To Nancy Ann Thomas,

Wishing you many more
wonderful beach memories…

As always, many thanks to the usual suspects around hearth
and home as well as my many supporters online.
You know who you are….

Table of Contents

Mermaids by Heidi Anne Heiner — 1
Notes About This Edition — 2

Articles

1. Melusina
   from *Curious Myths of the Middle Ages*
   by Sabine Baring-Gould — 4
2. Fables and Facts
   from *Wonders of the Deep*
   by Maximilian Schele de Vere — 26
3. A Chapter on Mermaids
   by Lieutenant Charles R. Low, I.N. — 41
4. Mermaids
   from *The Book of Days*
   edited by Robert Chambers — 54
5. Mermaid Balladry
   from *Old Ballad Folk-Lore*
   by James Napier — 58
6. Mermaids and Mermen
   from *Credulities Past and Present*
   by William Jones — 63
7. The Mermaid
   from *Sea Fables Explained*
   by Henry Lee — 74
8. Water Sprites and Mermaids
   by Fletcher S. Bassett — 105
9. Fictitious Creatures of the Sea
   from *Fictitious and Symbolic Creatures in Art*
   by John Vinycomb — 150

Tales & Pieces

10. Mermen and Mermaids in Iceland   *Iceland* — 168
11. Then Laughed the Merman   *Iceland* — 169
12. Then the Merman Laughed   *Iceland* — 170
13. Sea-People, or Mermen and Mermaids in Shetland
    Shetland Islands — 172
14. The Mermaid Wife   *Shetland Islands* — 174

15.	Clark Colven: Child Ballad 42A *United Kingdom*		176
16.	Clerk Colvill: Child Ballad 42B *United Kingdom*		179
17.	Clerk Colvin: Child Ballad 42C *United Kingdom*		180
18.	The Seamen's Distress: Child Ballad 289A *United Kingdom*		182
19.	The Stormy Winds Do Blow: Child Ballad 289B *United Kingdom*		184
20.	The Mermaid: Child Ballad 289C *United Kingdom*		185
21.	The Mermaid: Child Ballad 289D *United Kingdom*		186
22.	The Bonnie Mermaid: Child Ballad 289E *United Kingdom*		187
23.	Greenland: Child Ballad 289F *United Kingdom*		189
24.	Scottish Mermaids by R. J. Arnott *Scotland*		190
25.	The Mermaid by John Leyden *Scotland*		203
26.	Orcadian Water Spirits *Scotland*		215
27.	The Mermaid of Lochinver *Scotland*		216
28.	A' Mhaideann-mhara (The Mermaid) *Scotland*		217
29.	Another Legend of the Mermaid *Scotland*		218
30.	The Mermaid of Galloway by Allan Cunningham *Scotland*		219
31.	The Mermaid by James Hogg *Scotland*		226
32.	The Mermaiden by Robert Allan *Scotland*		229
33.	The Mermaiden by William Motherwell *Scotland*		230
34.	The Merrow-Maiden and Merrow-Man *Ireland*		231
35.	The Overflowing of Lough Neagh and Liban the Mermaid *Ireland*		234
36.	Liban, the Sea Woman *Ireland*		240
37.	Water Spirits and Mer Folk of Connacht, Ireland *Ireland*		241
38.	Children of the Mermaid *Ireland*		243
39.	The Fisherman Who Had Seven Sons *Ireland*		244
40.	Water Spirits and Mer-folk of County Clare *Ireland*		247
41.	The Lady of Gollerus *Ireland*		249
42.	Flory Cantillon's Funeral *Ireland*		257
43.	The Soul Cages *Ireland*		261
44.	The Lord of Dunkerron *Ireland*		273
45.	The Wonderful Tune *Ireland*		277
46.	Donald and the Mermaid *Ireland*		285
47.	White Cow, Red Cow, Black Cow *Ireland*		287
48.	Two Legends from County Meath *Ireland*		288
49.	The Captured Mermaid *Isle of Man*		289
50.	The Mermaid's Courtship *Isle of Man*		290

51.	The Mermaid's Revenge *Isle of Man*		291
52.	Dwellings under the Sea *Isle of Man*		292
53.	The Mermaid of Gob Ny Ooyl *Isle of Man*		294
54.	Teeval, Princess of the Ocean *Isle of Man*		295
55.	The City under Sea *Isle of Man*		297
56.	Mermaids and Mermen in Wales *Wales*		299
57.	Water Spirits in Shakespeare *England*		300
58.	Sabrina Fair		
	by John Milton *England*		301
59.	The Mermaid: A Ballad *England*		304
60.	The Mermaid of Martin Meer *England*		306
61.	Morva or Morveth (Sea-Daughters) *England*		319
62.	Merrymaids and Merrymen *England*		320
63.	The Mermaid of Padstow *England*		322
64.	The Mermaid of Padstow		
	by Richard Garnett *England*		323
65.	The Mermaid's Rock *England*		325
66.	The Mermaid of Seaton *England*		325
67.	The Old Man of Cury *England*		326
68.	The Mermaid's Vengence *England*		329
69.	The Mermaid of Zennor *England*		342
70.	Lutey and the Mermaid *England*		344
71.	The Mermaid's Song		
	by Anne Hunter for Haydn *England*		351
72.	The Mermaid of Margate		
	by Thomas Hood *England*		352
73.	The Merman		
	by Alfred, Lord Tennyson *England*		356
74.	The Mermaid		
	by Alfred, Lord Tennyson *England*		357
75.	The Forsaken Merman		
	by Matthew Arnold *England*		359
76.	The Neckan		
	by Matthew Arnold *England*		363
77.	The Fisherman and His Soul		
	by Oscar Wilde *England*		366
78.	The Mermaid (Windlass Song)		
	by Robert Buchanan *England & Scotland*		391
79.	Mermaids *Guernsey*		392
80.	The Entangled Mermaid *Netherlands*		394
81.	The Merman and the Mermaid in the Faeröes *Faroe Islands*		398
82.	The Mer-man and Marstig's Daughter *Denmark*		399
83.	Rosmer Havmand *Denmark*		404
84.	The Mermaid's Prophecy *Denmark*		408

85.	Agnete and the Merman	
	by Jens Baggesen *Denmark*	411
86.	Agnes	
	by Adam Gottlob Oehlenschläger *Denmark*	417
87.	The Little Mermaid	
	by Hans Christian Andersen *Denmark*	422
88.	Hans, the Mermaid's Son *Denmark*	437
89.	The Merman and Mermaid in Norway *Norway*	445
90.	The Fisher and the Merman *Norway*	446
91.	Necks, Mermen and Mermaids *Sweden*	447
92.	The Power of the Harp *Sweden*	449
93.	Duke Magnus and the Mermaid *Sweden*	453
94.	The King's Son and Messeria *Sweden*	455
95.	The King's Son and the Princess Singorra *Sweden*	466
96.	The Sea Nymph *Sweden*	484
97.	The Mermaid and the Boy *Lapland (Sweden & Finland)*	485
98.	The Merman and the Calf *Scandinavia*	493
99.	The Sea-Sprite *Scandinavia*	494
100.	The Shepherd and the Sea-Folk *Scandinavia*	495
101.	The Mermaid *Estonia*	496
102.	The Lake-Dwellers *Estonia*	505
103.	The Faithless Fisherman *Estonia*	507
104.	Russian Water Spirits *Russia*	509
105.	The Story of Tremsin, the Bird Zhar, and Nastasia, the	
	Lovely Maid of the Sea *Cossack (Russia & Ukraine)*	515
106.	The Fisherman *Germany*	520
107.	The Water-Woman *Germany*	521
108.	The Peasant and the Waterman *Germany*	522
109.	The Water-Smith *Germany*	524
110.	The Working Waterman *Germany*	525
111.	The Nix Labour *Germany*	526
112.	The Water Nix *Germany*	527
113.	The Nixie of the Mill-Pond *Germany*	528
114.	The Golden Mermaid *Germany*	532
115.	Undine	
	by Friedrich de la Motte Fouque *Germany*	538
116.	Slavonic Mermaids *Slavonic Region*	595
117.	Lidushka and the Water Demon's Wife *Bohemia (Czech Republic)*	598
118.	The Good Ferryman and the Water Nymphs *Poland*	601
119.	Mr. Cuttlefish's Love Story *Hungary*	608
120.	The Yellow Dwarf	
	by Madame d'Aulnoy *France*	614
121.	Fortunio and the Siren *Italy*	629
122.	An Impossible Enchantment *Italy*	639
123.	The Adventures of Bulukiya *Arabian Nights*	648

124.	Julnar the Sea-Born and her Son King Badr Basim of Persia *Arabian Nights*	669
125.	Abdullah the Fisherman and Abdullah the Merman *Arabian Nights*	707
126.	A Cairene Mermaid *Egypt*	727
127.	Ayuh, the Nigerian Mermaid *Nigeria*	727
128.	The Story of Tangalimlibo *South Africa*	728
129.	Chinese Mermaids *China*	735
130.	The Princess of the Tung-T'ing Lake *China*	737
131.	Ningyo *Japan*	744
132.	Toda, the Archer, and the Queen of the World under the Sea *Japan*	745
133.	The Boy of Urashima *Japan*	751
134.	How the Jelly-Fish Lost His Shell *Japan*	754
135.	Lord Cuttle-Fish's Concert *Japan*	757
136.	The Gamo-Gamo *Philippines*	761
137.	The Shark-Man, Nanaue *Hawaii, United States*	761
138.	The Mermaid of the Magdalenes *Canada*	768
139.	A Mermaid in Newfoundland *Canada*	771
140.	Sedna *Canada*	772
141.	Aboo-dom-k'n and Lampeg-win-wuk *United States*	774
142.	How Two Girls Were Changed to Water-Snakes, and of Two Others That Became Mermaids *United States*	775
143.	Ne Hwas, the Mermaid *United States*	776
144.	Mermaid of the Teton Tribe *United States*	778
145.	The Takelma Mermaid *United States*	779
146.	The Pascagoula River Mermaid *United States*	779
147.	The Mermaid: Child Ballad 289 *Vermont, United States*	781
148.	The Mermaid: Child Ballad 289 *Massachusetts, United States*	782
149.	Shipwreck: Child Ballad 289 *Missouri, United States*	784
150.	The Mermaid: Child Ballad 289 *United States*	785
151.	Little Girl, Mama Glau, and Humming-Bird *Trinidad*	786
152.	The Boy and the Mermaid *Jamaica*	788
153.	Sea-Mahmy *Jamaica*	789
154.	The Mermaid *Jamaica*	791
155.	The Mermaid's Lake *Guyana*	791
156.	Water Mamma *Guyana*	793
157.	Oiára, the Water-Maidens *Brazil*	794
158.	Yara *Brazil*	795
159.	The Story of the Yara *Brazil*	795
160.	The Mermaid of the Gocta Cataracts *Peru*	

Appendix

Bibliography 804
Index 810

Mermaids
by Heidi Anne Heiner

"It doubtless might please God to make a mermaid, but I don't believe God ever did make one."
—Sir Humphry Davy

APPEARING under many different guises, mermaids have a long, varied history dating back many centuries. Our modern day perception of mermaids is primarily based upon the mermaids and merrows of northern Europe, especially Scandinavia, Scotland and Ireland, as well as the sirens of ancient Greece. However, water spirits of some type exist in almost every culture situated near bodies of water, be they oceans, lakes, rivers or even wells and springs. Some are more deity than spirit and others share only a tenuous connection with the well-known mermaid.

This collection gathers together examples of the earliest scholarship concerning mermaids and their folkloric relatives, including several articles about their history from ancient times to the nineteenth century when mermaids captured the public's imagination during the folklore renaissance of the 1800s.

In addition to the articles, over 150 tales and ballads about mermaids and other water spirits from around the world are compiled into this volume. The emphasis is on the European mermaid in her many guises—especially in the aforementioned Scandinavia, Scotland and Ireland—but stories from Africa, Asia, and the Americas are also included. I did not include any Greek tales as they are discussed exhaustively in the various articles provided.

For most entries in the SurLaLune series I write a short introduction to provide an overview of the topic, but as I prepared one for this volume, I realized I was merely repeating what already appears in the book several times.

The best introduction—where I recommend starting—is "Melusina" from *Curious Myths of the Middle Ages* by Sabine Baring-Gould. This article became a touchstone for many scholars and offers the introduction I would have attempted to write for this volume. I also highly recommend "Water Sprites and Mermaids" by Fletcher S. Bassett which was written many years after Baring-Gould's piece. It successfully culls information from many sources and offers copious footnotes, some of which are not helpful, but most are. Many of the cited sources are offered in this current volume.

For the most part, the articles and tales included here are provided in their entirety with footnotes. Many materials are repeated from article to article, but each piece was carefully chosen for its validity, quality, and approach to the material. For the most part, the articles' authors are not believers in the mermaid mythos, but they are enthusiastic about the topic nevertheless.

Due to the nature of mermaid stories, many of the materials in this volume are not straightforward folktales, but are snippets and descripttions of the beliefs in various incarnations of water spirits. I chose to emphasize those materials gathered by folklorists and learned enthusiasts, over the news stories and sensationalized accounts offered in the popular media in times past.

During the course of my research, I gathered enough materials to fill two volumes, but for now, this collection with its heavy European influence made the most editorial sense. If this volume proves successful, I may offer a second in the future.

Despite pop culture's ongoing fascination with mermaids, not many informative books are available on the topic. Overall, the books published in the past several decades have fallen into three categories: Children's Literature, Art/Coffee Table, and Self-Help/New Age Studies. While the books in these categories are excellent for their intended audiences, they do not provide more than a cursory overview of the mermaid mythos from a folkloric viewpoint. Few provide extensive notes and resources for further reading and research.

Only one book stood out among the many offerings, *Sea Enchantress:The Tale of the Mermaid and Her Kin* by Gwen Benwell and Arthur Waugh. First published in 1961, it is long out of print, unfortunately, but I highly recommend it for those interested in the folkloric aspects of mermaids and other water spirits.

Notes About This Edition

THE text for this edition has been scanned and edited from the original published versions cited as the source materials. Original spelling and punctuation, sometimes considered antiquated to modern standards, has been maintained. Despite several proofreading sessions, other errata may appear that were part of the original publications or escaped detection through vigorous proofreading. All mistakes are unintentional and the best possible text has been offered for the reader's edification after countless hours of painstaking work.

Note that the materials were also originally published in a different period of history. Negative stereotypes and other "politically incorrect" usages and attitudes may appear within the text. They should be considered in their historical context and not interpreted as current views of the editor. They are not intended to be offensive but are representative of a time and place in the world's history.

Articles

1. Melusina
from *Curious Myths of the Middle Ages* by Sabine Baring-Gould

EMMERICK, Count of Poitou, was a nobleman of great wealth, and eminent for his virtues. He had two children, a son named Bertram, and a daughter Blaniferte. In the great forest which stretched away in all directions around the knoll on which stood the town and castle of Poictiers, lived a Count de la Forêt, related to Emmerick, but poor and with a large family. Out of compassion for his kinsman, the Count of Poitou adopted his youngest son Raymond, a beautiful and amiable youth, and made him his constant companion in hall and in the chase. One day the Count and his retinue hunted a boar in the forest of Colombiers, and distancing his servants, Emmerick found himself alone in the depths of the wood with Raymond. The boar had escaped. Night came on, and the two huntsmen lost their way. They succeeded in lighting a fire, and were warming themselves over the blaze, when suddenly the boar plunged out of the forest upon the Count, and Raymond, snatching up his sword, struck at the beast, but the blade glanced off and slew the Count. A second blow laid the boar at his side. Raymond then with horror perceived that his friend and master was dead. In despair he mounted his horse and fled, not knowing whither he went.

From Pucé Church (Gironde).

Presently the boughs of the trees became less interlaced, and the trunks fewer; next moment his horse, crashing through the shrubs, brought him out on a pleasant glade, white with rime, and illumined by the new moon; in the midst bubbled up a limpid fountain, and flowed away over a pebbly floor with a soothing murmur. Near the fountainhead sat three maidens in glimmering white dresses, with long waving golden hair, and faces of inexpressible beauty.

Raymond was riveted to the spot with astonishment. He believed that he saw a vision of angels, and would have prostrated himself at their feet, had not one of them advanced and stayed him. The lady inquired the cause of his manifest terror, and the young man, after a slight hesitation, told her of his dreadful misfortune. She listened with attention, and at the conclusion of his story, recommended him to remount his horse, and gallop out of the forest, and return to Poictiers, as though unconscious of what had taken place. All the huntsmen had that day lost themselves in the wood, and were returning singly, at intervals, to the castle, so that no suspicion would attach to him. The body of the count would be found, and from the proximity of the dead boar, it would be concluded that he had fallen before the tusk of the animal, to which he had given its death-blow.

Relieved of his anxiety, Raymond was able to devote his attention exclusively to the beauty of the lady who addressed him, and found means to prolong the conversation till daybreak. He had never beheld charms equal to hers, and the susceptible heart of the youth was completely captivated by the fair unknown. Before he left her, he obtained from her a promise to be his. She then told him to ask of his kinsman Bertram, as a gift, so much ground around the fountain where they had met, as could be covered by a stag's hide: upon this ground she undertook to erect a magnificent palace. Her name, she told him, was Melusina; she was a water-fay of great power and wealth. His she consented to be, but subject to one condition, that her Saturdays might be spent in a complete seclusion, upon which he should never venture to intrude.

Raymond then left her, and followed her advice to the letter. Bertram, who succeeded his father, readily granted the land he asked for, but was not a little vexed, when he found that, by cutting the hide into threads, Raymond had succeeded in making it include a considerable area.

Raymond then invited the young count to his wedding, and the marriage festivities took place, with unusual splendour, in the magnificent castle erected by Melusina. On the evening of the marriage, the bride, with tears in her beautiful eyes, implored her husband on no account to attempt an intrusion on her privacy upon Saturdays, for such an intrusion must infallibly separate them for ever. The enamoured Raymond readily swore to strictly observe her wishes in this matter.

Melusina continued to extend the castle, and strengthen its fortifications, till the like was not to be seen in all the country round. On its completion she named it after herself Lusinia, a name which has been corrupted into Lusignan, which it bears to this day.

In course of time, the Lady of Lusignan gave birth to a son, who was baptized Urian. He was a strangely shaped child: his mouth was large, his ears pendulous; one of his eyes was red, the other green.

A twelvemonth later she gave birth to another son, whom she called Cedes; he had a face which was scarlet. In thank-offering for his birth she erected and endowed the convent of Malliers; and, as a place of residence for her child, built the strong castle of Favent.

Melusina then bore a third son, who was christened Gyot. He was a fine, handsome child, but one of his eyes was higher up in his face than the other. For him his mother built La Rochelle.

Her next son Anthony, had long claws on his fingers, and was covered with hair; the next again had but a single eye. The sixth was Geoffry with the Tooth, so called from a boar's tusk which protruded from his jaw. Other children she had, but all were in some way disfigured and monstrous.

Years passed, and the love of Raymond for his beautiful wife never languished. Every Saturday she left him, and spent the twenty-four hours in the strictest seclusion, without her husband thinking of intruding on her privacy. The children grew up to be great heroes and illustrious warriors. One, Freimund, entered the Church, and became a pious monk, in the abbey of Malliers. The aged Count de la Forêt and the brothers of Raymond shared in his good fortune, and the old man spent his last years in the castle with his son, whilst the brothers were furnished with money and servants suitable to their rank.

One Saturday, the old father inquired at dinner after his daughter-in-law. Raymond replied that she was not visible on Saturdays. Thereupon one of his brothers, drawing him aside, whispered that strange gossiping tales were about relative to this sabbath seclusion, and that it behoved him to inquire into it, and set the minds of people at rest. Full of wrath and anxiety, the count rushed off to the private apartments of the countess, but found them empty. One door alone was locked, and that opened into a bath. He looked through the keyhole, and to his dismay beheld her in the water, her lower extremities changed into the tail of a monstrous fish or serpent.

Silently he withdrew. No word of what he had seen passed his lips; it was not loathing that filled his heart, but anguish at the thought that by his fault he must lose the beautiful wife who had been the charm and glory of his life. Some time passed by, however, and Melusina gave no token of consciousness that she had been observed during the period of her transformation. But one day news reached the castle that Geoffry with the Tooth had attacked the monastery of Malliers, and burned it; and that in the flames had perished Freimund, with the abbot and a hundred monks. On hearing of this disaster, the poor father, in a paroxysm of misery, exclaimed, as Melusina approached to comfort him, "Away, odious serpent, contaminator of my honourable race!"

At these words she fainted; and Raymond, full of sorrow for having spoken thus intemperately, strove to revive her. When she came to herself again, with streaming tears she kissed and embraced him for the last time. "O husband!" she said, "I leave two little ones in their cradle; look tenderly after them, bereaved of their mother. And now farewell for ever! yet know that thou, and those who succeed thee, shall see me hover over this fair castle of Lusignan, whenever a new lord is to come." And with a long wail of agony she swept from the window, leaving the impression of her foot on the stone she last touched.

The children in arms she had left were Dietrich and Raymond. At night, the nurses beheld a glimmering figure appear near the cradle of the babes, most like the vanished countess, but from her waist downwards terminating in a scaly fish-tail enamelled blue and white. At her approach the little ones extended their arms and smiled, and she took them to her breast and suckled them; but as the grey dawn stole in at the casement, she vanished, and the children's cries told the nurses that their mother was gone.

Long was it believed in France that the unfortunate Melusina appeared in the air, wailing over the ramparts of Lusignan before the death of one of its lords; and that, on the extinction of the family, she was seen whenever a king of France was to depart this life. Mézeray informs us that he was assured of the truth of the appearance of Melusina on the old tower of Lusignan, previous to the death of one of her descendants, or of a king of France, by people of reputation, and who were not by any means credulous. She appeared in a mourning dress, and continued for a long time to utter the most heart-rending lamentations.

Brantome, in his eulogium on the Duke of Montpensier, who in 1574 destroyed Lusignan, a Huguenot retreat, says:

"I heard, more than forty years ago, an old veteran say, that when the Emperor Charles V. came to France, they brought him by Lusignan for the sake of the recreation of hunting the deer, which were then in great abundance in the fine old parks of France; that he was never tired of admiring and praising the beauty, the size, and the chef d'œuvre of that house, built, which is more, by such a lady, of whom he made them tell him several fabulous tales, which are there quite common, even to the good old women who washed their linen at the fountains, whom Queen Catherine de Medicis, mother of the king, would also question and listen to. Some told her that they used sometimes to see her come to the fountain, to bathe in it, in the form of a most beautiful woman and in the dress of a widow. Others said that they used to see her, but very rarely, and that on Saturday evening (for in that state she did not let herself be seen), bathing, half her body being that of a very beautiful lady, the other half ending in a snake; others, that she used to appear a-top of the great tower in a very beautiful form, and as a snake. Some said, that when any great disaster was to come on the kingdom, or a change of reign, or a death, or misfortune among her relatives, who were the greatest people of France, and were kings, that three days before she was heard to cry, with a cry most shrill and terrible, three times.

"This is held to be perfectly true. Several persons of that place, who have heard it, are positive of it, and hand it from father to son; and say that, even when the siege came on, many soldiers and men of honour, who were there, affirmed it. But it was when order was given to throw down and destroy her castles, that she uttered her loudest cries and wails. Since then she has not been heard. Some old wives, however, say she has appeared to them, but very rarely."[1]

In 1387, Jean d'Arras, secretary to the Duke of Berry, received orders from his master to collect all information attainable with reference to Melusina, probably for the entertainment of the sister of the duke, the Countess de Bar. This he did, making considerable use of a history of the mysterious lady, written "by one of the race of Lusinia, William de Portenach (qu. Partenope), in Italian." This history if it ever existed, has not come down to us; the work of Jean d'Arras is a complete romance. According to him, Helmas, king of Albania (Scotland, or, as the German popular versions have it, Nordland), married a fay named Pressina, whom he found singing beside a fountain. She became his, after having exacted from him an oath never to visit her during her lying-in. She gave birth to three little girls at once, Melusina, Melior, and Plantina. A son of Helmas by a former wife hurried to his father with the joyful news, and the king, oblivious of his promise, rushed to his wife and found her bathing her three children. Pressina, on seeing him, exclaimed against his forgetfulness, and, taking her babes in her arms, vanished. She brought up the daughters until they were fifteen, when she unfolded to them the story of their father's breach of promise, and Melusina, the youngest, determined on revenge. She, in concert with her sisters, caught King Helmas and chained him in the heart of a mountain called Avalon, or, in the German books, Brunbelois, in Northubelon, *i.e.* Northumberland. At this unfilial act, the mother was so indignant, that she sentenced her daughter Melusina to spend the sabbath in a semi-fish form, till she should marry one who would never inquire into what became of her on that day. Jean d' Arras relates that Serville, who defended Lusignan for the English against the Duke de Berry, swore to that prince upon his faith and honour, "that three days before the surrender of the castle, there entered into his chamber, though the doors were shut, a large serpent, enamelled blue and white, which struck its tail several times against the foot of the bed whereon he was lying with his wife, who was not at all frightened at it, though he was very considerably so; and that when he seized his sword, the serpent changed all at once into a woman, and said to him: 'How, Serville, you, who have been in so many battles and sieges, are you afraid? Know that I am the mistress of this castle, which I erected, and that soon you will have to surrender it!' When she had ended these words, she resumed her serpent-shape, and glided away so swiftly that he could not perceive her."

---

[1] Keightley's *Fairy Mythology*, 1860, pp. 483, 484.

Stephan, a Dominican, of the house of Lusignan, developed the work of Jean d'Arras, and made the story so famous, that the families of Luxembourg, Rohan, and Sassenaye altered their pedigrees so as to be able to claim descent from the illustrious Melusina;[1] and the Emperor Henry VII. felt no little pride in being able to number the beautiful and mysterious lady among his ancestors. "It does not escape me," writes the chronicler Conrad Vecerius, in his life of that emperor, "to report what is related in a little work in the vernacular, concerning the acts of a woman, Melyssina, on one day of the week becoming a serpent from her middle downwards, whom they reckon among the ancestors of Henry VII. . . . . But, as authors relate, that in a certain island of the ocean, there are nine Sirens endowed with various arts, such, for instance, as changing themselves into any shape they like, it is no absurd conjecture to suppose that Melyssina came thence."[2]

The story became immensely popular in France, in Germany, and in Spain, and was printed and reprinted. The following are some of the principal early editions of it.

Jean d'Arras, "Le liure de Melusine en frācoys;" Geneva, 1478. The same, Lyons and Paris, without date; Lyons, 4to, 1500, and again 1544; Troyes, 4to, no date. "L'histoire de Melusine fille du roy d'Albanie et de dame Pressine, revue et mise en meilleur langage que par cy devant;" Lyons, 1597. "Le roman de Melusine, princesse de Lusignan, avec l'histoire de Geoffry, surnommé à la Grand Dent," par Nodot; Paris, 1700. An outline of the story in the "Bibliothèque des Romans," 1775, T. II. A Spanish version, "Historia de la linda Melosyna;" Tolosa, 1489. "La hystoria de la linda Melosina;" Sevilla, 1526. A Dutch translation, "Een san sonderlingke schone ende wonderlike historie, die men warachtich kout te syne ende autentick sprekende van eenre vrouwen gheheeten Melusine;" Tantwerpen, 1500. A Bohemian version, probably translated from the German, "Kronyke Kratochwilne, o ctné a slech netné Pannĕ Meluzijnĕ;" Prag, 1760, 1764, 1805. A Danish version, made about 1579, "Melusine;" Copenhagen, 1667, 1702, 1729. One in Swedish, without date. The original of these three last was the "History of Melusina," by Thüring von Ringoltingen, published in 1456; Augsburg, 1474; Strasburg, 1478. "Melosine-Geschicht," illustrated with woodcuts; Heidelberg, 1491. "Die Historia von Melusina;" Strasburg, 1506. "Die Histori oder Geschicht von der edle und schönen Melusina;" Augsburg, 1547; Strasburg, 1577, 1624. "Wunderbare Geschichte von der edeln und schönen Melusina, welche eine Tochter des Königs Helmus und ein Meerwunder gewesen ist;" Nürnberg, without date; reprinted in Marbach's "Volksbücher." Leipzig, 1838.

In the fable of Melusina, there are several points deserving of

---

[1] Bullet, *Dissertat. sur la Mythologie Française*. Paris, 1771, pp. 1-32.
[2] Urstisius, *Scriptores Germaniæ*. Frankfort, 1670.

consideration, as—the framework of the story, the half-serpent or fish-shape of Melusina, and her appearances as warnings of impending misfortune or death. The minor details, as, for instance, the trick with the hide, which is taken from the story of Dido, shall not detain us.

The framework of the myth is the story-radical corresponding with that of Lohengrin. The skeleton of the romance is this—
1. A man falls in love with a woman of supernatural race.
2. She consents to live with him, subject to one condition.
3. He breaks the condition and loses her.
4. He seeks her, and—α. recovers her; β. never recovers her.

In the story before us, the last item has dropped out, but it exists in many other stories which have sprung from the same root. The beautiful legend of Undine is but another version of the same story. A young knight marries a water-sprite, and promises never to be false to her, and never to bring her near a river. He breaks his engagement, and loses her. Then she comes to him on the eve of his second marriage and kisses him death. Fouqué's inimitable romance is found on the story as told by Theophrastus Paracelsus his "Treatise on Elemental Sprites;" but the bare bones of the myth related by the philosopher have been quickened into life and beauty by the heaven-drawn spark of poetry wherewith Fouqué endowed them.

In the French tale, Melusina seeks union a mortal solely that she may escape from enchantment; but in the German more earnest tale, Undine desires to become a bride that she may obtain an immortal soul. The corresponding Danish story is told by Hans Christian Andersen. A little mermaid sees a prince as she floats on surface of the sea, and saves him in her arms from drowning when the ship is wrecked. But from that hour her heart is filled with yearning love for the youth whose life she has preserved. She seeks earth of her own free will, leaving her native element, although the consequence is pain at every step she takes.

She becomes the constant attendant of the prince, till he marries a princess, when her heart breaks and she becomes a Light-Elf, with prospect of immortality.

Belonging to the same family is the pretty Indian tale of Urvaçî. Urvaçî was an "apsaras," or heavenly maiden; she loved Puravaras, a martial king, and became his wife, only, however, on condition that she should never behold him without his clothes. For some years they were together, till the heavenly companions of Urvaçî determined to secure her return to her proper sphere. They accordingly beguiled Puravaras into leaving his bed in the darkness of night, and then, with a lightning-flash, they disclosed him in his nudity to the wife, who was thereupon constrained to leave him. A somewhat similar story is told, in the Katha Sarit Sagara (Book iii. c. 18), of Vidûshaka, who loves and marries a beautiful Bhadrâ, but after a while she vanishes, leaving behind her a ring. The inconsolable husband wanders in search of her, and reaching the heavenly land, drops the ring in a goblet of water, which is taken to her. By this she recognizes him, and they are re-united.

The legend of Melusina, as it comes to us, is by no means in its original condition. Jean d'Arras, or other romancers, have considerably altered the simple tale, so as to make it assume the proportions of a romance. All that story of the fay Pressina, and her marriage with King Helmas, is but another version of the same story as Melusina.

Helmas finds Pressina near a fountain, and asks her to be his; she consents on condition that he does not visit her during her lying-in; he breaks the condition and loses her. This is the same as Raymond discovering Melusina near a spring, and obtaining her hand subject to the condition that he will not visit her one day of the week. Like Helmas, he breaks his promise and loses his wife. That both Pressina and Melusina are water-sprites, or nymphs, is unquestionable; both haunt a fountain, and the transformation of the lady of Lusignan indicates her aquatic origin. As Grimm has observed,[1] this is a Gallic, and therefore a Keltic myth, an opinion confirmed by the Banshee part played by the unfortunate nymph. For the Banshee superstition has no corresponding feature in Scandinavian, Teutonic, or Classic mythology, and belongs entirely to the Kelts. Among others there are death portents, but not, that I am aware of, spirits of women attached to families, by their bitter cries at night announcing the approach of the king of terrors.

The Irish Banshee is thus described: "We saw the figure of a tall, thin woman with uncovered head, and long hair that floated round her shoulders, attired in something which seemed either a loose white cloak or a sheet thrown hastily about her, uttering piercing cries.

"The most remarkable instance (of the Banshee) occurs in the MS memoirs of Lady Fanshawe, so exemplary for her conjugal affection. Her husband, Sir Richard, and she chanced, during their abode in Ireland, to visit a friend, the head of a sept, who resided in an ancient baronial castle surrounded with a moat. At midnight she was awakened by a ghastly and supernatural scream, and looking out of bed, beheld in the moonlight a female face and part of the form hovering at the window. The face was that of a young and rather handsome woman, but pale, and the hair, which was reddish, loose and dishevelled. The dress, which Lady Fanshawe's terror did not prevent her remarking accurately, was that of the ancient Irish. This apparition continued to exhibit itself for some time, and then vanished, with two shrieks similar to that which had first excited Lady Fanshawe's attention. In the morning, with infinite terror, she communicated to her host what she had witnessed, and found him prepared, not only to credit, but to account for the apparition:—

"'A near relation of my family,' said he, 'expired last night in this castle. We disguised our certain expectations of the event from you, lest

---

[1] *Deutsche Mythologie*, i. 405.

it should throw a cloud over the cheerful reception which was your due.[1] Now, before such an event happens in this family and castle, the female spectre whom ye have seen always is visible: she is believed to be the spirit of a woman of inferior rank, whom one of my ancestors degraded himself by marrying, and whom afterwards, to expiate the dishonour done to his family, he caused to be drowned in the castle moat.'"

A very remarkable story of the Banshee is given by Mr. Crofton Croker. The Rev. Charles Bunworth was rector of Buttevant, in the county Cork, about the middle of last century. He was famous for his performance on the national instrument, the Irish harp, and for his hospitable reception and entertainment of the poor harpers who travelled from house to house about the country; and in his granary were deposited fifteen harps, bequeathed to him by the last members of a race which has now ceased to exist.

The circumstances attending the death of Mr. Bunworth were remarkable; but, says Mr. Crofton Croker, there are still living credible witnesses who declare their authenticity, and who can be produced to attest most, if not all, of the following particulars. Shortly before his decease, a shepherd heard the Banshee keening and clapping her hands under a lightning-struck tree near the house. On the eve of his death the night was serene and moonlit, and nothing broke the stillness of the melancholy watch kept by the bedside of the sick man, who lay in the drawing-room, by his two daughters. The little party were suddenly roused by a sound at the window near the bed: a rose-tree grew outside the window, so closely as to touch the glass; this was forced aside with some noise, and a low moaning was heard, accompanied by clapping of hands, as if of some female in deep affliction. It seemed as if the sound proceeded from a person holding her mouth close to the window. The lady who sat by the bedside of Mr. Bunworth went into the adjoining room, where sat some male relatives, and asked, in a tone of alarm, if they had heard the Banshee. Sceptical of supernatural appearances, two of them rose hastily, and went out to discover the cause of these sounds, which they also distinctly heard. They walked all round the house, examining every spot of ground, particularly near the window from whence the voice had proceeded; the bed of earth beneath, in which the rose-tree was planted, had been recently dug, and the print of a footstep—if the tree had been forced aside by mortal hand—would have inevitably remained; but they could perceive no such impression, and an unbroken stillness reigned without. Hoping to dispel the mystery, they continued their search anxiously along the road, from the straightness of which, and the lightness of the night, they were enabled to see some distance around them; but all was silent and deserted, and they returned

---

[1] Like Admetus in the Alcestis of Euripides. This story of Lady Fanshawe is from a note to "The Lady of the Lake."

surprised and disappointed. How much more then were they astonished at learning that, the whole time of their absence, those who remained within the house had heard the moaning and clapping of hands even louder and more distinct than before they had gone out; and no sooner was the door of the room closed on them, than they again heard the same mournful sounds. Every succeeding hour the sick man became worse, and when the first glimpse of the morning appeared, Mr. Bunworth expired.

The Banshee is represented in Wales by the Gwrâch y Rhibyn, who is said to come after dusk, and flap her leathern wings against the window, giving warning of death, in a broken, howling tone, and calling on the one who is to quit mortality by his or her name several times. In Brittany, similar spirits are called Bandrhudes, and are attached to several of the ancient families. In other parts of France, they pass as Dames Blanches, who, however, are not to be confused with the Teutonic white ladies, which are spirits of a different order.

But, putting the Banshee part of the story of Melusina on one side, let us turn to the semi-fish or serpent form of Melusina. Jean d'Arras attributes this to a curse pronounced on her by the fay Pressina, but this is an invention of his own; the true conception of Melusina he did not grasp, and was therefore obliged to forge a legend which should account for her peculiar appearance. Melusina was a mermaid. Her presence beside the fountain, as well as her fishy tail, indicate her nature; she was not, perhaps, a native of the sea, but a stream-dweller, and therefore as closely related to the true mermaid of the briny deep as are the fresh-water fish to those of the salt sea.

The superstitious belief in mermaids is universal, and I frankly confess my inability to account for its origin in every case. In some particular cases the origin of the myth is clear, in others it is not so. Let me take one which can be explained—the Oannes of the Chaldæans, the Philistine Dagon.

Oannes and Dag-on (the fish On) are identical. According to an ancient fable preserved by Berosus, a creature half man and half fish came out of "that part of the Erythræan sea which borders upon Babylonia," where he taught men the arts of life, "to construct cities, to found temples, to compile laws, and, in short, instructed them in all things that tend to soften manners and humanize their lives;" and he adds that a representation of this animal Oannes was preserved in his day. A figure of him sporting in the waves, and apparently blessing a fleet of vessels, was discovered in a marine piece of sculpture, by M. Botta, in the excavations of Khorsabad.

At Nimroud, a gigantic image was found by Mr. Layard, representing him with the fish's head as a cap and the body of the fish depending over his shoulders, his legs those of a man, in his left hand holding a richly decorated bag, and his right hand upraised, as if in the act of presenting the mystic Assyrian fir-cone (British Museum, Nos. 29 and 30).

Oannes, from Khorsabad.

This Oannes is the Mizraimite On, and the Hebrew Aon, with a Greek case-termination, derived from a root signifying "to illumine." Aon was the original name of the god reverenced in the temple of Heliopolis, which in Scripture is called Beth-Aon, the house of On, as well as by its translation Beth-Shemesh, the house of the Sun. Not only does his name indicate his solar origin, but his representation with horned head-dress testifies to his nature. Ammon, Apis, Dionysos are sun-gods; Isis, Io, Artemis are moon-goddesses, and are all horned. Indeed, in ancient iconography horns invariably connect the gods represented with the two great sources of light. Apparent exceptions, such as the Fauns, are not so in reality, when subjected to close scrutiny. Civilizing gods, who diffuse intelligence and instruct barbarians, are also solar deities as the Egyptian Osiris, the Nabathæan Tammuz the Greek Apollo, and the Mexican Quetzalcoatl; beside these Oannes takes his place, as the sun-god, giving knowledge and civilization. According to the fable related by Berosus, he came on earth each morning, and at evening plunged into the sea; this is a mythical description of the rising and setting of the sun. His semi-piscine form was an expression of the idea that half his time was spent above ground, and half below the waves.

A Babylonish seal in the British Museum, from Munter's Babylonier.

In precisely similar manner the Semitic moon-goddess, who followed the course of the sun, at times manifesting herself to the eyes of men, at others seeking concealment in the western flood was represented as half woman, half fish, with characteristics which make her lunar origin indisputable. Her name was Derceto or Atergatis. On the coins of Ascalon, where she was held in great honour, is figured a goddess above whose head is a half-moon, and at her feet a woman with her lower extremities like a fish. This is Semiramis, who, according to a popular legend, was the child of Derceto. At Joppa she appears as a mermaid. The story was, that she fled from Typhon, and plunged into the sea, concealing herself under the form of a fish. According to Plutarch, the Syrian Tirgata, the Derceto of Palestine, was the goddess of moisture;[1] and Lucan (De dea Syra, c. 14) declares that she was represented as a woman with a fish-tail from her hips downward.

In every mythology, the different attributes of the deity in process of time became distinct gods, yet with sufficient impress of their origin still upon them to make that origin easy to be detected.

As On, the sun-god rising and setting in the sea, was supplied with a corresponding moon-goddess, Atergatis, and Bel or Baal, also a solar deity, had his lunar Baalti, so the fiery Moloch, "the great lord," was supplied with his Mylitta, "the birth-producer." Moloch was the fierce flame-god, and Mylitta the goddess of moisture. Their worst was closely united. The priests of Moloch wore female attire, the priestesses of Mylitta were dressed like men. Human sacrifices characterized the worship of the fire-god, prostitution that of the goddess of water. From her came the names of the hetaræ Melitta, Meleto, Milto, Milesia (Athenæus, lib. xiii.). Among the Carthaginians, this goddess was worshipped, as appears from their giving the name of Magasmelita (the tent of Mylitta) to one of the African provinces. Mylitta was identical with Atergatis; she was regarded as a universal mother, a source of life.

In Greece, the priestesses of Demeter we called Melissæ, the high-priest of Apollo was entitled κύριος των μελλισσων. A fable was invented to account for this name, and to connect them with bees and honey; but I have little doubt that it was corrupted from the Semitic designation of the servants of Mylitta. The Melissæ are sometimes spoken of as nymphs, but are not to be identified with the Meliadæ, Dryads sprung from the ash. Yet Melia, daughter of Oceanus, who plunges into the Haliacmon, strongly resembles the Syrian goddess. Selene, the moon, was also known by the name Melissa. Καί τὰς Δήμητρος ξερείας, ὡς τῆς χθονίας θεᾶς μυστίδας, μελίσσας οἱ παλαιοί ἐκάλουν, αὐτήν τε τὴν Κόρην μελισσώδη, Σελήνην τε, οὖσαν γενέσεως

---

[1] Plutarch, *Crass*, c. 17. According to Greek mythology, this goddess, under the name of Ceto, "with comely cheeks," is the daughter of Sea and Earth, and wife of Phorcys (Hesiod, *Theog.* v. 235. 270).

προστατίδα μέλισσαν ἐκάλουν.[1]

When we remember the double character of Mylitta, as a generative or all-mother, and as a moon-goddess, we are able to account for her name having passed into the Greek titles of priestesses of their corresponding goddesses Demeter and Selene.

The name Melissa was probably introduced into Gaul by the Phocian colony at Massilia, the modern Marseilles, and passed into the popular mythology of the Gallic Kelts as the title of nymphs, till it was finally appropriated by the Melusina of romance.

It may seem difficult at first sight to trace the connexion between the moon, a water-goddess, and a deity presiding over childbirth; yet it is certain that such a connexion does exist. The classic Venus was born of the sea-foam, and was unmistakably one with the moon. She was also the goddess of love, and was resorted to by barren women—as the Venus of Quimperle in Brittany is, to this day, sought by those who have no children.

On the Syrian coast, they told of their goddess plunging into the sea, because they saw the moon descend into the western waters; but the Cretans, who beheld her rise above the eastern horizon of sea, fabled of a foam-born goddess.

In classic iconography the Tritons, and in later art the Sirens, are represented half fish, half human. Originally the Sirens were winged, but after the fable had been accepted, which told of their strife with the Muses, and their precipitation into the sea, they were figured like mermaids; the fish-form was by them borrowed from Derceto. It is curious how widely-spread is the belief in fish-women. The prevalence of tales of mermaids among Celtic populations indicates these water-nymphs as having been originally deities of those peoples; and I cannot but believe that the circular mirror they are usually represented as holding is a reminiscence of the moon-disk. Bothe, in his "Kronecke der Sassen," in 1492, described a god, Krodo, worshipped in the Hartz, who was represented with his feet on a fish, a wheel to symbolize the moon in one hand, and a pail of water in the other. As among the Northern nations the moon is masculine, its deity was male. Probably the Mexican Coxcox or Teocipactli (*i.e.* Fish-god) was either a solar or lunar deity. He was entitled Huehueton-acateo-cateo-cipatli, or Fish-god-of-our-flesh, to give him his name in full; he somewhat resembled the Noah of Sacred Writ; for the Mexican fable related, that in a great time of flood, when the earth was covered with water, he rescued himself in a cypress trunk, and peopled the world with wise and intelligent beings.[2] The Babylonish Oannes was also identified with the flood.

---

[1] Schol. Theocr. xv. 94. Porphyr. de Antro Nymph. c. 18.
[2] Müller, *Geschichte der Amerikanischen Urreligionen.* Basel, 1855, p. 515.

The Peruvians had likewise their semi-fish gods, but the legend connected with them has not descended to our days.

The North-American Indians relate that they were conducted from Northern Asia by a man-fish. "Once upon a time, in the season of opening buds, the people of our nation were much terrified at seeing a strange creature, much resembling a man, riding upon the waves. He had upon his head long green hair, much resembling the coarse weeds which the mighty storms scatter along the margin of the strand. Upon his face, which was shaped like that of a porpoise, he had a beard of the same colour. But if our people were frightened at seeing a man who could live in the water like a fish or a duck, how much more were they frightened when they saw that from his breast down he was actually a fish, or rather two fishes, for each of his legs was a whole and distinct fish. And there he would sit for hours singing to the wondering ears of the Indians the beautiful things he saw in the depths of the ocean, always closing his strange stories with these words:—'Follow me, and see what I will show you.' For a great many suns, they dared not venture upon the water; but when they grew hungry, they at last put to sea, and following the man-fish, who kept close to the boat, reached the American coast."[1]

It is not impossible that the North-American Indians may have symbolized the sun in the same manner as the Syrians, and that this legend may signify that the early colonists, to reach the New Land, followed the fish-course of the sun, which as man goes from East to West, whereas when it dives it swims from West to East, the course taken by the Indians in their canoes. The wanderers in the Canadian forests have also their fish-woman, of whom a tale is related which bears a lively resemblance to that of Undine, and which is not a little like that of Melusina.

One day an Ottawa chief, whilst sitting by the water side, beheld a beautiful woman rise from the flood, her face exquisitely lovely, her eyes blue, her teeth white, and her locks floating over her shoulders. From her waist downwards she was fish, or rather two fishes. She entreated the warrior to permit her to live on earth, as she desired to win a human soul, which could only be acquired by union with a mortal. He consented and took her to his house, where she was to him as a daughter. Some years after an Andirondack youth beheld and loved her. He took her to wife, and she obtained that which she had desired—a human soul.

In the Undine story, a water-maiden, in like manner and for a like object, is adopted by an old fisherman, and becomes the bride of a youthful German knight. But the Andirondack tribe was ill-pleased at the marriage of their chief with the mysterious damsel, and they tore her from his arms, and drove her back to her original element. Then all the

---

[1] Epitomized from *Traditions of the North-American Indians*, by J. A. Jones. 1830, pp. 47-58.

water-spirits vowed revenge at the insult offered to one of their race; they stirred war between the Ottawas and Andirondacks, which led to the extermination of the latter; one only was rescued, and he was grasped by the fish-wife, and by her borne down to the watery depths below the Falls of S. Anthony. In the German story, the husband is weary with the taunts of those around at having married a water-sprite, and bids her return to her element. Then the spirits of the flood vow his destruction, and send Undine on earth to embrace her faithless lord, and kiss him to death. The name of the fish-woman is in German Meerfrau or Meriminni; in Danish, the Siren is Maremind; and in Icelandic and old Norse, Marmennill; in Irish she is the Merrow; with the Breton peasantry she is Marie-Morgan. In the legendary lore of all these people, there are stories of the loves of a mortal man and a mermaid. According to Mr. Crofton Croker, O'Sullivan More, Lord of Dunkerron, lost his heart to one of these beautiful water-sprites, and she agreed to be his, but her parents resented the union and killed her.

On the shore of Smerwick harbour, an Irishman, Dick Fitzgerald, caught a Merrow with her cohuleen driuth, or enchanted cap, lying on a rock beside her. He grasped the cap, and thereby possessed himself of the nymph, who, however, seemed nothing loth to obtain a mortal husband. They lived together happily for some years, and saw a family of beautiful children grow up at their knees. But one day the Lady of Gollerus, as she was called, discovered her old cap in a corner. She took it up and looked at it, and then thought of her father the king and her mother the queen, and felt a longing to go back to them. She kissed the babies, and then went down to the strand with the full intention of returning to Gollerus after a brief visit to her home. However, no sooner was the cohuleen driuth on her head, than all remembrance of her life on earth was forgotten, and she plunged into the sea, never to return. Similar tales are related in Shetland, the Faroes, in Iceland, and Norway.

Vade, the father of the famous smith Velund, was the son of King Vilkin and a mermaid whom he met in a wood on the sea-shore in Russia.[1] In the Saga of Half and his knights is an account of a merman who was caught and kept a little while on land. He sang the following entreaty to be taken back to his native element—

> "Cold water to the eyes
> Flesh raw to the teeth!
> A shroud to the dead!
> Flit me back to the sea!
> Henceforward never
> Men in ships sailing!
> Draw me to dry land

---

[1] *Vilkina Saga*, c. 18.

From the depth of the sea!"[1]

In the "Speculum Regale," an Icelandic work the twelfth century, is the following description a mermaid:—

"A monster is seen also near Greenland, which people call the Margygr. This creature appears like a woman as far down as her waist, with breast and bosom like a woman, long hands, and soft hair, the neck and head in all respects like those of a human being. The hands seem to people to be long, and the fingers not to be parted, but united by a web like that on the feet of water-birds. From the waist downwards, this monster resembles a fish, with scales, tail, and fins. This prodigy is believed to show itself especially before heavy storms. The habit of this creature is to dive frequently and rise again to the surface with fishes in its hands. When sailors see it playing with the fish, or throwing them towards the ship, they fear that they are doomed to lose several of the crew; but when it casts the fish, or, turning from the vessel, flings them away from her, then the sailors take it as a good omen that they will not suffer loss in the impending storm. This monster has a very horrible face, with broad brow and piercing eyes, a wide mouth, and double chin."[2] The Landnama, or Icelandic Doomsday book, speaks of a Marmennill, or merman, having been caught off the island of Grimsey; and the annals of the same country relate the appearance of these beings off the coast in 1305 and in 1329.

Megasthenes reported that the sea which washed Taprobane, the modern Ceylon, was inhabited by a creature having the appearance of a woman; and Ælian improved this account, by stating that there are whales having the form of Satyrs. In 1187, a merman was fished up off the coast of Suffolk. It closely resembled a man, but was not gifted with speech. One day, when it had the opportunity to escape, it fled to the sea, plunged in, and was never seen again. Pontoppidan records the appearance of a merman, which was deposed to on oath by the observers.

"About a mile from the coast of Denmark, near Landscrona, three sailors, observing something like a dead body floating in the water, rowed towards it. When they came within seven or eight fathoms, it still appeared as at first, for it had not stirred; but at that instant it sank, and came up almost immediately in the same place. Upon this, out of fear, they lay still, and then let the boat float, that they might the better examine the monster, which, by the help of the current, came nearer and nearer to them. He turned his face and stared at them, which gave them a good opportunity of examining him narrowly. He stood in the same place for seven or eight minutes, and was seen above the water breast-high. At last they grew apprehensive of some danger, and began to retire; upon

---

[1] *Halfs Saga ok rekum hans*, c. 7.
[2] Quoted in "Iceland, its Scenes and Sagas," p. 349.

which the monster blew up his cheeks and made a kind of lowing noise, and then dived from their view. In regard to his form, they declare in their affidavits, which were regularly taken and recorded, that he appeared like an old man, strong limbed, with broad shoulders, but his arms they could not see. His head was small in proportion to his body, and had short, curled black hair, which did not reach below his ears; his eyes lay deep in his head, and he had a meagre face, with a black beard; about the body downwards, this merman was quite pointed like a fish.[1]

In the year 1430, after a violent tempest, which broke down the dykes in Holland and flooded the low lands, some girls of the town of Edam in West Friesland, going in a boat to milk their cows, observed a mermaid in shallow water and embarrassed in the mud.

They took it into their boat and brought it into Edam, dressed it in female attire, and taught it to spin. It fed with them, but never could be taught to speak. It was afterwards brought to Haerlem, where it lived for several years, though still showing a strong inclination for water. Parival, in his "Délices de Hollande," relates that it was instructed in its duty to God, and that it made reverences before a crucifix. Old Hudson, the navigator, in his dry and ponderous narrative, records the following incident, when trying to force a passage to the pole near Nova Zembla, lat 75°, on the 15th June. "This morning, one of our company looking overboard saw a mermaid; and calling up some of the company to see her, one more came up, and by that time she was come close to the ship's side, looking earnestly at the men. A little after, a sea came and overturned her. From the navel upward, her back and breasts were like a woman's, as they say that saw her; her body as big as one of us, her skin very white, and long hair hanging down behind, of colour black. In her going down they saw her tail, which was like the tail of a porpoise, speckled like a mackerel. Their names that saw her were Thomas Hilles and Robert Rayner."

In 1560, near the island of Mandar, on the west of Ceylon, some fishermen entrapped in their net seven mermen and mermaids, of which several Jesuits, and Father Henriques, and Bosquez, physician to the Viceroy of Goa, were witnesses. The physician examined them with a great deal of care, and dissected them. He asserts that the internal and external structure resembled that of human beings. We have another account of a merman seen near the great rock Diamon, on the coast of Martinique. The persons who saw it gave a precise description of it before a notary; they affirmed that they saw it wipe its hands over its face, and even heard it blow its nose. Another creature of the same species was captured in the Baltic in 1531, and sent as a present to Sigismund, King of Poland, with whom it lived three days, and was seen by all the Court. Another was taken near Rocca de Sintra, as related by

---

[1] Pontoppidan's *Nat. Hist, of Norway*, p. 154.

Damian Goes. The King of Portugal and the Grand-Master of the Order of S. James are said to have had a suit at law, to determine which party the creature belonged to.

Captain Weddell, well known for his geographical discoveries in the extreme south of the globe, relates the following story:—"A boat's crew were employed on Hall's Island, when one of the crew, left to take care of some produce, saw an animal whose voice was even musical. The sailor had lain down, and about ten o'clock he heard a noise resembling human cries; and as daylight in these latitudes never disappears at this season, he rose and looked around, but, on seeing no person, returned to bed. Presently he heard the noise again, rose a second time, but still saw nothing. Conceiving, however, the possibility of a boat being upset, and that some of the crew might be clinging to some detached rocks, he walked along the beach a few steps, and heard the noise more distinctly, but in a musical strain. Upon searching round, he saw an object lying on a rock a dozen yards from the shore, at which he was somewhat frightened. The face and shoulders appear of human form, and of a reddish colour; over the shoulders hung long green hair; the tail resembled that of the seal, but the extremities of the arms he could not see distinctly. The creature continued to make a musical noise while he gazed about two minutes, and on perceiving him it disappeared in an instant. Immediately when the man saw his officer, he told this wild tale, and to add weight to his testimony (being a Romanist) he made a cross on the sand, which he kissed, as making oath to the truth of his statement. When I saw him, he told the story in so clear and positive a manner, making oath to its truth, that I concluded he must really have seen the animal he described, or that it must have been the effect of a disturbed imagination."[1]

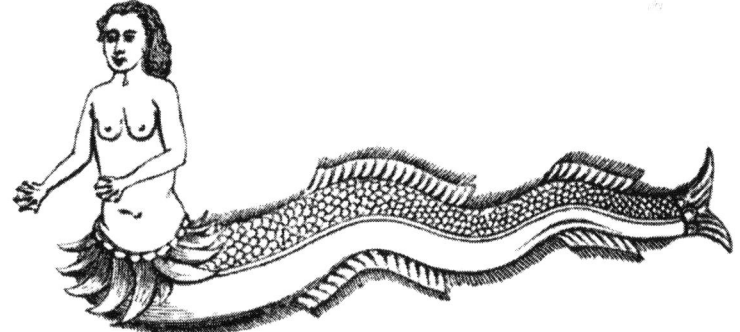

In a splendidly illustrated work with plates coloured by hand, "Poissons, écrevisses et crabes de diverses couleurs et figures

---

[1] *Voyage towards the South Pole*, p. 143, quoted by Goss: *Romance of Nat. Hist.*, 2nd Series.

extraordinaires, que l'on trouve autour des Isles Moluques," dedicated to King George of England, and published by Louis Renard at Amsterdam, in 1717, is a curious account of a mermaid. This book was the result of thirty years' labour, in the Indian seas, by Blatazar Coyett, Governor of the Islands of the Province of Amboine and President of the Commissioners in Batavia, and by Adrien Van der Stell, Governor Regent of the Province of Amboine. In the 2nd volume, p. 240, is the picture of a mermaid here reproduced, and the subjoined description:—

"See-wyf. A monster resembling a Siren, caught near the island of Borné, or Boeren, in the Department of Amboine. It was 59 inches long, and in proportion as an eel. It lived on land, in a vat full of water, during four days seven hours. From time to time it uttered little cries like those of a mouse. It would not eat, though it was offered small fish, shells, crabs, lobsters, &c. After its death, some excrement was discovered in the vat, like the secretion of a cat." The copy from which I have taken the representation for this work is thus coloured: hair, the hue of kelp; body, olive tint; webbed olive between the fingers, which each four joints; the fringe round the waist orange with a blue border; the fins green, face slate-grey; delicate row of pink hairs runs the length of the tail.

With such a portrait we may well ask with Tennyson—

> "Who would be
> A mermaid fair,
> Singing alone,
> Combing her hair
> Under the sea
> In a golden curl,
> With a comb of pearl,
> On a throne?"

The introduction to the book contains additional information.

The *Advertissement de l'Editeur* says:—"M. Baltazar Coyett is the first to whom the great discovery is due. Whilst governor, he encouraged the fishery of these fishes; and after having had about two hundred painted of those which were brought to his home by the Indians of Amboine and the neighbouring isles, as well as by the Dutch there settled, he formed of them two collections, the originals of which were brought by his son to M. Scott the Elder, who was then chief advocate, or prime minister, of the Company General of the East Indies at Amsterdam. He had them copied exactly. The second volume, less correct indeed in the exactitude of the drawings, but very curious on account of the novelties wherewith it is filled, and of the remarks accompanying each fish, was taken from the collection of M. Van der Stell, Governor of the Moluccas, by a painter named Gamael Fallours, who brought them to me from the Indies, and of which I have selected about 250. Moreover, to check incredulity in certain persons, I have thought fit to subjoin the following certificates." Among them, the most curious are those relating to the mermaid.

Letter from Renard, the publisher, to M. François Valentyn, minister of the Gospel at Dort, late superintendent of the churches in the colonies, dated Amsterdam, Dec. 17, 1716.

"Monsieur,

"His Majesty the Czar of Muscovy having done me the honour of visiting my house, and having had occasion to show the prince the work on the fishes of the Molucca islands, by the Sieur Fallours, in which, among other drawings, is the enclosed plate, representing a monster resembling a Siren, which this painter says that he saw alive for four days at Amboine, as you will be pleased to see in the writing with his own hand, which accompanies this picture, and as he believes that M. Van der Stell, the present Governor of Amboine, may have sent it to you, I remarked that his Majesty the Czar would be much gratified to have this fact substantiated; wherefore I shall be greatly obliged if you will favour me with a reply.

"I remain, &c."

REPLY.

"Dort, Dec. 18, 1716.

"Monsieur,

"It is not impossible that, since my departure from the Indies, Fallours may have seen at Amboine the monster whose picture you had the courtesy to send me, and which I return enclosed; but up to the present moment I have neither seen nor heard of the original. If I had the creature, I would with all my heart make a present of it to his Majesty the Czar, whose application in the research of objects of curiosity deserves the praise of all the world. But, sir, as evidence that there are monsters in nature resembling this Siren, I may say that I know for certain, that in the year 1652 or 1653 a lieutenant in the service of the Company saw two of these beings in the gulf, near the village of Hennetelo, near the islands of Ceram and Bœro, in the Department of Amboine. They were swimming side by side, which made him presume that one was male, the other female. Six weeks after they reappeared in the same spot, and were seen by more than fifty persons. These monsters were of a greenish grey colour, having precisely the shape of human beings from the head to the waist, with arms and hands, but their bodies tapered away. One was larger than the other; their hair was moderately long. I may add that, on my way back from the Indies, in which I resided thirty years, I saw, on the 1st May, 1714, long. 12° 18', and on the Meridian, during clear, calm weather, at the distance of three or four ship-lengths off, a monster, which was apparently a sort of marine-man, of a bluish grey (gris de mer). It was raised well above the surface, and seemed to have a sort of fisher's cap of moss on its head. All the ship's company saw it, as well as myself; but although its back was turned towards us, the monster seemed conscious that we were approaching too near, and it dived suddenly under water, and we saw it no more.

"I am, &c.,
"F. VALENTYN."

Letter from M. Parent, Pastor of the church of Amsterdam, written and exhibited before the notary Jacob Lansman.

"Amsterdam, July 15, 1717.

"Monsieur,

"I have seen with mingled pleasure and surprise the illuminated proofs of the beautiful plates which you have had engraved, representing the fishes of Molucca, which were painted from nature by the Sieur Samuel Fallours, with whom I was acquainted when at Amboine. I own, sir, that I was struck with astonishment at the sight of this work, the engravings of which closely resemble the fishes I have seen during my life, and which, or some of which, I have had the pleasure of eating during the thirteen years I resided at Amboine, from which I returned with the fleet in 1716. . . . Touching your inquiry, whether I ever saw a Siren in that country, I reply that, whilst making the circuit of our churches in the Molucca Isles (which is done twice in the year by the pastors who understand the language of the country), and navigating in an orambay, or species of galley, between the villages of Holilieuw and Karieuw, distant from one another about two leagues by water, it happened, whilst I was dozing, that the negro rowers uttered a shrill cry of astonishment, which aroused me with a start; and when I inquired the cause of their outcry, they replied unanimously that they had seen clearly and distinctly a monster like a Siren, with a face resembling that of a man, and long hair like that of a woman floating down its back; but at their cry it had replunged into the sea, and all I could see was the agitation of the water where this Siren had disturbed it by diving.

"I am, sir, &c.,
"Parent."

One of the most remarkable accounts of a mermaid is that in Dr. Robert Hamilton's "History of the Whales and Seals," in the "Naturalist's Library," he himself vouching for its general truth, from personal knowledge of some of the parties. "It was reported that a fishing-boat off the island of Yell, one of the Shetland group, had captured a mermaid by its getting entangled in the lines." The statement is, that the animal was about three feet long, the upper part of the body resembling the human, with protuberant mammæ, like a woman; the face, the forehead, and neck were short, and resembling those of a monkey; the arms, which were small, were kept folded across the breast; the fingers were distinct, not webbed; a few stiff, long bristles were on the top of the head, extending down to the shoulders, and these it could erect and depress at pleasure, something like a crest. The inferior part of the body was like a fish. The skin was smooth, and of a grey colour. It offered no resistance, nor attempted to bite, but uttered a low, plaintive sound. The crew, six in number, took it within their boat; but superstition getting the better of curiosity, they carefully disentangled it from the lines and from a hook which had accidentally fastened in its body, and return it to its native element. It instantly dived, descending in a perpendicular direction.

"After writing the above, (we are informed) the narrator had an interview with the skipper of the boat and one of the crew, from whom he learned the following additional particulars. They had the animal for three hours within the boat; the body was without scales or hair, was of a silver-grey colour above and white below, like the human skin; no gills were observed, nor fins on the back or belly; the tail was like that of the dog-fish; the mammæ were about as large as those of a woman; the mouth and lips were very distinct, and resembled the human. This communication was from Mr. Edmonton, a well-known and intelligent observer, to the distinguished professor of natural history in the Edinburgh University; and Mr. E. adds a few reflections, which are so pertinent that we shall avail ourselves of them. That a very peculiar animal has been taken, no one can doubt. It was seen and handled by six men on one occasion and for some time, not one of whom dreams of a doubt of its being a mermaid. If it were supposed that their fears magnified its supposed resemblance to the human form, it must at all events be admitted that there was some ground for exciting these fears. But no such fears were likely to be entertained; for the mermaid is not an object of terror to the fisherman: it is rather a welcome guest, and danger is to be apprehended only from its experiencing bad treatment. The usual resources of scepticism, that the seals and other sea-animals, appearing under certain circumstances, operating on an excited imagination, and so producing ocular illusion, cannot avail here. It is quite impossible that, under the circumstances, six Shetland fishermen could commit such a mistake."

One of these creatures was found in the belly of a shark, on the north-west coast of Iceland, and is thus described by Wernhard Guthmund's so priest of Ottrardale:—

"The lower part of the animal was entirely eaten away, whilst the upper part, from the epigastric and hypogastric region, was in some places partially eaten, in others completely devoured. The sternum, or breast-bone, was perfect. This animal appeared to be about the size of a boy eight or nine years old, and its head was formed like that of a man. The anterior surface of the occiput was very protuberant, and the nape of the neck had a considerable indentation or sinking. The alæ of the ears were very large, and extended a good way back. It had front teeth which were long and pointed, as were also the larger teeth. The eyes were lustreless, and resembled those of a codfish. It had on its head long black, coarse hair, very similar to the fucus filiformis; this hair hung over the shoulders. Its forehead was large and round. The skin above the eyelids was much wrinkled, scanty, and of a bright olive colour, which was indeed the hue of the whole body. The chin was cloven, the shoulders were high, and the neck uncommonly short. The arms were of their natural size, and each hand had a thumb and four fingers covered with flesh. Its breast was formed exactly like that of a man, and there was also to be seen something like nipples; the back was also like that of a man. It had very cartilaginous ribs; and in parts where the skin had been rubbed off, a black, coarse flesh was perceptible, very similar to that of the seal. This animal, after having been exposed about a week on the shore, was again thrown into the sea."[1]

To the manufactured mermaids which come from Japan, and which are exhibited at shows, it is not necessary to do more than allude; they testify to the Japanese conception of a sea-creature resembling the Tritons of ancient Greece, the Syrian On and Derceto, the Scandinavian Marmennill, and the Mexican Coxcox.

Source:
Baring-Gould, S[abine]. *Curious Myths of the Middle Ages, Second Series*. London: Rivingtons, 1868. pp. 206-258.

2. Fables and Facts from *Wonders of the Deep* by Maximilian Schele de Vere

"Whence and what art them, execrable shape."—MILTON.

THE great sea has its mountains and its deep valleys, with forests of weird, waving plants on the former, and, far down in the dark dells, masses of dismal debris, wrecks of vessels, and decaying bodies of men.

---

[1] Quoted in my "Iceland, its Scenes and Sagas."

There lies, half-covered with a crust of lime and hideous green slime, an ancient gun shining in sickly green; here, half-hidden, a quaint box filled with gold that was picked up amid the snows of the Peruvian Andes, and scattered over all a motley crowd of oddly-shaped shells. The empty skull of an old sea-captain has sunk down close to the broken armor of a huge turtle, and a deadly harpoon rusts and rots by the side of the enormous tooth of a walrus. Still farther down, "in the lower deep of the lowest," lie countless bales of Indian silks, in which large schools of fish dwell peacefully now; and over all, the silent currents of the ocean move incessantly to and fro, while millions of jelly fish throng every wave to feed the giant whales, and immense hosts of herring dash frightened through the waters to escape the voracious shark. Not only mountains and valleys, however, break the apparent monotony of the vast deep, but all that the surface of the earth can present of picturesque beauty or horrible hideousness is repeated below. In one place the waters foam and the waves break without rest or repose against oddly-shaped cliffs, which do not rise sufficiently high to be seen above; in another, they wash slowly and sadly against a wide desert of white sand. Where lofty mountains rise from the depth to a height not inferior to that of the tallest of Alpine summits, and vast forests of sea-tang clothe them in brilliant green, the sea circles mournfully all around in ceaseless windings, while farther on, where the valley sinks into the very bowels of the earth, and eternal darkness covers all with its mysterious mantle, the waters themselves are hushed and apparently motionless, as if awe-struck by the unbroken silence and the unfathomable night below.

The earth, it has been said, is one vast graveyard, and man can nowhere put down his foot without stepping on the remains of a brother. This is not less true with regard to the ocean. It is an ever-hungry grave, in which millions and millions of once living beings lie buried, and new hosts are added from year to year. It is the stage on which murder and maddest conflict are going on without ceasing. Immeasurable hatred dwells in those cold, unfeeling waters—and yet for a good purpose, since it is only through this unceasing destruction and change that life can be maintained in the crowded world that dwells in the "waters below the earth." The sea has its lions, its tigers, and wolves, as well as the earth above, its crocodiles and gigantic snakes, which daily sally forth to seek their prey and murder whole races; it has its medusæ and polypi, which spread their nets unceasingly for smaller fry; while whales, and their kindred, swallow millions of minute beings at a single gulp, swordfish and sea-bears hunt the giants of the lower world, and wretched parasites wait their opportunity to enter the fatty coats of huge monsters. Every thing is hunting, chasing, and murdering, but there is heard no merry "Tally Ho!" no war-cry encourages the weary combatants; no groan of pain, no shout of victory ever breaks the dread silence. The battles are fought in dumb passion, and no sound accompanies the fierce conflict but the splash of foaming waters and the last spasmodic effort of the wounded victim.

Can we wonder, then, that from time immemorial the sea has been peopled by the learned and the ignorant alike with marvels of every kind? It is the good fortune of travellers, and especially of those who "go down to the great deep," to be either determined that all they have seen must needs be unique, unheard of, and marvellous, or disposed to follow the nil admirari doctrine, and to insist that they have never met with any thing which was not perfectly familiar to them already from previous knowledge, or at least very easily accounted for by their superior mind. Vanity induces the former to magnify, self-love teaches the other to diminish all they have seen, and thus littleness of mind unfits both for correct observation and candid reports. The ancients, with their very limited knowledge of the sea and its life, very naturally transferred the features of the world above to that below the waters, and their lively imagination peopled the ocean with all the animals that were familiar to their eyes. There were sea-horses and sea-lions, poisonous sea-hares and ravenous sea-wolves, sea-swine, and even sea-locusts. There was the Chilon, with a man's head, living frugally on nothing but his own viscous humors; and there was the Balena, not so very like to a whale, and most cruel to its mate. There were those real wonders of the sea, the Dolphins, who swam about with their babies at the breast, and their eyes in their blade-bones, who dug graves for their deceased parents and friends, followed them in funeral procession, and buried them in submarine graveyards out of the way of the fishes. There was that strange fish, the Dies, with two wings and two legs, which in the perfect state lived only for a day. There was the Phoca, another oceanic brute, who was perpetually fighting with his wife until he killed her. Always remaining in the same spot, where he had murdered one wife, he disposed of her body and took another, thus playing Henry VIII. to a series of wives, until he either died himself or found a mate who was a match for him.

But these were only the teachings of that despised science, Natural History. Of far greater interest to the nation, and of deeper concern for their future welfare, were the legends of the god-like shepherds, a Proteus, a Nereus, and a Glaucus, who tended the aquatic flocks of Neptune, and were endowed with marvellous powers. We have all seen those classic bas-reliefs, in which the great Poseidon is accompanied by monsters, half-horses, half-fishes, while others wear partly the semblance of men, and blow trumpets made of huge shells with such terrible force, and such fearful sound, that their notes calmed the stormy sea! These hippocampi, sometimes provided with cloven feet and long tails, and then again covered all over with scales, and of the color of the sea, were favorite forms with some of the greatest sculptors of antiquity, like Myron and Scopas; and yet it is held doubtful whether they were altogether the offspring of poetic or artistic inspiration. Naturalists, as well as artists, have been led to think that extraordinary creatures of somewhat similar shape may have really peopled the seas in ancient times, and that they, like the giants of old, which are now reduced to the moderate proportions of our day, may have dwindled down into the diminutive hippocampi which abound in Southern waters. These little sea-horses, as they are familiarly called, have the perfect form of a horse's head, with prominent round eyes, and a steep, straight brow, while the gills float in exact imitation of a mane from the proudly-arched neck. They could not have copied the walrus, as that strange, monstrous animal, of which we shall presently have to say more, lives only in polar regions, to which the ancients did not have access. When the Tritons, on the other hand, were represented in human shape, they belonged, of course, simply to the realm of fables. And yet strong and frequent evidence is given by ancient authors of the real existence of beings whom they resembled. Demostratus, for instance, relates that such a Triton was still to be seen, imperfectly embalmed, in a temple of Bacchus at Tanagria.

It seems that there had been enmity for generations between these strange children of the sea, and the good people of Tanagria. One of the Tritons had been in the habit of coming forth every night from the waters to steal the cattle on shore, and all efforts to catch him on the part of the dwellers there had long been in vain. At last they placed a vessel, filled with strong wine, on the brow of a steep hill. When the Triton came, according to his custom, he noticed the vase, and was curious to ascertain its contents. He tasted, he liked it, and drank till he fell fast asleep on the edge of the precipice. During his disturbed slumbers, he rolled over and fell from the great height upon the rocks below, where the Tanagrians lay in wait, and wreaked their vengeance on the formidable robber.

Pausanias saw a smaller Triton at Rome, and from that time the annals of all countries of the world abound with strange legends of uncouth, horrible beings, born and bred in the sea, who entered into ill-fated relations with men, and almost invariably contrived their ruin. The White Lady of Scotland, the Nix or Undine of beautiful German lore, the Merminne of the Netherlands, and the Nech—our Old Nick—of the dismal North, are all children of the marine monsters of antiquity. Among the latter, some were great favorites with poet and priest, and their memory survives to our day. Thus the Ocean itself was represented as the son of the Heavens and the Earth, and the first of that gigantic race of Titans who stormed the abode of the gods, but the only one who did not join in the revolt of Saturn. How the briny deep was made to differ from the vast lakes with sweet water, their religion did not tell; but the distinction was made at an early date, for Hesiod already tells us that "ninetenths of the waters of the ocean, passing under the earth across dark night, fall in silvery showers upon the bed of the waves, around the earth, and on the back of the seas. One-tenth only, to the great injury of the gods, escaping from a lofty rock, forms the waters of the Styx, and by it the Immortals are fond of swearing."

Among the vast offspring of the ocean, again, the Nereids stand foremost by their number and by their beauty. They were all fair young maidens, nearly naked, and are often seen in the frescoes of Pompeii, and elsewhere, in most graceful positions, reclining on the back of sea-horses, or giving drink to thirsty monsters of the deep. It was only when the taste of artists became corrupt, and the fancy of men ran riot amid Eastern fictions, that they were represented as ending in fishtails, and as having hair of the color of the sea. Another sea-god, marrying the Muse of Lyric Poetry, was presented by her with three daughters, the Sirens, whom he called Blanche, Harmony, and Virgin Eye; but, unfortunately, he lost them soon after, when the infuriated Ceres punished them for having allowed the carrying off of her daughter Proserpina, and changed them into monsters, half women, half birds. The unfortunate maidens fled in despair, and hid themselves in the Islands which dot the waters between Sicily and Italy. But even there the curse pursued them still, for the decree had gone forth, that they were to die if ever man should pass them without stopping. Behold, now, the poor metamorphosed beauties straining their sweet voices, and blending them with the softest notes of their instruments, in order to attract hapless seamen, and to draw them into ruin. Surely, the ancients felt that sea and land alike are welcome stages for the fatal skill of the coquette! Only once the sad sirens were foiled in their attempts to win and to ruin the children of men. It was when the elite of Grecian heroes sallied forth on their great expedition in search of the Golden Fleece—in reality, a company of daring adventurers, who went to take possession of the gold mines in the Ural Mountains—and passed close to the islands on which the wretched sisters were living. They came down to the steep sides of the precipices, they displayed their unequalled charms, and sang their sweetest to cast their spell over all their senses. But Orpheus, who had joined the merry company with his lyre, raised his own sweet voice, and soon they were forced by its wondrous power to listen in their turn, and to let the Argo pass unharmed. Perhaps the godlike nature of the great singer was pleaded in their behalf, for they survived the future; and it was only when cunning Ulysses used the coarse trick of filling the ears of his companions with wax, and thus rendered them insensible to their enchantments, that they paid the penalty, and were changed into rocks. Even then one of them survived; for the compassionate waters refused to bury her; they sent her back to the surface, and she became fair Naples, the city of magic beauty, where so many have died from over-enjoyment, obeying literally the ancient saying: *Vedi Napoli e poi muori!*

Pliny seems still to have been in doubt as to the real existence of these marine monsters; at least, he defends himself against the suspicion of believing in them with an earnestness which goes far to prove the lingering doubt. "I do not believe in sirens," he says in his book on birds, "although Dino, father of Clearchus, a famous author, affirms that they exist in India and tempt men by their song, in order to tear them in pieces when they are asleep." In another place, again, he believes them to have been real fish, which recalled, in a vague manner, the features of human beings, and states that several such had been taken on the coast of Gaul.

The assertion is, strangely enough, supported by later evidence; for other portions of the earth, and later ages, have all faithfully repeated the legend, and pointed to actual beings in the sea as proof of their truth. Have not even the Arabs—who either ignore the sea altogether, or hate it as cursed by their great prophet—their weird beings, half men and half ostriches, who live on desolate islands, and devour the bodies of shipwrecked mariners brought to their rocks by the friendly waves? Near Rosetta and Alexandria, in Egypt, the waters are peopled with still stranger creatures, poetically called the Fathers of the Fair, who come only on shore for peaceful purposes, walk quietly about to enjoy the sweet air of heaven and the perfumes of flowers, and then return reluctantly to their dark homes in the great deep. A hundred of them were once captured, but they uttered such very sad sighs and unbearable groanings, that the hunters released them, and saw them plunge with delight into the cool waters. The Old Man of the Sea is familiar to all our readers through the Arabian Nights; but it is less generally known that he occasionally appeared near Damascus, and then promised a good harvest to the Syrians; the people were so grateful to him for his benevolence, that they caught him once and married him, fishtail and all, to a fair daughter of the land. The monster was well content, but not so the farmers, for his happy influence had left him as soon as he had found his master in his wife. Other Arabic authors tell us even the religion of one of those marine beings; he is called by them the Old Jew, and appears on the night preceding the Sabbath, with his white hair and shaggy coat, on the surface of the Mediterranean, and remains there, swimming about, plunging, and jumping high, and following the vessels as they pass near his home, till the Sabbath is over, and he sinks once more down under the waters.

These strange beings, reported to have been found or heard of with at least as much accuracy and as frequently as the Sea Serpent of our days, were evidently the ancestors of the mermen and mermaids, the ill-starred, God-forsaken dwellers in the kingdom of waters, the

> "Merman bold.
> Sitting alone,
> Sitting alone
> Under the sea,
> With a crown of gold.
> On a throne;
> And the mermaid fair,
> Singing alone.
> Combing her hair.
> Under the sea.
> In a golden curl

With a comb of pearl.
On a throne."

For a time Christian authors loved to revive the fables of pagan antiquity, or unconsciously repeated the weird fancies of older nations. Soon, however, certain features appear in their accounts, which show that they were either reports of real discoveries of marine monsters, dressed up, perhaps, in somewhat fanciful colors, or at least new inventions in harmony with the spirit of the age. The mermen soon cease to be mere monstrosities; they appear in a form resembling human beings, often scarcely to be distinguished from the people near whom they live, whence follows more frequent intercourse and a closer intimacy between the two races. One merman, found on the outermost point of Mauritania and brought to Spain, is reported as still having been in part a fish; but Theodore of Gaza already describes the mermaid, of which he saw several cast ashore on the coast of Greece, as fair and graceful; one of them he assisted in reaching the water, and immediately she plunged into the waves and was seen no more. Other authors, of such high repute that even the great Scaliger may be mentioned among them, tell of such wondrous beings, which they saw themselves or heard of through trustworthy friends. These accounts were, of course, valued only in proportion to the wonder they excited, and added nothing to our actual knowledge of the dwellers in the waters. They led, on the contrary, to new errors, and much amusement might be derived from the precepts given to unlucky sailors who should fall in with such sirens. They were advised to cast bottles into the sea, with which the monsters would play long enough to give them time to escape; to stop their ears carefully with wax and oakum, and to invoke aid from on high against their enchantments. The great Cabot, so intimately connected with the history of our continent, furnished the officers of the first vessel that ever attempted the voyage to the fantastic Cathay of those days, with a set of curious instructions. He recommended that prayers should be held twice every day, and all inventions of the Evil One, like dice, cards, and backgammon, should be strictly prohibited. By the side of such excellent suggestions are some of more doubtful morality. Thus he enjoins upon the officers to attract the natives of foreign lands, to bring them on board ship, and there to make them drunk with beer and wine till they had revealed all the secrets of their hearts. The rules contain at the end a recommendation "to take good care against certain creatures which, with the heads of men and the tails of fishes, swim about in the fiords and bays armed with bow and arrows, and feed upon human flesh."

The dark North, with its misty, murky atmosphere, which is reflected in the sombre legends of dismal superstitions, has its mermen above all others. They are mostly seen when fearful tempests threaten destruction, or sudden storms bring shipwreck to vessel and sailors alike. It is but here and there that they are painted in softer colors. In one of the legends, a famous giant of the seas, called Rosmer, carries off a Danish maiden of great beauty; she has to live with him in a great mountain, to which he comes every now and then from his home in the waters. Her brother, who had sallied forth to find her and to rescue her, lands at the desert rock, and is at first in great danger of being slain and devoured by the terrible monster. He succeeds, however, in pacifying the merman, and serves him faithfully for many years. At last he obtains leave to return home, and receives, as reward for his services, a large box filled with gold and precious stones. The giant even condescends to carry the box himself on board the ship, unconscious that the cunning maiden has first taken out all the treasures, and then concealed herself in the box, from which she comes forth as soon as the ship has reached the high seas.

It may readily be imagined that mariners who set out on long voyages to distant, unknown lands, with their minds filled with such images and marvellous stories, were ready to see sirens and other wonders of the deep to their hearts' content. Christopher Columbus even, when sailing along the coast of St. Domingo, met with three sirens, who were dancing on the water. They had, however, no sweet songs with which to allure him, and their silence, combined with their lack of beauty, made him think that they probably "regretted their absence from Greece." There can be little doubt that his sirens were Manatees, huge monsters so called because they carry their young with their flappers, or finlike hands, and give them suck on the breast—relations of the great Dugong of India, the only animal yet known that grazes at the bottom of the ocean. It has the strange power of suspending itself steadily in the water, and its jaws are bent in such a curious manner that the mouth is nearly vertical, by which means it is enabled to feed upon the sea-weeds down in the deep, very much as a cow does upon the herbage in the bright sunlight above. The Manatees serve to frighten the children of African slaves even now, when they suddenly rise like "spirits from the vasty deep," their large, gentle eyes looking anxiously around, and their young clasped tenderly to their bosom—a favorite position of theirs, which has earned them, with Spanish colonists, the name of Fish-Women.

The poor Brazilian natives, who still cherish the traditions of their forefathers, fondly believe in the existence of an immense lake in the interior which contains an enormous treasure, guarded and watched over by a siren whom they call the Mai das Aguas. They also believe still in the accounts given by early discoverers of strange beings met in their waters. Did not even brave John Smith, the valiant hero and daring navigator, when he came near our own continent, see a woman swimming gracefully near the vessel? Her eyes were large, beautiful, and full of expression, although rather round, the nose and ears well made, and the hair long and soft, but of sea-green color. His heart was near giving way to all these charms, when the strange being suddenly turned over, and showed to her disconcerted admirer a forked fish-tail!

Among South American Indians, it seems, tails of mermen are a favorite subject, though here and there these marine monsters are dreaded with instinctive abhorrence. Moravian missionaries have sent home strange reports of these superstitions, and yet found themselves unable, in their desire to honor the truth and to avoid misstatements, to deny positively all ground for these traditions. For not only the natives, but the ministers and agents of the pious Brethren themselves, firmly believed that they had met with men and women who lived in the water. They furnished statements, apparently made in full earnest and godly sincerity, that they had actually seen brownish beings with human faces and long hair rise suddenly from the water, and that the urgent intercession of the Indians alone had kept them from killing the supernatural beings. The natives looked upon them with superstitious awe, and insisted upon it that to kill one of them would be simply to bring dire calamities upon their settlements and the whole race. It must be presumed that we meet here with stray members of those aquatic tribes of Indians who live actually more in the water than on land. Martins, and other travellers, down to our day, tell us that the Indians who dwell near the upper branches of the Paraguay, the Maranhao, and other large rivers, remain for hours and hours in the water, and are such expert swimmers that they defy the most powerful current, and dive like waterfowl. A small bundle of leaf-stalks taken from the Buriti palm-tree is all they use ordinarily for their support; at other times they seize an oar, hold it between their feet, and use it as a rudder to steer with, and thus swim, holding their weapons in their muscular arms; or they leap with incredible agility upon a tree floating along on the swollen stream, sit down on it astride, and thus cross in a few minutes the most rapid current. No cayman or aquatic animal is safe from them, and they fight and defeat the huge capyvara, and the largest serpent, with great courage. They fear literally nothing except the Minhoças, a fabulous creature which is said to live in the rivers and still waters of Equatorial Brazil, and which naturalists believe to be either a giant eel endowed with powerful teeth, or perhaps a large variety of the famous gymnotus with its galvanic battery. These Canoeiros, as the Water-Indians are called, are true Ishmaelites; they are at war with all the other tribes, and are therefore hunted down like wild beasts; they have no home and no country of their own, and hence they may very well have given rise to the fabulous reports of mermen still rife among the credulous Indians of that continent.

In Germany, where folk lore abounds and superstition still has its strong hold on the minds of the masses, gruesome stories are told in the long winter nights of the Nixen, who dwell in the waters near the coast, in crystal-clear rivers, under the dark shadow of ancient trees, and in bright, babbling wells, in half-hidden glens. They are the sirens of the sunny South, and even here the ancient curse seems to follow the ill-fated race. For here, also, they are condemned to expiate some great and grievous sin committed by their forefathers, and to suffer long and miserably. As the whole creation groaneth, however, these sorrowful beings also yearn to be released, and of this longing many a touching tale is told in German legends. Thus one of them tells us, that the children of a Protestant minister were once playing on the banks of a river, when they saw a Nix rise from the waters, who, thinking himself unobserved, began to sing and to play on a strange, but ineffably sweet instrument. With the cruelty common to children, they at once rushed upon him and reproached him for his merriment, adding that as he was nothing but a condemned sinner, he had much better weep over his eternal wretchedness. The poor water-sprite, taken by surprise and distressed beyond measure, broke into tears; and the youthful tyrants, delighted with their success, went home to tell their father what had happened. But they were badly received here, and told that they had acted very wrongly and must return at once and comfort the poor being whom they had so grievously afflicted. They ran back, and as soon as they saw the Nix they cried out to him not to weep any longer, since their father had said that the Lord had died even for him, and he also might hope to be forgiven hereafter. Thereupon the poor Nix dried his tears, recovered his cheerfulness, and played with them all day long.

Holland, with its wondrous bulwarks and its lifelong conflict with the sea, abounds naturally in stories of every kind, in which mermen and mermaids play a prominent part. Sometimes they meet the intrepid sailor out on the high sea and sing of his joyous return, or warn him of his approaching end; at other times they come on shore, make themselves useful in a thousand ways, and vanish only when they are ill-treated or laughed at. There is hardly a town on the seacoast which has not its own legend of this kind; but generally the men are less interesting than the maidens, since the latter are prophets and play a prominent part in the sad history of that country. Such was the mermaid that once frequented the waters near Zevenbergen, a fortified town with massive walls and lofty towers, in which dwelt thousands of opulent citizens with their wives and children. But the people were as wicked as they were rich, and professed to believe neither in heaven nor hell. One fine day the Siren appeared in company with a sister mermaid, and with solemn, tearful voice both began to sing:

> "Zevenbergen must perish,
> And the tower of Lobbekens alone shall remain."

In spite of this warning the inhabitants continued their riotous living and sinful profanity. In a dark November night of the same year a fearful tempest arose; the wind blew from the northwest, and with such terrific force that the dykes gave way under the overwhelming pressure of the waters, and the Saint Elisabeth, as the inundation was called, overwhelmed not less than seventy-two towns and villages. Among these was the unfortunate town of Zevenbergen, and so thorough was its destruction in the deep waters, that when the morning broke, and people came from a distance in boats, they saw far beneath them the ruins of houses, and nothing standing but the one lofty tower of Lobbekens. Thus the prophecy of the mermaid had become true. Fortunately, man has triumphed over the evil prophet and the element alike. By an immense outlay of capital and the incessant labor of long years, the whole vast region has been once more laid dry, and from the midst of polders, or dyked meadows of surpassing fertility, there rises now a new town of Zevenbergen, richer and wiser than the doomed village of former days.

Holland is also the land which has originated the very peculiar faith in legends of sea-knights and sea-bishops, some of whom were captured from time to time and exhibited in the large cities. They were found afterwards in all the northern seas, and the works of those ages, down to the latter part of the sixteenth century, contain generally one or two so-called faithful likenesses of these very curious monsters of the deep. In 1305 already a sea-knight was caught out in the open sea to the north of Dockum, and carried from town to town; his fair appearance, and especially the complete suit of armor which he wore, excited universal admiration; but he died, unfortunately, in the third week, at Dockum.

A work of great scientific merit, and published as late as 1534, contains an engraving representing a sea-monk, whom the author, Rondelet, heard of in Norway, where it had been taken after a fearful tempest. It has the face of a man, but rough and repulsive, a bald, smooth head, the cowl of a monk hanging over the shoulders, two long fins instead of arms, and a body ending in a huge double-fluked tail. Other monks of the same kind appear in similar works, sometimes wearing a bishop's habit and mitre, and one of them is reported to have been sent in 1433 from the Baltic, where he was captured, to the king of Poland. The poor creature, however, refused steadfastly to utter a sound or to take any food; the king, moved with compassion, ordered him to be carried back to the sea, and the monster no sooner saw his own element than he gave signs of exuberant joy, leaped into the water and was never seen again. It may be added, that the Protestants made great capital out of these marine dignitaries of the church, and hence gave rise to the suspicion that the whole race of sea-monks and sea-bishops was artistically produced as a quaint revenge which the Reformation took on the persecuting Church of Rome.

The explanation is perhaps only an afterthought, but, as the proverb has it, that there is no smoke without fire, so here also, these countless and persistent traditions contain their grain of truth, which has been only half hid in a bushel of falsehoods. The fact is, that these fables could never have been invented, much less authenticated, even after the imperfect manner of early ages, if there were not certain animals living in the great deep which possess sufficient likeness to the human form to deceive careless and superstitious observers. If there are no real tritons and sirens to be met with in our waters, such as we see in ancient sculptures, or the coats of arms of noble families, there are at least seals and walrus, sea-lions and sea-cows, and similar monsters, whose faces and gestures, as seen on the surface of the waters, recall forcibly the features and movements of men. Unscrupulous cheats have occasionally taken great pains to manufacture actual sirens, and their remains are to this day carefully preserved in many a museum of European cities; like the well-known sirens of Leyden and the Hague. Nor is our own time exempt from these attempts to profit by the credulity of men. At the beginning of this century, a crafty fisherman on the coast of India skilfully joined the body of an ape to the lower part of a large fish, and dressed up the whole affair so cleverly that even experienced men were taken in, and bestowed much time and long research upon the extraordinary being. As the inventor attributed, moreover, healing powers to the touch of the siren, he was soon overrun, and could, after a short time, retire upon a competency. An European charlatan purchased the marine monster at a high price, and exhibited it in England and on the Continent. He met with great success for a time; then he and his siren were forgotten, only, however, to revive more brilliantly than ever in the hands of the master of his art, our own great Bamum. Another siren was, a couple of years ago, the marvel of the rural population all over England; nor was it, in this case, a mere mummy that was shown, but a living mermaid not unattractive in appearance, who discreetly plunged her fish-tail into the waters of a huge basin, and held the classic mirror and comb in her hands. At last public sympathy was aroused by some benevolent Quakers; an investigation was ordered by the authorities, and it was found that the poor woman had been forced for years to spend her days in the water, with an imitation fish-skin sewed on to her body!

There is, however, quite enough that is truly marvellous in some of the greater denizens of the deep, to engage our interest, and to find in them the originals of the fabled beings of whom we have spoken, without resorting to such gross and cruel deception. Pliny already speaks of a sea-elephant, so called at first, no doubt, mainly on account of his two enormous teeth, and of the peculiar shape of his head, which resembles somewhat the trunk of an elephant. A variety of these monsters seems to have been known to the Norwegian Olaus Magnus, who gives a most extraordinary description of the manner in which they were captured. "Sometimes," he says, "they fell asleep on the rocky coast, and then the fishermen went quickly to work, raising the fat along their tails, and attaching to it strong ropes, which they fastened to rocks and trees on the shore. Then they waked up the huge animal by throwing stones at it with a sling, and compelled it to return into the water, leaving its skin behind!" At present, the sea-elephant is found only in the Antarctic Ocean. On the confines of that world of ice, as far as the eye can reach, there appears nothing in sight but vast masses of ice, thrown in apparent disorder upon the immense plain, with here and there a colossal block rising on high and mimicking the shape of a great palace, with its walls and ramparts, towers and turrets, battlements and colonnades. Before these, smaller blocks dance in weird, wearisome motion up and down on the dusky waters, and gray mists hang from their sides, and break with their tatters and fragments the dreary prospect. At rare times the sun breaks through the dense fog, and then the whole world of ice begins to glitter and glare in the bright rays, and enchanted scenes dazzle the eye. Here is a snow landscape, with hamlets and trees; the larger blocks of ice resembling snow-covered houses, and the torn and tarnished masses appearing not unlike trees bending under the weight of hoarfrost, or bushes feathered with light crystals. The whole enchanted city, with its narrow canals, is buried in absolute stillness; gulls fly silently across the clear air, penguins rise and dive again in utter quiet, and even the sea-elephants lie voiceless, like colossal watchdogs, on the steps of the palaces. Only the low, mournful blowing of a whale, who sends up his airy fountain of foam, breaks occasionally upon the fearful silence of this magnificent city of ice.

In these inhospitable regions dwells the elephant of the seas, a monster not unfrequently thirty feet long, and measuring over sixteen feet in circumference! His powerful teeth are formidable enough in appearance, and above them he raises, when he is roused to anger, his inflated trunk, which ordinarily hangs loosely over the upper lip. His whole body is covered with stiff, shining hair, and underneath his fur coat he has a layer of fat at least a foot thick, which protects him effectually against the terrible cold of the polar regions. The two awkward feet, mere stumps encased in fin-like coverings, are of little avail to the giant when he moves on firm land; after a few yards he begins to groan and to rest, while the whole huge body shakes as if it were one vast mass of jelly-like fat. Here he falls an easy victim to the sailors, who come in search of his ivory and his oil; they walk fearlessly through the thick crowds, and knock them over by a single blow on the nose. The giant opens his enormous mouth and shows his formidable teeth, but, as he cannot move, he is virtually helpless. Very different are, however, his motions in his own element; as soon as he is under water, he swims with amazing rapidity, turns and twists like an eel, and is thus enabled to catch not only swift fish and sepias, bat even the web-footed penguins. He must find it difficult, at times, to provide his enormous body with sufficient food, for he swallows masses of tangled sea-tang, and large stones have been found in his stomach, to the number of twelve. When he wishes to sleep, he floats on the surface, and is rocked and cradled by the waves of the ocean.

What has, in all probability, led to their being taken for human beings by credulous and superstitious mariners of early ages, is the beauty of their eye, and the deep feeling they manifest at critical times. They not only never attack men, but, unlike the sympathetic seals, they also abandon their wounded companions, and purposely turn aside so as not to witness their sufferings and their agony. When they are mortally wounded, they drag themselves painfully inland, and hide behind a large rock to die in peace and unseen by others. If they are prevented from thus retiring, they shed tears, as they also weep bitterly when they are ill-treated by cruel sailors.

Very different in temper is the walrus, another of the great monsters of the deep, who, although by nature as gentle and peaceful as the sea-elephant, has become bitter and fierce by his constant warfare with man. It is the true type of the polar North: as all nature here is buried in sad, deathlike silence for several months, so the walrus also sleeps for the same time, deprived of all power and energy, while the fierce tempests and terrible ice-drifts of those regions are represented by their wild passions. They fight with indomitable courage for the fairest among the females, and many a bold knight among them leaves his life in the lists of the grim tournament. They defend their family and their race with intense rage, and know the strength that lies in union. Far up in the coldest ice regions of the Arctic seas they assemble in crowds of two thousand, and when their guards have been posted, they begin their sports in the half-frozen waters. They splash and splatter as they leap frantically or plunge their huge bodies into the foaming waves, and the noise they thus make, together with the trumpeting of their wide-open nostrils, and the mournful howl of their repulsive voice, fill the air with a stunning, confusing roar. Their appearance is in keeping with the whole scene: black heads, with red, staring eyes of great size, a broad-lipped, swollen mouth, and enormous beard, each hair of the thickness of a straw, adorned with snow-white teeth more than two feet long, and colossal, shapeless bodies, half horse and half whale, but weighing at times not less than three thousand pounds—surely nothing more was needed to strike terror into the hearts of ignorant seamen, and to lead to fancies wild and weird of man-resembling monsters of the deep.

Far greater, however, is the resemblance which certain varieties of seals bear to the human form. Their head, perfectly round and bald, their large bright eyes full of intelligence and tender feelings, their full beard on both sides of the face, and their broad shoulders, give to the upper part of their body a startling likeness, such as, in the foggy atmosphere of the northern seas, and with a predisposition to see what people expect to see, may very well have led to a sincere conviction that they were human beings. To this must be added their merry, playful disposition, and the peculiar manner in which they hold themselves almost perfectly upright when gambolling in the water. Naturally harmless, and even timid, they have a habit of following the small boats that go on shore, and of observing attentively all that is done; and if the crew remains longer at one and the same place, they become familiar, and fond of their company. They learn to know the people living on the shore near their playground, so that, in Corsica, flocks of them follow the fishing-boats, and modestly content themselves with the fish rejected after the nets have been hauled in. There can be little doubt that this intimacy has given rise to an account, given by Pliny, of a scene daily enacted near the town of

Mines, in southern France; and as here truth and fiction meet in striking relation to each other, we insert the words of the great naturalist:

"At a certain period of the year a prodigious number of mullets make their way to the sea through the narrow mouth of a swamp called Latera. These fish choose the moment of the incoming tide, which prevents the stretching out of nets and the taking them in vast quantities. By a similar instinct they tarn at once toward the open sea, and hasten to escape from the only place in which they are liable to be caught. The inhabitants, who know the period of the migration, and enjoy the pleasure of the sport, assemble on the shore. Spectators and fishermen all cry aloud: 'Simol Simo!' Immediately the dolphins know that they are needed. The north wind carries the sound of the voice to them. But whatever time it may be, these faithful allies never fail to appear at once. One might imagine it was an army, which instantly takes up its position in the opening where the action is to take place. They close the outlet to the mullets, who take fright, and throw themselves into shallow water. Then the fishermen surround them with their nets. But the mullets, with wonderful agility, leap over them. Now the dolphins fall upon them, and, content for the moment with having killed them, wait to devour them when the victory is assured. The action goes on, and, pressing the enemy closer and closer, the dolphins allow themselves to be imprisoned with the mullets, and, in order not to frighten them into desperate acts, they glide stealthily between the boats, the nets, and the swimming fishermen, so as to leave no passage open. When all are taken, they devour those they have killed. But knowing that they have labored hard enough to deserve more than a single day's wages, they reappear on the morrow, and not only receive as many fish as they desire, but are fed with bread soaked in wine!"

The talents of the seal are manifold: from the agility which he displays in catching fish for his master, to the capacity he has shown in learning actually to speak. More than one seal has been taught to utter distinctly the word Papa, and several animals of the kind are reported to have gone even beyond, and to have pronounced several words at a time. Nor must their love of music be forgotten, which is so great that they will rise from the water and remain nearly standing upright as long as the instrument is played, to which they listen with unmistakable pleasure. It is not so very long since one of this remarkable race came every day for six weeks from the waters of the Mediterranean, to take her rest under the divan of a custom-house officer in Smyrna. The latter had tamed her, and placed a few rough planks at the distance of about three feet from the water's edge under his couch, and on these boards the seal loved to rest for several hours, giving vent to her delight, oddly enough, in a profusion of sighs like those of a suffering man. She ate readily the rice and the bread which were offered her, though she seemed to have some trouble in softening the former sufficiently to swallow it with ease. After an absence of several days, the affectionate creature reappeared with a young one under the arm, but a month later she plunged one day, frightened, into the water, and was never seen again.

Nearly about the same time, another seal appeared suddenly in the very midst of the port of Constantinople undisturbed by the number of caiques dashing to and fro, and the noise of a thousand vessels with their crews and their passengers. One day the boat of the French legation was crossing over to Pera, loaded with wine for the ambassador. A drunken sailor was sitting astride on the cask, and singing boisterously, when all of a sudden the seal raised himself out of the water, seized the sailor with his left arm, and threw himself with his prey back into the waves. He reappeared at some distance, still holding the man under his fin, as if wishing to display his agility, and then sank once more, leaving the frightened, sobered sailor, to make his way back to the boat. Surely nothing more than one such occurrence was needed to give rise to the many romances of former ages; if the same, even, had happened in earlier days, the seal would have been a beautiful Nereid, who, having conceived a passion for the hapless sailor, had risen to take him down to her palace under the waves.

Source:
Schele de Vere, M[aximilian]. *Wonders of the Deep: A Companion to Stray Leaves from the Book of Nature*. New York: G.P. Putnam & Son, 1869.

3. A Chapter on Mermaids by Lieutenant Charles R. Low, I.N.

FROM the very earliest times, sailors, who are among the most superstitious of men, have credited the existence of mermaids, and indeed, were it not that there is absolutely no limit to the credulity of the human mind, so circumstantial have been some of the accounts, and so unimpeachable the credibility of the witnesses, that it would be impossible to have otherwise explained away or controverted the stories told of this fabulous animal. It is generally supposed, says a writer in the Asiatic Journal of 1822, in reference to a so-called mermaid exhibited in St. James' Street in that year, that various individuals of the cetaceous tribe, in particular, the sea-cow, have been mistaken by sailors for the mermaid, and that all the wonderful tales relate only to this animal, metamorphosed through the medium of a heated imagination; but he adds, we must allow that many travellers have attested its existence whose descriptions cannot be reconciled with that of the sea-cow, or of any other of the cetaceous tribe.

The ancient Syren, *Dulce malum in pelago*, was renowned for the bewitching charms of her voice, and Pliny, who speaks also of men who were half fishes, says that the Gallic ambassadors to Augustus Caesar declared that sea-women were often seen in their neighbourhood. Solinus and Aulus Gellius also bear testimony to their existence. The syrens of Homer possessed the attributes of gods, as it is mentioned that, to allure Ulysses, they offered him wisdom, a divine gift. They also lured mariners to their destruction, and the Argonauts only escaped the enchantment of their songs by the aid of the heavenly strains of Orpheus. Alexander the Great was also said to have thrown into the sea a golden cup as a propitiatory sacrifice to them.

According to the ancient poets the Syrens, like the Fates, were three in number—Parthenope, Lygea, and Leucosia—the daughters of the river-god Achelous, and one of the Muses. Allied to them, and possessed of similar dulcet voices, were the three Harpies, half women and half birds, of whom Pausanias says that, at the suggestion of Juno, they challenged the Muses to a trial of voices, but were vanquished, upon which the Muses plucked the golden leathers from the wings of the Harpies and formed them into crowns for the adornment of their heads.

We see these mermaids represented in the myths of many nations, and the sea-gods of Greek and Roman mythology find their counterpart in the kelpies of the Scotch. Dr. Hibbert, in his account of the Zetland Islands, gives particulars of the superstitions of the people in relation to mermen and mermaids, who carry off human beings to their submarine abodes. Georgius Trapanzantius also gravely states that he himself saw a mermaid rise many times out of the water, and he adds, that in Epirus, a merman came on shore and watched near a spring of water to inveigle young women, but was himself caught.

Artedi, in his "New System of Ichthyology," gives the name of syren to a class of animals which, he supposes, constitute a peculiar genus of the *plagiuri*, or cetaceous fishes. According to his account its characteristics are—the head, neck and breast, down to the navel, similar to the human body; only two fins, which are placed on the breast, and without the pinnated tail.

Perhaps the earliest account we have of the merman is that given by Larrey in his "Histoire d'Angleterre," where he speaks of one which was fished up on the Suffolk coast in the year 1187, and kept by the Governor for six months, when it managed to escape into the sea. This merman was quite dumb, and Larrey asserts that he exactly resembled a man, but that he never could be brought to understand his nature or position.

Johannes Hondius speaks of one that was caught in 1430, by some women in the meadows at Edam, in West Friesland, where it had been left by the sea, which entered through the broken dykes, during the great storms in that year. This mermaid, we are gravely told, was dressed in female attire, taught to spin, fed on cooked meat, had some notion of a deity, and bent in reverence when it passed a crucifix, and finally, after living some years at Haarlem, on its death received Christian burial. But it is added, this animal, like its fellow fished up on the coast of Suffolk in 1187, could never be taught to speak. In the year 1531, a creature of the same species was caught in the Baltic and sent as a present to Sigismund, King of Poland, but died after three days' confinement. In some tracts, published in 1650, by John Gregory, M.A., Chaplain of Christ Church, Oxford, it is described as a "huge animal of the human form, but very much resembling a bishop in his pontificals." It is slated that in the year 1560, near Manaar, on the coast of Ceylon, seven mermen and mermaids were caught by some fishermen in the presence of several Jesuits, who carefully examined and dissected the monsters, and "found the parts, external and internal, perfectly conformable to the human."

Purchas, in his account of the first voyage of Columbus, (see his "Pilgrimes" Book ii, Chap. 1,) says:—"After sayling from Port Nativitie, he saw three mermaids leaping a good height out of the sea, creatures, as he affirmed, not so faire as they are painted, somewhat resembling men in the face, of which at other times he said he had seene on the coast of Guinea." Christopher Turer, of Haimendorf, in his journal of his travels in Arabia, in 1556, says:—"On the 18th we came to Thora, which city is on the shoare of the Red Sea of no lustre; the haven small, in which ships laden with spices out of Arabia, Abassia and India resort. In this citie we saw a mermaid's skinne, taken there many yeares before, which in the lower part ends fish-fashion; of the upper part only the navill and breastes remaine, the arms and head being lost."

A remarkable reference to these fabulous creatures is contained in the following passage in the "Second Voyage or Employment of Master Henry Hudson, for finding a passage to the East Indies by the North-East," written by himself.—"June 15, 1608, lat. North, 75° 7'. This morning one of the companie looking overboard saw a mermaid, and calling up some of the companie to see her, one more came up, and by that time she was come close to the ship's side, looking earnestly on the men; a little after a sea came and overturned her; from the navill upward her back and breasts were like a woman's, (as they say that saw her,) her body as big as one of us, her skin verie white, and long haire and hanging downe behind, of colour blacke; in her going downe they saw her tayle, which was like the tayle of a porposs, and speckled like a macrell. Their names that saw her were Thomas Hilles and Robert Rayner."

Two years after this statement of the famous Arctic voyager, a Captain Richard Whitbourne gives the following circumstantial account of a mermaid he saw in the harbour of St. John's, in Newfoundland:— "Now, also, I will not omit to relate something of a strange creature that I first saw there in the year 1610, in a morning early, as I was standing by the waterside, in the harbour of St. John's, which I espied verie swiftly to come swimming towards me, looking cheerefully as it had beene a woman by the face, eyes, nose, mouth, chin, ears, necke and forehead; it seemed to be so beautifull, and in these parts so well proportioned, having round about upon the head all bleu straikes resembling hair deune to the necke, (but certainly it was haire,) for I beheld it lay, and another of my companie also, yet living, that was not then farre from me; and seeing the same comming so swiftly towards mee, I stepped backe, for it was come within the length of a long pike; which, when this strange creature saw that I went from it, it presently thereupon dived a little under water, and did swim to the place where before I landed; thereby I beheld the shoulders and backe doune to the middle to be as square, white and smooth as the backe of a man, and from the middle to the hinder parts pointing in proportion like a broad hooked arrow. How it was proportioned in the fore-part, from the necke and shoulders, I know not; but the same came shortly after to a boat, wherein one William Hawkridge, then my servant, was, that hath since bin a captain in a ship to the East Indies, and the same creature did put both his hands upon the side of the boate, and did strive to come in to him, and others taken in the said boate; whereat they were afraid, and one of them stroke it a full blow on the head, when it fell off from them, and afterwards came to two other boates in the harbour; the men in them fled for feare to land. This (I suppose) was a mermaid; now, because divers have written much of mermaids, I have presumed to relate what is most certaine of such a creature that was seene at Newfoundland; whether it was a mermaid or no, I know not; I leave it for others to judge, &c. R. W."

Harris, in his "Navigantium atque Itinerantium Bibliotheca," (Historical Repository of Sailors and Travellers) published early in the last century, commenting upon this narrative in the quaint language of the day, says—"This siren had a mind for the captain's company in some palace or other within the domains of Neptune, but he (though otherwise a man of good breeding) refused the favour and slighted her. What she would have done with him there, the Lord knows; however, he knew that there was no good wine in that country, but, on the other hand, a most confounded guzzling of salt water, such as would no way agree with his constitution. So he retired from her, and thereby, perhaps, escaped a drinking bout, which would have cost him his life and deprived him of Christian burial too. The siren let him go, and did not attempt by any further discovery of her charms, to seduce him. She had shown him those of her face, but thought him unworthy of the charms of her voice, those which poets through all antiquity have so wonderfully extolled....Upon the whole we can't see why this relation should not as effectually persuade all people that there are such creatures, as the voyage itself should that there is such a place as Newfoundland; for a man used to converse with the dangers and monsters of the sea, one may very easily believe not to be timorous. And a man can have no interest in forming a story of a mermaid, which is not at all adapted to serve any design in church or state. If the reader won't be convinced by this, there is no way for him but to follow the captain to St. John's harbour, and there wait for ocular demonstration."

We will not repeat the advice of Mr. Harris, that all disbelievers in the truth of this narrative, should proceed to St. John's harbour and "there wait for ocular demonstration," for were that counsel adopted, not only the reader, but the writer of this article, would be found waiting in that somewhat cheerless locality, and might fitly be classed among the fools of the period. But speaking gravely it does seem strange that so learned a writer as Harris, who was the editor of the first English Encyclopaedia, should be found expressing his belief in the existence of this fabulous denizen of the deep. And here we may observe that, in all probability, the creature seen by Captain Whitbourne, and also the mermaid described by Hudson, were either sea-cows or white porpoises, (*porcus-piscis*, or hog-fish) which may be seen in the gulf and river of St. Lawrence. The time of Hudson and Whitbourne was marked by many important discoveries by land as well as by sea, and travellers, no less than mariners, brought home strange stories of the wonderful animals, including the fabulous unicorn, having a "horne of three cubits," they had seen in the course of their peregrinations. Thus Purchas, who wrote his "Pilgrimes" nearly three centuries ago, says—"In Bengala are found great numbers of abadas or rhinocerotes, whose horne, (growing up from his snout) teeth, flesh, blood, clawes, and whatsoever he hath without and within his body, is good against poyson, and is much accounted of through all India. The skin upon the upper part of this beast is all wrinckled, as if he were armed with shields. It is a great enemie of the elephant. Some think that this is the right unicorne,[1] because as yet there is no other by late travellers found, but only by heare-say. Lodovicus Vertomannus saith he saw a couple of those other unicornes, at Mecca; one whereof had a horne of three cubits, being of the bignesse of a colt of two yeeres and a halfe old, the other was much lesse: both sent to the Sultan of Mecca, for a rare present out of Ethiopia. Gesner, in his booke of foure-footed beasts, citeth this testimony, and some others, whereby he persuadeth that there are divers sortes of these unicornes: but it cannot seem otherwise than strange, that in this last hundred of yeeres, wherein the world hath un-veiyled her face more than ever before, none of credit (that I have heard) hath affirmed himselfe to have seene the unicorne, but in picture." But to return to the mermaids, which will afford us quite sufficient matter for wonderment for one paper.

In the year 1714, one Valentyn averred that he saw a mermaid, while proceeding on his voyage from Batavia to Europe. It is described as "sitting on the surface of the water, with its back towards the ship. The body was of a grizzly colour, like the skin of a cod-fish; it had breasts,

---

[1] In the original text this was spelled "vnicorne" and has been changed by the present editor.~*HAH*

and was shaped like a woman to the waist, from which it went off tapering to a point." Eleven years later a mermaid was seen for some hours by the crew of a French ship off the coast of Newfoundland, and the account, subscribed with the names of all those who could write, was forwarded to M. de Maurepas, the French Minister of Marine, and is mentioned by Maillet in his 'Téliamède.'

In 1758, a living mermaid was exhibited at the fair of St. Germain, in France, "about two feet long, very active, and was seen sporting in a vessel of water, with great agility and seeming delight. Its position, when at rest, was always erect. It was a female, with ugly negro features; ears very large, and the back part and tail covered with scales." This mermaid fed on fish and bread. The next mermaid of which we hear, was one exhibited in London in the year 1775, but whether alive or dead "deponent sayeth not." The face of this creature is described as being "like that of a young female; its eyes a fine light blue, its nose small and handsome, its mouth small, its lips thin, with round edges like those of a cod-fish. Its teeth were small, regular and white, and its chin well-shaped; its ears were like those of an eel, but placed as in the human species, and behind them were gills for respiration, which appeared like curls. It had no hair on its head, but rolls instead of hair, which, at a distance, might have been taken for short curls. Its chief ornament was a beautiful membrane or fin, rising from the temples, and gradually diminishing till it ended pyramidically, forming a fore-top like a lady's head-dress. It had no fin on the back, but a bone like the human species. The breasts were fair and small, and the arms and hands well-proportioned, but without nails on the fingers. The belly was without a navel, and from the waist downwards, was in all respects like a codfish, but it had three sets of fins, one above and another below the waist, which enabled it to swim erect in the sea." Again there was exhibited in the neighbourhood of Covent Garden, in the year 1794, a mermaid described as having been taken in the North Sea, by a Captain Fortier. Like the preceding, "its figure, from the bead down to the lower part of the waist, was that of a woman, below the waist, that of a fish. It was three feet long, and had ears, gills, breasts, shoulders, arms, hands, fingers, and fins, and was covered with scales on the fish part." It is difficult to account for the physical economy of these creatures, which were exhibited, one of them at least, in a live state, in England and France, but in cases where specimens have been shown after death, there can be little doubt that the upper part of the figure of a monkey has been joined to the body of a fish, but so cleverly, from a mechanical point of view, that the closest inspection has failed to detect the line of junction.

The idea of such an artificial creature was not unknown to our ancestors, as the following suggestive lines denote:—

> "Who would not laugh, if Lawrence, hired to grace
> His costly canvas with each flattered face,

Abused his art, till Nature, with a blush,
Saw cits grow centaurs underneath his brush?
Or, should some limner join, for show or stale,
A maid of honour to a mermaid's tail?"

Three years after the exhibition of Captain Former's mermaid, a schoolmaster of Thurso, in Scotland, "affirmed that he had seen a mermaid, exactly resembling in every particular a woman, disporting herself in an erect position in the sea near the shore; and she was passing her fingers through her hair," which the schoolmaster doubtless knew from his classical studies, was the orthodox thing for a mermaid to do in such a situation, though we do not hear that she favoured him with the syren's song. We are further informed that twelve years afterwards, several persons beheld a similar creature near the same place, so probably she was waiting for the return of the schoolmaster. The next we hear of mermaids was on the 12th of January, 1809, when one was seen at Sandside, in the county of Caithness. Only the head and chest, the skin of which was of a "pink colour," were visible during the hour and a half that its motions were observed, but it remained within twenty yards of the shore. The breasts resembled those of a young woman; the arms were longer than in the human species and the eyes somewhat smaller. This Scotch mermaid, like the Thurso specimen, was observed when the waves displaced her hair, "which was of a seagreen colour," to replace it with her fingers. Had this lassie (if we may so call her, being Scotch) but sported a comb and looking-glass, she would be the veritable mermaid of British heraldry, worthy to be associated with that fabulous beast of the Roman naturalist, Pliny, the unicorn of the British arms, and with the phoenix and the griffin, not to speak of sphinxes and "chimaeras dire."

Two years after this appearance, one, John McIsaac, of Corphine, in Kintyre, stated on oath before the Sheriff-substitute, at Campbell Town, that on the 13th October, 1811, he saw, on a black rock on the sea-coast, an animal of which he gave the following description—"The upper half of its body was white, and of the human shape; the other half towards the tail was of a brindled or reddish colour, and apparently covered with scales. The extremity of the tail was of a shining reddish-green colour. The head was covered with long hair, which at times it would put back on both sides of its head. It would also spread its tail like a fan; and, while so extended, the tail was in a tremulous motion, but when drawn together again it remained motionless. The tail was about twelve or fourteen inches broad, and the hair long and of a light brown colour. The animal was between four or five feet long, and had a bead, hair, arms, and body down to the middle like a human being. The arms were short in proportion to the body, which appeared to be about the thickness of that of a young lad, tapering gradually to the point of the tail."

The chief thing remarkable in this description is the want of ingenuity of "the young man named John McIsaac," who had doubtless read the accounts of his countrymen of Thurso and Sandside, and, whether influenced by a heated imagination or a disregard for the requirements of truth, said the thing that was not. It is singular also that, as in the two previous cases, the enchantress of Corphine was engaged, while disporting herself on the rock, which she did for a period of nearly two hours, in putting back her hair with her hands, but the intruder on the privacy of the toilet could not see whether the hands were webbed or not, as the fingers were kept close together. As when under water, either at rest or swimming, the hair would naturally fall over the face much more than "when visiting the pale glimpses of the moon," it must be gathered that the greater part of the lives of these mermaids is passed in smoothing their hair, which all young ladies will agree must be an aggravating sort of existence without the toilet accompaniments of a comb and looking-glass, or even of a bit of ribbon of the shade most becoming the "sea-green" tint of the hair, and pink or white colour of the skin.

The deponent observed it for nearly two hours, during which time the rock on which the animal lay was dry, so that its whole figure was exposed, but when the tide had so far ebbed as to leave the rock four feet above the water, the animal tumbled itself clumsily into the sea, but rose again immediately to the surface. McIsaac now beheld clearly every feature of the face, which he describes as having the appearance of that of a human being, but with very hollow eyes. After a few minutes, during which it was "constantly stroking and washing its breast," the animal finally disappeared.

A very remarkable account is given by a Mr. Toupin, of Exmouth, in Devonshire, of a mermaid which he professes to have seen near the bar of the River Ex, on the 11th August, 1812, He says: "The day being very fine, I joined a party of ladies and gentlemen in a sailing excursion; when we had got about a mile to the south-east of Exmouth bar, our attention was suddenly arrested by a very singular noise, by no means unpleasant to the ears, but of which it is impossible to give any idea by mere description. It was not, however, unaptly compared by one of our ladies to the wild melodies of an Æolian harp, combined with a noise similar to that made by a stream of water falling gently on the leaves of a tree. In the meantime, we observed something about a hundred yards from us to windward. We all imagined it to be some human being, though, at the same time, we were at a loss to account for this at such a distance from the shore and no boat near. We hailed, but received no reply, and we made towards this creature as soon as possible, when, to the great astonishment of us all, it eluded our pursuit by plunging under the warter. In a few minutes it rose again, nearly at the same place, and by that time we had got sufficiently near for one of the boatmen to throw into the water a piece of boiled fish which he had in his locker. This seemed to alarm the animal, though it soon recovered from its fears, for we presently observed it to lay hold of the fish, which it ate with apparent relish. Several other pieces were thrown out, by which the creature was induced to keep a short distance from our boat, and afford us the opportunity of observing it with attention, and we found to our astonishment it was no other than a mermaid! As the sea was calm, and in a great degree transparent, every part of the animal's body became in turn visible. The head, from the crown to the chin, forms rather a long oval, and the face seems to resemble that of the seal, though, at the same time, it is far more agreeable, possessing a peculiar softness which renders the whole set of features very interesting. The upper and back part of the head appeared to be furnished with something like hair, and the forepart of the body with something like down, between a very light lawn and a very pale pink colour, which, at a distance, had the appearance of flesh, and may have given rise to the idea that the body of the mermaid is, externally, like that of the human being. This creature has two arms, each of which terminate in a hand with four fingers, connected to each other by means of a very thin elastic membrane. The animal used its arms with great agility, and its motions in general were very graceful. From the waist it gradually tapered, so as to form a tail, which had the appearance of being covered with strong, broad polished scales, which occasionally reflected the rays of the sun in a very beautiful manner; and, from the back and upper part of the neck down to the loins, the body also appeared covered with short, round broad feathers of the colour of the down on the forepart of the body. The whole length of the animal, from the crown of the head to the extremity of the tail, was supposed to be about five feet or five feet and a-half. In about ten minutes from the time we approached, the animal gave two or three plunges in quick succession as if it were at play. After this it gave a sudden spring and swam away from us very rapidly, and in a few minutes we lost sight of it."

If this animal were not a white porpoise or a sea-cow it is impossible to hazard an opinion as to its identity, unless we incline to the belief that Mr. Toupin was guilty of a flagrant falsehood. But similar creatures, and even more wonderful, have been seen in the River Ex, for it recorded that, more than a century ago, a mermaid was disporting itself close to the walls of Exeter, which resembled "the human form divine" from the head to the waist, but the nether man (or woman) bore a resemblance to a salmon. It had, however, "two legs placed below the waist," and, on these absolute novelties in the physical conformation of a respectable mermaid of the old-world type, it was seen to leave the shore of the Ex "and ran before its pursuers screaming with terror till it was knocked down and killed." We should have thought that the inhabitants of Exeter would have stuffed and preserved in the City Museum so unique a visitant after dispatching it in so barbarous a way, but whether this was so we know not.

In the autumn of 1819, an account appeared in the newspapers of an animal which was seen on the coast of Ireland, and which, on being fired at by a spectator, "plunged into the sea with a loud scream," and was seen no more. In size it was said to resemble a child of ten, with the figure of a girl of sixteen, together with long dark hair and full dark eyes. Unlike the Scotch mermaid, with their "pale green" and "light brown" hair, this mermaid was of Irish extraction, as anyone can vouch who has been in Tipperary and seen the veritable, barefooted syen of Milesian origin standing at the cottage door with "dark hair and eyes"—it is well it was so, or otherwise perhaps the Emerald Isle might have added this to the long list of "Irish grievances."

We now come to mermaids seen within the past century, in other parts of the world than the British Isles. Passing over a reference to a mermaid in the Red Sea, which M. Salamé, in a work published about the year 1822, says he saw leap a good height out of the water, we find repeated mention of these creatures having been seen in the Dutch settlement of Berbice in South America. Dr. Chisholm, in an Essay on the Malignant Fevers in the West Indies, publish in 1801, speaks of mermaids in the following terms:—"I probably hazard the implication of credulity by the following note: In the year 1797, happening to be at Governor Van Battenberg's plantations in Berbice, the conversation turned on a singular animal which had been repeatedly seen in Berbice river, and some smaller rivers. This animal is the famous mermaid, hitherto considered as a mere creature of the imagination. It is called by the Indians 'mene mamma' or 'mother of the waters.' The description given of it by the Governor is as follows: 'The upper portion resembles the human figure, the head smaller in proportion, sometimes, but oftener covered with a copious quantity of long black hair. The shoulders are broad, and the breasts large and well-formed. The lower portion resembles the tail portion of a fish, is of immense dimension, the tail forked, and not unlike that of a dolphin, as it is usually represented. The colour of the skin is either black or tawney. The animal is held in veneration and dread by the Indians, who imagine that the killing it would be attended with the most calamitous consequences. It is from this circumstance that none of these animals have been shot, and consequently not examined but at a distance. They have generally been observed in a sitting posture in the water, none of the lower extremity being discovered till disturbed; when, by plunging, the tail appears, and agitates the water to a considerable distance round. They have been always seen employed in smoothing their hair, or stroking their breasts with their hands, or something resembling hands. In this posture, and thus employed, they have frequently been taken for Indian women bathing.'" We fear that both Dr. Chisholm and Governor Van Battenberg "hazard the implication of credulity," in believing in the existence of these mermaids, though it is no doubt singular that in nearly all the accounts we have quoted the appearance and habits of the animals bear a striking similarity. The head is covered with long hair, the lower part of the body resembles a fish and the upper a woman, while their chief occupation, when absent from their families, presumably dwelling in a "cool grot" at the bottom of the sea, appears to consist in "smoothing their hair and stroking their breasts."

But Dr. Chisholm is not the only gentleman who reports the existence of these strange creatures. Dr. Pinckard, in his notes on the West Indies, (Vol. II. Letter 1), states that he has been present at conversations among natives in the same settlements, where the existence of mermaids of the above description was asserted; it may be noted that neither of these gentlemen was fortunate enough to see one, though Dr. Pinckard mentions that some Dutch planters corroborated the native account of the existence of mermaids, and declared that they had eaten their flesh.

The last mermaid of which we have any record was a dead one exhibited in the year 1822, in St. James Street in London. This creature was brought over to England by a Captain Eades, who purchased it in Batavia for 5,000 Spanish dollars, and stated that the natives regarded it as an object of worship. It had the head, arms, and shoulders resembling those of an ape, but from the breast, immediately below which there were fins, it resembled a fish. Its head was round, presenting a complete violation of all the mechanical principles to which nature conforms in the head of fishes and water-fowl; not only were the head and shoulders top heavy, so that undoubtedly the creature having the centre of gravity so high, could not have maintained the upright position universally ascribed to the mermaid, but in the descriptions no mention is made of gills, spiracles, and other physiological apparatus which we are accustomed to recognise as absolutely essential in the economy of submarine animals. Hence the opinion was held by the majority of the well-educated visitants to St. James Street, that the creature was a cleverly designed imposture, and that the head and shoulders where those of some animal of the *simia* class, and the remainder of the body that of a fish. As a mechanical contrivance the creature did credit to the ingenuity of its owners, for, notwithstanding the closest inspection, incredulous examiners were unable to detect the line of juncture.

The following description of this creature dated 26th April, 1822, is given by the Rev. Dr. Phillips, representative of the Church Missionary Society at Cape Town, where the ship in which Captain Eades was bringing it to England remained for a fortnight: "I have to-day seen a mermaid, now exhibiting in this town. I have always treated the existence of this creature as fabulous, but my scepticism is now removed. As it is probable no description of this extraordinary creature has yet reached England, the following particulars respecting it may gratify your curiosity and amuse you. The head is almost the size of that of a baboon. It is thinly covered with black hair, hanging down, and not inclined to frizzle. On the upper lip and on the chin there are a few hairs, resembling those upon the head. The cheek-bones are prominent, the forehead is low, but except in this particular the features are much better proportioned, and bear a more decided resemblance to those of the human countenance, than those of any of the baboon tribes. The head is turned back, and the countenance has an expression of terror, which gives it the appearance of a caricature of the human face; but I am disposed to think that both these circumstances are accidental, and have arisen from the manner in which the creature met its death. It bears the appearance of having died in great agony. The nose, ears, lips, chin, breasts and nipples, fingers and nails resemble those of a human figure. The spinous processes of the vertebrae are very prominent, and apparently arranged as in the human body. From the position of the arms, and the manner in which they are placed, and from such an examination as could be made in the circumstances in which I was placed at the time I saw it, I can have no doubt that it has clavicles, an appendage belonging to the human subject, which baboons are without. The appearance of the teeth afforded sufficient evidence that it is full grown, the incisors being worn on the upper surface. There are eight incisors, four canine, and eight molares. The canine teeth resemble those of a full grown dog; all the others resemble those of a human subject.

"The length of the animal is three feet, but not having been well preserved, it has shrunk considerably, and must have been both longer and thicker when alive than it is now. Its resemblance to the human species ceases immediately under the mammae. On the line of separation, and directly under the breast, are two fins. From the point where the human figure ceases, which is about twelve inches below the vertex of the head, it resembles a large fish of the salmon species. It is covered with scales all over. On the lower part of the animal the scales resemble those of a fish, but on that part of the animal which resembles the human form they are much less, and scarcely perceptible, except on a near inspection. On the lower part of the body it has six fins, one dorsal, two ventrical, two pectoral, and the tail. The pectoral fins are very remarkable; they are horizontal, and evidently formed as an apparatus to support the creature when in an erect posture, like that in which it has been sometimes represented combing its hair. The figure of the tail is exactly like that which is given in the usual representations of the mermaid."

Captain Eades, who hailed from Boston, after exhibiting this creature in London, took it to his own country, where doubtless his enterprise in giving 5,000 dollars for this latest of American "notions," and bringing it from the other side of the globe, reaped the reward he most coveted.

About that time this country was much excited by the intelligence of the discovery of the unicorn, and the *speciosa miracula rerum* appeared to be rising up in quick succession. A part of a skeleton, purporting to belong to this fabulous animal, was actually brought to England by a Mr. Campbell, and was examined by Sir Everard Hume, who published an account of it in the "Philosophical Transactions." In our time much is heard of the craken or sea-serpent, and a gigantic cuttle-fish, both of which have been seen by people above suspicion as regards their veracity, the latest and most remarkable appearance of the serpent being vouched for by the officers of one of Her Majesty's yachts.

Some years ago, a "manatee," as the creature found in the rivers of Guiana is called, was brought over to the Zoological Gardens in Regent's Park, but it only survived a few days. The only other specimen of this animal, which is the "Mene Mamma" of the natives of that South American state, and the nearest approach to the mermen and tnermaMs of antiquity, which has been exhibited in Europe, is the manatee now on view at the Royal Aquarium at Westminster.

In the Scandinavian mythology, the serpent Midgard surrounds the earth and lies at the bottom of the sea, and we are told by Mallet, in his "Antiquites du Nord," that the God Thor, on visiting the city of the giants, where all was illusion, so that he lost the sense of his own stupendous powers, went out fishing in one of the boats of the place. This, though far otherwise to his eyes, was really insufficient to carry the god, whose feet pierced its bottom, and rested on the serpent Midgard, which Thor mistook for the bed of the ocean. At another time, the legend has it, he was challenged by the giants to lift one of their gigantic cats, but found, with shame, that he could raise it little above the ground. The giants, however, subsequently confided to him that the cat had been no other than the great serpent Midgard, whose body surrounds the entire earth, and that they trembled with affright when they saw him lift it with his hands.

Scarcely less wonderful are the accounts we receive in our day of wonderful submarine and subterranean animals, such as the ancients, with all their avidity for the marvellous and powers of credulity, never imagined. We have all long been familiar with the sea-serpent in the various forms it has presented itself to "those who go down to the sea in ships," but yet more wonderful is the account of the latest addition to the list of terrestrial monsters. In a recent number of a German scientific journal devoted to zoological research, is a description of a gigantic "worm," known as the "Minhocas," which is said to frequent the marsh-lands in the highlands of Southern Brazil. It is described by those who have seen it, as a "black, armour-clad, serpent-like beast, some fifty yards long, five yards broad, and with two horns projecting from its forehead." Although seldom met with, the track of the minhocas is often found in the shape of great trenches cut deep into the earth, sometimes three or four yards wide and deep in proportion, sometimes trending downwards till they merged into regular tunnels, which are carried under the roots of trees and beneath streams, often causing serious land-slips and the complete diversion of the course of rivers. On some occasions a noise like distant thunder and a trembling of the earth, as if by volcanic force, have been experienced near the supposed dwelling-place of this phenomenon, before whose terrors all monsters, ancient and modern, marine or terrestrial, "pale their ineffectual fires."

Source:
Low, Lieutenant Charles R. "A Chapter on Mermaids." *The United Service Magazine*. Volume 147 (July 1878). pp. 339-351.

4. Mermaids from *The Book of Days* edited by Robert Chambers

The following appeared in the Chambers' A Book of Days, *a bestselling miscellany of popular antiquities connected to days of the year and a bestseller in the latter 1800s.*

MERMAIDS have had a legendary existence from very early ages; for the Syrens of the ancients evidently belonged to the same remarkable family. Mermen and mermaids and men of the sea, and women of the sea have been as stoutly believed in as the great sea serpent, and on very much the same kind of evidence. Sometimes, as expressed in Haydn's *Mermaid's Song*, there is a delightful bit of romance connected with the matter: as where the mermaid offers the tempting invitation:

> 'Come with me, and we will go
> Where the rocks of coral grow.'

But the romance is somewhat damped when the decidedly fishy tail is described. The orthodox mermaid is half woman, half fish; and the fishy half is sometimes depicted as being doubly-tailed. The heraldry of France and Germany often exhibits mermaids with two tails among the devices; and in the Basle edition of Ptolemy's Geography, dated 1540, a double tailed mermaid figures on one of the plates. Shakspeare makes many of his characters talk about mermaids. Thus, in the *Comedy of Errors*, Antipholus of Syracuse says:

> 'Oh, train me not, sweet mermaid, with the note!'

And in another place:

> 'I'll stop mine ears against the mermaid's song.'

In the *Midsummer Night's Dream*, Oberon says:

> 'I heard a mermaid on a dolphin's back.'

In *Hamlet*, the queen, speaking of Ophelia's death, says:

> 'Her clothes spread wide; and mermaid like,
> Awhile they bare her up.'

In two other passages, he makes his characters say:

> 'I'll drown more sailors than the mermaids shall.'

And:

> 'At the helm a seeming mermaid steers.'

But in all these cases Shakspeare, as was his wont, made his characters say what *they* were likely to think, in their several positions and periods of life.

Notices of mermaids are scattered abundantly in books of bygone times; sometimes in much detail, sometimes in a few vague words. In Merollo's *Voyage to Congo*, in 1682, mermaids are said to be very plentiful all along the river Zaire. A writer in *Notes and Queries*, in November 1858, lighted upon an old Scotch almanac, called the *Aberdeen Almanac, or New Prognostications for the Year 1688*; in which the following curious passage occurs: 'To conclude for this year 1688. Near the place where the famous Dee payeth his tribute to the German Ocean, if *curious observers of wonderful things in nature* will be pleased thither to resort the 1, 13, and 29 of May, and in divers other times in the ensuing summer, as also in the harvest time, to the 7 and 14 October, *they will undoubtedly see a pretty company of* MAR MAIDS, creatures of admirable beauty, and likewise hear their charming sweet melodious voices:

> "In well tun'd measures and harmonious lays,
> Extol their Maker and his bounty praise;
> That godly honest men, in everything,
> In quiet peace may live, GOD SAVE THE KING!"

The piety and loyalty of these predicted mermaids are certainly remarkable characteristics. In another part of Scotland, about the same period, a *real* mermaid was seen, if we are to believe *Brand's Description of Orkney and Shetland*, published in 1701. Two fishermen drew up with a hook a mermaid, having face, arms, breast, shoulders, &c., of a woman, and long hair hanging down the neck; but the nether part from below the waist hidden in the water. One of the fishermen, in his surprise, drew a knife and thrust it into her heart; where upon she cried, as they judged, "Alas!" and the hook giving way, she fell backwards, and was seen no more. In this case the evidence went thus Brand was told by a lady and gentleman, who were told by a bailie to whom the fishing boat belonged, who was told by the fishers; and thus we may infer as we please concerning the growth of the story as it travelled.

In 1775, there was a very circumstantial account given of a mermaid, which was captured in the Grecian Archipelago, in the preceding year, and exhibited in London. It has, as the *Annual Reviewer* of that day said, the features and complexion of a European. Its face is like that of a young female; its eyes of a fine light blue; its nose small and handsome; its mouth small; its lips thin, and the edges of them round like those of a codfish; its teeth small, regular, and white; its chin well shaped; its neck full; its ears like those of the eel, but placed like those of the human species; and behind them are the gills for respiration, which appear like curls. Some (mermaids) are said to have hair upon the head; but this has none, only rolls instead of hair, that at a distance may be mistaken for curls. But its chief ornament is a beautiful membrane or fin, rising from the temples, and gradually diminishing till it ends pyramidically, forming a foretop like that of a lady's headdress. It has no fin on the back, but a bone like that of the human species. Its breasts are fair and full, but without nipples; its arms and hands are well proportioned, but without nails on its fingers; its belly is round and swelling, but no navel. From the waist downwards, the body is in all respects like a codfish. It has three sets of fins, one above another, below the waist, which enables it to swim out upon the sea; and it is said to have an enchanting voice, which it never exerts except before a storm.' Here there is no great intricacy of evidence, for a writer in the *Gentlemen's Magazine* also said he saw this particular mermaid—which, however, he described as being only three feet long, tail and all. But a sad blow was afterwards given to its reputation, by a statement that it was craftily made up out of the skin of the angle shark.

In Mrs. Morgan's *Tour to Milford Haven* in the Year 1795, there is an equally circumstantial account of a mermaid observed by one Henry Reynolds, in 1782. Reynolds was a farmer of Pen-y-hold, in the parish of Castlemartin. One morning, just outside the cliff, he saw what seemed to him a person bathing, with the upper part of the body out of the water. Going a little nearer, to see who was bathing in so unusual a place, it seemed to him like a person sitting in a tub. Going nearer still, he found it to resemble a youth of sixteen or eighteen years of age, with a very white skin. The continuation of the body below the water, seemed to be a brownish substance, ending with a tail, which seemed capable of waving to and fro. The form of its body and arms was entirely human; but its arms and hands seemed rather thick and short in proportion to its body. The form of the head and all the features of the face were human also; but the nose rose high between the eyes, was pretty long, and seemed to terminate very sharp. Some peculiarities about the neck and back are then noticed, as also its way of washing its body. 'It looked attentively at him and at the cliffs, and seemed to take great notice of the birds flying over its head. Its looks were wild and fierce; but it made no noise, or did it grin, or in any way distort its face. When he left it, it was about a hundred yards from him; and when he returned with some others to look at it, it was gone.' We hear nothing further of this merman or merboy; but on looking at the roundabout evidence of the story, we find it to be thus—A paper containing the account was lent to Mrs. Morgan; the paper had been written by a young lady, pupil of Mrs. Moore, from an oral account given to her by that lady; Mrs. Moore had heard it from Dr. George Phillips; and he had heard it from Henry Reynolds himself from all of which statements we may infer that there were abundant means for converting some peculiar kind of fish into a merman without imputing intentional dishonesty to any one.

THE MERMAID.

Something akin to this kind of evidence is observable in the account of a mermaid seen in Caithness in 1809, the account of which attracted much attention in England as well as in Scotland, and induced the Philosophical Society of Glasgow to investigate the matter. The editor of a newspaper who inserted the statement had been told by a gentleman, who had been shown a letter by Sir John Sinclair, who had obtained it from Mrs. Innes, to whom it had been written by Miss Mackay, who had heard the story from the persons (two servant girls and a boy) who had seen the strange animal in the water.

So it is with all these stories of mermaids when investigated. There is always a fish at the bottom of it—either a living fish of peculiar kind, which an ignorant person thinks bears some resemblance to a human being; or a fish which becomes marvellous in the progress of its description from mouth to mouth; or a dead fish's skin manufactured into something that may accord with the popular notions regarding these beings. Mr. George Cruikshank, in 1822, made a drawing of a mermaid, which was exhibited in St. James's Street, and afterwards at Bartholomew Fair; it drew crowds by its ugliness, and showed what wretched things will suffice to gull the public—although, of course, *outside* the booth at the fair there was a picture of the orthodox mermaid, with beautiful features and hair, comb in one hand, mirror in the other, and so forth. This was probably the identical mermaid, respecting which the lord chancellor was called upon to adjudicate, towards the close of November 1822. There was a disputed ownership, and his lordship expressed his satisfaction that he was not called upon to decide whether the animal was man, woman, or mermaid, but only to say to whom it rightfully belonged.

Source:

Chambers, Robert, editor. *The Book of Days: A Miscellany of Popular Antiquities.* Vol. 2. Philadelphia: J. B. Lippincott & Co., 1879. pp. 612-613.

5. Mermaid Balladry from *Old Ballad Folk-Lore* by James Napier

THERE was a very old and wide-spread belief that there existed men and women who lived in the water. They were called mermen and mermaids, but from the varying descriptions given of these creatures in different ages and localities it is evident that imagination had a pretty free field, and was cultivated according to the fancy of those who described them. The following is from the song of the Niebelungen of the eleventh century:

"And when he saw the mermaids, he sped him silently;
But soon they heard his footseps, and quickly did they hie,
Glad and joyfull in their hearts, that they 'scaped the hero's arm:
From the ground he took their garments, did them none other harm.
Up then spake a mermaid, Hilburg was she hight,

Noble Hero Haghan, your fate will I reed aright,
At King Etzels' Court what adventures ye shall have,
If back thou give our garments, thou champion bold and brave.
Like birds they flew before him upon the watery flood,
And as they flew the mermaid's form thought him so fair and good,
That he believed full well what of his fate she spoke;
But for the hero's boldness she thought to be awroke."

Here we have the mermaids described as wearing garments, but for the time they had laid them aside upon the shore as young maidens did while bathing. Here also they fly naked over the surface of the water as do sea-fowls, and are endowed with power to tell fortunes. In another ballad called "Lady Grimild's Wrack," the hero, who is called Hogen, while walking along the sea-shore, came upon a mermaid sleeping and asked her to tell his fortune:

"It was the hero Hogen he dauner'd on the strand,
And there he found the mer-lady sleeping on the white sand;
Heal, heal to thee dear merlady thou art a cunning wife;
And I come to Hvenild's Land, it's may I brook my life?"

Her answer not satisfying the hero he was angry:

"'Twas then the hero Hogen his swerd swyth he drew,
And from the luckless mer-lady her head aff he hew.
Sae he has taken the bloody head, and cast it i' the sound,
The body's croppen after, and joined it at the ground."

In another ballad, called "Rosmer Hafmand," we find a merman much resembling, in character at least, the dwarf or elf-kings of other ballads. This merman gets possession of a betrothed maiden whom he loves and carries to his abode. Her human lover discovers her place of imprisonment and succeeds in getting to her. She, however, fearing that the merman will kill her lover, concocts a story wherewith to deceive her captor, and tells him that a near relative of hers has come to see her and bespeaks protection for him; the merman grants her request. The lovers then contrive a plan for escaping, and the merman is informed that her relation is prepared to return home. The merman engages to carry him across the water, together with a kist of luggage, the lady's gift to her relative. She herself goes into the kist:

"He took the man under his arm; the kist on his back took he;
Sae he can under the saut-sea gang, sae canny and sae free.
Now I hae born thee till the land thou seest baith sun and moon:
And I gae thee this kist o' goud, that is nae churlis boon."

When he returned to his abode and found the maiden gone:

"Now Rosmer waxt sae wroth and grim, when he nae Eline fand,
He turn'd into a whinstone gray, sic like he there does stand."

This ballad contains a vast amount of ancient notions concerning mermen and mermaids. But as we come nearer modern times we find great changes have taken place in this particular form of superstition. These changes were without doubt due to the commingling of eastern and northern streams of fable, which joined their currents at an early date, but did not coalesce into a homogeneous flood until a much later date. We must also remember, as I have already said, that Christianity acted as a controlling agent, rejecting what was discordant to its preconceptions, and introducing new material of its own, the product of a development differing considerably from the early forms, although the superstitions were about equal in quantity. In the later form mermen and mermaids have become prognosticated of evil, either of weather or to some persons, and when they speak, which they had the gift of doing in any language, it is always to predict evil or decoy some ill-fated individual to their destruction. This is illustrated in several ballads. Take the following, intitled "The Master of Weemys," by Motherwell, from *Minstrelsey Ancient and Modern*:

"They have hoisted sayle and left the land,
    They have saylit milis three,
When up their lap the bonnie mermayd,
    All in the norland sea.
'O whare saile ye,' quo the bonnie mermayd,
    Upon the saut sea faem,
It's we are bounde until norroway,
    God send us scaithless hame.
Down doukit then the mermayden,
    Deep intil the middil sea,
And merry leuch that master bauld
    With his jolly companie;
When lo' uplap shee the gude ships side
    The self same mermayden,
Shee hild a glass intil her richt hande,
    In the other shee held a kame,
And shee kembit her haire and aye shee sang
    As shee festerit on the faem,
And shee gliskit about and round about
    Upon the waters wan.
O nevir again on land or sea
    Shall be seen suk a fair woman.
And shee shed the haire off her milk white bree

> Wi' her fingers sae sma' and lang,
>   Sae louder was aye her sang.
> And aye shoo sang and aye shee sang,
>   As shee rade upon the sea,
> If ye bee men of christian moulde
>   Throwe the master out to mee.
> It's never a word spake the master baulde,
>   But a loud laugh leuch the crewe,
> And in the deep then the mermayden
>   Down drappit frae their viewe.
> Good Lord! there is a scaud o' fire
>   Fast coming out owre the sea,
> And fast therein that grim mermayden
>   Is sayling on to thee.
> Shee hailes the ship wi a shrill shrill cry,
>   Shee is coming alace more near,
> An woe is me now said the master baulde
>   For I baith do see and hear."

In a song entitled "The Mermaid," from *Legendary Ballads of England and Scotland*, the mermaid is identified with the Water Kelpie and the Elf. She decoys a knight to his destruction:

> "To yon fause stream, that, near the sea,
> Hides many an elf and plum,
> And rives wi fearful din the stanes,
> A witless knicht did come.
> Frae neath a rock, sune, sune she raise,
> And stately on she swam;
> Stopped i' the midst, and becked and sang
> To him to stretch his han'.
> The smile upon her bonnie cheek
> Was sweeter than the bee,
> Her voice excelled the burdies sang
> Upon the birchen tree.
> Sac couthie, couthie did she look,
> And meikle had she fleeched.
> Out shot his hand. Alas! alas!
> Fast in the swirl he screeched.
> The mermaid leuch, her brief was gane,
> And Kilpie's blast was blawin.
> Fu' low she duked, ne'er raise again,
> For deep deep was the fawin.
> Aboon the stream his wraith was seen,
> Warlocks tirled lang at gloamin,
> That e'en was coarse, the blast blew hoarse,

Ere lang the waves war foamin."

The following is an account of one that was caught in a net in a pool of the sea in Galloway, and her purpose is evident.[1] We have here more of the elf or the supernatural power of the dwarfs and witches:

"He spread his broad net, where 'tis said in the brine
The mermaidens sport mid the merry moonshine,
He drew it and laugh'd, for he found 'mongst the meshes
A fish and a maiden, with silken eye-lashes;
And she sang with a voice, like May Morley's of Larg,
'A maid and a salmon for young Sandy Harg.'
O white were her arms, and far whiter her neck,
Her long locks in armfuls oerflowed all the deck,
One hand on the rudder she pleasantly laid,
Another on Sandy, she merrily said:
'Thy halve net has wrought thee a gallant days darg,
Thou'rt monarch of Solway, my young Sandy Harg.'
O loud laugh'd young Sandy, and swore by the mass,
I'll never reign king but 'mid gowans and grass;
Oh loud laugh'd young Sandy and swore ' By thy hand,
My May Morley, I'm thine both by water and land:
Twere marvel if mer-woman slimy and slarg,
Could change the true love of young Sandy Harg;'
She knotted one ringlet, syne knotted she twain,
And sang—lo! thick darkness dropp'd down on the main—
She knotted three ringlets, syne knotted she nine,
A tempest stoop'd sudden and sharp on the brine.
And away flew the boat—there's a damsel in Larg
Will wonder what's came of thee, young Sandy Harg.
'The sky's spitting fire,' cried Sandy, 'and see,
Green Criffel reels round and will chocke up the sea,
From their bottles of tempest the fiends draw the corks,
Wild Solway is barmy like ale when it works,
There sits Satan's daughter who works the dread darg
To mar my blythe bridal,' quoth young Sandy Harg.
From his bosom a spell to work wonders he took,
Thrice kiss'd it and smiled, then triumphantly shook
The boat by the rudder, the maid by the hair;
With wailing and shrieks she bewildered the air;
He flung her far seaward, then sailed off to Larg,
There was mirth at the bridal of young Sandy Harg."

---

[1] *Historical and Traditional Tales connected with the South of Scotland.*

Many are the curious details existing in books and coming down to us by tradition of mermaids being seen, of their appearance, and the evil results which attended their appearance. In an Aberdeen almanac for 1488 there occurs the curious statement:

"Near the place where the Dee payeth its tribute to the German Ocean, *if curious observers of wonderful things in nature* will be pleased thither to resort on the 1st, 13th, and 29th of May, and in divers other times in the insueing summer; as also in the harvest time to the 7th and 14th of October *they will undoubtedly see a pretty company of mermaids*, creatures of admirable beauty, and likewise hear their charming sweet melodious voices:

"In well traced measure and harmonious lays
Extol their maker and his bounty praise,
That godly honest men in every thing
In quiet peace may live. God save the King."

Source:
Napier, James. "Old Ballad Folk-Lore." *The Folk-Lore Record.* Vol. 2 (1879). pp. 92-126.

6. Mermaids and Mermen from *Credulities Past and Present* by William Jones

THE superstitious belief in mermaids and mermen was universal, and dates from the earliest periods. In the excavations of Khorsabad, Botta found a figure of Oannes, a creature half man and half fish, identical with Dagon, who came out of that part of the Erythraeum sea, which borders upon Babylon. At Nimroud, a gigantic image was found by Layard, representing a fish's head as a cap, and the body of the fish depending over his shoulders, his legs those of a man; a richly decorated bag was in his left hand. On the coins of Ascalon is figured a goddess, above whose head is a half-moon, and at her feet a woman, with her lower extremities like a fish.

The tritons and the syrens are represented as half fish and half human. Originally, the syrens were winged, but after the fable had been accepted, which told of their strife with the Muses, and their precipitation into the sea, they were figured like mermaids.[1] It is curious how the prevalence of tales of mermaids exists among Celtic populations, indicating these water-nymphs as having been originally deities of those people. The Peruvians had, also, their semi-fish gods. The North American Indians relate, that they were conducted from Northern Asia by a man-fish. In the "Speculum Regali," an Icelandic work of the twelfth century, is the following description of a mermaid: "A monster is seen also near Greenland, which people call the Margyzr. This creature appears like a woman as far down as her waist, with breasts and bosom like a woman, long hands and soft hair; the neck and head in all respects like a human being. The hands seem to people to be long, and the fingers not to be parted, but united by a web like that on the feet of water birds. From the waist downwards, this monster resembles a fish with scales, tail, and fin. This prodigy is supposed to show itself more especially before heavy storms. The habit of this creature is to dive frequently, and rise again to the surface with fish in its hands. When sailors see it playing with the fish, or throwing them towards the ship, they fear they are doomed to lose several of the crew; but when it casts the fish, or turning from the vessel, flings them away from her, then the sailors take it as a good omen, that they will not suffer loss in the impending storm. The monster has a very horrible face, with broad brow and piercing eyes, a wide mouth and double chin."

The "Landnama," or Icelandic Doomsday Book, tells of a Marmennil, or merman, having been caught off the island of Grimsey, and the annals of the same country relate the appearance of these creatures off the coast in 1305, and 1329.

Megasthenes reported that the sea which washed Taprobana, the modern Ceylon, was inhabited by monsters having the appearance of a woman, and Ælian improved this account by stating that there were whales having the appearance of satyrs!

In 1187, a merman was stated to have been taken off the coast of Suffolk. It closely resembled a man, but was not gifted with speech. One day when it had the opportunity to escape, if fled to the sea, plunged in, and was never afterwards seen. Pontoppidan, in his "Natural History of

---

[1] In "The Eastern Travels of John of Hesse" (1389), amongst the perils of voyage we read: "We came to a smoky and stony mountain, where we heard Syrens singing, proprié meermaids, who draw ships into danger by their songs. We saw there many horrible monsters, and were in great fear."

As the ancient navigators pretended to have seen syrens, and poets sung of them, so, in later times, seamen declared they had beheld a fish, the head of which was crowned with a mitre, and the shoulders covered with a rich dalmatica. All believed in the bishop-fish, and a learned Jesuit wrote a book to attest its existence.

Norway," records the appearance of a merman, which was deposed to on oath by the observers. About a mile from the coast of Denmark, near Landscrona, three sailors observed something floating, like a dead body, in the water, and they rowed towards it. When they came within seven or eight fathoms, it still appeared as at first, for it had not stirred, but at that instant it sunk, and came up almost immediately in the same place. Upon this, out of fear, they lay still, and then let the boat float, so that they might better examine the monster, which, by the help of the current, came nearer and nearer to them. The creature turned its face, and stared at them, which gave them an opportunity of examining it narrowly. It stood in the same place for seven or eight minutes, and was seen in the water above breast-high. At last they grew apprehensive of some danger, and began to retire, upon which the monster blew out its cheeks, and made a kind of lowing noise, diving from their view. In regard to its form, it appeared like an old man, strong-limbed, with broad shoulders, but its arms they could not see. The head was small in proportion to the body, and it had short curled black hair, which did not reach below the ears; the eyes were deep in the head, and it had a meagre face, with a black beard, about the body downwards; this merman was quite pointed like a fish.

Old Hudson, the navigator, relates: "This morning, one of our company looking overboard, saw a mermaid, and calling up some of the company to see her, one more came up, and by that time she was come close to the ship's side, looking earnestly at the men. A little after, a sea came and overturned her. From the navel up, her back and breasts were like a woman's, as they say that saw her; her body as big as one of us; her skin very white, and long hair hanging down behind, of colour black. In her going down they saw her tail, which was like that of a porpoise, speckled like a mackerel."

The inhabitants of the Shetland Islands had a belief that these supernatural beings possess a sealskin, which serves them as a charm, and permits them to live in the depths of the ocean; had they not this talisman they would lose their amphibious qualities. A story is told of a man belonging to Unst, who, one day walking along the sands, saw a group of these singular beings dancing in the moonlight, and a considerable number of the sealskins lying near them on the shore. Each went to pick up its own, and the whole band of mermen and mermaids disappeared like magic in the sea; but the Shetlander noticed one of the skins at his feet, seized it, and hid it securely. On his return he found on the beach the loveliest maiden that mortal eyes had ever seen; she was bemoaning with many tears the theft which compelled her to remain an exile on land. In vain did she implore the restitution of her talisman, for the man was mad with love, and inexorable, offering, however, his protection, and a shelter beneath his roof as his wife. The mermaid, seeing there was no alternative but to accept, married him. This singular alliance lasted a few years, and some children were born, who had no other peculiarity of appearance, except that the fingers were slightly flattened. The wife, however, showed great coldness to her husband, and when occasion permitted, she wandered on the beach, and at a given signal some one appeared in the sea, with whom she kept up a restless conversation in an unknown tongue. One day it happened that one of her children accidentally found a sealskin hidden under a mill-wheel, and ran to show it to the mother. The latter started; her joy was only troubled when she looked at the boy, whom she was about to leave for ever. She kissed him, and ran at full speed across the sands. At this moment the husband returned home, and learned that the sealskin had been found, and ran to stop his wife; but he arrived only to see her transformation in the shape of a seal, and diving from a projecting rock into the sea.

In all the northern countries stories relating to mermen and mermaids are singularly prolific. One common in Sweden tells how one night as some fishermen from the farm of Kennare slept in their wooden huts, the door opened gently, and those who were awakened saw a woman's hand, nothing more. This was related to their friends the next day, when a reckless young fellow exclaimed: "Why did you not lay hold of it? I'll watch this evening myself." He did so, and when the hand appeared he seized it, but was drawn through the door and disappeared. Years afterwards his wife re-married. The young man now turned up again, and related how the hand of the mermaid (for such was the owner of it) had drawn him into the sea, and how he had lived with her under the water ever since, until one day she said: "To-night they dance at Kennare." Then he thought to himself that his wife must be re-married, and the mermaid telling him it was so, added: "Go and see your wife in her bridal wreath, but enter not beneath the roof." He went ashore, and stood some time looking at the festival, but could resist no longer, and entered. That night the roof of the farm buildings was carried off, and three days afterwards the fisherman died.

In the "History of the Netherlands" there is the following strange account of the sea-woman of Haarlem:

"At that time there was a great tempest at sea, with exceeding high tides, the which did drowne many villages in Friseland and Holland; by which tempest there came a sea-woman swimming in the Zuyderzee betwixt the towns of Campen and Edam, the which passing by the Purmeric, entered into the straight of a broken dyke in the Purmermer, where she remained a long time, and could not find the hole by which she entered, for that the breach had been stopped after that the tempest had ceased. Some country women and their servants, who did dayly pass the Pourmery, to milk their kine in the next pastures, did often see this woman swimming on the water, whereof at the first they were much afraid; but in the end being accustomed to see it very often, they viewed it neerer, and at last they resolved to take it if they could. Having discovered it they rowed towards it, and drew it out of the water by force, carrying it in one of their barkes unto the towne of Edam. When she had been well washed and cleansed from the sea-moss which was grown about her, she was like unto another woman; she was appareled, and began to accustome herself to ordinary meats like unto any other, yet she sought still means to escape, and to get into the water, but she was straightly guarded. They came from farre to see her. Those of Harlem made great sute to them of Edam to have this woman by reason of the strangenesse thereof. In the end they obtained her, where she did learn to spin, and lived many years (some say fifteen), and for the reverance which she bare unto the signe of the crosse whereunto she had beene accustomed, she was buried in the church-yarde. Many persons worthy of credit have justified in their writings that they had seene her in the said towne of Harlem."

On the western coast of Ireland, at certain rare conjunctions of wind and tide, there occurs what is called a "bore." The fishermen being totally ignorant of its actual cause, for it takes place in but one bay, and at remote intervals, called it an "avenging wave," and gave a terrible description of its rushing along crested with lightnings. Their account of its origin is this. A man of the name of Shea, a fisherman, once killed a mermaid, though she begged hard for mercy. The very next time that he sailed on the bay, the waves appeared in all their terrors. Struck by a guilty conscience he fled towards land; but the incredible speed of the "avenger" could not be baffled, he was overtaken, and not only he, but all in his boat perished. The punishment did not end there. Even to a later period the appearance of any of his direct descendants roused the same wave or "bore." Its desire of vengeance, or its power, somewhat diminished afterwards, for if the fishermen perceived it in time, and crossed the bar, they were secure.

In the Icelandic chronicles it is stated that there were seen in the sea of Greenland three sea-monsters of enormous size. The first, which some Norwegians saw from the waist upwards out of the water, was like a man about the neck, head, face, nose, and mouth, with the exception of the head being very much elevated and pointed towards the top. Its shoulders were broad, and at their extremity were two stumps of arms without hands. The body was slender below, and its look was chilling. There were heavy storms each time the monster appeared above the water. The second monster was formed down to the waist like a woman; it had large breasts, disheveled hair, and huge hands at the ends of the stumps of the arms, with long fingers, webbed like the feet of a duck. It was seen holding fish in its hand, and eating them. This phantom always preceded some storm. If it plunges in the water with its face towards the sailors, it is a sign they will not be shipwrecked; but if it turns its back to them, they are lost. The third monster had three large heads.

Scoresby, in his account of the Arctic Regions, says that when seen at a distance, the front part of the head of a young walrus without tusks is not unlike a human face. As this animal is in the habit of rearing its head above water to look at ships and other passing objects, it is not at all improbable that it may have afforded some foundation for the stories of mermaids. "I have myself," he remarks, "seen a sea-horse in such a position, and under such circumstances, that it required very little stretch of imagination to mistake it for a human being; so like indeed was it, that the surgeon of the ship actually reported to me his having seen a man with his head just appearing above the water."

Columbus in his "Journal" relates having seen three mermaids, which elevated themselves above the surface of the sea, and he adds that he had before seen such on the coast of Africa. They were by no means the beautiful beings that are generally represented, although they had some traces of the human countenance. It is supposed that these must have been manati, or sea-calves, seen indistinctly or at a distance, and that the imagination of Columbus, disposed to give a wonderful character to everything in this New World, had identified these misshapen animals with the syrens of ancient story.

The Russian popular mythology has, of course, its Vodyany, or water-sprite. "Here," remarks Mr. Ralston in his interesting work on the "Songs of the Russian Peasants," "is one of the stories about a mixed marriage beneath the waves. Except at the end, it is very like that which forms the groundwork of Mr. Matthew Arnold's exquisite romaunt of the 'Forsaken Merman.' "Once upon a time a girl was drowned, and she lived for many years after that with a water-sprite. But one fine day she swam to the shore, and saw the red sun and the green woods and fields, and heard the humming of insects and the distant sound of church-bells. Then a longing after her old life on earth came over her, and she could not resist the temptation. So she came out from the water, and went to her native village. But there, neither her relatives nor friends recognised her. Sadly did she return in the evening to the water-side, and passed once more to the power of the water-sprite. Two days later, her mutilated corse floated on the sands." When a water-sprite appears in a village, it is easy to recognise him; for water is always dripping from his left skirt, and the spot on which he sits becomes instantly wet. In his own realm he not only rules over all the fishes that swim, but he greatly influences the lot of fishers and mariners. Sometimes he brings them good-luck—sometimes he lures them to destruction. Sometimes he gets caught in nets; but he immediately tears them asunder, and all the fish that had been inclosed with him, swim after him.

In Bohemia, fishermen are afraid of assisting a drowning man, thinking the water-sprite will be offended, and will drive away the fish from their nets; and they say he often sits on the shore with a club in his hand, from which hang ribbons of various hues: with these he allures children, and those he gets hold of he drowns. The souls of his victims he keeps, making them his servants, but their bodies he allows to float to shore. Sometimes he changes himself into a fish, generally a pike. Sometimes, also, he is represented like the Western merman, with a fish's tail. In the Ukraine there is a tradition that, when the sea is rough, such half-fishy "marine people" appear on the surface of the water and sing songs. In other places they are called "Pharaohs," being supposed, like the seals in Iceland, to be the remains of that host of Pharaoh which perished in the Red Sea.

The tradition of the Russian peasants speak of the Tsar Moskoi, the Marine or Water-King, who dwells in the depths of the sea, or the lake, or the pool, and who rules over the subaqueous world. To this Slavonic Neptune a family of daughters is frequently attributed, maidens of exceeding beauty, who, when they don their feather dresses, become the Swan Maidens who figure in the popular legends of so many nations.

The following ballad of "Duke Magnus and the Mermaid," is from Smaland. Magnus was the youngest son of Gustavus Vasa. He died out of his mind. It is well known that insanity pervaded the Vasa family for centuries:

"Duke Magnus looked out from the castle window,
How the stream ran so rapidly;
And there he saw how upon the stream sat
A woman most fair and lovely.
    Duke Magnus, Duke Magnus, plight thee to me,
    I pray you still so freely;
    Say me not nay, but yes! yes!

"O, to you I will give a travelling ship,
The best that a knight would guide;
It goeth as well on water as on fair land,
And through the fields all so wide.
    Duke Magnus, etc.

"O, to you I will give a courser grey,
The best that a knight would ride;
He goeth as well on water as firm land,
And through the groves all so wide.
    Duke Magnus, etc.

"O, how shall I plight me to you?
I never any quiet get;
I serve the king and my native land,
But with woman I match me not yet.
    Duke Magnus, etc.

"To you I will give as much of gold
As far more than your life will endure;
And of pearls and precious stones handfuls,
And all shall be so pure.
    Duke Magnus, etc.

"O, gladly would I plight me to thee,
If thou wert of Christian kind;
But now thou art a vile sea-troll,
My love thou canst never win.
    Duke Magnus, etc.

"Duke Magnus, Duke Magnus, bethink thee well,
And answer not so haughtily;
For if thou wilt not plight me to thee,
Thou shalt ever crazy be.
    Duke Magnus, etc.

"I am a king's son so good,
How can I let you gain me?
You dwell not on land but in the flood,
Which would not with me agree.
    Duke Magnus, etc."

In one of the metrical romances of the Russians, the following story is told of a Novgorod trader, named Sadko: Once in a fit of dreariness, due to his being so poor that he had no possessions besides the gusli, on which he performed at festivals, he went down to the shore of Lake Ilmen, and there began to play. Presently the waters of the lake were troubled, and the Tsar Moskoi appeared, who thanked him for his music, and promised a rich reward. Thereupon Sadko flung a net into the lake, and drew a great treasure to land. Another of the poems tells how the same Sadko, after he had become a wealthy merchant, was sailing over the blue sea. Presently his ship stopped, and nothing would make it move on. Lots were cast to find out whose guilt was the cause of this delay, and they fixed the blame on Sadko. Then he confessed that he had now been sailing to and fro for twelve years, but had not remembered to pay fitting tribute to the King of the Waters—to offer bread and salt to the blue Caspian. Thereupon the sailors flung him overboard, and immediately the ship proceeded on its way. Sadko sank to the bottom of the sea, and there found a dwelling entirely made of wood. Inside lay the Tsar Moskoi, who said he had been expecting Sadko for twelve years, and told him to begin playing. Sadko obeyed and charmed the Tsar, who began to dance. Then the blue sea was troubled, the swift rivers overflowed, and many ships with their freight were submerged. The Ocean King was so pleased with the music that he offered the hand of any one of his thirty daughters to the musician, who married the nymph Volkhof; that being the name of the river which runs past Novgorod.

    Among the Indian tribes of Guiana, there is an important being in their mythology called the Orehu, a mysterious female inhabiting the waters. Though not decidedly malignant, she is very capricious, and consequently dreaded. Her supposed form agrees with that of the ordinary mermaid, but she sometimes presents herself above the water, with the head of a horse or other animal, as may suit her fancy or the object she has in view. She often amuses herself with terrifying mankind; but sometimes bears canoe and people to the bottom. There was a spot on the banks of the Pomeroon where the earth, being undermined by the current, had sunk, and the trees which formerly nourished there stood out of the water withered and bare, presenting a desolate appearance. That was supposed to be a favourite resort of the Orehu. Many, especially of the Warans, an Indian tribe, if compelled to pass the spot by night, would keep close to the opposite bank and glide with noiseless paddles past the place where the water-sprite was believed to have fixed her abode. The superstitious belief concerning this being prevailed also among the black people dwelling on the rivers of Guiana. One of the Obia dances of the blacks is commonly called the water-mama dance, from the appellation usually given by them to their adopted patroness, the Orehu of the Indians.

The occasional appearance above the surface of the waters of the Manati, or Water-Cow, is supposed to have given rise to this superstition in former days. But, however that may be, the Indians have for ages drawn a wide distinction between the "Orehu" and the "Koiamoora," or Manati, believing them to differ in nature as in name. The Orehu, according to their notions, may assume the figure of the Manati, as of any other animal, but the latter does not, in their belief, possess any supernatural power, and is eaten when captured.

Fairies, water-spirits, and kelpies had a share in bewildering the feeble minds of sailors in olden times. In Perthshire every lake had its kelpie, or water-horse, often seen dashing along the surface of the water. This malignant genius was supposed to allure women and children to his subaqueous haunts, there to be immediately devoured. He would also swell the torrent beyond its usual limits to overwhelm the hapless traveller.

The fishermen of Dieppe had a tradition that the fairies, at a certain season of the year, held a bazaar on the cliffs overhanging the sea, where articles of unequalled rarity and beauty were offered for sale. The passing fisherman on these occasions was accosted by these strange beings, who employed every art of fascination to draw his attention to their wares. If he had sufficient firmness to avert his gaze from the brilliant spectacle, he escaped uninjured; but if he yielded to the delusion, or listened to the delicious music that swelled around, all self-control was lost, and pursuing the glittering bait, which receded before him, he was drawn to the edge of the precipice, and hurled into the waves beneath.

I have ventured a ballad on this subject:

> 'Twas the eve of the bridal of Claude Deloraine,
> The boldest of fishers who travers'd the main,
> With the heart and the brow that had won him the hand

Of a maiden, the fairest and best in the land.

Still was the hour—the stars shone above,
As Claude bounded homeward, his thoughts full of love,
With a song on his lips, and a step light and free
As the waves that had rock'd him that day on the sea.

On, onward, he went; but it seem'd to his gaze
That the falaise grew longer; perchance 'twas the haze;
When, sudden, there gleam'd on his pathway a light,
That eclips'd the full moon in the glory of night.

And there rose in the midst, with a speed like the wind,
A mart of rich splendour, unmatch'd of its kind,
All the marvels of Stamboul in vain could compare
With the treasures of art that lay clustering there.

But bright though the jewels, how lovelier far
Shone the eyes of the elves—each the ray of a star,
As playful, and graceful, the gay creatures came
To the side of poor Claude, and breath'd softly his name.

"Come hither, young fisher, and buy from our store;
We have pearls from the deep, and earth's costliest ore:
Thy bride is awaiting some gift from thee now,
Take a chaplet of pearls to encircle her brow."

Soft fell the voice on the calm summer's even,
The herald of strains that seem'd wafted from heaven;
So thrilling, the heart of the sailor gave way,
And he look'd, with charm'd eyes, on the fairies' array!

"Ho! ho!" cried the elves, as the bridegroom drew near,
"The willows look greener when wet with a tear;
There's a boat on the wave, but no helmsman to guide,
There's an arm on the cold beach, but pulseless its pride!"

As the lights mov'd before him, Claude hasten'd along;
He marked not his footsteps; he heard but the song:
One moment—it ceas'd—'midst the silence of death
The sailor was hurl'd in the breakers beneath!

A droll legend of a fisherman and the piskies, or little people, how, with true Cornish keenness, he over-reached the fairies, is related by Mr. Couch, of Penzance. It seems that John Taprail, long since dead, moored his boat one evening beside a barge of much larger size, in which his neighbour John Rendle traded between Cornwall and Plymouth; and as the wind, though gusty, was not sufficient to cause any apprehension, he went to bed and slept soundly. In the middle of the night he was woke by a voice from without bidding him get up and "shift his rope over Rendle's," as his boat was in considerable danger. Now, as all Taprail's capital was invested in his boat and gear, we may be sure that he was not long in putting on his sea-clothes and going to its rescue. To his great chagrin he found that a joke had been played upon him, for the boat and barge were both riding quietly, at their rope. On his way back again, when within a few yards of his home, he observed a crowd of the little people congregated under the shelter of a boat that was lying high and dry upon the beach. They were sitting in a semicircle, holding their hats to one of their number, who was engaged in distributing a heap of money, pitching a gold piece into the hat of each in succession, after the manner in which cards are dealt. Now, John had a covetous heart, and the sight of so much cash made him forget the respect due to an assembly of piskies, and that they are not slow to punish any intrusion on their privacy; so he crept slily towards them, hidden by the boat, and reaching round, managed to introduce his hat without exciting any notice. When the heap was getting low, and Taprail was awaking to the dangers of detection, he craftily withdrew his hat, and made off with the prize. He had got a fair start before the trick was discovered, but the defrauded piskies were soon on his heels, and he barely managed to reach his house, and to close the door upon his pursuers. So narrow indeed was his escape that he had left the tails of his sea-coat in their hands.

Such is evidently the very imperfect version of an old legend as it is remembered by the Cornish fishermen of the present generation. We may suppose that John Taprail's door had a key-hole, and there would have been poetical justice in the story, if the elves had compelled the fraudulent fisherman to turn his hat, or his pocket, inside out.

The French sailors formerly dreaded the nocturnal visits of a goblin, a sort of mischievous Puck, who played his pranks on board while they slept: opened the knives in their pockets, singed their hair, tied up the cords that held the sails, drew up anchors in a calm, and tore in pieces the sails that had been carelessly tied by the sailors; in the latter case proving certainly a retributory monitor.

Sir George Grey, in his "Polynesian Mythology," observes that the New Zealanders learnt the art of netting mackerel from the fairies. It was a certain Kahakura, whose observation of the habits of his race was sufficiently acute to discover this device. Passing a place where some people had been cleaning mackerel, he remarked that the people who had been fishing must have been there in the night-time, and he said to himself, "These are no mortals who have been fishing here; spirits must have done this. Had they been men, some of the reeds and grass which they sit upon in their canoe would have been lying about." Keeping his own counsel, he returned to watch on the following night; and, sure enough there were the fairies, shouting out, "The net here—the net here!" and other encouraging cries. In the darkness, Kahakura managed to lend a hand in hauling in the nets; and in the collection and appropriation of the fish, availed himself of a crafty ruse to delay his companions from time to time, until the daylight broke. The fairies, when they saw that Kahakura was a man, dispersed in confusion, leaving their nets, the construction of which Kahakura could study at leisure. He thus taught his children to make nets, and by them the Maori race became acquainted with the art.

Source:
Jones, William. *Credulities Past and Present*. London: Chatto and Windus, 1880. pp 20-34.

7. The Mermaid from *Sea Fables Explained* by Henry Lee

NEXT to the pleasure which the earnest zoologist derives from study of the habits and structure of living animals, and his intelligent appreciation of their perfect adaptation to their modes of life, and the circumstances in which they are placed, is the interest he feels in eliminating fiction from truth, whilst comparing the fancies of the past with the facts of the present. As his knowledge increases, he learns that the descriptions by ancient writers of so-called "fabulous creatures" are rather distorted portraits than invented falsehoods, and that there is hardly one of the monsters of old which has not its prototype in Nature at the present day. The idea of the Lernean Hydra, whose heads grew again when cut off by Hercules, originated, as I have shown in another chapter, in a knowledge of the octopus; and in the form and movements of other animals with which we are now familiar we may, in like manner, recognise the similitude and archetype of the mermaid.

But we must search deeply into the history of mankind to discover the real source of a belief that has prevailed in almost all ages, and in all parts of the world, in the existence of a race of beings uniting the form of man with that of the fish. A rude resemblance between these creatures of imagination and tradition and certain aquatic animals is not sufficient to account for that belief. It probably had its origin in ancient mythologies, and in the sculptures and pictures connected with them, which were designed to represent certain attributes of the deities of various nations.

In the course of time the meaning of these was lost; and subsequent generations regarded as the portraits of existing beings effigies which were at first intended to be merely emblematic and symbolical.

Early idolatry consisted, first, in separating the idea of the One Divinity into that of his various attributes, and of inventing symbols and making images of each separately; secondly, in the worship of the sun, moon, stars, and planets, as living existences; thirdly, in the deification of ancestors and early kings; and these three forms were often mingled together in strange and tangled confusion.

Amongst the famous personages with whose history men were made acquainted by oral tradition was Noah. He was known as the second father of the human race, and the preserver and teacher of the arts and sciences as they existed before the Great Deluge, of which so many separate traditions exist among the various races of mankind. Consequently, he was an object of worship in many countries and under many names; and his wife and sons, as his assistants in the diffusion of knowledge, were sometimes associated with him.

FIG. I.—NOAH, HIS WIFE, AND THREE SONS, AS FISH-TAILED DEITIES.
From a Gem in the Florentine Gallery. After Calmet.

According to Berosus, of Babylon,—the Chaldean priest and astronomer, who extracted from the sacred books of "that great city" much interesting ancient lore, which he introduced into his 'History of Syria,' written, about B.C. 260, for the use of the Greeks,—at a time when men were sunk in barbarism, there came up from the Erythrean Sea (the Persian Gulf), and landed on the Babylonian shore, a creature named Oannes, which had the body and head of a fish. But above the fish's head was the head of a man, and below the tail of the fish were human feet. It had also human arms, a human voice, and human language. This strange monster sojourned among the rude people during the day, taking no food, but retiring to the sea at night; and it continued for some time thus to visit them, teaching them the arts of civilized life, and instructing them in science and religion.[1]

FIG. 2. — HEA, OR NOAH, THE GOD OF THE FLOOD. *Khorsabad.*

In this tale we have a distorted account of the life and occupation of Noah after his escape from the deluge which destroyed his home and drowned his neighbours. Oannes was one of the names under which he was worshipped in Chaldea, at Erech ("the place of the ark"), as the sacred and intelligent fish-god, the teacher of mankind, the god of science and knowledge. There he was also called Oes, Hoa, Ea, Ana, Anu, Aun, and Oan. Noah was worshipped, also, in Syria and Mesopotamia, and in Egypt, at "populous No,"[2] or Thebes—so named from "Theba," "the ark."

The history of the coffin of Osiris is another version of Noah's ark, and the period during which that Egyptian divinity is said to have been shut up in it, after it was set afloat upon the waters, was precisely the same as that during which Noah remained in the ark.

Dagon, also—sometimes called Odacon—the great fish-god of the Philistines and Babylonians, was another phase of Oannes. "Dag," in Hebrew, signifies "a male fish," and "Aun" and "Oan" were two of the names of Noah. "Dag-aun" or "Dagoan" therefore means "the fish Noah." He was portrayed in two ways. The more ancient image of him was that of a man issuing from a fish, as described of Oannes by Berosus; but in later times it was varied to that of a man whose upper half was human, and the lower parts those of a fish. The image of Dagon which fell upon its face to the ground before "the ark of the God of Israel," was probably of this latter form, for we read[3] that in its fall, "the head of Dagon and both the palms of his hands were cut off upon the

---

[1] Berosus, lib. i. p. 48.
[2] Nahum iii. 8.
[3] I Samuel v. 4.

threshold: only the stump (in the margin, "the fishy part") of Dagon was left to him. This was evidently Milton's conception of him:

"Dagon his name; sea-monster, upward man
And downward fish."[1]

In some of the Nineveh sculptures of the fish-god, the head of the fish forms a kind of mitre on the head of the man, whilst the body of the fish appears as a cloak or cape over his shoulders and back. The fish varies in length; in some cases the tail almost touches the ground; in others it reaches but little below the man's waist.

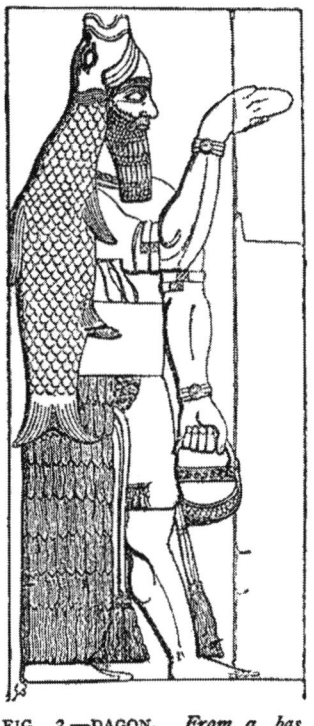

FIG. 3.—DAGON. *From a bas relief. Nimroud.*

FIG. 4.—DAGON. *After Calmet.*

In one of his "avatars," or incarnations, the god Vishnu "the Preserver," is represented as issuing from the mouth of a fish. He is celebrated as having miraculously preserved one righteous family, and, also, the Vedas, the sacred records, when the world was drowned. Not only is this legend of the Indian god wrought up with the history of

---

[1] 'Paradise Lost,' Book i. l. 462.

Noah, but Vishnu and Noah bear the same name—Vishnu being the Sanscrit form of "Ish-nuh," "the man Noah." The word "avatar" also means "out of the boat." In fact the whole mythology of Greece and Rome, as well as of Asia, is full of the history and deeds of Noah, which it is impossible to misunderstand. In all the representations of a deity having a combined human and piscine form, the original idea was that of

FIG. 5.—DAGON.
From an Agate Signet. Nineveh.

FIG. 6.—FISH AVATAR OF VISHNU.
After Calmet and Maurice.

a person coming out of a fish—not being part of one, but issuing from it, as Noah issued from the ark. In all of them the fish denoted "preservation," "fecundity," "plenty," and "diffusion of knowledge."[1] As the image was not the effigy of a divine personage, but symbolized

---

[1] Some writers are of the opinion that the legend of Oannes contains an allusion to the rising and setting of the sun, and that his semi-piscine form was the expression of the idea that half his time was spent above ground, and half below the waves. The same commentators also regard all the "civilizing" gods and goddesses as, respectively, solar and lunar deities. The attributes symbolized in the worship of Noah and the sun are so nearly alike that the two interpretations are not incompatible.

certain attributes of Divinity, its sex was comparatively unimportant, although it is possible that, combined with the fecundity of the fish, the idea of Noah's wife, as the second mother of all subsequent generations, according to the widely-spread and accepted traditions of the deluge, may have influenced the impersonation.

Atergatis, the far-famed goddess of the Syrians, was also a fish-divinity. Her image, like that of Dagon, had at first a fish's body with human extremities protruding from it; but in the course of centuries it was gradually altered to that of a being the upper portion of whose body was that of a woman and the lower half that of a fish. Gatis was a powerful queen of Sidon, and mother of Semiramis. She received the title of "Ater," or "Ader," "the Great," for the benefits she conferred on her people; one of these benefits being a strict conservation of their fisheries, both from their own imprudent use, and from foreign interference. She issued an edict that no fish should be eaten without her consent, and that no one should take fish in the neighbouring sea without a licence from herself. It is not improbable that she and her celebrated daughter, who is said by Ovid and others to have been the builder of the walls of Babylon, were worshipped together; for that Atergatis was the same as the fish-goddess Ashteroth, or Ashtoreth, "the builder of the encompassing wall," we have, amongst other proofs, a remarkable one in Biblical history. In the first book of Maccabees v. 43, 44, we read that "all the heathen being discomfited before him (Judas Maccabeus) cast away their weapons, and fled unto the temple that was at Carnaim. But they took the city, and burned the temple with all that were therein. Thus was Carnaim subdued, neither could they stand any longer before Judas." In the second book of Maccabees xii. 26, we are told that "Maccabeus marched forth to Carnion, and to the temple of Atargatis, and there he slew five and twenty thousand persons." In Genesis xiv. 5, this city and temple are referred to as "Ashteroth Karnaim."

Fig. 7 is a representation of Atergatis on a medal coined at Marseilles. It shows that when the Phoenecian colony from Syria, by whom that city was founded, settled there, they brought with them the worship of the gods of their country.

FIG. 7.—ATERGATIS.
From a Phœnician coin.

Atergatis was worshipped by the Greeks as Derceto and Astarte. Lucian writes:[1]—"In Phoenicia I saw the image of Derceto, a strange sight, truly! For she had the half of a woman, and from the thighs downwards a fish's tail." Diodorus Siculus describes (lib. ii.) the same deity, as represented at Ascalon, as "having the face of a woman, but all the rest of the body a fish's." And this very same image at Ascalon, which Diodorus calls Derceto, or Atergatis, is denominated by Herodotus[2] "the celestial Aphrodite," who was identical with the Cyprian and Roman Venus. Of all the sacred buildings erected to the goddess, this temple was by far the most ancient; and the Cyprians themselves acknowledged that their temple was built after the model of it by certain Phoenicians who came from that part of Syria.

FIG. 8.—VENUS RISING FROM THE SEA, SUPPORTED BY TRITONS.
After Calmet.

Thus the worship of Noah, as the second father of mankind, the repopulator of the earth, passed through various phases and transformations till it merged in that of Venus, who rose from the sea, and was regarded as the representative of the reproductive power of Nature—the goddess whom Lucretius thus addressed:

> "Blest Venus! Thou the sea and fruitful earth
> Peoplest amain; to thee whatever lives
> Its being owes, and that it sees the sun:"

---

[1] 'Opera Omnia,' tom. ii. p. 884, edit. Bened. de Dea Syr.
[2] Lib. i.cap. cv.

and to whom refers the passage in the Orphic hymn:

> "From thee are all things—all things thou producest
> Which are in heaven, or in the fertile earth,
> Or in the sea, or in the great abyss."

Under this latter phase—the impersonation of Venus—the fish portion of the body was discarded, and the cast-off form was allotted in popular credence to the Tritons—minor deities, who acknowledged the supremacy of the goddess, and were ready to render her homage and service by bearing her in their arms, drawing her chariot, etc., but who still possessed considerable power as sea-gods, and could calm the waves and rule the storm, at pleasure.

FIG. 9.   FIG. 10.

VENUS DRAWN IN HER CHARIOT BY TRITONS. *From two Corinthian coins.*

Figs. 9 and 10 are from two Corinthian medals, each shewing Venus in a car or chariot drawn by Tritons, one male, the other female. On the obverse of Fig. 9, is the head of Nero, and on that of Fig. 10, the head of his grandmother Agrippina.[1]

---

[1] It is worthy of note that the fish was also adopted as an emblem by the early Christians, and was frequently sculptured on their tombs as a private mark or sign of the faith in which the person there interred had died. It alluded to the letters which composed the Greek word ἰχθύς ("a fish") forming an anagram, the initials of words which conveyed the following sentiment: Ἰησούς, Jesus; Χριστός, Christ; Θεός, of God; Υἱός, Son; Σωτήρ, Saviour. But it doubtless bore, also, the older meaning of "preservation" and "reproduction," of which the fish was the symbol, and betokened a belief in a future resurrection, as Noah was preserved to dwell in, and populate, a new world. In 'Sea Monsters Unmasked,' page 55, I gave a figure, copied by permission from the Illustrated London News, of a rough sculpture in the Roman catacombs, of Jonah being disgorged by a sea-monster. Near to it was found, on another Christian tomb, one of these designs of the "fish;" and it is not a little curious that, whereas the animal depicted as casting forth Jonah is not a whale, but a

From the very earliest period of history, then, the conjoined human and fish form was known to every generation of men. It was presented to their sight in childhood by sculptures and pictures, and was a conspicuous object in their religious worship. By the lapse of time its original import was lost and debased; and, from being an emblem and symbol, it came to be accepted as the corporeal shape and structure of actually-existent sea deities, who might present themselves to the view of the mariner, in visible and tangible form, at any moment. Thus were men trained and prepared to believe in mermen and mermaids, to expect to meet with them at sea, and to recognise as one of them any animal the appearance and movements of which could possibly be brought into conformity with their pre-conceived ideas.

FIG. 11.—CHRISTIAN SYMBOL. *From the Catacombs at Rome.*

Accordingly, and very naturally, we find that from north to south this belief has been entertained. Megasthenes, who was a contemporary of Aristotle, but his junior, and whose geographical work was probably written at about the period of the great philosopher's death, reported that the sea which surrounded Taprobana, the ancient Ceylon, was inhabited by creatures having the appearance of women. Ælian stated that there were "whales," or "great fishes," having the form of satyrs. The early Portuguese settlers in India asserted that true mermen were found in the Eastern seas, and old Norse legends tell of submarine beings of conjoined human and piscine form, who dwell in a wide territory far below the region of the fishes, over which the sea, like the cloudy canopy of our sky, loftily rolls, and some of whom have, from time to time, landed on Scandinavian shores, exchanged their fishy extremities for human limbs, and acquired amphibious habits. Not only have poets sung of the wondrous and seductive beauty of the maidens of these aquatic tribes, but many a Jack tar has come home from sea prepared to affirm on oath that

---

sea-serpent, or dragon, the ichtheus in this instance is apparently not a fish, but a seal.

The article referred to appeared in the *Illustrated London News* of February 3rd, 1872, and the woodcut (fig. 11), an electrotype of which was most kindly presented to me by the proprietors of that paper, was one of the sketches that accompanied it.

he has seen a mermaid. To the best of his belief he has told the truth. He has seen some living being which looked wonderfully human, and his imagination, aided by an inherited superstition, has supplied the rest.

Before endeavouring to identify the object of his delusion, it may be well to mention a few instances of the supposed appearance of mermen and mermaidens in various localities.

Pliny writes:[1] "When Tiberius was emperor, an embassy was sent to him from Olysippo (Lisbon) expressly to inform him that a Triton, which was recognised as such by its form, had shown itself in a certain cave, and had been heard to produce loud sounds on a conch-shell. The Nereid, also, is not imaginary: its body is rough and covered with scales, but it has the appearance of a human being. For one was seen upon the same coast; and when it was dying those dwelling near at hand heard it moaning sadly for a long time. And the Governor of Gaul wrote to the divine Augustus that several Nereids had been found dead upon the shore. I have many informants—illustrious persons in high positions—who have assured me that they saw in the Sea of Cadiz a merman whose whole body was exactly like that of a man, that these mermen mount on board ships by night, and weigh down that end of the vessel on which they rest, and that if they are allowed to remain there long they will sink the ship."

Ælian in one of his short, jerky, disconnected chapters,[2] which rarely exceed a page in length, and some of which only contain two lines, writes: "It is reported that the great sea which surrounds the island of Taprobana (Ceylon) contains an immense multitude of fishes and whales, and some of them have the heads of lions, panthers, rams, and other animals; and (which is more wonderful still) some of the cetaceans have the form of satyrs. There are others which have the face of a woman, but prickles instead of hair. In addition to these, it is said there are other creatures of so strange and monstrous a kind that it would be impossible exactly to explain their appearance without the aid of a skilfully drawn picture: these have elongated and coiled tails, and, for feet, have claws[3] or fins. And I hear that in the same sea there are great amphibious beasts which are gregarious, and live on grain, and by night feed on the corn crops and grass, and are also very fond of the ripe fruit of the palms. To obtain these they encircle in their embrace the trees which are young and flexible, and, shaking them violently, enjoy the fruit which they thus cause to fall. When morning dawns they return to the sea, and plunge beneath the waves."

Ælian seems to have derived this information from Megasthenes,

---

[1] *Naturalis Historia*, Lib. ix. cap. v.
[2] *De Naturâ Animalium*, Lib. xvi. cap. xviii.
[3] "Forfices," literally "shears," or "nippers," like the claws of a lobster.

already referred to; but in another chapter,[1] he writes with greater certainty concerning these semi-human whales, and claims divine authority for his belief in the existence of tritons. "Although," he says, "we have no rational explanation nor absolute proof of that which fishermen are said to be able to affirm concerning the form of the tritons, we have the sworn testimony of many persons that there are in the sea cetaceans which from the head down to the middle of the body resemble the human species. Demostratus, in his works on fishing, says that an aged triton was seen near the town of Tanagra, in Boeotia, which was like the drawings and pictures of tritons, but its features were so obscured by age, and it disappeared so quickly, that its true character was not easily perceptible. But on the spot where it had rested on the shore were found some rough and very hard scales which had become detached from it. A certain senator—one of those selected by lot to carry on the administration of Achaia and the duties of the annual magistracy" (the mayor, in fact,) "being anxious to investigate the nature of this triton, put a portion of its skin on the fire. It gave out a most horrible odour; and those standing by were unable to decide whether it belonged to a terrestrial or marine animal. But the magistrate's curiosity had an evil ending, for very soon afterwards, whilst crossing a narrow creek in a boat, he fell overboard and was drowned; and the Tanagreans all regarded this as a judgment upon him for his crime of impiety towards the triton—an interpretation which was confirmed when his decomposing body was cast ashore, for it emitted exactly the same odour as had the burned skin of the triton. The Tanagreans and Demostratus explain whence the triton had strayed, and how it was stranded in this place. I believe," continues Ælian, "that tritons exist, and I reverentially produce as my witness a most veracious god—namely, Apollo Didymæus, whom no man in his senses would presume to regard as unworthy of credit. He sings thus of the triton, which he calls the sheep of the sea:

> 'Dum vocale maris monstrum natat œquore triton,
> Nepttini pecus, in funes forte incidit extra
> Demissos navim';"

which I venture to translate as follows:

> A triton, vocal monster of the deep,
> One of a flock of Neptune's scaly sheep,
> Was caught, whilst swimming o'er the watery plain,
> By lines which fishers from their boat had lain.

"Therefore," Ælian concludes, "if he, the omniscient god, pronounces

---

[1] Lib. xiii. cap. xxi.

that there are tritons, it does not behove us to doubt their existence."

Sir J. Emerson Tennent, in his 'Natural History of Ceylon,' quoting from the Histoire de la Compagnie de Jésus, mentions that the annalist of the exploits of the Jesuits in India gravely records that seven of these monsters, male and female, were captured at Manaar, in 1560, and carried to Goa, where they were dissected by Demas Bosquez, physician to the Viceroy, "and their internal structure found to be in all respects conformable to the human." He also quotes Valentyn, one of the Dutch colonial chaplains, who, in his account of the Natural History of Amboyna,[1] embodied in his great work on the Netherlands' possessions in India, published in 1727,[2] devoted the first section of his chapter on the fishes of that island to a minute description of the "Zee-Menschen," "Zee-Wyven," and mermaids, the existence of which he warmly insists on as being beyond cavil. He relates that in 1663, when a lieutenant in the Dutch service was leading a party of soldiers along the sea-shore in Amboyna, he and all his company saw the mermen swimming at a short

FIG. 12.—MERMAID AND FISHES OF AMBOYNA. *After Valentyn.*

distance from the beach. They had long and flowing hair of a colour between grey and green. Six weeks afterwards the creatures were again seen by him and more than fifty witnesses, at the same place, by clear daylight. "If any narrative in the world," adds Valentyn, "deserves credit it is this; since not only one, but two mermen together were seen by so many eye-witnesses. Should the stubborn world, however, hesitate to believe it, it matters nothing, as there are people who would even deny

---

[1] One of the Dutch spice-islands in the Banda Sea, between Celebes and Papua.
[2] *Beschrijving van Oud en Nieuw Oost-Indien*, etc., 5 vols, folio, Dordrecht and Amsterdam, 1727, vol. iii. p. 330.

that such cities as Rome, Constantinople, or Cairo, exist, merely because they themselves have not happened to see them. But what are such incredulous persons," he continues, "to make of the circumstance recorded by Albrecht Herport[1] in his account of India, that a merman was seen in the water near the church of Taquan on the morning of the 29th of April, 1661, and a mermaid at the same spot the same afternoon? Or what do they say to the fact that in 1714 a mermaid was not only seen but captured near the island of Booro, five feet, Rhineland measure, in height; which lived four days and seven hours, but, refusing all food, died without leaving any intelligible account of herself?" Valentyn, in support of his own faith in the mermaid, cites many other instances in which both "sea-men and seawomen" were seen and taken at Amboyna; especially one by a district visitor of the church, who presented it to the Governor Vanderstel. Of this "well-authenticated" specimen he gives an elaborate portrait amongst the fishes of the island,[2] with a minute description of each for the satisfaction of men of science.

The fame of this creature having reached Europe, the British minister in Holland wrote to Valentyn on the 28th of December, 1716, whilst the Emperor Peter the Great, of Russia, was his guest at Amsterdam, to communicate the desire of the Czar that the mermaid should be brought home from Amboyna for his inspection. To complete his proofs of the existence of mermen and merwomen, Valentyn points triumphantly to the historical fact that in Holland, in the year 1404, a mermaid was driven, during a tempest, through a breach in the dyke of Edam, and was taken alive in the lake of Purmer. Thence she was carried to Haarlem, where the Dutch women taught her to spin, and where several years after, she died in the Roman Catholic faith;—"but this," says the pious Calvinistic chaplain, "in no way militates against the truth of her story." The worthy minister citing the authority of various writers as proof that mermaids had in all ages been known in Gaul, Naples, Epirus, and the Morea, comes to the conclusion that as there are "sea-cows," "sea-horses," "sea-dogs," as well as "sea-trees," and "sea-flowers," which he himself had seen, there are no reasonable grounds for doubt that there may also be "sea-maidens "and "sea-men."

In an early account of Newfoundland,[3] Whitbourne describes a "maremaid or mareman," which he had seen "within the length of a pike," and which "came swimming swiftly towards him, looking cheerfully on his face, as it had been a woman. By the face, eyes, nose, mouth, chin, ears, neck and forehead, it appeared to be so beautiful, and

---

[1] *Itinerarium Indicum*, Berne, 1669.
[2] With the permission and assistance of Messrs. Longman, the accompanying wood-cut of this picture, and that of the Dugong are copied from Sir J. Emerson Tennent's book published in 1861.
[3] Whitbourne's 'Discourse of Newfoundland.'

in those parts so well proportioned, having round about the head many blue streaks resembling hair, but certainly it was no hair. The shoulders and back down to the middle were square, white, and smooth as the back of a man, and from the middle to the end it tapered like a broad-hooked arrow." The animal put both its paws on the side of the boat wherein its observer sat, and strove much to get in, but was repelled by a blow.

In 1676, a description was given by an English surgeon named Glover, of an animal of this kind. The author did not designate it by any name, but the incident has the honour of being recorded in the *Philosophical Transactions*.[1] About three leagues from the mouth of the river Rappahannock, in America, while alone in a vessel, he observed, at the distance of about half a stone-throw, he says, "a most prodigious creature, much resembling a man, only somewhat larger, standing right up in the water, with his head, neck, shoulders, breast and waist, to the cubits of his arms, above water, and his skin was tawny, much like that of an Indian; the figure of his head was pyramidal and sleek, without hair; his eyes large and black, and so were his eyebrows; his mouth very wide, with a broad black streak on the upper lip, which turned upwards at each end like mustachios. His countenance was grim and terrible. His neck, shoulders, arms, breast and waist, were like unto the neck, arms, shoulders, breast and waist of a man. His hands, if he had any, were under water. He seemed to stand with his eyes fixed on me for some time, and afterwards dived down, and, a little after, rose at somewhat a greater distance, and turned his head towards me again, and then immediately fell a little under water, that I could discern him throw out his arms and gather them in as a man does when he swims. At last, he shot with his head downwards, by which means he cast his tail above the water, which exactly resembled the tail of a fish, with a broad fane at the end of it."

Thormodus Torfæus[2] maintains that mermaids are found on the south coast of Iceland, and, according to Olafsen,[3] two have been taken in the surrounding seas, the first in the earlier part of the history of that island, and the second in 1733. The latter was found in the stomach of a shark. Its lower parts were consumed, but the upper were entire. They were as large as those of a boy eight or nine years old. Both the cutting teeth and grinders were long and shaped like pins, and the fingers were connected by a large web. Olafsen was inclined to believe that these were human remains, but the islanders all firmly maintained that they were part of "a marmennill," by which name the mermaid is known among them.

Of course the worthy bishop of Bergen, Pontoppidan, has something to tell us about mermaids in his part of the world. "Amongst the sea

---

[1] Glover's 'Account of Virginia,' ap. Phil. Trans, vol. xi. p. 625.
[2] *Historia rerum Norvegicarum*.
[3] *Voyage en Islande*, tom. iii. p. 223.

monsters," he says,[1] "which are in the North Sea, and are often seen, I shall give the first place to the Hav-manden, or merman, whose mate is called Hav-fruen, or mermaid. The existence of this creature is questioned by many, nor is it at all to be wondered at, because most of the accounts we have had of it are mixed with mere fables, and may be looked upon as idle tales." As such he regards the story told by Jonas Ramus in his 'History of Norway,' of a mermaid taken by fishermen at Hordeland, near Bergen, and which is said to have sung an unmusical song to King Hiorlief. In the same category he places an account given by Besenius in his life of Frederic II. (1577), of a mermaid that called herself Isbrandt, and held several conversations with a peasant at Samsoe, in which she foretold the birth of King Christian IV., "and made the peasant preach repentance to the courtiers, who were very much given to drunkenness." Equally "idle" with the above stories is, in his opinion, another, extracted from an old manuscript still to be seen in the University Library at Copenhagen, and quoted by Andrew Bussaeus (1619), of a merman caught by the two senators, Ulf Rosensparre and Christian Holch, whilst on their voyage home to Denmark from Norway. This sea-man frightened the two worshipful gentlemen so terribly that they were glad to let him go again; for as he lay upon the deck he spoke Danish to them, and threatened that if they did not give him his liberty "the ship should be cast away, and every soul of the crew should perish."

"When such fictions as these," says Pontoppidan, "are mixed with the history of the merman, and when that creature is represented as a prophet and an orator; when they give the mermaid a melodious voice, and tell us that she is a fine singer, we need not wonder that so few people of sense will give credit to such absurdities, or that they even doubt the existence of such a creature." The good prelate, however, goes on to say that "whilst we have no ground to believe all these fables, yet, as to the existence of the creature we may safely give our assent to it," and, "if this be called in question, it must proceed entirely from the fabulous stories usually mixed with the truth." Like Valentyn, he argues that as there are "sea-horses," "sea-cows," "sea-wolves," "sea-dogs," "sea-hogs," etc., it is probable from analogy, that "we should find in the ocean a fish or creature which resembles the human species more than any other." As for the objection "founded on self-love and respect to our own species which is honoured with the image of God, who made man lord of all creatures, and that, consequently, we may suppose he is entitled to a noble and heavenly form which other creatures must not partake of," he thinks "its force vanishes when we consider the form of apes, and especially of another African creature called 'Quoyas Morrov' described by Odoard Dapper" in his work on Africa, and which appears to have been a chimpanzee. Pontoppidan regarded it as being the Satyr of the ancients.

---

[1] 'Natural History of Norway,' vol. ii. p. 190.

He therefore claims that "if we will not allow our Norwegian Hastromber the honourable name of merman, we may very well call it the 'Sea-ape,' or the 'Sea-Quoyas-Morrov;' especially as the author already quoted says that, "in the Sea of Angola mermaids are frequently caught which resemble the human species. They are taken in nets, and killed by the negroes, and are heard to shriek and cry like women."

The Bishop adds that in the diocese of Bergen, as well as in the manor of Nordland, there were hundreds of persons who affirmed with the strongest assurances that they had seen this kind of creature; sometimes at a distance and at other times quite close to their boats, standing upright, and formed like a human creature down to the middle— the rest they could not see—but of those who had seen them out of water and handled them he had not been able to find more than one person of credit who could vouch it for truth. This informant, "the Reverend Mr. Peter Angel, minister of Vand-Elvens Gield, on Suderoe," assured his bishop, when he was on a visitation journey, that "in the year 1719, he (being then about twenty years old) saw what is called a merman lying dead on a point of land near the sea, which had been cast ashore by the waves along with several sea-calves (seals), and other dead fish. The length of this creature was much greater than what has been mentioned of any before, namely, above three fathoms. It was of a dark grey colour all over: in the lower part it was like a fish, and had a tail like that of a porpoise. The face resembled that of a man, with a mouth, forehead, eyes, etc. The nose was flat, and, as it were, pressed down to the face, in which the nostrils were very visible. The breast was not far from the head; the arms seemed to hang to the side, to which they were joined by a thin skin, or membrane. The hands were, to all appearance, like the paws of a sea-calf. The back of this creature was very fat, and a great part of it was cut off, which, with the liver, yielded a large quantity of train-oil." The author then quotes a description by Luke Debes[1] of a mermaid seen in 1670 at Faroe, westward of Qualboe Eide, by many of the inhabitants, as also by others from different parts of Suderoe. She was close to the shore, and stood there for two hours and a half, and was up to her waist in water. She had long hairs on her head, which hung down to the surface of the water all round about her, and she held a fish in her right hand.

Pontoppidan mentions other instances of similar appearances, and says that the latest he had heard of was of a merman seen in Denmark on the 20th of September, 1723, by three ferrymen who, at some distance from the land, were towing a ship just arrived from the Baltic. Having caught sight of something which looked like a dead body floating on the water, they rowed towards it, and there, resting on their oars, allowed it to drift close to them. It sank, but immediately came to the surface again,

---

[1] *Feroa Reserata, or Description of the Feroe Islands*. 8vo. Copenhagen, 1673.

and then they saw that it had the appearance of an old man, strong-limbed, and with broad shoulders, but his arms they could not see. His head was small in proportion to his body, and had short, curled, black hair, which did not reach below his ears; his eyes lay deep in his head, and he had a meagre and pinched face, with a black, coarse beard, that looked as if it had been cut. His skin was coarse, and very full of hair. He stood in the same place for half a quarter of an hour, and was seen above the water down to his breast: at last the men grew apprehensive of some danger, and began to retire; upon which the monster blew up his cheeks, and made a kind of roaring noise, and then dived under water, so that they did not see him any more. One of them, Peter Gunnersen, related (what the others did not observe) that this merman was, about the body and downwards, quite pointed, like a fish. This same Peter Gunnersen likewise deposed that "about twenty years before, as he was in a boat near Kulleor, the place where he was born, he saw a mermaid with long hair and large breasts." He and his two companions were, by command of the king, examined by the burgomaster of Elsineur, Andrew Bussæus, before the privy-councillor, Fridrich von Gram, and their testimony to the above effect was given on their respective oaths.

Brave old Henry Hudson, the sturdy and renowned navigator, who thrice, in three successive years, gave battle to the northern ice, and was each time defeated in his endeavour to discover a north-west or north-east passage to China, though he stamped his name on the title-page of a mighty nation's history, records the following incident: "This evening (June 15th) one of our company, looking overboard, saw a mermaid, and, calling up some of the company to see her, one more of the crew came up, and by that time she was come close to the ship's side, looking earnestly on the men. A little after a sea came and overturned her. From the navel upward, her back and breasts were like a woman's, as they say that saw her; her body as big as one of us, her skin very white, and long hair hanging down behind, of colour black. In her going down they saw her tail, which was like the tail of a porpoise and speckled like a mackarel's. Their names that saw her were Thomas Hilles and Robert Rayner."

Steller, who was a zoologist of some repute, reports having seen in Behrings Straits a strange animal, which he calls a "sea-ape," and in which one might almost recognise Pontoppidan's "Sea-Quoyas-Morrow." It was about five feet long, had sharp and erect ears and large eyes, and on its lips a kind of beard. Its body was thick and round, and it tapered to the tail, which was bifurcated, with the upper lobe longest. It was covered with thick hair, grey on the back, and red on the belly. No feet nor paws were visible. It was full of frolic, and sported in the manner of a monkey, swimming sometimes on one side of the ship and sometimes on the other. It often raised one-third of its body out of the water, and stood upright for a considerable time. It would frequently bring up a sea-plant, not unlike a bottle-gourd, which it would toss about and catch in its mouth, playing numberless fantastic tricks with it.

Somewhat similar accounts have been brought from the Southern Hemisphere, two, at least, of which are worth transcribing.

Captain Colnett, in his 'Voyage to the South Atlantic,' says:—"A very singular circumstance happened off the coast of Chili, in lat. 24° S., which spread some alarm amongst my people, and awakened their superstitious apprehensions. About 8 o'clock in the evening an animal rose alongside the ship, and uttered such shrieks and tones of lamentation, so much like those produced by the female human voice when expressing the deepest distress as to occasion no small degree of alarm among those who first heard it. These cries continued for upwards of three hours, and seemed to increase as the ship sailed from it. I never heard any noise whatever that approached so near those sounds which proceed from the organs of utterance in the human species."

Captain Weddell, in his 'Voyage towards the South Pole' (p. 143), writes that one of his men, having been left ashore on Hall's Island to take care of some produce, heard one night about ten o'clock, after he had lain down to rest, a noise resembling human cries. As daylight does not disappear in those latitudes at the season in which the incident occurred, the sailor rose and searched along the beach, thinking that, possibly, a boat might have been upset, and that some of the crew might be clinging to the detached rocks.

> "Roused by that voice of silver sound,
> From the paved floor he lightly sprung,
> And, glaring with his eyes around,
> Where the fair nymph her tresses wrung,"[1]

guided by occasional sounds, he at length saw an object lying on a rock a dozen yards from the shore, at which he was somewhat frightened. "The face and shoulders appeared of human form and of a reddish colour; over the shoulders hung long green hair; the tail resembled that of a seal, but the extremities of the arms he could not see distinctly."

> "As on the wond'ring youth she smiled,
> Again she raised the melting lay,"[2]

for the creature continued to make a musical noise during the two minutes he gazed at it, and, on perceiving him, disappeared in an instant.

The universality of the belief in an animal of combined human and fish-like form is very remarkable. That it exists amongst the Japanese we have evidence in their curious and ingeniously-constructed models which

---

[1] John Leyden.
[2] Also John Leyden.

are occasionally brought to this country. I have one of these which is so exactly the counterpart of that which my friend Mr. Frank Buckland described, originally in *Land and Water*, and which forms the subject of a chapter in his 'Curiosities of Natural History,'[1] that the portrait of the one (Fig. 13) will equally well represent the other. The lower half of the body is made of the skin and scales of a fish of the carp family, and fastened on to this, so neatly that it is hardly possible to detect where the joint is made, is a wooden body, the ribs of which are so prominent that the poor mermaid has a miserable and half-starved appearance. The upper part of the body is in the attitude of a Sphinx, leaning upon its elbows and fore-arms. The arms are thin and scraggy, and the fingers attenuated and skeleton-like. The nails are formed of small pieces of ivory or bone. The head is like that of a small monkey, and a little wool covers the crown, so thinly and untidily that if the mermaid possessed a crystal mirror she would see the necessity for the vigorous use of her comb of pearl. The teeth are those of some fish—apparently of the cat-fish, (*Anarchicas lupus*). These Japanese artificial mermaids have brought many a dollar into the pockets of Mr. Barnum and other showmen.

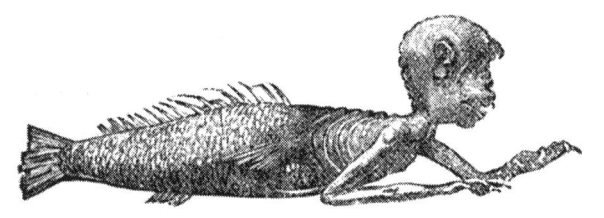

FIG. 13.—A JAPANESE ARTIFICIAL MERMAID.

Somewhat different in appearance from this, but of the same kind, was an artificial mermaid described in the *Saturday Magazine* of June 4th, 1836. Fig. 14 is a facsimile of the woodcut which accompanied it. This grotesque composition was exhibited in a glass case, some years previously, "in a leading street at the west end" of London. It was constructed "of the skin of the head and shoulders of a monkey, which was attached to the dried skin of a fish of the salmon kind with the head cut off, and the whole was stuffed and highly varnished, the better to deceive the eye." It was said to have been "taken by the crew of a Dutch vessel from on board a native Malacca boat, and from the reverence shown to it, it was supposed to be a representative of one of their idol gods." I am inclined to think that it was of Japanese origin.

Fig. 15 is described in the article above referred to as having been copied from a Japanese drawing, and as being a portrait of one of their deities. Its similarity to one of those of the Assyrians (Fig. 2) is

---

[1] Third Series, vol. ii. p. 134, 2nd ed.

remarkable. The inscription, however, does not indicate this. The Chinese characters in the centre—"*Nin giyo*"—signify "human fish;" those on the right in Japanese *Hira Kana*, or running-hand, have the same purport, and those on the left, in *Kata Kana*, the characters of the Japanese alphabet, mean "*Ichi hiru ike*"—"one day kept alive." The whole legend seems to pretend that this human fish was actually caught, and kept alive in water for twenty-four hours, but, as the box on which it is inscribed is one of those in which the Japanese showmen keep their toys, it was probably the subject of a "penny peep-show."

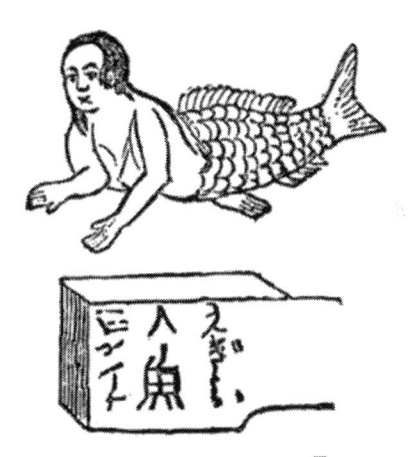

FIG. 14.—AN ARTIFICIAL MERMAID, PROBABLY JAPANESE.

FIG. 15.—A MERMAID. *From a Japanese picture.*

We need not travel from our own country to find the belief in mermaids yet existing. It is still credited in the north of Scotland that they inhabit the neighbouring seas: and Dr. Robert Hamilton, F.R.S.E., writing in 1839, expressed emphatically his opinion that there was then as much ignorance on this subject as had prevailed at any former period.[1]

In the year 1797, Mr. Munro, schoolmaster of Thurso, affirmed that he had seen "a figure like a naked female, sitting on a rock projecting into the sea, at Sandside Head, in the parish of Reay. Its head was covered with long, thick, light-brown hair, flowing down on the shoulders. The forehead was round, the face plump, and the cheeks ruddy. The mouth and lips resembled those of a human being, and the eyes were blue. The arms, fingers, breast, and abdomen were as large as those of a full-grown female," and, altogether,

---

[1] Naturalist's Library, Marine Amphibiæ, p. 291.

> "That sea-nymph's form of pearly light
> Was whiter than the downy spray,
> And round her bosom, heaving bright,
> Her glossy yellow ringlets play."[1]

"This creature," continued Mr. Munro, "was apparently in the act of combing its hair with its fingers, which seemed to afford it pleasure, and it remained thus occupied during some minutes, when it dropped into the sea." The Dominie

> "saw the maiden there,
> Just as the daylight faded,
> Braiding her locks of gowden hair
> An' singing as she braided,"[2]

but he did not remark whether the fingers were webbed. On the whole, he infers that this was a marine animal of which he had a distinct and satisfactory view, and that the portion seen by him bore a narrow resemblance to the human form. But for the dangerous situation it had chosen, and its appearance among the waves, he would have supposed it to be a woman. Twelve years later, several persons observed near the same spot an animal which they also supposed to be a mermaid.

A very remarkable story of this kind is one related by Dr. Robert Hamilton in the volume already referred to, and for the general truth of which he vouches, from his personal knowledge of some of the persons connected with the occurrence. In 1823 it was reported that some fishermen of Yell, one of the Shetland group, had captured a mermaid by its being entangled in their lines. The statement was that "the animal was about three feet long, the upper part of the body resembling the human, with protuberant mammae, like a woman; the face, forehead, and neck were short, and resembled those of a monkey; the arms, which were small, were kept folded across the breast; the fingers were distinct, not webbed; a few stiff, long bristles were on the top of the head, extending down to the shoulders, and these it could erect and depress at pleasure, something like a crest. The inferior part of the body was like a fish. The skin was smooth, and of a grey colour. It offered no resistance, nor attempted to bite, but uttered a low, plaintive sound. The crew, six in number, took it within their boat, but, superstition getting the better of curiosity, they carefully disentangled it from the lines and a hook which had accidentally become fastened in its body, and returned it to its native element. It instantly dived, descending in a perpendicular direction." Mr. Edmonston, the original narrator of this incident, was "a well-known and

---

[1] John Leyden.
[2] The Ettrick Shepherd.

intelligent observer," says Dr. Hamilton, and in a communication made by him to the Professor of Natural History in the Edinburgh University gave the following additional particulars, which he had learned from the skipper and one of the crew of the boat. "They had the animal for three hours within the boat: the body was without scales or hair; it was of a silvery grey colour above, and white below; it was like the human skin; no gills were observed, nor fins on the back or belly. The tail was like that of a dog-fish; the mammæ were about as large as those of a woman; the mouth and lips were very distinct, and resembled the human. Not one of the six men dreamed of a doubt of its being a mermaid, and it could not be suggested that they were influenced by their fears, for the mermaid is not an object of terror to fishermen: it is rather a welcome guest, and danger is apprehended from its experiencing bad treatment." Mr. Edmonston concludes by saying that "the usual resources of scepticism that the seals and other sea-animals appearing under certain circumstances, operating upon an excited imagination, and so producing ocular illusion, cannot avail here. It is quite impossible that six Shetland fishermen could commit such a mistake." It would seem that the narrator demands that his readers shall be silenced, if unconvinced; but

> "He that complies against his will
> Is of his own opinion still."

This incident is well-attested, and merits respectful and careful consideration; but I decline to admit any such impossibility of error in observation or description on the part of the fishermen, or the further impossibility of recognising in the animal captured by them one known to naturalists. The particulars given in this instance, and also of the supposed merman seen cast ashore dead in 1719 by the Rev. Peter Angel, are sufficiently accurate descriptions of a warm-blooded marine animal, with which the Shetlanders, and probably Mr. Edmonston also, were unacquainted, namely, the rytina, of which I shall have more to say presently; and these occurrences afford some slight hope that this remarkable beast may not have become extinct in 1768, as has been supposed, but that it may still exist somewhat further south than it was met with by its original describer, Steller.

Turning to Ireland, we find the same credence in the semi-human fish, or fish-tailed human being. In the autumn of 1819 it was affirmed that "a creature appeared on the Irish coast, about the size of a girl ten years of age, with a bosom as prominent as one of sixteen, having a profusion of long dark-brown hair, and full, dark eyes. The hands and arms were formed like those of a man, with a slight web connecting the upper part of the fingers, which were frequently employed in throwing back and dividing the hair. The tail appeared like that of a dolphin." This creature remained basking on the rocks during an hour, in the sight of numbers of people, until frightened by the flash of a musket, when

> "Away she went with a sea-gull's scream,
> And a splash of her saucy tail,"[1]

for it instantly plunged with a scream into the sea.

From Irish legends we learn that those sea-nereids, the "Merrows," or "Moruachs "came occasionally from the sea, gained the affections of men, and interested themselves in their affairs; and similar traditions of the "Morgan" (sea-women) and the "Morverch" (sea-daughters) are current in Brittany.

In English poetry the mermaid has been the subject of many charming verses, and Shakspeare alludes to it in his plays no less than six times. The head-quarters of these "daughters of the sea" in England, or of the belief in their existence, are in Cornwall. There the fisherman, many a time and

> "Oft, beneath the silver moon,
> Has heard, afar, the mermaid sing,"[2]

and has listened, so they say, to

> "The mermaid's sweet sea-soothing lay
> That charmed the dancing waves to sleep."[3]

Mr. Robert Hunt, F.R.S., in his collection of the traditions and superstitions of old Cornwall,[4] records several curious legends of the "merrymaids "and "merrymen "(the local name of mermaids), which he had gathered from the fisher-folk and peasants in different parts of that county.

And, in a pleasant article in 'All the Year Round,'[5] 1865, "A Cornish Vicar"[6] mentions some of the superstitions of the people in his neighbourhood, and the perplexing questions they occasionally put to him. One of his parishioners, an old man named Anthony Cleverdon, but who was popularly known as "Uncle Tony," having been the seventh son of his parents, in direct succession, was looked upon, in consequence, as a soothsayer. This "ancient augur" confided to his pastor many highly efficacious charms and formularies, and, in return, sought for information

---

[1] Tom Hood. 'The Mermaid at Margate.'
[2] John Leyden.
[3] John Leyden.
[4] 'Romances and Drolls of the West of England.' London: Hotten, 1871.
[5] Vol. xiii. p. 336.
[6] The "Cornish Vicar" was, evidently, the Rev. Robert Stephen Hawker, M.A., Vicar of Morwenstow, and author of 'Echoes from Old Cornwall,' 'Footprints of Former Men in Cornwall,' etc.

from him on other subjects. One day he puzzled the parson by a question which so well illustrates the local ideas concerning mermaids, and the sequel of which is, moreover, so humorously related by the vicar, that I venture to quote his own words, as follows:—

"Uncle Tony said to me, 'Sir, there is one thing I want to ask you, if I may be so free, and it is this: why should a merrymaid, that will ride about upon the waters in such terrible storms, and toss from sea to sea in such ruckles as there be upon the coast, why should she never lose her looking-glass and comb?' 'Well, I suppose,' said I, 'that if there are such creatures, Tony, they must wear their looking-glasses and combs fastened on somehow, like fins to a fish.' 'See!' said Tony, chuckling with delight, 'what a thing it is to know the Scriptures, like your reverence; I should never have found it out. But there's another point, sir, I should like to know, if you please; I've been bothered about it in my mind hundreds of times. Here be I, that have gone up and down Holacombe cliffs and streams fifty years come next Candlemas, and I've gone and watched the water by moonlight and sunlight, days and nights, on purpose, in rough weather and smooth (even Sundays, too, saving your presence), and my sight as good as most men's, and yet I never could come to see a merrymaid in all my life: how's that, sir?' 'Are you sure, Tony,' I rejoined, 'that there are such things in existence at all?' 'Oh, sir, my old father seen her twice! He was out one night for wreck (my father watched the coast, like most of the old people formerly), and it came to pass that he was down at the duck-pool on the sand at low-water tide, and all to once he heard music in the sea. Well, he croped on behind a rock, like a coastguardsman watching a boat, and got very near the music.... and there was the merrymaid, very plain to be seen, swimming about upon the waves like a woman bathing—and singing away. But my father said it was very sad and solemn to hear—more like the tune of a funeral hymn than a Christmas carol, by far—but it was so sweet that it was as much as he could do to hold back from plunging into the tide after her. And he an old man of sixty-seven, with a wife and a houseful of children at home. The second time was down here by Holacombe Pits. He had been looking out for spars—there was a ship breaking up in the Channel—and he saw some one move just at half-tide mark, so he went on very softly, step by step, till he got nigh the place, and there was the merrymaid sitting on a rock, the bootyfullest merrymaid that eye could behold, and she was twisting about her long hair, and dressing it, just like one of our girls getting ready for her sweetheart on the Sabbath-day. The old man made sure he should greep hold of her before ever she found him out, and he had got so near that a couple of paces more and he would have caught her by the hair, as sure as tithe or tax, when, lo and behold, she looked back and glimpsed him! So, in one moment she dived head-foremost off the rock, and then tumbled herself topsy-turvy about in the water, and cast a look at my poor father, and grinned like a seal.'" And a seal it probably was that Tony's "poor father" saw.

What, then, are these mermaids and mermen, a belief in whose existence has prevailed in all ages, and amongst all the nations of the earth? Have they, really, some of the parts and proportions of man, or do they belong to another order of mammals on which credulity and inaccurate observation have bestowed a false character?

Mr. Swainson, a naturalist of deserved eminence, has maintained on purely scientific grounds, that there must exist a marine animal uniting the general form of a fish with that of a man; that by the laws of Nature the natatorial type of the Quadrumana is most assuredly wanting, and that, apart from man, a being connecting the seals with the monkeys is required to complete the circle of quadrumanous animals.[1]

Mr. Gosse[2] argues that all the characters which Mr. Swainson selects as marking the natatorial type of animals belong to man, and that he being, in his savage state, a great swimmer, is the true aquatic primate, which Mr. Swainson regards as absent. Mr. Gosse admits, however, that "nature has an odd way of mocking at our impossibilities, and" that "it may be that green-haired maidens with oary tails, lurk in the ocean caves, and keep mirrors and combs upon their rocky shelves;" and the conclusion he arrives at is that the combined evidence "induces a strong suspicion that the northern seas may hold forms of life as yet uncatalogued by science."

That there are animals in the northern and other seas with which we are unacquainted, is more than probable: discoveries of animals of new species are constantly being made, especially in the life of the deep sea. But I venture to think that the production of an animal at present unknown is quite unnecessary to account for the supposed appearances of mermaids.

We have in the form and habits of the Phocidœ, or earless seals, a sufficient interpretation of almost every incident of the kind that has occurred north of the Equator—of those in which protuberant mammæ are described, we must presently seek another explanation. The round, plump, expressive face of a seal, the beautiful, limpid eyes, the hand-like fore-paws, the sleek body, tapering towards the flattened hinder fins, which are directed backwards, and spread out in the form of a broad fin, like the tail of a fish, might well give the idea of an animal having the anterior part of its body human and the posterior half piscine.

In the habits of the seals, also, we may trace those of the supposed mermaid, and the more easily the better we are acquainted with them. All seals are fond of leaving the water frequently. They always select the flattest and most shelving rocks which have been covered at high tide, and prefer those that are separated from the mainland. They generally go ashore at half-tide, and invariably lie with their heads towards the water,

---

[1] 'Geography and Distribution of Animals.'
[2] 'Romance of Natural History,' 2nd Series.

and seldom more than a yard or two from it. There they will often remain, if undisturbed, for six hours; that is, until the returning tide floats them off the rock. As for the sweet melody, "so melting soft," that must depend much on the ear and musical taste of the listener. I have never heard a seal utter any vocal sounds but a porcine grunt, a plaintive moan, and a pitiful whine. But another habit of the seals has, probably more than anything else, caused them to be mistaken for semi-human beings—namely, that of poising themselves upright in the water with the head and the upper third part of the body above the surface.

One calm sunny morning in August, 1881, a fine schooner-yacht, on board of which I was a guest, was slowly gliding out of the mouth of the river Maas, past the Hook of Holland, into the North Sea, when a seal rose just ahead of us, and assumed the attitude above described. It waited whilst we passed it, inspecting us apparently with the greatest interest; then dived, swam in the direction in which we were sailing, so as to intercept our course, and came up again, sitting upright as before. This it repeated three times, and so easily might it have been taken for a mermaid, that one of the party, who was called on deck to see it, thought, at first, that it was a boy who had swam off from the shore to the vessel on a begging expedition.

Laing, in his account of a voyage to the North, mentions having seen a seal under similar circumstances.

A young seal which was brought from Yarmouth to the Brighton Aquarium in 1873, habitually sat thus, showing his head and a considerable portion of his body out of water. His bath was so shallow in some parts that he was able to touch the bottom, and, with his after-flippers tucked under him, like a lobster's tail, and spread out in front, he would balance himself on his hind quarters, and look inquisitively at everybody, and listen attentively to everything within sight and hearing. When he was satisfied that no one was likely to interfere with him, and that it was unnecessary to be on the alert, he would half-close his beautiful, soft eyes, and either contentedly pat, stroke, and scratch his little fat stomach with his right paw, or flap both of them across his breast in a most ludicrous manner, exactly as a cabman warms the tips of his fingers on a wintry day, by swinging his arms vigorously across his chest, and striking his hands against his body on either side. He was very sensitive to musical sounds, as many dogs are, and when a concert took place in the building a high note from one of the vocalists would cause him to utter a mournful wail, and to dive with a splash that made the water fly, the audience smile, and the singer frown.

Captain Scoresby tells us that he had seen the walrus with its head above water, and in such a position that it required little stretch of imagination to mistake it for a human being, and that on one occasion of this kind the surgeon of his ship actually reported to him that he had seen a man with his head above water.

Peter Gunnersen's merman, who "blew up his cheeks and made a kind of roaring noise" before diving, was probably a "bladder-nose" seal. The males of that species have on the head a peculiar pad, which they can dilate at pleasure, and their voice is loud and discordant.

The appearance and behaviour of Steller's "sea-ape," may, I think, be attributed to one of the eared seals, the so-called sea-lions, or sea-bears. Every one who has seen these animals fed must have noticed the rapidity with which they will dive and swim to any part of their pond where they expect to receive food, and how, like a dog after a pebble, they will keenly watch their keeper's movements, and start in the direction to which he is apparently about to throw a fish, even before the latter has left his hand. This may be seen at the Zoological Gardens, Regent's Park, and, better than anywhere else in Europe, at the Jardin d'Acclimatation, Paris. It would be quite in accordance with their habits that one of these *Otaria* should dive under a ship, and rise above the surface on either side, eagerly surveying those on board, in hope of obtaining food, or from mere curiosity.

The seals and their movements account for so many mermaid stories, that all accounts of sea-women with prominent bosoms were ridiculed and discredited until competent observers recognised in the form and habits of certain aquatic animals met with in the bays and estuaries of the Indian Ocean, the Red Sea, the west coast of Africa, and sub-tropical America, the originals of these "travellers' tales." These were—first, the *manatee*, which is found in the West Indian Islands, Florida, the Gulf of Mexico, and Brazil, and in Africa in the River Congo, Senegambia, and the Mozambique Channel; second, the *dugong*, or *halicore*, which ranges along the east coast of Africa, Southern Asia, the Bornean Archipelago, and Australia; and, third, the *rytina*, seen on Behring's Island in the Kamschatkan Sea by Steller, the Russian zoologist and voyager, in 1741, and which is supposed to have become extinct within twenty-seven years after its discovery, by its having been recklessly and indiscriminately slaughtered.[1] Then science, in the person of Illeger, made the *amende honorable*, and frankly accepting Jack's introduction to his fish-tailed *innamorata*, classed these three animals together as a sub-order of the animal kingdom, and bestowed on them the name of the *Sirenia*. This was, of course, in allusion to the Sirens of classical mythology, who, in later art, were represented as having the body of a woman above the waist, and that of a fish below, although the lower portion of their body was originally described as being in the form of a bird.

---

[1] Almost all that is known of the living rytina is from an account published in 1751, in St. Petersburg, by Steller, who was one of an exploring party wrecked on Behring's Island in 1741. During the ten months the crew remained on the island they pursued this easily-captured animal so persistently, for food, that it was all but annihilated at the time. The last one there was killed in 1768.

It has been found difficult to determine to which order these *Manatidæ* are most nearly allied. In shape they most closely resemble the whales and seals. But the cetacea are all carnivorous, whereas the manatee and its relatives live entirely on vegetable food. Although, therefore, Dr. J. E. Gray, following Cuvier, classed them with the cetacea in his British Museum catalogue, other anatomists, as Professor Agassiz, Professor Owen, and Dr. Murie, regard their resemblance to the whales as rather superficial than real, and conclude from their organisation and dentition that they ought either to form a group apart or be classed with the pachyderms—the hippopotamus, tapir, etc.—with which they have the nearest affinities, and to which they seem to have been more immediately linked by the now lost genera, *Dinotherium* and *Halitherium*. With the opinion of those last-named authorities I entirely agree. I regard the manatee as exhibiting a wonderful modification and adaptation of the structure of a warm-blooded land animal which enables it to pass its whole life in water, and as a connecting link between the hippopotamus, elephant, etc., on the one side, and the whales and seals on the other.

FIG. 16.—THE DUGONG. *From Sir J. Emerson Tennent's 'Ceylon.'*

The *Halitherium* was a Sirenian with which we are only acquainted by its fossil remains found in the Miocene formation of Central and Southern Europe. These indicate that it had short hind limbs, and, consequently, approached more nearly the terrestrial type than either the manatee, the rytina, or the dugong, in which the hind limbs are absent. The two last named tend more than does the manatee to the marine mammals; but there is a strong likeness between these three recent forms. They all have a cylindrical body, like that of a seal, but instead of hind limbs there is in all a broad tail flattened horizontally; and the chief difference in their outward appearance is in the shape of this organ. In the manatee it is rounded, in the dugong forked like that of a whale, in the rytina crescent-shaped. The tail of the *Halitherium* appears to have been shaped somewhat like that of the beaver. The body of the manatee is broader in proportion to its length and depth than that of the dugong. In a paper read before the Royal Society, July 12th, 1821, on a manatee sent to London in spirits by the Duke of Manchester, then Governor of Jamaica, Sir Everard Home remarked of this greater lateral expansion that, as the manatee feeds on plants that grow at the mouths of great rivers, and the dugong upon those met with in the shallows amongst small islands in the Eastern seas, the difference of form would make the manatee more buoyant and better fitted to float in fresh water.

In all the *Manatidæ* the mammæ of the female, which are greatly distended during the period of lactation, are situated very differently from those of the whales, being just beneath the pectoral fins. These fins or paws are much more flexible and free in their movements than those of the cetæ, and are sufficiently prehensile to enable the animal to gather food between the palms or inner surfaces of both, and the female to hold her young one to her breast with one of them. Like the whales, they are warm-blooded mammals, breathing by lungs, and are therefore obliged to come to the surface at frequent intervals for respiration. As they breathe through nostrils at the end of the muzzle, instead of, like most of the whales, through a blow-hole on the top of the head, their habit is to rise, sometimes vertically, in the water, with the head and fore part of the body exposed above the surface, and often to remain in this position for some minutes. When seen thus, with head and breast bare, and clasping its young one to its body, the female presents a certain resemblance to a woman from the waist upward. When approached or disturbed it dives; the tail and hinder portion of the body come into view, and we see that if there was little of the "*mulier formosa superne*" at any rate "*desinit in piscem.*" The manatee has thence been called by the Spaniards and Portuguese the "woman-fish," and by the Dutch the "manetje," or mannikin. The dugong, having the muzzle bristly, is named by the latter the "baard-manetje," or "little bearded man." There are no bristles or whiskers on the muzzle of the manatee; all the portraits of it in which these are shown are in that respect erroneous. The origin of the word "manatee" has by some been traced to the Spanish, as indicating "an animal with hands." On the west coast of Africa it is called by the natives "Ne-hoo-le." By old writers it was described as the "sea-cow." Gesner depicts it in the act of bellowing; and Mr. Bates, in his work, "The Naturalist on the Amazon," says that its voice is something like the bellowing of an ox. The Florida "crackersx" or "mean whites," make the same statement. Although I have had opportunities of prolonged observation of it in captivity, I have not heard it give utterance to any sound—not even a grunt—and Mr. Bartlett, of the Zoological Gardens, tells me that his experience of it is the same. His son, Mr. Clarence Bartlett, says that a young one he had in Surinam used to make a feeble cry, or bleat, very much like the voice of a young seal. This is the only sound he ever heard from a manatee.[1]

I believe the dugong to be more especially the animal referred to by Ælian as the semi-human whale, and that which has led to this group having been supposed by southern voyagers to be aquatic human beings. In the first place, the dugong is a denizen of the sea, whereas the manatee is chiefly found in rivers and fresh-water lagoons; and secondly, the dugong accords with Ælian's description of the creature with a woman's face in that it has "prickles instead of hairs," whilst the manatee has no such stiff bristles.

FIG. 17.—THE MANATEE. ITS USUAL POSITION.

In the case of either of these two animals being mistaken for a mermaid, however, "distance" must "lend enchantment to the view," and

---

[1] For a full description of the habits of this animal in captivity, see an article by the present writer in the 'Leisure Hour' of September 28, 1878; from which the illustration, Fig. 17, is borrowed by the kind consent of the Editor of that publication.

a sailor must be very impressible and imaginative who, even after having been deprived for many months of the pleasure of females' society, could be allured by the charms of a bristly-muzzled dugong, or mistake the snorting of a wallowing manatee for the love-song of a beauteous sea-maiden.

Unfortunately both the dugong and the manatee are being hunted to extinction.

The flesh of the manatee is considered a great delicacy. Humboldt compares it with ham. Unlike that of the whales, which is of a deep and dark red hue, it is as white as veal, and, it is said, tastes very like it. It is remarkable for retaining its freshness much longer than other meat, which in a tropical climate generally putrefies in twenty-eight hours. It is therefore well adapted for pickling, as the salt has time to penetrate the flesh before it is tainted. The Catholic clergy of South America do not object to its being eaten on fast days, on the supposition that, with whales, seals, and other aquatic mammals, it may be liberally regarded as "fish." The "Indians" of the Amazon and Orinoco are so fond of it that they will spend many days, if necessary, in hunting for a manatee, and having killed one will cut it into slabs and slices on the spot, and cook these on stakes thrust into the ground aslant over a great fire, and heavily gorge themselves as long as the provision lasts. The milk of this animal is said to be rich and good, and the skin is valuable for its toughness, and is much in request for making leathern articles in which great strength and durability are required. The tail contains a great deal of oil, which is believed to be extremely nutritious, and has also the property of not becoming rancid. Unhappily for the dugong, its oil is in similarly high repute, and is greatly preferred as a nutrient medicine to cod-liver oil. As its flesh also is much esteemed, it is so persistently hunted on the Australian coasts that it will probably soon become extinct, like the rytina of Steller. The same fate apparently awaits the manatee, which is becoming perceptibly more and more scarce.

I fear that before many years have elapsed the Sirens of the Naturalist will have disappeared from our earth, before the advance of civilization, as completely as the fables and superstitions with which they have been connected, before the increase of knowledge; and that the mermaid of fact will have become as much a creature of the past as the mermaid of fiction. With regard to the latter—the Siren of the poets,—the water-maiden of the pearly comb, the crystal mirror, and the sea-green tresses,—there are few persons I suppose, at the present day who would not be content to be classed with Banks, the fine old naturalist and formerly ship-mate of Captain Cook. Sir Humphry Davy in his *Salmonia* relates an anecdote of a baronet, a profound believer in these fish-tailed ladies, who on hearing some one praise very highly Sir Joseph Banks, said that "Sir Joseph was an excellent man, but he had his prejudices—he did not believe in the mermaid." I confess to having a similar "prejudice;" and am willing to adopt the further remark of Sir Humphry

Davy:—"I am too much of the school of Izaac Walton to talk of impossibility. It doubtless might please God to make a mermaid, but I don't believe God ever did make one."

Source:
Lee, Henry. *Sea Fables Explained.* London: William Clowes and Sons, 1883.

8. Water Sprites and Mermaids by Fletcher S. Bassett

The following is one of the best overviews of several cultures and their mermaids available in this collection. The footnoting is also quite extensive. Please note that the unusual footnote formatting has been maintained from the original.

THE powerful deities and malignant demons described in a former chapter were not deemed the only inhabitants of the deep. In the traditions of many peoples, there existed below the waves races of mortals, some resembling the human dwellers on earth, others possessing varied forms and attributes. In the sea also abode huge giants, diminutive dwarfs, cunning fairies and wonderful goblins—beings analogous to those believed formerly to exist on land, and forming a link between the powerful deities and the ordinary inhabitants of the sea depths.

[1]Norse tradition says that when giants and trolls were driven from the earth by Christian priests, they took refuge in the sea, and are seen by mariners on distant strands.

Such an one is described in the old Norse "Book of Kings."[2] "It is tall and bulky, and stands right up out of the water. From the shoulder upward, it is like a man, while on the brows there is, as it were, a pointed helmet. It has no arms, and from the shoulders down it seems light and more slender. Nobody has ever been able to see whether its extremities end in a tail like that of a fish, or only in a point." This monster was called Hafstraub. "Its color was ice-blue color. Nor could any one discern whether it had scales or a skin like a man. When the monster appeared, the sailors knew it to be the presage of a storm. If it looked at a ship and

---

[1] Thorpe, *Northern Mythology.*
[2] In Jones' *Broad, Broad Ocean.*

then dived, a loss of life was certain, but if it looked away and then dived, people had a good hope that although they might encounter heavy storms, their lives would be saved."

[1]According to the Eddas, Hymir, a fabled giant, boiled his kettle when the storms raged. His name is from *humr*, the sea, and is connected with our word *humid*.

In the ancient Finnish Kalevala, a dwarf arises from the sea, and becomes a giant as high as the clouds.

These are like the giants (Jinns) in the Arabian nights, which are imprisoned in bottles, and which, says Lane,[2] were called in Arab-lore *El Ghowasah*, "divers in the sea."

Other giants, although not always abiding in the sea, were fabled to have more or less power therein.

[3]Ligur is a giant fabled in Helgoland as having separated the island from the mainland. Many stones strewn about the coast were dropped by him.

Walcheren, a Dutch giant, when pirates stole his flocks, waded out into the sea, sank the ships with his little finger, and recovered his sheep.

[4]A giant formerly lived in a cave near Portreath, England, who waded out and seized boats, dragging them in, and who seized drowning people sucked in by currents.

[5]More wonderful stories are told of Gargantua, whose deeds are renowned on many parts of the French coast. Many huge rocks and boulders on the coast, as at St. Just, St. Jacob, Plevenen, etc., were fabled to have been placed there by him. Others are said to be his tooth, his cradle, his bed, or the tombs of his limbs. Legends of his exploits are numerous. He drank of the sea, stepped over to Great Britain, and at numerous times swallowed ships, and even fleets. In some of these tales ships are blown up in his capacious stomach, and in others, whole fleets continue their combats, after he has swallowed them. An English fleet, thus absorbed, so disagreed with his gallic taste that he went in disgust to India, and threw them up.

[6]Mausthorpe, a famous Indian giant, was equally celebrated about Vineyard Sound. The rocks at Seaconnet are the remains of his wife, whom he threw into the sea there. He turned his children into fishes, and emptying out his pipe one day, formed Nantucket out of its ashes.

Dwarfs also went to sea. [7]St. Brandan met a dwarf a thumb long,

---

[1] Thorpe, *Northern Mythology*.
[2] Notes to *Arabian Nights*.
[3] Grimm.—*Teut. Mythology*, Vol. II, p. 536.
[4] Bottrell.—*Traditions of West Cornwall*.
[5] Sebillot.—*Gargantua dans les Traditions Populaires*, 1883.
[6] Drake.—*Legends and Folk-lore of New England*, p. 444.
[7] Grimm.—*Teut. Mythology*, Vol. II, p. 451.

floating in a bowl, during his wonderful voyage. [1]El Masudi tells us of the China Sea: "When a great storm comes on, black figures arise from the waters, about four or five spans long, and they look like little Abyssinians. They mount in the vessels; but, however numerous, they do no harm. When sailors observe them, they are sure that a storm is near, for their appearance is a certain sign of a gale."

Fairies figure in many tales of the sea and of seamen. Fishermen in the Tweed believe they affect their fishing. Nets are salted, and salt thrown into the water to blind the sea-fairies. Perthshire seamen believe in them.

[2]A Cornish tale says a fisherman found "piskies" playing, and watched them, but they detected him, and he was near being taken and destroyed. Another tale, that of John Taprail, is that he was awakened by a voice telling him that his boat, moored alongside another, was in danger. He arose to see to it, but found that a trick had been played on him, and his boat was all right. While on his way back he found a group of piskies distributing money in their hats. Slyly introducing his own, he obtained a share, was discovered, and barely had time to reach home, leaving the tails of his coat in the hands of the fairies.

According to the Irish Bardic legends, the King of Ulster was almost carried away by sea-fairies.

[3]Among Welsh fairies are the Gwragedd Annwn, or fairies of lakes and streams. These are not mermaids, nor are they sea-maidens. Some are said to inhabit Crumlyn Lake, and live in a fabled submerged town. They are said to be descendants of villagers condemned to sink below the waters for reviling St. Patrick on one of his visits. [4]Other localities are haunted by these subaqueous fairies, and a young farmer obtained one of them, who was in the habit of rowing about in a magic boat with golden oars, by dropping bread and cheese in the water. She left him on his striking her three times. Another lake-bride disappears when struck with iron. In another locality, lake-fairies inhabit beautiful gardens under the water.

In the Hebrides, sea-beans are supposed by some to be fairies' eggs.

In Holland it is said that elves are in the bubbles, seen on the surface of water, or that they will use eggshells thrown into the water, for boats.

[5]A French (Breton) story is told of a fairy who presented a sailor a rod that saved him from shipwreck, gave him a good breeze, and brought him a fortune.

---

[1] *Golden Meadows.*
[2] Jones.—*Credulities*, p. 30.
[3] Sikes—*British Goblins and Welsh Folk-lore*, 35.
[4] Sikes.—*British Goblins and Welsh Folk-lore*, 63.
[5] Sebillot.—*Contes des Paysauset des Péchems.*

[1]Dieppe fishermen say they hold an annual bazaar on the cliffs, and attempt to decoy men there. If one went, and listened to their music, he would be drowned from the cliffs.

Breton stories are told of fairies who dwell in the *Houles*, or grottoes in the cliffs. A fisherman once saw them rub their eyes with a salve, and then take the shape of mortals. Obtaining the ointment, he used it, and was thereafter able to distinguish these people, even when, in the shape of fish, they were robbing the nets.

The fairies sometimes married men. They have flocks and herds, sometimes obtaining those of mortals by theft. They are generally beneficent, bringing riches in return for favors, and possess supernatural powers. They are generally beautiful, but are invisible by day, except to those whose eyes are anointed with the magic salve. Some are clothed like human beings, others covered with barnacles or shells. In some tales, they are endowed with the powers of Circe, metamorphosing men into animals.

It was formerly said, in Ile et Vilaine, that a fairy inhabited a certain grotto, and was seen sailing on the river in a nautilus shell, accompanied by other fairies.

In Polynesian mythology, fairies taught them how to net fish, and make reels.

We also find at sea one of these familiar mischievous goblins, such as in German lore, under the name of Kobold, annoy the housewife and hostler. He is a beneficent demon, taking his turn at the capstan and grog-tub. [2]To French sailors, under the name of Gobelin, he is well known, and Norwegian sailors believe in his existence. He singes their hair in sleep, raises the anchor in a calm, tears carelesslyfurled sails, knots ropes, etc.

[3]In the fifteenth and sixteenth centuries, he was called Kobalos, in Germany. Now he is known as Klabautermann, or Klabautermannchen, as he is a small man, with large, fiery red head, and green teeth. He is dressed in yellow breeches, horseman's boots, and a steeple-crowned hat. He is a beneficent visitor, and is on good terms with the crew, as long as he is treated well, often assisting in their tasks.

These characteristics are aptly illustrated in the following lines:

"About Klaboterman
That Kobold of the sea, a sprite
Invisible to mortal sight.
Who o'er the rigging ran;
Sometime he hammered in the hold,

---

[1] Sebillot.—*Contes Pop. de la Haute Bretagne.*
[2] Jal.—*Glossaire Nautique*, "Gobelin."
[3] Grimm.—*Teut. Mythology.*

    Sometimes upon the mast;
    Sometimes abeam, sometimes abaft,
    Or at the bows, he sang and laughed.
    He helped the sailors at their work,
    And toil'd with jovial din.
    He helped them stow the casks and bales,
    And heave the anchor in;
    But woe unto the lazy louts,
    The idlers of the crew,
    Them to torment was his delight,
    And worry them by day and night,
    And pinch them black and blue.
    And woe to him whose mortal eyes
    Klaboterman beheld,
    It is a certain sign of death!"[1]

[2]In North Germany, it is said that his favor must be carefully courted. His favorite position is on the capstan, and he will occasionally take a glass of wine with the Captain, whose interests require him to be on favorable terms with this sprite. He is given food, but must not be offered old clothing. [3]Schmidt says Plymouth fishermen aver a belief in him, and say he was not always visible until the time of danger. Should a fisherman lose his luck, he saw Klabauterman go over the bows. On account of the noise he sometimes raised on board, he was called Klütermann (clatterman).

[4]In French accounts of him, he originally appeared on board of a ship in the Somme. He is there called Goguelin.

[5]Brewer says he is seen sitting on the bowsprit of the spectre ship, dressed in yellow, and smoking a short pipe.

In many places water-spirits assumed the shape of a horse, of a cow, or a bull. [6]"Mythic water-horses, waterbulls, or cows are to be found in the religious systems of many nations of old. And they still haunt the imagination of living men, in the shape of Scotch water-kelpies, or of dapple-gray stallions and brown steers, that still rise from some German lake."

In Iceland, Hnickur appears thus, but with hoofs turned backward. He tempts people to mount him, and is then off. [7]He was also called Vatua-

---

[1] Longfellow.—*Tales of a Wayside Inn.*
[2] Thorpe.—*Northern Mythology.*
[3] Seeman's *Sagen und Schiffer Märchen.*
[4] Jal.—*Glossaire Nautique.* "Gobelin."
[5] *Readers' Hand Book.* Klaboterman.
[6] Blind.—*Contemporary Review*, August, 1881.
[7] Blind.—*Contemporary Review*, August, 1881.

hestur, Nennir and Kumber. Gray was the usual color seen, and sometimes other shapes were assumed. One came through the ice, and had eight feel and ten heads. When the ice splits in the winter, it is said to be the sea-horse coming up.

He somtimes induces persons, especially young girls, to mount his back, when he rushes into the water. He can be caught and tamed, and the horses reared from him are stronger than others, but more mischievous. When tamed, his bridle must not be taken off, or he will rush into the river. [1]Arnanson tells a story of a water-horse who was caught and bridled by a young girl. Just as she was about to mount him she said, "I feel afraid; I'm half inclined not to mount him." He rushed forthwith into the water, not liking to be called Nennir, or "I'm not inclined," nor can he bear to be called by the Devil's name.

In the Orkneys, the water-sprite appears as a handsome little horse, with his mane covered with weeds; and one is described in Bevis's "Orkney." In Shetland, the handsome little horse is named Shoopiltree or Shoopultie. He aided Graham of Morphil to build his castle. When overloaded he said,—

> [2]"Sair back and sair banes
> Duven the Laird o' Morphil's stanes,
> The Laird o' Morphil'll never thrive
> So long's the kelpy is alive."

[3]Blind says an instance of a water-horse, yoked and worked during the day, is reported in the Landnama bok.

In Shetland, says Blind, he is also called Njuggle, Nyogle Neogle, or Niagle, all words of the same sort as Nöckel (Ger.), and derived from Nick, chief water demon. He is defined as "a horse, somewhat akin to the water kelpie." But in popular accounts, he differs from a horse in having a tail like a wheel. He is generally mischievous, stopping mills, etc. Stories are told in Shetland lore, of men mounting these water-horses, who were nearly being carried into the sea, only escaping by killing the horse.

[4]In Norway, when a thunder storm is brewing, the water-sprite comes in the shape of a horse.

[5]Numerous tales are told of the Scotch kelpie, who was usually black. He would, if possible, decoy travelers to mount him, then rush into the water with them. He could be caught by slipping over his head a bridle

---

[1] *Icelandic Legends.*
[2] *Scotch and Irish Legendary Ballads.*
[3] *Contemporary Review*, August, 1881.
[4] Faye—*Norsk Sagen*, p. 55.
[5] Gregor.—*Folk-lore of Scotland.*

on which the sign of the cross had been made, and then would work. A horseman saw one, attended by an old man. A blacksmith killed one with hot irons, by thrusting them in his side, when he became a heap of starch.

Burns says,—

> [1]"When thowes dissolve the snawy hoord,
> An' float the ginglin' icy-boord.
> Then water-kelpies haunt the foord."

Nearly every Scottish lake has its water-horse. [2]Gregor tells a story of a Scotchman who caught a kelpie, mounted his back, and nearly lost his life thereby, the water-horse rushing at once toward the lake. His rider escaped by striking the bridle from his head. [3]Another writer says of the water-sprite: "Sometimes it is described as wholly or partly human, as merman or mermaid, but more commonly the shape assigned to it, is that of a horse or a bull. The sounds of the kelpie, when heard during a storm, whether wild neighing, or hoarse bellowing, is reckoned a sure presage of misfortune."

Every lake in Perthshire has its kelpie, swelling the torrent to drown the traveler, and decoying women and children into the water.

[4]In Irish legend, water-horses are called Phookie and Aughisky, and are said to come up out of the lakes to graze; but some are carnivorous, one in Lough Mask destroying cattle when he came out. Another, that had been tamed, ran into the lake when he saw the water. Another in Loch Corub had a serpent's body, with a horse's head.

It is usually said of these water-horses, that their hoofs turn backward. Blind has pointed out that the wheel-shaped tail indicates the sun, or that here in these legends we have another phase of sun-worship, closely connected with water worship in many particulars. Bryant further argues that their backward-turned hoofs mean the crab, or the sun in the southern or Tartaric constellation; hence the water-horse is malicious and diabolic. His name, derived from Nick, indicates this character.

In the Isle of Man, we find the water-horse called Glashlan, Glashan, or Enach-I-Kibh, fairy stallion.

[5]In North Germany, Jagow is the water-horse, who, in a story, came out of the water, harnessed himself to a harrow, and worried the other horses nearly to death. It is generally said there that the water-sprites possess herds of cattle.

---

[1] *Tam O'Shanter.*

[2] *Folk-lore of Scotland.*

[3] Lt.-Col. Leslie.—*Early Races of Scotland and Their Monuments.*

[4] Blind.—Scottish and Shetland Water Tales, *Cont. Review*, August, 1882.

[5] Kuhn.—*Nord Deutsche Sagen.*

Near New Schlemnin, in Mecklenburg, is a lake called the Devil's lake, whence issue on St. John's day the cries of a man. He is a peasant, who called on the devil, when his horses were exhausted in traveling. A black horse came out of the lake, jumped to the harrow, and assisted in the task, but when the peasant mounted him, he rushed at once into the lake.

[1]The nixies that dwell in the waves are, in the Illyrian tales, of surpassing beauty. Often it happens that a youth inspires them with love, and then they change themselves into water-horses, in order to carry him on their backs into their crystal realm.

[2]Stories of sea-horses are found in eastern lore. King Mihraj's mares are visited by one producing a superior breed. El Kazwini says sea-horses are larger than those of the land, have cloven hoofs, and smaller mane and tail. Their colts are spotted, he says.

In the historical legends of the Indian Archipelago, Parar-al-Bahrri is a sea-horse who carries the hero over the waves.

The horse is connected with the sea in many legends, [3]Neptune created the horse, and Centaur, sprang from the sea. Perseus' horse, Pegasus, is supposed by many to have been a ship. Caxton, in the "Book of Troy," and Boccaccio, in the "Genealogia Deorum," say the same. [4]So Shakspeare likens a ship to Perseus' horse. The mother of Dyonisius was Hippos. Many heroes travel over the waves on the horse. Odin's horse Sleipnir thus conveyed his master, and various folk-lore tales make the hero imitate him. The ship is usually, in the Eddas, likened to a horse, and two of a famous Welsh triad of vessels were the black horse of the seas, and the horned horse. Sailors evidently recognized the analogies between the steed of the land and the courser of the seas, since we find nearly every part of the horse's anatomy, and much of his harness and fittings represented in nautical nomenclature. So with the cow. In Aryan mythology, cows represent clouds, and clouds were, as we shall see, widely represented as ships. "Die Bunte Kuh" was a famous German flag-ship in the middle ages. Certain marine mammals, as the walrus, sea-lion, etc., resembling cattle and horses in form, would aid the legend in its progress.

Water-cattle are also found in the folk-lore of many people. The Merovignan kings of France traced their descent from a water-bull, the direct ancestor of Merovaeus.

A shepherd, in a French story of the eleventh century, finds beautiful herds of cattle at the bottom of the sea, and drives them out.

An old Icelandic natural history reports that the bellowing of sea-

---

[1] Prof. Griesdorfer.—Letter to K. Blind., *Cont. Review*, August, 1881.
[2] Lane.—*Arabian Nights*.
[3] Cox.—*Aryan Mythology*, II, 263.
[4] *Troilus and Cressida*, Act I, scene 3.

cows and bulls makes people mad.

[1]Breton tales of the flocks and herds of the sea-fairies are numerous.

[2]In Scotch belief, water-bulls are friendly, and are inimical to the diabolic water-horses. In an old tale, a water-calf, who has grown into a young bull on shore, attacks a water-bull who has deluded a young girl into his power by assuming the shape of a young man, and kills him.

[3]There are many Welsh tales of water-cattle, issuing from the lakes, etc.

Kaffirs say the sea-people have cattle beneath the waves.

Clouds reflected in the waves were often thought to be sheep and cattle. So in the Norse story, "Big Peter and Little Peter,"[4] in the Gaelic tale, "The Three Widows," and in the German legend of the "Little Farmer." These are the Cattle of Helios, and Herds of Neptune; and such fancies doubtless aided in spreading these myths of water-horses and cattle.

But the water-sprites usually appeared in human form.

From the naiads, nereids, and nixies sprang a crowd of fabulous inhabitants of the ocean, lake, river, and stream.

We have seen that the ocean, the streams and lakes, and even the fountains were fabled, in ancient Greece, to be peopled by these semi-deities—the Oceanids, the Nereids, the Naiads, and the Nymphs. [5]These, with the sirens, the harpies, the centaurs, and other demi-gods and demons, were the undoubted ancestors of the host of forms, angelic and demoniac, that have been fabled to haunt the streams of the ocean and the air. The ancestry of many of these have been traced back to older Aryan days, and the nymphs found to be none other than the Apsaras, the centaurs but the Gaudharvas, and the harpies, or sirens, representatives of the Maruts. But the effects of the Greek conceptions of these inhabitants of sea and air were more marked than of the older primitive ideas.

[6]As Tylor says: "Through the ages of the classic world the river-gods and the water-nymphs held their places, till, within the bounds of Christendom, they came to be classed with ideal beings like them in the mythology of the Northern nations, the kindly sprites to whom offerings were given at springs and lakes, and the treacherous nixies who entice men to a watery death."

In spite of the opposition to water worship, made by the Christian priests, these beliefs prevailed, just as the belief in the more powerful sea-divinities endured, so that all the priests could do, was to degrade or maintain in their degraded position, the nymphs of the waves and the

---

[1] Sebillot.—*Litt. Orale de Haute Bretagne.*
[2] Gregor.—*Folk-lore of Scotland.*
[3] Sikes.—*British Goblins and Welsh Folk-lore*, p. 36.
[4] Dasent.—*Norse Tales.* Grimm, Campbell.
[5] Kelly.—*Curiosities of Indo-European Folk-lore.*
[6] *Primitive Culture.*

spirits of the deep.

The Sirens, at first bird-shaped, were afterwards, as we have seen, imagined beautiful maidens.[1] There finally grew up in mediaeval conception, two classes of sea-beings. The first, the water-sprite, appeared in human shape, but was endowed with the faculty of assuming other forms at will. The second, the mermaid, had always the fish tail which, ancient legends gave to many goddesses and water-beings.

Water-sprites were usually endowed with wisdom, often brought gifts or good luck, but were sometimes malicious, and even diabolic. All these qualities were inherited from their ancestors. Nick was diabolic, the nymphs often benefited mankind, and the Sirens were malicious and hurtful.

[2]According to the Eddas, Urda, who knew the past, Verande, skilled in present affairs, and Skulda, who prophesied the future, were all water-nymphs. Egeria of the fountain, who taught wisdom to Numa, had her representatives and followers in nearly every land.

Water-sprites appear in all countries, in ocean, lake, river and fountain.

[3]Wilkina, the Viking, found one in a forest, and carried her away. She afterwards appeared, climbing upon the poop of his ship at sea, and stopped it, by putting the helm hard over.

The sagas have other stories of water-sprites, and one sings,—

> "Cold water to the eyes,
> Flesh raw to the teeth,
> A shroud to the dead,
> Flit me back to the sea
> Henceforward never
> Men in ships sailing.
> Draw me to dry land
> From the depths of the sea."

The Drowning-Stol; a rock on the Norwegian coast, is fabled to have been the seat of a "Queen of the Sea," who used to sit there, combing her locks, and bringing luck to fishermen.

[4]In Norwegian story the Grim, or Fossegrim, is a mysterious water-fairy, a musical genius, who plays to every one, and requires a white kid every Thursday. In Norway, also, was the Roretrold, or Rorevand, sometimes appearing as a horse, at others as a human water-sprite.

---

[1] Chapter I.
[2] Thorpe.—*Northern Mythology*, Vol. II, p. 13.
[3] *Wilkina Saga*.
[4] Thorpe.—*Northern Mythology*, Vol. II, p. 23.

[1]When people drown at sea, a water-sprite appears, in the shape of a headless old man.

[2]The Swedish Strömkarl sits under bridges, playing wonderful melodies on the violin, which cause everybody hearing them to dance. He will teach his tunes to anyone, for a consideration.

He greatly desires salvation, an idea emanating undoubtedly from the priests.

[3]The "Lady of the Boundless Sea" figures in an old Norse fairy tale, bringing benefits with her.

In Icelandic legend, water-sprites make holes in the ice, called elf-holes. [4]Arnanson tells an Icelandic story of a fisherman, who is always granted good luck by a "sea-troll" whom he has benefited, so long as he waited to set out on his day's journey, until the troll had passed his hut. Other legends say these elves go out fishing, and their boats are seen.

[5]The Danish water-sprite has a long beard, green hat, green teeth, shaggy hair, and yellow curls and cap. He was often malicious.

> [6]"They launched the ship into the deep,
> The sea growled like a bear.
> The White Goose to the bottom sank,
> Some trold was surely there,"

says an old ballad. In another,—

> "The good King of Loffer had launched his ship,
> And sail'd the billowy main,
> There came a trold and his daughter seiz'd,
> And bitter his grief and pain."

In Holland, it is believed that water-sprites or elves float in bubbles, or in egg-shells that are thoughtlessly thrown into the water.

[7]A Dutch legend of 1305, reports that a knight who found a water-sprite, but afterwards killed it, died himself in consequence.

[8]In Germany, a crowd of various water-sprites is found. Frau Hulde, or Holde, is the spirit of fountains, and when the sun shines, she is combing her hair, and when it snows, she is making her bed. She is

---

[1] Grimm.—*Teutonic Mythology*, Vol. I, p. 491.
[2] Afzelius.—*Swedish Folk-Tales*.
[3] Dasent.—*Popular Tales from the Norse*.
[4] *Icelandic Legends*.
[5] Grimm.—*Teutonic Mythology*, Vol. I, p. 491.
[6] "Rosmer Hafmand."—*Northern Ballads*.
[7] Hagen.—*Deutsche Gedichte des Mittelalters*.
[8] Grimm.—*Teut. Myth.* Kuhn and Schwartz.—*Deutsche Sagen*.

frequently seen bathing at noon. She is thought to take all drowned persons. During the twelve days near Christmas, she joins the Wild Hunt with Odin and his gang. At Ilsensten, Ilse is seen often in long white robe and black hat, and she is also called Jungfern (maiden). In many places these water-sprites inhabited lakes, and raised storms, if stones were thrown in. These water-sprites inhabit every lake, river and pond in Germany, and innumerable stories are told of them. Some bring fortune, others ill luck. Many come on shore to dance with the peasants, and are known by the wet hem of their garments. Others are bloodthirsty and covetous. Should a water-maiden dally too long with the shore mortals, she is sure to suffer death on her return, and the waves appear red, above her abode. In Markland, children are told that the water-man will drag them in.

A party of fishermen found a lump of ice in the sea, and gave it to St. Theobald, their bishop, to cool his gouty feet. He heard a voice inside, and succeeded, by saying thirty masses, in saving and liberating the sprite within.

[1]Bohemian fishermen believe in a water-sprite, who sits on shore with a club, and destroys children. They fear to aid a drowning man, for fear of offending the water-sprite, who, in revenge, will draw the fish from their nets. These sprites are shaped like a fish, with human heads.

The folk tales of Austria, Bohemia and South Germany, are full of tales of these water-sprites, that inhabit every lake, river and stream. One comes out of the Teufel sea, in the shape of a white lady. The services of a midwife are often required beneath the waves, and such services are usually well rewarded. A young girl lost in the woods was found by a water-man from the Teufel sea. Water-men are sometimes beneficial, women always malicious.

[2]Boatmen say a water-sprite lives in the Traumsee, who requires a yearly sacrifice. A young miller, in love with a nun in a convent near by, was wont to swim the lake, to see his lady, but was claimed as a victim, along with the recreant nun. The deep and rock-bound lakes of the Tyrol are inhabited by maiden-sprites, whose songs are often heard. Offerings are frequently left on the banks of streams for them. They requite favors with benefits, and one struck dead the person who attempted to harm her. Water-sprites abound in the Danube and Vienna rivers, and old clothes are given to propitiate them.

[3]Bohemians will pray on the river-bank where a man has been drowned, and offer bread and wax candles to the spirit of the water. Duke Bresislaw forbade sacrifices, in Hungary, to water-spirits.

---

[1] Wuttke—*Deutsches Aberglauben*.

[2] Jones.—*Credulities*, p. 63.

[3] Tylor.—*Primitive Culture*. Vol. I.

[1]The Donaufürst (Danube prince) is a malicious sprite, dragging people below the waves. Eddies and whirlpools are caused by him.

[2]Bulgarians and Wallachians always throw a little water from each pail, as they believe that will spill out the water-spirit. In dipping water from a running stream, they are careful to hold the bucket down stream, to avoid catching the water-sprite, who dashes water in their faces.

[3]Russian traditions concerning water-sprites are abundant. Rusalkas are female water-sprites, and Vodyannies male spirits. The Rusalkas appear as beautiful maidens with long hair, bathing and sporting in the water. They tickle bathers to death. In many places, offerings of linen clothing are made to them, as they are thought fond of washing it. They cause storms and wind, are thought to influence the luck of sailors and fishermen, sometimes tearing nets and driving fish away. If game were dropped to the left of a path, a water-sprite would come to seek it. They drowned people in the overflow of rivers, especially about Whit-Sunday, when no one must bathe, for fear of offending them. During one week, called Rusalka week, relatives of drowned or shipwrecked people pour eggs and spirits on their graves. Offerings were made directly to the spirits, and in some places, a ceremony of expelling them with a straw figure is performed. Some are thought ghosts of still-born or unbaptized children, or of drowned persons. The wild-fire, or jack-o'-lantern, was thought to be lighted by them. At Astrakan, marine Rusalkas are thought to raise storms and destroy shipping. They can produce a flood by combing their hair. They come out and dance on St. Peter's day. Anyone treading on the linen which they spread out to dry, will be lamed. Anyone bathing on Whit-Sunday without praying first will be drowned, and these sprites sometimes drag people under with a long hook. They float in egg shells. They are desirous to save their souls, and one at Astrakan asked, "Is the end of the world come?"

A water-sprite came out of Lake Ladoga, and promised a fisherman great riches if he would subdue the "sprite of the third wave, by throwing his axe into it."

[4]The Vodyannies were rulers of fish, and influenced the weather and luck of fishermen. Their wives were drowned women. One of these wives is said in a popular story to have returned to visit her people, but, as in the case of Undine, her body floated up to the surface soon after her return. Another story is that a fisherman caught a Vodyanny child and returned him to the water on condition that he drive fish to the net, which he faithfully did. A fisherman once caught a dead body in his net, but hastily threw it overboard, finding it to be a Vodyanny. One must not

---

[1] Blind.—*Contemporary Review*, 1881.
[2] Tylor.—*Primitive Culture*.
[3] Ralston— *Songs of the Russian People*, pp. 139-146.
[4] Ralston.—*Songs of the Russian People*, 106, 129, 146.

bathe after sunset, nor without a cross about his neck. In the Ukraine, when the sea is rough, these water-sprites are seen on the surface, and their songs are heard. In some places a horse, smeared with honey and decked with flowers, is sacrificed, in others, oil is poured on the water to appease them.

Other traditions assert that they are fallen angels. They sit on the shore, or sport in the waters at night.

[1]They are also called Pharaohs, and are supposed to be the ghosts of the host drowned in the Red Sea. The chief water-sprite is Tsar Morskoi. A Russian folk-story is that a certain Ivan caught a fish, but liberated it, and in gratitude he was conveyed to the palace of the Tsar, where Ivan fell in love with his daughter. Both were driven out, and the fish guided them on shore. Another tale is told of Chudo Yudo, a water-sprite, who seizes people by the heard when they drink, and carries off a maiden to his palace and weds her.

The daughters of Tsar Morskoi appear as a pigeon, a duck, or a fish, and change into maidens, by shifting their coverings.

In one tale, a peasant chalks a cross on a water-sprite's back, preventing him from going into his natural element, until the cross is removed.

A story told of Sadko, relates that he charmed with his music the Tsar Morskoi from the waters of Lake Ilmen, and was thereupon promised a rich reward. He cast a net, and drew a rich treasure to land. He became rich, and went to sea with his fleet of thirty ships. They were mysteriously stopped at sea, when Sadko confessed he had not offered "bread and salt to the Caspian." He was thereupon flung overboard, his gusli, or harp, with him. Arriving at the palace of Tsar Morskoi, he plays for him, charms him, wrecks a fleet, and is finally saved by St. Nicholas.

[2]The Wends say water-sprites appear in the market in smock-frocks, with the bottom dripping.

Esthonian stories are told of water-sprites, and in one case one dwelt in a well, and a gun was fired down it to quell him. In another tale, the "Lady of the Water," goddess of winds and waves, figures.

Esthonians could see a churl with blue and yellow stockings in the sacred brook of Wöhaanda.

The "water-mother," or Wele-Ema, is the name given the water-maiden, and Aisstin Scheria, that applied to the water-man.

[3]Water-sprites, called Ahktaisset, are known in Finland, having their dwelling below the sea, and recognized by a dripping garment. One was accustomed to come to market, and indicate to a butcher the desired portion, but the butcher maliciously cut off his finger on one occasion,

---

[1] Ralston.—*Songs of the Russian People*, p. 171.
[2] Grimm.—*Teutonic Mythology*, Vol. I. p. 492.
[3] *Fraser's Mag.* Vol. LV, p. 528. *Folk-lore of Finland.*

and was soon after found dead with a red cloth about his throat.

Allatius says water-sprites, called Navagidae, abounded in Greek rivers and streams, in 1600.

Water-sprites are encountered in Italian folk-myths. Orlando and Rinaldo[1] are pursued by numerous emissaries of Fata Morgana, who lives in a beautiful palace below the sea. They escape all perils, and finally penetrate to her palace. Orlando also encounters a lake-siren, whom he kills. Tasso describes a water-sprite, seen in a fountain.

In another tale, the "Siren of the Sea," enters a ship through a hole bored to sink it, and carries off a maiden, whom she secures by binding her to the bottom with a golden chain.

[2]Gervase of Tilbury, writing in the twelfth century, says there were certain water-sprites in the south of France called Dracae, in human form, who inhabited caverns and recesses beneath the water, and inveigled persons into them. Men were devoured, and women taken as wives. They were thought to lure them by floating about in the shape of cups or rings of gold. A woman is said to have returned after living with them seven years.

[3]In Brittany, the water-women are called Korrigan. They are beautiful by night, but plain by daylight, with white hair, and red eyes. They are but two feet high, and wear only a veil, have beautiful voices, and are reputed the ghosts of Gallic princesses, who refused to become Christianized. They hate the priests, but are not otherwise harmful. Water-sprites and fountain maidens appear in many parts of France, and numerous tales are told of them.

[4]Walter Mapes tells a story of a Welshman who got a water-sprite for a wife, but one day she disappeared, having found, by accident, her sea-bridle in the market.

Taliesin, the Welsh bard, tells of a certain Gwillion, a water-sprite inhabiting lakes and ponds.

In a modern story, a cave near Pendine, Wales, is inhabited by two water-sprites, who lure ships to destruction, assuming various shapes, and even carrying ships on their backs.

A Celtic water-sprite brought stones to aid in building a certain church.

In Scotland, the most famous water-sprite is "Shellycoat," who appears covered with seaweed and shells.

[5]"Shelly-coat," says Scott, "a spirit who resides in the waters, and gives his name to many a rock and stone upon the Scottish coast."

---

[1] Ariosto.—*Orlando Furioso*.
[2] Dobeneck in Thorpe.—*N. Mythology*, Vol. II, p. 13.
[3] Sebillot.—*Litterature Orale de Haute Bretagne*.
[4] Walter Mapes, *Nuga Curialum* (1180).
[5] *Minstrelsy of the Scottish Border*.

Ramsay calls him "Spelly-coat," and mentions the belief that you must put running water between you and him.

Two men heard from a small stream a cry of "lost, lost!" apparently from some one in distress. On approaching, it went up the stream; then, as they followed, down again, laughing at them, and rattling its shelly coat.

[1]The Tees river has a water-sprite, Peg Porter, who lures people down below. Froth is "Peg Porter's suds," and foam "Peg Porter's cream." Children must not play near there, or the sprite will get them.

In another river it is Peg O'Nell. She requires a life every year; and if no dog, cat, or bird is thrown in, will have a human life. A certain traveler, bound to cross the river when it was high, was warned that she would get him, but persisted in crossing, and was drowned.

A man, riding on a brown horse with a black mane on the right side, caught a water-sprite. She was very restless in crossing a ford, and, on bringing her to the light, she dropped down, a mass of jelly. A shepherd caught another, but suddenly dropped her in the river, on observing her web-feet.

[2]In the Orkneys, the sprite is "Tangy," covered with seaweed, or tang.
[3]In Sutherland, Scotland, the Fualh-a-Banshee is a water-maiden with web-feet, and long yellow hair. She is mortal, and steel controls her. She is evil-minded, and much the same as the "water-wraith" of the old song,—

> "By this the storm grew loud apace,
> The water-wraith was shrieking."

A sprite, the Daoine-Shi, comes out of lakes in the Highlands, playing melodious music, and questioning the clergymen on the subject of her soul.

[4]In a Highland tale, "The Widow's Son," we meet with the "Princess of the realm beneath the sea," who conducts the son to her sub-marine home.

The kelpy has been described in Jamieson's ballad, and appears as half-man, half-fish.

> "The human schaip I sometimes aip,"

and says he rules the waves, to the salt sea.

Some years since, a boat's crew were drowned in Solway Firth,

---

[1] Stewart.—*Superstitions of the Highlands*, q. by Thorpe, *N. M.*, II, 18.
[2] Gregor.—*Folk-lore of Scotland*.
[3] Campbell.—*Tales of the West Highlands*.
[4] Campbell.—*Tales of the West Highlands*.

because their cries were thought to be those of kelpies, so no one would go to their assistance.

[1]Sometimes the water-sprite appeared in the shape of a bird. The aquatic bird called a "Bobbrie" is one of these.

But whatever shape the water-sprite assumed, its appearance boded disaster.

> [2]"The fishers have heard the water-sprite,
> Whose screams forbode that wreck is nigh."

We may remember that Ariel becomes a water-sprite. Prospero says,—

> [3]"Go make thyself like a nymph of the sea; be subject
> To no sight but thine and mine; invisible
> To every eyeball else."

Such sprites are not unknown even in modern England. [4]"There is scarcely a stream of any magnitude in either Lancashire or Yorkshire, which does not possess its presiding spirit in same part of its course." At Clitheroe is one which requires a sacrifice every seven years. Nor is our own practical land without them. Negroes of South Carolina[5] believe that the springs and subterranean rivers are inhabited by water-spirits, called by them "Cymbees,"—beings like the sprites of European tradition.

[6]Water-sprites figure in other parts of the world. In the Japanese story, "The Lost Fish-hook," a boy has his hook carried off by a large fish. To him appeared the "ruler of the tides," who set him afloat in a basket, in which he sank to the palace of the sea-dragon, saw and loved his daughter. The fishes are bled to find the hook, which is in the red-fish's mouth.

The rivers of India are haunted by these water-sprites, especially the Ganges,—the wife of Buddha.

Sea-sprites figure in stories in the "Arabian Nights." Gulnare is one of these, and Abdallah catches one in his net. Three daughters of the sea, beautiful and beneficent, appear in the tale of "Al Habib."

[7]Fishermen of Poyang lake, in Hunan, often miss their boats, which are temporarily borrowed for submarine purposes by the sprites of the

---

[1] Gregor.—*Folk-lore of Scotland.*
[2] Scott.—*Lay of the Last Minstrel.*
[3] *Tempest*, Act I; scene 3.
[4] Farrar.—*Primitive Civilization*, p. 306.
[5] *Popular Science Monthly*, 1875.
[6] Mitford.—*Tales of Old Japan.*
[7] *Chinese Tales.* By Pu Sing Ling—Giles' Translation.

lake. Music is always heard as these boats disappear, and they are safely returned to their anchorages after a time. Lin, a boatman, fell asleep in his boat, and on awakening, found his boat in the possession of these sprites. The Water King, who lives beneath the waves, appeared, and gave his subjects lists of people to be drowned, two hundred and twenty-eight in number. In the storm that ensued, Lin was saved by virtue of a crystal square, given him as a talisman. Lin afterwards married one of the sprites, and she was able to revisit her friends when desirous of it, always returning with rich presents.

[1]Esquimaux fear the spirits of the waters. A water-sprite haunted Pend d'Oreille lake, and in Lake Winnipeg, the Indians feared to speak for fear of offending them. Mexicans and Peruvians believed in water-beings, evil and beneficent. Algonquins believed in water-sprites, Nee-ban-aw-baigs.

[2]In Ottawa legend, the spirits of Lake Michigan caused great storms. An Ojibway tale relates the seizure of a woman by a water-sprite in Lake Superior, who appeared in the shape of a tiger, and carried her to his water wigwam.

[3]Among Guiana tribes, Orehue is the water-spirit. He is like a merman, but not always malignant. Sometimes he has the head of a horse or other animal. He sometimes seizes bathers, and drags them beneath the waves. He is believed especially to frequent a cove washed in the banks of the Pomeroon river. Many Indians would noiselessly row on the opposite banks at night. A dance in his favor is called, the water-mawa dance. They carefully distinguish between this imaginary being and the manatee. Among other South American tribes, Gamainha is a spirit of the water.

[4]Mae d'Acqua is a lovely female on shore, a fish in the water.

[5]Leewa is the water-ghost of Musquito Indians. The Suaranos say Wahua appears, rising from the water, and seizing maidens.

[6]Kaffirs say people live beneath the waves, and have herds and dwellings. Zulus also believe in semi-human beings, who live in the ocean.

Theal says Xosa Kaffirs believe in a water-spirit in the shape of a crocodile. A water-sprite, in a Kaffir tale, calls a woman and pulls her down.

[7]Ashango people say a water-sprite existed in the river Ngouyou, who

---

[1] Bancroft—*Native Races*, Vol. III, pp. 144-5.
[2] Schoolcraft.—*Algic Researches*, Vol. I, p. 131.
[3] Jones.—*Credulities*, p. 26.
[4] Verne.—*Giant Ruft*, ch. XI.
[5] Bancroft.—*Native Races*, Vol. III, p. 497.
[6] Theal.—*Kaffir Folk-lore*.
[7] Du Chaillu.—*Equatorial Africa*.

made the rapids. This spirit, Fougamon, is a worker in iron. Fanti negroes say people used to take iron and leave it near the river, for the spirits to work up into useful articles.

The water-sprite figures most in the guise of a sea-maiden, as her name, mermaid, literally signifies, whether we speak of the German Meerfrau, Danish Moremund, Icelandic Margyr, or Breton Marie Morgan, Welsh Morva or Morveth, Dutch Zee-wjf, Swedish Sjötrold, Anglo-Saxon Merewif, Cornish Morhuch, Irish Merrow, or by any of the special titles their class receives.

The idea of creatures beneath the wave, possessed of a man form with fish-like extremities, is not a modern one. Aside from the many fish-gods of antiquity, as Oannes, Dagon, and others, we are told by [1]Megasthenes that a creature like a woman inhabits the seas of Ceylon, and Lilian assures us there are whales formed like Satyrs. Tritons and Sirens were also figured half fish, in ancient representations. Demetrius says the Western islanders who died in hurricanes, were mermaids. Pliny says they came on board ships at night, and sunk them, and that Molos, making free with a sea-maiden, lost his head.

[2]That ancient naturalist gave more circumstantial accounts of them. "Nor are we," says he, "to disbelieve the stories told of Nereids, completely covered with rough scales, as one has actually been seen in the — —, and the inhabitants heard at a great distance her lamentations, whinings, and howlings, when she was dying, and his lieutenant wrote to Augustus that a number of Nereids had been found dead on the coast of Gaul. Several distinguished persons of Equestrian rank have assured me that they themselves have seen off the coast of Gades a merman, whose body was of a human form. He was accustomed to appear on board ships in the night time, and the part on which he stood gradually subsided, as if sunk down by his weight." He also asserts their existence in India, and Solinus and Aulus Gellius speak of them. These accounts of Pliny are the first of the appearance of the real mermaid, although he does not speak of the fish-tail. This idea, however, as we have seen, was not a new one.

[3]The Nereids, daughter of the Oceanid Doris, and of Nereus, and mothers of many heroes, were at first imagined; beautiful maidens. A mural painting in Pompeii shows such a one. Later they were given the fish-tail, thus becoming mermaids.

Achelous, brother of Nereus, and Calliope, were parents of the Sirens, and as we have seen, they, too, were gradually transformed from human-faced birds to fish-tailed maidens.

So also with the Tritons, offspring of Neptune and Amphitrite, who, at first regarded as men in form, were afterwards given the fish-tail and

---

[1] Jones.—*Credulities*, p. 25.
[2] *Nat. Hist.*, Vol. IV, p. 4.
[3] Landrin.—*Les Monstres Marins*, 262.

monstrous form, usually seen in art.

In the middle ages, stories of mermaids increased, and their characteristics were definitely settled.

Arabian writers often speak of them. [1]El-Kazwini says the Arabs believed that certain fish-men lived in islands in the Indian Ocean, and ate drowned men. Abou Muzaine says a Siren named the Old Man of the Sea, often appeared, prognosticating the good harvests. It spoke an unknown tongue. A similar animal caught a woman and married her, and their son spoke the language of both. Another similar animal, the Old Jew,[2] came to the surface in the Mediterranean, on Friday night, and played about ships all the Jewish Sabbath, Ibnala Bialsaths says sailors in his time caught on foreign shores marine women, with brown skin and black eyes, speaking a strange tongue. Ibn-Batuta, an old Arab writer, says he saw fish in the Persian Gulf with a human head as large as that of a child.

[3]Theodore de Gaza saw several Sirens on board ship, in the Peloponnessian sea, which were put back in the water, after being kept on board some time. They were beautiful maidens. George of Trebizonde saw one in the open sea. Gyllius says the skin of sea men taken in Dalmatia is so tough that it is used to make saddle covers.

[4]In the Nibelungen Lieb, Hagen steals a mermaid's garments, but she foretold him good luck if he would give them back again. Another story is that a mermaid told Hagen's fortune, but he, dissatisfied with it, cut off her head, which mysteriously joined the body again, and a storm thereupon ensued.

The old poets allude to them. Tasso makes two knights walk by a lake in a pleasure garden where,—

> "Two blooming damsels on the water lave
> And laugh and plunge beneath the lucid wave.

The blood of a mermaid was then thought a prophylactic. Ariosto relates that Orlando smeared his casque with the blood of a Siren;—

> "Naught resists his touch of flame e iron
> Save what has drunk the life blood of a Siren."

[5]Gower thus sings,—

---

[1] Landrin.—*Les Monstres Marins*, 282.
[2] Bochar.—*Hierozoicon*.
[3] Landrin.—*Les Monstres Marins*, 265 et seq.
[4] Ludlow.—*Popular Epics of Middle Ages*.
[5] *Confessio Amantis*, 1393.

> "Sirenes of a wonder kind
> Ben monstres as the bokes telleth
> And in the gret sea they dwelleth.
> Of body both and of visage
> Lik unto women of yonge age,
> Up fro' the navel on high they be,
> And down benethe as men may see
> They bene of fishes the figure.

[1]Spenser says they are,—

> "Transformed into fish for their bold surqueedry."

[2]And Guyon shows two maidens disporting in a fountain. An old verse of "Sir Patrick Spens" speaks of them,—

> "Upstarted the mermaid by the ship,
>   Wi' a glass and a kame in her hand,
> Says, 'reek about, reek about, my merry men,
>   Ye are not very far from land.'"

[3]Vincent de Beauvais says mermen were avoided by throwing a bottle overboard, when they will stop to play with them.

So learned a man as Joseph Scaliger believed in them. Two Epirote sailors told him they had seen a Siren. Valerio Tesio, a Valencian, told him one was taken in Spanish waters, but was restored to the sea soon after.

Many heroes, like the demi-gods of old, claimed descent from sea-maidens.

Wieland, or Waylund, a mythical Vulcan of the middle ages, is said to have descended from a mermaid.

So the French Counts of Lusignan, ancient kings of Cypress and Jerusalem, still claim as their ancestor and founder a water-maiden, Melusina, whom an ancestor saw bathing in a fountain, and whom he wedded.

The romances of the middle age often speak of them. Such are the maidens of the Rheingold, celebrated in Wagner's melodious strains.

[4]In the romantic legends of William of Orange, a mermaid is caught by a cavalier, but liberated. In gratitude therefore, she saves her captor, when his ship is wrecked. When mermaids appeared "then began they all

---

[1] *Faerie Queene.*
[2] *Bower of Bliss.*
[3] Landrin.—*Les Monstres Marins*, p. 266.
[4] Cox and Jones.—*Romances of the Middle Ages.*

to sing so high, so low, so sweet, and so clear, that the birds leave off flying, and the fish leave off swimming."

The ballads of Chivalry extolled their beauty. Doolin says, of a beautiful woman, "I thought she was an angel, or a sea-siren."

[1]In a Sicilian tale, a maiden treacherously thrown into the sea, is carried off by a merman, and chained to his tail. A similar story is told by Gubernatis, but the maiden is here liberated, her brother feeding the siren meat, while seven blacksmiths sever the chain.

These mermaids particularly desire a human soul—a thing denied them by the churchmen. [2]Paracelsus says: "So it follows that they woo men, to make them industrious and homelike, in the same way as a heathen wants baptism, to save his soul; and thus they create so great a love for men, that they are with men in the same union." This of the maidens, but mermen were not so friendly, often dragging people down, like Nick.

[3]In "The Eastern Travels of John of Hesse" (1389), we read: "We came to a smoky and stony mountain, where we heard sirens singing, proprie mermaids, who draw ships into danger by their songs. We saw there many horrible monsters, and were in great fear."

[4]In 1187, a merman is said to have been taken near Suffolk, England. It resembled a man, but could not speak. It escaped one day, fled into the sea, and was not again seen.

But the accounts of the early appearances of the mermaid are more circumstantial in northern countries. Here, where Nick dragged people down, where Ran sucked the breath of the drowned, and where the Strömkarl and the Kelpie flourished, the mermaid was often seen, sitting on the rocks, combing her hair, and predicting disaster to the mariner.

[5]Pontoppidan, Bishop of Norway, tells us much of the appearance of mermaids on the coasts of that country. Near Landscrona, on the Danish coast, three sailors in a boat saw something floating. On approaching it, it sank, then arose, and swam waist-deep. It appeared like an old man, with broad shoulders, small head, deep sunken eyes, thin face, black beard and hair, with fish-like extremities. A minister, Peter Angell, of Sundmoer parish, told the bishop that he saw a merman lying on the strand dead. It was about six feet long, dark gray in color, with the lower part like a fish, and a tail like a porpoise, a man's face, and arms joined by membranes to the body.

[6]We have earlier notices of them in the "Royal Mirror," which speaks

---

[1] Gubernatis.—*Zoological Mythology*, II.
[2] *Treatise of Elemental Spirits*.
[3] Jones.—*Credulities*, p. 20.
[4] *Histoire D'Angleterre*, in Jones' *Credulities*, p. 20.
[5] *Natural History of Norway*, q. Baring Gould.—*Curious Myths*, p. 508.
[6] *Konigs Skugg*. 1170.

of mermen and maids, calling the latter Margyra, and ascribing to them the attribute of a fish-tail, but saying nothing about its possession by the merman, or Hafstrambr.

[1]A later writer says: "Seamen and fishers in very tranquil waters sometimes see mermen and mermaids rise to the quiet top of the sea." These are described as fair maidens, with fish-tail, long yellow hair, etc. Their children are called Marmaëler, "Sea-talkers." "Sometimes the fishermen take them home, to get from them a knowledge of the future." "Seamen are very sorry to see these creatures, thinking they portend a storm."

[2]Norwegian stories are numerous. When the sea is calm they say the mermen (Marmenill) and mermaids (Margyr) rise to the surface. The mermen are described as being oldish men, with long beard and black hair, man from the waist upwards and fish downwards, and the mermaid is described as usual. The appearance of these beings forebodes a storm, and it is thought dangerous to hurt them. A sailor enticed one to his boat and cut off her hand as it lay on the gunwale. He nearly perished in the storm that arose in consequence. If in diving they turn toward a ship, it is a bad omen; if from the ship, no evil will result.

St. Olaf, on one of his piratical cruises, met one of these sirens, who was wont to lure sailors to destruction.

[3]Icelandic chronicles relate that three sea-monsters were seen near Greenland. The first, seen by Norwegian sailors in the water, had the body of a man, with broad shoulders, stumps of arms, and a pointed head. Heavy storms succeeded its appearance. The second was like a woman to the waist, with large breasts, disheveled hair, and large hands on the stumpy arms, webbed like a duck's foot. It held fish in its hand and ate them, and the usual signs with regard to the manner of its eating or using the fish are then told.

[4]The "Speculum Regali," an Icelandic work, tells us: "A monster is seen also near Greenland, which people call the Margyr. This creature appears like a woman as far down as her waist; long hands and soft hair, the neck and head in all respects like that of a human being. The hands seem to people to be long, and the fingers not to be parted, but united by a web, like that on the feet of water-birds. From the waist downward, this monster resembles a fish, with scales, tail, and fin. This prodigy is supposed to show itself more especially before heavy storms. The habit of this creature is to dive frequently, and rise again to the surface with fishes in its hands. When sailors see it playing with the fish, or throwing them toward the ship, they fear they are doomed to lose several of the

---

[1] Faye.—*Norsk Sagen.*
[2] Thorpe.—*N. Mythology.* Faye.—*Norsk Sagen.*
[3] *Iceland, Its Scenes and Saifas.*—B. Gould, p. 349.
[4] Jones.—*Broad, Broad Ocean*, p. 263.

crew; but when it casts the fish, or, turning from the vessel, flings them away from her, then the sailors take it as a good omen that they will not suffer loss, in an impending storm. The monster has a very horrible face, with broad brow and piercing eyes, a wide mouth, and double chin."

This excellent account embodies most of the traditions regarding the appearance and prognostications from the sight of the mermaid, current since that time. [1]The "Landnama," or Icelandic records of land, tells us of Marmenill, or mermen, caught off the island of Grimsey, and other annals tell us of their appearance there in 1305 and 1309.

[2]We also read in the Chronicle of Storlaformus, of the Hafstrambr: "It resembles a man from the neck, in its head, its nose, and its throat, except that the head is extraordinarily high, and elongated in front. It had shoulders like a man, and attached to them two stumps of arms without hands. The body tapers below, but it has never been seen how it is formed below the waist." He also describes the Marguguer. "It is formed like a woman, as far as the waist. It has a large bosom, thick hair, large hands, with lingers webbed like the foot of a goose, attached to its stumpy arms."

[3]Modern Icelandic folk-lore divides these beings into two classes. First, there are the Margyr, Hafgyr (Sea and Harbor-troll) or Haf-fru (Sea-maid), the seductive maidens of the sea, who have long yellow hair, often sleep in the boats, and occasionally drag them down, and who can be prevented from doing harm by the repetition of a sacred hymn. Then there are the Marmenill, or mermen, who never appear on the surface, but are occasionally caught in the nets, and who then become quite homesick, and earnestly beg to be put back into the water. [4]These make the millepora, coral, called in Iceland, Marmenill's Smi thi.

In a folk tale, a sea-troll appears in a stone boat, bringing luck to a ship, in good breezes and fine weather.

Mermaids are said still to be seen near Grimsey. They will pull men out of boats, but a credo will control them.

[5]Mermaids are seen on the Swedish coast, sitting on a rock combing their hair, with a glass in their hands, or spreading out linen to dry. They are said to be fatal and deceitful, and storms and tempests follow their appearance. If a fisherman sees one, he should not speak of it to his comrades. They are said to dwell at the bottom of the sea, and have castles, palaces, and herds of brindled cattle.

A certain knight, Gunnar, dwelt by a lake in Sweden (Anten). He fell

---

[1] Jones.—*Credulities*, p. 21.
[2] *Chronicle of Storlaformus* (1215), q. by Landrin, "*Les Monstres Marins*."
[3] Arnanson.—*Icelandic Legends*.
[4] Thorpe.—*Northern Mythology*, Vol. II. pp.27-8.
[5] Thorpe.—*Northern Mythology*, Vol. II. pp.27-8.

in one day, was rescued by a mermaid, and used thereafter to meet her weekly. Failing to do so once, the water rose and drowned him out of his castle, and he sank to the water-maiden's abode while escaping in a boat. The stone near which his boat traditionally sank, is still called Gunnar's stone. Fishermen rowing by it, salute by raising their hats, else they would have no luck.

These mermaids are said to entice young men, prognosticate storms, and foretell the future. Often they carry a harp. One flung away her harp on hearing that she would not be saved like a Christian.

[1]In Sweden, the door of a fisherman's hut was opened at night, and a woman's hand appeared. The next night a bold fellow watched, seized the hand, and disappeared. Some time afterward, when his wife remarried, he came back, saying that he had dwelt with the mermaid meanwhile, but was allowed to revisit the earth on condition of not entering the house. He did so, however, when the roof of the house was blown off, and the young man soon after died.[2]

Another legend, given in a poem by Smaland, is of Duke Magnus, son of Gustavus Vasa, who saw a mermaid, who promises him, if he will marry her, among other thing, a fine ship. But he resisted her importunities, whereupon she declared he would always be crazy. He died insane.

[3]It is deemed unlucky by Swedish fishermen to meet a meerwife. One story is told of a party of fishermen who were doubtingly joking about such beings, when one appeared and flung herself into the water. They caught no fish that day.

[4]These Hafsfru are said to appropriate the bodies of drowned men that do not rise to the surface. Swedish folktales concerning them are numerous. [5]In one, a maiden jumps overboard to save a ship in a gale, and is protected by the "mermaid who rules over all those that perish by sea." She is allowed to return to earth. In a variant, the "sea-troll" bores a hole in the ship, changes the maiden into a serpent, then into a mermaid, and thus obtains her. In another tale, the troll raises a storm and wrecks many ships. In another, a Havmand appears to Svend, closes his ears and eyes, and carries him down to his habitation below the waves. Another mermaid stops a ship, obtains from a queen the promise of one of her sons, and then only allows the ship to proceed. The prince is one day riding on his horse near the sea, when suddenly the animal plunges in, and carries his rider to the sea-palace. After performing many herculean feats, the hero returned to earth, whither the maiden follows. In a variant,

---

[1] Jones.—*Credulities*, p. 23.
[2] Jones.—*Credulities*, p. 26.
[3] Thorpe.—*Northern Mythology*, Vol. II, p. 76.
[4] Grimm.—*Teut. Myth.* II. 497.
[5] Dasent.—*Popular Tales from the Norse.*

it is a king who promises his son, and substitutes for him various animals, which are in turn cast on shore dead.

In other stories, people assume the forms of fish, to escape from pursuing mermaids.

[1]Danish legends are also numerous. In the neighborhood of Assen, many sea-people appeared on the strand, and fishermen often saw them with their children. In Nordstrand, a merwife grazing her cattle was captured by some people, and in revenge, covered the town with sand. In Aarhuus parish, a merman enticed a maiden to the bottom of the sea. But one day, after she had raised many children, she heard the bells and would go up. He allowed her to go on promise of returning, but she did not, and his wails from the depths are often heard. A ballad "Agnete og Harmandar," and two others, were written on this tale, which is the original of the "Forsaken Merman," of Matthew Arnold. An old Danish ballad says a mermaid foretold the death of Dagmar, queen of Frederick II., and the story goes: "In the year 1576 there came, late in the autumn, a simple old peasant from Samsö to the court, then being held at Kalundborg, who related that a beautiful female had more than once come to him, while working in his field by the sea-shore, whose figure from the waist downward resembled that of a fish, and who had repeatedly and strictly enjoined him to go and announce to the king that God had blessed his queen, so that she was progressed of a son (afterward Christian II.), and would be safely delivered of him."

H. C. Andersen tells a story of six mermaids, who were allowed to rise to the surface at sixteen years of age. The youngest saw a ship, and fell in love with a young prince on board. She was changed into an earth maiden by a water-witch, but the prince failed to marry her. Given a knife by her sisters to kill him, she fails to use it, plunges into the water, and is drowned herself.

[2]John Philip Abelinus related in the first volume of his "Theatre of Europe," that in the year 1619 two councillors of Christian IV., of Denmark, sailing between Norway and Sweden, discovered a merman swimming about with a bunch of grass on his head. They threw out a bait to him with a fish-hook concealed therein. The merman was fond of good living, it seems, and was caught with a slice of bacon. When caught, he threatened vengeance so loudly, that he was thrown back into the sea. Abelinus gives a picture of this merman.

In 1670, mermaids were seen on the islands off the Danish coast. [3]Resenius says a mermaid prophesied and preached against drunkenness.

Ferrymen testified in 1723, to having seen a merman between Hveen and Saedland. It was an old man, with black hair and beard, small head

---

[1] Thiele.—*Denmarks Folkes Sagen*.
[2] Thorpe.—*N. Mythology*, Vol. III, p. 170.
[3] *Life of Frederick II*.

and broad shoulders.

Popular tradition asserts that children frequently find little animals on the coast, a mixture between a man and a fish, but as soon as they have fed them, they set them into the water, for fear of misfortune, should the sea people be harmed.

The malignant character of the mermaid appears in an old ballad,—

> "Drowned at sea
> Seven ships of mine she has."

In another ballad, a mermaid steals a bride away, but her lover,—

> "Sail'd Norway's shore along,
> And there, at her cave, the mermaid found
> Who wrought so grievous wrong."

In the "Power of the Harp," Sir Peter loses his bride in crossing a stream, but calls for his golden harp, whose dulcet tones charm his mermaid bride and her two sisters from the waves.

A mermaid in a certain tale, assumes the human form, but warns her lover never to approach her while she becomes a fish, as she is then very fierce.

[1] In the Faröe Islands, there was a superstition that every ninth night, seals cast off their skins, assumed human forms, and danced on the beach. A fisherman found a skin one night, and obtained a wife thereby, but she got possession of the skin after years, and disappeared. Other stories similar to this are told, only it is a red cap, instead of a seal's skin. The possessor will be transported over seas by it.

[2] In 1670, mermaids were seen at the Faröe Islands.

[3] Among Shetlanders, there was a firm belief in mermaids, and the seal-skin story is there told as in the Faröe Islands. A fisherman of Unst saw a group dancing on the strand, picked up a seal-skin, and found a beautiful maiden in tears, who begged the skin, but perforce married him, when refused it. She often conversed with sea-people; one of her children found the seal-skin, showed it to her, and she was afterwards seen by her husband as a seal, diving from the rocks. They are thought to dwell in coral caves, resemble human beings, but are more beautiful. Wishing to come on earth, they cast off the hair garment. They are said particularly to love to revel about Ve Skerries (sacred rocks), are mortal, and are said to have been taken and killed by superstitious fishermen.

---

[1] *Folk-lore Record.*
[2] Gould.—*Curious Myths of the Middle Ages.*
[3] Hibbert's *Shetland.* Thorpe—*Northern Mythology*, Vol. II, p. 178.

[1]The mermen were, as Blind shows, known by the name of Finns, and were said to possess great nautical skill, rowing boats nine miles an hour. Sometimes they pursued ships, when nothing should be said to them, but silver pieces thrown overboard would prevent them from doing harm. Another authority says these men alone doffed the seal-skins, and could only resume the seal form by retaining possession of the skin. One tale is told of a merman caught by a fisherman, who grew larger and larger, until the fisherman complied with his request to throw him overboard, when he promised him luck. The stories of sea-brides obtained by mortals are numerous, and the mermaids are always endowed with a fish-tail.

Fishermen in the Hebrides are said to have caught a mermaid during the present century.

Scotch stories of them are not wanting. An old tale, the "Master of Weemys," is of a ship encountering one at sea,—

[2]"She held a glass with her richt hande,
    In the other she held a kame;
And she kembit her hair, and aye she sang.
    As she flotterit on the faem.

Sayle on. sayle on, said she;
    Sayle on, and ne'er bluine
The wind at will your sayles may fill
    But the land ye shall nevir win."

In another legend a mermaid decoys a knight out to sea with her. In another, a fisherman catches a mermaid in a net. She ties two knots, and darkness comes; three, and a tempest. He shakes her off by a spell, and the storm ceases. Here we have the magic storm-causing witch-knots. We find in an old Scotch poem these lines,—

"A mermaid from the water rose
And spaed Sir Sinclair ill."

A sea-maiden promised luck to a Scotch fisherman if he would give up his son in three years. She got him, but his mother finally obtained him from the sea-depths by playing music to the mermaid.

[3]Sometimes the visits of mermaids were considered beneficial. A mermaid is said to have asked a Scotchman, who was reading the Bible,

---

[1] Blind.—Scottish and Shetlandish Water-tales. *Contemporary Review*, August. 1881.
[2] *Scotch and English Legendary Ballads*.
[3] Gregor. *Folk-lore of Scotland*.

if there was comfort there for her. He said there was mercy for the sons and daughters of Adam, when she screamed and disappeared.

In the ballad, "Rosmer Hafmand," the merman carries a maiden to his sea-palaces, but she finally deceives him, and is carried back in a chest along with a young lover, whom she has passed off as a relative.

[1]A mermaid, who was accustomed to sing while seated on a stone in front of Knockdolin House, predicted disaster when the stone was removed, on account of her disturbing the young heir with her songs;—

> "Ye may-think on your cradle, I'll think on my stane.
> And there'll never be an heir to Knockdolin again."

Mermaids were often dangerous. The young Laird of Lorntie was about to rush into the water, to save a young creature whom he saw struggling there, but was restrained by his servant, who said, "That wailing madam was nae other, God sauf us, than the mermaid." As they rode off, she exclaimed:

> "Lorntie, Lorntie,
> Were it na for your man
> I had part your hairt's bluid
> Skirl in my pan!"

[2]Leyden's poem, "The Mermaid," is based on a tradition that a certain McPhail of Colonsay Isle, was carried off by a mermaid, and married her, but afterwards deserted her. She sang to him,—

> "The mermaids sweet sea-soothing lay
> That charmed the dancing waves to sleep,
> Before the Bark of Colonsay.
>
> And ever as the year returns
> The charm-bound sailors know the day
> For sadly still the mermaid mourns
> The lovely chief of Colonsay."

Many other ballads celebrate the adventures of these seamaidens, who entice mariners into the sea, are sometimes caught in nets, can raise storms by singing, or by knotting their hair, and can be conquered by certain spells.

[3]In the Aberdeen Almanac of 1688, it was predicted, that if people

---

[1] *Folk-lore Record.*
[2] Scott.—*Minstrelsy of the Scottish Border.*
[3] Baring Gould.—*Curious Myths.*

should go to the mouth of the Dee on the 1st, 13th, or 29th of May, they would see "a pretty company of mermaids."

A school-master of Thurso, testified in 1797, that he saw a mermaid on the rocks, combing her long hair, and twelve years afterward, others were seen in the same place. In 1871, John McIsaac, of Kintyre, whose testimony was supported by others, averred he saw one on the coast of Scotland. They are often seen, by the islanders, sitting on the rocks between Jura and Scarba.

[1]A Dr. Hamilton wrote to the Edinburg magazine, some years since, of the finding of a mermaid near the Shetland Islands, by two fishermen. They had it in the boat some two hours, but becoming superstitious, threw it overboard. It was gray in color, and had a fish tail, but neither scales nor hair on its body, nor webs nor fingers on its hands.

[2]Waldron says: "Mermen and Mermaids have been frequently seen. Many surprising stories of these amphibious creatures have I been told."

[3]A young mermaid fell in love with a Manx shepherd, and in embracing him, held him so tight, that he feared she would do him harm. He accordingly repulsed her, when she flung a stone at him, and mortally wounded him.

[4]Fishermen caught a sea maiden, but let her go, fearful of evil consequences. She was afterward asked what strange things she saw above the water, but the only thing she had particularly remarked, was that the water in which eggs were boiled was thrown away.

A Manx diver reported that he found "below the fishes," palaces of mother-of-pearl, with floors of inlaid stones, and inhabited by mermen and maids.

[5]Gervase of Tilbury reports the appearance of mermaids in English seas: "They attract sailors by their sweet songs, and lead them to wreck and destruction."

[6]Sir Thomas Browne says: "They are conceived to answer the shape of the ancient syren that attempted upon Ulysses, which, notwithstanding, were of another description, containing no fishy composition, but made up of man and bird."

[7]Coad says "The mermaid, I take it as I find it, whether it were a reality or a spectre. I can promise spectres are seen at sea some times, and I believe also that there are such Mockyuga of Humane Nature seen, as an ape is on the mountain."

---

[1] Gregor.—*Folk-lore of Scotland*.
[2] Waldron.—*History and Description of the Isle of Man*, 1744.
[3] Scott.—*Demonology and Witchcraft*.
[4] Scott.—*Minstrelsy of the Scottish Border*.
[5] Schindler.—*Aberglanben des Middelalters*, 20.
[6] *Pseudoxica Epidemica*.
[7] *Astro-Meteorologica* (1686), p. 204.

The early English poets occasionally allude to them. Shakspeare was well versed in the mermaid lore, as he speaks of them in many plays.[1]

[2]John Taylor, the "water-poet," thus sings of one,—

> "Four miles from land, we almost were aground,
> At last, unlook'd for, on our larboard side,
> A thick turmoyling in the sea we spyed,
> Like to a Merman, wading as he did,
> All in the sea his nether parts were hid,
> Whose brawny limbs and rough, neglected beard,
> And grim aspect, made us half afraid."

He spoke to them in good Kentish, and finally guided them out of danger.

Sabrina, goddess of the Severn river, was aided by them when she took refuge in the river depths,—

> [3] "The water-nymphs that in the bottom play'd,
> Held up their pearlèd wrists, and took her in."

The fish-exhibition alluded to by Autolycus, in "Winter Tale," "Here's another ballad of a fish that appeared upon the coast of a Wednesday, the fourscore of April, forty thousand fathoms above water, and sung this ballad against the hard hearts of maids. It was thought she was a woman, and was turned into a cold fish, for she would not exchange flesh with one that loved her," is paralleled by one in the "City Match,"[4]

> "Why, 'tis a man-fish,
> An ocean centaur, begot between a siren
> And a he stock-fish."

An old mariner's song runs thus,—

> "One Friday morning we set sail,
>   And, when not far from land,
> We all espied a fair mermaid
>   With a comb and a glass in her hand;

---

[1] *Midsummer Nights Dream*, Act III, scene 2. *Comedy of Errors*, Act III, scene 2. *Winters' Tale. Antony and Cleopatra*, Act II, scenes 2 and 3. *Henry VI*, Act III, scene 2.
[2] "A New Discovery by Sea," 1623.
[3] Milton.—*Poems*.
[4] Mayne.—*City Match*, 1639.

The stormy winds they did blow."

Thus embodying the storm-raising omens of sailing on Friday, and of seeing a mermaid

[1]The Stationers' Company published, in 1684, an account of "a strange reporte of a monstrous fish that appeared in the form of a woman from the waist upward, scene in the sea."

Early navigators chronicle their appearance. Columbus, in his "Journal," relates the appearance of three, raising themselves above the waves. He says he had previously seen them on the coast of Africa. He does not represent them as beautiful maidens, and they were probably rnanatee or dugongs. Hudson tells us: "This morning, one of our company looking overboard saw a mermaid, and calling up some of the company to see her, one more came up, and by that time she was come closely to the ship's side, looking earnestly at the men. A little after, a sea came and overturned her. From the navel up, her back and breasts were like a woman's, as they say that saw her, her body as big as one of us, her skin very white, and long hair hanging down behind, of color black. Seeing her go down, they saw her tail, which was like that of a porpoise, speckled like a mackerel."

In 1812, a gentleman of Exmouth saw a creature like a mermaid sporting in the water. One was seen on the Argleshire coast, on June 4, 1857, rising three or four times out of the water. Other appearances of them in 1817 and in 1863, near the Suffolk coast, are recorded. The skeleton of a so-called mermaid found on one of the islands, was ascertained to be that of a dugong.

[2]A story is told among seafaring men that a diver once saw a beautiful mermaid outside of his glass diving-bell. She told him she would protect him, if he would always recognize her in any shape. He promised, but, some days afterwards, he crushed a polypus with his foot. The next time he went down, the mermaid told him it was her whom he had injured, and he soon after met his death in consequence.

[3]Cornish fishermen call them merrymaids, or Morgan (sea-women). At a place on the coast, a sudden lifting of the fog disclosed seals on a rock, and these were said to be mermaids. Another rock on the Cornish coast, called Mermaid's Rock, is said to be a haunt of these maidens just before a wreck. Certain young men visited these rocks at such a time, but never reappeared. Senten Harbor was traditionally choked up by a mermaid. One is said to have been caught by an old man, and, in return for carrying her to sea, she gave him the power of dispelling witches, and also bestowed on him her comb. A family in Cornwall still display this

---

[1] Jones.—*Credulities.*

[2] Bottrell.—*Traditions of West Cornwall.*

[3] Hunt.—*Romance and Drolls of the West of England.*

comb (really a piece of a shark's jaw) in proof of this visit. A story entitled "The Mermaid's Revenge" tells us that a certain poor couple bathed their child daily in the sea. One day it slipped from their hands, was exchanged for a mermaid, which grew up in their family. She was afterwards betrayed by a lover, and he was dragged into the water, while walking on the strand, some time afterwards, as a punishment for his crime.

So-called mermaids have been exhibited several times in England. [1]In 1755, a carefully made imposture representing a mermaid, said to have been captured in the Grecian seas, was exhibited in London. Another, said to have been captured at sea by a Captain Forster, was shown at Covent Garden at the same time, and there is an account of the exhibition of one in Chamber's "Book of Days," in 1809. In 1822, a figure made in the East Indies, and brought to London, consisting of a fish-tail joined to an ape's body, was exhibited in London, purchased at a high figure by Barnum, and brought to America. I believe it is now in the Boston Museum. [2]Schele de Vere says a living mermaid was advertised in England, but was found to be a woman with a fish's tail sewn to her body.

Welsh tales of mermaids are told by Sikes, and by other writers.

[3]The story of the surgeons of Myddvai, relates that one of their ancestors, while sitting on the banks of the dark Lake Lyn y Van Vach, saw three maidens in the water, and courted them. They, however, called him "eater of baked bread," and refused to have anything to do with him. One day, however, he saw unbaked bread floating on the lake, ate it, and was thereby possessed of one of the mermaids. She declared that she would leave him, should he strike her thrice. He did so, in angry moments, and she left him. It is related that she visited her sons, and taught them medicine, in which their descendants are yet skilled. Welsh mermaids, however, are scarce, all the water-sprites and water-fairies of their stories being without the fishy tail that characterizes the mermaid proper.

A mermaid, looking like a maiden of seventeen years, was seen at Ren-y-hold in 1782.

[4]Gwenhidwy, whose sheep are the waves and who,

> "Drives her white flocks afield, and warns in time
> The wary fisherman,"

was fabled a mermaid. "Take the mermaid's advice, and save thyself;

---

[1] Gould.—*Myths of the Middle Ages.*
[2] *Wonders of the Deep.* p. 29.
[3] Choice Notes, *Notes and Queries*, p. 33 and 34.
[4] See Chapter I.

take shelter when you see the mermaid driving her flocks ashore," says an old Welsh poem.

[1]The Irish mermaid is called Merrow, or Moruach (sea-maid). Mermen have green hair, red eyes and nose, and are fond of brandy. A man obtained a sea-wife, but on returning home one night, he saw two seals on the beach, and found that one was his wife, who had obtained her seal-skin.

An old Celtic legend says Liban and her family were drowned in Lough Neagh, but she became a mermaid, married a knight, whom she fascinated, and was baptized.

[2]The first merman was Fintan, who came to Ireland before the deluge, was saved in the form of a fish, afterwards lived on shore, and was converted by St. Patrick, and became a saint himself. Old sculptures show him, like the Assyrian Dagon. In the cathedral of Omfert County, Ireland, a sculptured mermaid is seen, carrying a book in her hand.

A story of the Lady of Gollerus, given by Croker, relates that a mermaid was caught by getting possession of her enchanted cap (cohuleen druith). She says she is daughter of the king of the waves, marries her captor, but, as usual, finds the cap and disappears. The tale of the "Last of the Cantillons" relates that deceased members of that family were left on the sea-side to be carried away by sea-men, but that a curious fellow watched these people, and they declared no more should be thus carried away. In the story of the Lord of Dunkerron, he encounters a mermaid,—

> "For a beautiful spirit of ocean, 'tis said,
> The Lord of Dunkerron would win to his bed;
> When by moonlight the waters were hush'd to repose
> That beautiful spirit of ocean arose,
> Her hair, full of lustre, just floated and fell
> O'er her bosom that heav'd with a billowy swell."

He follows her to sea-caverns, but, after a time, on visiting the earth and returning, he finds that she is dead, killed by the enraged mermen.

[3]John Reid, of Cromarty, caught a mermaid, who begged to be put in the water, promising to fulfill three wishes. He did this, and obtained what he wished.

Rathlin Island is haunted by a mermaid:

> "'Tis said, at eve, when rude winds sleep,
> And hush'd is every turbid swell,

---

[1] Croker.—*Fairy Legends of the South of Ireland*.
[2] Popular Folk-lore of Ireland, *Eclectic Mag.*, 1873.
[3] Hugh Miller.—*Scenes and Legends*, p. 283.

> A mermaid rises from the deep
> And sweetly tunes her magic shell."

[1]In another legend, the daughter of the king of the land of youth appears to a young hunter, and he follows her to her courts beneath the waves.

A mermaid is said to have been found in a shark's belly in Ireland, and is minutely described as being of the size of a nine-year-old boy, with long hair, olive skin, one thumb, webbed fingers, etc. It was thrown into the sea.

[2]The Irish feared to kill seals, saying that they were the souls of those drowned at the flood, and that they can put aside their skin and appear in the guise of mortals, but cannot return to their watery element, if the skin is stolen.

Among the many legends of the famous piper, is that version in the tale of Maurice Connor, the Irish harper, who pipes a mermaid from the waters, but is in time charmed by her and accompanies her. So Arion, in danger of sacrifice by the Greek crew, plays first and charms the fish, until he is borne ashore to Corinth. The romantic historians of Ireland assert that Tuire, or sea-maidens, played about the Milesian ships on their way to Ireland.

[3]Breton stories of mermaids are abundant, and fishermen say they often see them on the coast. One (a "Siren") caught by a peasant, brought bread, clothing, silver and gold, to purchase her freedom, [4]Brantome says, "Nereids were abundant in French waters during the middle ages." The most celebrated one was Melusina, whose marriage to Raymond of Toulouse, was related above.

She was said afterwards to haunt the castle on the death of any one, becoming thus a banshee.

From the middle-age treatise of Paracelsus[5] comes the legend of Undine, whose story is so charmingly told by Fouque. She is really a water-sprite, who visits her foster-parents, and on one occasion sees and loves a wandering knight, who marries her, when she becomes the possessor of a soul, and various vicissitudes common to mortals await her. She once revisits the water-depths, and strange enough, returns unharmed, but the knight soon after dies.

There is a French legend of Poul Dahut, a rock on the Breton coast, where the daughter of a sea-king, Dahut, is said to sit in rough weather.

---

[1] Croker.—*Fairy Legends of the South of Ireland.*
[2] See Froude.—"Short Stories," p. 187.
[3] Sebillot.—*Litterature Orale de Haute Bretagne.*
[4] *Dictionnaire Historique.*
[5] *Treatise on Elementary Spirits.*

[1] A Breton tale is told of a lady, who found a mermaid on the beach, and put her into the water. The grateful sea-maiden brought her a shell, with a drink in it, telling her to give it to her son. Instead, she gave it to her cat, which became wise, but malicious, while her son was always half-witted.

In Provence, a gold ring is thrown into the water, and verses repeated, to charm the water king.

A negro mermaid was exhibited at St. Germain Fair in Paris, in 1758, and a shop in Ostend contained, in 1881, a figure said to be a mermaid, a cut of which was shown in Harper's Magazine.

[2] In an old "History of the Netherlands," we find this account of the appearance of one in 1493, at Haarlem: "At that time there was a great tempest at sea, with exceeding high tides, the which did drown many cities in Friseland and Holland; by which tempest there came a sea-woman swimming in the Zuyder-Zee, betwixt the towns of Campen and Edam, the which, passing by the Purmeric, entered into the strait of a broken dyke in the Purmermer, where she remained a long time, and could not find the hole by which she entered, for that the breach had been stopped after that the tempest had ceased. Some country women and their servants who did daily pass the Purmeric, to milk their kine in the next pastures, did often see this woman swimming on the water, whereof at the first they were much afraid; but in the end being accustomed to see it very often, they viewed it nearer, and at last they resolved to take it if they could. Having discovered it, they rowed toward it, and drew it out of the water by force, carrying it in one of their barks unto the town of Edam. When she had been well washed and cleansed from the sea-moss which was grown about her, she was alike unto another woman; she was apparalled, and began to accustom herself to ordinary meats like unto other mortals; yet she sought still means to escape, and to get into the water, but she was straightly guarded. They came from fare to see her. Those of Harlem made great sute to them of Edam to have this woman by reason of the strangenesse thereof. In the end they obtained her, where she did learn to spin, and lived many years (some say fifteen), and for the reverence which she bare unto the signe of the crosse whereupon she had been accustomed, she was buried in the churchyarde. Many persons worthy of credit have justified in their writings that they had seene her in the said towne of Harlem."

There is no fish-maiden here. If we are to believe the story at all, we may reasonably suspect this to be some outcast like Caspar Hauser, a human being trained to the shallow water of the pond, and placed to live there and be adopted by her finder, or we may account it the designed fraud of some sharp Hollander. In fact, more careful study has

---

[1] Gubernatis—*Zoological Mythology*.
[2] Baring Gould.—*Curious Myths*, p. 509.

demonstrated that the earliest accounts of her only described her as a water-woman, and the mermaid myth was afterward invented.

A mermaid is said to have appeared to Antwerp whalers and said,—

> [1]"Sailors, throw out a cask
> So soon you whales shall have."

[2]A mermaid prophesied the destruction of Zevenbergen, a wicked city of Holland, in 1721, and also of Minden,—

> "Zevenbergen must perish
> And Lobbeken's seven towers still remain."

[3]Gaspar Schott gives a curious sketch of a Triton with human body, arms and head, and fish tail.

[4]Ludovicus Vivus relates that in his time a mermaid was taken in Holland, and carefully kept for two years; that she began to speak, or at least to make a very disagreeable noise in imitation of speech; that she found an opportunity, and got into the sea. The same writer says that Lieutenant Transmale saw at the time he was sent with some men on an expedition in the Bay of Hodudela, as did all the people that were with him, in clear daytime, two mermaids, the one greater, the other smaller, which they took to be man and wife, swimming together, and the hair of their heads hung over their neck, and that it appeared between a green and grayish color; and that they could see that they had breasts. They were all above the waists shaped exactly as a human creature, but from thence downward they seemed to go off tapering to a point. About six weeks afterward, near the same place, a like appearance was seen by upward of fifty people.

Holland afterward became celebrated for its mermaids, so much so that in that country, and its colonies, the mermaid was deemed a native production.

[5]Valentin, a curate of Amboyna, published in the Dutch tongue a large collection of facts, in support of the existence of the mermaid. Many certificates accompanied his description, and the beautifully colored figures, in the curious work referred to.

[6]In 1611 it is said a mermaid or sea-woman was taken alive near the

---

[1] Landrin.—*Les Monstres Marins*.
[2] Schele de Vere.—*Wonders of the Deep*, p. 25.
[3] *Physica Curiosa*, 1662.
[4] Ruysch.—*Natural History*.
[5] *Poissons, Ecrivisses et Crabes de divers couleurs et figures extraordinaires, q'on a trouve dans les Iles Moluques, Amsterdam*, 1717.
[6] B. Gould.—*Curious Myths*.

island of Boro, which was fifty-nine inches long. She lived four days and seven hours and then died, as she would not eat anything. She was never heard to articulate any noise. One Samuel Falvers, in Amboyna, preserved the body for some time, and made out an exact description of it, by which it appears that her head was like a woman's, properly proportioned, with eyes, nose and mouth, only the eyes, which were light blue, seemed to differ a little from the human species. The hair, that just reached over the neck, appeared of sea-green and grayish color. She had breasts, long arms, hands, and all the upper parts of the body almost as white as a woman's, but leaning somewhat to the sea-gray. The lower part of her body appeared like the hinder part of a fish.

Dr. Kerschur, in one of his scientific reports, relates that another mermaid was caught in the Zuyder Zee, and dissected at Leyden by Professor Peter Pau, and in the same learned report, he makes mention of still another, who was found in Denmark, and who was taught to knit, and foretell future events. This mermaid had a pretty face, mild, sparkling eyes, a small, tiny nose; long, drooping arms; the fingers of her hands joined by a cartilage like a goose's foot; the breasts round and hard, and the skin covered with white shells. He asserted that the mermaids and mermen constitute a submarine population, which, partaking of the skill of the ape and the beaver, build their grottoes of stone in places inaccessible to all divers, and where they spread out their beds of sand, in which they lie, sleep and enjoy their loves.

The mermaid of the Royal Museum at the Hague was seen by Alexandre Dumas, during a visit there. He describes it as quite dried and withered, and in color very like the head of a Caribbee. Her eyes were shut, her nose flattened, her lips sticking to the teeth, of which only a few remained; her bosom was conspicuous, though sunk; a few short hairs stood out upon the head; finally, the lower part of the body terminated in a fish's tail. There was no opening for dispute. It was really and trully a siren, a mermaid, a sea-nymph. "If, after all this, there shall be found those who disbelieve the existence of such creatures as mermaids, let them please themselves. I shall give myself no more trouble about them."

[1]Dimas Bosque, physician to the viceroy of the island of Manara, relates in a letter inserted in Bartholdi's "History of Asia," that walking one day on the sea-shore with a Jesuit father, a party of fishermen came running up to them to invite the father to enter their barge, if he wished to behold a prodigy. There were sixteen fishes with human faces in the barge—nine females and seven males—all of which the fishermen had just drawn up with a single cast of their net. Their teeth were square and closely set together. The chest was broad and covered with a skin, singularly white, which left visible the blood-vessels. Their ears were elevated like our own, cartilaginous, and covered with a fine skin. Their

---

[1] Landrin.—*Les Monstres Marin.*

eyes were similar to ours in color, shape and position; they were inclosed in their orbits, below the forehead, furnished with lids, and did not possess, like fishes, different axes of vision. Their nose only differed from the human nose, by its being rather flatter, like the negro's, and partially slit up, like a bulldog's. In all of them the mouth and lips were perfectly similar to ours.

The females had round, full and firm bosoms, and some of them appeared to be suckling their young, as when the breasts were pressed upon, a very white and delicate milk jetted out. Their arms, two cubits in length, and much fuller and plumper than the men's, had no joints; their hands were joined to the cubitus. Lastly, the lower portion, beginning with the haunches and thighs, was divided into a double tail, as we see in ordinary fishes.

[1]German tales of the mermaid proper are not numerous. Goethe's "Waterman" is a pretty version of a Danish tale of a mermaid. A merman visits the church, and weds a maiden who falls in love with him. He brings a ship for her, and they embark,—

> "But when they were out in the midst of the sound,
> Down went they all in the deep profound."

In German legend, there is a queen of the sea, Merreimne (Norse Marmenille, mer-woman). She was fished up from the sea in a net, but the terrified fishermen hastily threw her overboard.

Three men are said to have caught a mermaid at Weningstede, in Schleswick-Holstein, but they put her back in the water, on hearing her cries. It is there believed that they foretell a storm, when seen about the bows of a ship. A "Waterman" is said to have stopped a ship at sea, and to have refused to let it go until the queen, a passenger thereon, should descend to his palace, where a midwife was needed.

Goethe's ballad, "Sir Peter of Stauffen," depicts the power of the mermaid's song; and there is another old ballad, where a waterman

> "Drags her down to his ocean cave
> The gentle Amelie."

The Lorelei, who is fabled to sit on the rocks in the Rhine, and lure boats to destruction, is celebrated in song by Heine and Doenninger, and mermaids are represented in Wagner's Rheingold.

An old German legend is told of a certain countess, who was seized while bathing, by mermaids and men, and stripped of her jewels. She expressed a great desire to recover her wedding-ring, at least, and on the seventh day thereafter, it was found in the stomach of a fish, caught near

---

[1] Baring Gould.—*Curious Myths*, 510.

the spot where she had bathed.

[1]A Hamburg skipper, Jan Schmidt, saw a mermaid in 1610, while at sea near Bayonne, just at daylight. He knew she would drag some one down, so had his men repulse her with long poles and pikes. When she found them prepared for her, she uttered a piercing cry, and dove down into the sea.

At Nidden, in West Prussia, a mermaid sits on the rocks and decoys persons to her, but they are drowned ere they reach her.

Frisians say there are but seven mermaids, and that a man devoting himself to one of them, will suffer death, should he ever abandon her.

In an Esthonian tale, a fisherman sees a daughter of the "Mother of the Seas," falls in love with her, and marries her. She leaves him on every Thursday, and, on watching her, he finds she has a fish-tail.

[2]In the Finnish Epic, the "Hostess of the Sea," rises at the sound of Wainamoïnen's harp (the wind), and combs her long locks by the seaside. That hero catches a mermaid, but as he is about to cut her open and eat her, she disappears.

Wallachian, Wendic, and Russian stories of water-sprites are told, some of whom assume the shape of birds, and fly through the air. Many of these are a kind of a cross between mermaids and sirens.

Mermaids are said to have been seen near Portugal in 1531, and Spanish and Italian stories of them are recorded.

[3]Lamia is a water-maiden in modern Greece, who is represented as malicious, greedy, and sensual, dragging people into the water. Mermaids are not, however, so abundant in southern waters, as in the colder seas of the north.

[4]Chinese say mermaids are of the shape of demons, and are ruled by a harpy, Nükira, who, when the heavens were torn, mended them, but left a hole in the northwest, whence emerge the cold winds. They call mermaids sea-women (hai-nü), and numerous stories are told of them. One is said to have been captured at Nanchow in 1800, and many saw her; and another was found at Nüshan. A cabinet councillor is said to have found one on the beach in Corea, and carried her to sea, putting her in it.

[5]In the Loochoo Islands also, one is said to have lived with a native ten years, but finally she climbed a tree, and disappeared. Here we have a nymph of the sky-sea.

Japan is, however, the headquarters of these coy maidens of the sea. Here an old Dutch navigator obtained the first "veritable" mermaid, and

---

[1] Schmidt.—Seeman's *Sagen und Schiller Märchen*.
[2] *Kalevala*.—Le Duc's Translation.
[3] Hahn.—*Greichishe Märchen*.
[4] Dennys.—*Folk-lore of China*.
[5] Conway.—*Demonology*, II, 218.

they may still be procured of ingenious natives. Numbers have been shown in museums, etc., deftly made by uniting a child's head to a fish's body. At Bartholomew fair, in 1825, there was exhibited a mermaid, obtained by a Dutch ship from Japan, and the Ottoman minister to Paris, in 1840, related that he had seen a veritable sea-woman, brought from Eastern seas.

A Japanese legend relates that a mermaid prophesied an epidemic.

[1]Ottawa Indians believed in the existence of a mermaid with two fish-like extremities, and called her daughter of the flood. Pascagoula Indians had traditions of a race emerging from the sea, who worshiped a mermaid.

An Ottawa tale is told of a certain Wassaur conveyed by a spirit-maiden to the "Spirit of the Sand Dunes," in Lake Superior.

[2]B. Gould tells a tale of an Ottawa chieftain who saw a beautiful woman arise from the water. She wished to have a human soul, but could only have one by marrying a mortal.

The tribe drove her away, and the result was a war of extermination with another tribe (Adirondacks), and finally one was left, who was carried down by the water-maiden at St. Anthony's Falls.

These maidens have often been seen on our shores.

[3]Captain John Smith saw, in 1614, off an island in the West Indies, a mermaid, with the upper part of the body perfectly resembling a woman. She was swimming about with all possible grace when he descried her near the shore. Her large eyes, rather too round, her finely-shaped nose, somewhat short, it is true, her well-formed ears, rather too long, however, made her a very agreeable person, and her long green hair imparted to her an original character by no means unattractive. Unfortunately the beautiful swimmer made a slip, and Captain Smith, who had already begun to experience the first effects of love, discovered that from below the waist the woman gave way to the fish.

[4]Jocelyn also tells of them: "One Mr. Miller, relates of a triton or mermaid, which he saw in Casco bay; the gentleman was a great forder, and used to go out with a small boat or canoe, and fetching a compass about a small island, there being many islands in the bay, he encountered with a triton, who, laying his hands upon the sides of the canoe, had one of them chopped off with a hatchet by Mr. Miller, which was in all respects like the hands of a man; the triton presently sunk, dyeing the water with his purple blood, and was no more seen."

The following account from a newspaper, of a similar occurrence, is given,—

---

[1] Gould.—*Myths of the Middle Ages.*
[2] Gould.—*Curious Myths*, p. 504.
[3] Landrin.—*Les Monstres Marins.*
[4] *Jocelyn's Voyages*, 1673, p. 23.

"John Dilercy related a curious story of some American fishermen: One night, it being a perfect calm, they observed a mermaid coming into their vessel, and fearing it to be some mischievous fish, in the fright of one of them, cut the creature's hand off with a hatchet, when it sank immediately, but soon came up again and gave a deep sigh as one feeling pain. The hand was found to have five fingers and nails like a woman's hand."

The Richmond *Dispatch*, of July, 1881, published an account of a negro woman who said that she, being pursued to death by some one in Cuba, jumped overboard, and was, after drifting for hours, rescued by a band of mermaids, who took her to their sea-caverns, and finally placed her on board a vessel bound for New Orleans.

In a daily (Boston) paper of October 31, 1881, is contained the following account of a mermaid captured in Aspinwall Bay and brought to New Orleans,—

"This wonder of the deep is in a fine state of preservation. The head and body of a woman are very plainly and distinctly marked. The features of the face, eyes, nose, mouth, teeth, arms, breasts and hair are those of a human being. The hair on its head is of a pale, silky blonde, several inches in length. The arms terminate in claws closely resembling an eagle's talons, instead of fingers with nails. From the waist up the resemblance to a woman is perfect, and from the waist down, the body is exactly the same as the ordinary mullet of our waters, with its scales, fins and tail perfect. Many old fishermen and amateur anglers who have seen it pronounce it unlike any fish they have ever seen. Scientists and savants alike are 'all at sea' respecting it, and say that if the mermaid be indeed a fabulous creature, they cannot class this strange comer from the blue waters."

Torquemada says that Mexican legends of the mermaid related that she, the tortoise and the whale, formed a bridge of their bodies for a man to pass the House of the Sun.

[1]Herbert Smith says there are stories on the lower Amazon, of water-maidens with long black hair, who sing and entice young men into the water. Uangaia, King of the Fishes, assumes many shapes, and entices women into the waters.

[2]Moravian missionaries in South America brought from thence wonderful stories of mermen and mermaids, some having seen these beings, with brown skin and long hair, in the water. The natives feared them and would not harm them, fearing disaster.

Negroes of Surinam told English officers, in 1801, that they often saw mermaids playing in the river on moonlight nights.

The tradition of the mermaid will long survive in nautical

---

[1] *Brazil*.
[2] Schele de Vera.—*Wonders of the Deep*, p. 22.

nomenclature. English fishermen call the frog-fish Meermaid, although no reference to the mermaid is intended. The Spongia palmata is called the mermaid's glove, and the outer covering of shark's eggs, as well as the hollow root of the sea-weed Fucus polyschides, are named the mermaid's purse.

Having thus traced the history of the mermaid, and given an account of her in all corners of the earth, we are prepared to believe her origin not an unnatural one, but a development of ideas originating in antiquity, and fostered during an age of credulity and superstition. Her origin is undoubtedly mythical, but various causes natural and legendary have assisted the myth in its growth. As before said, these maidens are originally cloud-nymphs. This ancestry has already been partially traced in the present chapter. Analogies between the mermaids and these ancient mythical beings have been given. Like Proteus, they may (at least the water-sprites can) change their forms at will. This is an attribute of their primitive form, that of the Apsaras, or "formless ones," whose cloud bodies arose from the vaporous deep. Like Nereus, they are possessed of great wisdom. This is also an attribute of all the primitive beings who arose from the deep, as Oannes, Hea, Viracocha, etc. Like the ancient sea-deities, they are benificent, since they possess great wealth. This latter characteristic is alleged of all the sea beings. The hoard of the Niflungs, the golden palace of Neptune, and of Œgir, the Rheingold, and other instances of this wealth, will be remembered. If they are malicious, or diabolic, they derive such a temperament from Nick, or from Typhon, from their ancestors the Sirens, or their prototypes, the harpies. The bad omen derived from their appearance may be traced at least to Melusina, who, after her death, becomes a banshee or evil apparition. Perhaps the Christian influence in the degradation of heathen deities may have aided in establishing a diabolic character. The song of the mermaid, by which she often lures to destruction listening mortals, is but the dangerous lay of the Sirens, or the sweet attractions of Circe. [1]The Myth is ancient, as Hylas was so charmed in the Argonautic voyages.

This lay is none other, as we have seen, than the sweet strains of Orpheus' harp, and here perhaps is the origin of the mermaid's comb, doubtless the ancient lyre. Being thus always malevolent, when seen at sea, and ominous in appearance, she would be naturally connected with the weather, a significant fact corroborating her cloud-parentage. The fish-tail peculiar to the mermaid is doubtless derived primarily from the Assyrian Oannes, and we have seen Tritons and Nereids thus represented. The Sirens, anciently birds, became, later, beauteous maidens, and were finally endowed with the scaly appendage.

[2]Price has thus embodied these ideas: "The Nereids of antiquity, the

---

[1] Ap. Rhodius.—"Argonauties," I.131.
[2] Introduction to Warton's *History of Poetry*.

daughters of the sea, born seers, are evidently the same with the mermaids of the British and Northern shores, the habitations of both are fixed in crystal caves or coral palaces, beneath the waters of the ocean; and they are alike distinguished for their partiality to the human race, and their prophetic power in disclosing the events of futurity. The Naiads differ only in name from the Nixen of Germany and Scandinavian Nissen, or the water-elves of our countrymen Aelfric."

Philologists find, however, that even this difference does not exist, since from a Sanskrit word Sna, to flow, are derived the names for Naiad, Nereid, Nymph, Nick, etc.

These beings require some recompense for their services, which represents the ancient sacrifices to the water-deities. The priestly influence is again visible in the notion that this gift is baptism, or salvation. The myth of marriage to mortals is of more difficult interpretation, and is closely connected with the legends of their having the power of changing their form, and of the possession of some mysterious garment whereby the change is effected. This garment was originally a swan's plumage, but is sometimes a peculiar cap, a seal-skin, or even a girdle. The swan story is first told in the Katha Sarit Sagatha.

[1]Svidatta saw a swan in the Ganges, plunged in, and followed the maiden to her palace beneath the waves. The story is common to many lands, and is even known among the Mongols and Tartars. Aeschylus says the Phorkides were swan-shaped. In the Hymn to Apollo, the clouds are swan-nymphs, attendant on Phoebus, the sun. "Here, then, we have the groundwork of all those tales which speak of men as wedded to fairies, nymphs, nixies, mermaids, swan-maidens or other supernatural beings." "From the thought which regarded the cloud as an eagle or swan, it was easy to pass to the idea that the birds were beautiful maidens; and hence that they could at will, or on the ending of the enchantment, assume their human form." "Then would follow the myth that the only way to capture these beings was to seize their garments of swan's or eagle's plumes, without which they were powerless."

But while we may acknowledge the mythical origin of these beings, there are many natural causes whose influence aided in the formation and perpetuation of the mermaid myth. Much of the testimony recorded above is too circumstantial to be accounted a mere trick of the imagination, or morbid fancy of the writers.

Species of existing sea-animals have certainly aided in perpetuating these many stories of maidens of the sea. The dugong and manatee especially have a human look, having large breasts and short, arm-like fins. [2]Scoresby says the front view of a young walrus without tusks resembles a human face. Speaking of their habit of rearing the head

---

[1] Gould.—*Myths of the Middle Ages*.
[2] *Voyages*.

above the water, he says, "I have myself seen a sea-horse in such a position, and under such circumstances, that it required very little stretch of the imagination to mistake it for a human being; so like, indeed, was it, that the surgeon of the ship actually reported to me his having seen a man with his head just appearing above the water." French and German heraldic signs represent mermaids with one or two tails.

The French call the manatee femme marine, and the Dutch name the dugong mannetje (little man) and Baardanetzee. (little beard). Professor Owen thinks these animals are the mermaids of fable.

In Oriental legend, the dugong is the mermaid of the Indian ocean, and their tears are pearls, and attract persons to them. Stories of mermaids singing or talking may also have arisen from hearing the cries of the seal, said by navigators to resemble those of an infant. The well-known friendliness of that animal to man, and its gentleness, would favor the current ideas concerning mermaids. Thus, while the mythical idea grew up in a superstitious age, the reports of mariners of these strange animals to a people equally ignorant in science, would foster and preserve the growths of the myths.

[1]Schele de Vere, in alluding to the accounts given of mermaids by the Moravian missionaries, in South America, conjectures these mermaids to be the Canthoeirus, a race of savages who almost live in the waters of the great rivers of the Amazon valley, often attack boats, and are greatly feared by the natives. Here would be a natural element in the growth of the mermaid myth. [2]Hone tells a story of a certain Vega, who, in 1674, leaped into the sea and was drawn ashore five years afterwards, covered with scales. He had forgotten his language, but was recognized by his family. He lived several years afterwards, but finally disappeared. [3]Tieck pronounces the story authentic.

These, along with the other phantoms of the deep, no longer appear to the intelligent mariner of this scientific age. Yet in remote corners, and to skeptical vision, such apparitions still are recorded.

But in spite of the occasional reports of such visions, we may reasonably conclude with the Swedish poet, Stagneli, that,—

> "The Neck no more upon the river sings,
> And no mermaid to bleach her linen plays
> Upon the waves in the wild solar rays."

---

[1] *Wonders of the Deep.*
[2] Hone.—*Table Book*, Vol. II, p. 188.
[3] *Das Wasserman*, 1831.

Source:
Bassett, Fletcher S. *Legends and Superstitions of the Sea and of Sailors in All Lands and at All Times*. Chicago and New York: Belford, Clarke & Co., 1885.

9. Fictitious Creatures of the Sea from *Fictitious and Symbolic Creatures in Art* by John Vinycomb

INTRODUCTORY NOTES

"The sea, that is
A world of waters heapèd up on high,
Rolling like mountains in wild wilderness,
Horrible, hideous, roaring with hoarse cry!"
            Spenser.

"I can call spirits from the vasty deep."
            Shakespeare.

MARINERS in all ages, prone to superstitious fears, have peopled the great deep with beings of the most dreadful kind, all the more wonderful and indescribable because of the mysterious and unknown regions in the sea depths which they were supposed to inhabit. Classic mythology in its wealth of imagery allotted a whole hierarchy of greater and lesser divinities to the government of the watery element, whose capricious ruling of the waves man altogether failed to comprehend. Their fancied terrors, begot in calms and storms, in darkness and in fogs, midst dangers of the most appalling kind, assumed those monstrous and fantastic shapes which their own fears created. The active forces of nature in unusual forms impressed them as the result of supernatural agency, or the "meddling of the gods," whose favours and protection the mariner, by prayers and supplications, endeavoured to propitiate; and whilst tremblingly he skirts the horizon's edge in timid ventures, new dangers impel him to promises of greater gifts to assuage the wrathful mood of his angry god or some other equally powerful or more spiteful.

The national god of the Philistines was represented with the face and hands of a man and the tail of a fish. It was but natural that a seafaring people should adopt a god of that form.

> "Dagon his name; sea-monster, upward man
> And downward fish: yet had his temple high
> Reared in Azotus, dreaded through the coast
> Of Palestine, in Gath and Ascalon,
> And Accaron and Gaza's frontier bounds."
> *Paradise Lost*, Book i. 462.

In the leviathan and behemoth of Scripture are darkly indicated monsters of the great deep. Scandinavian mythology, like that of all bold maritime peoples in old times, is rife with legends of certain great monsters of the sea. The kraken or sea-serpent of popular legend is a myth not yet laid to rest; there is still a lingering belief in the existence of the mermaid.

> "With a comb and a glass in her hand, her hand, her hand,
> With a comb and a glass in her hand."
> Popular sea-song.

Chief amongst the Grecian sea-divinities stands *Poseidon*, or *Neptune* as he was called by the Romans, the potent "ruler of the seas." He usually dwelt, not in Olympus, but at the bottom of the sea, in a magnificent golden palace in the neighbourhood of Ægæ. He is always represented with a trident, sometimes with a rudder—special symbols of his power over the sea. Accompanied by his wife, fair Amphitrite, he was frequently pictured in royal state in his chariot, drawn through the billows by wild sea-horses, attended by "Triton blowing loud his wreathed horn," Proteus, "the godlike shepherd of the sea," and other followers—dolphins leaping the waves and showing their high arched backs in wild gambolings.

Nereus and his fifty daughters, the *Nereides*, who dwelt in caves and grottos of the ocean—beneficent sea-nymphs,—win the hearts of the sailors, now by their merry sports and dances, now by their timely assistance in the hour of danger. Whilst Nereus and his lovely daughters represent the sea under its calm and pleasant aspect, Thaumas, Phorcys, Ceto present it as the world of wonders, under its more terrible conditions. The storm winds and all the terrors and dangers of the deep were typified under various strange and peculiar forms. Not the least dreaded were the *Sirens*, fatal sisters, who "spread o'er the silver waves their golden hair," basked near sunlit rocks, and lured all men to their ruin by their enchanting voices, save only the crafty Ulysses.

These and many others of lesser note, Proteus, Glaucus and the rest, make up the discordant influences that govern the watery element.

Many wonderful stories are told by classic writers concerning these old myths, and innumerable relics of antique art which embody the conceptions of the times are extant in our museums, by which we may judge to what a large extent such ideas influenced the common life and formed the beliefs of ancient peoples.

It is also worthy of observation to note in what manner the ancients sought to identify the various sea-deities and other mythical creatures with the element they lived in. Each was known by his form or the attributes by which he was accompanied. Modern heraldry repeats many of these old-world myths as new-coined fables, so that for their proper understanding and signification it will be necessary briefly to refer to ancient ideas respecting them. Lakes, rivers and fountains had each their impersonation peculiar to them, which will be found referred to in classic story.

Mediæval legend is equally rife with accounts of wonderful creatures of the sea. The change of one form of superstition for another alters but little the constitution of the mind to harbour fears, and the imagination will deceive even the wisest and best so long as Nature's laws are misunderstood.

Particular whirlpools, rocks and other dangerous places to navigation, are personated under the forms of monsters of various and awful shapes feared by the mariner, who dreads

"The loud yell of watery wolves to hear."

Scylla and Charybdis are two rocks which lie between Italy and Sicily. Ships which tried to avoid one were often wrecked on the other. The ancients feigned an interesting legend to account for their existence. It was Circe who changed Scylla into a frightful sea monster, and Jupiter who changed Charybdis into a whirlpool, the noise of which was likened to the loud barking of dogs; and the monster was therefore represented with savage dogs amidst her scaly folds, and loudly baying.

> "Far on the right her dogs foul Scylla hides;
> Charybdis roaring on the left presides,
> And in her greedy whirlpool sucks the tides,
> Then spouts them from below; with fury driven
> The waves mount up, and wash the face of heaven.
> But Scylla from her den with open jaws
> The sinking vessel in her eddy draws
> Then dashes on the rocks. A human face
> And virgin bosom hides her tail's disgrace;
> Her parts obscene below the waves descend,
> With dogs enclosed, and in a dolphin end."
> *Æneid*, Book iii.

Homer gives a vivid description of Ulysses passing the rocks and whirlpools:

> "Now through the rocks, appall'd with deep dismay,

> We bend our course, and stem the desperate way;
> Dire Scylla there a scene of horror forms;
> And here Charybdis fills the deep with storms.
> When the tide rushes from her rumbling caves,
> The rough rock roars, tumultuous boil the waves;
> They toss, they foam, a wild confusion raise,
> Like water bubbling o'er the fiery blaze;
> Eternal mists obscure the aërial plain,
> And high across the rocks she spouts the main:
> When in her gulfs the rushing sea subsides,
> She drains the ocean with the refluent tides:
> The rock rebellows with a thundering sound;
> Deep, wondrous deep, below appears the ground."
>
> *Odyssey*, Book xii.

The giants and ogres of romance were never so fearfully armed or clothed by the wildest fiction with so terrible an aspect as the cephalopods, the race to which the cuttlefish or octopus belongs. Eminently carnivorous, voracious and fierce; beneath staring eyes are spread eight strong fleshy arms furnished with tenacious suckers, which adhere with unrelenting pertinacity, and the arms are swiftly twined round the struggling prey, which vainly strives to disengage itself from so fearful and so fatal embrace. Cephalopods of enormous size are sometimes found with arms as thick as a man's thigh. Homer refers to its tenacity of grip in a simile.

The cuttlefish appears upon ancient Greek coins of Coressus, in allusion to the worship of Neptune, a deity much venerated as the protector of this island.

Amongst the veritable inhabitants of the ocean there are few more extraordinary mammals than the sea-unicorn, *Monodon monoceros*, the beaked whale of the Arctic seas, twenty to thirty feet from stern to snout. His length is increased about eight feet by his magnificent spirally twisted tusk of the purest ivory, which in reality is simply the canine tooth growing straight out of the upper jaw. One of the royal treasures of Denmark is the narwhal throne of the Castle of Rosenberg. It is the horn of this "strange fish" which has kept up the belief in the existence of the mythical unicorn.

Xiphias gladius, swordfish, is the largest of the thorny fishes, and belongs to the scombers or mackerel group. The sawfish, *Pristis antiquorum*, ranks by himself between the rays and sharks. He has the long body of a shark and the underside gill openings of a ray. His saw, like the sword of the Xiphias, is a long flattened bony snout, but is double-edged and serrated. It is well known as a weapon among the Polynesian islanders, and, like the sword of the Xiphias, is frequently found buried in the hulls of ocean-going ships.

There are two denizens of the deep which bear the name of sea-horse—one the tiny Hippocampus, the other the mighty walrus. The hippocampus of our public aquariums, a bony pipefish some six or eight inches in length, swimming upright, his favourite position in the water, with the general resemblance of his head to that of a horse, is very striking; anchored to the seaweed stems by their tails they dart on their prey with great quickness.

Hippocampus (ἵππος, *hippos*, a horse; κάμπη, *campe*, a bending), the steed of Neptune, had only the two forelegs of a horse, the hinder quarter being that of a dolphin. The word means "coiling horse."

The Sea-horse of the North, or walrus—the *Rossmareus* or *Morse* of the Scandinavians, the *Trichecus rosmarus* of science, is fifteen or twenty feet long, or even longer, and armed with huge canine teeth, sometimes measuring thirty inches in length—tusks which furnish no small amount of our commercial ivory. Many are the thrilling stories of the chase of these great sea-horses, for the walrus fights for his life as determinedly as any animal hunted by man. The walrus has had the honour assigned to it also of being the original of the mermaid, and Scoresby says the front part of the head of a young one without tusks might easily be taken at a little distance for a human face, especially as it has a habit of raising its head straight out of the water to look at passing ships.

The manatee, or sea-cow, found on the tropical coasts and streams of Africa and America, is called by the Portuguese and Spaniards the "woman-fish," from its supposed close resemblance. Its English name comes from the flipper resembling a human hand—*manus*—with which it holds its young to its breast. One of this species, which died at the Royal Aquarium in 1878, was as unlike the typical mermaid as one could possibly imagine, giving one a very startling idea of the difference between romance and reality; but if it was observed in its native haunts, and seen at some little distance, and then only by glimpses, it might possibly, as some have asserted, present a very striking resemblance to the human form.

Sir James Emerson Tennent, speaking of the *Dugong*, an herbivorous cetacean, says its head has a rude approach to the human outline, and the mother while suckling her young holds it to her breast with one flipper, as a woman holds an infant in her arm; if disturbed she suddenly dives under water and throws up her fish-like tail. It is this creature, he says, which has probably given rise to the tales about mermaids.

Seals differ from all other animals in having the toes of the feet included almost to the end in a common integument, converting them into broad fins armed with strong non-retractile claws. Of the many varieties of the seal family, from Kamchatka comes the noisy "Sea-lion" (*Otaria jubata*), so called from his curious mane. In the same neighbourhood we get the "Sea-leopard" (*Leptonyx weddellii*), and the "Sea-bear" (the *Etocephalus ursinus*), whose larger and better-developed limbs enable him to stand and walk on shore. But the most important of the seals, in a commercial sense, are the "Harp Seal" (*Phoca Grœnlandica*) and the Common Seal, or "Sea-dog" (*Phoca vitulina*), which yield the skins so valuable to the furrier. There are several other species, of which the most known are the Crested Seal, or *Neistsersoak* (*Stemmatopus cristatus*), and the Bearded Seal (*Phoca barbata*).

Apart from the seal having possibly given rise to legends of the mermaid, it has a distinguished position in superstition and mythology on its own account. In Shetland it is the "haff-fish," or selkie, a fallen spirit. Evil is sure to follow the unfortunate destroyer of one of these creatures. In the Faroe Islands there is a superstition that the seals cast off their skins every ninth night and appear as mortals, dancing until daybreak on the sands. Sometimes they are induced to marry, but if ever they recover their skins they betake themselves again to the water.

Stephen of Byzantium relates that the ships of certain Greek colonists were on their expeditions followed by an immense number of seals, and it was probably on this account that the city they founded in Asia received the name of Phocea, from φώκη (*Phoké*), the Greek name of a seal, and they also adopted that animal as the type or badge of the city upon their coinage. The gold pieces of the Phoceans were well known among the Greek States, and are frequently referred to by ancient writers. "Thus from a single coin," says Noel Humphreys,[1] "we obtain the corroboration of the legend of the swarm of seals, of the remote epoch of the emigration in question, the coin being evidently of the earliest period, most probably of the middle of the seventh century before the Christian era."

Luigi (+ 1598), brother to the Duke of Mantua, had for device a seal asleep upon a rock in a troubled sea, with the motto: "Sic quiesco" ("So rest I"). The seal, say the ancient writers, is never struck by lightning. The Emperor Augustus always wore a belt of seal-skin. "There is no living creature sleepeth more soundly," says Pliny,[2] "therefore when storms arise and the sea is rough the seal goes upon the rocks where it sleeps in safety unconscious of the storm."

The poet Spenser embodies many of the conceptions of his time in the description of the crowning adventures of the Knight Guyon. He here refers to "great sea monsters of all ugly shapes and horrible aspects" "such as Dame Nature's self might fear to see."

> "Spring-headed hydras, and sea-shouldering whales;
> Great whirlpools, which all fishes make to flee;
> Bright scolopendras arm'd with silver scales;
> Mighty monoceroses with unmeasured tails;

---

[1] "Coin Collector's Manual," Bohn.
[2] Book ix. ch. 13.

The dreadful fish that hath deserved the name
Of death, and like him looks in dreadful hue;
The grisly wasserman, that makes his game
The flying ships with swiftness to pursue;

The horrible sea-satyr that doth shew
His fearful face in time of greatest storm;
Huge Ziffius, whom mariners eschew
No less than rocks, as travellers inform;

And greedy rose-marines with visages deform;
All these, and thousand thousand many more
And more deformed monsters, thousandfold."
Faerie Queen, Book ii. cant. xii.

The early heralds took little account of these dreadful creatures—more easily imagined by fearful mariners or by poets than depicted by artists from their vague descriptions. The most imaginative of the tribe rarely ventured beyond such representations of marine monsters as appealed strongly and clearly to the universal sense of mankind—compounds of marine and land animals—either from a belief in the existence of such creatures, or because they used them as emblems or types of Qualities, combining for this purpose the attributes of certain inhabitants of the sea with those of the land or of the air to form the appropriate symbol.

In modern heraldry such bearings are usually adopted with special allusion to actions performed at sea, or they have reference in some way to the name or designation of the bearer, and hence termed allusive or canting heraldry. Some maritime towns bear nautical devices of the fictitious kind referred to. For instance, the City of Liverpool has for supporters Neptune with his trident, and a Triton with his horn. Cambridge and Newcastle-on-Tyne have sea-horses for supporters to their city's arms. Belfast has the sea-horse for sinister supporter and also for crest.

Many of the nobility also bear, either as arms or supporters, these mythical sea creatures, pointing in many instances to memorable events in their family history; indeed, as islanders and Britons, marine emblems—real and mythical—enter largely into our national heraldry.

POSEIDON OR NEPTUNE

POSEIDON or Neptune, the younger brother of Zeus (Jupiter), sometimes appears in heraldry, usually as a supporter. In the ancient mythology he was originally a mere symbol of the watery element, he afterwards became a distinct personality; the mighty ruler of the sea who with his powerful arms upholds and circumscribes the earth, violent and impetuous like the element he represents. When he strikes the sea with his trident, the symbol of his sovereignty, the waves rise with violence, as a word or look from him suffices to allay the fiercest tempest. Poseidon (Neptune) was naturally regarded as the chief patron and tutelary deity of the seafaring Greeks. To him they addressed their prayers before entering on a voyage, and to him they brought their offerings in gratitude for their safe return from the perils of the deep.

Dexter supporter of Baron Hawke.

In a famous episode of the "Faerie Queen" (Book iv. c. xi.) Spenser glowingly pictures the procession of all the water deities and their attendants:

> "First came great Neptune with his three-forked mace,
> That rules the seas and makes them rise and fall;
> His dewy locks did drop with brine apace
> Under his diadem imperial:
>
> "And by his side his Queen with coronal,
> Fair Amphitrite, most divinely fair,
> Whose ivory shoulders weren covered all,
> As with a robe, with her own silver hair,
> And decked with pearls which the Indian seas for her
>   prepare."

Amphitrite, his wife, one of the Nereids in ancient art, is represented as a slim and beautiful young woman, her hair falling loosely about her shoulders, and distinguished from all the other deities by the royal insignia. On ancient coins and gems she appears enthroned on the back of a mighty triton, or riding on a sea-horse, or dolphin.

Examples.—Baron Hawke bears for supporters to his shield an aggroupment of classic personations of a remarkable symbolic character, granted for the achievements of the renowned Admiral and Commander-in-Chief of the Fleet, Vice-Admiral of Great Britain, &c. &c., created Baron Hawke of Tarton, Yorks, 1776. *The dexter supporter is a figure of Neptune, his mantle vert, edged argent, crowned with an eastern crown, or, his dexter arm erect and holding a trident pointing downwards in the act of striking, sable, headea silver, and resting his left foot on a dolphin proper.*

Sir Isaac Heard, Somersetshire; Lancaster Herald, afterwards Garter. His arms, granted 1762, are thus blazoned in Burke's "General Armory" *Argent a Neptune crowned with an eastern crown of gold, his trident sable headed or, issuing from a stormy ocean, the sinister hand grasping the head of a ship's mast appearing above the waves, as part of a wreck, all proper; on a chief azure, the Arctic pole-star of the first between two water-bougets of the second.*

MERMAN OR TRITON

"Triton, who boasts his high Neptunian race
Sprung from the God by Solace's embrace."
Camoëns, "Lusiad."

"Triton his trumpet shrill before them blew
For goodly triumph and great jolliment
That made the rocks to roar as they were rent."
Spenser, "Faerie Queen."
(Procession of the Sea Deities.)

Merman or Triton.

Triton, with two tails. German.

TRITON was the only son of Neptune and Amphitrite. The poet Apollonius Rhodius describes him as having the upper parts of the body of a man, while the lower parts were those of a dolphin. Later poets and artists revelled in the conception of a whole race of similar tritons, who were regarded as a wanton, mischievous tribe, like the satyrs on land. Glaucus, another of the inferior deities, is represented as a triton, rough and shaggy in appearance, his body covered with mussels and seaweed; his hair and beard show that luxuriance which characterises sea-gods. Proteus, as shepherd of the seas, is usually distinguished with a crook. Triton, as herald of Neptune, is represented always holding, or blowing, his wreathed horn or conch shell. His mythical duties as attendant on the supreme sea-divinity would, as an emblem in heraldry, imply a similar duty or office in the bearer to a great naval hero.

Examples.—The City of Liverpool has for sinister supporter *a Triton blowing a conch shell and holding a flag in his right hand.*

Lord Lyttelton bears for supporters *two Mermen proper, in their exterior hands a trident or.*

Ottway, Bart.—Supporters on either side, *a Triton blowing his shell proper, navally crowned or, across the shoulder a wreath of red coral, and holding in the exterior hand a trident, point downward.*

Note.—In classic story, Triton and the Siren are distinct poetic creations, their vocation and attributes being altogether at variance—no relationship whatever existing between them. According to modern popular notions, however, the siren or mermaid, and triton, or merman as they sometimes term him, appear to be viewed as male and female of the same creature (in heraldic parlance baron and femme). They thus appear in companionship as supporters to the arms of Viscount Hood, and similarly in other achievements.

Mermaid and Triton supporters.

THE MERMAID OR SIREN

"Mermaid shapes that still the waves with ecstasies of song."
  T. Swan,
    "The World within the Ocean."

"And fair Ligea's golden comb,
Wherewith she sits on diamond rocks,
Sleeking her soft alluring hair."
  Milton, "Comus."

THIS fabulous creature of the sea, well known in ancient and modern times as the frequent theme of poets and the subject of numberless legends, has from a very early date been a favourite device. She is usually represented in heraldry as having the upper part the head and body of a beautiful young woman, holding a comb and glass in her hands, the lower part ending in a fish.

Ellis (Glasfryn, Merioneth).—*Argent, a mermaid gules, crined or, holding a mirror in her right hand and a comb in her left, gold. Crest, a mermaid as in the arms. Motto,* "Worth ein ffrwythau yn hadna byddir."

Another family of the same name, settled in Lancashire, bears the colours reversed, viz., *gules, a mermaid argent.*

Sir Josiah Mason.—Crest, *a mermaid, per fess wavy argent and azure, the upper part guttée de larmes, in the dexter hand a comb, and in the sinister a mirror, frame and hair sable.*

Balfour of Burleigh.—*On a rock, a mermaid proper, holding in her dexter hand an otter's head erased sable, and in the sinister a swan's head, erased proper.* The supporters of Baron Balfour are an otter and a swan, which will account for the heads appearing in the hands of the mermaid, instead of the traditional comb and mirror. In some other instances the like occurs, as in the mermaid crest of Cussack, *the mermaid sable crined or, holds in dexter hand a sword, and in the sinister a sceptre.*

Sir George Francis Bonham, Bart.—*Crest, a mermaid holding in dexter hand a wreath of coral, and in the sinister a mirror.*

Crest of Ellis.

Wallop, Earl of Portsmouth, bears for crest a mermaid proper, with her usual accompaniments, the comb and mirror. Another family of the same name and bearing the same arms has for crest *a mermaid with two tails extended proper, hair gold, holding her tails in her hands extended wide.*

In foreign heraldry the mermaid is generally termed *Mélusine*, and represented with two fishy extremities.

Die Ritter, of Nuremberg bears *per fess sable and or, a mermaid holding her two tails, vested gules, crowned or.*

The Austrian family of Estenberger bears for crest *a mermaid without arms, and having wings.*

A mermaid was the device of Sir William de Brivere, who died in 1226. It is the badge of the Berkeleys; in the monumental brass of Lord Berkeley, at Wolton-under-Edge, 1392 A.D., he bears a collar of mermaids over his camail. The Black Prince, in his will, mentions certain devices that he appears to have used as badges; among the rest we find "Mermaids of the Sea." It was the dexter supporter in the coat-of-arms of Sir Walter Scott, and the crest of Lord Byron. The supporters of Viscount

Boyne are mermaids. Skiffington, Viscount Marsereene, the Earl of Caledon, the Earl of Howth, Viscount Hood, and many other titled families bear it as crest or supporters. It is also borne by many untitled families.

Die Ritter, of Nuremberg.

The arms of the princely house of Lusignan, kings of Cyprus and Jerusalem, "Une sirène dans une cuvé," were founded on a curious mediæval legend of a mermaid or siren, termed Mélusine, a fairy, condemned by some spell to become on one day of the week only, half woman, half serpent. The Knight Roimoudin de Forez, meeting her in the forest by chance, became enamoured and married her, and she became the mother of several children, but she carefully avoided seeing her husband on the day of her change; one day, however, his curiosity led him to watch her, which led to the spell being broken, and the soul with which by her union with a Christian she hoped to have been endowed, was lost to her for ever.

This interesting myth is fully examined in Baring Gould's "Curious Myths of the Middle Ages."

The mermaid is represented as the upper half of a beautiful maiden joined to the lower half of a fish, and usually holding a comb in the right hand and a mirror in the left; these articles of the toilet have reference to the old fable that always when observed by man mermaids are found to be resting upon the waves, combing out their long yellow hair, while admiring themselves in the glass: they are also accredited with wondrous vocal powers, to hear which was death to the listener. It was long believed such creatures really did exist, and had from time to time been seen and spoken with; many, we are told, have fatally listened to "the mermaid's charmed speech," and have blindly followed the beguiling, deluding creature to her haunts beneath the wave, as did Sidratta, who, falling in the Ganges, became enamoured of one of these beautiful beings, the Upsaras, the swan-maidens of the Vedas.

All countries seem to have invented some fairylike story of the waters. The Finnish Nakki play their silver harps o' nights; the water imp or Nixey of Germany sings and dances on land with mortals, and the "Davy" (Deva), whose "locker" is at the bottom of the deep blue sea, are all poetical conceptions of the same description. The same may be said of the Merminne of the Netherlands, the White Lady of Scotland and the Silver Swan of the German legend, that drew the ship in which the Knight Lohengrin departed never to return.

In the "Bestiary" of Philip de Thaun he tells us that "Siren lives in the sea, it sings at the approach of a storm and weeps in fine weather; such is its nature: and it has the make of a woman down to the waist, and the feet of h falcon, and the tail of a fish. When it will divert itself, then it sings loud and clear; if then the steersman who navigates the sea hears it, he forgets his ship and immediately falls asleep."

The legendary mermaid still retains her place in popular legends of our sea coasts, especially in the remoter parts of our islands. The stories of the Mirrow, or Irish fairy, hold a prominent place among Crofton Croker's "Fairy Legends of the South of Ireland." Round the shores of Lough Neagh old people still tell how, in the days of their youth, mermaids were supposed to reside in the water, and with what fear and trepidation they would, on their homeward way in the twilight, approach some lonely and sequestered spot on the shore, expecting every moment to be captured and carried off by the witching mere-maidens. On the Continent the same idea prevails. Among the numerous legends of the Rhine many have reference to the same fabled creature.

As we know, mariners in all ages have delighted in tales of the marvellous, and in less enlightened times than the present, they were not unlikely to have found many willing listeners and sound believers. Early voyagers tell wonderful stories of these "fish-women," or "women-fish," as they termed them. The ancient chronicles indeed teem with tales of the capture of "mermaids," "mermen," and similar strange creatures; stories which now only excite a smile from their utter absurdity. So late as 1857 there appeared an article in the *Shipping Gazette*, under intelligence of June 4, signed by some Scotch sailors, and describing an object seen off the North British coast "in the shape of a woman, with full breast, dark complexion, comely face" and the rest. It is probable that some variety of the seal family may be the prototype of this interesting myth.

The myth of the mermaid is, however, of far older date; Homer and later Greek and Roman poets have said and sung a great deal about it.

THE SIRENS OF CLASSICAL MYTHOLOGY

THE Sirens (Greek, entanglers) enticed seamen by the sweetness of their song to such a degree that the listeners forgot everything and died of hunger. Their names were, Parthenope, Ligea, and Leucosia.

Parthenope, the ancient name of Neapolis (Naples) was derived from one of the sirens, whose tomb was shown in Strabo's time. Poetic legend states that she threw herself into the sea out of love for Ulysses, and was cast up on the Bay of Naples.

The celebrated Parthenon at Athens, the beautiful temple of Pallas Athenæ, so richly adorned with sculptures, likewise derives its name from this source.

Ulysses and the Sirens. Flaxman's "Odyssey."

Dante interviews the siren in "Purgatorio," xix. 7–33.

Flaxman, in his designs illustrating the "Odyssey," represents the sirens as beautiful young women seated on the strand and singing.

In the illustration from an ancient Greek vase gives a Grecian rendering of the story, and represents the Sirens as birds with heads of maidens.

The Sirens are best known from the story that Odysseus succeeded in passing them with his companions without being seduced by their song. He had the prudence to stop the ears of his companions with wax and to have himself bound to the mast. Only two are mentioned in Homer, but three or four are mentioned in later times and introduced into various legends. Demeter (*Ceres*) is said to have changed their bodies into those of birds, because they refused to go to the help of their companion, Persephone, when she was carried off by Pluto. "They are represented in Greek art like the harpies, as young women with the wings and feet of birds. Sometimes they appear altogether like birds, only with human faces; at other times with the bodies of women, in which case they generally hold instruments of music in their hands. As their songs are death to those subdued by them they are often depicted on tombs as spirits of death."

By the fables of the Sirens is represented the ensnaring nature of vain and deceitful pleasures, which sing and soothe to sleep, and never fail to destroy those who succumb to their beguiling influence.

Ulysses and the Sirens. From a painting on a Greek vase.

Spenser, in the "Faerie Queen," describes a place "where many mermaids haunt, making false melodies," by which the knight Guyon makes a somewhat "perilous passage." There were five sisters that had been fair ladies, till too confident in their skill in music they had ventured to contend with the Muses, when they were transformed in their lower extremities to fish:

> "But the upper half their hue retained still,
> And their sweet skill in wonted melody;
> Which ever after they abused to ill
> To allure weak travellers, whom gotten they did kill."
>
> Book ii. cant. cxii.

Shakespeare charmingly pictures Oberon in the moonlight, fascinated by the graceful form and the melodious strains of the mermaid half reclining on the back of the dolphin:

> "Oberon: . . . Thou rememberest
> Since once I sat upon a promontory,
> And heard a mermaid on a dolphin's back
> Uttering such dulcet and harmonious breath
> That the rude sea grew civil at her song
> And certain stars shot madly from their spheres
> To hear the sea-maid's music."

Commentators of Shakespeare find in this passage (and subsequent parts) certain references to Mary Queen of Scots, which they consider beyond dispute. She was frequently referred to in the poetry of the time under this title. She was married to the Dauphin (or Dolphin) of France. The rude sea means the Scotch rebels, and the shooting stars referred to were the Earls of Northumberland and Westmoreland, who, with others of lesser note, forgot their allegiance to Elizabeth out of love to Mary.

"Few eyes," says Sir Thomas Browne, "have escaped the picture of a mermaid with a woman's head above and a fish's extremity below." In those old days when reading and writing were rare accomplishments, pictured signboards served to give "a local habitation and a name" to hostelries and other places of business and resort. Among the most celebrated of the old London taverns bearing this sign,[1] that in Bread Street stands foremost.

We find this "Mermayde" mentioned as early as 1464. In 1603 Sir Walter Raleigh established a literary club in this house, and here Shakespeare, Ben Jonson, and the choice intellectual spirits of the time used to meet, and there took place those wit combats which Beaumont has commemorated and Fuller described. It is frequently alluded to by Beaumont and Fletcher in their comedies, but best known is that quotation from a letter of Beaumont to Ben Jonson:

> "What things have we seen
> Done at the Mermaid? heard words that have been
> So nimble and so full of subtle flame,
> As if that any one from whence they came
> Had meant to put his whole wit in a jest,
> And had resolved to live a fool the rest
> Of his dull life; then when there had been thrown
> Wit able enough to justify the town
> For three days past; wit that might warrant be
> For the whole city to talk foolishly,
> Till that were cancell'd; and when that was gone,
> We left an air behind us, which alone
> Was able to make the next two companies
> (Right witty, though but downright fools) more wise."

Source:
Vinycomb, John. *Fictitious and Symbolic Creatures in Art with Special Reference to Their Use in British Heraldry*. London: Chapman and Hall, 1906. pp. 225-253.

---

[1] The sign was also used by printers: John Rastall, brother-in-law to Sir Thomas More, "emprynted in the p. 253 Cheapesyde at the Sygne of the Mermayde; next to Powlsgate in 1572." Henry Binnemann, the Queen's printer, dedicated a work to Sir Thomas Gresham, in 1576, at the sign of the Mermaid, Knightrider Street. A representation of the creature was generally prefixed to his books.—"History of Sign-boards," p. 227.

Tales & Pieces

10. Mermen and Mermaids in Iceland

Iceland

THE mermaid is described as being golden-haired, and possessed of human shape down to the waist; below that she is like a fish, tail and all. Icelandic fishermen believe that they sometimes see her, for the most part north about Grímsey. She especially has her eye on young men, and comes on board the boat to them, if they happen to be nodding, but the 'Credo' in the old Graduale is a good defence against her.

The merman (marbendil) lives at the bottom of the sea, and never appears above the surface, unless when fished up. In Landnáma-bók it is told that Grím, one of the early colonists, went out fishing one winter with his thralls, taking with him his little son. The boy began to grow cold, so they put him into a seal-skin bag, which was drawn tight round his neck. Grím caught a merman, and said to him, "Tell us all our fortunes, and how long we have to live, otherwise you shall not get home again."

"It matters little for you to know," said the merman, "for you will be dead before spring; but your son will take land and settle, where your mare Skalm lies down under her load." More than this they could not get out of him.

Mermen have been caught in this way not unfrequently, and have also been found driven dead on shore, or in the stomachs of sharks. When they are caught alive, they always want to get back to the same spot as they were taken at; they are of few words, and give little heed to men. Once some fishermen from Höfdi on Latra-strönd caught a woman on one of their hooks, and took her home with them. She said she lived in the sea, and was busy screening her mother's kitchen chimney when they caught her. She continually entreated them to take her out to sea again, and let her down at the same place as they got her, but they would not. She remained there for a year, and sewed the vestments that have been in Lauf-ás ever since. At the end of the year she was taken out to sea again, for they saw that she would never be happy on land. She promised to send some cows up on shore, and told them to be ready to receive them whenever they appeared, and burst the bladder between their nostrils, otherwise they would immediately run back into the sea. Not long after this, twelve heifers came up out of the sea, and proceeded to Höfdi. They were all sea-grey in colour; six of them were caught and greatly prized, the other six escaped.

Source:
Craigie, William A. *Scandinavian Folk-Lore: Illustrations of the Traditional Beliefs of the Northern People.* London: Alexander Gardner, 1896.

11. Then Laughed the Merman

Iceland

This anthology offers two different versions of the following tale with marked differences between them, one ending with the fisherman's death and the other with his continued prosperity.

THERE is an old Icelandic saying, frequently made use of, "Then laughed the merman," the origin of which is said to be as follows. Once a fisherman caught a sea-creature, which called itself a "marbendil"; it had a big head and long arms, but resembled a seal from the waist downwards. The merman would give the fisher no information of any kind, so he took him ashore with him, sorely against the merman's will. His young wife came down to the sea to meet him, and kissed and caressed him, at which the man was delighted and gave her great praise, while at the same time he struck his dog for fawning on him. Then laughed the merman, and the fisherman asked the reason why he did so. "At folly," said the merman. As the man went homewards, he stumbled and fell over a little mound, whereupon he cursed it, and wondered why it had ever been made upon his land. Then laughed the merman, who was being taken along against his will, and said, "Unwise is the man." The man kept him prisoner for three nights, and during that time some packmen came with their wares. The man had never been able to get shoes with soles as thick as he wished them, and although these merchants thought they had them of the best, yet of all their stock the man said they were too thin, and would soon wear through. Then laughed the merman, and said, "Many a man is mistaken that thinks himself wise." Neither by fair means nor foul could the man get any more out of him, except on the condition that he should be taken out again to the same fishing bank where he was caught; there he would squat on the blade of an out-stretched oar, and answer all his questions, but not otherwise. The man took him out there, and after the merman had got out on the oar-blade, he asked him first what tackle fishermen should use, if they wished to have good catches. The merman answered, "Bitten iron and trodden shall they have for hooks, and make them where stream and sea can be heard, and harden them in horses' tire; have a grey bull's line and raw horseskin cord. For bait they shall have bird's crop and flounder bait, and man's flesh in the middle bight, and fey are you unless you fish. Froward shall the fisher's hook be."

The man then asked him what the folly was that he laughed at, when he praised his wife and struck his dog. "At your folly, man," said the merman, "for your dog loves you as its own life, but your wife wishes you were dead. The knoll that you cursed is your treasure-mound, with wealth in plenty under it; so you were unwise in that, and therefore I laughed. The shoes will serve you all your life, for you have but three days to live."

With that the merman dived off the oar-blade, and so they parted, but everything turned out true that he had said.

> "Well I mind that morning
> The merman laughed so low;
> The wife to wait her husband
> To water's edge did go;
> She kissed him there so kindly,
> Though cold her heart as snow;
> He beat his dog so blindly,
> That barked its joy to show."

Source:

Craigie, William A. *Scandinavian Folk-Lore: Illustrations of the Traditional Beliefs of the Northern People*. London: Alexander Gardner, 1896.

12. Then the Merman Laughed[1]

Iceland

LONG ago a farmer lived at Vogar, who was a mighty fisherman, and, of all the farms round about, not one was so well situated with regard to the fisheries as his.

---

[1] "The Merman" was the original title from Árnason's book, but the tale is most commonly known as "Then the Merman Laughed" and so was used here instead.

One day, according to custom, he had gone out fishing, and having cast down his line from the boat, and waited awhile, found it very hard to pull up again, as if there were something very heavy at the end of it. Imagine his astonishment when he found that what he had caught was a great fish, with a man's head and body! When he saw that this creature was alive, he addressed it and said, "Who and whence are you?"

"A merman from the bottom of the sea," was the reply.

The farmer then asked him what he had been doing when the hook caught his flesh.

The other replied, "I was turning the cowl of my mother's chimney-pot, to suit it to the wind. So let me go again, will you?"

"Not for the present," said the fisherman. "You shall serve me awhile first."

So without more words he dragged him into the boat and rowed to shore with him.

When they got to the boat-house, the fisherman's dog came to him and greeted him joyfully, barking and fawning on him, and wagging his tail. But his master's temper being none of the best, he struck the poor animal; whereupon the merman laughed for the first time.

Having fastened the boat, he went towards his house, dragging his prize with him, over the fields, and stumbling over a hillock, which lay in his way, cursed it heartily; whereupon the merman laughed for the second time.

When the fisherman arrived at the farm, his wife came out to receive him, and embraced him affectionately, and he received her salutations with pleasure; whereupon the merman laughed for the third time.

Then said the farmer to the merman, "You have laughed three times, and I am curious to know why you have laughed. Tell me, therefore."

"Never will I tell you," replied the merman, "unless you promise to take me to the same place in the sea wherefrom you caught me, and there to let me go free again." So the farmer made him the promise.

"Well," said the merman, "I laughed the first time because you struck your dog, whose joy at meeting you was real and sincere. The second time, because you cursed the mound over which you stumbled, which is full of golden ducats. And the third time, because you received with pleasure your wife's empty and nattering embrace, who is faithless to you, and a hypocrite. And now be an honest man and take me out to the sea whence you have brought me."

The farmer replied: "Two things that you have told me I have no means of proving, namely, the faithfulness of my dog and the faithlessness of my wife. But the third I will try the truth of, and if the hillock contain gold, then I will believe the rest."

Accordingly he went to the hillock, and having dug it up, found therein a great treasure of golden ducats, as the merman had told him. After this the farmer took the merman down to the boat, and to that place in the sea whence he had caught him. Before he put him in, the latter said to him:

"Farmer, you have been an honest man, and I will reward you for restoring me to my mother, if only you have skill enough to take possession of property that I shall throw in your way. Be happy and prosper."

Then the farmer put the merman into the sea, and he sank out of sight.

It happened that not long after, seven sea-grey cows were seen on the beach, close to the farmer's land. These cows appeared to be very unruly, and ran away directly the farmer approached them. So he took a stick and ran after them, possessed with the fancy that if he could burst the bladder which he saw on the nose of each of them, they would belong to him. He contrived to hit out the bladder on the nose of one cow, which then became so tame that he could easily catch it, while the others leaped into the sea and disappeared. The farmer was convinced that this was the gift of the merman. And a very useful gift it was, for better cow was never seen nor milked in all the land, and she was the mother of the race of grey cows so much esteemed now.

And the farmer prospered exceedingly, but never caught any more mermen. As for his wife, nothing farther is told about her, so we can repeat nothing.

Source:

Árnason, Jón. *Icelandic Legends*. Geo. E. J. Powell and Eiríkur Magnússon, translators. London: Richard Bentley, 1864.

13. Sea-People, or Mermen and Mermaids in Shetland

Shetland Islands

IT WAS believed that a light and beautiful land, underneath the watery wastes of the ocean, was inhabited by mar-men or mar-folk, who lived in beautiful halls and spacious caves of coral, amidst groves of aquatic trees and plants.

These beings were like people when in their homes; but when they were travelling through the sea, they became half man and half fish; their upper parts remaining man-like, while their nether parts became fish-like, or were enveloped in a fish-like covering. Without this fish-like covering, these people could not travel the seas; but, as it was of no use to them in other elements, they immediately discarded it upon arriving home, and also when they came ashore in the upper world.

They were about the size of the smallest people among us, and very well proportioned. Of a mild disposition, they were much attached to one another. They are known to have been fond of music, singing, dancing, and story-telling, when at home; and some of them played flutes and harp-like instruments.

The men were darker in complexion than the women, and had hair and beards of various colors; for instance, brown, black, gray, and reddish. Their beards and hair were generally rather long. The women had fine features, light skins, and very long yellow hair, which floated around them when they were in the water. They sometimes came ashore in fine moonlight nights and sat on the rocks, combing their hair. They could sing very sweetly, and their singing enchanted men, and perhaps other beings. If a man heard her song and saw her, he became spellbound. It is said that men became so insanely in love with mermaids, that they followed them into the sea, and were drowned. When a mermaid sang, seals also came crowding around, and remained listening as if spell-bound. Mermen, unlike mermaids, very rarely came ashore.

These sea-people occasionally played tricks on fishermen (especially when lines were set over their abodes) by fastening their hooks to the bottom or to seaweeds, or by taking the bait and sometimes the fish also off the hooks.

To see mermen at sea generally meant some kind of bad luck, bad weather, or danger. In fair weather, fishermen have seen what at first appeared to be a large seal rise out of the water and look intently at their boat. On further observing the creature, they would see that it had human features and long hair. Then they realized that it was one of the sea-people watching them; and this always foreboded a storm. If they were not noticed by the sea-being, no evil result need be predicted.

Stories are told of these people having been caught on hooks and hauled up to the surface or into boats. When thus caught, they begged to be released, and offered good luck or a reward for their release. Captors who had released them have afterwards been lucky, while those who retained them or harmed them have been drowned or have experienced bad luck. A story relates how a Norden man (North Shetlander), one of the crew of a boat engaged in haf-fishing (deep-sea fishing), found, when hauling in the lines, a mermaid (caught by the hand?) on one of the hooks. As she was brought alongside the boat, she begged not to be harmed, and prayed to be released; but before releasing her from the hook, the man stabbed her in the breast with a tolli ("sheath-knife") and she sank out of sight, moaning piteously. A severe storm came on shortly afterwards, and the boat barely made the land. The man was afterwards haunted, and eventually he was drowned.

It was believed that these people could foretell the future. Thus, when one was caught at sea, he (or she) was asked before being released to tell the fortunes of the men. The mar-folk according to some, could not live long ashore or in the sea, the atmosphere of their own element beneath the sea being different from either. Others say that they could live a long time ashore, but that they were always unhappy, and sooner or later died of grief, if not returned to the sea. There seems to be some confusion in Shetland folk-lore between these sea-people, or mar-folk, and the selki-folk; as some people say of the former that they could assume seal-form as well as fish-form when travelling in the sea, or that they could more frequently assume the shape of a seal than that of a fish. In both cases real transformations were not involved, but mere coverings were adjusted to enable them to roam the seas. To travel under water they enveloped themselves entirely in these contrivances; but on the surface of the sea their heads, necks, shoulders, and breast were uncovered, being out of water, and only the lower parts of necessity retained their fish or seal envelope. When they came ashore, they entirely discarded them, but never went very far; and in the case of alarm or some one approaching, they at once resumed their sea-forms and jumped into the sea. The loss of these possessions meant that they could no longer travel in the sea.

Some people even say that all had seal coverings, and that their body ended in hind flippers and that these have probably been mistaken for fish-tails. Stories are told of mermaids having married Shetlanders, and these narratives do not differ materially from similar ones referring to seal-folk. Sometimes the same narrative, in fact, refers to both kinds, the woman being a mermaid in one version, and a seal-woman in another.[1] It seems, however, that most people differentiate them quite clearly.

Source:
Teit, J. A. "Water-Beings in Shetlandic Folk-Lore, as Remembered by Shetlanders in British Columbia." *The Journal of American Folklore*. Vol. 31, No. 120 (Apr.-Jun. 1918). pp. 180-201.

14. The Mermaid Wife

Shetland Islands

ON A fine summer's evening, an inhabitant of Unst happened to be walking along the sandy margin of a voe.[2] The moon was risen, and by her light he discerned at some distance before him a number of the sea-

---

[1] In some cases there is still greater confusion, a Finn woman being spoken of instead of either a mermaid or seal-woman.
[2] A voe is a small bay.

people, who were dancing with great vigour on the smooth sand. Near them he saw lying on the ground several seal-skins.

As the man approached the dancers, all gave over their merriment, and flew like lightning to secure their garments; then clothing themselves, plunged in the form of seals into the sea. But the Shetlander, on coming up to the spot where they had been, and casting his eyes down on the ground, saw that they had left one skin behind them, which was lying just at his feet. He snatched it up, carried it swiftly away, and placed it in security.

On returning to the shore, he met the fairest maiden that eye ever gazed upon: she was walking backwards and forwards, lamenting m most piteous tones the loss of her seal-skin robe, without which she never could hope to rejoin her family and friends below the waters, but must remain an unwilling inhabitant of the region enlightened by the sun.

The man approached and endeavoured to console her, but she would not be comforted. She implored him in the most moving accents to restore her dress; but the view of her lovely face, more beautiful in tears, had steeled his heart. He represented to her the impossibility of her return, and that her friends would soon give her up; and finally, made an offer to her of his heart, hand, and fortune.

The sea-maiden, finding she had no alternative, at length consented to become his wife. They were married, and lived together for many years, during which time they had several children, who retained no vestiges of their marine origin, saving a thin web between their fingers, and a bend of their hands, resembling that of the fore paws of a seal; distinctions which characterise the descendants of the family to the present day.

The Shetlander's love for his beautiful wife was unbounded, but she made but a cold return to his affection. Often would she steal out alone and hasten down to the lonely strand, and there at a given signal, a seal of large size would make his appearance, and they would converse for hours together in an unknown language; and she would return home from this meeting pensive and melancholy.

Thus glided away years, and her hopes of leaving the upper world had nearly vanished, when it chanced one day, that one of the children, playing behind a stack of corn, found a seal-skin. Delighted with his prize, he ran with breathless eagerness to display it before his mother. Her eyes glistened with delight at the view of it; for in it she saw her own dress, the loss of which had cost her so many tears. She now regarded herself as completely emancipated from thraldom; and in idea she was already with her friends beneath the waves. One thing alone was a drawback on her raptures. She loved her children, and she was now about to leave them for ever. Yet they weighed not against the pleasures she had in prospect: so after kissing and embracing them several times, she took up the skin, went out, and proceeded down to the beach.

In a few minutes after the husband came in, and the children told him what had occurred. The truth instantly flashed across his mind, and he hurried down to the shore with all the speed that love and anxiety could give. But he only arrived in time to see his wife take the form of a seal, and from the ledge of a rock plunge into the sea.

The large seal, with whom she used to hold her conversations, immediately joined her, and congratulated her on her escape, and they quitted the shore together. But ere she went she turned round to her husband, who stood in mute despair on the, rock, and whose misery excited feelings of compassion in her breast. "Farewell," said she to him, "and may all good fortune attend you. I loved you well while I was with you, but I always loved my first husband better."

Source:

Keightley, Thomas. *The Fairy Mythology: Illustrative of the Romance and Superstition of Various Countries*. London: George Bell & Sons, 1905.

15. Clark Colven
Child Ballad 42A

Scotland & England

The following three ballads are variants of Child 42, commonly known as "Clerk Colvill," with an introduction excerpted in full from the 1904 edition. The original Part II 1884 edition offers over fifteen pages of analysis of this ballad as well as foreign variants from around Europe and is highly recommended further reading.

All the English versions are deplorably imperfect. Clerk Colvill is not, as his representative is or may be in other ballads, the guiltless and guileless object of the love or envy of a water-sprite or elf. It is clear that before his marriage with his gay lady he had been in the habit of resorting to this mermaid, and equally clear, from the impatient answer which he renders his dame, that he means to visit her again. His death is the natural penalty of his desertion of the water-nymph; for no point is better established than the fatal consequences of inconstancy in such connections. His history, were it fully told, would closely resemble that of the Knight of Staufenberg, as narrated in a German poem of about the year 1310. Clerk Colvill and the mermaid are represented by Sir Oluf and an elf in Scandinavian ballads to the number of about seventy. The oldest of these is derived from a Danish manuscript of 1550, two centuries and a half later than the Staufenberg poem, but two earlier than Clerk Colvill, the oldest ballad outside of the Scandinavian series (see Grundtvig, No. 47). The Breton 'Seigneur Nann' is closely akin to the Scandinavian versions, and the ballad has spread, apparently from Brittany, over all France ('Jean Renaud').

1. **CLARK COLVEN** and his gay ladie,
   As they walked to yon garden green,
   A belt about her middle gimp,
   Which cost Clark Colven crowns fifteen:

2. "O hearken weel now, my good lord,
   O hearken weel to what I say;
   When ye gang to the wall o Stream,
   O gang nae neer the well-fared may."

3. "O haud your tongue, my gay ladie,
   Tak nae sic care o me;
   For I nae saw a fair woman
   I like so well as thee."

4. He mounted on his berry-brown steed,
   And merry, merry rade he on,
   Till he came to the wall o Stream,
   And there he saw the mermaiden.

5. "Ye wash, ye wash, ye bonny may,
   And ay's ye wash your sark o silk:"
   "It's a' for you, ye gentle knight,
   My skin is whiter than the milk."

6. He's taen her by the milk-white hand,
   He's taen her by the sleeve sae green,
   And he's forgotten his gay ladie,
   And away with the fair maiden.

   * * * * * * * * * * * * * * * * *

7. "Ohon, alas!" says Clark Colven,
   "And aye sae sair's I mean my head!"
   And merrily leugh the mermaiden,
   "O win on till you be dead.

8. "But out ye tak your little pen-knife,
   And frae my sark ye shear a gare;

  Row that about your lovely head,
    And the pain ye'll never feel nae mair."

9. Out he has taen his little pen-knife,
    And frae her sark he's shorn a gare,
  Rowed that about his lovely head,
    But the pain increased mair and mair.

10. "Ohon, alas!" says Clark Colven,
    "An aye sae sair's I mean my head!"
  And merrily laughd the mermaiden,
    "It will ay be war till ye be dead."

11. Then out he drew his trusty blade,
    And thought wi it to be her dead,
  But she's become a fish again,
    And merrily sprang into the fleed.

12. He's mounted on his berry-brown steed,
    And dowy, dowy rade he home,
  And heavily, heavily lighted down
    When to his ladie's bower-door he came.

13. "Oh, mither, mither, mak my bed,
    And, gentle ladie, lay me down;
  Oh, brither, brither, unbend my bow,
    'Twill never be bent by me again."

14. His mither she has made his bed,
    His gentle ladie laid him down,
  His brither he has unbent his bow,
    'Twas never bent by him again.

NOTES

'Clark Colven,' from a transcript of No. 13 of William Tytler's Brown MS.

Source:
Child, Francis James, editor. *The English and Scottish Popular Ballads, Part II*. Boston: Houghton, Mifflin and Company, 1884.
Child, Francis James. *English and Scottish Popular Ballads: Student's Cambridge Edition*. Helen Child Sargent and George Lyman Kittredge, editors. Boston: Houghton, Mifflin and Company, 1904.

16. Clerk Colvill
Child Ballad 42B

Scotland & England

1. **CLERK COLVILL** and his lusty dame
    Were walking in the garden green;
   The belt around her stately waist
    Cost Clerk Colvill of pounds fifteen.

2. "O promise me now, Clerk Colvill,
    Or it will cost ye muckle strife,
   Ride never by the wells of Slane,
    If ye wad live and brook your life."

3. "Now speak nae mair, my lusty dame,
    Now speak nae mair of that to me;
   Did I neer see a fair woman,
    But I wad sin with her body?"

4. He's taen leave o his gay lady,
    Nought minding what his lady said,
   And he's rode by the wells of Slane,
    Where washing was a bonny maid.

5. "Wash on, wash on, my bonny maid,
    That wash sae clean your sark of silk;"
   "And weel fa you, fair gentleman,
    Your body whiter than the milk."

* * * * * * * * * * * * * * * * * *

6. Then loud, loud cry'd the Clerk Colvill,
    "O my head it pains me sair;"
   "Then take, then take," the maiden said,
    "And frae my sark you'll cut a gare."

7. Then she's gied him a little bane-knife,
    And frae her sark he cut a share;
   She's ty'd it round his whey-white face,
    But ay his head it aked mair.

8. Then louder cry'd the Clerk Colvill,
      "O sairer, sairer akes my head;"
   "And sairer, sairer ever will,"
      The maiden crys, "Till you be dead."

9. Out then he drew his shining blade,
      Thinking to stick her where she stood,
   But she was vanishd to a fish,
      And swam far off, a fair mermaid.

10. "O mother, mother, braid my hair;
       My lusty lady, make my bed;
    O brother, take my sword and spear,
       For I have seen the false mermaid."

NOTES

'Clerk Colvill, or, The Mermaid,' Herd's *Ancient and Modern Scots Songs*, 1769, p. 302; ed. 1776, I, 161.

Source:
Child, Francis James, editor. *The English and Scottish Popular Ballads, Part II*. Boston: Houghton, Mifflin and Company, 1884.

17. Clerk Colin
Child Ballad 42C

Scotland & England

1. **CLERK COLIN** and his mother dear
      Were in the garden green;
   The band that was about her neck
      Cost Colin pounds fifteen;
   The belt about her middle sae sma
      Cost twice as much again.

2. "Forbidden gin ye wad be, love Colin,
      Forbidden gin ye wad be,
   And gang nae mair to Clyde's water,
      To court yon gay ladie."

3. "Forbid me frae your ha, mother,
       Forbid me frae your bour,
   But forbid me not frae yon ladie;
       She's fair as ony flour.

4. "Forbidden I winna be, mother,
       Forbidden I winna be,
   For I maun gang to Clyde's water,
       To court yon gay ladie."

5. An he is on his saddle set,
       As fast as he could win,
   An he is on to Clyde's water,
       By the lee licht o the moon.

6. An when he cam to the Clyde's water
       He lichted lowly down,
   An there he saw the mermaiden,
       Washin silk upon a stane.

7. "Come down, come down, now, Clerk Colin,
       Come down an [fish] wi me;
   I'll row ye in my arms twa,
       An a foot I sanna jee."

   * * * * * * * * * * * * * * * * * *

8. "O mother, mother, mak my bed,
       And, sister, lay me doun,
   An brother, tak my bow an shoot,
       For my shooting is done."

9. He wasna weel laid in his bed,
       Nor yet weel fa'en asleep,
   When up an started the mermaiden,
       Just at Clerk Colin's feet.

10. "Will ye lie there an die, Clerk Colin,
        Will ye lie there an die?
    Or will ye gang to Clyde's water,
        To fish in flood wi me?"

11. "I will lie here an die," he said,
        "I will lie here an die;
    In spite o a' the deils in hell
        I will lie here an die."

NOTES

Notes and Queries, 4th Series, VIII, 510, from the recitation of a lady in Forfarshire.

Source:
Child, Francis James, editor. *The English and Scottish Popular Ballads, Part II*. Boston: Houghton, Mifflin and Company, 1884.

18. The Seamen's Distress
Child Ballad 289A

Scotland & England

The following seven ballads are variants of Child 289, most commonly known as "The Mermaid." Although seven variants are offered here, this ballad is not as wide-spread as the previous ballad group of Child 42: Clerk Colvill.

1. **AS** we lay musing in our beds,
      So well and so warm at ease,
   I thought upon those lodging-beds
      Poor seamen have at seas.

2. Last Easter day, in the morning fair,
      We was not far from land,
   Where we spied a mermaid on the rock,
      With comb and glass in hand.

3. The first came up the mate of our ship,
      With lead and line in hand,
   To sound and see how deep we was
      From any rock or sand.

4. The next came up the boatswain of our ship,
      With courage stout and bold:
   "Stand fast, stand fast, my brave lively lads,
      Stand fast, my brave hearts of gold!"

5. Our gallant ship is gone to wreck,
      Which was so lately trimmd;

        The raging seas has sprung a leak,
           And the salt water does run in.

6.   Our gold and silver, and all our cloths,
           And all that ever we had,
       We forced was to heave them overboard,
           Thinking our lives to save.

7.   In all, the number that was on board
           Was five hundred and sixty-four,
       And all that ever came alive on shore
           There was but poor ninety-five.

8.   The first bespoke the captain of our ship,
           And a well-spoke man was he;
       "I have a wife in fair Plymouth town,
           And a widow I fear she must be."

9.   The next bespoke the mate of our ship,
           And a well-bespoke man was he;
       "I have a wife in fair Portsmouth,
           And a widow I fear she must be."

10.   The next bespoke the boatswain of our ship,
           And a well-bespoke man was he;
       "I have a wife in fair Exeter,
           And a widow I fear she must be."

11.   The next bespoke the little cabbin-boy,
           And a well-bespoke boy was he;
       "I am as sorry for my mother dear
           As you are for your wives all three.

12.   "Last night, when the moon shin'd bright,
           My mother had sons five,
       But now she may look in the salt seas
           And find but one alive."

13.   "Call a boat, call a boat, you little Plymouth boys,
           Don't you hear how the trumpet[s] sound?
       [For] the want of our boat our gallant ship is lost,
           And the most of our merry men is drownd."

14.   Whilst the raging seas do roar,
           And the lofty winds do blow,

And we poor seamen do lie on the top,
　Whilst the landmen lies below.

NOTES

'The Seamen's Distress,' the second piece in *The Glasgow Lasses Garland*, British Museum, 11621. c. 3 (68). "Newcastle, 1765?"

Source:
Child, Francis James, editor. *The English and Scottish Popular Ballads, Part IX*. Boston: Houghton, Mifflin and Company, 1894.

19. The Stormy Winds Do Blow
Child Ballad 289B

Scotland & England

1.　**ONE** Friday morn when we set sail,
　　　Not very far from land,
　We there did espy a fair pretty maid
　　With a comb and a glass in her hand, her hand, her hand,
　　With a comb and a glass in her hand.
　　　While the raging seas did roar,
　　　　And the stormy winds did blow,
　　　While we jolly sailor-boys were up into the top,
　　　　And the land-lubbers lying down below, below, below,
　　　　And the land-lubbers lying down below.

2.　Then up starts the captain of our gallant ship,
　　　And a brave young man was he:
　"I've a wife and a child in fair Bristol town,
　　But a widow I fear she will be."
　　　For the raging seas, etc.

3.　Then up starts the mate of our gallant ship,
　　　And a bold young man was he:
　"Oh! I have a wife in fair Portsmouth town,
　　But a widow I fear she will be."
　　　For the raging seas, etc.

4.　Then up starts the cook of our gallant ship,

And a gruff old soul was he:
"Oh! I have a wife in fair Plymouth town,
But a widow I fear she will be."

5. And then up spoke the little cabin-boy,
And a pretty little boy was he;
"Oh! I am more grievd for my daddy and my mammy
Than you for your wives all three."

6. Then three times round went our gallant ship,
And three times round went she;
For the want of a life-boat they all went down,
And she sank to the bottom of the sea.

NOTES

A. 'The stormy winds do blow,' Chappell's *Popular Music of the Olden Time*, p. 742.
B. The same, p. 743, one stanza and the burden, contributed by Mr. Charles Sloman, in 1840.
C. *Notes and Queries*, 6th Series, VII, 276, communicated from memory by Mr. Thomas Bayne, Helensburgh, N.B., stanzas 1, 6.

Source:
Child, Francis James, editor. *The English and Scottish Popular Ballads, Part IX*. Boston: Houghton, Mifflin and Company, 1894.

20. The Mermaid
Child Ballad 289C

Scotland & England

1. ONE Friday morn as we'd set sail,
And our ship not far from land,
We there did espy a fair mermaid,
With a comb and a glass in her hand, her hand, her hand,
With a comb and a glass in her hand.
While the raging seas did roar,
And the stormy winds did blow,
And we jolly sailor-boys were up, up aloft,
And the landsmen were lying down below,

And the landlubbers all down below, below, below,
And the landlubbers all down below.

2. Then up spoke the captain of our gallant ship,
   Who at once did our peril see;
   "I have married a wife in fair London town,
   And tonight she a widow will be."

3. And then up spoke the litel cabin-boy,
   And a fair-haired boy was he;
   "I've a father and mother in fair Portsmouth town,
   And this night she will weep for me."

4. Now three times round goes our gallant ship,
   And three times round went she;
   For the want of a life-boat they all were drownd,
   As she went to the bottom of the sea.

NOTES

Communicated by Mr W. Chappell, as noted down by him from the singing of men dressed as sailors on Tower Hill. Subsequently printed, with a few variations, in *Old English Ditties*, Oxenford and Macfarren, 'The Mermaid,' I, 206.

Source:
Child, Francis James, editor. *The English and Scottish Popular Ballads, Part IX*. Boston: Houghton, Mifflin and Company, 1894.

21. The Mermaid
Child Ballad 289D

Scotland & England

1. 'TWAS a Friday morning when we set sail,
   And our ship was not far from land,
   When there we spied a fair pretty maid,
   With a comb and a glass in her hand.

   Oh, the raging seas they did roar,
   And the stormy winds they did blow,

       While we poor sailor-boys were all up aloft,
           And the land-lubbers lying down below, below, below,
           And the land-lubbers lying down below.

2.   Then up spoke the captain of our gallant ship,
           And a mariner good was he;
      "I have married a wife in fair London town,
           And this night a widow she will be."

3.   Then up spoke the cabin-boy of our gallant ship,
           And a brave little boy was he;
      "I've a father and a mother in old Portsmouth town,
           And this night they will both weep for me."

4.   Then up spoke a seaman of our gallant ship,
           And a well-spoken man was he;
      "For want of a long-boat we shall all be drowned,
           And shall sink to the bottom of the sea."

5.   Then three times round went that gallant ship,
           And down like a stone sank she;
      The moon shone bright, and the stars gave their light,
           But they were all at the bottom of the sea.

NOTES

A. Long, *Dictionary of the Isle of Wight Dialect*, 1886, p. 142.
B. Broadside, H. Such, 177 Union St., Boro'.

Source:
Child, Francis James, editor. *The English and Scottish Popular Ballads, Part IX*. Boston: Houghton, Mifflin and Company, 1894.

22. The Bonnie Mermaid Child Ballad 289E

Scotland & England

1.   UP and spoke the bonny mermaid,
           Wi the comb and the glass in her hand;
      Says, Cheer up your hearts, my mariners all,

You are not very far from the land.

> And the raging seas do foam, foam,
> And the stormy winds do blow,
> While we poor sailors must mount to the top,
> When the landsmen they lye low.

2. Out and spoke the captain of our ship,
    And a fine little man was he;
   "O I've a wife in fair London town,
    And a widow this night she shall be."

3. Out and spoke the mate of our ship,
    And a tight little man was he;
   "O I've a wife in Dublin city,
    And a widow this night she shall be."

4. Out and spoke our second mate,
    And a clever little man was he;
   "Oh I have a wife in Greenoch town,
    And a widow this night she shall be."

5. Out and spoke our little prentice boy,
    And a fine little boy was he;
   "Oh I am sorry for my mother," he said,
    "As you are for your wives all three."

6. Out and spoke the cook of our ship,
    And a rusty old dog was he;
   Says, I am as sorry for my pats and my pans
    As you are for your wives all three.

NOTES

A. Motherwell's MS., p. 145.
B. 'The Bonnie Mermaid,' *Motherwell's Minstrelsy*, Appendix, p. xxiii, No XXX, one stanza.

Source:
Child, Francis James, editor. *The English and Scottish Popular Ballads, Part IX*. Boston: Houghton, Mifflin and Company, 1894.

23. Greenland
Child Ballad 289F

Scotland & England

1. GREENLAND, Greenland, is a bonny, bonny place,
   Whare there's neither grief nor flowr,
   Whare there's neither grief nor tier to be seen,
   But hills and frost and snow.

2. Up starts the kemp o the ship,
   Wi a psalm-book in his hand:
   "Swoom away, swoom away, my merry old boys,
   For you'll never see dry land."

3. Up starts the gaucy cook,
   And a weil gaucy cook was he;
   "I wad na gie aw my pans and my kettles
   For aw the lords in the sea."

4. Up starts the kemp o the ship,
   Wi a bottle and a glass intil his hand;
   "Swoom away, swoom away, my merry old sailors,
   For you'll never see dry land."

5. O the raging seas they row, row, row,
   The stormy winds do blow,
   As sune as he had gane up to the tap,
   As . . . . .low.

NOTES

'Greenland,' Kinloch MSS, VII, 245. From the recitation of a little boy from Glasgow who sang it in Grove St., Edinburgh, July 1826.

Source:
Child, Francis James, editor. *The English and Scottish Popular Ballads, Part IX*. Boston: Houghton, Mifflin and Company, 1894.

24. Scottish Mermaids
by Mr R. J. Arnott, M.A.

Scotland

WHEREVER, in Europe at least, is to be found a people upon whom superstition and a fear of the supernatural have a hold the mermaid myth is sure to have a place in the popular traditional and legendary lore. Nor, curiously enough, are mermaids confined to the sea-board, for they have their haunts on the banks of rivers, and here and there on the shores of inland lakes, as well as in the caves or by the rocky bays and sandy beaches of the coasts. I have no intention of seeking to arrive at the origin of the myth, or of inquiring what was the name of the first mermaid, or where she was to be found, although it might not be an altogether impossible task; any more than, in connection with individual local legends, of speculating upon a possible explanation of how they came to exist or whether any substratum of truth may perchance underlie them. There is no particular occasion for dipping farther into classical mythology than to remark in passing that the Sybils, the Gorgons, and the Syrens of the ancient Greeks and Romans all had certain marked features in common, beauty of face and form and profusion of locks being as inseparable from them as from the more modern mermaid. While touching on these features, it may be noted that not only did both syrens and mermaids once have wings, but they did not always have tails. It is not necessary to turn to any of the "Just-so Stories" to learn how the mermaid lost the one or came by the other of these useful and ornamental appendages; for a full and faithful account of both phenomena may be found by those who care to put themselves to the trouble of a little research in the writings of various learned authors, whose earnestness of purpose and belief in the truth of what they are narrating are as far removed from the cheerful inconsequence of Mr Kipling's tales as are his object and style and treatment differ from theirs. It is not without significance of the persistency of the myth, and the perennial power it possesses of appealing to the fancy, that, even in these days when stolid matter-of-factness threatens to blight so much of the fruit of the imagination, the mermaid is still found capable of playing a leading part in the popular reading, just as in the literature of Greece and Rome. For, quite apart from the field of poetry, has not Mr H. C. Wells succeeded in giving us some idea of the perplexities and complications that are liable to arise when a "sea-lady" happens to find her way on shore?

The close similarity existing between the mermaid legends of different times and of various parts of the continent and those of our own islands is, of course, nothing to be surprised at. They all belong to that great body of folklore which is the common property of so many nations and peoples, owing to its having been in the possession of the original racial stock and becoming, through process of time, indigenous to the soil wherever members or offshoots settled.

Before proceeding to deal in detail with Scottish mermaid legends I may be permitted, in a few more introductory words, to indicate the general character of the various forms in which the myth prevails.

The mermaid of whom Tennyson has sung is, it is to be feared, a somewhat elementary, unsophisticated damsel in comparison with the most of her kind:—

> "I would be a mermaid fair.
> I would sing to myself the whole of the day;
> With a comb of pearl I would comb my hair;
> And still as I comb'd I would sing and say,
> 'Who is it loves me? who loves not me?'"

Charming, indeed, she is, but she is hardly the mermaid of the popular legend. Unfortunately for those mortals whose lot it has been to make the acquaintance of these sea-maidens, they are seldom content that

> "All the mermen under the sea
> Should feel their immortality
> Die in their hearts for the love of me."

More usually their song is that of the syrens of old—

> "Mariner, mariner, furl your sails,
> Come hither to me and to me:
> O hither, come hither, and be our lords,
> For merry brides are we:
> We will kiss sweet kisses and speak sweet words:
> O listen, listen, your eyes shall glisten
> When the sharp clear twang of the golden chords
> Runs up the ridged sea.
> Who can light on so happy a shore
> All the world o'er, all the world o'er?
> Whither away? listen and stay: mariner, mariner, fly no more."

But it is little wonder that the mariners "whisper to each other half in fear" when they hear that "shrill music." For while by reason of their partly human form these ocean dwellers are fated to seek intercourse with mortal men and women, it is seldom to the advantage of the latter that this should happen. Even where there appears to be love for love's sake, it never lasts. A mermaid may become the wife of a human being and make her home with him on land, but sooner or later the time comes when she cannot resist the temptation to return to her native element. And where a mortal is induced to consent to marriage with one of the sea-folk something generally happens after a while to sunder what may have proved to be a happy enough union. Such is, for instance, the case pictured in Matthew Arnold's beautiful poem, "The Forsaken Merman," with its haunting refrain:—

> "Here came a mortal,
> But faithless was she!
> And alone dwell for ever
> The kings of the sea"—

where "the sound of a far-off bell" at Easter-time is sufficient to bring about the return of the wife and mother to her kinsfolk.

Occasionally the mermaid will use her supernatural influence for the protection or the advantage of a human being; but more generally her appearance or intervention forebodes some impending disaster to those to whom she appears, and her purpose is rather to lure them to destruction than to warn them of the danger in which they stand.

Of most of these aspects of the mermaid's mission and character the following individual legends relating to different districts of Scotland will be found illustrative.

First let me cite, chiefly because of its typicalness of the nature and habits of the legendary mermaid, an example with which you are probably all familiar. It is the "Mermaid of Galloway," of whom we are told, in an almost faultless imitation of the old ballad, by Jean Walker, who was born in the village of Preston Mill, Kirkbean, and lived within sight and sound of the Solway until her marriage with the stonemason-poet, Allan Cunningham. As is the case with many others, I fancy, of these tales, the legend only seems to exist, or at least to survive, in the poem:—

> "There's a maid has sat on the green merse side
>   These ten lang years and mair;
> And every nicht o' the new moon
>   She kames her yellow hair.
>
> And aye while she sheds the yellow burning gowd,
>   Fu' sweet she sings an' hie,
> Till the fairest bird that wooes the green wood
>   Is charmed with her melodie.
>
> But wha e'er listens to that sweet sang,
>   Or gangs the dame to see,

Ne'er hears the sang o' the laverock again,
    Nor waukens an earthlie e'e.

It fell in aboot the sweet simmer month,
    I' the first come o' the moon,
That she sat o' the tap o' a seaweed rock,
    A-kaming her silk locks doon.

She kamed her locks owre her white shoulders,
    A fleece baith bonny an' lang;
An' ilka ringlet she shed frae her brows,
    She raised a lightsome sang.

****

'I hae dwelt on the Nith,' quo' the young Cowehill,
    'Thae twenty years an' three;
But the sweetest sang e'er brake frae a lip
    Come through the greenwood tree.

'O, is it a voice frae twa earthlie lips
    Whilk made sic melodie?
It wad wyle the lark frae the morning lift,
    An' weel may it wyle me!

'The simmer dew fa's soft, fair maid,
    Aneath the siller moon;
But eerie is thy seat i' the rock,
    Washed wi' the white sea foam.

'How rosie is thy parting lips,
    How lilie-white thy skin;
An' weel I wat thae kissing e'en
    Wad tempt a saint to sin.'

****

Then took she up his green mantle,
    Of lowing gowd the hem;
Then took she up his silken cap,
    Rich wi' a siller stem;
An' she threw them wi' her lilie hand
    Amang the white sea faem.

She took the bride-ring frae his finger,
    An' threw it in the sea:

> 'That hand shall mense nae ither ring,
>   But in the will o' me.'
>
> She faulded him in her lilie arms,
>   An' left her pearlie kame;
> His fleecy locks trailed owre the sand,
>   As she took the white sea faem.
>
> First raise the star out owre the hill,
>   An' neist the lovelier moon;
> While the beauteous bride o' Gallowa'
>   Looked for her blithe bridegroom."

Fortunate, it would seem, then, is he who can stand the sweet temptation. Narrow enough was the escape of the young laird of Lornty, in Perthshire. Riding home late one night, accompanied by his man, he heard what sounded like cries of distress from the direction of a loch near at hand, which lay hidden in a wood. Making his way quickly to the spot, he saw in the water a beautiful young woman, apparently in the last stages of exhaustion. Faintly she called for help, appealing to him by name. Without hesitation he plunged into the loch and was about to catch hold of the maiden by her long yellow locks, that "lay like hanks of gold upon the water," when a warning cry from his man arrested his action. "Bide, Lornty," he shouted, seizing his master by the arm and dragging him to the shore, "bide a blink; that waulin' madam was nae ither—God sauf us—than a mermaid." Fortunately the laird realised his danger in time. For as he prepared to mount his horse and ride off the woman rose in the water and addressed him in tones full of anger and baffled hate:—

> "Lornty, Lornty,
>   Were it na your man,
> I'd gart your heart's bluid
>   Skirl in my pan!"

That, however, the allurements of the mermaid do not always entail the ruin of their victims we are reminded by the story of Macphail of Colonsay and the mermaid of Corrievrekin (between the islands of Jura and Scarba), which Leyden adapted in his ballad, entitled "The Mermaid," from a Gaelic tradition. One day when Macphail is out in his boat there comes—

> "Floating o'er the deep
>   The mermaid's sweet, sea-soothing lay,
> That charmed the dancing waves to sleep
>   Before the bark of Colonsay.

> That sea-maid's form, all pearly light,
>   Was whiter than the downy spray,
> And round her bosom, heaving bright,
>   Her glossy, yellow ringlets play.
>
> Borne on a foamy-crested wave,
>   She reached amain the bounding prow,
> Then, clasping fast the chieftain brave,
>   She, plunging, sought the deep below."

He is carried down into a coral cave, and the mermaid asks him to forget his maid of Colonsay and marry her. At first Macphail refuses, but in a short time he yields to her entreaties. They live happily together for several years, in the course of which five children are born to them. After a while, however, Macphail begins to tire of his life beneath the waves, and prevailing upon his consort to carry him near the shore of Colonsay, he escapes to land.

> "And ever as the year returns,
>   The charm-bound sailors know the day,
> When sadly still the mermaid mourns
>   The lovely chief of Colonsay."

One peculiar power the mermaid of Corrievrekin possessed was that of laying aside at will her "scaly train;" only when she did divest herself of it she became so wild and ungentle in her bearing that means had to be taken, for obvious reasons, to prevent her lover from coming into her presence whenever the transformation took place.

Occasionally, as has been remarked, but not often, the appearance of a mermaid brings good fortune to those who encounter her. One Galloway mermaid is related to have come across a youth bewailing the illness of his sweetheart, who was suffering from consumption. Taking compassion on him, she cheered him with the adjuration:—

> "Wad ye let the bonnie Mary dee i' your hand,
> And the mugwort flowering i' the land?"

The lover followed her advice, and the restoration of the girl's health was effected by the administration of the mugwort (which, it may be explained, was supposed to be especially potent for the cure of ailments and diseases, even casting out madness, if gathered on St. John's Day).

A similar reminder, but one which, alas! came too late, was given by a mermaid who rose out of the Clyde, above Port Glasgow, as the funeral of a young woman who had died of consumption was passing along the high road by the side of the river:—

> "If they wad drink nettles in March,
>   And eat muggins in May,
>   Sae mony braw maidens
>   Wadna gang to the clay."

Generally when a mermaid places her knowledge at the disposal of a mortal it is in return for some service rendered to her. One day some Shetland fishermen out at the "haaf" fishing found a mermaid instead of a fish caught on one of their hooks. When dragged on board the boat she pleaded hard to be set free, promising in return that anything they might wish for would be granted them. This seemed a good enough bargain, and the mermaid was returned to her native element. As she was disappearing she sang:—

> "Muckle guid I wid ye gie,
>   An' mair I wid ye wish;
>   There's muckle evil in the sea:
>   Scoom weel your fish."

The skipper, thinking he was being merely jeered at for his pains, became very angry, and ejaculated—"Cheated, and by a mermaid!" Only one of the crew of the "sixern" paid any heed to the words of the mermaid. Accepting them literally, he "scoomed weel" his fish, with the result that he discovered among the "scoomings" a valuable pearl, for which he obtained a sum that made the voyage a highly profitable one.

Sometimes the good offices of the mermaid are to be purchased only at the cost of the performance of some feat of not a little difficulty. Hugh Miller tells a story of the Cromarty district in which such a task is required. Like Proteus, in classical mythology, the mermaid in question exerted the power she possessed by virtue of her connection with the invisible world, only when compelled to do so. Should she fall into mortal hands and be overpowered, her release must be purchased by the granting of any three wishes her captor might frame, concerning either his own fortunes or those of his friends. It was seldom, however, the opportunity came the way of any man, for her strength was such she generally emerged victorious from the struggle, and succeeded as well in carrying her assailant with her into the sea.

Early one morning John Reid, a young Cromarty shipmaster, was strolling aimlessly along the shore thinking moodily how badly his suit was faring with Helen Stuart, and how poor was the prospect of its happy issue. Suddenly his steps were arrested by the low notes of the sweetest singing he had ever heard. After listening for a moment or two, he crept noiselessly forward, and on turning the corner of a cliff he saw the musician, "apparently a young girl, who seemed bathing among the waves, and who was now sitting half on the rock, half in the water. Her long yellow hair fell in luxuriant profusion on her snow shoulders, and as she raised herself higher on the cliff, the sun shone on the parts below her waist with such dazzling brightness that the sailor raised his hands to his eyes, and a shivered speck of light, like the reflection of a mirror, went dancing over the shaded roughnesses of the opposite precipice." Then, realising that this was none other than the mermaid of whom he had heard so much, John dashed forward and seized her. Sturdy was her resistance, and a desperate struggle ensued; but eventually the mermaid had to yield. The price she offered for her freedom was that which John had heard tell of, and he at once stated the "wishes three," the fulfilment of which he desired. The first was that neither he himself nor any of his friends should perish by sea; the second, that he should be uninterruptedly fortunate in all his undertakings; the third wish he never communicated to anyone except the mermaid—and yet, somehow, nobody ever failed to guess it! These stated, "Quit and have!" exclaimed the mermaid, and as he released his hold, she sprang into the sea. John was soon able to put the genuineness of her promise to the test. Continuing his walk, he came upon Helen Stuart reclining on the grass, and setting himself beside her, he pursued his wooing with such success that not long afterwards she became his bride. And the mermaid proving as good as her word in every particular, it is needless to say that they lived happily ever afterwards.

The more terrible side of the mermaid's character is nowhere more grimly illustrated than in another of Hugh Miller's northern legends. Where the parish of Tarbat borders on that of Fearn is situated Loch Slin, "a dark, sluggish sheet of water, bordered on every side by thick, tangled hedges of reed and rushes." The very atmosphere is pervaded with the uncanniness of the story. A little girl from a cottage some distance off was passing by the loch one evening on her way home, just when the dusk had begun to draw round its shores, when she heard a strange sound as of continuous knocking. Then she discovered what seemed to be a tall female standing in the water, by the edge of the loch, engaged, apparently, in beating clothes on a stone with the sort of bludgeon still (or at least in Hugh Miller's time) used in the north country for the purpose. Something told the girl that this must be the mermaid of Loch Slin, of whom such eerie tales were told round the fires of a winter's night, and terror-stricken she took to her heels. But as she hurried past she could not help noticing that the woman "seemed to ply her work with a malignant pleasure, and that on the grass plot directly opposite where she stood there were spread out as if to dry thirty smocks and shirts all horribly dappled with blood." Breathless and horrified as she was, the girl was still able to relate her adventure when she arrived home, and there was much speculation as to what this strange spectacle might portend. It was but in keeping with the reputation of the mermaid that it should imply some impending calamity. This surmise proved only too true. On the following Sunday a terrible and mysterious explosion shattered the ancient Abbey of Fearn, bringing down the ponderous stone roof among the worshippers, and burying nearly half of them in the ruins. In all, thirty-six persons were killed on the spot, and many more were so frightfully injured that they never recovered. Among the victims were several relatives of the girl who had heard the uncanny knocking and witnessed the grim employment of the mermaid of Loch Slin.

There is often a vindictiveness, too, about the mermaid's nature, that leads her to wreak a terrible vengeance upon those who do her an injury or thwart her will or cross her path in any way. Close to the old house of Knockdalion, near the water of Eirvan, there used to be a block of stone on which a mermaid would sit at nightfall for hours at a time, singing her songs and combing her yellow hair. One day, however, the mistress of Knockdalion took it into her head that the singing was annoying her child and keeping him from sleeping, and she had the stone broken to pieces. Great was the mermaid's grief and anger when she appeared that night and found her favourite seat was no longer there. And this was what she sang:—

> "Ye may think on your cradle—I'll think on my stane,
> And there'll ne'er be an heir to Knockdalion again."

Soon after the cradle was found overturned, with the baby dead beneath it. And the mermaid's prophecy proved only too true, for the family became extinct with that generation.

One day some fishermen from Quarff, on the south-eastern coast of Shetland, caught a mermaid on one of their hooks. On seeing what was the nature of their prey, one of them drew his knife and stabbed the mermaid in the breast; whereupon the hook gave way, and she sank. Thenceforward the fisherman in question never prospered, and till the day of his death he was haunted by an evil spirit, in the form of an old man, who used to say to him—"Will ye still do such a thing, who killed a woman?"

Another Shetland story is of a somewhat similar character. A young fisherman one day caught a seal, which he skinned in the usual fashion, afterwards tossing the carcase into the sea. The animal, however, had only been stunned, and very soon revived. He naturally began to feel very cold in the absence of his outer covering, but what most made him disconsolate was the thought of his forlorn appearance. A mermaid who had observed the incident took pity on his plight, and her efforts to restore to him his lost skin resulted in a sad catastrophe. The mermaid became hooked on the fishing line of the boat to which the captor of the seal belonged. Although the latter, his conscience smiting him for what he had just done, pleaded for the release of the mermaid, she was hauled on board and placed in the bottom of the boat on the sealskin. In a few minutes a sudden squall arose and overturned the boat, drowning the whole of her crew. The seal was able to recover his skin; but, alas! he had to lament the loss of the friend through whose agency this was effected, for the mermaid had become so exhausted by her struggles that she was at her last gasp when she was precipitated back into her native element. Ever since this happened, the legend has it, the seals have constituted themselves the special guardians of the mermaid race.

A still closer relationship, however, than is generally recognised, subsists between the seals and the semi-human denizens of the ocean. In Orkney and Shetland "selkie" is the popular name for the seal; and those of the larger species are often called "selkie-folk," because they are supposed to have the power of turning into men and women. According to one statement, the original "selkie-folk" were fallen angels, who were condemned to this condition because of some fault, not serious enough to necessitate their consignment to the infernal regions. According to another version, they were human beings who, as a punishment for some wrong committed, were condemned to assume the form of the seal and to live in the sea, being only allowed to revert to their human character at certain periods and conditions of the tide, when they were on dry land. When they have doffed their sealskins, these "selkie-folk," of both sexes, are said to be particularly striking for their beauty of feature and fairness of form, and sad havoc have they been known to play with the affections of the sons and daughters of the coast. It is believed to this day in some parts of the islands of the north that a certain horny growth on the palms of the hands and the soles of the feet denotes descent from one of the "selkie-folk," this being the result of an attempt to cut away the webbed membrane appearing between the fingers and toes of the original offspring. There is, by the way, a beautiful legend that when a young and fair maiden is lost at sea she is not drowned, but taken captive by the "selkie-folk," and becomes the bride of one of them. One curious characteristic about these creatures is that they are never known to appear alone (as is almost invariably the case with the mermaid), but always in groups, basking in the sunshine or gambolling about on some sea-surrounded skerry, with their sealskins lying beside them on the rock. The moment the alarm is given of the approach of anyone, they make a dash for their furry garments, and donning them, are immediately seals again, and plunge into the sea and make off.

A typical story of an encounter with the "selkie-folk" and what came of it is that of the guidman of Wastness, in Shetland. This young fellow, who had successfully withstood the blandishments of the maidens of the country-side, and had escaped the toils of their mammas, one day came upon a group of "selkie-folk" sporting on a rock by the shore. Creeping forward, he secured the sealskin nearest him, before its proper owner could reach it, and set off home with it over his shoulder. Before he had gone far he heard a pitiful wailing behind him, and looking round, saw a beautiful girl following him, weeping dolefully. This, as he rightly conjectured, was the one of the "selkie-folk" whose sealskin he had seized, and who was unable to escape owing to the want of it. Timorously she approached, and tearfully she begged the restoration of property so necessary to her. The young crofter, struck by her beauty and winsomeness, refused to meet her wish unless she consented to become his wife. After some persuasion, he succeeded in wringing from the sea-maiden a reluctant consent, and she accompanied him home. A thrifty, frugal, and kindly goodwife, too, did she turn out, and the birth to them of seven children—four boys and three girls—seemed to leave nothing lacking for her happiness. But often the mother would turn away from her children and gaze with a longing, far-away look in her eyes, at the sea. The sealskin she had never seen since the day she came as an ocean bride. One day when her husband and eldest sons were away at the fishing, and she was left in the house with only the youngest child, who had been ill, an overpowering desire came over her. High and low she hunted for the missing skin, but she was unable to find it. She was on the point of giving up the search in despair, when the child said she knew where her father kept an old skin bundled up. Sure enough, this proved to be the identical article for which she was seeking, and slipping away from her child with it clasped close in her arms, she made quickly for the beach. Arrived at the water's edge, no time was lost in putting on the skin, and with a glad shout she sprang into the sea. Swimming rapidly towards a group of seals not far distant, she was greeted with warmth on her return to her kith and kin, the demonstrations of a large male seal which had been often noticed in the neighbourhood being particularly marked. Just then the guidman happened to be returning from the fishing, and as his boat sailed past what was his astonishment to hear himself addressed as follows:—

"Guidman o' Wastness, fareweel tae dee!
I liket dee weel; doo were guid tae me.
But I loo better my man o' da sea!"

When he arrived home he found it was no trick that was being played upon him; and what his youngest child had to tell soon enlightened him as to the manner in which he had lost his helpmeet. Distracted, he haunted the sea-shore for several days and nights; but never a trace did he again see of his "selkie" wife.

A story of a different kind is that relating the experience of a fisherman from Papa Stour who landed on the Ve Skerries with some others to secure some seals. A number had been stunned and skinned, when the rising of a tremendous swell caused the men to dash for their boat. In the hurry, one man was left behind. Realising that he had been deserted by his comrades, he returned to the spot where the carcases of the seals had been left lying. There, to his astonishment, he found what appeared to be a large number of human beings, busy attending to some others who lay on the ground. It was the "selkie-folk" who had come to the rescue of their stunned companions. The plight of the latter, even when they had recovered from their swoon, was a sad one, for the fishermen had not forgotten the skins in their haste. Instead of the marooned seal-hunter being, as he had expected, set upon by the "selkie-folk" and put to death for what had taken place, he was courteously approached and questioned concerning the possibility of the recovery of the skins. Ultimately a bargain was struck. One big seal, named Gioga, consented to convey the man to the mainland provided he would undertake to have them returned in as short a time as possible. Gioga even allowed him to cut holes in her shoulders and flanks for his hands and feet, to prevent his slipping off her back. In this fashion the voyage to Papa Stour was safely accomplished; and the Shetlander did not fail to fulfil his part of the bargain in securing the restoration of the captured skins. The truth of this tale is vouched for by the islanders by the fact that some time afterwards the body of a large seal which was washed ashore in that district was found to have holes cut in the skin corresponding to those spoken about by the fisherman in question.

We meet with a variant of the "selkie-folk" legend on the northern mainland. The story is told concerning a fisherman and seal-hunter who lived not far from John o' Groat's House. One day on returning home he was summoned by a stranger to accompany him to a person who was desirous of bargaining with him for sealskins. Mounting the horse that was standing at the door they rode till they came to a steep precipice. There they dismounted, and immediately the stranger seized the fisherman and leapt with him into the sea. How far they sank he could not tell, but ultimately they came to a door in the cliff. Entering, they came into the midst of a large assembly of "Roane" or seals, who were speaking and acting like human folk, but seemed very sad; and to his astonishment the fisherman perceived that both he and his companion had the appearance of seals themselves. The production of a large knife by one of the seals threw the hunter into a great state of fear, and his panic was in no wise diminished when he recognised it as one belonging to himself, which he had lost that very morning after stabbing a seal, which had escaped. He was assured, however, that he was in no danger. His guide explained that the seal that had been stabbed was really his (the guide's) old father, and he was at that very moment lying dangerously ill in an adjoining apartment. What the hunter had been brought for was in order that he might lend his aid towards bringing about the recovery of the invalid. When taken into the presence of the latter, he at once recognised him as the seal that had escaped him in the morning. He was now asked to cicatrise the wound he himself had inflicted—a tremendous cut in the hindquarter. The operation was performed without difficulty, and the seal arose from his couch in perfect health. The fisherman was then informed that he was free to return to his wife, on the express condition, however, that he would never again maim or kill a seal. On his assenting to this, not without some natural reluctance, he was conducted to the door of the cave, and he and his guide rose to the surface together, finding their former steed awaiting them, ready for a second gallop. Once on land, the guide breathed on the fisherman, and they both became like men again, and mounting, they were not long in reaching the door of the hut. And here, to his great delight, the fisherman was rewarded with a sum of money large enough to make his enforced abstention from seal-hunting a loss which he could afford to bear with perfect equanimity.

To conclude, let me borrow from "Fiona Macleod" an instance of another form assumed by one of these sirens of the sea. As might be expected from the narrator, the circumstances are invested with a supernatural eeriness such as is to be found only in an atmosphere of Celtic mysticism. Murdo MacIan of the Isle is made, in "Sea-Magic," to relate how "a woman often came out of the sea and said strange foreign words at the back of his door—and that in a whinnying voice like that of a foal—came white as foam, and went away grey as rain. And then," he adds, "she would go to that stroked rock yonder and put songs against me till my heart shook like a tallow-flaucht in the wind."

And once, he goes on to say, "a three-week back or so I came home in a thin, noiseless rain, and heard a woman-voice singing by the fire-flaucht, and stole up soft to the house-side; but she heard the beat of my pulse, and went out at the door, not looking once behind her. She was tall and white, with red hair, and though I did not see her face, I know it was like a rock in rain with the tears streaming on it. She was a woman till she was at the shore there, then she threw her arms into the winds, and was a gull, and flew away in the lowness of a cloud."

It is impossible to say in regard to questions such as these, where tradition based upon apparent fact merges into legend founded upon the frankest fiction. On that account, as well as from consideration of length, no attempt has here been made to inquire into, or even touch upon, any of the occasions on which mermaids are said, with more apparent matter-of-factness than is the case with most of the legends just brought to your notice, to have been seen on our coasts. The task would probably be as thankless as that of investigating the identity of the "mermaids" whose seizure has been recorded with full circumstantiality from time to time. It would probably also prove as futile as the oft-made attempt to grasp the elusive personality of that more up-to-date apparition of the vasty deep, the sea-serpent, whose actual capture, in spite of the growing frequency of its appearance even in our own waters, and the general agreement among those who have encountered it of at least the ferociousness of its aspect, has yet to be chronicled.

Source:

Arnott, R. J. "Scottish Mermaids: 5th April 1907." *The Transactions and Journal of Proceedings of the Dumfries and Galloway Natural History and Antiquarian Society*. Volume 19. Dumfries: Standard Office, 1908. pp.142-157.

25. The Mermaid
by John Leyden

Scotland

THE following poem is founded upon a Gaelic traditional ballad, called *Macphail of Colonsay, and the Mermaid of Corrivrekin*. The dangerous gulf of Corrivrekin lies between the islands of Jura and Scarba, and the superstition of the islanders has tenanted its shelves and eddies with all the fabulous monsters and demons of the ocean. Among these, according to a universal tradition, the Mermaid is the most remarkable. In her dwelling, and in her appearance, the Mermaid of the northern nations resembles the siren of the ancients. The appendages of a comb and mirror are probably of Celtic invention.

The Gaelic story bears, that Macphail of Colonsay was carried off by a Mermaid, while passing the gulf above mentioned: that they resided together in a grotto beneath the sea for several years, during which time she bore him five children; but finally, he tired of her society, and having prevailed upon her to carry him near the shore of Colonsay, he escaped to land.

The inhabitants of the Isle of Man have a number of such stories, which may be found in Waldron. One bears, that a very beautiful Mermaid fell in love with a young shepherd, who kept his flocks beside a creek much frequented by these marine people. She frequently caressed him, and brought him presents of coral, fine pearls, and every valuable production of the ocean. Once upon a time, as she threw her arms eagerly round him, he suspected her of a design to draw him into the sea, and, struggling hard, disengaged himself from her embrace, and ran away. But the Mermaid resented either the suspicion, or the disappointment, so highly, that she threw a stone after him, and flung herself into the sea, whence she never returned. The youth, though but slightly struck with the pebble, felt, from that moment, the most excruciating agony, and died at the end of seven days.—Waldron's *Works*, p. 176-7.

Another tradition of the same island affirms, that one of these amphibious damsels was caught in a net, and brought to land, by some fishers, who had spread a snare for the denizens of the ocean. She was shaped like the most beautiful female down to the waist, but below trailed a voluminous fish's tail, with spreading fins. As she would neither eat nor speak, (though they knew she had the power of language,) they became apprehensive that the island would be visited with some strange calamity, if she should die for want of food; and, therefore, on the third night, they left the door open, that she might escape. Accordingly she did not fail to embrace the opportunity; but, gliding with incredible swiftness to the sea-side, she plunged herself into the waters, and was welcomed by a number of her own species, who were heard to inquire what she had seen among the natives of the earth? "Nothing," she answered, "wonderful, except that they were silly enough to throw away the water in which they had boiled their eggs."

Collins, in his notes upon the line,

"Mona, long hid from those who sail the main,"

explains it, by a similar Celtic tradition. It seems, a mermaid had become so much charmed with a young man, who walked upon the beach, that she made love to him; and, being rejected with scorn, she excited, by enchantment, a mist which long concealed the island from all navigators.

I must mention another Mankish tradition, because, being derived from the common source of Celtic mythology, they appear the most natural illustrations of a Hebridean tale. About fifty years before Waldron went to reside in Man, (for there were living witnesses of the legend, when he was upon the island,) a project was undertaken to fish treasures up from the deep, by means of a diving-bell. A venturous fellow, accordingly, descended, and kept pulling for more rope, till all they had on board was expended. This must have been no small quantity, for a skilful mathematician who was on board, judging from the proportion of line let down, declared, that the adventurer must have descended at least double the number of leagues which the moon is computed to be distant from the earth. At such a depth, wonders might be expected, and wonderful was the account given by the adventurer, when drawn up to the air.

"After," said he, "I had passed the region of fishes, I descended into a pure element, clear as the air in the serenest and most unclouded day, through which, as I passed, I saw the bottom of the watery world, paved with coral, and a shining kind of pebbles, which glittered like the sunbeams, reflected on a glass. I longed to tread the delightful paths, and never felt more exquisite delight than when the machine I was enclosed in, grazed upon it.

"On looking through the little windows of my prison, I saw large streets and squares on every side, ornamented with huge pyramids of crystal, not inferior in brightness to the finest diamonds; and the most beautiful buildings, not of stone, nor brick, but of mother-of-pearl, and embossed in various figures, with shells of all colours, The passage, which led to one of those magnificent apartments, being open, I endeavoured, with my whole strength, to move my enclosure towards it; which I did, though with great difficulty, and very slowly. At last, however, I got entrance into a very spacious room, in the midst of which stood a large amber table, with several chairs round, of the same. The floor of it was composed of rough diamonds, topazes, emeralds, rubies, and pearls. Here I doubted not but to make my voyage as profitable as it was pleasant; for, could I have brought with me but a few of these, they would have been of more value than all we could hope for in a thousand wrecks; but they were so closely wedged in, and so strongly cemented by time, that they were not to be unfastened. I saw several chains, carcanets, and rings, of all manner of precious stones, finely cut, and set after our manner, which, I suppose, had been the prize of the winds and waves: these were hanging loosely on the jasper walls, by strings made of rushes, which I might easily have taken down; but as I had edged myself within half a foot reach of them, I was unfortunately drawn back through your want of line. In my return I saw several comely *mermen*, and beautiful *mermaids*, the inhabitants of this blissful realm, swiftly descending towards it; but they seemed frighted at my appearance, and glided at a distance from me, taking me, no doubt, for some monstrous and new-created species."—Waldson, *ibidem*.

It would be very easy to enlarge this introduction, by quoting a variety of authors concerning the supposed existence of these marine people. The reader may consult the *Telliamed* of M. Maillet, who, in support of the Neptunist system of geology, has collected a variety of legends, respecting mermen and mermaids, p. 230 *et sequen*. Much information may also be derived from Pontopiddan's *Natural History of Norway*, who fails not to people her seas with this amphibious race.[1] An older authority is to be found in the *Kongs skugg-sio*, or Royal Mirror, written, as it is believed, about 1170. The mermen, there mentioned, are termed *hafstrambur* (sea-giants,) and are said to have the upper parts resembling the human race; but the author, with becoming diffidence, declines to state, positively, whether they are equipped with a dolphin's tail. The female monster is called *Mar-Gyga* (sea-giantess,) and is averred certainly to drag a fish's train. She appears generally in the act of devouring fish, which she has caught. According to the apparent voracity of her appetite, the sailors pretend to guess what chance they had of saving their lives in the tempests, which always followed her appearance.—*Speculum Regale*, 1768, p. 166.

Mermaids were sometimes supposed to be possessed of supernatural powers. Resenius, in his Life of Frederick II., gives us an account of a siren, who not only prophesied future events, but, as might have been expected from the element in which she dwelt, preached vehemently against the sin of drunkenness.

---

[1] I believe something to the same purpose may be found in the school editions of Guthrie's *Geographical Grammar*; a work which, though in general as sober and dull as could be desired by the gravest preceptor, becomes of a sudden uncommonly lively, upon the subject of the seas of Norway; the author having thought meet to adopt the Right Reverend Brick Pontopiddan's account of Mermen, sea-snakes, and krakens.

The mermaid of Corrivrekin possessed the power of occasionally resigning her scaly train; and the Celtic tradition bears, that when, from choice or necessity, she was invested with that appendage, her manners were more stern and savage than when her form was entirely human. Of course, she warned her lover not to come into her presence when she was thus transformed. This belief is alluded to in the following ballad.

The beauty of the sirens is celebrated in the old romances of chivalry. Doolin, upon beholding, for the first time in his life, a beautiful female, exclaims, "*Par saint Marie, si belle creature ne vis je oncque en ma vie! Je crois que c'est un ange du del, on time seraine de mer; je crois que homme n'engendra oncque si belle creature.*"—*La Fleur des Battailles.*

I cannot help adding, that some late evidence has been produced, serving to show, either that imagination played strange tricks with the witnesses, or that the existence of mermaids is no longer a matter of question. I refer to the letters written to Sir John Sinclair, by the spectators of such a phenomenon, in the bay of Sandside, in Caithness.

[In 1811, a thin octavo volume was printed at Edinburgh, entitled, "*Description of the Spar Cave lately discovered in the Isle of Skye, &c, by K. Macleay*, M.D.," containing a copy of "The Mermaid," in which four additional stanzas appear, the first of which is inserted as stanza sixth in the text—the other three are given in small type at the bottom of a succeeding page. No portion of this ballad is connected with Border tradition; but it exhibits so much of Leyden's imaginative faculty, and his perfect mastery of the English language, that to withhold it would be doing injustice to his memory. Generally his pieces are deficient of that constructiveness and arrangement by which the effusions of Scott are often distinguished; but the great Minstrel's ability is chiefly conspicuous on scenes whereupon the sun is supposed to shine, and the wind to blow—where knight and damsel meet together—and where the aim of the author has been to develope and illustrate some obscure chapter in the history of his country. To Leyden, therefore, in this ballad, must be assigned the power of taking our attention down to the "yellow sands" at the bottom of the main, amid "sparry caves," and "chrystal halls set with rubies and emeralds," where a daughter of ocean, in her attempt to win a son of earth, found herself unable to compete with the "Maid of Colonsay."][1]

ON Jura's heath how sweetly swell
   The murmurs of the mountain bee!
How softly mourns the writhed shell
   Of Jura's shore, its parent sea!

---

[1] I have not included Leyden's dedicatory three stanza poem to Lady Charlotte Campbell which preceded the poem.~*HAH*

But softer, floating o'er the deep,
    The Mermaid's sweet sea-soothing lay,
That charm'd the dancing waves to sleep,
    Before the bark of Colonsay.

Aloft the purple pennons wave,
    As, parting gay from Crinan's shore,
From Morven's wars the seamen brave
    Their gallant chieftain homeward bore.

In youth's gay bloom, the brave Macphail
    Still blamed the lingering bark's delay;
For her he chid the flagging sail,
    The lovely maid of Colonsay.

And "Raise," he cried, "the song of love,
    The maiden sung with tearful smile,
When first o'er Jura's hills to rove,
    We left afar the lonely isle!

"I saw the tear-drops on her cheek
    Her eyes in dewy lustre shine,
And as she spoke, with pressure weak
    Her hand she fondly clasped in mine.

"'When on this ring of ruby red
    Shall die,' she said, 'the crimson hew,
Know that thy favourite fair is dead,
    Or proves to thee and love untrue.'"

Now, lightly poised, the rising oar
    Disperses wide the foamy spray,
And, echoing far o'er Crinan's shore,
    Resounds the song of Colonsay.

"Softly blow, thou western breeze,
    Softly rustle through the sail,
Soothe to rest the furrowy seas,
    Before my love, sweet western gale!

"Where the wave is tinged with red,
    And the russet sea-leaves grow,
Mariners, with prudent dread,
    Shun the shelving reefs below.

"As you pass through Jura's sound,
 Bend your course by Scarba's shore,
Shun, O shun, the gulf profound,
 Where Corrivrekin's surges roar!

"If, from that unbottom'd deep,
 With wrinkled form and wreathed train,
O'er the verge of Scarba's steep,
 The sea-snake heave his snowy mane,[1]

"Unwarp, unwind his oozy coils,
 Sea-green sisters of the main,
And, in the gulf, where ocean boils,
 The unwieldy wallowing monster chain![2]

---

[1] "They who, in works of navigation, on the coasts of Norway, employ themselves in fishing or merchandise, do all agree in this strange story, that there is a serpent there, which is of vast magnitude, namely, two hundred feet long, and moreover twenty feet thick; and is wont to live in rocks and caves, toward the sea coast about Berge; which will go alone from his holes, in a clear night in summer, and devour calves, lambs, and hogs; or else he goes into the sea to feed on polypus, locusts, and all sorts of sea-crabs. He hath commonly hair hanging from his neck a cubit long, and sharp scales, and is black, and he hath naming shining eyes. This snake disquiets the skippers, and he puts up his head on high, like a pillar, and catcheth away men, and he devours them; and this hapneth not but it signifies some wonderful change of the kingdom near at hand; namely, that the princes shall die, or be banished, or some tumultuous wars shall presentlie follow."—*Olaus Magnus*, London, 1558, rendered into English by J. S. Much more of the sea-snake may be learned from the credible witnesses cited by Pontoppidan, who saw it raise itself from the sea, twice as high as the mast of their vessel. The tradition probably originates in the immense snake of the Edda, whose folds were supposed to girdle the earth.

 A sort of sea-snake, of size immense enough to have given rise to this tradition, was thrown ashore upon one of the Orkney Isles, in 1808.—Walter Scott.

[2] Those three stanzes are from the copy of "The Mermaid" alluded to in the introduction.

   "Ne'er, my Love, in combat fierce
    Yield to foes the forward lance,
   Doom'd opposing breasts to pierce.
    Rapid as the lover's glance.

"Softly blow, thou western breeze,
    Softly rustle through the sail,
Soothe to rest the furrowed seas,
    Before my love, sweet western gale!"

Thus, all to soothe the Chieftain's woe,
    Far from the maid he loved so dear,
The song arose, so soft and slow,
    He seem'd her parting sigh to hear.

The lonely deck he paces o'er.
    Impatient for the rising day,
And still, from Crinan's moonlight shore,
    He turns his eyes to Colonsay.

The moonbeams crisp the curling surge,
    That streaks with foam the ocean green;
While forward still the rowers urge
    Their course, a female form was seen.

That sea-maid's form, of pearly light,
    Was whiter than the downy spray,
And round her bosom, heaving bright,
    Her glossy, yellow ringlets play.

Borne on a foamy-crested wave,
    She reach'd amain the bounding prow,
Then, clasping fast the Chieftain brave,
    She, plunging, sought the deep below.

Ah! long beside thy feigned bier,
    The monks the prayers of death shall say,
And long, for thee, the fruitless tear
    Shall weep the Maid of Colonsay!

"Ne'er, my Love, in fields of fight
    Yield thy temper'd keen claymore,
Till the splinters sparkle bright,
    Round them in the combat's roar.

"Ne'er my Love, by foes oppress'd,
    The dirk that pierces deep forego,
Till plunged within the warrior's breast,
    He stagg'ring sink beneath the blow."

But downwards, like a powerless corse,
    The eddying waves the Chieftain bear;
He only heard the moaning hoarse
    Of waters, murmuring in his ear.

The murmurs sink by slow degrees;
    No more the surges round him rave;
Lull'd by the music of the seas,
    He lies within a coral cave.

In dreamy mood reclines he long,
    Nor dares his tranced eyes unclose,
Till, warbling wild, the sea-maid's song,
    Far in the crystal cavern, rose;

Soft as that harp's unseen control,
    In morning dreams which lovers hear,
Whose strains steal sweetly o'er the soul,
    But never reach the waking ear.

As sunbeams through the tepid air,
    When clouds dissolve the dews unseen,
Smile on the flowers, that bloom more fair,
    And fields, that glow with livelier green—

So melting soft the music fell;
    It seem'd to soothe the fluttering spray—
"Say, heard'st thou not these wild notes swell?"—
    "Ah! 'tis the song of Colonsay."

Like one that from a fearful dream
    Awakes, the morning light to view,
And joys to see the purple beam,
    Yet fears to find the vision true,—

He heard that strain, so wildly sweet,
    Which bade his torbid langour fly;
He fear'd some spell had bound his feet,
    And hardly dared his limbs to try.

"This yellow sand, this sparry cave,
    Shall bend thy soul to beauty's sway;
Canst thou the maiden of the wave
    Compare to her of Colonsay?"

Roused by that voice, of silver sound,
    From the paved floor he lightly sprung,
And, glancing wild his eyes around,
    Where the fair nymph her tresses wrung,

No form he saw of mortal mould;
    It shone like ocean's snowy foam;
Her ringlets waved in living gold,
    Her mirror crystal, pearl her comb.

Her pearly comb the siren took,
    And careless bound her tresses wild;
Still o'er the mirror stole her look,
    As on the wondering youth she smiled.

Like music from the greenwood tree,
    Again she raised the melting lay;
—"Fair warrior, wilt thou dwell with me,
    And leave the Maid of Colonsay?

"Fair is the crystal hall for me,
    With rubies and with emeralds set,
And sweet the music of the sea
    Shall sing, when we for love are met.

"How sweet to dance, with gliding feet,
    Along the level tide so green,
Responsive to the cadence sweet,
    That breathes along the moonlight scene!

"And soft the music of the main
    Rings from the motley tortoise-shell,
While moonbeams, o'er the watery plain,
    Seem trembling in its fitful swell.

"How sweet, when billows heave their head,
    And shake their snowy crests on high,
Serene in Ocean's sapphire-bed,
    Beneath the tumbling surge, to lie;

"To trace, with tranquil step, the deep,
    Where pearly drops of frozen dew
In concave shells, unconscious, sleep,
    Or shine with lustre, silvery blue!

"Then shall the summer sun, from far,
    Pour through the wave a softer ray,
While diamonds, in a bower of spar,
    At eve shall shed a brighter day.

"Nor stormy wind, nor wintry gale,
    That o'er the angry ocean sweep,
Shall e'er our coral groves assail,
    Calm in the bosom of the deep.

"Through the green meads beneath the sea,
    Enamour'd, we shall fondly stray—
Then, gentle warrior, dwell with me,
    And leave the Maid of Colonsay!"—

"Though bright thy locks of glistering gold,
    Fair maiden of the foamy main!
Thy life-blood is the water cold,
    While mine beats high in every vein.

"If I, beneath thy sparry cave,
    Should in thy snowy arms recline,
Inconstant as the restless wave,
    My heart would grow as cold as thine."

As cygnet down, proud swell'd her breast;
    Her eye confest the pearly tear;
His hand she to her bosom press'd—
    "Is there no heart for rapture here?

"These limbs, sprung from the lucid sea,
    Does no warm blood their currents fill,
No heart-pulse riot, wild and free,
    To joy, to love's delirious thrill?"—

"Though all the splendour of the sea
    Around thy faultless beauty shine,
That heart, that riots wild and free,
    Can hold no sympathy with mine.

"These sparkling eyes, so wild and gay,
    They swim not in the light of love:
The beauteous Maid of Colonsay,
    Her eyes are milder than the dove!

"Even now, within the lonely isle,
    Her eyes are dim with tears for me;
And canst thou think that siren smile
    Can lure my soul to dwell with thee?"

An oozy film her limbs o'erspread;
    Unfolds in length her scaly train:
She toss'd, in proud disdain, her head,
    And lash'd, with webbed fin, the main.

"Dwell here, alone!" the mermaid cried,
    "And view far off the sea-nymphs play;
Thy prison-wall, the azure tide,
    Shall bar thy steps from Colonsay.

"Whene'er, like Ocean's scaly brood,
    I cleave, with rapid fin, the wave,
Far from the daughter of the flood,
    Conceal thee in this coral cave.

"I feel my former soul return;
    It kindles at thy cold disdain:
And has a mortal dared to spurn
    A daughter of the foamy main!"—

She fled,—around the crystal cave
    The rolling waves resume their road,
On the broad portal idly rave,
    But enter not the nymph's abode.

And many a weary night went by,
    As in the lonely cave he lay;
And many a sun roll'd through the sky,
    And pour'd its beams on Colonsay;

And oft, beneath the silver moon,
    He heard afar the mermaid sing,
And oft, to many a melting tune,
    The shell-formed lyres of ocean ring:

And when the moon went down the sky,
    Still rose, in dreams, his native plain,
And oft he thought his love was by,
    And charm'd him with some tender strain;

And heart-sick, oft he waked to weep,
    When ceased that voice of silver sound,
And thought to plunge him in the deep,
    That wall'd his crystal cavern round.

But still the ring, of ruby red,
    Retain'd it vivid crimson hue,
And each despairing accent fled,
    To find his gentle love so true.

When seven long lonely months were gone,
    The Mermaid to his cavern came,
No more misshapen from the zone,
    But like a maid of mortal frame.

"O give to me that ruby ring,
    That on thy finger glances gay,
And thou shalt hear the mermaid sing
    The song, thou lovest, of Colonsay."—

"This ruby ring, of crimson grain,
    Shall on thy finger glitter gay,
If thou wilt bear me through the main,
    Again to visit Colonsay."—

"Except thou quit thy former love,
    Content to dwell for aye with me,
Thy scorn my finny frame might move,
    To tear thy limbs amid the sea."—

"Then bear me swift along the main,
    The lonely isle again to see,
And, when I here return again,
    I plight my faith to dwell with thee."—

An oozy film her limbs o'erspread,
    While slow unfolds her scaly train,
With gluey fangs her hands were clad,
    She lash'd, with webbed fin, the main.

He grasps the mermaid's scaly sides,
    As, with broad fin, she oars her way;
Beneath the silent moon she glides,
    That sweetly sleeps on Colonsay.

Proud swells her heart! she deems, at last,
    To lure him with her silver tongue,
And, as the shelving rocks she past,
    She raised her voice, and sweetly sung.

In softer, sweeter strains she sung,
    Slow gliding o'er the moonlight bay,
When light to land the Chieftain sprung,
    To hail the Maid of Colonsay.

O sad the mermaid's gay notes fell,
    And sadly sink remote at sea!
So sadly mourns the writhed shell
    Of Jura's shore, its parent sea.

And ever as the year returns,
    The charm-bound sailors know the day;
For sadly still the mermaid mourns
    The lovely Chief of Colonsay.

1802-03

Source:
Leyden, John. *Poems and Ballads: With a Memoir of the Author by Sir Walter Scott*. Kelso: J. & J.H. Rutherford, 1858.

26. Orcadian Water Spirits

Orkney Islands, Scotland

SAILORS and fishermen are peculiarly superstitious. Our own North Sea is rich in legendary lore. Romans and Goths, Danes, Scandinavians, and Normans, blue-eyed Saxon maids, and ruthless invaders, mermen and mermaidens, trolls, water-wraiths, and genii of the caves have from earliest ages been associated with her shores, and have supplied material for many a thrilling tale of true history, and many a wild romance. In the moonlight nights of winter, and through the dreamy summer gloamings of the storm-swept Orcades, and the remote Ultima Thule, the mermaid combs her golden tresses, and by her witching strains lures the hapless mariner to destruction. The water-wraith, in the form of an old woman of majestic stature, haunts inland lochs and rivers, as well as firths, bays, and voes, and with loud shrieks gives warning of impending disaster.

Mermaids were believed to have the power, like the fairies, of kidnapping children. A woman, says an old legend, was one day bathing her infant in a pool on the sea-beach near a town, when suddenly, with a cry of joy, it jumped from her arms into the sea. She thought it was drowned, but in an instant it came to the surface, and she received it back again, more beautiful and bright than ever. She took it home, and cared for it as usual, never dreaming for a moment that it was not her own infant; but some old folks in the town knew that it was a mermaid's changeling. The child grew up a lovely woman, and the lord of the place fell in love with her. After a time he treated her very badly, and deserted her, and she died of a broken heart. But Nemesis was on his track. Returning late one moonlight night from a revel, by way of the sands, he saw a beautiful lady seated on a rock by the seaside. She bore such a striking resemblance to his lost love that he was frightened at first, but she smiled and beckoned to him, and when he went near her she clasped him in her arms, jumped with him into the sea, and held him beneath the waves till he was drowned. That same night a great storm arose, during which the mermaids, her sisters, choked up the harbour bar.

Source:
Laing, Jeanie M. *Notes on Superstition and Folk Lore*. Edinburgh: John Menzies & Co., 1885. pp. 71-72, 78.

27. The Mermaid of Lochinver

Sutherland, Scotland

A MERMAID fell in love with a fisherman of Lochinver. Her lover was enamoured, but he had heard how youths ensnared by mermaids had found a watery grave.

It became necessary then to make his own terms, and to arrange matters so as to secure himself. To rule a mermaid it is necessary to possess yourself, not of her person, but of the pouch and belt which mermaids wear. This carries the glass, comb, and other articles well-known to be indispensable to the lady's comfort, but also as a sort of life-preserver helps them to swim.

By fair means or foul this cautious swain got hold of the pouch, and the mermaid became in consequence his bride and his bondswoman.

There was little happiness in such a union for the poor little wife. She wearied of a husband, who, to tell the truth, thought more of himself than of her. He never took her out in his boat when the sun danced on the sea, but left her at home with the cows, and on a croft which was to her a sort of prison. Her silky hair grew tangled. The dogs teased her. Her tail was really in the way. She wept incessantly while rude people mocked at her. Nor was there any prospect of escape after nine months of this wretched life. Her powers of swimming depended on her pouch, and that was lost. What was more, she now suspected the fisherman of having cozened her out of it.

One day the fisherman was absent, and the labourers were pulling down a stack of corn. The poor mermaid watched them weeping, when to her great joy she espied her precious pouch and belt, which had been built in and buried among the sheaves. She caught it, and leapt into the sea, there to enjoy a delicious freedom.—(J. MacLeod, Laxford.)

Source:
Dempster, Miss. "The Folk-Lore of Sutherland-Shire." *The Folk-Lore Journal*. Vol. 6, No. 3 (1888). pp. 149-189.

28. A' Mhaideann-mhara (The Mermaid)

Hebrides, Scotland

THE sea-cattle—so says the legend—came ashore at Shawbost once upon a time. The mermaid followed them. When the people of the district saw them ashore, they hastened to get between them and the sea to sprinkle the landing-place with (Maighstir) urine. (Gun so a' dheanainh cha b' urrainn iad a bhi air an gleidheadh air tir.) Without performing this ceremony they could not be kept ashore. They then brought them to be housed at the nearest farmsteading. The mermaid followed them. They were kept ashore about a week. The mermaid was particularly reticent during her stay. She broke silence only once; the occasion was her observing the woman in whose house she stayed cleaning newly-caught fish. She said to her: "Nigh' us glan gu maith an tiasg a's ioma beast a tha 'sa mhuir" ("Wash and clean well the fish, there is many a monster in the sea"). These words are in frequent use as a proverb, with the addition "Mar a thub hairt a' mhaid-eann-mhar" ("As the mermaid said.") To prevent the sea-cattle running away to their native element it was a sine qua non to sprinkle them with (Maighstir) urine every morning before letting them out to graze. One morning, however, this ceremony was neglected by the herd. The mermaid observed his mistake and her chance. She immediately ran down to the sea and began to call the sea-cattle by their several names, as follows:

"Ho! gu'n tig 'Sìtheag.' Ho! gu'n tig 'Seòthag.' Ho! gu'n tig 'Crom-an-taoid'" (the Bend of the Rope). "Ho! gu'n tig Caòilteag-bhàn" (White Caoilteag). "Ho! gu'n tig Donnach-mhòr-a'-bhainne bhruich" (Big Donnach of the cooked milk). O may "Sìtheag" come, &c.

The sea-cattle ran down to the sea. When she saw them coming she exclaimed: "Tha mo chrodhsa'n so 'tighinn; ach ged thì'n crodh na thi'm buachaill." ("My cattle are here coming, but, though the cattle are coming let the herdman not come.") The herdman ran after them and caught the last of them by the tail as it plunged into the sea, but could not keep it. When the mermaid observed how the herd had behaved, she said:

> "Nach bu luath lòm Luram,
> (Mur be cruas arrainn,)
> 'Nam' be lite us bainne biadh Lurain,
> Cha bhiodh laogh na bò an diugh gun chumail."

> "How swift and nimble is Luran!
> (Were it not for the dryness of bread.)
> Had Luran's food been porridge and milk
> No calf or cow would have escaped to-day."

The legend says it was then that the people of that district began to use porridge as food.

Source:
MacPhail, Malcolm. "Folklore from the Hebrides. II." *Folklore*. Vol. 8, No. 4 (Dec. 1897). pp. 380-386.

29. Another Legend of the Mermaid

Hebrides, Scotland

THE crew of a Lewis boat were coming across the minch from Lochbroom. In mid-ocean they saw the mermaid rising at the helm. "Thubhairt fear de'n sgiopadh co luath s'a chunnaic i seun fala o'n à bheist," one of the crew said as soon as he saw her "blood-charm" from the monster. She went at once out of sight, but shortly thereafter rose

Tales From Around the World

again to the surface at the helm. "'Us' thubhairt i ris an stiureadair; le do churgair dubh air do lath-chrann cia do leth-rann," she said to the helmsman. ("With your little black hood on the side of your head, what is your half-stanza?") He replied: "Long a thig 'us a theid gu aithghearr, as e sin mo leth-rann" ("A ship which is in keen touch with the helm": literally a ship that goes and comes nimbly). "Is maith a chur sin ruit" ars ise, agus chaidh i fodha 'us chan fhac iad tuilledh i. ("It is well for you that you have so replied", said she, and disappeared, and they saw her no more). It was observed that when the mermaid was seen, under such circumstances as described above, it was a sure omen that drownings were to occur shortly in that neighbourhood, and so it happened our legend tells.

Source:
MacPhail, Malcolm. "Folklore from the Hebrides. II." *Folklore*. Vol. 8, No. 4 (Dec. 1897). pp. 380-386.

30. The Mermaid of Galloway by Allan Cunningham

Scotland

THERE'S a maid has sat on the green merse side
    These ten lang years and mair;
An' every first night o' the new moon
    She kames her yellow hair.

An' ay while she sheds the yellow burning gowd,
    Fu' sweet she sings an' hie,
Till the fairest bird that wooes the green wood,
    Is charm'd wi' her melodie.

But wha e'er listens to that sweet sang,
    Or gangs the dame to see,
Ne'er hears the sang o' the laverock again,
    Nor wakens an earthly ee.

It fell in about the sweet simmer month,
    I' the first come o' the moon,
That she sat o' the tap of a sea-weed rock,
    A-kaming her silk-locks down.

Her kame was o' the whitely pearl,
    Her hand like new-won milk;
Her breasts were all o' the snawy curd,
    In a net o' sea-green silk.

She kamed her locks owre her white shoulders,
    A fleece baith bonny and lang;
An' ilka ringlet she shed frae her brows,
    She raised a lightsome sang.

I' the very first lilt o' that sweet sang,
    The birds forsook their young;
An' they flew i' the gate o' the grey howlet,
    To listen the sweet maid's song.

I' the second lilt o' that sweet sang,
    Of sweetness it wes sae fu';
The tod leap'd out frae the frighted lambs,
    And dighted his red-wat mou'.

I' the very third lilt o' that sweet sang,
    Red lowed the new-woke moon;
The stars drapped blude on the yellow gowan tap,
    Sax miles that maiden roun'.

'I hae dwalt on the Nith,' quo' the young Cowehill,
    'These twenty years an' three,
But the sweetest sang e'er brake frae a lip,
    Comes thro' the green wood to me.

'O is it a voice frae twa earthly lips,
    Whilk makes sic melodie?
It wad wile the lark frae the morning lift,
    And weel may it wile me.'

'I dreamed a dreary thing, master,
    Whilk I am rad ye rede;
I dreamed ye kissed a pair o' sweet lips,
    That drapped o' red heart's-blede.'

'Come, haud my steed, ye little foot-page,
    Shod wi' the red gold roun';
Till I kiss the lips whilk sing sae sweet,'
    An' lightlie lap he down.

'Kiss nae the singer's lips, master,
    Kiss nae the singer's chin;
Touch nae her hand,' quo' the little foot-page,
    'If skaithless hame ye 'd win.

'O wha will sit on yere toom saddle,
    O wha will bruik yere gluve;
An' wha will fauld yere erled bride,
    I' the kindly clasps o' luve?'

He took aff his hat, a' gold i' the rim,
    Knot wi' a siller ban';
He seemed a' in lowe wi' his gold raiment,
    As thro' the green wood he ran.

'The simmer-dew fa's saft, fair maid,
    Aneath the siller moon;
But eerie is thy seat i' the rock,
    Washed wi' the white sea faem.

'Come, wash me wi' thy lilie white hand,
    Below and aboon the knee;
An' I'll kame thae links o' yellow burning gold,
    Aboon thy bonnie blue ee.

'How rosie are thy parting lips,
    How lilie-white thy skin,
An' weel I wat thae kissing een
    Wad tempt a saint to sin.'

'Tak aff thae bars an' bobs o' gold,
    Wi' thy gared doublet fine;
An' thraw me aff thy green mantle,
    Leafed wi' the siller twine.

'An' all in courtesie, fair knight,
    A maiden's love to win;
The gold lacing o' thy green weeds
    Wad harm her lilie skin.'

Syne coost he aff his green mantle,
    Hemm'd wi' the red gold roun';
His costly doublet coost he aff
    Wi' red gold flow'red down.

'Now ye maun kame my yellow hair,
    Down wi' my pearlie kame;
Then rowe me in thy green mantle,
    An' take me maiden hame.

'But first come take me 'neath the chin,
    An' syne come kiss my cheek;
An' spread my hanks o' wat'ry hair,
    I' the new-moon beam to dreep.'

Sae first he kissed her dimpled chin,
    Syne kissed her rosie cheek;
And lang he wooed her willin' lips,
    Like heather-hinnie sweet!

'O! if ye' ll come to the bonnie Cowehill,
    'Mang primrose banks to woo,
I'll wash thee ilk day i' the new-milked milk,
    An' bind wi' gold yere brow.

'An' a' for a drink o' the clear water
    Ye 'se hae the rosie wine,
An' a' for the water white lilie,
    Ye 'se hae these arms o' mine.'

'But what 'll she say, yere bonnie young bride
    Busked wi' the siller fine,
Whan the rich kisses ye kept for her lips,
    Are left wi' vows on mine?'

He took his lips frae her red-rose mou',
    His arms frae her waist sae sma';
'Sweet maiden, I'm in bridal speed,
    It's time I were awa'.

'O gie me a token o' luve, sweet May,
    A leal luve-token true;'
She crapped a lock o' yellow golden hair,
    An' knotted it roun' his brow.

'O tie nae it sae strait, sweet May,
    But with luve's rose-knot kind;
My head is full of burning pain,
    O saft ye maun it bind.'

His skin turned all o' the red-rose hue,
    Wi' draps o' bludie sweat;
An' he laid his head 'mang the water lilies:
    'Sweet maiden, I maun sleep.'

She tyed ae link of her wet yellow hair,
    Aboon his buruing bree;
Amang his curling haffet locks
    She knotted knurles three.

She weaved owre his brow the white lilie,
    Wi' witch-knots mae than nine;
'Gif ye were seven times bridegroom owre,
    This night ye shall be mine.'

O twice he turned his sinking head,
    An' twice he lifted his ee;
O twice he sought to loose the links
    Were knotted owre his bree.

'Arise, sweet knight, yere young bride waits,
    An' doubts her ale will sour;
An' wistly looks at the lilie-white sheets,
    Down spread in ladie bower.

'An' she has preened the broidered silk,
    About her white hause-bane;
Her princely petticoat is on,
    Wi' gold can stan' its lane.'

He faintlie, slowlie, turn'd his cheek,
    And faintly lift his ee,
And he strave to loose the witching bands
    Aboon his burning bree.

Then took she up his green mantle
    Of lowing gold the hem;
Then took she up his silken cap,
    Rich wi' a siller stem;
An' she threw them wi' her lilie hand
    Amang the white sea faem.

She took the bride ring frae his finger
    An' threw it in the sea;
'That hand shall mense nae ither ring
    But wi' the will o' me.'

She faulded him i' her lilie arms,
    An' took her pearlie kame;
His fleecy locks trailed owre the sand
    As she sought the white sea-faem.

First rose the star out owre the hill,
    An' neist the lovely moon;
While the beauteous bride o' Galloway
    Looked for her blythe bridegroom.

Lightlie she sang while the new moon rose,
    Blythe as a young bride May,
Whan the New Moon lights her lamp o' luve,
    An' blinks the bride away.

'Nithsdale, thou art a gay garden,
    Wi' monie a winsome flower;
But the princeliest rose o' that garden
    Maun blossom in my bower.

'O gentle be the wind on thy leaf,
    And gentle the gloaming dew;
And bonnie and balmy be thy bud,
    Of a pure and steadfast hue;
And she who sings this sang in thy praise,
    Shall love thee leal and true.'

An' ay she sewed her silken snood,
    An' sung a bridal sang;
But oft the tears drapt frae her ee,
    Afore the grey morn cam'.

The sun leamed ruddie 'mang the dew,
    Sae thick on bank and tree;
The plough-boy whistled at his darg,
    The milk-may answered hie;
But the lovely bride o' Galloway
    Sat wi' a tear-wet ee.

Ilk breath o' wind 'mang the forest leaves—
    She heard the bridegroom's tongue,
And she heard the bridal-coming lilt
    In every bird which sung.

She sat high on the tap tower stane,
    Nae waiting May was there;

She loosed the gold busk frae her breast,
    The kame frae 'mang her hair;
She wiped the tear-blobs frae her ee,
    An' looked lang and sair.

First sang to her the blythe wee bird,
    Frae aff the hawthorn green:
'Loose out the love curls frae yere hair,
    Ye plaited sae weel yestreen.'

An' the spreckled lark frae 'mang the clouds
    Of heaven came singing down:
'Take out the bride-knots frae yere hair
    An' let these lang locks down.'

'Come, bide wi' me, ye pair o' sweet birds,
    Come down and bide wi' me;
Ye sall peckle o' the bread an' drink o' the wine,
    And gold yere cage sall be.'

She laid the bride-cake 'neath her head,
    An' syne below her feet;
An' laid her down 'tween the lilie-white sheets,
    An' soundlie did she sleep!

It seemed i' the mid-hour o' the night,
    Her siller-bell did ring;
An' soun't as if nae earthlie hand
    Had pou'd the silken string.

There was a cheek touch'd that ladie's,
    Cauld as the marble stane;
An' a hand cauld as the drifting snaw
    Was laid on her breast-bane.

'O cauld is thy hand, my dear Willie,
    O cauld, cauld is thy cheek;
An' wring these locks o' yellow hair,
    Frae which the cauld draps dreep.'

'O seek anither bridegroom, Marie,
    On these bosom-faulds to sleep;
My bride is the yellow water lilie,
    Its leaves my bridal sheet!'

Originally published in 1810.

Source:
Cunningham, Allan. *Poems and Songs*. London: John Murray, 1847.

31. The Mermaid
by James Hogg

Scotland

"OH where won ye, my bonnie lass,
    Wi' look sae wild an' cheery?
There's something in that witching face
    That I lo'e wonder dearly."

"I live where the hare-bell never grew,
    Where the streamlet never ran,
Where the winds o' heaven never blew;
    Now find me gin you can."

"'Tis but your wild an' wily way,
    The gloaming maks you eirie,
For ye are the lass o' the Braken-Brae,
    An' nae lad maun come near ye:

"But I am sick, an' very sick
    Wi' a passion strange an' new,
For ae kiss o' thy rosy cheek
    An' lips o' the coral hue."

"O laith, laith wad a wanderer be
    To do your youth sic wrang;
Were you to reave a kiss from me
    Your life would not be lang.

"Go, hie you from this lonely brake,
    Nor dare your walk renew;
For I'm the Maid of the Mountain Lake,
    An' I come wi' the falling dew."

"Be you the Maid of the Crystal Wave,
    Or she of the Braken-Brae,
One tender kiss I mean to have;

You shall not say me nay.

"For beauty's like the daisy's vest
    That shrinks from the early dew,
But soon it opes its bonnie breast,
    An' sae may it fare wi' you."

"Kiss but this hand, I humbly sue,
    Even there I'll rue the stain;
Or the breath of man will dim its hue,
    It will ne'er be pure again.

"For passion's like the burning beal
    Upon the mountain's brow,
That wastes itself to ashes pale;
    An' sae will it fare wi' you."

"O mother, mother, make my bed,
    An' make it soft and easy;
An' with the cold dew bathe my head,
    For pains of anguish seize me:

"Or stretch me in the chill blue lake,
    To quench this bosom's burning;
An' lay me by yon lonely brake,
    For hope there's none returning.

"I've been where man should not have been,
    Oft in my lonely roaming;
And seen what man should not have seen,
    By greenwood in the gloaming.

"Oh, passion's deadlier than the grave,
    A' human things undoing!
The Maiden of the Mountain Wave
    Has lured me to my ruin!"

'Tis now an hundred years an' more,
    An' all these scenes are over,
Since rose his grave on yonder shore,
    Beneath the wild wood cover;

An' late I saw the Maiden there,
  Just as the day-light faded,
Braiding her locks of gowden hair,
  An' singing as she braided:

Mermaid's Song

Lie still, my love, lie still and sleep,
  Long is thy night of sorrow;
Thy Maiden of the Mountain deep
  Shall meet thee on the morrow.

But oh, when shall that morrow be,
  That my true love shall waken?
When shall we meet, refined an' free,
  Amid the moorland braken?

Full low and lonely is thy bed,
  The worm even flies thy pillow;
Where now the lips, so comely red,
  That kissed me 'neath the willow?

Oh I must laugh, do as I can,
  Even 'mid my song of mourning,
At all the fuming freaks of man
  To which there's no returning.

Lie still, my love, lie still an' sleep—
  Hope lingers o'er thy slumber;
What though thy years beneath the steep
  Should all its stones outnumber?

Though moons steal o'er an' seasons fly
  On time's swift wing unstaying,
Yet there's a spirit in the sky
  That lives o'er thy decaying.

In domes beneath the water-springs
  No end hath my sojourning;
An' to this land of fading things
  Far hence be my returning;

For spirits now have left the deep,
  Their long last farewell taken:
Lie still, my love, lie still an' sleep,
  Thy day is near the breaking!

When my loved flood from fading day
   No more its gleam shall borrow,
Nor heath-fowl from the moorland gray
   Bid the blue dawn good-morrow;

The Mermaid o'er thy grave shall weep,
   Without one breath of scorning:
Lie still, my love, lie still an' sleep,
   And fare thee well till morning!

Originally published in 1819.

Source:
Hogg, James. *The Works of the Ettrick Shepherd: Poems and Ballads.* London: Blackie & Son, 1874.

32. The Mermaiden by Robert Allan

Scotland

O HEARD you the Mermaid of the sea,
   When the ship by the rock was sinking;
Saw you the Maid with her coral cup,
   A health to the sea-nyraphs drinking.—
The morning was fair, and the ocean calm.
   Not a breath awoke the billow,
The foam that play'd in the clefted rock
   Was the Mermaid's resting pillow.

As round the cave, where the Mermaid slept,
   The vessel light was sailing,
A voice was heard in the gathering storm,
   Of Mariners deeply wailing;
And loud came the deep'ning thunder-peal,
   The white waves around were dashing,
And the light that illumin'd the pathless way,
   Was the gleam of light'ning flashing.

The sails are torn, the ship a wreck;
   The Mermaid sweet is singing,

And the crystal halls where the sea-nymphs bathe,
    Are merrily, merrily ringing.
And many a tear for these Mariners lost,
    From maidens' eyes are streaming,
While reckless they sleep in their wat'ry shroud,
    Nor of ought that's earthly dreaming.

Source:
Allan, Robert. "The Mermaid." *Beauties of the Scottish Poets; or, Harp of Renfrewshire: A Collection of Songs and Other Poetical Pieces*. William Motherwell, editor. Glasgow: William Turnbull, 1821.

33. The Mermaiden by William Motherwell

Scotland

"THE nicht is mirk, and the wind blaws schill,
    And the white faem weets my bree,
And my mind misgi'es me, gay maiden,
    That the land we sall never see!"
Then up and spak' the mermaiden,
    And she spak' blythe and free,
"I never said to my bonnie bridegroom,
    That on land we sud weddit be.

"Oh! I never said that ane erthlie priest
    Our bridal blessing should gi'e,
And I never said that a landwart bouir
    Should hauld my love and me."
"And whare is that priest, my bonnie maiden,
    If ane erthlie wicht is na he?"
"Oh! the wind will sough, and the sea will rair,
    When weddit we twa sall be?"

"And whare is that bouir, my bonnie maiden,
    If on land it sud na be?"
"Oh! my blythe bouir is low," said the mermaiden,
    "In the bonnie green howes of the sea:
My gay bouir is biggit o' the gude ship's keels,
    And the banes o' the drowned at sea;

The fisch are the deer that fill my parks,
  And the water waste my dourie.

"And my bouir is sklaitit wi' the big blue waves,
  And paved wi' the yellow sand,
And in my chaumers grow bonnie white flowers
  That never grew on land.
And have ye e'er seen, my bonnie bridegroom,
  A leman on earth that wud gi'e
Aiker for aiker o' the red plough'd land,
  As I'll gi'e to thee o' the sea?

"The mune will rise in half ane hour,
  And the wee bright starns will schine;
Then we'll sink to my bouir, 'neath the wan water
  Full fifty fathom and nine!"
A wild, wild skreich gi'ed the fey bridegroom,
  And a loud, loud lauch, the bride;
For the mune raise up, and the twa sank down
  Under the silver'd tide.

Source:
Motherwell, William. *The Poetical Works of William Motherwell*. 2nd edition. Glasgow: David Robertson, 1847.

34. The Merrow-Maiden and Merrow-Man

Ireland

"When, by moonlight, the waters were hush'd to repose,
That beautiful spirit of ocean arose;
Her hair, full of lustre, just floated and fell
O'er her bosom, that heaved with a billowy swell.

"The maiden she gazed on the creature of earth,
Whose voice in her breast to a feeling gave birth,
Then smil'd; and abash'd, as a maiden might be,
Looking down, gently sank to her home in the sea."
                              —Crofton Croker.

FROM generic notions of our native folk lore, certain strange and peculiar creations of fancy have received an imaginative form and existence. The Merrow, or, as it is written in Irish, *Morúadh*, or *Morúach*, is a sort of fantastic sea-nymph, corresponding with the prevailing conception of a mermaid. It is supposed to partake of semi-human nature and figure. From head to waist it appears in such shape; and thence to the extremities it is covered with greenish-tinted scales, having a fish-like termination. Those creatures are said to partake of a modest, affectionate, gentle, and beneficent disposition. Their name seems a compound of *muir*, the sea, and *oigh*, a maid. These marine objects are also called by the Irish, *Muir-gheilt, Samhghubha, Muidhucha'n,* and *Suire*. They would seem to have basked around our shores from the most remote period; for, according to bardic chroniclers, when the Milesian ships bore onwards in quest of a friendly harbour to our coasts, the *Suire*, or sea-nymphs, played around them on their passage. These fictitious imaginings are probably traceable to an Eastern origin. The merrow was capable of attachment to human beings, and is reported to have intermarried and lived with them for years in succession. Some allegory is probably concealed under the fiction of certain families or races, living on the southern and western coasts of Ireland, being partly descended from these marine creatures. Natural instincts, however, are found to prevail over their love. The merrow usually feels desirous of returning to her former haunts and companions under the sea waves. She is represented as the daughter of a king, whose gorgeous palace lies deep beneath the ocean. Sometimes mermaidens live under our lakes. In Moore's *Irish Melodies*, we have the fine conceit of a merrow being metamorphosed into the national instrument, to which allusion occurs in these opening lines,—

> "'Tis believed that this harp, which I now wake for thee,
> Was a syren of old, who sung under the sea;
> And who often, at eve, through the bright waters rov'd
> To meet, on the green shore, a youth whom she lov'd."

Mermaidens are said to allure youths of mortal mould to follow them beneath the waves, where they afterwards live in some enchanted state. Merrows wear a *cohuleen druith*, or little charmed cap, generally covered with feathers, and used for diving under water. If this be lost or stolen, they have no power to return beneath "waters of the vasty deep." Sometimes they are said to leave their outer skins behind, to assume others more magical and beauteous. The merrow has soft white webs between her fingers. She is often seen with a comb, parting her long green hair on either side of the head. Female merrows are represented as beautiful in features. Merrow music is frequently heard, coming up from the lowest depths of ocean, and sometimes floating over the surface Merrows often dance to it on the shore, strand, or waves. With all their fascinations, practised to seduce the sons of men, the mermaidens are occasionally found to be vengeful. An old tract, contained in the Book of Lecain, states that a king of the Fomorians, when sailing over the Ictian sea, had been enchanted by the music of mermaids, until he came within reach of these syrens. Then they tore his limbs asunder, and scattered them on the waves.

From Dr. O'Donovan's *Annals of the Four Masters*, at the year of Christ 887, we find a curious entry regarding a mermaid cast ashore by the sea in the country of Alba, the modern Scotland. One hundred and ninety-five feet was her length, we are told, eighteen feet was the length of her hair, seven feet was the length of the fingers of her hand, seven feet also was the length of her nose, while she was whiter than the swan all over. Hence, it would seem, that the merrows were thought to have attained extraordinary large proportions; if, indeed, this be not the actual record of a fact, illustrating the natural history of our coasts.

The valour of certain Fenian heroes is celebrated on behalf of a mariner-lady, in Miss Brooke's beautifully translated poem of *Moira Borb*. This we find in her *Reliques of Irish Poetry*. The chiefs met her coming into a harbour from the waves, over which her bark swiftly glided. Her beauty was faultless; and on being questioned as to her parentage, by the son of Comhal, she replies,—

> "Truth, O great chief! my artless story frames:
> A mighty king my filial duty claims.
> But princely birth no safety could bestow;
> And, royal as I am, I fly from woe."

Miss Brooke tells us, in a note, that she has not rendered this stanza literally, because she found it difficult to interpret the Irish words: *As mé ingean rig fo trinn*. They may be translated, *I am the daughter of the king under waves*; or the last words may be rendered, *king of waves*, or king of *Ton* (in the genitive), *Trin*, literally, *a wave*; but it may also mean some country, anciently bearing such name. It might even be a metaphorical phrase, implying either an island or some of the low countries.

Strange to say, the merrow is sometimes imagined to be a water-man; but in such case, he is deformed in shape and features. Meirow-men are also said to keep the spirits of drowned fishermen and sailors under cages, at the bottom of the sea. Doubtless, a belief in such fantasies and necromancy must have come down to us from the most remote times of Paganism.

Source:
O'Hanlon, John. *Irish Folk Lore: Traditions and Superstitions of the Country*. Glasgow: Cameron & Ferguson, [1870].

35. The Overflowing of Lough Neagh and Liban the Mermaid

Ireland

IN THE days of old a good king ruled over Muman,[1] whose name was Marid Mac Carido. He had two sons, Ecca and Rib. Ecca was restless and unruly, and in many ways displeased the king; and he told his brother Rib that he had made up his mind to leave his home, and win lands for himself in some far off part of the country. Rib tried hard to dissuade him; but though this delayed his departure for a while, he was none the less bent on going.

At last, Ecca, being wrought upon by his stepmother Ebliu (from whom Slieve Eblinne[2] was afterwards named), did a grievous wrong to his father, and fled from Muman with all his people; and his brother Rib and his stepmother Ebliu went with him. Ten hundred men they were in all, besides women and children; and they turned their faces toward the north.

After they had traveled for some time, their druids[3] told them that it was not fated for them to settle in the same place; and accordingly, when they had come to the Pass of the two Pillar Stones, they parted.

Rib and his people turned to the west, and they journeyed till they came to the plain of Arbthenn. And there the water of a fountain burst forth over the land, and drowned them all; and a great lake was formed, which to this day is called the Lake of Rib.[4]

Ecca continued his journey northwards; and he and his people fared slowly on till they came near to Bruga[5] of the Boyne, the palace of Mac Indoc, where they were fain to rest. No sooner had they halted, than a tall

---

[1] Muman, *i.e.* Munster.

[2] Slieve Eblinne, now Slieve Eelim or Slieve Phelim, in Tipperary, sometimes called the Twelve Hills of Evlinn. "Eblinne" is the genitive of "Ebliu."

[3] The Land of Promise: Fairyland: In ancient Gaelic romantic tales, mention is often made of *Tir Tairrngire*, the Land of Promise, Fairyland, as being one of the chief dwelling-places of the Dedannans or fairy host. In many passages this Land of Promise is identified with *Inis-Manann*, or the Isle of Man, which was ruled over by Mannanan Mac Lir, the sea-god, and named from him.

[4] Now Longh Ree, on the Shannon.

[5] Bruga of the Boyne, the palace of Angus, the great Dedannan magician, was situated on the north shore of the Boyne, not far from Slane.

man came forth from the palace, namely, Angus Mac Indoc of the Bruga, son of the Dagda, and commanded them to leave the place without delay. But they, being spent with the toil of travel, heeded not his words, and, pitching their tents, they rested on the plain before the palace. Whereupon, Angus being wroth that his commands were unheeded, killed all their horses that night.

Next day, he came forth again, and he said to them, "Your horses I slew last night; and now, unless ye depart from this place, I will slay your people to-night."

And Ecca said to him, "Much evil hast thou done to us already, for thou hast killed all our horses. And now we cannot go, even though we desire it, for without horses we cannot travel."

Then Angus brought to them a very large horse in full harness, and they put all their goods on him. And when they were about to go, he said to them—

"Beware that ye keep this great steed walking continually; not even a moment's rest shall ye give him, otherwise he will certainly be the cause of your death."

After this they set out again, one Sunday in the mid-month of autumn, and traveled on till they reached the Plain of the Grey Copse,[1] where they intended to abide. They gathered then round the great steed to take their baggage off him, and each was busy seeing after his own property, so that they forgot to keep the horse moving. And the moment he stood still, a magic well sprang up beneath his feet.

Now Ecca, when he saw the well spring up, was troubled, remembering Angus's warning. And he caused a house to be built round it, and near it he built his palace, for the better security. And he chose a woman to take care of the well, charging her strictly to keep the door locked, except when the people of the palace came for water.

After that the King of Ulad,[2] that is to say, Muridach, the son of Fiaca Findamnas (who was grandson of Conal Carna of the Red Branch[3]) came against Ecca to drive him forth from Ulad. But Ecca made a stout fight,

---

[1] The Plain of the Grey Copse, according to the legend, was the name of the plain now covered by Lough Neagh.

[2] Ulad, *i.e.* Ulster.

[3] The Red Branch Knights of Ulster, a sort of militia in the service of the monarch, much like the Feni of later date, flourished in the first century of the Christian era. Their home was the palace of Emania, near the city of Armagh; and they received their name from one of the houses of the palace in which they resided, which was called *Craebh-ruadh*, or Red Branch. They attained their greatest glory in the reign of Conor Mac Nessa, king of Ulster in the first century; and Conal Carna, mentioned in the story of "Liban the Mermaid," was one of their most illustrious champions.

so that he won the lordship of half of Ulad from Muridach. And after that his people settled down on the Plain of the Grey Copse.

Now Ecca had two daughters, Ariu and Liban, of whom Ariu was the wife of Curnan the Simpleton. And Curnan went about among the people, foretelling that a lake would flow over them from the well, and urging them earnestly to make ready their boats.

> Come forth, come forth, ye valiant men; build boats, and build ye fast!
> I see the water surging out, a torrent deep and vast;
> I see our chief and all his host o'erwhelmed beneath the wave;
> And Ariu, too, my best beloved, alas! I cannot save.
> But Liban east and west shall swim
> Long ages on the ocean's rim,
> By mystic shores and islets dim,
> And down in the deep sea cave!

And he ceased not to warn all he met, repeating this verse continually; but the people gave no heed to the words of the Simpleton.

Now the woman who had charge of the well, on a certain occasion forgot to close the door, so that the spell was free to work evil. And immediately the water burst forth over the plain, and formed a great lake, namely the Lake of the Copse. And Ecca and all his family and all his folk were drowned, save only his daughter Liban, and Conang, and Curnan the Simpleton. And they buried Ariu, and raised a mound over her, which is called from her Carn-Arenn.

Of Conang nothing more is told. But as to Curnan, he died of grief after his wife Ariu; and he was buried in a mound, which is called Carn-Curnan to this day in memory of him.

And thus the great Lake of the Copse was formed, which is now called Lough Necca,[1] in memory of Ecca, the son of Marid. And it was the overflow of this lake which, more than all other causes, scattered the Ultonians over Erin.

Now as to Liban. She also was swept away like the others; but she was not drowned. She lived for a whole year with her lap-dog, in her chamber beneath the lake, and God protected her from the water. At the end of the year she was weary; and when he saw the speckled salmon swimming and playing all round her, she prayed and said—

"O my Lord, I wish I were a salmon, that I might swim with the others through the clear green sea!"

And at the words she took the shape of a salmon, except her face and breast, which did not change. And her lap-dog was changed to an otter,

---

[1] Lough Necca, now Lough Neagh.

and attended her afterwards whithersoever she went, as long as she lived in the sea.

And so she remained swimming about from sea to sea for three hundred years; that is to say, from the time of Ecca, the son of Marid, to the time of Comgall of Bangor.[1]

Now on one occasion, Comgall sent Beoc, the son of Indli, from Bangor to Rome, to talk with Gregory[2] concerning some matters of order and rule. And when Beoc's curragh[3] was sailing over the sea, he and his crew heard sweet singing in the waters beneath them, as it were the chanting of angels.

And Beoc, having listened for a while, looked down into the water, and asked what the chant was for, and who it was that sang.

And Liban answered, "I am Liban, the daughter of Ecca, son of Marid; and it is I who sang the chant thou hast heard."

"Why art thou here?" asked Beoc.

And she replied, "Lo, I have lived for three hundred years beneath the sea; and I have come hither to fix a day and a place of meeting with thee. I shall now go westward; and I beseech thee, for the sake of the holy men of Dalaradia,[4] to come to Inver Ollarba,[5] to meet me, on this same day at the end of a year. Say also to Comgall and to the other holy men of Bangor, all that I say to thee. Come with thy boats and thy fishing-nets, and thou shalt take me from the waters in which I have lived."

"I shall not grant thee the boon thou askest," said Beoc, "unless you give me a reward."

"What reward dost thou seek?" asked Liban.

"That thou be buried in one grave with me in my own monastery," answered Beoc.

"That shall be granted to thee," said Liban.

Beoc then went on his way to Rome. And when he had returned, he

---

[1] This Marid was king of Munster about the beginning of the second century of the Christian era. St. Comgall, one of the greatest saints of the early Irish Church, flourished in the sixth century, and was the founder of the celebrated monastery of Bangor in the county of Down.

[2] Gregory, *i.e.* Pope Gregory.

[3] Boat. It would appear that in Ireland, and indeed in England and Scotland as well, navigation was carried on in ancient times chiefly by means of curraghs. The curragh was a boat or canoe, consisting of a light framework of wood, covered over with the skins of animals. Curraghs are still used on many parts of the western coast of Ireland; but they are now covered with tarred canvas instead of skins.

[4] Dalaradia, the old name of a territory which included the southern half of the county Antrim and a part of Down.

[5] Inver Ollarba, *i.e.* the inver, or mouth of the river Ollarba, which was the ancient name of the Larne Water, in Antrim.

related to Comgall and to the other saints of the monastery at Bangor, the story of the mermaid. And now the end of the year was nigh.

Then they made ready their nets, and on the day appointed they went in their boats to Inver Ollarba, a goodly company of the saints of Erin. And Liban was caught in the net of Fergus of Miluc:[1] and her head and shoulders were those of a maiden, but she had the body of a fish.

Now the boat in which she was brought to land was kept half-full of sea water, in which she remained swimming about. And many came to see her; and all were filled with wonder when they saw her strange shape and heard her story.

Among the rest came the chief of the tribe of Hua-Conang, wearing a purple cloak; and she kept gazing at him earnestly. The young chief, seeing this, said to her—

"Dost thou wish to have this cloak? If so, I will give it to thee willingly."

But she answered, "Not so: I desire not thy cloak. But it brings to my mind my father Ecca; for on the day he was drowned, he wore a cloak of purple like thine. But may good luck be on thee for thy gentleness, and on him who shall come after thee in thy place; and in every assembly where thy successor sits, may he be known to all without inquiry."

After that there came a large-bodied, dark-visaged, fierce hero, and killed her lap-dog. Whereupon she was grieved; and she told him that the heroism of himself and his tribe should be stained by the baseness of their minds, and that they should not be able to defend themselves against injuries till they should do penance, by fasting, for her sake.

Then the warrior repented what he had done, and humbled himself before her.

And now there arose a contention about her, as to whom she should belong. Comgall said she was his, forasmuch as she was caught in his territory. But Fergus urged that she belonged to him by right, as it was in his net she was taken. And Beoc said he had the best right of all to her, on account of the promise she had made to him.

And as no one could settle the dispute, these three saints fasted and prayed that God would give a judgment between them, to show who should own Liban.

And an angel said to one of the company: "Two wild oxen will come hither to-morrow from Carn-Arenn, that is to say, from the grave-mound of Liban's sister, Ariu. Yoke a chariot to them, and place the mermaid in it; and into whatsoever territory they shall bring her, she shall remain with the owner thereof."

The oxen came on the morrow, as the angel had foretold. And when

---

[1] Miluc, or Meelick, the name of an ancient ecclesiastical establishment in the county Antrim. See "Ecclesiastical Antiquities of Down, Connor, and Dromore" (page 3), by the Rev. William Reeves, M.B., M.R.I.A.

they were yoked, and when Liban was placed in the chariot, they brought her straightway to Beoc's church, namely to Tec-Da-Beoc.

Then the saints gave her a choice—either to die immediately after baptism, and go to heaven; or to live on earth as long as she had lived in the sea, and then to go to heaven after these long ages. And the choice she took was to die immediately. Whereupon Comgall baptized her; and he gave her the name of Murgen, that is, "Sea-born", or Murgelt, that is, "Mermaid."

And she is counted among the holy virgins, and held in honor and reverence, as God ordained for her in heaven; and wonders and miracles are performed through her means at Tec-Da-Beoc.

NOTES

"Leabhar na h-Uidhre," or "The Book of the Dun Cow," from which this tale is taken, is the oldest manuscript of miscellaneous Gaelic literature we possess. It was transcribed from older books by Maelmuire Mac Ceilechair, who died A.D. 1106; and it is now deposited in the Royal Irish Academy, Dublin—or rather, I should say, a large fragment of it, for the book has suffered much mutilation. This venerable book may now be said to be in the hands of the public, as it has been lately reproduced in lithograph facsimile, and published by the Council of the Royal Irish Academy, at the Government expense.

The story of "The Overflowing of Lough Neagh" (called in the original "The Destruction of Eocho Mac Mairedo") has been published, with text and literal translation, by the late J. O'Beirne Crowe, in the Kilkenny Archaeological Journal (volume for 1870-1).

In this story I have been obliged to make a few transpositions in the mere order of the incidents, for the narrative in the original is in some places very ill arranged.

It is now nearly eight hundred years since this story was transcribed from some old authority into "The Book of the Dun Cow;" and it is singular that the tradition of the formation of Lough Neagh, by the overflow of an enchanted well which was neglected by the woman in charge of it, still maintains a vivid existence among the peasantry. (See on this subject the author's "Origin and History of Irish Names of Places," Series I. 4th edition, page 176.)

Source:
Joyce, P. W. *Old Celtic Romances: Translated from the Gaelic*. London: C. Kegan Paul & Co., 1879.

36. Liban, the Sea Woman

Ireland

The following is an abbreviated version of the previous tale, "The Overflowing of Lough Neagh and Liban the Mermaid."

THE time Angus Og sent away Eochaid and Ribh from the plain of Bregia that was his playing ground, he gave them the loan of a very big horse to carry all they had northward. And Eochaid went on with the horse till he came to the Grey Thornbush in Ulster; and a well broke out where he stopped, and he made his dwelling-house beside it, and he made a cover for the well and put a woman to mind it. But one time she did not shut down the cover, and the water rose up and covered the Grey Thornbush, and Eochaid was drowned with his children; and the water spread out into a great lake that has the name of Loch Neach to this day.

But Liban that was one of Eochaid's daughters was not drowned, but she was in her sunny-house under the lake and her little dog with her for a full year, and God protected her from the waters. And one day she said, "O Lord, it would be well to be in the shape of a salmon, to be going through the sea the way they do." Then the one half of her took the shape of a salmon and the other half kept the shape of a woman; and she went swimming the sea, and her little dog following her in the shape of an otter and never leaving her or parting from her at all.

And one time Caoilte was out at a hunting near Beinn Boirche with the King of Ulster, and they came to the shore of the sea. And when they looked out over it they saw a young girl on the waves, and she swimming with the side-stroke and the foot-stroke. And when she came opposite them she sat up on a wave, as anyone would sit upon a stone or a hillock and she lifted her head and said, "Is not that Caolite Son of Ronan?"

"It is myself surely," said he.

"It is many a day," she said, "we saw you upon that rock, and the best man of Ireland or of Scotland with you, that was Finn son of Cumhal."

"Who are you so girl?" said Coalite.

"I am Liban daughter of Eochaid, and I never showed my face to anyone since the going away of the King of the Fianna to this day. And it is what led me to lift my head to-day," she said, "was to see yourself Caolite."

Just then the deer that were running before the hounds made for the sea and swam out into it. "Your spear to me Caolite!" said Liban.

Then he put the spear into her hand and she killed the deer with it, and sent them back to him where he was with the King of Ulster; and then she threw him back the spear and with that she went away.

And that is the way she was until the time Beoan son of Innle was sent by Comgall to Rome, to have talk with Gregory and to bring back rules and orders. And when he and his people were going over the sea they heard what was like the singing of angels under the currach.[1]

"What is that song?" said Beoan.

"It is I myself am making it," said Liban.

"Who are you?" said Beoan.

"I am Liban daughter of Eochaid son of Mairid, and I am going through the sea these three hundred years." Then she told him all her story, and how it was under the round hulls of ships she had her dwelling-place, and the waves were the roofing of her house, and the strands its walls. "And it is what I am come for now," she said, "to tell you that I will come to meet you on this day twelve-month at Inver Ollorba; and do not fail to meet me there for the sake of all the saints of Dalaradia."

And at the year's end the nets were spread along the coast where she said she would come, and it was in the net of Fergus from Miluic she was taken. And the clerks gave her her choice either to be baptized and go then and there to heaven, or to stay living through another three hundred years and at the end of that time to go to heaven; and the choice she made was to die. Then Comgall baptized her and the name he gave her was Muirgheis, the Birth of the Sea. So she died, and the messengers that came and that carried her to her burying place, were horned deer that were sent by the angels of God.

Source:

Gregory, Lady. *A Book of Saints and Wonders*. London: John Murray, 1907.

37. Water Spirits and Mer Folk of Connacht, Ireland

Connacht, Ireland

GREATEST of all the water spirits, the sea god, Manannán mac Lir, has occasionally appeared, usually on some errand of mercy on the coast of

---

[1] Curragh = boat.

Co. Mayo and he, or his son (or double), Oirbsen,[1] of Loch Oirbsen (Loch Corrib), on the coast of Galway Bay. He has sometimes come to warn of the approach of a storm. No doubt the pagan ancestors of the shore dwellers worshipped him of old; and his reverence lingered when his godhead was forgotten. The people live by the gifts of the sea, its fish, timber and seaweed, so naturally the gracious side of the god was most felt, but there are also suggestions that his fierce cruelty was once felt. Anything that falls into the sea should not be retrieved: a hat blows off and Aran boatmen have refused to go after it. A curious ceremony where young men naked on horseback are driven into Galway Bay and for some time kept from coming to land is very suggestive of a symbolic sacrifice. I am told that this has been in use near Spiddal, to the west of Galway, in very recent years. Some fifty years ago I heard from Lord Kilannin that his father and others had to go to the rescue of some shipwrecked men whom the peasantry would neither help nor permit to land. His relatives were eagerly warned of the disasters to which they might be liable for saving anyone from the sea.[2]

There are several tales about storm spirits collected by Lady Wilde and by Otway, but I found none in my journeyings on that coast.

Of the mer-folk, most of the tales merge into those about seals, under which heading they are best treated. A local wise woman, Biddy Toole, near Portacloy, living at the beginning of Queen Victoria's reign, used to tell how she got some fishermen to row her to a rocky islet to gather *duileasg* (edible seaweed, "dulse" or "dillisk"). They carried her out to sea for mischief and to enjoy her sarcastic and witty talk, she being a very merry and pleasant woman. They let down their lines, got a strong bite and pulled up a green "fishy looking child," a boy, in every respect save its colour like a human child. The terrified captor, when all had looked at his "catch," threw back the creature into the water, but, whether from imagination or some other cause, he pined and died before the end of the year, though apparently in robust health[3] on the ill-fated expedition. The fishermen at Lettermullen and Gorumna on Galway Bay tell much of a local merman.[4] He was a drowned fisherman, and more than one person claimed to have seen him. He had long black hair, a flat

---

[1] As in the case of the god Nuada Necht and his son Nechtan so Manannán and Oirbsen vary as father and son, or as the same person in the folk tales. I would refer to a note on Manannán in *Proc. R.I. Academy*, xxxiv. pp. 149-151.

[2] I have to thank Miss Matilda Redington of Kilcornan for several notes on the subject.

[3] Some fifty years since I often heard my mother argue girls among the Limerick peasantry into hope and recovery from some imagination or superstition, a simple "remedy" and much faith sufficed.

[4] Also from Miss Matilda Redington of Kilcornan.

face, a double chin and webbed hands. Far more attractive seems to have been a local mermaid who came to the more western coast to announce the coming of the three magic cows Bo finn (whence Inishbofin), Bo ruad (whence the "Red Cow's path," a spear's-cast wide, along the coast and the "Borua well"[1] on Ardillán), and the "Bo duff," of which I heard no local legends. She was very beautiful and named "Berooch."

At Inishark low music is heard under the water before an accident or a wreck. The best preservative is for the fishers to sing, or have music on board the boat, as the sea people love to hear men sing and forget to perform their spells till the fated moment has gone by.

Source:
Westropp, T. J. "A Study of Folklore on the Coasts of Connacht, Ireland (Continued)." *Folklore*. Vol. 32, No. 2 (Jun. 30, 1921). pp. 101-123.

38. Children of the Mermaid

County Sligo, Ireland

CROFTON Croker recounts a legend of human beings, metamorphosed by magic into stones, and in the townland of Scurmore, parish of Castleconnor, county Sligo, there are some large boulders, bearing the singular title of "Children of the Mermaid"; to them is attached a legend which accounts for their origin. It is as follows:—In olden days, a man walking along the sea shore, discovered amongst the rocks, a mermaid lying asleep. Now, everybody, or at least everybody in that locality, knows that if possession be obtained of an article of a sea nymph's costume, she at once loses her aquatic nature, both as regards form and disposition, and degenerates into an ordinary mortal. The man therefore approached stealthily, became the possessor of the magic garment, and led the metamorphosed nymph home as his bride. Retribution, however, finally overtook him. His seven children were nearly grown to maturity, when one day his youngest born saw him abstract the magic garment from its hiding-place, to deposit it where he imagined it would be still more secure. The youth ran off to describe what he had seen to his mother, who seized with a sudden yearning to return to her native element, resumed possession of her property, and bade her children

---

[1] "Brian Boru's well" is a surveyor's "little learning" foisted on to the maps both in Ardillán and near Corofin, Co. Clare.

follow her to the sea-shore. Being now re-endowed with all the attributes of a mermaid, she touched each in succession, changed them into seven stones, and then plunged into the ocean, and has never since been seen, but the boulders, seven in number, still stand on the circumference of a circular rampart surrounding a fine tumulus called Cruckancornia.

It appears to have been a very prevalent belief throughout Ireland, that some of the large stone circles were human beings, or giants, metamorphosed by magic into rocks.

Source:
Wood-Martin, W[illiam] G[regory]. *Traces of the Elder Faiths of Ireland, Volume 2*. London: Longmans, Green, and Co., 1902. pp. 212-213.

39. The Fisherman Who Had Seven Sons

County Mayo, Ireland

HE [the fisherman] had no land. His means of living was by fishing. He had four sets of nets. He himself, his three sons, and three other men of the neighbors, were out fishing. They were not catching any fish. They fell asleep, except the old man. It was not long until he saw a mermaid approaching him in the sea. She says to him, "You are not taking any fish to-night."

"I am not," says he.

"Well," says she, "if you will give me what I should ask of you, you would catch fish, and I would make you a rich man."

"Well," says he, "I do not know until I go home, or [until I learn] what you are asking of me."

"Your son," says she, "who is yet unborn, when he shall be twenty-one years [old]," says she. "Seven nights from to-night your wife shall have a son, and that is the son which I must get. Good-by!" says she, "be going home."

When the fisherman and his party went home, he told his wife the thing which the mermaid said to him; "and she said to me," says he, "that she would make a rich man of me."

"Good enough!" says the woman, "let it be a bargain."

The following night he and his party went out to the same place. They cast their nets. There were no fish in them. They fell backwards and forwards asleep, except the old man. It was not long until he saw the mermaid coming to him in the sea.

"I am glad," says she, "that you are up to your promise. Return," says she, "to the shore, and all you see there will be gold before you. Take with you enough of it; but the men who are with you will not believe you, and if they do not remain with you, tell them to look under your right arm, and then they will believe you."

They came in to the shore. Everything which was before them was yellow gold. Says the old man, "Do not go [away] from me until I take the load of my back with me."

"What will you take with you," say the other people, "if you do not take stones and water with you?"

"Look in under my right arm."

They looked.

"My soul from the devil!" say they. "Is the land yellow gold?"

They went off collecting and making little heaps. When the old man had collected as much as he thought he would carry home, he went, and his load with him. The others remained after him, collecting and making little heaps, until three waves came from the sea and took from them the little heaps. "We are now as badly off as ever," said one of the men. "We will follow the old devil until we see whether he has any penny [i.e., money] with him." They followed, and he was in the house before them.

"John, have you any penny?" say they.

"I have," says John. From that [time] he commenced buying lands and stock. There was not a man in that place half as rich as he. He was so for a long time. He and his seven sons were one day going to mass. "You would be a fine lot of sons," says the father, "but for one thing only."

"What is that, father?" says the youngest son.

"I will not tell you," says the father.

"You must tell me," says the son.

"Since you put the question to me, I must answer it. I sold you to the mermaid twenty-one years ago. The time is now nearly up."

"Well," says the son, "it is time for me to be going."

"Well," says the father, "I am greatly troubled that you are going."

He returned to the house. "Mother," says the son, "arise, prepare food and drink for me, and give me expenses for the long road which there is for me to go." She prepared and gave him everything which he required.

He struck the road. He was proceeding and continuously going until he turned into a wooded glen. He sat down and was tired. He saw a lion of the wood coming toward him. "As long as I have gone, I am dead at last."

The lion came up to him [and] looked at him. He commenced licking him. "You are tired," says he; "sit upon my back, and I will carry you out of the wood."

"You are good," says he. He sat up on his back, [and] they moved off. He did not stop or make any great delay until he brought him as far as the house of a shoemaker, which was built on the brink of a lake.

"Go in yonder," says the Lion, "and you will get lodging until morning there."

He went into the little house. "God bless all here!" says he.

"God and Mary bless you!" says the man of the house.

"Would I get lodging here until morning?" says he.

"You will, and welcome," says the man of the house, "and we consider the accommodation poor for you."

They sat down and ate supper in company.

"Now," says the shoemaker, "there will be a great meeting over yonder to-morrow. The great sea-monster is to be there, and the King's daughter will be tied there, and it must get her to swallow unless there shall be somebody to defend her; or would you go? If you do go there, we shall take the boat with us."

"I should like to go," says he, "but I should not like to go on the sea; but however that may be, I will go. But we should have arms of defence with us."

"There is a little old rusty sword outside there, which is for cutting turnips and cabbage," says the shoemaker.

"It will do well enough," says the stranger. "I will take it with me."

When they went over there in the boat and saw the great crowd which was before them, the King's daughter of the island was tied in a golden chair, and [the] sea-monster coming to eat her at the hour of twelve that day. There were kings, princes, and earls collected there to go to fight with the monster. At the hour of twelve they saw the sea moving and going mad, and the monster coming, putting the sea to the tops of the hills on each side of it, till it came to the place in which the young princess was sitting. There was no one there to go before it but this man. He arose with a leap and went on the back of the monster with his little rusty sword. He went for it until he killed it.

"I will not marry anyone," says the young princess, "but that man."

The two were married. A month from that time he was standing on the shore of the sea, and he saw the mermaid approaching him in the sea. Says she to him, "Twenty-one years ago to-day I bought you from your father and mother. It was not to kill you or drown you, and it is I who took you this way to be son-in-law to the King of the island. May you prosper henceforth," says she. "You are in a good way now. You will not see me again," says the mermaid.

NOTES

The story was taken down in 1898 from the lips of an old man in County Mayo, Connacht, by Mr. Stephen Barrett of Dublin, to whose kindness I am indebted for the text and a large part of the translation.

The tale is of peculiar interest, as it furnishes an excellent example of the preservation in Modern Irish folk-lore of a feature found in one of our earliest Celtic documents. In the Tochmarc Emire,[1] which probably dates in its earliest form from the eighth century, Cuchulainn is carried on the back of a friendly Lion to the border of the other world in much the same way as the hero of our folk-tale is carried to the house of the shoemaker. It may be added that in the same document Cuchulainn rescues a princess in somewhat the same way as does the fisherman's son here.[2]

Source:
Cross, Tom Peete. "An Irish Folk-Tale." *The Journal of American Folklore*. Vol. 23, No. 90 (Oct.-Dec. 1910). pp. 419-424.

40. Water Spirits and Mer-folk of County Clare

County Clare, Ireland

THE Shannon, according to the *Dindsenchas*, derived its name from a sea-lady, but evidently not a "water-breather." Sinenn, daughter of Lodan, came from *Tir-tairngire*, the Land of Youth, under the sea, to visit the well of Connla, under the river now called Shannon. She came to Linn na feile, but was drowned at Tarrchinn "on this side Shannon," and gave her name to the great river.[3] A water spirit, or mermaid, is remembered at Killone Lake and Newhall. The legend is preserved in several variants. In 1839 it was told how O'Brien of Killone saw a lovely girl in the lake, and caught her. Bringing her home, he found to his great disgust and disappointment that she had a fish's tail. He ordered her to be kept in a "crib," and fed and well-treated. As she never spoke, a local fool threw scalding water on her to make her say something. He was only too successful, for, after a wild, blood-curdling shriek, she cried:

---

[1] See *Archæological Review*, I (1888).

[2] Professor Kuno Meyer dates the later version, in which the episode of the rescued princess occurs, at the eleventh century (*Revue Celtique*, XI, pp. 435 ff.). On this saga see, further, Miss Hull, *Cuchullin Saga*, pp. 57 ff.; *On the Manners and Customs of the Ancient Irish*, III, p. 315; *Zeitschrift für Celtische Philologie*, III, pp. 229 ff; Haupt's *Zeitschrift*, XXXII, pp. 239 ff; Rhys, *Hibbert Lectures*, pp. 448 ff; *Philol. Soc. Trans.* (1891-94), pp. 514, 5; A. C. L. Brown, *Publications of the Modern Language Association of America*, XX (1905), pp. 688 ff.

[3] "The Dind Senchas," *Revue Celtique*, vol. xv. (1894), P. 456.

> "As the return of the salmon from the stream,
> A return without blood or flesh,
> May such be the departure of the O'Briens
> Like ears of wild corn from Killone."[1]

The legend recorded, almost at the same time (1840), by Crofton Croker was told to me by the old peasantry, about 1876, as follows:—A mermaid used to swim up a stream that flowed under the cellars of Newhall, in order to steal wine. The "master" (an O'Brien), or the butler, hid and stabbed her, (or threw her into a tub of scalding water where she became a big lump of jelly), and her blood ran down the stream and reddened all the lake. As the wounded being floated away she wailed:—

> "As the water maid floats weak and bloodless down the stream
> So the O'Brien shall go from Killone."

Prof. Brian O'Looney heard in his youth, and told me, a tale nearly identical:—

> "As the mermaid goes on the sea,
> A wretched victim devoid of flesh and blood,
> So shall the race of O'Brien pass away
> Till they leave Killone in wild weeds."

The lake, like the stream already noted at Caherminaun, turns red at times from iron scum and red clay after a dry summer. This is supposed to be caused by the local Undine's blood, and to foretell a change of occupants in Newhall. Strange to say, I saw it happen last when the place was let by the MacDonnells to the O'Briens. The cellar at Newhall has its outer section roofed with large slabs, and the inner consists of long, low, cross vaults. In the end of the innermost recess is a built-up square patch, which sounds hollow, and is said to show the opening closed to keep out the thievish mermaid. There seems no evidence of any stream running underneath the cellar, but local tradition tells of a vaulted passage down to the lake.

Sruhaunaglora (prattling brook), in Kilseily on the flank of the eastern hills, probably owes its name, as many brooks their legend, to the supposed talking of water-folk. There was some belief in mer-folk at Kilkee before 1879, but it has nowadays got touched-up for tourists. Such touching-up, however, cannot have affected the ugly, drunken, stupid merrow Coomara (sea-dog), who kept the souls of drowned sailors in magic lobster-pots in his house under the sea, off Killard, as related by

---

[1] *Ordnance Survey Letters*, (Co. Clare), vol. ii., p. III.

Crofton Croker.[1] The merrow's power of passing through the waves depended on a magic cap, and a duplicate of it enabled his human guest to visit him.

The last reported appearance of a mermaid is so recent as the end of April, 1910. Several people, including Martin Griffin, my informant, saw what they are firmly convinced was a mer-woman in a cove a little to the north of Spanish Point, near Miltown, Malbay. She was white-skinned and had well-shaped white hands. The party tried to make friends with her, giving her bread, which she ate. Then a Quilty fisherman got frightened, said she was "something bad," and threw a pebble at her, on which she plunged into the sea and disappeared. Soon afterwards King Edward died. An old man at Spanish Point said the last mermaid was seen the year of the Great Famine (1846), and that such an appearance foretells a public disaster.

Source:
Westropp, Thos. J. "A Folklore Survey of County Clare (Continued)." *Folklore.* Vol. 21, No. 3 (Sep. 1910). pp. 338-349.

41. The Lady of Gollerus

County Kerry, Ireland

ON THE shore of Smerwick harbor, one fine summer's morning, just at daybreak, stood Dick Fitzgerald "shoghing the dudeen," which may be translated, smoking his pipe. The sun was gradually rising behind the lofty Brandon, the dark sea was getting green in the light, and the mists clearing away out of the valleys went rolling and curling like the smoke from the corner of Dick's mouth.

"'Tis just the pattern of a pretty morning," said Dick, taking the pipe from between his lips, and looking towards the distant ocean, which lay as still and tranquil as a tomb of polished marble. "Well, to be sure," continued he, after a pause, "'tis mighty lonesome to be talking to one's self by way of company, and not to have another soul to answer one—nothing but the child of one's own voice, the echo! I know this, that if I had the luck, or maybe the misfortune," said Dick, with a melancholy

---

[1] *Fairy Legends of the South of Ireland*, Part II. (1828), pp. 30-58 ("The Soul Cages").

smile, "to have the woman, it would not be this way with me!—and what in the wide world is a man without a wife? He's no more, surely, than a bottle without a drop of drink in it, or dancing without music, or the left leg of a scissors, or a fishing line without a hook, or any other matter that is no ways complete.—Is it not so?" said Dick Fitzgerald, casting his eyes towards a rock upon the strand, which, though it could not speak, stood up as firm and looked as bold as ever Kerry witness did.

But what was his astonishment at beholding, just at the foot of that rock, a beautiful young creature combing her hair, which was of a sea-green color; and now the salt water shining on it, appeared, in the morning light, like melted butter upon cabbage.

Dick guessed at once that she was a merrow, although he had never seen one before, for he spied the *cohuleen druith*,[1] or little enchanted cap, which the sea people use for diving down into the ocean, lying upon the strand near her; and he had heard that if once he could possess himself of the cap, she would lose the power of going away into the water; so he seized it with all speed, and she, hearing the noise, turned her head about as natural as any Christian.

When the merrow saw that her little diving cap was gone, the salt tears—doubly salt, no doubt, from her—came trickling down her cheeks, and she began a low mournful cry with just the tender voice of a newborn infant. Dick, although he knew well enough what she was crying for, determined to keep the *cohuleen druith*, let her cry never so much, to see what luck would come out of it. Yet he could not help pitying her; and when the dumb thing looked up in his face, and her cheeks all moist with tears, 'twas enough to make anyone feel, let alone Dick, who had ever and always, like most of his countrymen, a mighty tender heart of his own.

"Don't cry, my darling," said Dick Fitzgerald; but the merrow, like any bold child, only cried the more for that.

Dick sat himself down by her side, and took hold of her hand, by way of comforting her. 'Twas in no particular an ugly hand, only there was a small web between the fingers, as there is in a duck's foot; but 'twas as thin and as white as the skin between egg and shell.

"What's your name, my darling?" says Dick, thinking to make her conversant with him; but he got no answer; and he was certain sure now, either that she could not speak, or did not understand him. He therefore squeezed her hand in his, as the only way he had of talking to her. It's the universal language; and there's not a woman in the world, be she fish or lady, that does not understand it.

The merrow did not seem much displeased at this mode of conversation; and, making an end of her whining all at once—"Man,"

---

[1] This is more commonly spelled *cohuleen druith*, but Croker's spelling has been retained.~*HAH*

says she, looking up in Dick Fitzgerald's face, "Man, will you eat me?"

"By all the red petticoats and check aprons between Dingle and Tralee," cried Dick, jumping up in amazement, "I'd as soon eat myself, my jewel! Is it I eat you, my pet?—Now, 'twas some ugly ill-looking thief of a fish put that notion into your own pretty head, with the nice green hair down upon it, that is so cleanly combed out this morning!"

"Man," said the merrow, "what will you do with me, if you won't eat me?"

Dick's thoughts were running on a wife. He saw, at the first glimpse, that she was handsome; but since she spoke, and spoke too like any real woman, he was fairly in love with her. 'Twas the neat way she called him "man" that settled the matter entirely.

"Fish," says Dick, trying to speak to her after her own short fashion. "Fish," says he, "here's my word, fresh and fasting, for you this blessed morning, that I'll make you Mistress Fitzgerald before all the world, and that's what I'll do."

"Never say the word twice." says she. "I'm ready and willing to be yours, Mister Fitzgerald; but stop, if you please, 'till I twist up my hair."

It was some time before she had settled it entirely to her liking, for she guessed, I suppose, that she was going among strangers, where she would be looked at. When that was done, the merrow put the comb in her pocket, and then bent down her head and whispered some words to the water that was close to the foot of the rock.

Dick saw the murmur of the words upon the top of the sea, going out towards the wide ocean, just like a breath of wind rippling along, and, says he, in the greatest wonder, "Is it speaking you are, my darling, to the salt water?"

"It's nothing else," says she, quite carelessly, "I'm just sending word home to my father, not to be waiting breakfast for me, just to keep him from being uneasy in his mind."

"And who's your father, my duck?" says Dick.

"What!" said the merrow, "Did you never hear of my father? He's the king of the waves, to be sure!"

"And yourself, then, is a real king's daughter?" said Dick, opening his two eyes to take a full and true survey of his wife that was to be.

"Oh, I'm nothing else but a made man with you, and a king your father. To be sure he has all the money that's down in the bottom of the sea!"

"Money," repeated the merrow, "what's money?"

"'Tis no bad thing to have when one wants it," replied Dick; "and maybe now the fishes have the understanding to bring up whatever you bid them?"

"Oh! yes," said the merrow, "they bring me what I want."

"To speak the truth," said Dick, "'tis a straw bed I have at home before you, and that, I'm thinking, is no ways fitting for a king's daughter; so if 'twould not be displeasing to you, just to mention, a nice featherbed, with a pair of new blankets—but what am I talking about? Maybe you have not such things as beds down under the water?"

"By all means," said she, "Mr. Fitzgerald—plenty of beds at your service. I've fourteen oyster beds of my own, not to mention one just planting for the rearing of young ones."

"You have," says Dick, scratching his head and looking a little puzzled. "'Tis a featherbed I was speaking of, but—clearly, yours is the very cut of a decent plan, to have bed and supper so handy to each other, that a person, when they'd have the one, need never ask for the other."

However, bed or no bed, money or no money, Dick Fitzgerald determined to marry the merrow, and the merrow had given her consent. Away they went, therefore, across the strand, from Gollerus to Ballinrunnig, where Father Fitzgibbon happened to be that morning.

"There are two words to this bargain, Dick Fitzgerald," said his Reverence, looking mighty glum. "And is it a fishy woman you'd marry? —the Lord preserve us!—send the scaly creature home to her own people, that's my advice to you, wherever she came from."

Dick had the *cohuleen driuth* in his hand, and was about to give it back to the merrow, who looked covetously at it, but he thought for a moment, and then, says he—

"Please your Reverence, she's a king's daughter."

"If she was the daughter of fifty kings," said Father Fitzgibbon, "I tell you, you can't marry her, she being a fish."

"Please your Reverence," said Dick again, in an undertone, "she is as mild and as beautiful as the moon."

"If she was as mild and as beautiful as the sun, moon, and stars, all put together, I tell you, Dick Fitzgerald," said the priest, stamping his right foot, "you can't marry her, she being a fish!"

"But she has all the gold that's down in the sea only for the asking, and I'm a made man if I marry her; and," said Dick, looking up slyly, "I can make it worth any one's while to do the job."

"Oh! That alters the case entirely," replied the priest. "Why there's some reason now in what you say. Why didn't you tell me this before? —marry her by all means, if she was ten times a fish. Money, you know, is not to be refused in these bad times, and I may as well have the hansel of it as another, that maybe would not take half the pains in counseling you as I have done."

So Father Fitzgibbon married Dick Fitzgerald to the merrow, and like any loving couple, they returned to Gollerus well pleased with each other. Everything prospered with Dick. He was at the sunny side of the world; the merrow made the best of wives, and they lived together in the greatest contentment.

It was wonderful to see, considering where she had been brought up, how she would busy herself about the house, and how well she nursed the children; for, at the end of three years, there were as many young Fitzgeralds—two boys and a girl.

In short, Dick was a happy man, and so he might have continued to the end of his days, if he had only the sense to take proper care of what he had got. Many another man, however, beside Dick, has not had wit enough to do that.

One day when Dick was obliged to go to Tralee, he left the wife minding the children at home after him, and thinking she had plenty to do without disturbing his fishing tackle.

Dick was no sooner gone than Mrs. Fitzgerald set about cleaning up the house, and chancing to pull down a fishing net, what should she find behind it in a hole in the wall but her own *cohuleen driuth*.

She took it out and looked at it, and then she thought of her father the king, and her mother the queen, and her brothers and sisters, and she felt a longing to go back to them.

She sat down on a little stool and thought over the happy days she had spent under the sea; then she looked at her children, and thought on the love and affection of poor Dick, and how it would break his heart to lose her. "But," says she, "he won't lose me entirely, for I'll come back to him again, and who can blame me for going to see my father and my mother after being so long away from them?"

She got up and went towards the door, but came back again to look once more at the child that was sleeping in the cradle. She kissed it gently, and as she kissed it a tear trembled for an instant in her eye and then fell on its rosy cheek. She wiped away the tear, and turning to the eldest little girl, told her to take good care of her brothers, and to be a good child herself until she came back. The merrow then went down to the strand.—The sea was lying calm and smooth, just heaving and glittering in the sun, and she thought she heard a faint sweet singing, inviting her to come down. All her old ideas and feelings came flooding over her mind. Dick and her children were at the instant forgotten, and placing the *cohuleen driuth* on her head, she plunged in.

Dick came home in the evening, and missing his wife, he asked Kathelin, his little girl, what had become of her mother, but she could not tell him. He then enquired of the neighbors, and he learned that she was seen going towards the strand with a strange looking thing like a cocked hat in her hand. He returned to his cabin to search for the *cohuleen driuth*. It was gone, and the truth now flashed upon him.

Year after year did Dick Fitzgerald wait, expecting the return of his wife, but he never saw her more. Dick never married again, always thinking that the merrow would sooner or later return to him, and nothing could ever persuade him but that her father the king kept her below by main force. "For," said Dick, "she surely would not of herself give up her husband and her children."

While she was with him, she was so good a wife in every respect, that to this day she is spoken of in the tradition of the country as the pattern for one, under the name of the Lady of Gollerus.

NOTES

The people of Feroe say, that the seal every ninth night puts off its skin and gets a human form, and then dances and sports like the "human mortals," till it resumes its skin and becomes a seal again. It once happened that a man came by while this took place, and seeing the skin, he seized it and hid it. When the seal, which was in the shape of a woman, could not find its skin to creep into, it was forced to remain in the human form, and, as she was fair to look upon, the same man took her to wife, had children by her, and lived right happy with her. After a long time, the wife found the skin that had been stolen and could not resist the temptation to creep into it, and so she became a seal again.—*Danske Folkesagn*, vol. 3. p. 51.

Mr. Hibbert, in his Description of the Shetland Islands, relates the same story in such a pleasing manner, that it is impossible to refrain from quoting his words. "Sometimes," he informs us, "Mermen and Merwomen have formed connubial attachments with the human race. A story is told of an inhabitant of Unst, who, in walking on the sandy margin of a voe, saw a number of these beings dancing by moonlight, and several seal-skins strewed beside them on the ground. At his approach, they immediately fled to secure their garbs, and taking upon themselves the form of seals, plunged immediately into the sea. But as the Shetlander perceived that one skin lay close to his feet, he snatched it up, bore it swiftly away, and placed it in concealment. On returning to the shore, he met the fairest damsel that was ever gazed upon by mortal eyes lamenting the robbery by which she should become an exile from her submarine friends and a tenant of the upper world. Vainly she implored the restitution of her property: the man had drunk deeply of love, and was inexorable, but offered her protection beneath his roof as his betrothed spouse. The Merlady perceiving that she must become an inhabitant of the earth, found that she could not do better than accept of the offer. This strange connubial attachment subsisted for many years, and several children were the fruits of it, who retained no farther marks of their origin, than in the resemblance which a sort of web between their fingers bore to the forefeet of a seal—this peculiarity being possessed by the descendants of the family to the present day. The Shetlander's love for his Merwife was unbounded, but his affection was coldly returned. The lady would often steal alone to the desert strand, and, on a signal being given, a large seal would make his appearance, with whom she would hold, in an unknown tongue, an anxious conference. Years had thus glided away, when it happened that one of the children, in the course of his play, found concealed beneath a stack of corn a seal's skin, and, delighted with the prize, ran with it to his mother. Her eyes glistened with rapture—she gazed upon it as her own—as the means by which she could pass through the ocean that led to her native home. She burst forth into an ecstasy of joy, which was only moderated when she beheld her children whom she was now about to leave, and after hastily embracing them, fled with all speed towards the sea side. The husband immediately returned—learned the discovery that had taken place—ran to overtake his wife, but only arrived in time to see her transformation of shape completed—to see her in the form of a seal, bound from the ledge of a rock into the sea. The large animal of the same kind with whom she had held a secret converse soon appeared, and evidently congratulated her in the most tender manner on her escape. But before she dived to unknown depth, she cast a parting glance at the wretched Shetlander, whose despairing looks excited in her breast a few transient feelings of commiseration. 'Farewell,' said she to him: 'I loved you very well when I resided upon earth, but I always loved my first husband much better.'"—Page 569.

Mr. Thiele tells us, in a note on the *Danske Folkesagn*, that there are still families who believe themselves to be descended from such marriages. A similar belief exists in Kerry respecting the O'Flaherty and the O'Sullivan families; and the Macnamaras, a Clare family, have their name from a tradition of the same nature. Morgan, according to Ussher, signified in the ancient British "*Born of the Sea.*" It was the real name of the celebrated Pelagius; and is at present a very common one in Wales.

Vade, the father of the famous smith Velent, was the son of king Vilkinus and a Mermaid whom he met in a wood on the sea shore in Russia.—*Vilkina Saga*, c. 18.

The stories of Peleus and Thetis in classical, and of king Beder and the fair Gulnare in oriental literature, may be referred to, as well as the ballad of *Rosmer Havmand* translated by Mr. Jamieson from the Kæmpe Viser, and many others.

"Paracelsus," says old Burton, "hath several stories of them" (Water devils), "how they have lived, and been married to mortal men, and so continued for several years with them, and after, upon some dislike, have forsaken them."—*Anatomie of Melancholy*, p. 47.

The Irish word Merrow, correctly written *Morúadh*, or *Morúach*, answers exactly to the English mermaid, aud is the compound of *muir*, the sea, and *oigh*, a maid. It is also used to express a sea monster, like the Armoric and Cornish *morhuch*, to which it evidently bears analogy. A mermaid is called in Basse Bretagne, *Mary Morgan*. Is Mary, Marie, or is it derived from the sea? Morgan has been already mentioned.

In Irish, *Murdhucha'n*, *Muir-gheilt*, *Sainhghubha*, and *Suire*, are various names for sea-nymphs or mermaids. The romantic historians of Ireland describe the *Suire*, or sea-nymphs, as playing round the ships of the Milesians when on their passage to that Island.

The poem of *Moira Borb* (to be found in Miss Brooke's Relics of Irish Poetry) celebrates the valour of the Finian heroes in the cause of a lady, who introduces herself in pretty nearly the words of the Merrow, in the foregoing story, *I am the daughter of the king under the waves*.

The *cohuleen driuth* bears some resemblance to the feather dresses of the ladies, in the oriental tales of Jahanshah, and Hassan of Bassora. There is something also of the same nature in a modern German Tale. It may be explained as an enchanted cap, from *cuthdarùn*, a sort of montera or monmouth cap; and *drùadh*, a charmer or magician.

In the tale, a rock on the shore is said to look as bold as ever Kerry witness did. A Kerry witness (no offence to MacGillicuddy) signifies a witness who will swear any thing.

"The dudeen," or the pipe, "the woman," and such expressions, are examples of the practice so common among the Irish of using the article instead of the possessive pronoun. In this, and the preceding volume, there are many instances. It agrees extremely with the Greek idiom; and the late bishop of Calcutta might have found in it a strong exemplification of some points of his doctrine respecting the article. It has, at all events, a better effect than the emphatically expressed my of the English.

Dick calls the echo the child of his voice: the daughter, according to General Vallancey, is a literal translation of the Irish compound name for Echo, and a convincing argument of our eastern origin. "What people in the world," says that fanciful antiquary, "the orientalists and the Irish excepted, called the copy of a book the son of a book, and echo the daughter of a voice?" The General here evidently alludes to the Rabbinical mode of divination by *the daughter of the voice*.

Mucalla is the Hibernian term for the "Jocosa Montis imago" of Horace, and is explained by Dr, O'Brien, in his Irish Dictionary, as *the pig of the rock or cliff*; query, if it be not *Macalla, son of the cliff*, which General Vallancey, with his usual ingenuity in the confounding of words, has translated daughter? *Allabhair*, another Irish name for echo, or rather a compound echo, is, literally, *the cliffs game at goal*, or the bounding and rebounding of the voice, as the ball in that game.

In Iceland they assign a supernatural origin to Echo, and call it *Dvergmal* or the voice of the Dvergs or Dwarfs.

Smerwick harbour, where the scene of the tale is laid, is situated on the north side of a little "tongue" of land, which the county Kerry shoots forth into the Atlantic, and which, to use the words of Camden, is "beaten on with barking billows on both sides." It is memorable in history, from the landing of some Spaniards and Italians, in 1579, under the pope's consecrated banner, who threw up a defence there, called Fort del Ore. Sir Walter Raleigh's butchery of the garrison in cold blood still remains a subject of execration in the mouths of the Irish peasantry, and a stain upon English history, which even the pens of Spenser and Camden fail in vindicating. To it, however, we are said to be indebted for the poet's truly valuable work, "a View of the State of Ireland," undertaken for the purpose of excusing his patron, lord Grey de Wilton, then lord deputy of Ireland.

A map of Smerwick harbour, illustrative of this event, is preserved in the State Paper Office, which that zealous and distinguished antiquary,

Mr. Lemon, conjectures, from the writing, to be the performance of the author of the "Faerie Queen."

Gollerus is a small village on the eastern side of the harbour, about a quarter of a mile from the shore, near which there is a very ancient stone cell or chapel, a building probably coeval with the round tower.

Source:
Croker, Thomas Crofton. *Fairy Legends and Traditions of the South of Ireland*. London: John Murray, 1828.

42. Flory Cantillon's Funeral

County Kerry, Ireland

THE ancient burial-place of the Cantillon family was on an island in Ballyheigh Bay. This island was situated at no great distance from the shore, and at a remote period was overflowed in one of the encroachments which the Atlantic has made on that part of the coast of Kerry. The fishermen declare they have often seen the ruined walls of an old chapel beneath them in the water, as they sailed over the clear green sea, of a sunny afternoon. However this may be, it is well known that the Cantillons were, like most other Irish families, strongly attached to their ancient burial-place; and this attachment led to the custom, when any of the family died, of carrying the corpse to the sea-side, where the coffin was left on the shore within reach of the tide. In the morning it had disappeared, being, as was traditionally believed, conveyed away by the ancestors of the deceased to their family tomb.

Connor Crowe, a county Clare man, was related to the Cantillons by marriage. "Connor Mac in Cruagh, of the seven quarters of Breintragh," as he was commonly called, and a proud man he was of the name. Connor, be it known, would drink a quart of salt water, for its medicinal virtues, before breakfast; and for the same reason, I suppose, double that quantity of raw whiskey between breakfast and night, which last he did with as little inconvenience to himself as any man in the barony of Moyferta; and were I to add Clanderalaw and Ibrickan, I don't think I should say wrong.

On the death of Florence Cantillon, Connor Crowe was determined to satisfy himself about the truth of this story of the old church under the sea: so when he heard the news of the old fellow's death, away with him to Ardfert, where Flory was laid out in high style, and a beautiful corpse he made.

Flory had been as jolly and as rollocking a boy in his day as ever was stretched, and his wake was in every respect worthy of him. There was all kind of entertainment and all sort of diversion at it, and no less than three girls got husbands there—more luck to them. Every thing was as it should be: all that side of the country, from Dingle to Tarbert, was at the funeral. The Keen was sung long and bitterly; and, according to the family custom, the coffin was carried to Ballyheigh strand, where it was laid upon the shore with a prayer for the repose of the dead.

The mourners departed, one group after another, and at last Connor Crowe was left alone: he then pulled out his whiskey bottle, his drop of comfort as he called it, which he required, being in grief; and down he sat upon a big stone that was sheltered by a projecting rock, and partly concealed from view, to await with patience the appearance of the ghostly undertakers.

The evening came on mild and beautiful; he whistled an old air which he had heard in his childhood, hoping to keep idle fears out of his head; but the wild strain of that melody brought a thousand recollections with it, which only made the twilight appear more pensive.

"If 'twas near the gloomy tower of Dunmore, in my own sweet county, I was," said Connor Crowe, with a sigh, "one might well believe that the prisoners, who were murdered long ago, there in the vaults under the castle, would be the hands to carry off the coffin out of envy, for never a one of them was buried decently, nor had as much as a coffin amongst them all. 'Tis often, sure enough, I have heard lamentations and great mourning coming from the vaults of Dunmore Castle; but," continued he, after fondly pressing his lips to the mouth of his companion and silent comforter, the whiskey bottle, "didn't I know all the time well enough, 'twas the dismal sounding waves working through the cliffs and hollows of the rocks, and fretting themselves to foam, Oh then, Dunmore Castle, it is you that are the gloomy looking tower on a gloomy day, with the gloomy hills behind you when one has gloomy thoughts on their heart, and sees you like a ghost rising out of the smoke made by the kelp burners on the strand, there is, the Lord save us! as fearful a look about you as about the Blue Man's Lake at midnight. Well then, any how," said Connor, after a pause, "is it not a blessed night, though surely the moon looks mighty pale in the face? St. Senan himself between us and all kinds of harm."

It was, in truth, a lovely moonlight night; nothing was to be seen around but the dark rocks, and the white pebbly beach, upon which the sea broke with a hoarse and melancholy murmur. Connor, notwithstanding his frequent draughts, felt rather queerish, and almost began to repent his curiosity. It was certainly a solemn sight to behold the black coffin resting upon the white strand. His imagination gradually converted the deep moaning of old ocean into a mournful wail for the dead, and from the shadowy recesses of the rocks he imaged forth strange and visionary forms.

As the night advanced, Connor became weary with watching; he caught himself more than once in the fact of nodding, when suddenly giving his head a shake, he would look towards the black coffin. But the narrow house of death remained unmoved before him.

It was long past midnight, and the moon was sinking into the sea, when he heard the sound of many voices, which gradually became stronger, above the heavy and monotonous roll of the sea: he listened, and presently could distinguish a Keen, of exquisite sweetness, the notes of which rose and fell with the heaving of the waves, whose deep murmur mingled with and supported the strain!

The Keen grew louder and louder, and seemed to approach the beach, and then fell into a low plaintive wail. As it ended, Connor beheld a number of strange, and in the dim light, mysterious looking figures, emerge from the sea, and surround the coffin, which they prepared to launch into the water.

"This comes of marrying with the creatures of earth," said one of the figures, in a clear, yet hollow tone.

"True," replied another, with a voice still more fearful, "our king would never have commanded his gnawing white-toothed waves to devour the rocky roots of the island cemetery, had not his daughter, Durfulla, been buried there by her mortal husband!"

"But the time will come," said a third, bending over the coffin.

"When mortal eye—our work shall spy,
And mortal ear—our dirge shall hear."

"Then," said a fourth, "our burial of the Cantillons is at an end for ever!"

As this was spoken, the coffin was borne from the beach by a retiring wave, and the company of sea people prepared to follow it; but at the moment, one chanced to discover Connor Crowe, as fixed with wonder and as motionless with fear as the stone on which he sat.

"The time is come," cried the unearthly being, "the time is come; a human eye looks on the forms of ocean, a human ear has heard their voices; farewell to the Cantillons; the sons of the sea are no longer doomed to bury the dust of the earth!"

One after the other turned slowly round, and regarded Connor Crowe, who still remained as if bound by a spell. Again arose their funeral song; and on the next wave they followed the coffin. The sound of the lamentation died away, and at length nothing was heard but the rush of waters. The coffin and the train of sea people sank over the old churchyard, and never, since the funeral of old Flory Cantillon, have any of the family been carried to the strand of Ballyheigh, for conveyance to their rightful burial-place, beneath the waves of the Atlantic.

NOTES

Another version of this wild and picturesque tradition has been communicated to the writer by Mr. Lynch, of the King's German legion. In both legends the locality is the same; but the name of the M'Ellicot family is substituted for that of the Cantillons. The latter, however, accords with the statement of Doctor Smith, in his History of Kerry, p. 210.

"The neighbouring inhabitants," says that writer, speaking of Ballyheigh, "show some rocks visible in this bay only at low tides, which they say are the remains of an island that was formerly the burial-place of the family of Cantillon, the ancient proprietors of Ballyheigh."

In the preceding note mention has been made of the conjugal union contracted between the human race and the inhabitants of the deep. An attachment, however, between the finny tribes and man has some foundation in fact, if we are to credit the testimony of the ancients. In the following story given by Athenteus, though dolphins do not exactly act as undertakers, they seem to have performed the part of mourners.

The dolphin, says Athenteus (Lib. 13. Cap. 8.), is of all animals the fondest of men, the most sensible, and one possessing the virtue of gratitude. Phylarchus relates, in his 12th Book, that Coiranus, the Milesian, seeing some fishermen who had caught a dolphin in their nets, and were about to cut him up, gave them some money, and prevailed on them to throw him back into the sea. Some time after happening to be shipwrecked near Myconos, all on board perished except Coiranus, who was saved by a dolphin. Coiranus died when an old man, in his own country; and the funeral happening to take place on the shore, by Miletus, a great number of dolphins appeared in the harbour on that day, and swam at a little distance along the shore after those who attended the funeral, joining, as it were, the procession, as mourners, and attending on the funeral of the man.

Pliny mentions a pretty anecdote of the friendship existing between a boy and a dolphin, which seems to have been a favourite tale, as it is also related both by Ælian and Aulus Gellius.

Connor Crowe will be recognised by those acquainted with the county Clare, as a faithful sketch from nature. The Blue Man's Lake mentioned in his soliloquy is situated in the Bog of Shragh, about four miles from Kilrush. It is so named from the tradition, that a spectral figure enveloped in a bluish flame haunts its melancholy waters.

Durfulla, the name of the sea-king's daughter, who married Flory Cantillon's ancestor, signifies *leaping water*. "Gnawing white toothed waves" is the literal translation of a common Irish epithet.

Source:
Croker, Thomas Crofton. *Fairy Legends and Traditions of the South of Ireland.* London: William Tegg, 1859.

43. The Soul Cages

County Kerry, Ireland

JACK Dogherty lived on the coast of the county Clare. Jack was a fisherman, as his father and grandfather before him had been. Like them, too, he lived all alone (but for the wife), and just in the same spot. People used to wonder why the Dogherty family were so fond of that wild situation, so far away from all human kind, and in the midst of huge shattered rocks, with nothing but the wide ocean to look upon. But they had their own good reasons for it.

The place was just the only spot on that part of the coast where anybody could well live. There was a neat little creek, where a boat might lie as snug as a puffin in her nest, and out from this creek a ledge of sunken rocks ran into the sea. Now when the Atlantic, according to custom, was raging with a storm, and a good westerly wind was blowing strong on the coast, many a richly-laden ship went to pieces on these rocks; and then the fine bales of cotton and tobacco, and such like things, and the pipes of wine and the puncheons of rum, and the casks of brandy, and the kegs of Hollands that used to come ashore! Dunbeg Bay was just like a little estate to the Doghertys.

Not but they were kind and humane to a distressed sailor, if ever one had the good luck to get to land; and many a time indeed did Jack put out in his little *corragh* (which, though not quite equal to honest Andrew Hennessy's canvas life-boat would breast the billows like any gannet), to lend a hand towards bringing off the crew from a wreck. But when the ship had gone to pieces, and the crew were all lost, who would blame Jack for picking up all he could find?

"And who is the worse of it?" said he. "For as to the king, God bless him! everybody knows he's rich enough already without getting what's floating in the sea."

Jack, though such a hermit, was a good-natured, jolly fellow. No other, sure, could ever have coaxed Biddy Mahony to quit her father's snug and warm house in the middle of the town of Ennis, and to go so many miles off to live among the rocks, with the seals and sea-gulls for next-door neighbours. But Biddy knew that Jack was the man for a woman who wished to be comfortable and happy; for to say nothing of the fish, Jack had the supplying of half the gentlemen's houses of the country with the *Godsends* that came into the bay. And she was right in her choice; for no woman ate, drank, or slept better, or made a prouder appearance at chapel on Sundays, than Mrs. Dogherty.

Many a strange sight, it may well be supposed, did Jack see, and many a strange sound did he hear, but nothing daunted him. So far was he from being afraid of Merrows, or such beings, that the very first wish of his heart was to fairly meet with one. Jack had heard that they were mighty like Christians, and that luck had always come out of an acquaintance with them. Never, therefore, did he dimly discern the Merrows moving along the face of the waters in their robes of mist, but he made direct for them; and many a scolding did Biddy, in her own quiet way, bestow upon Jack for spending his whole day out at sea, and bringing home no fish. Little did poor Biddy know the fish Jack was after!

It was rather annoying to Jack that, though living in a place where the Merrows were as plenty as lobsters, he never could get a right view of one. What vexed him more was that both his father and grandfather had often and often seen them; and he even remembered hearing, when a child, how his grandfather, who was the first of the family that had settled down at the creek, had been so intimate with a Merrow that, only for fear of vexing the priest, he would have had him stand for one of his children. This, however, Jack did not well know how to believe.

Fortune at length began to think that it was only right that Jack should know as much as his father and grandfather did. Accordingly, one day when he had strolled a little farther than usual along the coast to the northward, just as he turned a point, he saw something, like to nothing he had ever seen before, perched upon a rock at a little distance out to sea. It looked green in the body, as well as he could discern at that distance, and he would have sworn, only the thing was impossible, that it had a cocked hat in its hand. Jack stood for a good half-hour straining his eyes, and wondering at it, and all the time the thing did not stir hand or foot. At last Jack's patience was quite worn out, and he gave a loud whistle and a hail, when the Merrow (for such it was) started up, put the cocked hat on its head, and dived down, head foremost, from the rock.

Jack's curiosity was now excited, and he constantly directed his steps towards the point; still he could never get a glimpse of the sea-gentleman with the cocked hat; and with thinking and thinking about the matter, he began at last to fancy he had been only dreaming. One very rough day, however, when the sea was running mountains high, Jack Dogherty determined to give a look at the Merrow's rock (for he had always chosen a fine day before), and then he saw the strange thing cutting capers upon the top of the rock, and then diving down, and then coming up, and then diving down again.

Jack had now only to choose his time (that is, a good blowing day), and he might see the man of the sea as often as he pleased. All this, however, did not satisfy him—"much will have more"; he wished now to get acquainted with the Merrow, and even in this he succeeded. One tremendous blustering day, before he got to the point whence he had a view of the Merrow's rock, the storm came on so furiously that Jack was obliged to take shelter in one of the caves which are so numerous along the coast; and there, to his astonishment, he saw sitting before him a thing with green hair, long green teeth, a red nose, and pig's eyes. It had a fish's tail, legs with scales on them, and short arms like fins. It wore no clothes, but had the cocked hat under its arm, and seemed engaged thinking very seriously about something.

Jack, with all his courage, was a little daunted; but now or never, thought he; so up he went boldly to the cogitating fishman, took off his hat, and made his best bow.

"Your servant, sir," said Jack.

"Your servant, kindly, Jack Dogherty," answered the Merrow.

"To be sure, then, how well your honour knows my name!" said Jack.

"Is it I not know your name, Jack Dogherty? Why man, I knew your grandfather long before he was married to Judy Regan, your grandmother! Ah, Jack, Jack, I was fond of that grandfather of yours; he was a mighty worthy man in his time: I never met his match above or below, before or since, for sucking in a shellful of brandy. I hope, my boy," said the old fellow, with a merry twinkle in his eyes, "I hope you're his own grandson!"

'Never fear me for that," said Jack; "if my mother had only reared me on brandy, 'tis myself that would be a sucking infant to this hour!"

"Well, I like to hear you talk so manly; you and I must be better acquainted, if it were only for your grandfather's sake. But, Jack, that father of yours was not the thing! he had no head at all."

"I'm sure, said Jack, "since your honour lives down under the water, you must be obliged to drink a power to keep any beat in you in such a cruel, damp, could place. Well, I've often heard of Christians drinking like fishes; and might I be so bold as ask where you get the spirits?"

"Where do you get them yourself, Jack?" said the Merrow, twitching his red nose between his forefinger and thumb.

"Hubbubboo," cries Jack "now I see how it is; but I suppose, sir, your honour has got a fine dry cellar below to keep them in."

"Let me alone for the cellar," said the Merrow, with a knowing wink of his left eye.

"I'm sure," continued Jack, "it must be mighty well worth the looking at."

"You may say that, Jack," said the Merrow; "and if you meet me here next Monday, just at this time of the day, we will have a little more talk with one another about the matter."

Jack and the Merrow parted the best friends in the world. On Monday they met, and Jack was not a little surprised to see that the Merrow had two cocked hats with him, one under each arm.

"Might I take the liberty to ask, sir," said Jack, "why your honour has brought the two hats with you today? You would not, sure, be going to give me one of them, to keep for the curiosity of the thing?"

"No, no, Jack," said he, "I don't get my hats so easily, to part with them that way; but I want you to come down and dine with me, and I brought you that hat to dive with."

"Lord bless and preserve us!" cried Jack, in amazement, would you want me to go down to the bottom of the salt sea ocean? Sure, I'd be smothered and choked up with the water, to say nothing of being drowned! And what would poor Biddy do for me, and what would she say?"

"And what matter what she says, you *pinkeen*? Who cares for Biddy's squalling? It's long before your grandfather would have talked in that way. Many's the time he stuck that same hat on his head, and dived down boldly after me; and many's the snug bit of dinner and good shellful of brandy he and I have had together below, under the water."

"Is it really, sir, and no joke?" said Jack; "why, then, sorrow from me for ever and a day after, if I'll be a bit worse man nor my grandfather was! Here goes—but play me fair now. Here's neck or nothing!" cried Jack.

"That's your grandfather all over," said the old fellow; "so come along, then, and do as I do."

They both left the cave, walked into the sea, and then swam a piece until they got to the rock, The Merrow climbed to the top of it, and Jack followed him. On the far side it was as straight as the wall of a house, and the sea beneath looked so deep that Jack was almost cowed.

"Now, do you see, Jack," said the Merrow: "just put this hat on your head, and mind to keep your eyes wide open. Take hold of my tail, and follow after me, and you'll see what you'll see."

In he dashed, and in dashed Jack after him boldly. They went and they went, and Jack thought they'd never stop going. Many a time did he wish himself sitting at home by the fireside with Biddy. Yet where was the use of wishing now, when he was so many miles, as he thought, below the waves of the Atlantic? Still he held hard by the Merrow's tail, slippery as it was; and, at last, to Jack's great surprise, they got out of the water, and he actually found himself on dry land at the bottom of the sea. They landed just in front of a nice house that was slated very neatly with oyster shells! and the Merrow, turning about to Jack, welcomed him down.

Jack could hardly speak, what with wonder, and what with being out of breath with travelling so fast through the water. He looked about him and could see no living things, barring crabs and lobsters, of which there were plenty walking leisurely about on the sand. Overhead was the sea like a sky, and the fishes like birds swimming about in it.

"Why don't you speak, man?" said the Merrow: "I dare say you had no notion that I had such a snug little concern here as this? Are you smothered, or choked, or drowned, or are you fretting after Biddy, eh?"

"Oh! not myself indeed," said Jack, showing his teeth with a good-humoured grin—"but who in the world would ever have thought of seeing such a thing?"

"Well, come along, and let's see what they've got for us to eat?"

Jack really was hungry, and it gave him no small pleasure to perceive a fine column of smoke rising from the chimney, announcing what was going on within. Into the house he followed the Merrow, and there he saw a good kitchen, right well provided with everything. There was a noble dresser, and plenty of pots and pans, with two young Merrows cooking. His host then led him into the room, which was furnished shabbily enough. Not a table or a chair was there in it; nothing but planks and logs of wood to sit on, and eat off. There was, however, a good fire blazing upon the hearth—a comfortable sight to Jack.

"Come now, and I'll show you where I keep—you know what," said the Merrow, with a sly look; and opening a little door, he led Jack into a fine cellar, well filled with pipes, and kegs, and hogsheads, and barrels.

"What do you say to that, Jack Dogherty?—Eh!—may be a body can't live snug under the water?"

"Never the doubt of that," said Jack, with a convincing smack of his upper lip, that he really thought what he said.

They went back to the room, and found dinner laid. There was no tablecloth, to be sure—but what matter? It was not always Jack had one at home. The dinner would have been no discredit to the first house of the country on a fast day. The choicest of fish, and no wonder, was there. Turbots, and sturgeons, and soles, and lobsters, and oysters, and twenty other kinds, were on the planks at once, and plenty of the best of foreign spirits. The wines, the old fellow said, were too cold for his stomach.

Jack ate and drank till he could eat no more: then taking up a shell of brandy, "Here's to your honour's good health, sir," said he; "though, begging you pardon, it's mighty odd that as long as we've been acquainted I don't know your name yet."

"That's true, Jack," replied he; "I never thought of it before, but better late than never. My name's Coomara."

"And a mighty decent name it is," cried Jack, taking another shellfull: "here's to your good health, Coomara, and may ye live these fifty years to come!"

"Fifty years!" repeated Coomara; "I'm obliged to you, indeed! If you had said five hundred, it would have been something worth the wishing."

"By the laws, sir," cries Jack, "*youz* live to a powerful age here under the water! You knew my grandfather, and he's dead and gone better than these sixty years. I'm sure it must be a healthy place to live in."

"No doubt of it; but come, Jack, keep the liquor stirring."

Shell after shell did they empty, and to Jack's exceeding surprise, he found the drink never got into his head, owing, I suppose, to the sea being over them, which kept their noddles cool.

Old Coomara got exceedingly comfortable, and sung several songs; but Jack, if his life had depended on it, never could remember more than

"Rum fum boodle boo,

>   Ripple dipple nitty dob;
> Dumdoo doodle coo,
>   Raffle taffle chittibob!"

It was the chorus to one of them; and, to say the truth, nobody that I know has ever been able to pick any particular meaning out of it; but that, to be sure, is the case with many a song nowadays.

At length said he to Jack, "Now, my dear boy, if you follow me, I'll show you my curiosities!" He opened a little door, and led Jack into a large room, where Jack saw a great many odds and ends that Coomara had picked up at one time or another. What chiefly took his attention, however, were things like lobsterpots ranged on the ground along the wall.

"Well, Jack, how do you like my curiosities?" said old Coo.

"Upon my sowkins,[1] sir," said Jack, "they're mighty well worth the looking at; but might I make so bold as to ask what these things like lobster-pots are?"

"Oh! the Soul Cages, is it?"

"The what? sir!"

"These things here that I keep the souls in."

"*Arrah*! what souls, sir?" said Jack, in amazement; "sure the fish have no souls in them?"

"Oh! no," replied Coo, quite coolly, "that they have not; but these are the souls of drowned sailors."

"The Lord preserve us from all harm!" muttered lack, "how in the world did you get them?"

"Easily enough: I've only, when I see a good storm coming on, to set a couple of dozen of these, and then, when the sailors are drowned and the souls get out of them under the water, the poor things are almost perished to death, not being used to the cold; so they make into my pots for shelter, and then I have them snug, and fetch them home, and is it not well for them, poor souls, to get into such good quarters?"

Jack was so thunderstruck he did not know what to say, so he said nothing. They went back into the dining-room, and had a little more brandy, which was excellent, and then, as Jack knew that it must be getting late, and as Biddy might be uneasy, he stood up, and said he thought it was time for him to be on the road.

"Just as you like, Jack," said Coo, "but take a *duc an durrus*[2] before you go; you've a cold journey before you."

Jack knew better manners than to refuse the parting glass. "I wonder," said he, "will I be able to make out my way home?"

"What should ail you," said Coo, "when I'll show you the way?"

---

[1] Sowkins, diminutive of soul.

[2] *Recte, deoch án dorrus*—door-drink or stirrup-cup.

Out they went before the house, and Coomara took one of the cocked hats, and put it upon Jack's head the wrong way, and then lifted him up on his shoulder that he might launch him up into the water.

"Now," says he, giving him a heave, "you'll come up just in the same spot you came down in; and, Jack, mind and throw me back the hat."

He canted Jack off his shoulder, and up he shot like a bubble—whirr, whiff, whiz—away he went up through the water, till he came to the very rock he had jumped off where he found a landing-place, and then in he threw the hat, which sunk like a stone.

The sun was just going down in the beautiful sky of a calm summer's evening. *Feascor* was seen dimly twinkling in the cloudless heaven, a solitary star, and the waves of the Atlantic flashed in a golden flood of light. So Jack, perceiving it was late, set off home; but when he got there, not a word did he say to Biddy of where he had spent his day.

The state of the poor souls cooped up in the lobster-pots gave Jack a great deal of trouble, and how to release them cost him a great deal of thought. He at first had a mind to speak to the priest about the matter. But what could the priest do, and what did Coo care for the priest? Besides, Coo was a good sort of an old fellow, and did not think he was doing any harm. Jack had a regard for him, too, and it also might not be much to his own credit if it were known that he used to go dine with Merrows. On the whole, he thought his best plan would be to ask Coo to dinner, and to make him drunk, if he was able, and then to take the hat and go down and turn up the pots. It was, first of all, necessary, however, to get Biddy out of the way; for Jack was prudent enough, as she was a woman, to wish to keep the thing secret from her.

Accordingly, Jack grew mighty pious all of a sudden, and said to Biddy that he thought it would be for the good of both their souls if she was to go and take her rounds at Saint John's Well, near Ennis. Biddy thought so too, and accordingly off she set one fine morning at day dawn, giving Jack a strict charge to have an eye to the place.

The coast being clear, away went Jack to the rock to give the appointed signal to Coomara, which was throwing a big stone into the water. Jack threw, and up sprang Coo!

"Good morning, Jack," said he; "what do you want with me?"

"Just nothing at all to speak about, sir," returned Jack, "only to come and take a bit of dinner with me, if I might make so free as to ask you, and sure I'm now after doing so."

"It's quite agreeable, Jack, I assure you; what's your hour?"

"Any time that's most convenient to you, sir—say one o'clock, that you may go home, if you wish, with the daylight."

"I'll be with you," said Coo, "never fear me."

Jack went home, and dressed a noble fish dinner, and got out plenty of his best foreign spirits, enough, for that matter, to make twenty men drunk. Just to the minute came Coo, with his cocked hat under his arm. Dinner was ready, they sat down, and ate and drank away manfully. Jack, thinking of the poor souls below in the pots, plied old Coo well with brandy, and encouraged him to sing, hoping to put him under the table, but poor Jack forgot that he had not the sea over his head to keep it cool. The brandy got into it, and did his business for him, and Coo reeled off home, leaving his entertainer as dumb as a haddock on a Good Friday.

Jack never woke till the next morning, and then he was in a sad way. "'Tis to no use for me thinking to make that old Rapparee drunk," said Jack, "and how in this world can I help the poor souls out of the lobster-pots?" After ruminating nearly the whole day, a thought struck him. "I have it," says he, slapping his knee; "I'll be sworn that Coo never saw a drop of poteen, as old as he is, and that's the thing to settle him! Oh! then, is not it well that Biddy will not be home these two days yet; I can have another twist at him."

Jack asked Coo again, and Coo laughed at him for having no better head, telling him he'd never come up to his grandfather.

"Well, but try me again," said Jack, "and I'll be bail to drink you drunk and sober, and drunk again."

"Anything in my power," said Coo, "to oblige you."

At this dinner Jack took care to have his own liquor well watered, and to give the strongest brandy he had to Coo. At last says he, "Pray, sir, did you ever drink any poteen?—any real Mountain dew?"

"No," says Coo; "what's that, and where does it come from?"

"Oh, that's a secret," said Jack, "but it's the right stuff—never believe me again, if 'tis not fifty times as good as brandy or rum either. Biddy's brother just sent me a present of a little drop, in exchange for some brandy, and as you're an old friend of the family, I kept it to treat you with."

"Well, let's see what sort of thing it is," said Coomara.

The *poteen* was the right sort. It was first-rate, and had the real smack upon it. Coo was delighted: he drank and he sung *Rum bum boodle boo* over and over again; and he laughed and he danced, till he fell on the floor fast asleep. Then Jack, who had taken good care to keep himself sober, snapt up the cocked hat—ran off to the rock—leaped, and soon arrived at Coo's habitation.

All was as still as a churchyard at midnight—not a Merrow, old or young, was there. In he went and turned up the pots, but nothing did he see, only he heard a sort of a little whistle or chirp as he raised each of them. At this he was surprised, till he recollected what the priests had often said, that nobody living could see the soul, no more than they could see the wind or the air. Having now done all that he could for them, he set the pots as they were before, and sent a blessing after the poor souls to speed them on their journey wherever they were going. Jack now began to think of returning; he put the hat on, as was right, the wrong way; but when he got out he found the water so high over his head that he had no hopes of ever getting up into it, now that he had not old Coomara to give him a lift. He walked about looking for a ladder, but not one could he find, and not a rock was there in sight. At last he saw a spot where the sea hung rather lower than anywhere else, so he resolved to try there. Just as he came to it, a big cod happened to put down his tail. Jack made a jump and caught hold of it, and the cod, all in amazement, gave a bounce and pulled Jack up. The minute the hat touched the water away Jack was whisked, and up he shot like a cork, dragging the poor cod, that he forgot to let go, up with him tail foremost. He got to the rock in no time and without a moment's delay hurried home, rejoicing in the good deed he had done.

But, meanwhile, there was fine work at home; for our friend Jack had hardly left the house on his soul-freeing expedition, when back came Biddy from her soul-saving one to the well. When she entered the house and saw the things lying thrie-na-helah[1] on the table before her—

"Here's a pretty job!" said she; "that blackguard of mine—what ill-luck I had ever to marry him! He has picked up some vagabond or other, while I was praying for the good of his soul, and they've been drinking all the poteen that my own brother gave him, and all the spirits, to be sure, that he was to have sold to his honour."—Then hearing an outlandish kind of grunt, she looked down, and saw Coomara lying under the table.—"The Blessed Virgin help me," shouted she, "if he has not made a real beast of himself! Well, well, I've often heard of a man making a beast of himself with drink!—Oh hone—oh hone!—Jack, honey, what will I do with you, or what will I do without you? How can any decent woman ever think of living with a beast?"

With such like lamentations Biddy rushed out of the house, and was going she knew not where, when she heard the well-known voice of Jack singing a merry tune. Glad enough was Biddy to find him safe and sound, and not turned into a thing that was like neither fish nor flesh. Jack was obliged to tell her all, and Biddy, though she had half a mind to be angry with him for not telling her before, owned that he had done a great service to the poor souls. Back they both went most lovingly to the house, and Jack wakened up Coomara; and, perceiving the old fellow to be rather dull, he bid him not to be cast down, for 'twas many a good man's case; said it all came of his not being used to the *poteen*, and recommended him, by way of cure, to swallow a hair of the dog that bit him. Coo, however, seemed to think he had had quite enough. He got up, quite out of sorts, and without having the manners to say one word in the way of civility, he sneaked off to cool himself by a jaunt through the salt water.

Coomara never missed the souls. He and Jack continued the best friends in the world, and no one, perhaps, ever equalled Jack for freeing souls from purgatory; for he contrived fifty excuses for getting into the house below the sea, unknown to the old fellow, and then turning up the

---

[1] Tri-na-cheile, literally through other—*i.e.*, higgledy-piggledy.

pots and letting out the souls. It vexed him, to be sure, that he could never see them; but as he knew the thing to be impossible, he was obliged to be satisfied.

Their intercourse continued for several years. However, one morning, on Jack's throwing in a stone as usual, he got no answer. He flung another, and another, still there was no reply. He went away, and returned the following morning, but it was to no purpose. As he was without the hat, he could not go down to see what had become of old Coo, but his belief was, that the old man, or the old fish, or whatever he was, had either died, or had removed from that part of the country.

NOTES

In Grimm's *Deutche Sagan*, there is a story which has a striking resemblance to the foregoing; and it is accurately translated for the sake of comparison.

A waterman once lived on good terms with a peasant, who dwelt not far from his lake; he often visited him, and at last begged that the peasant would, in return, visit him in his house under the water. The peasant consented, and went with him. There was every thing below, in the water, as in a stately palace on the land,—halls, chambers, and cabinets, with costly furniture of every description. The waterman led his guest through the whole, and showed him every thing that was in it. They came at length to a little chamber, where there were standing several new pots turned upside down. The peasant asked what was in them. "They contain," said he, "the souls of drowned people which I put under the pots, and keep them close so that they cannot get away." The peasant said nothing, and came up again on the land. The affair of the souls caused him much uneasiness for a long time, and he watched till the waterman should be gone out. When this happened, the peasant who had marked the right road clown, descended into the water-house, and succeeded in finding again the little chamber; and when he was there, he turned up all the pots, one after another; immediately the souls of the drowned men ascended out of the water, and were again at liberty.

Grimm says that he was told the waterman is like any other man, only that when he opens his mouth, his green teeth may be seen; he also wears a green hat, and appears to the girls, as they go by the lake he dwells in, measures out ribbon and flings it to them.

Dunbeg Bay is situated on the coast of the county Clare, and may be readily found on any map of Ireland. Corragh, or currugh, is a small boat used by the fishermen of that part, and is formed of cow hides, or pitched cloth, strained on a frame of wickerwork. The boldness and confidence of the navigators of these fragile vessels often surprises the stranger. By the Irish poets they are invariably termed broad-chested or strong-bowed corraghs; "*Curraghaune aulin cleavorshin*," as it is pronounced. It is the *carabus* of the later Latin writers, thus described by Isidore: Carabus, parva scapha ex vimine facta, quæ contexta crudo corio genus navigii prabet."—Isidorus, Orig. l. xviii. c. I. It is also described in some pleasing verses by Festus Avienus. See Suidas and Et. Mag.

Of honest Andrew Hennessy's canvas life-boat it is only necessary to state, that the inventor, with a crew of five seamen, weathered the equinoctial gale of October 1823 (the severest remembered for many years), in an experimental passage from Cork to Liverpool. After so convincing a trial, it is to be regretted that Mr. Hennessy and his plans for the preservation of human life have not experienced more attention.

St. John's Well, whither Mrs. Dogherty journeyed to take her rounds, lies at the foot of a hill, about three miles from Ennis, and close to it is a rude altar, at which the superstitious offer up their prayers. The water of this, like other holy wells, is believed to possess the power of restoring the use of the limbs, curing defective vision, &c. Near the well there is a small lough, said to be the abode of a strange kind of fish or mermaid, which used to appear very frequently. This lady of the lake was observed resorting to the cellar of Newhall, the seat of Mr. M'Donall. The butler, perceiving the wine decrease rapidly, determined, with some of his fellow-servants, to watch for the thief, and at last they caught the mermaid in the fact of drinking it. The enraged butler threw her into a chaldron of boiling water, when she vanished, after uttering three piercing shrieks, leaving only a mass of jelly behind. Since that period, her appearances have been restricted to once in every seven years.

Merrows are said to be as fond of wine as snakes are of milk, and for the sake of it to steal on board of ships in the night time. Pausanias tells us, that the citizens of Tanagra were greatly annoyed by a Triton who frequented the neighbouring coast. By the advice of the oracle, they set a large vessel of wine on the beach, which the Triton emptied on his next visit; the liquor made him drunk, and the citizens cut off his head as he slept.

Coamara or *cú-mara*, means the sea-hound. The Irish family of Macnamara or Maconmara are, according to tradition, descended from *cúmara*, and hence their name from *mac* a son, *con* the genitive of *cu* a greyhound, and *mara* of the sea.

The Macnamara clan inhabited the western district of the county Clare, and were dependant on the O'Briens.

Cumara's song, if indeed it be not altogether the invention of the narrator, may be considered as an extremely curious lyrical fragment. But few will feel inclined to acknowledge its genuineness, as nothing appears to be more easy than to fabricate a short effusion of this kind, or even an entire language. Psalmanazar's Formosan language is well known. Rabelais abounds in specimens. Shakespeare, in "All's well that ends well," has tried his hand at it. Swift has given some morsels of Liliputian, Brobdignagian, and other tongues; and any one curious about fairy language has only to look into Giraldus Cambrensis. Even the inhabitants of the lower regions have had a dialect invented for them, as the following valuable extract from the Macaronica of the profound Merlinus Cocaius will prove. See the opening of the xxiv. book:

> "Cra era tif trafnot sgneflet canatanta riogna
> Ecce venit gridando Charon—"

which, in a marginal note, he kindly informs us—"nec Græcum nec Hebræum, sed diabolicum est." And perhaps even the well known line of Dante, of which it is an imitation—

> "Pape Satan, pape Satan Aleppè,"

is nec Latinum, nec Hebræum, sed diabolicum, also.

A translation of old Cu's song, however, it is expected, would add little to our stock of knowledge, as, judging from the indubitable specimens which exist, the remarks of the sea folk are not very profound, although they evince singular powers of observation.

Waldron, in his account of the Isle of Man, relates that an amphibious damsel was once caught, and after remaining three days on shore was allowed to escape. On plunging into the water she was welcomed by a number of her own species, who were heard to inquire what she had seen among the natives of earth.—"Nothing," she answered, "wonderful, except that they were silly enough to throw away the water in which they had boiled their eggs!"

Bochart tells us, on the authority of Alkazuinius, an Arabic author, that there is a sea-animal which exactly resembles a man, only that he has a tail; he has, moreover, a grey beard; hence he is called the old man of the sea. Once upon a time one of them was brought to a certain king, who, out of curiosity, gave him a wife. They had a son who could speak the languages of both his parents. The boy was asked one day what his father said; but as the reply must necessarily lose by translation, it is given in the original Greek.

On the Irishisms used in the Legend of "the Soul Cages" a few words. *Arrah* is a common exclamation of surprise. It is correctly written *ara*, and, according to Dr. O'Brien, signifies a conference. A popular phrase is, "Arrah come here now," *i.e.* come here and let us talk over the matter.

Duc an Durras, Anglicè, the stirrup cup, means literally, the drink at the door; from *Deoch*, to drink, and *Doras* or *Duras*, a door. In Devonshire and Cornwall it is called *Dash and Darras*, probably a corruption of the old Cornish expression.

Rapparee was the name given to certain freebooters in the times of James and William. It is used in the story rather as a term of regard, as we sometimes employ the word rogue.

Thrie-na-helah may be translated by the English word topsy-turvey.

Pinkeen and *Sowkin* are diminutives; the former of Penk or Pink, the name of the little fish more commonly called in England, Minnow.

Sowkin is evidently a contraction of *Soulkin*, the diminutive of soul. It answers to the German *Seelchen*, and is an old English expression, no longer, it is believed, to be met with in that country, but very common as a minor oath in Ireland.

By the Laws, is, as is well known, a softening down of a very solemn asseveration. If taken literally, people may fancy it an oath not very binding in the mouth of an Irishman, who is seldom distinguished by his profound veneration for the Statute Book. This, however, only proves that law and justice in Ireland were essentially different things; for sir John Davies, himself a lawyer, remarked, long since, how fond the natives were of justice; and it is to be hoped that a regular and impartial administration will speedily impress them as synonimes on the minds of the Irish peasantry.

Few need to be informed that the lower orders in Ireland, although their tone is different, speak the English language more grammatically than those of the same rank in England. The word *yez* or *youz* affords an instance of their attention to etymology; for as they employ *you* in speaking to a single person, they naturally enough imagined that it should be employed in the plural when addressed to more than one.

"A hair of the dog that bit him," is the common recommendation of an old toper to a young one, on the morning after a debauch.

"Shall we pluck a hair of the same wolf to-day, Proctor John?"—*Ben Jonson's Bartholomew Fair*, Act I. Scene I.

Source:
Croker, Thomas Crofton. *Fairy Legends and Traditions of the South of Ireland*. London: John Murray, 1828.

44. The Lord of Dunkerron

County Kerry, Ireland

THE lord of Dunkerron—O'Sullivan More,
   Why seeks he at midnight the sea-beaten shore?
His bark lies in haven, his bounds are asleep;
   No foes are abroad on the land or the deep.

Yet nightly the lord of Dunkerron is known
   On the wild shore to watch and to wander alone;
For a beautiful spirit of ocean, 'tis said,

The lord of Dunkerron would win to his bed.

When, by moonlight, the waters were hush'd to repose,
　　That beautiful spirit of ocean arose;
Her hair, full of lustre, just floated and fell
　　O'er her bosom, that heav'd with a billowy swell.

Long, long had he lov'd her—long vainly essay'd
　　To lure from her dwelling the coy ocean maid;
And long had he wander'd and watch'd by the tide,
　　To claim the fair spirit O'Sullivan's bride!

The maiden she gazed on the creature of earth,
　　Whose voice in her breast to a feeling gave birth;
Then smiled; and, abashed as a maiden might be,
　　Looking down, gently sank to her home in the sea.

Though gentle that smile, as the moonlight above,
　　O'Sullivan felt 'twas the dawning of love,
And hope came on hope, spreading over his mind,
　　Like the eddy of circles her wake left behind.

The lord of Dunkerron he plunged in the waves,
　　And sought through the fierce rush of waters, their caves;
The gloom of whose depth studded over with spars,
　　Had the glitter of midnight when lit up by stars.

Who can tell or can fancy the treasures that sleep
　　Intombed in the wonderful womb of the deep?
The pearls and the gems, as if valueless, thrown
　　To lie 'mid the sea-wrack concealed and unknown.

Down, down went the maid,—still the chieftain pursued;
　　Who flies must be followed ere she can be wooed.
Untempted by treasures, unawed by alarms,
　　The maiden at length he has clasped in his arms!

They rose from the deep by a smooth-spreading strand,
　　Whence beauty and verdure stretch'd over the land.
"Twas an isle of enchantment! and lightly the breeze,
　　With a musical murmur, just crept through the trees.

The haze-woven shroud of that newly born isle,
　　Softly faded away, from a magical pile,
A palace of crystal, whose bright-beaming sheen
　　Had the tints of the rainbow—red, yellow, and green.

And grottoes, fantastic in hue and in form,
    Were there, as flung up—the wild sport of the storm;
Yet all was so cloudless, so lovely, and calm,
    It seemed but a region of sunshine and balm.

"Here, here shall we dwell in a dream of delight,
    Where the glories of earth and of ocean unite!
Yet, loved son of earth! I must from thee away;
    There are laws which e'en spirits are bound to obey!

"Once more must I visit the chief of my race,
    His sanction to gain ere I meet thy embrace.
In a moment I dive to the chambers beneath:
    One cause can detain me—one only—'tis death!"

They parted in sorrow, with vows true and fond;
    The language of promise had nothing beyond.
His soul all on fire, with anxiety burns:
    The moment is gone—but no maiden returns.

What sounds from the deep meet his terrified ear—
    What accents of rage and of grief does he hear?
What sees he? what change has come over the flood—
    What tinges its green with a jetty of blood?

Can he doubt what the gush of warm blood would explain?
    That she sought the consent of her monarch in vain!
For see all around him, in white foam and froth,
    The waves of the ocean boil up in their wroth!

The palace of crystal has melted in air,
    And the dies of the rainbow no longer are there;
The grottoes with vapour and clouds are o'ercast,
    The sunshine is darkness—the vision has past!

Loud, loud was the call of his serfs for their chief;
    They sought him with accents of wailing and grief:
He heard, and he struggled—a wave to the shore,
    Exhausted and faint, bears O'Sullivan More!

Kenmare, 27th April, 1825.

NOTES

An attempt has been made at throwing into the ballad form one of the many tales told of the O'Sullivan family to the writer, by an old boatman, with whom he was becalmed an entire night in the Kenmare river, on his return from a pilgrimage to the Skellig Rocks.

Grimm relates precisely the same legend of the Elbe maid, who, it appears, in rather an unearthly fashion, used to come to the market at Magdeburg to buy meat. A young butcher fell in love with her, and followed her until he found whence she came and whither she returned. At last he went down into the water with her. They told a fisherman, who assisted them and - waited for them on the bank, that if a wooden trencher with an apple on it should come up through the water, all was well; if not, it was otherwise. Shortly after, a red streak shot up; a proof that the bridegroom had not pleased the kindred of the Elbe maid, and that they had put him to death. Another variation of this legend, and the one alluded to on account of its similarity, relates that the maid went down alone, and her lover remained sitting on the bank to wait her answer. She (dutiful girl) wished to get the consent of her parents to her marriage, or to communicate the affair to her brothers. However, instead of an answer, there only appeared a spot of blood upon the water, a sign that she had been put to death.

Mr. Barry St. Leger's tale of "the Nymph of the Lurley," in his clever work, "Mr. Blount's MSS.," hears a striking resemblance to another tradition related of the O'Sullivan family, and their strange intercourse with the "spirits of the vasty deep;" particularly in the circumstance of the attempt at wounding the mermaid, and the fate of the person making it.

A well known Manx legend relates that a sea maiden once carried off a beautiful youth, of whom she became enamoured, to the Isle of Man, and conjured up a mist around the island to prevent his escape; hence it has sometimes been called the Isle of Mists. Mermaid love is an extremely common fiction, and tales founded on it are abundant, although they contain little variety of incident. In the *Ballades el Chants populaires de la Provence*, lately published, there is a very pretty tale "of *La Fée aux Cheveux Verts*," who entices a fisherman to her palace beneath the sea. The amour, as is generally the case with fairy love, produces unhappy consequences.

The Annals of the Four Masters give us rather a gigantic idea of mermaids, although expressly mentioning the delicacy and beauty of their skin. According to this veritable record (which Irish historians are so fond of quoting as an authority J, Pontoppidan's Norway kraken is not without a fair companion: "A. D. 887. A mermaid of an enormous size was cast on the north-east coast of Scotland by the sea: her height was 195 feet; her hair was 18 feet; her fingers 7 feet; and her nose 7 feet: she was all over as white as a swan."

For an account of Dunkerron the reader is referred to Smith's History of Kerry, p. 88. The castle lies about a mile below the town of Kenmare, on the west side of the river. Its present remains are part of a square keep, and one side of a castellated mansion, which probably adjoined the keep, and was built at a more recent period. The Rev. Mr. Godfrey kindly pointed out to the writer two rudely sculptured stones, which had been removed from Dunkerron castle and placed in the boat-house at Lansdown lodge. One of these bears the following inscription:

> I. H. S. MARIA
> DEO GRATIAS
> • THIS WORK
> WAS MADE THE
> XX OF APRIEL
> 1596: BY OWEN
> OSULIVAN MORE
> • • • DONOGH
> MACCARTY RIEOGH.

The other, the O'Sullivan arms, in which a barbarous attempt to express the figure of a mermaid is evident above the "Manus Sullivanis."

In allusion to the galley which appears on the shield, it may be mentioned that a favourite name of the O'Sullivans is Morty or Murty (correctly written *Muireheartach* or *Muircheardach*), which literally means "expert at sea," or an able navigator. Murrough, a common Christian name of the O'Briens, signifies "the sea hound." Murphy, Murley, &c. have doubtless a marine origin.

Source:
Croker, Thomas Crofton. *Fairy Legends and Traditions of the South of Ireland.* London: John Murray, 1828.

45. The Wonderful Tune

County Kerry, Ireland

MAURICE Connor was the king, and that's no small word, of all the pipers in Munster. He could play jig and planxty without end, and Ollistrum's March, and the Eagle's Whistle, and the Hen's Concert, and odd tunes of every sort and kind. But he knew one, far more surprising than the rest, which had in it the power to set every thing dead or alive dancing.

In what way he learned it is beyond my knowledge, for he was mighty cautious about telling how he came by so wonderful a tune. At the very first note of that tune, the brogues began shaking upon the feet of all who heard it—old or young it mattered not—just as if their brogues had the ague; then the feet began going—going—going from under them, and at last up and away with them, dancing like mad!—whisking here, there, and everywhere, like a straw in a storm—there was no halting while the music lasted!

Not a fair, nor a wedding, nor a patron in the seven parishes round, was counted worth the speaking of with out "blind Maurice and his pipes." His mother, poor woman, used to lead him about from one place to another, just like a dog.

Down through Iveragh—a place that ought to be proud of itself for 'tis Daniel O'Connell's country—Maurice Connor and his mother were taking their rounds. Beyond all other places Iveragh is the place for stormy coast and steep mountains: as proper a spot it is as an in Ireland to get yourself drowned, or your neck broken on the land, should you prefer that. But, notwithstanding, in Ballinskellig bay there is a neat bit of ground, well fitted for diversion, and down from it, towards the water, is a clean smooth piece of strand—the dead image of a calm summer's sea on a moonlight night, with just the curl of the small waves upon it.

Here it was that Maurice's music had brought from all parts a great gathering of the young men and the young women—*O the darlints!*—for 'twas not every day the strand of Trafraska was stirred up by the voice of a bagpipe. The dance began; and as pretty a rinkafadda it was as ever was danced. "Brave music," said every body, "and well done," when Maurice stopped.

"More power to your elbow, Maurice, and a fair wind in the bellows," cried Paddy Dorman, a hump-backed dancing-master, who was there to keep order. "'Tis a pity," said he, "if we'd let the piper run dry after such music; 't would be a disgrace to Iveragh, that didn't come on it since the week of the three Sundays." So, as well became him, for he was always a decent man, says he: "Did you drink, piper?"

"I will, sir," says Maurice, answering the question on the safe side, for you never yet knew piper or schoolmaster who refused his drink.

"What will you drink, Maurice?" says Paddy.

"I'm no ways particular," says Maurice; "I drink any thing, and give God thanks, barring *raw* water: but if 'tis all the same to you, mister Dorman, may be you wouldn't lend me the loan of a glass of whiskey."

"I've no glass, Maurice," said Paddy; "I've only the bottle."

"Let that be no hindrance," answered Maurice; my mouth just holds a glass to the drop; often I've tried it, sure."

So Paddy Dorman trusted him with the bottle—more fool was he; and, to his cost, he found that though Maurice's mouth might not hold more than the glass at one time, yet, owing to the hole in his throat, it took many a filling.

"That was no bad whiskey neither," says Maurice, handing back the empty bottle.

"By the holy frost, then!" says Paddy, "'tis but could comfort there's in that bottle now; and 'tis your word we must take for the strength of the whiskey, for you've left us no sample to judge by:" and to be sure Maurice had not.

Now I need not tell any gentleman or lady with common understanding, that if he or she was to drink an honest bottle of whiskey at one pull, it is not at all the same thing as drinking a bottle of water; and in the whole course of my life, I never knew more than five men who could do so without being overtaken by the liquor. Of these Maurice Connor was not one, though he had a stiff head enough of his own—he was fairly tipsy. Don't think I blame him for it; 'tis often a good man's case; but true is the word that says, "when liquor's in sense is out;" and puff, at a breath, before you could say "Lord, save us!" out he blasted his wonderful tune.

'Twas really then beyond all belief or telling the dancing. Maurice himself could not keep quiet; staggering now on one leg, now on the other, and rolling about like a ship in a cross sea, trying to humour the tune. There was his mother too, moving her old bones as light as the youngest girl of them all: but her dancing, no, nor the dancing of all the rest, is not worthy the speaking about to the work that was going on down upon the strand. Every inch of it covered with all manner of fish jumping and plunging about to the music, and every moment more and more would tumble in out of the water, charmed by the wonderful tune. Crabs of monstrous size spun round and round on one claw with the nimbleness of a dancing-master, and twirled and tossed their other claws about like limbs that did not belong to them. It was a sight surprising to behold. But perhaps you may have heard of father Florence Conry, a Franciscan friar, and a great Irish poet; *bolg an dana*, as they used to call him—a wallet of poems. If you have not, he was as pleasant a man as one would wish to drink with of a hot summer's day; and he has rhymed out all about the dancing fishes so neatly, that it would be a thousand pities not to give you his verses; so here's my hand at an upset of them into English:

> The big seals in motion,
> Like waves of the ocean
>   Or gouty feet prancing,
> Came heading the gay fish,
> Crabs, lobsters, and cray fish,
>   Determined on dancing.
>
> The sweet sounds they follow'd,
> The gasping cod swallow'd;
>   'Twas wonderful, really!
> And turbot and flounder,

'Mid fish that were rounder,
   Just caper'd as gaily.

John-dories came tripping;
Dull hake by their skipping
   To frisk it seem'd given;
Bright mackrel went springing,
Like small rainbows winging
   Their flight up to heaven.

The whiting and haddock
Left salt water paddock
   This dance to be put in:
Where skate with flat faces
Edged out some odd plaices;
   But soles kept their footing.

Sprats and herrings in powers
Of silvery showers
   All number out-number'd.
And great ling so lengthy
Were there in such plenty
   The shore was encumber'd.

The scollop and oyster
Their two shells did roister,
   Like castanets fitting;
While limpets moved clearly,
And rocks very nearly
   With laughter were splitting.

Never was such an ullabulloo in this world, before or since; 'twas as if heaven and earth were coming together; and all out of Maurice Connor's wonderful tune!

In the height of all these doings, what should there be dancing among the outlandish set of fishes but a beautiful young woman—as beautiful as the dawn of day I She had a cocked hat upon her head; from under it her long green hair—just the colour of the sea—fell down behind, without hinderance to her dancing. Her teeth were like rows of pearl; her lips for all the world looked like red coral; and she had an elegant gown, as white as the foam of the wave, with little rows of purple and red sea weeds settled out upon it: for you never yet saw a lady, under the water or over the water, who had not a good notion of dressing herself out.

Up she danced at last to Maurice, who was flinging his feet from under him as fast as hops—for nothing in this world could keep still while that tune of his was going on—and says she to him, chaunting it out with a voice as sweet as honey—

> "I'm a lady of honour
> Who live in the sea;
> Come down, Maurice Connor,
> And be married to me.
> Sliver plates and gold dishes
> You shall have, and shall be
> The king of the fishes,
> When you're married to me."

Drink was strong in Maurice's head, and out he chaunted in return for her great civility. It is not every lady, may be, that would be after making such an offer to a blind piper; therefore 'twas only right in him to give her as good as she gave herself—so says Maurice,

> "I'm obliged to you, madam:
> Off a gold dish or plate,
> If a king, and I had 'em,
> I could dine in great state.
> With your own father's daughter
> I'd be sure to agree;
> But to drink the salt water
> Wouldn't do so with me!"

The lady looked at him quite amazed, and swinging her head from side to side like a great scholar, "Well," says she, "Maurice, if you're not a poet, where is poetry to be found?"

In this way they kept on at it, framing high compliments; one answering the other, and their feet going with the music as fast as their tongues. All the fish kept dancing too: Maurice heard the clatter, and was afraid to stop playing lest it might be displeasing to the fish, and not knowing what so many of them may take it into their heads to do to him if they got vexed.

Well, the lady with the green hair kept on coaxing of Maurice with soft speeches, till at last she overpersuaded him to promise to marry her, and be king over the fishes, great and small. Maurice was well fitted to be their king, if they wanted one that could make them dance; and he surely would drink, barring the salt water, with any fish of them all.

When Maurice's mother saw him, with that unnatural thing in the form of a green-haired lady as his guide, and he and she dancing down together so lovingly: to the water's edge, through the thick of the fishes, she called out after him to stop and come back. "Oh then," says she, "as if I was not widow enough before, there he is going away from me to be married to that scaly woman. And who knows but 'tis grandmother I may be to a hake or a cod—Lord help and pity me, but 'tis a mighty unnatural thing!—and may be 'tis boiling and eating my own grandchild I'll be, with a bit of salt butter, and I not knowing it!—Oh Maurice, Maurice, if there's any love or nature left in you, come back to your own ould mother, who reared you like a decent Christian!"

Then the poor woman began to cry and ullagoane so finely that it would do any one good to hear her.

Maurice was not long getting to the rim of the water; there he kept playing and dancing on as if nothing was the matter, and a great thundering wave coming in towards him' ready to swallow him up alive; but as he could not see it, he did not fear it. His mother it was who saw it plainly through the big tears that were rolling down her cheeks; and though she saw it, and her heart was aching as much as ever mother's heart ached for a son, she kept dancing, dancing, all the time for the bare life of her. Certain it was she could not help it, for Maurice never stopped playing that wonderful tune of his.

He only turned the bothered ear to the sound of his mother's voice, fearing it might put him out in his steps, and all the answer be made back was—

"Whisht with you, mother—sure I'm going to be king over the fishes down in the sea, and for a token of luck, and a sign that I'm alive and well, I'll send you in, every twelvemonth on this day, a piece of burned wood to Trafraska." Maurice had not the power to say a word more, for the strange lady with the green hair seeing the wave just upon them, covered him up with herself in a thing like a cloak with a big hood to it, and the wave curling over twice as high as their heads, burst upon the strand, with a rush and a roar that might be heard as far as Cape Clear.

That day twelvemonth the piece of burned wood came ashore in Trafraska. It was a queer thing for Maurice to think of sending all the way from the bottom of the sea. A gown or a pair of shoes would have been something like a present for his poor mother; but he had said it, and he kept his word. The bit of burned wood regularly came ashore on the appointed day for as good, ay, and better than a hundred years. The day is now forgotten, and may be that is the reason why people say how Maurice Connor has stopped sending the luck-token to his mother. Poor woman, she did not live to get as much as one of them; for what through the loss of Maurice, and the fear of eating her own grandchildren, she died in three weeks after the dance—some say it was the fatigue that killed her, but whichever it was, Mrs. Connor was decently buried with her own people.

Seafaring men have often heard, off the coast of Kerry, on a still night, the sound of music coming up from the water; and some, who have had good ears, could plainly distinguish Maurice Connor's voice singing these words to his pipes:—

> Beautiful shore, with thy spreading strand,

> Thy crystal water, and diamond sand;
> Never would I have parted from thee
> But for the sake of my fair ladie.[1]

NOTES

The wonderful effects of music on brutes, and even inanimate matter, have been the theme of traditions in all ages. Trees and rocks gave ear to the tones of the Orphean lyre; the stones of Thebes ranged themselves in harmony to the strains of Amphion; the dolphin, delighted by the music of Arion, bore him in safety through the seas; even

> "Rude Heiskar's seal through surges dark,
> Will long pursue the minstrel's bark."
> *Lord of the Isles*, c. i. st. 2.

The tales of Germany, and other countries, contain instances of magically endowed tunes. The effect of Oberon's horn is now well known in this country through Weber's opera, and Mr. Sotheby's elegant translation of Wieland's poem.

In Hogg's ballad of the Witch of Fife, the pipe of the "Wee wee man" makes

> "—the troutis laup out of the Leven Loch
> Charmit with the melodye."

And as to "fish out of water" feeling uncomfortable, Irish fish are said occasionally to prefer dry land. For this, if the language of nature be that of truth, we have no less an authority than Mr. Joseph Cooper Walker, the historian of the Irish bards, and a distinguished writer on matters of taste.

"Mr. O'Halloran informs me," says Mr. Walker, "that there is preserved in the Leabher Lecan, or Book of Sligo, a beautiful poem on the storm that arose on the second landing of the Milesians, which is attributed to Amergin. In this poem there appears a boldness of metaphor which a cold critic would despise, because it offends against the rules of Aristotle, though the Stagyrite was not then born: however, *it is the language of Nature!* The author, in order to heighten the horrors of the storm, represents the fish as being so much terrified, that they quit their element for dry land.

The odd tunes mentioned as being known to Maurice Connor are great favourites in Ireland. "The Eagle's Whistle" is a singularly wild

---

[1] This is almost a literal translation of a Rann in the well-known song of Deardra.

strain, which was a march or war-tune of the O'Donoghues, and is not to be met with in print. "The Hens' Concert" has been published in O'Farrell's Companion for the Pipes, and is a melodious imitation of the *tuc-tuc-a-tuc-too* of the barn-door gentry. "Ollistrum's March" may be found in Researches in the South of Ireland, p. 116.

The Rinka fada is a national dance mentioned in a note in the tale of "Master and Man," in the preceding volume. It is said to mean "the long dance," from the Irish words *Rinceadth*, a dance, and *fada*, long. In Ben Jonson's Irish Masque, the words *fading* and *faders* occur; on the former Mr. Gifford observes: "This word, which was the burthen of a popular Irish song, gave name to a dance frequently mentioned by our old dramatists. Both the song and the dance appear to have been of a licentious character, and merit no further elucidation." Notwithstanding the high critical reputation of the late editor of the Quarterly, the writer, in justice to his country, must state his ignorance of any such Irish song as that mentioned by Mr. Gifford; although, from the attention which he has paid to the subject, and his personal intercourse with the peasantry, it could hardly have escaped his acquaintance. He has frequently witnessed the Rinka fada performed, but has never observed the really graceful movements of that dance to partake of licentiousness. The mere explanation, that *Feadán* is the Irish for a pipe or reed, and *Feadánach*, a piper, appears to be all the comment which the passage in "rare Ben" requires. But Mr. Gifford was fond of volunteering incorrect information respecting Ireland: witness his note on "Harper," which occurs in the Masque of the Metamorphosed Gipsies, and where a reference to Simon's work on Coins would have prevented a series of inaccuracies uncalled for by the text.

"When liquor's in, the wit is out,"—a common Irish saying; resembles the old legend still to be seen over the cellar-door of Doddershall Park, Bucks, the venerable seat of colonel Pigott, where it was put up about the time of Elizabeth:

> "Welcome, my friende, drinke with a noble hearte,
> But pet, before you drinke too much, departe;
> For though good drinke will make a coward stout,
> Yet when too much is in the wit is out."

Father Conry's poem respecting the dancing fish is freely translated from the Irish. The concluding verse of the tale, which, it is said, Maurice Connor has been heard singing under the water, is almost a literal translation of a rann from the song of Deardra.

Source:
Croker, Thomas Crofton. *Fairy Legends and Traditions of the South of Ireland.* London: John Murray, 1828.

46. Donald and the Mermaid

County Kerry, Ireland

THEY entered a passage and saw before them, seated on a rock, a woman adjusting her tresses. As soon as she saw them, she was alarmed, and quick as lightning disappeared in the sea. In her haste she forgot her mantle, and Donald instantly seized it and held it in his grasp. "That was the mermaid, or sea nymph about whom we have heard so much," said Donald, "but this is the first time I have ever laid my eyes upon her: although I have been to sea, early and late." Scarcely had he spoken these words and while they were yet beneath the cliff, when the woman returned and demanded her cloak. With this request Donald refused to comply, and the mermaid threatened to send a mighty wave against the cliff that would overwhelm them, and sweep them into the ocean. This threat did not in the least daunt Donald, for he had often heard that a mermaid had no more power after she had parted with her mantle. When the men reached the road she was still following them, and imploring Donald to return the garment, but her cries and supplications did not in the least weaken his resolve to retain it, and he folded it inside his outer cloak. The woman's great distress moved the other men to pity,—pity perhaps not unmingled with fear. Old Donough acted as spokesman and remonstrated with Donald. "It is not lucky for you, Donald," said he, "to keep such a strange thing, and it is not safe or wise for you to bring it into your house, and the mermaid, the poor thing, will drop dead if you keep that mantle."

"Luck or ill luck," replied Donald, "I will not part with the mantle: and as soon as I reach home I will lock it in a trunk." The men were grieved at Donald's strange behavior, but save an exchange of ominous looks they did not venture any further persuasions. When the mermaid understood that there was no prospect of obtaining her garment she regained her composure, and followed Donald meekly to his house, where henceforth she took up her abode. Donald was at this time thirty years of age, and though there were hundreds of good-looking young women of his acquaintance he was yet a bachelor. For a man in his station in life he was the richest man in the barony. As already stated, the mermaid made Donald's home her abode, and there was not in his household any maid so skilful, so deft, or so zealous in the discharge of her duties. She was a beautiful woman and Donald became enamored with her when first he saw her seated on the rock beneath the cliff. The attachment of Donald for the mermaid was discussed far and near, and many predicted the mermaid would take Donald to Tirnanóg, as Niad had taken Ossian a thousand years before.

Donald and the mermaid were married, and there was not in all Kerry a more lovable couple than they. Nor had he any reason to regret his choice, for the mermaid was a good wife and an exemplary mother, and time only enhanced her in his esteem. They had now been married over thirty years, and were blessed with a large, grown up family. The daughters were like the mother, remarkably handsome, and there was not living at that time any woman who approached them for beauty. The sons were tall and stalwart, as they inherited their father's passion for the sea. They were leaders in every manly exercise, and there were not in all Ireland more skilled and fearless seamen. The sons and daughters were a credit to their parents and their happy home was the rendezvous of scholars, bards, poets, and musicians. Everything prospered with this worthy family, and with wealth came the desire for social distinction. To satisfy this desire they purchased a fine residence in the capital city of the province. All arrangements having been completed, the moving day arrived, and moving then was even a more formidable task than now, for the vans of over two hundred years ago were rather primitive and the ideal roads of to-day were then unknown. The family were seated in their coaches ready for the journey when the mother alighted from her coach and returned to the house presumably for something she had forgotten, or perhaps to take a look at the interior of a home in which she had lived so many years and where she had spent the happy days of her youth, where her children had been born, and where she had resided until she arrived at a serene and contented old age. On passing through one of the now almost empty rooms—empty of everything worth moving—she noticed that a large trunk containing miscellaneous old articles had fallen to pieces and the contents were scattered broadcast over the floor. She stooped and picked up what appeared to be an old dust-covered, well-worn garment. And no sooner did she grasp it than she laughed so loudly that her laugh was heard all over the village. If Donald had forgotten the magic mantle, not so had the mermaid. In an instant she regained her former youth and beauty. She no longer cared for husband and children, and swifter than the velocity of March winds she returned joyfully to her beloved Tirnanóg on the blue rim of the Western Ocean.

NOTES

This charming folk-tale was told and taken down forty years ago in New-Irish from the lips of a hedge-schoolmaster, a story-teller who knew Bearla lagair, in an ancient house on a large farm of five hundred acres, half-way between Cork and Killarney. It illustrates well the character of the myths which always have fascinated the Irish common people. Many of these story-tellers not only inherited the legends, but also the language of the old bards, who mystified the peasantry by their artificial learning, and retained it, as do the masons, as a secret tongue.

Source:
Sinclair, A. T. "The Secret Language of Masons and Tinkers." *The Journal of American Folklore*. Vol. 22, No. 86 (Oct.-Dec. 1909). pp. 353-364.

47. White Cow, Red Cow, Black Cow

County Cork, Ireland

LONG ages ago as some fishermen were strolling along the strand at Ballycronen, in the Barony of Imokilly, they observed a mermaid asleep on the water's edge. She was captured and carried to a farmer's house in the immediate vicinity, where she lived imparting instruction and foretelling future events. On the May Eve next succeeding her capture she gave directions that she should be carried back to the strand, and a great concourse of people assembled to witness her departure. She told them to assemble again on the same spot on the following May Eve, as three magical cows would emerge from the ocean, she then plunged into the billows, and was never seen again. On that day twelve months all the inhabitants of Ireland gathered on the cliffs, and about an hour after midday three enchanted cows suddenly emerged from the sea at Imokilly. The first was white; the second red, and the third black. They kept in company for about a mile; then the white cow went northwest towards the county Limerick, the red cow went westward, and passed around the coast of Ireland, the black cow going northeast towards the county Waterford. These roads are still pointed out in many places, and are known as "The White," "The Red," and "The Black Cow's Road."

Source:
Wood-Martin, W[illiam] G[regory]. *Traces of the Elder Faiths of Ireland, Volume 2*. London: Longmans, Green, and Co., 1902. p. 127.

48. Two Legends from County Meath

County Meath, Ireland

I.

A MAN who lived near Lough Sheelin, finding that something was eating his corn every night, sat up to see what it was. After some time, to his astonishment a number of horses came up out of the lake, driven by a most beautiful woman. So impressed was the man by this mermaid's beauty that he seized her in his arms and carried her to his house. Before very long he induced her to marry him, she making the stipulation that she was never to be allowed to see the lake again. For over twenty years they lived most happily together, and had several children. At last one day when the men were haymaking the mother strolled out to look at them and saw the distant lake. Giving a shriek she flew straight to it, and vanished for ever under the water.

II.

A man made a bet that he would go to the bottom of Lough Sheelin and bring up something from it, and one day he jumped in and went down. Below he found a house, which he entered, and saw in it an old woman sitting at a table, beneath which lay a gigantic eel coiled up. The old woman inquired, "In God's name what do you want down here?"

"Something to show that I was at the bottom of the lake."

"Then take that copper skillet and get away as quick as you can."

This he did, and swimming to the edge just got out of the water before the great eel, which was in pursuit of him, ploughed up the ground with its head exactly where he had landed.

NOTES

These short legends were communicated to me by letter by E. Crofton Rotherham, Esq.

Source:
Abercromby, John. "Notes and Queries: Legends from Co. Meath." *The Folk-Lore Journal*. Vol. 7, No. 4 (1889). pp. 313-322.

49. The Captured Mermaid

Isle of Man

> A mermaid from the water rose,
> A woman most fair and lovely.—Sinclair.

WALDRON was surprised to find that the Manx actually believed in mermaids, and he gave several stories that they told him about them, as follows:—"During the time that Oliver Cromwell usurped the Government of England, few ships resorted to this Island, and that uninterruption and solitude of the sea gave the mermen and mermaids (who are enemies to any company but those of their own species) frequent opportunities of visiting the shore, where, in moonlight nights, they have been seen to sit, combing their heads and playing with each other; but as soon as they perceived anybody coming near them, jumped into the water, and were out of sight immediately. Some people, who lived near the coast, having observed their behaviour, spread large nets made of small but very strong cords upon the ground, and watched at a convenient distance for their approach. The night they had laid this snare but one happened to come, who was no sooner sat down than those who held the strings of the net drew them with a sudden jerk, and enclosed their prize beyond all possibility of escaping. On opening the net, and examining their captive, by the largeness of her breasts and the beauty of her complexion, it was found to be a female. Nothing could be more lovely, more exactly formed in all parts above the waist, resembling a complete young woman, but below that all fish with fins and a huge spreading tail. She was carried to a house, and used very tenderly, nothing but liberty being denied. But though they set before her the best provision the place afforded, she would not be prevailed on to eat or drink, neither could they get a word from her, tho' they knew these creatures were not without the gift of speech, having heard them talk to each other, when sitting regaling themselves on the seaside. They kept her in this manner three days, but perceiving she began to look very ill with fasting, and fearing some calamity would befall the Island if they should keep her till she died, they agreed to let her return to the element she liked best, and the third night set open their door, which, as soon as she beheld, she raised herself from the place where she was then lying, and glided, with incredible swiftness, on her tail to the seaside. They followed at a distance, and saw her plunge into the water, where she was met by a great number of her own species, one of whom asked what she had observed among the people of the earth,—"Nothing very wonderful," answered she, "but that they are so very ignorant as to throw away the water they have boiled eggs in."

NOTES

The Mermaid, too, was well-known. She had no special name in Manx, being called simply *Ben-varry*, or "Woman of the sea," and had the same form, half fish, half woman, as represented in the tales of other countries. She was generally of an affectionate and gentle disposition, though terrible when angered, and she was greatly given to falling in love with young men. Of her mate, the Merman, *Dooiney-varrey*, "Man of the sea," or *Phollinagh*, as he is variously called, less is known.

Source:
Moore, A[rthur] W[illiam]. *The Folk-lore of the Isle of Man: Being an Account of Its Myths, Legends, Superstitions, Customs, & Proverbs.* London: D. Nutt, 1891.

50. The Mermaid's Courtship

Isle of Man

> Come to our rich and starry caves,
> Our home amid the ocean waves;
> Our coral caves are walled around
> With richest gems in ocean found,
> And crystal mirrors, clear and bright,
> Reflecting all in magic light.

A VERY beautiful mermaid became so much enamoured of a young man who used to tend his sheep upon the rocks, that she would frequently sit down by him, bring him pieces of coral, fine pearls, and what were yet greater curiosities, and of infinitely more value, had they fallen into the hands of a person who knew their worth, shells of various forms and figures, and so glorious in their colour and shine, that they even dazzled the eye that looked upon them. Her presents were accompanied with smiles, pattings of the cheek, and all the marks of a most sincere and tender passion. One day throwing her arms more than ordinarily eagerly about him, he began to be frightened that she had a design to draw him into the sea, and struggled till he disengaged himself, and then ran a good many paces from her; which behaviour she resented so highly, it seems, that she took up a stone, and after throwing it at him, glided into her more proper element, and was never seen on land again. But the poor youth, though but slightly hit with the stone, felt from that moment so excessive a pain in his bowels, that the cry was never out of his mouth for seven days, at the end of which he died.—Waldron.

Source:

Moore, A[rthur] W[illiam]. *The Folk-lore of the Isle of Man: Being an Account of Its Myths, Legends, Superstitions, Customs, & Proverbs.* London: D. Nutt, 1891.

51. The Mermaid's Revenge

Isle of Man

THERE is a tradition that a mermaid becoming enamoured of a young man of extraordinary beauty, took an opportunity of meeting him one day as he walked on the shore, and opened her passion to him, but was received with coldness occasioned by his horror and surprise at her appearance. This, however, was so misconstrued by the sea lady, that, in revenge for his treatment of her, she punished the whole Island, by covering it with mist; so that all who attempted to carry on any commerce with it, either never arrived at it, but wandered up and down the sea, or were on a sudden wrecked upon its cliffs, till the incantatory spell or pishag, as the Manks say, was broken by the fishermen stranded there, by whom notice was given to the people of their country, who sent ships in order to make a further discovery. On their landing, they had a fierce encounter with the little people, and having got the better of them, possessed themselves of Castle Rushen, and by degrees of the whole Island.—(Collins in a note to his "Ode to Liberty.")

Source:

Moore, A[rthur] W[illiam]. *The Folk-lore of the Isle of Man: Being an Account of Its Myths, Legends, Superstitions, Customs, & Proverbs.* London: D. Nutt, 1891.

52. Dwellings under the Sea[1]

Isle of Man

OF THE dwellings of these creatures under the sea, and of the treasure they have accumulated there, many tales are told. The notion of a land under the waves is very widely spread, and common to many nations. Manxmen formerly asserted that a splendid city, with many towers and gilded minarets, once stood near Langness, on a spot now covered by the sea, which, in peculiar states of the atmosphere, might have been occasionally seen in all its former magnificence.

Waldron gives the following marvellous account of dwellings under the sea, stocked with treasure, which he was assured had been attested by a whole ship's crew, and happened in the memory of some then living, but at which, nevertheless, "he was exceedingly surprised":—

There was, about some forty or fifty years since (1676), a project set on foot for searching for treasures in the sea. Vessels were got ready, and machines made of glass, and cased with a thick, tough leather, to let the person down who was to dive for the wealth. One of these ships happening to sail near to the Isle of Man, and having heard that great persons had formerly taken refuge there, imagined there could not be a more likely part of the ocean to afford the gain they were in search of, than this. They, therefore, let down the machine, and in it the person who had undertaken to go on this expedition; they let him down by a vast length of rope, but he still plucking it, which was the sign for those above to increase the quantity, they continued to do so, till they knew he must be descended an infinite number of fathoms. In fine, he gave the signal so long, that at last they found themselves out of cord, their whole stock being too little for his capacious inquisition. A very skilful mathematician being on board, said that he knew by the proportion of the line which was let down, he must have descended from the surface of the waters more than twice the number of leagues that the moon is computed to be distant from the earth. But having, as I said, no more cord, they were obliged to turn the wheel, which, by degrees, brought him up again; at their opening the machine, and taking him out, he appeared very much troubled, that his journey had so soon been stopped, at a period, telling them, that could he have gone a little further he should have brought discoveries well worth the search. It is not to be supposed but everybody

---

[1] Another rendition of this story is given in this collection as "The City under Sea."~*HAH*

was impatient to be informed of what kind they were, and being all gathered about him on the main deck, as soon as he had recruited himself with a hearty swill of brandy, he began to relate in this manner:—

After I had passed the region of fishes, I descended into a pure element—clear as the air in the serenest and most unclouded day, through which, as I passed, I saw the bottom of the watery world, paved with coral and a shining kind of pebbles, which glittered like the sunbeams reflected on a glass. I longed to tread the delightful paths, and never felt more exquisite delight, than when the machine I was enclosed in grazed upon it. On looking through the little windows of my prison, I saw large streets and squares on every side, ornamented with huge pyramids of crystal, not inferior in brightness to the finest diamonds; and the most beautiful buildings—not of stone, nor brick, but of mother of pearl, and embossed in various figures with shells of all colours. The passage which led to one of these magnificent apartments being open, I endeavoured with my whole strength to move my enclosure towards it, which I did, though with great difficulty, and very slowly. At last, however, I got entrance into a very spacious room, in the midst of which stood a large amber table, with several chairs round the same. The floor of it was composed of rough diamonds, topazes, emeralds, rubies, and pearls. Here I doubted not but to make my voyage as profitable as it was pleasant, for could I have brought with me but a few of these, they would have been of more value than all we could hope for in a thousand wrecks; but they were so closely wedged in, and so strongly cemented by time, that they were not to be unfastened. I saw several chains, carcanets, and rings, of all manner of precious stones, finely cut, and set after our manner, which, I suppose, had been the prize of the winds and waves. These were hanging loosely on the jasper walls, by strings made of rushes, which I might easily have taken down; but as I had edged myself within half a foot of them, I was unfortunately drawn back, through your want of line. In my return I met several comely mermen and beautiful mermaids, the inhabitants of this blissful realm, swiftly descending towards it, but they seemed frighted at my appearance, and glided at a distance from me, taking me, no doubt, for some monstrous and new created species.

Here he ended his account, but grew so melancholy, and so much enamoured of those regions he had visited, that he quite lost all relish for earthly pleasures, till continual pinings deprived him of his life; having no hope of ever descending there again, all design of prosecuting the diving project being soon after laid aside.

Source:
Moore, A[rthur] W[illiam]. *The Folk-lore of the Isle of Man: Being an Account of Its Myths, Legends, Superstitions, Customs, & Proverbs*. London: D. Nutt, 1891.

53. The Mermaid of Gob Ny Ooyl

Isle of Man

ONCE on a time there lived at the bottom end of Cornah gill a family of the name of Sayle, and the Mermaid who had her haunt up Bulgham way was a friend to them. They were always in luck's way and never seemed to be short of anything. Sure enough they were full of thrift, and to fill in odds of spare time they made lobster pots from the osier that grew around in plenty, and they always found a ready market. They kept a cow and a few sheep, just to give work to the women in the long winter nights, but their living was mostly got by the sea.

It was well known that Sayle had a strong liking for apples, and that he would often bring some with him out in the boat, but when he got well up in years he would be leaving a lot of the boat-work for the boys, and then the luck began to get less, and many a time one of them had to take a gun to keep something in the pot. Then the bigger ones took to the herrings. One, Evan, however, had to stay about to keep things going, and it happened that one day, after he had the creels set, just at Bulgham, that he pulled the boat in and went up the brow after eggs. On coming back to the boat he heard some one calling to him, and, looking round, he saw a fine-looking woman sitting on the edge of a rock.

"And how's your father?" said she. "It's seldom he's coming this way now."

Young Sayle was a bit frightened at first, but seeing a pleasant look on her face, he took courage and told her how things were at home. Then, saying she hoped to see him again, she slipped into the water and disappeared.

On getting home he told what had taken place, and the father, his face lighting up, declared:

"There will be luck on the house yet."

And he said:

"Take some apples with you the next time you go up that way, an' we'll see."

The very next time the young chap went, he took some apples with him, and when he got to the place where he had seen the beautiful woman, he went, as usual, on the hunt among the rocks. Then he heard sweet singing, and when he turned round what should he see but the Mermaid leaning over the boat and smiling pleasantly. She took an apple and began to eat and chant:

The luck o' the sea be with you, but don't forgetful be
Of bringing some sweet lan' eggs for the children of the sea.

From that time he was nearly living on the water until, at last, he was taken to task for being idle. Then he made up his mind to go sailing in foreign parts. The Mermaid was in great distress, so to please her, he went and planted an apple tree on the brow above her haunt, telling her that when he would be far away this tree would grow land-eggs which, when they would be sweet and ready for eating, would come of themselves to the water for her. And, sure enough, the luck of the family remained, though the boy was gone.

She seemed to bear up well for a long time and would often be seen sitting on the rocks in the evening, singing sad songs, and casting longing glances up to the apple tree above. She kept very shy of everyone coming her way, and at last, finding the apples slow in coming, made up her mind to go in search of young Sayle, hoping the apples would be ready for taking when they would come back.

But neither, of them ever came back, though for many a long year the apple tree bore fruit and marked the little creek where the Mermaid used to live.

Source:
Morrison, Sophia. *Manx Fairy Tales*. London: David Nutt, 1911.

54. Teeval, Princess of the Ocean

Isle of Man

IN THE old days Culain, the smith of the gods, was living in the Isle of Mann. It was the time when Conchubar was at the court of the King of Ulster, and had nothing but the sword in his hand. He was a fine handsome young man, and he had made up his mind to make himself a king. So he went one day to the Druid of Clogher to ask him what he had best do.

"Go thy way," said the Druid, "to the Isle of Mann. There thou wilt find the great smith Culain. Get him to make thee a sword and a spear and a shield, and with these thou shalt win the kingdom of Ulster."

Conchubar went away, and hired a boat and put out to sea. He landed in Mann and made straight for Culain's smithy. It was night when he got there, and the red glow of the furnace shone out into the dark. He could hear from inside the smithy the roar of the bellows and the clanging of the hammer on the anvil. When he came near, a great dog, as large as a calf, began to bay and to growl like thunder, and brought his master out.

"Who art thou, young man?" said he.

"Oh Culain!" cried Conchubar, "it is from the Druid of Clogher that I come, and he bade me ask thee to make me a sword and a spear and a shield, for only with weapons of thy making can I win the Kingdom of Ulster."

Culain's face grew black at first, but after he had gazed for a while at Conchubar, he saw that he had the look about him of one who would go far, and he said:

"It shall be done for thee, but thou must wait, for the work is long."

So Culain began to make the weapons, and Conchubar waited in the island.

Early one brave morning in May when the sun had just risen over Cronk-yn-Irree-Laa, he was walking on the strand, wondering to himself how much longer Culain would be making his weapons and thinking it was full time for him to return. The tide was going out, and the sun was shining on the wet sand. Suddenly he saw something flashing at the edge of the waves a few paces from him. He ran up to it and, behold, it was the most beautiful woman he had ever put sight on, fast asleep. Her hair was golden, like the gorse in bloom; her skin whiter than the foam of the sea, her lips red as the coral, and her cheeks rosy like the little clouds that were flying before the face of the rising sun. The fringe of her dress of many coloured seaweeds rose and fell with the ebb and flow of the waves. Pearls gleamed on her neck and arms. Conchubar stood and looked on her. He knew that she was a Mermaid and that as soon as she awoke she would slip back into the ocean and be lost to him. So he bound her fast with his girdle.

Then she awoke and opened her, eyes, which were blue as the sea, and when she saw that she was bound, she cried out with terror, "Loose me, man, loose me!"

Conchubar did not answer, so she said again, "Loose me, I beg thee!" in a voice as sweet as the music of Hom Mooar, the Fairy Fiddler.

By this time Conchubar was feeling that he would give all he had to keep her. He answered, trembling, "Woman, my heart, who art thou?"

"I am Teeval, Princess of the Ocean," said she. "Set me free, I pray thee."

"But if I set thee free," said Conchubar, "thou wilt leave me."

"I cannot stay with thee, Conchubar," she cried; "set me free, and I will give thee a precious gift."

"I will loose thee," answered Conchubar. "It is not for the gift, but because I cannot resist thee."

He unfastened the girdle from her and she said, "My gift to thee is this: Go now to Culain who is making thy shield, and tell him that Teeval, Princess of the Ocean, bids him to put her figure on the shield and round it to grave her name. Then thou shalt wear it always in battle, and when thou shalt look on my face and call my name, thy enemies' strength shall go from them and shall come into thee and thy men." When she had said this, she waved her white arm to Conchubar and plunged into the waves. He looked sadly for a long time at the spot where she had disappeared, and then walked slowly to the forge of Culain, and gave him the message.

Culain finished the mighty shield as the Princess had said, and forged also for Conchubar a golden-hilted magic sword, and a spear set with precious stones. Then Conchubar, in his crimson mantle and white gold-embroidered tunic, and armed with his great shield and his mighty weapons, went back to Ireland.

All that the Princess of the Ocean had said came true. When he went into battle he looked at the beautiful face in his shield and cried "Help, Teeval."

Then he felt strength come into him like the strength of a giant, and he cut his enemies down like grass. Before long he was famous all over Ireland for his great deeds, and in the end he became King of Ulster. Then he invited Culain to come and live in his kingdom, and gave him the plain of Murthemny to dwell in.

But he never again saw the lovely Mermaid.

Source:
Morrison, Sophia. *Manx Fairy Tales*. London: David Nutt, 1911.

55. The City under Sea

Isle of Man

NOW where Langness runs its long nose into the sea, and on a place now always covered by the waves, there was once a fine city with many towers and gilded domes. Great ships went sailing from its port to all parts of the world, and round it were well-grassed lands with cattle and sheep. Even now sailors sometimes see it through the clear, deep waters, and hear dimly the bleating of sheep, the barking of dogs, and the muffled chiming of bells "Nane, jees, three, kiare, queig." But no man can walk its streets.

For once upon a time, in the days when there were giants in the Isle of Mann, Finn Mac Cool had his home near this city. He lived at the Sound to keep his eye on Erinn and to watch the sea. But he was very seldom in Mann, and wherever he was he was always doing some mischief, so that his enemies were many. One, day he was in such a hurry to reach his home that he jumped from Erinn and landed in the island on the rocks above the Sound. He came down with such force that he left his footmarks in the hard stone, and the place has been called ever since, Slieu ynnyd ny Cassyn, or the Mountain of the place of the Feet. His first act when he reached home was to get in a red rage with the people of the city close by; his next act was to turn them all into blocks of granite. In his passion he struck the ground so hard with his club that he made a great dent in it—the waves rushed into the deep hollow and the roaring sea drowned the din of the city. Its towers and domes were covered by the green water; its streets and market-place, its harbour and its crowded quays, disappeared from sight. And. there it lies to this day.

But there is a strange story told of a man that went down to it more than two hundred years ago. A ship was searching for sunken treasure in those parts and this man was let down to the bottom of the sea in a kind of ancient diving bell. He was to pull the rope when he wished to be let down further. He pulled and pulled till the men on the ship knew that he was as deep down in the sea as the moon is high up in the sky; then there was no more rope and they had to draw him up again.

When on deck he told them that as if he could have gone further he would have made the most wonderful discoveries. They begged him to tell them what he had seen, and when he had drunk a cup of wine he told his story.

First he had passed through the waters in which the fishes live; then he came into the clear and peaceful region where storms never come, and saw the bottom of the World-under-Sea shining with coral and bright pebbles. When the diving bell rested on the ground he looked through its little windows and saw great streets decorated with pillars of crystal glittering like diamonds, and beautiful buildings made of mother-of-pearl, with shells of every colour set in it. He longed to go into one of these fine houses, but he could not leave his diving bell, or he would have been drowned. He managed to move it close to the entrance of a great hall, with a floor of pearls and rubies and all sorts of precious stones, and with a table and chair of amber. The walls were of jasper, and strings of lovely jewels were hanging upon them. The man wished to carry some away with him, but he could not reach them—the rope was at an end. As he rose up again towards the air he met many handsome Mermen and beautiful Mermaids, but they were afraid of him, and swam away as fast as they could.

That was the end of the man's story. After that he grew so sad with longing to go back to the World-under-Sea and stay there for ever, that he cared for nothing on earth, and soon died of grief.

Source:
Morrison, Sophia. *Manx Fairy Tales*. London: David Nutt, 1911.

56. Mermaids and Mermen in Wales

Wales

IT IS said that these fabulous beings frequented the sea-coasts of Wales to the great danger of the inhabitants. The description of the Welsh mermaid was just as it is all over the world; she is depicted as being above the waist a most lovely young woman, whilst below she is like a fish with fins and spreading tail. Both mermen and mermaids were fond, it is said, of combing their long hair, and the siren-like song of the latter was thought to be so seductive as to entice men to destruction. It was believed that beautiful mermaids fell in love with comely young men and even induced them to enter their abodes in the depth of the sea.

I heard the following tale, I believe in Carnarvonshire, but I have no notes of it, and write from memory.

A man captured a mermaid, and took her home to his house, but she did nothing but beg and beg to be allowed to return to the sea, but notwithstanding her entreaties her captor kept her safe enough in a room, and fastened the door so that she could not escape. She lingered several days, pitifully beseeching the man to release her, and then she died. But ever after that event a curse seemed to rest upon the man, for he went from bad to worse, and died miserably poor.

It was always considered most unlucky to do anything unkind to these beings. Fear acted as a powerful incentive, in days of old, to generous conduct. For it was formerly believed that vengeance ever overtook the cruel.

An Isle of Man legend, related by Waldron, in his account of the Isle of Man, and reproduced by Croker, vol. i., p. 56, states, that some persons captured a mermaid, and carried her to a house and treated her tenderly, but she refused meat and drink, neither would she speak, when addressed, though they knew these creatures could speak. Seeing that she began to look ill, and fearing some great calamity would befall the island if she died, they opened the door, after three days, and she glided swiftly to the sea side. Her keeper followed at a distance and saw her plunge into the sea, where she was met by a great number of her own species, one of whom asked her what she had seen among those on land, to which she answered, "Nothing, but that they are so ignorant as to throw away the very water they boil their eggs in."

Source:
Owen, Elias. *Welsh Folk-Lore: A Collection of the Folk-Tales and*

Legends of North Wales. Oswestry & Wrexham:Woodall, Minshall and Co., 1887.

57. Water Spirits in Shakespeare: Nymphs, Naiads, Nereids, Mermaids

England

NYMPHS, Naiads, Nereids, Mermaids: These form a class of supernatural beings which cannot well be explained, though they have formed the stock-in-trade of poets for many ages, as most of these poets held different views respecting them. They are described in classical dictionaries as goddesses and as inferior divinities. All are alluded to by Shakespeare, but they have little to do with genuine folklore, although from one point of view they are in touch with Ariel. There are nymphs of the hills, forests, and caves, of springs, streams, and rivers; and Ariel sings of "Sea-nymphs [who] hourly ring his knell" (*Tempest*, i. 2. 402). The sprite Iris, when she sings "You nymphs call'd naiads of the wandering brooks" (*Tempest*, iv. 128), is quite in accord with classical usage.

Nereids were nymphs of the sea, daughters of Nereus. They are described as attendant on Cleopatra:

> "Her gentlewomen, like the Nereids,
> So many mermaids."
> *Antony and Cleo*. ii. 2. 211.

The nereids were not mermaids, for a piece of statuary in the Naples Museum shows one borne along by a triton, and she has legs like an ordinary woman.

The sea captain tells Viola of her brother Sebastian:

> "Where, like Arion on the dolphin's back,
> I saw him hold acquaintance with the waves
> So long as I could see."
> *Twelfth Night*, i. 2. 15.

This refers to the story of Arion, the Greek musician, who was saved from drowning by dolphins drawn to him by his sweet singing. One of them, taking him on his back, carried him safe to land.

In *Midsumnmer Night's Dream* (i. 2. 15) Oberon says:

> "Since once I sat upon a promontory,
> And heard a mermaid, on a dolphin's back,
> Uttering such dulcet and harmonious breath
> That the rude sea grew civil at her song."

A mermaid might have worked upon the feelings of a dolphin by the sweetness of her voice, siren as she was, but one would suppose a mermaid could take care of herself on the sea without the help of a dolphin.

Both these references seem to have been suggested by Gascoigne's *Princely Pleasures at Kenilworth* in 1575. A triton, in likeness of a mermaid, came towards the Queen to declare the woeful distress of the Lady of the Lake; also Proteus appeared sitting on a dolphin's back, and then assumed the character of Arion.

Source:
Wheatley, Henry B. "The Folklore of Shakespeare." *Folklore*. Vol. 27, No. 4 (Dec. 31, 1916). pp. 378-407.

58. Sabrina Fair
by John Milton

England

Sabrina is a water nymph who appears in John Milton's **Comus: A Masque** *(1634). In the play, she is summoned by a helpful spirit to release a virtuous lady held captive in a chair. The following is excerpted from the masque and includes the summoning of Sabrina and her short appearance in the play. The "Song for Sabrina" has often been excerpted from the piece.*

Sabrina—also known as Sabre, Severn, Hafren, Habrena—first appears in Geoffrey of Monmouth's **Historia Regum Britanniae** *(c. 1136). A princess who drowned in the river Severn, she later became a goddess associated with the river.*

SPIRIT: There is a gentle Nymph not far from hence,
  That with moist curb sways the smooth Severn stream:
  Sabrina is her name: a virgin pure;
  Whilom she was the daughter of Locrine,
  That had the sceptre from his father Brute.
  She, guiltless damsel, flying the mad pursuit

Of her enraged stepdame, Guendolen,
Commended her fair innocence to the flood
That stayed her flight with his cross-flowing course.
The water-Nymphs, that in the bottom played,
Held up their pearled wrists, and took her in,
Bearing her straight to aged Nereus' hall;
Who, piteous of her woes, reared her lank head,
And gave her to his daughters to imbathe
In nectared lavers strewed with asphodil,
And through the porch and inlet of each sense
Dropt in ambrosial oils, till she revived.
And underwent a quick immortal change,
Made Goddess of the river. Still she retains
Her maiden gentleness, and oft at eve
Visits the herds along with twilight meadows,
Helping all urchin blasts, and ill-luck signs
That the shrewd meddling Elf delights to make,
Which she with pretious vialed liquors heals:
For which the Shepherds, at their festivals,
Carol her goodness loud in rustic lays,
And throw sweet garland wreaths into her stream,
Of pansies, pinks, and gaudy daffadils.
And, as the old Swain said, she can unlock
The clasping charm, and thaw the numbing spell,
If she be right invoked in warbled song;
For maidenhood she loves, and will be swift
To aid a virgin, such as was herself,
In hard-besetting need. This will I try,
And add the power of some adjuring verse.

Song for Sabrina

Sabrina fair,
    Listen where thou art sitting
Under the glassy, cool, translucent wave,
    In twisted braids of lilies knitting
The loose train of thy amber-dropping hair;
    Listen for dear honour's sake,
    Goddess of the silver lake,
      Listen and save!

Listen, and appear to us,
In name of great Oceanus,
By the earth-shaking Neptune's mace
And Tethys' grave majestic pace;
By hoary Nereus' wrinkled look,

And the Carpathian wizard's hook;
By scaly Triton's winding shell,
And old soothsaying Glaucus' spell;
By Leucothea's lovely hands,
And her son that rules the strands;
By Thetis' tinsel-slippered feet,
And the songs of Sirens sweet;
By dead Parthenope's dear tomb,
And fair Ligea's golden comb,
Wherewith she sits on diamond rocks
Sleeking her soft alluring locks;
By all the nymphs that nightly dance
Upon thy streams with wily glance;
Rise, rise, and heave thy rosy head
From thy coral-paven bed,
And bridle in thy headlong wave,
Till thou our summons answered have.
Listen and save!

Sabrina rises, attended by Water—nymphs, and sings.

SABRINA: By the rushy-fringed bank,
   Where grows the willow and the oiser dank,
     My sliding chariot stays,
   Thick set with agate, and the azurn sheen
     Of turkish blue, and emerald green,
     That in the channel strays:
   Whilst from off the waters fleet
   Thus I set my printless feet
   O'er the cowslip's velvet head,
     That bends not as I tread.
   Gentle swain, at thy request
     I am here!

SPIRIT: Goddess dear,
   We implore thy powerful hand
   To undo the charmed band
   Of true virgin here distressed
   Through the force and through the wile
   Of unblessed enchanter vile.

SABRINA: Shepherd, 'tis my office best
   To help insnared Chastity,
   Brightest Lady, look on me.
   Thus I sprinkle on thy breast
   Drops that from my fountain pure

I have kept of pretious cure;
Thrice upon thy finger's tip,
Thrice upon thy rubied lip:
Next this marble venomed seat,
Smeared with gums of glutinous heat,
I touch with chaste palms moist and cold.
Now the spell hath lost his hold;
And I must haste ere morning hour
To wait in Amphitrite's bower.

Sabrina descends, and the Lady rises out of her seat.

Source:
Milton, John. "Comus." *The Poetical Works of John Milton, Volume II.* Glasgow: Robert Malcolm, 1825.

59. The Mermaid: A Ballad

England

TO YON fause stream that, near the sea,
   Hides monie a shelve and plum,[1]
And rives wi' fearfu' din the stanes,
   A witless knicht did come.

The day shines clear—far in he's gane
   Whar shells are silver bricht,
Fishes war louping a' around,
   And sparkling to the licht.

Whan, as he lav'd, sounds cam sae sweet
   Frae ilka rock an' tree;
The brief[2] was out, 'twas him it doom'd
   The mermaid's face to see.[3]

---

[1] *Plum*, a deep hole in the river.

[2] *Brief*, literally a writ, here a sentence. In the account of Gourie's Conspiracy, appended to Gall's Gabions, it is used in the sense of "irresistible spell."

[3] *The Mermaid's face to see*. It appears that Mermaids could injure, even

Frae 'neath a rock, sune, sune she rase,
    And statelie on she swam,
Stopt in the midst, and beck'd[1] and sang
    To him to stretch his hand.

Gowden glist the yellow links,
    That round her neck she'd twine;
Her een war o' the skyie blue,
    Her lips did mock the wine.

The smile upon her bonnie cheek
    Was sweeter than the bee;
Her voice excelled the birdie's sang
    Upon the birchen tree.

Sae couthie, couthie[2] did she look,
    And meiklo had she fleech'd;[3]
Out shot[4] his hand, alas! alas!
    Fast in the swirl[5] he screech'd.

The mermaid leuch,[6] her brief was gane,
    And kelpie's blast was blawing,
Fu' low she duked, ne'er raise again,
    For deep, deep was the fawing.

Aboon the stream his wraith was seen,
    Warlocks tirl'd lang at gloamin';
That e'en was coarse, the blast blew hoarse,
    Ere lang the waves war foamin'.

NOTES

This beautiful piece of poetry was recovered from the recitation of a lady, who heard it sung by the servants in her father's family, about fifty years ago. It is believed, notwithstanding some modern expressions, to be very ancient. The lady mentions that it was very popular on the Carrick coast of Ayrshire. It bears a striking resemblance to a fragment written by Mr.

---

by a look; and on this circumstance turns the ballad of Clerk Colvin.

[1] *Beck'd*, beckoned.
[2] *Couthie*, kindly.
[3] *Fleech'd*, flattered.
[4] *Shot*, stretched.
[5] *Swirl*, whirlpool.
[6] *Leuch*, laughed.

Pinkerton, and to he found in his collection.

There is another piece to be found in Jamieson's Collection of Popular Ballads and Songs, called the Waterwoman, a translation from the German of Goethe, exactly similar in the story, and nearly so in description with the Mermaid. We do not know at what period the Waterwoman first made its appearance, but should be inclined to suppose, from internal evidence, that it was not imitated from "Pinkerton's fragment," which, among other things, wants the catastrophe.

Source:

Allan, Robert. "The Mermaid." *Beauties of the Scottish Poets; or, Harp of Renfrewshire: A Collection of Songs and Other Poetical Pieces.* William Motherwell, editor. Glasgow: William Turnbull, 1821.

60. The Mermaid of Martin Meer

Lancashire, England

"Now the dancing sunbeams play
O'er the green and glassy sea:
Come with me, and we will go
Where the rocks of coral grow."

LITTLE needs to be said by way of introduction or explanation of the following tale. Martin Meer is now in process of cultivation; the plough and the harrow leave more enduring furrows on its bosom. It is a fact, curious enough in connection with our story, that some years ago, in digging and draining, a canoe was found here. How far this may confirm our tradition, we leave the reader to determine. It is scarcely two miles from Southport; and the botanist, as well as the entomologist, would find themselves amply repaid by a visit.

Martin Meer, the scene of the following story, we have described in our first series of Traditions, where Sir Tarquin, a carnivorous giant, is slain by Sir Lancelot of the Lake. These circumstances, and more of the like purport on this subject, we therefore omit, as being too trite and familiar to bear repetition. We do not suppose the reader to be quite so familiar with the names and fortunes of Captain Harrington and Sir Ralph Molyneux, though they had the good fortune to be born eleven hundred years later, and to have seen the world, in consequence, eleven hundred years older—we wish we could say wiser and better tempered, less selfish and less disposed to return hard knocks, and to be corrupted with evil communications. But man is the same in all ages. The external habits and usages of society change his mode of action—clothe the person and passions in a different garb; but their form and substance, like the frame they inhabit, are unchanged, and will continue until this great mass of intelligence, this mischievous compound of good and evil, this round rolling earth, shall cease to swing through time and space—a mighty pendulum, whose last stroke shall announce the end of time, the beginning of eternity!

Our story gets on indifferently the while; but a willing steed is none the worse for halting. Harrington and his friend Sir Ralph were spruce and well-caparisoned cavaliers, living often about court towards the latter end of Charles the Second's reign. What should now require their presence in these extreme regions of the earth, far from society and civilisation, it is not our business to inquire. It sufficeth for our story that they were here, mounted, and proceeding at a shuffling trot along the flat, bare, sandy region we have described.

"How sweetly and silently that round sun sinks into the water!" said Harrington.

"But doubtless," returned his companion, "if he were fire, as thou sayest, the liquid would not bear his approach so meekly; why, it would boil if he were but chin-deep in yon great seething-pot."

"Thou art quicker at a jest than a moral, Molyneux," said the other and graver personage; "thou canst not even let the elements escape thy gibes. I marvel how far we are from our cousin Ireland's at Lydiate. My fears mislead me, or we have missed our way. This flat bosom of desolation hath no vantage-ground whence we may discern our path; and we have been winding about this interminable lake these two hours."

"Without so much as a blade of grass or a tree to say 'Good neighbour' to," said Molyneux, interrupting his companion's audible reverie. "Crows and horses must fare sumptuously in these parts."

"This lake, I verily think, follows us; or we are stuck to its side like a lady's bauble."

"And no living thing to say 'Good-bye,' were it fish or woman."

"Or mermaid, which is both." Scarcely were the words uttered when Harrington pointed to the water.

"Something dark comes upon that burning track left on the surface by the sun's chariot wheels."

"A fishmonger's skiff belike," said Sir Ralph.

They plunged through the deep sandy drifts towards the brink, hastening to greet the first appearance of life which they had found in this region of solitude. At a distance they saw a female floating securely, and apparently without effort, upon the rippling current. Her form was raised half-way above the water, and her long hair hung far below her shoulders. This she threw back at times from her forehead, smoothing it down with great dexterity. She seemed to glide on slowly, and without support; yet the distance prevented any very minute observation.

"A bold swimmer, o' my troth!" said Molyneux; "her body tapers to a fish's tail, no doubt, or my senses have lost their use."

Harrington was silent, looking thoughtful and mysterious.

"I'll speak to yon sea-wench."

"For mercy's sake, hold thy tongue. If, as I suspect—and there be such things, 'tis said, in God's creation—thou wilt"——

But the tongue of this errant knight would not be stayed; and his loud musical voice swept over the waters, evidently attracting her notice, and for the first time. She drew back her dark hair, gazing on them for a moment, when she suddenly disappeared. Harrington was sure she had sunk; but a jutting peninsula of sand was near enough to have deceived him, especially through the twilight, which now drew on rapidly.

"And thou hast spoken to her!" said he gravely; "then be the answer thine!"

"A woman's answer were easier parried than a sword-thrust, methinks; and that I have hitherto escaped."

"Let us be gone speedily. I like not yon angry star spying out our path through these wilds."

"Thou didst use to laugh at my superstitions; but thine own, I guess, are too chary to be meddled with."

"Laugh at me an' thou wilt," said Harrington: "when Master Lilly cast my horoscope he bade me ever to eschew travel when Mars comes to his southing, conjunct with the Pleiades, at midnight—the hour of my birth. Last night, as I looked out from where I lay at Preston, methought the red warrior shot his spear athwart their soft scintillating light; and as I gazed, his ray seemed to ride half-way across the heavens. Again he is rising yonder."

"And his meridian will happen at midnight?"

"Even so," replied Harrington.

"Then gallop on. I'd rather make my supper with the fair dames at Lydiate than in a mermaid's hall."

But their progress was a work of no slight difficulty, and even danger. Occasionally plunging to the knees in a deep bog, then wading to the girth in a hillock of sand and prickly bent grass (the Arundo arenaria, so plentiful on these coasts), the horses were scarcely able to keep their footing—yet were they still urged on. Every step was expected to bring them within sight of some habitation.

"What is yonder glimmer to the left?" said Molyneux. "If it be that hideous water again, it is verily pursuing us. I think I shall be afraid of water as long as I live."

"As sure as Mahomet was a liar, and the Pope has excommunicated him from Paradise, 'tis the same still, torpid, dead-like sea we ought to have long since passed."

"Then have our demonstrations been in a circle, in place of a right line, and we are fairly on our way back again."

Sure enough there was the same broad, still surface of the Meer, though on the contrary side, mocking day's last glimmer in the west. The bewildered travellers came to a full pause. They took counsel together while they rested their beasts and their spur-rowels; but the result was by no means satisfactory. One by one came out the glorious throng above them, until the heavens grew light with living hosts, and the stars seemed to pierce the sight, so vivid was their brightness.

"Yonder is a light, thank Heaven!" cried Harrington.

"And it is approaching, thank your stars!" said his companion. "I durst not stir to meet it, through these perilous paths, if our night's lodging depended on it."

The bearer of this welcome discovery was a kind-hearted fisherman, who carried a blazing splinter of antediluvian firewood dug from the neighbouring bog; a useful substitute for more expensive materials.

It appeared they were at a considerable distance from the right path, or indeed from any path that could be travelled with safety, except by daylight. He invited them to a lodging in a lone hut on the borders of the lake, where he and his wife subsisted by eel-catching and other precarious pursuits. The simplicity and openness of his manner disarmed suspicion. The offer was accepted, and the benighted heroes found themselves breathing fish-odours and turf-smoke for the night, under a shed of the humblest construction. His family consisted of a wife and one child only; but the strangers preferred a bed by the turf-embers to the couch that was kindly offered them.

The cabin was built of the most simple and homely materials. The walls were pebble-stones from the sea-beach, cemented with clay. The roof-tree was the wreck of some unfortunate vessel stranded on the coast. The whole was thatched with star-grass or sea-reed, blackened with smoke and moisture.

"You are but scantily peopled hereabouts," said Harrington, for lack of other converse.

"Why, ay," returned the peasant; "but it matters nought; our living is mostly on the water."

"And it might be with more chance of company than on shore; we saw a woman swimming or diving there not long ago."

"Have ye seen her?" inquired both man and dame with great alacrity.

"Seen whom?" returned the guest.

"The Meer-woman, as we call her."

"We saw a being, but of what nature we are ignorant, float and disappear as suddenly as though she were an inhabitant of yon world of waters."

"Thank mercy! Then she will be here anon."

Curiosity was roused, though it failed in procuring the desired intelligence. She might be half-woman half-fish for aught they knew. She always came from the water, and was very kind to them and the babe.

Such was the sum of the information; yet when they spoke of the child there was evidently a sort of mystery and alarm, calculated to awaken suspicion.

Harrington looked on the infant. It was on the woman's lap asleep, smiling as it lay; and an image of more perfect loveliness and repose he had never beheld. It might be about a twelvemonth old; but its dress did not correspond with the squalid poverty by which it was surrounded.

"Surely this poor innocent has not been stolen," thought he. The child threw its little hands towards him as it awoke; and he could have wept. Its short feeble wail had smitten him to the heart.

Suddenly they heard a low murmuring noise at the window.

"She is there," said the woman; "but she likes not the presence of strangers. Get thee out to her, Martin, and persuade her to come in."

The man was absent for a short time. When he entered, his face displayed as much astonishment as it was possible to cram into a countenance so vacant.

"She says our lives were just now in danger; and that the child's enemies are again in search; but she has put them on the wrong scent. We must not tarry here any longer; we must remove, and that speedily. But she would fain be told what is your business in these parts, if ye are so disposed."

"Why truly," said Harrington, "our names and occupation need little secrecy. We are idlers at present, and having kindred in the neighbourhood, are on our way to the Irelands at Lydiate, as we before told thee. Verily, there is but little of either favour or profit to be had about court now-a-days. Nought better than to loiter in hall and bower, and fling our swords in a lady's lap. But why does the woman ask? Hath she some warning to us? or is there already a spy upon our track?"

"I know not," said Martin; "but she seems mightily afeard o' the child."

"If she will entrust the babe to our care," said Harrington, after a long pause, "I will protect it. The shield of the Harringtons shall be its safeguard."

The fisherman went out with this message; and on his return it was agreed that, as greater safety would be the result, the child should immediately be given to Harrington. A solemn pledge was required by the unseen visitant that the trust should be surrendered whenever, and by whomsoever, demanded; likewise a vow of inviolable secrecy was exacted from the parties that were present. Harrington drew a signet from his finger; whoever returned it was to receive back the child. He saw not the mysterious being to whom it was sent; but the idea of the Meer-woman, the lake, and the untold mysteries beneath its quiet bosom, came vividly and painfully on his recollection.

Long after she had departed, the strange events of the evening kept them awake. Inquiries were now answered without hesitation. Harrington learned that the "Meer-woman's" first appearance was on a cold wintry day, a few months before. She did not crave protection from the dwellers in the hut, but seemed rather to command it. Leaving the infant with them, and promising to return shortly, she seemed to vanish upon the lake, or rather, she seemed to glide away on its surface so swiftly that she soon disappeared. Since then she had visited them thrice, supplying them with a little money and other necessaries; but they durst not question her, she looked so strange and forbidding.

In the morning they were conducted to Lydiate by the fisherman, who also carried the babe. Here they told a pitiable story of their having found the infant exposed, the evening before, by some unfeeling mother; and, strange to say, the truth was never divulged until the time arrived when Harrington should render up his trust.

Years passed on. Harrington saw the pretty foundling expand through every successive stage from infancy to childhood—lovelier as each year unfolded some hidden grace, and the bloom brightened as it grew. He had married in the interval, but was yet childless. His lady was passionately fond of her charge, and Grace Harrington was the pet and darling of the family. No wonder their love to the little stranger was growing deeper, and was gradually acquiring a stronger hold on their affections. But Harrington remembered his vow: it haunted him like a spectre. It seemed as though written with a sunbeam on his memory; but the finger of death pointed to its accomplishment. It will not be fulfilled without blood, was the foreboding that assailed him. His lady knew not of his grief, ignorant happily of its existence, and of its source.

Their mansion stood on a rising ground but a few miles distant from the lake. He thus seemed to hover instinctively on its precincts; though, in observance of his vow, he refrained from visiting that lonely hut, or inquiring about its inhabitants. Its broad smooth bosom was ever in his sight; and when the sun went down upon its wide brim his emotion was difficult to conceal.

One soft, clear evening, he sat enjoying the calm atmosphere, with his lady and their child. The sun was nigh setting, and the lake glowed like molten fire at his approach.

"'Tis said a mermaid haunts yon water," said Mrs Harrington; "I have heard many marvellous tales of her, a few years ago. Strange enough, last night I dreamed she took away our little girl, and plunged with her into the water. But she never returned."

"How I should like to see a mermaid!" said the playful girl. "Nurse says they are beautiful ladies with long hair and green eyes. But"—and she looked beseechingly towards them—"we are always forbidden to ramble towards the Meer."

"Harrington, the night wind makes you shiver. You are ill!"

"No, my love. But—this cold air comes wondrous keen across my bosom," said he, looking wistfully on the child, who, scarcely knowing why, threw her little arms about his neck, and wept.

"My dream, I fear, hath strange omens in it," said the lady

thoughtfully.

The same red star shot fiercely up from the dusky horizon; the same bright beam was on the wave; and the mysterious incidents of the fisherman's hut came like a track of fire across Harrington's memory.

"Yonder is that strange woman again that has troubled us about the house these three days," said Mrs Harrington, looking out from the balcony; "we forbade her yesterday. She comes hither with no good intent."

Harrington looked over the balustrade. A female stood beside a pillar, gazing intently towards him. Her eye caught his own; it was as if a basilisk had smitten him. Trembling, yet fascinated, he could not turn away his glance; a smile passed on her dark-red visage—a grin of joy at the discovery.

"Surely," thought he, "'tis not the being who claims my child!" But the woman drew something from her hand, which, at that distance, Harrington recognised as his pledge. His lady saw not the signal; without speaking, he obeyed. Hastening down-stairs, a private audience confirmed her demand, which the miserable Harrington durst not refuse.

Two days he was mostly in private. Business with the steward was the ostensible motive. He had sent an urgent message to his friend Molyneux, who, on the third day, arrived at H——, where they spent many hours in close consultation. The following morning Grace came running in after breakfast. She flung her arms about his neck.

"Let me not leave you to-day," she sobbed aloud.

"Why, my love?" said Harrington, strangely disturbed at the request.

"I do not know!" replied the child, pouting.

"To-day I ride out with Sir Ralph to the Meer, and as thou hast often wished—because it was forbidden, I guess—thou shalt ride with us a short distance; I will toss thee on before me, and away we'll gallop—like the Prince of Trebizond on the fairy horse."

"And shall we see the mermaid?" said the little maiden quickly, as though her mind had been running on the subject.

"I wish the old nurse would not put such foolery in the girl's head," said Mrs Harrington impatiently. "There be no mermaids now, my love."

"What! not the mermaid of Martin Meer?" inquired the child, seemingly disappointed.

Harrington left the room, promising to return shortly.

The morning was dull, but the afternoon broke out calm and bright. Grace was all impatience for the ride; and Rosalind, the favourite mare, looked more beautiful than ever in her eyes. She bounded down the terrace at the first sound of the horses' feet, leaving Mrs Harrington to follow.

The cavaliers were already mounted, but the child suddenly drew back.

"Come, my love," said Harrington, stretching out his hand; "look how your pretty Rosalind bends her neck to receive you."

Seeing her terror, Mrs Harrington soothed these apprehensions, and fear was soon forgotten amid the pleasures she anticipated.

"You are back by sunset, Harrington?"

"Fear not, I shall return," replied he; and away sprang the pawing beasts down the avenue. The lady lingered until they were out of sight. Some unaccountable oppression weighed down her spirits; she sought her chamber, and a heavy sob threw open the channel which hitherto had restrained her tears.

They took the nearest path towards the Meer, losing sight of it as they advanced into the low flat sands, scarcely above its level. When again it opened into view its wide waveless surface lay before them, reposing in all the sublimity of loneliness and silence. The rapture of the child was excessive. She surveyed with delight its broad unruffled bosom, giving back the brightness and glory of that heaven to which it looked; to her it seemed another sky and another world, pure and spotless as the imagination that created it.

They entered the fisherman's hut; but it was deserted. Years had probably elapsed since the last occupation. Half-burnt turf and bog-wood lay on the hearth; but the walls were crumbling down with damp and decay.

The two friends were evidently disappointed. At times they looked out anxiously, but in vain, as it might seem; for they again sat down, silent and depressed, upon a turf-heap by the window, while the child ran playing and gambolling towards the beach.

Harrington sat with his back to the window, when suddenly the low murmuring noise he had heard on his former visit was repeated. He turned pale.

"Thou art not alone; and where is the child?" or words to this purport were uttered in a whisper. He started aside; the sound, as he thought, was close to his ear. Molyneux heard it too.

"Shall I depart?" said he, cautiously; "I will take care to keep within call."

"Nay," said his friend, whispering in his ear, "thou must ride out of sight and sound too, I am afraid, or we shall not accomplish our plans for the child's safety. Depart with the attendants; I fear not the woman. Say to my lady I will return anon."

With some reluctance Sir Ralph went his way homewards, and Harrington was left to accomplish these designs without assistance.

Immediately he walked out towards the shore; but he saw nothing of the child, and his heart misgave him. He called her; but the sound died with its own echo upon the waters. The timid rabbit fled to its burrow, and the sea-gull rose from her gorge, screaming away heavily to her mate; but the voice of his child returned no more!

Almost driven to frenzy, he ran along the margin of the lake to a considerable distance, returning after a fruitless search to the hut, where he threw himself on the ground. In the agony of his spirit he lay with his face to the earth, as if to hide his anguish as he wept.

How long he remained was a matter of uncertainty. On a sudden, instantaneously with the rush that aroused him, he felt his arms pinioned, and that by no timid or feeble hand. At the same moment a bandage was thrown over his eyes, and he found himself borne away swiftly into a boat. He listened for some time to the rapid stroke of the oars. Not a word was spoken from which he could ascertain the meaning of this outrage. To his questions no reply was vouchsafed, and in the end he forbore inquiry—the mind wearied into apathy by excitement and its consequent exhaustion.

The boat again touched the shore, and he was carried out. The roar of the sea had for some time been rapidly growing louder as they neared the land. He was now borne along over hillocks of loose sand to the sea-beach, when he felt himself fairly launched upon the high seas. He heard the whistling of the cordage, the wide sail flap to the wind, with the groan of the blast as it rushed into the swelling canvas; then he felt the billows prancing under him, and the foam and spray from their huge necks as they swept by. It was not long ere he heard the sails lowered; and presently they were brought up alongside a vessel of no ordinary bulk. Harrington was conducted with little ceremony into the cabin; the bandage was removed from his eyes, and he found himself in the presence of a weather-beaten tar, who was sitting by a table, on which lay a cutlass and a pair of richly-embossed pistols.

"We have had a long tug to bring thee to," said the captain; "but we always grapple with the enemy in the long run. If thou hast aught to say why sentence of death should not pass on thee, ay, and be executed straightway too—say on. What! not a shot in thy locker? Then may all such land-sharks perish, say I, as thus I signify thy doom." He examined his pistols with great nicety as he spoke. Harrington was dumb with amazement, whilst his enemy surveyed him with a desperate and determined glance. At length he stammered forth—

"I am ignorant of thy meaning; much less can I shape my defence. Who art thou?"

The other replied, in a daring and reckless tone—

"I am the Free Rover, of whom thou hast doubtless heard. My good vessel and her gallant crew ne'er slackened a sky-raker in the chase, nor backed a mainsail astern of the enemy. But pirate as I am—hunted and driven forth like the prowling wolf, without the common rights and usages of my fellow men—I have yet their feelings. I had a child! Thy fell, unpitying purpose, remorseless monster, hath made me childless! But thou hast robbed the lioness of her whelp, and thou art in her gripe!"

"As my hope is to escape thy fangs, I am innocent of the crime."

"Maybe thou knowest not the mischief thou hast inflicted; but thy guilt and my bereavement are not the less. My child was ailing; we were off this coast, when we sent her ashore secretly until our return. A fisherman and his wife, to whom our messenger entrusted the babe, were driven forth by thee one bitter night without a shelter. The child perished; and its mother chides my tardy revenge."

"'Tis a falsehood!" cried Harrington, "told to cover some mischievous design. The child, if it be thine, was given to my care—by whom I know not. I have nurtured her kindly; not three hours ago, as I take it, she was in yonder hut; but she has been decoyed from me; and I am here thy prisoner, and without the means of clearing myself from this false and malicious charge."

The captain smiled incredulously.

"Thou art lord of yonder soil, I own; but thou shouldest have listened to the cry of the helpless. I have here a witness who will prove thy story false—the messenger herself. Call hither Oneida," said he, speaking to the attendants. But this personage could not be found.

"She has gone ashore in her canoe," said the pirate; "and the men never question her. She will return ere mid-watch. Prepare: thou showedst no mercy, and I have sworn!"

Harrington was hurried to a little square apartment, which an iron grating sufficiently indicated to be the state prison. The vessel lay at anchor; the intricate soundings on that dangerous coast rendered her perfectly safe from attack, even if she had been discovered. He watched the stars rising out, calm and silently, from the deep: "Ere yon glorious orb is on the zenith," thought he, "I may be—what?" He shrank from the conclusion. "Surely the wretch will not dare to execute his audacious threat?" He again caught that red and angry star gleaming portentously on him. It seemed to be his evil genius; its malignant eye appeared to follow out his track, to haunt him, and to beset his path continually with suffering and danger. He stood by the narrow grating, feverish and apprehensive; again he heard that low murmuring voice which he too painfully recognised. The mysterious being of the lake stood before him.

"White man"—she spoke in a strange and uncouth accent;—"the tree bows to the wing of the tempest—the roots look upward—the wind sighs past its withered trunk—the song of the warbler is heard no more from its branches, and the place of its habitation is desolate. Thine enemies have prevailed. I did it not to compass thine hurt: I knew not till now thou wert in their power; and I cannot prevent the sacrifice."

"Restore the child, and I am safe," said Harrington, trembling in his soul's agony at every point; "or withdraw thy false, thine accursed accusations."

"Thou knowest not my wrongs and my revenge! Thou seest the arrow, but not the poison that is upon it. The maiden, whose race numbers a thousand warriors, returns not to her father's tribe ere she wring out the heart's life-blood from her destroyer. Death were happiness to the torments I inflict on him and the woman who hath supplanted me. And yet they think Oneida loves them—bends like the bulrush when the wind blows upon her, and rises only when he departs. What! give back the child? She hath but taken my husband and my bed; as soon might ye tear the prey from the starved hunter. This night will I remove their child from them—to depart, when a few moons are gone—it may be to dwell again with my tribe in the wigwam and the forest."

"But I have not wronged thee!"

"Thou art of their detested race. Yet would I not kill thee."

"Help me to escape."

"Escape!" said this untamed savage, with a laugh which went with a shudder to his heart. "As soon might the deer dart from the hunter's rifle as thou from the cruel pirate who has pronounced thy death! I could tell thee such deeds of him and these bloody men as would freeze thy bosom, though it were wide and deep as the lakes of my country. Yet I loved him once! He came a prisoner to my father's hut. I have spilled my best blood for his escape. I have borne him where the white man's feet never trod—through forests, where aught but the Indian or the wild beast would have perished. I left my country and my kin—the graves of my fathers—and how hath he requited me? He gave the ring of peace to the red woman; but when he saw another and a fairer one of thy race, she became his wife; and from that hour Oneida's love was hate!—and I have waited and not complained, for my revenge was sure! And shall I now bind the healing leaf upon the wound?—draw the arrow from the flesh of mine enemies? Thou must die! for my revenge is sweet."

"I will denounce thee to him, fiend! I will reveal"——

"He will not believe thee. His eye and ear are sealed. He would stake his life on my fidelity. He knows not of the change."

"But he will discover it, monster, when thou art gone. He will track thee to the verge of this green earth and the salt sea, and thou shall not escape."

With a yell of unutterable scorn she cried—

"He may track the wild bee to its nest, and the eagle to his eyrie, but he discerns not one footprint of Oneida's path!"

The pangs of death seemed to be upon him. He read his doom in the kindling eye and almost demoniac looks of the being who addressed him. She seemed like some attendant demon waiting to receive his spirit. His brain grew dizzy. Death would have been welcome in comparison with the horrors of its anticipation. He would have caught her; but she glided from his grasp, and he was again left in that den of loneliness and misery. How long he knew not; his first returning recollection was the sound of bolts and the rude voices of his jailers.

In this extremity the remembrance of that Being in whom, and from whom, are all power and mercy, flashed on his brain like a burst of hope—like a sunbeam on the dark ocean of despair.

"God of my fathers, hear!" escaped from his lips in that appalling moment. His soul was calmed by the appeal. Vain was the help of man, but he felt as if supported and surrounded by the arm of Omnipotence, while silently, and with a firm step, he followed his conductors.

One dim light only was burning above. Some half-dozen of the crew stood armed on the quarter-deck behind their chief; their hard, forbidding faces looked without emotion upon this scene of unpitying, deliberate murder.

To some question from the pirate Harrington replied by accusing the Indian woman of treachery.

"As soon yonder star, which at midnight marks our meridian, would prove untrue in its course."

Harrington shuddered at this ominous reference.

"I cannot prove mine innocence," said he; "but I take yon orb to witness that I never wronged you or yours. The child is in her keeping."

"Call her hither, if she be returned," said the captain, "and see if he dare repeat this in her presence. He thinks to haul in our canvas until the enemy are under weigh, and then, Yoh ho, boys, for the rescue. But we shall be dancing over the bright Solway ere the morning watch, and thy carcase in the de'il's locker."

"If not for mine, for your own safety!"

"My safety! and what care I, though ten thousand teeth were grinning at me, through as many port-holes. My will alone bounds my power. Who shall question my sentence, which is death?"

He gnashed his teeth as he went on. "And your halls shall be too hot to hold your well-fed drones. Thy hearth, proud man, shall be desolate. I'll lay waste thy domain. Thy race, root and branch, will I extinguish; for thou hast made me childless!"

The messenger returned with the intelligence that Oneida was not in the ship.

"On shore again, the — —! If I were to bind her with the main-chains, and an anchor at each leg, she would escape me to go ashore. No heed; we will just settle the affair without her, and he shall drop quietly into a grave ready made, and older than Adam. I would we had some more of his kin; they should swing from the bowsprit, like sharks and porpoises, who devour even when they have had enough, and waste what they can't devour."

"Thou wilt not murder me thus, defenceless, and in cold blood."

"My child was more helpless, and had not injured thee! Ye give no quarter to the prowling beast, and yet, like me, he only robs and murders to preserve his life. How far is it from midnight?"

"Five minutes, and yon star comes to his southing," said the person he addressed.

"Then prepare; that moment marks thy death!"

The men looked significantly towards their rifles.

"Nay," cried this bloodthirsty freebooter, "my arm alone shall avenge my child."

He drew a pistol from his belt.

"Yonder is Oneida," sang out the man at the main-top; "she is within a cable's length."

"Heed her not. When the bell strikes, I have sworn thou shalt die!"

A pause ensued—a few brief moments in the lapse of time, but an age in the records of thought. Not a breath relieved the horror and intensity of that silence. The plash of a light oar was heard;—a boat touched the vessel. The bell struck.

"Once!" shouted the fierce mariner, and he raised his pistol with the sharp click of preparation.

"Twice!"

The bell boomed again.

"Thrice!"

"Hold!" cried a female, rushing between the executioner and the condemned: But the warning was too late;—the ball had sped, though not to its mark. Oneida was the victim. She fell, with a faint scream, bleeding on the deck. But Harrington was close locked in the arms of his little Grace. She had flown to him for protection, sobbing with joy.

The pirate seemed horror-struck at the deed. He raised Oneida, unloosing his neckcloth to staunch the wound.

"The Great Spirit calls me:" she spoke with great exertion: "the green woods, the streams, land of my forefathers. Oh! I come!" She raised herself suddenly with great energy, looking towards Harrington, who yet knelt, guarded and pinioned—the child still clinging to him.

"White man, I have wronged thee, and I am the sacrifice. Murderer, behold thy child!" She raised her eyes suddenly towards the pirate, who shook his head, supposing that her senses grew confused.

"It was for thy rescue!" again she addressed Harrington. "The Great Spirit appeared to me: he bade me restore what I had taken away, and I should be with the warriors and the chiefs who have died in battle. They hunt in forests from which the red-deer flies not, and fish in rivers that are never dry. But my bones shall not rest with my fathers!—I come. Lake of the woods, farewell!"

She threw one look of reproach on her destroyer, and the spirit of Oneida had departed.

The pirate stood speechless and bewildered. He looked on the child—a ray of recollection seemed to pass over his visage. Its expression was softened; and this man of outlawry and blood became gentle. The savage grew tame. The common sympathies of his nature, so long dried up, burst forth, and the wide deep flood of feeling and affection rolled on with it like a torrent, gathering strength by its own accumulation.

Years after, in a secluded cottage by the mansion of the Harringtons, dwelt an old man and his daughter. She soothed the declining hours of his sojourn. His errors and his crimes—and they were many and aggravated—were not unrepented of. She watched his last breath; and the richest lady of that land was "The Pirate's Daughter."

Source:

Roby, John. *Traditions of Lancashire*. Vol. II. Fifth Edition. London: George Routledge and Sons, 1872.

61. Morva or Morveth (Sea-Daughters)

Cornwall, England

> "You dwell not on land, but in the flood,
> Which would not with me agree."
> —*Duke Magnus and the Mermaid.*—SMALAND

THE parish of this name is situated on the north-west coast of Cornwall,—the parish of St Just being on its western borders, and that of Zennor on the east, between it and St Ives. The Cornish historian Tonkin says, "*Morva* signifies Locus Maritimus, a place near the sea, as this parish is. The name is sometimes written *Morveth*, implying much the same sense."

The similarity of this name to "Morgan," *sea-women*, and "Morverch," *sea-daughters*, which Mr Keightley has shown us is applied to the mermaids of the Breton ballads, is not a little curious. There are several stories current in this parish of ladies seen on the rocks, of *ladies going off from the shore to peculiar isolated rocks at special seasons, and of ladies sitting weeping and wailing on the shore*. Mr Blight, in his "Week at the Land's End," speaking of the church in the adjoining parish, Zennor, which still remains in nearly its primitive condition, whereas Morva church is a modern structure, says—"Some of the bench ends were carved; on one is a strange figure of a *mermaid*, which to many might seem out of character in a church." (Mr Blight gives a drawing of this bench end.) This is followed by a quotation bearing the initials R. S. H., which, it is presumed, are those of the Rev. R. S. Hawker, of Morwenstow:—

"The fishermen who were the ancestors of the Church, came from the Galilean waters to haul for men. We, born to God at the font, are children of the water. Therefore, all the early symbolism of the Church was of and from the sea. The carvure of the early arches was taken from the sea and its creatures. Fish, dolphins, mermen, and mermaids abound in the early types, transferred to wood and stone."

Surely the poet of "the Western Shore" might have explained the fact of the figures of mermaids being carved on the bench ends of some of the old churches with less difficulty, had he remembered that nearly all the churches on the coast of Cornwall were built by and for fishermen, to whom the superstitions of mermen and mermaidens had the familiarity of a creed.

The intimate connection between the inhabitants of Brittany, of

Cornwall, and of Wales, would appear to lead to the conclusion that the Breton word *Morverch*, or mermaid, had much to do with the name of this parish, Morva,—of Morvel, near Liskeard,—and probably of Morwenstow, of which the vicar, Mr Hawker, writes—"My glebe occupies a position of wild and singular beauty. Its western boundary is the sea, skirted by tall and tremendous cliffs, and near their brink, with the exquisite taste of ecclesiastical antiquity, is placed the church. The original and proper designation of the parish is *Morwen*-stow—that is, Morwenna's Stow, or station; but it has been corrupted by recent usage, like many other local names."

Source:
Hunt, Robert. *Popular Romances of the West of England: The Drolls, Traditions, and Superstitions of Old Cornwall*. 3rd edition. London: Chatto and Windus, 1903.

62. Merrymaids and Merrymen

Cornwall, England

THE "merry-maids" of the Cornish fishermen and sailors possess the well-recognised features of the mermaid. The Breton ballad, quoted by Mr Keightley, relating to the Morgan (sea-women) and the Morverch (sea-daughters), peculiarly adapts itself to the Cornish merry-maid.

"Fisher, hast thou seen the mermaid combing her hair, yellow as gold, by the noontide sun, at the edge of the water?"

"I have seen the fair mermaid; I have also heard her singing her songs plaintive as the waves."

The Irish legends make us acquainted with the amours of men with those sea-sirens. We learn that the Merrows, or Moruachs, came occasionally from the sea, and interested themselves in the affairs of man. Amongst the fragments which have been gathered, here a pebble and there a pebble, along the Western coast, will be found similar narratives.

The sirens of the Aegean Sea—probably the parents of the medieval mermaid—possess in a pre-eminent degree the beauty and the falsehood of all the race. Like all other things, even those mythical creations take colour from that they work in, like the dyer's hand. The Italian mermaid is the true creature of the romance of the sunny South; while the lady of our own southern seas, although she possesses much in common with her Mediterranean sister, has less poetry, but more human sympathy. The following stories, read in connection with those given by Mr Keightley and by Mr Croker, will show this.[1]

When, five-and-thirty years since, I spent several nights in a fisherman's cottage on a south-western coast, I was treated to many a "long yarn" respecting mermaids seen by the father and his sons in the southern ocean. The appearance of those creatures on our own shores, they said, was rare; but still they knew they had been seen. From them I learned of more than one family who have received mysterious powers from the sea-nymphs; and I have since heard that members of those families still live, and that they intimate to their credulous friends their firm belief that this power, which they say has been transmitted to them, was derived, by some one of their ancestors, from merman or mermaiden.

Usually those creatures are associated with some catastrophe; but they are now and then spoken of as the benefactors of man.

One word more. The story of "The Mermaid's Vengeance" has been produced from three versions of evidently the same legend, which differed in many respects one from the other, yet agreeing in the main with each other. The first I heard at the Lizard, or rather at Coverach; the second in Sennen Cove, near the Land's End; the third at Perranzabaloe. I have preferred the last locality, as being peculiarly fitted for the home of a mermaid story, and because the old man who told the tale there was far more graphic in his incidents; and these were strung more closely together than either of the other stories.

The following extract from a letter from an esteemed correspondent shows the existence of a belief in those fabled creations of the ocean amongst an extensive class of the labouring population of Cornwall. There is so much that is characteristic in my correspondent's letter that it is worth preserving as supporting the evidence of the existing belief:—

"I had the chance of seeing what many of our natives firmly believed to be that family. Some fourteen years ago I found myself, with about fifty emigrants in the Gulf of St Lawrence, on beard the old tub *Resolution*, Captain Davies, commander. We were shrouded in a fog so thick that you might cut it like a cheese, almost all the way from the Banks to Anticosti. One morning, soon after sunrise, when near that island, the fog as thick as night overhead, at times would rise and fall on the shore like the tantalising stage curtain. All at once there was a clear opening right through the dense clouds which rested on the water, that gave us a glimpse of the shore, with the rocks covered with what to us

---

[1] See "The Fairy Family: a Series of Ballads and Metrical Tales Illustrating the Fairy Mythology of Europe," Longman, 1857; "The Fairy Mythology, Illustrative of the Romance and Superstitions of Various Countries," by Thomas Keightley; and "Irish Fairy Legends," by Crofton Croker.

appeared very strange creatures. In a minute, the hue and cry from stem to stern, among all the cousin Johnnys, was 'What are they, you? What are they, you!' Somebody gave the word mermaids. Old men, women, and children, that hadn't been out of their bunks for weeks, tore on deck to see the mermaids, when, alas! the curtain dropped, or rather closed, and the fair were lost to sight, but to memory dear; for, all the way to Quebec, those not lucky enough to see the sight bothered the others out of their lives to know how they looked, and if we saw the comb and glass in their hands. The captain might as well save his breath as tell them that the creatures they saw on the rocks were seals, walruses, and sea-calves. 'Not yet, Captain dear, you won't come that over me at all; no, not by a long chalk! no, not at all, I can tell'e! I know there are mermaids in the sea; have heard many say so who have sees them too! but as for sea-calves, I ain't such a calf nor donkey neither as to believe ut. There may be a few of what we call soils (seals) for all I know; perhaps so, but the rest were flier-maidens.' No doubt, centuries hence, this story of the mermaidens will be handed down with many additions, in the log-huts of the Western States."

Source:
Hunt, Robert. *Popular Romances of the West of England: The Drolls, Traditions, and Superstitions of Old Cornwall*. 3rd edition. London: Chatto and Windus, 1903.

63. The Mermaid of Padstow

Cornwall, England

THE port of Padstow has a good natural harbour, so far as rocky area goes, but it is so choked up with drifting sands as to be nearly useless. A peasant recently thus explained the cause. He told how "it was once deep water for the largest vessel, and under the care of a *merry-maid*—as he called her; but one day, as she was sporting on the surface, a fellow with a gun shot at her. "She dived for a moment; but re-appearing, raised her right arm, and vowed that henceforth the harbour should be desolate."

"And," added the old man, "it always will be so. We have had commissions, and I know not what, about converting this place into a harbour of refuge. A harbour of refuge would be a great blessing, but not all the Government commissions in the world could keep the sand out, or make the harbour deep enough to swim a frigate, unless the parsons can find out the way to take up the merry-maid's curse."

Another tale refers the choking up of this harbour to the bad spirit Tregeagle.

Source:

Hunt, Robert. *Popular Romances of the West of England: The Drolls, Traditions, and Superstitions of Old Cornwall*. 3rd edition. London: Chatto and Windus, 1903.

64. The Mermaid of Padstow by Richard Garnett

England

IT IS long Tom Yeo of the town of Padstow,
    And he is a ne'er-do-weel:
"Ho, mates," cries he, "rejoice with me,
    For I have shot a seal."

Nay, Tom, by the mass thou art but an ass,
    No seal bestains this foam;
But the long wave rolls up a Mermaid's glass
    And a young Mermaiden's comb.

The sun has set, the night-clouds throng,
    The sea is steely grey.
They hear the dying Mermaid's song
    Peal from the outer bay.

"A curse with you go, ye men of Padstow!
    Ye shall not thrive or win,
Ye have seen the last ship from your haven slip,
    And the last ship enter in.

"For this deed I devote you to dwell without boat
    By the skirt of the oarèd blue,
And ever be passed by sail and by mast,
    And none with an errand for you."

And scarce had she spoke when the black storm broke
    With thunder and levin's might:

Three days did it blow, and none in Padstow
    Could tell the day from night.

Joy! the far thunder mutters soft,
    The wild clouds whirl o'erhead,
And from a ragged rift aloft
    A shaft of light is sped.

Now ho for him that waits to send
    The storm-bound bark to sea!
And ho for them that hither bend
    To crowd our busy quay!

Hath Ocean, think ye then, not heard
    His dying child deplore?
Are not his sandy deeps upstirred,
    And thrust against the shore?

Doth not a mighty ramp of sand
    Beleaguer all the bay,
Mocking the strength of mortal hand
    To pierce or sweep away?

The white-winged traders, all about,
    Fare o'er that bar to win:
But this one cries, I cannot out,
    And that, I may not in.

For thy dire woe, forlorn Padstow,
    What remedy may be?
Not all the brine of thy sad eyne
    Will float thy ships to sea.

The sighs that from thy seamen pass
    Might set a fleet a-sail,
And the faces that look in the Mermaid's glass
    Are as long as the Mermaid's tail.

Source:
Garnett, Richard. *Poems*. London: Elkin Mathews & John Lane, 1893.

65. The Mermaid's Rock

Cornwall, England

TO THE westward of the beautiful Cove of Lemorna is a rock which has through all time borne the above name. I have never been enabled to learn any special story in connection with this rock. There exists the popular fancy of a lady showing herself here previous to a storm—with, of course, the invariable comb and glass. She is said to have been heard singing most plaintively before a wreck, and that, all along the shore, the spirits have echoed her in low moaning voices.[1] Young men are said to have swam off to the rock, lured by the songs which they heard, but they have never returned. Have we not in this a dim shadow of the story of the Sirens?

Source:
Hunt, Robert. *Popular Romances of the West of England: The Drolls, Traditions, and Superstitions of Old Cornwall*. 3rd edition. London: Chatto and Windus, 1903.

66. The Mermaid of Seaton

Cornwall, England

NEAR Looe,—that is, between Down Derry and Looe,—there is a little sand-beach called "Seaton."

Tradition tells us that here once stood a goodly commercial town bearing this name, and that when it was in its pride, Plymouth was but a small fishing-village.

---

[1] The undulations of the air, travelling with more rapidity than the currents, reach our shores long before the tempest by which they have been established in the centre of the Atlantic, and by producing a low moaning sound, "the soughing of the wind," predicates the storms. The "moans of Tregeagle" is another expression indicating the same phenomenon.

The town of Seaton is said to have been overwhelmed with sand at an early period, the catastrophe having been brought about,—as in the case of the filling up of Padstow harbour,—by the curse of a mermaid, who had suffered some injury from the sailors who belonged to this port. Beyond this I have been unable to glean any story worth preserving.

Source:
Hunt, Robert. *Popular Romances of the West of England: The Drolls, Traditions, and Superstitions of Old Cornwall.* 3rd edition. London: Chatto and Windus, 1903.

67. The Old Man of Cury

Cornwall, England

MORE than a hundred years since, on a fine summer day, when the sun shone brilliantly from a cloudless sky, an old man from the parish of Cury, or, as it was called in olden time, Corantyn, was walking on the sands in one of the coves near the Lizard Point. The old man was meditating, or at least he was walking onward, either thinking deeply, or not thinking at all—that is, he was "lost in thought"—when suddenly he came upon a rock on which was sitting a beautiful girl with fair hair, so long that it covered her entire person. On the in-shore side of the rock was a pool of the most transparent water, which had been left by the receding tide in the sandy hollow the waters had scooped out. This young creature was so absorbed in her occupation,—arranging her hair in the watery mirror, or in admiration of her own lovely face, that she was unconscious of an intruder.

The old man stood looking at her for some time ere he made up his mind how to act. At length he resolved to speak to the maiden. "What cheer, young one?" he said; "what art thee doing there by thyself then, this time o' day?" As soon as she heard the voice, she slid off the rock entirely under the water.

The old man could not tell what to make of it. He thought the girl would drown herself, so he ran on to the rock to render her assistance, conceiving that in her fright at being found naked by a man she had fallen into the pool, and possibly it was deep enough to drown her. He looked into the water, and, sure enough, he could make out the head and shoulders of a woman, and long hair floating like fine sea-weeds all over the pond, hiding what appeared to him to be a fish's tail. He could not, however, see anything distinctly, owing to the abundance of hair floating around the figure. The old man had heard of mermaids from the fishermen of Gunwalloe; so he conceived this lady must be one, and he was at first very much frightened. He saw that the young lady was quite as much terrified as he was, and that, from shame or fear, she endeavoured to hide herself in the crevices of the rock, and bury herself under the sea-weeds.

Summoning courage, at last the old man addressed her, "Don't 'e be afraid, my dear. You needn't mind me. I wouldn't do ye any harm. I'm an old man, and wouldn't hurt ye any more than your grandfather."

After he had talked in this soothing strain for some time, the young lady took courage, and raised her head above the water. She was crying bitterly, and, as soon as she could speak, she begged the old man to go away.

"I must know, my dearie, something about ye, now I have caught ye. It is not every day that an old man catches a merry-maid, and I have heard some strange tales of you water-ladies. Now, my dear, don't 'e be afraid, I would not hurt a single hair of that beautiful head. How came ye here?" After some further coaxing she told the old man the following story:—

She and her husband and little ones had been busy at sea all the morning, and they were very tired with swimming in the hot sun; so the merman proposed that they should retire to a cavern, which they were in the habit of visiting in Kynance Cove. Away they all swam, and entered the cavern at mid-tide. As there was some nice soft weed, and the cave was deliciously cool, the merman was disposed to sleep, and told them not to wake him until the rise of the tide. He was soon fast asleep, snoring most lustily. The children crept out and were playing on the lovely sands; so the mermaid thought she should like to look at the world a little. She looked with delight on the children rolling to and fro in the shallow waves, and she laughed heartily at the crabs fighting in their own funny way. "The scent from the flowers came down over the cliffs so sweetly," said she, "that I longed to get nearer the lovely things which yielded those rich odours, and I floated on from rock to rock until I came to this one; and finding that I could not proceed any further, I thought I would seize the opportunity of dressing my hair." She passed her fingers through those beautiful locks, and shook out a number of small crabs, and much broken sea-weed. She went on to say that she had sat on the rock amusing herself until the voice of a mortal terrified her, and until then she had no idea that the sea was so far out, and a long dry bar of sand between her and it. "What shall I do? what shall I do? Oh! I'd give the world to get out to sea! Oh! oh! what shall I do?"

The old man endeavoured to console her; but his attempts were in vain. She told him her husband would "carry on" most dreadfully if he awoke and found her absent, and he would be certain of awaking at the turn of the tide, as that was his dinnertime. He was very savage when he was hungry, and would as soon eat the children as not, if there was no other food at hand. He was also dreadfully jealous, and if she was not at his side when he awoke, he would at once suspect her of having run off with some other merman. She begged the old man to bear her out to sea. If he would but do so, she would procure him any three things he would wish for. Her entreaties at length prevailed; and, according to her desire, the old man knelt down on the rock with his back towards her. She clasped her fair arms around his neck, and locked her long finny fingers together on his throat. He got up from the rock with his burthen, and carried the mermaid thus across the sands. As she rode in this way, she asked the old man to tell her what he desired.

"I will not wish," said he, "for silver and gold, but give me the power to do good to my neighbours: first, to break the spells of witchcraft; next, to charm away diseases; and thirdly, to discover thieves, and restore stolen goods."

All this she promised he should possess; but he must come to a half-tide rock on another day, and she would instruct him how to accomplish the three things he desired. They had reached the water, and taking her comb from her hair, she gave it to the old man, telling him he had but to comb the water and call her at any time, and she would come to him. The mermaid loosened her grasp, and sliding off the old man's back into the sea, she waved him a kiss and disappeared. At the appointed time the old man was at the half-tide rock,—known to the present time as the Mermaid's Rock,—and duly was he instructed in many mysteries. Amongst others, he learned to break the spells of witches from man or beast; to prepare a vessel of water, in which to show to any one who had property stolen the face of the thief; to charm shingles, tetters, St Antony's fire, and St Vitus's dance; and he learnt also all the mysteries of bramble leaves, and the like.

The mermaid had a woman's curiosity, and she persuaded her old friend to take her to some secret place, from which she could see more of the dry land, and of the funny people who lived on it, "and had their tails split, so that they could walk." On taking the mermaid back to the sea, she wished her friend to visit her abode, and promised even to make him young if he would do so, which favour the old gentleman respectfully declined. A family, well known in Cornwall, have for some generations exercised the power of charming, &c. They account for the possession of this power in the manner related. Some remote great-grandfather was the individual who received the mermaid's comb, which they retain to the present day, and show us evidence of the truth of their being supernaturally endowed. Some people are unbelieving enough to say the comb is only a part of a shark's jaw. Sceptical people are never lovable people.

Source:
Hunt, Robert. *Popular Romances of the West of England: The Drolls,*

Traditions, and Superstitions of Old Cornwall. 3rd edition. London: Chatto and Windus, 1903.

68. The Mermaid's Vengeance[1]

Cornwall, England

IN ONE of the deep valleys of the parish of Perranzabuloe, which are remarkable for their fertility, and especially for the abundance of fruit which the orchards produce, lived in days long ago, amidst a rudely-civilised people, a farmer's labourer, his wife, with one child, a daughter. The man and woman were equally industrious. The neatly white-washed walls of their mud-built cottage, the well-kept gravelled paths, and carefully-weeded beds of their small garden, in which flowers were cultivated for ornament, and vegetables for use, proclaimed at once the character of the inmates. In contrast with the neighbouring cottages, this one, although smaller than many others, had a superior aspect, and the occupiers of it exhibited a strong contrast to those peasants and miners amidst whom they dwelt.

Pennaluna, as the man was called, or Penna the Proud, as he was, in no very friendly spirit, named by his less thoughtful and more impulsive fellows, was, as we have said, a farmer's labourer. His master was a wealthy yeoman, and he, after many years' experience, was so convinced of the exceeding industry and sterling honesty of Penna, that he made him the manager of an outlying farm in this parish, under the hind (or hine—the Saxon pronunciation is still retained in the West of England), or general supervisor of this and numerous other extensive farms.

Penna was too great a favourite with the Squire to be a favourite of the hind's; he was evidently jealous of him, and from not being himself a man of very strict principles, he hated the unobtrusive goodness of his underling, and was constantly on the watch to discover some cause of complaint. It was not, however, often that he was successful in this. Every task committed to the care of Penna,—and he was often purposely overtasked,—was executed with great care and despatch. With the wife of Penna, however, the case was unfortunately different. Honour Penna

---

[1] Several versions of the following story have been given me. The general idea of the tale belongs to the north coast; but the fact of mermaidens taking innocents under their charge was common around the Lizard, and in some of the coves near the Land's End.

was as industrious as her husband, and to him she was in all respects a helpmate. She had, however, naturally a proud spirit, and this had been encouraged in her youth by her parents. Honour was very pretty as a girl, and, indeed, she retained much beauty as a woman. The only education she received was the wild one of experience, and this within a very narrow circle. She grew an ignorant girl, amongst ignorant men and women, few of them being able to write their names, and scarcely any of them to read. There was much native grace about her, and she was flattered by the young men, and envied by the young women, of the village,—the envy and the flattery being equally pleasant to her. In the same village was born, and brought up, Tom Chenalls, who had, in the course of years, become hind to the Squire. Tom, as a young man, had often expressed himself fond of Honour, but he was always distasteful to the village maiden, and eventually, while yet young, she was married to Pennaluna, who came from the southern coast, bringing with him the recommendation of being a stranger, and an exceedingly hard-working man, who was certain to earn bread, and something more, for his wife and family. In the relations in which these people were now placed towards each other, Chenalls had the opportunity of acting ungenerously towards the Pennas. The man bore this uncomplainingly, but the woman frequently quarrelled with him whom she felt was an enemy, and whom she still regarded but as her equal. Chenalls was a skilled farmer, and hence was of considerable value to the Squire; but although he was endured for his farming knowledge and his business habits, he was never a favourite with his employer. Penna, on the contrary, was an especial favourite, and the evidences of this were so often brought strikingly under the observation of Chenalls, that it increased the irritation of his hate, for it amounted to that. For years things went on thus. There was the tranquil suffering of an oppressed spirit manifested in Penna—the angry words and actions of his wife towards the oppressor,—and, at the same time, as she with much fondness studied to make their humble home comfortable for her husband, she reviled him not unfrequently for the meek spirit with which he endured his petty, but still trying, wrongs. The hind dared not venture on any positive act of wrong towards those people, yet he lost no chance of annoying them, knowing that the Squire's partiality for Penna would not allow him to venture beyond certain bounds, even in this direction.

Penna's solace was his daughter. She had now reached her eighteenth year, and with the well-developed form of a woman, she united the simplicity of a child. Selina, as she was named, was in many respects beautiful. Her features were regular, and had they been lighted up with more mental fire, they would have been beautiful; but the constant repose, the want of animation, left her face merely a pretty one. Her skin was beautifully white, and transparent to the blue veins which traced their ways beneath it, to the verge of that delicacy which indicates disease; but it did not pass that verge. Selina was full of health, as her well moulded form at once showed, and her clear blue eye distinctly told. At times there was a lovely tint upon the cheek—not the hectic of consumptive beauty,—but a pure rosy dye, suffused by the healthy life stream, when it flowed the fastest.

The village gossips, who were always busy with their neighbours, said strange things of this girl. Indeed, it was commonly reported that the real child of the Pennas was a remarkably plain child, in every respect a different being from Selina. The striking difference between the infant and the woman was variously explained by the knowing ones. Two stories were, however, current for miles around the country. One was, that Selina's mother was constantly seen gathering dew in the morning, with which to wash her child, and that the fairies on the Towens had, in pure malice, aided her in giving a temporary beauty to the girl, that it might lead to her betrayal into crime. Why this malice, was never clearly made out.

The other story was, that Honour Penna constantly bathed the child in a certain pool, amidst the arched rocks of Perran, which was a favourite resort of the mermaids; that on one occasion the child, as if in a paroxysm of joy, leapt from her arms into the water, and disappeared. The mother, as may well be supposed, suffered a momentary agony of terror; but presently the babe swam up to the surface of the water, its little face more bright and beautiful than it had ever been before. Great was the mother's joy, and also—as the gossips say—great her surprise at the sudden change in the appearance of her offspring. The mother knew no difference in the child whom she pressed lovingly to her bosom, but all the aged crones in the parish declared it to be a changeling. This tale lived its day; but, as the girl grew on to womanhood, and showed none of the special qualifications belonging either to fairies or mermaids, it was almost forgotten. The uncomplaining father had solace for all his sufferings in wandering over the beautiful sands with his daughter. Whether it was when the summer seas fell in musical undulations on the shore, or when, stirred by the winter tempests, the great Atlantic waves came up in grandeur, and lashed the resisting sands in giant rage, those two enjoyed the solitude. Hour after hour, from the setting sun time, until the clear cold moon flooded the ocean with her smiles of light, would the father and child walk these sands. They seemed never to weary of them and the ocean.

Almost every morning, throughout the milder seasons, Selina was in the habit of bathing, and wild tales were told of the frantic joy with which she would play with the breaking billows. Sometimes floating over, and almost dancing on the crests of the waves, at other times rushing under them, and allowing the breaking waters to beat her to the sands, as though they were loving arms, endeavouring to encircle her form. Certain it is, that Selina greatly enjoyed her bath, but all the rest must be regarded as the creations of the imagination. The most eager to give a construction unfavourable to the simple mortality of the maiden was, however, compelled to acknowledge that there was no evidence in her general conduct to support their surmises. Selina, as an only child, fared the fate of others who are unfortunately so placed, and was, as the phrase is, spoiled. She certainly was allowed to follow her own inclinations without any check. Still her inclinations were bounded to working in the garden, and to leading her father to the sea-shore. Honour Penna, sometimes, it is true, did complain that Selina could not be trusted with the most ordinary domestic duty. Beyond this, there was one other cause of grief, that was, the increasing dislike which Selina exhibited towards entering a church. The girl, notwithstanding the constant excuses of being sick, suffering from headache, having a pain in her side, and the like, was often taken, notwithstanding, by her mother to the church. It is said that she always shuddered as she passed the church-stile, and again on stepping from the porch into the church itself. When once within the house of prayer she evinced no peculiar liking or disliking, observing respectfully all the rules during the performance of the church-service, and generally sleeping, or seeming to sleep, during the sermon. Selina Pennaluna had reached her eighteenth year; she was admired by many of the young men of the parish, but, as if surrounded by a spell, she appeared to keep them all at a distance from her. About this time, a nephew to the Squire, a young soldier,—who had been wounded in the wars,—came into Cornwall to heal his wounds, and recover health, which had suffered in a trying campaign.

This young man, Walter Trewoofe, was a rare specimen of manhood. Even now, shattered as he was by the combined influences of wounds, an unhealthy climate, and dissipation, he could not but be admired for fineness of form, dignity of carriage, and masculine beauty. It was, however, but too evident, that this young man was his own idol, and that he expected every one to bow down with him, and worship it. His uncle was proud of Walter, and although the old gentleman could not fail to see many faults, yet he regarded them as the follies of youth, and trusted to their correction with the increase of years and experience. Walter, who was really suffering severely, was ordered by his surgeon, at first, to take short walks on the sea-shore, and, as he gained strength, to bathe. He was usually driven in his uncle's pony-carriage to the edge of the sands. Then dismounting he would walk for a short time, and quickly wearing, return in his carriage to the luxuriant couches at the manor-house.

On some of those occasions Walter had observed the father and daughter taking their solitary ramble. He was struck with the quiet beauty of the girl, and seized an early opportunity of stopping Penna to make some general inquiry respecting the bold and beautiful coast. From time to time they thus met, and it would have been evident to any observer that Walter did not so soon weary of the sands as formerly, and that Selina was not displeased with the flattering things he said to her. Although the young soldier had hitherto led a wild life, it would appear as if for a considerable period the presence of goodness had repressed every tendency to evil in his ill-regulated heart. He continued, therefore, for some time playing with his own feelings and those of the childlike being who presented so much of romance, combined with the most homely tameness, of character. Selina, it is true, had never yet seen Walter except in the presence of her father, and it is questionable if she had ever for one moment had a warmer feeling than that of the mere pleasure—a silent pride—that a gentleman, at once so handsome, so refined, and the nephew of her father's master, should pay her any attention. Evil eyes were watching with wicked earnestness the growth of passion, and designing hearts were beating quicker with a consciousness that they should eventually rejoice in the downfall of innocence. Tom Chenalls hoped that he might achieve a triumph, if he could but once asperse the character of Selina. He took his measures accordingly. Having noticed the change in the general conduct of his master's nephew, he argued that this was due to the refining influence of a pure mind, acting on one more than ordinarily impressionable to either evil or good.

Walter rapidly recovered health, and with renewed strength the manly energy of his character began to develop itself. He delighted in horse-exercise, and Chenalls had always the best horse on the farms at his disposal. He was a good shot, and Chenalls was his guide to the best shooting-grounds. He sometimes fished, and Chenalls knew exactly where the choicest trout and the richest salmon were to be found. In fact, Chenalls entered so fully into the tastes of the young man, that Walter found him absolutely necessary to him to secure the enjoyments of a country life.

Having established this close intimacy, Chenalls never lost an opportunity of talking with Walter respecting Selina Penna. He soon satisfied himself that Walter, like most other young men who had led a dissipated life, had but a very low estimate of women generally. Acting upon this, he at first insinuated that Selina's innocence was but a mask, and at length he boldly assured Walter that the cottage girl was to be won by him with a few words, and that then he might put her aside at any time as a prize to some low-born peasant. Chenalls never failed to impress on Walter the necessity of keeping his uncle in the most perfect darkness, and of blinding the eyes of Selina's parents. Penna was,—so thought Chenalls,—easily managed, but there was more to be feared from the wife. Walter, however, with much artifice, having introduced himself to Honour Penna, employed the magic of that flattery, which, being properly applied, seldom fails to work its way to the heart of a weak-minded woman. He became an especial favourite with Honour, and the blinded mother was ever pleased at the attention bestowed with so little assumption,—as she thought,—of pride, on her daughter, by one so much above them. Walter eventually succeeded in separating occasionally, though not often, Penna and his daughter. The witching whispers of unholy love were poured into the trusting ear. Guileless herself, this child-woman suspected no guile in others, least of all in one whom she had been taught to look upon as a superior being to herself. Amongst the villagers, the constant attention of Walter Trewoofe was the subject of gossip, and many an old proverb was quoted by the elder women, ill-naturedly, and implying that evil must come of this intimacy, Tom Chenalls was now employed by Walter to contrive some means by which he could remove Penna for a period from home. He was not long in doing this. He lent every power of his wicked nature to aid the evil designs of the young soldier, and thus he brought about that separation of father and child which ended in her ruin.

Near the Land's End the squire possessed some farms, and one of them was reported to be in such a state of extreme neglect, through the drunkenness and consequent idleness of the tenant, that Chenalls soon obtained permission to take the farm from this occupier, which he did in the most unscrupulous disregard for law or right. It was then suggested that the only plan by which a desirable occupier could be found, would be to get the farm and farm-buildings into good condition, and that Penna, of all men, would be the man to bring this quickly about. The squire was pleased with the plan. Penna was sent for by him, and was proud of the confidence which his master reposed in him. There was some sorrow on his leaving home. He subsequently said that he had had many warnings not to go, but he felt that he dared not disoblige a master who had trusted him so far—so he went.

Walter needed not any urging on the part of Chenalls, though he was always ready to apply the spur when there was the least evidence of the sense of right asserting itself in the young man's bosom. Week after week passed on. Walter had rendered himself a necessity to Selina. Without her admirer the world was cold and colourless. With him all was sunshine and glowing tints.

Three months passed thus away, and during that period it had only been possible for Penna to visit his home twice. The father felt that something like a spirit of evil stood between him and his daughter. There was no outward evidence of any change, but there was an inward sense—undefined, yet deeply felt—like an overpowering fear—that some wrong had been done. On parting, Penna silently but earnestly prayed that the deep dread might be removed from his mind. There was an aged fisherman, who resided in a small cottage built on the sands, who possessed all the superstitions of his class. This old man had formed a father's liking for the simple-hearted maiden, and he had persuaded himself that there really was some foundation for the tales which the gossips told. To the fisherman, Walter Trewoofe was an evil genius. He declared that no good ever came to him, if he met Walter when he was about to go to sea. With this feeling he curiously watched the young man and maiden, and he, in after days, stated his conviction that he had seen "merry maidens rising from the depth of the waters, and floating under the billows to watch Selina and her lover. He has also been heard to say that on more than one occasion Walter himself had been terrified by sights and sounds. Certain, however, it is, these were insufficient and the might of evil passions were more powerful than any of the protecting influences of the unseen world.

Another three months had gone by, and Walter Trewoofe had disappeared from Perranzabuloe. He had launched into the gay world of the metropolis, and rarely, if ever, dreamed of the deep sorrow which was weighing down the heart he had betrayed Penna returned home—his task was done—and Chenalls had no reason for keeping him any longer from his wife and daughter Clouds gathered slowly but unremittingly around him. His daughter retired into herself no longer as of old reposing her whole soul on her father's heart. His wife was somewhat changed too—she had some secret in her heart which she feared to tell The home he had left was not the home to which he had returned It soon became evident that some shock had shaken the delicate frame of his daughter. She pined rapidly; and Penna was awakened to a knowledge of the cause by the rude rejoicing of Chenalls, who declared "that all people who kept themselves so much above other people were sure to be pulled down." On one occasion he so far tempted Penna with sneers, at his having hope to secure the young squire for a son-in-law, that the long-enduring man broke forth and administered a severe blow upon his tormentor. This was duly reported to the squire, and added thereto was a magnified story of a trap which had been set by the Penna to catch young Walter; it was represented that even now they intended to press their claims, on account of grievous wrongs upon them, whereas it could be proved that Walter was guiltless—that he was indeed the innocent victim of designing people, who though to make money out of their assumed misfortune. The squire made his inquiries, and there were not a few who eagerly seized the opportunity to gain the friendship of Chenalls by representing this family to have been hypocrites of the deepest dye; and the poor girl especially was now loaded with a weight of iniquities of which she had no knowledge. All this ended in the dismissal of Penna from the Squire's service, and in his being deprived of the cottage in which he had taken so much pride. Although thrown out upon the world a disgraced man, Penna faced his difficulties manfully. He cast off, as it were, the primitive simplicity of his character, and evidently worked with a firm resolve to beat down his sorrows. He was too good a workman to remain long unemployed; and although his new home was not his happy home as of old, there was no repining heard from his lips. Weaker and weaker grew Selina, and it soon became evident to all, that if she came from a spirit-world, to a spirit-world she must soon return. Grief filled the hearts of her parents—it prostrated her mother, but the effects of severe labour, and the efforts of a settled mind, appeared to tranquillise the breast of her father. Time passed on, the wounds of the soul grew deeper, and there lay, on a low bed, from which she had not strength to move, the fragile form of youth with the countenance of age. The body was almost powerless, but there beamed from the eye the evidences of a spirit getting free from the chains of clay.

The dying girl was sensible of the presence of creations other than mortal, and with these she appeared to hold converse, and to derive solace from the communion. Penna and his wife alternately watched through the night hours by the side of their loved child, and anxiously did they mark the moment when the tide turned, in the full belief that she would be taken from them when the waters of the ocean began to recede from the shore. Thus days passed on, and eventually the sunlight of a summer morning shone in through the small window of this humble cottage,—on a dead mother—and a living babe.

The dead was buried in the churchyard on the sands, and the living went on their ways, some rejoicingly and some in sorrow.

Once more Walter Trewoofe appeared in Perran-on-the-sands. Penna would have sacrificed him to his hatred; he emphatically protested that he had lived only to do so; but the good priest of the Oratory contrived to lay the devil who had possession, and to convince Penna that the Lord would, in His own good time, and in His own way, avenge the bitter wrong. Tom Chenalls had his hour of triumph; but from the day on which Selina died everything went wrong. The crops failed, the cattle died, haystacks and corn-ricks caught fire, cows slipped their calves, horses fell lame, or stumbled and broke their knees,—a succession of evils steadily pursued him. Trials find but a short resting-place with the good; they may be bowed to the earth with the weight of a sudden sorrow, but they look to heaven, and their elasticity is restored. The evil-minded are crushed at once, and grovel on the ground in irremediable misery. That Chenalls fled to drink in his troubles appeared but the natural result to a man of his character. This unfitted him for his duties, and he was eventually dismissed from his situation. Notwithstanding that the Squire refused to listen to the appeals in favour of Chenalls, which were urged upon him by Walter, and that indeed he forbade his nephew to countenance "the scoundrel" in any way, Walter still continued his friend. By his means Tom Chenalls secured a small cottage on the cliff, and around it a little cultivated ground, the produce of which was his only visible means of support. That lonely cottage was the scene, however, of drunken carousals, and there the vicious young men, and the no less vicious young women, of the district, went after nightfall, and kept "high carnival" of sin. Walter Trewoofe came frequently amongst them; and as his purse usually defrayed the costs of a debauch, he was regarded by all with especial favour.

One midnight, Walter, who had been dancing and drinking for some hours, left the cottage wearied with his excesses, and although not drunk, he was much excited with wine. His pathway lay along the edge of the cliffs, amidst bushes of furze and heath, and through several irregular, zigzag ways. There were lateral paths striking off from one side of the main path, and leading down to the sea-shore. Although it was moonlight, without being actually aware of the error, Walter wandered into one of those; and before he was awake to his mistake, he found himself on the sands. He cursed his stupidity, and, uttering a blasphemous oath, he turned to retrace his steps.

The most exquisite music which ever flowed from human ups fell on his ear; he paused to listen, and collecting his unbalanced thoughts, he discovered that it was the voice of a woman singing a melancholy dirge:—

> "The stars are beautiful, when bright
>   They are mirror'd in the sea;
> But they are pale beside that light
>   Which was so beautiful to me.
> My angel child, my earth-born girl,
>   From all your kindred riven,
> By the base deeds of a selfish churl,
>   And to a sand-grave driven!
> How shall I win thee back to ocean?
>   How canst thou quit thy grave,
> To share again the sweet emotion
>   Of gliding through the wave?"

Walter, led by the melancholy song, advanced slowly along the sands. He discovered that the sweet, soft sounds proceeded from the other side of a mass of rocks, which project far out over the sands, and that now, at low-water, there was no difficulty in walking around it. Without hesitation he did so, and he beheld, sitting at the mouth of a cavern, one of the most beautiful women he had ever beheld. She continued her song, looking upwards to the stars, not appearing to notice the intrusion of a stranger. Walter stopped, and gazed on the lovely image before him with admiration and wonder, mingled with something of terror. He dared not speak, but fixed, as if by magic, he stood gazing on. After a few minutes, the maiden, suddenly perceiving that a man was near her, uttered a piercing shriek, and made as if to fly into the cavern. Walter sprang forward and seized her by the arm, exclaiming, "Not yet, my pretty maiden, not yet."

She stood still in the position of flight, with her arm behind her, grasped by Walter, and turning round her head, her dark eyes beamed with unnatural lustre upon him. Impressionable he had ever been, but never had he experienced anything so entrancing, and at the same time so painful, as that gaze. It was Selina's face looking lovingly upon him, but it seemed to possess some new power—a might of mind from which he felt it was impossible for him to escape. Walter slackened his hold, and slowly allowed the arm to fall from his hand. The maiden turned fully round upon him. "Go!" she said. He could not move. "Go, man!" she repeated. He was powerless.

"Go to the grave where the sinless one sleepeth!
Bring her cold corse where her guarding one weepeth;
Look on her, love her again, ay! betray her,
And wreath with false smiles the pale face of her slayer!
Go, go! now, and feel the full force of my sorrow!
For the glut of my vengeance there cometh a morrow."

Walter was statue-like, and he awoke from this trance-like state only when the waves washed his feet, and he became aware that even now it was only by wading through the waters that he could return around the point of rocks. He was alone. He called; no one answered. He sought wildly, as far as he now dared, amidst the rocks, but the lovely woman was nowhere to be discovered.

There was no real danger on such a night as this; therefore Walter walked fearlessly through the gentle waves, and recovered the pathway up from the sands. More than once he thought he heard a rejoicing laugh, which was echoed in the rocks, but no one was to be seen. Walter reached his home and bed, but he found no sleep; and in the morning he arose with a sense of wretchedness which was entirely new to him. He feared to make any one of his rough companions a confidant, although he felt this would have relieved his heart. He therefore nursed the wound which he now felt, until a bitter remorse clouded his existence. After some days, he was impelled to visit the grave of the lost one, and in the fullness of the most selfish sorrow, he sat on the sands and shed tears. The priest of the Oratory observed him, and knowing Walter Trewoofe, hesitated not to inquire into his cause of sorrow. His heart was opened to the holy man, and the strange tale was told—the only result being, that the priest felt satisfied it was but a vivid dream, which had resulted from a brain over-excited by drink. He, however, counselled the young man, giving him some religious instruction, and dismissed him with his blessing. There was relief in this. For some days Walter did not venture to visit his old haunt, the cottage of Chenalls. Since he could not be lost to his companions without greatly curtailing their vicious enjoyments, he was hunted up by Chenalls, and again enticed within the circle. His absence was explained on the plea of illness. Walter was, however, an altered man; there was not the same boisterous hilarity as formerly. He no longer abandoned himself without restraint to the enjoyments of the time. If he ever, led on by his thoughtless and rough-natured friends, assumed for a moment his usual mirth, it was checked by some invisible power. On such occasions he would turn deadly pale, look anxiously around, and fail back, as if ready to faint, on the nearest seat. Under these influences, he lost health. His uncle, who was really attached to his nephew, although he regretted his dissolute conduct, became now seriously alarmed. Physicians were consulted in vain; the young man pined, and the old gossips came to the conclusion that Walter Trewoofe was ill-wished, and there was a general feeling that Penna or his wife was at the bottom of it. Walter, living really on one idea, and that one the beautiful face which was, and yet was not, that of Selina, resolved again to explore the spot on which he had met this strange being, of whom nothing could be learned by any of the covert inquiries he made. He lingered long ere he could resolve on the task; but wearied, worn by the oppression of one undefined idea, in which an intensity of love was mixed with a shuddering fear, he at last gathered sufficient courage to seize an opportunity for again going to the cavern. On this occasion, there being no moon, the night was dark, but the stars shone brightly from a sky, cloudless, save a dark mist which hung heavily over the western horizon. Every spot of ground being familiar to him, who, boy and man, had traced it over many times, the partial darkness presented no difficulty. Walter had scarcely reached the level sands, which were left hard by the retiring tide, than he heard again the same magical voice as before. But now the song was a joyous one, the burthen of it being—

> "Join all hands—
>   Might and main,
> Weave the sands,
>   Form a chain,
> He, my lover,
>   Comes again!"

He could not entirely dissuade himself but that he heard this repeated by many voices; but he put the thought aside, referring it, as well he might, to the numerous echoes from the cavernous openings in the cliffs.

He reached the eastern side of the dark mass of rocks, from the point of which the tide was slowly subsiding. The song had ceased, and a low moaning sound—the soughing of the wind—passed along the shore. Walter trembled with fear, and was on the point of returning, when a most flute-like murmur rose from the other side of the rocky barrier, which was presently moulded into words:—

> "From your couch of glistering pearl,
>   Slowly, softly, come away;
> Our sweet earth-child, lovely girl,
>   Died this day,—died this day."

Memory told Walter that truly was it the anniversary of Selina Pennaluna's death, and to him every gentle wave falling on the shore sang, or murmured—

> "Died this day,—died this day."

The sand was left dry around the point of the rocks, and Walter impelled by a power which he could not control, walked onward. The moment he appeared on the western side of the rock, a wild laugh burst into the air, as if from the deep cavern before him, at the entrance of which sat the same beautiful being whom he had formerly met. There was now an expression of rare joy on her face, her eyes glistened with delight, and she extended her arms, as if to welcome him.

"Was it ever your wont to move so slowly towards your loved one?"

Walter heard it was Selina's voice. He saw it was Selina's features; but he was conscious it was not Selina's form.

"Come, sit beside me, Walter, and let us talk of love." He sat down without a word, and looked into the maiden's face with a vacant expression of fondness. Presently she placed her hand upon his heart; a shudder passed through his frame; but having passed, he felt no more pain, but a rare intensity of delight. The maiden wreathed her arm around his neck, drew Walter towards her, and then he remembered how often he had acted thus towards Selina. She bent over him and looked into his eyes. In his mind's mirror he saw himself looking thus into the eyes of his betrayed one.

"You loved her once?" said the maiden.

"I did indeed," answered Walter, with a sigh.

"As you loved her, so I love you," said the maiden, with a smile which shot like a poisoned dart through Walter's heart. She lifted the young man's head lovingly between her hands, and bending over him, pressed her lips upon and kissed his forehead, Walter curiously felt that although he was the kissed, yet that he was the kisser.

"Kisses," she said, "are as true at sea as they are false on land. You men kiss the earth-born maidens to betray them. The kiss of a sea-child is the seal of constancy. You are mine till death."

"Death!" almost shrieked Walter.

A full consciousness of his situation now broke upon Walter. He had heard the tales of the gossips respecting the mermaid origin of Selina; but he had laughed at them as an idle fancy. He now felt they were true. For hours Walter was compelled to sit by the side of his beautiful tormentor, every word of assumed love and rapture being a torture of the most exquisite kind to him. He could not escape from the arms which were wound around him. He saw the tide rising rapidly. He heard the deep voice of the winds coming over the sea from the far west. He saw that which appeared at first as a dark mist, shape itself into a dense black mass of cloud, and rise rapidly over the star-bedecked space above him. He saw by the brilliant edge of light which occasionally fringed the clouds that they were deeply charged with thunder. There was something sublime in the steady motion of the storm; and now the roll of the waves, which had been disturbed in the Atlantic, reached our shores, and the breakers fell thunderingly within a few feet of Walter and his companion. Paroxysms of terror shook him, and with each convulsion he felt himself grasped with still more ardour, and pressed so closely to the maiden's bosom, that he heard her heart dancing of joy.

At length his terrors gave birth to words, and he implored her to let him go.

"The kiss of the sea-child is the seal of constancy." Walter vehemently implored forgiveness. He confessed his deep iniquity. He promised a life of penitence.

"Give me back the dead," said the maiden bitterly, and she planted another kiss, which seemed to pierce his brain by its coldness, upon his forehead.

The waves rolled around the rock on which they sat; they washed their seat. Walter was .still in the female's grasp, and she lifted him to a higher ledge. The storm approached. Lightnings struck down from the heavens into the sands; and thunders roared along the iron cliffs. The mighty waves grew yet more rash, and washed up to this strange pair, who now sat on the highest pinnacle of the pile of rocks. Walter's terrors nearly overcame him; but he was roused by a liquid stream of fire, which positively hissed by him, followed immediately by a crash of thunder, which shook the solid earth. Tom Chenall's cottage on the cliff burst into a blaze, and Walter saw, from his place amidst the raging waters, a crowd of male and female roisterers rush terrified out upon the heath, to be driven back by the pelting storm. The climax of horrors appeared to surround Walter. He longed to end it in death, but he could not die. His senses were quickened. He saw his wicked companion and evil adviser struck to the ground, a blasted heap of ashes, by a lightning stroke, and at the same moment he and his companion were borne off the rock on the top of a mountainous wave, on which he floated; the woman holding him by the hair of his head, and singing in a rejoicing voice, which was like a silver bell heard amidst the deep base bellowings of the storm—

"Come away, come away,
  O'er the waters wild!
  Our earth-born child
Died this day, died this day.

"Come away, come away!
  The tempest loud
  Weaves the shroud
For him who did betray.

"Come away, come away!
  Beneath the wave
  Lieth the grave
Of him we slay, him we slay.

"Come away, come away!
  He shall not rest
  In earth's own breast

For many a day, many a day.

"Come away, come away!
   By billows to
   From coast to coast,
   Like deserted boat
   His corse shall float
Around the bay, around the bay."

Myriads of voices on that wretched night were heard amidst the roar of the storm. The waves were seen covered with a multitudinous host, who were tossing from one to the other the dying Walter Trewoofe, whose false heart thus endured the vengeance of the mermaid, who had, in the fondness of her soul, made the innocent child of humble parents the child of her adoption.

NOTES

"Inevitable death awaits the wretch who is seduced by their charms. They seize and drown the swimmer, and entice the child; and when they anticipate that their malevolence will be gratified, they are seen gaily darting over the surface of the waters."

   Since this tale has been in type, my attention has been called to an article on, the "Popular Mythology of the Middle Ages," by Sir F. Palgrave, in the *Quarterly Review*, No. 44, 1820. The Nixies, to whom the above quotation especially refers, are in most respects like the Cornish mermaids.

Source:
Hunt, Robert. *Popular Romances of the West of England: The Drolls, Traditions, and Superstitions of Old Cornwall*. 3rd edition. London: Chatto and Windus, 1903.

69. The Mermaid of Zennor

Cornwall, England

ZENNOR folks tell the following story, which, according to them, accounts for a singular carving on a bench-end in their Church.
   Hundreds of years ago a very beautiful and richly attired lady

attended service in Zennor Church occasionally—now and then she went to Morvah also;—her visits were by no means regular,—often long intervals would elapse between them.

Yet whenever she came the people were enchanted with her good looks and sweet singing. Although Zennor folks were remarkable for their fine psalmody, she excelled them all; and they wondered how, after the scores of years that they had seen her, she continued to look so young and fair. No one knew whence she came nor whither she went; yet many watched her as far as they could see from Tregarthen Hill.

She took some notice of a fine young man, called Mathey Trewella, who was the best singer in the parish. He once followed her, but he never returned; after that she was never more seen in Zennor Church, and it might not have been known to this day who or what she was but for the merest accident.

One Sunday morning a vessel cast anchor about a mile from Pendower Cove; soon after a mermaid came close alongside and hailed the ship. Rising out of the water as far as her waist, with her yellow hair floating around her, she told the captain that she was returning from church, and requested him to trip his anchor just for a minute, as the fluke of it rested on the door of her dwelling, and she was anxious to get in to her children.

Others say that while she was out on the ocean a-fishing of a Sunday morning, the anchor was dropped on the trap-door which gave access to her submarine abode. Finding, on her return, how she was hindered from opening her door, she begged the captain to have the anchor raised that she might enter her dwelling to dress her children and be ready in time for church.

However it may be, her polite request had a magical effect upon the sailors, for they immediately "worked with a will," hove anchor and set sail, not wishing to remain a moment longer than they could help near her habitation. Sea-faring men, who understood most about mermaids, regarded their appearance as a token that bad luck was near at hand. It was believed they could take such shapes as suited their purpose, and that they had often allured men to live with them.

When Zennor folks learnt that a mermaid dwelt near Pen-dower, and what she had told the captain, they concluded—it was, this sea-lady who had visited their church, and enticed Trewella to her abode. To commemorate these somewhat unusual events they had the figure she bore—when in her ocean-home—carved in holy-oak, which may still be seen.

Source:
Bottrell, William. *Traditions and Hearthside Stories of West Cornwall, Vol. 2*. Penzance: Beare and Son, 1873.

70. Lutey and the Mermaid

Cornwall, England

ONE lovely summer evening many, many years ago, an old man named Lutey was standing on the seashore not far from that beautiful bit of coast called the Lizard.

On the edge of the cliff above him stood a small farm, and here he lived, spending his time between farming, fishing, and, we must admit it, smuggling, too, whenever he got a chance. This summer evening he had finished his day's work early, and while waiting for his supper he strolled along the sands a little way, to see if there was any wreckage to be seen, for it was long since he had had any luck in that way, and he was very much put out about it.

This evening, though, he was no luckier than he had been before, and he was turning away, giving up his search as hopeless, when from somewhere out seaward came a long, low, wailing cry. It was not the melancholy cry of a gull, but of a woman or child in distress.

Lutey stopped, and listened, and looked back, but, as far as he could see, not a living creature was to be seen on the beach but himself. Even though while he listened the sound came wailing over the sand again, and this time left no doubt in his mind. It was a voice. Someone was in trouble, evidently, and calling for help.

Far out on the sands rose a group of rocks which, though covered at high water, were bare now. It was about half ebb, and spring tide, too, so the sea was further out than usual, so far, in fact, that a wide bar of sand stretched between the rocks and the sea. It was from these rocks that the cry seemed to come, and Lutey, feeling sure that someone was out there in distress, turned and walked back quickly to see if he could give any help.

As he drew near he saw that there was no one on the landward side, so he hurried round to the seaward,—and there, to his amazement, his eyes met a sight which left him almost speechless.

Lying on a ledge at the base of the rock, partially covered by the long seaweed which grew in profusion over its rough sides, and partially by her own hair, which was the most glorious you can possibly imagine, was the most beautiful woman his eyes had ever lighted upon. Her skin was a delicate pink and white, even more beautiful than those exquisite little shells one picks up sometimes on the seashore, her clear green eyes sparkled and flashed like the waves with the sun on them, while her hair was the colour of rich gold, like the sun in its glory, and with a ripple in it such as one sees on the sea on a calm day.

This wonderful creature was gazing mournfully out at the distant sea, and uttering form time to time the pitiful cry which had first attracted Lutey's attention. She was evidently in great distress, but how to offer her help and yet not frighten her he knew not, for the roar of the sea had deadened the sound of his footsteps on the soft sand, and she was quite unconscious of his presence.

Lutey coughed and hem'd, but it was of no use—she could not or did not hear; he stamped, he kicked the rock, but all in vain, and at last he had to go close to her and speak.

"What's the matter, missie?" he said. "What be doing all out here by yourself?" He spoke as gently as possible, but, in spite of his gentleness, the lovely creature shrieked with terror, and diving down into the deep pool at the base of the rock, disappeared entirely.

At first Lutey thought she had drowned herself, but when he looked closely into the pool, and contrived to peer through the cloud of hair which floated like fine seaweed all over the top of it, he managed to distinguish a woman's head and shoulders underneath, and looking closer he saw, he was sure, a fish's tail! His knees quaked under him, at that sight, for he realized that the lovely lady was no other than a mermaid!

She, though, seemed as frightened as he was, so he summoned up his courage to speak to her again, for it is always wise to be kind to mermaids, and to avoid offending them, for if they are angry there is no knowing what harm they may do to you.

"Don't be frightened, lady," he said coaxingly; "I wouldn't hurt 'ee for the world, I wouldn't harm a living creature. I only wants to know what your trouble is."

While he was speaking, the maiden had raised her head slightly above the water, and now was gazing at him with eyes the like of which he had never seen before. "I 'opes she understands Carnish," he added to himself, "for 'tis the only langwidge I'm fluent in."

"Beautiful sir," she replied in answer to his thoughts, "we sea-folk can understand all languages, for we visit the coast of every land, and all the tribes of the world sail over the kingdom, and oft-times come down through the waters to our home. The greatest kindness you can do me is to go away. You are accustomed to women who walk, covered with silks and laces. We could not wear such in our world, sporting in the waves, swimming into caverns, clambering into sunken ships. You cannot realize our free and untrammelled existence."

"Now, my lovely lady," said old Lutey, who did not understand a half of what she was saying, "don't 'ee think anything about such trifles, but stop your tears and tell me what I can do for 'ee. For, for sure, I can help 'ee somehow. Tell me how you come'd here, and where you wants to get to."

So the fair creature floated higher in the water, and, gradually growing braver, she presently climbed up and perched herself on the rock where Lutey had first seen her. Her long hair fell about her like a glorious mantle, and she needed no other, for it quite covered her. Holding in her hand her comb and mirror, and glancing from time to time at the latter, she told the old man her story.

"Only a few hours ago," she said sadly, "I was sporting about with my husband and children, as happy as a mermaiden could be. At length, growing weary, we all retired to rest in one of the caverns at Kynance, and there on a soft couch of seaweed my husband laid himself down to sleep. The children went off to play, and I was left alone. For some time I watched the crabs playing in the water, or the tiny fish at the bottom of the pools, but the sweet scent of flowers came to me from the gardens of your world, borne on the light breeze, and I felt I must go and see what these flowers were like whose breath was so beautiful, for we have nothing like it in our dominions. Exquisite sea-plants we have, but they have no sweet perfume.

"Seeing that my husband was asleep, and the children quite happy and safe, I swam off to this shore, but when here I found I could not get near the flowers; I could see them on the tops of the cliffs far, far beyond my reach, so I thought I would rest here for a time, and dress my hair, while breathing in their sweetness.

"I sat on, dreaming of your world, and trying to picture to myself what it was like, until I awoke with a start to find the tide far out, beyond the bar. I was so frightened I screamed to my husband to come and help me, but even if he heard me he could not get to me over that sandy ridge; and if he wakes before I am back, and misses me, he will be so angry, for he is very jealous. He will be hungry, too, and if he finds no supper prepared he will eat some of the children!"

"Oh, my dear!" cried Lutey, quite horrified, "he surely wouldn't never do such a dreadful thing!"

"Ah, you do not know Mermen," she said sorrowfully. "They are such gluttons, and will gobble up their children in a moment if their meals are a little late. Scores of my children have been taken from me. That is how it is," she explained, "that you do not oftener see us sea-folk. Poor children, they never learn wisdom! Directly their father begins to whistle or sing, they crowd about him, they are so fond of music, and he gets them to come and kiss his cheek, or whisper in his ear, then he opens wide his mouth, and in they go.—Oh dear, what shall I do! I have only ten little ones left, and they will all be gone if I don't get home before he wakes!"

"Don't 'ee take on so, my dear. The tide will be soon in, and then you can float off as quick as you like."

"Oh, but I cannot wait," she cried, tears running down her cheeks. "Beautiful mortal, help me! Carry me out to sea, give me your aid for ten minutes only, and I will make you rich and glorious for life. Ask of me anything you want, and it shall be yours."

Lutey was so enthralled by the loveliness of the mermaid, that he stood gazing at her, lost in wonder. Her voice, which sounded like a gentle murmuring stream, was to him the most lovely music he had ever heard. He was so fascinated that he would have done anything she asked him. He stooped to pick her up.

"First of all, take this," she said, giving him her pearl comb, "take this, to prove to you that you have not been dreaming, gentle stranger, and that I will do for you what I have said. When you want me, comb the sea three times with this, and call me by my name, 'Morwenna,' and I will come to you. Now take me to the sea."

Stooping again he picked her up in his arms. She clung tightly to him, twining her long, cool arms around his neck, until he felt half suffocated. "Tell me your wishes," she said sweetly, as they went along; "you shall have three. Riches will, of course, be one."

"No, lady," said Lutey thoughtfully, "I don't know that I'm so set on getting gold, but I'll tell 'ee what I should like. I'd dearly love to be able to remove the spells of the witches, to have power over the spirits to make them tell me all I want to know, and I'd like to be able to cure diseases."

"You are the first unselfish man I have ever met," cried the mermaid admiringly, "you shall have your wishes, and, in addition, I promise you as a reward, that your family shall never come to want."

In a state of great delight, Lutey trudged on with his lovely burthen, while she chatted gaily to him of her home, of the marvels and the riches of the sea, and the world that lay beneath it.

"Come with me, noble youth," she cried, "come with me to our caves and palaces; there are riches, beauty, and everything mortal can want. Our homes are magnificent, the roofs are covered with diamonds and other gems, so that it is ever light and sparkling, the walls are of amber and coral. Your floors are of rough, ugly rocks, ours are of mother-of-pearl. For statuary we have the bodies of earth's most beautiful sons and daughters, who come to us in ships, sent by the King of the Storms. We embalm them, so that they look more lovely even than in life, with their eyes still sparkling, their lips of ruby-red, and the delicate pink of the seashell in their cheeks. Come and see for yourself how well we care for them, and how reposeful they look in their pearl and coral homes, with sea-plants growing around them, and gold and silver heaped at their feet. They crossed the world to get it, and their journeys have not been failures. Will you come, noble stranger? Come to be one of us whose lives are all love, and sunshine, and merriment?"

"None of it's in my line, I'm thinking, my dear," said Lutey. "I'd rather come across some of the things that have gone down in the wrecks, wines and brandy, laces and silks; there's a pretty sight of it all gone to the bottom, one time and another, I'm thinking."

"Ah yes! We have vast cellars full of the choicest wines ever made, and caves stored with laces and silks. Come, stranger, come, and take all you want."

"Well," answered the old smuggler, who was thinking what a fine trade he could do, if only he could reach those caves and cellars, "I must say I'd like to, 'tis very tempting, but I should never live to get there, I'm thinking. I should be drownded or smothered before I'd got half-way."

"No, oh no, I can manage that for you. I will make two slits under your chin, your lovely countenance will not suffer, for your beard will hide them. Such a pair of gills is all you want, so do not fear. Do not leave me, generous-hearted youth. Come to the mermaid's home!"

They were in the sea by this time, and the breakers they wanted to reach were not far off. Lutey felt strangely tempted to go with this Siren; her flashing green eyes had utterly bewitched him by this time, and her promises had turned his head. She saw that he was almost consenting, almost in her power. She clasped her long, wet, finny fingers more closely round his neck, and pressed her cool lips to his cheeks.

Another instant, and Lutey would have gone to his doom, but at that moment there came from the shore the sound of a dog barking as though in distress. It was the barking of Lutey's own dog, a great favourite with its master. Lutey turned to look. At the edge of the water the poor creature stood; evidently frantic to follow its master, it dashed into the sea and out again, struggling, panting. Beyond, on the cliff, stood his home, the windows flaming against the sun, his garden, and the country looking green and beautiful; the smoke was rising from his chimney,—ah, his supper! The thought of his nice hot meal broke the spell, and he saw his danger.

"Let me go, let me go!" he shrieked, trying to lower the mermaid to the ground. She only clung the more tightly to him. He felt a sudden fear and loathing of the creature with the scaly body, and fish's tail. Her green eyes no longer fascinated him. He remembered all the tales he had heard of the power of mermaids, and their wickedness, and grew more and more terrified.

"Let me go!" he yelled again, "unwind your gashly great tail from about my legs, and your skinny fingers from off my throat, or I'll—I'll kill you!" and with the same he whipped his big clasp-knife from his pocket.

As the steel flashed before the mermaid's eyes she slipped from him and swam slowly away, but as she went she sang, and the words floated back to Lutey mournfully yet threateningly. "Farewell, farewell for nine long years. Then, my love, I will come again. Mine, mine, for ever mine!"

Poor Lutey, greatly relieved to see her disappear beneath the waves, turned and waded slowly back to land, but so shaken and upset was he by all that had happened, that it was almost more than he could accomplish. On reaching the shore he just managed to scramble to the shed where he kept many of the treasures he had smuggled from time to time, but having reached it he dropped down in a deep, overpowering sleep.

Poor old Ann Betty Lutey was in a dreadful state of mind when supper-time came and went and her husband had not returned. He had never missed it before. All through the night she watched anxiously for him, but when breakfast-time came, and still there was no sign of him, she could not rest at home another minute, and started right away in search of him.

She did not have to search far, though. Outside the door of the shed she found the dog sleeping, and as the dog was seldom seen far from his master, she thought she would search the shed first,—and there, of course, she found her husband.

He was still sound asleep. Ann Betty, vexed at once at having been frightened for nothing, shook him none too gently. "Here, Lutey, get up at once do you hear!" she cried, crossly. "Why ever didn't 'ee come in to supper,—such a beautiful bit of roast as I'd got, too! Where've 'ee been? What 'ave 'ee been doing? What 'ave 'ee been sleeping here for?"

Lutey raised himself into a sitting position. "Who are you?" he shouted. "Are you the beautiful maiden come for me? Are you Morwenna?"

"Whatever are you talking about? You haven't called me beautiful for the last thirty years, and I ain't called Morwenna. I'm Ann Betty Lutey, your own lawful wife, and if you don't know me, you must be gone clean out of your mind."

"Ann Betty Lutey," said the old man solemnly, "if you're my lawful wife you've had a narrow escape this night of being left a widow woman, and you may be thankful you've ever set eyes on me again."

"Come in and have some breakfast," said Ann Betty Lutey sternly, "and if you ain't better then I'll send for the doctor. It's my belief your brain is turned."

Lutey got up obediently and went in to his breakfast; indeed, he was glad enough of it, for he was light-headed from want of food. His breakfast did him good. Before he had finished it he was able to tell his wife about his adventure the night before, and he told it so gravely and sensibly that Ann Betty believed every word of it, and no longer thought his brain was turned.

Indeed, she was so much impressed by his story that before many hours had passed she had gone round to every house in the parish spreading the news, and to prove the truth of it she produced the pearl comb.

Then, oh dear, the gossiping that went on! It really was dreadful! The women neglected their homes, their children, and everything else for the whole of that week; and for months after old Lutey was besieged by all the sick and sorry for miles and miles around, who came to home to be cured. He did such a big business in healing people, that not a doctor for miles round could earn a living. Everyone went to old Lutey, and when it was found that he had power over witchcraft, too, he became the most important man in the whole country.

Lutey had been so rude and rough to the mermaiden when he parted from her, that no one would have been surprised if she had avenged herself on him somehow, and punished him severely. But no, she was true to all her promises. He got all his wishes, and neither he nor his descendants have ever come to want. Better far, though, would it have been for him had it been otherwise, for he paid dearly enough for his wishes in the end.

Nine years from that very time, on a calm moonlight night, Lutey, forgetting all about the mermaid and her threats, arranged to go out with a friend to do a little fishing. There was not a breath of wind stirring, and the sea was like glass, so that a sail was useless, and they had to take to the oars. Suddenly, though, without any puff of wind, or anything else to cause it, the sea rose round the boat in one huge wave, covered with a thick crest of foam, and in the midst of the foam was Morwenna!

Morwenna! as lovely as ever, her arms outstretched, her clear green eyes fixed steadily, triumphantly on Lutey. She did not open her lips, or make a sign, she only gazed and gazed at her victim.

For a moment he looked at her as though bewildered, then like one bereft of his senses by some spell, h rose in the boat, and turned his face towards the open sea. "My time is come," he said solemnly and sadly, and without another word to his frightened companion he sprang out of the boat and joined the mermaid. For a yard or two they swam in silence side by side, then disappeared beneath the waves, and the sea was as smooth again as though nothing had happened.

From that moment poor Lutey has never been seen, nor has his body been found. Probably he now forms one of the pieces of statuary so prized by the mermaiden, and stands decked with sea-blossoms, with gold heaped at his feet. Or, maybe, with a pair of gills slit under his chin, he swims about in their beautiful palaces, and revels in the cellars of shipwrecked wines. The misfortunes to his family did not end, though, with Lutey's disappearance, for, no matter how careful they are, how far they live from the sea, or what precautions they take to protect themselves, every ninth year one of old Lutey's descendants is claimed by the sea.

Source:
Quiller-Couch, Mabel. *Cornwall's Wonderland*. London & Toronto: J. M. Dent & Sons Ltd., n.d. [circa 1914].

71. The Mermaid's Song by Anne Hunter for Haydn

England

NOW the dancing sunbeams play
   On the green and glassy sea!
Come, and I will lead the way,
   Where the pearly treasures be.
Come with me, and we will go
Where the rocks of coral grow.
        Follow, follow, follow me!

Come, behold what treasures lie
   Far below the rolling waves,
Riches, hid from human eye,
   Dimly shine in ocean's caves.
Ebbing tides bear no delay,
Stormy winds are far away:
        Follow, follow, follow me!

NOTES

These words, as well as the others of the first six canzonets of Haydn [(Franz) Joseph Haydn (1732-1809)], were written for him by Mrs. John Hunter [Anne Hunter (1742-1821)], the wife of the most celebrated of English surgeons, and sister to a very distinguished one, the late Sir Everard Home. The music is Haydn's, the first from his set of six canzonets, composed during his visit to this country [England], in 1791.

Source:

Supplement to the Musical Library: March to December 1834. London:
   Charles Knight, 1834. pp. 15, 27.

72. The Mermaid of Margate
by Thomas Hood

England

>"Alas! what perils do environ
>That man who meddles with a siren!"
>   —Hudibrus

ON Margate beach, where the sick one roams,
    And the sentimental reads;
Where the maiden flirts, and the widow comes
    Like the ocean—to cast her weeds;—

Where urchins wander to pick up shells,
    And the Cit to spy at the ships,—
Like the water gala at Sadler's Wells,—
    And the Chandler for watery dips;—

There's a maiden sits by the ocean brim,
    As lovely and fair as sin!
But woe, deep water and woe to him,
    That she snareth like Peter Fin!

Her head is crowned with pretty sea-wares,
    And her locks are golden loose,
And seek to her feet, like other folks' heirs,
    To stand, of course, in her shoes!

And all day long she combeth them well,
    With a sea-shark's prickly jaw;
And her mouth is just like a rose-lipped shell,
    The fairest that man e'er saw!

And the Fishmonger, humble as love may be
    Hath planted his seat by her side;
"Good even, fair maid! Is thy lover at sea,
    To make thee so watch the tide?"

She turned about with her pearly brows,
    And clasped him by the hand;

"Come, love, with me; I've a bonny house
    On the golden Goodwin sand."

And then she gave him a siren kiss,
    No honeycomb e'er was sweeter;
Poor wretch! how little he dreamt for this
    That Peter should be salt-Peter:

And away with her prize to the wave she leapt,
    Not walking, as damsels do,
With toe and heel, as she ought to have stept,
    But she hopped like a Kangaroo;

One plunge, and then the victim was blind,
    Whilst they galloped across the tide;
At last, on the bank he waked in his mind,
    And the Beauty was by his side

One half on the sand, and half in the sea,
    But his hair began to stiffen;
For when he looked where her feet should be,
    She had no more feet than Miss Biffen!

But a scaly tail, of a dolphin's growth,
    In the dabbling brine did soak:
At last she opened her pearly mouth,
    Like an oyster, and thus she spoke:

"You crimpt my father, who was a skate,—
    And my sister you sold—a maid;
So here remain for a fish'ry fate,
    For lost you are, and betrayed!"

And away she went, with a sea-gull's scream,
    And a splash of her saucy tail;
In a moment he lost the silvery gleam
    That shone on her splended mail!

The sun went down with a blood-red flame,
    And the sky grew cloudy and black,
And the tumbling billows like leap-frog came,
    Each over the other's back!

Ah me! it had been a beautiful scene,
    With the safe terra-firma round;

But the green water-hillocks all seem'd to him
    Like those in a churchyard ground;

And Christians love in the turf to lie,
    Not in watery graves to be;
Nay, the very fishes will sooner die
    On the land than in the sea.

And whilst he stood, the watery strife
    Encroached on every hand,
And the ground decreased,—his moments of life
    Seemed measured, like Time's, by sand;

And still the waters foamed in, like ale,
    In front, and on either flank,
He knew that Goodwin and Co. must fail,
    There was such a run on the bank.

A little more, and a little more,
    The surges came tumbling in,
He sang the evening hymn twice o'er,
    And thought of every sin!

Each flounder and plaice lay cold at his heart,
    As cold as his marble slab;
And he thought he felt, in every part,
    The pincers of scalded crab.

The squealing lobsters that he had boiled,
    And the little potted shrimps,
All the horny prawns he had ever spoiled,
    Gnawed into his soul, like imps!

And the billows were wandering to and fro,
    And the glorious sun was sunk,
And Day, getting black in the face, as though
    Of the nightshade she had drunk!

Had there been but a smuggler's cargo adrift,
    One tub, or keg, to be seen,
It might have given his spirits a lift
    Or an *anker* where *Hope* might lean!

But there was not a box or a beam afloat,
    To raft him from that sad place;

Not a skiff, not a yawl, or a mackerel boat,
    Nor a smack upon Neptune's face.

At last, his lingering hopes to buoy,
    He saw a sail and a mast,
And called "Ahoy!"—but it was not a hoy,
    And so the vessel went past.

And with saucy wing that flapped in his face,
    The wild bird about him flew,
With a shrilly scream, that twitted his case,
    "Why, thou art a sea-gull too!"

And lo! the tide was over his feet;
    Oh! his heart began to freeze,
And slowly to pulse:—in another beat
    The wave was up to his knees!

He was deafened amidst the mountain tops,
    And the salt spray blinded his eyes,
And washed away the other salt drops
    That grief had caused to arise:—

But just as his body was all afloat,
    And the surges above him broke,
He was saved from the hungry deep by a boat
    Of Deal—(but builded of oak).

The skipper gave him a dram, as he lay,
    And chafed his shivering skin;
And the Angel returned that was flying away
    With the spirit of Peter Fin!

Source:
Hood, Thomas. *Whims and Oddities: In Prose and Verse*. London: Lupton Relfe, 1826.

73. The Merman
by Alfred, Lord Tennyson

England

Both this poem and its companion, "The Mermaid," which follows were originally published in 1830.

I.

WHO would be
A merman bold,
Sitting alone,
Singing alone
Under the sea,
With a crown of gold,
On a throne?

II.

    I would be a merman bold,
I would sit and sing the whole of the day;
I would fill the sea-halls with a voice of power;
But at night I would roam abroad and play
With the mermaids in and out of the rocks,
Dressing their hair with the white sea-flower;
And holding them back by their flowing locks
I would kiss them often under the sea,
And kiss them again till they kiss'd me
    Laughingly, laughingly;
And then we would wander away, away
To the pale-green sea-groves straight and high,
    Chasing each other merrily.

III.

There would be neither moon nor star;
But the wave would make music above us afar—
Low thunder and light in the magic night—
    Neither moon nor star.
We would call aloud in the dreamy dells,
Call to each other and whoop and cry

    All night, merrily, merrily;
They would pelt me with starry spangles and shells,
Laughing and clapping their hands between,
    All night, merrily, merrily:
But I would throw to them back in mine
Turkis and agate and almondine:
Then leaping out upon them unseen
I would kiss them often under the sea,
And kiss them again till they kiss'd me
    Laughingly, laughingly.
Oh! what a happy life were mine
Under the hollow-hung ocean green!
Soft are the moss-beds under the sea;
We would live merrily, merrily.

Source:
Tennyson, Lord Alfred. *The Complete Poetical Works of Alfred, Lord Tennyson, Poet Laureate.* New York: Harper & Brothers, 1884.

74. The Mermaid by Alfred, Lord Tennyson

England

This poem is the companion to Tennyson's "The Merman."

I.

WHO would be
A mermaid fair,
Singing alone,
Combing her hair
Under the sea,
In a golden curl
With a comb of pearl,
On a throne?

II.

    I would be a mermaid fair;
I would sing to myself the whole of the day;

With a comb of pearl I would comb my hair;
And still as I comb'd I would sing and say,
"Who is it loves me? who loves not me?"
I would comb my hair till my ringlets would fall
      Low adown, low adown,
From under my starry sea-bud crown
      Low adown and around,
And I should look like a fountain of gold
        Springing alone
     With a shrill inner sound,
      Over the throne
     In the midst of the hall;
Till that great sea-snake under the sea
From his coiled sleeps in the central deeps
Would slowly trail himself sevenfold
Round the hall where I sate, and look in at the gate
With his large calm eyes for the love of me.
And all the mermen under the sea
Would feel their immortality
Die in their hearts for the love of me.

III.

But at night I would wander away, away,
    I would fling on each side my low-flowing locks,
And lightly vault from the throne and play
    With the mermen in and out of the rocks;
We would run to and fro, and hide and seek,
    On the broad sea-wolds in the crimson shells,
    Whose silvery spikes are nighest the sea.
But if any came near I would call, and shriek,
And adown the steep like a wave I would leap
    From the diamond-ledges that jut from the dells;
For I would not be kiss'd by all who would list,
Of the bold merry mermen under the sea;
They would sue me, and woo me, and flatter me,
In the purple twilights under the sea;
But the king of them all would carry me,
Woo me, and win me, and marry me,
In the branching jaspers under the sea;
Then all the dry pied things that be
In the hueless mosses under the sea
Would curl round my silver feet silently,
All looking up for the love of me.
And if I should carol aloud, from aloft
All things that are forked, and horned, and soft

Would lean out from the hollow sphere of the sea,
All looking down for the love of me.

Source:

Tennyson, Lord Alfred. *The Complete Poetical Works of Alfred, Lord Tennyson, Poet Laureate.* New York: Harper & Brothers, 1884.

75. The Forsaken Merman by Matthew Arnold

England

COME, dear children, let us away;
Down and away below!
Now my brothers call from the bay;
Now the great winds shorewards blow;
Now the salt tides seawards flow;
Now the wild white horses play,
Champ and chafe and toss in the spray.
Children dear, let us away.
This way, this way.

Call her once before you go—
Call once yet.
In a voice that she will know:
"Margaret! Margaret!"
Children's voices should be dear
(Call once more) to a mother's ear:
Children's voices, wild with pain—
Surely she will come again.
Call her once and come away.
This way, this way.
"Mother dear, we cannot stay.
The wild white horses foam and fret."
Margaret! Margaret!

Come, dear children, come away down,
Call no more.
One last look at the white-wall'd town,
And the little grey church on the windy shore.
Then come down!

She will not come though you call all day;
Come away, come away!

Children dear, was it yesterday
We heard the sweet bells over the bay?
In the caverns where we lay,
Through the surf and through the swell,
The far-off sound of a silver bell?
Sand-strewn caverns, cool and deep,
Where the winds are all asleep;
Where the spent lights[1] quiver and gleam;
Where the salt weed sways in the stream;
Where the sea-beasts rang'd all round
Feed in the ooze[2] of their pasture-ground;
Where the sea-snakes coil and twine,
Dry their mail and bask[3] in the brine;
Where great whales come sailing by,
Sail and sail, with unshut eye,
Round the world for ever and aye?
When did music come this way?
Children dear, was it yesterday?

Children dear, was it yesterday
(Call yet once) that she went away?
Once she sate with you and me,
On a red gold throne in the heart of the sea,
And the youngest sate on her knee.
She comb'd its bright hair, and she tended it well,
When down swung the sound of the far-off bell.
She sigh'd, she look'd up through the clear green sea.
She said; "I must go, for my kinsfolk pray
In the little grey church on the shore to-day.
'Twill be Easter-time in the world—ah me!
And I lose my poor soul, Merman, here with thee."
I said; "Go up, dear heart, through the waves;
Say thy prayer, and come back to the kind sea-caves."

---

[1] *The spent lights*: the lights are fainter down below and broken up into many quivering rays by the movement of the water.

[2] *Ooze*, properly 'moisture,' but it is especially used for the soft mud at the bottom of deep water.

[3] *Bask*. The word means originally to 'bathe oneself,' being a reflexive form of 'bathe'; hence it is used of bathing in the sunshine. Here the sense is, of course, the usual one of basking in the sun.

She smil'd, she went up through the surf in the bay.
Children dear, was it yesterday?

    Children dear, were we long alone?
"The sea grows stormy, the little ones moan.
Long prayers," I said, "in the world they say.
Come," I said, and we rose through the surf in the bay.
We went up the beach, by the sandy down[1]
Where the sea-stocks bloom, to the white-wall'd town.
Through the narrow pav'd streets, where all was still,
To the little grey church on the windy hill.
From the church came a murmur of folk at their prayers,
But we stood without in the cold blowing airs.
We climb'd on the graves, on the stones, worn with rains,
And we gazed up the aisle through the small leaded panes.
She sate by the pillar; we saw her clear:
"Margaret, hist! come quick, we are here!
Dear heart," I said, "we are long alone.
The sea grows stormy, the little ones moan."
But, ah, she gave me never a look,
For her eyes were seal'd to the holy book!
"Loud prays the priest; shut stands the door."
Come away, children, call no more!
Come away, come down, call no more!

    Down, down, down!
Down to the depths of the sea!
She sits at her wheel in the humming town,
Singing most joyfully.
Hark, what she sings; "O joy, O joy,
For the humming street, and the child with its toy!
For the priest, and the bell, and the holy well.
For the wheel where I spun,
And the blessed light of the sun!"
And so she sings her fill,
Singing most joyfully,
Till the spindle drops[2] from her hand,
And the whizzing wheel stands still.

---

[1] *We went up the beach, etc.* The original Teutonic idea of a sea-spirit does not include the notion of a fish-like form, and consequently Mermen and Mermaids (but they are commonly conceived as male) can, and often do, come on shore and associate with men.

[2] *Till the spindle drops.* The first edition had by an oversight, "Till the shuttle falls," as if the work had been weaving.

She steals to the window, and looks at the sand;
And over the sand at the sea;
And her eyes are set in a stare;
And anon there breaks a sigh,
And anon there drops a tear,
From a sorrow-clouded eye,
And a heart sorrow-laden,
A long, long sigh,
For the cold strange eyes of a little Mermaiden,
And the gleam of her golden hair.

   Come away, away children;
Come children, come down!
The hoarse wind blows colder;[1]
Lights shine in the town.
She will start from her slumber
When gusts shake the door;
She will hear the winds howling,
Will hear the waves roar.
We shall see, while above us[2]
The waves roar and whirl,
A ceiling of amber,
A pavement of pearl.
Singing, "Here came a mortal,
But faithless was she!
And alone dwell for ever
The kings of the sea."

But, children, at midnight,
When soft the winds blow;
When clear falls the moonlight;
When spring-tides are low:
When sweet airs come seaward
From heaths starr'd with broom;
And high rocks throw mildly
On the blanch'd sands a gloom:
Up the still, glistening beaches,
Up the creeks we will hie;[3]
Over banks of bright seaweed
The ebb-tide leaves dry.
We will gaze, from the sand-hills,

---

[1] "The salt tide rolls seaward" in 1849 edition.
[2] *We shall see, etc.* Note the picturesque quality of these four lines.
[3] *Hie*, 'hasten.'

At the white, sleeping town;
At the church on the hill-side—
And then come back down.
Singing, "There dwells a lov'd one,
But cruel is she.
She left lonely for ever
The kings of the sea."

NOTES

In this poem, published in 1849, the same idea occurs as in Arnold's "The Neckan," [Offered next in the present anthology.] of sea-creatures who intermarry with mortals and complain of the hard-heartedness of their human mates, from whom they are separated by barriers of religion. It is the gem of these shorter narrative poems, admirable for its simple pathos as well as for the picturesqueness of the descriptions.

Source:
Arnold, Matthew. *Poems by Matthew Arnold*. G. C. Macauley, editor. London: Macmillan and Co., 1896.

76. The Neckan
by Matthew Arnold

England

IN summer, on the headlands,
    The Baltic Sea along,
Sits Neckan with his harp of gold,
    And sings his plaintive song.

Green rolls beneath the headlands,
    Green rolls the Baltic Sea.
And there, below the Neckan's feet,
    His wife and children be.

He sings not of the ocean,
    Its shells and roses pale.
Of earth, of earth the Neckan sings;
    He hath no other tale.

He sits upon the headlands,
    And sings a mournful stave
Of all he saw and felt on earth,
    Far from the green sea wave.

Sings how, a knight, he wander'd
    By castle, field, and town.—
But earthly knights have harder hearts
    Than the Sea Children own.

Sings of his earthly bridal—
    Priest, knights, and ladies gay.
"And who art thou," the priest began,
    "Sir Knight, who wedd'st to-day?"—

"I am no knight," he answer'd;
    "From the sea waves I come."—
The knights drew sword, the ladies scream'd,
    The surplic'd priest stood dumb.

He sings how from the chapel
    He vanish'd with his bride,
And bore her down to the sea halls,
    Beneath the cold[1] sea tide.

He sings how she sits weeping
    'Mid shells that round her lie.
"False Neckan shares my bed," she weeps;
    "No Christian mate have I."—

He sings how through the billows
    He rose to earth again,
And sought a priest to sign the cross,
    That Neckan Heaven might gain.

He sings how, on an evening,
    Beneath the birch trees cool,
He sate and play d his harp of gold,
    Beside the river pool.

Beside the pool sate Neckan—
    Tears fill'd his mild[2] blue eye.

---

[1] *Cold*: salt in 1853, 1854.
[2] 'Cold' instead of 'mild' in later versions.

On his white mule, across the bridge,
    A cassock'd priest rode by.

"Why sitt'st thou there, O Neckan,
    And play'st thy harp of gold?
Sooner shall this my staff bear leaves,
    Than thou shalt Heaven behold."—

But, lo, the staff, it budded![1]
    It green'd, it branch'd, it waved.
"O ruth[2] of God," the priest cried out,
    "This lost sea-creature saved!"

The cassock'd priest rode onwards,
    And vanish'd with his mule.
And Neckan in the twilight grey[3]
    Wept by the river pool.

He wept: "The earth hath kindness,
    The sea, the starry poles;
Earth, sea, and sky, and God above—
    But, ah, not human souls!"

In summer, on the headlands,
    The Baltic Sea along,
Sits Neckan with his harp of gold,
    And sings this plaintive song.

NOTES

The 'Nichus,' 'Necker,' or 'Nek,' is the water-spirit of Teutonic mythology; hence the modern German *Nixe*. Such creatures were conceived to have special delight in music and song. The popular idea about them was that, though doomed to perdition, they might under certain circumstances be saved. In Grimm's *Teutonic Mythology* we have the following story: "Two boys were playing by the riverside; the Neck sat there touching his harp, and the children cried to him, 'What do you sit and

---

[1] *But, lo, the staff.* A similar incident occurs in the legend of Tannhauser, when the Pope declares the impossibility of the sinner obtaining pardon.
[2] *Ruth*, i.e. 'pity,' 'mercy.'
[3] *But Neckan, etc.* There is perhaps some inconsistency between the new stanzas and the old: after the assurance of salvation given by the miracle of the budding staff, the grief ought to have been abated.

Slay here for, Neck? You know you will never be saved.' The feck began to weep bitterly, threw his harp away, and sank to the bottom. When the boys got home, they told their father what had happened. The father, who was a priest, said, 'You have sinned against the Neck; go back and comfort him, and tell him he may be saved.' When they returned to the river, the Neck sat on the bank, weeping and wailing. The children said, 'Do not cry so, poor Neck; father says that your Redeemer liveth too.' Then the Neck exclaimed joyfully, and played charmingly till long after sunset." Grimm adds, "I do not know that anywhere in our legends it is so pointedly expressed how badly the heathen stand in need of the Christian religion, and how mildly it ought to meet them" (Vol. II., p. 494, English translation). The idea of water-spirits wandering among men, and endeavouring to become one of them by intermarriage or otherwise, occurs often in German tales.

This poem has undergone some interesting changes since it was first published in 1853. Two whole stanzas have been added, and they are those which most definitely strike the note of hope for the 'lost sea-creature,' viz. the fourteenth, beginning, "But, lo, the staff it budded," and the sixteenth, "He wept: 'The earth hath kindness,'" etc.

Source:
Arnold, Matthew. *Poems by Matthew Arnold*. G. C. Macauley, editor. London: Macmillan and Co., 1896.

77. The Fisherman and His Soul by Oscar Wilde

England

EVERY evening the young Fisherman went out upon the sea, and threw his nets into the water.

When the wind blew from the land he caught nothing, or but little at best, for it was a bitter and black-winged wind, and rough waves rose up to meet it. But when the wind blew to the shore, the fish came in from the deep, and swam into the meshes of his nets, and he took them to the market-place and sold them.

Every evening he went out upon the sea, and one evening the net was so heavy that hardly could he draw it into the boat. And he laughed, and said to himself "Surely I have caught all the fish that swim, or snared some dull monster that will be a marvel to men, or some thing of horror that the great Queen will desire," and putting forth all his strength, he tugged at the coarse ropes till, like lines of blue enamel round a vase of bronze, the long veins rose up on his arms. He tugged at the thin ropes, and nearer and nearer came the circle of flat corks, and the net rose at last to the top of the water.

But no fish at all was in it, nor any monster or thing of horror, but only a little Mermaid lying fast asleep.

Her hair was as a wet fleece of gold, and each separate hair as a thread of line gold in a cup of glass. Her body was as white ivory, and her tail was of silver and pearl. Silver and pearl was her tail, and the green weeds of the sea coiled round it; and like sea-shells were her ears, and her lips were like sea-coral. The cold waves dashed over her cold breasts, and the salt glistened upon her eyelids.

So beautiful was she that when the young Fisherman saw her he was filled with wonder, and he put out his hand and drew the net close to him, and leaning over the side he clasped her in his arms. And when he touched her, she gave a cry like a startled sea-gull and woke, and looked at him in terror with her mauve-amethyst eyes, and struggled that she might escape. But he held her tightly to him, and would not suffer her to depart.

And when she saw that she could in no way escape from him, she began to weep, and said, "I pray thee let me go, for I am the only daughter of a King, and my father is aged and alone."

But the young Fisherman answered, "I will not let thee go save thou makest me a promise that whenever I call thee, thou wilt come and sing to me, for the fish delight to listen to the song of the Sea-folk, and so shall my nets be full."

"Wilt thou in very truth let me go, if I promise thee this?" cried the Mermaid.

"In very truth I will let thee go," said the young Fisherman. So she made him the promise he desired, and sware it by the oath of the Sea-folk. And he loosened his arms from about her, and she sank down into the water, trembling with a strange fear.

Every evening the young Fisherman went out upon the sea, and called to the Mermaid, and she rose out of the water and sang to him. Round and round her swam the dolphins, and the wild gulls wheeled above her head.

And she sang a marvellous song. For she sang of the Sea-folk who drive their flocks from cave to cave, and carry the little calves on their shoulders; of the Tritons who have long green beards, and hairy breasts, and blow through twisted conchs when the King passes by; of the palace of the King which is all of amber, with a roof of clear emerald, and a pavement of bright pearl; and of the gardens of the sea where the great filigrane fans of coral wave all day long, and the fish dart about like silver birds, and the anemones cling to the rocks, and the pinks bourgeon in the ribbed yellow sand. She sang of the big whales that come down from the north seas and have sharp icicles hanging to their fins; of the

Sirens who tell of such wonderful things that the merchants have to stop their ears with wax lest they should hear them, and leap into the water and be drowned; of the sunken galleys with their tall masts, and the frozen sailors clinging to the rigging, and the mackerel swimming in and out of the open portholes; of the little barnacles who are great travellers, and cling to the keels of the ships and go round and round the world; and of the cuttlefish who live in the sides of the cliffs and stretch out their long black arms, and can make night come when they will it. She sang of the nautilus who has a boat of her own that is carved out of an opal and steered with a silken sail; of the happy Mermen who play upon harps and can charm the great Kraken to sleep; of the little children who catch hold of the slippery porpoises and ride laughing upon their backs; of the Mermaids who lie in the white foam and hold out their arms to the mariners; and of the sea-lions with their curved tusks, and the sea-horses with their floating manes.

And as she sang, all the funny-fish came in from the deep to listen to her, and the young Fisherman threw his nets round them and caught them, and others he took with a spear. And when his boat was well-laden, the Mermaid would sink down into the sea, smiling at him.

Yet would she never come near him that he might touch her. Often times he called to her and prayed of her, but she would not; and when he sought to seize her she dived into the water as a seal might dive, nor did he see her again that day. And each day the sound of her voice became sweeter to his ears. So sweet was her voice that he forgot his nets and his cunning, and had no care of his craft. Vermilion-finned and with eyes of bossy gold, the tunnies went by in shoals, but he heeded them not. His spear lay by his side unused, and his baskets of plaited osier were empty. With lips parted, and eyes dim with wonder, he sat idle in his boat and listened, listening till the sea-mists crept round him, and the wandering moon stained his brown limbs with silver.

And one evening he called to her, and said: "Little Mermaid, little Mermaid, I love thee. Take me for thy bridegroom, for I love thee."

But the Mermaid shook her head. "Thou hast a human soul," she answered. "If only thou would'st send away thy soul, then could I love thee."

And the young Fisherman said to himself "Of what use is my soul to me? I cannot see it. I may not touch it. I do not know it. Surely I will send it away from me, and much gladness shall be mine." And a cry of joy broke from his lips, and standing up in the painted boat, he held out his arms to the Mermaid. "I will send my soul away," he cried, "and you shall be my bride, and I will be the bridegroom, and in the depth of the sea we will dwell together, and all that thou hast sung of thou shalt show me, and all that thou desirest I will do, nor shall our lives be divided."

And the little Mermaid laughed for pleasure, and hid her face in her hands.

"But how shall I send my soul from me?" cried the young Fisherman.

"Tell me how I may do it, and lo! it shall be done."

"Alas! I know not," said the little Mermaid: "the Sea-folk have no souls." And she sank down into the deep, looking wistfully at him.

Now early on the next morning, before the sun was the span of a man's hand above the hill, the young Fisherman went to the house of the Priest and knocked three times at the door.

The novice looked out through the wicket, and where he saw who it was, he drew back the latch and said to him, "Enter."

And the young Fisherman passed in, and knelt down on the sweet-smelling rushes of the floor, and cried to the Priest who was reading out of the Holy Book and said to him, "Father, I am in love with one of the Sea-folk, and my soul hindereth me from having my desire. Tell me how I can send my soul away from me, for in truth I have no need of it. Of what value is my soul to me? I cannot see it. I may not touch it. I do not know it."

And the Priest beat his breast, and answered, "Alack, Alack, thou art mad, or hast eaten of poisonous herb, for the soul is the noblest part of man, and was given to us by God that we should nobly use it. There is no thing more precious than a human soul, nor any earthly thing that can be weighed with it. It is worth all the gold that is in the world, and is more precious than the rubies of the kings. Therefore, my son, think not any more of this matter, for it is a sin that may not be forgiven. And as for the Seafolk, they are lost, and they who would traffic with them are lost also. They are as the beasts of the field that know not good from evil, and for them the Lord has not died."

The young Fisherman's eyes filled with tears when he heard the bitter words of the Priest, and he rose up from his knees and said to him, "Father, the Fauns live in the forest and are glad, and on the rocks sit the Mermen with their harps of red gold. Let me be as they are, I beseech thee, for their days are as the days of flowers. And as for my soul, what doth my soul profit me, if it stand between me and the thing that I love?"

"The love of the body is vile," cried the Priest, knitting his brows, "and vile and evil are the pagan things God suffers to wander through His world. Accursed be the Fauns of the woodland, and accursed be the singers of the sea! I have heard them at night-time, and they have sought to lure me from my beads. They tap at the window, and laugh. They whisper into my ears the tale of their perilous joys. They tempt me with temptations, and when I would pray they make mouths at me. They are lost, I tell thee, they are lost. For them there is no heaven nor hell, and in neither shall they praise God's name."

"Father," cried the young Fisherman, "thou knowest not what thou sayest. Once in my net I snared the daughter of a King. She is fairer than the morning star, and whiter than the moon. For her body I would give my soul, and for her love I would surrender heaven. Tell me what I ask of thee, and let me go in peace."

"Away! Away!" cried the Priest: "thy leman is lost, and thou shalt be lost with her." And he gave him no blessing, but drove him from his door.

And the young Fisherman went down into the market-place, and he walked slowly, and with bowed head, as one who is in sorrow.

And when the merchants saw him coming, they began to whisper to each other, and one of them came forth to meet him, and called him by name, and said to him, "What hast thou to sell?"

"I will sell thee my soul," he answered: "I pray thee buy it off me, for I am weary of it. Of what use is my soul to me? I cannot see it. I may not touch it. I do not know it."

But the merchants mocked at him, and said, "Of what use is a man's soul to us? It is not worth a clipped piece of silver. Sell us thy body for a slave, and we will clothe thee in sea-purple, and put a ring upon thy finger, and make thee the minion of the great Queen. But talk not of the soul, for to us it is nought, nor has it any value for our service."

And the young Fisherman said to himself: "How strange a thing this is! The Priest telleth me that the soul is worth all the gold in the world, and the merchants say that it is not worth a clipped piece of silver." And he passed out of the market-place, and went down to the shore of the sea, and began to ponder on what he should do.

And at noon he remembered how one of his companions, who was a gatherer of samphire, had told him of a certain young Witch who dwelt in a cave at the head of the bay and was very cunning in her witcheries. And he set to and ran, so eager was he to get rid of his soul, and a cloud of dust followed him as he sped round the sand of the shore. By the itching of her palm the young Witch knew his coming, and she laughed and let down her red hair. With her red hair falling around her, she stood at the opening of the cave, and in her hand she had a spray of wild hemlock that was blossoming.

"What d'ye lack? What d'ye lack?" she cried, as he came panting up the steep, and bent down before her. "Fish for thy net, when the wind is foul? I have a little reed-pipe, and when I blow on it the mullet come sailing into the bay. But it has a price, pretty boy, it has a price. What d'ye lack? What d'ye lack? A storm to wreck the ships, and wash the chests of rich treasure ashore? I have more storms than the wind has, for I serve one who is stronger than the wind, and with a sieve and a pail of water I can send the great galleys to the bottom of the sea. But I have a price, pretty boy, I have a price. What d'ye lack? What d'ye lack? I know a flower that grows in the valley, none knows it but I. It has purple leaves, and a star in its heart, and its juice is as white as milk. Should'st thou touch with this flower the hard lips of the Queen, she would follow thee all over the world. Out of the bed of the King she would rise, and over the whole world she would follow thee. And it has a price, pretty boy, it has a price. What d'ye lack? What d'ye lack? I can pound a toad in a mortar, and make broth of it, and stir the broth with a dead man's hand. Sprinkle it on thine enemy while he sleeps, and he will turn into a black viper, and hid own mother will slay him. With a wheel I can draw the Moon from heaven, and in a crystal I can show thee Death. What d'ye lack? What d'ye lack? Tell me thy desire, and I will give it thee, and thou shalt pay me a price, pretty boy, thou shalt pay me a price."

"My desire is but for a little thing," said the young Fisherman, "yet hath the Priest been wroth with me, and driven me forth. It is but for a little thing, and the merchants have mocked at me, and denied me. Therefore am I come to thee, though men call thee evil, and whatever be thy price I shall pay it."

"What would'st thou?" asked the Witch, coming near to him.

"I would send my soul away from me," answered the young Fisherman.

The Witch grew pale, and shuddered, and hid her face in her blue mantle. "Pretty boy, pretty boy," she muttered, "that is a terrible thing to do."

He tossed his brown curls and laughed. "My soul is nought to me," he answered. "I cannot see it. I may not touch it. I do not know it."

"What wilt thou give me if I tell thee?" asked the Witch looking down at him with her beautiful eyes.

"Five pieces of gold," he said, "and my nets, and the wattled house where I live, and the painted boat in which I sail. Only tell me how to get rid of my soul, and I will give thee all that I possess."

She laughed mockingly at him, and struck him with the spray of hemlock. "I can turn the autumn leaves into gold," she answered, "and I can weave the pale moonbeams into silver if I will it. He whom I serve is richer than all the kings of this world and has their dominions."

"What then shall I give thee," he cried, "if thy price be neither gold nor silver?"

The Witch stroked his hair with her thin white hand. "Thou must dance with me, pretty boy," she murmured, and she smiled at him as she spoke.

"Nought but that?" cried the young Fisherman in wonder, and he rose to his feet.

"Nought but that," she answered, and she smiled at him again.

"Then at sunset in some secret place we shall dance together," he said, "and after that we have danced thou shalt tell me the thing which I desire to know."

She shook her head. "When the moon is full, when the moon is full," she muttered. Then she peered all round, and listened. A blue bird rose screaming from its nest and circled over the dunes, and three spotted birds rustled through the coarse grey grass and whistled to each other. There was no other sound save the sound of a wave fretting the smooth pebbles below. So she reached out her hand, and drew him near to her and put her dry lips close to his ear.

"To-night thou must come to the top of the mountain," she whispered. "It is a Sabbath, and He will be there." The young Fisherman started and looked at her, and she showed her white teeth and laughed.

"Who is He of whom thou speakest?" he asked.

"It matters not," she answered. "Go thou to-night, and stand under the branches of the hornbeam, and wait for my coming. If a black dog run towards thee, strike it with a rod of willow, and it will go away. If an owl speak to thee, make it no answer. When the moon is full I shall be with thee, and we will dance together on the grass."

"But wilt thou swear to me to tell me how I may send my soul from me?" he made question.

She moved out into the sunlight, and through her red hair rippled the wind. "By the hoofs of the goat I swear it," she made answer.

"Thou art the best of the witches," cried the young Fisherman, "and I will surely dance with thee to-night on the top of the mountain. I would indeed that thou hadst asked of me either gold or silver. But such as thy price is thou shalt have it, for it is but a little thing." And he doffed his cap to her, and bent his head low, and ran back to the town filled with a great joy.

And the Witch watched him as he went, and when he had passed from her sight she entered her cave, and having taken a mirror from a box of carved cedarwood, she set it up on a frame, and burned vervain on lighted charcoal before it, and peered through the coils of the smoke. And after a time she clenched her hands in anger. "He should have been mine," she muttered, "I am as fair as she is."

And that evening, when the moon had risen, the young Fisherman climbed up to the top of the mountain, and stood under the branches of the hornbeam. Like a targe of polished metal the round sea lay at his feet, and the shadows of the fishing boats moved in the little bay. A great owl, with yellow sulphurous eyes, called to him by his name, but he made it no answer. A black dog ran towards him and snarled. He struck it with a rod of willow, and it went away whining. At midnight the witches came flying through the air like bats. "Phew!" they cried, as they lit upon the ground, "there is someone here we know not!" and they sniffed about, and chattered to each other, and made signs.

Last of all came the young Witch, with her red hair streaming in the wind. She wore a dress of gold tissue embroidered with peacocks' eyes, and a little cap of green velvet was on her head.

"Where is he, where is he?" shrieked the witches when they saw her, but she only laughed, and ran to the hornbeam, and taking the Fisherman by the hand she led him out into the moonlight and began to dance. Round and round they whirled, and the young Witch jumped so high that he could see the scarlet heels of her shoes. Then right across the dancers came the sound of the galloping of a horse, but no horse was to be seen, and he felt afraid.

"Faster," cried the Witch, and she threw her arms about his neck, and her breath was hot upon his face. "Faster, faster!" she cried, and the earth seemed to spin beneath his feet, and his brain grew troubled, and a great terror fell on him, as of some evil thing that was watching him, and at last he became aware that under the shadow of a rock there was a figure that had not been there before. It was a man dressed in a suit of black velvet, cut in the Spanish fashion. His face was strangely pale, but his lips were like a proud red flower. He seemed weary, and was leaning back toying in a listless manner with the pommel of his dagger. On the grass beside him lay a plumed hat, and a pair of riding gloves gauntleted with gilt lace, and sewn with seed-pearls wrought into a curious device. A short cloak lined with sables hung from his shoulder, and his delicate white hands were gemmed with rings. Heavy eyelids drooped over his eyes. The young Fisherman watched him, as one snared in a spell. At last their eyes met, and wherever he danced it seemed to him that the eyes of the man were upon him. He heard the Witch laugh, and caught her by the waist, and whirled her madly round and round.

Suddenly a dog bayed in the wood, and the dancers stopped, and going up two by two, knelt down, and kissed the man's hands. As they did so, a little smile touched his proud lips, as a bird's wing touches the water and makes it laugh. But there was disdain in it. He kept looking at the young Fisherman.

"Come! let us worship," whispered the Witch, and she led him up, and a great desire to do as she besought him seized on him, and he followed her. But when he came close, and without knowing why he did it, he made on his breast the sign of the Cross, and called upon the holy name.

No sooner had he done so than the witches screamed like hawks and flew away, and the pallid face that had been watching him twitched with a spasm of pain. The man went over to a little wood, and whistled. A jennet with silver trappings came running to meet him. As he leapt upon the saddle he turned round, and looked at the young Fisherman sadly.

And the Witch with the red hair tried to fly away also, but the Fisherman caught her by her wrists, and held her fast. "Loose me," she cried, "and let me go. For thou hast named what should not be named, and shown the sign that may not be looked at."

"Nay," he answered, "but I will not let thee go till thou hast told me the secret."

"What secret?" said the Witch, wrestling with him like a wild cat, and biting her foam-flecked lips.

"Thou knowest," he made answer.

Her grass-green eyes grew dim with tears, and she said to the Fisherman, "Ask me anything but that!"

He laughed, and held her all the more tightly.

And when she saw that she could not free herself she whispered to him, "Surely I am as fair as the daughters of the sea, and as comely as those that dwell in the blue waters," and she fawned on him and put her face close to his.

But he thrust her back frowning, and said to her, "If thou keepest not the promise that thou madest to me I will slay thee for a false witch."

She grew grey as a blossom of the Judas tree, and shuddered. "Be it so," she muttered. "It is thy soul and not mine. Do with it as thou wilt." And she took from her girdle a little knife that had a handle of green viper's skin, and gave it to him.

"What shall this serve me?" he asked of her wondering.

She was silent for a few moments, and a look of terror came over her face. Then she brushed her hair back from her forehead, and smiling strangely she said to him, "What men call the shadow of the body is not the shadow of the body, but is the body of the soul. Stand on the seashore with thy back to the moon, and cut away from around thy feet thy shadow, which is thy soul's body, and bid thy soul leave thee, and it will do so."

The young Fisherman trembled. "Is this true?" he murmured.

"It is true, and I would that I had not told thee of it," she cried, and she clung to his knees weeping.

He put her from him and left her in the rank grass, and going to the edge of the mountain he placed the knife in his belt, and began to climb down.

And his Soul that was within him called out to him and said, "Lo! I have dwelt with thee for all these years, and have been thy servant. Send me not away from thee now, for what evil have I done thee?"

And the young Fisherman laughed. "Thou has done me no evil, but I have no need of thee," he answered. "The world is wide, and there is Heaven also, and Hell, and that dim twilight house that lies between. Go wherever thou wilt, but trouble me not, for my love is calling to me."

And his Soul besought him piteously, but he heeded it not, but leapt from crag to crag, being sure-footed as a wild goat, and at last he reached the level ground and the yellow shore of the sea.

Bronze-limbed and well-knit, like a statue wrought by a Grecian, he stood on the sand with his back to the moon, and out of the foam came white arms that beckoned to him, and out of the waves rose dim forms that did him homage. Before him lay his shadow, which was the body of his soul, and behind him hung the moon in the honey-coloured air.

And his Soul said to him, "If indeed thou must drive me from thee, send me not forth without a heart. The world is cruel, give me thy heart to take with me."

He tossed his head and smiled. "With what should I love my love if I gave thee my heart?" he cried.

"Nay, but be merciful," said his Soul: "give me thy heart, for the world is very cruel, and I am afraid."

"My heart is my love's," he answered, "therefore tarry not, but get thee gone."

"Should I not love also?" asked his Soul.

"Get thee gone, for I have no need of thee," cried the young Fisherman, and he took the little knife with its handle of green viper's skin, and cut away his shadow from around his feet, and it rose up and stood before him, and looked at him, and it was even as himself.

He crept back, and thrust the knife into his belt, and a feeling of awe came over him. "Get thee gone," he murmured, "and let me see thy face no more."

"Nay, but we must meet again," said the Soul. Its voice was low and flute-like, and its lips hardly moved while it spake.

"How shall we meet?" cried the young Fisherman. "Thou wilt not follow me into the depths of the sea?"

"Once every year I will come to this place, and call to thee," said the Soul. "It may be that thou wilt have need of me."

"What need should I have of thee?" cried the young Fisherman, "but be it as thou wilt," and he plunged into the water, and the Tritons blew their horns, and the little Mermaid rose up to meet him, and put her arms around his neck and kissed him on the mouth.

And the Soul stood on the lonely beach and watched them. And when they had sunk down into the sea, it went weeping away over the marshes.

And after a year was over the Soul came down to the shore of the sea and called to the young Fisherman, and he rose out of the deep, and said, "Why dost thou call to me?"

And the Soul answered, "Come nearer, that I may speak with thee, for I have seen marvellous things."

So he came nearer, and couched in the shallow water, and leaned his head upon his hand and listened.

And the Soul said to him, "When I left thee I turned my face to the East and journeyed. From the East cometh everything that is wise. Six days I journeyed, and on the morning of the seventh day I came to a hill that is in the country of the Tartars. I sat down under the shade of a tamarisk tree to shelter myself from the sun. The land was dry, and burnt up with the heat. The people went to and fro over the plain like flies crawling upon a disk of polished copper.

"When it was noon a cloud of red dust rose up from the flat rim of the land. When the Tartars saw it, they strung their painted bows, and having leapt upon their little horses they galloped to meet it. The women fled screaming to the waggons, and hid themselves behind the felt curtains.

"At twilight the Tartars returned, but five of them were missing, and of those that came back not a few had been wounded. They harnessed their horses to the waggons and drove hastily away. Three jackals came out of a cave and peered after them. Then they sniffed up the air with their nostrils, and trotted off in the opposite direction.

"When the moon rose I saw a camp-fire burning on the plain, and went towards it. A company of merchants were seated round it on carpets. Their camels were picketed behind them, and the negroes who were their servants were pitching tents of tanned skin upon the sand, and making a high wall of the prickly pear.

"As I came near them, the chief of the merchants rose up and drew his sword, and asked me my business.

"I answered that I was a Prince in my own land, and that I had escaped from the Tartars, who had sought to make me their slave. The chief smiled, and showed me five heads fixed upon long reeds of bamboo.

"Then he asked me who was the prophet of God, and I answered him Mohammed.

"When he heard the name of the false prophet, he bowed and took me by the hand, and placed me by his side. A negro brought me some mare's milk in a wooden-dish, and a piece of lamb's flesh roasted.

"At daybreak we started on our journey. I rode on a red-haired camel by the side of the chief, and a runner ran before us carrying a spear. The men of war were on either hand, and the mules followed with the merchandise. There were forty camels in the caravan, and the mules were twice forty in number.

"We went from the country of the Tartars into the country of those who curse the Moon. We saw the Gryphons guarding their gold on the white rocks, and the scaled Dragons sleeping in their caves. As we passed over the mountains we held our breath lest the snows might fall on us, and each man tied a veil of gauze before his eyes. As we passed through the valleys the Pygmies shot arrows at us from the hollows of the trees, and at night time we heard the wild men beating on their drums. When we came to the Tower of Apes we set fruits before them, and they did not harm us. When we came to the Tower of Serpents we gave them warm milk in bowls of brass, and they let us go by. Three times in our journey we came to the banks of the Oxus. We crossed it on rafts of wood with great bladders of blown hide. The river-horses raged against us and sought to slay us. When the camels saw them they trembled.

"The kings of each city levied tolls on us, but would not suffer us to enter their gates. They threw us bread over the walls, little maize-cakes baked in honey and cakes of fine flour filled with dates. For every hundred baskets we gave them a bead of amber.

"When the dwellers in the villages saw us coming, they poisoned the wells and fled to the hill-summits. We fought with the Magadae who are born old, and grow younger and younger every year, and die when they are little children; and with the Laktroi who say that they are the sons of tigers, and paint themselves yellow and black; and with the Aurantes who bury their dead on the tops of trees, and themselves live in dark caverns lest the Sun, who is their god, should slay them; and with the Krimnians who worship a crocodile, and give it earrings of green glass, and feed it with butter and fresh fowls; and with the Agazonbae, who are dog-faced; and with the Sibans, who have horses' feet, and run more swiftly than horses. A third of our company died in battle, and a third died of want. The rest murmured against me, and said that I had brought them an evil fortune. I took a horned adder from beneath a stone and let it sting me. When they saw that I did not sicken they grew afraid.

"In the fourth month we reached the city of Illel. It was night time when we came to the grove that is outside the walls, and the air was sultry, for the Moon was travelling in Scorpion. We took the ripe pomegranates from the trees, and brake them and drank their sweet juices. Then we lay down on our carpets and waited for the dawn.

"And at dawn we rose and knocked at the gate of the city. It was wrought out of red bronze, and carved with sea-dragons and dragons that have wings. The guards looked down from the battlements and asked us our business. The interpreter of the caravan answered that we had come from the island of Syria with much merchandise. They took hostages, and told us that they would open the gate to us at noon, and bade us tarry till then.

"When it was noon they opened the gate, and as we entered in the people came crowding out of the houses to look at us, and a crier went round the city crying through a shell. We stood in the market-place, and the negroes uncorded the bales of figured cloths and opened the carved chests of sycamore. And when they had ended their task, the merchants set forth their strange wares, the waxed linen from Egypt and the painted linen from the country of the Ethiops, the purple sponges from Tyre and the blue hangings from Sidon, the cups of cold amber and the fine vessels of glass and the curious vessels of burnt clay. From the roof of a house a company of women watched us. One of them wore a mask of gilded leather.

"And on the first day the priests came and bartered with us, and on the second day came the nobles, and on the third day came the craftsmen and the slaves. And this is their custom with all merchants as long as they tarry in the city.

"And we tarried for a moon, and when the moon was waning, I wearied and wandered away through the streets of the city and came to the garden of its god. The priests in their yellow robes moved silently through the green trees, and on a pavement of black marble stood the rose-red house in which the god had his dwelling. Its doors were of powdered lacquer, and bulls and peacocks were wrought on them in raised and polished gold. The tiled roof was of sea-green porcelain, and the jutting eaves were festooned with little bells. When the white doves flew past, they struck the bells with their wings and made them tinkle.

"In front of the temple was a pool of clear water paved with veined onyx. I lay down beside it, and with my pale fingers I touched the broad leaves. One of the priests came towards me and stood behind me. He had sandals on his feet, one of soft serpent-skin and the other of birds' plumage. On his head was a mitre of black felt decorated with silver crescents. Seven yellows were woven into his robe, and his frizzed hair was stained with antimony.

"After a little while he spake to me, and asked me my desire.

"I told him that my desire was to see the god.

"'The god is hunting,' said the priest, looking strangely at me with his small slanting eyes.

"'Tell me in what forest, and I will ride with him,' I answered.

"He combed out the soft fringes of his tunic with his long pointed nails. 'The god is asleep,' he murmured.

"'Tell me on what couch, and I will watch by him,' I answered.

"'The god is at the feast,' he cried.

"'If the wine be sweet I will drink it with him, and if it be bitter I will drink it with him also,' was my answer.

"He bowed his head in wonder, and, taking me by the hand, he raised me up, and led me into the temple.

"And in the first chamber I saw an idol seated on a throne of jasper bordered with great orient pearls. It was carved out of ebony, and in stature was of the stature of a man. On its forehead was a ruby, and thick oil dripped from its hair on to its thighs. Its feet were red with the blood of a newly-slain kid, and its loins girt with a copper belt that was studded with seven beryls.

"And I said to the priest, 'Is this the god?' And he answered me, 'This is the god.'

"'Show me the god,' I cried, 'or I will surely slay thee.' And I touched his hand, and it became withered.

"And the priest besought me, saying, 'Let my lord heal his servant, and I will show him the god.'

"So I breathed with my breath upon his hand, and it became whole again, and he trembled and led me into the second chamber, and I saw an idol standing on a lotus of jade hung with great emeralds. It was carved out of ivory, and in stature was twice the stature of a man. On its forehead was a chrysolite, and its breasts were smeared with myrrh and cinnamon. In one hand it held a crooked sceptre of jade, and in the other a round crystal. It ware buskins of brass, and its thick neck was circled with a circle of selenites.

"And I said to the priest, 'Is this the god?' And he answered me. 'This is the god.'

"'Show me the god,' I cried, 'or I will surely slay thee.' And I touched his eyes, and they became blind.

"And the priest besought me, saying, 'Let my lord heal his servant, and I will show him the god.'

"So I breathed with my breath upon his eyes, and the sight came back to them, and he trembled again, and led me into the third chamber, and lo! there was no idol in it, nor image of any kind, but only a mirror of round metal set on an altar of stone.

"And I said to the priest, 'Where is the god?'

"And he answered me: 'There is no god but this mirror that thou seest, for this is the Mirror of Wisdom. And it reflecteth all things that are in heaven and on earth, save only the face of him who looketh into it. This it reflecteth not, so that he who looketh into it may be wise. Many other mirrors are there, but they are mirrors of Opinion. This only is the

Mirror of Wisdom. And they who possess this mirror know everything, nor is there anything hidden from them. And they who possess it not have not Wisdom. Therefore is it the god, and we worship it.' And I looked into the mirror, and it was even as I he had said to me.

"And I did a strange thing, but what I did matters not, for in a valley that is but a day's journey from this place have I hidden the Mirror of Wisdom. Do but suffer me to enter into thee again and be thy servant, and thou shalt be wiser than all the wise men, and Wisdom shall be thine. Suffer me to enter into thee, and none will be as wise as thou."

But the young Fisherman laughed. "Love is better than Wisdom," he cried, "and the little Mermaid loves me."

"Nay, but there is nothing better than Wisdom," said the Soul.

"Love is better," answered the young Fisherman, and he plunged into the deep, and the Soul went weeping away over the marshes.

And after the second year was over the Soul came down to the shore of the sea, and called to the young Fisherman, and he rose out of the deep and said, "Why dost thou call to me?"

And the Soul answered, "Come nearer that I may speak with thee, for I have seen marvellous things."

So he came nearer, and couched in the shallow water, and leaned his head upon his hand and listened.

And the Soul said to him, "When I left thee, I turned my face to the South and journeyed. From the South cometh every thing that is precious. Six days I journeyed along the highways that lead to the city of Ashter, along the dusty red-dyed highways by which the pilgrims are wont to go did I journey, and on the morning of the seventh day I lifted up my eyes, and lo! the city lay at my feet, for it is in a valley.

"There are nine gates to this city, and in front of each gate stands a bronze horse that neighs when the Bedouins come down from the mountains. The walls are cased with copper, and the watch-towers on the walls are roofed with brass. In every tower stands an archer with a bow in his hand. At sunrise he strikes with an arrow on a gong, and at sunset he blows through a horn of horn.

"When I sought to enter, the guards stopped me and asked of me who I was. I made answer that I was a Dervish and on my way to the city of Mecca, where there was a green veil on which the Koran was embroidered in silver letters by the hands of the angels. They were filled with wonder, and entreated me to pass in.

"Inside it is even as a bazaar. Surely thou should'st have been with me. Across the narrow streets the gay lanterns of paper flutter like large butterflies. When the wind blows over the roofs they rise and fall as painted bubbles do. In front of their booths sit the merchants on silken carpets. They have straight black beards, and their turbans are covered with golden sequins, and long strings of amber and carved peach-stones glide through their cool fingers. Some of them sell galbanum and nard, and curious perfumes from the islands of the Indian Sea, and the thick oil of red roses and myrrh and little nail-shaped cloves. When one stops to speak to them, they throw pinches of frankincense upon a charcoal brazier and make the air sweet. I saw a Syrian who held in his hands a thin rod like a reed. Grey threads of smoke came from it, and its odour as it burned was as the odour of the pink almond in spring. Others sell silver bracelets embossed all over with creamy blue turquoise stones, and anklets of brass wire fringed with little pearls, and tigers' claws set in gold, and the claws of that gilt cat, the leopard, set in gold also, and earrings of pierced emerald, and finger-rings of hollowed jade. From the tea-houses comes the sound of the guitar, and the opium-smokers with their white smiling faces look out at the passers-by.

"Of a truth thou should'st have been with me. The wine-sellers elbow their way through the crowd with great black skins on their shoulders. Most of them sell the wine of Schiraz, which is as sweet as honey. They serve it in little metal cups and strew rose leaves upon it. In the market-place stand the fruitsellers, who sell all kinds of fruit: ripe figs, with their bruised purple flesh, melons, smelling of musk and yellow as topazes, citrons and rose-apples and clusters of white grapes, round red-gold oranges, and oval lemons of green gold. Once I saw an elephant go by. Its trunk was painted with vermilion and turmeric, and over its ears it had a net of crimson silk cord. It stopped opposite one of the booths and began eating the oranges, and the man only laughed. Thou canst not think how strange a people they are. When they are glad they go to the bird-sellers and buy of them a caged bird, and set it free that their joy may be greater, and when they are sad they scourge themselves with thorns that their sorrow may not grow less.

"One evening I met some negroes carrying a heavy palanquin through the bazaar. It was made of gilded bamboo, and the poles were of vermilion lacquer studded with brass peacocks. Across the windows hung thin curtains of muslim embroidered with beetles' wings and with tiny seed-pearls, and as it passed by a pale-faced Circassian looked out and smiled at me. I followed behind, and the negroes hurried their steps and scowled. But I did not care. I felt a great curiosity come over me.

"At last they stopped at a square white house. There were no windows to it, only a little door like the door of a tomb. They set down the palanquin and knocked three times with a copper hammer. An Armenian in a caftan of green leather peered through the wicket, and when he saw them he opened, and spread a carpet on the ground, and the woman stepped out. As she went in, she turned round and smiled at me again. I had never seen anyone so pale.

"When the moon rose I returned to the same place and sought for the house, but it was no longer there. When I saw that, I knew who the woman was, and wherefore she had smiled at me.

"Certainly thou should'st have been with me. On the feast of the New Moon the young Emperor came forth from his palace and went into the mosque to pray. His hair and beard were dyed with rose-leaves, and his cheeks were powdered with a fine gold dust. The palms of his feet and hands were yellow with saffron.

"At sunrise he went forth from his palace in a robe of silver, and at sunset he returned to it again in a robe of gold. The people flung themselves on the ground and hid their faces, but I would not do so. I stood by the stall of a seller of dates and waited. When the Emperor saw me, he raised his painted eyebrows and stopped. I stood quite still, and made him no obeisance. The people marvelled at my boldness, and counsel-led me to flee from the city. I paid no heed to them, but went and sat with the sellers of strange gods, who by reason of their craft are abominated. When I told them what I had done, each of them gave me a god and prayed me to leave them.

"That night, as I lay on a cushion in the tea-house that is in the Street of Pomegranates, the guards of the Emperor entered and led me to the palace. As I went in they closed each door behind me, and put a chain across it. Inside was a great court with an arcade running all round. The walls were of white alabaster, set here and there with blue and green tiles. The pillars were of green marble, and the pavement of a kind of peach-blossom marble. I had never seen anything like it before.

"As I passed across the court two veiled women looked down from a balcony and cursed me. The guards hastened on, and the butts of the lances rang upon the polished floor. They opened a gate of wrought ivory, and I found myself in a watered garden of seven terraces. It was planted with tulip-cups and moonflowers, and silver-studded aloes. Like a slim reed of crystal a fountain hung in the dusky air. The cypress-trees were like burnt-out torches. From one of them a nightingale was singing.

"At the end of the garden stood a little pavilion. As we approached it two eunuchs came out to meet us. Their fat bodies swayed as they walked, and they glanced curiously at me with their yellow-lidded eyes. One of them drew aside the captain of the guard, and in a low voice whispered to him. The other kept munching scented pastilles, which he took with an affected gesture out of an oval box of lilac enamel.

"After a few moments the captain of the guard dismissed the soldiers. They went back to the palace, the eunuchs following slowly behind and plucking the sweet mulberries from the trees as they passed. Once the elder of the two turned round, and smiled at me with an evil smile.

"Then the captain of the guard motioned me towards the entrance of the pavilion. I walked on without trembling, and drawing the heavy curtain aside I entered in.

"The young Emperor was stretched on a couch of dyed lion skins, and a ger-falcon perched upon his wrist. Behind him stood a brass-turbaned Nubian, naked down to the waist, and with heavy earrings in his split ears. On a table by the side of the couch lay a mighty scimitar of steel.

"When the Emperor saw me he frowned, and said to me, 'What is thy name? Knowest thou not that I am Emperor of this city?' But I made him no answer.

"He pointed with his finger at the scimitar, and the Nubian seized it, and rushing forward struck at me with great violence. The blade whizzed through me, and did me no hurt. The man fell sprawling on the floor, and, when he rose up, his teeth chattered with terror and he hid himself behind the couch.

"The Emperor leapt to his feet, and taking a lance from a stand of arms, he threw it at me. I caught it in its flight, and brake the shaft into two pieces. He shot at me with an arrow, but I held up my hands and it stopped in mid-air. Then he drew a dagger from a belt of white leather, and stabbed the Nubian in the throat lest the slave should tell of his dishonour. The man writhed like a trampled snake, and a red foam bubbled from his lips.

"As soon as he was dead the Emperor turned to me, and when he had wiped away the bright sweat from his brow with a little napkin of purfled and purple silk, he said to me, 'Art thou a prophet, that I may not harm thee, or the son of a prophet that I can do thee no hurt? I pray thee leave my city to night, for while thou art in it I am no longer its lord.'

"And I answered him, 'I will go for half of thy treasure. Give me half of thy treasure, and I will go away.'

"He took me by the hand, and led me out into the garden. When the captain of the guard saw me, he wondered. When the eunuchs saw me, their knees shook and they fell upon the ground in fear.

"There is a chamber in the palace that has eight walls of red porphyry, and a brass-scaled ceiling hung with lamps. The Emperor touched one of the walls and it opened, and we passed down a corridor that was lit with many torches. In niches upon each side stood great wine-jars filled to the brim with silver pieces. When we reached the centre of the corridor the Emperor spake the word that may not be spoken, and a granite door swung back on a secret spring, and he put his hands before his face lest his eyes should be dazzled.

"Thou could'st not believe how marvellous a place it was. There were huge tortoise-shells full of pearls, and hollowed moonstones of great size piled up with red rubies. The gold was stored in coffers of elephant-hide, and the gold-dust in leather bottles. There were opals and sapphires, the former in cups of crystal, and the latter in cups of jade. Round green emeralds were ranged in order upon thin plates of ivory, and in one corner were silk bags filled, some with turquoise-stones and others with beryls. The ivory horns were heaped with purple amethysts, and the horns of brass with chalcedonies and sards. The pillars, which were of cedar, were hung with strings of yellow lynx-stones. In the flat oval shields there were carbuncles, both wine-coloured and coloured like grass. And yet I have told thee but a tithe of what was there.

"And when the Emperor had taken away his hands from before his face he said to me: 'This is my house of treasure, and half that is in it is thine, even as I promised to thee. And I will give thee camels and camel drivers, and they shall do thy bidding and take thy share of the treasure to whatever part of the world thou desirest to go. And the thing shall be done to night, for I would not that the Sun, who is my father, should see that there is in my city a man whom I cannot slay.'

"But I answered him, 'The gold that is here is thine, and the silver also is thine, and thine are the precious jewels and the things of price. As for me, I have no need of these. Nor shall I take aught from thee but that little ring that thou wearest on the finger of thy hand.'

"And the Emperor frowned. 'It is but a ring of lead,' he cried, 'nor has it any value. Therefore take thy half of the treasure and go from my city.'

"'Nay,' I answered, 'but I will take nought but that leaden ring, for I know what is written within it, and for what purpose.'

"And the Emperor trembled, and besought me and said, 'Take all the treasure and go from my city. The half that is mine shall be thine also.'

"And I did a strange thing, but what I did matters not, for in a cave that is but a day's journey from this place have I hidden the Ring of Riches. It is but a day's journey from this place, and it waits for thy coming. He who has this Ring is richer than all the kings of the world. Come therefore and take it, and the world's riches shall be thine."

But the young Fisherman laughed. "Love is better than Riches," he cried, "and the little Mermaid loves me."

"Nay, but there is nothing better than Riches," said the Soul. "Love is better," answered the young Fisherman, and he plunged into the deep, and the Soul went weeping away over the marshes.

And after the third year was over, the Soul came down to the shore of the sea, and called to the young Fisherman, and he rose out of the deep and said, "Why dost thou call to me?"

And the Soul answered, "Come nearer, that I may speak with thee, for I have seen marvellous things."

So he came nearer, and couched in the shallow water, and leaned his head upon his hand and listened.

And the Soul said to him, "In a city that I know of there is an inn that standeth by a river. I sat there with sailors who drank of two different coloured wines, and ate bread made of barley, and little salt fish served in bay leaves with vinegar. And as we sat and made merry, there entered to us an old man bearing a leathern carpet and a lute that had two horns of amber. And when he had laid out the carpet on the floor, he struck with a quill on the wire strings of his lute, and a girl whose face was veiled ran in and began to dance before us. Her face was veiled with a veil of gauze, but her feet were naked. Naked were her feet, and they moved over the carpet like little white pigeons. Never have I seen anything so marvellous, and the city in which she dances is but a day's journey from this place."

Now when the young Fisherman heard the words of his soul, he remembered that the little Mermaid had no feet and could not dance. And a great desire came over him, and he said to himself, "It is but a day's journey, and I can return to my love," and he laughed, and stood up in the shallow water, and strode towards the shore.

And when he had reached the dry shore he laughed again, and held out his arms to his Soul. And his Soul gave a great cry of joy and ran to meet him, and entered into him, and the young Fisherman saw stretched before him upon the sand that shadow of the body that is the body of the Soul.

And his Soul said to him, "Let us not tarry, but get hence at once, for the Sea-gods are jealous, and have monsters that do their bidding."

So they made haste, and all that night they journeyed beneath the moon, and all the next day they journeyed beneath the sun, and on the evening of the day they came to a city.

And the young Fisherman said to his Soul, "Is this the city in which she dances of whom thou did'st speak to me?"

And his Soul answered him, "It is not this city, but another. Nevertheless let us enter in."

So they entered in and passed through the streets, and as they passed through the Street of the Jewellers the young fisherman saw a fair silver cup set forth in a booth. And his Soul said to him, "Take that silver cup and hide it."

So he took the cup and hid it in the fold of his tunic, and they went hurriedly out of the city.

And after that they had gone a league from the city, the young Fisherman frowned, and flung the cup away, and said to his Soul, "Why did'st thou tell me to take this cup and hide it, for it was an evil thing to do?"

But his Soul answered him, "Be at peace, be at peace."

And on the evening of the second day they came to a city, and the young Fisherman said to his Soul, "Is this the city in which she dances of whom thou did'st speak to me?"

And his Soul answered him, "It is not this city, but another. Nevertheless let us enter in."

So they entered in and passed through the streets, and as they passed through the Street of the Sellers of Sandals, the young Fisherman saw a child standing by a jar of water. And his Soul said to him, "Smite that child." So he smote the child till it wept, and when he had done this they went hurriedly out of the city.

And after that they had gone a league from the city the young Fisherman grew wroth, and said to his Soul, "Why did'st thou tell me to smite the child, for it was an evil thing to do?"

But his Soul answered him, "Be at peace, be at peace."

And on the evening of the third day they came to a city, and the young Fisherman said to his Soul, "Is this the city in which she dances of whom thou did'st speak to me?"

And his Soul answered him, "It may be that it is this city, therefore let us enter in."

So they entered in and passed through the streets, but nowhere could the young Fisherman find the river or the inn that stood by its side. And the people of the city looked curiously at him, and he grew afraid and said to his Soul, "Let us go hence, for she who dances with white feet is not here."

But his Soul answered, "Nay, but let us tarry, for the night is dark and there will be robbers on the way."

So he sat him down in the market-place and rested, and after a time there went by a hooded merchant who had a cloak of cloth of Tartary, and bare a lantern of pierced horn at the end of a jointed reed. And the merchant said to him, "Why dost thou sit in the market-place, seeing that the booths are closed and the bales corded?"

And the young Fisherman answered him, "I can find no inn in this city, nor have I any kinsman who might give me shelter."

"Are we not all kinsmen?" said the merchant. "And did not one God make us? Therefore come with me, for I have a guest-chamber."

So the young Fisherman rose up and followed the merchant to his house. And when he had passed through a garden of pomegranates and entered into the house, the merchant brought him rose-water in a copper dish that he might wash his hands, and ripe melons that he might quench his thirst, and set a bowl of rice and a piece of roasted kid before him.

And after that he had finished, the merchant led him to the guest-chamber, bade him sleep and be at rest. And the young Fisherman gave him thanks, and kissed the ring that was on his hand, and flung himself down on the carpets of dyed goat's-hair. And when he had covered himself with a covering of black lambs-wool he fell asleep.

And three hours before dawn, and while it was still night, his Soul waked him, and said to him, "Rise up and go to the room of the merchant, even to the room in which he sleepeth, and slay him, and take from him his gold, for we have need of it."

And the young Fisherman rose up and crept towards the room of the merchant, and over the feet of the merchant there was lying a curved sword, and the tray by the side of the merchant held nine purses of gold. And he reached out his hand and touched the sword, and when he touched it the merchant started and awoke, and leaping up seized himself the sword and cried to the young Fisherman, "Dost thou return evil for good, and pay with the shedding of blood for the kindness that I have shown thee?"

And his Soul said to the young Fisherman, "Strike him," and he struck him so that he swooned, and he seized then the nine purses of gold, and fled hastily through the garden of pomegranates, and set his face to the star that is the star of morning.

And when they had gone a league from the city, the young Fisherman beat his breast, and said to his Soul, "Why didst thou bid me slay the merchant and take his gold? Surely thou art evil."

But his Soul answered him, "Be at peace, be at peace."

"Nay," cried the young Fisherman, "I may not be at peace, for all that thou hast made me to do I hate. Thee also I hate, and I bid thee tell me wherefore thou hast wrought with me in this wise."

And his Soul answered him, "When thou didst send me forth into the world thou gavest me no heart, so I learned to do all these things and love them."

"What sayest thou?" murmured the young Fisherman.

"Thou knowest," answered his Soul, "thou knowest it well. Hast thou forgotten that thou gavest me no heart? I trow not. And so trouble not thyself nor me, but be at peace, for there is no pain that thou shalt not give away, nor any pleasure that thou shalt not receive."

And when the young Fisherman heard these words he trembled and said to his Soul, "Nay, but thou art evil, and hast made me forget my love, and hast tempted me with temptations, and hast set my feet in the ways of sin." And his Soul answered him, "Thou hast not forgotten that when thou didst send me forth into the world thou gavest me no heart. Come, let us go to another city, and make merry, for we have nine purses of gold."

But the young Fisherman took the nine purses of gold, and flung them down, and trampled on them.

"Nay," he cried, "but I will have nought to do with thee, nor will I journey with thee anywhere, but even as I sent thee away before, so will I send thee away now, for thou hast wrought me no good." And he turned his back to the moon, and with the little knife that had the handle of green viper's skin he strove to cut from his feet that shadow of the body which is the body of the Soul.

Yet his Soul stirred not from him, nor paid heed to his command, but said to him, "The spell that the Witch told thee avails thee no more, for I may not leave thee, nor mayest thou drive me forth. Once in his life may a man send his Soul away, but he who receiveth back his Soul must keep it with him for ever, and this is his punishment and his reward."

And the young Fisherman grew pale and clenched his hands and cried, "She was a false Witch in that she told me not that."

"Nay," answered his Soul, "but she was true to Him she worships, and whose servant she will be ever."

And when the young Fisherman knew that he could no longer get rid of his Soul, and that it was an evil Soul and would abide with him always, he fell upon the ground weeping bitterly.

And when it was day the young Fisherman rose up and said to his Soul, "I will bind my hands that I may not do thy bidding, and close my lips that I may not speak thy words, and I will return to the place where she whom I love has her dwelling. Even to the sea will I return, and to the little bay where she is wont to sing, and I will call to her and tell her the evil I have done and the evil thou hast wrought on me."

And his Soul tempted him and said, "Who is thy love that thou should'st return to her? The world has many fairer than she is. There are the dancing-girls of Samaris who dance in the manner of all kinds of birds and beasts. Their feet are painted with henna, and in their hands they have little copper bells. They laugh while they dance, and their laughter is as clear as the laughter of water. Come with me and I will show them to thee. For what is this trouble of thine about the things of sin? Is that which is pleasant to eat not made for the eater? Is there poison in that which is sweet to drink? Trouble not thyself, but come with me to another city. There is a little city hard by in which there is a garden of tulip-trees. And there dwell in this comely garden white peacocks and peacocks that have blue breasts. Their tails when they spread them to the sun are like disks of ivory and like gilt disks. And she who feeds them dances for their pleasure, and sometimes she dances on her hands and at other times she dances with her feet. Her eyes are coloured with stibium, and her nostrils are shaped like the wings of a swallow. From a hook in one of her nostrils hangs a flower that is carved out of a pearl. She laughs while she dances, and the silver rings that are about her ankles tinkle like bells of silver. And so trouble not thyself any more, but come with me to this city."

But the young Fisherman answered not his Soul, but closed his lips with the seal of silence and with a tight cord bound his hands, and journeyed back to the place from which he had come, even to the little bay where his love had been wont to sing. And ever did his Soul tempt him by the way, but he made it no answer, nor would he do any of the wickedness that it sought to make him to do, so great was the power of the love that was within him.

And when he had reached the shore of the sea, he loosed the cord from his hands, and took the seal of silence from his lips, and called to the little Mermaid. But she came not to his call, though he called to her all day long and besought her.

And his Soul mocked him and said, "Surely thou hast but little joy out of thy love. Thou art as one who in time of dearth pours water into a broken vessel. Thou givest away what thou hast, and nought is given to thee in return. It were better for thee to come with me, for I know where the Valley of Pleasure lies, and what things are wrought there."

But the young Fisherman answered not his Soul, but in a cleft of the rock he built himself a house of wattles, and abode there for the space of a year. And every morning he called to the Mermaid, and every noon he called to her again and at night-time he spake her name. Yet never did she rise out of the sea to meet him, nor in any place of the sea could he find her, though he sought for her in the caves and in the green water, in the pools of the tide and in the wells that are at the bottom of the deep.

And ever did his Soul tempt him with evil, and whisper of terrible things. Yet did it not prevail against him, so great was the power of his love.

And after the year was over, the Soul thought within himself, "I have tempted my master with evil, and his love is stronger than I am. I will tempt him now with good, and it may be that he will come with me."

So he spake to the young Fisherman and said, "I have told thee of the joy of the world, and thou hast turned a deaf ear to me. Suffer me now to tell thee of the world's pain, and it may be that thou wilt hearken. For of a truth, pain is the Lord of this world, nor is there anyone who escapes from its net. There be some who lack raiment, and others who lack bread. There be widows who sit in purple, and widows who sit in rags. To and fro over the fens go the lepers, and they are cruel to each other. The beggars go up and down on the highways, and their wallets are empty. Through the streets of the cities walks Famine, and the Plague sits at their gates. Come, let us go forth and mend these things, and make them not to be. Wherefore should'st thou tarry here calling to thy love, seeing she comes not to thy call? And what is love, that thou should'st set this high store upon it?"

But the young Fisherman answered it nought, so great was the power of his love. And every morning he called to the Mermaid, and every noon he called to her again, and at night-time he spake her name. Yet never did she rise out of the sea to meet him, nor in any place of the sea could he find her, though he sought for her in the rivers of the sea, and in the valleys that are under the waves, in the sea that the night makes purple, and in the sea that the dawn leaves grey.

And after the second year was over, the Soul said to the young Fisherman at night-time, and as he sat in the wattled house alone, "Lo! now I have tempted thee with evil, and I have tempted thee with good, and thy love is stronger than I am. Wherefore will I tempt thee no longer, but I pray thee to suffer me to enter thy heart, that I may be one with thee even as before."

"Surely thou mayest enter," said the young Fisherman, "for in the days when with no heart thou didst go through the world thou must have much suffered."

"Alas!" cried his Soul, "I can find no place of entrance, so compassed about with love is this heart of thine."

"Yet I would that I could help thee," said the young Fisherman.

And as he spake there came a great cry of mourning from the sea, even the cry that men hear when one of the Sea-folk is dead. And the young Fisherman leapt up, and left his wattled house, and ran down to the shore. And the black waves came hurrying to the shore, bearing with them a burden that was whiter than silver. White as the surf it was, and like a flower it tossed on the waves. And the surf took it from the waves, and the foam took it from the surf, and the shore received it, and lying at his feet the young Fisherman saw the body of the little Mermaid. Dead at his feet it was lying.

Weeping as one smitten with pain he flung himself down beside it, and he kissed the cold red of the mouth, and toyed with the wet amber of the hair. He flung himself down beside it on the sand, weeping as one trembling with joy, and in his brown arms he held it to his breast. Cold were the lips, yet he kissed them. Salt was the honey of the hair, yet he tasted it with a bitter joy. He kissed the closed eyelids, and the wild spray that lay upon their cups was less salt than his tears.

And to the dead thing he made confession. Into the shells of its ears he poured the harsh wine of his tale. He put the little hands round his neck, and with his fingers he touched the thin reed of the throat. Bitter, bitter was his joy, and full of strange gladness was his pain.

The black sea came nearer, and the white foam moaned like a leper. With white claws of foam the sea grabbled at the shore. From the palace of the Sea-King came the cry of mourning again, and far out upon the sea the great Tritons blew hoarsely upon their horns.

"Flee away, said his Soul, "for ever doth the sea come nigher, and if thou tarriest it will slay thee. Flee away, for I am afraid, seeing that thy heart is closed against me by reason of the greatness of thy love. Flee away to a place of safety. Surely thou wilt not send me without a heart into another world?"

But the young Fisherman listened not to his Soul, but called on the little Mermaid and said, "Love is better than wisdom, and more precious than riches, and fairer than the feet of the daughters of men. The fires cannot destroy it, nor can the waters quench it. I called on thee at dawn, and thou didst not come to my call. The moon heard thy name, yet hadst thou no heed of me. For evilly had I left thee, and to my own hurt had I wandered away. Yet ever did thy love abide with me, and ever was it strong, nor did aught prevail against it, though I have looked upon evil and looked upon good. And now that thou art dead, surely I will die with thee also."

And his Soul besought him to depart, but he would not, so great was his love. And the sea came nearer, and sought to cover him with its waves, and when he knew that the end was at hand he kissed with mad lips the cold lips of the Mermaid and the heart that was within him brake. And as through the fulness of his love his heart did break, the Soul found an entrance and entered in, and was one with him even as before. And the sea covered the young Fisherman with its waves.

And in the morning the Priest went forth to bless the sea, for it had been troubled. And with him went the monks and the musicians, and the candle-bearers, and the swingers of censers, and a great company.

And when the Priest reached the shore he saw the young Fisherman lying drowned in the surf, and clasped in his arms was the body of the little Mermaid. And he drew back frowning, and having made the sign of the cross, he cried aloud and said, "I will not bless the sea nor anything that is in it. Accursed be the Sea-folk, and accursed be all they who traffic with them. And as for him who for love's sake forsook God, and so lieth here with his leman slain by God's judgment, take up his body and the body of his leman, and bury them in the corner of the Field of the Fullers, and set no mark above them, nor sign of any kind, that none may know the place of their resting. For accursed were they in their lives, and accursed shall they be in their deaths also."

And the people did as he commanded them, and in the corner of the Field of the Fullers, where no sweet herbs grew, they dug a deep pit, and laid the dead things within it.

And when the third year was over, and on a day that was a holy day, the Priest went up to the chapel, that he might show to the people the wounds of the Lord, and speak to them about the wrath of God.

And when he had robed himself with his robes, and entered in and bowed himself before the altar, he saw that the altar was covered with strange flowers that never had he seen before. Strange were they to look at, and of curious beauty, and their beauty troubled him, and their odour was sweet in his nostrils. And he felt glad, and understood not why he was glad.

And after that he had opened the tabernacle, and incensed the monstrance that was in it, and shown the fair wafer to the people, and hid it again behind the veil of veils, he began to speak to the people, desiring to speak to them of the wrath of God. But the beauty of the white flowers troubled him, and their odour was sweet in his nostrils, and there came another word into his lips, and he spake not of the wrath of God, but of the God whose name is Love. And why he so spake, he knew not.

And when he had finished his word the people wept, and the Priest went back to the sacristy, and his eyes were full of tears. And the deacons came in and began to unrobe him, and took from him the alb and the girdle, the maniple and the stole. And he stood as one in a dream.

And after that they had unrobed him, he looked at them and said, "What are the flowers that stand on the altar, and whence do they come?"

And they answered him, "What flowers they are we cannot tell, but they come from the corner of the Fullers' Field." And the Priest trembled, and returned to his own house and prayed.

And in the morning, while it was still dawn, he went forth with the monks and the musicians, and the candle-bearers and the swingers of censers, and a great company, and came to the shore of the sea, and blessed the sea, and all the wild things that are in it. The Fauns also he blessed, and the little things that dance in the woodland, and the bright-eyed things that peer through the leaves. All the things in God's world he blessed, and the people were filled with joy and wonder. Yet never again in the corner of the Fullers' Field grew flowers of any kind, but the field remained barren even as before. Nor came the Sea-folk into the bay as they had been wont to do, for they went to another part of the sea.

Source:
Wilde, Oscar. *A House of Pomegranates*. London: James R. Osgood McIlvaine, 1891.

78. The Mermaid (Windlass Song) by Robert Buchanan

England & Scotland

I.

I'LL tell you, mates, how she came to sea!
    (Heave at the windlass! heave ho! cheerily)
She loved me, and I loved she,
    For she was the gel for a Sailor!
She hailed from Wapping, her name was Sue,
    And she was the daughter of a tailor,
We parted at last, but without ado
She bought both jacket and breeches blue,
And aboard she came for to join our crew
    And live the life of a Sailor!

CHORUS.

    Heave at the windlass! yeo heave ho!
    Up with the anchor! away we go!
    The wind's off the shore, boys,—let it blow,—
        Hurrah for the life of a Sailor!
                YEO—HO!

II.

Our Captain he eyed her from stem to starn
    (Heave at the windlass! heave ho! cheerily)
But nought of her secret could he discarn,
    For his savage jib couldn't quail her.
But when she went for'ard among the res
    Her heart began for to fail her,
So she took me aside and the truth confess'd,
With her face a-blushing on this 'ere breast,
And I stared and stared, and says I, "I'm blest!
    My Sue turn'd into a Sailor!"

III.

Now we hadn't got far away from land

  (Heave at the windlass, heave ho! cheerily)
When a Mermaid rose with a glass in her hand,
  And our ship hove to for to hail her.
Says she, "Each wessel that looks on me,
  Man-o'-war, merchantman, or whaler,
Must sink right down to the bottom of the sea,
Where the dog-fish flies and the sea-snakes flee,
Unless a Wirgin on board there be
  To plead for the life of a Sailor!"

IV.

Then up jumped Sue with the breeches on!
  (Heave at the windlass, heave ho! cheerily)
"You nasty hussy!" says she, "begone!"
  And the Mermaid's cheeks grew paler!
"There's a gel aboard and her name is Sue!
  A Wirgin, the daughter of a tailor,
Who's more than a match for the likes of you! "
At this the Mermaid looked werry blue,
And then, with a splash of her tail, withdrew,
  While Sue she embraced her Sailor!

Source:
Buchanan, Robert. *The Complete Poetical Works of Robert Buchanan, Volume II*. London: Chatto & Windus, 1901.

79. Mermaids

Guernsey

  "I'll drown more sailors than the mermaid shall."
   —Shakespeare

  "Thou rememb'rest
  Since once I sat upon a promontory,
  And heard a mermaid on a dolphin's back,
  Uttering such dulcet and harmonious breath,
  That the rude sea grew civil at her song."
   —Shakespeare.

A belief in the existence of mermaids is not quite extinct, although no tales relating to them appear to have been preserved among the people. An old man, living in the parish of the Forest, of the name of Matthieu Tostevin, whose word might be implicitly relied on, affirmed to Mr. Denys Corbet, the master of the parochial school, that on one occasion, being on the cliffs over-looking Petit-Bôt Bay, he saw a company of six mermaids, or, as he termed them "seirênes," disporting themselves on the sands below. He described them as usually depicted, half woman, half fish. He hastened down to the beach as fast as he could, to get a nearer sight of them, but, on his approaching them, they took to the sea, and were immediately out of sight.

It was doubtless a flock of seals which he saw, for, although these animals are no longer found in numbers on our coasts, a stray one is occasionally, though very rarely, to be seen. They are known to exist on the opposite shores of Brittany and Normandy, and the few specimens that have been taken in our seas are of the same variety as those found on the French coast. It is not improbable that they may have been more common in former days; and it is possible that "Le Creux du Chien," a large cavern at the foot of the cliffs to the eastward of Petit-Bôt Bay, may have been so named from being the resort of one of these amphibians.

From Mr. Denys Corbet.

NOTES

In Sark as well as in Guernsey they still believe in sirens, and an old man there, who had been a fisherman in his youth, told me of these women who used to sit on the rocks and sing before a storm. In Sark they are considered young and beautiful, but Guernsey fishermen talk of old women who sit on the rocks and sing, and the ships are brought closer to the rocks by the curiosity of those on board to hear this mysterious music, and then the storm comes, and the ships go to pieces on the rocks, and the sirens,—whether young or old,—carry down the sailors to the bottom of the sea, and eat them. So the tradition goes.

Source:
MacCulloch, Sir Edgar. *Guernsey Folk Lore.* Edith F. Carey, editor. London: Elliot Stock, 1903.

80. The Entangled Mermaid

Netherlands

LONG AGO, in Dutch Fairy Land, there lived a young mermaid who was very proud of her good looks. She was one of a family of mere or lake folks dwelling not far from the sea. Her home was a great pool of water that was half salt and half fresh, for it lay around an island near the mouth of a river. Part of the day, when the sea tides were out, she splashed and played, dived and swam in the soft water of the inland current. When the ocean heaved and the salt water rushed in, the mermaid floated and frolicked and paddled to her heart's content. Her father was a gray-bearded merryman and very proud of his handsome daughter. He owned an island near the river mouth, where the young mermaids held their picnics and parties and received the visits of young merrymen.

Her mother and two aunts were merwomen. All of these were sober folks and attended to the business which occupies all well brought up mermaids and merrymen. This was to keep their pool clean and nice. No frogs, toads or eels were allowed near, but in the work of daily housecleaning, the storks and the mermaids were great friends.

All water-creatures that were not thought to be polite and well behaved were expected to keep away. Even some silly birds, such as loons and plovers and all screaming and fighting creatures with wings, were warned off the premises, because they were not wanted. This family of merry folks liked to have a nice, quiet time by themselves, without any rude folks on legs, or with wings or fins from the outside. Indeed they wished to make their pool a model, for all respectable mermaids and merrymen, for ten leagues around. It was very funny to see the old daddy merman, with a switch made of reeds, shooing off the saucy birds, such as the sandpipers and screeching gulls. For the bullfrogs, too big for the storks to swallow, and for impudent fishes, he had a whip made of seaweed.

Of course, all the mermaids in good society were welcome, but young mermen were allowed to call only once a month, during the week when the moon was full. Then the evenings were usually clear, so that when the party broke up, the mermen could see their way in the moonlight to swim home safely with their mermaid friends. For, there were sea monsters that loved to plague the merefolk, and even threatened to eat them up! The mermaids, dear creatures, had to be escorted home, but they felt safe, for their mermen brothers and daddies were so fierce that, except sharks, even the larger fish, such as porpoises and dolphins were afraid to come near them.

One day daddy and the mother left to visit some relatives near the island of Urk. They were to be gone several days. Meanwhile, their daughter was to have a party, her aunts being the chaperones.

The mermaids usually held their picnics on an island in the midst of the pool. Here they would sit and sun themselves. They talked about the fashions and the prettiest way to dress their hair. Each one had a pocket mirror, but where they kept these, while swimming, no mortal ever found out. They made wreaths of bright colored seaweed, orange and black, blue, gray and red and wore them on their brows like coronets. Or, they twined them, along with sea berries and bubble blossoms, among their tresses. Sometimes they made girdles of the strongest and knotted them around their waists.

Every once in a while they chose a queen of beauty for their ruler. Then each of the others pretended to be a princess. Their games and sports often lasted all day and they were very happy.

Swimming out in the salt water, the mermaids would go in quest of pearls, coral, ambergris and other pretty things. These they would bring to their queen, or with them richly adorn themselves. Thus the Mermaid Queen and her maidens made a court of beauty that was famed wherever mermaids and merrymen lived. They often talked about human maids.

"How funny it must be to wear clothes," said one.

"Are they cold that they have to keep warm?" It was a little chit of a mermaid, whose flippers had hardly begun to grow into hands, that asked this question.

"How can they swim with petticoats on?" asked another.

"My brother heard that real men wear wooden shoes! These must bother them, when on the water, to have their feet floating," said a third, whose name was Silver Scales. "What a pity they don't have flukes like us," and then she looked at her own glistening scaly coat in admiration.

"I can hardly believe it," said a mermaid, that was very proud of her fine figure and slender waist. "Their girls can't be half as pretty as we are."

"Well, I should like to be a real woman for a while, just to try it, and see how it feels to walk on legs," said another, rather demurely, as if afraid the other mermaids might not like her remark.

They didn't. Out sounded a lusty chorus, "No! No! Horrible! What an idea! Who wouldn't be a mermaid?"

"Why, I've heard," cried one, "that real women have to work, wash their husband's clothes, milk cows, dig potatoes, scrub floors and take care of calves. Who would be a woman? Not I"—and her snub nose—since it could not turn up—grew wide at the roots. She was sneering at the idea that a creature in petticoats could ever look lovelier than one in shining scales.

"Besides," said she, "think of their big noses, and I'm told, too, that girls have even to wear hairpins."

At this—the very thought that any one should have to bind up their tresses—there was a shock of disgust with some, while others clapped their hands, partly in envy and partly in glee.

But the funniest things the mermaids heard of were gloves, and they laughed heartily over such things as covers for the fingers. Just for fun, one of the little mermaids used to draw some bag-like seaweed over her hands, to see how such things looked.

One day, while sunning themselves in the grass on the island, one of their number found a bush on which foxgloves grew. Plucking these, she covered each one of her fingers with a red flower. Then, flopping over to the other girls, she held up her gloved hands. Half in fright and half in envy, they heard her story.

After listening, the party was about to break up, when suddenly a young merman splashed into view. The tide was running out and the stream low, so he had had hard work to get through the fresh water of the river and to the island. His eyes dropped salt water, as if he were crying. He looked tired, while puffing and blowing, and he could hardly get his breath. The queen of the mermaids asked him what he meant by coming among her maids at such an hour and in such condition.

At this the bashful merman began to blubber. Some of the mergirls put their hands over their mouths to hide their laughing, while they winked at each other and their eyes showed how they enjoyed the fun. To have a merman among them, at that hour, in broad daylight, and crying, was too much for dignity.

"Boo-hoo, boo-hoo," and the merman still wept salt water tears, as he tried to catch his breath. At last, he talked sensibly. He warned the Queen that a party of horrid men, in wooden shoes, with pickaxes, spades and pumps, were coming to drain the swamp and pump out the pool. He had heard that they would make the river a canal and build a dyke that should keep out the ocean.

"Alas! alas!" cried one mermaid, wringing her hands. "Where shall we go when our pool is destroyed? We can't live in the ocean all the time." Then she wept copiously. The salt water tears fell from her great round eyes in big drops.

"Hush!" cried the Queen. "I don't believe the merman's story. He only tells it to frighten us. It's just like him."

In fact, the Queen suspected that the merman's story was all a sham and that he had come among her maids with a set purpose to run off with Silver Scales. She was one of the prettiest mermaids in the company, but very young, vain and frivolous. It was no secret that she and the merman were in love and wanted to get married.

So the Queen, without even thanking him, dismissed the swimming messenger. After dinner, the company broke up and the Queen retired to her cave to take a long nap! She was quite tired after entertaining so much company. Besides, since daddy and mother were away, and there were no beaus to entertain, since it was a dark night and no moon shining on the water, why need she get up early in the morning?

So the Mermaid Queen slept much longer than ever before. Indeed, it was not till near sunset the next day that she awoke. Then, taking her comb and mirror in hand, she started to swim and splash in the pool, in order to smooth out her tresses and get ready for supper.

But oh, what a change from the day before! What was the matter? All around her things looked different. The water had fallen low and the pool was nearly empty. The river, instead of flowing, was as quiet as a pond. Horrors! when she swam forward, what should she see but a dyke and fences! An army of horrid men had come, when she was asleep, and built a dam. They had fenced round the swamp and were actually beginning to dig sluices to drain the land. Some were at work, building a windmill to help in pumping out the water.

The first thing she knew she had bumped her pretty nose against the dam. She thought at once of escaping over the logs and into the sea. When she tried to clamber over the top and get through the fence, her hair got so entangled between the bars that she had to throw away her comb and mirror and try to untangle her tresses. The more she tried, the worse became the tangle. Soon her long hair was all twisted up in the timber. In vain were her struggles to escape. She was ready to die with fright, when she saw four horrid men rush up to seize her. She attempted to waddle away, but her long hair held her to the post and rails. Her modesty was so dreadfully shocked that she fainted away.

When she came to herself, she found she was in a big long tub. A crowd of curious little girls and boys were looking at her, for she was on show as a great curiosity. They were bound to see her and get their money's worth in looking, for they had paid a stiver [two cents] admission to the show. Again, before all these eyes, her modesty was so shocked that she gave one groan, flopped over and died in the tub.

Woe to the poor father and mother at Urk! They came back to find their old home gone. Unable to get into it, they swam out to sea, never stopping till they reached Spitzbergen.

What became of the body of the Mermaid Queen?

Learned men came from Leyden to examine what was now only a specimen, and to see how mermaids were made up. Then her skin was stuffed, and glass eyes put in, where her shining orbs had been. After this, her body was stuffed and mounted in the museum, that is, set up above a glass case and resting upon iron rods. Artists came to Leyden to make pictures of her and no fewer than nine noblemen copied her pretty form and features into their coats of arms. Instead of the Mermaid's Pool is now a cheese farm of fifty cows, a fine house and barn, and a family of pink-cheeked, yellow-haired children who walk and play in wooden shoes.

So this particular mermaid, all because of her entanglement in the fence, was more famous when stuffed than when living, while all her young friends and older relatives were forgotten.

Source:
Griffis, William Elliot. *Dutch Fairy Tales For Young Folks*. New York: Thomas Y. Crowell Co., 1919.

81. The Merman and the Mermaid in the Faeröes

Faroe Islands

THE merman (marmennil) is like a human being, but considerably smaller in growth, and with very long fingers. He lives at the bottom of the sea, and annoys fishers by biting the bait off the hooks and fixing these in the bottom, so that they have to cut the line. If he is caught, he is so dexterous that he can loose the thread that ties the hooks to the line, and so escape from being brought up, and taken on board like any other fish. One time when he tried to play his tricks at the bottom of the sea, he was rather unlucky, for just as he was about to lay hold of the line of Anfinn from Eldu-vík, with intent to make it fast, Anfinn gave a pull, and caught the merman by the right hand. With one hand he could not free himself from the line, and so was drawn up; a cross was made upon him, and he was taken home. Anfinn kept him in his house on the hearth-stone, but had to remember every evening to make a cross on the four corners of this. He would eat nothing but fish-bait. When they went out to fish, they took the merman with them, and had to recollect to make the mark of the cross on him, when they took him on board the boat. When they rowed over a shoal of fish, he began to laugh and play in the boat, and they were sure of a good catch, if they put out their lines then, especially if he dipped his finger into the sea. Anfinn had the merman with him for a long time, but one day the sea was pretty stormy when they launched the boat, and they forgot to make the cross on him. When they had got out from land, he slipped overboard, and was never seen again.

The mermaid is like a human being above the waist, and has long brown hair like a woman, which floats round about her on the sea, but her arms are shorter. Below the waist she is like a fish, with a scaly tail. If she turns towards the boat when she comes up out of the water, a storm is sure to come, and then it is a case of rowing home as fast as possible, and so try to escape being drowned. But if the merman comes up beside her, it will be good weather. The mermaid sings so sweetly that men lose their senses with listening to her song, and so they must thrust the thumbs of their gloves into their ears, else in their madness and frenzy they will leap out of the boat into the sea to her.

Source:
Craigie, William A. *Scandinavian Folk-Lore: Illustrations of the Traditional Beliefs of the Northern People.* London: Alexander Gardner, 1896.

82. The Mer-man and Marstig's Daughter

Denmark

NOW rede me, dear mither, a sonsy rede;
    A sonsy rede swythe rede to me,
How Marstig's daughter I may fa',
    My love and lemman gay to be."

She's made him a steed o' the clear water;
    A saddle and bridle o' sand made she;
She's shap'd him into a knight sae fair,
    Syne into Mary's kirk-yard rade he.

He's tied his steed to the kirk-stile,
    Syne wrang-gaites[1] round the kirk gaed he;
When the Mer-Man entered the kirk-door,
    Awa the sma' images turned their e'e.

The priest afore the altar stood:
    "O what for a gude knight may this be?"
The may leugh till hersell,[2] and said,

---

[1] "*Wrong gaites;*" in the Dan. *avet om, i.e. wrong-ways about.* This may signify either *backward*, or what the Scots call *widdershins*, in a direction contrary to the apparent motion of the sun; a kind of motion of mighty efficacy in all incantations.

[2] "*Leugh till hersell;*" in the orig. *smiler under skind, i.e.* smiled under *her covering*, or dress; a form of speech constantly occurring in the Danish ballads, as does *unther weed*, and *unther kell*, &c. in the old English romances.

"God gif that gude knight were for me!"

The Mer-man he stept o'er ae deas,[1]
    And he has steppit over three:
"O maiden, pledge me faith and troth!
    O Marstig's daughter, gang wi' me!"

And she raught out her lily hand,
    And pledged it to the knight sae free:
"Hae; there's my faith and troth, sir knight,
    And willingly I'll gang wi' thee."

Out frae the kirk gaed the bridal train,
    And on they danced wi' fearless glee:
And down they danced unto the strand,
    Till twasome now alane they be:
"O Marstig's daughter, haud my steed,
    And the bonniest ship I'll bigg for thee."

And whan they came to the white sand,
    To shore the sma' boats turning came;
And whan they came to the deep water,
    The maiden sank in the saut sea faem.

The shriek she shriek'd amang the waves
    Was heard far up upo' the land:
"I rede gude ladies, ane and a',
    They dance wi' nae sic mica man."[2]

---

[1] "*Deas,*" in the Dan. *stole*, which, among other things, denominates a *pew* in church, which, in the north of Scotland, is still called a *deas*; as is also the long *settle*, or *sittee*, commonly met with in old farm-houses in England and Scotland. *Deas* was, perhaps, at first, only a corruption of the Latin *sedes*, a seat.

I remember having seen in the hall of the ruined castle of Elan Stalker, in the district of Appin, an old oaken deas, which was so contrived as to serve for a sittee; at meal-times the back was turned over, rested upon the arms, and became a table; and at night the seat was raised up, and displayed a commodious bed for four persons, two and two, feet to feet, to sleep in.

I was told, that this kind of deas was formerly common in the halls of great houses, where such economy, with respect to bed-room, was very necessary.

[2] "They dance," &c. in the orig. "They dance not with *much pride*;" *i.e.* be not so fond of shewing off their fine dancing, as to let their heels run

NOTES

Translated from the Danish.—See *Kæmpe Viser.* ed. 1695, p. 759.

It is my purpose to offer it to my countrymen as nearly as possible in the exact state in which it grew amid the rocks of Norway, and in the vallies of Jutland. I have therefore endeavoured to do for these ballads no more than seems to have been done in "The North Countries" for such tales as the Cimbri left behind them, or composed, in that quarter. I have merely adapted their dialect to the usage of the day. This seems to me to be the proper manner of Albinizing Scandinavian poetry. Let Regner Lodbrog still drink his *ale, to sweel his halse, out of a harn-shell*; for a goblet of cut glass would be out of character in so robust a hand.

So scrupulous have I been in faithfully rendering these pieces, that I have commonly preserved most of the original words, with only a slight alteration of the orthography, and sometimes of the arrangement; so that my version, may be nearly as intelligible to a Dane or Swede, as to a Scotsman. Nor have I the least apprehension, that this affirmation will provoke any judicious and liberal critic to be witty at the expence of my perspicuity. No one, that has not a radical knowledge of the Scotish dialect, can be a fair and competent judge in this case; and those who have, will, I flatter myself, easily comprehend all I have written; and, if they have never made the Cimbric language the subject of particular attention, they will be surprised to find, that, after such a series of years and of events, it has undergone so little change as it has done in Scotland.

I am sensible that some little stiffness may be observed in the translations; but that was unavoidable, as I studied to illustrate, and not to embellish. As the occasional irregularities of the measure, and inaccuracies of the rhymes, are studiously copied from the originals, I hope they will bring no unfavourable imputation upon my taste, judgement, or industry.

"These mer-men," says the editor of the *K. Viser*, "who were formerly said to carry off people and drown them, were called Nycker. But, through the knowledge of the Gospel, such goblins disappear ay more and more, so that people now hear nothing of them."

This mer-man. who so slyly nick'd Marstig's daughter, cannot, with propriety, be deemed a water-king, water-sprite, or water-fiend. Although an inhabitant of the waters, he was not the sole lord of the element; and although mer-men and mer-women were endowed with long life and supernatural powers, their substance was neither serial nor aqueous. Their power of assuming different forms, was no more than is enjoyed by every old woman, who can turn herself into a cat or a magpie. Danish ballad authority is all that we are concerned with at present; and if that

---

away with their heads, and get beyond their depth, as Marstig's daughter did.—"*I rede gude ladies, one and a'*," not to forget this!

may be admitted, they were of flesh and blood like men, with human feelings and affections; and their malignity was chiefly experienced by those, who either slighted their love, or provoked their resentment. That they were often friendly to mankind, and that, even when grossly injured, they were not always, in the opinion of their historians, destitute of principle and honour, will appear from the following legends.

The Hero Hogen, ("K. Viser," p. 55.) setting out on an expedition, as he is about to step on board, finds a mer-maid sleeping on the beech. He wakes her, flatters her, calls her a fair and lovely female, and soothsaying woman; and requests her to *spae* his fortune. She gives him very sensible and friendly advice to avoid his fate, but dissuades him from his intended expedition, *dim canens fata*, if he persists. Enraged and disappointed, be draws his sword, and strikes off her head. The bloody head rolls into the water, the body crawls after, and they are united again at the bottom of the sea. The event verifies her predictions.

Proud Ellen-lille, ("K. Viser," p. 161.) the king of Iceland's daughter, was stolen away from her mother. A ship was built, and Young Roland, her youngest brother, sets out in search of her. After sailing eight years, the ship founders in a storm, and all are drowned except Young Roland, who lands on a green island, where was a castle, in which he finds his sister. She tells him, if he had a hundred and a thousand lives, they will all be lost when the mer-man Rosmer comes in. Young Roland hides himself in a corner.

> Rosmer hame frae Zealand came,
> And he took on to bann;
> "I smell fu' well, by my right hand.
> That here is a Christian man!"

> "There flew a craw out o'er the house,
> Wi' a man's leg in his mouth;
> He coost it in, and I coost it out.
> As fast as e'er I couth."

> But wilyly she can Rosmar win.
> And clapping him tenderlie:
> "It's here is come my sister's son;
> Gin I lose him, I'll die!

> "It's here is come my sister's son,
> Frae baith our father's land:
> My lord, I've gi'en him faith and troth,
> That ye will not him bann."

> "And is he come, thy sister-son,
> Frae thy father's land to thee?

>   Then I will swear my highest aith,
>   He's dree nae skaith frae me."

Rosmer takes the poor shivering shipwrecked Roland on his knee, dandles him like a baby before the fire, and claps him till he is black and blue. Fear keeps Young Roland quiet; but Ellen interferes, to prevent the consequences of such clumsy kindness, and tells Rosmer to "remember that he has not small fingers, to clap so little a child." Rosmer desists; and Young Roland lives very happily in the castle during two years, at the end of which Proud Ellen finds herself with child by him. It would seem that no sexual intercourse subsisted between Ellen and the gigantic mer-man with the great fingers, or that such intercourse could not be productive; for she entertains the most terrible apprehensions from Rosmer's wrath when her situation is discovered. To avoid this, she tells the mer-man, (who appears to have been an unsuspecting, good-natured sort of a devil, and much the best Christian of the three,) that her nephew is tired of living so long in the sea, and longs to return to his country; and persuades the complaisant Hafmand to give him a chest full of gold, in which she afterwards secrets herself, and carry him to the land. Rosmer Hafmand takes" young Roland under his arm, and the chest in his mouth," and sets them down on their native coast. Young Roland now tells him, that, as he is such a good fellow, and has given him a chest of gold, and carried him back to his country, he will tell him as a piece of news, that Proud Ellen is with bairn. Rosmer is furiously enraged, and swears, that if he had not pledged his oath for his safety, he would drown him. "Rosmer sprang into the sea, and dashed the water up to the sky." When he returned to his castle, and found that Ellen was gone, "the tears ran, like a stream, down his cheeks;" and, through grief and amazement, he became (poetically, I suppose,) "a whin-stane grey, and stood an insensible object."

Such is the outline of the story of three different, ballads in the "Kæmpe Viser," on the subject of Rosmer Hafmand, which I intend to translate; as well as three concerning Hero Hogen, and the Mer-woman; and two or three in which the Gam, Valrafn, and Verner Rafn, are introduced. Of these I mean to get a few copies printed for the curious, with such illustrations as I can procure.

It may be observed, that there is a striking resemblance between the story of Rosmer Hafmand, and the romance of Child Rowland (not yet entirely lost in Scotland), which is quoted by *Mad Tom* in Shakespeare.

The British story is much finer, in every respect, than the Danish; and the conduct of Child Rowland (the youngest son of King Arthur of merry Carlisle,) much more honourable and manly than that of his Icelandic namesake. Instead of creeping into a corner to hide himself, he starts upon his legs, draws his father's good sword Excalibar, (or, as the Scots not very improperly recite it, his father's gude claymore), and exclaims, "Strike then, bogle of hell, if thou darest!" A short, but furious combat ensues, and the elf-king is felled to the ground. Child Rowland spares him, on condition that he will liberate his sister, Fair Ellen, and restore to life his two elder brothers, who lie dead in a corner of the hall: so they all four return in triumph to merry Carlisle. The failure of the two elder brothers was owing to their not having strictly observed the instructions given them by Myrddin Wyldt, whom they had consulted.

But of this romance I shall speak more at large, when I set about illustrating the story of Rosmer Hafmand.

As to the Danish term *Nycke*, I have long been of opinion, that both the Scotish and Danish *Nick* was originally no more than a playful abbreviation of the Latin *Niger*, which has for many ages been understood all over Europe to mean, *a black*. Ainsworth has derived the Latin, in his usual way, from the Greek *mortuus*; *mortui enim nigrescunt*: but this seems to be putting the cart before the horse. The Greek is more likely to have been derived from *strife, war*, and like the Latin *necatus*, most probably at first signified a person that had died by violence. Be this as it may, it appears that the appellation of Nick, applied indiscriminately by the Scots to Black Sanctus, the Prince of Darkness and Father of Necromancy, is by the Danes appropriated exclusively to that description of demi-gods of the waters, who, in many particulars, approach very near to the character of the Water Kelpie. Yet it may be observed, that although the Water Kelpie is never called Nick; the term Auld Nick is generally applied with some allusion to such whimsical pranks and merry mischief as the Kelpie also, when in good humour, is fond of indulging in.

Source:
Jamieson, Robert, editor. *Popular Ballads and Songs, Volume I.* Edinburgh: Archibald Constable and Co., 1806.

83. Rosmer Hafmand; or, The Mer-Man Rosmer

Denmark

THERE dwalls a lady in Danmarck,
　　Lady Hillers lyle men her ca';
And she's gar'd bigg a new castell,
　　That shines o'er Danmarck a'.

Her dochter was stown awa frae her;

She sought for her wide-whare;
But the mair she sought, and the less she fand,—
   That wirks her sorrow and care.

And she's gar'd bigg a new ship,
   Wi' vanes o' flaming goud,
Wi' mony a knight and mariner,
   Sae stark in need bestow'd.

She's followed her sons down to the strand,
   That chaste and noble fre;
And wull and waif for eight lang years
   They sail'd upon the sea.

And eight years wull and waif they sail'd,
   O' months that seem'd sae lang;
Syne they sail'd afore a high castell,
   And to the land can gang.

And the young lady Svanè lyle,
   In the bower that was the best,
Says, "Wharfrae cam thir frem swains,
   Wi' us this night to guest?"

Then up and spak her youngest brither,
   Sae wisely ay spak he;
"We are a widow's three poor sons,
   Lang wilder'd on the sea.

"In Danmarck were we born and bred,
   Lady Hillers lyle was our mither;
Our sister frae us was stown awa,
   We findna whare or whither."

"In Danmarck were ye born and bred?
   Was Lady Hillers your mither?
I can nae langer heal frae thee,
   Thou art my youngest brither.

"And hear ye this, my youngest brither,
   Why bade na ye at hame?
Had ye a hunder and thousand lives,
   Ye canna brook ane o' them."

She's set him in the weiest nook
   She in the house can meet;

She's bidden him for the high God's sake
    Nouther to laugh ne greet.

Rosmer hame frae Zealand came,
    And he took on to bann:
"I smell fu' weel, by my right hand,
    That here is a Christian man."

"There flew a bird out o'er the house,
    Wi' a man's bane in his mouth;
He coost it in, and I cast it out,
    As fast as e'er I couth."

But wilyly she can Rosmer win;
    And clapping him tenderly,
"It's here is come my sister-son;—
    Gin I lose him, I'll die.

"It's here is come, my sister-son,
    Frae baith our fathers' land;
And I ha'e pledged him faith and troth,
    That ye will not him bann."

"And is he come, thy sister-son,
    Frae thy father's land to thee?
Then I will swear my highest aith,
    He's dree nae skaith frae me."

'Twas then the high king Rosmer,
    He ca'd on younkers twae:
"Ye bid proud Svanè lyle's sister-son
    To the chalmer afore me gae."

It was Svanè lyle's sister-son,
    Whan afore Rosmer he wan,
His heart it quook, and his body shook,
    Sae fley'd, he scarce dow stand.

Sae Rosmer took her sister-son,
    Set him upon his knee;
He clappit him sae luifsomely,
    He turned baith blue and blae.

And up and spak she, Svanè lyle;
    "Sir Rosmer, ye're nae to learn
That your ten fingers arena sma,

To clap sae little a bairn."

There was he till, the fifthen year,
    He green'd for hame and land:
"Help me now, sister Svanè lyle,
    To be set on the white sand."

It was proud Lady Svanè lyle,
    Afore Rosmer can stand:
"This younker sae lang in the sea has been,
    He greens for hame and land."

"Gin the younker sae lang in the sea has been,
    And greens for hame and land,
Then I'll gie him a kist wi' goud,
    Sae fitting till his hand."

"And will ye gi'e him a kist wi' goud,
    Sae fitting till his hand?
Then hear ye, my noble heartis dear,
    Ye bear them baith to land."

Then wrought proud Lady Svanè lyle
    What Rosmer little wist;
For she's tane out the goud sae red,
    And laid hersel i' the kist.

He's ta'en the man upon his back;
    The kist in his mouth took he;
And he has gane the lang way up
    Frae the bottom o' the sea.

"Now I ha'e borne thee to the land;
    Thou seest baith sun and moon;
Namena Lady Svane for thy highest God,
    I beg thee as a boon."

Rosmer sprang i' the saut sea out,
    And jawp'd it up i' the sky;
But whan he cam till the castell in,
    Nae Svanè lyle could he spy.

Whan he came till the castell in,
    His dearest awa was gane;
Like wood he sprang the castell about,
    On the rock o' the black flintstane.

Glad they were in proud Hillers lyle's house,
　Wi' welcome joy and glee;
Hame to their friends her bairns were come,
　That had lang been in the sea.

NOTES

From Jamieson: Translated from the Danish. See "Kæmper Viser," p. 161. [This piece, being the first in order of those mentioned, vol. i, p. 208, has been received from the Editor in Riga, since this work went to the press.]

From Child: The ballad of Rosmer is found in Danish, Swedish, Faroish, and Norse. All the questions bearing upon its origin, and the relations of the various forms in which the story exists, are amply discussed by Grundtvig, vol. ii. p. 72. Three versions of the Danish ballad are given by Vedel, all of which Jamieson has translated. The following is No. 31 in Abrahamson.

Source:
Child, Francis James, editor. *English and Scottish Ballads, Volume 1*.
　London: Sampson Low, Son, & Co., 1861.
Jamieson, Robert, editor. *Popular Ballads and Songs, Volume II*.
　Edinburgh: Archibald Constable and Co., 1806.

84. The Mermaid's Prophecy

Denmark

The following ballad concerns a mermaid predicting the death of Dagmar of Bohemia, the Queen consort and first wife of King Valdemar II of Denmark. Queen Dagmar died in childbirth in 1212/1213. The original source of the translated ballad is not provided so it has been placed under Denmark since its story is set there.

THE King he has caught the fair mermaid, and deep
　(The mermaid dances the floor upon)
In the dungeon has placed her, to pine and to weep,
　Because his will she had not done.

The Queen of the Danes addressed two of her band:
    (The mermaid dances the floor upon)
"To come to my presence the mermaid command,
    For my will by her it shall be done."

The mermaid came in, to the Queen she up went:
    (The mermaid dances the floor upon)
"What wilt thou, O Queen, that for me thou hast sent?
    By me thy will can never be done."

The Queen the blue cushion stroked down with a smile:
    (The mermaid dances the floor upon)
"Sit down pretty mermaid and rest thee awhile,
    My will by thee must now be done."

"Why seek'st thou, O Queen, to betray my young life?
    (The mermaid dances the floor upon)
For under that cushion is stuck a sharp knife,
    By me thy will can never be done."

"If thou knowest that, then much more thou dost know,
    (The mermaid dances the floor upon)
So do thou my destiny unto me show,
    And thus by thee shall my will be done."

"If I should thy destiny to thee announce,
    (The mermaid dances the floor upon)
On a fire of faggots thou d'st burn me at once!
    By me unwilling your will is done.

"Three babes thou shalt bear, each a beautiful boy,
    (The mermaid dances the floor upon)
And in leaving thy womb they thy life shall destroy,
    And thus fair Queen thy will is done."

"If with me, luckless me, it no better shall speed,
    (The mermaid dances the floor upon)
Inform me what fortune for them is decreed,
    For thus by thee can my will be done."

"The first shall be King in old Denmark of them,
    (The mermaid dances the floor upon)
The next shall succeed to the gold diadem,
    By me can thus thy will be done.

"The third as the wisest of mortals shall shine,

(The mermaid dances the floor upon)
And for him thou art doomed thy young life to resign,
    Thus all your will, fair Queen, I've done."

In her mantle of azure the Queen wrapt her head,
    (The mermaid dances the floor upon)
And unto the hall to the Monarch she sped,
    For she her will had fairly done.

"Now hear my entreaty, my heart's belov'd Lord,
    (The mermaid dances the floor upon)
To my own disposal this mermaid award,
    For she my will has fairly done."

"I'll not give her thee, nor her life shalt thou save,
    (The mermaid dances the floor upon)
For my seven brave vessels she swamped in the wave,
    My pleasure thus she has not done."

Black, black as a clod grew the Queen at that word,
    (The mermaid dances the floor upon)
And down she fell senseless before the King's board,
    Because her will she had fairly clone.

"My Queen and my dearest! thy heart shall not break,
    (The mermaid dances the floor upon)
Thou art free to the strand the fair mermaid to take,
    Because thy will she has fairly done."

The mermaid in scarlet so fine she array'd,
    (The mermaid dances the floor upon)
Although she had heard her own death by her spaed,
    For thus, for thus, her will she'd done.

The Queen gave command to the maids in her train:
    (The mermaid dances the floor upon)
"Convey ye the mermaid hence down to the main,
    For she my will has fairly done."

Upon the blue billows the mermaid they place,
    (The mermaid dances the floor upon)
The Queen fell to weeping, and sad was each face,
    For she her will, alack! had done.

"O prythee don't weep, and O prythee don't grieve,
    (The mermaid dances the floor upon)

Heaven's portals stand open thy soul to receive,
   Now I thy will have fairly done.

"In the mansions of Heaven thou aye shalt remain,
   (The mermaid dances the floor upon)
And there perfect quiet and rest thou shalt gain—
   Now all thy will, fair Queen, I've done!"

Source:
Borrow, George, translator. *The Mermaid's Prophecy and Other Songs Relating to Queen Dagmar*. London: Printed for Private Circulation, 1913.

85. Agnete and the Merman by Jens Baggesen

Denmark

AGNETE she was guileless.
   She was beloved and true,
But solitude, it charm'd her,
   And mirth she never knew—
      She never knew
She made the joy of all around
   Yet never felt it too.

Over the dark blue waves,
   Agnete, gazing, bends,
When lo! a merman rising there
   From ocean's depths ascends;
      Up he ascends.
Yet still, Agnete's bending form
   With the soft billows blends.

His glossy hair, it seemed as spun
   Out of the purest gold,
His beaming eye, it brightly glow'd
   With warmest love untold—
      With love untold!
And his scale-cover'd bosom held
   A heart that was not cold.

The song he sang Agnete,
  On love and sorrow rang;
His voice it was so melting soft,
  So sadly sweet he sang—
    Sadly he sang.
It seemed as if his beating heart
  Upon his lips it sprang.

"And hearken, dear Agnete!
  What I shall say to thee—
My heart, oh! it is breaking, sweet!
  With longing after thee!
    Still after thee!
Oh! wilt thou ease my sorrow, love,
  Oh! wilt thou smile on me?"

Two silver buckles lay
  Upon the rocky shore,
And aught more rich, or aught more bright,
  No princess ever wore,
    No, never wore.
"My best beloved,"—so sang he—
  "Add these unto thy store!"

Then drew he from his breast
  A string of pearls so rare—
None richer, no, or none more pure
  Did princess ever wear—
    Oh! ever wear.
"My best beloved," so sang he,
  "Accept this bracelet fair!"

Then from his finger drew he
  A ring of jewels fine—
And none more brilliant, none more rich,
  Midst princely gems might shine;
    "Here, here from mine,
My best beloved," so sang he,
  "Oh, place this upon thine!"

Agnete, on the deep sea
  Beholds the sky's soft hue,
The waves they were so crystal clear,
  The ocean 'twas so blue!
    Oh! so blue!
The merman smiled, and thus he sang,

As near to her he drew:—

"Ah! hearken, my Agnete,
    What I to thee shall speak:
For thee my heart is burning, love,
    For thee, my heart will break!
        Oh! 'twill break!
Say, sweet, wilt thou be kind to me,
    And grant the love I seek?"

"Dear merman! hearken thou,
    Yes, I will list to thee!
If deep beneath the sparkling waves
    Thou'lt downward carry me—
        Take thou me!
And bear me to thine ocean bow'r
    There, I will dwell with thee."

Then stoppeth he her ears,
    Her mouth then stoppeth he;
And with the lady he hath fled,
    Deep, deep beneath the sea!
        Beneath the sea!
There kiss'd they, and embraced they,
    So fond, and safe, and free!

For full two years and more,
    Agnete, she lived there,
And warm, untiring, faithful love
    They to each other bear;
        Such love they bear.
Within the merman's shelly bower
    Are born two children fair.

Agnete—she sat tranquilly,
    And to her boys she sang;
When hark! a sound of earth she hears,
    How solemnly it rang!
        Ding—dong—dang!
It was the church's passing bell
    In Holmé Vale that clang.

Agnete, from the cradle,
    Springs suddenly away,
She hastes to seek her merman dear,
    "Loved merman, say I may—

　　　　　Say—Oh say,
That I, ere midnight's hour, may take
　　To Holmé's church my way?"

"Thou wishest ere the midnight
　　To Holmé church to go?
See then that thou, ere day, art back
　　Here, to thy boys below—
　　　　　Go—go—go!
But ere the morning light return
　　Come to thy sons below!"

He stoppeth then her ears,
　　Her mouth then stoppeth he;
And upwards they together rise
　　Till Holmé Vale they see.
　　　　　"Now part we!"
They part, and he descends again
　　Beneath the deep blue sea.

Straight on to the churchyard,
　　Agnete's footsteps hie:
She meets—O God! her mother there,
　　And turns again to fly.
　　　　　"Why—O why?"
Her mother's voice her steps arrests
　　Thus speaking with a sigh:—

"Oh hearken, my Agnete,
　　What I shall say to thee,
Where has thy distant dwelling been
　　So long away from me?
　　　　　Away from me!
Say, where hast thou, my child, been hid
　　So long and secretly?"

"O mother! I have dwelt
　　Beneath the boundless main,
Within a merman's coral bower,
　　And we have children twain,
　　　　　Beneath the main.
I came to pray—and then I go
　　Back to the deep again!"

"But hearken thou, Agnete,
　　What I to thee shall say—

Here thy two little daughters weep
    Because thou art away;
        By night, by day,
Thy little girls bemoan and grieve;
    With them thou'lt surely stay?"

"Well—let my daughters small
    For me both grieve and long,
My ears are closed—I cannot hear
    Their cries yon waves among!
        Oh! I belong
To my dear sons, and they will die
    If I my stay prolong."

"Have pity on thy babes—
    Let them not pine away!
Oh! think upon thy youngest child
    Who in her cradle lay!
        With them oh stay!
Forget yon elves, and with thine own,
    Thy lawful children stay!"

"Nay, let them bloom or fade—
    The two—as Heav'n may will!
My heart is closed—their cries no more
    Can now my bosom thrill—
        Oh! no more thrill!
For now my merman's sons alone
    All my affections fill."

"Alas! though thou canst thus
    Thy smiling babes forget;
Yet think upon their father's faith,
    Thy noble lord's regret,
        The fate he met!
As soon as thou wert lost to him
    His sun of joy was set.

"Long—long he search'd for thee,
    He went a weary way;
At last from yonder shelving rock
    He cast himself one day—
        One dismal day.
His corpse upon the pebbly strand
    In the dim twilight lay!

"And here—'twas not long since—
    His coffin they did bring;
Ha! list, my daughter, hearest thou?
    The midnight bells they ring!
        Ding—dong—ding!"
Away her mother hastens then
    As loud the church bells ring.

Agnete, o'er the church-door
    Stepp'd softly from without,
When all the little images
    They seem'd to turn about;
        Round about.
Within the church, the images
    They seem'd to turn about.

Agnete gazes on
    The altar-piece so fair;
The altar-piece it seem'd to turn,
    And the altar with it there.
        All where'er
Her eye it fell within the church,
    Seem'd turning, turning there!

Agnete, on the ground
    She gazed in thoughtful mood,
When lo! she saw her mother's name
    That on a tomb-stone stood.
        There it stood!
Then, sudden from her bursting heart,
    Flow'd back her chill'd life's blood.

Agnete—first she stagger'd back,
    She fainted, then she fell.
Now may her children long in vain
    For her they loved so well.
        Oh, so well!
Now, neither sons nor daughters more
    To her their wants may tell.

Ay! Let them weep, and let them long,
    And seek her o'er and o'er!
Dark, dark, are now her eyes so bright,
    They ne'er shall open more!
        Oh, never more!

And crush'd is now that death-cold heart,
  So warm with love before.

Source:
Bushby, Mrs. *The Danes: Sketched by Themselves, A Series of Popular Stories by the Best Danish Authors.* Vol. 1. London: Richard Bentley, 1864.

86. Agnes
by Adam Gottlob Oehlenschläger

Denmark

MAID AGNES musing sat alone
  Upon the lonely strand;
The breaking waves sighed soft and low
  Upon the white sea-sand.

Watching the thin white foam, that broke
  Upon the wave, sat she,
When up a beauteous merman rose
  From the bottom of the sea.

And he was clad unto the waist
  With scales like silver white,
And on his breast the setting sun
  Put rosy gleams of light.

The merman's spear a boat-mast was,
  With crook of coral brown,
His shield was made of turtle-shell,
  Of mussel-shells his crown.

His hair upon his shoulders fell,
  Of bright and glittering tang;
And sweeter than the nightingale's
  Sounded the song he sang.

"And tell to me, sweet merman,
  Fresh from the deep, deep sea,

When will a tender husband come
    To woo and marry me?"

"O hearken, sweetest Agnes,
    To the words I say to thee—
All for the sake of my true heart,
    Let me thy husband he.

"Far underneath the deep, deep sea,
    I reign in palace halls,
And all around, of crystal clear,
    Uprise the wondrous walls.

"And seven hundred handmaids wait,
    To serve my slightest wish—
A hove the waist like milk-white maids,
    Below the waist, like fish.

"Like mother-of-pearl the sea-sledge gleams,
    Wherein I journey crowned,
Along the sweet green path its goes,
    Dragged by the great seal-hound.

"And all along the green, green deeps
    Grow flowers wondrous fair;
They drink the wave, and grow as tall
    As those that breathe the air."

Fair Agnes smiled, and stretched her arms,
    And leapt into the sea,
And down beneath the tall sea-plants
    He led her tenderlie.

Eight happy years fair Agnes dwelt
    Under the green sea-wave,
And seven beauteous little ones
    She to the merman gave.

She sat beneath the tall sea-plants,
    Upon a throne of shells,
And from the far-off land she heard
    The sound of sweet kirk bells.

Unto her gentle lord she stept,
    And softly took his hand:

"And may I once, and only once,
    Go say my prayers on land?"

"Then hearken, sweet wife Agnes,
    To the words I say to thee—
Fail not in twenty hours and four
    To hasten home to me."

A thousand times "Good night" she said
    Unto her children small,
And ere she went away she stooped,
    And softly kissed them all;

And, old and young, the children wept
    As Agnes went away,
And loud as any cried the babe
    Who in the cradle lay.

Now Agnes sees the sun again,
    And steps upon the strand—
She trembles at the light, and hides
    Her eyes with her white hand.

Among the folk she used to know,
    As they walk to kirk, steps she.
"We know thee not, thou woman wild,
    Come from a far countree."

The kirk bells chime, and into kirk
    And up the aisle she flies;
The images upon the walls
    Are turning away their eyes!

The silver chalice to her lips
    She lifteth tremblinglie,
For that her lips were all athirst,
    Under the deep, deep sea.

She tried to pray, and could not pray,
    And still the kirk bells sound;
She spills the cup of holy wine
    Upon the cold, cold ground.

When smoke and mist rose from the sea,
    And it was dark on land,

She drew her robe about her face,
    And stood upon the strand.

Then folded she her thin, thin hands,
    The merman's weary wife:
"Heaven help me in my wickedness,
    And take away my life!"

She sank among the meadow grass,
    As white and cold as snow;
The roses growing round about
    Turned white and cold also.

The small birds sang upon the bough,
    And their song was sad and deep—
"Now, Agnes, it is gloaming hour,
    And thou art going to sleep."

All in the twilight, when the sun
    Sank down behind the main,
Her hands were pressed upon her heart,
    And her heart had broke in twain.

The waves creep up across the strand,
    Sighing so mournfullie,
And tenderly they wash the corse
    To the bottom of the sea.

Three days she stayed beneath the sea,
    And then came back again,
And mournfully, so mournfully,
    Upon the sand was lain.

And, sweetly decked by tender hands,
    She lay a-sleeping there,
And all her form is wreathed with weeds,
    And a flower was in her hair.

The little herd-boy drove his geese
    Seaward at peep o' day,
And there, her hands upon her breast,
    Sweet Agnes sleeping lay.

He dug a grave behind a stone,
    All in the soft sea-sand,

And there the maiden's bones are dry,
  Though the waves creep up the strand.

Each morning and each evening,
  The stone is wet above;
The merman hath wept (the town girls say)
  Over his lost true-love.

NOTES

From Buchanan's preface: Another ballad, "Agnete and the Merman," begins—

> "On the high tower Agnete is pacing slow,
>   Sudden a Merman upsprings from below,
>   Ho! ho! ho!
>   A Merman upsprings from the water below."

"Agnete! Agnete!" he cries, "wilt thou be my true-love—my all-dearest?" "Yea, if thou takest me with thee to the bottom of the sea." They dwell together eight years, and have seven sons. One day, Agnete, as she sits singing under the blue water, "hears the clocks of England clang," and straightway asks and receives permission to go on shore to church. She meets her mother at the church door. "Where hast thou been these eight years, my daughter?" "I have been at the bottom of the sea," replies Agnete, "and have seven sons by the Merman." The Merman follows her into the church, and all the small images turn away their eyes from him. "Hearken, Agnete! thy small bairns are crying for thee." "Let them cry as long as they will;—I shall not return to them." And the cruel one cannot be persuaded to go back. This pathetic story, so capable of poetic treatment, has been exquisitely paraphrased by Oehlenschläger, whose poem I have here translated in preference to the original. The Danish Mermen, by the way, seem to have been good fellows, and badly used. One Rosmer Havmand does many kindly acts, but is rewarded with base ingratitude by everybody. The tale of Rosmer bears a close resemblance to the romance of Childe Rowland, quoted by Edgar in "Lear."

Source:
Buchanan, Robert. *Ballad Stories of the Affections: From the Scandinavian.* London: George Routledge & Sons, [1866].

87. The Little Mermaid by Hans Christian Andersen

Denmark

FAR out in the ocean, where the water is as blue as the prettiest cornflower, and as clear as crystal, it is very, very deep; so deep, indeed, that no cable could fathom it: many church steeples, piled one upon another, would not reach from the ground beneath to the surface of the water above. There dwell the Sea King and his subjects. We must not imagine that there is nothing at the bottom of the sea but bare yellow sand. No, indeed; the most singular flowers and plants grow there; the leaves and stems of which are so pliant, that the slightest agitation of the water causes them to stir as if they had life. Fishes, both large and small, glide between the branches, as birds fly among the trees here upon land. In the deepest spot of all, stands the castle of the Sea King. Its walls are built of coral, and the long, gothic windows are of the clearest amber. The roof is formed of shells, that open and close as the water flows over them. Their appearance is very beautiful, for in each lies a glittering pearl, which would be fit for the diadem of a queen.

The Sea King had been a widower for many years, and his aged mother kept house for him. She was a very wise woman, and exceedingly proud of her high birth; on that account she wore twelve oysters on her tail; while others, also of high rank, were only allowed to wear six. She was, however, deserving of very great praise, especially for her care of the little sea-princesses, her grand-daughters. They were six beautiful children; but the youngest was the prettiest of them all; her skin was as clear and delicate as a rose-leaf, and her eyes as blue as the deepest sea; but, like all the others, she had no feet, and her body ended in a fish's tail. All day long they played in the great halls of the castle, or among the living flowers that grew out of the walls. The large amber windows were open, and the fish swam in, just as the swallows fly into our houses when we open the windows, excepting that the fishes swam up to the princesses, ate out of their hands, and allowed themselves to be stroked. Outside the castle there was a beautiful garden, in which grew bright red and dark blue flowers, and blossoms like flames of fire; the fruit glittered like gold, and the leaves and stems waved to and fro continually. The earth itself was the finest sand, but blue as the flame of burning sulphur. Over everything lay a peculiar blue radiance, as if it were surrounded by the air from above, through which the blue sky shone, instead of the dark depths of the sea. In calm weather the sun could be seen, looking like a purple flower, with the light streaming from the calyx. Each of the young princesses had a little plot of ground in the garden, where she might dig and plant as she pleased. One arranged her flower-bed into the form of a whale; another thought it better to make hers like the figure of a little mermaid; but that of the youngest was round like the sun, and contained flowers as red as his rays at sunset. She was a strange child, quiet and thoughtful; and while her sisters would be delighted with the wonderful things which they obtained from the wrecks of vessels, she cared for nothing but her pretty red flowers, like the sun, excepting a beautiful marble statue. It was the representation of a handsome boy, carved out of pure white stone, which had fallen to the bottom of the sea from a wreck. She planted by the statue a rose-colored weeping willow. It grew splendidly, and very soon hung its fresh branches over the statue, almost down to the blue sands. The shadow had a violet tint, and waved to and fro like the branches; it seemed as if the crown of the tree and the root were at play, and trying to kiss each other. Nothing gave her so much pleasure as to hear about the world above the sea. She made her old grandmother tell her all she knew of the ships and of the towns, the people and the animals. To her it seemed most wonderful and beautiful to hear that the flowers of the land should have fragrance, and not those below the sea; that the trees of the forest should be green; and that the fishes among the trees could sing so sweetly, that it was quite a pleasure to hear them. Her grandmother called the little birds fishes, or she would not have understood her; for she had never seen birds.

"When you have reached your fifteenth year," said the grand-mother, "you will have permission to rise up out of the sea, to sit on the rocks in the moonlight, while the great ships are sailing by; and then you will see both forests and towns."

In the following year, one of the sisters would be fifteen: but as each was a year younger than the other, the youngest would have to wait five years before her turn came to rise up from the bottom of the ocean, and see the earth as we do. However, each promised to tell the others what she saw on her first visit, and what she thought the most beautiful; for their grandmother could not tell them enough; there were so many things on which they wanted information. None of them longed so much for her turn to come as the youngest, she who had the longest time to wait, and who was so quiet and thoughtful. Many nights she stood by the open window, looking up through the dark blue water, and watching the fish as they splashed about with their fins and tails. She could see the moon and stars shining faintly; but through the water they looked larger than they do to our eyes. When something like a black cloud passed between her and them, she knew that it was either a whale swimming over her head, or a ship full of human beings, who never imagined that a pretty little mermaid was standing beneath them, holding out her white hands towards the keel of their ship.

As soon as the eldest was fifteen, she was allowed to rise to the surface of the ocean. When she came back, she had hundreds of things to talk about; but the most beautiful, she said, was to lie in the moonlight, on a sandbank, in the quiet sea, near the coast, and to gaze on a large town nearby, where the lights were twinkling like hundreds of stars; to listen to the sounds of the music, the noise of carriages, and the voices of human beings, and then to hear the merry bells peal out from the church steeples; and because she could not go near to all those wonderful things, she longed for them more than ever. Oh, did not the youngest sister listen eagerly to all these descriptions? and afterwards, when she stood at the open window looking up through the dark blue water, she thought of the great city, with all its bustle and noise, and even fancied she could hear the sound of the church bells, down in the depths of the sea.

In another year the second sister received permission to rise to the surface of the water, and to swim about where she pleased. She rose just as the sun was setting, and this, she said, was the most beautiful sight of all. The whole sky looked like gold, while violet and rose-colored clouds, which she could not describe, floated over her; and, still more rapidly than the clouds, flew a large flock of wild swans towards the setting sun, looking like a long white veil across the sea. She also swam towards the sun; but it sunk into the waves, and the rosy tints faded from the clouds and from the sea.

The third sister's turn followed; she was the boldest of them all, and she swam up a broad river that emptied itself into the sea. On the banks she saw green hills covered with beautiful vines; palaces and castles peeped out from amid the proud trees of the forest; she heard the birds singing, and the rays of the sun were so powerful that she was obliged often to dive down under the water to cool her burning face. In a narrow creek she found a whole troop of little human children, quite naked, and sporting about in the water; she wanted to play with them, but they fled in a great fright; and then a little black animal came to the water; it was a dog, but she did not know that, for she had never before seen one. This animal barked at her so terribly that she became frightened, and rushed back to the open sea. But she said she should never forget the beautiful forest, the green hills, and the pretty little children who could swim in the water, although they had not fish's tails.

The fourth sister was more timid; she remained in the midst of the sea, but she said it was quite as beautiful there as nearer the land. She could see for so many miles around her, and the sky above looked like a bell of glass. She had seen the ships, but at such a great distance that they looked like sea-gulls. The dolphins sported in the waves, and the great whales spouted water from their nostrils till it seemed as if a hundred fountains were playing in every direction.

The fifth sister's birthday occurred in the winter; so when her turn came, she saw what the others had not seen the first time they went up. The sea looked quite green, and large icebergs were floating about, each like a pearl, she said, but larger and loftier than the churches built by men. They were of the most singular shapes, and glittered like diamonds.

She had seated herself upon one of the largest, and let the wind play with her long hair, and she remarked that all the ships sailed by rapidly, and steered as far away as they could from the iceberg, as if they were afraid of it. Towards evening, as the sun went down, dark clouds covered the sky, the thunder rolled and the lightning flashed, and the red light glowed on the icebergs as they rocked and tossed on the heaving sea. On all the ships the sails were reefed with fear and trembling, while she sat calmly on the floating iceberg, watching the blue lightning, as it darted its forked flashes into the sea.

When first the sisters had permission to rise to the surface, they were each delighted with the new and beautiful sights they saw; but now, as grown-up girls, they could go when they pleased, and they had become indifferent about it. They wished themselves back again in the water, and after a month had passed they said it was much more beautiful down below, and pleasanter to be at home. Yet often, in the evening hours, the five sisters would twine their arms round each other, and rise to the surface, in a row. They had more beautiful voices than any human being could have; and before the approach of a storm, and when they expected a ship would be lost, they swam before the vessel, and sang sweetly of the delights to be found in the depths of the sea, and begging the sailors not to fear if they sank to the bottom. But the sailors could not understand the song, they took it for the howling of the storm. And these things were never to be beautiful for them; for if the ship sank, the men were drowned, and their dead bodies alone reached the palace of the Sea King.

When the sisters rose, arm-in-arm, through the water in this way, their youngest sister would stand quite alone, looking after them, ready to cry, only that the mermaids have no tears, and therefore they suffer more. "Oh, were I but fifteen years old," said she: "I know that I shall love the world up there, and all the people who live in it."

At last she reached her fifteenth year. "Well, now, you are grown up," said the old dowager, her grandmother; "so you must let me adorn you like your other sisters;" and she placed a wreath of white lilies in her hair, and every flower leaf was half a pearl. Then the old lady ordered eight great oysters to attach themselves to the tail of the princess to show her high rank.

"But they hurt me so," said the little mermaid.

"Pride must suffer pain," replied the old lady. Oh, how gladly she would have shaken off all this grandeur, and laid aside the heavy wreath! The red flowers in her own garden would have suited her much better, but she could not help herself: so she said, "Farewell," and rose as lightly as a bubble to the surface of the water. The sun had just set as she raised her head above the waves; but the clouds were tinted with crimson and gold, and through the glimmering twilight beamed the evening star in all its beauty. The sea was calm, and the air mild and fresh. A large ship, with three masts, lay becalmed on the water, with only one sail set; for not a breeze stiffed, and the sailors sat idle on deck or amongst the rigging. There was music and song on board; and, as darkness came on, a hundred colored lanterns were lighted, as if the flags of all nations waved in the air. The little mermaid swam close to the cabin windows; and now and then, as the waves lifted her up, she could look in through clear glass window-panes, and see a number of well-dressed people within. Among them was a young prince, the most beautiful of all, with large black eyes; he was sixteen years of age, and his birthday was being kept with much rejoicing. The sailors were dancing on deck, but when the prince came out of the cabin, more than a hundred rockets rose in the air, making it as bright as day. The little mermaid was so startled that she dived under water; and when she again stretched out her head, it appeared as if all the stars of heaven were falling around her, she had never seen such fireworks before. Great suns spurted fire about, splendid fireflies flew into the blue air, and everything was reflected in the clear, calm sea beneath. The ship itself was so brightly illuminated that all the people, and even the smallest rope, could be distinctly and plainly seen. And how handsome the young prince looked, as he pressed the hands of all present and smiled at them, while the music resounded through the clear night air.

It was very late; yet the little mermaid could not take her eyes from the ship, or from the beautiful prince. The colored lanterns had been extinguished, no more rockets rose in the air, and the cannon had ceased firing; but the sea became restless, and a moaning, grumbling sound could be heard beneath the waves: still the little mermaid remained by the cabin window, rocking up and down on the water, which enabled her to look in. After a while, the sails were quickly unfurled, and the noble ship continued her passage; but soon the waves rose higher, heavy clouds darkened the sky, and lightning appeared in the distance. A dreadful storm was approaching; once more the sails were reefed, and the great ship pursued her flying course over the raging sea. The waves rose mountains high, as if they would have overtopped the mast; but the ship dived like a swan between them, and then rose again on their lofty, foaming crests. To the little mermaid this appeared pleasant sport; not so to the sailors. At length the ship groaned and creaked; the thick planks gave way under the lashing of the sea as it broke over the deck; the mainmast snapped asunder like a reed; the ship lay over on her side; and the water rushed in. The little mermaid now perceived that the crew were in danger; even she herself was obliged to be careful to avoid the beams and planks of the wreck which lay scattered on the water. At one moment it was so pitch dark that she could not see a single object, but a flash of lightning revealed the whole scene; she could see every one who had been on board excepting the prince; when the ship parted, she had seen him sink into the deep waves, and she was glad, for she thought he would now be with her; and then she remembered that human beings could not live in the water, so that when he got down to her father's palace he would be quite dead. But he must not die. So she swam about among the beams and planks which strewed the surface of the sea, forgetting that they could crush her to pieces. Then she dived deeply under the dark waters, rising and falling with the waves, till at length she managed to reach the young prince, who was fast losing the power of swimming in that stormy sea. His limbs were failing him, his beautiful eyes were closed, and he would have died had not the little mermaid come to his assistance. She held his head above the water, and let the waves drift them where they would.

In the morning the storm had ceased; but of the ship not a single fragment could be seen. The sun rose up red and glowing from the water, and its beams brought back the hue of health to the prince's cheeks; but his eyes remained closed. The mermaid kissed his high, smooth forehead, and stroked back his wet hair; he seemed to her like the marble statue in her little garden, and she kissed him again, and wished that he might live. Presently they came in sight of land; she saw lofty blue mountains, on which the white snow rested as if a flock of swans were lying upon them. Near the coast were beautiful green forests, and close by stood a large building, whether a church or a convent she could not tell. Orange and citron trees grew in the garden, and before the door stood lofty palms. The sea here formed a little bay, in which the water was quite still, but very deep; so she swam with the handsome prince to the beach, which was covered with fine, white sand, and there she laid him in the warm sunshine, taking care to raise his head higher than his body. Then bells sounded in the large white building, and a number of young girls came into the garden. The little mermaid swam out farther from the shore and placed herself between some high rocks that rose out of the water; then she covered her head and neck with the foam of the sea so that her little face might not be seen, and watched to see what would become of the poor prince. She did not wait long before she saw a young girl approach the spot where he lay. She seemed frightened at first, but only for a moment; then she fetched a number of people, and the mermaid saw that the prince came to life again, and smiled upon those who stood round him. But to her he sent no smile; he knew not that she had saved him. This made her very unhappy, and when he was led away into the great building, she dived down sorrowfully into the water, and returned to her father's castle. She had always been silent and thoughtful, and now she was more so than ever. Her sisters asked her what she had seen during her first visit to the surface of the water; but she would tell them nothing. Many an evening and morning did she rise to the place where she had left the prince. She saw the fruits in the garden ripen till they were gathered, the snow on the tops of the mountains melt away; but she never saw the prince, and therefore she returned home, always more sorrowful than before. It was her only comfort to sit in her own little garden, and fling her arm round the beautiful marble statue which was like the prince; but she gave up tending her flowers, and they grew in wild confusion over the paths, twining their long leaves and stems round the branches of the trees, so that the whole place became dark and gloomy. At length she could bear it no longer, and told one of her sisters all about it. Then the others heard the secret, and very soon it became known to two mermaids whose intimate friend happened to know who the prince was. She had also seen the festival on board ship, and she told them where the prince came from, and where his palace stood.

"Come, little sister," said the other princesses; then they entwined their arms and rose up in a long row to the surface of the water, close by the spot where they knew the prince's palace stood. It was built of bright yellow shining stone, with long flights of marble steps, one of which reached quite down to the sea. Splendid gilded cupolas rose over the roof, and between the pillars that surrounded the whole building stood life-like statues of marble. Through the clear crystal of the lofty windows could be seen noble rooms, with costly silk curtains and hangings of tapestry; while the walls were covered with beautiful paintings which were a pleasure to look at. In the centre of the largest saloon a fountain threw its sparkling jets high up into the glass cupola of the ceiling, through which the sun shone down upon the water and upon the beautiful plants growing round the basin of the fountain. Now that she knew where he lived, she spent many an evening and many a night on the water near the palace. She would swim much nearer the shore than any of the others ventured to do; indeed once she went quite up the narrow channel under the marble balcony, which threw a broad shadow on the water. Here she would sit and watch the young prince, who thought himself quite alone in the bright moonlight. She saw him many times of an evening sailing in a pleasant boat, with music playing and flags waving. She peeped out from among the green rushes, and if the wind caught her long silvery-white veil, those who saw it believed it to be a swan, spreading out its wings. On many a night, too, when the fishermen, with their torches, were out at sea, she heard them relate so many good things about the doings of the young prince, that she was glad she had saved his life when he had been tossed about half-dead on the waves. And she remembered that his head had rested on her bosom, and how heartily she had kissed him; but he knew nothing of all this, and could not even dream of her. She grew more and more fond of human beings, and wished more and more to be able to wander about with those whose world seemed to be so much larger than her own. They could fly over the sea in ships, and mount the high hills which were far above the clouds; and the lands they possessed, their woods and their fields, stretched far away beyond the reach of her sight. There was so much that she wished to know, and her sisters were unable to answer all her questions. Then she applied to her old grandmother, who knew all about the upper world, which she very rightly called the lands above the sea.

"If human beings are not drowned," asked the little mermaid, "can they live forever? do they never die as we do here in the sea?"

"Yes," replied the old lady, "they must also die, and their term of life is even shorter than ours. We sometimes live to three hundred years, but when we cease to exist here we only become the foam on the surface of the water, and we have not even a grave down here of those we love. We have not immortal souls, we shall never live again; but, like the green sea-weed, when once it has been cut off, we can never flourish more. Human beings, on the contrary, have a soul which lives forever, lives after the body has been turned to dust. It rises up through the clear, pure air beyond the glittering stars. As we rise out of the water, and behold all the land of the earth, so do they rise to unknown and glorious regions which we shall never see."

"Why have not we an immortal soul?" asked the little mermaid mournfully; "I would give gladly all the hundreds of years that I have to live, to be a human being only for one day, and to have the hope of knowing the happiness of that glorious world above the stars."

"You must not think of that," said the old woman; "we feel ourselves to be much happier and much better off than human beings."

"So I shall die," said the little mermaid, "and as the foam of the sea I shall be driven about never again to hear the music of the waves, or to see the pretty flowers nor the red sun. Is there anything I can do to win an immortal soul?"

"No," said the old woman, "unless a man were to love you so much that you were more to him than his father or mother; and if all his thoughts and all his love were fixed upon you, and the priest placed his right hand in yours, and he promised to be true to you here and hereafter, then his soul would glide into your body and you would obtain a share in the future happiness of mankind. He would give a soul to you and retain his own as well; but this can never happen. Your fish's tail, which amongst us is considered so beautiful, is thought on earth to be quite ugly; they do not know any better, and they think it necessary to have two stout props, which they call legs, in order to be handsome."

Then the little mermaid sighed, and looked sorrowfully at her fish's tail. "Let us be happy," said the old lady, "and dart and spring about during the three hundred years that we have to live, which is really quite long enough; after that we can rest ourselves all the better. This evening we are going to have a court ball."

It is one of those splendid sights which we can never see on earth. The walls and the ceiling of the large ball-room were of thick, but transparent crystal. May hundreds of colossal shells, some of a deep red, others of a grass green, stood on each side in rows, with blue fire in them, which lighted up the whole saloon, and shone through the walls, so that the sea was also illuminated. Innumerable fishes, great and small, swam past the crystal walls; on some of them the scales glowed with a purple brilliancy, and on others they shone like silver and gold. Through the halls flowed a broad stream, and in it danced the mermen and the mermaids to the music of their own sweet singing. No one on earth has such a lovely voice as theirs. The little mermaid sang more sweetly than them all. The whole court applauded her with hands and tails; and for a moment her heart felt quite gay, for she knew she had the loveliest voice of any on earth or in the sea. But she soon thought again of the world above her, for she could not forget the charming prince, nor her sorrow that she had not an immortal soul like his; therefore she crept away silently out of her father's palace, and while everything within was gladness and song, she sat in her own little garden sorrowful and alone. Then she heard the bugle sounding through the water, and thought—"He is certainly sailing above, he on whom my wishes depend, and in whose hands I should like to place the happiness of my life. I will venture all for him, and to win an immortal soul, while my sisters are dancing in my father's palace, I will go to the sea witch, of whom I have always been so much afraid, but she can give me counsel and help."

And then the little mermaid went out from her garden, and took the road to the foaming whirlpools, behind which the sorceress lived. She had never been that way before: neither flowers nor grass grew there; nothing but bare, gray, sandy ground stretched out to the whirlpool, where the water, like foaming mill-wheels, whirled round everything that it seized, and cast it into the fathomless deep. Through the midst of these crushing whirlpools the little mermaid was obliged to pass, to reach the dominions of the sea witch; and also for a long distance the only road lay right across a quantity of warm, bubbling mire, called by the witch her turfmoor. Beyond this stood her house, in the centre of a strange forest, in which all the trees and flowers were polypi, half animals and half plants; they looked like serpents with a hundred heads growing out of the ground. The branches were long slimy arms, with fingers like flexible worms, moving limb after limb from the root to the top. All that could be reached in the sea they seized upon, and held fast, so that it never escaped from their clutches. The little mermaid was so alarmed at what she saw, that she stood still, and her heart beat with fear, and she was very nearly turning back; but she thought of the prince, and of the human soul for which she longed, and her courage returned. She fastened her long flowing hair round her head, so that the polypi might not seize hold of it. She laid her hands together across her bosom, and then she darted forward as a fish shoots through the water, between the supple arms and fingers of the ugly polypi, which were stretched out on each side of her. She saw that each held in its grasp something it had seized with its numerous little arms, as if they were iron bands. The white skeletons of human beings who had perished at sea, and had sunk down into the deep waters, skeletons of land animals, oars, rudders, and chests of ships were lying tightly grasped by their clinging arms; even a little mermaid, whom they had caught and strangled; and this seemed the most shocking of all to the little princess.

She now came to a space of marshy ground in the wood, where large, fat water-snakes were rolling in the mire, and showing their ugly, drab-colored bodies. In the midst of this spot stood a house, built with the bones of shipwrecked human beings. There sat the sea witch, allowing a toad to eat from her mouth, just as people sometimes feed a canary with a piece of sugar. She called the ugly water-snakes her little chickens, and allowed them to crawl all over her bosom.

"I know what you want," said the sea witch; "it is very stupid of you, but you shall have your way, and it will bring you to sorrow, my pretty princess. You want to get rid of your fish's tail, and to have two supports instead of it, like human beings on earth, so that the young prince may fall in love with you, and that you may have an immortal soul." And then the witch laughed so loud and disgustingly, that the toad and the snakes fell to the ground, and lay there wriggling about. "You are but just in time," said the witch; "for after sunrise to-morrow I should not be able to help you till the end of another year. I will prepare a draught for you, with which you must swim to land tomorrow before sunrise, and sit down on the shore and drink it. Your tail will then disappear, and shrink up into what mankind calls legs, and you will feel great pain, as if a sword were passing through you. But all who see you will say that you are the prettiest little human being they ever saw. You will still have the same floating gracefulness of movement, and no dancer will ever tread so lightly; but at every step you take it will feel as if you were treading upon sharp knives, and that the blood must flow. If you will bear all this, I will help you."

"Yes, I will," said the little princess in a trembling voice, as she thought of the prince and the immortal soul.

"But think again," said the witch; "for when once your shape has become like a human being, you can no more be a mermaid. You will never return through the water to your sisters, or to your father's palace again; and if you do not win the love of the prince, so that he is willing to forget his father and mother for your sake, and to love you with his whole soul, and allow the priest to join your hands that you may be man and wife, then you will never have an immortal soul. The first morning after he marries another your heart will break, and you will become foam on the crest of the waves."

"I will do it," said the little mermaid, and she became pale as death.

"But I must be paid also," said the witch, "and it is not a trifle that I ask. You have the sweetest voice of any who dwell here in the depths of the sea, and you believe that you will be able to charm the prince with it also, but this voice you must give to me; the best thing you possess will I have for the price of my draught. My own blood must be mixed with it, that it may be as sharp as a two-edged sword."

"But if you take away my voice," said the little mermaid, "what is left for me?"

"Your beautiful form, your graceful walk, and your expressive eyes; surely with these you can enchain a man's heart. Well, have you lost your courage? Put out your little tongue that I may cut it off as my payment;

then you shall have the powerful draught."

"It shall be," said the little mermaid.

Then the witch placed her cauldron on the fire, to prepare the magic draught.

"Cleanliness is a good thing," said she, scouring the vessel with snakes, which she had tied together in a large knot; then she pricked herself in the breast, and let the black blood drop into it. The steam that rose formed itself into such horrible shapes that no one could look at them without fear. Every moment the witch threw something else into the vessel, and when it began to boil, the sound was like the weeping of a crocodile. When at last the magic draught was ready, it looked like the clearest water. "There it is for you," said the witch. Then she cut off the mermaid's tongue, so that she became dumb, and would never again speak or sing. "If the polypi should seize hold of you as you return through the wood," said the witch, "throw over them a few drops of the potion, and their fingers will be torn into a thousand pieces." But the little mermaid had no occasion to do this, for the polypi sprang back in terror when they caught sight of the glittering draught, which shone in her hand like a twinkling star.

So she passed quickly through the wood and the marsh, and between the rushing whirlpools. She saw that in her father's palace the torches in the ballroom were extinguished, and all within asleep; but she did not venture to go in to them, for now she was dumb and going to leave them forever, she felt as if her heart would break. She stole into the garden, took a flower from the flower-beds of each of her sisters, kissed her hand a thousand times towards the palace, and then rose up through the dark blue waters. The sun had not risen when she came in sight of the prince's palace, and approached the beautiful marble steps, but the moon shone clear and bright. Then the little mermaid drank the magic draught, and it seemed as if a two-edged sword went through her delicate body: she fell into a swoon, and lay like one dead. When the sun arose and shone over the sea, she recovered, and felt a sharp pain; but just before her stood the handsome young prince. He fixed his coal-black eyes upon her so earnestly that she cast down her own, and then became aware that her fish's tail was gone, and that she had as pretty a pair of white legs and tiny feet as any little maiden could have; but she had no clothes, so she wrapped herself in her long, thick hair. The prince asked her who she was, and where she came from, and she looked at him mildly and sorrowfully with her deep blue eyes; but she could not speak. Every step she took was as the witch had said it would be, she felt as if treading upon the points of needles or sharp knives; but she bore it willingly, and stepped as lightly by the prince's side as a soap-bubble, so that he and all who saw her wondered at her graceful-swaying movements. She was very soon arrayed in costly robes of silk and muslin, and was the most beautiful creature in the palace; but she was dumb, and could neither speak nor sing.

Beautiful female slaves, dressed in silk and gold, stepped forward and sang before the prince and his royal parents: one sang better than all the others, and the prince clapped his hands and smiled at her. This was great sorrow to the little mermaid; she knew how much more sweetly she herself could sing once, and she thought, "Oh if he could only know that! I have given away my voice forever, to be with him."

The slaves next performed some pretty fairy-like dances, to the sound of beautiful music. Then the little mermaid raised her lovely white arms, stood on the tips of her toes, and glided over the floor, and danced as no one yet had been able to dance. At each moment her beauty became more revealed, and her expressive eyes appealed more directly to the heart than the songs of the slaves. Every one was enchanted, especially the prince, who called her his little foundling; and she danced again quite readily, to please him, though each time her foot touched the floor it seemed as if she trod on sharp knives.

The prince said she should remain with him always, and she received permission to sleep at his door, on a velvet cushion. He had a page's dress made for her, that she might accompany him on horseback. They rode together through the sweet-scented woods, where the green boughs touched their shoulders, and the little birds sang among the fresh leaves. She climbed with the prince to the tops of high mountains; and although her tender feet bled so that even her steps were marked, she only laughed, and followed him till they could see the clouds beneath them looking like a flock of birds travelling to distant lands. While at the prince's palace, and when all the household were asleep, she would go and sit on the broad marble steps; for it eased her burning feet to bathe them in the cold sea-water; and then she thought of all those below in the deep.

Once during the night her sisters came up arm-in-arm, singing sorrowfully, as they floated on the water. She beckoned to them, and then they recognized her, and told her how she had grieved them. After that, they came to the same place every night; and once she saw in the distance her old grandmother, who had not been to the surface of the sea for many years, and the old Sea King, her father, with his crown on his head. They stretched out their hands towards her, but they did not venture so near the land as her sisters did.

As the days passed, she loved the prince more fondly, and he loved her as he would love a little child, but it never came into his head to make her his wife; yet, unless he married her, she could not receive an immortal soul; and, on the morning after his marriage with another, she would dissolve into the foam of the sea.

"Do you not love me the best of them all?" the eyes of the little mermaid seemed to say, when he took her in his arms, and kissed her fair forehead.

"Yes, you are dear to me," said the prince; "for you have the best heart, and you are the most devoted to me; you are like a young maiden whom I once saw, but whom I shall never meet again. I was in a ship that was wrecked, and the waves cast me ashore near a holy temple, where several young maidens performed the service. The youngest of them found me on the shore, and saved my life. I saw her but twice, and she is the only one in the world whom I could love; but you are like her, and you have almost driven her image out of my mind. She belongs to the holy temple, and my good fortune has sent you to me instead of her; and we will never part."

"Ah, he knows not that it was I who saved his life," thought the little mermaid. "I carried him over the sea to the wood where the temple stands: I sat beneath the foam, and watched till the human beings came to help him. I saw the pretty maiden that he loves better than he loves me;" and the mermaid sighed deeply, but she could not shed tears. "He says the maiden belongs to the holy temple, therefore she will never return to the world. They will meet no more: while I am by his side, and see him every day. I will take care of him, and love him, and give up my life for his sake."

Very soon it was said that the prince must marry, and that the beautiful daughter of a neighboring king would be his wife, for a fine ship was being fitted out. Although the prince gave out that he merely intended to pay a visit to the king, it was generally supposed that he really went to see his daughter. A great company were to go with him. The little mermaid smiled, and shook her head. She knew the prince's thoughts better than any of the others.

"I must travel," he had said to her; "I must see this beautiful princess; my parents desire it; but they will not oblige me to bring her home as my bride. I cannot love her; she is not like the beautiful maiden in the temple, whom you resemble. If I were forced to choose a bride, I would rather choose you, my dumb foundling, with those expressive eyes." And then he kissed her rosy mouth, played with her long waving hair, and laid his head on her heart, while she dreamed of human happiness and an immortal soul. "You are not afraid of the sea, my dumb child," said he, as they stood on the deck of the noble ship which was to carry them to the country of the neighboring king. And then he told her of storm and of calm, of strange fishes in the deep beneath them, and of what the divers had seen there; and she smiled at his descriptions, for she knew better than any one what wonders were at the bottom of the sea.

In the moonlight, when all on board were asleep, excepting the man at the helm, who was steering, she sat on the deck, gazing down through the clear water. She thought she could distinguish her father's castle, and upon it her aged grandmother, with the silver crown on her head, looking through the rushing tide at the keel of the vessel. Then her sisters came up on the waves, and gazed at her mournfully, wringing their white hands. She beckoned to them, and smiled, and wanted to tell them how happy and well off she was; but the cabin-boy approached, and when her sisters dived down he thought it was only the foam of the sea which he saw.

The next morning the ship sailed into the harbor of a beautiful town belonging to the king whom the prince was going to visit. The church bells were ringing, and from the high towers sounded a flourish of trumpets; and soldiers, with flying colors and glittering bayonets, lined the rocks through which they passed. Every day was a festival; balls and entertainments followed one another.

But the princess had not yet appeared. People said that she was being brought up and educated in a religious house, where she was learning every royal virtue. At last she came. Then the little mermaid, who was very anxious to see whether she was really beautiful, was obliged to acknowledge that she had never seen a more perfect vision of beauty. Her skin was delicately fair, and beneath her long dark eye-lashes her laughing blue eyes shone with truth and purity.

"It was you," said the prince, "who saved my life when I lay dead on the beach," and he folded his blushing bride in his arms. "Oh, I am too happy," said he to the little mermaid; "my fondest hopes are all fulfilled. You will rejoice at my happiness; for your devotion to me is great and sincere."

The little mermaid kissed his hand, and felt as if her heart were already broken. His wedding morning would bring death to her, and she would change into the foam of the sea. All the church bells rung, and the heralds rode about the town proclaiming the betrothal. Perfumed oil was burning in costly silver lamps on every altar. The priests waved the censers, while the bride and bridegroom joined their hands and received the blessing of the bishop. The little mermaid, dressed in silk and gold, held up the bride's train; but her ears heard nothing of the festive music, and her eyes saw not the holy ceremony; she thought of the night of death which was coming to her, and of all she had lost in the world. On the same evening the bride and bridegroom went on board ship; cannons were roaring, flags waving, and in the centre of the ship a costly tent of purple and gold had been erected. It contained elegant couches, for the reception of the bridal pair during the night. The ship, with swelling sails and a favorable wind, glided away smoothly and lightly over the calm sea. When it grew dark a number of colored lamps were lit, and the sailors danced merrily on the deck. The little mermaid could not help thinking of her first rising out of the sea, when she had seen similar festivities and joys; and she joined in the dance, poised herself in the air as a swallow when he pursues his prey, and all present cheered her with wonder. She had never danced so elegantly before. Her tender feet felt as if cut with sharp knives, but she cared not for it; a sharper pang had pierced through her heart. She knew this was the last evening she should ever see the prince, for whom she had forsaken her kindred and her home; she had given up her beautiful voice, and suffered unheard-of pain daily for him, while he knew nothing of it. This was the last evening that she would breathe the same air with him, or gaze on the starry sky and the deep sea; an eternal night, without a thought or a dream, awaited her:

she had no soul and now she could never win one. All was joy and gayety on board ship till long after midnight; she laughed and danced with the rest, while the thoughts of death were in her heart. The prince kissed his beautiful bride, while she played with his raven hair, till they went arm-in-arm to rest in the splendid tent. Then all became still on board the ship; the helmsman, alone awake, stood at the helm. The little mermaid leaned her white arms on the edge of the vessel, and looked towards the east for the first blush of morning, for that first ray of dawn that would bring her death. She saw her sisters rising out of the flood: they were as pale as herself; but their long beautiful hair waved no more in the wind, and had been cut off.

"We have given our hair to the witch," said they, "to obtain help for you, that you may not die to-night. She has given us a knife: here it is, see it is very sharp. Before the sun rises you must plunge it into the heart of the prince; when the warm blood falls upon your feet they will grow together again, and form into a fish's tail, and you will be once more a mermaid, and return to us to live out your three hundred years before you die and change into the salt sea foam. Haste, then; he or you must die before sunrise. Our old grandmother moans so for you, that her white hair is falling off from sorrow, as ours fell under the witch's scissors. Kill the prince and come back; hasten: do you not see the first red streaks in the sky? In a few minutes the sun will rise, and you must die." And then they sighed deeply and mournfully, and sank down beneath the waves.

The little mermaid drew back the crimson curtain of the tent, and beheld the fair bride with her head resting on the prince's breast. She bent down and kissed his fair brow, then looked at the sky on which the rosy dawn grew brighter and brighter; then she glanced at the sharp knife, and again fixed her eyes on the prince, who whispered the name of his bride in his dreams. She was in his thoughts, and the knife trembled in the hand of the little mermaid: then she flung it far away from her into the waves; the water turned red where it fell, and the drops that spurted up looked like blood. She cast one more lingering, half-fainting glance at the prince, and then threw herself from the ship into the sea, and thought her body was dissolving into foam. The sun rose above the waves, and his warm rays fell on the cold foam of the little mermaid, who did not feel as if she were dying. She saw the bright sun, and all around her floated hundreds of transparent beautiful beings; she could see through them the white sails of the ship, and the red clouds in the sky; their speech was melodious, but too ethereal to be heard by mortal ears, as they were also unseen by mortal eyes. The little mermaid perceived that she had a body like theirs, and that she continued to rise higher and higher out of the foam. "Where am I?" asked she, and her voice sounded ethereal, as the voice of those who were with her; no earthly music could imitate it.

"Among the daughters of the air," answered one of them. "A mermaid has not an immortal soul, nor can she obtain one unless she wins the love of a human being. On the power of another hangs her eternal destiny. But the daughters of the air, although they do not possess an immortal soul, can, by their good deeds, procure one for themselves. We fly to warm countries, and cool the sultry air that destroys mankind with the pestilence. We carry the perfume of the flowers to spread health and restoration. After we have striven for three hundred years to all the good in our power, we receive an immortal soul and take part in the happiness of mankind. You, poor little mermaid, have tried with your whole heart to do as we are doing; you have suffered and endured and raised yourself to the spirit-world by your good deeds; and now, by striving for three hundred years in the same way, you may obtain an immortal soul."

The little mermaid lifted her glorified eyes towards the sun, and felt them, for the first time, filling with tears. On the ship, in which she had left the prince, there were life and noise; she saw him and his beautiful bride searching for her; sorrowfully they gazed at the pearly foam, as if they knew she had thrown herself into the waves. Unseen she kissed the forehead of her bride, and fanned the prince, and then mounted with the other children of the air to a rosy cloud that floated through the aether.

"After three hundred years, thus shall we float into the kingdom of heaven," said she. "And we may even get there sooner," whispered one of her companions. "Unseen we can enter the houses of men, where there are children, and for every day on which we find a good child, who is the joy of his parents and deserves their love, our time of probation is shortened. The child does not know, when we fly through the room, that we smile with joy at his good conduct, for we can count one year less of our three hundred years. But when we see a naughty or a wicked child, we shed tears of sorrow, and for every tear a day is added to our time of trial!"

Source:

Andersen, Hans Christian. *Hans Andersen's Fairy Tales*. Mrs. Henry H. B. Paull, translator. Wilhelm Petersen and Lorenz Frolich, illustrators. London: Frederick Warne & Co., [1872, 1883].

88. Hans, the Mermaid's Son

Denmark

IN A VILLAGE there once lived a smith called Basmus, who was in a very poor way. He was still a young man, and a strong handsome fellow to boot, but he had many little children and there was little to be earned by his trade. He was, however, a diligent and hard-working man, and when he had no work in the smithy he was out at sea fishing, or gathering wreckage on the shore.

It happened one time that he had gone out to fish in good weather, all alone in a little boat, but he did not come home that day, nor the following one, so that all believed he had perished out at sea. On the third day, however, Basmus came to shore again and had his boat full of fish, so big and fat that no one had ever seen their like. There was nothing the matter with him, and he complained neither of hunger or thirst. He had got into a fog, he said, and could not find land again. What he did not tell, however, was where he had been all the time; that only came out six years later, when people got to know that he had been caught by a mermaid out on the deep sea, and had been her guest during the three days that he was missing. From that time forth he went out no more to fish; nor, indeed, did he require to do so, for whenever he went down to the shore it never failed that some wreckage was washed up, and in it all kinds of valuable things. In those days everyone took what they found and got leave to keep it, so that the smith grew more prosperous day by day.

When seven years had passed since the smith went out to sea, it happened one morning, as he stood in the smithy, mending a plough, that a handsome young lad came in to him and said, "Good-day, father; my mother the mermaid sends her greetings, and says that she has had me for six years now, and you can keep me for as long."

He was a strange enough boy to be six years old, for he looked as if he were eighteen, and was even bigger and stronger than lads commonly are at that age.

"Will you have a bite of bread?" said the smith.

"Oh, yes," said Hans, for that was his name.

The smith then told his wife to cut a piece of bread for him. She did so, and the boy swallowed it at one mouthful and went out again to the smithy to his father.

"Have you got all you can eat?" said the smith.

"No," said Hans, "that was just a little bit."

The smith went into the house and took a whole loaf, which he cut into two slices and put butter and cheese between them, and this he gave to Hans. In a while the boy came out to the smithy again.

"Well, have you got as much as you can eat?" said the smith.

"No, not nearly," said Hans; "I must try to find a better place than this, for I can see that I shall never get my fill here."

Hans wished to set off at once, as soon as his father would make a staff for him of such a kind as he wanted.

"It must be of iron," said he, "and one that can hold out."

The smith brought him an iron rod as thick as an ordinary staff, but

Tales From Around the World 439

Hans took it and twisted it round his finger, so that wouldn't do. Then the smith came dragging one as thick as a waggon-pole, but Hans bent it over his knee and broke it like a straw. The smith then had to collect all the iron he had, and Hans held it while his father forged for him a staff, which was heavier than the anvil. When Hans had got this he said, "Many thanks, father; now I have got my inheritance." With this he set off into the country, and the smith was very pleased to be rid of that son, before he ate him out of house and home.

Hans first arrived at a large estate, and it so happened that the squire himself was standing outside the farmyard.

"Where are you going?" said the squire.

"I am looking for a place," said Hans, "where they have need of strong fellows, and can give them plenty to eat."

"Well," said the squire, "I generally have twenty-four men at this time of the year, but I have only twelve just now, so I can easily take you on."

"Very well," said Hans, "I shall easily do twelve men's work, but then I must also have as much to eat as the twelve would."

All this was agreed to, and the squire took Hans into the kitchen, and told the servant girls that the new man was to have as much food as the other twelve. It was arranged that he should have a pot to himself, and he could then use the ladle to take his food with.

It was in the evening that Hans arrived there, so he did nothing more that day than eat his supper—a big pot of buck-wheat porridge, which he cleaned to the bottom and was then so far satisfied that he said he could sleep on that, so he went off to bed. He slept both well and long, and all the rest were up and at their work while he was still sleeping soundly. The squire was also on foot, for he was curious to see how the new man would behave who was both to eat and work for twelve.

But as yet there was no Hans to be seen, and the sun was already high in the heavens, so the squire himself went and called on him.

"Get up, Hans," he cried; "you are sleeping too long."

Hans woke up and rubbed his eyes. "Yes, that's true," he said, "I must get up and have my breakfast."

So he rose and dressed himself, and went into the kitchen, where he got his pot of porridge; he swallowed all of this, and then asked what work he was to have.

He was to thresh that day, said the squire; the other twelve men were already busy at it. There were twelve threshing-floors, and the twelve men were at work on six of them—two on each. Hans must thresh by himself all that was lying upon the other six floors. He went out to the barn and got hold of a flail. Then he looked to see how the others did it and did the same, but at the first stroke he smashed the flail in pieces. There were several flails hanging there, and Hans took the one after the other, but they all went the same way, every one flying in splinters at the first stroke. He then looked round for something else to work with, and found a pair of strong beams lying near. Next he caught sight of a horse-hide nailed up on the barn-door. With the beams he made a flail, using the skin to tie them together. The one beam he used as a handle, and the other to strike with, and now that was all right. But the barn was too low, there was no room to swing the flail, and the floors were too small. Hans, however, found a remedy for this—he simply lifted the whole roof off the barn, and set it down in the field beside. He then emptied down all the corn that he could lay his hands on and threshed away. He went through one lot after another, and it was all the same to him what he got hold of, so before midday he had threshed all the squire's grain, his rye and wheat and barley and oats, all mixed through each other. When he was finished with this, he lifted the roof up on the barn again, like setting a lid on a box, and went in and told the squire that the job was done.

The squire opened his eyes at this announcement; and came out to see if it was really true. It was true, sure enough, but he was scarcely delighted with the mixed grain that he got from all his crops. However, when he saw the flail that Hans had used, and learned how he had made room for himself to swing it, he was so afraid of the strong fellow, that he dared not say anything, except that it was a good thing he had got it threshed; but it had still to be cleaned.

"What does that mean?" asked Hans.

It was explained to him that the corn and the chaff had to be separated; as yet both were lying in one heap, right up to the roof. Hans began to take up a little and sift it in his hands, but he soon saw that this would never do. He soon thought of a plan, however; he opened both barn-doors, and then lay down at one end and blew, so that all the chaff flew out and lay like a sand-bank at the other end of the barn, and the grain was as clean as it could be. Then he reported to the squire that that job also was done. The squire said that that was well; there was nothing more for him to do that day. Off went Hans to the kitchen, and got as much as he could eat; then he went and took a midday nap which lasted till supper-time.

Meanwhile the squire was quite miserable, and made his moan to his wife, saying that she must help him to find some means to getting rid of this strong fellow, for he durst not give him his leave. She sent for the steward, and it was arranged that next day all the men should go to the forest for fire-wood, and that they should make a bargain among them, that the one who came home last with his load should be hanged. They thought they could easily manage that it would be Hans who would lose his life, for the others would be early on the road, while Hans would certainly oversleep himself. In the evening, therefore, the men sat and talked together, saying that next morning they must set out early to the forest, and as they had a hard day's work and a long journey before them, they would, for their amusement, make a compact, that whichever of them came home last with his load should lose his life on the gallows. So Hans had no objections to make.

Long before the sun was up next morning, all the twelve men were on foot. They took all the best horses and carts, and drove off to the forest. Hans, however, lay and slept on, and the squire said, "Just let him lie."

At last, Hans thought it was time to have his breakfast, so he got up and put on his clothes. He took plenty of time to his breakfast, and then went out to get his horse and cart ready. The others had taken everything that was any good, so that he had a difficulty in scraping together four wheels of different sizes and fixing them to an old cart, and he could find no other horses than a pair of old hacks. He did not know where it lay, but he followed the track of the other carts, and in that way came to it all right. On coming to the gate leading into the forest, he was unfortunate enough to break it in pieces, so he took a huge stone that was lying on the field, seven ells long, and seven ells broad, and set this in the gap, then he went on and joined the others. These laughed at him heartily, for they had laboured as hard as they could since daybreak, and had helped each other to fell trees and put them on the carts, so that all of these were now loaded except one.

Hans got hold of a woodman's axe and proceeded to fell a tree, but he destroyed the edge and broke the shaft at the first blow. He therefore laid down the axe, put his arms round the tree, and pulled it up by the roots. This he threw upon his cart, and then another and another, and thus he went on while all the others forgot their work, and stood with open mouths, gazing at this strange woodcraft. All at once they began to hurry; the last cart was loaded, and they whipped up their horses, so as to be the first to arrive home.

When Hans had finished his work, he again put his old hacks into the cart, but they could not move it from the spot. He was annoyed at this, and took them out again, twisted a rope round the cart, and all the trees, lifted the whole affair on his back, and set off home, leading the horses behind him by the rein. When he reached the gate, he found the whole row of carts standing there, unable to get any further for the stone which lay in the gap.

"What!" said Hans, "can twelve men not move that stone?" With that he lifted it and threw it out of the way, and went on with his burden on his back, and the horses behind him, and arrived at the farm long before any of the others. The squire was walking about there, looking and looking, for he was very curious to know what had happened. Finally, he caught sight of Hans coming along in this fashion, and was so frightened that he did not know what to do, but he shut the gate and put on the bar. When Hans reached the gate of the courtyard, he laid down the trees and hammered at it, but no one came to open it. He then took the trees and tossed them over the barn into the yard, and the cart after them, so that every wheel flew off in a different direction.

When the squire saw this, he thought to himself, "The horses will come the same way if I don't open the door," so he did this.

"Good day, master," said Hans, and put the horses into the stable, and went into the kitchen, to get something to eat. At length the other men came home with their loads. When they came in, Hans said to them, "Do you remember the bargain we made last night? Which of you is it that's going to be hanged?"

"Oh," said they, "that was only a joke; it didn't mean anything."

"Oh well, it doesn't matter, "said Hans, and there was no more about it.

The squire, however, and his wife and the steward, had much to say to each other about the terrible man they had got, and all were agreed that they must get rid of him in some way or other. The steward said that he would manage this all right. Next morning they were to clean the well, and they would use of that opportunity. They would get him down into the well, and then have a big mill-stone ready to throw down on top of him—that would settle him. After that they could just fill in the well, and then escape being at any expense for his funeral. Both the squire and his wife thought this a splendid idea, and went about rejoicing at the thought that now they would get rid of Hans.

But Hans was hard to kill, as we shall see. He slept long next morning, as he always did, and finally, as he would not waken by himself, the squire had to go and call him. "Get up, Hans, you are sleeping too long," he cried. Hans woke up and rubbed his eyes. "That's so," said he, "I shall rise and have my breakfast." He got up then and dressed himself, while the breakfast stood waiting for him. When he had finished the whole of this, he asked what he was to do that day. He was told to help the other men to clean out the well. That was all right, and he went out and found the other men waiting for him. To these he said that they could choose whichever task they liked—either to go down into the well and fill the buckets while he pulled them up, or pull them up, and he alone would go down to the bottom of the well. They answered that they would rather stay above-ground, as there would be no room for so many of them down in the well.

Hans therefore went down alone, and began to clean out the well, but the men had arranged how they were to act, and immediately each of them seized a stone from a heap of huge blocks, and threw them down above him, thinking to kill him with these. Hans, however, gave no more heed to this than to shout up to them, to keep the hens away from the well, for they were scraping gravel down on the top of him.

They then saw that they could not kill him with little stones, but they had still the big one left. The whole twelve of them set to work with poles and rollers and rolled the big mill-stone to the brink of the well. It was with the greatest difficulty that they got it thrown down there, and now they had no doubt that he had got all that he wanted. But the stone happened to fall so luckily that his head went right through the hole in the middle of the mill-stone, so that it sat round his neck like a priest's collar. At this, Hans would stay down no longer. He came out of the well, with the mill-stone round his neck, and went straight to the squire and complained that the other men were trying to make a fool of him. He would not be their priest, he said; he had too little learning for that. Saying this, he bent down his head and shook the stone off, so that it crushed one of the squire's big toes.

The squire went limping in to his wife, and the steward was sent for. He was told that he must devise some plan for getting rid of this terrible person. The scheme he had devised before had been of no use, and now good counsel was scarce.

"Oh, no," said the steward, "there are good enough ways yet. The squire can send him this evening to fish in Devilmoss Lake: he will never escape alive from there, for no one can go there by night for Old Eric."

That was a grand idea, both the squire and his wife thought, and so he limped out again to Hans, and said that he would punish his men for having tried to make a fool of him. Meanwhile, Hans could do a little job where he would be free from these rascals. He should go out on the lake and fish there that night, and would then be free from all work on the following day.

"All right," said Hans; "I am well content with that, but I must have something with me to eat—a baking of bread, a cask of butter, a barrel of ale, and a keg of brandy. I can't do with less than that."

The squire said that he could easily get all that, so Hans got all of these tied up together, hung them over his shoulder on his good staff, and tramped away to Devilmoss Lake.

There he got into the boat, rowed out upon the lake, and got everything ready to fish. As he now lay out there in the middle of the lake, and it was pretty late in the evening, he thought he would have something to eat first, before starting to work. Just as he was at his busiest with this, Old Eric rose out of the lake, caught him by the cuff of the neck, whipped him out of the boat, and dragged him down to the bottom. It was a lucky thing that Hans had his walking-stick with him that day, and had just time to catch hold of it when he felt Old Eric's claws in his neck, so when they got down to the bottom he said, "Stop now, just wait a little; here is solid ground." With that he caught Old Eric by the back of the neck with one hand, and hammered away on his back with the staff, till he beat him out as flat as a pancake. Old Eric then began to lament and howl, begging him just to let him go, and he would never come back to the lake again.

"No, my good fellow," said Hans, "you won't get off until you promise to bring all the fish in the lake up to the squire's courtyard, before to-morrow morning."

Old Eric eagerly promised this, if Hans would only let him go; so Hans rowed ashore, ate up the rest of his provisions, and went home to bed.

Next morning, when the squire rose and opened his front door, the fish came tumbling into the porch, and the whole yard was crammed full of them. He ran in again to his wife, for he could never devise anything himself, and said to her, "What shall we do with him now? Old Eric hasn't taken him. I am certain that all the fish are out of the lake, for the yard is just filled with them."

"Yes, that's a bad business," said she; "you must see if you can't get him sent to Purgatory, to demand tribute." The squire therefore made his way to the men's quarters, to speak to Hans, and it took him all his time to push his way along the walls, under the eaves, on account of the fish that filled the yard. He thanked Hans for having fished so well, and said that now he had an errand for him, which he could only give to a trusty servant, and that was to journey to Purgatory, and demand three years tribute, which, he said, was owing to him from that quarter.

"Willingly," said Hans; "but what road do I go, to get there?"

The squire stood, and did not know what to say, and had first to go in to his wife to ask her.

"Oh, what a fool you are!" said she, "can't you direct him straight forward, south through the wood? Whether he gets there or not, we shall be quit of him."

Out goes the squire again to Hans.

"The way lies straight forward, south through the wood," said he.

Hans then must have his provisions for the journey; two bakings of bread, two casks of butter, two barrels of ale, and two kegs of brandy. He tied all these up together, and got them on his shoulder hanging on his good walking-stick, and off he tramped southward.

After he had got through the wood, there was more than one road, and he was in doubt which of them was the right one, so he sat down and opened up his bundle of provisions. He found he had left his knife at home, but by good chance, there was a plough lying close at hand, so he took the coulter of this to cut the bread with. As he sat there and took his bite, a man came riding past him.

"Where are you from?" said Hans.

"From Purgatory," said the man.

"Then stop and wait a little," said Hans; but the man was in a hurry, and would not stop, so Hans ran after him and caught the horse by the tail. This brought it down on its hind legs, and the man went flying over its head into a ditch. "Just wait a little," said Hans; "I am going the same way." He got his provisions tied up again, and laid them on the horse's back; then he took hold of the reins and said to the man, "We two can go along together on foot."

As they went on their way Hans told the stranger both about the errand he had on hand and the fun he had had with Old Eric. The other said but little but he was well acquainted with the way, and it was no long time before they arrived at the gate. There both horse and rider disappeared, and Hans was left alone outside. "They will come and let me in presently," he thought to himself; but no one came. He hammered at the gate; still no one appeared. Then he got tired of waiting, and smashed at the gate with his staff until he knocked it in pieces and got inside. A whole troop of little demons came down upon him and asked what he wanted. His master's compliments, said Hans, and he wanted three years' tribute. At this they howled at him, and were about to lay hold of him and drag him off; but when they had got some raps from his walking-stick they let go again, howled still louder than before, and ran in to Old Eric, who was still in bed, after his adventure in the lake. They told him that a messenger had come from the squire at Devilmoss to demand three years' tribute. He had knocked the gate to pieces and bruised their arms and legs with his iron staff.

"Give him three years! give him ten!" shouted Old Eric, "only don't let him come near me."

So all the little demons came dragging so much silver and gold that it was something awful. Hans filled his bundle with gold and silver coins, put it on his neck, and tramped back to his master, who was scared beyond all measure at seeing him again.

But Hans was also tired of service now. Of all the gold and silver he brought with him he let the squire keep one half, and he was glad enough, both for the money and at getting rid of Hans. The other half he took home to his father the smith in Furreby. To him also he said, "Farewell;" he was now tired of living on shore among mortal men, and preferred to go home again to his mother. Since that time no one has ever seen Hans, the Mermaid's son.

Source:
Lang, Andrew, editor. *The Pink Fairy Book*. London: Longmans, Green, and Co., 1897.

89. The Merman and Mermaid in Norway

Norway

WHEN the weather is calm, sailors and fishermen sometimes see mermen and mermaids rise up out of the sea. The former are of a dusky hue, have a long beard and black hair, and resemble a human being above the waist, but below it are like a fish. The latter, on the other hand, are fair and like a beautiful woman above, but below they have also the shape of a fish. The fishers sometimes catch their children, whom they call Marmaeler, and take them home with them to get knowledge of the future from them, for they, as well as the old ones, can foretell things to come. Now-a-days, however, it is very rare to hear mermaids speak or sing. Sailors dislike to see these beings, as they forebode storm and tempest. To try to do them harm is dangerous. A sailor who once enticed a mermaid so near that she laid her hand on the gunwale, and then hacked it off, was punished for his cruelty with a terrible storm, from which he only escaped with the greatest difficulty.

Source:
Craigie, William A. *Scandinavian Folk-Lore: Illustrations of the Traditional Beliefs of the Northern People*. London: Alexander Gardner, 1896.

90. The Fisher and the Merman

Norway

ONE cold winter day a fisherman had gone out to sea. It began to grow stormy when he was about to return, and he had trouble enough to clear himself. He then saw, near his boat, an old man with a long gray beard, riding on a wave. The fisherman knew well that it was the merman he saw before him, and knew also what it meant. "Uh, then, how cold it is!" said the merman as he sat and shivered, for he had lost one of his hose. The fisherman pulled off one of his, and threw it out to him. The merman disappeared with it, and the fisherman came safe to land. Some time after this the fisherman was again out at sea, far from land. All at once the merman stuck his head over the gunwale, and shouted out to the man in the boat,

> "Hear, you man that gave the hose,
> Take your boat and make for shore,
> It thunders under Norway."

The fisherman made all the haste he could to get to land, and there came a storm the like of which had never been known, in which many were drowned at sea.

Source:
Craigie, William A. *Scandinavian Folk-Lore: Illustrations of the Traditional Beliefs of the Northern People*. London: Alexander Gardner, 1896.

91. Necks, Mermen and Mermaids

Sweden[1]

The following three stories are extracted from Thomas Keightley's **The Fairy Mythology** *originally published in 1833 in two volumes.*

> Ei Necken mer i flodens vågor quäder,
> Och ingen Hafsfru bleker sina kläder
> Pas böljans rygg i milda solars glans.
> —STAGNELIUS.
>
> The Neck no more upon the river sings,
> And no Mermaid to bleach her linen flings
> Upon the waves in the mild solar ray.

IT IS a prevalent opinion in the North that all the various beings of the popular creed were once worsted in a conflict with superior powers, and condemned to remain till doomsday in certain assigned abodes. The Dwarfs, or Hill (*Berg*) trolls, were appointed the hills; the Elves the groves and leafy trees; the Hill-people (*Högfolk*)[2] the caves and caverns; the Mermen, Mermaids, and Necks, the sea, lakes, and rivers; the Riverman (*Strömkarl*) the small waterfalls. Both the Catholic and Protestant clergy have endeavoured to excite an aversion to these beings, but in vain. They are regarded as possessing considerable power over man and nature, and it is believed that though now unhappy, they will be eventually saved, or *faa förlossning* (get salvation), as it is expressed.

The NECK (in Danish Nökke)[3] is the river-spirit. The ideas

---

[1] While this section discusses tales from Scandanavia in general, I elected to place it under Sweden geographically for convenience since the longest portion is about Sweden.~*HAH*

[2] *Berg* signifies a larger eminence, mountain, hill; *Hög*, a height, hillock. The *Hög-folk* are Elves and musicians.

[3] The Danish peasantry in Wormius' time described the Nökke (Nikke) as a monster with a human head, that dwells both in fresh and salt water. When any one was drowned, they said, *Nökken tog ham bort* (the Nökke took him away); and when any drowned person was found with the nose red, they said the Nikke has sucked him: *Nikken har suet ham.*— Magnusen, Eddalaere. Denmark being a country without any streams of magnitude, we meet in the Danske Folkesagn no legends of the Nökke;

respecting him are various. Sometimes he is represented as sitting, of summer nights, on the surface of the water, like a pretty little boy, with golden hair hanging in ringlets, and a red cap on his head; sometimes as above the water, like a handsome young man, but beneath like a horse;[1] at other times, as an old man with a long beard, out of which he wrings the water as he sits on the cliffs. In this last form, Odin, according to the Icelandic sagas, has sometimes revealed himself.

The Neck is very severe against any haughty maiden who makes an ill return to the love of her wooer; but should he himself fall in love with a maid of human kind, he is the most polite and attentive suitor in the world.

Though he is thus severe only against those who deserve it, yet country people when they are upon the water use certain precautions against his power. Metals, particularly steel, are believed "to bind the Neck," (*binda Necken*); and when going on the open sea, they usually put a knife in the bottom of the boat, or set a nail in a reed. In Norway the following charm is considered effectual against the Neck:—

> Nyk, nyk, naal i vatn!
> Jomfru Maria kastet staal i vatn
> Du sök, äk flyt!

> Neck, neck, nail in water!
> The virgin Mary casteth steel in water!
> Do you sink, I flit!

The Neck is a great musician. He sits on the water and plays on his gold harp, the harmony of which operates on all nature. To learn music of him, a person must present him with a black lamb, and also promise him resurrection and redemption.

The following story is told in all parts of Sweden:—

"Two boys were one time playing near a river that ran by their father's house. The Neck rose and sat on the surface of the water, and played on his harp; but one of the children said to him, 'What is the use, Neck, of your sitting there and playing? you will never be saved.' The Neck then began to weep bitterly, flung away his harp, and sank down to the bottom. The children went home, and told the whole story to their father, who was the parish priest. He said they were wrong to say so to the Neck, and desired them to go immediately back to the river, and

---

and in ballads, such as a "The Power of the Harp," what in Sweden is ascribed to the Neck, is in Denmark imputed to the Havmand or Merman.

[1] The Neck is also believed to appear in the form of a complete horse, and can be made to work at the plough, if a bridle of a particular description be employed.—*Kalm's Vestgötha Resa.*

console him with the promise of salvation. They did so; and when they came down to the river the Neck was sitting on the water, weeping and lamenting. They then said to him, 'Neck, do not grieve so; our father says that your Redeemer liveth also.' The Neck then took his harp and played most sweetly, until long after the sun was gone down."

This legend is also found in Denmark, but in a less agreeable form. A clergyman, it is said, was journeying one night to Roeskilde in Zealand. His way led by a hill in which there was music and dancing and great merriment going forward. Some dwarfs jumped suddenly out of it, stopped the carriage, and asked him whither he was going. He replied to the synod of the church. They asked him if he thought they could be saved. To that, he replied, he could not give an immediate answer. They then begged that he would give them a reply by next year. When he next passed, and they made the same demand, be replied, "No, you are all damned." Scarcely had be spoken the word, when the whole hill appeared in flames.

In another form of this legend, a priest says to the Neck, "Sooner will this cane which I hold in my hand grow green flowers than thou shalt attain salvation." The Neck in grief flung away his harp and wept, and the priest rode on. But soon his cane began to put forth leaves and blossoms, and he then went back to communicate the glad tidings to the Neck who now joyously played on all the entire night.[1]

Source:
Keightley, Thomas. *The Fairy Mythology: Illustrative of the Romance and Superstition of Various Countries*. London: George Bell & Sons, 1905.

92. The Power of the Harp

Sweden (West Gothland and Vermland)

LITTLE Kerstin she weeps in her bower all the day;
Sir Peter in his courtyard is playing so gay.
    My heart's own dear!
    Tell me wherefore you grieve?

"Grieve you for saddle, or grieve you for steed?

---

[1] Afzelius, *Sago-häfdar*, ii. 156.

Or grieve you for that I have you wed?"
    My heart's own dear!
    Tell me wherefore you grieve?

"And grieve do I not for saddle or for steed:
And grieve do I not for that I have you wed.
    My heart's own dear!
    Tell me wherefore you grieve?

"Much more do I grieve for my fair gold hair,
Which in the blue waves shall be stained to-day.
    My heart's own dear!
    Tell me wherefore you grieve?

"Much more do I grieve for Ringfalla flood,
In which have been drowned my two sisters proud.
    My heart's own dear!
    Tell me wherefore you grieve?

"It was laid out for me in my infancy,
That my wedding-day should prove heavy to me."
    My heart's own dear!
    Tell me wherefore you grieve?

"And I shall make them the horse round shoe,
He shall not stumble on his four gold shoes.
    My heart's own dear!
    Tell me wherefore you grieve?

"Twelve of my courtiers shall before thee ride,
Twelve of my courtiers upon each side."
    My heart's own dear!
    Tell me wherefore you grieve?

But when they were come to Ringfalla wood,
There sported a hart with gilded horns prowl.
    My heart's own dear!
    Tell me wherefore you grieve?

And all the courtiers after the hart are gone;
Little Kerstin, she must proceed alone.
    My heart's own dear!
    Tell me wherefore you grieve?

And when on Ringfalla bridge she goes,
Her steed he stumbled on his four gold shoes.

My heart's own dear!
Tell me wherefore you grieve?

Four gold shoes, and thirty gold nails,
And the maiden into the swift stream falls.
    My heart's own dear!
    Tell me wherefore you grieve?

Sir Peter he spake to his footpage so—
"Thou must for my gold harp instantly go."
    My heart's own dear!
    Tell me wherefore you grieve?

The first stroke on his gold harp he gave
The foul ugly Neck sat and laughed on the wave.
    My heart's own dear!
    Tell me wherefore you grieve?

The second time the gold harp he swept,
The foul ugly Neck on the wave sat and wept.
    My heart's own dear!
    Tell me wherefore you grieve?

The third stroke on the gold harp rang,
Little Kerstin reached up her snow-white arm.
    My heart's own dear!
    Tell me wherefore you grieve?

He played the bark from off the high trees;
He played Little Kerstin back on his knees.
    My heart's own dear!
    Tell me wherefore you grieve?

And the Neck he out of' the waves came there,
And a proud maiden on each arm be bare.
    My heart's own dear!
    Tell me wherefore you grieve?[1]

NOTES

The STRÖMKARL, called in Norway Grim or Fosse-Grim[2] (*Waterfall-Grim*) is a musical genius like the Neck. Like him too, when properly

---

[1] As sung in West Gothland and Vermland.
[2] *Fosse* is the North of England *force*.

propitiated, he communicates his art. The sacrifice also is a black lamb[1] which the offerer must present with averted head, and on Thursday evening. If it is poor the pupil gets no further than to the tuning of the instruments; if it is fat the Strömkarl seizes the votary by the right hand, and swings it backwards and forwards till the blood runs out at the finger-ends. The aspirant is then enabled to play in such a masterly manner that the trees dance and waterfalls stop at his music.[2]

The Havmand, or Merman, is described as of a handsome form, with green or black hair and beard. He dwells either in the bottom of the sea, or in the cliffs and hills near the sea shore, and is regarded as rather a good and beneficent kind of being.[3]

The Havfrue, or Mermaid, is represented in the popular tradition sometimes as a good, at other lames as an evil and treacherous being. She is beautiful in her appearance. Fishermen sometimes see her in the bright summer's sun, when a thin mist hangs over the sea, sitting on the surface of the water, and combing her long golden hair with a golden comb, or driving up her snow-white cattle to feed on the strands and small islands. At other times she comes as a beautiful maiden, chilled and shivering with the cold of the night, to the fires the fishers have kindled, hoping by this means to entice them to her love.[4] Her appearance prognosticates both storm and ill success in their fishing. People that are drowned, and whose bodies are not found, are believed to be taken into the dwellings of the Mermaids. These beings are also supposed to have the power of foretelling future events. A Mermaid, we are told, prophesied the birth of Christian IV. of Denmark, and

>En Havfrue op af Vandet steg,
>Og spaade Herr Sinklar ilde.
>—SINCLAR'S VISA.

---

[1] Or a white kid, Faye *ap*. Grimm, *Deut. Mythol.*, p. 461.
[2] The Strömkarl has eleven different measures, to ten of which alone people may dance; the eleventh belongs to the night spirit his host. If any one plays it, tables and benches, cans and cups, old men and women, blind and lame, even the children in the cradle, begin to dance.—Arndt. *ut sup*.
[3] In the Danske Viser and Folkesagn there are a few stories of Mermen, such as Rosmer Havmand and Marstig's Daughter, both translated by Dr. Jamieson, and Agnete and the Merman, which resembles Proud Margaret. It was natural, says Afzelius, that what in Sweden was related of a Hill King, should, in Denmark, be ascribed to a Merman.
[4] The appearance of the Wood-woman (*Skogsfru*) or Elve-woman, is equally unlucky for hunters. She also approaches the fires, and seeks to seduce young men.

> A mermaid from the water rose,
> And spaed Sir Sinclar ill.

Fortune-telling has been in all countries a gift of the sea-people. We need hardly mention the prophecies of Nereus and Proteus.

A girl one time fell into the power of a Havfrue and passed fifteen years in her submarine abode without ever seeing the sun. At length her brother went down in quest of her, and succeeded in bringing her back to the upper world. The Havfrue waited for seven years expecting her return, but when she did not come back, she struck the water with her staff and made it boil up and cried—

> Hade jag trott att du varit så falsk,
> Så skulle jag kreckt dig din tiufvehals!
>
> Had I but known thee so false to be,
> Thy thieving neck I'd have cracked for thee.[1]

Source:

Keightley, Thomas. *The Fairy Mythology: Illustrative of the Romance and Superstition of Various Countries*. London: George Bell & Sons, 1905.

93. Duke Magnus and the Mermaid

Sweden (Småland)

DUKE MAGNUS looked out through the castle window,
How the stream ran so rapidly;
And there he saw how upon the stream sat
A woman most fair and lovelie,
> Duke Magnus, Duke Magnus, plight thee to me,
> I pray you still so freely;
> Say me not nay, but yes, yes!

"O, to you I will give a travelling ship,
The best that a knight would guide;
It goeth as well on water as on firm land,

---

[1] Arvidsson, ii. 320, ap. Grimm, p. 463.

And through the fields all so wide.
>Duke Magnus, Duke Magnus, plight thee to me,
>I pray you still so freely;
>Say me not nay, but yes, yes!

"O, to you will I give a courser gray,
The best that a knight would ride;
He goeth as well on water as on firm land,
And through the groves all so wide."
>Duke Magnus, Duke Magnus, plight thee to me,
>I pray you still so freely;
>Say me not nay, but yes, yes!

"O, how should I plight me to you?
I never any quiet get;
I serve the king and my native land,
But with woman I match me not yet."
>Duke Magnus, Duke Magnus, plight thee to me,
>I pray you still so freely;
>Say me not nay, but yes, yes!

"To you will I give as much of gold
As for more than your life will endure;
And of pearls and precious stones handfuls;
And all shall be so pure."
>Duke Magnus, Duke Magnus, plight thee to me,
>I pray you still so freely;
>Say me not nay, but yes, yes!

"O gladly would I plight me to thee,
If thou wert of Christian kind;
But now thou art a vile sea-troll,
My love thou canst never win."
>Duke Magnus, Duke Magnus, plight thee to me,
>I pray you still so freely;
>Say me not nay, but yes, yes!

"Duke Magnus, Duke Magnus, bethink thee well,
And answer not so haughtily;
For if thou wilt not plight thee to me,
Thou shalt ever crazy be."
>Duke Magnus, Duke Magnus, plight thee to me,
>I pray you still so freely;
>Say me not nay, but yes, yes!

"I am a king's son so good,
How can I let you gain me?
You dwell not on land, but in the flood,
Which would not with me agree."
    Duke Magnus, Duke Magnus, plight thee to me,
    I offer you still so freely;
    Say me not nay, but yes, yes!

NOTES

This is a ballad from Småland. Magnus was the youngest son of Gustavus Vass [Gustavus I]. He died out of his mind. It is well known that insanity pervaded the Vass family for centuries.

Source:

Keightley, Thomas. *The Fairy Mythology: Illustrative of the Romance and Superstition of Various Countries*. London: George Bell & Sons, 1905.

94. The King's Son and Messeria

Sweden (South Småland)

THERE was once a king and a queen who were childless. At this they were much grieved; for the king desired nothing so fervently as to have an heir to his crown and kingdom; but year after year passed away, and there seemed no hope that his wish should ever be realized.

The queen, the king's consort, found her chief pleasure in sailing about on the sea, whenever the weather permitted. It happened once that her bark suddenly stood still, so that the sailors were unable to move it either backwards or forwards. Now every one may easily imagine that there was some one in the water, who held the vessel fast. The queen, therefore, went on deck, and demanded who it was that hindered their course, when, from under the keel, a voice was heard, saying: "Never again shalt thou tread the green earth, unless thou wilt give me what thou bearest under thy girdle." To this the queen readily consented, for she knew not that she was pregnant; and then cast her bunch of keys, which hung at her girdle, into the deep. Instantly the bark was again afloat, and began gliding over the billows, until it reached a port in the king's territory.

Some time after, the queen found that she was pregnant. Great joy was thereupon spread over the whole country, and the king was the gladdest of all, that now his fondest wish would be gratified. But the queen was not glad; for she feared within herself that she had unwittingly promised away her own offspring. When the king observed her Secret sorrow, he thought it extraordinary, and asked her why she alone was afflicted, while every one else was full of joy. The queen now imparted to him what had befallen her on her marine excursion. But the king bade her be comforted and cast off her grief, adding that he would take such measures, that the Mermaid should never get their child into her hands.

When the time arrived, the queen gave birth to a boy. The young prince increased in age and strength, and became stronger and comelier than all other children. At this the king and queen were rejoiced at heart, and regarded the child as the apple of their eye. Thus passed the time until the prince attained his twelfth year. It then happened that the king received a visit from his brother, who reigned over another kingdom, accompanied by his two sons. The three royal children found their greatest delight in playing together. One day the two stranger princes were amusing themselves with riding in the court before the palace, while their cousin stood within observing their sport; when on a sudden he was seized with an irresistible desire to partake in it. Stealing therefore from his attendants, he ran into the court and mounted on horseback. The youths then went down to the beach to water their horses; but scarcely had the prince's horse touched the water, when it ran out into the sea and disappeared among the billows. The two cousins, on witnessing this disaster, instantly returned to the palace and related what had happened. Now, as it is easy to imagine, there were weeping and sorrow. The king sent his men to seek after the prince; but all their search was vain: the youth was away and remained away.

At the bottom of the ocean the young prince found a green path, which led to a fair palace, that glittered all over with gold and precious stones, so that the like was never seen. In this palace dwelt the Mermaid, who rules over the wind and waves. When the prince entered the palace, the crone looked at him with eyes of benevolence, and said: "Welcome, fair youth! for these twelve years have I been expecting thee. Thou shalt now stay here, and be my little page. If thou servest me faithfully and well, thou shalt be allowed to return to thy relations; but if thou doest not as I command thee, thou shalt forfeit thy life." At this speech the youth felt ill at ease; for he longed after home and his parents, as is usual with boys of that age; but he was obliged to reconcile himself to his fate, and live awhile with the Mermaid in the fair palace at the bottom of the sea.

One day the Mermaid ordered the young prince to appear before her, and said to him: "It is time that thou beginnest thy duties, and this shall be thy first trial. Here are two bundles of yarn, one white and one black. Now thou shalt wash the white one black, and the black one white. But the whole must be ready betimes to-morrow, when I wake; otherwise thy life is at stake." The youth then took the two bundles, as the Mermaid had commanded, went down to the beach, and began washing with all his might. But let him do as he would, the white yarn was and would be white, and the black black. When the prince saw that he could not perform his task, he was sadly disheartened, and wept bitterly. In the same moment a young and beautiful maiden appeared before him, who greeted him in a friendly tone, and asked him why he was so afflicted. The prince answered: "I may well be afflicted; for the Mermaid has commanded me to wash this white yarn black, and the black yarn white; and if I have not done it by the morning, when she wakes, my life is at stake." The damsel then said: "If thou wilt promise to be true to me, I will help thee, and will always be true to thee in return." To this proposal the youth gladly assented; for the maiden was so fair that no one can imagine how fair she was. So they promised ever to be faithful to each other. The damsel then went to a stone, on which she struck, saying: "Come forth, all my Lady Mother's Pysslings, and help to wash this white yarn black, and the black yarn till it becomes white." At the same moment a whole multitude of little people, or Pysslings, came up, whose number no one could tell; and each Pyssling, taking a little end of thread, began to wash so diligently, so diligently, and did not leave off until the white yarn was washed black, and the black yam white. When the work was done, the Pysslings crept down under the stone, and no more of them was seen. The young damsel then sat down to converse with the king's son, and related to him that she was a princess, and her name Messeria. She, at the same time, warned him not to let any one know how they had met with each other.

Early in the morning, before sunrise, the prince went to his mistress, as he had been commanded. As soon as he entered, the Mermaid asked him whether he had executed her orders. The youth answered in the affirmative, and showed her the two bundles of yarn. At the sight of them, the Mermaid was greatly astonished, and said: "How has this been accomplished? Hast thou met with any of my daughters?" The youth answered, that he had seen no one; and so they parted for that time.

Some time after, the Mermaid again ordered the youth to be called before her, and said: "I will now put thee to another trial. Here are a barrel of wheat and a barrel of barley mingled together. Thou shalt separate these from each other, so that the barley may be parted from the wheat, and the wheat from the barley. But all must be done tomorrow by the time I wake; otherwise thy life is forfeited." So the youth took the wheat and barley, as he had been commanded, and began picking as well as he could; but let him do as he might, when night approached, he had separated only a very small portion. He was now sadly downcast and wept bitterly, when Messeria on a sudden appeared before him, greeted him kindly, and asked him the cause of his great affliction. The prince answered: "I may well weep and be sad. The Mermaid has commanded me to separate all this grain according to its different kinds, so that the barley be parted from the wheat, and the wheat from the barley. But if I have not done it by to-morrow when she wakes, my life is forfeited." The maiden said: "If thou wilt promise to be true to me, I will help thee, and always be true to thee in return." The prince assured her that he would never love any other in the world; but her only. The damsel then went to a stone, on which she struck, saying: "Come forth, all my Lady Mother's Pysslings, and help to separate the barley from the wheat, and the wheat from the barley." Instantly there came up a countless multitude of Pysslings, each of whom took a grain, and they picked so diligently, so diligently, until all the grain was sorted, the barley by itself, and the wheat by itself. When all was done, the Pysslings crept down again under the stone, and were no more seen. Messeria also went her way; but warned the king's son not to let any one know how they had met with each other.

Early in the morning, before dawn, the prince appeared before his mistress, as he had been commanded. On seeing him, the Mermaid asked him whether he had performed his task. The youth answered in the affirmative, and showed her the grain separated, each kind by itself. The crone was greatly surprised, and said: "How has this been accomplished? Hast thou met with one of my daughters?" The prince answered that he had not seen any one; and so they parted for that time.

When some time had again passed, the Mermaid sent a message to the young prince. On his appearing before her, she said: "I will now put thee to a third trial. In my stalls there are a hundred oxen, and the stalls have not been cleansed for twenty years. Thou shalt go and cleanse them. If thou hast finished the work by to-morrow, when I wake, I will give thee one of my daughters, and permission to return home to thy kindred. But if thou hast not finished it, thy life is forfeited." The youth then went to the Mermaid's stalls, and began throwing and throwing out the dung; but let him toil as he might, it was easy to see that he would never perform his task, as the heap seemed rather to increase than diminish. The prince was now ill at ease, and wept bitterly; but on a sudden the beautiful Messeria appeared before him, and inquired the cause of his great affliction. The youth answered: "I may well weep and be sorrowful. The Mermaid has ordered me to cleanse the stalls, in which she has a hundred oxen. If I have done it by to-morrow, when she wakes, she will give me one of her daughters; but if I have not done it, my life is forfeited." The damsel said: "If thou wilt promise to be true to me, I will help thee, and always be true to thee in return." The king's son reiterated the assurance, that he would never love any other in all the world. Messeria then went to a large stone, on which she struck, saying: "Come forth, all my Lady Mother's Pysslings, and help to cleanse the Mermaid's stalls." Instantly there came up such a multitude of Pysslings, that the place swarmed with them; and the little men laboured so sedulously and incessantly, that the stalls were soon cleansed. When all was done, the Pysslings crept again under the stone, and were no more seen. But

Messeria sat down and conversed with the prince, and warned him not to let any one know that they had met together. She further informed him that the Mermaid's daughters were in reality the children of kings, who had been transformed into all kinds of animals. "But," continued she, "if thou art resolved to be true to me, bear in remembrance that I am changed into a little cat with yellow sides and one of my ears cropped." The youth treasured all this up in his memory, and said he would never forget her instructions. They then took a loving farewell of each other.

In the morning betimes, with the first dawn, the prince appeared before his mistress, as he had been ordered. When the Mermaid saw him, she asked him whether he had executed her commission. The youth answered "Yes," and they went to the stalls together. On seeing that all was done as she had commanded, she was indeed surprised, and asked how it could be, and whether no one had helped him. The king's son answered that he had seen no one. The Mermaid then said: "If such be the case, I will stand by the word and promise that I have given. Thou shalt choose one of my daughters, and then return home to thy family."

The prince now accompanied the Mermaid, and they came to a spacious saloon, in which he had never before been. The saloon was extremely beautiful, and adorned most sumptuously with gold and silver, and in it was assembled a large collection of animals of all kinds: serpents, toads, lizards, weasels, and others out of number. The Mermaid said to him: "Here thou seest all my daughters; choose now which thou wilt have." But when the youth looked at the ugly animals, he felt painfully embarrassed, and knew not which way to turn, so disgusting did they appear to him. While in this state of anxiety, he chanced to cast his eyes on a little cat, that had yellow sides, and one ear cropped, and walked about the apartment wagging its tail and looking very disconsolate. At the sight of the little animal, the prince instantly thought of what Messeria had told him; therefore, going up to it, he stroked it with his hand, and said: "This I will have, and no other." In a moment the animal changed its form, a fair maiden rose before him, in whom he recognised the beautiful damsel who had helped him. But the Mermaid was greatly disconcerted, and said: "Why hast thou chosen her? she was the dearest to me of all my daughters."

When some time had elapsed, the Mermaid sent for the prince, and said: "I will now make preparations for thy marriage; but first thou must go and get wedding clothes for thy young bride. Go, therefore, to my sister and greet her from me, and thou wilt get all that is requisite." When the prince heard that he must go to the Mermaid's sister, he was greatly troubled; for he knew that it was a perilous journey; so he sat down and wept bitterly. While he was thus sitting, the fair Messeria came to him and inquired why he was so afflicted. The prince answered: "I may well weep and be afflicted. The Mermaid has commanded me to go to her sister for wedding clothes; and I can easily imagine it will be a dangerous journey." Messeria said: "If thou wilt promise to be true to me, I will help thee, and will always be true to thee in return." The king's son again assured her that he would never violate his faith and promise to her. The damsel then continued: "When thou hast travelled for some time, thou wilt come to a gate, which stands on the boundary where the Mermaid's territory ends. The gate is old and heavy; but grease it with the grease out of this grease-horn. Thou wilt next come to two men engaged in hewing an oak by the way-side. They have wooden axes; give them these iron ones. Then thou wilt come to two other men who are thrashing. They have iron flails; give them these wooden ones. Afterwards thou wilt come to two eagles, which will swell and threaten when thou approachest them; give them these pieces of meat. At the Mermaid's sister's I have never been; and therefore cannot counsel thee. Only be cautious and eat nothing." The prince thanked her warmly for her good advice, and promised to follow it. He then bade Messeria farewell, and set out on his journey.

After travelling for some distance, he came to the gate, as described by Messeria; and, as she had directed him, smeared the hinges, and then continued his journey till he came to the two men, who were hewing the oak. They had wooden axes, but the king's son gave an iron axe to each. He then came to where the two men stood thrashing. They had heavy flails of iron, but the prince gave them wooden flails. Going further, he came to the two eagles, which swelled up, and threatened him as he approached; but the prince gave to each of them a piece of meat, and so, without hindrance, reached the place to which his steps were directed.

When the king's son entered, he went directly to the Mermaid's sister and delivered his message. His reception was the best imaginable; but the crone had a sinister countenance, and the youth could plainly perceive that she did not mean all that she said. She bade him sit down, while she went and prepared the things for the wedding, and ordered refreshments to be brought in that he might eat. But the prince, bearing Messeria's injunctions in his memory, would taste no food; but watching his opportunity, concealed it under the couch. When a little time had elapsed, the Mermaid came in, and inquired whether her guest had eaten. The youth answered that he had, at which the crone laughed in her sleeve, saying:—

"Man's head, where art thou?"

The meat answered:—

"I'm here at the foot of the couch,
I'm here at the foot of the couch."

The youth now felt ill at ease; for he perceived the crone's wickedness; but the Mermaid was angry, sought after the food, and said that the prince should eat of it, whether he would or not.

She then went out a second time, and the youth looked about him for a new hiding-place. He now thrust the meat into the mouth of the stove, and thus concealed it as well as he could. But ere long the mermaid returned, and asked whether he had eaten. The prince answered in the affirmative, and the crone laughed in her false heart, and said:—

"Man's head, where art thou?"

The meat answered:—

"I'm in the mouth of the stove;
I'm in the mouth of the stove."

When the Mermaid perceived that the youth was on his guard against her artifices, she became highly exasperated, sought after the meat, and said that the prince should eat of it, or forfeit his life.

She then went away for the third time. The prince was now quite at a loss where to hide the meat; but at length concealed it in his bosom under his clothes. So when the Mermaid returned, she asked him, as before, whether he had eaten. He answered that he had. Then said the crone:—

"Man's head, where art thou?"

The meat answered:—

"I lie in his bosom,
I lie in his bosom."

Now the Mermaid laughed and said:—

"If thou liest in his breast,
Thou'lt be soon in his maw."

She then gave him many greetings for her sister, and a box containing the things for the wedding, wished him a pleasant journey, and so they parted.

The youth was now on his return, and glad was he, which will seem wonderful to no one. But "it is not wise to cry out hurrah before one has crossed the brook," as the old proverb tells us; for the prince had not got further than to the two eagles, when the crone cried out:—

"Eagles! tear him in pieces."

He was now dreadfully terrified; but when the eagles saw who it was, they did him no harm, but answered:—

"No, he has given us food,
He has given us food."

So the prince passed by them, and came to where the men were thrashing. The Mermaid then cried out:—

"Thrashers! beat him to death."

The youth now again trembled for his life; but when the men saw who it was, they would not do him any harm, and answered:—

"No, he gave us wooden flails for iron ones,
Wooden flails for iron ones."

Thus the king's son passed unscathed by the thrashers, and came to the men who were hewing the tree. Then the Mermaid cried out:—

"Hewers! hew him in pieces."

But when the men saw who it was, they did him no injury, saying:—

"No, he gave us iron axes for wooden ones,
Iron axes for wooden ones."

The prince now took to his heels, and ran at full speed till he came to the boundary, when the Mermaid cried:—

"Gate, squeeze him to death."

But the gate answered:—

"No, he has greased me,
He has greased me."

Thus the youth again entered his mistress's domain, and no one will wonder that he was very tired after such a journey.

When he had rested a while, he continued his journey homewards. While thus travelling along the road, it entered his mind that it might be as well to know what wedding gear was contained in the box; for he thought of his dear Messeria and her warnings; and, as is wont to be the case, "youth and wisdom do not accompany each other," the more he pondered the greater grew his curiosity; till at last he could no longer control his inquisitiveness, but opened the lid just a little at one edge. But a great wonder now met his eyes: for it appeared to him that the box was full of sparks, and a stream of fire issued from the opening; the sparks of which flew in all directions. The prince now repented of his rashness; but it was too late; so that at last he could go neither back nor forwards, but sat down and wept bitterly. At length it occurred to him that he would try whether Messeria's Pysslings would help him, and he went to a large stone, struck on it and cried: "Come forth, all my Lady Mother's little Pysslings, and help me to replace the wedding gear." Instantly there came forth an innumerable multitude of Pysslings, and the little men spread themselves in all directions, and ran after the sparks over hill and dale. After a while the whole swarm returned, each having caught a spark, which he replaced in the box. The Pysslings then crept down again under the stone. The king's son now resolved, that another time he would be more cautious, and continued his journey to the palace where his mistress dwelt.

When the Mermaid saw him, and heard that he had passed through all the dangers, she was greatly astonished, and gave him a kind reception. She then caused the prince's marriage to be celebrated with great state and rejoicings, and all her daughters were present at the feast. But Messeria was the fairest among all the king's daughters, and the bridegroom regarded her as more precious than all the jewels he had seen in the beautiful palace.

When the marriage was concluded, the prince and his fair bride got leave to depart. They bade the Mermaid farewell, heartily wishing never again to set eyes on her. Then placing themselves in a gilded chariot, they travelled over many green plains, till they rose up from the sea not far from the king's palace. Now the youth was seized with a violent longing to see how all things were at home among his kindred. Messeria was opposed to this wish, and said it would be better if they first drove to her father, who was likewise a king. But the prince adhered to his determination, and prevailed. When about to separate, Messeria received her husband's promise that he would taste no food during his absence from her, but would instantly return. The prince promised to obey her in this, and took his departure. But the young bride sat down and wept bitterly, for she could well foresee the consequences of his journey.

When the youth entered his father's palace, there were great rejoicings, as it is easy to imagine, but greatest of all was the joy of the king and queen. A sumptuous feast was then prepared, and all wished the prince welcome home. But the youth would neither eat nor drink, saying he must instantly depart. This to the queen seemed very singular, and she would not allow him to go away fasting. So the prince was at length with many prayers persuaded, and at length prevailed on himself, to taste a peppercorn. From that moment his mind became changed, so that he forgot his fair bride, and all that had passed while he was with the Mermaid. He began then to eat and drink and make merry with his relations. But Messeria sat in the forest till the sun went down, and then, in deep sorrow, betook herself to a little cottage, and begged for shelter of the poor people who dwelt in it.

When some time had elapsed, the king wished his son to marry. The prince had no objection, and set out for another kingdom, to pay his court to a fair young princess. A feast was afterwards prepared, at which the healths of bridegroom and bride were drunk, with all kinds of rejoicings and plays. But the fair Messeria journeyed to the palace and prayed to be received as a waiting-maid. Thus she passed in and out of the festive hall, and it may easily be imagined that it was with a heavy heart. But she suppressed her tears, and amid the general joy there was no one that noticed her sorrow.

While the wedding was in progress, the table was spread for the guests, and Messeria aided in bringing in the viands. She had with her two doves, that flew to and fro in the hall. When the first course was brought in, she took three grains of wheat and threw them to the doves; but the cock was foremost, and pecked up all the three grains, leaving nothing for his mate. Then said the little dove:—

> "Out upon thee!
> Thou hast served me
> As the king's son served Messeria."

There was now silence in the hall, and the guests were struck with wonder at the little birds. But the bridegroom grew very thoughtful, enticed the doves to him and caressed them.

After some time another course was set on the table, and Messeria helped to bring in the viands. She again cast three grains of wheat to the doves; but, as on the former occasion, the cock pecked up all the three grains, and left nothing for his mate. Then said the little dove:—

> "Out upon thee!
> Thou hast served me
> As the king's son served Messeria."

Silence again prevailed in the hall, and all the guests listened to the words of the bird; but the prince was singularly affected, and again enticed the little birds and caressed them.

When the third course was brought in, Messeria again cast three grains of wheat to her doves, and the cock was again foremost, and pecked up all the three grains, leaving not one for his mate. Then said the little dove:—

> "Out upon thee!
> Thou hast served me
> As the king's son served Messeria."

Now a deep silence reigned over all the festive hall, and no one knew what to think of this miracle. But when the king's son heard the words of the dove, he awoke as from a dream, and it rushed into his memory how he had rewarded the fair Messeria for all her love. He sprang up from the table, clasped the young serving-maid to his breast, and said that she and no other should be his bride. He then related all the faith and affection that Messeria had proved to him, and everything besides that he had undergone while with the Mermaid.

When the king and queen and the several guests had heard his story, they could hardly recover from their astonishment. The stranger princess was now sent back to her family; but Messeria was adorned as a bride, and wedded to the young prince. They lived together for many happy years, virtuously and honourably. But the prince never again forgot the fair Messeria.

NOTES

The following list of variants of this tale came from the table of contents of the collection. Usually these tales do not contain water spirits but are variants of the tale's plot. To read about more Swedish variants, see the notes to the following tale, "The King's Son and the Princess Singorra."~HAH

1. The Norwegians.—See Asbjörnsen og Moe, *ut sup.*, ii. No. 47. "Mestermö."
2. The Danes.—See a Fragment in Winther, *ut sup.*, 1st Samling, pp. 31-35. "Prindsen og Havmanden."
3. The Irish.—See Carleton, "Traits and Stories of the Irish Peasantry." Dublin, 1842, pp. 23-47. "The Three Tasks."
4. The Germans.—a. See Feen-Märchen, Braunschweig, 1801, pp. 40, *seqq.* "Der Riesenwald." b. *Ibid.* pp.122, *seqq.* "Die Drei Gürtel." c. Grimm, K. und H. M. i. No. 51. "Funde-vogel" (*Cf.* iii. p. 88). d. Grimm, i. No. 56. "Der Liebste Roland (*Cf.* iii. pp. 99-101). e. *Ibid.* i. No. 79. "Die Wasser-nix." f. *Ibid.* ii. No. 113. "De beiden Künigeskinner." g. *Ibid.* ii. No. 186. "Die wahre Braut." h. *Ibid.* ii. No. 193. "Der Trommler." i. Kuhn, "Märkisehe Sagen und Märchen." Berlin, 1843, pp. 263-267. "Die Königstochter beim Popanz."
5. The Italians.—a. See Basile, Il Pentam. ii. No. 7. "La Palomma." b. *Ibid.* iii. No. 9. "Rosella." c. *Ibid.* v. No. 4. The latter part of "Lo Turzo d'Oro."
6. The French.—a. See Mad. D'Aulnoy, Contes des Fées; "Gracieuse et Percinet." b. *Ibid.* "L'Oranger et l'Abeille."
7. The Magyars.—See Gaal, "Märchen der Magyaren." Wien, 1822. No. 3. "Die Gläserne Hacke."
8. The Poles.—See Woycicki, Pomische Volkssagen, iii. No. 10.
9. The Russians.—See Kletke, Märchensaal, ii. pp. 70-79. "Kojata."

Source:
Thorpe, Benjamin. *Yule-Tide Stories*. London: Henry G. Bohn, 1853.

95. The King's Son and the Princess Singorra

Sweden (Skåne)

THERE was once a king who ruled over a powerful kingdom. He was a great warrior, and often lived in the camp, both summer and winter. It happened once, when he was at sea, that his bark stood still on the billowy ocean, and could not be made to move in any direction; though no one knew what held the vessel fast. The king thereupon went to the prow, and saw the Mermaid sitting on the waves by the bow of the ship, and now well knew it was she that stopped its course. He addressed her, and asked her what she required. The Mermaid answered: "Thou shalt never go hence until thou hast promised me the first living being thou meetest on thy own shore." As the king had no other means of releasing his ship, he agreed to the Mermaid's condition, when the bark was instantly free again, the wind filled the sails and was favourable, until the king again landed in his own country.

The king had an only son, just fifteen years old, a youth of excellent promise. The young prince was fondly attached to his father, and anxiously longed for his return. When he saw the pendant of his parent's ship fluttering in the breeze, he was overjoyed, and ran down to the strand to bid his father welcome. But when the king saw his son he was sorely grieved; for he remembered the promise he had made to the Mermaid. He, therefore, cast his eyes first on a hog, and then on a goose, that were wandering about on the sea-shore. On entering his castle, he ordered the hog to be thrown into the sea, which was done.

The next day, a violent storm arose, the sea raged mountains high, and the hog was cast dead on the shore, close by the king's residence. The king now plainly perceived that the Mermaid was angry, and, therefore, ordered the goose to be thrown into the ocean; but the same took place again, a storm arose, and the dead bird was thrown by the waves upon the strand. The king was now sensible that the Mermaid was resolved to have his only son. But the youth was his father's chief delight, who would not lose him for half his kingdom.

But however long the time that elapsed, the king must at last experience the truth of the old proverb, that "no one is stronger than his fate." For it happened one day that the youth went down to the strand, to play with other boys of his own age, when suddenly a snow-white hand, with a gold ring on each finger, rose out of the water. The hand seized on the king's son, where he was playing on the shore, and drew him down amid the blue billows. The prince was then conducted through the waters, over many green ways, and rested not until he came to the Mermaid's dwelling. Now we are told that the Mermaid has her abode deep in the bottom of the ocean, and that it is so splendid that it glitters with gold and precious stones, both within and without.

The youth now dwelt in the fair mansion, and found there many other royal children. But among the Mermaid's attendants there was a young princess named Singorra. She had resided there for seven long years, and possessed much hidden knowledge. The king's son contracted a strong affection for the fair maiden, and they vowed to each other love and faith, as long as they lived in the world.

One day the Mermaid called the youth to her, and said: "I have observed that thy inclination is turned to my attendant Singorra. I will, therefore, propose three labours to thee. If thou performest them all, I will bestow on thee the fair maiden, and grant thee permission to return home to thy family. But if thou failest to do what I propose, thou shalt stay here and serve me for the rest of thy days." The youth was unable to say much in answer. The Mermaid then led him to a large meadow, that was thickly overgrown with green sea-grass, and said to him: "Thy first labour shall be to mow all this grass, and set it up again, each blade on its root, so that it may thrive and grow as before. But the whole must be done this evening by sunset." Having thus spoken, she went her way, leaving the youth by himself. The prince now began cutting and cutting; but he had not laboured long before he could very well see that he would never get through his task. So he sat down in the meadow and wept bitterly.

While the youth thus sat weeping, the fair Singorra appeared before him, and asked him why he was so afflicted. The king's son answered: "I cannot but weep. The Mermaid has commanded me to mow the whole meadow, and set every blade on its root again. If I have not done it by the time the sun sinks in the forest, I shall lose thee and all the pleasure I have in the world." The maiden replied: "I will help thee, if thou wilt promise to be true to me; for I will never deceive thee." The prince gladly made the promise, adding that he would never break his faith and vow. Singorra then took the sithe, and with it touched the grass, when, in one instant, the whole meadow was mowed and every little blade of grass fell at once to the ground. She then touched the grass again, and lo! every blade raised itself upon its root, and the meadow was as before. The princess then went her way; but the youth was delighted, and went to his mistress, and announced to her that he had performed the task which she had set him.

The next day, the Mermaid called the youth to her again, and said: "I will give thee another work to perform. In my stable there stand a hundred horses, and it has not been cleansed within the memory of man. Thou shalt now go thither, and make it clean. If thou hast done it this evening by sunset, I will stand firm to my promise." Having so spoken, she went her way, and left the youth alone. When he came to the stable, he could very well see that he should never perform the task; and, therefore, sat down and wept bitterly.

He had not sat long, when the fair Singorra appeared before him, and inquired the cause of his sorrow. The king's son answered: "I cannot refrain from weeping. The Mermaid has commanded me to cleanse her stable, if I will not lose thee and every other joy. But the stable must be cleansed this evening by sunset." The maiden said: "I will help thee, if thou wilt promise to be true to me; for thee I will never deceive." The youth gladly made the promise, and said he would never love any but her. Thereupon Singorra went to the stable door, took down a gold whip that hung on the wall, and with it struck the horse that stood in the farthest corner. The horse instantly got loose, and began scraping the ground with his hoofs, until the whole stable was clean; so that all the hundred horses neighed and stamped for joy. When all was done, the princess went her way; but the youth was delighted, and went to his mistress, to announce to her that he had performed her command.

On the third day, the Mermaid again sent for the king's son, and said: "I will yet assign thee another labour. If thou accomplishest also that, I will adhere to the promise I have given thee; but if thou dost not perform it, thou shalt stay here and serve me all thy days." The prince asked what his mistress required. The Mermaid answered: "In my sty there are some thousands of swine, and the soil has not been removed for a hundred years. Thou shalt cleanse the pig-sty, and it shall be done this evening by sunset." Having thus spoken, she conducted the prince to a vast pig-sty, wherein lay more swine than any one could count, and the filth rose to a high mount, which no one could traverse, except over a narrow bridge. The Mermaid then went her way, and thought for certain that the youth would never complete the task. The prince, too, was of the same mind, and, therefore, sat down with his head in his hand, and wept bitterly.

While he was thus sitting and weeping, the fair Singorra again appeared before him, and inquired the cause of his sorrow. The prince answered: "I may well be sad. The Mermaid has commanded me to cleanse the hog-sty. If I have not finished it before evening, when the sun goes down, I shall lose thee and every other joy." The maiden replied: "Be of good cheer; I will help thee, if thou wilt promise to be true to me; for thee will I never deceive." The king's son gladly said "yes," adding that while he lived he would never forget her. Singorra then mounted up on the dunghill, and proceeded cautiously over the bridge, until she came to an old grey hog, that lay concealed in the mire. The king's daughter said:—

> "Hog, hog! make all clean after thee,
> So shalt thou henceforth be free."

And scarcely were the words uttered before the hog sprang up, ran hastily about the sty, poked with his snout, and kicked with his feet, and ceased not until the whole place was as clean as a drawing-room floor. He then went his way, and never returned. The prince was overjoyed, and could never sufficiently praise the beautiful damsel for all her aid.

The king's son now again appeared before his mistress, and said that he had performed the task she had given him. The Mermaid was ready to burst with anger, and resolved that she would try which was the stronger, her craft or the youth's good luck. She therefore concealed her displeasure; but in the morning, at sunrise, she summoned the youth, and told him that he should go to her sister to get necessaries for the wedding; at the same time giving him a box to put them in. But the prince, nevertheless, thought he could perceive from her manner that she did not expect to see him return unscathed from the journey.

When the time for the youth's departure was at hand, the fair Singorra came to him, and said: "I understand that thou art going to the Mermaid's sister, and, if thou doest not as I tell thee, we shall most probably never meet again. Here are two iron knives, two iron-axes, two woollen caps, and two cakes. These thou must take with thee, and dispose of on the way, wherever thou seest occasion. When thou art arrived, be careful where thou sittest. In the Troll's apartment there are five chairs of different colours. If thou sittest on the white chair, thou wilt sink down to the nethermost abyss of the ocean, and never rise again. If thou sittest on the red, thou wilt burn, and never be cool again. If thou sittest on the blue chair, thou wilt be stricken with palsy and sudden death, and we shall never see each other again. If thou sittest on the yellow, thou wilt get consumption, and wilt waste and fade away, and never be well again. But on the black chair thou mayest sit, for on that thou wilt remain unscathed." She then added: "Here is a silken cushion, which thou must lay under the serpent that creeps about the floor. But, above all things, eat no food that is proffered thee; otherwise thou wilt die, and we shall never meet again."

The king's son thanked her fervently for her good counsel, and departed from his dear Singorra; and no one will wonder that they parted with heartfelt sorrow on both sides. He then began his journey, but no particulars of his course have reached us, until he came to where two men were occupied in cutting and carving; but they had only one knife, and that by no means a good one, for it was of wood. Now it occurred to the prince what Singorra had told him; so he took forth his iron knives, and gave one to each of the men.

The youth now went on, and came to two woodcutters; but their labour proceeded very slowly; for they had only one axe, and that but a poor one, for it was also of wood. Singorra's words now again occurred to the prince, and he gave to each an iron axe. He then continued his journey, and came to two men, who were standing by the way and grinding at a mill; but the wind blew cold, and the men were bareheaded. The prince had pity on them, and gave to each a woollen cap. After travelling a while longer, he came to the castle gate. Here a wolf and a bear rushed forth, and the wolf extended his jaws, and the bear growled, as if they would swallow him up. The youth was, however, in nowise at a loss; but taking a cake, he broke it in halves, and gave the wolf and the bear each a portion. The beasts then crept back into their dens, and left the way free, so that the prince, without any further adventures, arrived at the Troll's habitation.

When the youth entered and appeared before the Troll-queen, he greeted her from her sister, and delivered his message. His reception was of the best kind, and the crone promised to furnish the wedding things that were required. She then ordered the white chair to be set, and requested the youth to rest himself after his long journey. But the prince, bearing Singorra's caution in his mind, answered that he was not weary. The Troll-queen then ordered the red chair to be set out; but the prince answered, as before, that he was well able to stand. Then the crone ordered the blue chair to be brought; but still the youth would not sit down. And in like manner also with the yellow chair. But as the Troll-queen did not desist from her importunity, the youth walked to the other end of the apartment, sat down on the black chair, and said: "Here I think a little rest may be of service to me." The crone could now plainly see that the prince was on his guard, and it may easily be imagined that she was not a whit the more well-disposed on that account.

The Troll-queen now had a sausage brought forth, and invited the prince to partake of it, saying he must needs require something after so long a journey. But the youth excused himself by saying that he was not at all hungry; but his excuse availed nothing; for he should eat, whether he would or not. The crone then went away to prepare the things for the wedding; but first said to the serpent that lay in a corner of the room:—

> "Serpent mine!
> Watch thou him."

When now the youth looked about, and perceived the serpent curled up on the floor, he recollected the words of Singorra; so running to the monster, he stroked him with his hand, and laid the silken cushion under his head, with which the serpent seemed well pleased. The prince then withdrew to a corner, hid the sausage under the broom, and returned to his seat.

He had hardly done so before the crone returned, and asked whether he had eaten of the food she had given him. The king's son answered that he had. Then said the Troll:—

> "Sausage mine!
> Where art thou now?"

The sausage answered:—

> "Here under the broom,
> Here under the broom."

The Troll-queen was now highly displeased, fetched the sausage, and said that the prince should eat it all by the time she returned. She then went out, but first said to the serpent:—

> "Serpent mine!
> Watch thou him."

While the crone was away, the prince could not, for his life, hit on any place where to hide the foul refection. At last it occurred to him to conceal it in his bosom, under his clothes. A few minutes only had passed when the Troll came in, and asked whether he had eaten the food. The youth answered that he had. Then said the Troll-queen:—

> "Sausage mine!
> Where art thou now?"

The sausage answered:—

> "Here, in his breast,
> Here, in his breast."

The crone was now quite satisfied, and said:—

> "If thou art in his breast,
> Thou'lt soon be in his maw."

The king's son then received the box with the requisites for the wedding, took leave of the Troll-queen, and set out for home. But scarcely had he got into the court-yard, before the sausage began to move under his clothes, and became changed into a horrid dragon, that spread its wings, and flew aloft in the air. The youth was terrified, and hurried on as fast as he was able. When he came to the castle gate, the crone cried out:—

> "My bear!
> Tear him in a thousand pieces."

The bear instantly rushed forth; but the youth took half a cake, and threw it into the animal's mouth. The bear then said:—

> "I was hungry!
> Now I am satisfied,"

and withdrew into his den. But the youth pursued his way till he came to the wolf; when the Troll again cried out:—

> "My wolf!
> Tear him in a thousand pieces."

Instantly the wolf rushed forth with extended jaws; but the king's son took the other half of the cake, and threw it into his mouth. The wolf then retired into his den, saying:—

> "I was hungry!
> Now I am satisfied."

The king's son now thought it advisable not to delay, and therefore began to run with all his speed, and came to where the two men were grinding at the mill. The Troll-queen then cried out:—

> "Millers twain!
> Grind him in a thousand pieces."

But when the millers saw who it was, they refused to do him any harm, and said: "We will not reward good with evil. He gave us woollen caps, when we were standing bareheaded." They then continued to grind without intermission. But the youth ran on till he came to the men who were cutting wood. The crone then again cried out:—

> "Wood-cutters twain!
> Cut him in a thousand pieces."

But when the cutters saw who it was, they refused to do him any harm, and said: "We will not reward good with evil. We were cutting with a wooden knife, when he gave us iron knives." They then resumed their labour; but the king's son hastened on, and came to where the men were hewing, when the Troll again cried out:—

> "Hewers twain!
> Hew him in a thousand pieces."

When the hewers saw who it was, they would not do him any harm, and said: "We will not reward good with evil. We had an axe of wood, and he gave us iron ones." The men then went on with their work; but the king's son ran on, and stopped not before he reached the Mermaid's abode.

The youth now appeared before his mistress, gave her the wedding things, and rendered an account of his journey. When the Mermaid saw him safe and sound, she was much astonished, and, it was easy to see, not a little angry. In the evening, when people are about to betake themselves to rest, the fair Singorra came to the prince, greeted him with great kindness, and said: "The crone is in a rage, and we must instantly flee from hence, if we value our lives." The prince answered: "How is that to be done? We shall never be able to leave the Mermaid's abode without her consent." The damsel replied: "Be of good cheer; I will devise means, if thou wilt promise to be true to me; for to thee I will never be faithless." The king's son assured her, over and over, that he would never love any other in the world but her. Then said Singorra: "Go down to the stable, and place the golden saddle on the black stallion, and the silver saddle on the black mare. At the hour of midnight we will flee hence." The prince did as the king's daughter had directed him. But Singorra went to her chamber, rolled some clothes together, and made of them three small dolls, one of which she placed by her bed, one in the middle of the floor, and the third on the threshold. She then cut the little finger of her left hand, let three drops of blood fall on each doll, and said: "Ye shall answer for me when I am away."

At midnight the prince and princess stole down to the stable, mounted their horses, and soon left the Mermaid's mansion far behind them. But when the hour of matins drew nigh, and the cocks began to crow, the Mermaid awoke, and called out:—

"Singorra mine!
Art thou yet sleeping?"

"No, my lady," answered the puppet, that stood by the bedpost. When some time had elapsed, the Mermaid again called out:—

"Singorra mine!
What art thou doing?"

"I am kindling the fire, my lady," answered the puppet that stood in the middle of the floor. After another interval the crone cried a third time:—

"Singorra mine!
Does it burn yet?"

"Yes, my lady," answered the third puppet that stood at the threshold. But when daylight approached, the Mermaid herself went to Singorra's chamber, and we can easily conceive that she was far from pleased on finding it empty, and no one in it but the dolls, standing on the floor staring at her. She then ran down to the stable, to see after her horses: but there also she found no comfort, for the black stallion and the black mare were both away; whence the crone could well conclude that the prince and princess had taken their departure.

Her anger now knew no bounds, and she resolved that the two fugitives should not have acted with impunity. She therefore called her serving-man, and said: "In all haste saddle my own goat, which goes a hundred miles at a step. Then ride away and seize both little and great!" The servant was instantly ready, saddled the crone's goat, mounted on its back, and rode off, as when the wind skims over the ocean. When Singorra heard the noise and clattering behind her, she at once divined the cause. Turning, therefore, to the prince, she said: "Dost thou hear that clattering? Now we shall do well to take care of ourselves; for the Mermaid's goat is out and after us." She then changed herself and her lover into two little rats, that ran playing along the way. Scarcely had she done this when the Mermaid's man came travelling through the air, so that it resounded around him. On seeing the two rats, he thought within himself: "It can hardly be those that my mistress means." He then rode on, and at length turned back without finding any one or anything. When he came home, the Mermaid was out in her court-yard: she said: "Well, hast thou seen them?" "No," answered the servant, "I saw nothing but a couple of small rats, sporting along the way." "Them thou shouldst have taken," said the mermaid, and was very angry. "Go back now, and take both great and small."

The man then mounted again on the swift-footed goat, and set off with the speed of lightning. But when Singorra heard the noise behind her, she said to her companion: "Dost thou hear that buzzing? It is best that we take care of ourselves; for the Mermaid's goat is out and after us." She then transformed herself and her lover into two little birds, that flew to and fro in the air. At this moment the serving-man came up riding on his goat, and passed by like a flash of lightning. When he saw the two birds flying in the air, he thought to himself: "It cannot be those that my mistress means," and rode on; but at length returned without having found anything. When he came home, the Mermaid, who was standing in her court-yard, said: "Well, hast thou seen them?" "No," answered the servant, "I saw nothing but two little birds fluttering about in the air. "Them thou shouldst just have taken," said the Mermaid, highly incensed; "Now go back and take both great and small."

The serving-man now again mounted on the swift-footed goat, and was away like thought. When Singorra heard the noise behind her, she said to the king's son: "Dost thou hear what a buzzing there is? It is advisable that we take care of ourselves; for the Mermaid's goat is again out and after us." She then changed herself and her lover into two trees standing by the wayside; but the trees had no roots. Scarcely had this been done, when the servant came riding up on his goat, and hastened forward with such speed that he caused a whistling through the air. When he saw the two trees, he thought to himself: "They can hardly be what my mistress means," and then rode past them, but at length turned back, after a fruitless errand. When he came home, the Mermaid was again standing out in her court-yard, and questioned him: "Well, hast thou seen them?" "No," answered he," I saw nothing but two trees standing by the way." "They are just what thou shouldst have taken," said the Mermaid. "Did I not command thee to take both small and great?" The crone was now almost beside herself with rage, and set off in pursuit of the fugitives. But Singorra had made good use of the time, so that when the Mermaid drew nigh, both she and the prince were already across the boundary, and she had no longer power over them.

The king's son and the fair Singorra now travelled on, and emerged from the sea not far from the king's palace. When the youth recognized his father's abode, he was seized with an irresistible longing to go and see how all his family were, whether they were yet living. Singorra opposed his wish with all her power; for she could plainly foresee how it would all end. But the youth entreated her so fervently, that she was at length unable to withstand his prayers. It was, therefore, agreed that the prince should go up to the palace; but that Singorra should remain behind and await his return. When on the point of separating, the princess said: "One promise thou must make me, for all the faith and devotion that I have shown to thee. Thou must not speak to any one in thy father's palace; for if thou dost, thou wilt forget the word and promises thou hast given to me." The prince promised accordingly and took his departure. But the princess sat by the wayside and wept; for it seemed to her hard to lose him, whom she held so dear, before everything else in the world.

When the youth came riding to his father's palace, there was great joy among all his kindred, who went out to meet him with gladness of heart. But the prince seemed in a strange state of mind, and would neither speak, nor answer when spoken to, but was impatient to ride away again. This appeared very unaccountable to his family; but they could not detain him. When he was in the act of passing through the palace gate, the dogs came rushing towards him barking violently. Now the youth forgot his promise, and cried out: "Away! away!" In the same instant his whole mind was changed, so that he forgot his dear Singorra and everything else; and the past appeared to him only as an oppressive dream. He therefore turned back to his family, and was by every one received with heartfelt affection. And there was joy in all the king's palace, and over the whole kingdom, that the king had recovered his only son, who had been so long absent.

We will now return and see how it fared with Singorra, while she sat waiting for her lover. She waited and waited, but no prince appeared. She was now but too well convinced how matters stood, and was therefore deeply afflicted; so leaving the public road, she went and sat by a little fountain and wept. Towards morning, just as the sun was rising, a young girl came to the spring to fetch water. As she bent forwards and saw the reflection of Singorra's beautiful countenance in the fountain, she was delighted, and felt fully persuaded that it was her own face which she saw. Then clasping her hands together, she exclaimed: "What! am I so beautiful? Then am I no longer fit to sit in a hut with my blind father." With these words she left her pitcher and ran off. Singorra now took up the pitcher of water, went to the hut to the blind man, and attended him as assiduously as if he had been her father. Nor did the old man think otherwise than that it was his daughter; although it struck him as remarkable that on a sudden her conduct was so altered.

In the meanwhile a report of the beauty of the old man's daughter was spread about the neighbourhood; it was said that a lovelier female could nowhere be found. This report reached the ears of the courtiers in the royal palace, and they resolved to ascertain whether what was said were true, that the young maiden was as proud as she was fair. They, therefore, agreed that one after another should endeavour to win her good graces, and thought they would at last make good the old saw, that the "dove always looks on while the bow is bending."

When a short time had elapsed, the first courtier thought he would try his luck. He therefore proceeded to the old man's cot, sat down to chat with the fair damsel, and helped her in her household avocations, as young men are wont to do. When it grew late, and people were about retiring to rest, the courtier was loth to depart, and begged for permission to remain the night over. Singorra made semblance to accede to his wish; but at the same moment exclaimed: "Ah! that is true, I have forgotten to shut the shutter, and it will be so cold in the night." The courtier was instantly ready, and offered to go in her stead. The maiden thanked him, and said: "Tell me when you have hold on the bar." "Well, I am now holding it," answered the courtier. Whereupon the princess cried out:—

> "Bar hold man, and man hold bar,
> Until the lightsome day."

The courtier was now fast, and could not move backwards or forwards; but stood by the shutter pulling and pulling through the whole night. At dawn he became free, and sneaked off abashed to the royal palace; and who will wonder that he told no one how ridiculously his enterprise had terminated?

The next evening it was another courtier's turn to try his fortune. He went accordingly to the old man's cot, sat down by the young damsel, and vented forth an abundance of flattering chitchat, as young men are wont to do. When it grew late, and people were retiring to rest, the courtier was unwilling to depart, but begged for permission to stay the night over. The maiden granted his request, and seemed very friendly; but on a sudden she exclaimed: "Ah! that is true, I have forgotten to lock the door, and it will be so cold in the night." The courtier was instantly ready, and offered to go for her. The maiden thanked him, and said: "Tell me when you have hold on the lock." "Well, I am holding it now," answered the courtier. The princess then cried out:—

> "Door hold man, and man hold door,
> Until the lightsome day."

The courtier was now fast at the door, and stood there tugging and tugging till daylight. He then got loose, and sneaked away abashed home to the palace. But he took particularly good care that no one should know of the adventure he had in the night.

On the third evening another courtier went to try his luck. He went to the old man's cot, sat down by the young damsel, and extolled her beauty, as females, for the most part, readily listen to the praise of their own charms. The princess affected to hear all this trifling prattle with great pleasure, and seemed very friendly. When it grew late, and people were retiring for the night, the courtier would positively not go away, but begged for permission to remain. Singorra yielded to his wish, but on a sudden exclaimed: "Ah! now I recollect that I have not shut the calf in; and that I must not forget." The courtier was instantly ready, and offered to do it for her. She thanked him, and said: "The calf is difficult to catch; tell me when you have got him fast." "Well, I have got him now," answered the courtier, holding the calf by the tail. The princess then cried out:—

> "Calf hold man, and man hold calf,
> And ran over hill, and run over dale,
> Until the lightsome day."

Now a ludicrous race began; the calf bounding over both hill and dale, and the courtier behind him, with his hands fastened to the calf's tail. In this fashion they ran the whole night until sunrise, when the courtier was so weary that he could hardly move. He then returned to the palace, and thought it would not greatly redound to his honour, if it were known how his expedition had terminated.

While all this was taking place the king and queen, after consulting with each other, resolved that the prince should marry. The prince willingly acceded to the proposal, departed for a foreign land, and betrothed himself to a fair princess. Preparations were afterwards made for the marriage, and all was pleasure and glee over the whole palace. It one day so happened that the prince was out with his fair young bride, and came to the hut where Singorra abode with the old blind man. As they were driving by, the horses became restive, broke the pole, dashed the chariot in pieces, and ran off, so that no one could catch them. Now there was no lack of puzzling and considering how the young couple were to get back to the royal palace; and the three courtiers beforementioned stared at each other. At length one of them said: "I know where we can get a new pole. If the young lass who dwells in this cottage will lend us the shutter-bar which lies on the roof, I am sure it would do for a pole." Another said: "I know how we can repair the chariot. If the same young girl will lend us the door of her cot, I am certain it would answer the purpose." The third said: "The worst is how to get horses. But if the young lass will lend us her calf, I am pretty sure that he is able to draw the whole chariot, be it ever so heavy." As now no other course seemed to present itself, the prince sent to the young maiden, and begged the loan of the shutter-bar, the cottage-door, and the calf. With this request the princess instantly complied, but with the condition that she should be present at the prince's wedding. This he promised her. The bar was now turned into a pole, and fitted admirably; the door was likewise placed in the chariot, and also fitted. Last of all the calf was harnessed to the vehicle; and so the prince and his young bride rode home to the king's palace with pleasure and merriment.

On the day fixed for the wedding, Singorra arrayed herself in a silk-embroidered kirtle, adorned herself with costly ornaments, and proceeded to the palace. Her kirtle was resplendent with red gold at every seam, and she herself so lovely that all were wonderstruck, and thought that she must be the daughter of a king. The wedding-guests then sat down to table, and the eyes of all were turned to the stranger damsel, to see how she would act. When a short time had elapsed, Singorra drew forth a box, in which were three little birds and three small gold corns. When the maiden raised the lid, the birds hopped out, and flew over the middle of the table to where the bridegroom was sitting. Two of them had each a gold corn in its mouth; but the third had forgotten its corn. Thereupon the other two birds said to it, "See, thou hast forgotten thy gold corn, as the king's son forgot Singorra." At the same instant there rose as it were a light in the prince's memory, and it rushed into his mind how he had forfeited both truth and honour to his beloved Singorra. He started up from the table, clasped her to his breast, and said: "Thee, or no one in all the world, will I have; for thou art my betrothed."

At this incident great confusion arose in the hall, and the guests looked with surprise at each other. The bridegroom then related all that had taken place from the day on which he was carried off by the mermaid, and what great devotion the young maiden had constantly shown him. The stranger princess was then sent back to her father with great pomp and every mark of honour. But the prince celebrated his marriage with the fair Singorra, the festivities of which lasted many days.

NOTES

1. In a variation from South Småland, it is related that there was a king and a queen who had no children. On this account the king was sorely grieved, and consulted an aged woman who came to the palace. The woman comforted him, saying: "It is well that thou hast no son, for he would be destined to be taken by the Mermaid." But the king would not be content. Then said the fortune-teller: "As thou art so anxious to have a son, know that the queen is pregnant; but be careful not to let the prince go near any water before he is twelve years old, else the Mermaid will have power over him." Having so spoken, the old woman went her way.

It came to pass exactly as the old woman had predicted; for the queen found herself pregnant, and gave birth to a son who was called Anesidei.

The king was overjoyed at this event, and caused a tower to be built, in which the young prince should be reared until he was grown up. When he had attained his twelfth year the king ordered a grand feast to be prepared, and fetched his son from the tower with great solemnity. But as the prince was crossing over a bridge, he was changed to a drop of blood, and fell into the water. Thus the king experienced the truth of the aged crone's prediction.

It is afterwards related how Anesidei came to the Mermaid, and met with a beautiful handmaiden named Meserimei. This young girl helped him in his tasks, and they vowed to each other eternal faith and affection. When the prince had undergone all the Mermaid's trials, and fetched things for the wedding from her sister, the young couple resolved on taking flight together. Then said Meserimei: "Go and sit on the high stone, and call the palfrey on which the crone rode when she was a bride." The prince did so, and returned with the horse, which they both mounted and rode away; but the Mermaid, who had observed their flight, went in pursuit of them. When she caught sight of them, she transformed the land before them into a large sea; but Meserimei had skill to turn it again into land. So the Mermaid was forced to return; but the prince came up out of the sea, not far from his father's palace.

The conclusion accords with story No. II. The king's son rides to his father's palace; but is persuaded to drink a bowl of milk, and so forgets his beloved and everything that had befallen him. He then courts a fair princess in a foreign land. But Meserimei gets employment in the palace as dairy-maid, and befools the three courtiers, as above related.

At the prince's wedding Meserimei is present, clad in most splendid attire. During dinner she casts three gold pearls on the table for her two doves; but the cock takes all three, and leaves nothing for the hen. The little dove thereupon says: "Out upon thee! thou deceivest thy mate, as Anesidei deceived Meserimei." When the king's son hears this the third time, he wakes as from a dream, and recognises his true betrothed.

2. According to a variation from Roslagen, the young princess is named Solfålla. The story has, moreover, the following deviations from the foregoing, No. II.

The prince's second trial consists in his being set to cut down all the trees in the sea-forest, and set them on their roots again. The prince and Solfålla then take flight, and are pursued first by one of the puppets that is changed into a tap-shaped cloud, and travels through the air. The princess then transforms herself and her lover into two rats, playing by the wayside. The Mermaid now sends the second puppet, in the same form; but Solfålla transforms herself and her lover into a duck and a drake. The Mermaid next sends the third puppet, but to no better purpose; the princess changes herself and bridegroom into two trees, and the puppet passes them unnoticed. At last the Troll herself goes after them, and traverses the air like a thick cloud. Solfålla then transforms herself and the prince into a goose and a gander. But the Mermaid perceives her artifice, and transforms herself into a fox, and is on the point of snapping up the goose; but at the same instant the sun rises, at which the goose cries out: "Ha! ha! master Reynard, look behind you, there is a beautiful girl coming." The Mermaid turns about, and, on seeing the sun, is split in two through the middle, and so gets her death.

When the prince returns home to the palace he forgets Solfålla's injunction not to kiss his mother, and so forgets his bride and everything that had befallen him. But the king's daughter takes shelter in. a cottage in the forest, and befools the prince, as is above related of the courtiers. The conclusion of the story accords, in other respects, with what is given above.

3. In a variation from South Småland, the prince is named Flod, and the princess Flodina. They have both been carried off by the Mermaid, and agree to escape together. In their flight they are pursued by their mistress, but transform themselves first into a thorn-bush with a bird in it, then into a church with a priest, and, lastly, into two ducks. When the Mermaid sees the ducks, she lies down to drink the water out of the sea; but drinks too much, and bursts in pieces.

4. A version from Östergötland relates, that there was a queen who encountered a violent storm at sea, and was forced to promise what she carried under her girdle. Shortly after she gave birth to a son, who was named Tobe. But hardly was the child born, when the Mermaid assumed an eagle's plumage, flew into the queen's chamber, and carried him off.

Tobe now grew up in the Mermaid's mansion, where he met with a fair young handmaiden, named Sara. The children contracted a reciprocal affection, and resolved to flee together. Sara then spat on the hearth, on the pile of wood, and in the cellar, bidding them answer for her. She took with her a stone, a brush, and a horsecloth, and so fled with her lover. When the Mermaid was aware of their flight she pursued them in a dense cloud. Sara then cast the stone behind her, which grew to a large mountain, so that the Troll could not pass it, but had to go home for her rock-springer. Tobe and Sara in the meanwhile continued their flight with all speed. But the Mermaid came after them again, when the young maiden threw the brush, and a thick forest sprang up, so that the Troll could not proceed, and now had to go home for her wood-cutter. After a little while she was again after them, when Sara threw the horsecloth, and a large lake arose. The Troll was now obliged to return home for her dog, that was named Glufsa. The Troll and Glufsa then lay down to drink the lake dry, but, drinking too much, they both burst.

When Tobe was about to solemnize his marriage with the foreign princess, Sara threw corn to the fowls in the yard; but the cock pecked up all that was thrown; at which the hens cried out: "The cock serves us as Tobe served Sara." The prince instantly recognises his true bride, and makes her his queen.

5. In a version from Westergötland, it is told that there was a king's son, named Andreas, who had a wicked stepmother. The Troll-wife

wished to destroy the young prince, but he was saved by a young maiden, named Messeria, and at length fled with her. Before they began their flight the maiden cut herself in the little finger of the left hand, and let three drops of blood fall on the floor, saying that they should answer for her when she was away.

The queen now sent her men to catch the two fugitives; but Messeria formed a little church by the way, transformed the prince into a priest, and herself into the sexton. So the men, being unable to find them, turned back. The queen then went herself after them; but Messeria formed a lake, and changed herself and her lover into two large fishes. When the queen reached the shore the fishes came forth, and would swallow her up; for they well knew that if she only got to taste a drop of water, she would have them again in her power.

6. In a very remarkable version from North Småland, the scene of the story is removed from the sea to a hill on land; and for the Mermaid we have an ordinary Mountain-troll. The following is an outline of the story. There was once a king's son, who one day in summer was out gathering strawberries, when a Troll came and enticed him into a mount. There he met with a young maiden, who in like manner had been enticed, and had lived seven long years with the Troll-crone. The young girl helped the youth to perform his tasks, and they promised ever to love each other.

One day the Troll said to the youth: "Thou shalt go and cleanse my stable, which has not been cleansed these four and twenty years." The youth was at a loss how to proceed, and was so sad, so sad. At this moment the young maiden came to him, and said: "Do not weep! If thou wilt promise ever to be faithful-to me, I will give thee counsel. Mount up on that high stone, and call out:—

> "All mother's shovellers, come forth!
> All mother's sweepers, come forth!"

The prince did so, when instantly there came forth a countless multitude of Pysslings, and began to shovel up and sweep, and ceased not until the stable was cleansed.

When that was done, the Troll said: "Here is a bushel of corn. This thou shalt sow in the field; then thou shalt plough and harrow it, and afterwards gather up every grain again." The youth felt completely bewildered, and was so sad, so sad. At this moment the young maiden came to him, and said: "Do not weep! If thou wilt promise ever to be faithful to me, I will help thee. Mount up on that high stone, and call out:—

> "All mother's sowers, come forth!
> All mother's ploughers, come forth!
> All mother's harrowers, come forth!
> All mother's gatherers, come forth!"

The prince did so, when instantly there came forth an innumerable swarm of little, little old men, who began to sow, plough, harrow, and gather, and so great was their number that they fought for every single grain. When the corn was all gathered, the prince carried it into the mount: but the young maiden took away three grains, without any one knowing what she purposed doing with them.

Some time after, the Troll-wife said: "I am now going to a wedding. Go, therefore, and fetch my palfrey, on which I rode when I myself went to be married, just four and twenty years since." The prince was now sorely puzzled, for he did not know where to find the Troll's palfrey. At this moment the young maiden appeared before him, and inquired why he was so sad. The prince answered: "The crone has ordered me to go for her palfrey, on which she rode to be married, four and twenty years ago; and I don't know where to find it." The maiden answered: "If thou wilt promise ever to be faithful to me, I will help thee in this, and also in more." The youth made the desired promise. Then said the maiden: "Go first for the bridle, that hangs nearest the door in the stable." The prince did so. The maiden continued: "Here is a loaf; when thou comest far, far in the forest, thou must violently shake the bridle, when thou wilt hear a great noise and neighing. Then mount up into the highest tree thou canst see; but when thou art half up the tree, thou must shake the bridle yet more violently, and then hasten up to the very top. The horse will then come running at full speed, and will snort and be very untractable. But thou must throw the loaf on his neck, when he will become tame and docile, so that thou mayst catch him, as mother has ordered." The prince thanked her warmly for this good counsel, and they separated for that time.

The prince then went to the forest, having with him the bridle and loaf. When he had proceeded a considerable distance he shook the bridle violently, and climbed up into the highest tree he could see. Instantly he heard a hideous noise and neighing, so that the whole forest resounded. When he had ascended half-way in the tree, he shook the bridle again yet more violently than before, and climbed, as fast as he could, up to the top of the tree. At the same instant he heard a noise, as if the earth were rent, and the horse came running at full speed, so that the trees and shrubs were broken down wherever he came. The horse was large, and as high as the loftiest pine, and gaped so formidably as if he would swallow the prince at a single mouthful. But the youth did not yield to fear, but was instantly ready, and cast the loaf, into his mouth. The animal then became as gentle as a lamb, and patiently waited while the prince put the bridle on him. The youth then vaulted on his back, and rode back to the mount, as the Troll had commanded him.

When the Troll saw that the prince returned safe and sound, she was highly displeased, and meditated in what other manner she might deprive him of life. For this purpose she commanded her handmaid to kill the youth and bake him, while she herself was absent at the wedding. The maiden promised to do as she was ordered; but when the crone was gone the girl made three dolls of cloth, placed them, one at the threshold, one on the hearth, and one by the bed, and commanded them to answer for her. Then she and the youth took all the chattels and gold that were in the mount, and fled. When the Troll-wife returned from the wedding she was very tired, and lay down to sleep, and slept the whole twenty-four hours. When she woke she called to her handmaid: "Dost thou hear, girl? hast thou baked the lad yet?" Then the puppet that was placed at the threshold answered: "I am just now heating the oven." The crone then turned round, went to sleep again, and slept another twenty-four hours. When she woke she again asked: "Dost thou hear, girl? hast thou baked the lad yet?" The doll that stood on the hearth answered: "I am now just putting him in." The Troll turned round again, went fast to sleep, and slept for another twenty-four hours. When she woke she cried out again: "Dost thou hear, girl? is the boy baked yet?" The doll which stood by the bed answered: "Yes, I am just now taking him out." The Troll-wife then rose, and went to the maiden's chamber; but when she entered she saw no one there, except the three rag-dolls staring at her.

The crone was now pretty well aware how matters stood, and was wroth beyond all bounds. She called her men, and ordered them instantly to go in pursuit of the fugitives. Now the king's son and his companion hear a great noise in the air, and the maiden says: "Dost thou hear that noise? Mother has sent all her people after us." She then transformed the prince into a thorn-bush, and herself into a rose growing on it. The men took no notice of the bush and flower, but passed by with all speed. When they returned, the crone said: "Well, have you seen anything?" The men answered: "We saw nothing but a little thorn-bush, with a rose in it, that stood by the wayside." The Troll-wife was sorely displeased at this answer, and said: "Those are just what you should have taken; I must now go in pursuit of them myself."

The Troll then set out in chase of the fugitives, and travelled with such speed that the air whined and whistled. The maiden then said to her companion: "Dost thou hear that hideous din? It is mother herself that is out after us." She then changed herself and her lover into two ducks, and they swam across the lake that lay before them. But when the crone approached and saw them on the opposite side, she laid herself down, and drank up the whole lake. At that moment the sun rose, and the young maiden cried out: "See! what a beautiful damsel is running up yonder." When the crone turned round to look, she split in pieces; for, as is well known, Trolls have not the power of looking at the sun.

The prince on his return home, as usual, forgets his bride, and is about to marry a foreign princess. When the wedding-day arrived, the deserted damsel applied for employment as a servant. She had with her a duck and a drake that waddled up and down the festive hall. While the guests were all at table, and all was mirth and glee, the maiden drew forth three grains of corn, and threw them on the floor. Instantly the drake hastened forward and picked up all the three. Thereupon the maiden struck him with her hand, saying: "Out upon thee! that thus castest aside thy mate." When the prince heard these words he recognised his right bride, and remembered all the fidelity and devotion she had shown him, &c.

To see a list of other European variants of this tale—most of which do not contain water spirits—see the notes to the previous tale, "The King's Son and Messeria."~HAH

Source:
Thorpe, Benjamin. *Yule-Tide Stories*. London: Henry G. Bohn, 1853.

96. The Sea Nymph

Sweden (Gotland)

ONE night a number of fishermen quartered themselves in a hut by a fishing village on the northwest shores of an island. After they had gone to bed, and while they were yet awake, they saw a white, dew-besprinkled woman's hand reaching in through the door. They well understood that their visitor was a sea nymph, who sought their destruction, and feigned unconsciousness of her presence.

The following day their number was added to by the coming of a young, courageous and newly married man from Kinnar, in Lummelund. When they related to him their adventure of the night before, he made fun of their being afraid to take a beautiful woman by the hand, and boasted that if he had been present he would not have neglected to grasp the proffered hand.

That evening when they laid themselves down in the same room, the late arrival with them, the door opened again, and a plump, white woman's arm, with a most beautiful hand, reached in over the sleepers.

The young man arose from his bed, approached the door and seized the outstretched hand, impelled, perhaps, more by the fear of his comrades scoffing at his boasted bravery, than by any desire for a closer acquaintance with the strange visitor.

Immediately his comrades witnessed him drawn noiselessly out through the door, which closed softly after him. They thought he would return soon, but when morning approached and he did not appear, they set out in search of him. Far and near the search was pursued, but without success. His disappearance was complete.

Three years passed and nothing had been heard of the missing man. His young wife, who had mourned him all this time as dead, was finally persuaded to marry another. On the evening of the wedding day, while the mirth was at its highest, a stranger entered the cottage. Upon closer observation some of the guests thought they recognized the bride's former husband.

The utmost surprise and commotion followed.

In answer to the inquiries of those present as to where he came from and where he had been, he related that it was a sea nymph whose hand he had taken that night when he left the fisherman's hut; and that he was dragged by her down into the sea. In her pearly halls he forgot his wife, parents, and all that was loved by him until the morning of that day, when the sea nymph exclaimed, "There will be a dusting out in Kinnar this evening."

Then his senses immediately returned, and, with anxiety, he asked, "Then it is my wife who is to be the bride?"

The sea nymph replied in the affirmative.

At his urgent request, she allowed him to come up to see his wife as a bride, stipulating that when he arrived at the house he should not enter. When he came and saw her adorned with garland and crown he could, nevertheless, not resist the desire to enter. Then came a tempest and took away half the roof of the house, whereupon the man fell sick and three days later died.

Source:
Hofberg, Herman. *Swedish Fairy Tales*. W. H. Myers, translator. Chicago: Belford-Clarke Company, 1890.

97. The Mermaid and the Boy

Lapland (Sweden & Finland)[1]

LONG, long ago, there lived a king who ruled over a country by the sea. When he had been married about a year, some of his subjects, inhabiting a distant group of islands, revolted against his laws, and it became needful for him to leave his wife and go in person to settle their disputes.

---

[1] Andrew Lang credits his source as *Lappländische Märchen*, stories from historical Lapland which now is part of the northern regions of Sweden and Finland.~*HAH*

The queen feared that some ill would come of it, and implored him to stay at home, but he told her that nobody could do his work for him, and the next morning the sails were spread, and the king started on his voyage.

The vessel had not gone very far when she ran upon a rock, and stuck so fast in a cleft that the strength of the whole crew could not get her off again. To make matters worse, the wind was rising too, and it was quite plain that in a few hours the ship would be dashed to pieces and everybody would be drowned, when suddenly the form of a mermaid was seen dancing on the waves which threatened every moment to overwhelm them.

"There is only one way to free yourselves," she said to the king, bobbing up and down in the water as she spoke, "and that is to give me your solemn word that you will deliver to me the first child that is born to you."

The king hesitated at this proposal. He hoped that some day he might have children in his home, and the thought that he must yield up the heir to his crown was very bitter to him; but just then a huge wave broke with great force on the ship's side, and his men fell on their knees and entreated him to save them.

So he promised, and this time a wave lifted the vessel clean off the rocks, and she was in the open sea once more.

The affairs of the islands took longer to settle than the king had expected, and some months passed away before he returned to his palace. In his absence a son had been born to him, and so great was his joy that he quite forgot the mermaid and the price he had paid for the safety of his ship. But as the years went on, and the baby grew into a fine big boy, the remembrance of it came back, and one day he told the queen the whole story. From that moment the happiness of both their lives was ruined. Every night they went to bed wondering if they should find his room empty in the morning, and every day they kept him by their sides, expecting him to be snatched away before their very eyes.

At last the king felt that this state of things could not continue, and he said to his wife:

"After all, the most foolish thing in the world one can do is to keep the boy here in exactly the place in which the mermaid will seek him. Let us give him food and send him on his travels, and perhaps, if the mermaid ever blocs come to seek him, she may be content with some other child." And the queen agreed that his plan seemed the wisest.

So the boy was called, and his father told him the story of the voyage, as he had told his mother before him. The prince listened eagerly, and was delighted to think that he was to go away all by himself to see the world, and was not in the least frightened; for though he was now sixteen, he had scarcely been allowed to walk alone beyond the palace gardens. He began busily to make his preparations, and took off his smart velvet coat, putting on instead one of green cloth, while he refused a beautiful bag which the queen offered him to hold his food, and slung a leather knapsack over his shoulders instead, just as he had seen other travellers do. Then he bade farewell to his parents and went his way.

All through the day he walked, watching with interest the strange birds and animals that darted across his path in the forest or peeped at him from behind a bush. But as evening drew on he became tired, and looked about as he walked for some place where he could sleep. At length he reached a soft mossy bank under a tree, and was just about to stretch himself out on it, when a fearful roar made him start and tremble all over. In another moment something passed swiftly through the air and a lion stood before him.

"What are you doing here?" asked the lion, his eyes glaring fiercely at the boy.

"I am flying from the mermaid," the prince answered, in a quaking voice.

"Give me some food then," said the lion, "it is past my supper time, and I am very hungry."

The boy was so thankful that the lion did not want to eat him, that he gladly picked up his knapsack which lay on the ground, and held out some bread and a flask of wine.

"I feel better now," said the lion when he had done, "so now I shall go to sleep on this nice soft moss, and if you like you can lie down beside me." So the boy and the lion slept soundly side by side, till the sun rose.

"I must be off now," remarked the lion, shaking the boy as he spoke; "but cut off the tip of my ear, and keep it carefully, and if you are in any danger just wish yourself a lion and you will become one on the spot. One good turn deserves another, you know."

The prince thanked him for his kindness, and did as he was bid, and the two then bade each other farewell.

"I wonder how it feels to be a lion," thought the boy, after he had gone a little way; and he took out the tip of the ear from the breast of his jacket and wished with all his might. In an instant his head had swollen to several times its usual size, and his neck seemed very hot and heavy; and, somehow, his hands became paws, and his skin grew hairy and yellow. But what pleased him most was his long tail with a tuft at the end, which he lashed and switched proudly. "I like being a lion very much," he said to himself, and trotted gaily along the road.

After a while, however, he got tired of walking in this unaccustomed way—it made his back ache and his front paws felt sore. So he wished himself a boy again, and in the twinkling of an eye his tail disappeared and his head shrank, and the long thick mane became short and curly. Then he looked out for a sleeping place, and found some dry ferns, which he gathered and heaped up.

But before he had time to close his eyes there was a great noise in the trees near by, as if a big heavy body was crashing through them. The boy rose and turned his head, and saw a huge black bear coming towards him.

"What are you doing here?" cried the bear.

"I am running away from the mermaid," answered the boy; but the bear took no interest in the mermaid, and only said: "I am hungry; give me something to eat."

The knapsack was lying on the ground among the fern, but the prince picked it up, and, unfastening the strap, took out his second flask of wine and another loaf of bread. "We will have supper together," he remarked politely; but the bear, who had never been taught manners, made no reply, and ate as fast as he could. When he had quite finished, he got up and stretched himself.

"You have got a comfortable-looking bed there," he observed. "I really think that, bad sleeper as I am, I might have a good night on it. I can manage to squeeze you in," he added; "you don't take up a great deal of room." The boy was rather indignant at the bear's cool way of talking; but as he was too tired to gather more fern, they lay down side by side, and never stirred till sunrise next morning.

"I must go now," said the bear, pulling the sleepy prince on to his feet; "but first you shall cut off the tip of my ear, and when you are in any danger just wish yourself a bear and you will become one. One good turn deserves another, you know." And the boy did as he was bid, and he and the bear bade each other farewell.

"I wonder how it feels to be a bear," thought he to himself when he had walked a little way; and he took out the tip from the breast of his coat and wished hard that he might become a bear. The next moment his body stretched out and thick black fur covered him all over. As before, his hands were changed into paws, but when he tried to switch his tail he found to his disgust that it would not go any distance. "Why it is hardly worth calling a tail!" said he. For the rest of the day he remained a bear and continued his journey, but as evening came on the bear-skin, which had been so useful when plunging through brambles in the forest, felt rather heavy, and he wished himself a boy again. He was too much exhausted to take the trouble of cutting any fern or seeking for moss, but just threw himself down under a tree, when exactly above his head he heard a great buzzing as a bumble-bee alighted on a honeysuckle branch. "What are you doing here?" asked the bee in a cross voice; "at your age you ought to be safe at home."

"I am running away from the mermaid," replied the boy; but the bee, like the lion and the bear, was one of those people who never listen to the answers to their questions, and only said: "I am hungry. Give me something to eat."

The boy took his last loaf and flask out of his knapsack and laid them on the ground, and they had supper together. "Well, now I am going to sleep," observed the bee when the last crumb was gone, "but as you are not very big I can make room for you beside me," and he curled up his wings, and tucked in his legs, and he and the prince both slept soundly till morning. Then the bee got up and carefully brushed every scrap of dust off his velvet coat and buzzed loudly in the boy's ear to waken him.

"Take a single hair from one of my wings," said he, "and if you are in danger just wish yourself a bee and you will become one. One good turn deserves another, so farewell, and thank you for your supper." And the bee departed after the boy had pulled out the hair and wrapped it carefully in a leaf.

"It must feel quite different to be a bee from what it does to be a lion or bear," thought the boy to himself when he had walked for an hour or two. "I dare say I should get on a great deal faster," so he pulled out his hair and wished himself a bee.

In a moment the strangest thing happened to him. All his limbs seemed to draw together, and his body to become very short and round; his head grew quite tiny, and instead of his white skin he was covered with the richest, softest velvet. Better than all, he had two lovely gauze wings which carried him the whole day without getting tired.

Late in the afternoon the boy fancied he saw a vast heap of stones a long way off, and he flew straight towards it. But when he reached the gates he saw that it was really a great town, so he wished himself back in his own shape and entered the city.

He found the palace doors wide open and went boldly into a sort of hall which was full of people, and where men and maids were gossiping together. He joined their talk and soon learned from them that the king had only one daughter who had such a hatred to men that she would never suffer one to enter her presence. Her father was in despair, and had had pictures painted of the handsomest princes of all the courts in the world, in the hope that she might fall in love with one of them; but it was no use; the princess would not even allow the pictures to be brought into her room.

"It is late," remarked one of the women at last; "I must go to my mistress." And, turning to one of the lackeys, she bade him find a bed for the youth.

"It is not necessary," answered the prince, "this bench is good enough for me. I am used to nothing better." And when the hall was empty he lay down for a few minutes. But as soon as everything was quiet in the palace he took out the hair and wished himself a bee, and in this shape he flew upstairs, past the guards, and through the keyhole into the princess's chamber. Then he turned himself into a man again.

At this dreadful sight the princess, who was broad awake, began to scream loudly. "A man! a man!" cried she; but when the guards rushed in there was only a bumble-bee buzzing about the room. They looked under the bed, and behind the curtains, and into the cupboards, then came to the conclusion that the princess had had a bad dream, and bowed themselves out. The door had scarcely closed on them than the bee disappeared, and a handsome youth stood in his place.

"I knew a man was hidden somewhere," cried the princess, and screamed more loudly than before. Her shrieks brought back the guards, but though they looked in all kinds of impossible places no man was to be seen, and so they told the princess.

"He was here a moment ago—I saw him with my own eyes," and the guards dared not contradict her, though they shook their heads and whispered to each other that the princess had gone mad on this subject, and saw a man in every table and chair. And they made up their minds that—let her scream as loudly as she might—they would take no notice.

Now the princess saw clearly what they were thinking, and that in future her guards would give her no help, and would perhaps, besides, tell some stories about her to the king, who would shut her up in a lonely tower and prevent her walking in the gardens among her birds and flowers. So when, for the third time, she beheld the prince standing before her, she did not scream but sat up in bed gazing at him in silent terror.

"Do not be afraid," he said, "I shall not hurt you"; and he began to praise her gardens, of which he had heard the servants speak, and the birds and flowers which she loved, till the princess's anger softened, and she answered him with gentle words. Indeed, they soon became so friendly that she vowed she would marry no one else, and confided to him that in three days her father would be off to the wars, leaving his sword in her room. If any man could find it and bring it to him he would receive her hand as a reward. At this point a cock crew, and the youth jumped up hastily saying: "Of course I shall ride with the king to the war, and if I do not return, take your violin every evening to the seashore and play on it, so that the very sea-kobolds who live at the bottom of the ocean may hear it and come to you."

Just as the princess had foretold, in three days the king set out for the war with a large following, and among them was the young prince, who had presented himself at court as a young noble in search of adventures. They had left the city many miles behind them, when the king suddenly discovered that he had forgotten his sword, and though all his attendants instantly offered theirs, he declared that he could fight with none but his own.

"The first man who brings it to me from my daughter's room," cried he, "shall not only have her to wife, but after my death shall reign in my stead."

At this the Red Knight, the young prince, and several more turned their horses to ride as fast as the wind back to the palace. But suddenly a better plan entered the prince's head, and, letting the others pass him, he took his precious parcel from his breast and wished himself a lion. Then on he bounded, uttering such dreadful roars that the horses were frightened and grew unmanageable, and he easily outstripped them, and soon reached the gates of the palace. Here he hastily changed himself into a bee, and flew straight into the princess's room, where he became a man again. She showed him where the sword hung concealed behind a curtain, and he took it down, saying as he did so: "Be sure not to forget what you have promised to do."

The princess made no reply, but smiled sweetly, and slipping a golden ring from her finger she broke it in two and held half out silently to the prince, while the other half she put in her own pocket. He kissed it, and ran down the stairs bearing the sword with him. Some way off he met the Red Knight and the rest, and the Red Knight at first tried to take the sword from him by force. But as the youth proved too strong for him, he gave it up, and resolved to wait for a better opportunity.

This soon came, for the day was hot and the prince was thirsty. Perceiving a little stream that ran into the sea, he turned aside, and, unbuckling the sword, flung himself on the ground for a long drink. Unluckily, the mermaid happened at that moment to be floating on the water not very far off, and knew he was the boy who had been given her before he was born. So she floated gently in to where he was lying, she seized him by the arm, and the waves closed over them both. Hardly had they disappeared, when the Red Knight stole cautiously up, and could hardly believe his eyes when he saw the king's sword on the bank. He wondered what had become of the youth, who an hour before had guarded his treasure so fiercely; but, after all, that was no affair of his! So, fastening the sword to his belt, he carried it to the king.

The war was soon over, and the king returned to his people, who welcomed him with shouts of joy. But when the princess from her window saw that her betrothed was not among the attendants riding behind her father, her heart sank, for she knew that some evil must have befallen him. and she feared the Red Knight. She had long ago learned how clever and how wicked he was, and something whispered to her that it was he who would gain the credit of having carried back the sword, and would claim her as his bride, though he had never even entered her chamber. And she could do nothing; for although the king loved her, he never let her stand in the way of his plans.

The poor princess was only too right, and everything came to pass exactly as she had foreseen it. The king told her that the Red Knight had won her fairly, and that the wedding would take place next day, and there would be a great feast after it.

In those days feasts were much longer and more splendid than they are now; and it was growing dark when the princess, tired out with all she had gone through, stole up to her own room for a little quiet. But the moon was shining so brightly over the sea that it seemed to draw her towards it, and taking her violin under her arm, she crept down to the shore.

"Listen! listen! said the mermaid to the prince, who was lying stretched on a bed of seaweeds at the bottom of the sea. "Listen! that is your old love playing, for mermaids know everything that happens upon earth."

"I hear nothing," answered the youth, who did not look happy. "Take me up higher, where the sounds can reach me."

So the mermaid took him on her shoulders and bore him up midway to the surface. "Can you hear now?" she asked.

"No," answered the prince, "I hear nothing but the water rushing; I must go higher still."

Then the mermaid carried him to the very top. "You must surely be able to hear now?" said she.

"Nothing but the water," repeated the youth. So she took him right to the land.

"At any rate you can hear now?" she said again.

"The water is still rushing in my ears," answered he; "but wait a little, that will soon pass off." And as he spoke he put his hand into his breast, and seizing the hair wished himself a bee, and flew straight into the pocket of the princess. The mermaid looked in vain for him, and coated all night upon the sea; but he never came back, and never more did he gladden her eyes. But the princess felt that something strange was about her, though she knew not what, and returned quickly to the palace, where the young man at once resumed his own shape. Oh, what joy filled her heart at the sight of him! But there was no time to be lost, and she led him right into the hall, where the king and his nobles were still sitting at the feast. "Here is a man who boasts that he can do wonderful tricks," said she, "better even than the Red Knight's! That cannot be true, of course, but it might be well to give this impostor a lesson. He pretends, for instance, that he can turn himself into a lion; but that I do not believe. I know that you have studied the art of magic," she went on, turning to the Red Knight, "so suppose you just show him how it is done, and bring shame upon him."

Now the Red Knight had never opened a book of magic in his life; but he was accustomed to think that he could do everything better than other people without any teaching at all. So he turned and twisted himself about, and bellowed and made faces; but he did not become a lion for all that.

"Well, perhaps it is very difficult to change into a lion. Make yourself a bear," said the princess. But the Red Knight found it no easier to become a bear than a lion.

"Try a bee," suggested she. "I have always read that anyone who can do magic at all can do that." And the old knight buzzed and hummed, but he remained a man and not a bee.

"Now it is your turn," said the princess to the youth. "Let us see if you can change yourself into a lion." And in a moment such a fierce creature stood before them, that all the guests rushed out of the hall, treading each other underfoot in their fright. The lion sprang at the Red Knight, and would have torn him in pieces had not the princess held him back, and bidden him to change himself into a man again. And in a second a man took the place of the lion.

"Now become a bear," said she; and a bear advanced panting and stretching out his arms to the Red Knight, who shrank behind the princess.

By this time some of the guests had regained their courage, and returned as far as the door, thinking that if it was safe for the princess perhaps it was safe for them. The king, who was braver than they, and felt it needful to set them a good example besides, had never left his seat, and when at a new command of the princess the bear once more turned into a man, he was silent from astonishment, and a suspicion of the truth began to dawn on him. "Was it he who fetched the sword?" asked the king.

"Yes, it was," answered the princess; and she told him the whole story, and how she had broken her gold ring and given him half of it. And the prince took out his half of the ring, and the princess took out hers, and they fitted exactly. Next day the Red Knight was hanged, as he richly deserved, and there was a new marriage feast for the prince and princess.

Lappländische Märchen.

Source:
Lang, Andrew, editor. *The Brown Fairy Book*. London and New York: Longmans, Green, and Company, 1904.

98. The Merman and the Calf

Scandinavia

AN OLD woman in Stradil tells the following story after her grandmother. Once, when no ship had been wrecked for a long time, and the merman thus had not got his victim, he went up on shore, and cast his hook into the cows which went about on the sandhills. Just beside the sea there lived a peasant, who had two pretty red calves that he did not want to lose, so he coupled them together with rowan tree, and the merman had no power over them. All the same he fixed his hook in them, but he could not drag them down into the sea, and had to let go his hook, with which the calves came home in the evening. The man took it, guessing it was the merman's, and hung it up beside the stove, where it hung till one day, when only an old woman was left in the house. Then the merman came and took his hook, and turning about to the old woman, said in his own imperfect speech, "Two red cows' first calves; rowan tree to couple;

man couldn't drag them; man has lost many good catch since." With that he went away with the hook, and never tried to take cattle on the beach again.

Source:
Craigie, William A. *Scandinavian Folk-Lore: Illustrations of the Traditional Beliefs of the Northern People.* London: Alexander Gardner, 1896.

99. The Sea-Sprite

Scandinavia

THE sea-sprite is seen after sunset standing on out-lying reefs, and when men row out to fish he calls upon them and asks to be taken on board the boat. Sometimes they have taken him on board, and set him on one of the seats to row with the others; during the darkest part of the night he can row against two at the least, so strong is he. He is good at finding the fishing-ground when it is not clear enough to see the land-marks, but he grows smaller and smaller as day approaches, and fades away into nothing when the sun rises out of the sea. They have made the sign of the cross on him, but as the eastern sky grew redder and redder before the sun, he begged more and more piteously to be let go. One time they would not let him away, but when the sun rose he disappeared, and his pelvis was left lying on the seat, for the sea-sprite is said to take to himself a human pelvis, and this is left behind if the sprite himself disappears. He can also produce ocular deceptions: sometimes he seems like a man, sometimes like a dog. He is of a dark-red colour, and hoots and howls so that it can be heard a far way off. Fire flies from him when he is on shore. He has only one foot (or tail), but can hop a long way with it, and his tracks have been seen in the snow. When he meets a man on land he tries to drive him out into the sea.

Source:
Craigie, William A. *Scandinavian Folk-Lore: Illustrations of the Traditional Beliefs of the Northern People.* London: Alexander Gardner, 1896.

100. The Shepherd and the Sea-Folk

Scandinavia

ONE time there was a rich yeoman who had a large and splendid house, with a sitting room all panelled from floor to ceiling, but it had the defect that any one who stayed there on Christmas eve was found dead next morning. It was, therefore, difficult to get any one to stay there, for no one wished to remain at home that night, and yet it was necessary for some one to do so. Once the yeoman had got a new shepherd, as he did frequently, for he had many sheep and required an active man to look after them. The yeoman told the man honestly of this bad point about the farm, but the shepherd said he did not mind such trifles, and was quite as willing to come to him for all that. He came to him accordingly, and they got on very well together. Time passed until Christmas came, and the yeoman and all his household went to evensong on Christmas eve, except the shepherd, who was not making ready to go to church. His master asked why this was. The shepherd said he meant to stay at home, as it was impossible to leave the farm to itself, and let the cattle want their food so long. The farmer told him never to mind that, no one could venture to stay there on Christmas eve, as he had said before, for every living thing then about the house was killed, and he would not have him risk it on any account. The shepherd professed to think this all nonsense, and said he would try it. When his master found he could not persuade him, he went away with the others, and left him there alone.

The shepherd, when left to himself, began to think over his design, and decided that he had better be prepared for all emergencies, as there was plainly something wrong. He kindled a light in the sitting-room, and made it quite bright. Then he looked for a place to hide himself, and loosening two planks of the panelling at the end of the room, he crept in there, drawing them into their places again so as to leave no trace. There he stood between the panelling and the wall, being able to see all that went on in the room through a chink in the boards.

No long time after he had thus disposed of himself, he saw two unknown and very grim-looking men enter the room, and look all round it. Then one of them said, "The smell of man! the smell of man!" "No," said the other, "there is no man here." They then took lights, and looked everywhere in the room, high and low, till at last they found a dog that was lying below one of beds. Him they took and wrung his neck, and threw him out at the door. The shepherd saw then that it would not have done for him to come in contact with these fellows, and thanked his good fortune that he was where he was. After this the room began to fill with people, who proceeded to lay the table, and had all their table-service of silver—dishes, spoons, and knives. Food was then served up, and they sat down to it, making great noise and mirth, and were there eating, drinking and dancing all night. Two, however, were set to watch and tell if they saw any man on the move outside, and whether day was about to dawn. Thrice during the night they went out and said they saw no one coming, and that it was not yet day. When the shepherd thought that it must be dawn, he seized both the loose boards, sprang out into the floor with the greatest violence, clapped the boards together, and yelled with all his might, "Day! Day!" The strangers were so startled at this that they tumbled out, heads over heels, leaving all their belongings—table, table-service, and clothes which they had put off during the night to be all the lighter for dancing. Some were hurt and some trodden under foot, while the shepherd continued to chase them, clapping his boards and shouting "Day! Day!" till they reached a lake a little way from the farm, into which they all dived, and then he saw that they were "sea-folk" or "water-dwellers." After that he went back home, dragged out the dead ones, and killed the half-dead, and then burned up the bodies. When his master came home, he and the shepherd divided between them all that the visitors had left, and from that time forward nothing strange happened there on Christmas Eve.

Source:
Craigie, William A. *Scandinavian Folk-Lore: Illustrations of the Traditional Beliefs of the Northern People*. London: Alexander Gardner, 1896.

101. The Mermaid[1]

Estonia

IN THE happy days of old, better men lived on earth than now, and the Heavenly Father revealed many wonders to them which are now quite concealed, or but rarely manifested to a child of fortune. It is true that the

---

[1]Schiefner considers the name of this story (*Näki Neitsi*) to indicate a Swedish origin; but this seems to be very doubtful evidence, and the incidental allusion to the Swedes in the course of the narrative seems opposed to such an idea.

birds sing and the beasts converse as of old, but unhappily we no longer comprehend their speech, and what they say brings us neither profit nor wisdom.

In old days a fair mermaid dwelt on the shores of the province of Lääne. She often appeared to the people, and my grandfather's father, who was reared in the neighbourhood, sometimes saw her sitting on a rock, but the little fellow did not venture to approach her. The maiden appeared in various forms, sometimes as a foal or a calf, and sometimes under the form of some other animal. In the evening she often came among the children, and let them play with her, until some little boy mounted her back, when she would vanish as suddenly as if she had sunk into the ground.

At that time old people said that in former days the maiden was to be seen on the borders of the sea almost every fine evening in the summer, sitting on a rock, and combing her long fair hair with a golden comb, and she sang such beautiful songs that it melted the hearts of her listeners. But she could not endure the gaze of men, and vanished from their sight or fled into the sea, where she rocked on the waves like a swan. We will now relate the cause of her flying from men, and no longer meeting them with her former confidence.

In old times, long before the invasion of the Swedes, a rich farmer lived on the coast of Lääne with his wife and four sons. They obtained their food more from the sea than from the land, for fishing was a very productive industry in their days. The youngest son was very different from his brothers, even from a child. He avoided the companionship of men, and wandered about on the sea-shore and in the forest. He talked much to himself and to the birds, or to the winds and waves, but when he was in the company of others he hardly opened his mouth, but stood like one dreaming. When the storms raged over the sea in autumn, and the waves swelled up as high as a house and broke foaming on the beach, the boy could not contain himself in the house, but ran like one possessed, and often half-naked, to the shore. Neither wind nor weather harmed his robust body. He sprang into his boat, seized the oars, and drove like a wild goose over the crest of the raging billows far out to sea, without incurring any harm by his rashness. In the morning, when the storm had spent its fury, he was found sound asleep on the beach. If he was sent anywhere on an errand, to herd cattle in summer, or to do any other easy employment, he gave his parents only trouble. He lay down under the shadow of a bush without minding the animals, and they strayed away or trampled down the meadows and cornfields, and his brothers had often to work for hours before they could find the lost animals. The father often let the boy feel the rod severely enough, but it had no more effect than water poured on the back of a goose. When the boy grew up into a youth, he did not mend his ways. No work prospered in his negligent hands; he hacked and broke the tools, wearied out the draught cattle, and yet never did anything right.

His father sent him to neighbouring farmers to work, hoping that a stranger's whip might improve the sloven, but whoever had the fellow for one week on trial sent him back again on the next. His parents rated him for a sluggard, and his brothers dubbed him "Sleepy Tony." This soon became his nickname with everybody, though he had been christened Jüri.[1] Sleepy Tony brought no one any good, but was only a nuisance to his parents and relatives, so that they would gladly have given a sum of money if anybody would have rid them of the lazy fellow. As nobody would put up with him any longer, his father engaged him as servant to a foreign captain, because he could not run away at sea, and because he had always been so fond of the water from a child. However, after a few weeks, nobody knows how, he escaped from the ship, and again set his lazy feet on his native soil. But he was ashamed to enter his father's house, where he could not expect to meet with a friendly reception, so he wandered about from one place to another, and sought to get his living as he could, without working. He was a strong handsome fellow, and could talk very agreeably if he liked, although he had never been accustomed to talk much in his father's house. He was now obliged to use his handsome appearance and fine tongue to ingratiate himself with the women and girls.

One fine summer evening after sunset it happened that he was wandering alone on the beach when the clear song of the mermaid reached his ears. Sleepy Tony thought to himself, "She is a woman, at any rate, and won't do me any harm." He did not hesitate to approach nearer, to take a view of the beautiful bird. He climbed the highest hill, and saw the mermaid some distance off, sitting on a rock, combing her hair with a golden comb, and singing a ravishing song. The youth would have wished for more ears to listen to her song, which pierced his heart like a flame, but when he drew nearer he saw that he would have needed just as many eyes to take in the beauty of the maiden. The mermaid must have seen him coming, but she did not fly from him, as she was always wont to do when men approached. Sleepy Tony advanced to within ten paces of her, and then stopped, undecided whether to go nearer. And oh, wonderful! the mermaid rose from the stone and came to meet him with a friendly air. She gave him her hand in greeting, and said, "I have expected you for many days, for a fateful dream warned me of your arrival. You have neither house nor home among those of your own race. Why should you be dependent upon strangers when your parents refuse to receive you into their house? I have known you from a child, and better than men have known you, for I have often watched over and protected you when your rashness would otherwise have destroyed you. I have often guarded the rocking boat with my hands, when it would otherwise have sunk in the depths. Come with me, and you shall enjoy

---

[1] George.

every happiness which your heart can desire, and you shall want for nothing. I will watch over and protect you as the apple of my eye, so that neither wind nor rain nor frost shall touch you."

Sleepy Tony stood for a time uncertain what to answer, though every word of the maiden was like a flaming arrow in his heart. At last he stammered out an inquiry as to whether her home was very far away. "We can reach it with the speed of the wind, if you have confidence in me," answered the mermaid. Then Sleepy Tony remembered many sayings which he had heard about the mermaid, and his heart failed him, and he asked for three days to make up his mind. "I will agree to your wish," said the mermaid, "but lest you should again be doubtful, I will put my gold ring on your finger before we part, that you may not forget to return. When we are better acquainted, this pledge may serve as an engagement ring." She then drew off the ring, placed it on the youth's little finger, and vanished as if she had melted into air. Sleepy Tony stood staring with wide-open eyes, and would have supposed it was all a dream, if the sparkling ring on his finger had not been proof to the contrary. But the ring seemed like a strange spirit, which left him no peace or rest anywhere. He wandered aimlessly about the shore all night, and always returned to the rock on which the maiden had been sitting; but the stone was cold and vacant. In the morning he lay down for a short time, but uneasy dreams disturbed his sleep. When he awoke, he felt neither hunger nor thirst, and all his thoughts were directed towards the evening, when he hoped to see the mermaid again. The day waned at last, and evening approached, the wind sank, the birds in the alder-bushes left off singing and tucked their tired heads under their wings, but that evening he saw the mermaid nowhere.

He wept bitter tears of sorrow and trouble, and reflected bitterly on his folly in having hesitated to seize the good fortune offered to him the evening before, when a cleverer fellow would have grasped at it with both hands. But regret and complaint were useless now. The night and the day which followed were equally painful to him, and his trouble weighed upon him so much that he never felt hunger. Towards sunset he sat down with an aching heart on the rock where the mermaid had sat two evenings ago. He began to weep bitterly, and exclaimed, sobbing, "If she does not come back to me, I will live no longer, but either die of hunger on this rock, or cast myself headlong into the waves, and end my miserable life in the depths of the sea."

I know not how long he sat thus on the rock in his distress, but at last he felt a soft warm hand laid upon his forehead. When he looked up, he saw the maiden before him, and she said tenderly, "I have seen your bitter suffering and heard your longing sighs, and could not withdraw myself longer, though the time does not expire till to-morrow night."

"Forgive me, forgive me, dear maiden," stammered Sleepy Tony. "Forgive me; I was a mad fool not to accept the proffered happiness. The devil only knows what folly came into my head two nights ago. Carry me whither you please. I will oppose you no longer, and would joyfully give up my very life for your sake."

The mermaid answered smiling, "I do not desire your death, but I will take you living as my dear companion." She took the youth by the hand, led him a few paces nearer to the sea, and bound a silk handkerchief over his eyes. Immediately Sleepy Tony felt himself embraced by two strong arms, which raised him up as if in flight, and then plunged headlong into the sea. The moment the cold water touched his body, he lost all consciousness, and knew nothing more of what was happening around him; nor was he afterwards able to tell how long this insensibility lasted.

When he awoke, he was to experience something stranger still.

He found himself lying on soft cushions in a silken bed, which stood in a beautiful chamber, with walls of glass covered on the inside with curtains of red satin, lest the glaring light should wake the sleeper. Some time passed before he could make out whether he was still alive, or whether he was in some unknown region of the dead. He rocked his limbs to and fro, took the end of his nose between his fingers, and behold, he was quite unchanged. He was dressed in a white shirt, and handsome clothes lay in a chair in front of his bed. After lying in bed for some time, and feeling himself all over to make sure that he was really alive, he got up and dressed himself.

Presently he coughed, when two maids entered, who greeted him as "his lordship," and wished to know what he would like for breakfast. One laid the table, and the other went to prepare the food. In a short time the table was loaded with dishes of pork, sausage, black puddings, and honey, with jugs of beer and mead, just the same as at a grand wedding-feast. Sleepy Tony, who had eaten nothing for several days before, now set to work in earnest, and ate his fill, after which he laid down on the bed to digest it. When he got up again, the waiting-maids came back, and invited his lordship to take a walk in the garden while her ladyship was dressing. He heard himself called "your lordship" so often, that he already began to feel himself such in reality, and forgot his former station.

In the garden he met with beauty and elegance at every step; gold and silver apples glittered among the green leaves, and even the fir and pine cones were of gold, while birds of golden plumage hopped among the twigs and branches. Two maids came from behind a bush, who were commissioned to show his lordship round the garden, and to point out all its beauties. They went farther, and reached the edge of a pond where silver-feathered geese and swans were swimming. A rosy flush as of dawn filled all the sky, but the sun was not visible. The bushes were covered with flowers which exhaled a delicious odour, and bees as large as hornets flew among the flowers. All the flowers and shrubs which our friend beheld here were far more beautiful than he had ever seen before. Presently two elegantly dressed girls appeared, who invited his lordship to meet her ladyship, who was expecting him. But first they threw a blue silken shawl over his shoulders. Who would have recognised the former Sleepy Tony in such a guise?

In a beautiful hall, as large as a church, and built of glass like the bedroom, sat twelve fair maidens on silver chairs. Against the wall behind them was a dais on which two golden thrones were placed. On one throne sat the august queen, and the other was unoccupied. When Sleepy Tony crossed the threshold, all the maidens rose from their seats and saluted him respectfully, and did not sit down again until desired to do so. The lady herself remained seated, bent her head to the youth in salutation, and signed with her finger, upon which Sleepy Tony's attendants took him between them, and conducted him to their mistress. The youth advanced with faltering steps, and did not venture to lift his eyes, for he was dazzled with all the unaccustomed splendour and magnificence. He was shown to his place on the golden throne next to the lady, and she said, "This young man is my beloved bridegroom, to whom I have plighted myself and whom I have accepted as my consort. You must show him every respect, and obey him as you obey me. Whenever I leave the house, you must amuse him and look after him and guard him as the apple of my eye. You will be severely punished if you neglect to carry out my orders exactly."

Sleepy Tony looked round him like one dazed, for he did not know what to make of the adventures of the night, which were more wonderful than wonder itself. He continually turned the question over in his mind as to whether he was awake or dreaming. The lady noticed his confusion, and rose from her throne, took him by the hand, and led him from one room to another, all of which were untenanted. At last they arrived at the twelfth chamber, which was rather smaller, but handsomer than the others. Here the lady took her crown from her head, cast aside the gold-embroidered mantle, and when Sleepy Tony ventured to raise his eyes, he recognised that it was the mermaid at his side, and no strange lady. Oh, how quickly his courage rose and his hopes revived! He cried out joyfully, "O dear mermaid!"—but the maiden laid her hand on his mouth, and spoke very earnestly, "If you have any regard for your own happiness or for mine, never call me by that name, which has only been given to me in mockery. I am one of the daughters of the Water-Mother. There are many sisters of us, but we all live apart, each in her own place, in the sea, or in lakes and rivers, and we only see each other occasionally by some fortunate chance." She then explained to him that she had hitherto remained unmarried, but now that she was an established ruler, she must assume the dignity of a royal matron. Sleepy Tony was so bewildered with this unimagined good fortune that he did not know how to express his happiness. His tongue seemed paralysed, and he could not manage to say more than Yes or No. But while he was enjoying a capital dinner and delicious beverages, his tongue was loosened, and he was not only able to talk as well as before, but to indulge in many pleasant jests.

This agreeable life was continued on the next and on the third day, and Sleepy Tony thought he had been exalted to heaven in his living body. But before retiring to rest the mermaid said to him, "To-morrow will be Thursday, and every week I am bound by a vow to fast, and to remain apart from every one. You cannot see me at all on Thursdays until the cock has crowed thrice in the evening. My attendants will sing to you to pass the time away, and will see that you want for nothing."

Next morning Sleepy Tony could not find his consort anywhere. He remembered what she had told him the evening before, that he must pass this and all future Thursdays without her. The waiting-maids exerted themselves to amuse him in every possible manner; they sang, played, and performed elegant dances, and then set before him such food and drink that no prince by birthright could have enjoyed better, and the day passed quicker than he had expected. After supper he laid himself to rest, and when the cock had crowed three times, the fair one returned to him. The same thing happened on every following Thursday. He often implored his beloved to allow him to fast with her on Thursdays, but all to no purpose. He troubled his consort again on a Wednesday with this request, and allowed her no rest; but the mermaid said, with tears in her eyes, "Take my life, if you please; I would lay it down cheerfully; but I cannot and dare not yield to your wish to take you with me on my fast-days."

A year or more might have passed in this manner, when doubts arose in the mind of Sleepy Tony, which became always more tormenting, and allowed him no peace. His food became distasteful to him and his sleep refreshed him not. He feared lest the mermaid might have some other lover in secret besides himself, in whose arms she passed every Thursday, while he was obliged to pass his time with the waiting-maids. He had long ago discovered the room in which the mermaid hid herself on Thursdays, but how did that help him? The door was always locked, and the windows were so closely hung with double curtains on the inside that there was not an opening left as large as a needle's eye through which a sunbeam, much less a human eye, could penetrate. But the more impossible it seemed to penetrate this secret, the more eager grew his longing to get to the very bottom of it. Although he never breathed a word of the weight upon his mind to the mermaid, she could see from his altered manner that all was not as it should be. Again and again she implored him with tears in her eyes not to torment both himself and her with evil thoughts. "I am free from every fault against you," she declared, "and I have no secret love nor any other sin against you on my conscience. But your false suspicion makes us both miserable, and will destroy the peace of our hearts. I would gladly give up every moment of my life to you if you wished it, but I cannot allow you to come near me on my fast-days. It cannot be, for it would put an end to our love and happiness for ever. We are able to live quietly and happily together for six days in the week, and how should the separation of one day be so heavy that you cannot bear it?"

She talked in this sensible way for six days, but when the following Thursday came, and the mermaid did not show herself, Sleepy Tony lost his wits, and behaved as if he was half-mad. He knew no peace, and at last one Thursday he refused to have any one with him. He ordered the waiting-maids to bring him his food and drink, and then to leave him directly, so that he remained alone like a spectre.

This great alteration in his conduct astonished everybody, and when the mermaid heard of the matter, she almost wept her eyes out of her head, though she only gave way to her grief when no one was present. Sleepy Tony hoped that when he was alone he might have a better opportunity of inspecting the secret fasting chamber, and perhaps he might find some crack through which he could spy upon what was going on. The more he tormented himself, the more depressed became the mermaid, and although she still maintained a cheerful countenance, her friendliness no longer came from the heart as before.

Some weeks passed by, and matters remained at a standstill, neither worse nor better, when one Thursday Sleepy Tony found a small space near the window where the curtains had slightly shifted, so that he could look into the chamber. The secret chamber had no floor, but looked like a great square tank, filled with water many feet deep. Herein swam his much-loved mermaid. From her head to her middle she was a beautiful woman, but from the navel downwards she was wholly a fish, covered with scales and provided with fins. Sometimes she threshed the water with her broad fish's tail and it dashed high up.

The spy shrunk back confounded and made his way home very sorrowfully. What would he not have given to have blotted the sight from his memory! He thought of one thing and another, but could not decide on what to do.

In the evening the cock crowed three times as usual, but the mermaid did not come back to him. He lay awake all night, but the fair one never came. She did not return till morning, when she was clad in black mourning garments and her face was covered with a thin silk handkerchief. Then she said, weeping, "O thou unhappy one! to have brought our happy life to an end by thy folly! Thou seest me to-day for the last time, and must return to thy former condition, and this thou hast brought upon thyself. Farewell, for the last time."

There was a sudden crash and a tremendous noise, as if the floor was giving way beneath his feet, and Sleepy Tony was hurled down stunned, and could not perceive what was happening to himself or about him.

No one knows how long afterwards it may have been when he recovered from his swoon, and found himself on the sea-shore close to the rock on which the fair mermaid had sat when she entered into the bond of friendship with him. Instead of the magnificent robes which be had worn every day in the dwelling of the mermaid, he found himself dressed in his old clothes, which were now much older and more ragged than he could possibly have supposed. Our friend's happy days were over, and no remorse, however bitter, could bring them back.

He walked on till he reached the first houses of his village. They were standing in the same places, but yet looked different. But what appeared to him much more wonderful when he looked round, was that the people were all strangers, and he did not meet a single face which he knew.

The people all looked strangely at him, too, as though he was a monster. Sleepy Tony went on to the farm of his parents, but here too he encountered only strangers, who knew him not, and whom he did not know. He asked in amazement for his father and brothers, but no one could tell him anything about them. At length an infirm old man came up, leaning on a stick, and said, "Peasant, the farmer whom you ask after has been sleeping in the ground for more than thirty years, and his sons must be dead too. How comes it, my good old man, that you ask after people who have been so long forgotten?" The words "old man" took Sleepy Tony so much aback that he was unable to ask another question. He felt his limbs trembling, turned his back on the strange people, and went out at the gate. The expression "old man" left him no peace; it fell upon him with a crushing weight, and his feet refused him their office.

He hurried to the nearest spring and gazed in the water. The pale sunken cheeks, the hollow eyes, the long grey beard and grey hair, confirmed what he had heard. This worn-out, withered form no longer bore the slightest resemblance to the youth whom the mermaid had chosen as her consort. Now he fully realised his misery for the first time, and knew that the few years that he appeared to have been absent had comprised the greater part of his life, for he had entered the mermaid's house as a vigorous youth, and had returned as a spectre-like old man. There he had felt nothing of the course of time or of the wasting of his body, and he could not comprehend how the burden of old age had fallen upon him so suddenly, like the passing of a bird's wing. What could he do now, when he was a grey stranger among strangers?

He wandered about on the beach for a few days, from one farm to another, and good people gave him a piece of bread out of charity. He chanced to meet with a friendly young fellow, to whom he related all the adventures of his life, but the same night he disappeared. A few days afterwards the waves cast up his body on the shore. It is not known whether he threw himself into the sea, or was drowned by accident.

After this the behaviour of the mermaid towards mankind entirely changed. She sometimes appears to children only, most often in another form, but she does not permit grown-up people to approach her, but shuns them like fire.

Kreutzwald.

Source:
Kirby, W. F. *The Hero of Esthonia, Volume 2.* London: John C. Nimmo, 1895.

102. The Lake-Dwellers

Estonia

MANY years ago a man was driving over a lake with his little son before the ice was properly formed. It broke, and they all sank in the water, when an old man with silver-grey hair came up, and upbraided them for breaking through the winter roof of his palace. He told the man that he must stay with him, but he would give him a grey horse and a sledge with golden runners, that he might drive about under the ice in autumn, and make a noise to warn others that it was unsafe until Father Taara had strengthened it sufficiently. But he would help the boy and the horse above the ice, for they were not to blame. When the water-god had brought them from under the ice, he told the boy to go home, and not to mourn for his father, who would be very happy under the water, and to be careful not to drop anything out of the sledge. On reaching home, be found two lumps of ice in the sledge, and threw them out, but when they struck against a stone and did not break, he discovered that they were lumps of pure silver. He had now plenty to live upon comfortably; but every autumn when the lake was covered with young ice, he went to it, hoping to see or hear something of his father. The ice often cracked and heaved just before his footsteps, as if his father was trying to speak to him, but there was no other sign.

Many years passed by, and the son grew old and grey. One day he went to the lake as usual, and sat down sorrowfully on a stone, just where the river falls into it, and great tears rolled down his cheeks. Suddenly he saw, on raising his eyes, a great door of silver with golden lattice-work close to the mouth of the river. He rose up and went to it, and he had scarcely touched it when it sprang open. He hesitated a moment and then entered, and found himself in a gloomy gallery of bronze. He went some distance, and presently reached a second door like the former, but much higher. Before it stood a dwarf with a broad stone hat on his head and bronze armour. He wore a copper girdle round his waist, and held in his hand a copper halbert about six feet long. "I suppose you have come to see your father?" he said in a friendly manner.

"Yes, indeed, my good man," answered the other. "Can you not help me to see him or meet him? I am already an old man myself, and my life grows ever more lonely."

"I must not make any promises," said the dwarf, "and it is about time for your father to fulfil his office. Hark, he is just driving off in his golden sledge with the grey horse, to warn mortals against treading incautiously on our delicate silver roof. But as you have once before been our guest, and have ventured to come again, I will show you the house and grounds of the water-world. None of our people are at home to-day, neither the gentry nor the household, so that we can go through the rooms without interference."

As he spoke he touched the door, and the old man and his guide entered a vast and splendid palace of crystal. There they saw a great crowd of men, women, and children walking about, or sitting talking, or amusing themselves; but none of them noticed or addressed the newcomers. Presently the dwarf led the old man farther into the hall. All the fittings were of bright gold and silver, and the floor was of copper, and the farther they advanced the brighter everything shone, without any apparent end.

At last the old man asked to turn back, and the dwarf said, "It is well that you mentioned it, for a little farther on the gold shines so brilliantly that the eyes of mortal men cannot endure it. And there dwells our good and mighty king, with his noble consort, surrounded by the bold heroes and lovely dames of our realm."

"You told me the gentry and dependants were not at home," said the old man, "but who were all the people who were talking and laughing near the door, and the children who were playing with all manner of costly toys of gold and silver? Don't they belong to your people?"

"Half-way indeed, but not quite," said the dwarf. "They are, if I may be permitted to tell you, people from your world, who all sank into our kingdom, sooner or later. But they live a very pleasant life here, and have no wish to return to your world, even if they were permitted. For whoever comes to our kingdom must stay with us."

"Must I stay here too?" asked the old man startled, not knowing what preparations he had to make for the life below.

"Do you find our home so bad?" asked the dwarf. "But fear nothing, and don't alarm yourself. This day you can go or stay, as you please. I led you in freely, and will lead you out freely. But this is the first time that a mortal man has been permitted to leave our abode."

Then the old man asked, "Shall I never see my father again?" and tears stood in his eyes once more.

The dwarf answered, "You would not see him again till after three weeks, when the ice has become strong and firm. Your father will then have finished his work for the year, and can pass his time pleasantly with us till another year has passed, and he must again perform his office for a month."

"Must he then do this work for ever, and remember his misfortune every year?" asked the old man sadly.

The dwarf answered, "He must perform this duty till another mortal accidentally damages our roof and sinks down himself. Then is the first man released from his journeying under the young ice, and the other must henceforth take the work upon himself."

As they were thus conversing, the old man and his guide reached the gate. Then they looked in each other's faces, and the dwarf gave the old man two rods of copper with a friendly smile, and said, "If you ever come to this gate, and don't find me on guard, but some one whom you don't know, strike these rods together, and I will do what you wish, as far as I can."

Then he led his guest through the lofty gate, and accompanied him through the bronze passage to the outer gate, and opened it. Then the old man found himself standing again on the banks of the lake near the mouth of the river, as if he had fallen from the clouds. The door had vanished, but the rods in his hand showed him that what he had seen was a reality. He put them in his pocket, and wandered home sunk in deep thought, and dazed like a drunken man. But here he found no rest or pleasure in anything. He went to the mouth of the river on the lake daily for three weeks, and sat on the rock as if in a dream; and at last he disappeared, and never came home again.

Jannsen.

NOTES

Kreutzwald relates that every autumn a little grey man, who lives in the Ülemiste järv, rises from it to see if the new buildings are sufficiently decorated. When he has finished his inspection, he returns to the lake; but if he was so dissatisfied as to turn his head in the opposite direction, evil would come on Tallin (Revel), for the low-lying country would be inundated, and the town would be destroyed.

Source:
Kirby, W. F. *The Hero of Esthonia, Volume 2.* London: John C. Nimmo, 1895.

103. The Faithless Fisherman

Estonia

A FISHERMAN was sleeping on the sand, by the Baltic, when a stranger roused him, telling him that the sea was full of fish. They fished together all day, when the boat was filled, and the stranger sent the fisherman to sell the fish, insisting that he should bring him half the profits, and give the other half to his own wife. Next day they would go fishing again. This went on day after day, and the stranger regularly received half the proceeds of the work, giving back a trifle to the fisherman in return for the use of the boat and tackle. When everything was arranged, he used to disappear behind a large stone.

Thus the fisherman became rich. He built himself a cottage, and bought a new boat, and sometimes he indulged in a glass to quench his thirst.

One day it occurred to him to give his partner less than his due; but next day the results of their fishing were much smaller, and the stranger looked at him sorrowfully. In the evening the fisherman went to sell the fish, but gave his partner still less than the day before. Next day, when they cast the nets, they did not take a single fish, and the stranger said, "You have cheated me two days running, and now you must die." He then threw the fisherman overboard, and two days afterwards his body was found on the beach and buried. As his wife stood weeping by his grave, a tall, strong man approached, who told her to dry her tears; for if he had not drowned her husband, he would have died on the gallows. He then gave her a bag of money, telling her that her husband had gained it honestly, and that he was the water-sprite. Then he disappeared, leaving the money, and the widow went home and lived happily with her children.

Jannsen.

NOTES

Another curious story relative to water-sprites is that of the mermaid and the lord of Pahlen (Kreutzwald). The latter found the maiden sitting on a stone by the sea-shore, and lamenting because her father, the king of the sea, compelled her to raise storms, in which many people perished, in order to please the Mother of the Winds. The nobleman freed her from her trouble by breaking the ring with which she raised the storms with his teeth, and she rewarded him with two large barrels of gold.

Source:
Kirby, W. F. *The Hero of Esthonia, Volume 2*. London: John C. Nimmo, 1895.

104. Russian Water Spirits
by W.R.S. Ralston

Russia

THE Rusalkas are female water-spirits, who occupy a position which corresponds in many respects with that filled by the elves and fairies of Western Europe. The origin of their name seems to be doubtful, but it appears to be connected with *rus*, an old Slavonic word for a stream, or with *ruslo*, the bed of a river, and with several other kindred words, such as *rosá*, dew, which have reference to water. They are generally represented under the form of beauteous maidens with full and snow-white bosoms, and with long and slender limbs. Their feet are small, their eyes are wild, their faces are fair to see, but their complexion is pale, their expression anxious. Their hair is long and thick and wavy, and green as is the grass. Their dress is either a covering of green leaves, or a long white shift, worn without a girdle. At times they emerge from the waters of the lake or river in which they dwell, and sit upon its banks, combing and plaiting their flowing locks, or they cling to a mill-wheel; and turn round with it amid the splash of the stream. If any one happens to approach, they fling themselves into the waters, and there divert themselves, and try to allure him to join them. Whomsoever they get hold of they tickle to death.[1] Witches alone can bathe with them unhurt.

In certain districts bordering on the sea the people believe, or used to believe, in marine Rusalkas, who are supposed, in some places, as, for instance, about Astrakhan, to raise storms and vex shipping. But as a general rule the Rusalkas are looked upon in Russia as haunting lakes and streams, at the bottom of which they usually dwell in crystal halls, radiant with gold and silver and precious stones. Sometimes, however, they are not so sumptuously housed, but have to make for themselves nests out of straw and feathers collected during the "Green Week," the seventh after Easter. If a Rusalka's hair becomes dry she dies, and therefore she is generally afraid of going far from the water, unless, indeed, she has a comb with her. So long as she has a comb she can always produce a flood by passing it through her waving locks.

In some places they are fond of spinning, in others they are given to washing linen. During the week before Whitsuntide, as many songs testify, they sit upon trees, and ask for linen garments. Up to the present

---

[1] The verb *Shchekotat'* originally meant to utter loud, piercing sounds, to laugh shrilly, and afterwards acquired the sense of to do what produces shrill laughter, to tickle. See Afanasief, P. V. S. II. 339.

day, in Little-Russia, it is customary to hang on the boughs of oaks and other trees, at that time of year, shifts and rags and skeins of thread, all intended as a present to the Rusalkas. In White-Russia the peasants affirm that during that week the forests are traversed by naked women and children, and whoever meets them, if he wishes to escape a premature death, must fling them a handkerchief, or some scrap torn from his dress.

On the approach of winter the Rusalkas disappear, and do not show themselves again until it is over. In Little-Russia they are supposed to appear on the Thursday in Holy Week, a day which in olden times was dear to them, as well as to many other spiritual beings. In the Ukraine the Thursday before Whitsuntide is called the Great Day, or Easter Sunday, of the Rusalkas. During the days called the "Green Svyatki," at Whitsuntide, when every home is adorned with boughs and green leaves, no one dares to work for fear of offending the Rusalkas. Especially must women abstain from sewing or washing linen; and men from weaving fences and the like, such occupations too closely resembling those of the supernatural weavers and washers. It is chiefly at that time that the spirits leave their watery abodes, and go strolling about the fields and forests, continuing to do so until the end of June. All that time their voices may be heard in the rustling or sighing of the breeze, and the splash of running water betrays their dancing feet. At that time the peasant-girls go into the woods, and throw garlands to the Rusalkas, asking for rich husbands in return, or float them down a stream, seeing in their movements omens of future happiness or sorrow.

After St. Peter's day, June 29, the Rusalkas dance by night beneath the moon, and in Little-Russia and Galicia, where Rusalkas (or Mavki as they are there called) have danced, circles of darker, and of richer grass are found in the fields. Sometimes they induce a shepherd to play to them. All night long they dance to his music: in the morning a hollow marks the spot where his foot has beaten time. Sometimes a man encounters Rusalkas who begin to writhe and contort themselves after a strange fashion. Involuntarily he imitates their gestures, and for the rest of his life he is deformed, or is a victim to St. Vitus' dance. Any one who treads upon the linen which the Rusalkas have laid out to dry loses all his strength, or becomes a cripple; those who desecrate the *Rusalnaya* (or Rusalkas') week by working are punished by the loss of their cattle and poultry. At times the Rusalkas entice into their haunts both youths and maidens, and tickle them to death, or strangle or drown them.

The Rusalkas have much to do with the harvest, sometimes making it plenteous, and at other times ruining it by rain and wind. The peasants in White-Russia say that the Rusalkas dwell amid the standing corn; and in Little-Russia it is believed that on Whit-Sunday Eve they go out to the corn-fields, and there, with joyous singing and clapping of hands, they scamper through the rye or hang on to its stalks, and swing to and fro, so that the corn undulates as if beneath a strong wind.

In some parts of Russia there is performed, immediately after the end of the Whitsuntide festival, the ceremony of expelling the Rusalkas. On the first Monday of the "Peter's Fast" a figure made of straw is draped in woman's clothes, so as to represent a Rusalka. Afterwards a Khorovod is formed, and the assembled company go out to the fields with dance and song, she who holds the straw Rusalka in her hand bounding about in the middle of the choral circle. On arriving at the fields the singers form two bodies, one of which attacks the figure, while the other defends it. Eventually it is torn to pieces, and the straw of which it was made is thrown to the winds, after which the performers return home, saying they have expelled the Rusalka. In the Government of Tula the women and girls go out to the fields during the "Green Week," and chase the Rusalka, who is supposed to be stealing the grain. Having made a straw figure, they take it to the banks of a stream and fling it into the water. In some districts the young people run about the fields on Whit-Sunday Eve, waving brooms, and crying, "Pursue! pursue!" There are people who affirm that they have seen the hunted Rusalkas running out of the corn-fields into the woods, and have heard their sobs and cries.

Besides the full-grown Rusalkas there are little ones, having the appearance of seven-year-old girls. These are supposed, by the Russian peasants, to be the ghosts of still-born children, or such as have died before there was time to baptize them. Such children the Rusalkas are in the habit of stealing after death, taking them from their graves, or even from the cottages in which they lie, and carrying them off to their subaqueous dwellings. Every Whitsuntide, for seven successive years, the souls of these children fly about, asking to be christened. If any person who hears one of them lamenting will exclaim, "I baptize thee in the name of the Father, and of the Son, and of the Holy Ghost," the soul of that child will be saved, and will go straight to heaven. A religious service, annually performed on the first Monday of the "Peter's Fast," in behalf of an unbaptized child will be equally efficacious. But if the stray soul, during seven years, neither hears the baptismal formula pronounced, nor feels the effect of the divine service, it becomes enrolled for ever in the ranks of the Rusalkas. The same fate befalls those babes whom their mothers have cursed before they were born, or in the interval between their birth and their baptism. Such small Rusalkas, who abound among the Little-Russian Mavki, are evidently akin to our own fairies. Like them they make the grass grow richly where they dance, they float on the water in egg-shells, and some of them are sadly troubled by doubts about a future state. At least it is believed in the Government of Astrakhan that the sea Rusalkas come to the surface and ask mariners, "Is the end of the world near at hand?" Besides the children of whom mention has been made, women who kill themselves, and all those who are drowned, choked, or strangled, and who do not obtain Christian burial, are liable to become Rusalkas. During the Rusalka week the relatives of drowned or strangled persons go out to their graves, taking with them pancakes, and spirits, and red eggs. The eggs are broken, and the spirits poured over the graves, after which the remnants are left for the Rusalkas, these lines being sung:—

> Queen Rusalka,
> Maiden fair,
> Do not destroy the soul,
> Do not cause it to be choked,
> And we will make obeisance to thee.

On the people who forget to do this the Rusalkas will wreak their vengeance.[1] In the Saratof Government the Rusalkas are held in bad repute. There they are described as hideous, humpbacked, hairy creatures, with sharp claws, and an iron hook with which they try to seize on passers-by. If any one ventures to bathe in a river on Whit-Sunday, without having uttered a preliminary prayer, they instantly drag him down to the bottom. Or if he goes into a wood without taking a handful of wormwood (*Poluin*), he runs a serious risk, for the Rusalkas may ask him, "What have you got in your hands? is it *Poluin* or *Petrushka* (Parsley)." If he replies *Poluin*, they cry, "Hide under the tuin (hedge)," and he is safe. But if he says, *Petrushka*, they exclaim affectionately, "Ah! my *dushka*," and begin tickling him till he foams at the mouth. In either case they seem to be greatly under the influence of rhyme.

In the vicinity of the Dnieper the peasants believe that the wild-fires which are sometimes seen at night flickering above graves, or around the tumuli called Kurgáns, or in woods and swampy places, are lighted by the Rusalkas, who wish thereby to allure incautious travellers to their ruin; but in many places these wandering "Wills o' the Wisp" are regarded as being the souls of unbaptized children, and so small Rusalkas themselves. In many parts of Russia the Rusalkas are represented in the songs of the people as propounding riddles to girls, and tickling and teasing those who cannot answer them. Sometimes the Rusalkas are asked similar questions, which they answer at once, being very sharp-witted.

****

The traditions of the Russian peasants people the waters with other spiritual inhabitants besides the Rusalkas. Their songs and stories often speak of the Tsar Morskoi, the Marine or Water King, who dwells in the depths of the sea, or the lake, or the pool, and who rules over the subaqueous world. To this Slavonic Neptune a family of daughters is frequently attributed, maidens of exceeding beauty, who, when they don

---

[1] Afanasief, P. V. S. III. 244.

their feather dresses, become the Swan Maidens who figure in the popular literature of so many nations. These graceful creatures, however, as well as their royal parent, belong to the realm of the peasant's imagination rather than to that of his belief. But this is not the case with the spirits who are called *Vodyanuie*, the male counterparts of the Rusalkas. In them he still believes, and of them he often stands in considerable awe.

The Vodyany, or Water-sprite, like his kin spirit the Domovoy, is affectionately called *Dyedushka*, or Grandfather, by the peasants. He generally inhabits the depths of rivers, lakes, or pools; but sometimes he dwells in swamps, and he is specially fond of taking up his quarters in a mill-stream, close to the wheel. Every mill is supposed to have a Vodyany attached to it, or several if it has more wheels than one. Consequently millers are generally obliged to be well-versed in the black art, for if they do not understand how to treat the water-spirits all will go ill with them.

The Vodyany is represented by the people as a naked old man, with a great paunch and a bloated face. He is much given to drinking, and delights in carouses and card-playing. He is a patron of bee-keeping, and it is customary to enclose the first swarm of the year in a bag, and to throw it, weighted with a stone, into the nearest river, as an offering to him. He who does this will flourish as a bee-master, especially if he takes a honeycomb from a hive on St. Zosima's day, and flings it at midnight into a millstream.

The water-sprites have their subaqueous dwellings well-stocked with all sorts of cattle, which they drive out into the fields to graze by night. They have wives and children too, under the waves, the former sometimes being women who have been drowned, or whom a parent's curse has placed within the power of the Evil One. Many a girl who has drowned herself has been turned into a Rusalka or some such being, and then has married a Vodyany. On the occasion of such a marriage, or indeed of any subaqueous wedding, the Vodyanies indulge in such revels and mad pranks that the waters are wildly agitated, and often carry away bridges or mill-dams; at least, that is how the peasants explain such accidents as arise when the snows melt and the streams wax violent. When a water-sprite's wife is about to bear a child he assumes the appearance of an ordinary mortal, and fetches a midwife from some neighbouring village to attend her. Once a water-baby was caught by some fishermen in their nets. It splashed about joyously as long as it was in the water, but wailed sorely when it was taken into a cottage. Its capturers returned it to its father on his promising to drive plenty of fish into their nets in future—a promise which he conscientiously fulfilled. Here is one of the stories about a mixed marriage beneath the waves. Except at the end, it is very like that which forms the groundwork of Mr. Matthew Arnold's exquisite romaunt of "The Forsaken Merman." "Once upon a time a girl was drowned, and she lived for many years after that with a water-sprite. But one fine day she swam to the shore, and saw the red sun, and the green woods and fields, and heard the humming of insects and the distant sound of church-bells. Then a longing after her old life on earth came over her, and she could not resist the temptation. So she came out from the water, and went to her native village. But there neither her relatives nor her friends recognized her. Sadly did she return in the evening to the water-side, and passed once more into the power of the water-sprite. Two days later her mutilated corpse floated on to the sands, while the river roared and was wildly agitated. The remorseful water-sprite was lamenting his irrevocable loss."[1]

When a Vodyany appears in a village it is easy to recognize him, for water is always dripping from his left skirt, and the spot on which he sits instantly becomes wet. In his own realm he not only rules over all the fishes that swim, but he greatly influences the lot of fishers and mariners. Sometimes he brings them good luck; sometimes he lures them to destruction. Sometimes he gets caught in nets, but he immediately tears them asunder, and all the fish that had been enclosed in them swim out after him. A fisherman once found a dead body floating about in the water, so he took it into his boat. But to his horror the corpse suddenly came to life, uttered a wild laugh, and jumped overboard. That was one of the Vodyany's pranks. A sportsman once waded into a river after a wounded duck. The Vodyany got hold of him by the neck, and would have pulled him under if he had not cut himself loose with his axe. When he got home his neck was all over blue marks left by the Vodyany's fingers. Sometimes the Vodyany will jump on a horse and ride it to death; so, to keep him away while horses are fording a river, the peasants sign a cross on the water with a knife or a scythe. One should not bathe, say the peasants, without a cross round one's neck, or after sunset. Especially dangerous is it to bathe during the week in which falls the feast of the Prophet Ilya (Elijah, formerly Rerun, the Thunderer), for then the Vodyany is on the look out for victims. During the day he generally lies at the bottom of the deep pools, but at night he sits on the shore combing his hair, or he sports in the water, diving with a splash and coming up far away; sometimes, also, he fights with the wood-sprites, the noise of their combats being heard afar off. In Bohemia fishermen are afraid of assisting a drowning man, thinking the Vodyany will be offended and will drive away the fish from their nets; and they say he often sits on the shore with a club in his hand, from which hang ribbons of various hues: with these he allures children, and those whom be gets bold of be drowns, The souls of his victims the Vodyany keeps, making them his Servants, but their bodies he allows to float to shore.

Sometimes he changes himself into a fish, generally a pike. Sometimes, also, he is represented, like the western Merman, with a

---

[1] Afanasief, P. V. S. II. 239.

fish's tail. In the Ukraine there is a tradition that, when the sea is rough, such half-fishy "marine people" appear on the surface of the water and sing songs. The *Chumaki* (local carriers) go down at such times to the sea-side, and there hear those wonderful songs which they afterwards sing in the towns and villages. In other places these "sea people" are called "Pharaohs," being supposed, like the seals in Iceland, to be the remains of that host of Pharaoh which perished in the Red Sea.

During the winter the Vodyany sleeps, but with the early spring he awakes, wrathful and hungry, and manifests his anger by various spiteful actions. In order to propitiate him the peasants in some places buy a horse, which they feed well for three days; then they tie its legs together, smear its head with honey, adorn its mane with red ribbons, attach two millstones to its neck, and at midnight fling it into an ice-hole, or, if the frost has broken up, into the middle of a river. Three days long has the Vodyany awaited his present, manifesting his impatience by groanings and upheavings of water. After he has received his due he becomes quiet. Fishermen propitiate him at the same season of the year by pouring oil on the water, begging him, as they do so, to be good to them; and millers once a year sacrifice a black pig to him. A goose, also, is generally presented to him in the middle of September, as a return for his having watched over the farmer's ducks and geese during the summer months.

Source:
Ralston, W. R. S. *The Songs of the Russian People*. 2nd edition. London: Ellis & Green, 1872.

105. The Story of Tremsin, the Bird Zhar, and Nastasia, the Lovely Maid of the Sea

Cossack (Russia & Ukraine)

THERE was once upon a time a man and a woman, and they had one little boy. In the summertime they used to go out and mow corn in the fields, and one summer when they had laid their little lad by the side of a sheaf, an eagle swooped down, caught up the child, carried him into a forest, and laid him in its nest. Now in this forest three bandits chanced to be wandering at the same time. They heard the child crying in the eagle's nest: "Oo-oo! oo-oo! oo-oo!" so they went up to the oak on which was the nest and said one to another, "Let us hew down the tree and kill the child!"

"No," replied one of them, "it were better to climb up the tree and bring him down alive." So he climbed up the tree and brought down the lad, and they nurtured him and gave him the name of Tremsin. They brought up Tremsin until he became a youth, and then they gave him a horse, set him upon it, and said to him, "Now go out into the wide world and search for thy father and thy mother!" So Tremsin went out into the wide world and pastured his steed on the vast steppes, and his steed spoke to him and said, "When we have gone a little farther, thou wilt see before thee a plume of the Bird Zhar;[1] pick it not up, or sore trouble will be thine!" Then they went on again. They went on and on, through ten tsardoms they went, till they came to another empire in the land of Thrice Ten where lay the feather. And the youth said to himself, "Why should I not pick up the feather when it shines so brightly even from afar?" And he went near to the feather, and it shone so that the like of it cannot be expressed or conceived or imagined or even told of in tales. Then Tremsin picked up the feather and went into the town over against him, and in that town there lived a rich nobleman. And Tremsin entered the house of this nobleman and said, "Sir, may I not take service with thee as a labourer?"

The nobleman looked at him, and seeing that he was comely and stalwart, "Why not? Of course thou mayst," said he. So he took him into his service. Now this nobleman had many servants, and they curried his horses for him, and made them smart and glossy against the day he should go a-hunting. And Tremsin began to curry his horse likewise, and the servants of the nobleman could not make the horses of their master so shining bright as Tremsin made his own horse. So they looked more closely, and they perceived that when Tremsin cleaned his horse he stroked it with the feather of the Bird Zhar, and the coat of the good steed straightway shone like burnished silver. Then those servants were filled with envy, and said among themselves, "How can we remove this fellow from the world? We'll saddle him with a task he is unable to do, and then our master will drive him away."

So they went to their master and said, "Tremsin has a feather of the Bird Zhar, and he says that if he likes he can get the Bird Zhar itself." Then the nobleman sent for Tremsin and said to him, "O Tremsin! my henchmen say that thou canst get the Bird Zhar if thou dost choose."

"Nay, but I cannot," replied Tremsin.

"Answer me not," said the nobleman, "for so sure as I've a sword, I'll slice thy head off like a gourd."

Then Tremsin fell a-weeping and went away to his horse. "My master," said he, "hath given me a task to do that will clean undo me."

"What task is that?" asked the horse.

"Why, to fetch him the Bird Zhar."

"Why that's not a task, but a trifle," replied the horse. "Let us go to

---

[1] *i.e.* Burning bright.

the steppes," it continued, "and let me go a-browsing; but do thou strip thyself stark-naked and lie down in the grass, and the Bird Zhar will straightway swoop down to feed. So long as she only claws about thy body, touch her not; but as soon as she begins to claw at thine eyes, seize her by the legs."

So when they got to the wild steppes, Tremsin stripped himself naked and flung himself in the grass, and, immediately, the Bird Zhar swooped down and began pecking all about him, and at last she pecked at his eyes. Then Tremsin seized her by both legs, and mounted his horse and took the Bird Zhar to the nobleman. Then his fellow-servants were more envious than ever, and they said among themselves, "How shall we devise for him a task to do that cannot be done, and so rid the world of him altogether?" So they bethought them, and then they went to the nobleman and said, "Tremsin says that to get the Bird Zhar was nothing, and that he is also able to get the thrice-lovely Nastasia of the sea." Then the nobleman again sent for Tremsin and said to him, "Look now! thou didst get for me the Bird Zhar, see that thou now also gettest for me the thrice-lovely Nastasia of the sea."

"But I cannot, sir!" said Tremsin.

"Answer me not so!" replied the nobleman, "for so sure as I've a sword, I'll slice thy head off like a gourd an thou bring her not."

Then Tremsin went out to his horse and fell a-weeping.

"Wherefore dost thou weep?" asked the faithful steed.

"Wherefore should I not weep?" he replied. "My master has given me a task that cannot be done."

"What task is that?"

"Why, to fetch him the thrice-lovely Nastasia of the sea!"

"Oh-ho!" laughed the horse, "that is not a task, but a trifle. Go to thy master and say, 'Cause white tents to be raised by the sea-shore, and buy wares of sundry kinds, and wine and spirits in bottles and flasks,' and the thrice-lovely Nastasia will come and purchase thy wares, and then thou mayst take her."

And the nobleman did so. He caused white tents to be pitched by the sea-shore, and bought kerchiefs and scarves and spread them out gaily, and made great store of wine and brandy in bottles and flasks. Then Tremsin rode toward the tents, and while he was on the way his horse said to him, "Now when I go to graze, do thou lie down and feign to sleep. Then the thrice-lovely Nastasia will appear and say, 'What for thy wares?' but do thou keep silence. But when she begins to taste of the wine and the brandy, then she will go to sleep in the tent, and thou canst catch her easily and hold her fast!" Then Tremsin lay down and feigned to sleep, and forth from the sea came the thrice-lovely Nastasia, and went up to the tents and asked, "Merchant, merchant, what for thy wares?" But he lay there, and moved never a limb. She asked the same thing over and over again, but, getting no answer, went into the tents where stood the flasks and the bottles. She tasted of the wine. How good it was! She tasted of the brandy. That was still better. So from tasting she fell to drinking. First she drank a little, and then she drank a little more, and at last she went asleep in the tent. Then Tremsin seized the thrice-lovely Nastasia and put her behind him on horseback, and carried her off to the nobleman. The nobleman praised Tremsin exceedingly, but the thrice-lovely Nastasia said, "Look now! since thou hast found the feather of the Bird Zhar, and the Bird Zhar herself, since also thou hast found me, thou must now fetch me also my little coral necklace from the sea!" Then Tremsin went out to his faithful steed and wept sorely, and told him all about it. And the horse said to him, "Did I not tell thee that grievous woe would come upon thee if thou didst pick up that feather?" But the horse added, "Come! weep not! after all 'tis not a task, but a trifle." Then they went along by the sea, and the horse said to him, "Let me out to graze, and then keep watch till thou seest a crab come forth from the sea, and then say to him, 'I'll catch thee.'"

So Tremsin let his horse out to graze, and he himself stood by the seashore, and watched and watched till he saw a crab come swimming along. Then he said to the crab, "I'll catch thee."

"Oh! seize me not!" said the crab, "but let me get back into the sea, and I'll be of great service to thee."

"Very well," said Tremsin, "but thou must get me from the sea the coral necklace of the thrice-lovely Nastasia," and with that he let the crab go back into the sea again. Then the crab called together all her young crabs, and they collected all the coral and brought it ashore, and gave it to Tremsin. Then the faithful steed came running up, and Tremsin mounted it, and took the coral to the thrice-lovely Nastasia. "Well," said Nastasia, "thou hast got the feather of the Bird Zhar, thou hast got the Bird Zhar itself, thou hast got me my coral, get me now from the sea my herd of wild horses!"

Then Tremsin was sore distressed, and went to his faithful steed and wept bitterly, and told him all about it. "Well," said the horse, "this time 'tis no trifle, but a real hard task. Go now to thy master, and bid him buy twenty hides, and twenty poods[1] of pitch, and twenty poods of flax, and twenty poods of hair."

So Tremsin went to his master and told him, and his master bought it all. Then Tremsin loaded his horse with all this, and to the sea they went together. And when they came to the sea the horse said, "Now lay upon me the hides and the tar and the flax, and lay them in this order—first a hide, and then a pood of tar, and then a pood of flax, and so on, laying them thus till they are all laid." Tremsin did so. "And now," said the horse, "I shall plunge into the sea, and when thou seest a large red wave driving toward the shore, run away till the red wave has passed and thou dost see a white wave coming, and then sit down on the shore and keep

---

[1] A pood = 40 lb.

watch. I shall then come out of the sea, and after me the whole herd; then thou must strike with the horsehair the horse which gallops immediately after me, and he will not be too strong for thee."

So the faithful steed plunged into the sea, and Tremsin sat down on the shore and watched. The horse swam to a bosquet that rose out of the sea, and there the herd of sea-horses was grazing. When the strong charger of Nastasia saw him and the hides he carried on his back, it set off after him at full tilt, and the whole herd followed the strong charger of Nastasia. They drove the horse with the hides into the sea, and pursued him. Then the strong charger of Nastasia caught up the steed of Tremsin and tore off one of his hides, and began to worry it with his teeth and tear it to fragments as he ran. Then he caught him up a second time, and tore off another hide, and began to worry that in like manner till he had torn it also to shreds; and thus he ran after Tremsin's steed for seventy miles, till he had torn off all the hides, and worried them to bits. But Tremsin sat upon the sea-shore till he saw the large white billow bounding in, and behind the billow came his own horse, and behind his own horse came the thrice-terrible charger of the thrice-lovely Nastasia, with the whole herd at his heels. Tremsin struck him full on the forehead with the twenty poods of hair, and immediately he stood stock still. Then Tremsin threw a halter over him, mounted, and drove the whole herd to the thrice-lovely Nastasia. Nastasia praised Tremsin for his prowess, and said to him, "Well, thou hast got the feather of the Bird Zhar, thou hast got the Bird Zhar itself, thou hast got me my coral and my herd of horses, now milk my mare and put the milk into three vats, so that there may be milk hot as boiling water in the first vat, lukewarm milk in the second vat, and icy cold milk in the third vat." Then Tremsin went to his faithful steed and wept bitterly, and the horse said to him, "Wherefore dost thou weep?"

"Why should I not weep?" cried he; "the thrice-lovely Nastasia has given me a task to do that cannot be done. I am to fill three vats with the milk from her mare, and the milk must be boiling hot in the first vat, and lukewarm in the second, and icy cold in the third vat."

"Oh-ho!" cried the horse, "that is not a task, but a trifle. I'll caress the mare, and then go on nibbling till thou hast milked all three vats full." So Tremsin did so. He milked the three vats full, and the milk in the first vat was boiling hot, and in the second vat warm, and in the third vat freezing cold. When all was ready the thrice-lovely Nastasia said to Tremsin, "Now, leap first of all into the cold vat, and then into the warm vat, and then into the boiling hot vat!"

Tremsin leaped into the first vat, and leaped out again an old man; he leaped into the second vat, and leaped out again a youth; he leaped into the third vat, but when he leaped out again, he was so young and handsome that no pen can describe it, and no tale can tell of it. Then the thrice-lovely Nastasia herself leaped into the vats. She leaped into the first vat, and came out an old woman; she leaped into the second vat, and came out a young maid; but when she leaped out of the third vat, she was so handsome and goodly that no pen can describe it, and no tale can tell of it. Then the thrice-lovely Nastasia made the nobleman leap into the vats. He leaped into the first vat, and became quite old; he leaped into the second vat, and became quite young; he leaped into the third vat, and burst to pieces. Then Tremsin took unto himself the thrice-lovely Nastasia to wife, and they lived happily together on the nobleman's estate, and the evil servants they drove right away.

Source:
Nisbet, R. *Cossack Fairy Tales and Folk Tales*. London: George G. Harrap & Co., 1916.

106. The Fisherman

Germany

THE water rush'd, the water swell'd,
    A fisherman sat nigh;
Calm was his heart, and he beheld
    His line with watchful eye:

While thus he sits with tranquil look,
    In twain the water flows;
Then, crown'd with reeds, from out the brook,
    A lovely, woman rose.

To him she sung, to him she said,
    —"Why tempt'st thou from the flood,
"By cruel arts of man betray'd,
    "Fair youth, my scaly brood?

"Ah! knew'st thou how we find it sweet
    "Beneath the waves to go,
"Thyself would leave the hook's deceit,
    "And live with us below.

"Love not their splendour in the main
    "The sun and moon to lave?
"Look not their beams as bright again,
    "Reflected on the wave?

"Tempts not this river's glassy blue,
   "So crystal, clear and bright?
"Tempts not thy shade, which bathes in dew,
   "And shares our cool delight?"—

The water rush'd, the water swell'd,
   The fisherman sat nigh;
With wishful glance the flood beheld,
   And long'd the wave to try.

To him she said, to him she sung,
   The river's guileful queen:
Half in he fell, half in he sprung,
   And never more was seen.

From the German of Goethe translated by M. G. Lewis.

Source:
Lewis, M[atthew] G[regory]. *Tales of Wonder, Volume I.* London: W. Bulmer and Co., 1801.

107. The Water-Woman

Germany

THE water roared, the water swelled;
   A fisherman sat by;
And calm and cool at heart, he watch'd
   His line with steady eye.

And while he sat, and while he look'd,
   The heaving waves unclose;
And out a humid female from
   The troubled water rose.

She sang to him—she said to him,
   "Why dost thou wyle my brood
For your thin element of death
   To quit the genial flood?"

"O knewst thou but how happy here
    The little fishes dwell,
Thou wouldst come down e'en as thou art,
    And then wouldst first be well!

"Do not the sun and moon delight
    Their beauties here to lave?
Seem not their beauties doubly fresh
    Enliven'd by the wave?

"Does not the sky, within the deep,
    More lovely tempt thy view?
And thy own shade, that woo's thee in
    To the everlasting dew?"

The water roar'd, the water swell'd;
    It bathed his naked feet;
His heart did yearn as it had yearn'd
    His love's embrace to meet.

She spoke to him, she sang to him;
    Sae fey he grew, bedeen,
That half she drew him, half he sank,
    And never more was seen.

From the German of Goethe translated by Robert Jamieson.

Source:
Jamieson, Robert, editor. *Popular Ballads and Songs, Volume I.* Edinburgh: Archibald Constable and Co., 1806.

108. The Peasant and the Waterman

Germany

The following four stories are extracted from Thomas Keightley's **The Fairy Mythology** *originally published in 1833 in two volumes.*

      Kennt ihr der Nixen, munt're Schaar?
      Von Auge schwarz und grün von Haar

> Sie lauscht am Schilfgestade.
> —MATTHISSON.

> Know you the Nixes, gay and fair?
> Their eyes are black, and green their hair—
> They lurk in sedgy shores.

THE Nixes, or Water-people, inhabit lakes and rivers. The man is like any other man, only he has green teeth. He also wears a green hat. The female Nixes appear like beautiful maidens. On fine sunny days they may be seen sitting on the banks, or on the branches of the trees, combing their long golden locks. When any person is shortly to be drowned, the Nixes may be previously seen dancing on the surface of the water. They inhabit a magnificent region below the water, whither they sometimes convey mortals. A girl from a village near Leipzig was one time at service in the house of a Nix. She said that everything there was very good; all she had to complain of was that she was obliged to eat her food without salt. The female Nixes frequently go to the market to buy meat: they are always dressed with extreme neatness, only a corner of their apron or some other part of their clothes is wet. The man has also occasionally gone to market. They are fond of carrying off women whom they make wives of, and often fetch an earthly midwife to assist at their labour. Among the many tales of the Nixes we select the following:—

The Peasant and the Waterman

A WATER-MAN once lived on good terms with a peasant who dwelt not far from his lake. He often visited him, and at last begged that the peasant would visit him in his house under the water. The peasant consented, and went down with him. There was everything down under the water as in a stately palace on the land,—halls, chambers, and cabinets, with costly furniture of every description. The Water-man led his guest over the whole, and showed him everything that was in it. They came at length to a little chamber, where were standing several new pots turned upside down. The peasant asked what was in them. "They contain," was the reply, "the souls of drowned people, which I put under the pots and keep them close, so that they cannot get away." The peasant made no remark, and he came up again on the land. But for a long time the affair of the souls continued to give him great trouble, and be watched to find when the Water-man should be from home. When this occurred, as he had marked the right way down, he descended into the water-house, and, having made out the little chamber, he turned up all the pots one after another, and immediately the souls of the drowned people ascended out of the water, and recovered their liberty.

NOTES

This legend seems to be connected with the ancient idea of the water-deities taking the souls of drowned persons to themselves. In the Edda, this is done by the sea-goddess Ran.

Source:
Keightley, Thomas. *The Fairy Mythology: Illustrative of the Romance and Superstition of Various Countries*. London: George Bell & Sons, 1905.

109. The Water-Smith

Germany

THERE is a little lake in Westphalia called the Darmssen, from which the peasants in the adjacent village of Epe used to hear all through the night a sound as if of hammering upon an anvil. People who were awake used also to see something in the middle of the lake. They got one time into a boat and went to it, and there they found that it was a smith, who, with his body raised over the water, and a hammer in his hand, pointed to an anvil, and bid the people bring him something to forge. Prom that time forth they brought iron to him, and no people had such good plough-irons as those of Epe.

One time as a man from this village was getting reeds at the Darmssen, he found among them a little child that was rough all over his body. The smith cried out, "Don't take away my son!" but the man put the child on his back, and ran home with it. Since that time the smith has never more been seen or heard. The man reared the Roughy, and he became the cleverest and best lad in the place. But when he was twenty years old he said to the farmer, "Farmer, I must leave you. My father has called me!" "I am sorry for that," said the farmer. "Is there no way that you could stay with me?" "I will see about it," said the water-child. "Do you go to Braumske and fetch me a little sword; but you must give the seller whatever he asks for it, and not haggle about it." The farmer went to Braumske and bought the sword; but he haggled, and got something off the price. They now went together to the Darmssen, and the Roughy said, "Now mind. When I strike the water, if there comes up blood, I must go away; but if there comes milk, then I may stay with you." He struck the water, and there came neither milk nor blood. The Roughy was annoyed, and said, "You have been bargaining and haggling, and so there comes neither blood nor milk. Go off to Braumske and buy another sword." The farmer went and returned; but it was not till the third time that he bought a sword without haggling. When the Roughy struck the water with this it became as red as blood, and he threw himself into the lake, and never was seen more.[1]

Source:

Keightley, Thomas. *The Fairy Mythology: Illustrative of the Romance and Superstition of Various Countries.* London: George Bell & Sons, 1905.

110. The Working Waterman

Germany

AT Seewenweiher, in the Black-Forest, a little Water-man (Seemänlein) used to come and join the people, work the whole day long with them, and in the evening go back into the lakes. They used to set his breakfast and dinner apart for him. When, in apportioning the work, the rule of "Not too much and not too little" was infringed, he got angry, and knocked all the things about. Though his clothes were old and worn, he steadily refused to let the people get him new ones. But when at last they would do so, and one evening the lake-man was presented with a new coat, be said, "When one is paid off, one must go away. After this day I'll come no more to you." And, unmoved by the excuses of the people, he never let himself be seen again.[2]

Source:

Keightley, Thomas. *The Fairy Mythology: Illustrative of the Romance and Superstition of Various Countries.* London: George Bell & Sons, 1905.

---

[1] Grimm, *ut sup.* p. 463.
[2] Grimm, *ut sup.* p. 453.

111. The Nix Labour

Germany

A **MIDWIFE** related that her mother was one night called up, and desired to make haste and come to the aid of a woman in labour. It was dark, but notwithstanding she got up and dressed herself, and went down, where she found a man waiting. She begged of him to stay till she should get a lantern, and she would go with him; but he was urgent, said he would show her the way without a lantern, and that there was no fear of her going astray.

He then bandaged her eyes, at which she was terrified, and was going to cry out; but he told her she was in no danger, and might go with him without any apprehension. They accordingly went away together, and the woman remarked that he struck the water with a rod, and that they went down deeper and deeper till they came to a room, in which there was no one but the lying-in woman.

Her guide now took the bandage off her eyes, led her up to the bed, and recommending her to his wife, went away. She then helped to bring the babe into the world, put the woman to bed, washed the babe, and did everything that was requisite.

The woman, grateful to the midwife, then secretly said to her: "I am a Christian woman as well as you; and I was carried off by a Water-man, who changed me. Whenever I bring a child into the world he always eats it on the third. day. Come on the third day to your pond, and you will see the water turned to blood. When my husband comes in now and offers you money, take no more from him than you usually get, or else he will twist your neck. Take good care!"

Just then the husband came in. He was in a great passion, and he looked all about; and when he saw that all had gone on properly he bestowed great praise on the midwife. He then threw a great heap of money on the table, and said, "Take as much as you will!" She, however, prudently answered, "I desire no more from you than from others, and that is a small sum. If you give me that I am content; if you think it too much, I ask nothing from you but to take me home again." "It is God," says he, "has directed you to say that." He paid her then the sum she mentioned, and conducted her home honestly. She was, however, afraid to go to the pond at the appointed day.

There are many other tales in Germany of midwives, and even ladies of rank, who have been called in to assist at Nix or Dwarf labours. The Ahnfrau von Ranzau, for example, and the Frau von Alvensleben—the

Ladies Bountiful of Germany—were waked up in the night to attend the little women in their confinement. There is the same danger in touching anything in the Dwarf as in the Nix abodes, but the Dwarfs usually bestow rings and other articles, which will cause the family to flourish. We have seen tales of the same kind in Scandinavia, and shall meet with them in many other countries.

NOTES

A tale of this kind is to be seen in Luther's Table-talk, told by die frau doctorin, his wife. The scene of it was the river Mulda.

Source:
Keightley, Thomas. *The Fairy Mythology: Illustrative of the Romance and Superstition of Various Countries*. London: George Bell & Sons, 1905.

112. The Water-Nix

Germany

A LITTLE brother and sister were once playing by a well, and while they were thus playing, they both fell in. A water-nix lived down below, who said, "Now I have got you, now you shall work hard for me!" and carried them off with her. She gave the girl dirty tangled flax to spin, and she had to fetch water in a bucket with a hole in it, and the boy had to hew down a tree with a blunt axe, and they got nothing to eat but dumplings as hard as stones. Then at last the children became so impatient, that they waited until one Sunday, when the nix was at church, and ran away. But when church was over, the nix saw that the birds were flown, and followed them with great strides. The children saw her from afar, and the girl threw a brush behind her which formed an immense hill of bristles, with thousands and thousands of spikes, over which the nix was forced to scramble with great difficulty; at last, however, she got over. When the children saw this, the boy threw behind him a comb which made a great hill of combs with a thousand times a thousand teeth, but the nix managed to keep herself steady on them, and at last crossed over that. Then the girl threw behind her a looking-glass which formed a hill of mirrors, and was so slippery that it was impossible for the nix to cross it. Then she thought, "I will go home quickly and fetch my axe, and cut the hill of glass in half." Long before she returned, however, and had hewn through the glass, the children had escaped to a great distance, and the water-nix was obliged to betake herself to her well again.

NOTES

From Hanau. It is a pursuit of the children by the witch, as in the story of Dearest Roland No. 56; she is at the same time Frau Holle, and the wicked one who makes people spin entangled flax, and gives them stones to eat instead of food. For the whole, compare J. Grimm's *Irmenstrasse*.

Source:
Grimm, Jacob and Wilhelm. *Household Tales*. Margaret Hunt, translator. London: George Bell, 1884, 1892.

113. The Nixie of the Mill-Pond

Germany

THERE was once upon a time a miller who lived with his wife in great contentment. They had money and land, and their prosperity increased year by year more and more. But ill-luck comes like a thief in the night, as their wealth had increased so did it again decrease, year by year, and at last the miller could hardly call the mill in which he lived, his own. He was in great distress, and when he lay down after his day's work, found no rest, but tossed about in his bed, full of care.

One morning he rose before daybreak and went out into the open air, thinking that perhaps there his heart might become lighter. As he was stepping over the mill-dam the first sunbeam was just breaking forth, and he heard a rippling sound in the pond. He turned round and perceived a beautiful woman, rising slowly out of the water. Her long hair, which she was holding off her shoulders with her soft hands, fell down on both sides, and covered her white body. He soon saw that she was the Nix of the Mill-pond, and in his fright did not know whether he should run away or stay where he was. But the nix made her sweet voice heard, called him by his name, and asked him why he was so sad?

The miller was at first struck dumb, but when he heard her speak so kindly, he took heart, and told her how he had formerly lived in wealth and happiness, but that now he was so poor that he did not know what to do.

"Be easy," answered the nix, "I will make thee richer and happier than thou hast ever been before, only thou must promise to give me the young thing which has just been born in thy house."

"What else can that be," thought the miller, "but a young puppy or kitten?" and he promised her what she desired. The nix descended into the water again, and he hurried back to his mill, consoled and in good spirits. He had not yet reached it, when the maid-servant came out of the house, and cried to him to rejoice, for his wife had given birth to a little boy. The miller stood as if struck by lightning; he saw very well that the cunning nix had been aware of it, and had cheated him. Hanging his head, he went up to his wife's bedside and when she said, "Why dost thou not rejoice over the fine boy?" he told her what had befallen him, and what kind of a promise he had given to the nix.

"Of what use to me are riches and prosperity?" he added, "if I am to lose my child; but what can I do?" Even the relations, who had come thither to wish them joy, did not know what to say.

In the meantime prosperity again returned to the miller's house. All that he undertook succeeded, it was as if presses and coffers filled themselves of their own accord, and as if money multiplied nightly in the cupboards. It was not long before his wealth was greater than it had ever been before. But he could not rejoice over it untroubled, for the bargain which he had made with the nix tormented his soul. Whenever he passed the mill-pond, he feared she might ascend and remind him of his debt. He never let the boy himself go near the water.

"Beware," he said to him, "if thou dost but touch the water, a hand will rise, seize thee, and draw thee down." But as year after year went by and the nix did not show herself again, the miller began to feel at ease.

The boy grew up to be a youth and was apprenticed to a huntsman. When he had learnt everything, and had become an excellent huntsman, the lord of the village took him into his service. In the village lived a beautiful and true-hearted maiden, who pleased the huntsman, and when his master perceived that, he gave him a little house, the two were married, lived peacefully and happily, and loved each other with all their hearts.

One day the huntsman was chasing a roe; and when the animal turned aside from the forest into the open country, he pursued it and at last shot it. He did not notice that he was now in the neighbourhood of the dangerous mill-pond, and went, after he had disembowelled the stag, to the water, in order to wash his blood-stained hands. Scarcely, however, had he dipped them in than the nix ascended, smilingly wound her dripping arms around him, and drew him quickly down under the waves, which closed over him.

When it was evening, and the huntsman did not return home, his wife became alarmed. She went out to seek him, and as he had often told her that he had to be on his guard against the snares of the nix, and dared not venture into the neighbourhood of the mill-pond, she already suspected what had happened. She hastened to the water, and when she found his hunting-pouch lying on the shore, she could no longer have any doubt of the misfortune. Lamenting her sorrow, and wringing her hands, she called on her beloved by name, but in vain. She hurried across to the other side of the pond, and called him anew; she reviled the nix with harsh words, but no answer followed. The surface of the water remained calm, only the crescent moon stared steadily back at her. The poor woman did not leave the pond. With hasty steps, she paced round and round it, without resting a moment, sometimes in silence, sometimes uttering a loud cry, sometimes softly sobbing. At last her strength came to an end, she sank down to the ground and fell into a heavy sleep.

Presently a dream took possession of her. She was anxiously climbing upwards between great masses of rock; thorns and briars caught her feet, the rain beat in her face, and the wind tossed her long hair about. When she had reached the summit, quite a different sight presented itself to her; the sky was blue, the air soft, the ground sloped gently downwards, and on a green meadow, gay with flowers of every colour, stood a pretty cottage. She went up to it and opened the door; there sat an old woman with white hair, who beckoned to her kindly. At that very moment, the poor woman awoke, day had already dawned, and she at once resolved to act in accordance with her dream. She laboriously climbed the mountain; everything was exactly as she had seen it in the night. The old woman received her kindly, and pointed out a chair on which she might sit.

"Thou must have met with a misfortune," she said, "since thou hast sought out my lonely cottage." With tears, the woman related what had befallen her. "Be comforted," said the old woman, "I will help thee. Here is a golden comb for thee. Tarry till the full moon has risen, then go to the mill-pond, seat thyself on the shore, and comb thy long black hair with this comb. When thou hast done, lay it down on the bank, and thou wilt see what will happen." The woman returned home, but the time till the full moon came, passed slowly.

At last the shining disc appeared in the heavens, then she went out to the mill-pond, sat down and combed her long black hair with the golden comb, and when she had finished, she laid it down at the water's edge. It was not long before there was a movement in the depths, a wave rose, rolled to the shore, and bore the comb away with it. In not more than the time necessary for the comb to sink to the bottom, the surface of the water parted, and the head of the huntsman arose. He did not speak, but looked at his wife with sorrowful glances. At the same instant, a second wave came rushing up, and covered the man's head. All had vanished, the mill-pond lay peaceful as before, and nothing but the face of the full moon shone on it. Full of sorrow, the woman went back, but again the dream showed her the cottage of the old woman.

Next morning she again set out and complained of her woes to the wise woman. The old woman gave her a golden flute, and said, "Tarry till the full moon comes again, then take this flute; play a beautiful air on it, and when thou hast finished, lay it on the sand; then thou wilt see what will happen." The wife did as the old woman told her. No sooner was the flute lying on the sand than there was a stirring in the depths, and a wave rushed up and bore the flute away with it. Immediately afterwards the water parted, and not only the head of the man, but half of his body also arose. He stretched out his arms longingly towards her, but a second wave came up, covered him, and drew him down again.

"Alas, what does it profit me?" said the unhappy woman, "that I should see my beloved, only to lose him again!"

Despair filled her heart anew, but the dream led her a third time to the house of the old woman. She set out, and the wise woman gave her a golden spinning-wheel, consoled her and said, "All is not yet fulfilled, tarry until the time of the full moon, then take the spinning-wheel, seat thyself on the shore, and spin the spool full, and when thou hast done that, place the spinning-wheel near the water, and thou wilt see what will happen."

The woman obeyed all she said exactly; as soon as the full moon showed itself, she carried the golden spinning-wheel to the shore, and span industriously until the flax came to an end, and the spool was quite filled with the threads. No sooner was the wheel standing on the shore than there was a more violent movement than before in the depths of the pond, and a mighty wave rushed up, and bore the wheel away with it. Immediately the head and the whole body of the man rose into the air, in a water-spout. He quickly sprang to the shore, caught his wife by the hand and fled. But they had scarcely gone a very little distance, when the whole pond rose with a frightful roar, and streamed out over the open country. The fugitives already saw death before their eyes, when the woman in her terror implored the help of the old woman, and in an instant they were transformed, she into a toad, he into a frog. The flood which had overtaken them could not destroy them, but it tore them apart and carried them far away.

When the water had dispersed and they both touched dry land again, they regained their human form, but neither knew where the other was; they found themselves among strange people, who did not know their native land. High mountains and deep valleys lay between them. In order to keep themselves alive, they were both obliged to tend sheep.

For many long years they drove their flocks through field and forest and were full of sorrow and longing. When spring had once more broken forth on the earth, they both went out one day with their flocks, and as chance would have it, they drew near each other. They met in a valley, but did not recognize each other; yet they rejoiced that they were no longer so lonely. Henceforth they each day drove their flocks to the same place; they did not speak much, but they felt comforted.

One evening when the full moon was shining in the sky, and the sheep were already at rest, the shepherd pulled the flute out of his pocket, and played on it a beautiful but sorrowful air. When he had finished he saw that the shepherdess was weeping bitterly.

"Why art thou weeping?" he asked.

"Alas," answered she, "thus shone the full moon when I played this air on the flute for the last time, and the head of my beloved rose out of the water."

He looked at her, and it seemed as if a veil fell from his eyes, and he recognized his dear wife, and when she looked at him, and the moon shone in his face she knew him also. They embraced and kissed each other, and no one need ask if they were happy.

NOTES

From a story current in Upper Lusatia, in Haupt's *Zeitschrift*, 257, 267. Here again we have a malicious Nix, while in other stories of this kind, as in No. 34 [Clever Elsie], the Devil takes her place, but the benevolent old woman who helps the unfortunate is not lacking.

Source:
Grimm, Jacob and Wilhelm. *Household Tales*. Margaret Hunt, translator. London: George Bell, 1884, 1892.

114. The Golden Mermaid

Germany

A POWERFUL king had, among many other treasures, a wonderful tree in his garden, which bore every year beautiful golden apples. But the King was never able to enjoy his treasure, for he might watch and guard them as he liked, as soon as they began to get ripe they were always stolen. At last, in despair, he sent for his three sons, and said to the two eldest, "Get yourselves ready for a journey. Take gold and silver with you, and a large retinue of servants, as beseems two noble princes, and go through the world till you find out who it is that steals my golden apples, and, if possible, bring the thief to me that I may punish him as he deserves." His sons were delighted at this proposal, for they had long wished to see something of the world, so they got ready for their journey with all haste, bade their father farewell, and left the town.

The youngest Prince was much disappointed that he too was not sent out on his travels; but his father wouldn't hear of his going, for he had always been looked upon as the stupid one of the family, and the King was afraid of something happening to him. But the Prince begged and implored so long, that at last his father consented to let him go, and furnished him with gold and silver as he had done his brothers. But he gave him the most wretched horse in his stable, because the foolish youth hadn't asked for a better. So he too set out on his journey to secure the thief, amid the jeers and laughter of the whole court and town.

His path led him first through a wood, and he hadn't gone very far when he met a lean-looking wolf who stood still as he approached. The Prince asked him if he were hungry, and when the wolf said he was, he got down from his horse and said, "If you are really as you say and look, you may take my horse and eat it."

The wolf didn't wait to have the offer repeated, but set to work, and soon made an end of the poor beast. When the Prince saw how different the wolf looked when he had finished his meal, he said to him, "Now, my friend, since you have eaten up my horse, and I have such a long way to go, that, with the best will in the world, I couldn't manage it on foot, the least you can do for me is to act as my horse and to take me on your back."

"Most certainly," said the wolf, and, letting the Prince mount him, he trotted gaily through the wood. After they had gone a little way he turned round and asked his rider where he wanted to go to, and the Prince proceeded to tell him the whole story of the golden apples that had been stolen out of the King's garden, and how his other two brothers had set forth with many followers to find the thief. When he had finished his story, the wolf, who was in reality no wolf but a mighty magician, said he thought he could tell him who the thief was, and could help him to secure him. "There lives," he said, "in a neighbouring country, a mighty emperor who has a beautiful golden bird in a cage, and this is the creature who steals the golden apples, but it flies so fast that it is impossible to catch it at its theft. You must slip into the Emperor's palace by night and steal the bird with the cage; but be very careful not to touch the walls as you go out."

The following night the Prince stole into the Emperor's palace, and found the bird in its cage as the wolf had told him he would. He took hold of it carefully, but in spite of all his caution he touched the wall in trying to pass by some sleeping watchmen. They awoke at once, and, seizing him, beat him and put him into chains. Next day he was led before the Emperor, who at once condemned him to death and to be thrown into a dark dungeon till the day of his execution arrived.

The wolf, who, of course, knew by his magic arts all that had happened to the Prince, turned himself at once into a mighty monarch with a large train of followers, and proceeded to the Court of the Emperor, where he was received with every show of honour. The Emperor and he conversed on many subjects, and, among other things, the stranger asked his host if he had many slaves. The Emperor told him he had more than he knew what to do with, and that a new one had been captured that very night for trying to steal his magic bird, but that as he had already more than enough to feed and support, he was going to have this last captive hanged next morning.

"He must have been a most daring thief," said the King, "to try and steal the magic bird, for depend upon it the creature must have been well guarded. I would really like to see this bold rascal." "By all means," said the Emperor; and he himself led his guest down to the dungeon where the unfortunate Prince was kept prisoner. When the Emperor stepped out of the cell with the King, the latter turned to him and said, "Most mighty Emperor, I have been much disappointed. I had thought to find a powerful robber, and instead of that I have seen the most miserable creature I can imagine. Hanging is far too good for him. If I had to sentence him I should make him perform some very difficult task, under pain of death. If he did it so much the better for you, and if he didn't, matters would just be as they are now and he could still be hanged."

"Your counsel," said the Emperor, "is excellent, and, as it happens, I've got the very thing for him to do. My nearest neighbour, who is also a mighty Emperor, possesses a golden horse which he guards most carefully. The prisoner shall be told to steal this horse and bring it to me." The Prince was then let out of his dungeon, and told his life would be spared if he succeeded in bringing the golden horse to the Emperor. He did not feel very elated at this announcement, for he did not know how in the world he was to set about the task, and he started on his way weeping bitterly, and wondering what had made him leave his father's house and kingdom. But before he had gone far his friend the wolf stood before him and said, "Dear Prince, why are you so cast down? It is true you didn't succeed in catching the bird; but don't let that discourage you, for this time you will be all the more careful, and will doubtless catch the horse." With these and like words the wolf comforted the Prince, and warned him specially not to touch the wall or let the horse touch it as he led it out, or he would fail in the same way as he had done with the bird.

After a somewhat lengthy journey the Prince and the wolf came to the kingdom ruled over by the Emperor who possessed the golden horse. One evening late they reached the capital, and the wolf advised the Prince to set to work at once, before their presence in the city had aroused the watchfulness of the guards. They slipped unnoticed into the Emperor's stables and into the very place where there were the most guards, for there the wolf rightly surmised they would find the horse. When they came to a certain inner door the wolf told the Prince to remain outside, while he went in. In a short time he returned and said, "My dear Prince, the horse is most securely watched, but I have bewitched all the guards, and if you will only be careful not to touch the wall yourself, or let the horse touch it as you go out, there is no danger and the game is yours. The Prince, who had made up his mind to be more than cautious this time, went cheerfully to work. He found all the guards fast asleep, and, slipping into the horse's stall, he seized it by the bridle and led it out; but, unfortunately, before they had got quite clear of the stables a gadfly stung the horse and caused it to switch its tail, whereby it touched the wall. In a moment all the guards awoke, seized the Prince and beat him mercilessly with their horse-whips, after which they bound him with chains, and flung him into a dungeon. Next morning they brought him before the Emperor, who treated him exactly as the King with the golden bird had done, and commanded him to be beheaded on the following day.

When the wolf-magician saw that the Prince had failed this time too, he transformed himself again into a mighty king, and proceeded with an even more gorgeous retinue than the first time to the Court of the Emperor. He was courteously received and entertained, and once more after dinner he led the conversation on to the subject of slaves, and in the course of it again requested to be allowed to see the bold robber who had dared to break into the Emperor's stable to steal his most valuable possession. The Emperor consented, and all happened exactly as it had done at the court of the Emperor with the golden bird; the prisoner's life was to be spared only on condition that within three days he should obtain possession of the golden mermaid, whom hitherto no mortal had ever approached.

Very depressed by his dangerous and difficult task, the Prince left his gloomy prison; but, to his great joy, he met his friend the wolf before he had gone many miles on his journey. The cunning creature pretended he knew nothing of what had happened to the Prince, and asked him how he had fared with the horse. The Prince told him all about his misadventure, and the condition on which the Emperor had promised to spare his life. Then the wolf reminded him that he had twice got him out of prison, and that if he would only trust in him, and do exactly as he told him, he would certainly succeed in this last undertaking. Thereupon they bent their steps towards the sea, which stretched out before them, as far as their eyes could see, all the waves dancing and glittering in the bright sunshine. "Now," continued the wolf, "I am going to turn myself into a boat full of the most beautiful silken merchandise, and you must jump boldly into the boat, and steer with my tail in your hand right out into the open sea. You will soon come upon the golden mermaid. Whatever you do, don't follow her if she calls you, but on the contrary say to her, 'The buyer comes to the seller, not the seller to the buyer.' After which you must steer towards the land, and she will follow you, for she won't be able to resist the beautiful wares you have on board your ship."

The Prince promised faithfully to do all he had been told, whereupon the wolf changed himself into a ship full of most exquisite silks, of every shade and colour imaginable. The astonished Prince stepped into the boat, and, holding the wolf's tail in his hand, he steered boldly out into the open sea, where the sun was gilding the blue waves with its golden rays. Soon he saw the golden mermaid swimming near the ship, beckoning and calling to him to follow her; but, mindful of the wolf's warning, he told her in a loud voice that if she wished to buy anything she must come to him. With these words he turned his magic ship round and steered back towards the land. The mermaid called out to him to stand still, but he refused to listen to her and never paused till he reached the sand of the shore. Here he stopped and waited for the mermaid, who had swum after him. When she drew near the boat he saw that she was far more beautiful than any mortal he had ever beheld. She swam round the ship for some time, and then swung herself gracefully on board, in order to examine the beautiful silken stuffs more closely. Then the Prince seized her in his arms, and kissing her tenderly on the cheeks and lips, he told her she was his for ever; at the same moment the boat turned into a wolf again, which so terrified the mermaid that she clung to the Prince for protection.

So the golden mermaid was successfully caught, and she soon felt quite happy in her new life when she saw she had nothing to fear either from the Prince or the wolf—she rode on the back of the latter, and the Prince rode behind her. When they reached the country ruled over by the Emperor with the golden horse, the Prince jumped down, and, helping the mermaid to alight, he led her before the Emperor. At the sight of the beautiful mermaid and of the grim wolf, who stuck close to the Prince this time, the guards all made respectful obeisance, and soon the three stood before his Imperial Majesty. When the Emperor heard from the Prince how he had gained possession of his fair prize, he at once recognized that he had been helped by some magic art, and on the spot gave up all claim to the beautiful mermaid. "Dear youth," he said, "forgive me for my shameful conduct to you, and, as a sign that you pardon me, accept the golden horse as a present. I acknowledge your power to be greater even than I can understand, for you have succeeded in gaining possession of the golden mermaid, whom hitherto no mortal has ever been able to approach." Then they all sat down to a huge feast, and the Prince had to relate his adventures all over again, to the wonder and astonishment of the whole company.

But the Prince was wearying now to return to his own kingdom, so as soon as the feast was over he took farewell of the Emperor, and set out on his homeward way. He lifted the mermaid on to the golden horse, and swung himself up behind her—and so they rode on merrily, with the wolf trotting behind, till they came to the country of the Emperor with the golden bird. The renown of the Prince and his adventure had gone before him, and the Emperor sat on his throne awaiting the arrival of the Prince and his companions. When the three rode into the courtyard of the palace, they were surprised and delighted to find everything festively illuminated and decorated for their reception. When the Prince and the golden mermaid, with the wolf behind them, mounted the steps of the palace, the Emperor came forward to meet them, and led them to the throne room. At the same moment a servant appeared with the golden bird in its golden cage, and the Emperor begged the Prince to accept it with his love, and to forgive him the indignity he had suffered at his hands. Then the Emperor bent low before the beautiful mermaid, and, offering her his arm, he led her into dinner, closely followed by the Prince and her friend the wolf; the latter seating himself at table, not the least embarrassed that no one had invited him to do so.

As soon as the sumptuous meal was over, the Prince and his mermaid took leave of the Emperor, and, seating themselves on the golden horse, continued their homeward journey. On the way the wolf turned to the Prince and said, "Dear friends, I must now bid you farewell, but I leave you under such happy circumstances that I cannot feel our parting to be a sad one." The Prince was very unhappy when he heard these words, and begged the wolf to stay with them always; but this the good creature refused to do, though he thanked the Prince kindly for his invitation, and called out as he disappeared into the thicket, "Should any evil befall you, dear Prince, at any time, you may rely on my friendship and gratitude." These were the wolf's parting words, and the Prince could not restrain his tears when he saw his friend vanishing in the distance; but one glance at his beloved mermaid soon cheered him up again, and they continued on their journey merrily.

The news of his son's adventures had already reached his father's Court, and everyone was more than astonished at the success of the once despised Prince. His elder brothers, who had in vain gone in pursuit of the thief of the golden apples, were furious over their younger brother's good fortune, and plotted and planned how they were to kill him. They hid themselves in the wood through which the Prince had to pass on his way to the palace, and there fell on him, and, having beaten him to death, they carried off the golden horse and the golden bird. But nothing they could do would persuade the golden mermaid to go with them or move from the spot, for ever since she had left the sea, she had so attached herself to her Prince that she asked nothing else than to live or die with him.

For many weeks the poor mermaid sat and watched over the dead body of her lover, weeping salt tears over his loss, when suddenly one day their old friend the wolf appeared and said, "Cover the Prince's body with all the leaves and flowers you can find in the wood." The maiden did as he told her, and then the wolf breathed over the flowery grave, and, lo and behold! the Prince lay there sleeping as peacefully as a child. "Now you may wake him if you like," said the wolf, and the mermaid bent over him and gently kissed the wounds his brothers had made on his forehead, and the Prince awoke, and you may imagine how delighted he was to find his beautiful mermaid beside him, though he felt a little depressed when he thought of the loss of the golden bird and the golden horse. After a time the wolf, who had likewise fallen on the Prince's neck, advised them to continue their journey, and once more the Prince and his lovely bride mounted on the faithful beast's back.

The King's joy was great when he embraced his youngest son, for he had long since despaired of his return. He received the wolf and the beautiful golden mermaid most cordially too, and the Prince was made to tell his adventures all over from the beginning. The poor old father grew very sad when he heard of the shameful conduct of his elder sons, and had them called before him. They turned as white as death when they saw their brother, whom they thought they had murdered, standing beside them alive and well, and so startled were they that when the King asked them why they had behaved so wickedly to their brother they could think of no lie, but confessed at once that they had slain the young Prince in order to obtain possession of the golden horse and the golden bird. Their father's wrath knew no bounds, and he ordered them both to be banished, but he could not do enough to honour his youngest son, and his marriage with the beautiful mermaid was celebrated with much pomp and magnificence. When the festivities were over, the wolf bade them all farewell, and returned once more to his life in the woods, much to the regret of the old King and the young Prince and his bride.

And so ended the adventures of the Prince with his friend the wolf.

Grimm.[1]

Source:
Lang, Andrew, editor. *The Green Fairy Book*. London: Longmans, Green, and Company, 1892.

115. Undine
by Friedrich de la Motte Fouque

Germany

DEDICATION.

UNDINE, thou image fair and blest,
    Since first thy strange mysterious glance,

---

[1] Lang attributed "The Golden Mermaid" to the Brothers Grimm, but the tale as it appears here does not appear in the Grimms' collection. The tale closely resembles their tale, "The Golden Bird," with noticeable differences such as the mermaid who is simply a maiden in "The Golden Bird." However, during my research I discovered the tale in *Fancy Tales from the German* edited by J. S. Laurie (London, n.d.), a reprint of an 1861 publication in which "The Golden Mermaid" appears and is credited to Straparola, placing Lang's original source in question.~*HAH*

Shone on me from some old romance,
How hast thou sung my heart to rest!

How hast thou clung to me and smiled,
    And wouldest, whispering in my ear,
    Give vent to all thy miseries drear,
A little half-spoiled timorous child!

Yet hath my zither caught the sound,
    And breathed from out its gates of gold,
    Each gentle word thy lips have told,
Until their fame is spread around.

And many a heart has loved thee well,
    In spite of every wayward deed,
    And many a one will gladly read,
The pages which thy history tell.

I catch the whispered hope expressed,
    That thou should'st once again appear;
    So cast aside each doubt and fear,
And come, Undine! thou spirit blest!

Greet every noble in the hall,
    And greet 'fore all, with trusting air,
    The beauteous women gathered there;
I know that thou art loved by all.

And if one ask thee after me,
    Say: he's a true and noble knight,
    Fair woman's slave in song and fight
And in all deeds of chivalry.

CHAPTER I.
HOW THE KNIGHT CAME TO THE FISHERMAN.

There was once, it may be now many hundred years ago, a good old fisherman, who was sitting one fine evening before his door, mending his nets. The part of the country in which he lived was extremely pretty. The greensward, on which his cottage stood, ran far into the lake, and it seemed as if it was from love for the blue clear waters that the tongue of land had stretched itself out into them, while with an equally fond embrace the lake had encircled the green pasture rich with waving grass and flowers, and the refreshing shade of trees. The one welcomed the other, and it was just this that made each so beautiful. There were indeed few human beings, or rather none at all, to be met with on this pleasant spot, except the fisherman and his family. For at the back of this little promontory there lay a very wild forest, which, both from its gloom and pathless solitude as well as from the wonderful creatures and illusions with which it was said to abound, was avoided by most people except in cases of necessity.

The pious old fisherman, however, passed through it many a time undisturbed, when he was taking the choice fish, which he had caught at his beautiful home, to a large town situated not far from the confines of the forest. The principal reason why it was so easy for him to pass through this forest was because the tone of his thoughts was almost entirely of a religious character, and besides this, whenever he set foot upon the evil reputed shades, he was wont to sing some holy song, with a clear voice and a sincere heart.

While sitting over his nets this evening, unsuspicious of any evil, a sudden fear came upon him, at the sound of a rustling in the gloom of the forest, as of a horse and rider, the noise approaching nearer and nearer to the little promontory. All that he had dreamed, in many a stormy night, of the mysteries of the forest, now flashed at once through his mind; foremost of all, the image of a gigantic snow-white man, who kept unceasingly nodding his head in a portentous manner. Indeed, when he raised his eyes toward the wood it seemed to him as if he actually saw the nodding man approaching through the dense foliage. He soon, however, reassured himself, reflecting that nothing serious had ever befallen him even in the forest itself, and that upon this open tongue of land the evil spirit would be still less daring in the exercise of his power. At the same time he repeated aloud a text from the Bible with all his heart, and this so inspired him with courage that he almost smiled at the illusion he had allowed to possess him. The white nodding man was suddenly transformed into a brook long familiar to him, which ran foaming from the forest and discharged itself into the lake. The noise, however, which he had heard, was caused by a knight beautifully apparelled, who, emerging from the deep shadows of the wood, came riding toward the cottage. A scarlet mantle was thrown over his purple gold-embroidered doublet; a red and violet plume waved from his golden-colored head-gear; and a beautifully and richly ornamented sword flashed from his shoulder-belt. The white steed that bore the knight was more slenderly formed than war-horses generally are, and he stepped so lightly over the turf that this green and flowery carpet seemed scarcely to receive the slightest injury from his tread.

The old fisherman did not, however, feel perfectly secure in his mind, although he tried to convince himself that no evil was to be feared from so graceful an apparition; and therefore he politely took off his hat as the knight approached, and remained quietly with his nets.

Presently the stranger drew up, and inquired whether he and his horse could have shelter and care for the night. "As regards your horse, good sir," replied the fisherman. "I can assign him no better stable than this shady pasture, and no better provender than the grass growing on it. Yourself, however, I will gladly welcome to my small cottage, and give you supper and lodging as good as we have." The knight was well satisfied with this; he alighted from his horse, and, with the assistance of the fisherman, he relieved it from saddle and bridle, and turned it loose upon the flowery green. Then addressing his host, he said: "Even had I found you less hospitable and kindly disposed, my worthy old fisherman, you would nevertheless scarcely have got rid of me to-day, for, as I see, a broad lake lies before us, and to ride back into that mysterious wood, with the shades of evening coming on, heaven keep me from it!"

"We will not talk too much of that," said the fisherman, and he led his guest into the cottage.

There, beside the hearth, from which a scanty fire shed a dim light through the cleanly-kept room, sat the fisherman's aged wife in a capacious chair. At the entrance of the noble guest she rose to give him a kindly welcome, but resumed her seat of honor without offering it to the stranger. Upon this the fisherman said with a smile: "You must not take it amiss of her, young sir, that she has not given up to you the most comfortable seat in the house; it is a custom among poor people, that it should belong exclusively to the aged."

"Why, husband," said the wife, with a quiet smile, "what can you be thinking of? Our guest belongs no doubt to Christian men, and how could it come into the head of the good young blood to drive old people from their chairs? Take a seat, my young master," she continued, turning toward the knight; "over there, there is a right pretty little chair, only you must not move about on it too roughly, for one of its legs is no longer of the firmest." The knight fetched the chair carefully, sat down upon it good-humoredly, and it seemed to him as if he were related to this little household, and had just returned from abroad.

The three worthy people now began to talk together in the most friendly and familiar manner. With regard to the forest, about which the knight made some inquiries, the old man was not inclined to be communicative; he felt it was not a subject suited to approaching night, but the aged couple spoke freely of their home and former life, and listened also gladly when the knight recounted to them his travels, and told them that he had a castle near the source of the Danube, and that his name was Sir Huldbrand of Ringstetten. During the conversation, the stranger had already occasionally heard a splash against the little low window, as if some one were sprinkling water against it. Every time the noise occurred, the old man knit his brow with displeasure; but when at last a whole shower was dashed against the panes, and bubbled into the room through the decayed casement, he rose angrily, and called threateningly from the window: "Undine! will you for once leave off these childish tricks? and to-day, besides, there is a stranger knight with us in the cottage." All was silent without, only a suppressed laugh was audible, and the fisherman said as he returned: "You must pardon it in her, my honored guest, and perhaps many a naughty trick besides; but she means no harm by it. It is our foster-child, Undine, and she will not wean herself from this childishness, although she has already entered her eighteenth year. But, as I said, at heart she is thoroughly good."

"You may well talk," replied the old woman, shaking her head; "when you come home from fishing or from a journey, her frolics may then be very delightful, but to have her about one the whole day long, and never to hear a sensible word, and instead of finding her a help in the housekeeping as she grows older, always to be obliged to be taking care that her follies do not completely ruin us, that is quite another thing, and the patience of a saint would be worn out at last."

"Well, well," said her husband with a smile, "you have your troubles with Undine, and I have mine with the lake. It often breaks away my dams, and tears my nets to pieces, but for all that, I have an affection for it, and so have you for the pretty child, in spite of all your crosses and vexations. Isn't it so?"

"One can't be very angry with her, certainly," said the old woman, and she smiled approvingly.

Just then the door flew open, and a beautiful, fair girl glided laughing into the room, and said "You have only been jesting, father, for where is your guest?"

At the same moment, however, she perceived the knight, and stood fixed with astonishment before the handsome youth, Huldbrand was struck with her charming appearance, and dwelt the more earnestly on her lovely features, as he imagined it was only her surprise that gave him this brief enjoyment, and that she would presently turn from his gaze with increased bashfulness. It was, however, quite otherwise; for after having looked at him for some time, she drew near him confidingly, knelt down before him, and said, as she played with a gold medal which he wore on his breast, suspended from a rich chain: "Why, you handsome, kind guest, how have you come to our poor cottage at last? Have you been obliged then to wander through the world for years, before you could find your way to us? Do you come out of that wild forest, my beautiful knight?" The old woman's reproof allowed him no time for reply. She admonished the girl to stand up and behave herself and to go to her work. Undine, however, without making any answer drew a little footstool close to Huldbrand's chair, sat down upon it with her spinning, and said pleasantly: "I will work here." The old man did as parents are wont to do with spoiled children. He affected to observe nothing of Undine's naughtiness and was beginning to talk of something else. But this the girl would not let him do; she said: "I have asked our charming guest whence he comes, and he has not yet answered me."

"I come from the forest, you beautiful little vision," returned Huldbrand; and she went on to say:—

"Then you must tell me how you came there, for it is usually so feared, and what marvellous adventures you met with in it, for it is impossible to escape without something of the sort."

Huldbrand felt a slight shudder at this remembrance, and looked involuntarily toward the window, for it seemed to him as if one of the strange figures he had encountered in the forest were grinning in there; but he saw nothing but the deep dark night, which had now shrouded everything without. Upon this he composed himself and was on the point of beginning his little history, when the old man interrupted him by saying: "Not so, sir knight! this is no fit hour for such things." Undine, however, sprang angrily from her little stool, and standing straight before the fisherman with her fair arms fixed in her sides, she exclaimed: "He shall not tell his story, father? He shall not? but it is my will. He shall! He shall in spite of you!" and thus saying she stamped her pretty little foot vehemently on the floor, but she did it all with such a comically graceful air that Huldbrand now felt his gaze almost more riveted upon her in her anger than before in her gentleness.

The restrained wrath of the old man, on the contrary, burst forth violently. He severely reproved Undine's disobedience and unbecoming behavior to the stranger, and his good old wife joined with him heartily. Undine quickly retorted: "If you want to chide me, and won't do what I wish, then sleep alone in your old smoky hut!" and swift as an arrow she flew from the room, and fled into the dark night.

CHAPTER II.
IN WHAT WAY UNDINE HAD COME TO THE FISHERMAN.

Huldbrand and the fisherman sprang from their seats and were on the point of following the angry girl. Before they reached the cottage door, however, Undine had long vanished in the shadowy darkness without, and not even the sound of her light footstep betrayed the direction of her flight. Huldbrand looked inquiringly at his host; it almost seemed to him as if the whole sweet apparition, which had suddenly merged again into the night, were nothing else than one of that band of the wonderful forms which had, but a short time since, carried on their pranks with him in the forest. But the old man murmured between his teeth: "This is not the first time that she has treated us in this way. Now we have aching hearts and sleepless eyes the whole night through; for who knows, that she may not some day come to harm, if she is thus out alone in the dark until daylight."

"Then let us for God's sake follow her," cried Huldbrand, anxiously.

"What would be the good of it?" replied the old man. "It would be a sin were I to allow you, all alone, to follow the foolish girl in the solitary night, and my old limbs would not overtake the wild runaway, even if we knew in what direction she had gone."

"We had better at any rate call after her, and beg her to come back," said Huldbrand; and he began to call in the most earnest manner: "Undine! Undine! Pray come back!" The old man shook his head, saying, that all that shouting would help but little, for the knight had no idea how self-willed the little truant was. But still he could not forbear often calling out with him in the dark night: "Undine! Ah! dear Undine, I beg you to come back—only this once!"

It turned out, however, as the fisherman had said. No Undine was to be heard or seen, and as the old man would on no account consent that Huldbrand should go in search of the fugitive, they were at last both obliged to return to the cottage. Here they found the fire on the hearth almost gone out, and the old wife, who took Undine's flight and danger far less to heart than her husband, had already retired to rest. The old man blew up the fire, laid some dry wood on it, and by the light of the flame sought out a tankard of wine, which he placed between himself and his guest. "You, sir knight," said he, "are also anxious about that silly girl, and we would both rather chatter and drink away a part of the night than keep turning round on our rush mats trying in vain to sleep. Is it not so?" Huldbrand was well satisfied with the plan; the fisherman obliged him to take the seat of honor vacated by the good old housewife, and both drank and talked together in a manner becoming two honest and trusting men. It is true, as often as the slightest thing moved before the windows, or even at times when nothing was moving, one of the two would look up and say: "She is coming!" Then they would be silent for a moment or two, and as nothing appeared, they would shake their heads and sigh and go on with their talk.

As, however, neither could think of anything but of Undine, they knew of nothing better to do than that the old fisherman should tell the story, and the knight should hear, in what manner Undine had first come to the cottage. He therefore began as follows:—

"It is now about fifteen years ago that I was one day crossing the wild forest with my goods, on my way to the city. My wife had stayed at home, as her wont is, and at this particular time for a very good reason, for God had given us, in our tolerably advanced age, a wonderfully beautiful child. It was a little girl; and a question already arose between us, whether for the sake of the new-comer, we would not leave our lovely home that we might better bring up this dear gift of heaven in some more habitable place. Poor people indeed cannot do in such cases as you may think they ought, sir knight, but, with God's blessing, every one must do what he can. Well, the matter was tolerably in my head as I went along. This slip of land was so dear to me, and I shuddered when, amid the noise and brawls of the city, I thought to myself, 'In such scenes as these, or in one not much more quiet, thou wilt also soon make thy abode!' But at the same time I did not murmur against the good God; on the contrary, I thanked him in secret for the new-born babe; I should be telling a lie, too, were I to say, that on my journey through the wood, going or returning, anything befell me out of the common way, and at that time I had never seen any of its fearful wonders. The Lord was ever with me in those mysterious shades."

As he spoke he took his little cap from his bald head, and remained for a time occupied with prayerful thoughts; he then covered himself again, and continued:—

"On this side the forest, alas! a sorrow awaited me. My wife came to meet me with tearful eyes and clad in mourning. 'Oh! Good God!' I groaned, 'where is our dear child? speak!'—'With him on whom you have called, dear husband,' she replied; and we now entered the cottage together weeping silently. I looked around for the little corpse, and it was then only that I learned how it had all happened."

"My wife had been sitting with the child on the edge of the lake, and as she was playing with it, free of all fear and full of happiness, the little one suddenly bent forward, as if attracted by something very beautiful in the water. My wife saw her laugh, the dear angel, and stretch out her little hands; but in a moment she had sprung out of her mother's arms, and had sunk beneath the watery mirror. I sought long for our little lost one; but it was all in vain; there was no trace of her to be found."

"The same evening we, childless parents, were sitting silently together in the cottage; neither of us had any desire to talk, even had our tears allowed us. We sat gazing into the fire on the hearth. Presently, we heard something rustling outside the door: it flew open, and a beautiful little girl three or four years old, richly dressed, stood on the threshold smiling at us. We were quite dumb with astonishment, and I knew not at first whether it were a vision or a reality. But I saw the water dripping from her golden hair and rich garments, and I perceived that the pretty child had been lying in the water, and needed help. 'Wife,' said I, 'no one has been able to save our dear child; yet let us at any rate do for others what would have made us so blessed.' We undressed the little one, put her to bed, and gave her something warm; at all this she spoke not a word, and only fixed her eyes, that reflected the blue of the lake and of the sky, smilingly upon us. Next morning we quickly perceived that she had taken no harm from her wetting, and I now inquired about her parents, and how she had come here. But she gave a confused and strange account. She must have been born far from here, not only because for these fifteen years I have not been able to find out anything of her parentage, but because she then spoke, and at times still speaks, of such singular things that such as we are cannot tell but that she may have dropped upon us from the moon. She talks of golden castles, of crystal domes, and heaven knows what besides. The story that she told with most distinctness was, that she was out in a boat with her mother on the great lake, and fell into the water, and that she only recovered her senses here under the trees where she felt herself quite happy on the merry shore. We had still a great misgiving and perplexity weighing on our heart. We had, indeed, soon decided to keep the child we had found and to bring her up in the place of our lost darling; but who could tell us whether she had been baptized or not? She herself could give us no information on the matter. She generally answered our questions by saying that she well knew she was created for Gods praise and glory, and that she was ready to let us do with her whatever would tend to His honor and glory."

"My wife and I thought that if she were not baptized, there was no time for delay, and that if she were, a good thing could not be repeated too often. And in pursuance of this idea, we reflected upon a good name for the child, for we now were often at a loss to know what to call her. We agreed at last that Dorothea would be the most suitable for her, for I once heard that it meant a gift of God, and she had surely been sent to us by God as a gift and comfort in our misery. She, on the other hand, would not hear of this, and told us that she thought she had been called Undine by her parents, and that Undine she wished still to be called. Now this appeared to me a heathenish name, not to be found in any calendar, and I took counsel therefore of a priest in the city. He also would not hear of the name of Undine, but at my earnest request he came with me through the mysterious forest in order to perform the rite of baptism here in my cottage. The little one stood before us so prettily arrayed and looked so charming that the priest's heart was at once moved within him, and she flattered him so prettily, and braved him so merrily, that at last he could no longer remember the objections he had had ready against the name of Undine. She was therefore baptized 'Undine,' and during the sacred ceremony she behaved with great propriety and sweetness, wild and restless as she invariably was at other times. For my wife was quite right when she said that it has been hard to put up with her. If I were to tell you"—

The knight interrupted the fisherman to draw his attention to a noise, as of a rushing flood of waters, which had caught his ear during the old man's talk, and which now burst against the cottage-window with redoubled fury. Both sprang to the door. There they saw, by the light of the now risen moon, the brook which issued from the wood, widely overflowing its banks, and whirling away stones and branches of trees in its sweeping course. The storm, as if awakened by the tumult, burst forth from the mighty clouds which passed rapidly across the moon; the lake roared under the furious lashing of the wind; the trees of the little peninsula groaned from root to topmost bough, and bent, as if reeling, over the surging waters. "Undine! for Heaven's sake, Undine." cried the two men in alarm. No answer was returned, and regardless of every other consideration, they ran out of the cottage, one in this direction, and the other in that, searching and calling.

CHAPTER III.
HOW THEY FOUND UNDINE AGAIN.

The longer Huldbrand sought Undine beneath the shades of night, and failed to find her, the more anxious and confused did he become.

The idea that Undine had been only a mere apparition of the forest, again gained ascendancy over him; indeed, amid the howling of the waves and the tempest, the cracking of the trees, and the complete transformation of a scene lately so calmly beautiful, he could almost have considered the whole peninsula with its cottage and its inhabitants as a mocking illusive vision; but from afar he still ever heard through the tumult the fisherman's anxious call for Undine, and the loud praying and singing of his aged wife. At length he came close to the brink of the swollen stream, and saw in the moonlight how it had taken its wild course directly in front of the haunted forest, so as to change the peninsula into an island. "Oh God!" he thought to himself, "if Undine has ventured a step into that fearful forest, perhaps in her charming wilfulness, just because I was not allowed to tell her about it; and now the stream may be rolling between us, and she may be weeping on the other side alone, among phantoms and spectres!"

A cry of horror escaped him, and he clambered down some rocks and overthrown pine-stems, in order to reach the rushing stream and by wading or swimming to seek the fugitive on the other side. He remembered all the awful and wonderful things which he had encountered, even by day, under the now rustling and roaring branches of the forest. Above all it seemed to him as if a tall man in white, whom he knew but too well, was grinning and nodding on the opposite shore; but it was just these monstrous forms which forcibly impelled him to cross the flood, as the thought seized him that Undine might be among them in the agonies of death and alone.

He had already grasped the strong branch of a pine, and was standing supported by it, in the whirling current, against which he could with difficulty maintain himself; though with a courageous spirit he advanced deeper into it. Just then a gentle voice exclaimed near him: "Venture not, venture not, the old man, the stream, is full of tricks!" He knew the sweet tones; he stood as if entranced beneath the shadows that duskily shrouded the moon, and his head swam with the swelling of the waves, which he now saw rapidly rising to his waist. Still he would not desist.

"If thou art not really there, if thou art only floating about me like a mist, then may I too cease to live and become a shadow like thee, dear, dear Undine!" Thus exclaiming aloud, he again stepped deeper into the stream. "Look round thee, oh! look round thee, beautiful but infatuated youth!" cried a voice again close beside him, and looking aside, he saw by the momentarily unveiled moon, a little island formed by the flood, on which he perceived under the interweaved branches of the overhanging trees, Undine smiling and happy, nestling in the flowery grass.

Oh! how much more gladly than before did the young man now use the aid of his pine-branch!

With a few steps he had crossed the flood which was rushing between him and the maiden, and he was standing beside her on a little spot of turf, safely guarded and screened by the good old trees. Undine had half-raised herself, and now under the green leafy tent she threw her arms round his neck, and drew him down beside her on her soft seat.

"You shall tell me your story here, beautiful friend," said she, in a low whisper; "the cross old people cannot hear us here: and our roof of leaves is just as good a shelter as their poor cottage."

"It is heaven itself!" said Huldbrand, embracing the beautiful girl and kissing her fervently.

The old fisherman meanwhile had come to the edge of the stream, and shouted across to the two young people; "Why, sir knight, I have received you as one honest-hearted man is wont to receive another, and now here you are caressing my foster-child in secret, and letting me run hither and thither through the night in anxious search of her."

"I have only just found her myself, old father," returned the knight.

"So much the better," said the fisherman; "but now bring her across to me without delay upon firm ground."

Undine, however, would not hear of this; she declared she would rather go with the beautiful stranger, into the wild forest itself, than return to the cottage, where no one did as she wished, and from which the beautiful knight would himself depart sooner or later. Then, throwing her arms round Huldbrand, she sang with indescribable grace:—

> "A stream ran out of the misty vale
> Its fortunes to obtain,
> the ocean's depths it found a home
> And ne'er returned again."

The old fisherman wept bitterly at her song, but this did not seem to affect her particularly. She kissed and caressed her new friend, who at last said to her: "Undine, if the old man's distress does not touch your heart, it touches mine—let us go back to him."

She opened her large blue eyes in amazement at him, and spoke at last, slowly and hesitatingly: "If you think so—well, whatever you think is right to me. But the old man yonder must first promise me that he will let you, without objection, relate to me what you saw in the wood, and—well, other things will settle themselves."

"Come, only come," cried the fisherman to her, unable to utter another word: and at the same time he stretched out his arms far over the rushing stream toward her, and nodded his head as if to promise the fulfilment of her request, and as he did this, his white hair fell strangely over his face, and reminded Huldbrand of the nodding white man in the forest. Without allowing himself, however, to grow confused by such an idea the young knight took the beautiful girl in his arms, and bore her over the narrow passage which the stream had forced between her little island and the shore.

The old man fell upon Undine's neck and could not satisfy the exuberance of his joy; his good wife also came up and caressed the newly-found in the heartiest manner. Not a word of reproach passed their lips; nor was it thought of, for Undine, forgetting all her waywardness, almost overwhelmed her foster-parents with affection and fond expressions.

When at last they had recovered from the excess of their joy, day had already dawned, and had shed its purple hue over the lake; stillness had followed the storm, and the little birds were singing merrily on the wet branches. As Undine now insisted upon hearing the knight's promised story, the aged couple smilingly and readily acceded to her desire. Breakfast was brought out under the trees which screened the cottage from the lake, and they sat down to it with contented hearts—Undine on the grass at the knight's feet, the place chosen by herself.

Huldbrand then proceeded with his story.

CHAPTER IV.
OF THAT WHICH THE KNIGHT ENCOUNTERED IN THE WOOD.

"It is now about eight days ago since I rode into the free imperial city, which lies on the other side of the forest. Soon after my arrival, there was a splendid tournament and running at the ring, and I spared neither my horse nor my lance. Once when I was pausing at the lists, to rest after my merry toil, and was handing back my helmet to one of my squires, my attention was attracted by a female figure of great beauty, who was standing richly attired on one of the galleries allotted to spectators."

"I asked my neighbor, and learned from him, that the name of the fair lady was Bertalda, and that she was the foster-daughter of one of the powerful dukes living in the country. I remarked that she also was looking at me, and, as it is wont to be with us young knights, I had already ridden bravely, and now pursued my course with renovated confidence and courage. In the dance that evening I was Bertalda's partner, and I remained so throughout the festival."

A sharp pain in his left hand, which hung down by his side, here interrupted Huldbrand's narrative, and drew his attention to the aching part. Undine had fastened her pearly teeth upon one of his fingers, appearing at the same time very gloomy and angry. Suddenly, however, she looked up in his eyes with an expression of tender melancholy, and whispered in a soft voice: "It is your own fault." Then she hid her face, and the knight, strangely confused and thoughtful, continued his narrative.

"This Bertalda was a haughty, wayward girl. Even on the second day she pleased me no longer as she had done on the first, and on the third day still less. Still I continued about her, because she was more pleasant to me than to any other knight, and thus it was that I begged her in jest to give me one of her gloves. 'I will give it you when you have quite alone explored the ill-famed forest,' said she, 'and can bring me tidings of its wonders.' It was not that her glove was of such importance to me, but the word had been said, and an honorable knight would not allow himself to be urged a second time to such a proof of valor."

"I think she loved you," said Undine, interrupting him.

"It seemed so," replied Huldbrand.

"Well," exclaimed the girl, laughing, "she must be stupid indeed. To drive away any one dear to her. And moreover, into an ill-omened wood. The forest and its mysteries might have waited long enough for me!"

"Yesterday morning." continued the knight, smiling kindly at Undine, "I set out on my enterprise. The stems of the trees caught the red tints of the morning light which lay brightly on the green turf, the leaves seemed whispering merrily with each other, and in my heart I could have laughed at the people who could have expected anything to terrify them in this pleasant spot. 'I shall soon have trotted through the forest there and back again,' I said to myself, with a feeling of easy gayety, and before I had even thought of it I was deep within the green shades, and could no longer perceive the plain which lay behind me. Then for the first time it struck me that I might easily lose my way in the mighty forest, and that this perhaps was the only danger which the wanderer had to fear. I therefore paused and looked round in the direction of the sun, which in the mean while had risen somewhat higher above the horizon. While I was thus looking up I saw something black in the branches of a lofty oak. I thought it was a bear and I grasped my sword; but with a human voice, that sounded harsh and ugly, it called to me from above: 'If I do not nibble away the branches up here, Sir Malapert, what shall we have to roast you with at midnight?' And so saying it grinned and made the branches rustle, so that my horse grew furious and rushed forward with me before I had time to see what sort of a devil it really was."

"You must not call it so," said the old fisherman as he crossed himself; his wife did the same silently. Undine looked at the knight with sparkling eyes and said: "The best of the story is that they certainly have not roasted him yet; go on now, you beautiful youth!"

The knight continued his narration: "My horse was so wild that he almost rushed with me against the stems and branches of trees; he was dripping with sweat, and yet would not suffer himself to be held in. At last he went straight in the direction of a rocky precipice; then it suddenly seemed to me as if a tall white man threw himself across the path of my wild steed; the horse trembled with fear and stopped: I recovered my hold of him, and for the first time perceived that my deliverer was no white man, but a brook of silvery brightness, rushing down from a hill by my side and crossing and impeding my horse's course."

"Thanks, dear Brook," exclaimed Undine, clapping her little hands. The old man, however, shook his head and looked down in deep thought.

"I had scarcely settled myself in the saddle," continued Huldbrand. "and seized the reins firmly, when a wonderful little man stood at my side, diminutive, and ugly beyond conception. His complexion was of a yellowish brown, and his nose not much smaller than the rest of his entire person. At the same time he kept grinning with stupid courtesy, exhibiting his huge mouth, and making a thousand scrapes and bows to me. As this farce was now becoming inconvenient to me, I thanked him briefly and turned about my still trembling steed, thinking either to seek another adventure, or in case I met with none, to find my way back, for during my wild chase the sun had already passed the meridian; but the little fellow sprang round with the speed of lightning and stood again before my horse. 'Room!' I cried, angrily; 'the animal is wild and may easily run over you.'—'Ay, ay!' snarled the imp, with a grin still more horribly stupid. 'Give me first some drink-money, for I have stopped your horse; without me you and your horse would be now both lying in the stony ravine; ugh!'—'Don't make any more faces,' said I, 'and take your money, even if you are telling lies; for see, it was the good brook there that saved me, and not you, you miserable wight! And at the same time I dropped a piece of gold into his grotesque cap, which he had taken off in his begging. I then trotted on; but he screamed after me, and suddenly with inconceivable quickness was at my side. I urged my horse into a gallop; the imp ran too, making at the same time strange contortions with his body, half-ridiculous, half-horrible, and holding up the gold-piece, he cried, at every leap, 'False money! false coin!, false coin!, false money!'—and this he uttered with such a hollow sound that one would have supposed that after every scream he would have fallen dead to the ground."

"His horrid red tongue moreover hung far out of his mouth. I stopped, perplexed, and asked: 'What do you mean by this screaming? take another piece of gold, take two, but leave me.' He then began again his hideous burlesque of politeness, and snarled out: 'Not gold, not gold, my young gentleman. I have too much of that trash myself, as I will show you at once?'"

"Suddenly it seemed to me as if I could see through the solid soil as though it were green glass and the smooth earth were as round as a ball; and within, a multitude of goblins were ranking sport with silver and gold; head over heels they were rolling about, pelting each other in jest with the precious metals, and provokingly blowing the gold-dust in each other's eyes. My hideous companion stood partly within and partly without; he ordered the others to reach him up heaps of gold, and showing it to me with a laugh, he then flung it back again with a ringing noise into the immeasurable abyss."

"He then showed the piece of gold I had given him to the goblins below, and they laughed themselves half-dead over it and hissed at me. At last they all pointed at me with their metal-stained fingers, and more and more wildly, and more and more densely, and more and more madly, the swarm of spirits came clambering up to me. I was seized with terror as my horse had been before: I put spurs to him, and I know not how far I galloped for the second time wildly into the forest."

"At length, when I again halted, the coolness of evening was around me. Through the branches of the trees I saw a white foot-path gleaming, which I fancied must lead from the forest toward the city. I was anxious to work my way in that direction; but a face perfectly white and indistinct, with features ever changing, kept peering at me between the leaves; I tried to avoid it, but wherever I went it appeared also. Enraged at this, I determined at last to ride at it, when it gushed forth volumes of foam upon me and my horse, obliging us half-blinded to make a rapid retreat. Thus it drove us step by step ever away from the foot-path, leaving the way open to us only in one direction. When we advanced in this direction, it kept indeed close behind us, but did not do us the slightest harm."

"Looking around at it occasionally, I perceived that the white face that had besprinkled us with foam belonged to a form equally white and of gigantic stature. Many a time I thought that it was a moving stream, but I could never convince myself on the subject. Wearied out, the horse and his rider yielded to the impelling power of the white man, who kept nodding his head, as if he would say, 'Quite right, quite right!' And thus at last we came out here to the end of the forest, where I saw the turf, and the lake, and your little cottage, and where the tall white man disappeared."

"It's well that he's gone," said the old fisherman; and now he began to talk of the best way by which his guest could return to his friends in the city. Upon this Undine began to laugh slyly to herself; Huldbrand observed it, and said: "I thought you were glad to see me here; why then do you now rejoice when my departure is talked of?"

"Because you cannot go away," replied Undine. "Just try it once, to cross that overflowed forest stream with a boat, with your horse, or alone, as you may fancy. Or rather don't try it, for you would be dashed to pieces by the stones and trunks of trees which are carried down by it with the speed of lightning. And as to the lake, I know it well; father dare not venture out far enough with his boat."

Huldbrand rose, smiling, in order to see whether things were as Undine had said; the old man accompanied him, and the girl danced merrily along by their side. They found every thing, indeed, as Undine had described, and the knight was obliged to submit to remain on the little tongue of land, that had become an island, till the flood should subside. As the three were returning to the cottage after their ramble, the knight whispered in the ear of the little maiden "Well, how is it, my pretty Undine—are you angry at my remaining?"

"Ah!" she replied, peevishly, "let me alone. If I had not bitten you, who knows how much of Bertalda would have appeared in your story?"

CHAPTER V.
HOW THE KNIGHT LIVED ON THE LITTLE PROMONTORY.

After having been much driven to and fro in the world, you have perhaps, my dear reader, reached at length some spot where all was well with thee; where the love for home and its calm peace, innate to all, has again sprung up within thee; where thou hast thought that this home was rich with all the flowers of childhood and of the purest, deepest love that rests upon the graves of those that are gone, and thou hast felt it must be good to dwell here and to build habitations. Even if thou hast erred in this, and hast had afterward bitterly to atone for the error, that is nothing to the purpose now, and thou wouldst not, indeed, voluntarily sadden thyself with the unpleasant recollection. But recall that inexpressibly sweet foreboding, that angelic sense of peace, and thou wilt know somewhat of the knight Huldbrand's feelings during his abode on the little promontory.

He often perceived with hearty satisfaction that the forest stream rolled along every day more wildly, making its bed ever broader and broader, and prolonging his sojourn on the island to an indefinite period. Part of the day he rambled about with an old cross-bow, which he had found in a corner of the cottage and had repaired; and, watching for the water-fowl, he killed all that he could for the cottage kitchen. When he brought his booty home, Undine rarely neglected to upbraid him with having so cruelly deprived the happy birds of life; indeed she often wept bitterly at the sight he placed before her. But if he came home another time without having shot anything she scolded him no less seriously, since now, from his carelessness and want of skill, they had to be satisfied with living on fish. He always delighted heartily in her graceful little scoldings, all the more as she generally strove to compensate for her ill-humor by the sweetest caresses.

The old people took pleasure in the intimacy of the young pair; they regarded them as betrothed, or even as already united in marriage, and living on this isolated spot, as a succor and support to them in their old age. It was this same sense of seclusion that suggested the idea also to Huldbrand's mind that he was already Undine's accepted one. He felt as if there were no world beyond these surrounding waters, or as if he could never recross them to mingle with other men; and when at times his grazing horse would neigh as if inquiringly to remind him of knightly deeds, or when the coat of arms on his embroidered saddle and horse-gear shone sternly upon him, or when his beautiful sword would suddenly fall from the nail on which it was hanging in the cottage, gliding from the scabbard as it fell, he would quiet the doubts of his mind by saving: "Undine is no fisherman's daughter; she belongs in all probability to some illustrious family abroad." There was only one thing to which he had a strong aversion, and this was, when the old dame reproved Undine in his presence. The wayward girl, it is true, laughed at it for the most part, without attempting to conceal her mirth; but it seemed to him as if his honor were concerned, and yet he could not blame the old fisherman's wife, for Undine always deserved at least ten times as many reproofs as she received; so, in his heart he felt the balance in favor of the old woman, and his whole life flowed onward in calm enjoyment.

There came, however, an interruption at last. The fisherman and the knight had been accustomed at their mid-day meal, and also in the evening when the wind roared without, as it was always wont to do toward night, to enjoy together a flask of wine. But now the store which the fisherman had from time to time brought with him from the town, was exhausted, and the two men were quite out of humor in consequence.

Undine laughed at them excessively all day, but they were neither of them merry enough to join in her jests as usual. Toward evening she went out of the cottage to avoid, as she said, two such long and tiresome faces. As twilight advanced, there were again tokens of a storm, and the water rushed and roared. Full of alarm, the knight and the fisherman sprang to the door, to bring home the girl, remembering the anxiety of that night when Huldbrand had first come to the cottage. Undine, however, met them, clapping her little hands with delight. "What will you give me," she said, "to provide you with wine?" or rather, "you need not give me anything," she continued, "for I am satisfied if you will look merrier and be in better spirits than you have been throughout this whole wearisome day. Only come with me; the forest stream has driven ashore a cask, and I will be condemned to sleep through a whole week if it is not a wine-cask." The men followed her, and in a sheltered creek on the shore, they actually found a cask, which inspired them with the hope that it contained the generous drink for which they were thirsting.

They at once rolled it as quickly as possible toward the cottage, for the western sky was overcast with heavy storm-clouds, and they could observe in the twilight the waves of the lake raising their white, foaming heads, as if looking out for the rain which was presently to pour down upon them. Undine helped the men as much as she was able, and when the storm of rain suddenly burst over them, she said, with a merry threat to the heavy clouds: "Come, come, take care that you don't wet us; we are still some way from shelter." The old man reproved her for this, as simple presumption, but she laughed softly to herself, and no mischief befell any one in consequence of her levity. Nay, more: contrary to all expectation, they reached the comfortable hearth with their booty perfectly dry, and it was not till they had opened the cask, and had proved that it contained some wonderfully excellent wine, that the rain burst forth from the dark cloud, and the storm raged among the tops of the trees, and over the agitated billows of the lake.

Several bottles were soon filled from the great cask, which promised a supply for many days, and they were sitting drinking and jesting round the glowing fire, feeling comfortably secured from the raging storm without. Suddenly the old fisherman became very grave and said: "Ah, great God! here we are rejoicing over this rich treasure, and he to whom it once belonged, and of whom the floods have robbed it, has probably lost this precious life in their waters."

"That he has not," declared Undine, as she smilingly filled the knight's cup to the brim.

But Huldbrand replied: "By my honor, old father, if I knew where to find and to rescue him, no knightly errand and no danger would I shirk. So much, however, I can promise you, that if ever again I reach more inhabited lands, I will find out the owner of this wine or his heirs, and requite it twofold, nay, threefold."

This delighted the old man; he nodded approvingly to the knight, and drained his cup with a better conscience and greater pleasure.

Undine, however, said to Huldbrand: "Do as you will with your gold and your reimbursement; but you spoke foolishly about the venturing out in search; I should cry my eyes out, if you were lost in the attempt, and isn't it true, that you would yourself rather stay with me and the good wine."

"Yes, indeed," answered Huldbrand, smiling.

"Then," said Undine, "you spoke unwisely. For charity begins at home, and what do other people concern us?"

The old woman turned away sighing and shaking her head; the fisherman forgot his wonted affection for the pretty girl and scolded her.

"It sounds exactly," said he, as he finished his reproof, "as if Turks and heathens had brought you up; may God forgive both me and you, you spoiled child."

"Well," replied Undine, "for all that, it is what I feel, let who will hate brought me up, and all your words can't help that."

"Silence!" exclaimed the fisherman, and Undine, who, in spite of her pertness, was exceedingly fearful, shrank from him, and moving tremblingly toward Huldbrand, asked him in a soft tone: "Are you also angry, dear friend?"

The knight pressed her tender hand and stroked her hair. He could say nothing, for vexation at the old man's severity toward Undine closed his lips: and thus the two couples sat opposite to each other, with angry feelings and embarrassed silence.

CHAPTER VI.
OF A NUPTIAL CEREMONY.

A low knocking at the door was heard in the midst of this stillness, startling all the inmates of the cottage; for there are times when a little circumstance, happening quite unexpectedly, can unduly alarm us. But there was here the additional cause of alarm that the enchanted forest lay so near, and that the little promontory seemed just now inaccessible to human beings. They looked at each other doubtingly, as the knocking was repeated accompanied by a deep groan, and the knight sprang to reach his sword. But the old man whispered softly: "If it be what I fear, no weapon will help us."

Undine meanwhile approached the door and called out angrily and boldly: "Spirits of the earth, if you wish to carry on your mischief, Kuhleborn shall teach you something better."

The terror of the rest was increased by these mysterious words; they looked fearfully at the girl, and Huldbrand was just regaining courage enough to ask what she meant, when a voice said without: "I am no spirit of the earth, but a spirit indeed still within its earthly body. You within the cottage, if you fear God and will help me, open to me." At these words, Undine had already opened the door, and had held a lamp out in the stormy night, by which they perceived an aged priest standing there, who stepped back in terror at the unexpected sight of the beautiful maiden. He might well think that witchcraft and magic were at work when such a lovely form appeared at such an humble cottage door: he therefore began to pray: "All good spirits praise the Lord!"

"I am no spectre," said Undine, smiling; "do I then look so ugly? Besides you may see the holy words do not frighten me. I too know of God and understand how to praise Him; every one to be sure in his own way, for so He has created us. Come in, venerable father; you come among good people."

The holy man entered, bowing and looking round him, with a profound, yet tender demeanor. But the water was dropping from every fold of his dark garment, and from his long white beard and from his gray locks. The fisherman and the knight took him to another apartment and furnished him with other clothes, while they gave the women his own wet attire to dry. The aged stranger thanked them humbly and courteously, but he would on no account accept the knight's splendid mantle, which was offered to him; but he chose instead an old gray overcoat belonging to the fisherman. They then returned to the apartment, and the good old dame immediately vacated her easy-chair for the reverend father, and would not rest till he had taken possession of it. "For," said she, "you are old and exhausted, and you are moreover a man of God." Undine pushed under the stranger's feet her little stool, on which she had been wont to sit by the side of Huldbrand, and she showed herself in every way most gentle and kind in her care of the good old man. Huldbrand whispered some raillery at it in her ear, but she replied very seriously: "He is a servant of Him who created us all; holy things are not to be jested with." The knight and the fisherman then refreshed their reverend guest with food and wine, and when he had somewhat recovered himself, he began to relate how he had the day before set out from his cloister, which lay far beyond the great lake, intending to travel to the bishop, in order to acquaint him with the distress into which the monastery and its tributary villages had fallen on account of the extraordinary floods.

After a long, circuitous route, which these very floods had obliged him to take, he had been this day compelled, toward evening, to procure the aid of a couple of good boatmen to cross an arm of the lake, which had overflowed its banks.

"Scarcely however," continued he, "had our small craft touched the waves, than that furious tempest burst forth which is now raging over our heads. It seemed as if the waters had only waited for us, to commence their wildest whirling dance with our little boat. The oars were soon torn out of the hands of my men, and were dashed by the force of the waves further and further beyond our reach. We ourselves, yielding to the resistless powers of nature, helplessly drifted over the surging billows of the lake toward your distant shore, which we already saw looming through the mist and foam. Presently our boat turned round and round as in a giddy whirlpool; I know not whether it was upset, or whether I fell overboard. In a vague terror of inevitable death I drifted on, till a wave cast me here, under the trees on your island."

"Yes, island!" cried the fisherman; "a short time ago it was only a point of land; but now, since the forest-stream and the lake have become well-nigh bewitched, things are quite different with us."

"I remarked something of the sort," said the priest, "as I crept along the shore in the dark, and hearing nothing but the uproar around me. I at last perceived that a beaten foot-path disappeared just in the direction from which the sound proceeded. I now saw the light in your cottage, and ventured hither, and I cannot sufficiently thank my heavenly Father that after preserving me from the waters, He has led me to such good and pious people as you are; and I feel this all the more, as I do not know whether I shall ever behold any other beings is this world, except those I now address."

"What do you mean?" asked the fisherman.

"Do you know then how long this commotion of the elements is to last?" replied the holy man. "And I am old in years. Easily enough may the stream of my life run itself out before the overflowing of the forest-stream may subside. And indeed it were not impossible that more and more of the foaming waters may force their way between you and yonder forest, until you are so far sundered from the rest of the world that your little fishing-boat will no longer be sufficient to carry you across, and the inhabitants of the continent in the midst of their diversions will have entirely forgotten you in your old age."

The fisherman's wife started at this, crossed herself and exclaimed. "God forbid." But her husband looked at her with a smile, and said "What creatures we are after all! even were it so, things would not be very different—at least not for you, dear wife—than they now are. For have you for many years been further than the edge of the forest? and have you seen any other human beings than Undine and myself? The knight and this holy man have only come to as lately. They will remain with us if we do become a forgotten island; so you would even be a gainer by it after all."

"I don't know," said the old woman; "it is somehow a gloomy thought, when one imagines that one is irrecoverably separated from other people, although, were it otherwise, one might neither know nor see them."

"Then you will remain with us! then you will remain with us!" whispered Undine, in a low, half-singing tone, as she nestled closer to Huldbrand's side. But he was absorbed in the deep and strange visions of his own mind.

The region on the other side of the forest-river seemed to dissolve into distance during the priest's last words: and the blooming island upon which he lived grew more green, and smiled more freshly in his mind's vision. His beloved one glowed as the fairest rose of this little spot of earth, and even of the whole world, and the priest was actually there. Added to this, at that moment an angry glance from the old dame was directed at the beautiful girl, because even in the presence of the reverend father she leaned so closely on the knight, and it seemed as if a torrent of reproving words were on the point of following. Presently, turning to the priest, Huldbrand broke forth: "Venerable father, you see before you here a pair pledged to each other: and if this maiden and these good old people have no objection, you shall unite us this very evening." The aged couple were extremely surprised. They had, it is true, hitherto often thought of something of the sort, but they had never yet expressed it, and when the knight now spoke thus, it came upon them as something wholly new and unprecedented.

Undine had become suddenly grave, and looked down thoughtfully while the priest inquired respecting the circumstances of the case, and asked if the old people gave their consent. After much discussion together, the matter was settled; the old dame went to arrange the bridal chamber for the young people, and to look out two consecrated tapers which she had had in her possession for some time, and which she thought essential to the nuptial ceremony. The knight in the mean while examined his gold chain, from which he wished to disengage two rings, that he might make an exchange of them with his bride.

She, however, observing what he was doing, started up from her reverie, and exclaimed: "Not so! my parents have not sent me into the world quite destitute; on the contrary, they must have anticipated with certainty that such an evening as this would come." Thus saving, she quickly left the room and reappeared in a moment with two costly rings, one of which she gave to her bridegroom, and kept the other for herself. The old fisherman was extremely astonished at this, and still more so his wife, who just then entered, for neither had ever seen these jewels in the child's possession.

"My parents," said Undine, "sewed these little things into the beautiful frock which I had on, when I came to you. They forbid me, moreover, to mention them to anyone before my wedding evening, so I secretly took them, and kept them concealed until now."

The priest interrupted all further questionings by lighting the consecrated tapers, which he placed upon a table, and summoned the bridal pair to stand opposite to him. He then gave them to each other with a few short solemn words; the elder couple gave their blessing to the younger, and the bride, trembling and thoughtful, leaned upon the knight. Then the priest suddenly said: "You are strange people after all. Why did you tell me you were the only people here on the island? and during the whole ceremony, a tall stately man, in a white mantle, has been looking at me through the window opposite. He must still be standing before the door, to see if you will invite him to come into the house."

"God forbid," said the old dame with a start; the fisherman shook his head in silence, and Huldbrand sprang to the window. It seemed even to him as if he could still see a white streak, but it soon completely disappeared in the darkness. He convinced the priest that he must have been absolutely mistaken, and they all sat down together round the hearth.

CHAPTER VII.
WHAT FURTHER HAPPENED ON THE EVENING OF THE WEDDING.

Both before and during the ceremony, Undine had shown herself gentle and quiet; but it now seemed as if all the wayward humors which rioted within her, burst forth all the more boldly and unrestrainedly. She teased her bridegroom and her foster-parents, and even the holy man whom she had so lately reverenced, with all sorts of childish tricks; and when the old woman was about to reprove her, she was quickly silenced by a few grave words from the knight, speaking of Undine now as his wife. Nevertheless, the knight himself was equally little pleased with Undine's childish behavior: but no signs, and no reproachful words were of any avail. It is true, whenever the bride noticed her husband's dissatisfaction—and this occurred occasionally—she became more quiet, sat down by his side, caressed him, whispered something smilingly into his ear, and smoothed the wrinkles that were gathering on his brow. But immediately afterward, some wild freak would again lead her to return to her ridiculous proceedings, and matters would be worse than before. At length the priest said in a serious and kind tone: "My fair young maiden, no one indeed can look at you without delight; but remember so to attune your soul betimes, that it may ever harmonize with that of your wedded husband."

"Soul!" said Undine, laughing; "that sounds pretty enough, and may be a very edifying and useful caution for most people. But when one hasn't a soul at all, I beg you, what is there to attune then? and that is my case." The priest was silent and deeply wounded, and with holy displeasure he turned his face from the girl. She, however, went up to him caressingly, and said: "No! listen to me first, before you look angry, for your look of anger gives me pain, and you must not give pain to any creature who has done you no wrong—only have patience with me, and I will tell you properly what I mean."

It was evident that she was preparing herself to explain something in detail, but suddenly she hesitated, as if seized with an inward shuddering, and burst out into a flood of tears. They none of them knew what to make of this ebullition, and filled with various apprehensions they gazed at her in silence. At length, wiping away her tears, and looking earnestly at the reverend man, she said: "There must be something beautiful, but at the same time extremely awful, about a soul. Tell me, holy sir, were it not better that we never shared such a gift?" She was silent again as if waiting for an answer, and her tears had ceased to flow. All in the cottage had risen from their seats and had stepped back from her with horror. She, however, seemed to have eyes for no one but the holy man; her features wore an expression of fearful curiosity, which appeared terrible to those who saw her. "The soul must be a heavy burden," she continued, as no one answered her, "very heavy! for even its approaching image overshadows me with anxiety and sadness. And, ah! I was so light-hearted and so merry till now!" And she burst into a fresh flood of tears, and covered her face with the drapery she wore. Then the priest went up to her with a solemn air, and spoke to her, and conjured her by the name of the Most Holy to cast aside the veil that enveloped her, if any spirit of evil possessed her. But she sank on her knees before him, repeating all the sacred words he uttered, praising God, and protesting that she wished well with the whole world.

Then at last the priest said to the knight: "Sir bridegroom, I will leave you alone with her whom I have united to you in marriage. So far as I can discover there is nothing of evil in her, but much indeed that is mysterious. I commend to you—prudence, love, and fidelity." So saying, he went out, and the fisherman and his wife followed him, crossing themselves.

Undine had sunk on her knees: she unveiled her face and said, looking timidly round on Huldbrand: "Alas! you will surely now not keep me as your own; and yet I have done no evil, poor child that I am!" As she said this, she looked so exquisitely graceful and touching, that her bridegroom forgot all the horror he had felt, and all the mystery that clung to her, and hastening to her he raised her in his arms. She smiled through her tears; it was a smile like the morning-light playing on a little stream.

"You cannot leave me," she whispered, with confident security, stroking the knight's cheek with her tender hand. Huldbrand tried to dismiss the fearful thoughts that still lurked in the background of his mind, persuading him that he was married to a fairy or to some malicious and mischievous being of the spirit world, only the single question half unawares escaped his lips: "My little Undine, tell me this one thing, what was it you said of spirits of the earth and of Kuhleborn, when the priest knocked at the door?"

"It was nothing but fairy tales!—children's fairy tales!" said Undine, with all her wonted gayety; "I frightened you at first with them, and then you frightened me, that's the end of our story and of our nuptial evening."

"Nay! that it isn't," said the knight, intoxicated with love, and extinguishing the tapers, he bore his beautiful beloved to the bridal chamber by the light of the moon which shone brightly through the windows.

CHAPTER VIII.
THE DAY AFTER THE WEDDING.

The fresh light of the morning awoke the young married pair. Wonderful and horrible dreams had disturbed Huldbrand's rest; he had been haunted by spectres, who, grinning at him by stealth, had tried to disguise themselves as beautiful women, and from beautiful women they all at once assumed the faces of dragons, and when he started up from these hideous visions, the moonlight shone pale and cold into the room; terrified he looked at Undine, who still lay in unaltered beauty and grace. Then he would press a light kiss upon her rosy lips, and would fall asleep again only to be awakened by new terrors. After he had reflected on all this, now that he was fully awake, he reproached himself for any doubt that could have led him into error with regard to his beautiful wife. He begged her to forgive him for the injustice he had done her, but she only held out to him her fair hand, sighed deeply, and remained silent. But a glance of exquisite fervor beamed from her eyes such as he had never seen before, carrying with it the full assurance that Undine bore him no ill-will. He then rose cheerfully and left her, to join his friends in the common apartment.

He found the three sitting round the hearth, with an air of anxiety about them, as if they dared not venture to speak aloud. The priest seemed to be praying in his inmost spirit that all evil might be averted. When, however, they saw the young husband come forth so cheerfully the careworn expression of their faces vanished.

The old fisherman even began to jest with the knight, so pleasantly, that the aged wife smiled good-humoredly as she listened to them. Undine at length made her appearance. All rose to meet her and all stood still with surprise, for the young wife seemed so strange to them and yet the same. The priest was the first to advance toward her with paternal arms affection beaming in his face, and, as he raised his hand to bless her, the beautiful woman sank reverently on her knees before him. With a few humble and gracious words she begged him to forgive her for any foolish things she might have said the evening before, and entreated him in an agitated tone to pray for the welfare of her soul. She then rose, kissed her foster-parents, and thanking them for all the goodness they had shown her, she exclaimed: "Oh! I now feel in my innermost heart, how much, how infinitely much, you have done for me, dear, kind people!" She could not at first desist from her caresses, but scarcely had she perceived that the old woman was busy in preparing breakfast, than she went to the hearth, cooked and arranged the meal, and would not suffer the good old mother to take the least trouble.

She continued thus throughout the whole day, quiet, kind, and attentive—at once a little matron and a tender, bashful girl. The three who had known her longest expected every moment to see some whimsical vagary of her capricious spirit burst forth. But they waited in vain for it. Undine remained as mild and gentle as an angel. The holy father could not take his eyes from her, and he said repeatedly to the bridegroom: "The goodness of heaven, sir, has intrusted a treasure to you yesterday through me, unworthy as I am; cherish it as you ought, and it will promote your temporal and eternal welfare."

Toward evening Undine was hanging on the knight's arm with humble tenderness, and drew him gently out of the door, where the declining sun was shining pleasantly on the fresh grass, and upon the tall, slender stems of the trees. The eyes of the young wife were moist, as with the dew of sadness and love, and a tender and fearful secret seemed hovering on her lips, which, however, was only disclosed by scarcely audible sighs. She led her husband onward and onward in silence; when he spoke, she only answered him with looks, in which, it is true, there lay no direct reply to his inquiries, but whole heaven of love and timid devotion. Thus they reached the edge of the swollen forest stream, and the knight was astonished to see it rippling along in gentle waves, without a trace of its former wildness and swell. "By the morning it will be quite dry," said the beautiful wife, in a regretful tone, "and you can then travel away wherever you will, without anything to hinder you."

"Not without you, my little Undine," replied the knight, laughing: "remember, even if I wished to desert you, the church, and the spiritual powers, and the emperor, and the empire would interpose and bring the fugitive back again."

"All depends upon you, all depends upon you," whispered his wife, half-weeping and half-smiling. "I think, however, nevertheless, that you will keep me with you: I love you so heartily. Now carry me across to that little island that lies before us. The matter shall be decided there. I could easily indeed glide through the rippling waves, but it is so restful in your arms, and if you were to cast me off, I shall have sweetly rested in them once more for the last time." Huldbrand, full as he was of strange fear and emotion, knew not what to reply. He took her in his arms and carried her across, remembering now for the first time that this was the same little island from which he had borne her back to the old fisherman on that first night. On the further side he put her down on the soft grass, and was on the point of placing himself lovingly near his beautiful burden, when she said: "No, there opposite to me! I will read my sentence in your eyes, before your lips speak; now, listen attentively to what I will relate to you." And she began:—

"You must know, my loved one, that there are beings in the elements which almost appear like mortals, and which rarely allow themselves to become visible to your race. Wonderful salamanders glitter and sport in the flames; lean and malicious gnomes dwell deep within the earth; spirits, belonging to the air, wander through the forests, and a vast family of water-spirits live in the lakes, and streams, and brooks. In resounding domes of crystal, through which the sky looks in with its sun and stars, these latter spirits find their beautiful abode; lofty trees of coral with blue and crimson fruits gleam in their gardens; they wander over the pure sand of the sea, and among lovely variegated shells, and amid all exquisite treasures of the old world, which the present is no longer worthy to enjoy; all these the floods have covered with their secret veils of silver, and the noble monuments sparkle below, stately and solemn, and bedewed by the loving waters which allure from them many a beautiful moss-flower and entwining cluster of sea-grass. Those, however, who dwell there are very fair and lovely to behold, and for the most part are more beautiful than human beings. Many a fisherman has been so fortunate as to surprise some tender mermaid as she rose above the waters and sang. He would tell afar of her beauty, and such wonderful beings have been given the name of Undines. You, however, are now actually beholding an Undine."

The knight tried to persuade himself that his beautiful wife was under the spell of one of her strange humors, and that she was taking pleasure in teasing him with one of her extravagant inventions. But repeatedly as he said this to himself, he could not believe it for a moment; a strange shudder passed through him; unable to utter a word, he stared at the beautiful narrator with an immovable gaze. Undine shook her head sorrowfully, drew a deep sigh, and then proceeded as follows:—

"Our condition would be far superior to that of other human beings—for human beings we call ourselves, being similar to them in form and culture—but there is one evil peculiar to us. We and our like in the other elements, vanish into dust and pass away, body and spirit, so that not a vestige of us remains behind; and when you mortals hereafter awake to a purer life, we remain with the sand and the sparks and the wind and the waves. Hence we have also no souls; the element moves us, and is often obedient to us while we live, though it scatters us to dust when we die; and we are merry, without having aught to grieve us—merry as the nightingales and the little gold-fishes and other pretty children of nature. But all things aspire to be higher than they are. Thus, my father, who is a powerful water-prince in the Mediterranean Sea, desired that his only daughter should become possessed of a soul, even though she must then endure many of the sufferings of those thus endowed. Such as we are, however, can only obtain a soul by the closest union of affection with one of your human race. I am now possessed of a soul, and my soul thanks you, my inexpressibly beloved one, and it will ever thank you, if you do not make my whole life miserable. For what is to become of me, if you avoid and reject me? Still, I would not retain you by deceit. And if you mean to reject me, do so now, and return alone to the shore. I will dive into this brook, which is my uncle; and here in the forest, far removed from other friends, he passes his strange and solitary life. He is, however, powerful, and is esteemed and beloved by many great streams; and as he brought me hither to the fisherman, a light-hearted, laughing child, he will take me back again to my parents, a loving, suffering, and soul-endowed woman."

She was about to say still more, but Huldbrand embraced her with the most heartfelt emotion and love, and bore her back again to the shore. It was not till he reached it, that he swore amid tears and kisses, never to forsake his sweet wife, calling himself more happy than the Greek Pygmalion, whose beautiful statue received life from Venus and became his loved one. In endearing confidence, Undine walked back to the cottage, leaning on his arm; feeling now for the first time, with all her heart, how little she ought to regret the forsaken crystal palaces of her mysterious father.

CHAPTER IX.
HOW THE KNIGHT TOOK HIS YOUNG WIFE WITH HIM.

When Huldbrand awoke from his sleep on the following morning, and missed his beautiful wife from his side, he began to indulge again in the strange thoughts, that his marriage and the charming Undine herself were but fleeting and deceptive illusions. But at the same moment she entered the room, sat down beside him, and said: "I have been out rather early to see if my uncle keeps his word. He has already led all the waters back again into his own calm channel, and he now flows through the forest, solitarily and dreamily as before. His friends in the water and the air have also returned to repose: all will again go on quietly and regularly, and you can travel homeward when you will, dry-shod." It seemed to Huldbrand as though he were in a waking dream, so little could he reconcile himself to the strange relationship of his wife. Nevertheless he made no remark on the matter, and the exquisite grace of his bride soon lulled to rest every uneasy misgiving. When he was afterward standing before the door with her, and looking over the green peninsula with its boundary of clear waters, he felt so happy in this cradle of his love, that he exclaimed: "Why shall we travel so soon as to-day? We shall scarcely find more pleasant days in the world yonder than those we have spent in this quiet little shelter. Let us yet see the sun go down here twice or thrice more."

"As my lord wills," replied Undine, humbly. "It is only that the old people will, at all events, part from me with pain, and when they now for the first time perceive the true soul within me, and how I can now heartily love and honor, their feeble eyes will be dimmed with plentiful tears. At present they consider my quietness and gentleness of no better promise than before, like the calmness of the lake when the air is still;

and, as matters now are, they will soon learn to cherish a flower or a tree as they have cherished me. Do not, therefore, let me reveal to them this newly-bestowed and loving heart, just at the moment when they must lose it for this world; and how could I conceal it, if we remain longer together?"

Huldbrand conceded the point; he went to the aged people and talked with them over the journey, which he proposed to undertake immediately. The holy father offered to accompany the young married pair, and, after a hasty farewell, he and the knight assisted the beautiful bride to mount her horse, and walked with rapid step by her side over the dry channel of the forest-stream into the wood beyond. Undine wept silently but bitterly, and the old people gave loud expression to their grief. It seemed as if they had a presentiment of all they were now losing in their foster-child.

The three travellers had reached in silence the densest shades of the forest. It must have been a fair sight, under that green canopy of leaves, to see Undine's lovely form, as she sat on her noble and richly ornamented steed, with the venerable priest in the white garb of his order on one side of her, and on the other the blooming young knight in his gay and splendid attire, with his sword at his girdle. Huldbrand had no eyes but for his beautiful wife Undine, who had dried her tears, had no eyes but for him, and they soon fell into a mute, voiceless converse of glance and gesture, from which they were only roused at length by the low talking of the reverend father with a fourth traveller, who in the mean while had joined them unobserved.

He wore a white garment almost resembling the dress of the priests order, except that his hood hung low over his face, and his whole attire floated round him in such vast folds that he was obliged every moment to gather it up, and throw it over his arm, or dispose of it in some way, and yet it did not in the least seem to impede his movements. When the young couple first perceived him, he was just saying "And so, venerable sir. I have now dwelt for many years here in the forest, and yet no one could call me a hermit, in your sense of the word. For, as I said, I know nothing of penance, and I do not think I have any especial need of it. I lose the forest only for this reason, that its beauty is quite peculiar to itself, and it amuses me to pass along in my flowing white garments among the eases and dusky shadows, while now and then a sweet sunbeam shines down unexpectedly upon me."

"You are a very strange man," replied the priest, "and I should like to be more closely acquainted with you."

"And to pass from one thing to another, who may you be yourself?" asked the stranger.

"I am called Father Heilmann," said the holy man; "and I come from the monastery of 'our Lady' which lies on the other side of the lake."

"Indeed," replied the stranger; "my name is Kuhleborn, and so far as courtesy is concerned I might claim the title of Lord of Kuhleborn, or free Lord of Kuhleborn; for I am as free as the birds in the forest and perhaps a little more so. For example, I have now something to say to the young lady there." And before they were aware of his intention, he was at the other side of the priest, close beside Undine, stretching himself up to whisper something in her ear.

But she turned from him with alarm, and exclaimed: "I have nothing more to do with you."

"Ho, ho," laughed the stranger, "what is this immensely grand marriage you have made, that you don't know your own relations any longer? Have you forgotten your uncle Kuhleborn, who so faithfully bore you on his back through this region?"

"I beg you, nevertheless," replied Undine, "not to appear in my presence again. I am now afraid of you; and suppose my husband should learn to avoid me when he sees me in such strange company and with such relations!"

"My little niece," said Kuhleborn, "you must not forget that I am with you here as a guide; the spirits of earth that haunt this place might otherwise play some of their stupid pranks with you. Let me therefore go quietly on with you; the old priest there remembered me better than you appear to have done, for he assured me just now that I seemed familiar to him, and that I must have been with him in the boat, out of which he fell into the water. I was so, truly enough; for I was the water-spout that carried him out of it and washed him safely ashore for your wedding."

Undine and the knight turned toward Father Heilmann; but he seemed walking on, as in a sort of dream, and no longer to be conscious of all that was passing. Undine then said to Kuhleborn, "I see yonder the end of the forest. We no longer need your help, and nothing causes us alarm but yourself. I beg you, therefore, in all love and good-will, vanish, and let us proceed in peace."

Kuhleborn seemed to become angry at this; his countenance assumed a frightful expression, and he grinned fiercely at Undine, who screamed aloud and called upon her husband for assistance. As quick as lightning, the knight sprang to the other side of the horse, and aimed his sharp sword at Kuhleborn's head. But the sword cut through a waterfall, which was rushing down near them from a lofty crag; and with a splash, which almost sounded like a burst of laughter, it poured over them and wet them through to the skin.

The priest, as if suddenly awaking, exclaimed "I have long been expecting that, for the stream ran down from the height so close to us. At first it really seemed to me like a man, and as if it could speak." As the waterfall came rushing down, it distinctly uttered these words in Huldbrand's ear:—

> "Rash knight,
> Brave knight,
> Rage, feel I not,

Chide, will I not.
But ever guard thy little wife as well,
Rash knight, brave knight! Protect her well!"

A few footsteps more, and they were upon open ground. The imperial city lay bright before them, and the evening sun, which gilded its towers, kindly dried the garments of the drenched wanderers.

CHAPTER X.
HOW THEY LIVED IN THE CITY.

The sudden disappearance of the young knight, Huldbrand von Ringstetten, from the imperial city, had caused great sensation and solicitude among those who had admired him, both for his skill in the tournament and the dance, and no less so for his gentle and agreeable manners. His servants would not quit the place without their master, although not one of them would have had the courage to go in quest of him into the shadowy recesses of the forest. They therefore remained in their quarters, inactively hoping, as men are wont to do, and keeping alive the remembrance of their lost lord by their lamentations. When, soon after, the violent storms and floods were observed, the less doubt was entertained as to the certain destruction of the handsome stranger; and Bertalda openly mourned for him and blamed herself for having allured the unfortunate knight into the forest. Her foster-parents, the duke and duchess, had come to fetch her away, but Bertalda entreated them to remain with her until certain intelligence had been obtained of Huldbrand's fate. She endeavored to prevail upon several young knights, who were eagerly courting her, to follow the noble adventurer to the forest. But she would not pledge her hand as a reward of the enterprise, because she always cherished the hope of belonging to the returning knight, and no glove, nor riband, nor even kiss, would tempt any one to expose his life for the sake of bringing back such a dangerous rival.

When Huldbrand now suddenly and unexpectedly appeared, his servants. and the inhabitants of the city, and almost every one, rejoiced. Bertalda alone refused to do so; for agreeable as it was to the others that he should bring with him such a beautiful bride, and Father Heilmann as a witness of the marriage, Bertalda could feel nothing but grief and vexation. In the first place, she had really loved the young knight with all her heart, and in the next, her sorrow at his absence had proclaimed this far more before the eyes of all, than was now befitting. She still, however, conducted herself as a wise maiden, reconciled herself to circumstances, and lived on the most friendly terms with Undine, who was looked upon throughout the city as a princess whom Huldbrand had rescued in the forest from some evil enchantment. When she or her husband were questioned on the matter, they were wise enough to be silent or skilfully to evade the inquiries. Father Heilmann's lips were sealed to idle gossip of any kind, and moreover, immediately after Huldbrand's arrival, he had returned to his monastery; so that people were obliged to be satisfied with their own strange conjectures, and even Bertalda herself knew no more of the truth than others.

Day by day, Undine felt her affection increase for the fair maiden. "We must have known each other before," she often used to say to her, "or else, there must be some mysterious connection between us, for one does not love another as dearly as I have loved you from the first moment of our meeting without some cause—some deep and secret cause." And Bertalda also could not deny the fact that she felt drawn to Undine with a tender feeling of confidence, however much she might consider that she had cause for the bitterest lamentation at this successful rival. Biassed by this mutual affection, they both persuaded—the one her foster-parents, the other her husband—to postpone the day of departure from time to time; indeed, it was even proposed that Bertalda should accompany Undine for a time to castle Ringstetten, near the source of the Danube.

They were talking over this plan one beautiful evening, as they were walking by starlight in the large square of the Imperial city, under the tall trees that enclose it. The young married pair had incited Bertalda to join them in their evening walk, and all three were strolling up and down under the dark-blue sky, often interrupting their familiar talk to admire the magnificent fountain in the middle of the square, as its waters rushed and bubbled forth with wonderful beauty. It had a soothing happy influence upon them; between the shadows of the trees there stole glimmerings of light from the adjacent houses; a low murmur of children at play, and of others enjoying their walk, floated around them; they were so alone, and yet in the midst of the bright and living world; whatever had appeared difficult by day, now became smooth as of itself; and the three friends could no longer understand why the slightest hesitation had existed with regard to Bertalda's visit to Ringstetten. Presently, just as they were on the point of fixing the day for their common departure, a tall man approached them from the middle of the square, bowed respectfully to the company, and said something in the ear of the young wife. Displeased as she was at the interruption and its cause, she stepped a little aside with the stranger, and both began to whisper together, as it seemed, in a foreign tongue. Huldbrand fancied he knew the strange man, and he stared so fixedly at him that he neither heard nor answered Bertalda's astonished inquiries.

All at once Undine, clapping her hands joyfully, and laughing, quitted the stranger's side, who, shaking his head, retired hastily and discontentedly, and vanished in the fountain. Huldbrand now felt certain on the point, but Bertalda asked: "And what did the master of the fountain want with you, dear Undine?"

The young wife laughed within herself, and replied: "The day after to-morrow, my dear child, on the anniversary of your name-day, you shall know it." And nothing more would she disclose. She invited

Bertalda and sent an invitation to her foster-parents, to dine with them on the appointed day, and soon after they parted.

"Kuhleborn? was it Kuhleborn?" said Huldbrand, with a secret shudder, to his beautiful bride, when they had taken leave of Bertalda, and were now going home through the darkening streets.

"Yes, it was he," replied Undine, "and he was going to say all sorts of nonsensical things to me. But, in the midst, quite contrary to his intention, he delighted me with a most welcome piece of news. If you wish to hear it at once, my dear lord and husband, you have but to command, and I will tell it you without reserve. But if you would confer a real pleasure on your Undine, you will wait till the day after to-morrow, and you will then have your share too in the surprise."

The knight gladly complied with his wife's desire, which had been urged so sweetly, and as she fell asleep, she murmured smilingly to herself: "Dear, dear Bertalda! How she will rejoice and be astonished at what her master of the fountain told me!"

CHAPTER XI.
THE ANNIVERSARY OF BERTALDA'S NAME-DAY.

The company were sitting at dinner; Bertalda, looking like some goddess of spring with her flowers and jewels, the presents of her foster-parents and friends, was placed between Undine and Huldbrand. When the rich repast was ended, and the last course had appeared, the doors were left open, according to a good old German custom, that the common people might look on, and take part in the festivity of the nobles. Servants were carrying round cake and wine among the spectators. Huldbrand and Bertalda were waiting with secret impatience for the promised explanation, and sat with their eyes fixed steadily on Undine. But the beautiful wife still continued silent, and only kept smiling to herself with secret and hearty satisfaction. All who knew of the promise she had given could see that she was every moment on the point of betraying her happy secret, and that it was with a sort of longing renunciation that she withheld it, just as children sometimes delay the enjoyment of their choicest morsels. Bertalda and Huldbrand shared this delightful feeling, and expected with fearful hope the tidings which were to fall from the lips of Undine. Several of the company pressed Undine to sing. The request seemed opportune, and ordering her lute to be brought, she sang the following words:—

>Bright opening day,
>Wild flowers so gay,
>Tall grasses their thirst that slake,
>On the banks of the billowy lake!
>
>What glimmers there so shining

The reedy growth entwining?
Is it a blossom white as snow
Fallen from heav'n here below?

It is an infant, frail and dear!
With flowerets playing in its dreams
And grasping morning's golden beams;
Oh! whence, sweet stranger, art thou here?

From some far-off and unknown strand,
The lake has borne thee to this land.

Nay, grasp not tender little one,
With thy tiny hand outspread;
No hand will meet thy touch with love,
Mute is that flowery bed.

The flowers can deck themselves so fair
And breathe forth fragrance blest,
Yet none can press thee to itself,
Like that far-off mother's breast.

So early at the gate of life,
With smiles of heav'n on thy brow,
Thou hast the best of treasures lost,
Poor wand'ring child, nor know'st it now.

A noble duke comes riding by,
And near thee checks his courser's speed,
And full of ardent chivalry
He bears thee home upon his steed.

Much, endless much, has been thy gain!
Thou bloom'st the fairest in the land!
Yet ah! the priceless joy of all,
Thou'st left upon an unknown strand.

Undine dropped her lute with a melancholy smile, and the eyes of Bertalda's foster-parents were filled with tears. "Yes, so it was on the morning that I found you, my poor sweet orphan," said the duke, deeply agitated; "the beautiful singer is certainly right; we have not been able to give you that 'priceless joy of all.'"

"But we must also hear how it fared with the poor parents," said Undine, as she resumed her lute, and sang:—

Thro' every chamber roams the mother,

> Moves and searches everywhere,
> Seeks, she scarce knows what, with sadness,
> And finds an empty house is there.
>
> An empty house! Oh, word of sorrow,
> To her who once had been so blest,
> Who led her child about by day
> And cradled it at night to rest.
>
> The beech is growing green again,
> The sunshine gilds its wonted spot,
> But mother, cease thy searching vain!
> Thy little loved one cometh not.
>
> And when the breath of eve blows cool,
> And father in his home appears,
> The smile he almost tries to wear
> Is quenched at once by gushing tears.
>
> Full well he knows that in his home
> He naught can find but wild despair,
> He hears the mother's grieved lament
> And no bright infant greets him there.

"Oh! for God's sake, Undine, where are my parents?" cried the weeping Bertalda; "you surely know; you have discovered them, you wonderful being, for otherwise you would not have thus torn me heart. Are they perhaps already here? Can it be?" Her eye passed quickly over the brilliant company and lingered on a lady of high rank who was sitting next her foster-father. Undine, however, turned toward the door, while her eyes overflowed with the sweetest emotion. "Where are the poor waiting parents?" she inquired, and, the old fisherman and his wife advanced hesitatingly from the crowd of spectators. Their glance rested inquiringly now on Undine, now on the beautiful girl who was said to be their daughter "It is she," said the delighted benefactress, in a faltering tone, and the two old people hung round the neck of their recovered child, weeping and praising God.

But amazed and indignant, Bertalda tore herself from their embrace. Such a recognition was too much for this proud mind, at a moment when she had surely imagined that her former splendor would even be increased, and when hope was deluding her with a vision of almost royal honors. It seemed to her as if her rival had devised all this on purpose signally to humble her before Huldbrand and the whole world. She reviled Undine, she reviled the old people, and bitter invectives, such as "deceiver" and "bribed impostors," fell from her lips. Then the old fisherman's wife said in a low voice to herself: "Ah me, she is become a wicked girl; and yet I feel in my heart that she is my child."

The old fisherman, however, had folded his hands, and was praying silently that this might not be his daughter. Undine, pale as death, turned with agitation from the parents to Bertalda, and from Bertalda to the parents; suddenly cast down from that heaven of happiness of which she had dreamed, and overwhelmed with a fear and a terror such as she had never known even in imagination. "Have you a soul? Have you really a soul, Bertalda?" she cried again and again to her angry friend, as if forcibly to rouse her to consciousness from some sudden delirium or maddening nightmare. But when Bertalda only became more and more enraged, when the repulsed parents began to weep aloud, and the company, in eager dispute, were taking different sides, she begged in such a dignified and serious manner to be allowed to speak in this her husband's hall, that all around were in a moment silenced. She then advanced to the upper end of the table, where Bertalda has seated herself, and with a modest and yet proud air, while every eye was fixed upon her, she spoke as follows:—

"My friends, you look so angry and disturbed and you have interrupted my happy feast by your disputings. Ah! I knew nothing of your foolish habits and your heartless mode of thinking, and I shall never all my life long become accustomed to them. It is not my fault that this affair has resulted in evil; believe me, the fault is with yourselves alone, little as it may appear to you to be so. I have therefore but little to say to you, but one thing I must say: I have spoken nothing but truth. I neither can nor will give you proofs beyond my own assertion, but I will swear to the truth of this. I received this information from the very person who allured Bertalda into the water, away from her parents, and who afterward placed her on the green meadow in the duke's path."

"She is an enchantress!" cried Bertalda, "a witch, who has intercourse with evil spirits. She acknowledges it herself."

"I do not," said Undine, with a whole heaven innocence and confidence beaming, in her eyes. "I am no witch; only look at me."

"She is false and boastful," interrupted Bertalda, "and she cannot prove that I am the child of these low people. My noble parents, I beg you to take me from this company and out of this city, where they are only bent on insulting me."

But the aged and honorable duke remained unmoved, and his wife, said: "We must thoroughly examine how we are to act. God forbid that we should move a step from this hall until we have done so."

Then the old wife of the fisherman drew near, and making a low reverence to the duchess, she said: "Noble, god-fearing lady, you have opened my heart. I must tell you, if this evil-disposed young lady is my daughter, she has a mark, like a violet, between her shoulders, and another like it on the instep of her left foot. If she would only go out of the hall with me!"

"I shall not uncover myself before the peasant woman!" exclaimed

Bertalda, proudly turning her back on her.

"But before me you will." rejoined the duchess, very gravely. "Follow me into that room, girl, and the good old woman shall come with us." The three disappeared, and the rest of the company remained where they were, in silent expectation. After a short time they returned; Bertalda was pale as death. "Right is right." said the duchess; "I must therefore declare that our hostess has spoken perfect, truth. Bertalda is the fisherman's daughter, and that is as much as it is necessary to inform you here."

The princely pair left with their adopted daughter; and at a sign from the duke, the fisherman and his wife followed them. The other guests retired in silence or with secret murmurs, and Undine sank weeping into Huldbrand's arms.

CHAPTER XII.
HOW THEY DEPARTED FROM THE IMPERIAL CITY.

The lord of Ringstetten would have certainly preferred the events of this day to have been different; but even as they were, he could scarcely regret them wholly, as they had exhibited his charming wife under such a good and sweet and kindly aspect. "If I have given her a soul," he could not help saying to himself, "I have indeed given her a better one than my own;" and his only thought now was to speak soothingly to the weeping Undine, and on the following morning to quit with her a place which, after this incident, must have become distasteful to her. It is true that she was not estimated differently to what she had been. As something mysterious had long been expected of her, the strange discovery of Bertalda's origin had caused no great surprise, and every one who had heard the story and had seen Bertalda's violent behavior, was disgusted with her alone. Of this, however, the knight and his lady knew nothing as yet; and, besides, the condemnation or approval of the public was equally painful to Undine, and thus there was no better course to pursue than to leave the walls of the old city behind them with all the speed possible.

With the earliest beams of morning a pretty carriage drove up to the entrance gate for Undine: the horses which Huldbrand and his squires were to ride stood near, pawing the ground with impatient eagerness. The knight was leading his beautiful wife from the door, when a fisher-girl crossed their way. "We do not need your fish," said Huldbrand to her, "we are now starting on our journey." Upon this the fisher-girl began to weep bitterly, and the young couple perceived for the first time that it was Bertalda. They immediately returned with her to their apartment, and learned from her that the duke and duchess were so displeased at her violent and unfeeling conduct on the preceding way, that they had entirely withdrawn their protection from her, though not without giving her a rich portion.

The fisherman, too, had been handsomely rewarded, and had the evening before set out with his wife to return to their secluded home.

"I would have gone with them," she continued, "but the old fisherman, who is said to be my father"—

"And he is so indeed, Bertalda," interrupted Undine. "Look here, the stranger, whom you took for the master of the fountain, told me the whole story in detail. He wished to dissuade me from taking you with me to castle Ringstetten, and this led him to disclose the secret."

"Well, then," said Bertalda, "if it must be so, my father said, 'I will not take you with me until you are changed. Venture to come to us alone through the haunted forest; that shall be the proof whether you have any regard for us. But do not come to me as a lady; come only as a fisher-girl!' So I will do just as he has told me, for I am forsaken by the whole world, and I will live and die in solitude as a poor fisher-girl, with my poor parents. I have a terrible dread though of the forest. Horrible spectres are said to dwell in it, and I am so fearful. But how can I help it? I only came here to implore pardon of the noble lady of Ringstetten for my unbecoming behavior yesterday. I feel sure, sweet lady, you meant to do me a kindness, but you knew not how you would wound me, and in my agony and surprise, many a rash and frantic expression passed my lips. Oh forgive, forgive! I am already so unhappy. Only think yourself what I was yesterday morning, yesterday at the beginning of your banquet, and what I am now!"

Her voice became stifled with a passionate flood of tears, and Undine, also weeping bitterly, fell on her neck. It was some time before the deeply agitated Undine could utter a word; at length she said:—

"You can go with us to Ringstetten; everything shall remain as it was arranged before; only do not speak to me again as 'noble lady.' You see, we were exchanged for each other as children; our faces even then sprang as it were from the same stem, and we will now so strengthen this kindred destiny that no human power shall be able to separate it. Only, first of all, come with us to Ringstetten. We will discuss there how we shall share all things as sisters."

Bertalda looked timidly toward Huldbrand. He pitied the beautiful girl in her distress, and offering her his hand he begged her tenderly to intrust herself with him and his wife. "We will send a message to your parents," he continued, "to tell them why you are not come;" and he would have added more with regard to the worthy fisherman and his wife, but he saw that Bertalda shrunk with pain from the mention of their name, and he therefore refrained from saying more.

He then assisted her first into the carriage, Undine followed her; and he mounted his horse and trotted merrily by the side of them, urging the driver at the same time to hasten his speed, so that very soon they were beyond the confines of the imperial city and all its sad remembrances; and now the ladies began to enjoy the beautiful country through which their road lay.

After a journey of some days, they arrived one exquisite evening, at castle Ringstetten. The young knight had much to hear from his overseers and vassals, so that Undine and Bertalda were left alone.

They both repaired to the ramparts of the fortress, and were delighted with the beautiful landscape which spread far and wide through fertile Swabia.

Presently a tall man approached them, greeting them respectfully, and Bertalda fancied she saw a resemblance to the master of the fountain in the imperial city. Still more unmistakable grew the likeness, when Undine angrily and almost threateningly waved him off, and he retreated with hasty steps and shaking head, as he had done before, and disappeared into a neighboring copse. Undine, however, said:

"Don't be afraid, dear Bertalda, this time the hateful master of the fountain shall do you no harm." And then she told her the whole story in detail, and who she was herself, and how Bertalda had been taken away from the fisherman and his wife, and Undine had gone to them. The girl was at first terrified with this relation; she imagined her friend must be seized with sudden madness, but she became more convinced that all was true, for Undine's story was so connected, and fitted so well with former occurrences, and still more she had that inward feeling with which truth never fails to make itself known to us. It seemed strange to her that she was now herself living, as it were, in the midst of one of those fairy tales to which she had formerly only listened.

She gazed upon Undine with reverence, but she could not resist a sense of dread that seemed to come between her and her friend, and at their evening repast she could not but wonder how the knight could behave so lovingly and kindly toward a being who appeared to her, since the discovery she had just made, more of a phantom than a human being.

CHAPTER XIII.
HOW THEY LIVED AT CASTLE RINGSTETTEN.

The writer of this story, both because it moves his own heart, and because he wishes it to move that of others, begs you, dear reader, to pardon him, if he now briefly passes over a considerable space of time, only cursorily mentioning the events that marked it. He knows well that he might portray skilfully, step by step, how Huldbrand's heart began to turn from Undine to Bertalda; how Bertalda more and more responded with ardent affection to the young knight, and how they both looked upon the poor wife as a mysterious being rather to be feared than pitied; how Undine wept, and how her tears stung the knight's heart with remorse without awakening his former love, so that though he at times was kind and endearing to her, a cold shudder would soon draw him from her, and he would turn to his fellow-mortal, Bertalda. All this the writer knows might be fully detailed, and perhaps ought to have been so; but such a task would have been too painful, for similar things have been known to him by sad experience, and he shrinks from their shadow even in remembrance. You know probably a like feeling, dear reader, for such is the lot of mortal man. Happy are you if you have received rather than inflicted the pain, for in such things it is more blessed to receive than to give. If it be so, such recollections will only bring a feeling of sorrow to your mind, and perhaps a tear will trickle down your cheek over the faded flowers that once caused you such delight. But let that be enough. We will not pierce our hearts with a thousand separate things, but only briefly state, as I have just said, how matters were.

Poor Undine was very sad, and the other two were not to be called happy. Bertalda especially thought that she could trace the effect of jealousy on the part of the injured wife whenever her wishes were in any way thwarted by her. She had therefore habituated herself to an imperious demeanor, to which Undine yielded in sorrowful submission, and the now blinded Huldbrand usually encouraged this arrogant behavior in the strongest manner. But the circumstance that most of all disturbed the inmates of the castle, was a variety of wonderful apparitions which met Huldbrand and Bertalda in the vaulted galleries of the castle, and which had never been heard of before as haunting the locality. The tall white man, in whom Huldbrand recognized only too plainly Uncle Kuhleborn, and Bertalda the spectral master of the fountain, often passed before them with a threatening aspect, and especially before Bertalda; so much so, that she had already several times been made ill with terror, and had frequently thought of quitting the castle. But still she stayed there, partly because Huldbrand was so dear to her, and she relied on her innocence, no words of love having ever passed between them, and partly also because she knew not whither to direct her steps. The old fisherman, on receiving the message from the lord of Ringstetten that Bertalda was his guest, had written a few lines in an almost illegible hand, but as good as his advanced age and long dis- would admit of.

"I have now become," he wrote, "a poor old widower, for my dear and faithful wife is dead. However lonely I now sit in my cottage, Bertalda is better with you than with me. Only let her do nothing to harm my beloved Undine! She will have my curse if it be so." The last words of this letter, Bertalda flung to the winds, but she carefully retained the part respecting her absence from her father—just as we are all wont to do in similar circumstances.

One day, when Huldbrand had just ridden out, Undine summoned together the domestics of the family, and ordered them to bring a large stone, and carefully to cover with it the magnificent fountain which stood in the middle of the castle-yard. The servants objected that it would oblige them to bring water from the valley below. Undine smiled sadly. "I am sorry, my people," she replied, "to increase your work. I would rather myself fetch up the pitchers, but this fountain must be closed. Believe me that it cannot be otherwise, and that it is only by so doing that we can avoid a greater evil."

The whole household were glad to be able to please their gentle mistress; they made no further inquiry, but seized the enormous stone. They were just raising it in their hands, and were already poising it over the fountain, when Bertalda came running up, and called out to them to stop, as it was from this fountain that the water was brought which was so good for her complexion, and she would never consent to its being closed. Undine, however, although gentle as usual, was more than usually firm. She told Bertalda that it was her due, as mistress of the house, to arrange her household as she thought best, and that, in this, she was accountable to no one but her lord and husband. "See, oh, pray see," exclaimed Bertalda, in an angry, yet uneasy tone, "how the poor beautiful water is curling and writhing at being shut out from the bright sunshine and from the cheerful sight of the human face, for whose mirror it was created!"

The water in the fountain was indeed wonderfully agitated and hissing; it seemed as if something within were struggling to free itself, but Undine only the more earnestly urged the fulfilment of her orders. The earnestness was scarcely needed. The servants of the castle were as happy in obeying their gentle mistress as in opposing Bertalda's haughty defiance; and in spite of all the rude scolding and threatening of the latter the stone was soon firmly lying over the opening of the fountain. Undine leaned thoughtfully over it, and wrote with her beautiful fingers on its surface. She must, however, have had something very sharp and cutting in her hand, for when she turned away, and the servants drew near to examine the stone, they perceived various strange characters upon it, which none of them had seen there before.

Bertalda received the knight, on his return home in the evening, with tears and complaints of Undine's conduct. He cast a serious look at his poor wife, and she looked down as if distressed. Yet she said with great composure: "My lord and husband does not reprove even a bondslave without a hearing, how much less then, his wedded wife?"

"Speak," said the knight with a gloomy countenance, "what induced you to act so strangely?"

"I should like to tell you when we are quite alone," sighed Undine.

"You can tell me just as well in Bertalda's presence," was the rejoinder.

"Yes, if you command me," said Undine; "but command it not. Oh pray, pray command it not!"

She looked so humble, so sweet, and obedient, that the knight's heart felt a passing gleam from better times. He kindly placed her arm within his own, and led her to his apartment, when she began to speak as follows:—

"You already know, my beloved lord, something of my evil uncle, Kuhleborn, and you have frequently been displeased at meeting him in the galleries of this castle. He has several times frightened Bertalda into illness. This is because he is devoid of soul, a mere elemental mirror of the outward world, without the power of reflecting the world within. He sees, too, sometimes, that you are dissatisfied with me; that I, in my childishness, am weeping at this, and that Bertalda perhaps is at the very same moment laughing. Hence he imagines various discrepancies in our home life, and in many ways mixes unbidden with our circle. What is the good of reproving him? What is the use of sending him angrily away? He does not believe a word I say. His poor nature has no idea that the joys and sorrows of love have so sweet a resemblance, and are so closely linked that no power can separate them. Amid tears a smile shines forth, and a smile allures tears from their secret chambers."

She looked up at Huldbrand, smiling and weeping; and he again experienced within his heart all the charm of his old love. She felt this, and pressing him more tenderly to her, she continued amid tears of joy:—

"As the disturber of our peace was not to be dismissed with words, I have been obliged to shut the door upon him. And the only door by which he obtains access to us is that fountain. He is cut off by the adjacent valleys from the other water-spirits in the neighborhood, and his kingdom only commences further off on the Danube, into which some of his good friends direct their course. For this reason I had the stone placed over the opening of the fountain, and I inscribed characters upon it which cripple all my uncle's power, so that he can now neither intrude upon you, nor upon me, nor upon Bertalda. Human beings, it is true, can raise the stone again with ordinary effort, in spite of the characters inscribed on it. The inscription does not hinder them. If you wish, therefore, follow Bertalda's desire, but, truly! she knows not what she asks. The rude Kuhleborn has set his mark especially upon her; and if much came to pass which he has predicted to me, and which might, indeed, happen without your meaning any evil, ah! dear one, even you would then be exposed to danger!"

Huldbrand felt deeply the generosity of his sweet wife, in her eagerness to shut up her formidable protector, while she had even been chided for it by Bertalda. He pressed her in his arms with the utmost affection, and said with emotion: "The stone shall remain, and all shall remain, now and ever, as you wish to have it, my sweet Undine."

She caressed him with humble delight, as she heard the expressions of love so long withheld, and then at length she said: "My dearest husband, you are so gentle and kind to-day, may I venture to ask a favor of you? See now, it is just the same with you as it is with summer. In the height of its glory, summer puts on the flaming and thundering crown of mighty storms, and assumes the air of a king over the earth. You, too, sometimes, let your fury rise, and your eyes flash and your voice is angry, and this becomes you well, though I, in my folly, may sometimes weep at it. But never, I pray you, behave thus toward me on the water, or even when we are near it. You see, my relatives would then acquire a right over me. They would unrelentingly tear me from you in their rage;

because they would imagine that one of their race was injured, and I should be compelled all my life to dwell below in the crystal palaces, and should never dare to ascend to you again; or they would send me up to you—and that, oh God, would be infinitely worse. No, no, my beloved husband, do not let it come to that, if your poor Undine is dear to you."

He promised solemnly to do as she desired, and they both returned from the apartment, full of happiness and affection. At that moment Bertalda appeared with some workmen, to whom she had already given orders, and said in a sullen tone, which she had assumed of late: "I suppose the secret conference is at an end, and now the stone may be removed. Go out, workmen, and attend to it."

But the knight, angry at her impertinence, desired in short and very decisive words that the stone should be left: he reproved Bertalda, too, for her violence toward his wife. Whereupon the workmen withdrew, smiling with secret satisfaction: while Bertalda, pale with rage, hurried away to her room.

The hour for the evening repast arrived, and Bertalda they waited for in vain. They sent after her, but the domestic found her apartments empty, and only brought back with him a sealed letter addressed to the knight. He opened it with alarm, and read: "I feel with shame that I am only a poor fisher-girl. I will expiate my fault in having forgotten this for a moment by going to the miserable cottage of my parents. Farewell to you and your beautiful wife."

Undine was heartily distressed. She earnestly entreated Huldbrand to hasten after their friend and bring her back again. Alas! she had no need to urge him. His affection for Bertalda burst forth again with vehemence. He hurried round the castle, inquiring if any one had seen which way the fugitive had gone. He could learn nothing of her, and he was already on his horse in the castle-yard, resolved at a venture to take the road by which he had brought Bertalda hither. Just then a page appeared, who assured him that he had met the lady on the path to the Black Valley. Like an arrow the knight sprang through the gateway in the direction indicated, without hearing Undine's voice of agony, as she called to him from the window:—

"To the Black Valley! Oh, not there! Huldbrand, don't go there! or, for heaven's sake, take me with you!" But when she perceived that all her calling was in vain, she ordered her white palfrey to be immediately saddled, and rode after the knight, without allowing any servant to accompany her.

CHAPTER XIV.
HOW BERTALDA RETURNED HOME WITH THE KNIGHT.

The Black Valley lies deep within the mountains. What it is now called we do not know. At that time the people of the country gave it this appellation on account of the deep obscurity in which the low land lay, owing to the shadows of the lofty trees, and especially firs, that grew there. Even the brook which bubbled between the rocks wore the same dark hue, and dashed along with none of that gladness with which streams are wont to flow that have the blue sky immediately above them. Now, in the growing twilight of evening, it looked wild and gloomy between the heights. The knight trotted anxiously along the edge of the brook, fearful at one moment that by delay he might allow the fugitive to advance too far, and at the next that by too great rapidity he might overlook her in case she were concealing herself from him. Meanwhile he had already penetrated tolerably far into the valley, and might soon hope to overtake the maiden, if he were on the right track. The fear that this might not be the case made his heart beat with anxiety. Where would the tender Bertalda tarry through the stormy night, which was so fearful in the valley, should he fail to find her? At length he saw something white gleaming through the branches on the slope of the mountain. He thought he recognized Bertalda's dress, and he turned his course in that direction. But his horse refused to go forward; it reared impatiently; and its master, unwilling to lose a moment, and seeing moreover that the copse was impassable on horseback, dismounted; and, fastening his snorting steed to an elm-tree, he worked his way cautiously through the bushes. The branches sprinkled his forehead and cheeks with the cold drops of the evening dew; a distant roll of thunder was heard murmuring from the other side of the mountains; everything looked so strange that he began to feel a dread of the white figure, which now lay only a short distance from him on the ground. Still he could plainly see that it was a female, either asleep or in a swoon, and that she was attired in long white garments, such as Bertalda had worn on that day. He stepped close up to her, made a rustling with the branches, and let his sword clatter, but she moved not. "Bertalda!" he exclaimed, at first in a low voice, and then louder and louder—still she heard not. At last, when he uttered the dear name with a more powerful effort, a hollow echo from the mountain-caverns of the valley indistinctly reverberated "Bertalda!" but still the sleeper woke not. He bent down over her; the gloom of the valley and the obscurity of approaching night would not allow him to distinguish her features.

Just as he was stooping closer over her, with a feeling of painful doubt, a flash of lightning shot across the valley, and he saw before him a frightfully distorted countenance, and a hollow voice exclaimed: "Give me a kiss, you enamoured swain!"

Huldbrand sprang up with a cry of horror, and the hideous figure rose with him. "Go home!" it murmured; "wizards are on the watch. Go home! or I will have you!" and it stretched out its long white arms toward him.

"Malicious Kuhleborn!" cried the knight, recovering himself, "What do you concern me, you goblin? There, take your kiss!" And he furiously hurled his sword at the figure. But it vanished like vapor, and a gush of water which wetted him through left the knight no doubt as to the foe with whom he had been engaged.

"He wishes to frighten me back from Bertalda," said he aloud to himself; "he thinks to terrify me with his foolish tricks, and to make me give up the poor distressed girl to him, so that he can wreak his vengeance on her. But he shall not do that, weak spirit of the elements as he is. No powerless phantom can understand what a human heart can do when its best energies are aroused." He felt the truth of his words, and that the very expression of them had inspired his heart with fresh courage. It seemed too as if fortune were on his side, for he had not reached his fastened horse, when he distinctly heard Bertalda's plaintive voice not far distant, and could catch her weeping accents through the ever-increasing tumult of the thunder and tempest. He hurried swiftly in the direction of the sound, and found the trembling girl just attempting to climb the steep, in order to escape in any way from the dreadful gloom of the valley. He stepped, however, lovingly in her path, and bold and proud as her resolve had before been, she now felt only too keenly the delight, that the friend whom she so passionately loved should rescue her from this frightful solitude, and that the joyous life in the castle should be again open to her. She followed almost unresisting, but so exhausted with fatigue that the knight was glad to have brought her to his horse, which he now hastily unfastened, in order to lift the fair fugitive upon it; and then, cautiously holding the reins, he hoped to proceed through the uncertain shades of the valley.

But the horse had become quite unmanageable from the wild apparition of Kuhleborn. Even the knight would have had difficulty in mounting the rearing and snorting animal, but to place the trembling Bertalda on its back was perfectly impossible. They determined, therefore, to return home on foot. Drawing the horse after him by the bridle, the knight supported the tottering girl with his other hand. Bertalda exerted all her strength to pass quickly through the fearful valley, but weariness weighed her down like lead, and every limb trembled, partly from the terror she had endured when Kuhleborn had pursued her, and partly from her continued alarm at the howling of the storm and the pealing of the thunder through the wooded mountain.

At last she slid from the supporting arm of her protector, and sinking down on the moss, she exclaimed: "Let me lie here, my noble lord; I suffer the punishment due to my folly, and I must now perish here through weariness and dread."

"No, sweet friend, I will never leave you!" cried Huldbrand, vainly endeavoring to restrain his furious steed; for, worse than before, it now began to foam and rear with excitement, until at last the knight was glad to keep the animal at a sufficient distance from the exhausted maiden lest her fears should be increased. But scarcely had he withdrawn a few paces with the wild steed, than she began to call after him in the most pitiful manner, believing that he was really going to leave her in this horrible wilderness. He was utterly at a loss what course to take. Gladly would he have given the excited beast its liberty and have allowed it to rush away into the night and spend its fury, had he not feared that is this narrow defile it might come thundering with its iron-shod hoofs over the very spot where Bertalda lay.

In the midst of this extreme perplexity and distress, he heard with delight the sound of a vehicle driving slowly down the stony road behind them. He called out for help; and a man's voice replied, bidding him have patience, but promising assistance; and soon after, two gray horses appeared through the bushes, and beside them the driver in the white smock of a carter; a great white linen cloth was next visible, covering the goods apparently contained in the wagon. At a loud shout from their master, the obedient horses halted. The driver then came toward the knight, and helped him in restraining his foaming animal.

"I see well," said he, "what ails the beast. When I first travelled this way, my horses were no better. The fact is, there is an evil water-spirit haunting the place, and he takes delight in this sort of mischief. But I have learned a charm; if you will let me whisper it in your horse's ear, he will stand at once just as quiet as my gray beasts are doing there."

"Try your luck then, only help us quickly!" exclaimed the impatient knight. The wagoner then drew down the head of the rearing charger close to his own, and whispered something in his ear. In a moment the animal stood still and quiet, and his quick panting and reeking condition was all that remained of his previous unmanageableness. Huldbrand had no time to inquire how all this had been effected. He agreed with the carter that he should take Bertalda on his wagon, where, as the man assured him, there were a quantity of soft cotton-bales, upon which she could be conveyed to castle Ringstetten, and the knight was to accompany them on horseback. But the horse appeared too much exhausted by its past fury to be able to carry its master so far, so the carter persuaded Huldbrand to get into the wagon with Bertalda. The horse could be fastened on behind. "We are going down hill," said he, "and that will make it light for my gray beasts."

The knight accepted the offer and entered the wagon with Bertalda; the horse followed patiently behind, and the wagoner, steady and attentive, walked by the side.

In the stillness of the night, as its darkness deepened and the subsiding tempest sounded more and more remote, encouraged by the sense of security and their fortunate escape, a confidential conversation arose between Huldbrand and Bertalda. With flattering words he reproached her for her daring flight; she excused herself with humility and emotion, and from every word she said a gleam shone forth which disclosed distinctly to the lover that the beloved was his. The knight felt the sense of her words far more than he regarded their meaning, and it was the sense alone to which he replied. Presently the wagoner suddenly shouted with loud voice,—

"Up, my grays, up with your feet, keep together! remember who you are!"

The knight leaned out of the wagon and saw that the horses were stepping into the midst of a foaming stream or were already almost swimming, while the wheels of the wagon were rushing round and gleaming like mill-wheels, and the wagoner had got up in front, in consequence of the increasing waters.

"What sort of a road is this? It goes into the middle of the stream." cried Huldbrand to his guide.

"Not at all, sir." returned the other, laughing, "it is just the reverse, the stream goes into the very middle of our road. Look round and see how everything is covered by the water."

The whole valley indeed was suddenly filled with the surging flood, that visibly increased. "It is Kuhleborn, the evil water-spirit, who wishes to drown us!" exclaimed the knight. "Have you no charm, against him, my friend?"

"I know indeed of one," returned the wagoner, "but I cannot and may not use it until you know who I am."

"Is this a time for riddles?" cried the knight. "The flood is ever rising higher, and what does it matter to me to know who you are?"

"It does matter to you, though," said the wagoner, "for I am Kuhleborn."

So saying, he thrust his distorted face into the wagon with a grin, but the wagon was a wagon no longer, the horses were not horses—all was transformed to foam and vanished in the hissing waves, and even the wagoner himself, rising as a gigantic billow, drew down the vainly struggling horse beneath the waters, and then swelling higher and higher, swept over the heads of the floating pair, like some liquid tower, threatening to bury them irrecoverably.

Just then the soft voice of Undine sounded through the uproar, the moon emerged from the clouds, and by its light Undine was seen on the heights above the valley. She rebuked, she threatened the floods below; the menacing, tower-like wave vanished, muttering and murmuring, the waters flowed gently away in the moonlight, and like a white dove, Undine flew down from the height, seized the knight and Bertalda, and bore them with her to a fresh, green, turfy spot on the hill, where with choice refreshing restoratives, she dispelled their terrors and weariness; then she assisted Bertalda to mount the white palfrey, on which she had herself ridden here, and thus all three returned back to castle Ringstetten.

CHAPTER XV.
THE JOURNEY TO VIENNA.

After this last adventure, they lived quietly and happily at the castle. The knight more and more perceived the heavenly goodness of his wife, which had been so nobly exhibited by her pursuit, and by her rescue of them in the Black Valley, where Kuhleborn's power again commenced; Undine herself felt that peace and security, which is never lacking to a mind so long as it is distinctly conscious of being on the right path, and besides, in the newly-awakened love and esteem of her husband, many a gleam of hope and joy shone upon her. Bertalda, on the other hand, showed herself grateful, humble and timid, without regarding her conduct as anything meritorious. Whenever Huldbrand or Undine were about to give her any explanation regarding the covering of the fountain or the adventure in the Black Valley, she would earnestly entreat them to spare her the recital, as she felt too much shame at the recollection of the fountain, and too much fear at the remembrance of the Black Valley. She learned therefore nothing further of either; and for what end was such knowledge necessary? Peace and joy had visibly taken up their abode at castle Ringstetten. They felt secure on this point, and imagined that life could now produce nothing but pleasant flowers and fruits.

In this happy condition of things, winter had come and passed away, and spring, with its fresh green shoots and its blue sky, was gladdening the joyous inmates of the castle. Spring was in harmony with them, and they with spring. What wonder then, that its storks and swallows inspired them also with a desire to travel? One day when they were taking a pleasant walk to one of the sources of the Danube, Huldbrand spoke of the magnificence of the noble river, and how it widened as it flowed through countries fertilized by its waters, how the charming city of Vienna shone forth on its banks, and how with every step of its course it increased in power and loveliness.

"It must be glorious to go down the river as far as Vienna!" exclaimed Bertalda, but immediately relapsing into her present modesty and humility, she paused and blushed deeply.

This touched Undine deeply, and with the liveliest desire to give pleasure to her friend, she said: "What hinders us from starting on the little voyage?"

Bertalda exhibited the greatest delight, and both she and Undine began at once to picture the tour of the Danube in the brightest colors. Huldbrand also gladly agreed to the prospect; only he once whispered anxiously in Undine's ear,—

"But Kuhleborn becomes possessed of his power again out there!"

"Let him come," she replied with a smile, "I shall be there, and he ventures upon none of his mischief before me." The last impediment was thus removed; they prepared for the journey, and soon after set out upon it with fresh spirits and the brightest hopes.

But wonder not, oh man, if events always turn out different to what we have intended. That malicious power, lurking for our destruction, gladly lulls its chosen victim to sleep with sweet songs and golden delusions; while on the other hand the rescuing messenger from Heaven often knocks sharply and alarmingly at our door.

During the first few days of their voyage down the Danube they were extremely happy. Everything grew more and more beautiful as they sailed further and further down the proudly flowing stream. But in a region otherwise so pleasant, and in the enjoyment of which they had promised themselves the purest delight, the ungovernable Kuhleborn began, undisguisedly, to exhibit his power of interference. This was indeed manifested in mere teasing tricks, for Undine often rebuked the agitated waves, or the contrary winds, and then the violence of the enemy would be immediately humbled; but again the attacks would be renewed, and again Undine's reproofs would become necessary, so that the pleasure of the little party was completely destroyed. The boatmen too were continually whispering to each other in dismay, and looking with distrust at the three strangers, whose servants even began more and more to forebode something uncomfortable, and to watch their superiors with suspicious glances. Huldbrand often said to himself: "This comes from like not being linked with like, from a man uniting himself with a mermaid!" Excusing himself as we all love to do, he would often think indeed as he said this: "I did not really know that she was a sea-maiden, mine is the misfortune, that every step I take is disturbed and haunted by the wild caprices of her race, but mine is not the fault." By thoughts such as these, he felt himself in some measure strengthened, but on the other hand, he felt increasing ill-humor, and almost animosity toward Undine. He would look at her with an expression of anger, the meaning of which the poor wife understood well. Wearied with this exhibition of displeasure, and exhausted by the constant effort to frustrate Kuhleborn's artifices, she sank one evening into a deep slumber, rocked soothingly by the softly gliding bark.

Scarcely, however, had she closed her eyes than every one in the vessel imagined he saw, in whatever direction he turned, a most horrible human head; it rose out of the waves, not like that of a person swimming, but perfectly perpendicular as if invisibly supported upright on the watery surface, and floating along in the same course with the bark. Each wanted to point out to the other the cause of his alarm, but each found the same expression of horror depicted on the face of his neighbor, only that his hands and eyes were directed to a different point where the monster, half-laughing and half-threatening, rose before him. When, however, they all wished to make each other understand what each saw, and all were crying out: "Look there! No, there!" the horrible heads all at one and the same time appeared to their view, and the whole river around the vessel swarmed with the most hideous apparitions. The universal cry raised at the sight awoke Undine. As she opened her eyes, the wild crowd of distorted visages disappeared. But Huldbrand was indignant at such unsightly jugglery. He would have burst forth in uncontrolled imprecations had not Undine said to him with a humble manner and a softly imploring tone: "For God's sake, my husband, we are on the water, do not be angry with me now."

The knight was silent, and sat down absorbed in revery. Undine whispered in his ear: "Would it not be better, my love, if we gave up this foolish journey, and returned to castle Ringstetten in peace?"

But Huldbrand murmured moodily: "So I must be a prisoner in my own castle, and only be able to breathe so long as the fountain is closed! I would your mad kindred"—Undine lovingly pressed her fair hand upon his lips. He paused, pondering in silence over much that Undine had before said to him.

Bertalda had meanwhile given herself up to a variety of strange thoughts. She knew a good deal of Undine's origin, and yet not the whole, and the fearful Kuhleborn especially had remained to her a terrible but wholly unrevealed mystery. She had indeed never even heard his name. Musing on these strange things, she unclasped, scarcely conscious of the act, a gold necklace, which Huldbrand had lately purchased for her of a travelling trader; half dreamingly she drew it along the surface of the water, enjoying the light glimmer it cast upon the evening-tinted stream. Suddenly a huge hand was stretched out of the Danube, it seized the necklace and vanished with it beneath the waters. Bertalda screamed aloud, and a scornful laugh resounded from the depths of the stream. The knight could now restrain his anger no longer. Starting up, he inveighed against the river; he cursed all who ventured to interfere with his family and his life, and challenged them, be they spirits or sirens, to show themselves before his avenging sword.

Bertalda wept meanwhile for her lost ornament, which was so precious to her, and her tears added fuel to the flame of the knight's anger, while Undine held her hand over the side of the vessel, dipping it into the water, softly murmuring to herself, and only now and then interrupting her strange mysterious whisper, as she entreated her husband: "My dearly loved one, do not scold me here; reprove others if you will, but not me here. You know why!" And indeed, he restrained the words of anger that were trembling on his tongue. Presently in her wet hand which she had been holding under the waves, she brought up a beautiful coral necklace of so much brilliancy that the eyes of all were dazzled by it.

"Take this," said she, holding it out kindly to Bertalda; "I have ordered this to be brought for you as a compensation, and don't be grieved any more, my poor child."

But the knight sprang between them. He tore the beautiful ornament from Undine's hand, hurled it again into the river, exclaiming in passionate rage: "Have you then still a connection with them? In the name of all the witches, remain among them with your presents, and leave us mortals in peace, you sorceress!"

Poor Undine gazed at him with fixed but tearful eyes, her hand still stretched out, as when she had offered her beautiful present so lovingly to Bertalda. She then began to weep more and more violently, like a dear innocent child bitterly afflicted. At last, wearied out she said:

"Alas, sweet friend, alas! farewell! They shall do you no harm; only remain true, so that I may be able to keep them from you. I must, alas! go away; I must go hence at this early stage of life. Oh woe, woe! what have you done! Oh woe, woe!"

She vanished over the side of the vessel. Whether she plunged into the stream, or flowed away with it, they knew not; her disappearance was like both and neither. Soon, however, she was completely lost sight of in the Danube; only a few little waves kept whispering, as if sobbing, round the boat, and they almost seemed to be saying: "Oh woe, woe! oh remain true! oh woe!"

Huldbrand lay on the deck of the vessel, bathed in hot tears, and a deep swoon soon cast its veil of forgetfulness over the unhappy man.

CHAPTER XVI.
HOW IT FARED FURTHER WITH HULDBRAND.

Shall we say it is well or ill, that our sorrow is of such short duration? I mean that deep sorrow which affects the very well-spring of our life, which becomes so one with the lost objects of our love that they are no longer lost, and which enshrines their image as a sacred treasure, until that final goal is reached which they have reached before us! It is true that many men really maintain these sacred memories, but their feeling is no longer that of the first deep grief. Other and new images have thronged between; we learn at length the transitoriness of all earthly things, even to our grief, and, therefore. I must say "Alas, that our sorrow should be of such short duration?"

The lord of Ringstetten experienced this whether for his good, we shall hear in the sequel to this history. At first he could do nothing but weep, and that as bitterly as the poor gentle Undine had wept when he had torn from her hand that brilliant ornament with which she had wished to set everything to rights. And then he would stretch out his hand, as she had done, and would weep again, like her. He cherished the secret hope that he might at length dissolve in tears; and has not a similar hope passed before the mind of many a one of us, with painful pleasure, in moments of great affliction? Bertalda wept also, and they lived a long while quietly together at Castle Ringstetten, cherishing Undine's memory, and almost wholly forgetful of their former attachment to each other. And, therefore, the good Undine often visited Huldbrand in his dreams; caressing him tenderly and kindly, and then going away, weeping silently, so that when he awoke he often scarcely knew why his cheeks were so wet; whether they had been bathed with her tears, or merely with his own?

These dream-visions became, however, less frequent as time passed on, and the grief of the knight was less acute; still he would probably have cherished no other wish than thus to think calmly of Undine and to talk of her, had not the old fisherman appeared one day unexpectedly at the castle, and sternly insisted on Bertalda's returning with him as his child. The news of Undine's disappearance had reached him, and he had determined on no longer allowing Bertalda to reside at the castle with the widowed knight.

"For," said he, "whether my daughter love me or no, I do not care to know, but her honor is at stake, and where that is concerned, nothing else is to be thought of."

This idea of the old fisherman's, and the solitude which threatened to overwhelm the knight in all the halls and galleries of the desolate castle, after Bertalda's departure, brought out the feelings that had slumbered till now and which had been wholly forgotten in his sorrow for Undine; namely, Huldbrand's affection for the beautiful Bertalda. The fisherman had many objections to raise against the proposed marriage. Undine had been very dear to the old fisherman, and he felt that no one really knew for certain whether the dear lost one were actually dead. And if her body were truly lying cold and stiff at the bottom of the Danube, or had floated away with the current into the ocean, even then Bertalda was in some measure to blame for her death, and it was unfitting for her to step into the place of the poor supplanted one. Yet the fisherman had a strong regard for the knight also; and the entreaties of his daughter, who had become much more gentle and submissive, and her tears for Undine, turned the scale, and he must at length have given his consent, for he remained at the castle without objection, and a messenger was despatched to Father Heilmann, who had united Undine and Huldbrand in happy days gone by, to bring him to the castle for the second nuptials of the knight.

The holy man, however, had scarcely read the letter from the knight of Ringstetten, than he set out on his journey to the castle, with far greater expedition than even the messenger had used in going to him. Whenever his breath failed in his rapid progress, or his aged limbs ached with weariness, he would say to himself: "Perhaps the evil may yet be prevented; fail not, my tottering frame, till you have reached the goal!" And with renewed power he would then press forward, and go on and on without rest or repose, until late one evening he entered the shady courtyard of castle Ringstetten.

The betrothed pair were sitting side by side under the trees, and the old fisherman was near them, absorbed in thought. The moment they recognized Father Heilmann, they sprang up, and pressed round him with warm welcome. But he, without making much reply, begged Huldbrand to go with him into the castle; and when the latter looked astonished, and hesitated to obey the grave summons, the reverend father said to him:—

"Why should I make any delay in wishing to speak to you in private, Herr von Ringstetten? What I have to say concerns Bertalda and the fisherman as much as yourself, and what a man has to hear, he may prefer to hear as soon as possible. Are you then so perfectly certain, Knight Huldbrand, that your first wife is really dead? It scarcely seems so to me. I will not indeed say anything of the mysterious condition in which she may be existing, and I know, too, nothing of it with certainty. But she was a pious and faithful wife, that is beyond all doubt; and for a fortnight past she has stood at my bedside at night in my dreams, wringing her tender hands in anguish and sighing out: 'Oh, prevent him, good father! I am still living! oh, save his life! save his soul!' I did not understand what this nightly vision signified; when presently your messenger came, and I hurried thither, not to unite, but to separate, what ought not to be joined together. Leave her, Huldbrand! Leave him, Bertalda! He yet belongs to another; and do you not see grief for his lost wife still written on his pale cheek? No bridegroom looks thus, and a voice tells me that if you do not leave him, you will never be happy."

The three listeners felt in their innermost heart that Father Heilmann spoke the truth, but they would not believe it. Even the old fisherman was now so infatuated that he thought it could not be otherwise than they had settled it in their discussions during the last few days. They therefore all opposed the warnings of the priest with a wild and gloomy rashness, until at length the holy father quitted the castle with a sad heart, refusing to accept even for a single night the shelter offered, or to enjoy the refreshments brought him. Huldbrand, however, persuaded himself that the priest was full of whims and fancies, and with dawn of day he sent for a father from the nearest monastery, who, without hesitation, promised to perform the ceremony in a few days.

CHAPTER XVII.
THE KNIGHT'S DREAM.

It was between night and dawn of day that the knight was lying on his couch, half-waking, half-sleeping. Whenever he was on the point of falling asleep a terror seemed to come upon him and scare his rest away, for his slumbers were haunted with spectres. If he tried, however, to rouse himself in good earnest he felt fanned as by the wings of a swan, and he heard the soft murmuring of waters, until soothed by the agreeable delusion, he sunk back again into a half-conscious state. At length he must have fallen sound asleep, for it seemed to him as if he were lifted up upon the fluttering wings of the swans and borne by them far over land and sea, while they sang to him their sweetest music. "The music of the swan! the music of the swan!" he kept saying to himself; "does it not always portend death?" But it had yet another meaning. All at once he felt as if he were hovering over the Mediterranean Sea. A swan was singing musically in his ear that this was the Mediterranean Sea. And while he was looking down upon the waters below they became clear as crystal, so that he could see through them to the bottom. He was delighted at this, for he could see Undine sitting beneath the crystal arch. It is true she was weeping bitterly, and looking much sadder than in the happy days when they had lived together at the castle of Ringstetten, especially at their commencement, and afterward also, shortly before they had begun their unhappy Danube excursion. The knight could not help thinking upon all this very fully and deeply, but it did not seem as if Undine perceived him.

Meanwhile Kuhleborn had approached her, and was on the point of reproving her for her weeping. But she drew herself up, and looked at him with such a noble and commanding air that he almost shrunk back with fear. "Although I live here beneath the waters," said she, "I have yet brought down my soul with me; and therefore I may well weep, although you can not divine what such tears are. They too are blessed, for everything is blessed to him in whom a true soul dwells."

He shook his head incredulously, and said, after some reflection: "And yet, niece, you are subject to the laws of our element, and if he marries again and is unfaithful to you, you are in duty bound to take away his life."

"He is a widower to this very hour," replied Undine, "and his sad heart still holds me dear."

"He is, however, at the same time betrothed," laughed Kuhleborn, with scorn; "and let only a few days pass, and the priest will have given the nuptial blessing, and then you will have to go upon earth to accomplish the death of him who has taken another to wife."

"That I cannot do," laughed Undine in return; "I have sealed up the fountain securely against myself and my race."

"But suppose he should leave his castle," said Kuhleborn, "or should have the fountain opened again! for he thinks little enough of these things."

"It is just for that reason," said Undine, still smiling amid her tears, "it is just for that reason, that he is now hovering in spirit over the Mediterranean Sea, and is dreaming of this conversation of ours as a warning. I have intentionally arranged it so."

Kuhleborn, furious with rage, looked up at the knight, threatened, stamped with his feet, and then swift as an arrow shot under the waves. It seemed as if he were swelling in his fury to the size of a whale. Again the swans began to sing, to flap their wings, and to fly. It seemed to the knight as if he were soaring away over mountains and streams, and that he at length reached the castle Ringstetten, and awoke on his couch.

He did, in reality, awake upon his couch, and his squire coming in at that moment informed him that Father Heilmann was still lingering in the neighborhood; that he had met him the night before in the forest, in a hut which he had formed for himself of the branches of trees, and covered with moss and brushwood. To the question what he was doing here, since he would not give the nuptial blessing, he had answered: "There are other blessings besides those at the nuptial altar, and though I have not gone to the wedding, it may be that I shall be at another solemn ceremony. We must be ready for all things. Besides, marrying and mourning are not so unlike, and every one not wilfully blinded must see that well."

The knight placed various strange constructions upon these words, and upon his dream, but it is very difficult to break off a thing which a man has once regarded as certain, and so everything remained as it had been arranged.

CHAPTER XVIII.
HOW THE KNIGHT HULDBRAND IS MARRIED.

If I were to tell you how the marriage-feast passed at castle Ringstetten, it would seem to you as if you saw a heap of bright and pleasant things, but a gloomy veil of mourning spread over them all, the dark hue of which would make the splendor of the whole look less like happiness than a mockery of the emptiness of all earthly joys. It was not that any spectral apparitions disturbed the festive company, for we know that the castle had been secured from the mischief of the threatening water-spirits. But the knight and the fisherman and all the guests felt as if the chief personage were still lacking at the feast, and that this chief personage could be none other than the loved and gentle Undine. Whenever a door opened, the eyes of all were involuntarily turned in that direction, and if it was nothing but the butler with new dishes, or the cup-bearer with a flask of still richer wine, they would look down again sadly, and the flashes of wit and merriment which had passed to and fro, would be extinguished by sad remembrances. The bride was the most thoughtless of all, and therefore the most happy; but even to her it sometimes seemed strange that she should be sitting at the head of the table, wearing a green wreath and gold-embroidered attire, while Undine was lying at the bottom of the Danube, a cold and stiff corpse, or floating away with the current into the mighty ocean. For, ever since her father had spoken of something of the sort, his words were ever ringing in her ear, and this day especially they were not inclined to give place to other thoughts.

The company dispersed early in the evening, not broken up by the bridegroom himself, but sadly and gloomily by the joyless mood of the guests and their forebodings of evil. Bertalda retired with her maidens, and the knight with his attendants; but at this mournful festival there was no gay, laughing train of bridesmaids and bridesmen.

Bertalda wished to arouse more cheerful thoughts; she ordered a splendid ornament of jewels which Huldbrand had given her, together with rich apparel and veils, to be spread out before her, in order that from these latter she might select the brightest and most beautiful for her morning attire. Her attendants were delighted at the opportunity of expressing their good wishes to their young mistress, not failing at the same time to extol the beauty of the bride in the most lively terms. They were more and more absorbed in these considerations, till Bertalda at length, looking in a mirror, said with a sigh: "Ah, but don't you see plainly how freckled I am growing here at the side of my neck?"

They looked at her throat, and found the freckles as their fair mistress had said, but they called them beauty-spots, and mere tiny blemishes only, tending to enhance the whiteness of her delicate skin. Bertalda shook her head and asserted that a spot was always a defect.

"And I could remove them," she sighed a last, "only the fountain is closed from which I used to have that precious and purifying water. Oh! if I had but a flask of it to-day!"

"Is that all?" said an alert waiting-maid, laughing, as she slipped from the apartment.

"She will not be mad," exclaimed Bertalda, in a pleased and surprised tone, "she will not be so mad as to have the stone removed from the fountain this very evening!" At the same moment they heard the men crossing the courtyard, and could see from the window how the officious waiting-woman was leading them straight up to the fountain, and that they were carrying levers and other instruments on their shoulders. "It is certainly my will," said Bertalda, smiling, "if only it does not take too long." And, happy in the sense that a look from her now was able to effect what had formerly been so painfully refused her, she watched the progress of the work in the moonlit castle-court.

The men raised the enormous stone with an effort; now and then indeed one of their number would sigh, as he remembered that they were destroying the work of their former beloved mistress. But the labor was far lighter than they had imagined. It seemed as if a power within the spring itself were aiding them in raising the stone.

"It is just," said the workmen to each other in astonishment, "as if the water within had become a springing fountain." And the stone rose higher and higher, and almost without the assistance of the workmen, it rolled slowly down upon the pavement with a hollow sound. But from the opening of the fountain there rose solemnly a white column of water; at first they imagined it had really become a springing fountain, till they perceived that the rising form was a pale female figure veiled in white. She was weeping bitterly, raising her hands wailingly above her head and wringing them, as she walked with a slow and serious step to the castle-building. The servants fled from the spring; the bride, pale and stiff with horror, stood at the window with her attendants. When the figure had now come close beneath her room, it looked moaningly up to her, and Bertalda thought she could recognize beneath the veil the pale features of Undine. But the sorrowing form passed on, sad, reluctant, and faltering, as if passing to execution.

Bertalda screamed out that the knight was to be called, but none of her maids ventured from the spot; and even the bride herself became mute, as if trembling at her own voice.

While they were still standing fearfully at the window, motionless as statues, the strange wanderer had reached the castle, had passed up the well-known stairs, and through the well-known halls, ever in silent tears. Alas! how differently had she once wandered through them!

The knight, partly undressed, had already dismissed his attendants, and in a mood of deep dejection he was standing before a large mirror; a taper was burning dimly beside him. There was a gentle tap at his door. Undine used to tap thus when she wanted playfully to tease him "It is all fancy," said he to himself; "I must seek my nuptial bed."

"So you must, but it must be a cold one!" he heard a tearful voice say from without, and then he saw in the mirror his door opening slowly—slowly—and the white figure entered, carefully closing it behind her. "They have opened the spring," said she softly, "and now I am here, and you must die."

He felt in his paralyzed heart that it could not be otherwise, but covering his eyes with his hands he said: "Do not make me mad with terror in my hour of death. If you wear a hideous face behind that veil, do not raise it, but take my life, and let me see you not."

"Alas!" replied the figure, "will you then not look upon me once more? I am as fair as when you wooed me on the promontory."

"Oh, if it were so!" sighed Huldbrand, "and if I might die in your fond embrace!"

"Most gladly, my loved one," said she; and throwing her veil back, her lovely face smiled forth divinely beautiful. Trembling with love and with the approach of death, she kissed him with a holy kiss; but not relaxing her hold she pressed him fervently to her, and as if she would weep away her soul. Tears rushed into the knight's eyes, and seemed to surge through his heaving breast, till at length his breathing ceased, and he fell softly back from the beautiful arms of Undine, upon the pillows of his couch—a corpse.

"I have wept him to death," said she to some servants who met her in the ante-chamber; and, passing through the affrighted group, she went slowly out toward the fountain.

CHAPTER XIX.
HOW THE KNIGHT HULDBRAND WAS BURIED.

Father Heilmann had returned to the castle as soon as the death of the lord of Ringstetten had been made known in the neighborhood, and he appeared at the very same moment that the monk who had married the unfortunate couple was fleeing from the gates overwhelmed with fear and terror.

"It is well," replied Heilmann, when he was informed of this; "now my duties begin, and I need no associate."

Upon this he began to console the bride, now a widow, small result as it produced upon her worldly thoughtless mind. The old fisherman, on the other hand, although heartily grieved, was far more resigned to the fate which had befallen his daughter and son-in-law, and while Bertalda could not refrain from abusing Undine as a murderess and sorceress, the old man calmly said: "It could not be otherwise after all; I see nothing in it but the judgment of God, and no one's heart has been more deeply grieved by Huldbrand's death than that of her by whom it was inflicted—

the poor forsaken Undine!"

At the same time he assisted in arranging the funeral solemnities as befitted the rank of the deceased.

The knight was to be interred in the village churchyard which was filled with the graves of his ancestors. And this church had been endowed with rich privileges and gifts both by these ancestors and by himself. His shield and helmet lay already on the coffin, to be lowered with it into the grave, for Sir Huldbrand, of Ringstetten, had died the last of his race; the mourners began their sorrowful march, singing requiems under the bright, calm canopy of heaven; Father Heilmann walked in advance, bearing a high crucifix, and the inconsolable Bertalda followed, supported by her aged father. Suddenly, in the midst of the black-robed attendants in the widow's train, a snow-white figure was seen, closely veiled, and wringing her hands with fervent sorrow. Those near whom she moved felt a secret dread, and retreated either backward or to the side, increasing by their movements the alarm of the others near to whom the white stranger was now advancing, and thus a confusion in the funeral-train was well-nigh beginning. Some of the military escort were so daring as to address the figure, and to attempt to remove it from the procession; but she seemed to vanish from under their hands, and yet was immediately seen advancing again amid the dismal cortege with slow and solemn step. At length, in consequence of the continued shrinking of the attendants to the right and to the left, she came close behind Bertalda. The figure now moved so slowly that the widow did not perceive it, and it walked meekly and humbly behind her undisturbed.

This lasted till they came to the churchyard, where the procession formed a circle round the open grave. Then Bertalda saw her unbidden companion, and starting up half in anger and half in terror, she commanded her to leave the knight's last resting-place. The veiled figure, however, gently shook her head in refusal, and raised her hands as if in humble supplication to Bertalda, deeply agitating her by the action, and recalling to her with tears how Undine had so kindly wished to give her that coral necklace on the Danube. Father Heilmann motioned with his hand and commanded silence, as they were to pray in mute devotion over the body, which they were now covering with the earth. Bertalda knelt silently, and all knelt, even the grave-diggers among the rest, when they had finished their task. But when they rose again, the white stranger had vanished; on the spot where she had knelt there gushed out of the turf a little silver spring, which rippled and murmured away till it had almost entirely encircled the knight's grave; then it ran further and emptied itself into a lake which lay by the side of the burial-place. Even to this day the inhabitants of the village show the spring, and cherish the belief that it is the poor rejected Undine, who in this manner still embraces her husband in her loving arms.

Source:
Motte-Fouqué, Friedrich de La. *Undine and Other Tales*. Fanny Elizabeth Bunnett, translator. London: Sampson Low, Son, and Marston, 1867.

116. Slavonic Mermaids

Slavonic Region of Europe

THE mermaid beliefs of the Slavonians and the Cornu-British Celt were not dissimilar save that in the Slavonian peasant tales the Undine is usually a lake or river spirit, or rather personage, in Celtic usually an inhabitant of the ocean. The reason is obvious. The Celts were a maritime people for the most part, the Slavonians accustomed to great lakes and to rivers, larger in some cases than any in our British Isles. The Slavonic lakes have often a very picturesque and weird aspect, bordered by huge primeval forests, and are rarely navigated. Most of them have indeed now-a-days a boat or two, but these are only used occasionally for fishing and rarely by night. Some of the smaller ones even now have no boats on their shores, and thus are rarely if ever crossed by man. Strange stories arise about them therefore quite as naturally as the wild mermaid legends which amused the fireside evenings of the Cornish fishing-folk of days of yore, about the fair Circes, half-fish, half-women, who were at times seen combing their hair on the rocks, and who could lure to death, or, if they were pleased, bestow fairy gifts on those who approached them. The thought of the waste and unprofitableness of the ocean is a thought as old as Homer, and the peasant mind has been wont to fill the void by dreams of ocean dwellers, men-fish in crystal palaces, rulers of the waters as man is of the land. The waste of the mysterious lake was as suggestive to the Slavonic peasant as the waste of the ocean to the Celtic fishermen. It was perhaps more so, for the fishermen lived by the harvest of the deep, and in fine weather could traverse almost every creek of his rocky shore; the peasant as a landsman rarely pushed out in a boat on the wide expanses of his mysterious lakes. So the unknown lake had even a better claim to its Undines than the fairly known sea to its mermaids.

A curious contrast, however, exists in the nature of the Slavonic water demon with the Celtic. He might seem like a reptile—a frog for instance, as well as a fish. He thus appears in the Bohemian story of Lidushka and the water demon. Here Lidushka becomes the godmother of the children of the Undine, and is admitted to her crystal palace, and shares in the fish feasts of the water spirits. She finds a shelf on which are many jars turned upside down. She lifts one of these, a white dove flutters forth; so she does with the others,[1] and from each a dove flutters forth. They are the souls of those drowned by the water demon. A variant of the same sort of story appears in Yanechek. Here the mother seeks the soul of her son in the subaqueous palace, and in doing so lets all the spirits free, each spirit being in a silver jar.

One story I have had narrated to me in the country about Gniezn, about a haunted lake, which I believe has never yet been published, and which is interesting to Englishmen as being in one point similar to a folk-belief of South Devon, *i.e.*, as embodied in the proverb, "The River Dart every year claims its heart," *i.e.*, somebody or other is yearly drowned in the Dart.

A peasant was once cutting wood in a forest near Mogilno (the "town of tombs" or tumuli as its name implies). He penetrated into depths of the forest glade never yet traversed by man. Suddenly, between the glinting foliage, he perceived a castle-towers, massive walls, battlements-grander than he had ever seen even in his unfrequent visits to the "sacred city of the rest," Gniezn, or even to Posen, the other ancient capital, "the city of the recognition." In fact he had never before seen anything so grand.

The unselfish thought struck him, "Perhaps the lord of this grand castle is in want of workmen, and some of the men of my village might find good employment and pay with him." So with a parting glance at the noble towers of the forest palace he turned homewards and told the gossips of the village at the karczma or village inn that night of the grand castle he had seen and the excellent opening for well-paid work which it probably offered.

In the morning the village was early awake; the young men came out in numbers to seek new employment with the rich seigneur who had settled in their neighbourhood. They started into the forest. They followed the path pointed out by their guide. Lo! to their chagrin and grief only a deep blue lake appeared. The castle was a magic castle of the nymph of the lake, only visible in twilight.

Their hopes were disappointed, but the mystic lake was no longer unknown or unfrequented. A path was made through the forest near it, linking two villages. Then the spell worked. Year after year some benighted peasant was caught in its deep blue waters, the more mysterious because half shrouded by the green foliage. The Rusialka claimed her offering of a human heart, some human life sacrificed to her Circe charms. But this could not be endured. The magic lake was held accursed. Again and again, in broad daylight, did the peasant try to sound its depths, just as the Cornish moorsmen say they have tried Dosmary

---

[1] This and some of the following stories are narrated by Mr. Naake, to whose book I refer my readers.—*Slavonic Fairy Tales*, 1874.

Pool, in vain. At length something, every one felt, must be done. A deputation of peasants waited on the parish priest. It was a scandal to the Church that this demon of the waters should thus hold sway in the parish. Persuaded by his parishioners he sallied forth with all the paraphernalia of exorcism to exorcise the spirit. He came with a long procession of villagers to the lake. He solemnly adjured the Rusialka to depart for ever. The service of exorcism was performed. Since then the peasants say the fatality of the lake has diminished, if not ceased. The story of the exorcism was, I was credibly assured, no legend but an historic fact.

As to the story itself, it may be explained easily on natural grounds. The evening twilight has strange effects in forest glades. Perhaps the mists of the lake in warm weather might have produced an effect on the mind of the peasant, full of fancy and folk-lore, to make him imagine a castle. Day dispelled the delusion. The idea of its being fathomless here as at Dosmary was due to no better sounding instruments than long poles being available. The exorcism was a fact. Its result possibly was due to peasants now avoiding the dreaded spot.

It is curious that the symbol of the plague should be the same both in Slavonic and Celtic lands, the tall gaunt woman in her long white dress. I remember once twelve years ago a Cornish mining village being quite disturbed by the story of a tall woman in white having been seen on the moors, and prophesying to some miners that a pestilence was coming. Fortunately it remained a mere apparition, the prophesy not being fulfilled.

In the Polish tale of the plague the pestilence appears personified also as a tall woman in white garments, with her hair floating about her, and is hunted by dogs.

In another Polish variant of the same myth, the plague fixes on the back of a poor peasant whom she compels to carry her like the old man in Sinbad the Sailor, and forces the wretched fellow to carry her about from place to place. He bears with many a sight of misery which she works. At last he beholds his native village. He will not carry the plague there, but drowns himself in the Pruth.

This evidently is a myth of the carrying of the seeds of infection. Many may carry the infection to others even without catching the disease themselves.

The proportion of moral tales in Slavonic collections to the rest is far larger than in our Cornish or indeed general English collections. These moral tales the folk-tale student is inclined to regard with suspicion as probably of modern origin, and possibly the work of some well-meaning country parson, who has composed them for the edification of the junior members of his flock, by whom they have been handed down to their descendants. Perhaps the very singularity of these highly-moral tales to western ears may be evidences of their modern origin. If they were really ancient they would portray perhaps their common Aryan origin, traced from those remote pre-historic times when the ancestors of the Slav and the Celt were living in the same regions; their diversity from all western sentiment and thought perhaps shows that they are merely Slavonic, and Slavonic in the most modern phase. Of these stories are the warning stories about naughty boys so common in Slav folk-lore; one of these is the tale of Yarechek and the water-demon; but here, as I mentioned, though the preface is modern, the latter part is a variant of an ancient Slav myth of drowned souls in jars, the "Davy Jones's locker," it may be, of our British seamen.

The Servian story of "Right and Wrong" has an antique ring, and also that of "Wisdom and Fortune," from the Bohemian, related by Mr. Naake, are of this style. Not a few of the peasant tales in their chapbooks, which form an interesting collection of folk-tales, are of this moralizing order.

Source:
Lach-Szyrma, W. S. "Slavonic Folk-Lore." *The Folk-Lore Record*. Vol. 4 (1881). pp. 52-70.

117. Lidushka and the Water Demon's Wife

Bohemia (Czech Republic)[1]

IN A certain place lived a young housewife, whose name was Lidushka. One day, as she was washing linen in a rivulet, a large, swollen frog swam towards her, looking so ugly that Lidushka, alarmed at the sight of it, jumped back a pace or two. The ugly looking frog approached nearly to the spot where Lidushka had just been washing, spread its legs out on the top of the water, and opening its mouth as if it wished to say something, stood perfectly still.

"You great, fat frog," said Lidushka to herself; "what do you want here, and why do you open your mouth at me so?"

She then threw a piece of linen that she happened to have in her hand at the frog, wishing to drive it away that she might go on with her washing. The frog dived, and before Lidushka had time to look about her, it reappeared at the other side of the water, and began to swim directly towards her. Lidushka again drove it away; but the frog would

---

[1] The source material credits Bohemia as the location of the tale which today is a region in the west of the former Czechoslovakia and present-day Czech Republic.~*HAH*

persist in swimming towards her, opening its mouth all the time; it would not be driven away, but continued to interrupt her in her work.

"Go away, you great, fat thing!" cried Lidushka at last, quite angrily. "Let me know when you have got your baby, and I will come and be its godmother;" and she threw another piece of linen at the frog.

"Very good, very good!" croaked the frog. Then it disappeared under the water, and disturbed Lidushka no more at her washing.

Not long afterwards, Lidushka came again to the rivulet to wash her linen at the usual place, when suddenly, the same frog she had before seen, only that it was much thinner now, swam towards her.

"I have got my children now," croaked the frog, "and have come to ask you to be their godmother, as you promised."

Lidushka remembered that she had said, not long before, that if the frog had a little one, and would let her know, she would be its godmother; she therefore, although alarmed, did not refuse to do what she had once promised.

"But you silly thing," said Lidushka full of anxiety, "where am I to go with you to gratify your wish, and to fulfill my promise?"

"Come, come, come!" croaked the frog, spreading out its legs and swimming on the water.

The promised godmother followed it sorrowfully along the bank of the rivulet. The frog swam on until it came to a dam, when it stopped and croaked, "Fear not, fear not! Remove that stone, and under it you will see a flight of stairs; they will lead you down to my house. Come, come! I will go before you."

Having thus croaked, the frog disappeared under water, and the good-natured Lidushka saw no other way to get out of her trouble than simply to do what the frog told her. She removed the stone, and saw that there was really a flight of stairs leading under the dam. They were most wonderful stairs; neither of wood nor of stone, but as if made of the purest crystal, clear and transparent, like layers of water placed one below the other. Lidushka went timidly down a few steps, when the frog appeared hopping and croaking joyfully before her, because she was about to fulfill her promise of becoming godmother to its little ones. Lidushka, without further hesitation, descended the remainder of the beautiful steps. They soon reached the object they had in view—the frog's house. It also was built entirely of crystal water. Like the stairs, by which they had come down, was the whole house—bright, sparkling, and transparent as crystal. The frog, full of joy, hopped about Lidushka, and took her to her little ones.

When the ceremony was over, Lidushka, in fulfillment of her promise, having taken her part in it as a godmother, a splendid entertainment followed, to which many frogs from far and near had been invited. They all hopped about Lidushka, and croaked with great joy. There were various courses—boiled and pickled, roast and fried—but they all consisted of fish: the finest carp, jack, chad, trout, whiting, perch, and many other fish which Lidushka did not know even by name. She was amazed at the sight of all this. The dinner at an end, she took a walk about the house to see everything more closely.

In the course of her walk, she came to a small room, which looked like the kitchen. It was full of long shelves, and on the shelves stood rows of little jars. Lidushka was much surprised when she noticed that all the jars stood upside down. She was curious to know what was under them, and lifted one up. In a moment a little white dove flew from under it, joyfully fluttered its wings, rose up and disappeared. Lidushka lifted another jar, and, oh, wonderful! there flew from it another beautiful white dove, which joyfully fluttered its wings, and also disappeared. Then Lidushka lifted a third jar, and a third white dove flew out of it, fluttered its wings with joy, rose up in the air and vanished from her sight. She wondered greatly why these little doves were here confined: for Heaven has given an immortal soul to man, that he may live forever; and wings to the birds, that they may fly freely over the earth.

"Oh, how cruel!" said Lidushka to herself, "to keep you here in everlasting darkness. Wait a moment, you dear little doves, and I will give you all your liberty." Thus saying she began to raise the little jars, one after another, and as from the first three, there flew from each successive jar a white dove. As if wishing to thank her for their release from their dark prison, each of them fluttered its wings with joy, then rose up and disappeared in the air.

Scarcely had Lidushka finished lifting up the little jars, when the mistress of the house, the ugly looking frog, hopped up to her croaking in a most dismal manner. She could see from afar what Lidushka was doing with the little jars.

"Unhappy woman!" cried the frog; "why did you let those souls free? Quick! make haste and fly! Search for a lump of dry earth or a piece of toasted bread. There comes my husband! Quick! or he will rob you of your soul!"[1]

When the amiable Lidushka heard this dreadful croaking, she turned round to see from what quarter the husband was coming; but she could see nothing of him. Only at a distance she observed a few buds of a beautiful red water-plant floating towards her on the top of the water. Suddenly she remembered what she had often heard before, that the Water Demon sometimes shows himself on the surface of the water in the shape of a cluster of red flowers. He does this especially to young girls as they are haymaking near a stream or pond, to induce them to try to reach the flowers with their rakes. He then pulls them in and drowns them.

---

[1] It is said that the Water Demon has no power over those who hold, either a handful of dry earth or a piece of toasted bread; but that he can drown a man in even a spoonful of water.

Lidushka dashed up the stairs as fast as she could run, and fortunately reached the dry land in time. She was overjoyed at having released all the little white doves; they were the souls of the unfortunate people whom the Water Demon had drawn into his power, and had cruelly drowned. Each soul had been kept in a separate dark prison, in the shape of a little jar. Lidushka was the deliverer of them all.

Source:

Naaké, John Theophilus. *Slavonic Fairy Tales: Collected and Translated From the Russian, Polish, Servian, and Bohemian.* London: Henry S. King & Co., 1874.

118. The Good Ferryman and the Water Nymphs

Poland

THERE was once an old man, very poor, with three sons. They lived chiefly by ferrying people over a river; but he had had nothing but ill-luck all his life. And to crown all, on the night he died, there was a great storm, and in it the crazy old ferry-boat, on which his sons depended for a living, was sunk.

As they were lamenting both their father and their poverty, an old man came by, and learning the reason of their sorrow said:

"Never mind; all will come right in time. Look! there is your boat as good as new."

And there was a fine new ferry-boat on the water, in place of the old one, and a number of people waiting to be ferried over.

The three brothers arranged to take turns with the boat, and divide the fares they took.

They were however very different in disposition. The two elder brothers were greedy and avaricious, and would never take anyone over the river, without being handsomely paid for it.

But the youngest brother took over poor people, who had no money, for nothing; and moreover frequently relieved their wants out of his own pocket.

One day, at sunset, when the eldest brother was at the ferry the same old man, who had visited them on the night their father died, came, and asked for a passage.

"I have nothing to pay you with, but this empty purse," he said.

"Go and get something to put in it then first," replied the ferry-man;

"and be off with you now!"

Next day it was the second brother's turn; and the same old man came, and offered his empty purse as his fare. But he met with a like reply.

The third day it was the youngest brother's turn; and when the old man arrived, and asked to be ferried over for charity, he answered:

"Yes, get in, old man."

"And what is the fare?" asked the old man.

"That depends upon whether you can pay or not," was the reply; "but if you cannot, it is all the same to me."

"A good deed is never without its reward," said the old man: "but in the meantime take this empty purse; though it is very worn, and looks worth nothing. But if you shake it, and say:

> 'For his sake who gave it, this purse I hold,
> I wish may always be full of gold;'

it will always afford you as much gold as you wish for."

The youngest brother came home, and his brothers, who were sitting over a good supper, laughed at him, because he had taken only a few copper coins that day, and they told him he should have no supper. But when he began to shake his purse and scatter gold coins all about, they jumped up from the table, and began picking them up eagerly.

And as it was share and share alike, they all grew rich very quickly. The youngest brother made good use of his riches, for he gave away money freely to the poor. But the greedy elder brothers envied him the possession of the wonderful purse, and contrived to steal it from him. Then they left their old home; and the one bought a ship, laded it with all sorts of merchandize, for a trading voyage. But the ship ran upon a rock, and every one on board was drowned. The second brother was no more fortunate, for as he was travelling through a forest, with an enormous treasure of precious stones, in which he had laid out his wealth, to sell at a profit, he was waylaid by robbers, who murdered him, and shared the spoil among them.

The youngest brother, who remained at home, having lost his purse, became as poor as before. But he still did as formerly, took pay from passengers who could afford it, ferried over poor folks for nothing, and helped those who were poorer than himself so far as he could.

One day the same old man with the long white beard came by; the ferry-man welcomed him as an old friend, and while rowing him over the river, told him all that had happened since he last saw him.

"Your brothers did very wrong, and they have paid for it," said the old man; "but you were in fault yourself. Still, I will give you one more chance. Take this hook and line; and whatever you catch, mind you hold fast, and not let it escape you; or you will bitterly repent it."

The old man then disappeared, and the ferry-man looked in wonder at

Tales From Around the World

his new fishing-tackle—a diamond hook, a silver line, and a golden rod.

All at once the hook sprang of itself into the water; the line lengthened out along the river current, and there came a strong pull upon it. The fisherman drew it in, and beheld a most lovely creature, upwards from the waist a woman, but with a fish's tail.

"Good ferry-man, let me go," she said; "take your hook out of my hair! The sun is setting, and after sunset I can no longer be a water-nymph again."

But without answering, the ferry-man only held her fast, and covered her over with his coat, to prevent her escaping. Then the sun set, and she lost her fish-tail.

"Now," she said: "I am yours; so let us go to the nearest church and get married."

She was already dressed as a bride, with a myrtle garland on her head, in a white dress, with a rainbow-coloured girdle, and rich jewels in her hair and on her neck. And she held in her hand the wonderful purse, that was always full of gold.

They found the priest and all ready at the church; were married in a few minutes; and then came home to their wedding-feast, to which all the neighbours were invited. They were royally entertained, and when they were about to leave the bride shook the wonderful purse, and sent a shower of gold pieces flying among the guests; so they all went home very well pleased.

The good ferry-man and his marvellous wife lived most happily together; they never wanted for anything, and gave freely to all who came. He continued to ply his ferry-boat; but he now took all passengers over for nothing, and gave them each a piece of gold into the bargain.

Now there was a king over that country, who a year ago had just succeeded to his elder brother. He had heard of the ferry-man, who was so marvellously rich, and wishing to ascertain the truth of the story he had heard, came on purpose to see for himself. But when he saw the ferry-man's beautiful young wife, he resolved to have her for himself, and determined to get rid of her husband somehow.

At that time there was an eclipse of the sun; and the king sent for the ferry-man, and told him he must find out the cause of this eclipse, or be put to death.

He came home in great distress to his wife; but she replied:

"Never mind, my dear. I will tell you what to do, and how to gratify the king's curiosity."

So she gave him a wonderful ball of thread, which he was to throw before him, and follow the thread as it kept unwinding—towards the East.

He went on a long way, over high mountains, deep rivers, and wide regions. At last he came to a ruined city, where a number of corpses were lying about unburied, tainting the air with pestilence.

The good man was sorry to see this, and took the pains to summon men from the neighbouring cities, and get the bodies properly buried. He then resumed his journey.

He came at last to the ends of the earth. Here he found a magnificent golden palace, with an amber roof, and diamond doors and windows.

The ball of thread went straight into the palace, and the ferry-man found himself in a vast apartment, where sat a very dignified old lady, spinning from a golden distaff.

"Wretched man! what are you here for?" she exclaimed, when she saw him. "My son will come back presently and burn you up."

He explained to her how he had been forced to come, out of sheer necessity.

"Well, I must help you," replied the old lady, who was no less than the Mother of the Sun, "because you did Sol that good turn some days ago, in burying the inhabitants of that town, when they were killed by a dragon. He journeys every day across the wide arch of heaven, in a diamond car, drawn by twelve grey horses, with golden manes, giving heat and light to the whole world. He will soon be back here, to rest for the night. . . . But . . . here he comes; hide yourself, and take care to observe what follows."

So saying she changed her visitor into a lady-bird, and let him fly to the window.

Then the neighing of the wonderful horses and the rattling of chariot wheels were heard, and the bright Sun himself presently came in, and stretching himself upon a coral bed, remarked to his mother:

"I smell a human being here!"

"What nonsense you talk!" replied his mother. "How could any human being come here? You know it is impossible."

The Sun, as if he did not quite believe her, began to peer anxiously about the room.

"Don't be so restless," said the old lady; "but tell me why you suffered eclipse a month or two ago."

"How could I help it?" answered the Sun; "When the dragon from the deep abyss attacked me, and I had to fight him? Perhaps I should have been fighting with the monster till now, if a wonderful mermaid had not come to help me. When she began to sing, and looked at the dragon with her beautiful eyes, all his rage softened at once; he was absorbed in gazing upon her beauty, and I meanwhile burnt him to ashes, and threw them into the sea."

The Sun then went to sleep, and his mother again touched the ferry-man with her spindle; he then returned to his natural shape, and slipped out of the palace. Following the ball of thread he reached home at last, and next day went to the king, and told him all.

But the king was so enchanted at the description of the beautiful sea-maiden, that he ordered the ferry-man to go and bring her to him, on pain of death.

He went home very sad to his wife, but she told him she would manage this also. So saying she gave him another ball of thread, to show him which way to go, and she also gave him a carriage-load of costly lady's apparel and jewels, and ornaments—told him what he was to do, and they took leave of one another.

On the way the ferry-man met a youth, riding on a fine grey horse, who asked:

"What have you got there, man?"

"A woman's wearing apparel, most costly and beautiful"—he had several dresses, not simply one.

"I say, give me some of those as a present for my intended, whom I am going to see. I can be of use to you, for I am the Storm-wind. I will come, whenever you call upon me thus:

'Storm-wind! Storm-wind! come with speed!
Help me in my sudden need!'"

The ferry-man gave him some of the most beautiful things he had, and the Storm-wind passed.

A little further on he met an old man, grey-haired, but strong and vigorous-looking, who also said:

"What have you got there?"

"Women's garments costly and beautiful."

"I am going to my daughter's wedding; she is to marry the Storm-wind; give me something as a wedding present for her, and I will be of use to you. I am the Frost; if you need me call upon me thus:

'Frost, I call thee; come with speed;
Help me in my sudden need!'"

The ferry-man let him take all he wanted and went on.

And now he came to the sea-coast; here the ball of thread stopped, and would go no further.

The ferry-man waded up to his waist into the sea, and set up two high poles, with cross-bars between them, upon which he hung dresses of various colours, scarves, and ribbons, gold chains, and diamond earrings and pins, shoes, and looking-glasses, and then hid himself, with his wonderful hook and line ready.

As soon as the morning rose from the sea, there appeared far away on the smooth waters a silvery boat, in which stood a beautiful maiden, with a golden oar in one hand, while with the other she gathered together her long golden hair, all the while singing so beautifully to the rising sun, that, if the ferry-man had not quickly stopped his ears, he would have fallen into a delicious reverie, and then asleep.

She sailed along a long time in her silver boat, and round her leaped and played golden fishes with rainbow wings and diamond eyes. But all at once she perceived the rich clothes and ornaments, hung, up on the poles, and as she came nearer, the ferry-man called out:

> "Storm-wind! Storm-wind! come with speed!
> Help me in my sudden need!"

"What do you want?" asked the Storm-wind.
The ferry-man without answering him, called out:

> "Frost, I call thee; come with speed,
> Help me in my sudden need!"

"What do you want?" asked the Frost.
"I want to capture the sea-maiden."
Then the wind blew and blew, so that the silver boat was capsized, and the frost breathed on the sea till it was frozen over.

Then the ferryman rushed up to the sea-maiden, entangling his hook in her golden hair; lifted her on his horse, and rode off as swift as the wind after his wonderful ball of thread.

She kept weeping and lamenting all the way; but as soon as they reached the ferry-man's home, and saw his wife, all her sorrow changed into joy; she laughed with delight, and threw herself into her arms.

And then it turned out that the two were sisters.

Next morning the ferry-man went to court with both his wife and sister-in-law, and the king was so delighted with the beauty of the latter, that he at once offered to marry her. But she could give him no answer until he had the Self-playing Guitar.

So the king ordered the ferry-man to procure him this wonderful guitar, or be put to death.

His wife told him what to do, and gave him a handkerchief of hers, embroidered with gold, telling him to use this in case of need.

Following the ball of thread he came at last to a great lake, in the midst of which was a green island.

He began to wonder how he was to get there, when he saw a boat approaching, in which was an old man, with a long white beard, and he recognized him with delight, as his former benefactor.

"How are you, ferry-man?" he asked. "Where are you going?"

"I am going wherever the ball of thread leads me, for I must fetch the Self-playing Guitar."

"This guitar," said the old man, "belongs to Goldmore, the lord of that island. It is a difficult matter to have to do with him; but perhaps you may succeed. You have often ferried me over the water; I will ferry you now."

The old man pushed off, and they reached the island.

On arriving the ball of thread went straight into a palace, where Goldmore came out to meet the traveller, and asked him where he was going and what he wanted.

He explained:

"I am come for the Self-playing Guitar."

"I will only let you have it on condition that you do not go to sleep for three days and nights. And if you do, you will not only lose all chance of the Self-playing Guitar; but you must die."

What could the poor man do, but agree to this?

So Goldmore conducted him to a great room, and locked him in. The floor was strewn with sleepy-grass, so he fell asleep directly.

Next morning in came Goldmore, and on waking him up said:

"So you went to sleep! Very well, you shall die!"

And he touched a spring in the floor, and the unhappy ferry-man fell down into an apartment beneath, where the walls were of looking-glass, and there were great heaps of gold and precious stones lying about.

For three days and nights he lay there; he was fearfully hungry. And then it dawned upon him that he was to be starved to death!

He called out, and entreated in vain; nobody answered, and though he had piles of gold and jewels about him, they could not purchase him a morsel of food.

He sought in vain for any means of exit. There was a window, of clearest crystal, but it was barred by a heavy iron grating. But the window looked into a garden whence he could hear nightingales singing, doves cooing, and the murmur of a brook. But inside he saw only heaps of useless gold and jewels, and his own face, worn and haggard, reflected a thousand times.

He could now only pray for a speedy death, and took out a little iron cross, which he had kept by him since his boyhood. But in doing so he also drew out the gold-embroidered handkerchief, given him by his wife, and which he had quite forgotten till now.

Goldmore had been looking on, as he often did, from an opening in the ceiling to enjoy the sight of his prisoner's sufferings. All at once he recognized the handkerchief, as belonging to his own sister, the ferry-man's wife.

He at once changed his treatment of his brother-in-law, as he had discovered him to be; took him out of prison, led him to his own apartments, gave him food and drink, and the Self-playing Guitar into the bargain.

Coming home, the ferry-man met his wife half-way.

"The ball of thread came home alone," she explained; "so I judged that some misfortune had befallen you, and I was coming to help you."

He told her all his adventures, and they returned home together.

The king was all eagerness to see and hear the Self-playing Guitar; so he ordered the ferry-man, his wife, and her sister to come with it to the palace at once.

Now the property of this Self-playing Guitar was such that wherever its music was heard, the sick became well, those who were sad merry, ugly folks became handsome, sorceries were dissolved, and those who had been murdered rose from the dead, and slew their murderers.

So when the king, having been told the charm to set the guitar playing, said the words, all the court began to be merry, and dance—except the king himself! . . . For all at once the door opened, the music ceased, and the figure of the late king stood up in his shroud, and said:

"I was the rightful possessor of the throne! and you, wicked brother, who caused me to be murdered, shall now reap your reward!"

So saying he breathed upon him, and the king fell dead—on which the phantom vanished.

But as soon as they recovered from their fright, all the nobility who were present acclaimed the ferry-man as their king.

The next day, after the burial of the late king, the beautiful sea-maiden, the beloved of the Sun, went back to the sea, to float about in her silvery canoe, in the company of the rainbow fishes, and to rejoice in the sunbeams.

But the good ferry-man and his wife lived happily ever after, as king and queen. And they gave a grand ball to the nobility and to the people. . . . The Self-playing Guitar furnished the music, the wonderful purse scattered gold all the time, and the king entertained all the guests right royally.

Source:
Gliński, Antoni Józef. *Polish Fairy Tales*. Maude Ashurst Biggs, translator. London: John Lane, 1920.

119. Mr. Cuttlefish's Love Story

Hungary

Despite the source,* Old Hungarian Fairy Tales *by Baroness Orczy, claiming the tale to be older, this rendition is definitely a literary fairy tale, most likely with great embellishment by Orczy, most famous for her* The Scarlet Pimpernel *series.

THERE was a great commotion in the Coral Palace of the Queen of the Sea. It was very plain that something unusual was happening in the otherwise peaceful dwelling at the bottom of the deep blue sea. As a rule, on hot summer evenings, the Queen reclined lazily on a bed of pink sea-shell, while her two mermaids-in-waiting stood near her, fanning her with tall fans, made of sharks' fins, and telling her all the latest news that occurred among the upper ten of the fish kingdom. Everything had to be kept very quiet during that time, as the Queen objected to every kind of noise that might disturb her, if she chose to take a nap, which she usually did.

But on this particular evening the royal palace wore a totally different aspect; the bed of sea-shell was deserted, the fans of sharks' fins lay idle on the ground, and not a fish was visible in any of the pink coral halls.

Stay, that is not quite correct. When I say not a fish could be seen, I mean not a whole fish, for at every crevice, every window, and every door, there were rows and rows of tails, the heads and bodies of their owners being thrust as far out as possible. Apparently they were intent on watching a most amusing spectacle, for every now and then these tails shook with suppressed laughter, making the water foam and bubble all around.

The Queen herself so far forgot her dignity as to sit at a half-opened window, and gaze out into the blue depths, and clap her hands with glee, and laugh till the tears streamed down her cheeks.

What so evidently excited the mirth of her Majesty and all her subjects was certainly, to any impartial observer, a most amusing sight. Under the shades of the giant sea-weed, in the grounds of the Coral Palace, Mr. Cuttlefish was making love to dear little Marina, the Queen's favourite mermaid, whose amorous glances quite equalled his own. He rolled his great goggle eyes at her, and surrounded her graceful little form with five of his long arms.

"My dearest, I am afraid we must part," she was saying to him, "and I don't think I can possibly meet you out here again. I am sure some one will see us; the Palace is so near and the windows of the great hall look out on this part of the grounds, and," she added, kissing his great puffy cheek, "I know the Queen will never consent to our marriage; you have no appointment at court, and your business compels you to live in quite another part of the sea. I must remain near the Queen, or by our laws I should lose the human half of my body and become a fish altogether, probably a sole, or some other nasty flat thing. What a cone-down for me, dear. I have always been accounted so sharp."

Mr. Cuttlefish did not appreciate jokes which were not his own, and would have adminstered a severe rebuke to Marina for venturing to make one at so serious a moment. She, however, looked so pretty, and was evidently so much in love with him, poor dear, that he merely withdrew two or three of his arms from round her waist to show his displeasure. This act of unnecessary cruelty brought tears to the eyes of poor little Marina.

"Well, my dear," he said, when harmony was once more restored between them, "you must try and find out whether there is not some good appointment vacant at Court, and I will immediately apply for and obtain it. There were several reasons why I withdrew myself from Court life altogether . . . Ahem! . . . I will leave you to guess these reasons, dear

Marina . . . As a matter of fact Her Majesty herself . . . ahem! . . . lately intimated to her subjects her desire for a fitting helpmate through the cares of State . . . ahem! . . . and when she announced this intention in public . . . ahem! . . . ahem!"

"Well! well!"

"Well! ahem! . . . you won't be jealous, dear Marina?"

"Jealous? Why?"

"Well! the fact is," said Mr. Cuttle-fish, now blushing to the tips of his fingers, or rather suckers, "that Her Majesty deigned to cast eyes of approval on one of her subjects whom modesty forbids me to name."

"Oh," said Marina, clasping her hands in awed reverence, "then you would be king of us all."

"Well; yes! my dear, I believe that would have been my position," said Mr. Cuttlefish, modestly covering his eyes with an arm or two and wiping a humble tear. "What was that?" he added, in sudden alarm, as a loud peal of irrepressible laughter from the hidden spectators of this dainty scene echoed through the grounds.

"Nothing, my dearest, only a difference of opinion, I expect, between two pikes in Her Majesty's kitchen; they never can agree over the way in which a minnow should be sliced, and quarrel over it in a most rowdy manner."

Mr. Cuttlefish thought to himself that he would not even slice a pike for that matter, but said nothing. Suddenly little Marina had an idea.

"I'll tell you what, dear Mr. Cuttlefish, I believe there is a vacant appointment at Court, it is a very lucrative one I know, and one to which, I think, you are peculiarly suited. Her Majesty's Royal Musician died the other day; one of the choir swallowed him accidentally while singing a bass solo. I know you have great talent for music, and, you see, none of your choir could possibly succeed in swallowing you."

"That is so," said Mr. Cuttlefish, "and how do you think I could best succeed in obtaining this appointment?"

"By thoroughly convincing the Queen of your musical capabilities. I should say if you could get an orchestra together, and a few soloists, you might obtain permission to perform before Her Majesty—that is," added little Marina, "if your modesty will allow you to stand once more before her after the forward advances she made to you."

At this point the laughter in the palace became so uproarious, that all the sea around became a wilderness of foam and bubbles. Little Marina ran home in dismay, terrified lest she should have been seen; and Mr. Cuttlefish sailed away more rapidly than dignity generally allows. Modesty had now got the better of him and he thought it prudent to retire for the night to his cavern between the rocks.

The next day all was quiet and peaceful in the beautiful kingdom under the sea. The light shone like brilliant emeralds through the water, illuminating the coral grottoes, and lighting their fantastic forms with innumerable points of glittering sparks. The great branches of giant seaweed waved to and fro with slow rhythmic cadence, and the ribbon-weed floated gracefully, forming myriads of little ripples.

There was a general air of festivity pervading the whole of the royal palace. Every little fish seemed to have donned his gayest colours, and all the crabs and the lobsters seemed to have assumed an air of being very busy and pressed for time.

Suddenly a most singular sound echoed through all the neighbouring caverns, and caused a general commotion in the waters. It penetrated as far as the Queen's bed-chamber, where her Majesty was enjoying a quiet rest while reflecting over the events of the night before. She had forbidden all her Court to make the slightest allusion to them before her little mermaid, as it might distress her to feel that she and her lover had been so openly laughed at. She was a dear, kind-hearted sort of Queen, and really very fond of little Marina, so she determined to smooth the path of true love as much as lay in her power.

In the meantime the noise was growing louder and louder, and more and more distinct. Now it resembled a grampus blowing through his nose, and now it seemed like a hundred engines letting steam off all at once. At last an unusually discordant note resounded through the royal bedchamber, and Her Majesty, now fully aroused, and not at all pleased at being disturbed in her nap, dispatched an attendant crab to inquire the cause of this extraordinary commotion. He came back with the startling news that Mr. Cuttlefish was preparing for a grand concert, which he proposed to give that very afternoon.

"But," said the Queen, addressing no once in particular, "I did not know the gentleman was musical."

"He is not," said an old thornback, spitefully, "but he fancies he is, and likes to be thought a distinguished amateur and musical critic. He wrote a very severe article in the 'Fly Fancier's Gazette' on the subject of your Majesty's choir."

"In which," said the nautilus, indignantly, "he disapproved of my voice."

"And distinctly hinted that we sang flat," exclaimed the chorus of crabs.

"And," added the oysters, opening their shells, and looking defiantly round, "that we have no notion of time."

A wail of indignation rose at these complaints against Mr. Cuttlefish. However, the Queen was determined to try and make matters as pleasant for Marina as possible, and influence public opinion in her lover's favour as far as she could. She wished to hear more about the concert.

"May it please your Majesty," said a little bony fish, who seemed well posted up in all the news, "Mr. Cuttlefish issued cards of invitation early this morning, but the Grand Chamberlain, the Right Honourable Tortoise, who is offended with him about something or other, has evidently withheld your Majesty's card. As for me, I shall certainly not go, he does not mention the word supper, and I don't believe there will be any." While all this was going on poor little Marina felt on thorns, she grew hot and cold alternately, and hardly knew how to hold herself erect on her tail, while fanning the Queen. The concert was evidently now in full swing, the waters around were continually disturbed by crowds of fishes trooping to join in it, and carrying their cards of invitation under their fins; the Queen was now quite unable to check her curiosity any longer, and announced her gracious intention to honour the concert by her august presence.

Lord Chamberlain Tortoise, who had been simply dying to go himself, but, of course, did not dare show his eagerness before Her Majesty, now stalked off in high glee to order the royal mermen, who always conveyed the Queen, to be in readiness.

Her Majesty mounted one of them while another swam in front, both blowing a shell trumpet; Marina and the other little seamaids brought up the rear, carrying the fans, handkerchiefs and smelling salts. On seeing the Queen approach, Mr. Cuttlefish bade the music cease, then rose with great ceremony and bowed three times, as did all the other fishes present, while the oysters, whose absence of legs forbade them to bow, clapped their shells respectfully. Mr. Cuttlefish extended one of his arms and, taking the queen's hand, led her to a seat on a large green rock, covered with beautiful anemones. Seating himself, with a look at Marina, which conveyed to her the expression of his endless love, he took a great trumpet in one hand, seized a drumstick in another, a pair of cymbals and a concertina in four more. A large lobster then gravely announced that Mr. Cuttlefish would play a grand march, composed by himself, entitled "The good old Sharks," and would be assisted in the performance by a full choir, selected and trained by himself.

The words and music were alike impressive, the orchestration eminently modern, and the chorus written in four parts. Three huge frogs, rolling their goggle eyes, rolled out the bass, the herrings sang alto in sentimental style, the whiting were high treble, and as they sang with their tails in their mouths—as all well-regulated whiting do—their voices had an additional charm. The moonfish, the trunkfish, the gurnard were all tenors, but as they had been unavoidably prevented from attending the rehearsals, their parts did not go very well; however, the sword-fish, who sang baritone, and the fire-fish, who sang contralto, managed to drown their mistakes pretty effectually.

The conductor was a great green crab, who endeavoured to keep time by waving his claws; he found this fairly easy while the slow part of the march was being performed, but in the more rapid movements no one paid any attention to him, which somewhat marred the harmony of the whole effect, but in no way interfered with the enjoyment of the performers. As for Mr. Cuttlefish's trumpet and big drum, nothing seemed to drown them, he never ceased blowing the one or beating the other; though he sometimes disengaged an available arm to administer an impressive rebuke to any of the chorus who appeared to slacken energy.

In fact the whole affair was a brilliant success, and when the piece was over, everybody clapped his shell or his fins, and congratulated the composer, who took all these honours with the indifference characteristic of genius.

Her Majesty desired his presence.

Mr. Cuttlefish advanced, and bending exceedingly low, humbly waited her gracious pleasure.

"We are very pleased with the extraordinary talent, sir, displayed by you this afternoon; in fact, our royal ears have never been struck by so large a volume of sound. We will therefore appoint you our Royal Musician, with a fitting salary, and give you the hand of our favourite sea-maiden, Marina, in marriage."

Mr. Cuttlefish cast a grateful look at his Sovereign, who taking a shark's fin fan in her hand and smiting him on top of his bald head, added:

"Rise, Sir Cuttlefish. We confer this honour upon you for your distinguished talents, and for the pleasure you have given us this afternoon."

Sir Cuttlefish wished to raise a modest protest against so much honour, but eventually thought better of it, and accepted it all with the noble resignation of the really great.

The lobster now announced a dance, Sir Cuttlefish opened the ball by standing on his head and whirling all his arms about till the water foamed, while everybody did their best to make the evening lively, by turning over and over and round and round. The shrimps waltzed together, while the eels curled themselves up first one way and then the other.

When they were all tired out the supper was brought in by five and twenty green tortoises. It was the most magnificent repast, consisting of crayfish, minnows, and some deliciously prepared carp; Sir Cuttlefish ate five hundred of these, which proved to be an injudicious quantity. There was a slight stir towards the end of the supper, caused by the sharks, who had not been invited, gobbling up some of the company, but, on the whole, the evening passed off very pleasantly. After supper the gathering broke up, Sir Cuttlefish seeing the Queen home.

Next day the great composer was suffering from a detestable fit of indigestion. The poor Queen had a fearful headache, but, nevertheless, she had never enjoyed herself so much in all her life.

The wedding of Sir Cuttlefish and Marina was fixed for an early date, and the Queen did the bride the great honour of not only being present at the ceremony, but of holding a reception at the Palace. All the Court officials were ordered to be present, and the poor Lord Chamberlain Tortoise had his hands full, what with issuing the invitation cards, settling the order of precedence, and making arrangements for the breakfast. The Queen ordered that everything should be conducted in the best style, and expense should be no obstacle to the success of the entertainment.

Meanwhile, Sir Cuttlefish was busy. He chose the leader of his choir for his "best fish." Then he ordered the lobsters to make the ring of pearl, and it took no little ingenuity on their part to round off and polish it to Sir Cuttlefish's satisfaction. The happy bridegroom also presented his bride with a brooch made of sea diamonds, in shape like a big drum—a perfect work of art—in commemoration of the great concert that had proved such a triumph.

Needless to add, I think, that the deep sea orchestra and choir played and sang the wedding march and hymns, the new R. M.—Royal Musician—having drilled them himself most carefully. On the great day, Sir Cuttlefish got himself up in most sumptuous style; he had ordered four pairs of white gloves—you see he had eight arms; this was looked upon as a piece of most extravagant folly, and the shark (who had not yet got over his annoyance at not being asked to the concert) made some very unpleasant remarks on the subject in his paper, "The Fisherman's Foe."

The gorgeousness of the ceremony and the splendour of the wedding breakfast it were vain to attempt to relate, for they even threw the glories of the Cuttlefish's concert and fête into the shade.

The bridegroom borrowed a most beautiful grotto in which to pass his honeymoon, and also spent much time in having his own house thoroughly done up and repaired, and in that newly decorated house under the sea, dear little readers, we will leave the happy pair, for in it they have lived in joy and prosperity from that day to this.

Source:
Orczy, Baroness Emmuska. *Old Hungarian Fairy Tales*. London: Dean & Son, [1895].

120. The Yellow Dwarf by Madame d'Aulnoy

France

THERE was once a queen who had lost all her children except one daughter, who was all the world to her. But, being a widow, and loving the young princess as the dearest thing on earth, she was so fearful of losing her that she never corrected her faults. Thus the maiden, whose beauty was extraordinary and divine rather than mortal, and who was destined to wear a crown one day, became so headstrong and so vain of her budding charms that she looked down on everybody.

Her mother, by her caresses and indulgence, encouraged her in the belief that there was nobody worthy of her. She was nearly always dressed as Pallas or Diana, attended by the greatest ladies of the court attired as nymphs. And, to put the finishing stroke to her vanity, the queen called her Toutebelle: and having had her picture painted by the most skilled artists, sent it to several kings with whom she kept up a close friendship. When they gazed on the picture, not one of them was proof against the irresistible power of her charms. Some fell ill, others went out of their mind, and the more fortunate who reached her side in good health, no sooner set eyes on her than they became her slaves.

Never was there such gallantry and courtesy at any court. Twenty kings vied with each other to please her; and, after spending three and four hundred millions on a single fête, they thought themselves only too well recompensed if they obtained from her a word, such as "How pretty!" Their adoration delighted the queen. Not a day passed but there came to her court seven or eight thousand sonnets, and as many elegies, madrigals, and songs, sent by all the poets of the universe. Toutebelle was the one and only subject of the prose and verse of the authors of the time. Yet these poems served for nothing but lighting bonfires, and they sparkled and burned better than any kind of fuel.

The princess was fifteen years old, but no one dared aspire to the honour of becoming her husband; and yet there was no one who did not desire to be the happy man. But how were they to touch a heart like hers? They would have thought little of being hanged five or six times a-day just to please her, but she would have regarded it as a mere trifle. Her lovers murmured loudly against her cruelty, and the queen, who wished her to marry, did not know how to persuade her to make up her mind. "Will you not," she used sometimes to say, "lay aside a little of the intolerable pride that causes you to look with con tempt on all the kings who come to our court? I want you to marry one of them. You have no desire to please me."

"I am so happy," replied Toutebelle. "Allow me, madam, to remain as I am, calm and indifferent. If I once lost my peace of mind you would be sorry."

"Yes," replied the queen; "I should be sorry if you loved some one beneath you; but consider those who ask you, and learn that nowhere are others to be found like them."

That was true; but the princess's idea of her own merits was such that she thought herself worth something better still; and by degrees her obstinacy in remaining single began deeply to grieve her mother, who repented, but too late, of having been so indulgent.

Uncertain what she ought to do, she determined to go all by herself to see a celebrated fairy called the Fairy of the Desert. But it was no easy matter to get at her, for she was guarded by lions. The queen would have found it impossible had she not long since learnt that you had to throw them a cake made of millet seed, sugar candy, and crocodiles' eggs. She kneaded the cake herself, and put it in a little basket which she carried on her arm. Unaccustomed to so much walking, she became tired, and lay down at the foot of a tree to take some rest. Before she was aware of it she had fallen asleep, and on awaking found that the cake was no longer in the basket; and, to complete her misfortune, she heard the lions approaching. They had scented her, and were making a great noise.

"Alas!" she cried, sorrowfully, "what will become of me? I shall be eaten up." She wept, and, having no strength to run away, remained by the tree where she had slept. At the same time she heard a sound like "Chet! Chet! Hem! Hem!" Raising her eyes, she looked all round her, and saw on the tree a little man no bigger than your arm, eating oranges. "Oh! queen," he said to her, "I know you well, and I know the fright you are in lest the lions should eat you up; and you have every reason to be afraid, for they have eaten many others. To add to your misfortune, you have no cake."

"I must make up my mind to die," said the queen, sighing. "Alas, I should be less distressed if my dear daughter were married!"

"What? You have a daughter!" cried the yellow dwarf, who was so called from the colour of his complexion and the orange tree in which he lived. "Truly, I rejoice, for I have been seeking a wife over sea and land. Come now, if you promise to give her to me I will under take to protect you from lions, tigers, and bears." The queen looked at him, and was scarcely less afraid of his hideous little face than of the lions. She seemed to be pondering, and she answered not a word. "What! you hesitate, madam?" he cried. "Then you do not care much for your life?" At the same moment the queen saw the lions on the top of a hill running towards her.

They had each two heads, eight feet, four rows of teeth, and their skin was as hard as shell, and as red as morocco leather. At that sight the poor queen, more fearful than a dove at the sight of a kite, exclaimed with all her might: "Sir Dwarf! Toutebelle is yours". "Oh!" he said, with a contemptuous air, "Toutebelle is too beautiful; I don't want her; keep her."

"Ah, sir," continued the distressed queen, "do not refuse her. She is the most charming princess in the world."

"Well," he replied, "I will take her out of charity; but remember the gift you make me." The orange tree immediately opened; the queen rushed headlong inside. It closed again, and the lions caught nothing.

The queen was so upset that she did not notice a door which had been contrived in this tree. At last she saw it, and opened it. It looked on a field of nettles and thistles, and was surrounded by a muddy ditch, while a little further off was a low thatched hut, out of which came the yellow dwarf with a sprightly air. He wore wooden shoes and a yellow frieze jacket. He had no hair on his head, big ears, and looked a perfect little villain.

"I am delighted, mother-in-law," he said to the queen, "for you to see the little castle in which your Toutebelle will live with me. With the nettles and thistles she can feed an ass to ride on. Under this rustic roof she will be protected from stress of weather. She will drink of this water and feed on the fat frogs that live in it; and then she will have me beside her day and night, handsome, lively, and gallant as you see me; for I should be sorry if her shadow were a closer companion to her than I."

The unhappy queen, suddenly realising the miserable existence the dwarf promised her beloved daughter, and unable to endure so terrible a thought, fell prostrate on the floor, unconscious and without strength enough to utter a single word. While in this condition, she was put to bed with the greatest care, and in the finest night-cap, trimmed with the prettiest ribbon knots she had ever worn in her life. The queen, when she awoke, remembered what had happened, but she thought it must have been a delusion, for, finding herself in her palace in the midst of her ladies with her daughter by her side, there seemed no evidence of her having been in the desert, of her having encountered such great danger, nor of the dwarf having saved her on the hard condition of Toutebelle's hand in marriage. And yet this night-cap of valuable lace and the knot of ribbons were quite as surprising as the dream she thought she had dreamt. These things preyed on her mind to such an extent that she could scarcely speak, eat, or sleep for the extraordinary melancholy that took possession of her.

The princess, who loved her with all her heart, was exceedingly uneasy, and entreated her over and over again to tell her what was the matter. But the queen would put her off by telling her sometimes that it was caused by her bad health, sometimes that one of her neighbours was threatening her with a great war. Toutebelle saw that these replies were plausible enough, but that there was something more behind which the queen was trying to hide from her. Unable to endure her anxiety any longer, she determined to seek the celebrated Fairy of the Desert, whose wisdom was known far and wide. She was also desirous of asking her advice as to whether she should remain single or marry; for everybody was strongly urging her to choose a husband. She took care to knead with her own hands the cake which was to appease the fury of the lions; and, pretending to go to bed early in the evening, she went out by a little secret stair-case, her face covered with a long white veil that reached to her feet; and thus, alone, she took her way towards the grotto where the wise fairy lived.

But reaching the fateful orange tree, of which I have already spoken, she saw that it was full of fruit and flowers, and was seized with a longing to pluck some. Placing her basket on the ground, she gathered and ate a few oranges. But when she wished to pick up her basket and her cake it was no longer there. As she stood there uneasy and unhappy at her loss, she suddenly saw in front of her the hideous little dwarf I mentioned before. "What is the matter with you, my fine maiden? Why do you weep?" said he. "Alas! who would not weep?" she replied. "I've lost my basket and my cake, and I can never reach the Fairy of the Desert safely without them."

"Well, and what do you want with her, pretty maid?" said the ugly little man. "I am her relative, her friend, and, to say the least, as clever as she is."

"The queen, my mother," replied the princess, "has for some time been so terribly melancholy that I fear for her life. I cannot help thinking that I am perhaps the cause, for she wants me to marry. I confess to you that as yet I have found no one worthy of me. All these reasons make me desirous of speaking with the fairy."

"Don't take the trouble, princess," said the dwarf; "I am better able than she to explain these matters to you. The queen is in trouble because she has promised you in marriage."

"The queen has promised me!" she said, interrupting him. "Ah, doubtless you are mistaken; she would have told me, and I have too much interest in the matter for her to have pledged me without my consent."

"Beautiful princess," said the dwarf, suddenly falling on his knees, "I flatter myself that this choice will not be displeasing to you when I tell you that it is I who am destined to such happiness."

"My mother wishes you to be her son-in-law!" exclaimed Toutebelle, falling back a step or two; "was ever any one so mad as you?"

"I care very little for the honour," said the dwarf, testily. "Here come the lions. In three bites they will avenge me for your unjust contempt."

At the same moment the princess heard them coming with loud roars. "What is to become of me?" she exclaimed. "Am I thus to end my fair days?" The wicked dwarf looked at her, and smiled contemptuously. "You will at least have the satisfaction of dying unmarried," said he, "and of not allying your shining merit with a miserable dwarf like myself."

"Do not be angry, I beg of you," said the princess, clasping her beautiful hands; "I would rather marry all the dwarfs in the world than perish in this frightful way."

"Look at me well, princess, before pledging your word," he replied, "for I have no desire to entrap you."

"I have looked at you enough and to spare. The lions are on me; my terror grows. Save me! save me! or I shall die of fear." Indeed, scarcely had she uttered these words before she swooned; and, without knowing how, she found herself in her own bed in the most beautiful night gown trimmed with the prettiest ribbons, and a little ring made of a single red hair which clung so closely that it would have been easier to have torn off her skin than to have removed the ring from her finger.

When the princess saw these things and remembered what had happened in the night, she fell into a melancholy that surprised and alarmed the whole court. The queen was the most distressed of all, and asked her hundreds and hundreds of times what was the matter. But she persisted in concealing her adventure. At length the estates of the realm, impatient to see their princess married, after holding a council, came to the queen begging her to choose a husband. She said that was exactly what she wished to do, but that her daughter showed so much repugnance that she advised them to go and talk to her themselves. They did so without delay. Since her adventure with the yellow dwarf Toutebelle's pride had been greatly humbled, and she could conceive no better way of getting out of the difficulty than by marrying some great king, with whom the ugly little man would be in no position to dispute so glorious a prize. Thus she replied more favourably than could have been expected: that, although she should have considered herself happy in remaining single all her life, she consented to marry the King of the Gold Mines. He was a powerful, handsome prince, who had loved her with the utmost passion for some years, and who, so far, had had no reason to flatter himself that his love was returned.

When he learned the delightful news his supreme joy can be easily imagined, and also the rage of all his rivals at losing forever the hope that fed their passion. But Toutebelle could not marry twenty kings; it had given her trouble enough to choose one, for her vanity did not fail her, and she was entirely persuaded that no one in the world could be compared with her.

Everything necessary for the greatest fête imaginable was prepared. The King of the Gold Mines sent such enormous sums that the whole sea was covered with the ships that brought them. He sent to the most elegant and brilliant courts, and especially to that of France, to procure the most valuable things to adorn the princess, although her beauty was so perfect that she had little need of ornaments to set it off. The King of the Gold Mines, seeing himself on the point of becoming happy, never left the side of the charming princess.

It was to her interest to know him well, and, studying him with care, she discovered in him so much merit and intelligence, such lively and delicate feelings—in short, so beautiful a soul in so perfect a body—that she began to feel for him something of what he felt for her. These were happy times for both, when, in the loveliest gardens in the world, they were free to speak to each other all their passion. Those delights were often accompanied by music. The king, always gallant and loving, made poems and songs for the princess. Here is one which pleased her very much:—

> "These woods and meadows don their gayest dress,
> Shine out their best to greet your loveliness;
> And west winds blow and fairest flowers up-spring,
> While loving birds their sweetest roundels sing.
>   All nature hastes, in humour gay,
>   Homage to love's own queen to pay."

They were at the height of their joy. The king's rivals, disconsolate at his good fortune, returned to their homes overwhelmed with the keenest sorrow, Unable to be present at Toutebelle's wedding. They bade her farewell in so touching a manner that she could not but pity them. "Ah, madam," said the King of the Gold Mines, "of what are you robbing me? You grant your pity to lovers who are only too well paid for their distresses by a single one of your glances."

"I should be sorry," replied Toutebelle, "if you had not observed the compassion I show these princes, who are losing me forever; it is a proof of your delicacy which I prize. But, sir, their condition is so different from yours. You have so much reason to be pleased with me, and they have so little, that you should not carry your jealousy further." The King of the Gold Mines, ashamed at the kindly way in which the princess took a thing that might have annoyed her, threw himself at her feet, and, kissing her hands, asked her pardon a thousand times.

At last the long-expected and much-desired day arrived: when everything was ready for Toutebelle's wedding, musical instruments and trumpets announced the great fête through the city. The streets were laid with red cloth, strewn with flowers, and the people rushed in crowds to the great courtyard of the palace. The queen was so excited that she had scarcely been to bed at all; and she rose before the dawn to give the necessary instructions and to choose the precious stones with which the princess was to be decked. She was covered with diamonds to her very shoes, which were made of them. Her gown of silver brocade was trimmed with a dozen sunbeams, of countless price indeed; but there! what could have been more brilliant?—only the beauty of the princess herself. A magnificent crown adorned her head; her hair hung down to her feet; and her dignified bearing marked her out from all the ladies attending her. The King of the Gold Mines was no less perfectly appointed and magnificent. His joy appeared in his countenance and in all his actions. No one went to greet him without returning loaded with gifts; for round his banqueting hall he had had placed a thousand casks filled with gold, and big velvet bags embroidered with pearls filled with gold pieces. Each one held a hundred thousand. They were given indiscriminately to all who came for them; so that this little ceremony, which was not the least useful and pleasant part of the wedding, attracted many persons who would scarcely have appreciated the other entertainments.

As the queen and the princess were on their way to join the king they saw two big turkey cocks, dragging a very ill-made box, enter the long gallery where they were. Behind them came a tall old woman, whose advanced age and decrepitude were not less surprising than her exceeding ugliness. She leaned on a crutch, and wore a black silk ruff, a red velvet hood, and a ragged farthingale. She went three times round with the turkey cocks without saying a word; then, stopping in the middle of the gallery and brandishing her crutch in a threatening manner: "Ho!

ho queen!—Ho! ho! princess!" she shouted. "You think you can break with impunity the promise you gave m friend the yellow dwarf! I am the Fairy of the Desert. Without him, without his orange tree, do you not know my big lions would have eaten you up? Such insults are not endured in Fairyland. Consider quickly what you intend to do; for I swear by the cap on my head that you shall marry him or I will burn my crutch."

"Ah! princess," said the queen, in tears, "do I hear? What have you promised?"

"Ah! mother," replied Toutebelle, sorrowfully, "what did you promise yourself?" The King of the Gold Mines, angry at what was going on and because the wicked old woman had come in the way of his happiness, approached her, sword in hand, pointing it at her throat. "Wretched woman," he said, "depart from this place for ever, or your life shall pay for your wickedness."

He had scarcely spoken these words when the lid of the box jumped right up to the ceiling with a fearful noise, and out came the yellow dwarf, mounted on a big Spanish cat. He placed himself between the Fairy of the Desert and the King of the Gold Mines. "Rash youth," he said, "do not seek to injure this most distinguished fairy. It is with me that you have to reckon. I am your rival; I am your enemy. The faithless princess who intends to marry you has given me her promise, and accepted mine. Look if she has not a ring made of one of my hairs. Try to take it from her, and even by that slight test you will see that your power is less than mine."

"Wretched monster," said the king, "you are actually bold enough to call yourself the adorer of this divine princess, and to lay claim to so splendid a possession? Consider, you are an ugly little imp, whose hideous face hurts one's eyes. I should have already taken your life had you been worthy of so glorious a death." The yellow dwarf, mortally offended, struck his spurs into the cat, which set up a horrible mewing, and, jumping first to one side and then to the other, frightened every one except the brave king. He was grappling with the dwarf when the creature drew a large cutlass with which he was armed, and, challenging the king to a combat, with a strange noise rushed down into the courtyard of the palace.

With hasty strides the wrathful king followed him. Hardly were they face to face, and the whole court on the balconies, than the sun growing suddenly red as if stained with blood, darkness came on so that they could scarcely distinguish each other. Thunder and lightning seemed bent on the destruction of the world; and the two turkey cocks looked by the side of the wicked dwarf like two giants, taller than the mountains, casting forth fire from their mouths and eyes in such quantities that you might have taken them for a fiery furnace. All these things would not have terrified the brave heart of the young monarch. The boldness of his look and actions reassured all who were anxious for his preservation, and even, perhaps, somewhat troubled the yellow dwarf. But his courage was not equal to seeing the condition to which his beloved princess was reduced. The Fairy of the Desert, like Tisiphone her head covered with long snakes, was mounted on a winged griffin and armed With a spear, with which she struck the princess such cruel blows that she fell into the queen's arms bathed in blood. The tender mother, more hurt by the blow than her daughter, uttered the most piteous cries and laments. At this the king lo his courage and his presence of mind, and, giving up the combat, ran to help the princess, and to die with her. But the yellow dwarf did not give him time to reach her. With his Spanish cat he sprang on to the balcony where she was tore her from the hands of the queen and of all her ladies, and, jumping on to the roof of the palace, disappeared with his prey.

The king, stupefied and motionless was regarding with the uttermost despair so extraordinary an event, and one in which he had the misfortune to be quite powerless when, to add to his ill-luck, he felt a veil come over his eyes, which deprived him of all sense of sight; while some one with remarkable strength carried him away into the Vast region of air. What a tale of misfortunes! Love, cruel love! is it thus you treat those who own you for their conqueror? The wicked Fairy of the Desert, who had come to help the yellow dwarf to carry off the princess, had scarcely looked at the King of the Gold Mines when, her savage heart feeling the worth of the young prince, she wished to make him her prey. So she carried him to the depths of a horrible cave and loaded him with chains which she had fastened to a rock, hoping that the fear of a speedy death would make him forget Toutebelle, and induce him to do whatever she wished. As soon as they arrived she restored his sight without giving him his liberty, and, borrowing from the fairies' art the grace and charm nature had denied her, she appeared before him as a lovely nymph whom chance had led to that spot.

"Whom do I see here?" she cried. "What! it is you, charming prince? What ill fortune has come upon you and keeps you in so sorry an abode?" The king, deceived by these false appearances, replied: "Alas, lovely nymph, I have no idea what the fiendish fury who brought me here wants of me. Although she deprived me of the use of my eyes when she carried me off and has not appeared since, I did not fail to recognise, by the Sound of her voice, that she was the Fairy of the Desert."

"Ah, sir," cried the pretended nymph, "if you are in the power of that woman you will not get free until she has married you. She has played this trick on more than one hero, and she is the least manageable person in the world with regard to her infatuations" While she was pretending to sympathise with the king's distress, he looked at the nymph's feet, and saw that they resembled those of a griffin. The fairy, in her various metamorphoses, might always be recognised by these; for she was unable to change that part of her griffin nature.

The king took no notice, and went on speaking in a confidential tone:

"I have no aversion," he said, "for the Fairy of the Desert, but I cannot brook that she should protect the yellow dwarf from me and keep me chained like a criminal. What have I done to her? I loved a charming princess; but, if she restores me my liberty, I feel that gratitude would oblige me to love only her."

"Are you speaking sincerely?" asked the deluded nymph. "Do not doubt it," replied the king; "the art of feigning is unknown to me, and I confess that the idea of a fairy flatters my vanity more than a mere princess; hut, even were I dying of love for her, I should always show her nothing but hatred until I was set free,"

The Fairy of the Desert, deceived by these words, resolved to carry the king away to a place as delightful as the present solitude was horrible. Forcing him to get into her chariot, to which she had yoked swans instead of the bats that usually drew her, she flew from one end of the earth to the other.

But what were the prince's feelings when, traversing the vast region of air, he saw his beloved princess in a castle of steel, whose walls, struck by the sun's rays, formed glowing mirrors that burned all who attempted to approach them! She was in a grove, lying by the side of a stream. One of her hands supported her head, while with the other she seemed to be wiping away her tears. As she lifted her eyes to heaven, as if to ask its aid, she saw the king pass with the Fairy of the Desert, who, employing the fairy art in which she was skilled to appear beautiful in the eyes of the young monarch, seemed, in fact, in those of the princess the most wondrously fair lady in the world. "What!" she exclaimed, "am I not wretched enough in this inaccessible castle to which the horrible yellow dwarf has brought me? To add to my misfortunes, must I be persecuted by the demon of jealousy? By so strange an adventure must I learn the faithlessness of the King of the Gold Mines? He thought in losing sight of me that he was freed from all the oaths he made me. But who is this formidable rival, whose fatal beauty surpasses mine?"

While she was speaking thus the amorous king felt sick at heart at flying with such speed from the beloved object of his vows. If he had had less know ledge of the fairy's power he would have tried everything to get away from her, either by killing her, or by any other means his love and courage might have suggested. But what could he do against so powerful a personage? Only time and cunning could free him from her clutches.

The fairy had seen Toutebelle, and sought to discover in the king's eyes the effect of the sight on his heart. "I am better able than any one," he said, "to tell you what you desire to know. The unexpected meeting with an un fortunate princess, to whom I was attached before I knew you, has somewhat moved me, but you rank so far above her in my heart that rather than be faith less to you I would die."

"Ah, prince," she said, "may I flatter myself that I have inspired in you such a strong affection?"

"Time will convince you, madam," he said; "but, if you wish to prove to me that I have found favour with you, do not refuse me your assistance for Toutebelle."

"Think what you are asking," said the fairy, frowning and looking askance at him. "You wish me to use my skill against the yellow dwarf, who is my best friend, and take out of his hands a haughty princess, whom I cannot but regard as my rival?" The king sighed, and answered never a word. What could he have replied to this keen-sighted person?

They reached a vast meadow brilliant with a thousand different flowers. A deep river surrounded it, and many a rivulet flowed gently under the thick-spreading trees, in whose shade it was always cool. In the distance rose a magnificent palace, the walls of which were of transparent emerald. Immediately the swans that drew the fairy alighted under a portico with a pavement of diamonds and a roof of rubies. Then appeared on all sides a thousand beautiful ladies, who received her with great shouts of joy, singing these words:—

> "When love would fain subdue a heart
> Resistance but augments the smart:
> The warrior, most famed in fight,
> Must soonest yield to Cupid's might."

The Fairy of the Desert was charmed to hear them sing the story of her love. She led the king into the most magnificent chamber ever seen within the memory of fairy; and, that he should not think himself absolutely a prisoner, left him there a few minutes. He felt pretty certain that she was not far off, and that, hidden in some place, she was watching what he did. So he went up to a large mirror, and, addressing it, said: "Faithful counsellor, show me what I can do to make myself agreeable to the charming Fairy of the Desert, for the desire to please her is never out of my mind". Then he combed and powdered his hair, put on a patch, and, seeing on a table a coat more splendid than his own, hastily put it on. The fairy entered, so carried away by her joy, that she was unable to restrain it. "I see," she said, "the care you take to please me; without any effort you have discovered the secret; judge then, sir, if, when you wish it, it will be difficult."

The king, who had his reasons for saying pretty things to the old fairy, was not sparing of them, and, little by little, gained permission to walk along the sea-shore. By her art she had made the sea so terrible and stormy that there were no pilots bold enough to sail it. Thus she had nothing to fear from the indulgence she showed her prisoner; and he found some consolation for his troubles in being able to dream in solitude, without the interruptions of his wicked gaoler.

After walking for some time on the sand, he bent down and wrote these lines with a stick he carried in his hand:—

> "Here am I free
> To ease my grief with pouring out my tears,
> For that my loved one never more appears.
> O wind-toss'd sea!
> That scal'st heaven's height,
> Searchest hell's night,
> Driving poor mortals from this churlish shore!—
> The winds torment thee with an endless strife,
> Yet my heart struggleth more.
> O cruel fate, that bore Toutebelle away,
> O heaven, that said my loved one might not stay,
> Wilt thou not take my life?
> Fair goddess of the wave,
> If that thou ever yet hast felt love's power,
> Come from thy deepest cave,
> And help the lover in his darkest hour!"

While he was writing he heard a voice, which, in spite of himself, attracted his whole attention, and, seeing that the waves began to swell, he looked all around, and saw a woman of extraordinary beauty. Her only covering was her long hair, which, gently stirred by zephyrs, floated on the water. She held a mirror in one hand and a comb in the other. Her body ended in a long fish's tail with fins. The king was very much surprised at so strange an encounter. As soon as she was within speaking distance, she said to him: "I know the sad plight to which you are reduced by the loss of your princess, and by the strange passion the Fairy of the Desert has for you. If you like, I will take you away from this fatal place, where, it may be, you will languish for more than thirty years." The king did not know what reply to make to the proposal: not from any lack of desire for his liberty, but because he feared the Fairy of the Desert had only borrowed this shape to deceive him. As he hesitated the mermaid, who divined his thoughts, said: "Do not think I am setting a trap for you; I am too sincere to wish to serve your enemies. The doings of the Fairy of the Desert and of the yellow dwarf have incensed me against them. I see your beautiful princess every day. Her beauty and merit alike make me Pity her. I again repeat that, if you have Confidence in me, I will save you." trust you so entirely," cried the king, "that I will do everything you command, but, since you have seen my princess, give me news of her."

"We should lose too much time talking," said she. "Come with me; I will take you to the castle of steel, and leave on this shore a figure so nearly resembling you that the fairy will be deceived."

She then cut some sea rushes, made a big bundle of them, and, breathing on them three times, said "Sea rushes, my friends, I command you to remain stretched out on the sand, Without moving, until the Fairy of the Desert con to carry you off". The sea rushes had all the appearance of being covered with skin, and were so like the King of the Gold Mines that nothing more wonderful was ever seen. They were dressed in a coat like his, and were pale and feeble to look like the drowned king. Then the good mermaid made the king seat himself on her big fish tail, and both, equally pleased, sailed out to sea.

"I will now tell you," said she, "that when the wicked yellow dwarf carried off Toutebelle, notwithstanding the wound the Fairy of the Desert had inflicted on her, he put her behind him on his terrible Spanish cat. She lost so much blood and was so disturbed by the adventure that her strength failed, and she remained in a Swoon the whole way. But the yellow dwarf would not stop to restore her to consciousness until he was safely arrived in his terrible castle of steel. There he was received by the most beautiful ladies in the world, whom he had stolen away. Each vied with the other in her eagerness to serve the princess. She was placed in a bed made of cloth of gold, embroidered with pearls bigger than nuts."

"Ah," exclaimed the King of the Gold Mines, interrupting the mermaid. "He has married her. I am faint; I shall die."

"No, sir," said she, "make yourself easy; Toutebelle's firmness preserved her from the violence of the horrid dwarf."

"Go on, I beg of you," said the king. "What more have I to tell you?" replied the mermaid. "She was in the wood when you passed. She saw you with the Fairy of the Desert, who was so disguised that she seemed her superior in beauty. Her despair cannot be imagined; she thinks you love the fairy."

"She thinks I love her Oh, ye gods "cried the king, "into how fatal an error has she fallen! and how shall I undeceive her?"

"Consult your heart," replied the mermaid, with a charming smile. "When a man is so passionately in love he has no need of advice." By this time they had reached the castle of steel. The side looking seawards was the only part that the yellow dwarf had not fortified with the formidable walls that burned up everybody.

"I know," said the mermaid to the king, "that Toutebelle is by the side of the same stream where you saw her when you passed; but, since you will have foes to vanquish before reaching her, here is a sword with which, provided you do not let it fall, you can undertake anything and brave the greatest dangers. Farewell; I shall betake myself to the shade of the rock you see there. If you have need of me to help you further with your beloved princess, I shall not fail you; for the queen is my best friend, and it was to serve her that I came to your aid." So saying, she gave the king a sword made of a single diamond, brighter than the sun's rays. He well understood its use; and, unable to find words strong enough to express his gratitude, he begged her to supply those that would describe what a grateful heart is capable of feeling for such good service.

We must now tell something of what has been happening to the Fairy of the Desert. Since her charming lover did not return, she hastened in search of him, betaking herself to the shore with a hundred damsels of her suite, all bearing magnificent presents for him. Some carried large baskets filled with diamonds, others golden vases wonderfully wrought, several containing amber-gris, coral, and pearls. Others bore on their heads bales of stuffs of inconceivable richness; others, again, fruits, flowers and even birds. But what were the feelings of the fairy, who was following this fine and numerous company, when she saw the sea rushes so like the King of the Gold Mines that no difference could be discovered? At the sight, struck with astonishment and the keenest sorrow, she uttered a terrible cry, which pierced the heavens and made the mountains tremble and re-echo even to the depths of hell. The faces of the furies, Megara, Alecto, and Tisiphone themselves, could not have been more terrible to look on than hers. Throwing herself on the king's body, she wept, she howled, she tore in pieces fifty of the most beautiful damsels who had ac companied her, sacrificing them to the spirit of her dead lover. Afterwards she summoned eleven of her sisters, fairies like herself begging them to aid her building a magnificent mausoleum for the young hero. There was not one who was not deceived by the sea rushes. This may seem surprising, for the fairies knew everything; but the clever mermaid knew even more than they did.

While they were Providing the porphyry, the jasper, the agate, and the marble, the statues, the inscriptions the gold, and the bronze to immortalise the memory of the king whom they thought dead, he was thanking the good mermaid and imploring her to grant him her protection. She promised with the best grace in the world, and vanished from his sight. Nothing remained but to advance towards the castle of steel.

So, guided by his love, he walked with great strides, looking about eagerly for his adored princess. But he was not long without occupation Four terrible sphinxes surrounded him, and, sticking their sharp claws into him, would have torn him in pieces, had not the diamond sword been as useful as the mermaid had foretold. It scarcely glittered in the eyes of the monsters before they fell helpless at his feet. Giving each a mortal wound, he advanced further and saw six dragons covered with scales harder to pierce than iron. However alarming the encounter was he did not Jose heart, and, making use of his formidable sword, cut each one of them in half. He hoped he had now overcome the greatest difficulties; but there still remained an embarrassing one. He met four-and-twenty nymphs, beautiful and charming, holding long wreaths of flowers, and by their means barring his passage. "Where do you wish to go, sir?" said they. "We are the guardians of this place; if we let you pass endless disasters will happen to you and to us. We entreat you not to persist. Would you stain your victorious hand with the blood of four innocent damsels who have never done you any harm?" At this sight the king remained dumbfounded and undecided, not knowing what to do. He, who professed to respect the fair sex and to be their knight to the death, must, on this occasion, destroy them. But a voice that he heard suddenly gave him strength. Strike! strike! spare no one," said the voice, "or you will lose the princess forever!"

Then, without answering the nymphs, he rushed into their midst, broke their wreaths, attacked them without quarter, and scattered them in a moment, it was one of the last obstacles he was to find, and he at length entered the little wood where he had seen Toutebelle she was beside the stream, pale and languishing. He approached her trembling, and would have thrown himself at her feet, but she drew back as quickly as if he had been the yellow dwarf. "Do not condemn me unheard, madam," he said; "I am neither faithless nor guilty; I am unfortunate enough to have displeased you without intending it."

"Ah! cruel one!" she exclaimed, "I saw you ride through the air with a woman of extra ordinary beauty. Did you set out on that journey against your will?" Yes, princess," he replied, "it was against my will. The wicked Fairy of the Desert, not satisfied with chaining me to a rock, carried me off in a chariot to one of the ends of the earth, where, if it had not been for the unexpected aid of a good mermaid who brought me here, I should be languishing now. I come, princess, to snatch you from the hand that keeps you captive. Do not refuse the help of the most faithful of all lovers.' He threw himself at her feet, but in laying hold of her gown unfortunately dropped his famous sword. The yellow dwarf, who was hidden under a lettuce, no sooner saw it out of the king's hands than, knowing its power, he threw himself upon it and seized it.

The princess uttered a heartrending cry on seeing the dwarf; hut her lamentations only served to exasperate the little monster. Uttering two words in his own jargon, two giants appeared, who loaded the king with chains and irons. "Now," said the dwarf to the princess, "I am master of my rival's destiny; but I will grant him his life and permission to leave this place, if you will agree to marry me without delay."

"Ah! Let me rather die a thousand deaths!" said the love-stricken king. "Alas!" cried the princess. "What more terrible than that you should die?"

"And what more frightful," replied the king, "than that you should become the victim of this monster?"

"Let us then die together," continued she. "Let me, my princess, have the consolation of dying for you."

"Nay, rather do I consent," she said to the dwarf, "to your wishes."

"In my sight," replied the king; "in my sight, you would take him for your husband, cruel princess? Life would be hateful to me."

"No," said the yellow dwarf. "The betrothal will not take place in your presence; I dread too much a favoured rival."

At these words, in spite of the tears and cries of Toutebelle, he stabbed the king to the heart and stretched him at his feet. The princess, who could not live after her lover's death, fell on his body, and it was not long before her soul joined his. Thus perished the unhappy prince and princess; and the mermaid could give them no help, for all the power of her magic lay in the diamond sword.

The wicked dwarf was better pleased to see the princess dead than in the arms of another; and the Fairy of the Desert, having heard what had happened destroyed the mausoleum she had built, conceiving for the memory of the King of the Gold Mines as great a hatred as she had felt affection for his person before. The only favour the good mermaid, in despair at the ill-fortune, could obtain from Destiny was to change the lovers into palm trees. The two perfect bodies became two beautiful trees, bearing ever a faithful love one to the other, embracing each other with their intertwined branches, and in this tender union immortalising their loves.

Source:

d'Aulnoy, [Marie Catherine Baronne]. *The Fairy Tales of Madame d'Aulnoy*. Miss Annie Macdonell and Miss Lee, translators. Clinton Peters, illustrator. London: Lawrence and Bullen, 1892.

121. Fortunio and the Siren
Night the Third, Fourth Fable

Italy

Fortunio, on account of an injury done to him by his supposed father and mother, leaves them, and after much wandering, comes to a wood, where he finds three animals, who do him good service. Afterwards he goes to Polonia, where he gets to wife Doralice, the king's daughter, as a reward for his prowess.

THERE is a saying, very frequent in the mouths of common people, that it is not seemly to jest at affliction nor to make a mock at the truth; forasmuch as he who keeps his eyes and ears open, and holds his tongue, is not likely to injure his fellows, and may hope himself to live in peace.

Once upon a time there lived in one of the remoter districts of Lombardy a man called Bernio, who, although he was not over well endowed with the gifts of fortune, was held to be in no way wanting with respect to good qualities of head and heart. This man took to wife a worthy and amiable woman named Alchia, who, though she chanced to be of low origin, was nevertheless of good parts and exemplary conduct, and loved her husband as dearly as any woman could. This married pair greatly desired to have children, but such a gift of God was not granted to them, peradventure for the reason that man often, in his ignorance, asks for those things which would not be to his advantage. Now, forasmuch as this desire for offspring still continued to possess them, and as fortune obstinately refused to grant their prayer, they determined at last to adopt a child whom they would nurture and treat in every way as if he were their own legitimate son. So one morning early they betook themselves to a certain spot where young children who had been cast off by their parents were often left, and, having seen there one who appeared to them more seemly and attractive than the rest, they took him home with them, and brought him up with the utmost care and good governance. Now after a time it came to pass (according to the good pleasure of Him who rules the universe and tempers and modifies everything according to His will) that Alchia became with child, and when her time of delivery was come, was brought to bed with a boy who resembled his father exactly. On this account both father and mother rejoiced exceedingly, and called their son by the name of Valentino.

The infant was well nurtured, and grew up strong and healthy and well-mannered; moreover, he loved so dearly his brother—to whom the name of Fortunio had been given—that he was inclined almost to fret himself to death whenever they chanced to be separated the one from the other. But the genius of discord, the foe of everything that is good, becoming aware of their warm and loving friendship, and being able no longer to suffer their good understanding to continue, one day interposed between them, and worked her evil will so effectively that before long the two friends began to taste her bitter fruits. Wherefore as they were sporting together one day (after the manner of boys) they grew somewhat excited over their game, and Valentino, who could not bear that Fortunio should get any advantage over him in their play, became inflamed with violent anger, and more than once called his companion a bastard and the son of a vile woman. Fortunio, when he heard these words, was much astonished, and perturbed as well, and turning to Valentin he said to him, "And why am I a bastard?" In reply, Valentino, muttering angrily between his teeth, repeated what he had already said, and even more. Whereupon Fortunio, greatly grieved and disturbed in mind, gave over playing and went forthwith to his so-called mother, and asked her whether he was in sooth the son of Bernio and herself. Alchia answered that he was, and, having learned that Fortunio had been insulted by Valentino, she rated the latter soundly, and declared that she would give him heavy chastisement if he should repeat his offence. But the words which Alchia had spoken roused fresh suspicion in Fortunio, and made him well nigh certain that he was not her legitimate son; indeed, there often came upon him the desire to put her to the test, to see whether she really was his mother or not, and thus discover the truth. In the end he questioned and importuned her so closely that she acknowledged he was not born of her, but that he had been adopted and brought up in their house for the love of God and for the alleviation of the misfortune which had been sent upon herself and her husband. These words were as so many dagger-thrusts in the young man's heart, piling up one sorrow upon another, and at last his grief grew beyond endurance; but, seeing that he could not bring himself to seek refuge from his trouble by a violent death, he determined to depart from Bernio's roof, and, in wandering up and down the world, to seek a better fortune.

Alchia, when she perceived that Fortunio's desire to quit the house grew stronger every day, was greatly incensed against him, and, as she found herself powerless to dissuade him from his purpose, she heaped all sorts of curses upon him, praying that if ever he should venture upon the sea he might be engulfed in the waves and swallowed up by the sirens, as ships are often swallowed up by storms. Fortunio, driven on by a headlong access of rage, took no heed of Alchia's malediction, and, without saying any further words of farewell, either to her or to Bernio, departed, and took his way towards the east. He journeyed on, passing by marshes, by valleys, by rocks, and all kinds of wild and desert spots, and at last, one day between sext and none, he came upon a thick and densely-tangled forest, in the midst of which, by strange chance, he found a wolf and an eagle and an ant, who were engaged in a long and sharp contention over the body of a stag which they had lately captured, without being able to agree as to how the venison should be divided amongst themselves. When Fortunio came upon the three animals they were in the midst of their stubborn dispute, and not one was disposed in any way to yield to the others; but after a while they agreed that this young man, who had thus unexpectedly come amongst them, should adjudicate the matter in question, and assign to each one of them such part of the spoil as he might deem most fitting. Then, when they had assented to these preliminaries, and had promised that they would be satisfied with and observe the terms of any award he might make, even though it might seem to be unjust, Fortunio readily undertook the task, and after he had carefully considered the case, he divided the prey amongst them in the following manner. To the wolf, as to a voracious animal and one very handy with his sharp teeth, he gave, as the guerdon of his toil in the chase, all the bones of the deer and all the lean flesh. To the eagle, a rapacious fowl, but furnished with no teeth, he gave the entrails, and all the fat lying round the lean parts and the bones. To the provident and industrious ant, which had none of that strength which nature had bestowed up on the wolf and the eagle, he gave the soft brains as her share of reward for the labour she had undergone. When the three animals understood the terms of this just and carefully considered decision, they were fully satisfied, and thanked Fortunio as well as they could for the courtesy he had shown them.

Now these three animals held—and with justice—that, of all the vices, ingratitude was the most reprehensible; so with one accord they insisted that the young man should not depart until they have fully rewarded him for the great service he had done them. Wherefore the wolf, speaking first, said: "My brother, I give you the power, if at any time the desire should come upon you to be a wolf instead of a man, to become one forthwith, merely by saying the words, 'Would that I were a wolf!' At the same time you will be able to return to your former shape whenever you may desire." And in like manner both the eagle and the ant endowed him with power to take upon him their form and similitude.

Then Fortunio, rejoicing greatly at the potent virtues thus given to him, and rendering to all three of the animals the warmest gratitude for their boon, took his leave and wandered far abroad, until at last he came to Polonia, a populous city of great renown, which was at that time under the rule of Odescalco, a powerful and valorous sovereign, who had but one child, a daughter called Doralice. Now the king was ambitious to find a noble mate for this princess, and it chanced that, at the time when Fortunio arrived in Polonia, he had proclaimed throughout his kingdom that a grand tournament should be held in the city, and that the Princess Doralice should be given in marriage to the man who should be the victor in the jousts. And already many dukes and marquises and other powerful nobles had come together from all parts to contend for this noble prize, and on the first day of the tournament, which had already passed, the honours of the tilting were borne off by a foul Saracen of hideous aspect and ungainly form, and with a face as black as pitch. The king's daughter, when she viewed the deformed and unseemly figure of the conqueror of the day, was overwhelmed with grief that fate should have awarded to such a one the victory in the joust, and, burying her face, which was crimson with shame, in her tender delicate hands, she wept and lamented sore, execrating her cruel and malignant destiny, and begging that death might take her rather than that she should become the wife of this misshapen barbarian. Fortunio, when he entered the city gate, noted the festal array on all sides and the great concourse of people about the streets, and when he learned the cause of all this magnificent display he was straightway possessed with an ardent desire to prove his valour by contending in the tournament, but when he came to consider that he was lacking in all the apparel needful in such honourable contests, his heart fell and heavy sorrow came over him. While he was in this doleful mood it chanced that his steps led him past the palace of the king, and raising his eyes from the ground he espied Doralice, the daughter of the king, who was leaning out of one of the windows of her apartment. She was surrounded by a group of lovely and highborn dames and maidens, but she shone out amongst them all on account of her beauty, as the radiant glorious sun shines out amidst the lesser lights of heaven.

By-and-by, when the dark night had fallen, and all the ladies of the court had retired to their apartments, Doralice, restless and sad at heart, betook herself alone to a small and exquisitely ornamented chamber and gazed once more out into the night, and there below, as luck would have it, was Fortunio. When the youth saw her standing solitary at the open window, he was so overcome by the charms of her beauty that he forth with whispered to himself in an amorous sigh: "Ah! wherefore am I not an eagle?" Scarcely had these words issued from his lips when he found himself transformed into an eagle, whereupon he flew at once into the window of the chamber, and, having willed to become a man again, was restored to his own shape. He went forward with a light and joyful air to greet the princess, but she, as soon as she saw him, was filled with terror and began to cry out in a loud voice, just as if she were being attacked and torn by savage dogs. The king, who happened to be in an apartment not far distant from his daughter's, heard her cries of alarm and ran immediately to seek the cause thereof, and, having heard from her that there was a young man in the room, he at once ordered it to be searched in every part. But nothing of the sort was found, because Fortunio had once more changed himself into an eagle and had flown out of the window. Hardly, however, had the father gone back to his chamber when the maiden began to cry aloud just the same as before, because, forsooth, Fortunio had once more come into her presence.

But Fortunio, when he again heard the terrified cries of the maiden, began to fear for his life, and straightway changed himself into an ant, and crept into hiding beneath the blond tresses of the lovely damsel's hair. Odescalco, hearing the loud outcries of his daughter, ran to her succour, but when he found nothing more this second time than he had found before, he was greatly incensed against her, and threatened her harshly that if she should cry out again and disturb him he would play her some trick which would not please her, and thus he left her with angry words, suspecting that what had caused her trouble was some vision of one or other of the youths who for love of her had met their deaths in the tournament. Fortunio listened attentively to what the king said to his daughter, and, as soon as he had left the apartment, once more put off the shape of an ant and stood revealed in his own form. Doralice, who in the meanwhile had gone to bed, was so terror-stricken when she saw him that she tried to spring from her couch and to give the alarm, hut she was not able to do this, because Fortunio placed one of his hands on her lips, and thus spake: "Signora, fear not that I have come here to despoil you of your honour, or to steal aught that be longs to you. I am come rather to succour you to the best of my power, and to proclaim myself your most humble servant. If you cry out, one or other of two misfortunes will befall us, either your honour and fair name will be tarnished, or you will be the cause of your death and of my own. Therefore, dear lady of my heart, take care lest at the same time you cast a stain upon your reputation and imperil the lives of us both."

While Fortunio was thus speaking, Doralice was weeping bitterly, her presence of mind being completely over thrown by this unexpected declaration on his part, and the young man, when he perceived how powerfully agitated she was, went on addressing her in words gentle and persuasive enough to have melted the heart of a stone. At last, conquered by his words and tender manner, she softened towards him, and consented to let him make his peace with her. And after a little, when she saw how handsome the youth was in face, and how strong and well knit in body and limb, she fell a-thinking about the ugliness and deformity of the Saracen, who, as the conqueror in the jousts, must before long be the master of her person. While these thoughts were passing through her mind the young man said to her: "Dear lady, if I had the fitting equipment, how willingly would I enter the jousts to tilt on your behalf; and my heart tells me that, were I to contend, I should surely conquer." Whereupon the damsel in reply said: "If this, indeed, were to come to pass, if you should prove victorious in the lists, I would give myself to you alone." And when she saw what a well-disposed youth he was, and how ardent in her cause, she brought forth a great quantity of gems and a heavy purse of gold, and bade him take them. Fortunio accepted them with his heart full of joy, and inquired of her what garb she wished him to wear in the lists to-morrow. And she bade him array himself in white satin, and in this matter he did as she commanded him.

On the following day Fortunio, encased in polished armour, over which he wore a surcoat of white satin richly embroidered with the finest gold, and studded with jewels most delicately carven, rode into the piazza unknown to anybody there present. He was mounted on a powerful and fiery charger, which was caparisoned and decked in the same colours as its rider. The crowd, which had already come together to witness the grand spectacle of the tournament, no sooner caught sight of the gallant un known champion, with lance in hand all ready for the fray, than every person was lost in wonderment at so brave a sight, and each one, gazing fixedly at Fortunio, and astonished at his grace, began to inquire of his neighbour: "Ah! who can this knight be who rides so gallantly and splendidly arrayed into the lists? Know you not what is his name?" In the meantime Fortunio, having entered the lists, called upon some rival to advance, and for the first course the Saracen presented himself; whereupon the two champions, keeping low the points of their trusty lances, rushed one upon the other like two lions loosened from their bonds, and so shrewd was the stroke dealt by Fortunio upon the head of the Saracen, that the latter was driven right over the crupper of his horse, and fell dead upon the bare earth, mangled and broken up as a fragile glass is broken when it is thrown against a wall. And Fortunio ran his course just as victoriously in encountering every other champion who ventured to oppose him in the lists. The damsel, when she saw how the fortune of the day was going, was greatly rejoiced, and kept her eyes steadily fixed on Fortunio in deepest admiration, and, thanking God in her heart for having thus graciously delivered her from the bondage of the Saracen, prayed to Him that this brave youth might be the final victor.

When the night had come they bade Doralice come to supper with the rest of the court; but to this bidding she made demur, and commanded them bring her certain rich viands and delicate wines to her chamber, feigning that she had not yet any desire for food, but would eat, perchance, later on if any appetite should come upon her. Then, having locked herself in her chamber and opened the window thereof, she watched with ardent desire for the coming of her lover, and when he had gained admittance to the chamber by the same means as he had used the previous day, they supped joyfully together. Then Fortunio demanded of her in what fashion she would that he should array himself for the morrow, and she made answer that he must bear a badge of green satin all embroidered with the finest thread of silver and gold, and that his horse should be caparisoned in like manner. On the following morning Fortunio appeared, attired as Doralice had directed, and, having duly presented himself in the piazza at the appointed time, he entered the lists and proved himself again as valiant a champion as he had proved to be on the day before. So great was the admiration of the people of his prowess, that the shout went up with one voice that he had worthily won the gracious princess for his bride.

On the evening of that day the princess, full of merriment and happiness and joyous expectations, made the same pre text for absenting herself from supper as she had made the day before, and, having locked the door of her chamber, awaited there the coming of her lover, and supped pleasantly with him. And when he asked her once more with what vestments he should clothe himself on the following day, she answered that she wished him to wear a surcoat of crimson satin, all worked and embroidered with gold and pearls, and to see that the trappings of his horse were made in the same fashion; adding that she herself would, on the morrow, be clad in similar wise. "Lady," replied Fortunio, "if by any chance I should tarry somewhat in making my entry into the lists, be not astonished, for I shall not be late without good cause."

When the morning of the third day had come, the spectators awaited the issue of the momentous strife with the most earnest expectation, but, on account of the inexhaustible valour of the gallant unknown champion, there was no opponent found who dared to enter the lists against him, and he himself for some hidden reason did not appear. After a time the spectators began to grow impatient at his non-appearance, and injurious words were dropped. Even Doralice herself was assailed by suspicions as to his worth, although she had been warned by Fortunio himself that probably his coming would be delayed: so, overcome by this hidden trouble of hers—concerning which no one else knew anything—she well nigh swooned with grief. At last, when it was told to her that the unknown knight was advancing into the piazza, her failing senses began to revive. Fortunio was clad in a rich and sumptuous dress, and the trappings of his horse were of the finest cloth of gold, all embroidered with shining rubies and emeralds and sapphires and great pearls. When the people saw these they affirmed that the price of them would be equal to a great kingdom, and when Fortunio came into the piazza, every one cried out in a loud voice: "Long live the unknown knight!" and after this they all applauded vigorously and clapped their hands. Then the jousting began, and Fortunio once more carried himself so valiantly that he bore to earth all those who dared to oppose him, and in the end was hailed as the victor in the tournament. And when he had dismounted from his noble horse, the chief magnates and the wealthy citizens of the town bore him aloft on their shoulders, and to the sound of trumpets and all other kinds of musical instruments, and with loud shouts which went up to the heavens, they carried him into the presence of the king. When they had taken off his helmet and his shining armour the king perceived what a seemly graceful youth he was, and, having called his daughter into his presence, he betrothed them forthwith, and celebrated the nuptials with the greatest pomp, keeping open table at the court for the space of a month.

After Fortunio had lived for a certain space of time in loving dalliance with his fair wife, he was seized one day with the thought that he was playing the part of an unworthy sluggard in thus passing the days in indolence, merely counting the hours as they sped by, after the manner of foolish folk, and of those who consider not the duties of a man. Wherefore he made up his mind to go afield into certain regions, where there might be found due scope and recognition for his valour and enterprise; so, having got ready a galley and taken a large treasure which his father-in-law had given him, he embarked after taking leave of his wife and of King Odescalco. He sailed away, wafted on by gentle and favourable breezes, until he came into the Atlantic Ocean, but before he had gone more than ten miles thereon, there arose from the waves the most beautiful Siren that ever was seen, and singing softly, she began to swim towards the ship. Fortunio, who was reclining by the side of the galley, bent his head low down over the water to listen to her song, and straightway fell asleep, and, while he thus slept, the Siren drew him gently from where he lay, and, bearing him in her arms, sank with him headlong into the depths of the sea. The mariners, after having vainly essayed to save him, broke out into loud lamentations over his sad fate, and, weeping and mourning, they decked the galley with black ensigns of grief, and returned to the unfortunate Odescalco to tell him of the terrible mischance which had befallen them during their voyage. The king and Doralice, when the sad news was brought to them, were overwhelmed with the deepest grief—as indeed was everyone else in the city—and all put on garments of mourning black.

Now at the time of Fortunio's departure Doralice was with child, and when the season of her delivery had come she gave birth to a beautiful boy, who was delicately and carefully nurtured until he came to be two years of age. At this time the sad and despairing Doralice, who had always brooded over her unhappy fate in losing the company of her beloved husband, began to abandon all hope of ever seeing him again; so she, like a brave and great-souled woman, resolved to put her fortune to the test and go to seek for him upon the deep, even though the king her father should not consent to let her depart. So she caused to be set in order for her voyage an armed galley, well fitted for such a purpose, and she took with her three apples, each one a master piece of handicraft, of which one was fashioned out of golden bronze, another of silver, and the last of the finest gold. Then, having taken leave of her father the king, she embarked with her child on board the galley, and sailed away before a prosperous wind into the open sea.

After the sad and woe-stricken lady had sailed a certain time over the calm sea, she bade the sailors steer the ship forthwith towards the spot where her husband had been carried off by the Siren, and this command they immediately obeyed. And when the vessel had been brought to the aforesaid spot, the child began to cry fretfully, and would in no wise be pacified by his mother's endearments; so she gave him the apple which was made of golden bronze to appease him. While the child was thus sporting with the apple, he was espied by the Siren, who, having come near to the galley and lifted her head a little space out of the foaming waves, thus spake to Doralice: "Lady, give me that apple, for I desire greatly to have it." But the princess answered her that this thing could not be done, inasmuch as the apple was her child's plaything. "If you will consent to give it to me," the Siren went on, "I will show you the husband you have lost as far as his breast." Doralice, when she heard these words, at once took the apple from the child and handed it courteously to the Siren, for she longed above all things else to get sight of her beloved husband.

The Siren was faithful to her promise, and after a little time brought Fortunio to the surface of the sea and showed him as far as the breast to Doralice, as a reward for the gift of the apple, and then plunged with him once more into the depths of the ocean, and disappeared from sight.

Doralice, who had naturally feasted her eyes upon the form of her husband what time he was above the water, only felt the desire to see him once more grow stronger after he was gone under again, and, not knowing what to do or to say, she sought comfort in the caresses of her child, and when the little one began to cry once more, the mother gave to it the silver apple to soothe its fancy. Again the Siren was on the watch and espied the silver apple in the child's hand, and having raised her head above the waves, begged Doralice to give her the apple, but the latter, shrugging her shoulders, said that the apple served to divert the child, and could not be spared. Whereupon the Siren said: "If only you will give me this apple, which is far more beautiful than the other, I promise I will show you your husband as far as his knees." Poor Doralice, who was now consumed with desire to see her beloved husband again, put aside the satisfaction of the child's fancy, and, having taken away from him the silver apple, handed it eagerly to the Siren, who, after she had once more brought Fortunio to the surface and exhibited him to Doralice as far as his knees (according to her promise), plunged again beneath the waves.

For a while the princess sat brooding in silent grief and suspense, trying in vain to hit upon some plan by which she might rescue her husband from his piteous fate, and at last she caught up her child in her arms and tried to comfort herself with him and to still his weeping. The child, mindful of the fair apple he had been playing with, continued to cry; so the mother, to appease him, gave him at last the apple of fine gold. When the covetous Siren, who was still watching the galley, saw this apple, and perceived that it was much fairer than either of the others, she at once demanded it as a gift from Doralice, and she begged so long and persistently, and at last made a promise to the princess that, in return for the gift of this apple, she would bring Fortunio once more into the light, and show him from head to foot; so Doralice took the apple from the boy, in spite of his chiding, and gave it to the Siren. Where upon the latter, in order to carry out her promise, came quite close to the galley, bearing Fortunio upon her back, and having raised herself somewhat above the surface of the water, showed the person of Fortunio from head to foot. Now, as soon as Fortunio felt that he was quite clear of the water, and resting free upon the back of the Siren, he was filled with great joy in his heart, and, without hesitating for a moment, he cried out, "Ah! would that I were an eagle," and scarcely had he ceased speaking when he was forthwith trans formed into an eagle, and, having poised himself for flight, he flew high above the sail yards of the galley, from whence—all the shipmen looking on the while in wonder—he descended into the ship and returned to his proper shape, and kissed and embraced his wife and his child and all the sailors on the galley.

Then, all of them rejoicing at the rescue of Fortunio, they sailed back to King Odescalco's kingdom, and as soon as they entered the port they began to play upon the trumpets and tabors and drums and all the other musical instruments they had with them, so that the king, when he heard the sound of these, was much astonished, and in the greatest suspense waited to learn what might be the meaning thereof. And before very long time had elapsed the herald came before him, and announced to the king how his dear daughter, having rescued her husband from the Siren, had come back. When they were disembarked from the galley, they all repaired to the royal palace, where their return was celebrated by sumptuous banquets and rejoicings. But after some days had passed, Fortunio betook himself for a while to his old home, and there, after having transformed himself into a wolf, he devoured Alchia, his adoptive mother, and Valentino her son, in revenge for the injuries they had worked him. Then, after he had returned to his rightful shape, he mounted his horse and rode back to his father-in-law's kingdom, where, with Doralice his dear wife, he lived in peace for many years to the great delight of both of them.

As soon as Alteria had brought to an end her long and interesting story the Signora bade her at once to set forth her enigma, and she, smiling pleasantly, obeyed the command.

       Far from this our land doth dwell
       One who by turns is fair or fell;

Springing from a twofold root,
One part woman, one part brute.
Now like beauty's fairest jewel,
Now a monster fierce and cruel.
Sweetest song on vocal breath,
To lead men down to shameful death.

Alteria's most fitting and noteworthy enigma was answered in divers fashion by the listeners, some giving one interpretation of it and some another, but not one of them came upon its exact meaning. Therefore, when the fair Alteria saw there was little chance of anyone finding the true answer, she said: "Ladies and gentlemen, the real subject of my enigma is the fascinating Siren who is fabled to dwell in the deep sea. She is very fair to look upon, for her head and breast and body and arms are those of a beautiful damsel, but all the rest of her form is scaly like a fish, and in her nature she is cunning and cruel. She sings so sweetly that the mariners, when they hear her song, are soothed to slumber, and while they sleep she drowns them in the sea." When the listeners heard this clever and subtle solution given by Alteria, they praised it warmly with one accord, declaring the while that it was most ingenious. And she, smiling with pleasure and gratitude, rose from her chair and thanked them for their kindness in thus lending their attention to her story.

Source:
Straparola, Giovanni Francesco. *The Facetious Nights by Straparola*. Volume 2 of 4. W. G. Waters, translator. London: Privately Printed for Members of the Society of Bibliophiles, 1901.

122. An Impossible Enchantment

Italy

The following tale is from Andrew Lang's **Grey Fairy Book.** *Lang does not credit a source for this tale and so its source has proved elusive. The current editor has designated it as an Italian tale based upon the character names and plot, but this educated guess may be wrong. The tale may be French, Italian, Spanish or Portuguese.*

THERE once lived a king who was much loved by his people, and he, too, loved them warmly. He led a very happy life, but he had the greatest dislike to the idea of marrying, nor had he ever felt the slightest wish to fall in love. His subjects begged him to marry, and at last he promised to try to do so. But as, so far, he had never cared for any woman he had seen, he made up his mind to travel in hopes of meeting some lady he could love.

So he arranged all the affairs of state in an orderly manner, and set out, attended by only one equerry, who, though not very clever, had most excellent good sense. These people indeed generally make the best fellow travellers.

The king explored several countries, doing all he could to fall in love, but in vain; and at the end of two years' journeys he turned his face towards home, with as free a heart as when he set out.

As he was riding along through a forest he suddenly heard the most awful miawing and shrieking of cats you can imagine. The noise drew nearer, and nearer, and at last they saw a hundred huge Spanish cats rush through the trees close to them. They were so closely packed together that you could easily have covered them with a large cloak, and all were following the same track. They were closely pursued by two enormous apes, dressed in purple suits, with the prettiest and best made boots you ever saw.

The apes were mounted on superb mastiffs, and spurred them on in hot haste, blowing shrill blasts on little toy trumpets all the time.

The king and his equerry stood still to watch this strange hunt, which was followed by twenty or more little dwarfs, some mounted on wolves, and leading relays, and others with cats in leash. The dwarfs were all dressed in purple silk liveries like the apes.

A moment later a beautiful young woman mounted on a tiger came in sight. She passed close to the king, riding at full speed, without taking any notice of him; but he was at once enchanted by her, and his heart was gone in a moment.

To his great joy he saw that one of the dwarfs had fallen behind the rest, and at once began to question him.

The dwarf told him that the lady he had just seen was the princess Mutinosa, the daughter of the king in whose country they were at that moment. He added that the princess was very fond of hunting, and that she was now in pursuit of rabbits.

The king then asked the way to the court, and having been told it, hurried off, and reached the capital in a couple of hours.

As soon as he arrived, he presented himself to the king and queen, and on mentioning his own name and that of his country, was received with open arms. Not long after, the princess returned, and hearing that the hunt had been very successful, the king complimented her on it, but she would not answer a word.

Her silence rather surprised him, but he was still more astonished when he found that she never spoke once all through supper-time. Sometimes she seemed about to speak, but whenever this was the case her father or mother at once took up the conversation. However, this silence did not cool the king's affection, and when he retired to his rooms at night he confided his feelings to his faithful equerry. But the equerry was by no means delighted at his king's love affair, and took no pains to hide his disappointment.

"But why are you vexed?" asked the king. "Surely the princess is beautiful enough to please anyone?"

"She is certainly very handsome," replied the equerry, "but to be really happy in love something more than beauty is required. To tell the truth, sire," he added, "her expression seems to me hard."

"That is pride and dignity," said the king, "and nothing can be more becoming."

"Pride or hardness, as you will," said the equerry; "but to my mind the choice of so many fierce creatures for her amusements seems to tell of a fierce nature, and I also think there is something suspicious in the care taken to prevent her speaking."

The equerry's remarks were full of good sense; but as opposition is only apt to increase love in the hearts of men, and especially of kings who hate being contradicted, this king begged, the very next day, for the hand of the princess Mutinosa. It was granted him on two conditions.

The first was that the wedding should take place the very next day; and the second, that he should not speak to the princess till she was his wife; to all of which the king agreed, in spite of his equerry's objections, so that the first word he heard his bride utter was the "Yes' she spoke at their marriage.

Once married, however, she no longer placed any check on herself, and her ladies-in-waiting came in for plenty of rude speeches—even the king did not escape scolding; but as he was a good-tempered man, and very much in love, he bore it patiently. A few days after the wedding the newly married pair set out for their kingdom without leaving many regrets behind.

The good equerry's fears proved only too true, as the king found out to his cost. The young queen made herself most disagreeable to all her court, her spite and bad temper knew no bounds, and before the end of a month she was known far and wide as a regular vixen.

One day, when riding out, she met a poor old woman walking along the road, who made a curtsy and was going on, when the queen had her stopped, and cried: "You are a very impertinent person; don't you know that I am the queen? And how dare you not make me a deeper curtsy?"

"Madam," said the old woman, "I have never learnt how to measure curtsies; but I had no wish to fail in proper respect."

"What!" screamed the queen; "she dares to answer! Tie her to my horse's tail and I'll just carry her at once to the best dancing-master in the town to learn how to curtsy."

The old woman shrieked for mercy, but the queen would not listen, and only mocked when she said she was protected by the fairies. At last the poor old thing submitted to be tied up, but when the queen urged her horse on he never stirred. In vain she spurred him, he seemed turned to bronze. At the same moment the cord with which the old woman was tied changed into wreaths of flowers, and she herself into a tall and stately lady.

Looking disdainfully at the queen, she said, "Bad woman, unworthy of your crown; I wished to judge for myself whether all I heard of you was true. I have now no doubt of it, and you shall see whether the fairies are to be laughed at."

So saying the fairy Placida (that was her name) blew a little gold whistle, and a chariot appeared drawn by six splendid ostriches. In it was seated the fairy queen, escorted by a dozen other fairies mounted on dragons.

All having dismounted, Placida told her adventures, and the fairy queen approved all she had done, and proposed turning Mutinosa into bronze like her horse.

Placida, however, who was very kind and gentle, begged for a milder sentence, and at last it was settled that Mutinosa should become her slave for life unless she should have a child to take her place.

The king was told of his wife's fate and submitted to it, which, as he could do nothing to help it, was the only course open to him.

The fairies then all dispersed, Placida taking her slave with her, and on reaching her palace she said: "You ought by rights to be scullion, but as you have been delicately brought up the change might be too great for you. I shall therefore only order you to sweep my rooms carefully, and to wash and comb my little dog."

Mutinosa felt there was no use in disobeying, so she did as she was bid and said nothing.

After some time she gave birth to a most lovely little girl, and when she was well again the fairy gave her a good lecture on her past life, made her promise to behave better in future, and sent her back to the king, her husband.

Placida now gave herself up entirely to the little princess who was left in her charge. She anxiously thought over which of the fairies she would invite to be godmothers, so as to secure the best gift, for her adopted child.

At last she decided on two very kindly and cheerful fairies, and asked them to the christening feast. Directly it was over the baby was brought to them in a lovely crystal cradle hung with red silk curtains embroidered with gold.

The little thing smiled so sweetly at the fairies that they decided to do all they could for her. They began by naming her Graziella, and then Placida said: "You know, dear sisters, that the commonest form of spite or punishment amongst us consists of changing beauty to ugliness, cleverness to stupidity, and oftener still to change a person's form altogether. Now, as we can only each bestow one gift, I think the best plan will be for one of you to give her beauty, the other good understanding, while I will undertake that she shall never be changed into any other form."

The two godmothers quite agreed, and as soon as the little princess had received their gifts, they went home, and Placida gave herself up to the child's education. She succeeded so well with it, and little Graziella grew so lovely, that when she was still quite a child her fame was spread abroad only too much, and one day Placida was surprised by a visit from the fairy Queen, who was attended by a very grave and severe-looking fairy.

The queen began at once: "I have been much surprised by your behaviour to Mutinosa; she had insulted our whole race, and deserved punishment. You might forgive your own wrongs if you chose, but not those of others. You treated her very gently while she was with you, and I come now to avenge our wrongs on her daughter. You have ensured her being lovely and clever, and not subject to change of form, but I shall place her in an enchanted prison, which she shall never leave till she finds herself in the arms of a lover whom she herself loves. It will be my care to prevent anything of the kind happening."

The enchanted prison was a large high tower in the midst of the sea, built of shells of all shapes and colours. The lower floor was like a great bathroom, where the water was let in or off at will. The first floor contained the princess's apartments, beautifully furnished. On the second was a library, a large wardrobe-room filled with beautiful clothes and every kind of linen, a music-room, a pantry with bins full of the best wines, and a store-room with all manner of preserves, bonbons, pastry and cakes, all of which remained as fresh as if just out of the oven.

The top of the tower was laid out like a garden, with beds of the loveliest flowers, fine fruit trees, and shady arbours and shrubs, where many birds sang amongst the branches.

The fairies escorted Graziella and her governess, Bonnetta, to the tower, and then mounted a dolphin which was waiting for them. At a little distance from the tower the queen waved her wand and summoned two thousand great fierce sharks, whom she ordered to keep close guard, and not to let a soul enter the tower

The good governess took such pains with Graziella's education that when she was nearly grown up she was not only most accomplished, but a very sweet, good girl.

One day, as the princess was standing on a balcony, she saw the most extraordinary figure rise out of the sea. She quickly called Bonnetta to ask her what it could be. It looked like some kind of man, with a bluish face and long sea-green hair. He was swimming towards the tower, but the sharks took no notice of him.

"It must be a merman," said Bonnetta.

"A man, do you say?" cried Graziella; "let us hurry down to the door and see him nearer."

When they stood in the doorway the merman stopped to look at the princess and made many signs of admiration. His voice was very hoarse and husky, but when he found that he was not understood he took to signs. He carried a little basket made of osiers and filled with rare shells, which he presented to the princess.

She took it with signs of thanks; but as it was getting dusk she retired, and the merman plunged back into the sea.

When they were alone, Graziella said to her governess: "What a dreadful-looking creature that was! Why do those odious sharks let him come near the tower? I suppose all men are not like him?"

"No, indeed," replied Bonnetta. "I suppose the sharks look on him as a sort of relation, and so did not attack him."

A few days later the two ladies heard a strange sort of music, and looking out of the window, there was the merman, his head crowned with water plants, and blowing a great sea-shell with all his might.

They went down to the tower door, and Graziella politely accepted some coral and other marine curiosities he had brought her. After this he used to come every evening, and blow his shell, or dive and play antics under tile princess's window. She contented herself with bowing to him from the balcony, but she would not go down to the door in spite of all his signs.

Some days later he came with a person of his own kind, but of another sex. Her hair was dressed with great taste, and she had a lovely voice. This new arrival induced the ladies to go down to the door. They were surprised to find that, after trying various languages, she at last spoke to them in their own, and paid Graziella a very pretty compliment on her beauty.

The mermaid noticed that the lower floor was full of water. "Why," cried she, "that is just the place for us, for we can't live quite out of water." So saying, she and her brother swam in and took up a position in the bathroom, the princess and her governess seating themselves on the steps which ran round the room.

"No doubt, madam," said the mermaid, "you have given up living on land so as to escape from crowds of lovers; but I fear that even here you cannot avoid them, for my brother is already dying of love for you, and I am sure that once you are seen in our city he will have many rivals."

She then went on to explain how grieved her brother was not to be able to make himself understood, adding: "I interpret for him, having been taught several languages by a fairy."

"Oh, then, you have fairies, too?" asked Graziella, with a sigh.

"Yes, we have," replied the mermaid; "but if I am not mistaken you have suffered from the fairies on earth."

The princess, on this, told her entire history to the mermaid, who assured her how sorry she felt for her, but begged her not to lose courage; adding, as she took her leave: Perhaps, some day, you may find a way out of your difficulties."

The princess was delighted with this visit and with the hopes the mermaid held out. It was something to meet someone fresh to talk to.

"We will make acquaintance with several of these people," she said to her governess, "and I dare say they are not all as hideous as the first one we saw. Anyhow, we shan't be so dreadfully lonely."

"Dear me," said Bonnetta, "how hopeful young people are to be sure! As for me I feel afraid of these folk. But what do you think of the lover you have captivated?"

"Oh, I could never love him," cried the princess; "I can't bear him. But, perhaps, as his sister says they are related to the fairy Marina, they may be of some use to us."

The mermaid often returned, and each time she talked of her brother's love, and each time Graziella talked of her longing to escape from her prison, till at length the mermaid promised to bring the fairy Marina to see her, in hopes she might suggest something.

Next day the fairy came with the mermaid, and the princess received her with delight. After a little talk she begged Graziella to show her the inside of the tower and let her see the garden on the top, for with the help of crutches she could manage to move about, and being a fairy could live out of water for a long time, provided she wetted her forehead now and then.

Graziella gladly consented, and Bonnetta stayed below with the mermaid.

When they were in the garden the fairy said: "Let us lose no time, but tell me how I can be of use to you." Graziella then told all her story and Marina replied: "My dear princess, I can do nothing for you as regards dry land, for my power does not reach beyond my own element. I can only say that if you will honour my cousin by accepting his hand, you could then come and live amongst us. I could teach you in a moment to swim and dive with the best of us. I can harden your skin without spoiling its colour. My cousin is one of the best matches in the sea, and I will bestow so many gifts on him that you will be quite happy."

The fairy talked so well and so long that the princess was rather impressed, and promised to think the matter over.

Just as they were going to leave the garden they saw a ship sailing nearer the tower than any other had done before. On the deck lay a young man under a splendid awning, gazing at the tower through a spy-glass; but before they could see anything clearly the ship moved away, and the two ladies parted, the fairy promising to return shortly.

As soon as she was gone Graziella told her governess what she had said. Bonnetta was not at all pleased at the turn matters were taking, for she did not fancy being turned into a mermaid in her old age. She thought the matter well over, and this was what she did. She was a very clever artist, and next morning she began to paint a picture of a handsome young man, with beautiful curly hair, a fine complexion, and lovely blue eyes. When it was finished she showed it to Graziella, hoping it would show her the difference there was between a fine young man and her marine suitor.

The princess was much struck by the picture, and asked anxiously whether there could be any man so good looking in the world. Bonnetta assured her that there were plenty of them; indeed, many far handsomer.

"I can hardly believe that," cried the princess; "but, alas! If there are, I don't suppose I shall ever see them or they me, so what is the use? Oh, dear, how unhappy I am!"

She spent the rest of the day gazing at the picture, which certainly had the effect of spoiling all the merman's hopes or prospects.

After some days, the fairy Marina came back to hear what was decided; but Graziella hardly paid any attention to her, and showed such dislike to the idea of the proposed marriage that the fairy went off in a regular huff.

Without knowing it, the princess had made another conquest. On board the ship which had sailed so near was the handsomest prince in the world. He had heard of the enchanted tower, and determined to get as near it as he could. He had strong glasses on board, and while looking through them he saw the princess quite clearly, and fell desperately in love with her at once. He wanted to steer straight for the tower and to row off to it in a small boat, but his entire crew fell at his feet and begged him not to run such a risk. The captain, too, urged him not to attempt it. "You will only lead us all to certain death," he said. "Pray anchor nearer land, and I will then seek a kind fairy I know, who has always been most obliging to me, and who will, I am sure, try to help your Highness."

The prince rather unwillingly listened to reason. He landed at the nearest point, and sent off the captain in all haste to beg the fairy's advice and help. Meantime he had a tent pitched on the shore, and spent all his time gazing at the tower and looking for the princess through his spyglass.

After a few days the captain came back, bringing the fairy with him. The prince was delighted to see her, and paid her great attention. "I have heard about this matter," she said; "and, to lose no time, I am going to send off a trusty pigeon to test the enchantment. If there is any weak spot he is sure to find it out and get in. I shall bid him bring a flower back as a sign of success; and if he does so I quite hope to get you in too."

"But," asked the prince, "could I not send a line by the pigeon to tell the princess of my love?"

"Certainly," replied the fairy, "it would be a very good plan."

So the prince wrote as follows:—

"Lovely Princess,—I adore you, and beg you to accept my heart, and to believe there is nothing I will not do to end your misfortunes.
—BLONDEL."

This note was tied round the pigeon's neck, and he flew off with it at once. He flew fast till he got near the tower, when a fierce wind blew so hard against him that he could not get on. But he was not to be beaten, but flew carefully round the top of the tower till he came to one spot which, by some mistake, had not been enchanted like the rest. He quickly slipped into the arbour and waited for the princess.

Before long Graziella appeared alone, and the pigeon at once fluttered to meet her, and seemed so tame that she stopped to caress the pretty creature. As she did so she saw it had a pink ribbon round its neck, and tied to the ribbon was a letter. She read it over several times and then wrote this answer:—

> "You say you love me; but I cannot promise to love you without seeing you. Send me your portrait by this faithful messenger. If I return it to you, you must give up hope; but if I keep it you will know that to help me will be to help yourself.
> —GRAZIELA.

Before flying back the pigeon remembered about the flower, so, seeing one in the princess's dress, he stole it and flew away.

The prince was wild with joy at the pigeon's return with the note. After an hour's rest the trusty little bird was sent back again, carrying a miniature of the prince, which by good luck he had with him.

On reaching the tower the pigeon found the princess in the garden. She hastened to untie the ribbon, and on opening the miniature case what was her surprise and delight to find it very like the picture her governess had painted for her. She hastened to send the pigeon back, and you can fancy the prince's joy when he found she had kept his portrait.

"Now," said the fairy, "let us lose no more time. I can only make you happy by changing you into a bird, but I will take care to give you back your proper shape at the right time."

The prince was eager to start, so the fairy, touching him with her wand, turned him into the loveliest humming-bird you ever saw, at the same time letting him keep the power of speech. The pigeon was told to show him the way.

Graziella was much surprised to see a perfectly strange bird, and still more so when it flew to her saying, "Good-morning, sweet princess."

She was delighted with the pretty creature, and let him perch on her finger, when he said, "Kiss, kiss, little birdie," which she gladly did, petting and stroking him at the same time.

After a time the princess, who had been up very early, grew tired, and as the sun was hot she went to lie down on a mossy bank in the shade of the arbour. She held the pretty bird near her breast, and was just falling asleep, when the fairy contrived to restore the prince to his own shape, so that as Graziella opened her eyes she found herself in the arms of a lover whom she loved in return!

At the same moment her enchantment came to an end. The tower began to rock and to split. Bonnetta hurried up to the top so that she might at least perish with her dear princess. Just as she reached the garden, the kind fairy who had helped the prince arrived with the fairy Placida, in a car of Venetian glass drawn by six eagles.

"Come away quickly," they cried, "the tower is about to sink!" The prince, princess, and Bonnetta lost no time in stepping into the car, which rose in the air just as, with a terrible crash, the tower sank into the depths of the sea, for the fairy Marina and the mermen had destroyed its foundations to avenge themselves on Graziella. Luckily their wicked plans were defeated, and the good fairies took their way to the kingdom of Graziella's parents.

They found that Queen Mutinosa had died some years ago, but her kind husband lived on peaceably, ruling his country well and happily. He received his daughter with great delight, and there were universal rejoicings at the return of the lovely princess.

The wedding took place the very next day, and, for many days after, balls, dinners, tournaments, concerts and all sorts of amusements went on all day and all night.

All the fairies were carefully invited, and they came in great state, and promised the young couple their protection and all sorts of good gifts. Prince Blondel and Princess Graziella lived to a good old age, beloved by every one, and loving each other more and more as time went on.

Source:
Lang, Andrew, editor. *The Grey Fairy Book*. London: Longmans, Green, and Co., 1900.

123. The Adventures of Bulukiya

Arabian Nights

"KNOW thou, O Hasib, there was once in the city of Cairo a King of the Banu Isra'íl, a wise and a pious, who was bent double by poring over books of learning, and he had a son named Bulúkiyá. When he grew old and weak and was nigh upon death, his Grandees and Officers of state came up to salute him, and he said to them, 'O folk, know that at hand is the hour of my march from this world to the next, and I have no charge to lay on you, save to commend to your care my son Bulukiya.' Then said he, 'I testify that there is no god save the God;' and, heaving one sigh, departed the world the mercy of Allah be upon him! They laid him out and washed him and buried him with a procession of great state. Then they made his son Bulukiya Sultan in his stead; and he ruled the kingdom justly and the people had peace in his time. Now it befell one day that he entered his father's treasuries, to look about him, and coming upon an inner compartment and finding the semblance of a door, opened it and passed in. And lo! he found himself in a little closet, wherein stood a column of white marble, on the top of which was a casket of ebony; he opened this also and saw therein another casket of gold, containing a book. He read the book and found in it an account of our lord Mohammed (whom Allah bless and preserve!) and how he should be sent in the latter days[1] and be the lord of the first Prophets and the last. On seeing the personal description Bulukiya's heart was taken with love of him, so he at once assembled all the notables of the Children of Israel, the Cohens or diviners, the scribes and the priests, and acquainted them with the book, reading portions of it to them and, adding, 'O folk, needs must I bring my father out of his grave and burn him.' The lieges asked, 'Why wilt thou burn him?'; and he answered, 'Because he hid this book from me and imparted it not to me.' Now the old King had excerpted it from the Torah or Pentateuch and the Books of Abraham; and had set it in one of his treasuries and concealed it from all living. Rejoined they, 'O King, thy father is dead; his body is in the dust and his affair is in the hands of his Lord; thou shalt not take him forth of his tomb.' So he knew that they would not suffer him to do this thing by his sire and leaving them he repaired to his mother, to whom said he, 'O my mother, I have found, in one of my father's treasuries, a book containing a description of Mohammed (whom Allah bless and keep!), a prophet who shall be sent in the latter days; and my heart is captivated with love of him. Wherefore am I resolved to wander over the earth, till I foregather with him; else I shall die of longing for his love.' Then he doffed his clothes and donned an Aba gown of goat's hair and coarse sandals, saying, 'O my mother, forget me not in thy prayers.' She wept over him and said, 'What will become of us after thee?'; but Bulukiya answered, 'I can endure no

---

[1] "Akhir al-Zamán." As old men praise past times, so prophets prefer to represent themselves as the last. The early Christians caused much scandal amongst the orderly law-loving Romans by their wild and mistaken predictions of the end of the world being at hand. The catastrophe is a fact for each man under the form of death; but the world has endured for untold ages and there is no apparent cause why it should not endure as many more. The "latter days," as the religious dicta of most "revelations" assure us, will be richer in sinners than in sanctity: hence "End of Time" is a facetious Arab title for a villain of superior quality. My Somali escort applied it to one thus distinguished: in 1875, I heard at Aden that he ended life by the spear as we had all predicted.

longer, and I commit my affair and thine to Allah who is Almighty.' Then he set out on foot Syria wards without the knowledge of any of his folk, and coming to the sea board found a vessel whereon he shipped as one of the crew. They sailed till he made an island, where Bulukiya landed with the crew, but straying away from the rest he sat down under a tree and sleep got the better of him. When he awoke, he sought the ship but found that she had set sail without him, and in that island he saw serpents as big as camels and palm trees, which repeated the names of Allah (be He extolled and exalted!) and blessed Mohammed (whom the Lord assain and save!), proclaiming the Unity and glorifying the Glorious; whereat he wondered."—And Shahrazad perceived the dawn of day and ceased saying her permitted say.

When it was the Four Hundred and Eighty-seventh Night,

She said, It hath reached me, O auspicious King, that "when Bulukiya saw the serpents glorifying God and proclaiming the Unity, he wondered with extreme wonder. When they saw him, they flocked to him and one of them said to him, 'Who and whence art thou and whither goest thou. and what is thy name?' Quoth he, 'My name is Bulukiya; I am of the Children of Israel and, being distracted for love of Mohammed (whom Allah bless and keep!), I come in quest of him. But who are ye, O noble creatures?' Answered they, 'We are of the dwellers in the Jahannam-hell; and Almighty Allah created us for the punishment of Kafirs.' 'And how came ye hither?' asked he, and the Serpents answered, 'Know, O Bulukiya, that Hell[1] of the greatness of her boiling, breatheth twice a year, expiring in the summer and inspiring in the winter, and hence the summer heat and winter cold. When she exhaleth, she casteth us forth of her maw, and we are drawn in again with her inhaled breath.' Quoth Bulukiya, 'Say me, are there greater serpents than you in Hell?'; and they said, 'Of a truth we are cast out with the expired breath but by reason of our smallness; for in Hell every serpent is so great, that were the biggest of us to pass over its nose it would not feel us.'[2] Asked Bulukiya, 'Ye sing the praises of Allah and invoke blessings on Mohammed, whom the Almighty assain and save! Whence wot ye of Mohammed?'; and they answered, 'O Bulukiya, verily his name is written on the gates of Paradise; and, but for him, Allah had not created the worlds[3] nor

---

[1] Jahannam and the other six Hells are personified as feminine; and (woman-like) they are somewhat addicted to prolix speechification.
[2] These puerile exaggerations are fondly intended to act as nurses frighten naughty children.
[3] Alluding to an oft-quoted saying "Lau lá-ka, etc. Without thee (O Mohammed) We (Allah) had not created the spheres," which may have been suggested by "Before Abraham was, I am" (John viii. 58); and by

Paradise, nor heaven nor hell nor earth, for He made all things that be, solely on his account, and hath conjoined his name with His own in every place; wherefore we love Mohammed, whom Allah bless and preserve!' Now hearing the serpents' converse did but inflame Bulukiya's love for Mohammed and yearning for his sight; so he took leave of them; and, making his way to the sea-shore, found there a ship made fast to the beach; he embarked therein as a seaman and sailed nor ceased sailing till he came to another island. Here he landed and walking about awhile found serpents great and small, none knoweth their number save Almighty Allah, and amongst them a white Serpent, clearer than crystal, seated in a golden tray borne on the back of another serpent as big as an elephant. Now this, O Hasib, was the Serpent-queen, none other than myself." Quoth Hasib, "And what answer didst thou make him?" Quoth she, "Know, O Hasib, that when I saw Bulukiya, I saluted him with the salam, and he returned my salutation, and I said to him, 'Who and what art thou and what is thine errand and whence comest thou and whither goest thou?' Answered he, 'I am of the Children of Israel; my name is Bulukiya, and I am a wanderer for the love of Mohammed, whose description I have read in the revealed scriptures, and of whom I go in search. But what art thou and what are these serpents about thee?' Quoth I, 'O Bulukiya, I am the Queen of the Serpents; and when thou shalt foregather with Mohammed (whom Allah assain and save!) bear him my salutation.' Then Bulukiya took leave of me and journeyed till he came to the Holy City which is Jerusalem. Now there was in that stead a man who was deeply versed in all sciences, more especially in geometry and

---

Gate xci. of Zoroastrianism "O Zardusht for thy sake I have created the world" (Dabistan i. 344). The sentiment is by no means "Shi'ah," as my learned friend Prof. Aloys Springer supposes. In his Mohammed (p. 220) we find an extract from a sectarian poet, "For thee we dispread the earth; for thee we caused the waters to flow; for thee we vaulted the heavens." As Baron Alfred von Kremer, another learned and experienced Orientalist, reminds me, the "Shi'ahs" have always shown a decided tendency to this kind of apotheosis and have deified or quasi-deified Ali and the Imams. But the formula is first found in the highly orthodox Burdah poem of Al–Busiri:—

> "But for him (Lau lá-hu) the world had never come out of nothingness."

Hence it has been widely diffused. See Les Aventures de Kamrup (pp. 146–7) and Les Œuvres de Wali (pp. 51–52), by M. Garcin de Tassy and the Dabistan (vol. i. pp. 2–3).

astronomy and mathematics, as well as in white magic[1] and Spiritualism; and he had studied the Pentateuch and the Evangel and the Psalms and the Books of Abraham. His name was Affan; and he had found in certain of his books, that whoso should wear the seal ring of our lord Solomon, men and Jinn and birds and beasts and all created things would be bound to obey him. Moreover, he had discovered that our lord Solomon had been buried in a coffin which was miraculously transported beyond the Seven Seas to the place of burial;"—And Shahrazad perceived the dawn of day and ceased to say her permitted say.

When it was the Four Hundred and Eighty-eighth Night,

She said, It hath reached me, O auspicious King, that "Affan had found in certain books that none, mortal or spirit, could pluck the seal ring from the lord Solomon's finger; and that no navigator could sail his ship upon the Seven Seas over which the coffin had been carried. Moreover, he had found out by reading that there was a herb of herbs and that if one express its juice and anoint therewith his feet, he should walk upon the surface of any sea that Allah Almighty had created without wetting his soles, but none could obtain this herb, without he had with him the Serpent-queen. When Bulukiya arrived at the Holy City, he at once sat down to do his devotions and worship the Lord; and, whilst he was so doing, Affan came up and saluted him as a True Believer. Then seeing him reading the Pentateuch and adoring the Almighty, he accosted him saying, 'What is thy name, O man; and whence comest thou and whither goest thou?' He answered, 'My name is Bulukiya; I am from the city of Cairo and am come forth wandering in quest of Mohammed, whom Allah bless and preserve!' Quoth Affan, 'Come with me to my lodging that I may entertain thee.' 'To hear is to obey,' replied Bulukiya So the devotee took him by the hand and carried him to his house where he entreated him with the utmost honour and presentry said to him, 'Tell me thy history, O my brother, and how thou camest by the knowledge of Mohammed (whom Allah assain and save!) that thy heart hath been taken with love of him and compelled thee to fare forth and seek him; and lastly tell me who it was directed thee in this road.' So he related to him his tale in its entirety; whereupon Affan, who well nigh lost his wits for wonder, said to him, 'Make tryst for me with the Queen of the Serpents and I will bring thee in company with Mohammed, albeit the date of his mission is yet far distant. We have only to prevail upon the Queen and

---

[1] Arab. "Símiyá" from the Pers., a word apparently built on the model of "Kámiyá" = alchemy, and applied, I have said, to fascination, minor miracles and white magic generally like the Hindu "Indrajal." The common term for Alchemy is Ilm al-Káf (the K-science) because it is not safe to speak of it openly as Alchemy.

carry her in a cage to a certain mountain where the herbs grow; and, as long as she is with us, the plants as we pass them will parley with human speech and discover their virtues by the ordinance of Allah the Most High. For I have found in my books that there is a certain herb and all who express its juice and anoint therewith their feet shall walk upon whatsoever sea Almighty Allah hath made, without wetting sole. When we have found the magical herb, we will let her go her way; and then will we anoint our feet with the juice and cross the Seven Seas, till we come to the burial place of our lord Solomon. Then we will take the ring off his finger and rule even as he ruled and win all our wishes; we will enter the Main of Murks[1] and drink of the Water of Life, and so the Almighty will let us tarry till the End of Time and we shall foregather with Mohammed, whom Allah bless and preserve!' Hearing these words Bulukiya replied, 'O Affan, I will make tryst for thee with the Serpent-queen and at once show thee her abiding place.' So Affan made him a cage of iron; and, providing himself with two bowls, one full of wine and the other of milk, took ship with Bulukiya and sailed till they came to the island, where they landed and walked upon it. Then Affan set up the cage, in which he laid a noose and withdrew after placing in it the two bowls; when he and Bulukiya concealed themselves afar off. Presently, up came the Queen of the Serpents (that is, myself) and examined the cage. When she (that is I) smelt the savour of the milk, she came down from the back of the snake which bore her tray and, entering the cage, drank up the milk. Then she went to the bowl of wine and drank of it, whereupon her head became giddy and she slept. When Affan saw this, he ran up and locking the cage upon her, set it on his head and made for the ship, he and Bulukiya. After awhile she awoke and finding herself in a cage of iron on a man's head and seeing Bulukiya walking beside the bearer, said to him, 'This is the reward of those who do no hurt to the sons of Adam.' Answered he, 'O Queen, have no fear of us, for we will do thee no hurt at all. We wish thee only to show us the herb which, when pounded and squeezed yieldeth a juice, and this rubbed upon the feet conferreth the power of walking dryshod upon what sea soever Almighty Allah hath created; and when we have found that, we will return thee to thy place and let thee wend thy way.' Then Affan and Bulukiya fared on for the hills where grew the herbs; and, as they went about with the Queen, each plant they passed began to speak and avouch its virtues by permission of Allah the Most High. As they were thus doing and the herbs speaking right and left, behold, a plant spoke out and said, 'I am the herb ye seek, and all who gather and crush me and anoint their feet with my juice, shall fare over what sea soever Allah Almighty hath created and yet ne'er wet sole.' When Affan heard this, he set down the cage from his head and,

---

[1] Mare Tenebrarum = Sea of Darknesses; usually applied to the "mournful and misty Atlantic."

gathering what might suffice them of the herb, crushed it and filling two vials with the juice kept them for future use; and with what was left they anointed their feet. Then they took up the Serpent-queen's cage and journeyed days and nights, till they reached the island, where they opened the cage and let out her that is me. When I found myself at liberty, I asked them what use they would make of the juice; and they answered, 'We design to anoint our feet and to cross the Seven Seas to the burial place of our lord Solomon[1] and take the seal ring from his finger.' Quoth I, 'Far, far is it from your power to possess yourselves of the ring!' They enquired, 'Wherefore?' and I replied, 'Because Almighty Allah vouchsafed unto our lord Solomon the gift of this ring and distinguished him thereby, for that he said to him, 'O Lord, give me a kingdom which may not be obtained after me; for Thou verily art the Giver of kingdoms.'[2] 'So that ring is not for you.' And I added, 'Had ye twain taken the herb, whereof all who eat shall not die until the First Blast,[3] it had better availed you than this ye have gotten; for ye shall nowise come at your desire thereby.' Now when they heard this, they repented them with exceeding penitence and went their ways."—And Shahrazad perceived the dawn of day and ceased saying her permitted say.

When it was the Four Hundred and Eighty-ninth Night,

She said, It hath reached me, O auspicious King, that "when Bulukiya and Affan heard these words, they repented them with exceeding penitence and went their ways. Such was their case; but as regards myself" (continued the Serpent-queen) "I went in quest of my host and found it fallen in piteous case, the stronger of them having grown weak in my absence and the weaker having died. When they saw me, they rejoiced and flocking about me, asked, 'What hath befallen thee, and where hast thou been?' So I told them what had passed, after which I

---

[1] Some Moslems hold that Solomon and David were buried in Jerusalem, others on the shore of Lake Tiberias. Mohammed, according to the history of Al–Tabari (p. 56 vol. i. Duleux's "Chronique de Tabari") declares that the Jinni bore Solomon's corpse to a palace hewn in the rock upon an island surrounded by a branch of the "Great Sea" and set him on a throne, with his ring still on his finger, under a guard of twelve Jinns. "None hath looked upon the tomb save only two, Affan who took Bulukiya as his companion: with extreme pains they arrived at the spot, and Affan was about to carry off the ring when a thunderbolt consumed him. So Bulukiya returned."
[2] Koran xxxviii. 34, or, "art the liberal giver."
[3] *i.e.* of the last trumpet blown by the Archangel Israfil: an idea borrowed from the Christians. Hence the title of certain churches—*ad Tubam.*

gathered my forces to "ether and repaired with them to the mountain Kaf, where I was wont to winter, summer-freshing in the place where thou now seest me, O Hasib Karim al-Din. This, then, is my story and what befell me." Thereupon Hasib marvelled at her words and said to her, "I beseech thee, of thy favour, bid one of thy guards bear me forth to the surface of the earth, that I may go to my people." She replied, "O Hasib, thou shalt not have leave to depart from us till winter come, and needs must thou go with us to the Mountain Kaf and solace thyself with the sight of the hills and sands and trees and birds magnifying the One God, the Victorious; and look upon Marids and Ifrits and Jinn, whose number none knoweth save Almighty Allah." When Hasib heard this, he was sore chafed and chagrined: then he said to her, "Tell me of Affan and Bulukiya; when they departed from thee and went their way, did they cross the Seven Seas and reach the burial-place of our lord Solomon or not; and if they did had they power to take the ring or not?" Answered she, "Know, that when they left me, they anointed their feet with the juice; and, walking over the water, fared on from sea to sea, diverting themselves with the wonders of the deep, nor ceased they faring till they had traversed the Seven Seas and came in sight of a mountain, soaring high in air, whose stones were emeralds and whose dust was musk; and in it was a stream of running water. When they made it they rejoiced, saying each to the other, 'Verily we have won our wish'; and they entered the passes of the mountain and walked on, till they saw from afar a cavern surmounted by a great dome, shining with light. So they made for the cavern, and entering it beheld therein a throne of gold studded with all manner jewels, and about it stools whose number none knoweth save Allah Almighty. And they saw lying at full length upon the throne our lord Solomon, clad in robes of green silk inwoven with gold and broidered with jewels and precious minerals: his right hand was passed over his breast and on the middle finger was the seal ring whose lustre outshone that of all other gems in the place. Then Affan taught Bulukiya adjurations and conjurations galore and said to him, 'Repeat these conjurations and cease not repeating until I take the ring.' Then he went up to the throne; but, as he drew near unto it lo! a mighty serpent came forth from beneath it and cried out at him with so terrible a cry that the whole place trembled and sparks flew from its mouth, saying, 'Begone, or thou art a dead man' But Affan busied himself with his incantations and suffered himself not to be startled thereby. Then the serpent blew such a fiery blast at him, that the place was like to be set on fire, and said to him, Woe to thee! Except thou turn back, I will consume thee' Hearing these words Bulukiya left the cave, but Affan, who suffered himself not to be troubled, went up to the Prophet: then he put out his hand to the ring and touched it and strove to draw it off the lord Solomon's finger; and behold, the serpent blew on him once more and he became a heap of ashes. Such was his case; but as regards Bulukiya he fell down in a swoon."—And Shahrazad perceived the dawn of day and ceased to say her permitted say.

When it was the Four Hundred and Ninetieth Night,

She said, It hath reached me, O auspicious King, that the Queen continued: "When Bulukiya saw Affan burnt up by the fire and become a heap of ashes, he fell down in a swoon. Thereupon the Lord (magnified be His Majesty!) bade Gabriel descend earthwards and save him ere the serpent should blow on him. So Gabriel descended without delay and, finding Affan reduced to ashes and Bulukiya in a fit, aroused him from his trance and saluting him asked, 'How camest thou hither?' Bulukiya related to him his history from first to last, adding, 'Know that I came not hither but for the love of Mohammed (whom Allah assain and save!), of whom Affan informed me that his mission would take place at the End of Time; moreover that none should foregather with him but those who endured to the latter days by drinking of the Water of Life through means of Solomon's seal. So I companied him hither and there befell him what befell; but I escaped the fire and now it is my desire that thou inform me where Mohammed is to be found.' Quoth Gabriel, 'O Bulukiya, go thy ways, for the time of Mohammed's coming is yet far distant.' Then he ascended up to heaven forthright, and Bulukiya wept with sore weeping and repented of that which he had done, calling to mind my words, whenas I said to them, 'Far is it from man's power to possess himself of the ring.' Then he descended from the mountain and returned in exceeding confusion to the sea shore and passed the night there, marvelling at the mountains and seas and islands around him. When morning dawned, he anointed his feet with the herb-juice and descending to the water, set out and fared on over the surface of the seas days and nights, astonied at the terrors of the main and the marvels and wonders of the deep, till he came to an island as it were the Garden of Eden. So he landed and, finding himself in a great and pleasant island, paced about it and saw with admiration that its dust was saffron and its gravel carnelian and precious minerals; its hedges were of jessamine, its vegetation was of the goodliest of trees and of the brightest of odoriferous shrubs; its brushwood was of Comorin and Sumatran aloes-wood and its reeds were sugar-canes. Round about it were roses and narcissus and amaranths and gilly-flowers and chamomiles and white lilies and violets, and other flowers of all kinds and colours. Of a truth the island was the goodliest place, abounding in space, rich in grace, a compendium of beauty material and spiritual. The birds warbled on the boughs with tones far sweeter than chaunt of Koran and their notes would console a lover whom longings unman. And therein the gazelle frisked free and fain and wild cattle roamed about the plain. Its trees were of tallest height; its streams flowed bright; its springs welled with waters sweet and light; and all therein was a delight to sight and sprite. Bulukiya marvelled at the charms of the island but knew that he had strayed from the way he had first taken in company with Affan. He wandered about the place and solaced him with various spectacles until nightfall, when he climbed into a tree to sleep; but as he sat there, musing over the beauty of the site, behold, the sea became troubled and there rose up to the surface a great beast, which cried out with a cry so terrible that every living thing upon the isle trembled. As Bulukiya gazed upon him from the tree and marvelled at the bigness of his bulk, he was presently followed unexpectedly by a multitude of other sea beasts in kind manifolds, each holding in his fore-paw a jewel which shone like a lamp, so that the whole island became as light as day for the lustre of the gems. After awhile, there appeared, from the heart of the island, wild beasts of the land, none knoweth their number save Allah the Most High; amongst which Bulukiya noted lions and panthers and lynxes and other ferals; and these land beasts flocked down to the shore; and, foregathering with the sea beasts, conversed with them till daybreak, when they separated and each went his own way. Thereupon Bulukiya, terrified by what he had seen, came down from the tree and, making the sea shore, anointed his feet with the magical juice, and set out once more upon the surface of the water. He fared on days and nights over the Second Sea, till he came to a great mountain skirting which ran a Wady without end, the stones whereof were magnetic iron and its beasts, lions and hares and panthers. He landed on the mountain foot and wandered from place to place till nightfall, when he sat down sheltered by one of the base hills on the sea side, to eat of the dried fish thrown up by the sea. Presently, he turned from his meal and behold, a huge panther was creeping up to rend and ravin him; so he anointed his feet in haste with the juice and, descending to the surface of the water, fled walking over the Third Sea, in the darkness, for the night was black and the wind blew stark. Nor did he stay his course till he reached another island, whereon he landed and found there trees bearing fruits both fresh and dry.[1] So he took of these fruits and ate and praised Allah Almighty; after which he walked for solace; about the island till eventide."—And Shahrazad perceived the dawn of day and ceased saying her permitted say.

When it was the Four Hundred and Ninety-first Night,

She said, It hath reached me, O auspicious King, that "Bulukiya (continued the Queen) walked for solace about the island till eventide, when he lay down to sleep. As soon as day brake, he began to explore the place and ceased not for ten days, after which he again made the shore and anointed his feet and, setting out over the Fourth Sea, walked upon it

---

[1] This may mean that the fruits were fresh and dried like dates or tamarinds (a notable wonder), or soft and hard of skin like grapes and pomegranates.

many nights and days, till he came to a third island of fine white sand without sign of trees or grass. He walked about it awhile but, finding its only inhabitants sakers which nested in the sand, he again anointed his feet and trudged over the Fifth Sea, walking night and day till he came to a little island, whose soil and hills were like crystal. Therein were the veins wherefrom gold is worked; and therein also were marvellous trees whose like he had never seen in his wanderings, for their blossoms were in hue as gold. He landed and walked about for diversion till it was nightfall, when the flowers began to shine through the gloom like stars. Seeing this sight, he marvelled and said, 'Assuredly, the flowers of this island are of those which wither under the sun and fall to the earth, where the winds smite them and they gather under the rocks and become the Elixir[1] which the folk collect and thereof make gold.' He slept there all that night and at sunrise he again anointed his feet and, descending to the shore, fared on over the Sixth Sea nights and days, till he came to a fifth island. Here he landed and found, after walking an hour or so, two mountains covered with a multitude of trees, whose fruits were as men's heads hanging by the hair, and others whose fruits were green birds hanging by the feet; also a third kind, whose fruits were like aloes, if a drop of the juice fell on a man it burnt like fire; and others, whose fruits wept and laughed, besides many other marvels which he saw there. Then he returned to the sea shore and, finding there a tall tree, sat down beneath it till supper time when he climbed up into the branches to sleep. As he sat considering the wonderful works of Allah behold, the waters became troubled, and there rose therefrom the daughters of the sea, each mermaid holding in her hand a jewel which shone like the morning. They came ashore and, foregathering under the trees, sat down and danced and sported and made merry whilst Bulukiya amused himself with watching and wondering at their gambols, which were prolonged till the morning, when they returned to the sea and disappeared. Then he came down and, anointing his feet, set out on the surface of the Seventh Sea, over which he journeyed two whole months, without getting sight of highland or island or broadland or lowland or shoreland, till he came to the end thereof. And so doing he suffered exceeding hunger, so that he was forced to snatch up fishes from the surface of the sea and devour them raw, for stress of famine. In such case he pushed on till in early forenoon he came to the sixth island, with trees a-growing and rills a flowing, where he landed and walked about, looking right and left, till he came to an apple tree and put forth his hand to pluck of the fruit, when lo! one cried out to him from the tree, saying, 'An thou draw near to this tree and cut of it aught, I will cut thee in twain.' So he looked and saw a giant forty cubits high, being the cubit of the people of that day; whereat he feared with sore fear and refrained from that tree. Then said he to the

---

[1] Arab. "Ai-lksír" meaning lit. an essence; also the philosopher's stone.

giant, 'Why cost thou forbid me to eat of this tree?' Replied the other, 'Because thou art a son of Adam and thy father Adam forgot the covenant of Allah and sinned against Him and ate of the tree.' Quoth Bulukiya, 'What thing art thou and to whom belongeth this island, with its trees, and how art thou named?' Quoth the tall one, 'My name is Sharáhiyá and trees and island belong to King Sakhr;[1] I am one of his guards and in charge of his dominion,' presently adding, 'But who art thou and whence comest thou hither?' Bulukiya told him his story from beginning to end and Sharahiya said, 'Be of good cheer,' and brought him to eat. So he ate his fill and, taking leave of the giant, set out again and ceased not faring on over the mountains and sandy deserts for ten days; at the end of which time he saw, in the distance, a dust cloud hanging like a canopy in air; and, making towards it, he heard a mighty clamour, cries and blows and sounds of mellay. Presently he reached a great Wady, two months' journey long; and, looking whence the shouts came, he saw a multitude of horse men engaged in fierce fight and the blood running from them till it railed like a river. Their voices were thunderous and they were armed with lance and sword and iron mace and bow and arrow, and all fought with the utmost fury. At this sight he felt sore affright"—And Shahrazad perceived the dawn of day and ceased to say her permitted say.

When it was the Four Hundred and Ninety-second Night,

She said, It hath reached me, O auspicious King, that the Queen continued: "When Bulukiya saw the host in fight, he felt sore affright and was perplexed about his case; but whilst he hesitated, behold, they caught sight of him and held their hands one from other and left fighting. Then a troop of them came up to him, wondering at his make, and one of the horsemen said to him, 'What art thou and whence camest thou hither and whither art wending; and who showed thee the way that thou hast come to our country?' Quoth he, 'I am of the sons of Adam and am come out, distracted for the love of Mohammed (whom Allah bless and preserve!); but I have wandered from my way.' Quoth the horseman, 'Never saw we a son of Adam till now, nor did any ever come to this land.' And all marvelled at him and at his speech. 'But what are ye, O creatures?' asked Bulukiya; and the rider replied, 'We are of the Jánn.' So he said, 'O Knight, what is the cause of the fighting amongst you and where is your abiding place and what is the name of this valley and this land?' He replied, 'Our abiding-place is the White Country; and, every year, Allah Almighty commandeth us to come hither and wage war upon the unbelieving Jann.' Asked Bulukiya, 'And where is the White Country?'

---

[1] Name of the Jinni whom Solomon imprisoned in Lake Tiberias (See vol. i., 41).

and the horseman answered, 'It is behind the mountain Kaf, and distant seventy-five years journey from this place which is termed the Land of Shaddád son of 'Ád: we are here for Holy War; and we have no other business, when we are not doing battle, than to glorify God and hallow him. More over, we have a ruler, King Sakhr hight, and needs must thou go with us to him, that he may look upon thee for his especial delight.' Then they fared on (and he with them) till they came to their abiding place; where he saw a multitude of magnificent tents of green silk, none knoweth their number save Allah the Most High, and in their midst a pavilion of red satin, some thousand cubits in compass, with cords of blue silk and pegs of gold and silver. Bulukiya marvelled at the sight and accompanied them as they fared on and behold, this was the royal pavilion. So they carried him into the presence of King Sakhr, whom he found seated upon a splendid throne of red gold, set with pearls and studded with gems; the Kings and Princes of the Jann being on his right hand, and on his left his Councillors and Emirs and Officers of state, and a multitude of others. The King seeing him bade introduce him, which they did; and Bulukiya went up to him and saluted him after kissing the ground before him. The King returned his salute and said, 'Draw near me, O mortal!' and Bulukiya went close up to him. Hereupon the King, commanding a chair to be set for him by his royal side, bade him sit down and asked him 'Who art thou?'; and Bulukiya answered, 'I am a man, and one of the Children of Israel.' 'Tell me thy story,' cried King Sakhr, 'and acquaint me with all that hath befallen thee and how thou camest to this my land.' So Bulukiya related to him all that had occurred in his wanderings from beginning to end."—And Shahrazad perceived the dawn of day and ceased saying her permitted say.

When it was the Four Hundred and Ninety-third Night,

She said, It hath reached me, O auspicious King, that the Queen continued: "When Bulukiya related to Sakhr what befell him in his wanderings, he marvelled thereat. Then he bade the servants bring food and they spread the tables and set on one thousand and five hundred platters of red gold and silver and copper, some containing twenty and some fifty boiled camels, and others some fifty head of sheep; at which Bulukiya marvelled with exceeding marvel. Then they ate and he ate with them, till he was satisfied and returned thanks to Allah Almighty; after which they cleared the tables and set on fruits, and they ate thereof, glorifying the name of God and invoking blessings on His prophet Mohammed (whom Allah bless and preserve!) When Bulukiya heard them make mention of Mohammed, he wondered and said to King Sakhr, 'I am minded to ask thee some questions.' Rejoined the King, 'Ask what thou wilt,' and Bulukiya said, 'O King, what are ye and what is your origin and how came ye to know of Mohammed (whom Allah assain and save!) that ye draw near to him and love him?' King Sakhr answered, 'O

Bulukiya, of very sooth Allah created the fire in seven stages, one above the other, and each distant a thousand years journey from its neighbour. The first stage he named Jahannam[1] and appointed the same for the punishment of the transgressors of the True-believers, who die unrepentant; the second he named Lazá and appointed for Unbelievers: the name of the third is Jahím and is appointed for Gog and Magog.[2] The fourth is called Sa'ír and is appointed for the host of Iblis. The fifth is called Sakar and is prepared for those who neglect prayer. The sixth is called Hatamah and is appointed for Jews and Christians. The seventh is named Háwiyah and is prepared for hypocrites. Such be the seven stages.' Quoth Bulukiya, 'Haply Jahannam hath least of torture for that it is the uppermost.' 'Yes,' quoth King Sakhr, 'the most endurable of them all is Jahannam; natheless in it are a thousand mountains of fire, in each mountain seventy thousand cities of fire, in each city seventy thousand castles of fire, in each castle seventy thousand houses of fire, in each house seventy thousand couches of fire and in each couch seventy thousand manners of torment. As for the other hells, O Bulukiya, none knoweth the number of kinds of torment that be therein save Allah Most Highest.' When Bulukiya heard this, he fell down in a fainting-fit, and when he came to himself, he wept and said, 'O King what will be my case?' Quoth Sakhr, 'Fear not, and know thou that whoso loveth Mohammed (whom Allah bless and keep!) the fire shall not burn him, for he is made free therefrom for his sake; and whoso belongeth to his Faith the fire shall fly him. As for us, the Almighty Maker created us of the fire for the first that he made in Jahannam were two of His host whom he called Khalít and Malít. Now Khalít was fashioned in the likeness of a lion, with a tail like a tortoise twenty years' journey in length and ending in a member masculine; while Malít was like a pied wolf whose tail was furnished with a member feminine. Then Almighty Allah commanded the tails to couple and copulate and do the deed of kind, and of them were born serpents and scorpions, whose dwelling is in the fire, that

---

[1] Vulgarly pronounced "Jahannum." The second hell is usually assigned to Christians. As there are seven Heavens (the planetary orbits) so, to satisfy Moslem love of symmetry, there must be as many earths and hells under the earth. The Egyptians invented these grim abodes, and the marvellous Persian fancy worked them into poem.

[2] Arab. "Yájúj and Majuj," first named in Gen. x. 2, which gives the ethnology of Asia Minor, circ. B.C. 800. "Gomer" is the Gimri or Cymmerians; "Magog" the original Magi, a division of the Medes, "Javan" the Ionian Greeks, "Meshesh" the Moschi; and "Tires" the Turusha, or primitive Cymmerians. In subsequent times, "Magog" was applied to the Scythians, and modern Moslems determine from the Koran (chaps. xviii. and xxi.) that Yajuj and Majuj are the Russians, whom they call Moska or Moskoff from the Moskwa River.

Allah may there with torment those whom He casteth therein; and these increased and multiplied. Then Allah commanded the tails of Khalit and Malit to couple and copulate a second time, and the tail of Malit conceived by the tail of Khalit and bore fourteen children, seven male and seven female, who grew up and intermarried one with the other. All were obedient to their sire, save one who disobeyed him and was changed into a worm which is Iblis (the curse of Allah be upon him!). Now Iblis was one of the Cherubim, for he had served Allah till he was raised to the heavens and cherished[1] by the especial favour of the Merciful One, who made him chief of the Cherubim.'"—And Shahrazad perceived the dawn of day and ceased to say her permitted say.

When it was the Four Hundred and Ninety-fourth Night,

She said, It hath reached me, O auspicious King, that the Queen continued: "'Iblis served God and became chief of Cherubim. When, however, the Lord created Adam (with whom be peace!), He commanded Iblis to prostrate himself to him, but he drew back; so Allah Almighty expelled him from heaven and cursed him.[2] This Iblis had issue and of his lineage are the devils; and as for the other six males, who were his elders, they are the ancestors of the true believing Jann, and we are their descendants. Such, O Bulukiya is our provenance.'[3] Bulukiya marvelled at the King's words and said, 'O King, I pray thee bid one of thy guards bear me back to my native land.' 'Naught of this may we do,' answered Sakhr, 'save by commandment of Allah Almighty; however, an thou desire to leave us and return home, I will mount thee on one of my mares and cause her carry thee to the farthest frontiers of my dominions, where thou wilt meet with the troops of another King, Barákhiyá hight, who will recognize the mare at sight and take thee off her and send her back to us; and this is all we can do for thee, and no more.' When Bulukiya heard these words he wept and said, 'Do whatso thou wilt.' So King Sakhr caused bring the mare and, setting Bulukiya on her back, said to him,

---

[1] I attempt to preserve the original pun; "Mukarrabin" (those near Allah) being the Cherubim, and the Creator causing Iblis to draw near Him (karraba).
[2] A vulgar version of the Koran (chaps. vii.), which seems to have borrowed from the Gospel of Barnabas. Hence Adam becomes a manner of God-man.
[3] These wild fables are caricatures of Rabbinical legends which began with "Lilith," the Spirit-wife of Adam: Nature and her counterpart, Physis and Antiphysis, supply a solid basis for folk-lore. Amongst the Hindus we have Brahma (the Creator) and Viswakarmá, the anti-Creator: the former makes a horse and a bull and the latter caricatures them with an ass and a buffalo, and so forth.

'Beware lest thou alight from her or strike her or cry out in her face; for if thou do so she will slay thee; but abide quietly riding on her back till she stop with thee; then dismount and wend thy ways.' Quoth Bulukiya, 'I hear and I obey;' he then mounted and setting out, rode on a long while between the rows of tents; and stinted not riding till he came to the royal kitchens where he saw the great cauldrons, each holding fifty camels, hung up over the fires which blazed fiercely under them. So he stopped there and gazed with a marvel ever increasing till King Sakhr thinking him to be anhungered, bade bring him two roasted camels; and they carried them to him and bound them behind him on the mare's crupper. Then he took leave of them and fared on, till he came to the end of King Sakhr's dominions, where the mare stood still and Bulukiya dismounted and began to shake the dust of the journey from his raiment. And behold, there accosted him a party of men who, recognising the mare, carried her and Bulukiya before their King Barakhiya. So he saluted him, and the King returned his greeting and seated him beside himself in a splendid pavilion, in the midst of his troops and champions and vassal Princes of the Jann ranged to right and left; after which he called for food and they ate their fill and pronounced the Alhamdolillah. Then they set on fruits, and when they had eaten thereof, King Barakhiya, whose estate was like that of King Sakhr, asked his guest, 'When didst thou leave King Sakhr?' And Bulukiya answered, 'Two days ago.' Quoth Barakhiya, 'Dost thou know, how many days' journey thou hast come in these two days?' Quoth he, 'No,' and the King rejoined, 'Thou hast come a journey of threescore and ten months.'"—And Shahrazad perceived the dawn of day and ceased saying her permitted say.

When it was the Four Hundred and Ninety-fifth Night,

She said, It hath reached me, O auspicious King, that the Queen continued: "Barakhiya said to Bulukiya, 'In two days thou hast come a journey of threescore and ten months; moreover when thou mountedst the mare, she was affrighted at thee, knowing thee for a son of Adam, and would have thrown thee; so they bound on her back these two camels by way of weight to steady her.' When Bulukiya heard this, he marvelled and thanked Allah Almighty for safety. Then said the King, 'Tell me thy adventures and what brought thee to this our land.' So he told him his story from first to last, and the King marvelled at his words, and kept Bulukiya with him two months." Upon this Hasib Karim al-Din after he had marvelled at her story, again besought the Serpent-queen saying, "I pray thee of thy goodness and graciousness command one of thy subjects conduct me to the surface of the earth, that I may return to my family;" but she answered, "O Hasib, I know that the first thing thou wilt do, after seeing the face of the earth will be to greet thy family and then repair to the Hammam bath and bathe; and the moment thou endest thine ablutions will see the last of me, for it will be the cause of my death." Quoth Hasib,

"I swear that I will never again enter the Hammam bath so long as I live, but when washing is incumbent on me, I will wash at home." Rejoined the Queen, "I would not trust thee though thou shouldst swear to me an hundred oaths; for such abstaining is not possible, and I know thee to be a son of Adam for whom no oath is sacred. Thy father Adam made a covenant with Allah the most High, who kneaded the clay whereof He fashioned him forty mornings and made His angels prostrate themselves to him; yet after all his promise did he forget and his oath violate, disobeying the commandment of his Lord." When Hasib heard this, he held his peace and burst into tears; nor did he leave weeping for the space of ten days, at the end of which time he said to the Queen, "Prithee acquaint me with the rest of Bulukiya's adventures." Accordingly, she began again as follows: "Know, O Hasib, that Bulukiya, after abiding two months with King Barakhiya, farewelled him and fared on over wastes and deserts nights and days' till he came to a high mountain which he ascended. On the summit he beheld seated a great Angel glorifying the names of God and invoking blessings on Mohammed. Before him lay a tablet covered with characters, these white and those black,[1] whereon his eyes were fixed, and his two wings were outspread to the full, one to the western and the other to the eastern horizon. Bulukiya approached and saluted the Angel, who returned his salam adding, 'Who art thou and whence comest thou and whither wendest thou and what is thy story?' Accordingly, he repeated to him his history, from first to last, and the Angel marvelled mightily thereat, whereupon Bulukiya said to him, 'I pray thee in return acquaint me with the meaning of this tablet and what is writ thereon; and what may be thine occupation and thy name.' Replied the Angel, 'My name is Michael, and I am charged with the shifts of night and day; and this is my occupation till the Day of Doom.' Bulukiya wondered at his words and at his aspect and the vastness of his stature and, taking leave of him, fared onwards, night and day, till he came to a vast meadow over which he walked observing that it was traversed by seven streams and abounded in trees. He was struck by its beauty and in one corner thereof he saw a great tree and under it four Angels. So he drew near to them and found the first in the likeness of a man, the second in the likeness of a wild beast, the third in the likeness of a bird and the fourth in the likeness of a bull, engaged in glorifying Almighty Allah, and saying, 'O my God and my Master and my Lord, I conjure Thee, by Thy truth and by the decree of Thy Prophet Mohammed (on whom be blessings and peace!) to vouchsafe Thy mercy and grant Thy forgiveness to all things created in my likeness; for Thou

---

[1] This is the "Lauh al-Mahfúz," the Preserved Tablet, upon which are written all Allah's decrees and the actions of mankind good (white) and evil (black). This is the "perspicuous Book" of the Koran, chaps. vi. 59. The idea again is Guebre.

over all things art Almighty!' Bulukiya marvelled at what he heard but continued his journey till he came to another mountain and ascending it, found there a great Angel seated on the summit, glorifying God and hallowing Him and invoking blessings on Mohammed (whom Allah assain and save!), and he saw that Angel continually opening and shutting his hands and bending and extending his fingers. He accosted him and saluted him; whereupon the Angel returned his salam and enquired who he was and how he came thither. So Bulukiya acquainted him with his adventures including his having lost the way; and besought him to tell him, in turn, who he was and what was his function and what mountain was that. Quoth the Angel, 'Know, O Bulukiya, that this is the mountain Kaf, which encompasseth the world; and all the countries the Creator hath made are in my grasp. When the Almighty is minded to visit any land with earthquake or famine or plenty or slaughter or prosperity, He biddeth me carry out His commands and I carry them out without stirring from my place; for know thou that my hands lay hold upon the roots of the earth,'"—And Shahrazed perceived the dawn of day and ceased to say her permitted say.

When it was the Four Hundred and Ninety-sixth Night,

She said, It hath reached me, O auspicious King, that the Queen continued: "When the angel said, 'And know thou that my hands lay hold upon the roots of the earth,' he asked, 'And hath Allah created other worlds than this within the mountain Kaf?' The Angel answered, 'Yes, He hath made a world white as silver, whose vastness none knoweth save Himself, and hath peopled it with Angels, whose meat and drink are His praise and hallowing and continual blessings upon His Prophet Mohammed (whom Allah bless and keep!). Every Thursday night[1] they repair to this mountain and worship in congregation Allah until the morning, and they assign the future recompense of their lauds and litanies to the sinners of the Faith of Mohammed (whom Allah assain and save!) and to all who make the Ghusl ablution of Friday; and this is their function until the Day of Resurrection.' Asked Bulukiya, 'And hath Allah created other mountains behind the mountain Kaf?'; whereto he answered, 'Yes, behind this mountain is a range of mountains five hundred years' journey long, of snow and ice, and this it is that wardeth off the heat of Jahannam from the world, which verily would else be consumed thereby. Moreover, behind the mountain Kaf are forty worlds, each one the bigness of this world forty times told, some of gold and some of silver and others of carnelian. Each of these worlds hath its own colour, and Allah hath peopled them with angels, that know not Eve nor

---

[1] *i.e.* the night before Friday which in Moslem parlance would be Friday night.

Adam nor night nor day, and have no other business than to celebrate His praises and hallow Him and make profession of His Unity and proclaim His Omnipotence and supplicate Him on behalf of the followers of Mohammed (whom Allah bless and keep!). And know, also, O Bulukiya, that the earths were made in seven stages, one upon another, and that Allah hath created one of His Angels, whose stature and attributes none knoweth but Himself and who beareth the seven stages upon his shoulders. Under this Angel Almighty Allah hath created a great rock, and under the rock a bull, and under the bull a huge fish, and under the fish a mighty ocean.[1] God once told Isa (with whom be peace!) of this fish, and he said, 'O Lord show me the fish, that I may look upon it.' So the Almighty commanded an angel to take Isa and show him the fish. Accordingly, he took him up and carried him (with whom be peace!) to the sea, wherein the fish dwelt, and said, 'Look, O Isa, upon the fish.' He looked but at first saw nothing, when, suddenly, the fish darted past like lightning. At this sight Isa fell down aswoon, and when he came to himself, Allah spake to him by inspiration, saying, 'O Isa, hast thou seen the fish and comprehended its length and its breadth?' He replied, 'By Thy honour and glory, O Lord, I saw no fish; but there passed me by a great bull, whose length was three days' journey, and I know not what manner of thing this bull is.' Quoth Allah, 'O Isa, this that thou sawest and which was three days in passing by thee, was but the head of the fish;[2] and know that every day I create forty fishes like unto this.' And Isa hearing this marvelled at the power of Allah the Almighty. Asked Bulukiya, 'What hath Allah made beneath this sea which containeth the fish?'; and the Angel answered, 'Under the sea the Lord created a vast abyss of air, under the air fire, and under the fire a mighty serpent, by name Falak; and were it not for fear of the Most Highest, this serpent would assuredly swallow up all that is above it, air and fire and the Angel and his burden, without sensing it.'"—And Shahrazed perceived the dawn of day and ceased saying her permitted say.

When it was the Four Hundred and Ninety-seventh Night,

She said, It hath reached me, O auspicious King, that the angel said to Bulukiya when describing the serpent, "'And were it not for fear of the Most Highest, this serpent would assuredly swallow up all that is above it, air and fire, and the Angel and his burden, without sensing it. When Allah created this serpent He said to it by inspiration, 'I will give thee somewhat to keep for me, so open thy mouth.' The serpent replied, 'Do whatso Thou wilt;' and opened his mouth and God placed Hell into his

---

[1] Again Persian "Gáw-i-Zamín" = the Bull of the Earth. "The cosmogony of the world," etc., as we read in the Vicar of Wakefield.
[2] The Calc. Edit. ii. 614. here reads by a clerical error "bull."

maw, saying, 'Keep it until the Day of Resurrection. When that time comes, the Almighty will send His angels with chains to bring Hell and bind it until the Day when all men shall meet; and the Lord will order Hell to go open its gates and there will issue therefrom sparks bigger than the mountains.' When Bulukiya heard these things he wept with sore weeping and, taking leave of the Angel, fared on westwards, till he came in sight of two creatures sitting before a great shut gate. As he drew near, he saw that one of the gatekeepers had the semblance of a lion and the other that of a bull; so he saluted them and they returned his salam and enquired who and whence he was and whither he was bound. Quoth he, 'I am of the sons of Adam, a wanderer for the love of Mohammed (whom Allah assain and save!) and I have strayed from my way.' Then he asked them what they were and what was the gate before which they sat, and they answered, 'We are the guardians of this gate thou seest and we have no other business than the praise and hallowing of Allah and the invocation of blessings on Mohammed (whom may He bless and keep!).' Bulukiya wondered and asked them, 'What is within the gate?'; and they answered, 'We wot not.' Then quoth he, 'I conjure you, by the truth of your glorious Lord, open to me the gate, that I may see that which is therein.' Quoth they, 'We cannot, and none may open this gate, of all created beings save Gabriel, the Faithful One, with whom be peace!' Then Bulukiya lifted up his voice in supplication to Allah, saying, 'O Lord, send me thy messenger Gabriel, the Faithful One, to open for me this gate that I may see what be therein;' and the Almighty gave ear unto his prayer and commanded the Archangel to descend to earth and open to him the gate of the Meeting-place of the Two Seas. So Gabriel descended and, saluting Bulukiya, opened the gate to him, saying, 'Enter this door, for Allah commandeth me to open to thee.' So he entered and Gabriel locked the gate behind him and flew back to heaven. When Bulukiya found himself within the gate, he looked and beheld a vast ocean, half salt and half fresh, bounded on every side by mountain ranges of red ruby whereon he saw angels singing the praises of the Lord and hallowing Him. So he went up to them and saluted them and having received a return of his salam, questioned them of the sea and the mountains. Replied they, 'This place is situate under the Arsh or empyreal heaven; and this Ocean causeth the flux and flow of all the seas of the world; and we are appointed to distribute them and drive them to the various parts of the earth, the salt to the salt and the fresh to the fresh,[1] and this is our employ until the Day of Doom. As for the mountain ranges they serve to limit and to contain the waters. But thou, whence comest thou and whither art thou bound?' So he told them his story and asked them of the road. They bade him traverse the surface of the ocean which lay before him: so he anointed his feet with the juice of the herb he had with him,

---

[1] *i.e.* Lakes and rivers.

and taking leave of the angels, set out upon the face of the sea and sped on over the water nights and days; and as he was faring, behold, he met a handsome youth journeying along like himself, whereupon he greeted him and he returned his greeting. After they parted he espied four great Angels wayfaring over the face of the sea, and their going was like the blinding lightning; so he stationed himself in their road, and when they came up to him, he saluted them and said to them, 'I ask you by the Almighty, the Glorious, to tell me your names and whither are ye bound?' Replied the first Angel, 'My name is Gabriel and these my companions are called Isráfíl and Míká'íl and Azrá'íl. There hath appeared in the East a mighty dragon, which hath laid waste a thousand cities and devoured their inhabitants; wherefore Allah Almighty hath commanded us to go to him and seize him and cast him into Jahannam.' Bulukiya marvelled at the vastness of their stature and fared on, as before, days and nights, till he came to an island where he landed and walked about for a while,"—And Shahrazad perceived the dawn of day and ceased to say her permitted say.

When it was the Four Hundred and Ninety-eighth Night,

She said, It hath reached me, O auspicious King, that "Bulukiya landed on the island and walked about for a while, till he saw a comely young man with light shining from his visage, sitting weeping and lamenting between two built tombs. So he saluted him and he returned his salutation, and Bulukiya said to him, 'Who art thou and what are these two built tombs between which thou sittest, and wherefore this wailing?' He looked at him and wept with sore weeping, till he drenched his clothes with his tears; then said, 'Know thou, O my brother, mine is a marvellous story and a wondrous; but I would have thee sit by me and first tell me thy name and thine adventures and who thou art and what brought thee hither; after which I will, in turn, relate to thee my history.' So Bulukiya sat down by him and related to him all that had befallen him from his father's death,[1] adding, 'Such is my history, the whole of it, and Allah alone knoweth what will happen to me after this.' When the youth heard his story, he sighed and said, 'O thou unhappy! How few things thou hast seen in thy life compared with mine. Know, O Bulukiya, that unlike thyself I have looked upon our lord Solomon, in his life, and have seen things past count or reckoning. Indeed, my story is strange and my case out of range, and I would have thee abide with me, till I tell thee my history and acquaint thee how I come to be sitting here.'" Hearing this much Hasib again interrupted the Queen of the Serpents and said to her, "Allah upon thee, O Queen, release me and command one of thy servants

---

[1] Here some abridgement is necessary, for we have another recital of what has been told more than once.

carry me forth to the surface of the earth, and I will swear an oath to thee that I will never enter the Hammam-bath as long as I live." But she said, "This is a thing which may not be nor will I believe thee upon thine oath." When he heard this, he wept and all the serpents wept on his account and took to interceding for him with their Queen, saying, "We beseech thee, bid one of us carry him forth to the surface of the earth, and he will swear thee an oath never to enter the bath his life long." Now when Yamlaykhá (for such was the Queen's name) heard their appeal, she turned to Hasib and made him swear to her an oath; after which she bade a serpent carry him forth to the surface of the earth. The serpent made ready, but as she was about to go away with him, he turned to Queen Yamlaykha and said, "I would fain have thee tell me the history of the youth whom Bulukiya saw sitting between two tombs." So she said: "Know, O Hasib, that when Bulukiya sat down by the youth and told him his tale, from first to last, in order that the other might also recount his adventures and explain the cause of his sitting between the two tombs."—And Shahrazad perceived the dawn of day and ceased saying her permitted say.

When it was the Four Hundred and Ninety-ninth Night,

She said, It hath reached me, O auspicious King, that the Queen continued: "When Bulukiya ended his recount, the youth said, 'How few things of marvel hast thou seen in thy life, O unhappy! Now I have looked upon our lord Solomon while he was yet living and I have witnessed wonders beyond compt and conception.'

Source:
Burton, Sir Richard. *Lady Burton's Edition of Her Husband's Arabian Nights, Vol. 3.* Lady Isabel Burton and Justin Huntly McCarthy, editors. London: Waterlow & Sons, 1887.

124. Julnar the Sea-Born and her Son King Badr Basim of Persia

Arabian Nights

THERE was once in days of yore and in ages and times long gone before, in Ajam-land a King Shahrimán[1] hight, whose abiding place was Khorásán. He owned an hundred concubines, but by none of them had he been blessed with boon of child, male or female, all the days of his life. One day, among the days, he bethought him of this and fell lamenting for that the most part of his existence was past and he had not been vouchsafed a son to inherit the kingdom after him, even as he had inherited it from his fathers and forebears; by reason whereof there betided him sore cark and care and chagrin exceeding. As he sat thus one of his Mamelukes came in to him and said, "O my lord, at the door is a slave girl with her merchant, and fairer than she eye hath never seen." Quoth the King, "Hither to me with merchant and maid!"; and both came in to him. Now when Shahriman beheld the girl, he saw that she was like a Rudaynian lance, and she was wrapped in a veil of gold-purfled silk. The merchant uncovered her face, whereupon the place was illumined by her beauty and her seven tresses hung down to her anklets like horses' tails. She had Nature kohl'd eyes, heavy hips and thighs and waist of slenderest guise, her sight healed all maladies and quenched the fire of sighs, for she was even as the poet cries,

> "I love her madly for she is perfect fair,
> Complete in gravity and gracious way;
> Nor overtall nor overshort, the while
> Too full for trousers are those hips that sway:
>
> Her shape is midmost 'twixt o'er small and tall;
> Nor long to blame nor little to gainsay:
> O'erfall her anklets tresses black as night
> Yet in her face resplends eternal day."

The King seeing her marvelled at her beauty and loveliness, her symmetry and perfect grace and said to the merchant, "O Shaykh, how much for this maiden?" Replied the merchant, "O my lord, I bought her for two thousand diners of the merchant who owned her before myself, since when I have travelled with her three years and she hath cost me, up to the time of my coming hither, other three thousand gold pieces; but she is a gift from me to thee." The King robed him with a splendid robe of honour and ordered him ten thousand ducats, whereupon he kissed his hands, thanking him for his bounty and beneficence, and went his ways. Then the King committed the damsel to the tire women, saying, "Amend ye the case of this maiden[2] and adorn her and furnish her a bower and set her therein." And he bade his chamberlains carry her everything she

---

[1] In the Mac. Edit. "Shahzamán," a corruption of Sháh Zamán = King of the Age. (See vol. i. 2)

[2] *i.e.* bathe her and apply cosmetics to remove ail traces of travel.

needed and shut all the doors upon her. Now his capital wherein he dwelt was called the White City and was seated on the sea shore; so they lodged her in a chamber, whose latticed casements overlooked the main.—And Shahrazad perceived the dawn of day and ceased saying her permitted say.

When it was the Seven Hundred and Thirty-ninth Night,

She said, It hath reached me, O auspicious King, that the King after taking the maiden, committed her to the tire women bidding them amend her case and set her in a bower, and ordered his chamberlains to shut all the doors upon her when they had lodged her in a chamber whose latticed casements overlooked the main. Then Shahriman went in to her; but she spake not to him neither took any note of him.[1] Quoth he, 'Twould seem she hath been with folk who have not taught her manners." Then he looked at the damsel and saw her surpassing beauty and loveliness and symmetry and perfect grace, with a face like the rondure of the moon at its full or the sun shining in the sheeny sky. So he marvelled at her charms of favour and figure and he praised Allah the Creator (magnified be His might!), after which he walked up to her and sat him down by her side; then he pressed her to his bosom and seating her on his thighs, sucked the dew of her lips' which he found sweeter than honey. Presently he called for trays spread with richest viands of all kinds and ate and fed her by mouthfuls, till she had enough; yet she spoke not one word. The King began to talk to her and asked her of her name; but she abode still silent and uttered not a syllable nor made him any answer, neither ceased to hang down her head groundwards, and it was but the excess of her beauty and loveliness and the amorous grace that saved her from the royal wrath. Quoth he to himself, "Glory be to God, the Creator of this girl! How charming she is, save that she speaketh not! But perfection belongeth only to Allah the Most High." And he asked the slave girls whether she had spoken, and they said, "From the time of her coming until now she hath not uttered a word nor have we heard her address us." Then he summoned some of his women and concubines and bade them sing to her and make merry with her, so haply she might speak. Accordingly they played before her all manner instruments of music and

---

[1] These pretentious and curious displays of coquetry are not uncommon in handsome slave-girls when newly bought; and it is a kind of pundonor to humour them. They may also refuse their favours and a master who took possession of their persons by brute force would be blamed by his friends, men and women. Even the most despotic of despots, Fath Ali Shah of Persia, put up with refusals from his slave-girls and did not, as would the mean-minded, marry them to the grooms or cooks of the palace.

sports and what not and sang, till the whole company was moved to mirth, except the damsel, who looked at them in silence, but neither laughed nor spoke. The King's breast was straitened; thereupon he dismissed the women and abode alone with that damsel: after which he doffed his clothes and disrobing her with his own hand, looked upon her body and saw it as it were a silvern ingot. So he loved her with exceeding love and falling upon her, took her maidenhead and found her a pure virgin; whereat he rejoiced with excessive joy and said in himself, "By Allah, 'tis a wonder that a girl so fair of form and face should have been left by the merchants a clean maid as she is!"[1] Then he devoted himself altogether to her, heeding none other and forsaking all his concubines and favourites, and tarried with her a whole year as it were a single day. Still she spoke not till, one morning he said to her (and indeed the love of her and longing waxed upon him), "O desire of souls, verily passion for thee is great with me, and I have forsaken for thy sake all my slave girls and concubines and women and favourites and I have made thee my portion of the world and had patience with thee a whole year; and now I beseech Almighty Allah, of His favour, to soften thy heart to me, so thou mayst speak to me. Or, an thou be dumb, tell me by a sign, that I may give up hope of thy speech. I pray the Lord (extolled be He!) to vouchsafe me by thee a son child, who shall inherit the kingdom after me; for I am old and lone and have none to be my heir. Wherefore, Allah upon thee, an thou love me, return me a reply." The damsel bowed her head awhile in thought, and presently raising it, smiled in his face, whereat it seemed to him as if lightning filled the chamber. Then she said, "O magnanimous liege lord, and valorous lion, Allah hath answered thy prayer, for I am with child by thee and the time of my delivery is near at hand, though I know not if the unborn babe be male or female.[2] But, had I not conceived by thee, I had not spoken to thee one word." When the King heard her speech, his face shone with joy and gladness and he kissed her head and hands for excess of delight, saying Alhamdolillah— laud to Lord—who hath vouchsafed me the things I desired!, first, thy speech, and secondly, thy tidings that thou art with child by me." Then he rose up and went forth from her and, seating himself on the throne of his kingship, in an ecstasy of happiness, bade his Wazir distribute to the poor and needy and widows and others an hundred thousand dinars, by way of thank offering to Allah Most High and alms on his own account. The Minister did as bidden by the King who, returning to the damsel, sat with her and embraced and pressed her to his breast, saying, "O my lady, my

---

[1] Such continence is rarely shown by the young Jallabs or slave-traders; when older they learn how much money is lost with the chattel's virginity.
[2] Midwives in the East, as in the less civilised parts of the West, have many nostrums for divining the sex of the unborn child.

queen, whose slave I am, prithee what was the cause of this thy silence? Thou hast been with me a whole year, night and day, waking and sleeping, yet hast not spoken to me till this day." She replied, "Hearken, O King of the Age, and know that I am a wretched exile, broken hearted and far parted from my mother and my family and my brother." When the King heard her words, he knew her desire and said, "As for thy saying that thou art wretched, there is for such speech no ground, inasmuch as my kingdom and good and all I possess are at thy service and I also am become thy bondman; but, as for thy saying, 'I am parted from my mother and brother and family', tell me where they are and I will send and fetch them to thee." There' upon she answered, "Know, then, O auspicious King, that I am called Julnár[1] the Sea born and that my father was of the Kings of the Main. He died and left us his reign, but while we were yet unsettled, behold, one of the other Kings arose against us and took the realm from our hands. I have a brother called Sálih, and my mother also is a woman of the sea; but I fell out with my brother 'The Pious' and swore that I would throw myself into the hands of a man of the folk of the land. So I came forth of the sea and sat down on the edge of an island in the moonshine,[2] where a passer by found me and, carrying me to his house, besought me of love liesse; but I smote him on the head, so that he all but died; whereupon he carried me forth and sold me to the merchant from whom thou hadst me, and this was a good man and a virtuous; pious, loyal and generous. Were it not that thy heart loved me and that thou promotedest me over all thy concubines, I had not remained with thee a single hour, but had cast myself from this window into the sea and gone to my mother and family; but I was ashamed to fare

---

[1] Arabic (which has no written "g") from Pers. Gulnár (Gul-i-anár) pomegranate-flower the Gulnare" of Byron who learnt his Orientalism at the Mekhitarist (Armenian) Convent, Venice. I regret to see the little honour now paid to the gallant poet in the land where he should be honoured the most. The systematic depreciation was begun by the late Mr. Thackeray, perhaps the last man to value the noble independence of Byron's spirit; and it has been perpetuated, I regret to see, by better judges. These critics seem wholly to ignore the fact that Byron founded a school which covered Europe from Russia to Spain, from Norway to Sicily, and which from England passed over to the two Americas. This exceptional success, which has not yet fallen even to Shakespeare's lot, was due to genius only, for the poet almost ignored study and poetic art. His great misfortune was being born in England under the Gerogium Sidus. Any Continental people would have regarded him s one of the prime glories of his race.

[2] Arab. "Fí al-Kamar," which Lane renders "in the moonlight" It seems to me that the allusion is to the Comorin Islands; but the sequel speaks simply of an island.

themwards, being with child by thee; for they would have deemed evilly of me and would not have credited me, even although I swore to them, an I told them that a King had bought me with his gold and made me his portion of the world and preferred me over all his wives and every thing that his right hand possessed. This then is my story and—the Peace!"— And Shahrazad perceived the dawn of day and ceased to say her permitted say.

When it was the Seven Hundred and Fortieth Night,

She resumed, It hath reached me, O auspicious King, that when Julnar[1] the Sea-born, answering the question of King Shahriman, told him her past from first to last, the King thanked her and kissed her between the eyes, saying, "By Allah, O my lady and light of mine eyes" I cannot bear to be parted from thee one hour; and given thou leave me, I shall die forthright. What then is to be done?" Replied she "O my lord, the time of my delivery is at hand and my family needs must be present, that they may tend me; for the women of the land know not the manner of child bearing of the women of the sea, nor do the daughters of the ocean know the manner of the daughters of the earth; and when my people come, I shall be reconciled to them and they will be reconciled to me." Quoth the King, "How do the people of the sea walk therein, without being wetted?"; and quoth she, "O King of the Age, we walk in the waters with our eyes open, as do ye on the ground, by the blessing of the names graven upon the seal-ring of Solomon Davidson (on whom be peace!). But, O King, when my kith and kin come, I will tell them how thou boughtest me with thy gold, and hast entreated me with kindness and benevolence. It behoveth that thou confirm my words to them and that they witness thine estate with their own eyes and they learn that thou art a King, son of a King." He rejoined, "O my lady, do what seemeth good to thee and what pleaseth thee and I will consent to thee in all thou wouldst do." The damsel continued, yes, we walk in the sea and see what is therein and behold the sun, moon, stars and sky, as it were on the surface of earth and this irketh us naught. Know also that there be many peoples in the main and various forms and creatures of all kinds that are on the land, and that all that is on the land compared with that which is in the main is but a very small matter." And the King marvelled at her words. Then she pulled out from her bosom two bits of Comorin lign-

---

[1] The Mac. Edit. misprints Julnár as Julnáz (so the Bul Edit. ii. 233), and Lane's Jullanár is an Egyptian vulgarism. He is right in suspecting the "White City" to be imaginary, but its sea has no apparent connection with the Caspian. The mermen and mermaids appear to him to be of an inferior order of the Jinn, termed Al–Ghawwásah, the Divers, who fly through air and are made of fire which at times issues from their mouths.

aloes and, kindling fire in a chafing dish, chose somewhat of them and threw it in, then she whistled a loud whistle and spake words none understood. Thereupon arose a great smoke and she said to the King, who was looking on, "O my lord, arise and hide thyself in a closet, that I may show thee my brother and mother and family, whilst they see thee not; for I design to bung them hither, and thou shalt presently espy a wondrous thing and shalt marvel at the several creatures and strange shapes which Almighty Allah hath created." So he arose without stay or delay and entering a closet, fell a-watching what she should do. She continued her fumigations and conjurations till the sea foamed and frothed turbid and there rose from it a handsome young man of a bright favour, as he were the moon at its full, with brow flower-white, cheeks of ruddy light and teeth like the marguerite. He was the likest of all creatures to his sister and the tongue of the case spoke in his praise these two couplets,

> "The full moon groweth perfect once a month
> But thy face each day we see perfected.
> And the full moon dwelleth in single sign,
> But to thee all hearts be a dwelling stead."

After him there came forth of the sea an ancient dame with hair speckled gray and five maidens, as they were moons, bearing a likeness to the damsel hight Julnar. The King looked upon them as they all walked upon the face of the water, till they drew near the window and saw Julnar, whereupon they knew her and went in to her. She rose to them and met them with joy and gladness, and they embraced her and wept with sore weeping. Then said they to her, "O Julnar, how couldst thou leave us four years, and we unknowing of thine abiding place? By Allah the world hath been straitened upon us for stress of severance from thee, and we have had no delight of food or drink; no, not for one day, but have wept with sore weeping night and day for the excess of our longing after thee!" Then she fell to kissing the hands of the youth her brother and her mother and cousins, and they sat with her awhile, questioning her of her case and of what had betided her, as well as of her present estate. "Know," replied she, "that, when I left you, I issued from the sea and sat down on the shore of an island, where a man found me and sold me to a merchant, who brought me to this city and sold me for ten thousand diners to the King of the country, who entreated me with honour and forsook all his concubines and women and favourites for my sake and was distracted by me from all he had and all that was in his city." Quoth her brother, "Praised be Allah, who hath reunited us with thee! But now, O my sister, 'tis my purpose that thou arise and go with us to our country and people." When the King heard these words, his wits fled him for fear lest the damsel accept her brother's words and he himself avail not to stay her, albeit he loved her passionately, and he became distracted with fear of losing her. But Julnar answered, "By Allah, O my brother, the mortal who bought me is lord of this city and he is a mighty King and a wise man, good and generous with extreme generosity. Moreover, he is a personage of great worth and wealth and hath neither son nor daughter. He hath entreated me with honour and done me all manner of favour and kindness; nor, from the day of his buying me to this time have I heard from him an ill word to hurt my heart: but he hath never ceased to use me courteously; doing nothing save with my counsel, and I am in the best of case with him and in the perfection of fair fortune. Furthermore, were I to leave him, he would perish; for he cannot endure to be parted from me an hour; and if I left him, I also should die, for the excess of the love I bear him, by reason of his great goodness to me during the time of my sojourn with him; for, were my father alive, my estate with him would not be like my estate with this great and glorious and puissant potentate. And verily, ye see me with child by him and praise be to Allah, who hath made me a daughter of the Kings of the sea, and my husband the mightiest of the Kings of the land, and Allah, in very sooth, he hath compensated me for whatso I lost."—And Shahrazad perceived the dawn of day and ceased saying her permitted say.

When it was the Seven Hundred and Forty-first Night,

She said, It hath reached me, O auspicious King, that Julnar the Sea born told her brother all her tale, adding "Allah hath not cut me off, but hath compensated me for whatso I lost. Now this King hath no issue, male or female, so I pray the Almighty to vouchsafe me a son who shall inherit of this mighty sovran that which the Lord hath bestowed upon him of lands and palaces and possessions." Now when her brother and the daughters of her uncle heard this her speech, their eyes were cooled thereby and they said, 'O Julnar, thou knowest thy value with us and thou wottest the affection we bear thee and thou art certified that thou art to us the dearest of all creatures and thou art assured that we seek but ease for thee, without travail or trouble. Wherefore, an thou be in unease, arise and go with us to our land and our folk but, an thou be at thine ease here, in honour and happiness, this is our wish and our will; for we desire naught save thy welfare in any case.''[1] Quoth she, "By Allah, I am here in the utmost ease and solace and honour and grace!" When the King heard what she said, he joyed with a heart set at rest and thanked her silently for this; the love of her redoubled on him and entered his heart core and he knew that she loved him as he loved her and that she desired to abide with him, that she might see his child by her. Then Julnar bade her women lay the tables and set on all sorts of viands, which had been

---

[1] Arab. "lá Kulli hál," a popular phrase, like the Anglo–American "anyhow."

cooked in kitchen under her own eyes, and fruits and sweetmeats, whereof she ate, she and her kinsfolk. But, presently, they said to her, "O Julnar, thy lord is a stranger to us, and we have entered his house, without his leave or weeting. Thou hast extolled to us his excellence and eke thou hast set before us of his victual whereof we have eaten; yet have we not companied with him nor seen him, neither hath he seen us nor come to our presence and eaten with us, so there might be between us bread and salt." And they all left eating and were wroth with her, and fire, issued from their mouths, as from cressets; which when the King saw, his wits fled for excess of fear of them. But Julnar arose and soothed them and going to the closet where was the King her lord, said to him, "O my lord, hast thou seen and heard how I praised thee and extolled thee to my people and hast thou noted what they said to me of their desire to carry me away with them?" Quoth he, "I both heard and saw: May the Almighty abundantly requite thee for me! By Allah, I knew not the full measure of thy fondness until this blessed hour, and now I doubt not of thy love to me!" Quoth she, "O my lord, is the reward of kindness aught but kindness? Verily, thou hast dealt generously with me and hast entreated me with worship and I have seen that thou lovest me with the utmost love, and thou hast done me all manner of honour and kindness and preferred me above all thou lovest and desirest. So how should my heart be content to leave thee and depart from thee, and how should I do thus after all thy goodness to me? But now I desire of thy courtesy that thou come and salute my family, so thou mayst see them and they thee and pure love and friendship may be between you; for know, O King of the Age, that my brother and mother and cousins love thee with exceeding love, by reason of my praises of thee to them, and they say, 'We will not depart from thee nor go to our homes till we have foregathered with the King and saluted him.' For indeed they desire to see thee and make acquaintance with thee." The King replied, "To hear is to obey, for this is my very own wish." So saying, he rose and went in to them and saluted them with the goodliest salutation; and they sprang up to him and received him with the utmost worship, after which he sat down in the palace and ate with them; and he entertained them thus for the space of thirty days. Then, being desirous of returning home, they took leave of the King and Queen and departed with due permission to their own land, after he had done them all possible honour. Awhile after this, Julnar completed the days of her pregnancy and the time of her delivery being come, she bore a boy, as he were the moon at its full, whereat the utmost joy betided the King, for that he had never in his life been vouchsafed son or daughter. So they held high festival and decorated the city seven days, in the extreme of joy and jollity: and on the seventh day came Queen Julnar's mother, Farásha hight,[1] and

---

[1] In the text the name does not appear till near the end of the tale.

brother and cousins, whenas they knew of her delivery.—And Shahrazad perceived the light of day and ceased to say her permitted say.

When it was the Seven Hundred and Forty-second Night,

She said, It hath reached me, O auspicious King, that when Julnar was brought to bed and was visited by her people, the King received them with joy at their coming and said to them, "I said that I would not give my son a name till you should come and name him of your knowledge." So they named him Badr Básim,[1] and all agreed upon this name. Then they showed the child to his uncle Salih, who took him in his arms and arising began to walk about the chamber with him in all directions right and left. Presently he carried him forth of the palace and going down to the salt sea, fared on with him, till he was hidden from the King's sight. Now when Shahriman saw him take his son and disappear with him in the depth of the sea, he gave the child up for lost and fell to weeping and wailing; but Julnar said to him, "O King of the Age, fear not, neither grieve for thy son, for I love my child more than thou and he is with my brother, so reck thou not of the sea neither fear for him drowning. Had my brother known that aught of harm would betide the little one, he had not done this deed; and he will presently bring thee thy son safe, Inshallah—an it please the Almighty." Nor was an hour past before the sea became turbid and troubled and King Salih came forth and flew from the sea till he came up to them with the child lying quiet and showing a face like the moon on the night of fulness. Then, looking at the King he said, "Haply thou fearedst harm for thy son, whenas I plunged into the sea with him?" Replied the father, "Yes, O my lord, I did indeed fear for him and thought he would never be saved therefrom." Rejoined Salih, "O King of the land, we pencilled his eyes with an eye powder we know of and recited over him the names graven upon the seal-ring of Solomon David son (on whom be the Peace!), for this is what we use to do with children newly born among us; and now thou needst not fear for him drowning or suffocation in all the oceans of the world, if he should go down into them; for, even as ye walk on the land, so walk we in the sea." Then he pulled out of his pocket a casket, graven and sealed and, breaking open the seals, emptied it; whereupon there fell from it strings of all manner jacinths and other jewels, besides three hundred bugles of emerald and other three hundred hollow gems, as big as ostrich eggs, whose light dimmed that of sun and moon. Quoth Salih, "O King of the Age, these jewels and jacinths are a present from me to thee. We never yet brought thee a gift, for that we knew not Julnar's abiding place neither had we of her any tidings or trace; but now that we see thee to be united with her and we are all become one thing, we have brought thee

---

[1] *i.e.* Full moon smiling.

this present; and every little while we will bring thee the like thereof, Inshallah! for that these jewels and jacinths are more plentiful with us than pebbles on the beach and we know the good and the bad of them and their whereabouts and the way to them, and they are easy to us." When the King saw the jewels, his wits were bewildered and his sense was astounded and he said, "By Allah, one single gem of these jewels is worth my realm!" Then he thanked for his bounty Salih the Sea born and, looking towards Queen Julnar, said, "I am abashed before thy brother, for that he hath dealt munificently by me and bestowed on me this splendid gift, which the folk of the land were unable to present." So she thanked her brother for his deed and he said, "O King of the Age, thou hast the prior claim on us and it behoves us to thank thee, for thou hast entreated our sister with kindness and we have entered thy dwelling and eaten of thy victual; and the poet saith,[1]

> 'Had I wept before she did in my passion for Saada,
> I had healed my soul before repentance came.
> But she wept before I did: her tears drew mine; and I said,
> The merit belongs to the precedent.'"

"And" (resumed Salih the Pious) "if we stood on our faces in thy service, O King of the Age, a thousand years, yet had we not the might to requite thee, and this were but a scantling of thy due." The King thanked him with heartiest thanks and the Merman and Merwomen abode with him forty days' space, at the end of which Salih arose and kissed the ground before his brother in law, who asked ' What wantest thou, O Salih?" He answered, "O King of the Age, indeed thou hast done us overabundant favours, and we crave of thy bounties that thou deal charitably with us and grant us permission to depart; for we yearn after our people and country and kinsfolk and our homes; so will we never forsake thy service nor that of my sister and my nephew; and by Allah, O King of the Age, 'tis not pleasant to my heart to part from thee; but how shall we do, seeing that we have been reared in the sea and that the sojourn of the shore liketh us not?" When the King heard these words he rose to his feet and farewelled Salih the Sea born and his mother and his cousins, and all wept together, because of parting and presently they said to him, "Anon we will be with thee again, nor will we forsake thee, but will visit thee every few days." Then they flew off and descending into the sea, disappeared from sight.—And Shahrazad perceived the dawn of day and ceased saying her permitted say.

When it was the Seven Hundred and Forty-third Night,

---

[1] These lines have occurred in vol. iii. 264,. so I quote Lane ii. 499.

She continued, It hath reached me, O auspicious King, that the relations of Julnar the Sea-born farewelled the King and her, weeping together because of parting; then they flew off and descending into the depths disappeared from sight. After this King Shahriman showed the more kindness to Julnar and honoured her with increase of honour; and the little one grew up and flourished, whilst his maternal uncle and grandam and cousins visited the King every few days and abode with him a month or two months at a time. The boy ceased not to increase in beauty and loveliness with increase of years, till he attained the age of fifteen and was unique in his perfection and symmetry. He learnt writing and Koran reading; history, syntax and lexicography; archery, spearplay and horsemanship and what not else behoveth the sons of Kings; nor was there one of the children of the folk of the city, men or women, but would talk of the youth's charms, for he was of surpassing beauty and perfection, even such an one as is praised in the saying of the poet,[1]

> "The whiskers write upon his cheek, with ambergris on pearl,
> Two lines, as 'twere with jet upon an apple, line for line.
> Death harbours in his languid eye and slays with every glance,
> And in his cheek is drunkenness, and not in any wine."

And in that of another,

> "Upsprings from table of his lovely cheeks[2]
> A growth like broidery my wonder is:
> As 'twere a lamp that burns through night hung up
> Beneath the gloom[3] in chains of ambergris."

And indeed the King loved him with exceeding love, and summoning his Wazir and Emirs and the Chief Officers of state and Grandees of his realm, required of them a binding oath that they would make Badr Basim King over them after his sire; and they sware the oath gladly, for the sovran was liberal to the lieges, pleasant in parley and a very compend of goodness, saying naught but that wherein was advantage for the people. On the morrow Shahriman mounted, with all his troops and Emirs and Lords, and went forth into the city and returned. When they drew near the palace, the King dismounted, to wait upon his son who abode on horseback, and he and all the Emirs and Grandees bore the saddlecloth of honour before him, each and every of them bearing it in his turn, till they

---

[1] These lines occurred in vol. ii. 301. I quote Mr. Payne.
[2] Arab. "Khadd" = cheek from the eye-orbit to the place where the beard grows; also applied to the side of a rough highland, the side-planks of a litter, etc. etc.
[3] The black hair of youth.

came to the vestibule of the palace, where the Prince alighted and his father and the Emirs embraced him and seated him on the throne of Kingship, whilst they (including his sire) stood before him. Then Badr Basim judged the people, deposing the unjust and promoting the just and continued so doing till near upon noon, when he descended from the throne and went in to his mother, Julnar the Sea-born, with the crown upon his head, as he were the moon. When she saw him, with the King standing before him, she rose and kissing him, gave him joy of the Sultanate and wished him and his sire length of life and victory over their foes. He sat with her and rested till the hour of mid afternoon prayer, when he took horse and repaired, with the Emirs before him, to the Maydan plain, where he played at arms with his father and his lords, till night fall, when he returned to the palace, preceded by all the folk. He rode forth thus every day to the tilting ground, returning to sit and judge the people and do justice between earl and churl; and thus he continued doing a whole year, at the end of which he began to ride out a-hunting and a-chasing and to go round about in the cities and countries under his rule, proclaiming security and satisfaction and doing after the fashion of Kings; and he was unique among the people of his day for glory and valour and just dealing among the subjects. And it chanced that one day the old King fell sick and his fluttering heart forebode him of translation to the Mansion of Eternity. His sickness grew upon him till he was nigh upon death, when he called his son and commended his mother and subjects to his care and caused all the Emirs and Grandees once more swear allegiance to the Prince and assured himself of them by strongest oaths; after which he lingered a few days and departed to the mercy of Almighty Allah. His son and widow and all the Emirs and Wazirs and Lords mourned over him, and they built him a tomb and buried him therein. They ceased not ceremonially to mourn for him a whole month, till Salih and his mother and cousins arrived and condoled with their grieving for the King and said, "O Julnar, though the King be dead, yet hath he left this noble and peerless youth, and not dead is whoso leaveth the like of him, the rending lion and the shining moon."—And Shahrazad perceived the dawn of day and ceased to say her permitted say.

When it was the Seven Hundred and Forty-fourth Night,

She pursued, It hath reached me, O auspicious King, that Salih brother of Julnar and her mother and cousins said to her, "Albeit the King be dead, yet hath he left behind him as successor this noble and peerless youth, the rending lion and the shining moon." Thereupon the Grandees and notables of the Empire went in to King Badr Basim and said to him, "O King, there is no harm in mourning for the late sovran: but overmourning beseemeth none save women; wherefore occupy thou not thy heart and our hearts with mourning for thy sire; inasmuch as he hath left thee behind him, and whoso leaveth the like of thee is not dead." Then they comforted him and diverted him and lastly carried him to the bath. When he came out of the Hammam, he donned a rich robe, purfled with gold and embroidered with jewels and jacinths; and, setting the royal crown on his head, sat down on his throne of kingship and ordered the affairs of the folk, doing equal justice between strong and weak, and exacting from the prince the dues of the pauper; wherefore the people loved him with exceeding love. Thus he continued doing for a full year, whilst, every now and then. his kinsfolk of the sea visited him, and his life was pleasant and his eye was cooled. Now it came to pass that his uncle Salih went in one night of the nights to Julnar and saluted her; whereupon she rose and embracing him seated him by her side and asked him, "O my brother, how art thou and my mother and my cousins?" He answered, "O my sister, they are well and glad and in good case, lacking naught save a sight of thy face." Then she set somewhat of food before him and he ate, after which talk ensued between the twain and they spake of King Badr Basim and his beauty and loveliness, his symmetry and skill in cavalarice and cleverness and good breeding. Now Badr was propped upon his elbow hard by them; and, hearing his mother and uncle speak of him, he feigned sleep and listened to their talk.[1] Presently Salih said to his sister, "Thy son is now seventeen years old and is unmarried, and I fear lest mishap befal him and he have no son; wherefore it is my desire to marry him to a Princess of the princesses of the sea, who shall be a match for him in beauty and loveliness." Quoth Julnar, "Name them to me for I know them all." So Salih proceeded to enumerate them to her, one by one, but to each she said, "I like not this one for my son; I will not marry him but to one who is his equal in beauty and loveliness and wit and piety and good breeding and magnanimity and dominion and rank and lineage."[2] Quoth Salih, "I know none other of the daughters of the Kings of the sea, for I have numbered to thee more than an hundred girls and not one of them pleaseth thee: but see, O my sister, whether thy son be asleep or no." So she felt Badr and finding on him the signs of slumber said to Salih, "He is asleep; what hast thou to say and what is thine object in making sure his sleeping?" Replied he, "O my sister, know that I have bethought me of a Mermaid of the mermaids who befitteth thy son; but I fear to name her, lest he be awake and his heart be taken with her love and maybe we shall be unable to win to her; so should he and we and the Grandees of the realm be wearied in vain and trouble betide us through this; for, as saith the poet,

---

[1] This manner of listening is not held dishonourable amongst Arabs or Easterns generally; who, however, hear as little good of themselves as Westerns declare in proverb.

[2] Arab. "Hasab wa nasab," before explained as inherited degree and acquired dignity. See vol. iv. 171.

'Love, at first sight, is a spurt of spray;[1]
But a spreading sea when it gaineth sway.'"

When she heard these words, she cried, "Tell me the condition of this girl, and her name for I know all the damsels of the sea, Kings' daughters and others; and, if I judge her worthy of him, I will demand her in marriage for him of her father, though I spend on her whatso my hand possesseth. So recount to me all anent her and fear naught, for my son sleepeth." Quoth Salih, "I fear lest he be awake; and the poet saith,

'I loved him, soon as his praise I heard;
For ear oft loveth ere eye survey.'"

But Julnar said, "Speak out and be brief and fear not, O my brother." So he said, "By Allah, O my sister, none is worthy of thy son save the Princess Jauharah, daughter of King Al-Samandal,[2] for that she is like unto him in beauty and loveliness and brilliancy and perfection; nor is there found, in sea or on land, a sweeter or pleasanter of gifts than she; for she is prime in comeliness and seemlihead of face and symmetrical shape of perfect grace; her cheek is ruddy dight, her brow flower white, her teeth gem bright, her eyes blackest black and whitest white, her hips of heavy weight, her waist slight and her favour exquisite. When she turneth she shameth the wild cattle[3] and the gazelles and when she walketh, she breedeth envy in the willow branch: when she unveileth her face outshineth sun and moon and all who look upon her she enslaveth soon: sweet lipped and soft sided indeed is she." Now when Julnar heard what Salih said, she replied, "Thou sayest sooth, O my brother! By Allah, I have seen her many and many a time and she was my companion, when we were little ones but now we have no knowledge of each other, for constraint of distance; nor have I set eyes on her for eighteen years. By Allah none is worthy of my son but she!" Now Badr heard all they said and mastered what had passed, first and last, of these praises bestowed on Jauharah daughter of King Al-Samandal; so he fell in love with her on hearsay, pretending sleep the while, wherefore fire was kindled in his heart on her account full sore and he was drowned in a sea without bottom or shore.—And Shahrazad perceived the dawn of day and ceased

---

[1] Arab. "Mujájat" = spittle running from the mouth: hence Lane, "is like running saliva," which, in poetry is not pretty.

[2] Arab. and Heb. "Salmandra" from Pers. Samandal (—dar—duk—dun, etc.), a Salamander, a mouse which lives in fire, some say a bird in India and China and others confuse with the chameleon (Bochart Hiero. Part ii. chapt. vi).

[3] Arab. "Mahá" one of the four kinds of wild cows or bovine antelopes, bubalus, Antelope defassa, A. Ieucoryx, etc.

saying her permitted say.

When it was the Seven Hundred and Forty-fifth Night,

She resumed, It hath reached me, O auspicious King, that when King Badr Basim heard the words of his uncle Salih and his mother Julnar, praising the daughter of King Al–Samandal, a flame of fire burnt in his heart full sore and he was drowned in a sea which hath nor bottom nor shore. Then Salih, looking at his sister, exclaimed, "By Allah, O my sister, there is no greater fool among the Kings of the sea than her father nor one more violent of temper than he! So name thou not the girl to thy son, till we demand her in marriage of her father. If he favour us with his assent, we will praise Allah Almighty; and if he refuse us and will not give her to thy son to wife, we will say no more about it and seek another match." Answered Julnar, "Right is thy rede;" and they parleyed no more: but Badr passed the night with a heart on fire with passion for Princess Jauharah. However he concealed his case and spake not of her to his mother or his uncle, albeit he was on coals of fire for love of her. Now when it was morning, the King and his uncle went to the Hammam-bath and washed, after which they came forth and drank wine and the servants set food before them, whereof they and Julnar ate their sufficiency, and washed their hands. Then Salih rose and said to his nephew and sister, "With your leave, I would fain go to my mother and my folk for I have been with you some days and their hearts are troubled with awaiting me." But Badr Basim said to him, "Tarry with us this day;" and he consented. Then quoth the King, "Come, O my uncle, let us go forth to the garden." So they sallied forth and promenaded about the pastures and took their solace awhile, after which King Badr lay down under a shady tree, thinking to rest and sleep; but he remembered his uncle's description of the maiden and her beauty and loveliness and shed railing tears, reciting these two couplets,[1]

> "Were it said to me while the flame is burning within me,
> And the fire blazing in my heart and bowels,
> 'Wouldst thou rather that thou shouldest behold them
> Or a draught of pure water?'—I would answer, 'Them.'"

Then he sighed and wept and lamented, reciting these verses also,

> "Who shall save me from love of a lovely gazelle,
> Brighter browed than the sunshine, my bonnibel!
> My heart, erst free from her love, now burns

---

[1] These lines have occurred in vol. iii. 279; so I quote Lane (iii. 274) by way of variety; although I do not like his "bowels."

With fire for the maid of Al–Samandal."

When Salih heard what his nephew said, he smote hand upon hand and said, "There is no god but the God! Mohammed is the Apostle of God and there is no Majesty and there is no Might save in Allah, the Glorious, the Great!" adding, "O my son, heardest thou what passed between me and thy mother respecting Princess Jauharah?" Replied Badr Basim, "Yes, O my uncle, and I fell in love with her by hearsay through what I heard you say. Indeed, my heart cleaveth to her and I cannot live without her." Rejoined his uncle, "O King, let us return to thy mother and tell her how the case standeth and crave her leave that I may take thee with me and seek the Princess in marriage of her sire; after which we will farewell her and I and thou will return. Indeed, I fear to take thee and go without her leave, lest she be wroth with me; and verily the right would be on her side, for I should be the cause of her separation from us. Moreover, the city would be left without king and there would be none to govern the citizens and look to their affairs, so should the realm be disordered against thee and the kingship depart from thy hands." But Badr Basim, hearing these words, cried, "O my uncle, if I return to my mother and consult her on such matter, she will not suffer me to do this; wherefore I will not return to my mother nor consult her." And he wept before him and presently added, "I will go with thee and tell her not and after will return." When Salih heard what his nephew said, he was confused anent his case and said, "I crave help of the Almighty in any event." Then, seeing that Badr Basim was resolved to go with him, whether his mother would let him or no, he drew from his finger a seal ring, whereon were graven certain of the names of Allah the Most High, and gave it to him, saying, "Put this on thy finger, and thou shalt be safe from drowning and other perils and from the mischief of sea beasts and great fishes." So King Badr Basim took the ring and set it on his finger. Then they dove into the deep—And Shahrazad perceived the dawn of day and ceased to say her permitted say.

When it was the Seven Hundred and Forty-sixth Night,

She said, It hath reached me, O auspicious King, that Badr Basim and his uncle, after diving into the deep, fared on till they came to Salih's palace, where they found Badr Basim's grandmother, the mother of his mother, seated with her kinsfolk and, going in to them, kissed their hands. When the old Queen saw Badr, she rose to him and embracing him, kissed him between the eyes and said to him, "A blessed coming, O my son! How didst thou leave thy mother Julnar?" He replied, "She is well in health and fortune, and saluteth thee and her uncle's daughters." Then Salih related to his mother what had occurred between him and his sister and how King Badr Basim had fallen in love with the Princess Jauharah daughter of Al-Samandal by report and told her the whole tale from beginning to end adding, "He hath not come save to demand her in wedlock of her sire;" which when the old Queen heard, she was wroth against her son with exceeding wrath and sore troubled and concerned and said, "O Salih, O my son, in very sooth thou diddest wrong to name the Princess before thy nephew, knowing, as thou dost, that her father is stupid and violent, little of wit and tyrannical of temper, grudging his daughter to every suitor; for all the Monarchs of the Main have sought her hand, but he rejected them all; nay, he would none of them, saying, 'Ye are no match for her in beauty or in loveliness or in aught else.' Wherefore we fear to demand her in wedlock of him, lest he reject us, even as be hath rejected others; and we are a folk of high spirit and should return broken-hearted." Hearing these words Salih answered, "O my mother what is to do? For King Badr Basim saith, 'There is no help but that I seek her in marriage of her sire, though I expend my whole kingdom'; and he avoucheth that, an he take her not to wife, he will die of love for her and longing." And Salih continued, "He is handsomer and goodlier than she; his father was King of all the Persians, whose King he now is, and none is worthy of Jauharah save Badr Basim. Wherefore I purpose to carry her father a gift of jacinths and jewels befitting his dignity, and demand her of him in marriage. An he object to us that he is a King, behold, our man also is a King and the son of a King; or, if he object to us her beauty, behold our man is more beautiful than she; or, again, if he object to us the vastness of his dominion, behold our man's dominion is vaster than hers and her father's and numbereth more troops and guards, for that his kingdom is greater than that of Al-Samandal. Needs must I do my endeavour to further the desire of my sister's son, though it relieve me of my life; because I was the cause of whatso hath betided; and, even as I plunged him into the ocean of her love, so will I go about to marry him to her, and may Almighty Allah help me thereto!" Rejoined his mother, "Do as thou wilt, but beware of giving her father rough words, whenas thou speakest with him; for thou knowest his stupidity and violence and I fear lest he do thee a mischief, for he knoweth not respect for any." And Salih answered, "Hearkening and obedience." Then he sprang up and taking two bags full of gems such as rubies and bugles of emerald, noble ores and all manner jewels gave them to his servants to carry and set out with his nephew for the palace of Al–Samandal. When they came thither, he sought audience of the King and being admitted to his presence, kissed ground before him and saluted him with the goodliest Salam. The King rose to him and honouring him with the utmost honour, bade him be seated. So he sat down and presently the King said to him, "A blessed coming: indeed thou hast desolated us, O Salih! But what bringeth thee to us? Tell me thine errand that we may fulfil it to thee." Whereupon Salih arose and, kissing the ground a second time, said, "O King of the Age, my errand is to Allah and the magnanimous liege lord and the valiant lion, the report of whose good qualities the caravans far and near have dispread and whose renown for benefits and beneficence and clemency and graciousness and liberality to all climes and countries hath sped." Thereupon he opened the two bags and, displaying their contents before Al–Samandal, said to him, "O King of the Age, haply wilt thou accept my gift and by showing favour to me heal my heart."—And Shahrazad perceived the dawn of day and ceased saying her permitted say.

When it was the Seven Hundred and Forty-seventh Night,

She continued, It hath reached me, O auspicious King, that when Salih offered his gift to the King, saying, "My aim and end is that the Sovran show favour to me and heal my heart by accepting my present," King Al–Samandal asked, "With what object dost thou gift me with this gift? Tell me thy tale and acquaint me with thy requirement. An its accomplishment be in my power I will straightway accomplish it to thee and spare thee toil and trouble; and if I be unable thereunto, Allah compelleth not any soul aught beyond its power."[1] So Salih rose and kissing ground three times, said, "O King of the Age, that which I desire thou art indeed able to do; it is in thy power and thou art master thereof; and I impose not on the King a difficulty, nor am I Jinn-demented, that I should crave of the King a thing whereto he availeth not; for one of the sages saith, 'An thou wouldst be complied with ask that which can be readily supplied'. Wherefore, that of which I am come in quest, the King (whom Allah preserve!) is able to grant." The King replied, "Ask what thou wouldst have, and state thy case and seek thy need." Then said Salih,[2] "O King of the Age, know that I come as a suitor, seeking the unique pearl and the hoarded jewel, the Princess Jauharah, daughter of our lord the King; wherefore, O King disappoint thou not thy suitor." Now when the King heard this, he laughed till he fell backwards, in mockery of him and said, "O Salih, I had thought thee a man of worth and a youth of sense, seeking naught save what was reasonable and speaking not save advisedly. What then hath befallen thy reason and urged thee to this monstrous matter and mighty hazard, that thou seekest in marriage daughters of Kings, lords of cities and climates? Say me, art thou of a rank to aspire to this great eminence and hath thy wit failed thee to this extreme pass that thou affrontest me with this demand?" Replied Salih, "Allah amend the King! I seek her not for myself (albeit, an I did, I am her match and more than her match, for thou knowest that my father was King of the Kings of the sea, for all thou art this day our King), but I seek her for King Badr Basim, lord of the lands of the Persians and son of King Shahriman, whose puissance thou knowest. An thou object that

---

[1] The last verse (286) of chapt. ii. The Cow: "compelleth" in the sense of "burdeneth."

[2] Salih's speeches are euphuistic.

thou art a mighty great King, King Badr is a greater; and if thou object thy daughter's beauty King Badr is more beautiful than she and fairer of form and more excellent of rank and lineage; and he is the champion of the people of his day. Wherefore, if thou grant my request, O King of the Age thou wilt have set the thing in its stead; but, if thou deal arrogantly with us, thou wilt not use us justly nor travel with us the 'road which is straight'.[1] Moreover, O King, thou knowest that the Princess Jauharah, the daughter of our lord the King must needs be wedded and bedded, for the sage saith, a girl's lot is either grace of marriage or the grave.[2] Wherefore, an thou mean to marry her, my sister's son is worthier of her than any other man." Now when King Al–Samandal heard Salih's words, he was wroth with exceeding wrath; his reason well nigh fled and his soul was like to depart his body for rage, and he cried, "O dog, shall the like of thee dare to bespeak me thus and name my daughter in the assemblies,[3] saying that the son of thy sister Julnar is a match for her? Who art thou and who is this sister of thine and who is her son and who was his father,[4] that thou durst say to me such say and address me with such address? What are ye all, in comparison with my daughter, but dogs?" And he cried out to his pages, saying, "Take yonder gallows bird's head!" So they drew their swords and made for Salih but he fled and for the palace gate sped; and reaching the entrance, he found of his cousins and kinsfolk and servants, more than a thousand horse armed cap-à-pie in iron and close knitted mail-coats, hending in hand spears and naked swords glittering white. And these when they saw Salih come running out of the palace (they having been sent by his mother to his succour), questioned him and he told them what was to do; whereupon they knew that the King was a fool and violent tempered to boot. So they dismounted and baring their blades, went in to the King Al–Samandal, whom they found seated upon the throne of his Kingship, unaware of their coming and enraged against Salih with furious rage; and they beheld his eunuchs and pages and officers unprepared. When the King saw them enter, drawn brand in hand, he cried out to his people, saying "Woe to you! Take me the heads of these hounds!" But ere an hour had sped Al–Samandal's party were put to the route and relied upon flight, and Salih and his kinsfolk seized upon the King and pinioned him.—And Shahrazad perceived the dawn of day and ceased to say her permitted say.

---

[1] From the Fátihah.
[2] A truly Eastern saying, which ignores the "old maids" of the West.
[3] *i.e.* naming her before the lieges as if the speaker were her and his superior. It would have been more polite not to have gone beyond "the unique pearl and the hoarded jewel:" the offensive part of the speech was using the girl's name.
[4] Meaning emphatically that one and all were nobodies.

When it was the Seven Hundred and Forty-eighth Night,

She pursued, It hath reached me, O auspicious King, that when Salih and his kinsfolk pinioned the King, Princess Jauharah awoke and knew that her father was a captive and his guards slain. So she fled forth the palace to a certain island, and climbing up into a high tree, hid herself in its summit. Now when the two parties came to blows, some of King Al–Samandal's pages fled and Badr Basim meeting them, questioned them of their case and they told him what had happened. But when he heard that the King was a prisoner, Badr feared for himself and fled, saying in his heart, "Verily, all this turmoil is on my account and none is wanted but I." So he sought safety in flight, security to sight, knowing not whither he went; but destiny from Eternity fore-ordained crave him to the very island where the Princess had taken refuge, and he came to the very tree whereon she sat and threw himself down, like a dead man, thinking to lie and repose himself and knowing not there is no rest for the pursued, for none knoweth what Fate hideth for him in the future. As he lay down, he raised his eyes to the tree and they met the eyes of the Princess. So he looked at her and seeing her to be like the moon rising in the East, cried, "Glory to Him who fashioned yonder perfect form, Him who is the Creator of all things and who over all things is Almighty! Glory to the Great God, the Maker, the Shaper and Fashioner! By Allah, if my presentiments be true, this is Jauharah, daughter of King Al–Samandal! Methinks that, when she heard of our coming to blows with her father, she fled to this island and, happening upon this tree, hid herself on its head; but, if this be not the Princess herself, 'tis one yet goodlier than she." Then he bethought himself of her case and said in himself, "I will arise and lay hands on her and question her of her condition; and, if she be indeed the she, I will demand her in wedlock of herself and so win my wish." So he stood up and said to her, "O end of all desire, who art thou and who brought thee hither?" She looked at Badr Basim and seeing him to be as the full moon,[1] when it shineth from under the black cloud, slender of shape and sweet of smile answered, "O fair of fashion, I am Princess Jauharah, daughter of King Al–Samandal, and I took refuge in this place, because Salih and his host came to blows with my sire and slew his troops and took him prisoner, with some of his men, wherefore I fled, fearing for my very life," presently adding, "And I weet not what fortune hath done with my father." When King Badr Basim heard these words he marvelled with exceeding marvel at this strange chance, and thought: "Doubtless I have won my wish by the capture of her sire." Then he looked at Jauharah and said to her, "Come down, O my lady; for I am slain for love of thee and thine eyes have captivated me. On my account and thine are all these broils and battles; for thou must know that

---

[1] Arab Badr, the usual pun.

I am King Badr Basim, Lord of the Persians and Salih is my mother's brother and he it is who came to thy sire to demand thee of him in marriage. As for me, I have quitted my kingdom for thy sake, and our meeting here is the rarest coincidence. So come down to me and let us twain fare for thy father's palace, that I may beseech uncle Salih to release him and I may make thee my lawful wife." When Jauharah heard his words, she said in herself, "'Twas on this miserable gallows bird's account, then, that all this hath befallen and that my father hath fallen prisoner and his chamberlains and suite have been slain and I have been departed from my palace, a miserable exile and have fled for refuge to this island. But, an I devise not against him some device to defend myself from him, he will possess himself of me and take his will of me; for he is in love and for aught that he doeth a lover is not blamed.'" Then she beguiled him with winning words and soft speeches, whilst he knew not the perfidy against him she purposed, and asked him, "O my lord and light of my eyes, say me, art thou indeed King Badr Basim, son of Queen Julnar?" And he answered, "Yes, O my lady."—And Shahrazad perceived the dawn of day and ceased saying her permitted say.

When it was the Seven Hundred and Forty-ninth Night,

She resumed, It hath reached me, O auspicious King, that Jauharah, daughter of King Al–Samandal, asked the youth, "Art thou in very sooth King Badr Basim, son of Queen Julnar?" And he answered, "Yes, O my lady!" Then she, "May Allah cut off my father and gar his kingdom cease from him and heal not his heart neither avert from him strangerhood, if he could desire a comelier than thou or aught goodlier than these fair qualities of thine! By Allah, he is of little wit and judgment!" presently adding, "But, O King of the Age, punish him not for that he hath done; more by token that an thou love me a span, verily I love thee a cubit. Indeed, I have fallen into the net of thy love and am become of the number of thy slain. The love that was with thee hath transferred itself to me and there is left thereof with thee but a tithe of that which is with me." So saying, she came down from the tree and drawing near him strained him to her bosom and fell to kissing him; whereat passion and desire for her redoubled on him and doubting not but she loved him, he trusted in her, and returned her kisses and caresses. Presently he said to her, "By Allah, O Princess, my uncle Salih set forth to me not a fortieth part of thy charms; no, nor a quarter-carat[1] of the four and twenty." Then

---

[1] Arab. "Kirát" (χεράτιον) the bean of the Abrus precatorius, used as a weight in Arabia and India and as a bead for decoration in Africa. It is equal to four Kamhahs or wheat grains and about 3 grs. avoir.; and being the twenty fourth of a miskal, it is applied to that proportion of

Jauharah pressed him to her bosom and pronounced some unintelligible words; then spat on his face, saying, "Quit this form of man and take shape of bird, the handsomest of birds, white of robe, with red bill and legs." Hardly had she spoken, when King Badr Basim found himself transformed into a bird, the handsomest of birds, who shook himself and stood looking at her. Now Jauharah had with her one of her slave girls, by name Marsinah;[1] so she called her and said to her, "By Allah, but that I fear for the life of my father, who is his uncle's prisoner, I would kill him! Allah never requite him with good! How unlucky was his coming to us; for all this trouble is due to his hard headedness! But do thou, O slave girl, bear him to the Thirsty Island and leave him there to die of thirst." So Marsinah carried him to the island in question and would have returned and left him there but she said in herself, "By Allah, the lord of such beauty and loveliness deserveth not to die of thirst!" So she went forth from that island and brought him to another abounding in trees and fruits and rills and, setting him down there, returned to her mistress and told her, "I have left him on the Thirsty Island." Such was the case with Badr Basim; but as regards King Salih he sought for Jauharah after capturing the King and killing his folk; but, finding her not, returned to his palace and said to his mother, "Where is my sister's son, King Badr Basim?" "By Allah, O my son," replied she, "I know nothing of him! For when it reached him that you and King Al–Samandal had come to blows and that strife and slaughter had betided between you, he was affrighted and fled." When Salih heard this, he grieved for his nephew and said, "O my mother, by Allah, we have dealt negligently by King Badr and I fear lest he perish or lest one of King Al-Samandal's soldiers or his daughter Jauharah fall in with him. So should we come to shame with his mother and no good betide us from her, for that I took him without her leave." Then he despatched guards and scouts throughout the sea and elsewhere to seek for Badr; but they could learn no tidings of him; so they returned and told King Salih, wherefore cark and care redoubled on him and his breast was straitened for King Badr Basim. So far concerning nephew and uncle, but as for Julnar the Sea-born, after their departure she abode in expectation of them, but her son returned not and she heard no report of him. So when many days of fruitless waiting had gone by, she arose and going down into the sea, repaired to her mother, who sighting her rose to her and kissed her and embraced her, as did the Mermaids her cousins. Then she questioned her mother of King Badr Basim, and she answered, saying, "O my daughter, of a truth he came hither with his

---

everything. Thus the Arabs say of a perfect man, "He is of four-and-twenty Kirát" *i.e.* pure gold. See vol. iii. 239.

[1] The (she) myrtle: Kazimirski (A. de Biberstein) Dictionnaire Arabe–Francais (Pairs Maisonneuve 1867) gives Marsín = Rose de Jericho: myrte.

uncle, who took jacinths and jewels and carrying them to King Al–Samandal, demanded his daughter in marriage for thy son but he consented not and was violent against thy brother in words. Now I had sent Salih nigh upon a thousand horse and a battle befel between him and King Al–Samandal; but Allah aided thy brother against him, and he slew his guards and troops and took himself prisoner. Meanwhile, tidings of this reached thy son, and it would seem as if he feared for himself; wherefore he fled forth from us, without our will, and returned not to us, nor have we heard any news of him." Then Julnar enquired for King Salih, and his mother said, "He is seated on the throne of his kingship, in the stead of King Al–Samandal, and hath sent in all directions to seek thy son and Princess Jauharah." When Julnar heard the maternal words, she mourned for her son with sad mourning and was highly incensed against her brother Salih for that he had taken him and gone down with him into the sea without her leave; and she said, "O my mother, I fear for our realm; as I came to thee without letting any know; and I dread tarrying with thee, lest the state fall into disorder and the kingdom pass from our hands. Wherefore I deem best to return and govern the reign till it please Allah to order our son's affair for us. But look ye forget him not neither neglect his case; for should he come to any harm, it would infallibly kill me, since I see not the world save in him and delight but in his life." She replied, "With love and gladness, O my daughter. Ask not what we suffer by reason of his loss and absence." Then she sent to seek for her grandson, whilst Julnar returned to her kingdom, weeping-eyed and heavy-hearted, and indeed the gladness of the world was straitened upon her.—And Shahrazad perceived the dawn of day and ceased to say her permitted say.

When it was the Seven Hundred and Fiftieth Night,

She said, It hath reached me, O auspicious King, that when Queen Juluar returned from her mother to her own realm, her breast was straitened and she was in ill-case. So fared it with her; but as regards King Badr Basim, after Princess Jauharah had ensorcelled him and had sent him with her handmaid to the Thirsty Island, saying, "Leave him there to die of thirst," and Marsinah had set him down in a green islet, he abode days and nights in the semblance of a bird eating of its fruits and drinking of its waters and knowing not whither to go nor how to fly; till, one day, there came a certain fowler to the island to catch somewhat wherewithal to get his living. He espied King Badr Basim in his form of a white robed bird, with red bill and legs, captivating the sight and bewildering the thought; and, looking thereat, said in himself "Verily, yonder is a beautiful bird: never saw I its like in fairness or form." So he cast his net over Badr and taking him, carried him to the town, mentally resolved to sell him for a high price. On his way one of the townsfolk accosted him and said, "For how much this fowl, O fowler?" Quoth the fowler, "What wilt thou do with him an thou buy him?" Answered the other, "I will cut his throat and eat him;" whereupon said the birder, "Who could have the heart to kill this bird and eat him? Verily, I mean to present him to our King, who will give me more than thou wouldest give me and will not kill him, but will divert himself by gazing upon his beauty and grace, for in all my life, since I have been a fowler, I never saw his like among land game or water fowl. The utmost thou wouldst give me for him, however much thou covet him, would be a dirham, and, by Allah Almighty I will not sell him!" Then he carried the bird up to the King's palace and when the King saw it, its beauty and grace pleased him and the red colour of its beak and legs. So he sent an eunuch to buy it, who accosted the fowler and said to him, "Wilt thou sell this bird?" Answered he, "Nay, 'tis a gift from me to the King."[1] So the eunuch carried the bird to the King and told him what the man had said; and he took it and gave the fowler ten dinars, whereupon he kissed ground and fared forth. Then the eunuch carried the bird to the palace and placing him in a fine cage, hung him up after setting meat and drink by him. When the King came down from the Divan, he said to the eunuch, "Where is the bird? Bring it to me, that I may look upon it; for, by Allah, 'tis beautiful!" So the eunuch brought the cage and set it between the hands of the King, who looked and seeing the food untouched, said, "By Allah, I wis not what it will eat, that I may nourish it!" Then he called for food and they laid the tables and the King ate. Now when the bird saw the flesh and meats and fruits and sweet meats, he ate of all that was upon the trays before the King, whereat the Sovran and all the bystanders marvelled and the King said to his attendants, eunuchs and Mamelukes, "In all my life I never saw a bird eat as doth this bird!" Then he sent an eunuch to fetch his wife that she might enjoy looking upon the bird, and he went in to summon her and said, "O my lady, the King desireth thy presence, that thou mayst divert thyself with the sight of a bird he hath bought. When we set on the food, it flew down from its cage and perching on the table, ate of all that was thereon. So arise, O my lady, and solace thee with the sight for it is goodly of aspect and is a wonder of the wonders of the age." Hearing these words she came in haste; but, when she noted the bird, she veiled her face and turned to fare away. The King rose up and looking at her, asked, "Why dost thou veil thy face when there is none in presence save the women and eunuchs who wait on thee and thy husband?" Answered she, "O King, this bird is no bird, but a man like thyself." He rejoined, "Thou liest, this is too much of a jest. How should he be other than a bird?"; and she "O King, by Allah, I do not jest with thee nor do I tell thee aught but the truth; for verily this bird is King Badr Basim, son of

---

[1] Needless to note that the fowler had a right to expect a return present worth double or treble the price of his gift. Such is the universal practice of the East: in the West the extortioner says, "I leave it to you, sir!"

King Shahriman, Lord of the land of the Persians, and his mother is Julnar the Sea-born."—And Shahrazad perceived the dawn of day and ceased saying her permitted say.

When it was the Seven Hundred and Fifty-first Night,

She continued, It hath reached me, O auspicious King, that when the King's wife said to the King, "Verily, this is no bird but a man like thyself: he is King Badr Basim son of King Shariman and his mother is Julnar the Sea born," quoth the King, "And how came he in this shape?"; and quoth she, "Princess Jauharah, daughter of King Al–Samandal, hath enchanted him:" and told him all that had passed with King Badr Basim from first to last.[1] The King marvelled exceedingly at his wife's words and conjured her, on his life, to free Badr from his enchantment (for she was the notablest enchantress of her age), and not leave him in torment, saying, "May Almighty Allah cut off Jauharah's hand, for a foul witch as she is! How little is her faith and how great her craft and perfidy!" Said the Queen, "Do thou say to him, 'O Badr Basim, enter yonder closet!'" So the King bade him enter the closet and he went in obediently. Then the Queen veiled her face and taking in her hand a cup of water,[2] entered the closet where she pronounced over the water certain incomprehensible words ending with, "By the virtue of these mighty names and holy verses and by the majesty of Allah Almighty, Creator of heaven and earth, the Quickener of the dead and Appointer of the means of daily bread and the terms determined, quit this thy form wherein thou art and return to the shape in which the Lord created thee!" Hardly had she made an end of her words, when the bird trembled once and became a man; and the King saw before him a handsome youth, than whom on earth's face was none goodlier. But when King Badr Basim found himself thus restored to his own form he cried, "There is no god but the God and Mohammed is the Apostle of God! Glory be to the Creator of all creatures and Provider of their provision, and Ordainer of their life terms preordained!" Then he kissed the King's hand and wished him long life, and the King kissed his head and said to him, "O Badr Basim, tell me thy history from commencement to conclusion." So he told him his whole tale, concealing naught; and the King marvelled thereat and said to him, "O Badr Basim, Allah hath saved thee from the spell: but what hath thy judgment decided and what thinkest thou to do?" Replied he, "O King of the Age, I desire

---

[1] And she does tell him all that the reader well knows.
[2] This was for sprinkling him, but the texts omit that operation. Arabic has distinct terms for various forms of metamorphosis. "Naskh" is change from a lower to a higher, as beast to man; "Maskh" (the common expression) is the reverse, "Raskh" is from animate to inanimate (man to stone) and "Faskh" is absolute wasting away to corruption.

thy bounty that thou equip me a ship with a company of thy servants and all that is needful; for 'tis long since I have been absent and I dread lest the kingdom depart from me. And I misdoubt me my mother is dead of grief for my loss, and this doubt is the stronger for that she knoweth not what is come of me nor whether I am alive or dead. Wherefore, I beseech thee, O King, to crown thy favours to me by granting me what I seek." The King, after beholding the beauty and grace of Badr Basim and listening to his sweet speech, said, "I hear and obey." So he fitted him out a ship, to which he transported all that was needful and which he manned with a company of his servants; and Badr Basim set sail in it, after having taken leave of the King. They sailed over the sea ten successive days with a favouring wind; but, on the eleventh day, the ocean became troubled with exceeding trouble, the ship rose and fell and the sailors were powerless to govern her. So they drifted at the mercy of the waves, till the craft neared a rock in mid-sea which fell upon her[1] and broke her up and all on board were drowned, save King Badr Basim who got astride one of the planks of the vessel, after having been nigh upon destruction. The plank ceased not to be borne by the set of the sea, whilst he knew not whither he went and had no means of directing its motion, as the wind and waves wrought for three whole days. But on the fourth the plank grounded with him on the sea shore where he sighted a white city, as it were a dove passing white, built upon a tongue of land that jutted out into the deep and it was goodly of ordinance, with high towers and lofty walls against which the waves beat. When Badr Basim saw this, he rejoiced with exceeding joy, for he was well-nigh dead of hunger and thirst, and dismounting from the plank, would have gone up the beach to the city; but there came down to him mules and asses and horses, in number as the see sends and fell to striking at him and staying him from landing. So he swam round to the back of the city, where he waded to shore and entering the place, found none therein and marvelled at this, saying, "Would I knew to whom cloth this city belong, wherein is no lord nor any liege, and whence came these mules and asses and horses that hindered me from landing." And he mused over his case. Then he walked on at hazard till he espied an old man, a grocer.[2] So he saluted him and the other returned his salam and seeing him to be a handsome young man, said to him, "O youth, whence comest thou and what brought thee

---

[1] I render this improbable detail literally: it can only mean that the ship was dashed against a rock.

[2] Who was probably squatting on his shop counter. The "Bakkál" (who must not be confounded with the épicier), lit. "vender of herbs" = greengrocer, and according to Richardson used incorrectly for Baddál (?) vendor of provisions. Popularly it is applied to a seller of oil, honey, butter and fruit, like the Ital. "Pizzicagnolo" = Salsamentarius, and in North–West Africa to an inn-keeper.

to this city?" Badr told him his story; at which the old man marvelled and said, "O my son, didst thou see any on thy way?" He replied, "Indeed, O my father, I wondered in good sooth to sight a city void of folk." Quoth the Shaykh, my son, come up into the shop, lest thou perish." So Badr Basim went up into the shop and sat down; whereupon the old man set before him somewhat of food, saying, "O my son, enter the inner shop; glory be to Him who hath preserved thee from yonder she-Sathanas!" King Badr Basim was sore affrighted at the grocer's words; but he ate his fill and washed his hands then glanced at his host and said to him, "O my lord, what is the meaning of these words? Verily thou hast made me fearful of this city and its folk." Replied the old man, "Know, O my son that this is the City of the Magicians and its Queen is as she were She-Satan, a sorceress and a mighty enchantress, passing crafty and perfidious exceedingly. All thou sawest of horses and mules and asses were once sons of Adam like thee and me; they were also strangers, for whoever entereth this city, being a young man like thyself this miscreant witch taketh him and hometh him for forty days, after which she enchanteth him, and he becometh a mule or a horse or an ass, of those animals thou sawest on the sea-shore."—And Shahrazad perceived the dawn of day and ceased to say her permitted say.

When it was the Seven Hundred and Fifty-second Night,

She pursued, It hath reached me, O auspicious King, that the old grocer related to King Badr Basim the history of the enchantress ending with, "All these people hath she spelled; and, when it was thy intent to land they feared lest thou be transmewed like themselves; so they counselled thee by signs that said, 'Land not,' of their solicitude for thee, fearing that haply she should do with thee like as she had done with them. She possessed herself of this city and seized it from its citizens by sorcery and her name is Queen Lab, which being interpreted, meaneth in Arabic 'Almanac of the Sun.'"[1] When Badr Basim heard what the old man said, he was affrighted with sore affright and trembled like reed in wind saying in himself, "Hardly do I feel me free from the affliction wherein I was by reason of sorcery, when Destiny casteth me into yet sorrier case!" And he fell a-musing over his condition and that which had betided him. When the Shaykh looked at him and saw the violence of his terror, he said to him, "O my son, come, sit at the threshold of the shop and look upon yonder creatures and upon their dress and complexion and that wherein

---

[1] Here the Shaykh is mistaken: he should have said, "The Sun in old Persian." "Almanac" simply makes nonsense of the Arabian Circe's name. In Arab. it is "Takwím," whence the Span. and Port. "Tacuino:" in Heb. Hakamathá-Takunah = sapientia dis positionis astrorum (Asiat. Research. iii.120).

they are by reason of gramarye and dread not; for the Queen and all in the city love and tender me and will not vex my heart or trouble my mind." So King Badr Basim came out and sat at the shop door, looking out upon the folk; and there passed by him a world of creatures without number. But when the people saw him, they accosted the grocer and said to him, "O elder, is this thy captive and thy prey gotten in these days?" The old man replied, "He is my brother's son, I heard that his father was dead; so I sent for him and brought him here that I might quench with him the fire of my home sickness." Quoth they, "Verily, he is a comely youth; but we fear for him from Queen Lab, lest she turn on thee with treachery and take him from thee, for she loveth handsome young men." Quoth the Shaykh, "The Queen will not gainsay my commandment, for she loveth and tendereth me; and when she shall know that he is my brother's son, she will not molest him or afflict me in him neither trouble my heart on his account." Then King Badr Basim abode some months with the grocer, eating and drinking, and the old man loved him with exceeding love. One day, as he sat in the shop according to his custom, behold, there came up a thousand eunuchs, with drawn swords and clad in various kinds of raiment and girt with jewelled girdles: all rode Arabian steeds and bore in baldrick Indian blades. They saluted the grocer, as they passed his shop and were followed by a thousand damsels like moons, clad in various raiments of silks and satins fringed with gold and embroidered with jewels of sorts, and spears were slung to their shoulders. In their midst rode a damsel mounted on a Rabite mare, saddled with a saddle of gold set with various kinds of jewels and jacinths; and they reached in a body the Shaykh's shop. The damsels saluted him and passed on, till, lo and behold! up came Queen Lab, in great state, and seeing King Badr Basim sitting in the shop, as he were the moon at its full, was amazed at his beauty and loveliness and became passionately enamoured of him, and distraught with desire of him. So she alighted and sitting down by King Badr Basim said to the old man, "Whence hadst thou this handsome one?"; and the Shaykh replied, "He is my brother's son, and is lately come to me." Quoth Lab, "Let him be with me this night, that I may talk with him;' and quoth the old man, "Wilt thou take him from me and not enchant him?" Said she, "Yes," and said he, Swear to me." So she sware to him that she would not do him any hurt or ensorcell him, and bidding bring him a fine horse, saddled and bridled with a golden bridle and decked with trappings all of gold set with jewels, gave the old man a thousand dinars saying, "Use this."[1] Then she took Badr Basim and carried him off, as he were the full moon on its fourteenth night, whilst all the folk, seeing his beauty, were grieved for him and said, "By Allah, verily, this youth deserveth not to be bewitched by yonder sorceress, the accursed!" Now King Badr Basim

---

[1] *i.e.* for thy daily expenses.

heard all they said, but was silent, committing his case to Allah Almighty, till they came to—And Shahrazad perceived the dawn of day and ceased saying her permitted say.

When it was the Seven Hundred and Fifty-third Night,

She resumed, It hath reached me, O auspicious King, that King Badr Basim ceased not faring with Queen Lab and her suite till they came to her palace-gate, where the Emirs and eunuchs and Lords of the realm took foot and she bade the Chamberlains dismiss her Officers and Grandees, who kissed ground and went away, whilst she entered the palace with Badr Basim and her eunuchs and women. Here he found a place, whose like he had never seen at all, for it was builded of gold and in its midst was a great basin brimfull of water midmost a vast flower-garden. He looked at the garden and saw it abounding in birds of various kinds and colours, warbling in all manner tongues and voices pleasurable and plaintive. And everywhere he beheld great state and dominion and said, "Glory be to God, who of His bounty and long suffering provideth those who serve other than Himself!" The Queen sat down at a latticed window overlooking the garden on a couch of ivory, whereon was a high bed, and King Badr Basim seated himself by her side. She kissed him and pressing him to her breast, bade her women bring a tray of food. So they brought a tray of red gold, inlaid with pearls and jewels and spread with all manner of viands and he and she ate, till they were satisfied, and washed their hands; after which the waiting women set on flagons of gold and silver and glass, together with all kinds of flowers and dishes of dried fruits. Then the Queen summoned the singing-women and there came ten maidens, as they were moons, bending all manner of musical instruments. Queen Lab crowned a cup and drinking it off, filled another and passed it to King Badr Basim, who took and drank; and they ceased not to drink till they had their sufficiency. Then she bade the damsels sing, and they sang all manner modes till it seemed to Badr Basim as if the palace danced with him for joy. His sense was ecstasied and his breast broadened, and he forgot his strangerhood and said in himself, "Verily, this Queen is young and beautiful[1] and I will never leave her; for her kingdom is vaster than my kingdom and she is fairer than Princess Jauharah." So he ceased not to drink with her till even tide came, when they lighted the lamps and waxen candles and diffused censer-perfumes; nor did they leave drinking, till they were both drunken, and the singing women sang the while. Then Queen Lab, being in liquor, rose from her

---

[1] Un adolescent aime toutes les femmes. Man is by nature polygamic whereas woman as a rule is monogamic and polyandrous only when tired of her lover. For the man, as has been truly said, loves the woman, but the love of the woman is for the love of the man.

seat and lay down on a bed and dismissing her women called to Badr Basim to come and sleep by her side. So he lay with her, in all delight of life till the morning.—And Shahrazad perceived the dawn of day and ceased to say her permitted say.

When it was the Seven Hundred and Fifty-fourth Night,

She said, It hath reached me, O auspicious King, that when the Queen awoke she repaired to the Hammam-bath in the palace, King Badr Basim being with her, and they bathed and were purified; after which she clad him in the finest of raiment and called for the service of wine. So the waiting women brought the drinking-gear and they drank. Presently, the Queen arose and taking Badr Basim by the hand, sat down with him on chairs and bade bring food, whereof they ate, and washed their hands. Then the damsels fetched the drinking gear and fruits and flowers and confections, and they ceased not to eat and drink,[1] whilst the singing-girls sang various airs till the evening. They gave not over eating and drinking and merry-making for a space of forty days, when the Queen said to him, "O Badr Basim, say me whether is the more pleasant, this place or the shop of thine uncle the grocer?" He replied, "By Allah, O Queen, this is the pleasenter, for my uncle is but a beggarly man, who vendeth pot-herbs." She laughed at his words and the twain lay together in the pleasantest of case till the morning, when King Badr Basim awoke from sleep and found not Queen Lab by his side, so he said, "Would Heaven I knew where can she have gone!" And indeed he was troubled at her absence and perplexed about the case, for she stayed away from him a great while and did not return; so he donned his dress and went seeking her but not finding her, and he said to himself, "Haply, she is gone to the flower-garden." Thereupon he went out into the garden and came to a running rill beside which he saw a white she-bird and on the stream-bank a tree full of birds of various colours, and he stood and watched the birds without their seeing him. And behold, a black bird flew down upon that white-she bird and fell to billing her pigeon-fashion, then he leapt on her and trod her three consecutive times, after which the bird changed and became a woman. Badr looked at her and lo! it was Queen Lab. So he knew that the black bird was a man transmewed and that she was enamoured of him and had transformed herself into a bird, that he might enjoy her; wherefore jealousy got hold upon him and he was wroth with the Queen because of the black bird. Then he returned to his place and

---

[1] I have already noted that the heroes and heroines of Eastern love-tales are always bonne fourchettes: they eat and drink hard enough to scandalise the sentimental amourist of the West; but it is understood that this abundant diet is necessary to qualify them for the Herculean labours of the love night.

lay down on the carpet-bed and after an hour or so she came back to him and fell to kissing him and jesting with him; but being sore incensed against her he answered her not a word. She saw what was to do with him and was assured that he had witnessed what befel her when she was a white bird and was trodden by the black bird; yet she discovered naught to him but concealed what ailed her. When he had done her need, he said to her, "O Queen, I would have thee give me leave to go to my uncle's shop, for I long after him and have not seen him these forty days." She replied, "Go to him but tarry not from me, for I cannot brook to be parted from thee, nor can I endure without thee an hour." He said, "I hear and I obey," and mounting, rode to the shop of the Shaykh, the grocer, who welcomed him and rose to him and embracing him said to him, "How hast thou fared with yonder idolatress?" He replied, "I was well in health and happiness till this last night," and told him what had passed in the garden with the black bird.[1] Now when the old man heard his words, he said, "Beware of her, for know that the birds upon the tree were all young men and strangers, whom she loved and enchanted and turned into birds. That black bird thou sawest was one of her Mamelukes whom she loved with exceeding love, till he cast his eyes upon one of her women, wherefore she changed him into a black bird";—And Shahrazad perceived the dawn of day and ceased saying her permitted say.

When it was the Seven Hundred and Fifty-fifth Night,

She continued, It hath reached me, O auspicious King, that when Badr Basim acquainted the old grocer with all the doings of Queen Lab and what he had seen of her proceedings, the Shaykh gave him to know that all the birds upon the tree were young men and strangers whom she had enchanted, and that the black bird was one of her Mamelukes whom she had transmewed. "And," continued the Shaykh, "whenas she lusteth after him she transformeth herself into a she-bird that he may enjoy her, for she still loveth him with passionate love. When she found that thou knewest of her case, she plotted evil against thee, for she loveth thee not wholly. But no harm shall betide thee from her, so long as I protect thee; therefore fear nothing; for I am a Moslem, by name Abdallah, and there is none in my day more magical than I; yet do I not make use of gramarye save upon constraint. Many a time have I put to naught the sorceries of yonder accursed and delivered folk from her, and I care not for her, because she can do me no hurt: nay, she feareth me with exceeding fear, as do all in the city who, like her, are magicians and serve the fire, not the Omnipotent Sire. So to-morrow, come thou to me and tell me what she doth with thee; for this very night she will cast about to

---

[1] Here again a little excision is necessary; the reader already knows all about it.

destroy thee, and I will tell thee how thou shalt do with her, that thou mayst save thyself from her malice." Then King Badr Basim farewelled the Shaykh and returned to the Queen whom he found awaiting him. When she saw him, she rose and seating him and welcoming him brought him meat and drink and the two ate till they had enough and washed their hands; after which she called for wine and they drank till the night was well nigh half spent, when she plied him with cup after cup till he was drunken and lost sense[1] and wit. When she saw him thus, she said to him, "I conjure thee by Allah and by whatso thou worshippest, if I ask thee a question wilt thou inform me rightly and answer me truly?" And he being drunken, answered, "Yes, O my lady." Quoth she, "O my lord and light of mine eyes, when thou awokest last night and foundest me not, thou soughtest me, till thou sawest me in the garden under the guise of a white she-bird, and also thou sawest the black bird leap on me and tread me. Now I will tell the truth of this matter. That black bird was one of my Mamelukes, whom I loved with exceeding love; but one day he cast his eyes upon a certain of my slave-girls, wherefore jealousy gat hold upon me and I transformed him by my spells into a black bird and her I slew. But now I cannot endure without him a single hour, so, whenever I lust after him, I change myself into a she—bird and go to him, that he may leap me and enjoy me, even as thou hast seen. Art thou not therefore incensed against me, because of this, albeit by the virtue of Fire and Light, Shade and Heat, I love thee more than ever and have made thee my portion of the world?" He answered (being drunken), "Thy conjecture of the cause of my rage is correct, and it had no reason other than this." With this she embraced him and kissed him and made great show of love to him; then she lay down to sleep and he by her side Presently about midnight she rose from the carpet-bed and King Badr Basim was awake; but he feigned sleep and watched stealthily to see what she would do. She took out of a red bag a something red, which she planted a-middlemost the chamber, and it became a stream, running like the sea; after which she took a handful of barley and strewing it on the ground, watered it with water from the river; whereupon it became wheat in the ear, and she gathered it and ground it into flour. Then she set it aside and returning to bed, lay down by Badr Basim till morning when he arose and washed his face and asked her leave to visit the Shaykh his uncle. She gave him permission and he repaired to Abdallah and told him what had passed. The old man laughed and said, "By Allah, this miscreant witch plotteth mischief against thee; but reck thou not of her ever!" Then he gave him a pound of parched corn[2] and said to him, "Take this with thee

---

[1] Arab. "Hiss," prop. speaking a perception (as of sound or motion) as opposed to "Hades," a surmise or opinion without proof.
[2] Arab. "Sawík," the old and modern name for native frumenty, green grain (mostly barley) toasted, pounded, mixed with dates or sugar and

and know that, when she seeth it, she will ask thee, 'What is this and what wilt thou do with it?' Do thou answer, 'Abundance of good things is good'; and eat of it. Then will she bring forth to thee parched grain of her own and say to thee, 'Eat of this Sawik; and do thou feign to her that thou eatest thereof, but eat of this instead, and beware and have a care lest thou eat of hers even a grain; for, an thou eat so much as a grain thereof, her spells will have power over thee and she will enchant thee and say to thee, 'Leave this form of a man.' Whereupon thou wilt quit thine own shape for what shape she will. But, an thou eat not thereof, her enchantments will be null and void and no harm will betide thee therefrom; whereat she will be shamed with shame exceeding and say to thee, 'I did but jest with thee!' Then will she make a show of love and fondness to thee; but this will all be but hypocrisy in her and craft. And do thou also make a show of love to her and say to her, 'O my lady and light of mine eyes, eat of this parched barley and see how delicious it is.' And if she eat thereof, though it be but a grain, take water in thy hand and throw it in her face, saying, 'Quit this human form' (for what form soever thou wilt have her take). Then leave her and come to me and I will counsel thee what to do." So Badr Basim took leave of him and returning to the palace, went in to the Queen, who said to him, "Welcome and well come and good cheer to thee!" And she rose and kissed him, saying, "Thou hast tarried long from me, O my lord." He replied, "I have been with my uncle, and he gave me to eat of this Sawik." Quoth she, "We have better than that." Then she laid his parched Sawik in one plate and hers in another and said to him, "Eat of this, for 'tis better than thine." So he feigned to eat of it and when she thought he had done so, she took water in her hand and sprinkled him therewith, saying, "Quit this form, O thou gallows—bird, thou miserable, and take that of a mule one-eyed and foul of favour." But he changed not; which when she saw, she arose and went up to him and kissed him between the eyes, saying, "O my beloved, I did but jest with thee; bear me no malice because of this." Quoth he, "O my lady, I bear thee no whit of malice; nay, I am assured that thou lovest me: but eat of this my parched barley." So she ate a mouthful of Abdallah's Sawik; but no sooner had it settled in her stomach than she was convulsed; and King Badr Basim took water in his palm and threw it in her face, saying, "Quit this human form and take that of a dapple mule." No sooner had he spoken than she found herself changed into a she-mule, whereupon the tears rolled down her cheeks and she fell to rubbing her muzzle against his feet. Then he would have bridled her, but

---

eaten on journeys when cooking is impracticable. M. C. de Perceval (iii. 54), gives it a different and now unknown name; and Mr. Lane also applies it to "ptisane." It named the "Day of Sawaykah" (for which see Pilgrimage ii. 19), called by our popular authors the "War of the Meal-sacks."

she would not take the bit; so he left her and, going to the grocer, told him what had passed. Abdallah brought out for him a bridle and bade him rein her forthwith. So he took it to the palace, and when she saw him, she came up to him and he set the bit in her mouth and mounting her, rode forth to find the Shaykh. But when the old man saw her, he rose and said to her, "Almighty Allah confound thee, O accursed woman!" Then quoth he to Badr, "O my son, there is no more tarrying for thee in this city; so ride her and fare with her whither thou wilt and beware lest thou commit the bridle[1] to any." King Badr thanked him and farewelling him, fared on three days, without ceasing, till he drew near another city and there met him an old man, gray headed and comely, who said to him, "Whence comest thou, O my son?" Badr replied, "From the city of this witch"; and the old man said, "Thou art my guest to-night." He consented and went with him; but by the way behold, they met an old woman, who wept when she saw the mule, and said, "There is no god but the God! Verily, this mule resembleth my son's she-mule, which is dead, and my heart acheth for her; so, Allah upon thee, O my lord, do thou sell her to me!" He replied, "By Allah, O my mother, I cannot sell her." But she cried, "Allah upon thee, do not refuse my request, for my son will surely be a dead man except I buy him this mule." And she importuned him, till he exclaimed, "I will not sell her save for a thousand dinars," saying in himself, "Whence should this old woman get a thousand gold pieces?" Thereupon she brought out from her girdle a purse containing a thousand ducats, which when King Badr Basim saw, he said, "O my mother, I did but jest with thee; I cannot sell her." But the old man looked at him and said, "O my son, in this city none may lie, for whoso lieth they put to death." So King Badr Basim lighted down from the mule.—And Shahrazad perceived the dawn of day and ceased to say her permitted say.

When it was the Seven Hundred and Fifty-sixth Night,

She pursued, It hath reached me, O auspicious King, that when Badr Basim dismounted from and delivered the mule to the old woman, she drew the bit from her mouth and, taking water in her hand, sprinkled the mule therewith, saying, "O my daughter, quit this shape for that form

---

[1] Mr. Keightley (H. 122–24 Tales and Popular Fictions, a book now somewhat obsolete) remarks, "There is nothing said about the bridle in the account of the sale (infra), but I am sure that in the original tale, Badr's misfortunes must have been owing to his having parted with it. In Chaucer's Squier's Tale the bridle would also appear to have been of some importance. "He quotes a story from the Notti Piacevoli of Straparola, the Milanese, published at Venice in 1550. And there is a popular story of the kind in Germany.

wherein thou wast aforetime!" Upon this she was straightway restored to her original semblance and the two women embraced and kissed each other. So King Badr Basim knew that the old woman was Queen Lab's mother and that he had been tricked and would have fled; when, lo! the old woman whistled a loud whistle and her call was obeyed by an Ifrit as he were a great mountain, whereat Badr was affrighted and stood still. Then the old woman mounted on the Ifrit's back, taking her daughter behind her and King Badr Basim before her, and the Ifrit flew off with them; nor was it a full hour ere they were in the palace of Queen Lab, who sat down on the throne of kingship and said to Badr, "Gallows-bird that thou art, now am I come hither and have attained to that I desired and soon will I show thee how I will do with thee and with yonder old man the grocer! How many favours have I shown him! Yet he cloth me frowardness; for thou hast not attained thine end but by means of him." Then she took water and sprinkled him therewith, saying, "Quit the shape wherein thou art for the form of a foul-favoured fowl, the foulest of all fowls"; and she set him in a cage and cut off from him meat and drink; but one of her women seeing this cruelty, took compassion on him and gave him food and water without her knowledge. One day, the damsel took her mistress at unawares and going forth the palace, repaired to the old grocer, to whom she told the whole case, saying, "Queen Lab is minded to make an end of thy brother's son." The Shaykh thanked her and said, "There is no help but that I take the city from her and make thee Queen thereof in her stead." Then he whistled a loud whistle and there came forth to him an Ifrit with four wings, to whom he said, "Take up this damsel and carry her to the city of Julnar the Sea-born and her mother Faráshah[1] for they twain are the most powerful magicians on face of earth." And he said to the damsel, "When thou comest thither, tell them that King Badr Basim is Queen Lab's captive." Then the Ifrit took up his load and, flying off with her, in a little while set her down upon the terrace roof of Queen Julnar's palace. So she descended and going in to the Queen, kissed the earth and told her what had passed to her son, first and last, whereupon Julnar rose to her and entreated her with honour and thanked her. Then she let beat the drums in the city and acquainted her lieges and the lords of her realm with the good news that King Badr Basim was found after which she and her mother Farashah and her brother Salih assembled all the tribes of the Jinn and the troops of the main; for the Kings of the Jinn obeyed them since the taking of King Al-Samandal. Presently they all flew up into the air and lighting down on the city of the sorceress, sacked the town and the palace and slew all the

---

[1] Here, for the first time we find the name of the mother who has often been mentioned in the story. Faráshah is the fem. or singular form of "Farásh," a butterfly, a moth. Lane notes that his Shaykh gives it the very unusual sense of "a locust."

Unbelievers therein in the twinkling of an eye. Then said Julnar to the damsel, "Where is my son?" And the slave girl brought her the cage and signing to the bird within, cried, "This is thy son." So Julnar took him forth of the cage and sprinkled him with water, saying, "Quit this shape for the form wherein thou wast aforetime;" nor had she made an end of her speech ere he shook and became a man as before: whereupon his mother, seeing him restored to human shape, embraced him and he wept with sore weeping. On like wise did his uncle Salih and his grandmother and the daughters of his uncle and fell to kissing his hands and feet. Then Julnar sent for Shaykh Abdallah and thanking him for his kind dealing with her son, married him to the damsel, whom he had despatched to her with news of him, and made him King of the city. Moreover, she summoned those who survived of the citizens (and they were Moslems), and made them swear fealty to him and take the oath of loyalty, whereto they replied, "Hearkening and obedience!" Then she and her company farewelled him and returned to their own capital. The townsfolk came out to meet them, with drums beating, and decorated the place three days and held high festival, of the greatness of their joy for the return of their King Badr Basim. After this Badr said to his mother, "O my mother, naught remains but that I marry and we be all united." She replied, "Right is thy rede, O my son, but wait till we ask who befitteth thee among the daughters of the Kings." And his grandmother Farashah, and the daughters of both his uncles said, "O Badr Basim, we will help thee to win thy wish forthright." Then each of them arose and fared forth questing in the lands, whilst Julnar sent out her waiting women on the necks of Ifrits, bidding them leave not a city nor a King's palace without noting all the handsome girls that were therein. But, when King Badr Basim saw the trouble they were taking in this matter, he said to Julnar, "O my mother, leave this thing, for none will content me save Jauharah, daughter of King Al–Samandal; for that she is indeed a jewel,[1] according to her name." Replied Julnar, "I know that which thou seekest;" and bade forthright bring Al–Samandal the King. As soon as he was present, she sent for Badr Basim and acquainted him with the King's coming, whereupon he went in to him. Now when Al–Samandal was aware of his presence, he rose to him and saluted him and bade him welcome; and King Badr Basim demanded of him his daughter Jauharah in marriage. Quoth he, "She is thine handmaid and at thy service and disposition," and despatched some of his suite bidding them seek her abode and, after telling her that her sire was in the hands of King Badr Basim, to bring her forthright. So they flew up into the air and disappeared and they returned after a while, with the Princess who, as soon as she saw her father, went up to him and threw her arms round his neck. Then looking at her he

---

[1] Punning upon Jauharah = "a jewel" a name which has an Hibernian smack.

said, "O my daughter, know that I have given thee in wedlock to this magnanimous Sovran, and valiant lion King Badr Basim, son of Queen Julnar the Sea-born, for that he is the goodliest of the folk of his day and most powerful and the most exalted of them in degree and the noblest in rank; he befitteth none but thee and thou none but him." Answered she, "I may not gainsay thee, O my sire do as thou wilt, for indeed chagrin and despite are at an end, and I am one of his handmaids." So they summoned the Kazi and the witnesses who drew up the marriage contract between King Badr Basim and the Princess Jauharah, and the citizens decorated the city and beat the drums of rejoicing, and they released all who were in the jails, whilst the King clothed the widows and the orphans and bestowed robes of honour upon the Lords of the Realm and Emirs and Grandees: and they made bride-feasts and held high festival night and morn ten days, at the end of which time they displayed the bride, in nine different dresses, before King Badr Basim who bestowed an honourable robe upon King Al-Samandal and sent him back to his country and people and kinsfolk. And they ceased not from living the most delectable of life and the most solaceful of days, eating and drinking and enjoying every luxury, till there came to them the Destroyer of delights and the Sunderer of Societies; and this is the end of their story,[1] may Allah have mercy on them all! Moreover, O auspicious King, a tale is also told anent

Source:
Burton, Sir Richard. *Lady Burton's Edition of Her Husband's Arabian Nights, Vol. 4.* Lady Isabel Burton and Justin Huntly McCarthy, editors. London: Waterlow & Sons, 1886.

---

[1] In the old version "All the lovers of the Magic Queen resumed their pristine forms as soon as she ceased to live;" moreover, they were all sons of kings, princes, or persons of high degree.

125. Abdullah the Fisherman and Abdullah the Merman[1]

Arabian Nights

THERE was once a Fisherman named Abdullah, who had a large family, to wit, nine children and their mother, so was he poor, very poor, owning naught save his net. Every day he used to go to the sea a-fishing, and if he caught little, he sold it and spent the price on his children, after the measure of that which Allah vouchsafed him of provision; but if he caught much, he would cook a good mess of meat and buy fruit and spend without stint till nothing was left him, saying to himself, "The daily bread of to-morrow will come to-morrow." Presently, his wife gave birth to another child, making a total of ten, and it chanced that day that he had nothing at all; so she said to him, "O my master, see and get me somewhat wherewithal I may sustain myself." Quoth he, "I am going (under favour of Almighty Allah) this day seawards to fish on the luck of this new-born child, that we may see its fair fortune;" and quoth she, "Put thy trust in Allah!" So he took his net and went down to the sea-shore, where he cast it on the luck of the little one, saying, "O my God, make his living of ease not of unease, and abundant, not scant!" Then he waited awhile and drew in the net, which came up full of rubbish and sand and pebbles and weeds, and he saw therein no sign of fish neither muchel nor little. He cast it again and waited, then drew it in, but found no catch in it, and threw it a third and a fourth and a fifth time still not a single fish came up. So he removed to another place beseeching his daily bread of Allah Almighty and thus he kept working till the end of the day, but caught not so much as a minnow;[2] whereat he fell a-marvelling in

---

[1] The tale begins upon the model of "Júdar and his Brethren," vi. 213. Its hero's full name is Abdu'lláhi = Slave of Allah, which vulgar Egyptians pronounce Abdallah and purer speakers, Badawin and others, Abdullah: either form is therefore admissible. It is more common among Moslems but not unknown to Christians especially Syrians who borrow it from the Syriac Alloh. Mohammed is said to have said, "The names most approved by Allah are Abdu'llah, Abd al-Rahmán (Slave of the Compassionate) and such like" (Pilgrimage i. 20).

[2] Arab. "Sírah" here probably used of the Nile-sprat (Clupea Sprattus Linn.) or Sardine of which Forsk says, "Sardinn in Al–Yaman is applied to a Red Sea fish of the same name." Hasselquist the Swede notes that Egyptians stuff the Sardine with marjoram and eat it fried even when half putrid.

himself and said self-communing, "Hath Allah then created this new-born child without lot of provision? This may never, never be. He who slitteth the corners of the lips hath pledged Himself for its provision, because Almighty Allah is the Bountiful, the Provider!"[1] So saying, he shouldered his net and turned him homewards, broken-spirited and heavy at heart about his family, for that he had left them without food, more by token that his wife was in the straw. And as he continued trudging along and saying in himself, "How shall I do and what shall I say to the children to-night?" he came to a baker's oven and saw a crowd about it; for the season was one of dearth and in those days food was scant with the folk; so people were proffering the baker money, but he paid no heed to any of them, by reason of the dense crowd. The fisherman stood looking and snuffing he smell of the hot bread (and indeed his soul longed for it, by reason of his hunger), till the baker caught sight of him and cried out to him, "Come hither, O fisherman!" So he went up to him, and the baker said, "Dost thou want bread?" But he was silent. Quoth the baker, "Speak out and be not ashamed, for Allah is bountiful. An thou have no silver, I will give thee bread and have patience with thee till weal betide thee." And quoth the fisherman, "By Allah, O master, I have indeed no money! But give me bread enough for my family, and I will leave thee this net in pawn till the morrow." Rejoined the baker, "Nay, my poor fellow, this net is thy shop and the door of thy daily subsistence; so an thou pawn it, wherewithal wilt thou fish? Tell me how much will suffice thee?"; and replied the fisherman, "Ten half-dirhams' worth."[2] So he gave him ten Nusfs worth of bread and ten in silver saying, "Take these ten Nusfs and cook thyself a mess of meat therewith; so wilt thou owe me twenty, for which bring me fish to-morrow; but, an thou catch nothing again, come and take thy bread and thy ten Nusfs, and I will have patience with thee till better luck betide thee,"—And Shahrazad perceived the dawn of day and ceased saying her permitted say.

When it was the Nine Hundred and Forty-first Night,

She pursued, It hath reached me, O auspicious King, that the baker said to the fisherman, "Take whatso thou needest and I will have patience with thee till better luck betide thee, after the which thou shalt bring me fish for all thou owest me." Said the fisherman, Almighty Allah reward thee, and requite thee for me with all good!" Then he took the bread and the coins and went away, glad at heart, and buying what he could returned to his wife whom he found sitting up, soothing the children, who

---

[1] *i.e.* by declaring in the Koran (lxvii. 14; lxxiv. 39; lxxviii. 69; lxxxviii. 17), that each creature hath its appointed term and lot; especially "Thinketh man that he shall be left uncared for?" (xl. 36).

[2] Arab. "Nusf," see vol. ii. 37.

were weeping for hunger, and saying to them, "At once your father will be here with what ye may eat." So he set the bread before them and they ate, whilst he told his wife what had befallen him, and she said, "Allah is bountiful."[1] On the morrow, he shouldered his net and went forth of his house, saying, "I beseech thee, O Lord, to vouchsafe me this day that which shall whiten my face with the baker!"[2] When he came to the seashore, he proceeded to cast his net and pull it in; but there came up no fish therein; and he ceased not to toil thus till ended day but he caught nothing. Then he set out homewards, in great concern, and the way to his house lay past the baker's oven; so he said to himself, "How shall I go home? But I will hasten my pace that the baker may not see me." When he reached the shop, he saw a crowd about it and walked the faster, being ashamed to face his creditor; but the baker raised his eyes to him and cried out to him, saying, "Ho, fisherman! Come and take thy bread and spending-money. Meseems thou forgettest." Quoth Abdullah, "By Allah, I had not forgotten; but I was ashamed to face thee, because I have caught no fish this day;" and quoth the baker, "Be not ashamed. Said I not to thee, At thy leisure,[3] till better luck betide thee?" Then he gave him the bread and the ten Nusfs and he returned and told his wife, who said, "Allah is bountiful. Better luck shall yet betide thee and thou shalt give the baker his due, Inshallah." He ceased not doing on this wise forty days, betaking himself daily to the sea, from the rising of the sun to the going down thereof, and returning home without fish; and still he took bread and spending-money of the baker, who never once named the fish to him nor neglected him nor kept him waiting like the folk,[4] but gave him the bread and the ten half-dirhams without delay. Whenever the fisherman said to him, "O my brother, reckon with me," he would say, "Be off:[5] this is no time for reckoning. Wait till better luck betide thee, and then I will reckon with thee." And the fisherman would bless him and go away thanking him. On the one-and-fortieth day, he said to his

---

[1] Arab. "Allah Karím" (which Turks pronounce Kyerím) a consecrated formula used especially when a man would show himself resigned to "small mercies." The fisherman's wife was evidently pious as she was poor; and the description of the pauper household is simple and effective.
[2] This is repeated in the Mac. Edit. pp. 496–97; an instance amongst many of most careless editing.
[3] Arab. "Alà mahlak" (vulg.), a popular phrase, often corresponding with our "Take it coolly."
[4] For "He did not keep him waiting, as he did the rest of the folk." Lane prefers "nor neglected him as men generally would have done." But we are told supra that the baker "paid no heed to the folk by reason of the dense crowd."
[5] Arab. "Ruh!" the most abrupt form, whose sound is coarse and offensive as the Turkish yell, "Gyel!" = come here.

wife, "I have a mind to tear up the net and be quit of this life." She asked, "Why wilt thou do this?"; and he answered, "Meseems there is an end of my getting my daily bread from the waters. How long shall this last? By Allah, I burn with shame before the baker and I will go no more to the sea, so I may not pass by his oven, for I have none other way home; and every time I pass he calleth me and giveth me the bread and the ten silvers. How much longer shall I run in debt to him?" The wife replied, "Alhamdolillah—lauded be the Lord, the Most High, who hath inclined his heart to thee, so that he giveth thee our daily bread! What dislikest thou in this?"; and the husband rejoined, "I owe him now a mighty great sum of dirhams, and there is no doubt but that he will demand his due." "Hath he vexed thee with words?" "No, on the contrary, he still refuseth to reckon with me, saying, 'Wait till better luck betide thee.'" "If he press thee, say to him, 'Wait till there come the good luck for which we hope, thou and I.'" "And when will the good luck come that we hope for?" "Allah is bountiful." "Sooth thou speakest!" So saying he shouldered his net and went down to the sea-side, praying, "O Lord provide thou me, though but with one fish, that I may give it to the baker!" And he cast his net into the sea and pulling it in, found it heavy; so he tugged at it till he was tired with sore travail. But when he got it ashore, he found in it a dead donkey swollen and stinking; whereat his senses sickened and he freed it from the net, saying, "There is no Majesty and there is no Might save in Allah, the Glorious, the Great! Indeed, I can no more! I say to that wife of mine, 'There is no more provision for me in the waters; let me leave this craft.' And she still answereth me, 'Allah is bountiful: good will presently betide thee.' Is this dead ass the good whereof she speaketh?" And he grieved with the sorest grief. Then he turned to another place, so he might remove from the stench of the dead donkey, and cast his net there and waited a full hour: then he drew it in and found it heavy. Thereupon quoth he, "Good; we are hauling up all the dead donkeys in the sea and ridding it of its rubbish."[1] However he gave not over tugging at the net, till blood came from the palms of his hands, and when he got it ashore, he saw a man[2] in it and took him for one of the

---

[1] Bresl. Edit. xi. 50–51.
[2] Arab. "Ádami" = an Adamite, one descended from the mythical and typical Adam for whom see Philo Judæus. We are told in one place a few lines further on that the merman is of humankind; and in another that he is a kind of fish (Night dccccxlv). This belief in mermen, possible originating with the caricatures of the human face in the intelligent seal and stupid manatee, is universal. Al–Kazwini declares that a waterman with a tail was dried and exhibited, and that in Syria one of them was married to a woman and had by her a son "who understood the languages of both his parents." The fable was refined to perfect beauty by the Greeks: the mer-folk of the Arabs, Hindus and Northerners

Ifrits of the lord Solomon, whom he was wont to imprison in cucurbits of brass and cast him into the main, believing that the vessel had burst for length of years and that the Ifrit had come forth and fallen into the net; wherefore he fled from him, crying out and saying, "Mercy, mercy, O Ifrit of Solomon!" But the Adamite called out to him from within the net and said, "Come hither, O fisherman, and flee not from me; for I am human like thyself. Release me, so thou mayst get a recompense for me of Allah." Whenas he heard these words, the fisherman took heart and coming up to him, said to him, "Art thou not an Ifrit of the Jinn?"; and replied the other, "No: I am a mortal and a believer in Allah and His Apostle." Asked the fisherman, "Who threw thee into the sea?"; and the other answered, "I am of the children of the sea, and was going about therein, when thou castest the net over me. We are people who obey Allah's commandments and show loving-kindness unto the creatures of the Almighty, and but that I fear and dread to be of the disobedient, I had torn thy net; but I accept that which the Lord hath decreed unto me; wherefore by setting me free thou becomest my owner and I thy captive. Wilt thou then set me free for the love[1] of Almighty Allah and make a covenant with me and become my comrade? I will come to thee every day in this place, and do thou come to me and bring me a gift of the fruits of the land. For with you are grapes and figs and water-melons and peaches and pomegranates and so forth, and all thou bringest me will be acceptable unto me. Moreover, with us are coral and pearls and chrysolites and emeralds and rubies and other gems, and I will fill thee the basket, wherein thou bringest me the fruit, with precious stones of the jewels of the sea.[2] What sayest thou to this, O my brother?" Quoth the fisherman, "Be the Opening Chapter of the Koran between thee and me upon this!" So they recited together the Fátihah, and the fisherman loosed the Merman from the net and asked him, "What is thy name?" He replied, "My name is Abdullah of the sea; and if thou come hither and see me not, call out and say, 'Where are thou, O Abdullah, O Merman?' and I will be with thee."—And Shahrazad perceived the dawn of day and ceased to say her permitted say.

(Scandinavians, etc) are mere grotesques with green hair, etc. Art in its highest expression never left the shores of the Mediterranean, and there is no sign that it ever will.

[1] Here Lane translates "Wajh" lit. "the desire of seeing the face of God," and explains in a note that a "Muslim holds this to be the greatest happiness that can be enjoyed in Paradise." But I have noted that the tenet of seeing the countenance of the Creator, except by the eyes of spirit, is a much disputed point amongst Moslems.

[2] Artful enough is this contrast between the squalid condition of the starving fisherman and the gorgeous belongings of the Merman.

When it was the Nine Hundred and Forty-second Night,

She resumed, It hath reached me, O auspicious King, that Abdullah of the sea thus enjoined the other, "An thou come hither and see me not, call out and say, 'Where art thou, O Abdullah, O Merman?' and I will be with thee forthwith. But thou, what is thy name?" Quoth the fisherman, "My name also is Abdullah;" and quoth the other, "Thou art Abdullah of the land and I am Abdullah of the Sea; but tarry here till I go and fetch thee a present." And the fisherman repented him of having released him and said to himself, "How know I that he will come back to me? Indeed, he beguiled me, so that I loosed him, and now he will laugh at me.[1] Had I kept him, I might have made a show of him for the diversion of the city-folk and taken silver from all men and gone with him to the houses of the great." And he repented him of having set him free and said, "Thou hast let thy prey from thy hand away." But, as he was thus bemoaning his folly in releasing the prisoner, behold, Abdullah the merman returned to him, with both hands full of pearls and coral and smaragds and rubies and other gems, and said to him, "Take these, O my brother, and excuse me; had I a fish-basket[2] I would have filled it for thee." Abdullah the fisherman rejoiced and took the jewels from the Merman who said to him, "Every day come hither, before sunrise," and farewelling him, went down into the sea; whilst the other returned to the city, rejoicing, and stayed not walking till he came to the baker's oven and said to him, "O my brother, good luck is come to us at last; so do thou reckon with me." Answered the baker, "There needeth no reckoning. An thou have aught, give it me: and if thou have naught, take thy bread and spending-money and begone, against weal betide thee." Rejoined the fisherman, "O my friend, indeed weal hath betided me of Allah's bounty, and I owe thee much money; but take this." So saying, he took for him a handful of the pearls and coral and rubies and other jewels he had with him (the handful being about half of the whole), and gave them to the baker, saying, "Give me some ready money to spend this day, till I sell these jewels." So the baker gave him all the money he had in hand and all the bread in his basket and rejoiced in the jewels, saying, "I am thy slave and thy servant." Then he set all the bread on his head and following the fisherman home, gave it to his wife and children, after which he repaired to the market and brought meat and greens and all manner fruit. Moreover, he left his oven and abode with Abdullah all that day, busying himself in his service and fulfilling all his affairs. Said the fisherman, "O my brother, thou weariest thyself;" and the baker replied, "This is my

---

[1] Lit. "Verily he laughed at me so that I set him free." This is a fair specimen of obscure conciseness.

[2] Arab. "Mishannah," which Lane and Payne translate basket: I have always heard it used of an old gunny-bag or bag of plaited palm-leaves.

duty, for I am become thy servant and thou hast overwhelmed me with thy boons." Rejoined the fisherman, "'Tis thou who wast my benefactor in the days of dearth and distress." And the baker passed that night with him enjoying good cheer and became a faithful friend to him. Then the fisherman told his wife what had befallen him with the Merman, whereat she rejoiced and said, "Keep thy secret, lest the government come down upon thee;" but he said, "Though I keep my secret from all men, yet will I not hide it from the baker." On the morrow, he rose betimes and, shouldering a basket which he had filled in the evening with all manner fruits, repaired before sunrise to the sea-shore, and setting down the crate on the water-edge called out, "Where art thou, O Abdullah, O Merman?" He answered, "Here am I, at thy service;" and came forth to him. The fisherman gave him the fruit and he took it and plunging into the sea with it, was absent a full hour, after which time he came up, with the fish-basket full of all kinds of gems and jewels. The fisherman set it on his head and went away; and, when he came to the oven, the baker said to him, "O my lord, I have baked thee forty buns[1] and have sent them to thy house; and now I will bake some firsts and as soon as all is done, I will bring it to thy house and go and fetch thee greens and meat." Abdullah handed to him three handfuls of jewels out of the fish-basket and going home, set it down there. Then he took a gem of price of each sort and going to the jewel-bazar, stopped at the Syndic's shop and said to him, "Buy these precious stones of me." "Show them to me," said the Shaykh. So he showed them to him and the jeweller said, "Hast thou aught beside these?"; and Abdullah replied, "I have a basket-full at home." The Syndic asked, "And where is thine house?" and the fisherman answered, "In such a quarter"; whereupon the Shaykh took the jewels from him and said to his followers, "Lay hold of him, for he is the thief who stole the jewellery of the Queen, the wife of our Sultan." And he bade beat him. So they bastinadoed him and pinioned him; after which the Syndic and all the people of the jewel-market arose and set out for the palace, saying, "We have caught the thief." Quoth one, "None robbed such an one but this villain," and quoth another, "'Twas none but he stole all that was in such an one's house;" and some said this and others said that. All this while he was silent and spake not a word nor returned a reply, till they

---

[1] Arab. "Kaff Shurayk" applied to a single bun. The Shurayk is a bun, an oblong cake about the size of a man's hand (hence the term "Kaff" = palm) with two long cuts and sundry oblique crosscuts, made of leavened dough, glazed with egg and Samn (clarified butter) and flavoured with spices (cinnamon, curcuma, artemisia and prunes mahalab) and with aromatic seeds, (Rihat al-'ajin) of which Lane (iii. 641) specifies aniseed, nigella, absinthium, (Artemisia arborescens) and Káfúrah (A. camphorata Monspeliensis) etc. The Shurayk is given to the poor when visiting the tombs and on certain fêtes.

brought him before the King, to whom said the Syndic, "O King of the age, when the Queen's necklace was stolen, thou sentest to acquaint us of the theft, requiring of us the discovery of the culprit; wherefore I strove beyond the rest of the folk and have taken the thief for thee. Here he standeth before thee, and these be the jewels we have recovered from him." Thereupon the King said to the chief eunuch, "Carry these jewels for the Queen to see, and say to her, 'Are these thy property thou hast lost?'" So the eunuch took the jewels and went in with them to the Queen, who seeing their lustre marvelled at them and sent to the King to say, "I have found my necklace in my own place and these jewels are not my property; nay, they are finer than those of my necklace. So oppress not the man;"—And Shahrazad perceived the dawn of day and ceased saying her permitted say.

When it was the Nine Hundred and Forty-third Night,

She said, It hath reached me, O auspicious King, that when the King's wife sent to the King to say, "These are not my property; nay, these gems are finer than those of my necklace. So oppress not this man; but, if he will sell them, buy them for thy daughter Umm al-Su'úd,[1] that we may set them in a necklace for her." When the eunuch returned and told the King what the Queen said, he damned the Syndic of the jewellers, him and his company, with the damnation of Ád and Thamúd,[2] and they said to him, "O King of the age, we knew this man for a poor fisherman and deemed such things too much for him,[3] so we supposed that he had stolen them." Cried the King, "O ye filthy villains, begrudge ye a True Believer good fortune? Why did ye not make due enquiry of him? Haply Allah Almighty hath vouchsafed him these things from a source whereupon he reckoned not. Why did ye make him out a thief and disgrace him amongst the folk? Begone, and may Allah never bless you!" So they went out affrighted and the King said to Abdullah, "O man (Allah bless thee in all He hath bestowed on thee!), no harm shall befal thee; but tell me truly, whence gottest thou these jewels; for I am a King yet have I not the like of them." The fisherman replied, "O King of the age, I have a fish-basket full of them at home and the case is thus and thus." Then he told him of his friendship with the Merman, adding, "We have made a covenant together that I shall bring him every day a basket full of fruit and that he shall fill me the basket with these jewels." Quoth the King, O man this is thy lucky lot; but wealth needeth rank,[4] I will defend thee for

---

[1] "Mother of Prosperities."
[2] Tribes of pre-historic Arabs who were sent to Hell for bad behaviour to Prophets Sálih and Húd. See vol. iii. 294.
[3] "Too much for him to come by lawfully."
[4] To protect it. The Arab. is "Jáh" = high station, dignity.

the present against men's domineering; but haply I shall be deposed or die and another rule in my stead, and he shall slay thee because of his love of the goods of this world and his covetousness. So I am minded to marry thee to my daughter and make thee my Wazir and bequeath thee the kingdom after me, so none may hanker for thy riches when I am gone. Then said he, "Hie with this man to the Hammam." So they bore him to the Baths and bathed his body and robed him in royal raiment, after which they brought him back to the King, and he made him his Wazir and sent to his house couriers and the soldiers of his guard and all the wives of the notables, who clad his wife and children in Kingly costume and mounting the woman in a horse-litter, with the little child in her lap, walked before her to the palace, escorted by the troops and couriers and officers. They also brought her elder children in to the King who made much of them, taking them in his lap and seating them by his side; for they were nine children male and the King had no son and heir nor had he been blessed with any child save this one daughter, Umm al-Su'ud hight. Meanwhile the Queen entreated Abdullah's wife with honour and bestowed favours on her and made her Waziress to her. Then the King bade draw up the marriage contract between his daughter and Abdullah of the Land[1] who assigned to her, as her dower, all the gems and precious stones in his possession, and they opened the gates of festival. The King commanded by proclamation to decorate the city, in honour of his daughter's wedding. Then Abdullah went in unto the Princess and abated her maidenhead. Next morning the King looked out of the lattice and saw Abdullah carrying on his head a fish-crate full of fruit. So he called to him, "What hast thou there, O my son-in-law, and whither wendest thou?" The fisherman replied, "To my friend, Abdullah the Merman;" and the King said, "O my son-in-law, this is no time to go

---

[1] The European reader, especially feminine, will think this a hard fate for the pious first wife but the idea would not occur to the Moslem mind. After bearing ten children a woman becomes "Umm al-banáti w'al-banín" = a mother of daughters and sons, and should hold herself unfit for love-disport. The seven ages of womankind are thus described by the Arabs and I translate the lines after a well-known (Irish) model:—

From ten years to twenty—	From forty to fifty—
Of beauty there's plenty.	An old'un and shifty.
From twenty to thirty—	From fifty to sixty—
Fat, fair and alert t'ye.	A sorrow that sticks t'ye.
From thirty to forty—	From sixty to seventy—
Lads and lasses she bore t'ye.	A curse of God sent t'ye.

For these and other sentiments upon the subject of women and marriage see Pilgrimage ii. 285–87.

to thy comrade." Quoth Abdullah, "Indeed, I fear to break tryst with him, lest he reckon me a liar and say, 'The things of the world have diverted thee from me,'" and quoth the King, "Thou speakest sooth: go to thy friend and God help thee!" So he walked through the city on his way to his companion; and, as he went, he heard the folk who knew him say, "There goeth the King's son-in-law to exchange fruit for gems;" whilst those who knew him not said, "Ho, fellow, how much a pound? Come, sell to me." And he answered, saying, "Wait till I come back to thee," for that he would not hurt the feelings of any man. Then he fared on till he came to the sea-shore and foregathered with his friend Abdullah the Merman, to whom he delivered the fruit, receiving gems in return. He ceased not doing thus till one day, as he passed by the baker's oven, he found it closed; and so he did ten days, during which time the oven remained shut and he saw nothing of the baker. So he said to himself, "This is a strange thing! Would I wot whither the baker went!" Then he enquired of his neighbour, saying, "O my brother, where is thy neighbour the baker and what hath Allah done with him?"; and the other responded, "O my lord, he is sick and cometh not forth of his house." "Where is his house?" asked Abdullah; and the other answered, "In such a quarter." So he fared thither and enquired of him; but, when he knocked at the door, the baker looked out of window and seeing his friend the fisherman, full basket on head, came down and opened the door to him. Abdullah entered and throwing himself on the baker embraced him and wept, saying, "How dost thou, O my friend? Every day, I pass by thine oven and see it unopened; so I asked thy neighbour, who told me that thou wast sick; therefore I enquired for thy house, that I might see thee." Answered the baker, "Allah requite thee for me with all good! Nothing aileth me; but it reached me that the King had taken thee, for that certain of the folk had lied against thee and accused thee of being a robber wherefore I feared and shut shop and hid myself." "True," said Abdullah and told him all that had befallen him with the King and the Shaykh of the jewellers' bazar, adding "Moreover, the King hath given me his daughter to wife and made me his Wazir;" and, after a pause, "So do thou take what is in this fish-basket to thy share and fear naught." Then he left him, after having done away from his affright, and returned with the empty crate to the King, who said to him, "O my son-in-law, 'twould seem thou hast not foregathered with thy friend the Merman to-day." Replied Abdullah, "I went to him but that which he gave me I gave to my gossip the baker, to whom I owe kindness." "Who may be this baker?" asked the King; and the fisherman answered, "He is a benevolent man, who did with me thus and thus in the days of my poverty and never neglected me a single day nor hurt my feelings." Quoth the King, "What is his name?"; and quoth the fisherman "His name is Abdullah the Baker;

Tales From Around the World

and my name is Abdullah of the Land and that of my friend the Merman Abdullah of the Sea." Rejoined the King, "And my name also is Abdullah; and the servants of Allah[1] are all brethren. So send and fetch thy friend the baker, that I may make him my Wazir of the left."[2] So he sent for the baker who speedily came to the presence, and the King invested him with the Wazirial uniform and made him Wazir of the left, making Abdullah of the Land his Wazir of the right.—And Shahrazad perceived the dawn of day and ceased to say her permitted say.

When it was the Nine Hundred and Forty-fourth Night,

She continued, It hath reached me, O auspicious King, that the King made his son-in-law, Abdullah of the Land, Wazir of the right and Abdullah the baker Wazir of the left. In such condition the fisherman abode a whole year, every day carrying for the Merman the crate full of fruit and receiving it back, full of jewels; and when fruit failed from the gardens, he carried him raisins and almonds and filberts and walnuts and figs and so forth; and all that he brought for him the Merman accepted and returned him the fish-basket full of jewels according to his custom. Now it chanced one day that he carried him the crate, full of dry[3] fruits as was his wont, and his friend took them from him. Then they sat down to converse, Abdullah the fisherman on the beach and Abdullah the Merman in the water near the shore, and discoursed; and the talk went round between them, till it fell upon the subject of sepulchres; whereat quoth the Merman, "O my brother, they say that the Prophet (whom Allah assain and save!) is buried with you on the land. Knowest thou his tomb?" Abdullah replied, "Yes; it lieth in a city called Yathrib."[4] Asked the Merman, "And do the people of the land visit it?" "Yes," answered the fisherman, and the other said, "I give you joy, O people of the land,

---

[1] Abdullah, as has been said, means "servant or rather slave of Allah."

[2] Again the "Come to my arms, my slight acquaintance," of the Anti–Jacobin.

[3] Arab. "Nukl," e.g. the quatre mendicants as opposed to "Fákihah" = fresh fruit. The Persians, a people who delight in gross practical jokes, get the confectioner to coat with sugar the droppings of sheep and goats and hand them to the bulk of the party. This pleasant confection is called "Nukl-i-peshkil"— dung-dragées.

[4] The older name of Madínat al-Nabi, the city of the Prophet; vulg. called Al–Medinah per excellentiam. See vol. iv. 114. In the Mac. and Bul. texts we have "Tayyibah" = the goodly, one of the many titles of that Holy City: see Pilgrimage ii. 119.

of visiting[1] that noble Prophet and compassionate, which whoso visiteth meriteth his intercession! Hast thou made such visitation, O my brother?" Replied the fisherman, "No: for I was poor and had not the necessary sum[2] to spend by the way, nor have I been in easy case but since I knew thee and thou bestowedst on me this good fortune. But such visitation behoveth me after I have pilgrimed to the Holy House of Allah[3] and naught withholdeth me therefrom but my love to thee, because I cannot leave thee for one day." Rejoined the Merman, "And dost thou set the love of me before the visitation of the tomb of Mohammed (whom Allah assain and save!), who shall intercede for thee on the Day of Review before Allah and shall save thee from the Fire and through whose intercession thou shalt enter Paradise? And dost thou, for the love of the world, neglect to visit the tomb of thy Prophet[4] Mohammed, whom God bless and preserve?" Replied Abdullah, "No, by Allah, I set the visitation of the Prophet's tomb above all else, and I crave thy leave to pray before it this year." The Merman rejoined, "I grant thee leave, on condition that when thou shalt stand by his sepulchre thou salute him for me with the Salam. Furthermore I have a trust to give thee; so come thou with me into the sea, that I may carry thee to my city and entertain thee in my house and give thee a deposit; which when thou takest thy station by the Prophet's tomb, do thou lay thereon, saying, 'O apostle of Allah, Abdullah the Merman saluteth thee, and sendeth thee this present,

---

[1] Not "visiting the tomb of," etc. but visiting the Prophet himself, who is said to have declared that "Ziyárah" (visitation) of his tomb was in religion the equivalent of a personal call upon himself.

[2] Arab. "Nafakah"; for its conditions see Pigrimage iii. 224. I have again and again insisted upon the Anglo–Indian Government enforcing the regulations of the Faith upon pauper Hindi pilgrims who go to the Moslem Holy Land as beggars and die of hunger in the streets. To an "Empire of Opinion" this is an unmitigated evil (Pilgrimage iii. 256); and now, after some thirty-four years, there are signs that the suggestions of common sense are to be adopted. England has heard of the extraordinary recklessness and inconsequence of the British–Indian "fellow-subject."

[3] The Ka'abah of Meccah.

[4] When Moslems apply "Nabí!" to Mohammed it is in the peculiar sense of "prophet" = one who speaks before the people, not one who predicts, as such foresight was adjured by the Apostle. Dr. A. Neubauer (The Athenæum No. 3031) finds the root of "Nabí!" in the Assyrian Nabu and Heb. Noob (occurring in Exod. vii. 1. "Aaron thy brother shall be thy prophet." *i.e.* orator, speaker before the people), and holds it to be a Canaanite term which supplanted "Roeh" (the Seer) e.g. 1 Samuel ix. 9. The learned Hebraist traces the cult of Nebo, a secondary deity in Assyria to Palestine and Phœnicia, Palmyra, Edessa (in the Nebok of Abgar) and Hierapolis in Syria or Mabug (Nabog?).

imploring thine intercession to save him from the Fire.'" Said the fisherman, "O my brother, thou wast created in the water and water is thy abiding-place and doth thee no hurt, but, if thou shouldst come forth to the land, would any harm betide thee?" The Merman replied, "Yes; my body would dry up and the breezes of the land would blow upon me and I should die." Rejoined the fisherman, "And I, in like manner, was created on the land and the land is my abiding-place; but, an I went down into the sea, the water would enter my belly and choke me and I should die." Retorted the other, "Have no fear for that, for I will bring thee an ointment, wherewith when thou hast anointed thy body, the water will do thee no hurt, though thou shouldst pass the lave of thy life going about in the great deep: and thou shalt lie down and rise up in the sea and naught shall harm thee." Quoth the fisherman, "An the case by thus, well and good; but bring me the ointment, so that I may make trial of it;" and quoth the Merman, "So be it;" then, taking the fish-basket disappeared in the depths. He was absent awhile, and presently returned with an unguent as it were the fat of beef, yellow as gold and sweet of savour. Asked the fisherman, "What is this, O my brother?"; and answered the Merman, "'Tis the liver-fat of a kind of fish called the Dandan,[1] which is the biggest of all fishes and the fiercest of our foes. His bulk is greater than that of any beast of the land, and were he to meet a camel or an elephant, he would swallow it at a single mouthful." Abdullah enquired, "O my brother, what doth this baleful beast?"; and the Merman replied, "He eateth of the beasts of the sea. Hast thou not heard the saying, 'Like the fishes of the sea: forcible eateth feeble?'"[2] "True; but have you many of these Dandans in the sea?" "Yes, there be many of them with us. None can tell their tale save Almighty Allah." "Verily, I fear lest, if I go down with thee into the deep a creature of this kind fall in with me and devour me." "Have no fear: when he seeth thee, he will know thee for a son of Adam and will fear thee and flee. He dreadeth none in the sea as he dreadeth a son of Adam; for that an he eateth a man he dieth forthright, because human fat is a deadly poison to this kind of creature; nor do we collect its liver-speck save by means of a man, when he falleth into the sea and is drowned; for that his semblance becometh changed and ofttimes his flesh is torn; so the Dandan eateth him, deeming him the same of the denizens of the deep, and dieth. Then we light upon our enemy dead and take the speck of his liver and grease ourselves so that

---

[1] I cannot find "Dandán" even in Lib. Quintus de Aquaticis Animalibus of the learned Sam. Bochart's "Hierozoïcon" (London, 1663) and must conjecture that as "Dandán" in Persian means a tooth (vol. ii. 83) the writer applied it to a sun-fish or some such well-fanged monster of the deep.

[2] A favourite proverb with the Fellah, when he alludes to the Pasha and to himself.

we can over-wander the main in safety. Also, wherever there is a son of Adam, though there be in that place an hundred or two hundred or a thousand or more of these beasts, all die forthright an they but hear him,—And Shahrazad perceived the dawn of day and ceased saying her permitted say.

When it was the Nine Hundred and Forty-fifth Night,

She pursued, It hath reached me, O auspicious King, that Abdullah of the sea said to Abdullah of the Land, "And if a thousand or more of this kind hear an Adamite cry a single cry, forthright all die nor hath one of them power to remove from his place; so, whenever a son of Adam falleth into the sea, we take him and anoint him with this fat and go round about the depths with him, and whenever we see a Dandan or two or three or more, we bid him cry out and they all die forthright for his once crying." Quoth the fisherman, "I put my trust in Allah;" and, doffing his clothes, buried them in a hole which he dug in the beach; after which he rubbed his body from head to heels which that ointment. Then he descended into the water and diving, opened his eyes and the brine did him no hurt. So he walked right and left, and if he would, he rose to the sea-face, and if he would, he sank to the base. And he beheld the water as it were a tent over his head; yet it wrought him no hurt. Then said the Merman to him, "What seest thou, O my brother?"; and said he, "O my brother, I see naught save weal;[1] and indeed thou spakest truth in that which thou saidst to me; for the water doth me no hurt." Quoth the Merman, "Follow me." So he followed him and they ceased not faring on from place to place, whilst Abdullah discovered before him and on his right and left mountains of water and solaced himself by gazing thereon and on the various sorts of fish, some great and some small, which disported themselves in the main. Some of them favoured buffaloes[2] others oxen and others dogs and yet others human beings; but all to which they drew near fled, whenas they saw the fisherman, who said to the Merman, "O my brother, how is it that I see all the fish, to which we draw near, flee from us afar?" Said the other, "Because they fear thee, for all things that Allah hath made fear the son of Adam."[3] The fisherman ceased not to

---

[1] An euphemistic answer, unbernfen as the Germans say.

[2] It is a temptation to derive this word from bœuf à l'eau, but I fear that the theory will not hold water. The "buffaloes" of Alexandria laughed it to scorn.

[3] Here the writer's zoological knowledge is at fault. Animals, which never or very rarely see man, have no fear of him whatever. This is well-known to those who visit the Gull-fairs at Ascension Island, Santos and many other isolated rocks; the hen birds will peck at the intruder's ankles but they do not rise from off their eggs. For details concerning the "Gull-

divert himself with the marvels of the deep, till they came to a high mountain and fared on beside it. Suddenly, he heard a mighty loud cry and turning, saw some black thing, the bigness of a camel or bigger, coming down upon him from the liquid mountain and crying out. So he asked his friend, "What is this, O my brother?"; and the Merman answered, "This is the Dandan. He cometh in search of me, seeking to devour me; so cry out at him, O my brother, ere he reach us; else he will snatch me up and devour me." Accordingly Abdullah cried out at the beast and behold, it fell down dead; which when he saw, he said, "Glorified be the perfection of God and His praise! I smote it not with the sword nor knife; how cometh it that, for all the vastness of the creature's bulk, it could not bear my cry, but died?" Replied the Merman, "Marvel not, for, by Allah, O my brother, were there a thousand or two thousand of these creatures, yet could they not endure the cry of a son of Adam." Then they walked on, till they made a city, whose inhabitants the fisherman saw to be all women, there being no male among them; so he said to his companion, "O my brother, what city is this and what are these women?" "This is the city of women; for its inhabitants are of the women of the sea." "Are there any males among them?" "No!" "Then how do they conceive and bear young, without males?"[1] "The King of the sea banisheth them hither and they conceive not neither bear children. All the women of the sea, with whom he is wroth, he sendeth to this city, and they cannot leave it; for, should one of them come forth therefrom, any of the beasts of the sea that saw her would eat her. But in other cities of the main there are both males and females." Thereupon asked the fisherman, "Are there then other cities than this in the sea?"; and the Merman answered, "There are many." Quoth the fisherman, "And is there a Sultan over you in the sea?" "Yes," quoth the Merman. Then said Abdullah "O my brother, I have indeed seen many marvels in the main!"

---

fair" of the Summer Islands consult p. 4 "The History of the Bermudas," edited by Sir J. H. Lefroy for the Hakluyt Society, 1882. I have seen birds on Fernando Po peak quietly await a second shot; and herds of antelopes, the most timed of animals, in the plains of Somali-land only stared but were not startled by the report of the gun. But Arabs are not the only moralists who write zoological nonsense: witness the notable verse,

"Birds in their little nests agree,"

when the feathered tribes are the most pugnacious of breathing beings.
[1] Lane finds these details "silly and tiresome or otherwise objectionable," and omits them.

But the Merman said, "And what hast thou seen of its marvels?[1] Hast thou not heard the saying, 'The marvels of the sea are more manifold than the marvels of the land?'" "True," rejoined the fisherman and fell to gazing upon those women, whom he saw with faces like moons and hair like women's hair, but their hands and feet were in their middle and they had tails like fishes' tails. Now when the Merman had shown him the people of the city, he carried him forth therefrom and forewalked him to another city, which he found full of folk, both males and females, formed like the women aforesaid and having tails; but there was neither selling nor buying amongst them, as with the people of the land, nor were they clothed, but went all naked and with their same uncovered. Said Abdullah "O my brother, I see males and females alike with their shame exposed,"[2] and the other said, "This is because the folk of the sea have no clothes." Asked the fisherman, "And how do they when they marry?" The Merman answered, "They do not marry; but every one who taketh a liking to a female doth his will of her." Quoth Abdullah, "This is unlawful! Why doth he not ask her in marriage and dower her and make her a wedding festival and marry her, in accordance with that which is pleasing to Allah and His Apostle?"; and quoth the other, "We are not all of one religion: some of us are Moslems, believers in The Unity, others Nazarenes and what not else; and each marrieth in accordance with the ordinances of his creed; but those of us who marry are mostly Moslems." The fisherman continued, "Ye are naked and have neither buying nor selling among you: of what then is your wives' dowry? Do ye give them jewels and precious stones?" The Merman rejoined, "Gems with us are only stones without worth: but upon the Moslem who is minded to marry they impose a dowry of a certain number of fishes of various kinds that he must catch, a thousand or two thousand, more or less, according to the agreement between himself and the bride's father. As soon as he bringeth the amount required, the families of the bride and bridegroom assemble and eat the marriage-banquet; after which they bring him in to his bride, and he catcheth fish and feedeth her; or, if he be unable, she catcheth fish and feedeth him." Enquired the fisherman, "And how if a woman commit adultery?"; and the other replied, "If a woman be convicted of this case, they banish her to the City of Women; and if she be with child by her gallant, they leave her till she be delivered; then, if she give birth to a

---

[1] Meaning, "Thou hast as yet seen little or nothing." In most Eastern tongues a question often expresses an emphatic assertion. See vol. i. 37.

[2] Easterns wear as a rule little clothing but it suffices for the essential purposes of decency and travellers will live amongst them for years without once seeing an accidental "exposure of the person." In some cases, as with the Nubian thong-apron, this demand of modesty requires not a little practice of the muscles; and we all know the difference in a Scotch kilt worn by a Highlander and a cockney sportsman.

girl, they banish her with her, calling her adulteress, daughter of adulteress, and she abideth a maid till she die; but, if the woman give birth to a male child, they carry it to the Sultan of the Sea, who putteth it to death." Abdullah marvelled at this and the Merman carried him to another city and thence to another and yet another, till he had diverted him with the sight of eighty cities, and he saw the people of each city unlike those of every other. Then said he to the Merman, "O my brother, are there yet other cities in the main?"; whereto said the other, "And what hast thou seen of the cities of the sea and its wondrous spectacles? By the virtue of the noble Prophet, the benign, the compassionate, were I to show thee every day a thousand cities for a thousand years, and in each city a thousand marvels, I should not have shown thee one carat of the four-and-twenty carats of the cities of the sea and its miracles! I have but shown thee our own province and country, nothing more." The fisherman thus resumed, "O my brother, since this is the case, what I have seen sufficeth me, for I am a-weary of eating fish, and these fourscore days I have been in thy company, thou hast fed me, morning and night, upon nothing but raw fish, neither broiled nor boiled." "And what is broiled or boiled?" "We broil fish with fire and boil it in water and dress it in various ways and make many dishes of it." "And how should we come by fire in the sea? We know not broiled nor boiled nor aught else of the kind." "We also fry it in olive-oil and oil of sesame."[1] How should be come by olive-oil and oil of sesame in the sea? Verily we know nothing of that thou namest." "True, but O my brother, thou hast shown me many cities; yet hast thou not shown me thine own city." "As for mine own city, we passed it a long way, for it is near the land whence we came, and I left it and came with thee hither, thinking only to divert thee with the sight of the greater cities of the sea." "That which I have seen of them sufficeth me; and now I would have thee show me thine own city." "So be it," answered Abdullah of the Sea; and, returning on his traces, carried him back thither and said to him, "This is my city." Abdullah of the Land looked and saw a city small by comparison with those he had seen; then he entered with his comrade of the deep and they fared on till they came to a cave. Quoth the Merman, "This is my house and all the houses in the city are like this, caverns great and small in the mountains; as are also those of every other city of the sea. For whoso is minded to make him a house must repair to the King and say to him, 'I wish to make me a house

---

[1] Arab. "Shíraj" = oil extracted from rape seed but especially from sesame. The Persians pronounce it "Síraj" (apparently unaware that it is their own word "Shírah" = juice in Arabic garb) and have coined a participle "Musayrij" e.g., Bú-i-musayrij, taint of sesame-oil applied especially to the Jews who very wisely prefer, in Persia and elsewhere, oil which is wholesome to butter which is not. The Moslems, however, declare that its immoderate use in cooking taints the exudations of the skin.

in such a place.' Whereupon the King sends with him a band of the fish called 'Peckers,'[1] which have beaks that crumble the hardest rock, appointing for their wage a certain quantum of fish. They betake themselves to the mountain chosen by the intended owner and therein pierce the house, whilst the owner catcheth fish for them and feedeth them, till the cave is finished, when they wend their ways and the house-owner taketh up his abode therein. On such wise do all the people of the sea; they traffic not one with other nor serve each other save by means of fish; and their food is fish and they themselves are a kind of fish."[2] Then he said to him, "Enter!" So Abdullah entered and the Merman cried out, saying, "Ho, daughter mine!" when behold, there came to him a damsel with a face like the rondure of the moon and hair long, hips heavy, eyes black-edged and waist slender; but she was naked and had a tail. When she saw Abdullah of the Land she said to her sire, "O my father, what is this No-tail[3] thou hast brought with thee?" He replied, "O my daughter this is my friend of the land, from whom I used to bring thee the fruits of the ground. Come hither and salute him with the salam." So she came forward and saluted the fisherman with loquent tongue and eloquent speech; and her father said to her, "Bring meat for our guest, by whose visit a blessing hath betided us:"[4] whereupon she brought him two great fishes, each the bigness of a lamb, and the Merman said to him, "Eat." So he ate for stress of hunger, despite himself; because he was tired of eating fish and they had naught else save fish. Before long, in came the Merman's wife, who was beautiful of form and favour and with her two children, each having in his hand a young fish, which he craunched as a man would craunch a cucumber. When she saw the fisherman with her husband, she said, "What is this No-tail?" And she and her sons and their sister came up to him and fell to examining the back parts of Abdullah of the Land, and saying, "Yea, by Allah, he is tailless!"; and they laughed at him. So he said to the Merman, "O my brother, hast thou brought me hither to make me a butt and a laughing-stock for thy children and thy consort?"—And Shahrazad perceived the dawn of day and ceased to say her permitted say.

When it was the Nine Hundred and Forty-sixth Night,

She resumed, It hath reached me, O auspicious King, that Abdullah of the Land said to Abdullah of the sea, "O my brother, hast thou brought

---

[1] Arab. "Nakkárún" probably congeners of the redoubtable "Dandán."
[2] Bresl. Edit. xi. 78. The Mac. says "They are all fish" (Kullu-hum) and the Bul. "Their food (aklu-hum) is fish."
[3] Arab. "Az'ar," usually = having thin hair. The general term for tailless is "abtar." See Koran cviii. 3, when it means childless.
[4] A common formula of politeness.

me hither to make me a butt and a laughing-stock for thy children and thy consort?" Cried the Merman, "Pardon, O my brother! Those who have no tails are rare among us, and whenever one such is found, the Sultan taketh him, to make fun of him, and he abideth a marvel amongst us, and all who see him laugh at him. But, O my brother, excuse these young children and this woman, for they lack wits." Then he cried out to his family, saying, "Silence!"; so they were afraid and held their peace; whilst he went on to soothe Abdullah's mind. Presently, as they were talking, behold, in came some ten Merman, tall and strong and stout, and said to him, "O Abdullah, it hath reached the King that thou hast with thee a No-tail of the No-tails of the earth." Answered the Merman, "Yes; and this is he; but he is not of us nor of the children of the sea. He is my friend of the land and hath come to me as a guest and I purpose to carry him back to the land." Quoth they, "We cannot depart but with him; so, an thou have aught to say, arise and come with him before the King; and whatso thou wouldst say to us, say thou that same to the King." Then quoth the Merman to the fisherman, "O my brother, my excuse is manifest, and we may not disobey the King: but go thou with me to him and I will do my best to deliver thee from him, Inshallah! Fear not, for he deemeth thee of the children of the sea; but, when he seeth thee, he will know thee to be of the children of the land, and he will surely entreat thee honourably and restore thee to the land." And Abdullah of the Land replied, "'Tis thine to decide, I will trust in Allah and wend with thee." So he took him and carried him to the King, who, when he saw him, laughed at him and said, "Welcome to the No-tail!" And all who were about the King began to laugh at him and say, "Yea, by Allah, he is tailless!" Then Abdullah of the Sea came forward and acquainted the King with the fisherman's case, saying, "This man is of the children of the land and he is my comrade and cannot live amongst us, for that he loveth not the eating of fish, except it be fried or boiled; wherefore I desire that thou give me leave to restore him to the land." Whereto the King replied, "Since the case is so, and he cannot live among us, I give thee leave to restore him to his place, after due entertainment," presently adding, "Bring him the guest-meal." So they brought him fish of various kinds and colours and he ate, in obedience to the royal behest; after which the King said to him, "Ask a boon of me." Quoth he, "I ask of thee that thou give me jewels;" and the King said, "Carry him to the jewel-house and let him choose that whereof he hath need." So his friend carried him to the jewel-house and he picked out whatso he would, after which the Merman brought him back to his own city and pulling out a purse, said to him, "Take this deposit and lay it on the tomb of the Prophet, whom Allah save and assain!" And he took it, knowing not what was therein. Then the Merman went forth with him, to bring him back to land, and by the way he heard singing and merrymaking and saw a table spread with fish and folk eating and singing and holding mighty high festival. So Abdullah of the Land said to his friend, "What aileth these people to rejoice thus? Is there a wedding among them?" Replied Abdullah of the Sea, "Nay; one of them is dead." Asked the fisherman, "Then do ye, when one dieth amongst you, rejoice for him and sing and feast?"; and the Merman answered, "Yes: and ye of the land, what do ye?" Quoth Abdullah of the Land, "When one dieth amongst us, we weep and keen for him and the women beat their faces and rend the bosoms of their raiment, in token of mourning for the dead." But Abdullah the Merman stared at him with wide eyes and said to him, "Give me the deposit!" So he gave it to him. Then he set him ashore and said to him, "I have broken off our companionship and our amity; wherefore from this day forward thou shalt no more see me, nor I see thee." Cried the fisherman, "Why sayst thou this?"; and the other said, "Are ye not, O folk of the land, a deposit of Allah?" "Yes." "Why then," asked the Merman, "is it grievous to you that Allah should take back His deposit and wherefore weep ye over it? How can I entrust thee with a deposit for the Prophet (whom Allah save and assain!), seeing that, when a child is born to you, ye rejoice in it, albeit the Almighty setteth the soul therein as a deposit; and yet, when he taketh it again, it is grievous to you and ye weep and mourn? Since it is hard for thee to give up the deposit of Allah, how shall it be easy to thee to give up the deposit of the Prophet?[1] Wherefore we need not your companionship." Saying thus he left him and disappeared in the sea. Thereupon Abdullah of the Land donned his dress and taking the jewels, went up to the King, who met him lovingly and rejoiced at his return saying, "How dost thou, O my son-in-law, and what is the cause of thine absence from me this while?" So he told him his tale and acquainted him with that which he had seen of marvels in the sea, whereat the King wondered. Then he told him what Abdullah the Merman had said;[2] and the King replied, "Indeed 'twas thou wast at fault to tell him this." Nevertheless, he continued for some time to go down to the shore and call upon Abdullah of the Sea, but he answered him not nor came to him; so, at last, he gave up all hope of him and abode, he and the King his father-in-law and the families of them both in the happiest of case and the practice of righteous ways, till there came to them the Destroyer of delights and the Severer of societies and they died all. Wherefore glory be to the Living, who dieth not, whose is the empire of the Seen and the Unseen, who over all things is Omnipotent and is gracious to His servants and knowth their every intent! And amongst the tales they tell is one anent

---

[1] Bresl. Edit. xi. 82; meaning, "You will probably keep it for yourself." Abdullah of the Sea is perfectly logical; but grief is not. We weep over the deaths of friends mostly for our own sake: theoretically we should rejoice that they are at rest; but practically we are afflicted by the thought that we shall never again see their pleasant faces.

[2] *i.e.* about rejoicing over the newborns and mourning over the dead.

Source:
Burton, Sir Richard. *Lady Burton's Edition of Her Husband's Arabian Nights, Vol. 6.* Lady Isabel Burton and Justin Huntly McCarthy, editors. London: Waterlow & Sons, 1886.

126. A Cairene Mermaid

Egypt

IN THE sea there lives a creature half fish and half woman, the woman's half extending to the waist. When steamers were first invented they had no whistles, and orders were conveyed by word of mouth. But one day the order was shouted by the mermaid, and on its being replied to the pilot was told to lower his hand. The mermaid seized it immediately and dragged him into the water. Since then the steam-whistle has been employed.

Source:
Sayce, A. H. "Cairene Folklore." *Folklore.* Vol. 11, No. 4 (Dec. 1900). pp. 354-395.

127. Ayuh, the Nigerian Mermaid

Nigeria

THE most characteristic and most remarkable mammal on the Niger was the amphibious *ayuh*, a mammal which the natives say is half-woman, half-fish, and is described as a mermaid by early travellers on the Niger. Near Gao there was a family of these *ayuh*, and I believe they were common enough further south and in some of the tributaries of the Niger. They resembled a large seal. The head and upper portion of the body had some sort of a resemblance to a human being. The females, they say—I never saw one myself—had well-developed breasts, like women. I possess pieces of the hide of one of the *ayuh*, or *lamantin*, as the French call them. The thickness and elasticity is amazing; of a light amber colour, it becomes quite transparent when trimmed and polished, and can be made into beautiful walking-sticks.

There were many legends among the natives about these mammals.

Source:
Landor, A[rnold] Henry Savage. *Across Widest Africa: An Account of the Country and People of Eastern, Central and Western Africa*. Vol. II. London: Hurst and Blackett Ltd., 1907. pp. 399-400.

128. The Story of Tangalimlibo

Xhosa People, South Africa

Be sure to read the notes at the end of this tale which describe the Xhosa people's belief in water spirits that cause drowning.

THERE was once a man who had two wives, one of whom had no children. She grieved much about that, till one day a bird came to her and gave her some little pellets. The bird said she must eat of these always before she partook of food, and then she would bear a child. She was very glad, and offered the bird some millet.
But the bird said: "No, I do not want millet."
The woman then offered an isidanga,[1] but the bird said it had no use for that. Then she got some very fine gravel and placed before the bird, which it received at her hands.
After this the woman had a daughter. Her husband knew nothing of what had happened, because he never went to her house. He did not love her at all, for the reason that she bore no children. So she said:
"I will keep my daughter in the house till my husband comes; he will surely love me when he sees I have such a beautiful child."
The name given to the girl was Tangalimlibo.
The man went always to the house of the other wife, and so it happened that Tangalimlibo was grown to be a young woman when her father first saw her. He was very much pleased, and said:
"My dear wife, you should have told me of this before."
The girl had never been out of the house in the daytime. Only in the night-time she had gone out, when people could not see her.

---

[1] An ornamental breast-band which women wear.

The man said to his wife:

"You must make much beer, and invite many people to come and rejoice with me over this that has happened."

The woman did so. There was a big tree in front of the kraal, and the mats were spread under it. It was a fine sunny day, and very many men came. Among them was the son of a certain chief, who fell in love with Tangalimlibo as soon as he saw her.

When the young chief went home he sent a message to the father of the girl that he must send her to him to be married. The man told all his friends about that. He told them also to be ready at a certain time to conduct his daughter to the chief. So they came and took her, and the marriage feast was very great. The oxen were many which were killed that day. Tangalimlibo had a large and beautiful ox given to her by her father. That ox was called by her own name. She took off a piece of her clothing and gave it to the ox, which ate it.

After she had been married some time, this woman had a son. She was loved very much by her husband, because she was pretty and industrious; only this thing was observed of her, that she never went out in the daytime. Therefore she received the name of Sihamba Ngenyanga.[1]

One day her husband went to a distant place to hunt with other men. There were left at his home with this woman only her father-in-law, her mother-in-law, and a girl who nursed the little child.

The father-in-law said:

"Why does she not work during the day?

He pretended to become thirsty, and sent the girl to Tangalimlibo to ask for water, saying:

"I die with thirst."

The woman sent water to her father-in-law, but he threw it on the ground, saying:

"It is water from the river I desire."

She said:

"I never go to the river in the daytime."

He continued to ask, saying again

"I die with thirst."

Then she took a milk-basket and a calabash ladle, and went weeping to the river. She dipped the ladle in the water, and it was drawn out of her hand. She dipped the milk-basket in the water, and it was drawn away from her. Then she tried to take some water in her mantle, and she was drawn under the surface. After a little time the girl was sent to look for her, but she came back, saying:

"I found her not who is accustomed to draw water only in the night."

Her father-in-law drove oxen quickly to the river. He took the big ox that was called by her name and killed it. He put all the flesh and

---

[1] The walker by moonlight.

everything else that was of that ox into the river, saying:

"Let this be instead of my child."

A voice was heard saying:

"Go to my father and my mother and say to them that I am taken by the river."

That evening the little child of Tangalimlibo, was crying very bitterly. Its father was not yet home. Its grandmother tried by every means to keep it from crying, but in vain. Then she gave it to the nurse, who fastened it on her back. Still the child continued to cry. In the middle of the night the nurse went down to the river with the child, singing this song:

> "It is crying, it is crying,
> The child of Sihamba Ngenyanga;
> It is crying, it will not be pacified."

Then the mother of the child came out of the river, and wailed this song:

> "It is crying, it is crying,
> The child of the walker by moonlight.
> It was done intentionally by people whose names are unmentionable.
> They sent her for water during the day.
> She tried to dip with the milk-basket, and then it sank.
> Tried to dip with the ladle, and then it sank.
> Tried to dip with the mantle, and then it sank."

With the name as a chorus at the end of each line.

Then she took her child and put it to her breast to suck.

When the child had finished sucking, she gave it back to the nurse, telling her to take it home. She commanded the nurse never to say to any one that she came out of the water, and told her that when people asked where the child got food she must say she gave it berries to eat.

This continued for some days. Every night the nurse took the child to the river, when its mother came out and suckled it. She always looked round to see that no one was present, and always put the same command on the girl.

After a time the father of the child returned from hunting. They told him of Tangalimlibo's going to the river and not returning. Then the nurse brought the child to him. He inquired what it ate, and was told that berries were given to it.

He said: "That cannot be so; go and get some berries, and let me see my child eat them."

The girl went and brought some berries, but they were not eaten by the child. Then the father of the child beat the girl until she told the truth. She said she went at night to the river, when the mother came out and caressed her child and gave it of her milk.

Then they made a plan that the husband of Tangalimlibo should hide himself in the reeds and try and catch his wife when she came out of the water. He took the skin of an ox and cut it into a long riem,[1] one end of which he fastened round his waist. The other end he gave to the men of that village, telling them to hold it fast and to pull hard when they felt it being drawn from them.

At night the man hid himself in the reeds. Tangalimlibo came out of the water and looked all round while she was singing her song. She asked the girl if any one was there, and when the girl replied that there was no one she took her child. Then her husband sprang upon her, clasping her very tight. She tried to pull back, but the men at the village drew upon the riem. She was drawn away, but the river followed her, and its water turned into blood. When it came close to the village, the men who were pulling at the riem saw it, and became frightened. They let the riem go, when the river at once went back, taking Tangalimlibo with it.

After that her husband was told of the voice which came from the water, saying:

"Go to my father and my mother and tell them I am taken by the river."

He called his racing ox, and said:

"Will you, my ox, take this message to the father and mother of Tangalimlibo?"

The ox only bellowed.

He called his dog and said:

"Will you, my dog, take this message to the father and mother of Tangalimlibo?"

The dog only barked.

Last of all he called the cock.

He said: "Will you, my cock, take this message to the father and mother of Tangalimlibo?"

The cock answered: "I will do so, my master."

He said: "Let me hear what you will say."

The cock answered: "I will sing—

> "I am a cock that ought not to be killed—Cock-a-doodle-doo!
> I have come to intimate about Tangalimlibo—Cock-a-doodle-doo!
> Tangalimlibo is dead—Cock-a-doodle-doo!
> She dipped water for a person that cannot be named—Cock-a-doodle-doo!
> It was tried to send an ox; it bellowed—Cock-a-doodle-doo!
> It was tried to send a dog; it barked—Cock-a-doodle-doo!"

---

[1] Intambo, a riem, or thong of untanned oxhide.

The chief said: "That is good, my cock, go now."

As the cock was going on his way, some boys who were tending calves saw him.

One of them said to the others: "Come here, come here, boys; there is a cock for us to kill."

Then the cock stood up, and sang his song.

The boys said: "Sing again, we did not hear you plainly."

So he sang again:

> "I am a cock that ought not to be killed—Cock-a-doodle-doo!
> I have come to intimate about Tangalimlibo—Cock-a-doodle-doo!
> Tangalimlibo is dead—Cock-a-doodle-doo!
> She dipped water for a person that cannot be named—Cock-a-doodle-doo!
> It was tried to send an ox; it bellowed—Cock-a-doodle-doo!
> It was tried to send a dog; it barked—Cock-a-doodle-doo!"

Then the boys let him go on his way.

He travelled far from that place and came to a village, where the men were sitting in the kraal. He flew up on the back of the kraal to rest himself, and the men saw him.

They said: "Where does this cock come from? We thought all the cocks here were killed. Make haste, boys, and kill him."

The cock began to sing his song.

Then the men said: "Wait, boys, we wish to hear what he says."

They said to him: "Begin again, we did not hear you."

The cock said: "Give me some food, for I am very hungry."

The men sent a boy for some millet, and gave it to him. When he had eaten, he sang his song.

The men said: "Let him go;" and he went on his way.

Then he came to the village of the father of Tangalimlibo, to the house of those he was seeking. He told the message he was sent to carry. The mother of Tangalimlibo was a woman skilful in the use of medicines.

She said to her husband: "Get a fat ox to go with us."

They arrived at the river, and killed the ox.

Then that woman worked with her medicines while they put the meat in the water. There was a great shaking and a rising up of the river, and Tangalimlibo came out. There was great joy among those people when they took her home to her husband.

NOTES

This is a favourite story, and is therefore very widely known. Sometimes it happens that native girls are employed as nurses by Europeans, and that little children are taught by them to sing, or rather chant the song of the cock, so that this story may even be like "an old acquaintance with a cheerful face" to many of our own race who have grown up on the frontier,

The original of the first song is:—

> Uyalila, uyalila, umta ka Sihamba Ngenyanga.
> Wenziwe ngabomu Sihamba Ngenyanga,
> Ngabantu abantloni. Sihamba Ngenyanga.
> Bamtuma amanzi emini. Sihamba Ngenyanga.
> Waba kuka ngetunga, laza latshona. Sihamba Ngenyanga.
> Waba kuka ngomcepe, waza watshona. Sihamba Ngenyanga.
> Waba kuka ngexakato, laza latshona. Sihamba Ngenyanga.

That of the second is:—

> Ndiyi nkuku nje ndingebulawe. Kukulu ku-u-u.
> Ndize kubika u-Tangalimlibo. Kukulu ku-u-u.
> U-Tangalimlibo ufile. Kukulu ku-u-u.
> Ukelele umntu ntloni amanzi. Kukulu ku-u-u.
> Ibe kutunywa inkomo, yakonya. Kukulu ku-u-u.
> Yaba kutunywa inja, yakonkota. Kukulu ku-u-u.

Among the Kaffirs a childless woman finds little or no favour. In many cases she would be treated by her husband in exactly the manner described in this tale, so that by becoming a mother she might say from the bottom of her heart, with Elizabeth of old, that "her reproach was taken away from among men." Sometimes she is returned by her husband to her parents, a proceeding commonly adopted when she has a marriageable sister who can be given to him in exchange. The husband is required, however, before repudiating his wife, to go through the customary ceremonies, which are described in the following case tried before me when acting as a border magistrate in 1881:—A, a Kaffir, sued B, another Kaffir, to recover the value of a heifer lent to him two years before under these circumstances. B's wife, who was distantly related to A, had been married more than a year without bearing a child. B thereupon applied to him for a heifer, the hair of the tail of which was needed by the doctor of the clan to make a charm to put round the woman's neck. He had lent him one for the purpose, and now wanted payment for it. The defence was that A, being the woman's nearest relative who had cattle, was bound to furnish a heifer for the purpose. The hair of the tail was needed, the doctor had made a charm of it and hung it round the woman's neck, and she had thereafter given birth to a son. The heifer could not be returned after being so used. In this case, if the plaintiff had been so nearly related to defendant's wife as to have participated in the benefit of the cattle given by her husband for her, he could not have justified his claim under Kaffir law; but as he was very distantly connected, he got judgment. The feeling entertained by the Kaffirs about the court in this instance was that B had acted very ungratefully towards A, who had not even been present at the woman's marriage feast, but who had cheerfully acted in conformity with the custom which requires that a charm must be made out of the hair of the tail of a heifer belonging to a relative of a childless wife, in order to cause her to bear children.

It will be observed that the woman speaks of those whose names are unmentionable. According to Kaffir custom no woman may pronounce the names of any of her husband's male relatives in the ascending line. She is bound to show them the greatest respect, and implicitly to obey their commands. She may not sit in the house where her father-in-law is seated, she may not even pronounce any word in which the principal syllable of his name occurs. Thus, a woman who sang the song of Tangalimlibo for me used the word angoca instead of amanzi for water, because this last contained the syllable nzi, which she would not on any account pronounce. She had therefore manufactured another word, the meaning of which had to be judged of by the context, as standing alone it is meaningless.

The beer-drinking company on the mats under a tree, the escort of the bride to her husband, and the wedding feast are true to the life.

The idea of the Kaffir with regard to drowning is also shown very distinctly in this tale. He believes that a spirit pulls the person under water, and that this spirit is willing sometimes to accept an ox as a ransom for the human victim. How this belief works practically may be illustrated by facts which have come under my own cognizance.

Some time in 1875, a party of Kaffir girls went to bathe in a little stream not far from the place where I was then living There was a deep hole in the stream, into which one of them lot, and she was drowned. The others ran away home as fast as they could, and there told a story how their companion had been lured away from their side by the spirit calling her. She was with them, they said, in a shallow part, when suddenly she stood upright and said, "It is calling." She then walked straight into the deep place, and would not allow any of them to touch her. One of them heard her saying, "Go and tell my father and my mother that it took me." Upon this, the father collected his cattle as quickly as possible, and set off for the stream. The animals were driven into the water while the man stood on the bank imploring the spirit to take the choicest of them and restore his daughter. The failure to get the exchange effected is still attributed by the relatives of the drowned girl to the absence of one skilful to work with medicines.

On another occasion, a Kaffir was trying to cross one of the fords of a river when it was in flood. He was carried away by the current, but succeeded in getting safely to land sonic quarter of a mile or so further down. Eight or ten lusty fellows saw him carried off his feet, but not one made the slightest effort to help him. On the contrary, they all rushed away frantically, shouting out to the herd boys on the hill sides to drive down the cattle. As might be supposed, the escape of the man from being drowned was then attributed to his being in possession of a powerful charm.

Besides these spirits, according to the belief of the Kaffirs, there are people living under the water, pretty much as those do who are in the upper air. They have houses and furniture, and even cattle, all of their domestic animals being, however, of a dark colour. They are wiser than other people, and from them the most skilful witchfinders are supposed to obtain a portion of the knowledge of their art. This is not a fancy of children, but the implicit belief of grown-up men and women at the present day. A knowledge of this is of great service to those who have to do with Kaffirs. As an instance, a woman came to me in July, 1881, to beg assistance. A child had died in her village, and the witchfinder had pointed her out as the person who had caused its death. Her husband was absent, and the result of her being "smelt out" was that no one would enter her hut, share food with her, or so much as speak to her. If she was in a path every one fled out of her way, and even her own children avoided her. Being in the colony she could not be otherwise punished, but such treatment as this would of itself, in course of time, have made her insane. She denied most emphatically having been concerned in the death of the child, though she did not doubt that some one had caused it by means of witchcraft. The witchfinder was sent for, and, as the matter was considered an important one, a larger number of Kaffirs than usual appeared at the investigation. On putting the ordinary tests to the witchfinder he failed to meet them, and when he was compelled, reluctantly, to admit that he had never held converse with the people under the water, it was easy to convince the bystanders that he was only an impostor.

Source:
Theal, Georg McCall. *Kaffir Folk-Lore*. London: S. Sonnenschein, Le Bas & Lowrey, 1886.

129. Chinese Mermaids

China

SOME of my readers may perchance be interested to learn that the original home of the mermaid (Ch. sea-woman *hai nü*) is almost within sight of the room in which these notes are being written. The only specimen of a veritable mermaid I ever saw was Barnum's celebrated purchase from Japan, which, so far as could be judged, consisted of a monkey's body most artistically joined to a fish's tail. But the author of a work entitled *Yueh chung chieh wên*, or "Jottings on the South of China," compiled in 1801, narrates how a man of the district of Sin-an (locally *Sin-on*) captured a mermaid on the shore of Ta-yü-shan or Namtao Island. "Her features and limbs were in all respects human, except that her body was covered with fine hair of many beautiful colours. The fisherman took home his prize and married her, though she was unable to talk and could only smile. She however learned to wear clothes like ordinary mortals. When the fisherman died the sea-maiden was sent back to the spot where she was first found, and she disappeared beneath the waves." The narrator quaintly adds, "This testifies that a man-fish does no injury to human beings," and he moreover informs us that these creatures are frequently to be found near Yü-shan and the Ladrone Island—so that any adventurous Hongkong canoeist may still have a chance of making a novel acquaintance. Another case recorded by the same writer speaks of a mermaid of more conventional form than the lady already noticed. "The Cabinet Councillor Cha Tao being despatched on a mission to Corea, and lying at anchor in his ship at a bay upon the coast, saw a woman stretched upon the beach, with her face upwards, her hair short and streaming loose, and with webbed feet and hands. He recognised this being as a mermaid (or man fish) and gave orders that she should be carried to the sea. This being done, the creature clasped her hands with an expression of loving gratitude and sank beneath the waters."

The Straits of Hainan are regarded by the Chinese as the chief habitat of monstrous fishes of strange shape, ruled over by the God of the waters, a sort of Chinese Neptune. And it is quite possible that the opening of the principal port of the island to foreign trade may (on the ground that nearly all such legends have a faint substratum of truth) reveal to the eyes of the naturalist new and undreamt-of inhabitants of the deep. It is but a few years since the ridicule excited by M. Victor Hugo's "devil fish" has given way to a sober recognition of the fact that the octopus of real life is a monster but little differing from the fanciful sketch given of his congener. And he would now-a-days be rash who ventured to assert that the Chinese have less ground for asserting the existence of very real monsters to our eyes than is possessed by the hardy fishermen of the coasts of Northern Europe.

Source:
Dennys, N[icholas] B[elfield]. *The Folk-Lore of China*. London: Trübner and Co., 1876. pp. 114-115.

130. The Princess of the Tung-T'ing Lake

China

CH'EN PI-CHIAO was a Pekingese; and being a poor man he attached himself as secretary to the suite of a high military official named Chia. On one occasion, while anchored on the Tung-t'ing lake, they saw a dolphin[1] floating on the surface of the water; and General Chia took his bow and shot at it, wounding the creature in the back. A fish was hanging on to its tail, and would not let go; so both were pulled out of the water together, and attached to the mast. There they lay gasping, the dolphin opening its mouth as if pleading for life, until at length young Ch'en begged the General to let them go again; and then he himself half jokingly put a piece of plaster upon the dolphin's wound, and had the two thrown back into the water, where they were seen for some time afterwards diving and rising again to the surface. About a year afterwards, Ch'en was once more crossing the Tung-t'ing lake on his way home, when the boat was upset in a squall, and he himself only saved by clinging to a bamboo crate, which finally, after floating about all night, caught in the overhanging branch of a tree, and thus enabled him to scramble on shore. By-and-by, another body floated in, and this turned out to be his servant; but on dragging him out, he found life was already extinct. In great distress, he sat himself down to rest, and saw beautiful green hills and waving willows, but not a single human being of whom he could ask the way. From early dawn till the morning was far advanced he remained in that state; and then, thinking he saw his servant's body move, he stretched out his hand to feel it, and before long the man threw up several quarts of water and recovered his consciousness. They now dried their clothes in the sun, and by noon these were fit to put on; at which period the pangs of hunger began to

---

[1] Literally, a "pig old-woman dragon." Porpoise (Fr. *porc-poisson*) suggests itself at once; but I think fresh-water dolphin is the best term, especially as the Tung-t'ing lake is many hundred miles inland. The commentator explains it by *t'o*, which would be "alligator" or "cayman," and is of course out of the question. My friend, Mr. L. C. Hopkins, has taken the trouble to make some investigations for me on this subject. He tells me that this fish, also called the "river pig," has first to be surrounded and secured by a strong net. Being too large to be hauled on board a boat, it is then driven ashore, where oil is extracted from the carcase and used for giving a gloss to silk thread, &c.

assail them, and accordingly they started over the hills in the hope of coming upon some habitation of man. As they were walking along, an arrow whizzed past, and the next moment two young ladies dashed by on handsome palfreys. Each had a scarlet band round her head, with a bunch of pheasant's feathers stuck in her hair, and wore a purple riding-jacket with small sleeves, confined by a green embroidered girdle round the waist. One of them carried a cross-bow for shooting bullets, and the other had on her arm a dark-coloured bow-and-arrow case. Reaching the brow of the hill, Ch'en beheld a number of riders engaged in beating the surrounding cover, all of whom were beautiful girls and dressed exactly alike. Afraid to advance any further, he inquired of a youth who appeared to be in attendance, and the latter told him that it was a hunting party from the palace; and then, having supplied him with food from his wallet, he bade him retire quickly, adding that if he fell in with them he would assuredly be put to death. Thereupon Ch'en hurried away; and descending the hill, turned into a copse where there was a building which he thought would in all probability be a monastery. On getting nearer, he saw that the place was surrounded by a wall, and between him and a half-open red-door was a brook spanned by a stone bridge leading up to it. Pulling back the door, he beheld within a number of ornamental buildings circling in the air like so many clouds, and for all the world resembling the Imperial pleasure-grounds; and thinking it must be the park of some official personage, he walked quietly in, enjoying the delicious fragrance of the flowers as he pushed aside the thick vegetation which obstructed his way. After traversing a winding path fenced in by balustrades, Ch'en reached a second enclosure, wherein were a quantity of tall willow-trees which swept the red eaves of the buildings with their branches. The note of some bird would set the petals of the flowers fluttering in the air, and the least wind would bring the seed vessels down from the elm-trees above; and the effect upon the eye and heart of the beholder was something quite unknown in the world of mortals. Passing through a small kiosque, Ch'en and his servant came upon a swing which seemed as though suspended from the clouds, while the ropes hung idly down in the utter stillness that prevailed.[1] Thinking by this that they were approaching the ladies' apartments,[2] Ch'en would have turned back, but

---

[1] Literally, in the utter absence of anybody.

[2] In passing near to the women's quarters in a friend's house, it is etiquette to cough slightly, that inmates may be warned and withdraw from the doors or windows in time to escape observation. Over and over again at interviews with mandarins of all grades I have heard the rustling of the ladies' dresses from some coigne of vantage, whence every movement of mine was being watched by an inquisitive crowd; and on one occasion I actually saw an eye peering through a small hole in the partition behind me.

at that moment he heard sounds of horses' feet at the door, and what seemed to be the laughter of a bevy of girls. So he and his servant hid themselves in a bush; and by-and-by, as the sounds came nearer, he heard one of the young ladies say, "We've had but poor sport to-day;" whereupon another cried out, "If the princess hadn't shot that wild goose, we should have taken all this trouble for nothing." Shortly after this, a number of girls dressed in red came in escorting a young lady, who went and sat down under the kiosque. She wore a hunting costume with tight[1] sleeves, and was about fourteen or fifteen years old. Her hair looked like a cloud of mist at the back of her head, and her waist seemed as though a breath of wind might snap it[2]—incomparable for beauty, even among the celebrities of old. Just then the attendants handed her some exquisitely fragrant tea, and stood glittering round her like a bank of beautiful embroidery. In a few moments the young lady arose and descended the kiosque; at which one of her attendants cried out, "Is your Highness too fatigued by riding to take a turn in the swing?" The princess replied that she was not; and immediately some supported her under the shoulders, while others seized her arms, and others again arranged her petticoats, and brought her the proper shoes.[3] Thus they helped her into the swing, she herself stretching out her shining arms, and putting her feet into a suitable pair of slippers; and then—away she went, light as a flying-swallow, far up into the fleecy clouds. As soon as she had had enough, the attendants helped her out, and one of them exclaimed, "Truly, your Highness is a perfect angel!" At this the young lady laughed, and walked away, Ch'en gazing after her in a state of semi-consciouness, until, at length, the voices died away, and he and his servant crept forth. Walking up and down near the swing, he suddenly espied a red handkerchief near the paling, which he knew had been dropped by one of the young ladies; and, thrusting it joyfully into his sleeve, he walked up and entered the kiosque. There, upon a table, lay writing materials, and taking out the handkerchief he indited upon it the following lines:—

> "What form divine was just now sporting nigh?—
> 'Twas she, I trow of 'golden lily' fame;
> Her charms the moon's fair denizens might shame,
> Her fairy footsteps bear her to the sky."

---

[1] Literally, "bald"—*i.e.*, without the usual width and ornamentation of a Chinese lady's sleeve.

[2] Small waists are much admired in China, but any such artificial aids as stays and tight lacing are quite unknown. A certain Prince Wei admitted none but the possessors of small waists into his harem; hence his establishment came to be called the *Palace of Small Waists*.

[3] Probably of felt or some such material, to prevent the young lady from slipping as she stood, not sat, in the swing.

Humming this stanza to himself, Ch'en walked along seeking for the path by which he had entered; but every door was securely barred, and he knew not what to do. So he went back to the kiosque, when suddenly one of the young ladies appeared, and asked him in astonishment what he did there. "I have lost my way," replied Ch'en; "I pray you lend me your assistance."

"Do you happen to have found a red handkerchief?" said the girl. "I have, indeed," answered Ch'en, "but I fear I have made it somewhat dirty;" and, suiting the action to the word, he drew it forth, and handed it to her. "Wretched man!" cried the young lady, "you are undone. This is a handkerchief the princess is constantly using, and you have gone and scribbled all over it; what will become of you now?" Ch'en was in a great fright, and begged the young lady to intercede for him; to which she replied, "It was bad enough that you should come here and spy about; however, being a scholar, and a man of refinement, I would have done my best for you; but after this, how am I to help you?" Off she then ran with the handkerchief, while Ch'en remained behind in an agony of suspense, and longing for the wings of a bird to bear him away from his fate. By-and-by, the young lady returned and congratulated him, saying, "There is some hope for you. The Princess read your verses several times over, and was not at all angry. You will probably be released; but, meanwhile, wait here, and don't climb the trees, or try to get through the walls, or you may not escape after all." Evening was now drawing on, and Ch'en knew not, for certain, what was about to happen; at the same time he was very empty, and, what with hunger and anxiety, death would have been almost a happy release. Before long, the young lady returned with a lamp in her hand, and followed by a slave-girl bearing wine and food, which she forthwith presented to Ch'en. The latter asked if there was any news about himself; to which the young lady replied that she had just mentioned his case to the Princess who, not knowing what to do with him at that hour of the night, had given orders that he should at once be provided with food, "which, at any rate," added she, "is not bad news." The whole night long Ch'en walked up and down unable to take rest; and it was not till late in the morning that the young lady appeared with more food for him. Imploring her once more to intercede on his behalf, she told him that the Princess had not instructed them either to kill or to release him, and that it would not be fitting for such as herself to be bothering the Princess with suggestions. So there Ch'en still remained until another day had almost gone, hoping for the welcome moment; and then the young lady rushed hurriedly in, saying, "You are lost! Some one has told the Queen, and she, in a fit of anger, threw the handkerchief on the ground, and made use of very violent language. Oh dear! oh dear! I'm sure something dreadful will happen." Ch'en threw himself on his knees, his face as pale as ashes, and begged to know what he should do; but at that moment sounds were heard outside, and the young lady waved her hand to him, and ran away. Immediately a crowd came pouring in through the door, with ropes ready to secure the object of their search; and among them was a slave-girl, who looked fixedly at our hero, and cried out, "Why, surely you are Mr. Ch'en, aren't you?" at the same time stopping the others from binding him until she should have reported to the Queen. In a few minutes she came back, and said the Queen requested him to walk in and in he went, through a number of doors, trembling all the time with fear, until he reached a hall, the screen before which was ornamented with green jade and silver. A beautiful girl drew aside the bamboo curtain at the door, and announced, "Mr. Ch'en;" and he himself advanced, and fell down before a lady, who was sitting upon a dais at the other end, knocking his head upon the ground, and crying out, "Thy servant is from a far-off country; spare, oh! spare his life."

"Sir!" replied the Queen, rising hastily from her seat, and extending a hand to Ch'en, "but for you, I should not be here to-day. Pray excuse the rudeness of my maids." Thereupon a splendid repast was served, and wine was poured out in chased goblets, to the no small astonishment of Ch'en, who could not understand why he was treated thus. "Your kindness," observed the Queen, "in restoring me to life, I am quite unable to repay; however, as you have made my daughter the subject of your verse, the match is clearly ordained by fate, and I shall send her along to be your handmaid." Ch'en hardly knew what to make of this extraordinary accomplishment of his wishes, but the marriage was solemnized there and then; bands of music struck up wedding-airs, beautiful mats were laid down for them to walk upon, and the whole place was brilliantly lighted with a profusion of coloured lamps. Then Ch'en said to the Princess, "That a stray and unknown traveller like myself, guilty of spoiling your Highness's handkerchief, should have escaped the fate he deserved, was already more than could be expected; but now to receive you in marriage—this, indeed, far surpasses my wildest expectations."

"My mother," replied the Princess, "is married to the King of this lake, and is herself a daughter of the River Prince. Last year, when on her way to visit her parents, she happened to cross the lake, and was wounded by an arrow; but you saved her life, and gave her plaster for the wound. Our family, therefore, is grateful to you, and can never forget your good act. And do not regard me as of another species than yourself; the Dragon King has bestowed upon me the elixir of immortality, and this I will gladly share with you." Then Ch'en knew that his wife was a spirit, and by-and-by he asked her how the slave-girl had recognised him; to which she replied, that the girl was the small fish which had been found hanging to the dolphin's tail. He then inquired why, as they didn't intend to kill him, he had been kept so long a prisoner. "I was charmed with your literary talent," answered the Princess, "but I did not venture to take the responsibility upon myself; and no one saw how I tossed and turned the livelong night."

"Dear friend," said Ch'en; "but, come, tell me who was it that brought my food."

"A trusty waiting-maid of mine," replied the Princess; "her name is A-nien." Ch'en then asked how he could ever repay her, and the Princess told him there would be plenty of time to think of that; and when he inquired where the king, her father, was, she said he had gone off with the God of War to fight against Ch'ih-yu,[1] and had not returned. A few days passed, and Ch'en began to think his people at home would be anxious about him; so he sent off his servant with a letter to tell them he was safe and sound, at which they were all overjoyed, believing him to have been lost in the wreck of the boat, of which event news had already reached them. However, they were unable to send him any reply, and were considerably distressed as to how he would find his way home again. Six months afterwards Ch'en himself appeared, dressed in fine clothes, and riding on a splendid horse, with plenty of money, and valuable jewels in his pocket—evidently a man of wealth. From that time forth he kept up a magnificent establishment; and in seven or eight years had become the father of five children. Every day he kept open house, and if any one asked him about his adventures, he would readily tell them without reservation. Now a friend of his, named Liang, whom he had known since they were boys together, and who, after holding an appointment for some years in Nan-fu, was crossing the Tung-t'ing Lake, on his way home, suddenly beheld an ornamental barge, with carved wood-work and red windows, passing over the foamy waves to the sound of music and singing from within. Just then a beautiful young lady leant out of one of the windows, which she had pushed open, and by her side Liang saw a young man sitting, in a négligé attitude, while two nice-looking girls stood by and shampooed[2] him. Liang, at first, thought it must be the party of some high official, and wondered at the scarcity of attendants;[3] but, on looking more closely at the young man, he saw it was

---

[1] A rebel chieftain of the legendary period of China's history, who took up arms against the Emperor Huang Ti (B.C. 2697-2597), but was subsequently defeated in what was perhaps the first decisive battle of the world.

[2] This favourite process consists in gently thumping the person operated upon all over the back with the soft part of the closed fists. Compare Lane, *Arabian Nights*, Vol. I., p. 551:—"She then pressed me to her bosom, and laid me on the bed, and continued gently kneading my limbs until slumber overcame me."

[3] The *retinue* of a high mandarin is composed as follows:—First, gong-bearers, then banner-men, tablet-bearers (on which tablets are inscribed the titles of the official), a large red umbrella, mounted attendants, a box containing a change of clothes, bearers of regalia, a second gong, a small umbrella or sunshade, a large wooden fan, executioners, lictors from hell,

no other than his old friend Ch'en. Thereupon he began almost involuntarily to shout out to him; and when Ch'en heard his own name, he stopped the rowers, and walked out towards the figurehead,[1] beckoning Liang to cross over into his boat, where the remains of their feast was quickly cleared away, and fresh supplies of wine, and tea, and all kinds of costly foods spread out by handsome slave-girls. "It's ten years since we met," said Liang, "and what a rich man you have become in the meantime."

"Well," replied Ch'en, "do you think that so very extraordinary for a poor fellow like me?" Liang then asked him who was the lady with whom he was taking wine, and Ch'en said she was his wife, which very much astonished Liang, who further inquired whither they were going. "Westwards," answered Ch'en, and prevented any further questions by giving a signal for the music, which effectually put a stop to all further conversation.[2] By-and-by, Liang found the wine getting into his head, and seized the opportunity to ask Ch'en to make him a present of one of his beautiful slave-girls. "You are drunk,[3] my friend," replied Ch'en;

---

who wear tall hats; a mace (called a "golden melon"), bamboos for "bambooing," incense-bearers, more attendants, and now the great man himself, followed by a body-guard of soldiers and a few personal attendants, amounting in all to nearly one hundred persons, many of whom are mere street-rowdies or beggars, hired at a trifling outlay when required to join what might otherwise be an imposing procession. The scanty *retinues* of foreign officials in China still continue to excite the scorn of the populace, who love to compare the rag-tag and bob-tail magnificence of their own functionaries with the modest show even of H.B.M.'s Minister at Pekin. A considerable number of the attendants there mentioned would accompany any high official, some in the same, the rest in another barge.

[1] Generally known as the "cut-wave God."

[2] At all great banquets in China a theatrical troupe is engaged to perform while the dinner, which may last from four to six hours, drags its slow length along.

[3] I have already discussed the subject of drunkenness in China (*Chinese Sketches*, pp. 113, 114), and shall not return to it here, further than to quote a single sentence, to which I adhere as firmly now as when the book in question was published:—"Who ever sees in China a tipsy man reeling about a crowded thoroughfare, or lying with his head in a ditch by the side of some country road?"

It is not, however, generally known that the Chinese, with their usual quaintness, distinguish between five kinds of drunkenness, different people being differently affected, according to the physical constitution of each. Wine may fly (1) to the heart, and produce maudlin emotions; or (2) to the liver, and incite to pugnacity; or (3) to the stomach, and cause "however, I will give you the price of one as a pledge of our old friendship." And, turning to a servant, he bade him present Liang with a splendid pearl, saying, "Now you can buy a Green Pearl;[1] you see I am not stingy;" adding forthwith, "but I am pressed for time, and can stay no longer with my old friend." So he escorted Liang back to his boat, and, having let go the rope, proceeded on his way. Now, when Liang reached home, and called at Ch'en's house, whom should he see but Ch'en himself drinking with a party of friends. "Why, I saw you only yesterday," cried Liang, "upon the Tung-t'ing. How quickly you have got back!" Ch'en denied this, and then Liang repeated the whole story, at the conclusion of which, Ch'en laughed, and said, "You must be mistaken. Do you imagine I can be in two places at once?" The company were all much astonished, and knew not what to make of it; and subsequently when Ch'en, who died at the age of eighty, was being carried to his grave, the bearers thought the coffin seemed remarkably light, and on opening it to see, found that the body had disappeared.

Source:
Giles, Herbert A., translator. *Strange Stories from a Chinese Studio, Volume 2*. London: Thos. De La Rue & Co., 1880.

131. Ningyo

Japan

NINGYO: Sort of mermaids, inhabitants of the Taiyan island waters, who are represented with a human bust attached to the body of a fish, and listening in shells to the secrets of the sea. The shell is usually a haliotis. The mermaid proper is usually represented with forelegs. There was a curious specimen in the Dresser collection (sold 1905), consisting of the dried body of a fish the head of which had been replaced by a carved head and forelegs with claws.

Sometimes the Ningyo holds a Tama [jewel].

Other creatures, generally females, with a scanty covering perhaps of seaweed around the loins, but with legs and no tail, and carrying a scythe-shaped knife in the right hand, are often met with as netsuké, the

---

drowsiness, accompanied by a flushing of the face; or (4) to the lungs, and induce hilarity; or (5) to the kidneys, and excite desire.

[1] The name of a celebrated beauty.

left hand carrying to the ear a shell; they are Awabi divers.

But one type of old netsuké, very often rudely carved out of deer horn, with large protruding abdomen is said to represent the Empress Jingo Kogo, who retarded her accouchement during the Korean war.

Source:
Joly, Henri L. *Legend in Japanese Art*. London: John Lane, The Bodley Head, 1908.

132. Toda, the Archer, and the Queen of the World under the Sea[1]

Japan

RIGHT in the heart of the main island of Japan, surrounded by mountains and mulberry fields, lies the lovely lake of Biwa. It is sixty miles long, and as blue as the bright sky, whose mirror it is. All around, nature is beautiful; for in the neighborhood lie the sacred city of Kioto, and the ten most beautiful views of scenery in Japan.

Of this scenery, many a Japanese book, with its crooked worm-like letters, tells; of it every child in Japan learns; and to see it, people travel from all parts of the empire. Four lovely islands dot the lake's surface, like cut and polished emeralds on a rock of turquoise. From amid groves of pine trees, temples and monasteries peep out, with their red gates and belfries. The dense foliage is whitened by vast flocks of white heron, which whirr and sail and tremble and alight continually. Skimming over the lake, or following unharmed after the farmer in the furrows, to pick up worms by day, they all assemble at night and lie asleep and quiet, like masses of snow on the grand old pine-trees of the islands. When the great temple bell of Miidera booms and quivers over the lake, they rise and soar and separate—all save the nestlings left at home with the old

---

[1] This story, which is a very ancient and famous one, has been put into its present English dress, by Prof. William E. Griffis, the author of "The Mikado's Empire"—the latest and the most complete work on Japan. Besides treating of the history, mythology, manners, customs, literature, and ideas underlying Japanese art, it also contains a chapter on "Folk Lore and Fireside Stories;" and in these latter will be found a fuller description of the "Queen of the World Under the Sea," and of "Kai Riu Ō, the Dragon-monarch of the Deep." Prof. Griffis spent four years in Japan, in the educational service of the Japanese government.

grannies and patriarchs of the flocks. Tame deer also roam the islands; for Japanese children are taught not to harm either bird or beast, and they obey. On the edge of the lake, at Karasaki, is the great pine-tree planted long, long ago, before Toda the archer was born, and when the oldest stork or tortoise was young.[1] It is not tall; but its branches are many of them seventy feet long, and it covers a space of over four hundred square feet. Its old limbs are propped up on crutches, or recline, supported on a lattice-work of bamboo like a mattress. Underneath it, you can walk knee-deep in a level heap of brown pine needles, which have fallen for centuries. Further up the lake is the Bridge of Seta, and on its western shore are the white walls and pagoda towers of the Castle of Hikoné.

The name Biwa—what does it mean, and how came it?

A biwa is a lute, or three-stringed guitar, which Japanese ladies play. It is almost exactly like those used in Italy, by the troubadours; only the strings are struck with an ivory stick or plectrum. The biwa is wide and round at one end, long and narrow at the other; and this is the shape of the lake.

Wonderful to tell, this lake was not always where it is now. It was born in a night. Long, long ago—two thousand years or more, they say—there was a mighty earthquake during the night. People said that Kai Riu Ō, the Dragon-king of the World under the Sea, caused it. Suddenly, amid the awful rocking, the land sunk, and formed the lake. At the same time, sixty miles distant, a vast mass of earth rose up, and became the sacred mountain Fuji. This glorious cone is twelve thousand feet high, robed with forests and crowned with snow.

When the astonished people came to look at the newborn lake, they were delighted with mother earth's new-born baby.[2] After a while, some rowers over the lake found out its shape, and in delight called it Lake Biwa, after the guitar with which plays Benten—the earthly name of the Queen of the World under the Sea.

In this under-world, dwell Kai Riu Ō, the Dragon-king of the Deep, and his consort, the Queen. Their palace is of shells and coral, marble and gems. All the bright colors of moving life on the ocean floor—such as only the diver ever sees—adorn its gates and walls and ceilings. The light in this under-world is like that in a glass aquarium, through which the sun is shining; and the water is to the inhabitants like the air to us—no more trouble to them, and just as pleasant. However, there are no winds or tempests, or drafts of hot or chilly air; and so people never catch cold in those regions. The King rules this water-world by a host of vassal lords. All the fishes and monsters of the deep are his servants. The

---

[1] The popular belief in Japan is, that the crane and tortoise live to be a thousand years old; or, as some say, ten thousand.

[2] In Japanese mythology, the various mountains, rivers, islands, etc, are conceived of and called the children, born of the gods who created Japan.

dragon is his messenger to do his commands. Sometimes he is the king's courser, and, with him on his back, careers over the sea and through the air at lightning speed. The dragon holds in his claws the two crystal jewel balls which govern the ebb and flow of the tides. The dragon sends and withholds the rain, spouts out the flood, breathes out the tempest, and, with his tail, lashes the ocean waves into foam and fury.

Rarely does the Dragon-king rise above the waves into the earth-world. He comes only to endow a king's son,[1] or to arrange matters of importance between the sea and clouds, or to keep his dragons in order; for there are many kinds of these monsters, and sometimes they fight and quarrel dreadfully with each other. Kai Riu Ō is always known by his helmet, the crest and back of which is a living dragon, the chief of the dragons.

His Queen, however, likes to visit the earth often. When she comes, she assumes the form of, and dresses like, one of the ladies of the palace in the Mikado's (emperor's) court. She rides on the clouds and waves, on her favorite green dragon. Often she cultivates the earth and gathers the crops and fruit which are ripened by the showers from her watery domains. Dressed in crimson and white robes, with the two fashionable sable spots on her forehead, with long fan with silken cords of many colors, she walks the earth like one of the court beauties.

But even this mighty Queen—so powerful in her own Under-world—is only a woman on earth, and is glad to be protected by a brave samurai (knight). Her chief enemy is the great snake-centipede, named Ja. This is no common milleped, or "thousand legger," such as crawls over our bricks and damp places. Oh no! the Japanese Ja had a head like a dragon, eyes that blazed red like fire, horrible curling mustaches like writhing adders, horny scales like iron armor, and a long snaky body with a million legs. It was so immense that it coiled its serpentine folds seven times and a half round the mountain of Mikami. This mountain lies a little to the northeast of Lake Biwa, at its outlet to the river, which is crossed by the Bridge of Séta.

Now the Queen had built herself a summer palace under the Lake, and near by, on its land borders, she planted a garden, grain fields, and mulberry plantations, to provide food for her silk-worms. But when her crops were nearly ripe, down came the wicked centipede, and ate up all the fruit and grain, and tore up the ground. As for the laborers—the men and women whom the Queen hired—he swallowed them all up at one gulp, and spat out their bones. Thus he scattered misery and destruction

---

[1] At the Centennial Exposition at Philadelphia, in the main aisle in the Japanese Section, Main Hall, there was a spirited representation in bronze, and gold and silver, of Kai Riu Ō, rising up from the deeps with a casket of jewels in his hand, to endow Ojin, the infant son of the queen Jingu.

all around.

Coming one day to visit her fields, the Queen saw, with horror and dismay, the awful ruin. She began to weep bitterly, because on earth she was so helpless, and no one could destroy the awful Ja.

Now it happened that the famous warrior Toda, all in armor, with his trusty bow, was passing by. To him she applied for help, telling him her misfortunes. Toda did not know the lady; but, ever ready to help the weak, he resolved to fight Ja. He knew that a common arrow could wound, but not kill the centipede; but that a barb, well moistened with saliva, would mortally wound the monster. Human saliva was the only thing the great Ja feared.

Advancing cautiously over the bridge, bow in hand, with an arrow ready fitted to the string, Toda could see nothing, till casting his eyes upon the mountain, he saw two lurid round lights—the eyes of the centipede. It was now quite dark, and the orbs glowered on him with such frightful brilliancy that, in his excitement, he forgot to wet the steel barb of the arrow with his tongue. He shot; and the arrow struck the eye of the centipede, whose terrible groan made the mountains echo, and the earth tremble. In a moment more, the bow twanged a second time, and a twin arrow buried itself in the other eye of the monster,' whose howls were now deafening. Maddened with pain, the Ja began to uncoil his folds, to rush upon Toda and destroy him. Suddenly, the archer remembered to wet his next arrow well in his mouth. He took aim between the eyes, and let fly. The moistened barb sank deep into his forehead, and the great monster slowly stiffened out dead. In the morning, they found that his body lay coiled seven times and a half round the mountain. Toda hacked the hideous corpse to pieces, and the buzzards held a great feast over his carcase.

Now came his reward. The lady revealed herself to him as the Queen of the Under-world; thanked him, and invited him to her palace under the lake. They went together to the island of Chikubu, in the lake. The Queen clapped her hands, and Toda could see rising up through the limpid depths, a boat like a large shell. Into this they stepped, and, in a few minutes, passed down under the earth, even far below the roots of the mountains. The shell-boat stopped near the palace of the Queen.

Toda was surprised at the wonders all around him. The creatures of this sea-world, appeared to be human—like human beings—yet there seemed to be a good deal of the nature of fishes in them. It was not dark, but the light was like the sunlight when it comes through globes of water. The palace was of white coral, with decorations, in many colors, of the same materials. Gardens of sea-weeds of the rarest tints bloomed all around him, while some of the loveliest ladies of the sea-world sat chatting together on banks of sponge of all hues. Groves of marine plants were planted at intervals, while in pools in the bottom were fishes of every kind, many of which Toda had never seen. A vast archway leading off in one direction was, so Toda was told, the tunnel or highway leading to the ocean-palace of Kai Riu Ō.

But what struck Toda with the greatest surprise, and more than the gold and jewels, music, feasting, banners and bells, and amber throne of the Queen, was the strange sort of head-dresses which these people wore. He liked to think of them as people, though he was sure they were fairies. Like a polite Japanese courtier, however, he asked no questions.

In the first place, their clothing was cut in the fashion of long, long ago—in the old days before the pine-tree of Karasaki was planted. It reminded him of the time when the first emperor came to Japan, and the fairies lived on the earth. As for the material, it seemed to be woven of shells and coral and amber. The edges and fringes of the robes were of mother of pearl, and the rainbow tints of nacre, and changeable silk. The Queen wore a diadem composed of amber, jade, crystal, coral, and rarest shells, with a plume of "spun-glass coral."[1]

But the head-dresses were the most curious of all. The pages wore bonnets of living sea-anemones, with their tentacles all twirling, with their vivid purple, orange, scarlet and blue colors. Each of the musicians had on a cuttle-fish, with its big-eyed lumpy body on his head, and the long pulpy legs, full of sucking-cups, dangling down the wearer's back. Some had flounders for skull-caps. One had a sea-horse for the crest of his helmet; another wore a conch. Toda noticed on others, sturgeon, sea-bass, stars, crawfish, lobsters, jelly-fish etc., etc. A whole fish-market could be seen made into hats and bonnets, and all alive. As for the cooks, scullions, laborers, and porters, they did not wear much clothing of any sort—but none were bare-headed. They had on caps made of clam shells, oyster shells, sea-ears, limpets, gudgeons, sardines, sculpins, shrimps, king-crabs, squids, and such baser sort of water-vermin.

Strange to say, all these head-dresses were alive; yet the cat-fish did not stick with his fins, nor the lobster snap his claws, nor the cuttle-fish suck, nor the sword-fish stab, nor the squid squirt ink on any one. They only winked and blinked and wagged tails and fins, and twirled their feelers, and yawned or gaped sometimes, but behaved each one like a well-trained monkey on its master's shoulders. The kin-giyo, or goldfish, seemed, however, to be specially anxious to show its triple lace-like tail.

As for the people, they did not think themselves or their dress curious, but they gazed politely on Toda, whose helmet, brocade dress, armor, bow and arrows, were never-failing objects of wonder. They could not talk Japanese, but only make signs that showed them well-bred

---

[1] The Hyalonema Mirabilis (wonderful Glass-cable Sponge) which grows only on the deep-sea bottoms; first found only in the seas of Japan, but now proved by the Challenger researches to flourish in many parts of the "world under the sea." It is composed of a silicious sponge, anchored by the finest filaments of pure silex, like spun glass, arranged in concentric layers.

in under-world etiquette, which made Toda suspect all the more that they were half fish and half fairy—their motions were so much like fins.

After dancing, with music and feasting, and shows of all kinds, Toda wished to return home. Then the Queen, in presence of all her court, in the Hall of Red Coral, presented him with rare and curious presents—the chief of all being a massive bronze bell. A great procession escorted the hero to that part of the under-world situated beneath Chikubu island.

First, came two fish-headed heralds bearing banners of pearl inscribed with the blazon of Kai Riu Ō. Next, two trumpeters, a gong-beater, a flute-blower, and one other with a cuttle-fish head and tsutsumi, or hand drum. Next followed Toda, with the Queen, her maid of honor, and her prime minister with his dragon-helmet on. Seven fish-headed grandees followed, preceding the great bell and the royal gifts. These included a sword, silk robes, jars of wine, casks of rice, and bags of money. Next came more banner men, and behind them a long train of lesser lords and ladies and vassals, all in robes of pink shell and crowns of fish, such as trout, tunny, stickleback, skate, hammerheads, roach, mullet, dace, and many other sorts belonging to both fresh and salt water. On arriving at the shell-boat, Toda bade his friends sayonara (good bye). In a few minutes he rose out of the water at Chikubu island, where his presents were landed, and he was left all alone.

Not long alone, however; for his own servants, alarmed at his absence, had been searching for him, and rejoiced to find their master alive. They bore him and his presents, except the bell, home to Kioto, where all welcomed the brave destroyer of the Ja.

The best part of the reward was to come. Toda knew that he would grow old, and that he might become poor. He felt gloomy, when lo! he discovered that the casks of rice never got empty before they filled themselves again, and the jars of wine brimmed as fast as they were tapped. The silk dress never wore out, nor did its gold embroidery ever dim. The sword conquered all it touched. The money bag never became empty, but always kept fat and full. So Toda feasted his friends and lived a jolly life, to a good old age.

As for the great bronze bell, Toda gave it as a thank-offering to the temple of Miidera. There it still hangs and swings and quivers and booms. Night and morning, its mellow notes roll over the lake, and echo in the mountains, waking up at once the white herons, the farmer folks, the mulberry and tea-pickers, and the monks, to the labors of the day.

Still smiles the blue lake of Biwa to the bluer sky, though now seven little steamboats ply over its bosom, scare the snowy heron with their whistle, and blacken the white castle walls with coal smoke. Still, in autumn, the maple leaves turn red on the slope of Mikami mountain. Still the traveler crosses the Bridge of Séta, and looks up to the heights where the eyes of the Ja once glared. Often, the little Japanese child leans over the side of the boat which his father sculls over Lake Biwa, and gazes far down into the clear depths, hoping to catch a glimpse of the Sea-queen's palaces. The descendants of Toda still live in Japan, and are the renowned Fujiwara[1] family, from which have come so many of the empresses of the one hundred and twenty-three Mikados of Japan. Still in Japanese art—on fans, screens and pictures; in ivory, bronze, porcelain and lacquered work, as well as by aunts and grandmothers—is told the story of Toda, the brave archer, and how he was rewarded by the Queen of the Under-world, in the regions of Kai Riu Ō.

Source:
Pabke, Marie, and Margery Deane. *Wonder-World Stories*. New York: G. P. Putnam's Sons, 1877.

133. The Boy of Urashima

Japan

IN THE reign of the Empress Suiko (A.D. 593-628) there lived, on a small island off the coast of Tango, a poor fisherman and his wife. Though too poor to provide more than the barest necessaries of life, they managed, being pious folks, to keep the lamp always burning in the shrine of Riu Jin, the sea-god, their patron. Night and morning they offered up their prayers, and, though their meals might be scanty, they never failed to burn a stick of incense at the shrine.

To this good couple a dear son was born, who grew up to be pious and dutiful, and to be the staff of his aged parents. When they were too old to go out to fish, Tarō, the son, caught enough fish to Support himself and them. Now, it happened that one day in autumn Tarō was out, as usual, in his boat, though the sea was rough and the waves high. The increasing storm finally compelled him to seek shelter in his hut. He uttered a prayer to the sea-god, and turned his prow homeward. Suddenly there appeared, on the crest of the waves, a divine being, robed in white, riding upon a large tortoise. Approaching the wearied fisherman, he greeted him kindly, and said, "Follow me, and I will make you a happy man."

Tarō, leaving his boat, and mounting the tortoise with his august companion, the tortoise sped away with marvelous celerity; and on they journeyed for three days, passing some of the most wonderful sights

---

[1] Fujiwara means, "meadow of Wistaria blossoms;" the Fuji or Wistaria being indigenous to Japan.

human being ever beheld. There were ponds of perfectly transparent water filled with the fish lie daily caught, and others with strange species. The roads were lined with rare and fragrant trees laden with golden fruit, and flowers more beautiful than he had ever Seen or imagined. Finally, they came to a great gate of white marble, of rare design and imposing proportion. Richly dressed ladies and pages were waiting to welcome him. He entered a golden palanquin, and amidst trains of courtiers was borne to the palace of the king, and treated with honor and courtesy. The splendors of this palace it is not possible to describe in the language of earth. Tarō was assigned to one of the fairest apartments, and beautiful girls waited upon him, and a host of servants were ready to do his bidding. Feasts, music, songs, dancing, gay parties, were given in his honor. Many of the people around him seemed very remarkable beings. Some had heads made of shells, some of coral. All the lovely colors of nacre, the rarest tints which man can see beneath the deep-blue sea when the ocean's floor is visible, appeared on their dresses and ornaments. Their jewels of pearls and precious stones and gold and silver were profuse, but wrought in exquisite art. Tarō could scarcely tell whether the fascinating creatures were human or not; but he was very happy, and his hosts so kind that he did not stop to notice their peculiarities. That he was in fairy-land he knew, for such wealth was never seen, even in king's palaces, on earth.

After Tarō had spent, as he supposed, seven days at the king's palace, he wished to go and see his parents. He felt it was wrong to be happy when he was uncertain of their fate in the upper world. The king allowed his request, and, on parting with him, gave him a box. "This," said he, "I give you on condition that you never open it, nor show it to any one, under any circumstances whatever." Tarō, wondering, received it, and bid adieu to the king. He was escorted to the white marble gate, and, mounting the same tortoise, reached the spot where he had left his boat. The tortoise then left him.

Tarō was all alone. He looked round, and saw nothing on the strand. The mountains and rocks were familiar, but no trace of his parents' but was seen. He began to make inquiries, and finally learned from an old gray-headed fisherman that, centuries before, the persons he described as his parents had lived there, but had been buried so long ago that their names could be read only by scraping the moss and lichens off the very oldest stones of the grave-yard in the valley yonder. Thither Tarō hied, and after long search found the tomb of his dear parents. He now, for the first time since he had left his boat—as he thought, a few days ago—felt the pangs of sorrow. He felt an irresistible longing to open the box. He did so. A purple vapor, like a cloud, issued and suffused his head for a moment. A cold shiver ran through him. He tried to rise; his limbs were stiff and bent. His face was wrinkled; his teeth dropped out; his limbs trembled; he was an old man, with the weight of four centuries on him. His infirmities were too great for flesh to bear; he died a few days afterward.

I have given the story as it was current in Echizen. I have also heard it told with the location on the shores of the Bay of Yedo. Another version makes the strand of a river in Shinano the place of Tarō's departure and return. In another form of the story, Tarō returns to find his parents dwelling in a glorious mansion. After greetings are over, the old folks are curious to know what the box contains. Tarō, persuaded, opens it, to find himself, alone and old, on a desolate shore. The story is undoubtedly very old. It is found in several books, and has been often made the subject of art. The fishermen in various parts of Japan worship the good boy of Urashima, who, even in the palaces of the sea-gods, forgot not his old parents.

NOTES

The Sea-god rising out of the Deep.—Riu Jin (Dragon-god), or Kai Riu Ō (Dragon-king of the Sea), is the personification of the dragon; and the monarch of the world under the sea appears in many fairy tales and very ancient legends, his palaces being located under the ocean, the Inland Sea, or Lake Biwa. He is a reality still to millions of Japanese people. He is represented in terrible majesty, and of awful mien, rising out of the deep. His helmet and mail it a living dragon—the symbol of irresistible might, motion, and ubiquity. His robes are gold and jewels. Around him the waves mount, part, roll, and churn into white foam-edges, their translucent green curves flecked with silvery foam-bells. He holds in his hands a casket, in which are the jewels that control the ebb and flow of the tides (the powers of the sun and moon[?]), significant of victory, longevity, valor, and invulnerability to Ōjin, the infant god of war, whom he offers to endow with them. "Quick; take this casket: the opportunity is brief. I deign not long to remain in this upper world," is the expression on his face. In pictures, Takénouchi is holding the infant god when the Dragon-king appears. In several bronzes and ivory carvings his queen is represented in robes of shell and coral, with diadem of rare shells.

Source:
Griffis, William E. *The Mikado's Empire*. New York: Harper & Brothers, 1876, 1883.

134. How the Jelly-Fish Lost His Shell

Japan

IN THE days of old, the Jelly-fish was one of the retainers in waiting upon the Queen of the World under the Sea. In those days he had a shell, and as his head was hard, no one dared to insult him, or stick him with their horns, or pinch him with their claws, or scratch him with their nails, or brush rudely by him with their fins. In short, this fish instead of being a lump of jelly, as white and helpless as a pudding, as we see him now, was a lordly fellow that could get his back up and keep it high when he wished to. He waited on the Queen and right proud was he of his office. He was on good terms with the King's Dragon, which often allowed him to play with his scaly tail, but never hurt him in the least. One day the Queen fell sick, and every hour grew worse. The King became anxious, and her subjects talked about nothing else but her sickness. There was grief all through the waterworld; from the mermaids on their beds of sponge, and the dragons in the rocky caverns, down to the tiny gudgeons in the rivers, that were considered no more than mere bait. The jolly Cuttle-fish stopped playing his drums and guitar, folded his six arms and hid away moping in his hole. His servant the Lobster in vain lighted his candle at night, and tried to induce him to come out of his lair. The dolphins and porpoises wept tears, but the clams, oysters, and limpets shut up their shells and did not even wiggle. The flounders and skates lay flat on the ocean's floor, never even lifting up their noses. The Squid wept a great deal of ink, and the Jelly-fish nearly melted to pure water. The Tortoise was patient and offered to do anything for the relief of the Queen.

But nothing could be done. The Cuttle-fish who professed to be "a kind of a" doctor, offered the use of all his cups to suck out the poison, if that were the trouble.

But it wasn't. It was internal, and nothing but medicine that could be swallowed would reach the disease.

At last some one suggested that the liver of a Monkey would be a specific for the royal sickness, and it was resolved to try it. The Tortoise, who was the Queen's messenger, because he could live on both land and water, swim or crawl, was summoned. He was told to go upon earth to a certain mountain, catch a monkey and bring him alive to the Underworld.

Off started the Tortoise on his journey to the earth, and going to a mountain where the monkeys lived, squatted down at the foot of a tree and pretended to be asleep though keeping his claws and tail out. There he waited patiently, well knowing that curiosity and the monkey's love of tricks would bring one within reach of his talons. Pretty soon, a family of chattering monkeys came running along among the branches overhead, when suddenly a young fellow caught sight of the sleeping Tortoise.

"Is it possible?" said the long-handed fellow, "here's fun! Let's tickle the old fellow's back and pull his tail."

All agreed, and forthwith a dozen monkeys, joining hand over hand, made a long ladder of themselves until they just reached the Tortoise's back. They didn't use their tails, for Japanese monkeys have none, except stumps two inches long. However, he who was to be the tail end of this living rope, when all was ready, crawled along and slipped over the whole line, whispering as he slid:

"'Sh! don't chatter or laugh, you'll wake him up."

Now the Monkey expected to hold on the living pendulum by one long hand, and swinging down with the other, to pull the Tortoise's tail, and see how near he could come to his snout without being snapped up. For he well knew that a tortoise could neither jump off its legs nor climb a tree.

One! Two! The monkey pendulum swung back and forth without touching.

Three! Four! The Monkey's fingernails scratched the Tortoise's back. Yet old Hard Shell pretended to be sound asleep.

Five! Six! The Monkey caught hold of the Tortoise's tail and jerked it hard. Old Tortoise now moved out its head a little, as if still only half awake.

Seven! Eight! This time the Monkey intended to pull the Tortoise's head, when just as he came within reach, the Tortoise snapped him, held him in his claws, and as the monkey pendulum swung back he lost his hold. In an instant he was jerked loose, and fell head-foremost to the ground, half stunned.

Frightened at the loss of their end link, the other monkeys of the chain wound themselves up like a windlass over the branches, and squatting on the trees, set up a doleful chattering.

"Now," said the Tortoise, "I want you to go with me. If you don't, I'll eat you up. Get on my back and I'll carry you; but I must hold your paw in my mouth so you will not try to run away."

Half frightened to death, the Monkey obeyed, and the Tortoise trotted off to the sea, swam to the spot over the Queen's palace, and in a fillip of the finger was down in the gardens of the Under World.

The Queen hearing of the Monkey's arrival thanked the Tortoise, and commanded her cook and baker to feed him well and treat him kindly, for the Queen felt really sorry because he was to lose his liver.

As for the unsuspecting Monkey he enjoyed himself very much, and ran around everywhere amusing the star-fishes, clams, oysters, and other pulpy creatures that could not run, by his rapid climbing of the rocks and coral bushes, and by rolling over the sponge beds and cutting all manner of antics. They had never before seen anything like it. Poor fellow! he would not have been so frolicsome if he had known what was in store for him.

All this time however the Jelly-fish pitied him in his heart, and could hardly keep what he knew to himself. Seeing the Monkey in one of his gayest moods, the Jelly-fish squeezed up near him and said:

"Excuse my addressing you, but I feel very sorry for you because you are to be put to death."

"Why?" said the Monkey. "What have I done?"

"Oh, nothing," said the Jelly-fish, "only our Queen is sick and she wants your liver for medicine."

Then if ever any one saw a sick looking monkey it was this one. As the Japanese still say, "His liver was smashed." He felt dreadfully afraid. He put his hands over his eyes, and immediately began to plan how to save both life and liver!

After a while the clever fellow began to see a way out. Clapping his hand to his stomach he ran into the hall of the Queen's palace and began to weep bitterly. Just then the Tortoise, passing by, saw his captive.

"What are you crying about?" he asked.

"Boohoo!" cried the Monkey. "When I left my home on the earth, I forgot to bring my liver with me, but hung it upon a tree, and now my liver will decay and I'll die. Boo-hoo-hoo!" and the poor Monkey's eyes became red as a fish's and streamed with tears.

When the Tortoise told the Queen's courtiers what the Monkey had said, their faces fell.

"Why, here's a pretty piece of business! The Monkey is of no use without his liver. We must send him after it."

So they dispatched the Tortoise to the earth again, the Monkey sitting a-straddle of his back. They came to the mountain again, and the Tortoise being a little lazy waited at the foot while the Monkey scampered off, saying he would be back in an hour. The two creatures had become so well acquainted that the old Hard Shell fully trusted the lively little fellow.

But instead of an hour the Tortoise waited till evening. No Monkey came. So finding himself fooled, and knowing all the monkeys would take the alarm, he waddled back and told the Queen all about it.

"Then," said the Queen after reprimanding her messenger for his silly confidence, "the Monkey must have got wind of our intention to use his liver, and what is more, some one of my servants must have told him."

So the Queen issued an order commanding all her subjects to appear before the Dragon-King of the World under the Sea. Whoever did this wicked thing, must be punished speedily.

Obedient to this command, the fish and sea animals of all sorts, that swam, crawled, rolled, or moved in any way, appeared before the Dragon-King, and his Queen—all except the Jelly-fish. This convinced the Queen that the Jelly-fish was the guilty one. She ordered the culprit to be brought into her presence, and before all her retainers, she cried out:

"You leaky-tongued wretch, for your crime of betraying the confidence of your sovereign, you shall no longer remain among shell-fish. I condemn you to lose your shell."

Then she stripped off his shell, and left the poor Jelly-fish entirely naked and ashamed.

"Be off, you telltale!" she ended. "Hereafter all your children shall be as soft and defenceless as yourself."

The poor Jelly-fish blushed crimson, squeezed himself out, and swam off out of sight. Since that time all jelly-fishes have had no shells.

Source:
Griffis, William E. *Fairy Tales of Old Japan*. London: George G. Harrap & Co., 1911.

135. Lord Cuttle-Fish's Concert

Japan

DESPITE the loss of the Monkey's liver, the Queen of the World under the Sea, after careful attention and long rest, got well again, and was able to be about her duties and govern her kingdom. The news of her recovery created the wildest joy in the Under-world, and from tears and gloom and silence, the caves echoed with laughter, and the sponge-beds with music. Every one had on a "white face." Drums, flutes and banjos, which had been hung up on coral branches, or packed away in shell boxes, were taken down, or brought out, and right merrily were they thrummed. The pretty maids of the Queen put on their ivory thimble-nails, and the Queen again listened to the sweet melodies on the harp, while down among the smaller fry of fishy retainers and the scullions of the kitchen, were heard the constant thump of the shoulder-drum, the bang of the big drum, and the loud cries of the dancers as they struck all sorts of attitudes with hands, feet and head.

No allusion was openly made either to monkeys, tortoises, or jelly-fish. This would not have been polite. But the Jelly-fish, in a distant pool in the garden, could hear a merry mocking song which he felt to be directed against himself.

But none of these musical performances were worthy of the Queen's notice although as evidences of the joy of her subjects they did very well.

A great many entertainments were gotten up to amuse the finny people, but the Queen was present at none of them except the one about to be described. How and why she became a spectator shall also be told.

One night the Queen was sitting in the pink drawing-room, arrayed in her queenly robes, for she was almost recovered and expected to walk out in the evening. Everything in the room, except a vase of green and golden colored sponge-plant, and a plume of glass-thread, was of a pink color. Then there was a pretty rockery made of a pyramid of pumice, full of embossed rosettes of living sea-anemones of scarlet, orange, gray, and black colors, which were trained to fold themselves up like an umbrella, or blossom out like chrysanthemums, at certain hours of the day, or when touched, behaving just like four o'clocks and sensitive plants.

All the furniture and hangings of the rooms were pink. The floor was made of mats woven from strips of mother-of-pearl, bound at the sides with an inch border of pink coral. The ceiling was made of the rarest of pink shells wrought into flowers and squares. The walls were decorated with the same material, representing sea-scenes, jewels, and tortoise-shell patterns. In the alcove was a bouquet of seaweed of richest dyes, and in the nooks was an open cabinet holding several of the Queen's own treasures, such as a tiara which looked like woven threads of crystal and a toilet box and writing case made of solid pink coral. The gem of all was a screen having eight folds, on which were depicted her palace and throne-room, the visit of Toda, and the procession of the Queen, nobles, and grandees that escorted the brave archer, when he took his farewell to return to earth.

The Queen sat on the glistening sill of the wide window looking out over her gardens, her two maids sitting at her feet. Presently the sound of music wafted through the coral groves and crystal grottoes reached her ear.

"How wonderful this is!" exclaimed the Queen, half aloud. "What strange music is it I hear? It is neither guitar nor drum nor singing. It seems to be a mixture of all. Harken! It sounds as if a band with many instruments were playing, and a chorus were singing."

True enough! It was the most curious music ever heard in the Underworld, for to tell the truth the voices were not in perfect accord, though all kept good time. The sound seemed to issue from the mansion of Lord Cuttle-fish, the palace physician. The Queen's curiosity was roused.

"I shall go and see what it is," said she, as she rose up. Then she recollected, and exclaimed: "O, no, it would not be proper for me to be seen in public at this hour of the evening, and if it is in Lord Cuttle-fish's mansion, I could not enter without a retinue. No, it would be beneath my dignity."

Curiosity, however, got the better of the Queen and off she started with only her two maids who held aloft over her head the long pearl-handled fans made of white shark's fins. She had decided to go incognito.

"Besides," thought she, "perhaps the concert is outside, in the garden. If so, I can look down and see from the great green rock that overlooks it, and my lord the King need not know of it."

The Queen walked over her pebbled garden walk, avoiding the great high road. The sound of the drums and voices grew louder as she advanced, until when she reached the top of a green rock back of Lord Cuttle-fish's garden, the whole performance was open to her view.

It was so funny, and the Queen was so overcome at the comical sight, that she nearly fell down in her merriment. She utterly forgot her dignity, and laughed till the tears ran down her face. She was so afraid she would scream out, that she nearly choked herself with her sleeve, while her alarmed maids, though meaning nothing by their acts but friendly help, slapped her on the back to give her breath. And this is what she saw.

There, at the top of a high green rock all covered with barnacles, on a huge tuft of sponge, sat Lord Cuttle-fish, playing on three musical instruments at once. His great speckled head, six feet high, like a huge bag upside down, was bent forward to read the notes of his music book by the light of a wax candle, which was stuck in the feelers of a prickly Lobster, and patiently held. Of his six pulpy arms one long one ran down like the trunk of an elephant, fingering along the pages of a music book. Two others were used to play the guitar. The small double drum was held by one arm on his shoulder and neck, while still another arm curled up in a bunch, punched it like a fist. Below him was a bass drum, set in a frame, and in his last arm was clutched a heavy drumstick which pounded out a tremendous noise. There the old fellow sat with his head bobbing, and all his six cuppy arms in motion, his rolling blue eyes ogling the notes, and his mouth like an elephant's, screeching out the words of the song.

All this time, in front of Lord Cuttle-fish, sat the Lobster holding up the light, and nodding his head in time to the music.

But the audience, or rather the orchestra, was the funniest part of all. They could not be called listeners, for they were all performers. On the left was the lusty red-faced Bream with its gills wide open, singing at the top, or rather at the bottom, of its throat, and beating time by flapping its wide fins. A little Gudgeon, just behind silent and fanning itself with a blue flat fan, had disgracefully broken down on a high note. Next on the right was a long-nosed Gar-fish singing alto, and proud of its slender form. In the foreground squatted a great fat Frog with big bulging eyes, singing bass, and leading the choir by flapping his webbed fingers up and down, with his frightful cavern of a mouth wide open. Next, sat the stately and dignified Mackerel, rather scandalized at the whole affair, who kept very still, refusing to join in. At the Mackerel's right fin, squeaked out the stupid flat-headed Globe-fish with her big eye impolitely winking at the servant-maid just bringing in refreshments; for the truth was, all were very thirsty after so much vocal exercise.

Just behind the Herring, with one eye on Lord Cuttle-fish and one on the coming refreshments, was the Skate. The truth must be told that the entire right wing of the orchestra was very much demoralized by the smell of the steaming tea and eatables just about to be served. The Tortoise though continuing to sing, impolitely turned its head away from Lord Cuttle-fish, and its back to the Frog that acted as precentor. The Sucker, though very homely and bloated with fat, kept on in the chorus, and pretended not to notice the waiter and the tray and cups. Indeed, Madame Sucker thought it quite vulgar in the Tortoise to be so eager after the cakes and wine.

Suddenly the music ceased to the relief of all the hungry ones. Lord Cuttle-fish kicked over his drum, unscrewed his guitar, and packed it away in his music box. He then slid along to the refreshment table, and actually amused the company by standing on his head and twirling his six cuppy arms around in the air like a windmill.

At this Miss Mackerel was quite shocked, and whispered under her fan to the Gar-fish, "It is quite undignified! What would the Queen say if she saw it?" not knowing that the Queen was looking on.

Then all sat down on their tails, propped upright on one fin, and produced their fans to cool themselves off. The Lobster pulled off the candle stump and ate it up, wiped his feelers, and joined the party.

The liquid refreshments consisted of sweet and clear saké, tea, and cherry-blossom water. The solids were thunder-cakes, egg-cracknels, boiled rice, radishes, macaroni, lotus-root, and sweet potatoes. Side-dishes were piled up with flies, worms, bugs and all kinds of bait for the small fry—the finny brats that were to eat at the second table. The tea was poured by the servants of Lord Cuttle-fish.

The Queen did not wait to see the end of the feast, but laughing heartily, returned to her palace and went to sleep.

After helping himself with all the cups of his arms out of the tub of boiled rice, until Miss Mackerel made up her mind that he was a glutton, and drinking like a shoal of fishes, Lord Cuttle-fish went home, coiled himself up into a ball, and fell asleep. He had a headache next morning. But the concert and feast had done the Queen more good than all her medicine.

Source:
Griffis, William E. *Fairy Tales of Old Japan*. London: George G. Harrap & Co., 1911.

136. The Gamo-Gamo

Philippines

CERTAIN interesting water-gods, known as Gamo-Gamo, are distinguished in bodily aspect by mermaid characters, though they behave in a different manner from the traditional mermaid. The female gamo-gamo are divinities of little streams, while the gamo-gamo men are in charge of large rivers. Both sexes are human down to the waist; below that, fish—resembling a big fish called mungagat. In the test for theft, these river-people seize the guilty one, and torment him with pricks from their sharp iron punches. Another type of gamo-gamo is a good manobo who lives in the ocean, and takes care of large vessels. He is said to be of enormous height, with a head as high as a Bagobo man's full stature.

There is also a family of gods—a male deity, his wife, and two children—known as Olu k'Waig, and associated with the mountain streams. All of them are said to be extremely small in size, but otherwise they are not definitely described, although it is currently reported that Datu Yting once caught sight of them on the mountain trails. In spite of the identity in name, they do not appear to be traditionally associated with the Malaki t'Olu k'Waig.

Source:
Benedict, Laura Watson. *A Study of Bagobo Ceremonial, Magic and Myth*. New York: The New York Academy of Sciences, 1916.

137. The Shark-Man, Nanaue

Hawaii, United States

KAMOHOALII, the King-shark of Hawaii and Maui, has several deep sea caves that he uses in turn as his habitat. There are several of these at the bottom of the palisades, extending from Waipio toward Kohala, on the island of Hawaii. A favorite one was at Koamano, on the mainland, and another was at Maiaukiu, the small islet just abreast of the valley of Waipio. It was the belief of the ancient Hawaiians that several of these shark gods could assume any shape they chose, the human form even, when occasion demanded.

In the reign of Umi, a beautiful girl, called Kalei, living in Waipio, was very fond of shellfish, and frequently went to Kuiopihi for her favorite article of diet. She generally went in the company of other women, but if the sea was a little rough, and her usual companion was afraid to venture out on the wild and dangerous beach, she very often went alone rather than go without her favorite sea-shells.

In those days the Waipio River emptied over a low fall into a basin partly open to the sea; this basin is now completely filled up with rocks from some convulsion of nature, which has happened since then. In this was a deep pool, a favorite bathing-place for all Waipio. The King shark god, Kamohoalii, used to visit this pool very often to sport in the fresh waters of the Waipio River. Taking into account the many different tales told of the doings of this shark god, he must have had quite an eye for human physical beauty.

Kalei, as was to be expected from a strong, well-formed Hawaiian girl of those days, was an expert swimmer, a good diver, and noted for the neatness and grace with which she would lelekawa (jump from the rocks into deep water) without any splashing of water, which would happen to unskilful divers, from the awkward attitudes they would assume in the act of jumping.

It seems Kamohoalii, the King-shark, had noted the charms of the beautiful Kalei, and his heart, or whatever answers in place of it with fishes, had been captured by them. But he could not expect to make much of an impression on the maiden's susceptibilities *in propria persona*, even though he was perfectly able to take her bodily into his capacious maw; so he must needs go courting in a more pleasing way. Assuming the form of a very handsome man, he walked on the beach one rather rough morning, waiting for the girl's appearance.

Now the very wildness of the elements afforded him the chance he desired, as, though Kalei was counted among the most agile and quick of rock-fishers, that morning, when she did come, and alone, as her usual companions were deterred by the rough weather, she made several unsuccessful springs to escape a high threatening wave raised by the god himself; and apparently, if it had not been for the prompt and effective assistance rendered by the handsome stranger, she would have been swept out into the sea.

Thus an acquaintance was established. Kalei met the stranger from time to time, and finally became his wife.

Some little time before she expected to become a mother, her husband, who all this time would only come home at night, told her his true nature, and informing her that he would have to leave her, gave orders in regard to the bringing up of the future child. He particularly cautioned the mother never to let him be fed on animal flesh of any kind, as he would be born with a dual nature, and with a body that he could change at will.

In time Kalei was delivered of a fine healthy boy, apparently the same as any other child, but he had, besides the normal mouth of a human being, a shark's mouth on his back between the shoulder blades. Kalei had told her family of the kind of being her husband was, and they all agreed to keep the matter of the shark-mouth on the child's back a secret, as there was no knowing what fears and jealousies might be excited in the minds of the King or high chiefs by such an abnormal being, and the babe might be killed.

The old grandfather, far from heeding the warning given by Kamohoalii in the matter of animal diet, as soon as the boy, who was called Nanaue, was old enough to come under the taboo in regard to the eating of males, and had to take his meals at the mua house with the men of the family, took especial pains to feed him on dog meat and pork. He had a hope that his grandson would grow up to be a great, strong man, and become a famous warrior; and there was no knowing what possibilities lay before a strong, skilful warrior in those days. So he fed the boy with meat, whenever it was obtainable. The boy thrived, grew strong, big, and handsome as a young lama (Maba sandwicensis) tree.

There was another pool with a small fall of the Waipio River very near the house of Kalei, and the boy very often went into it while his mother watched on the banks. Whenever he got into the water he would take the form of a shark and would chase and eat the small fish which abounded in the pool. As he grew old enough to understand, his mother took especial pains to impress on him the necessity of concealing his shark nature from other people.

This place was also another favorite bathing-place of the people, but Nanaue, contrary to all the habits of a genuine Hawaiian, would never go in bathing with the others, but always alone; and when his mother was able, she used to go with him and sit on the banks, holding the kapa scarf, which he always wore to hide the shark-mouth on his back.

When he became a man, his appetite for animal diet, indulged in childhood, had grown so strong that a human being's ordinary allowance would not suffice for him. The old grandfather had died in the meantime, so that he was dependent on the food supplied by his stepfather and uncles, and they had to expostulate with him on what they called his shark-like voracity. This gave rise to the common native nickname of a manohae (ravenous shark) for a very gluttonous man, especially in the matter of meat.

Nanaue used to spend a good deal of his time in the two pools, the one inland and the other opening into the sea. The busy-bodies (they had some in those days as well as now) were set to wondering why he always kept a kihei, or mantle, on his shoulders; and for such a handsomely shaped, athletic young man, it was indeed a matter of wonder and speculation, considering the usual attire of the youth of those days. He also kept aloof from all the games and pastimes of the young people, for fear that the wind or some active movement might displace the kapa mantle, and the shark-mouth be exposed to view.

About this time children and eventually grown-up people began to disappear mysteriously.

Nanaue had one good quality that seemed to redeem his apparent unsociability; he was almost always to be seen working in his mother's taro or potato patch when not fishing or bathing. People going to the sea beach would have to pass these potato or taro patches, and it was Nanaue's habit to accost them with the query of where they were going. If they answered, "To bathe in the sea," or, "Fishing," he would answer, "Take care, or you may disappear head and tail." Whenever he so accosted any one it would not be long before some member of the party so addressed would be bitten by a shark.

If it should be a man or woman going to the beach alone, that person would never be seen again, as the shark-man would immediately follow, and watching for a favorable opportunity, jump into the sea. Having previously marked the whereabouts of the person he was after, it was an easy thing for him to approach quite close, and changing into a shark, rush on the unsuspecting person and drag him or her down into the deep, where he would devour his victim at his leisure. This was the danger to humanity which his king-father foresaw when he cautioned the mother of the unborn child about feeding him on animal flesh, as thereby an appetite would be evoked which they had no means of satisfying, and a human being would furnish the most handy meal of the kind that he would desire.

Nanaue had been a man grown some time, when an order was promulgated by Umi, King of Hawaii, for every man dwelling in Waipio to go to koele work, tilling a large plantation for the King. There were to be certain days in an anahulu (ten days) to be set aside for this work, when every man, woman, and child had to go and render service, excepting the very old and decrepit, and children in arms.

The first day every one went but Nanaue. He kept on working in his mother's vegetable garden to the astonishment of all who saw him. This was reported to the King, and several stalwart men were sent after him. When brought before the King he still wore his kapa kihei or mantle.

The King asked him why he was not doing koele work with every one else. Nanaue answered he did not know it was required of him. Umi could not help admiring the bold, free bearing of the handsome man, and noting his splendid physique, thought he would make a good warrior, greatly wanted in those ages, and more especially in the reign of Umi, and simply ordered him to go to work.

Nanaue obeyed, and took his place in the field with the others, and proved himself a good worker, but still kept on his kihei, which it would be natural to suppose that he would lay aside as an encumbrance when engaged in hard labor. At last some of the more venturesome of the younger folks managed to tear his kapa off, as if accidentally, when the shark-mouth on his back was seen by all the people near.

Nanaue was so enraged at the displacement of his kapa and his consequent exposure, that he turned and bit several of the crowd, while the shark-mouth opened and shut with a snap, and a clicking sound was heard such as a shark is supposed to make when baulked by its prey.

The news of the shark-mouth and his characteristic shark-like actions were quickly reported to the King, with the fact of the disappearance of so many people in the vicinity of the pools frequented by Nanaue; and of his pretended warnings to people going to the sea, which were immediately followed by a shark bite or by their being eaten bodily, with every one's surmise and belief that this man was at the bottom of all those disappearances. The King believed it was even so, and ordered a large fire to be lighted, and Nanaue to be thrown in to be burnt alive.

When Nanaue saw what was before him, he called on the shark god, his father, to help him; then, seeming to be endowed with superhuman strength in answer to his prayer, he burst the ropes with which he had been bound in preparation for the burning, and breaking through the throng of Umi's warriors, who attempted to detain him, he ran, followed by the whole multitude, toward the pool that emptied into the sea. When he got to the edge of the rocks bordering the pool, he waited till the foremost persons were within arm's length, when he leaped into the water and immediately turned into a large shark on the surface of the water, in plain view of the people who had arrived, and whose numbers were being continually augmented by more and more arrivals.

He lay on the surface some little time, as if to recover his breath, and then turned over on his back, and raising his head partly out of the water, snapped his teeth at the crowd who, by this time, completely lined the banks, and then, as if in derision or defiance of them, turned and flirted his tail at them and swam out to sea.

The people and chiefs were for killing his mother and relatives for having brought up such a monster. Kalei and her brothers were seized, bound, and dragged before Umi, while the people clamored for their immediate execution, or as some suggested, that they be thrown into the fire lighted for Nanaue.

But Umi was a wise king and would not consent to any such summary proceedings, but questioned Kalei in regard to her fearful offspring. The grieved and frightened mother told everything in connection with the paternity and bringing up of the child, and with the warning given by the dread sea-father.

Umi considered that the great sea god Kamohoalii was on the whole a beneficent as well as a powerful one. Should the relatives and mother of that shark god's son be killed, there would then be no possible means of checking the ravages of that son, who might linger around the coast and creeks of the island, taking on human shape at will, for the purpose of travelling inland to any place he liked, and then reassume his fish form and lie in wait in the many deep pools formed by the streams and springs.

Umi, therefore, ordered Kalei and her relatives to be set at liberty, while the priests and shark kahunas were requested to make offerings and invocations to Kamohoalii that his spirit might take possession of one of his hakas (mediums devoted to his cult), and so express to humanity his desires in regard to his bad son, who had presumed to eat human beings, a practice well known to be contrary to Kamohoalii's design.

This was done, whereupon the shark god manifested himself through a haka, and expressed his grief at the action of his wayward son. He told them that the grandfather was to blame for feeding him on animal flesh contrary to his orders, and if it were not for that extenuating circumstance, he would order his son to be killed by his own shark officers; but as it was, he would require of him that he should disappear forever from the shores of Hawaii. Should Nanaue disregard that order and be seen by any of his father's shark soldiers, he was to be instantly killed.

Then the shark god, who it seems retained an affection for his human wife, exacted a promise that she and her relatives were to be forever free from any persecutions on account of her unnatural son, on pain of the return and freedom from the taboo of that son.

Accordingly Nanaue left the island of Hawaii, crossed over to Maui, and landing at Kipahulu, resumed his human shape and went inland. He was seen by the people, and when questioned, told them he was a traveller from Hawaii, who had landed at Hana and was going around sightseeing. He was so good looking, pleasant, and beguiling in his conversation that people generally liked him. He was taken as aikane by one of the petty chiefs of the place, who gave his own sister for wife to Nanaue. The latter made a stipulation that his sleeping house should be separated from that of his wife, on account of a pretended vow, but really in order that his peculiar second mouth might escape detection.

For a while the charms of the pretty girl who had become his wife seem to have been sufficient to prevent him from trying to eat human beings, but after a while, when the novelty of his position as a husband had worn off, and the desire for human flesh had again become very strong, he resumed the old practice for which he had been driven away from Hawaii.

He was eventually detected in the very act of pushing a girl into the sea, jumping in after her, then turning into a shark, and commencing to devour her, to the horror of some people who were fishing with hook and rod from some rocks where he had not observed them. These people raised the alarm, and Nanaue seeing that he was discovered, left for Molokai where he was not known.

He took up his residence on Molokai at Poniuohua, adjoining the ahupuaa of Kainalu, and it was not very long before he was at his old practice of observing and accosting people, giving them his peculiar warning, following them to the sea in his human shape, then seizing one of them as a shark and pulling the unfortunate one to the bottom, where he would devour his victim. In the excitement of such an occurrence, people would fail to notice his absence until he would reappear at some distant point far away from the throng, as if engaged in shrimping or crabbing.

This went on for some time, till the frightened and harassed people in desperation went to consult a shark kahuna, as the ravages of the man-eating shark had put a practical taboo on all kinds of fishing. It was not safe to be anywhere near the sea, even in the shallowest water.

The kahuna told them to lie in wait for Nanaue, and the next time he prophesied that a person would be eaten head and tail, to have some strong men seize him and pull off his kapa mantle, when a shark mouth would be found on his back. This was done, and the mouth seen, but the shark-man was so strong when they seized him and attempted to bind him, that he broke away from them several times. He was finally overpowered near the seashore and tightly bound. All the people then turned their attention to gathering brush and firewood to burn him, for it was well known that it is only by being totally consumed by fire that a man-shark can be thoroughly destroyed, and prevented from taking possession of the body of some harmless fish shark, who would then be incited to do all the pernicious acts of a man-shark.

While he lay there on the low sandy beach, the tide was coming in, and as most of the people were returning with fagots and brush, Nanaue made a supreme effort and rolled over so that his feet touched the water, when he was enabled at once to change into a monster shark. Those who were near him saw it, but were not disposed to let him off so easily, and they ran several rows of netting makai, the water being very shallow for quite a distance out. The shark's flippers were all bound by the ropes with which the man Nanaue had been bound, and this with the shallowness of the water prevented him from exerting his great strength to advantage. He did succeed in struggling to the breakers, though momentarily growing weaker from loss of blood, as the people were striking at him with clubs, spears, stone adzes and anything that would hurt or wound, so as to prevent his escape.

With all that, he would have got clear, if the people had not called to their aid the demigod Unauna, who lived in the mountains of upper Kainalu. It was then a case of Akua vs. Akua, but Unauna was only a young demigod, and not supposed to have acquired his full strength and supernatural powers, while Nanaue was a full-grown man and shark. If it had not been for the latter's being hampered by the cords with which he was bound, the nets in his way, as well as the loss of blood, it is fully believed that he would have got the better of the young local presiding deity; but he was finally conquered and hauled up on the hill slopes of Kainalu to be burnt.

The shallow ravine left by the passage of his immense body over the light yielding soil of the Kainalu Hill slope can be seen to this day, as also a ring or deep groove completely around the top of a tall insulated rock very near the top of Kainalu Hill, around which Unauna had thrown the rope, to assist him in hauling the big shark uphill. The place was ever afterwards called Puumano (Shark Hill), and is so known to this day.

Nanaue was so large, that in the attempt to burn him, the blood and water oozing out of his burning body put out the fire several times. Not to be outwitted in that way by the shark son of Kamohoalii, Unauna ordered the people to cut and bring for the purpose of splitting into knives, bamboos from the sacred grove of Kainalu. The shark flesh was then cut into strips, partly dried, and then burnt, but the whole bamboo grove had to be used before the big shark was all cut. The god Mohoalii (another form of the name of the god Kamohoalii), father of Unauna, was so angered by the desecration of the grove, or more likely on account of the use to which it was put, that he took away all the edge and sharpness from the bamboos of this grove forever, and to this day they are different from the bamboos of any other place or grove on the islands, in this particular, that a piece of them cannot cut any more than any piece of common wood.

Source:

Nakuina, Mrs. E. M. "The Shark-Man, Nanaue." *Hawaiian Folk Tales: A Collection of Native Legends*. Thos. G. Thrum, compiler. Chicago: The Lakeside Press, 1907.

138. The Mermaid of the Magdalenes

Canada

FAR off the north-east coast of Canada is a group of rugged islands called the Magdalenes. They are a lonely, barren group, where grass and flowers and trees grow scantily. There, the northern storms rage with their wildest fury, and the sea breaks with its greatest force upon the bleak rocks. Numberless birds of strange cries and colours fly constantly about. On days when the storm dashes the sea white and angry against the coast, even the thunder of the surf is almost shut out by the screaming of countless gulls; and on clear days the sun is hidden when the birds rise in clouds from their nests. The "Isle of Birds," the Jesuits called one of the islands when they first visited the group hundreds of years ago, and it is an "Isle of Birds" still. It is a wild and rock-bound desolate land.

But although the islands are barren of grass and flowers and trees, the waters around and between them are rich in fish. "The Kingdom of Fish," men call the place, for adventurous traders grow wealthy there reaping the harvest of the sea. The greatest product of the waters is the lobster. He always inhabited these northern seas, and about his power in olden times strange tales are told. Away off the coast of one of the islands, you can still see on fine moonlight nights in May, and also during the day once a year, a maiden holding a glass in her hand, combing her long hair, and looking wistfully to the land. Sometimes, too, on calm nights you can still hear her strange song above the murmur of the waves. She is the phantom lady of the Island over whom the Lobster in far away days used his power. She is now a prisoner in the deep, held there as a punishment for her deeds.

Now, it happened that long ago when fish were first canned for food there was a great slaughter of sardines—the tiny fish of the sea—by cruel money-greedy traders who caught them, packed them in small boxes, and shipped them to far countries, just as they do to-day. These traders received large money rewards for their labour, for people all over the world liked the little fish and paid a high price for them. The sardines saw their number slowly growing smaller, for, being little, they were helpless against their captors, and among all their family there was great sorrow. In despair they asked the big fish of the sea to help them. At last, in answer to their appeal, a meeting of all the fish in the sea was called. Here the big fish took an oath to help their small cousins in their struggle with man, and to punish when they could all who ate or fished the sardine family. And the little fish rejoiced greatly.

One May day a large ship loaded with packed fish was wrecked on the sunken rocks of the Magdalene Islands. Soon the ship was broken up by the heavy surf on the sharp reef, and her cargo was strewn along the shore. It happened that in the cargo were many boxes of sardines, and they too were washed up on the beach by the tide. In the evening, after the sea had calmed, a fair maiden who lived on the Island with her father, a fish trader, walked along the shore alone to view the wreckage of the broken ship. She found, to her delight, one of the boxes in which the sardines were packed. She resolved at once to eat the contents, for she too, like all the world at that time, liked the little fish. But although she tried as hard as she could, she was unable to open the box. She sat by the side of the sea and sang a song of lament, calling on anyone who could to open the box for her. She sang:

> "I love sardines when they're boiled with beans
> And mixed with the sands of the sea."

Away out from the beach a skate-fish was resting on a sand-bar. Hearing the song of the maiden, he quickly swam towards the shore. When he came close enough to hear the words of the song and to know what the box contained, he swam away in great disgust, for he was cousin to the sardines in the box, and came from the same family tree as they. But he was too timid to try to punish the maiden. Then a bold merman heard the song. He had long looked for a land wife to live with him in his home under the sea; now he said, "Here at last is a shore maiden for me," for the voice of the singer was beautiful to him. So he went to his looking-glass to dress himself in the most genteel fashion. From bright clean sea-weeds and sea-leaves he quickly made himself a new suit, all green and yellow; and he covered his feet with bright-coloured shells, and his neck with pearls which the oyster gave him; and dressing himself carefully, he hastened in the direction of the song. But when he came close enough to hear the words and to know what the box contained, he remembered his oath at the great gathering of the fish, and although he loved the singer he swam hurriedly away. For, like the skate-fish, he too feared to try to punish the maiden.

The maiden was now sore distressed, for it was growing late and the moon was already far up in the sky. The box was still unopened, and the girl was hungry for the fish. Going to the edge of the sea, she knocked the box hard against a large rock that lay in the water, hoping thereby to break it open. But the box would not break. Now, it chanced that under the rock a large black lobster lay sleeping quietly after a long battle with an enemy in the sea. The tapping on the roof of his sleeping-place awoke him, and he rubbed his eyes and listened. The maiden was again singing her song:—

> "Oh I love sardines when they're boiled with beans,
> And mixed with the sands of the sea.
> I am dying for some. Will nobody come
> And open this box for me?"

Then the lobster remembered his oath at the great gathering of the fish. Unlike the skate-fish and the merman, he had no fear of the maiden, for he knew his power. He determined to punish her, and he resolved at once upon a crafty trick. He came out of his hiding place, and waving his claw politely he said, "Fair lady, I can open the box for you; give it to me and let me try." But when, in answer, she held the box out towards him in her hand, he grasped her by the wrist with his strong claw, and, holding her fast, he swam with her far out to sea. Where he went and what he did with her, no man knows. It is believed that he sold her to the merman who had long sought a shore-wife, and that she is still being slowly changed into a fish. One thing is certain,—she never came back to land. But on the first day of May she always appears on the water away off the coast of the Island; and if that day is fine and clear you can still always see her there. She holds in her hand a looking-glass in which in the sunlight she looks at herself to see if she is nearer to a fish than she was on May Day the year before when she last appeared in the sun; and she is combing her long hair, which is now covered with pearls; and she looks with longing eyes to the shore and her old home. And sometimes on moonlight nights in May, when the wind is still and the sea is calm, the fishermen hear her strange sad song across the waters. They know then that she is lonely, and that she is singing her song to lure land-comrades for company to her side. And on these nights they stay on shore, for they know that if they venture out to sea she will seize them and carry them off for playmates to her home of bright shells far under the sea.

Source:
MacMillian, Cyrus. *Canadian Wonder Tales*. London: John Lane, The Bodley Head, 1918.

139. A Mermaid in Newfoundland

Canada

A LADY supplies me with the following:

"An old fisherman told me of a locality which was formerly inhabited by Frenchmen. There is a good beach for landing, but no boat will remain tied on it. Fasten the painter as you will, ghostly hands untie the knots again and again. (By the by, most of the ghosts are supposed to be Frenchmen.) That old man has had some other strange experiences. He saw a mermaid sitting on a rock as plainly as he ever saw anything, and was within a couple of boat's lengths of her when she dived to her crystal caves below and was lost to sight."

Source:
Patterson, George. "Notes on the Folk-Lore of Newfoundland." *The Journal of American Folklore*. Vol. 8, No. 31 (Oct.-Dec. 1895). pp. 285-290.

140. Sedna

Canada

There are several Inuit legends concerning Sedna, the goddess of the sea and marine animals. Many of the tales such as the following tell of how Sedna came to rule over Adlivun, the Inuit underworld.

THE old stories which mothers relate during the long winter evenings to their timidly listening children tell of Sedna. Once upon a time there lived a Jnnung, with his daughter Sedna, on the solitary shore. His wife had been dead for some time, and the two led a quiet existence. Sedna grew up to be a handsome girl, and the youth came in from all around to sue for her hand, but none of them could touch her proud heart. Finally, at the breaking up of the ice in the spring, a fulmar flew from over the sea and wooed Sedna with enticing song. "Come to me," it said; "come into the land of birds, where there is never hunger, where my tent is made of the most beautiful skins. You shall rest on soft deer-skins. My fellows, the storm-birds, shall bring you all your heart may desire; their feathers shall clothe you thickly; your lamp shall always be filled with oil, your pot with meat." Sedna could not long resist such wooing, and they went together over the vast sea. When at last they reached the country of the fulmar, after a long and hard journey, Sedna discovered that her spouse had shamefully deceived her. Her new home was not built of beautiful pelts, but was covered with wretched fish-skins, full of holes that gave free entrance to wind and snow. Instead of white reindeer-skins, her bed was made of hard walrus-hides; and she had to live on miserable fish which the birds brought her. Too soon she discovered that she had thrown her fortune away when, in her foolish pride, she had rejected the Innuit youth. In her woe she sang:

"Aya! father, if you knew how wretched I am, you would come to me, and we would hurry away in your boat over the waters. These strange birds look unkindly upon me. The cold winds roar around my bed; they give me miserable food—oh, come and take me back home! Aya!"

When a year had passed, and the sea was again stirred with warmer winds, the father left his land to visit Sedna. His daughter greeted him joyfully, and besought him to take her back home. The father, pitying his daughter, took her in his boat while the birds were out hunting, and they quickly left the country which had brought so much sorrow to Sedna. When the fulmar came home in the evening, and found his wife not there, he was very angry. He called his fellows around him, and they all flew away in search of the fugitives. They soon discerned them, and stirred up a great storm. The sea rose in immense waves, that threatened the pair with destruction. In his mortal peril the father determined to offer Sedna up to the birds, and threw her overboard. She clung with a death-hold to the edge of the boat. The cruel father then took a knife and cut off the first joints of her fingers. Falling into the sea, they were changed into seals. Sedna, holding to the boat more tightly, the second finger-joints fell under the sharp knife, and swam around as ground-seals; when the father cut off the stumps of the fingers, they became whales.

In the mean time the storm subsided, for the storm-birds thought Sedna was drowned. The father then allowed her to come into the boat again. But she from that time cherished a deadly hatred against him, and swore bitter revenge. After they got ashore, she called up two dogs, and let them eat the feet and hands of her father while he was asleep. Upon this he cursed himself, his daughter, and the dogs which had maimed him, when the earth opened and swallowed hut, father, daughter, and dogs. They have since lived in the land of Adliwun, of which Sedna is the mistress.

The seals, ground-seals, and whales, which grew from Sedna's fingers, increased rapidly, and soon filled all the waters, affording choice food to the Innuit. But Sedna has always hated those people, whom she despised when on the earth, because they hunt and kill the creatures which have arisen from her flesh and blood. Her father, who has to get along by creeping, appears to the dying; and the wizards often see his crippled hand seizing and taking away the dead. The dead have to stay a year in Sedna's dismal abode. The two great dogs lie on the threshold, and only move aside to let the dead come in. It is dark and cold inside. No bed of reindeer-skins invites to rest; but the new-comer has to lie on hard walrus-hides.

Only those who have been good and brave on the earth escape Sedna, and lead happy lives in the upper-land of Kudliwun. This land is full of reindeer; it is never cold there, and snow and ice never visit it. Those, also, who have died a violent death may go into the fields of the blessed. But whoever has been with Sedna must always stay in the land of Adliwun, and hunt whales and walruses. With all the other evil spirits, Sedna now lingers in the fall among the Innuit. But, while the others fill the air and the water, she rises from under the ground.

It is then a busy season for the wizards. In every hut we may hear singing and praying, and conjuring of the spirits is going on in every house. The lamps burn low. The wizard sits in a mystic gloom in the back part of the hut. He has thrown off his outer coat and drawn the hood of his inner garment over his head. Muttering undistinguishable words, he throws his arras feverishly around his body. He utters sounds which it is hard to ascribe to a human voice. At last the guardian spirit responds to the invocation. The Angeko lies in a trance, and when he comes to himself he promises, in incoherent phrases, the help of the good spirit against the Tupilak, and informs the credulous, affrighted Innuit how they can escape the dreaded evil.

The hardest task, that of driving away Sedna, is reserved for the most powerful wizards. A rope is coiled on the floor of a large hut, in such a manner as to leave a small opening at the top, which represents the breathing-hole of a seal. Two wizards stand by the side of it, one of them holding the seal-spear in his hand as if he were watching at the seal-hole in the winter, the other holding the harpoon-rope. Another Angeko sits in the back of the hut, whose office it is to lure Sedna up with magic song. At last Sedna comes up through the hard earth, and the Angeko hears her heavy breathing; now she emerges from the ground, and meets the wizards waiting at the hole. She is harpooned, and sinks away in angry haste, drawing after her the harpoon, to which the two men hold with all their strength. Only by a desperate effort does she tear herself away from it and return to her dwelling in Adliwun. Nothing is left with the two men but the blood-sprinkled harpoon, which they proudly show to the Innuit.

Sedna and the other evil spirits are at last driven away, and a great festival for young and old is celebrated on the next day in honor of the event. But they must still be careful, for the wounded Sedna is greatly enraged, and will seize any one whom she can find out of his hut. So, on this day, they all wear protecting amulets en the tops of their hoods.

Source:
Boas, Dr. Franz. "Cumberland Sound and Its Eskimos." *The Popular Science Monthly*. Apr 1885. pp. 768-779.

141. Aboo-dom-k'n and Lampeg-win-wuk

Passamaquoddy Tribe, United States

ABOO-DOM-K'N is an evil sprite that is believed to live in the water, to cast evil spells upon Indians who may stroll along the shore, or even to seize or devour children who may be playing in the water. *Aboo-dom-k'n* is supposed to have a fish's body and tail, with a woman's head and hair, and corresponds to our idea of a mermaid, if we have any. The *Lampeg-win-wuk* are sprites who live under the water, and sometimes dance in the waves. It is probable that these are really the phosphorescent gleams made by animalculae in the sea.

Source:
"Superstitions of the Passamaquoddies." *The Journal of American Folklore*. Vol. 2, No. 6 (Jul.-Sep. 1889). pp. 229-231.

142. How Two Girls Were Changed to Water-Snakes, and of Two Others That Became Mermaids

Passamaquoddy Tribe, United States

POCUMKWESS, or Thoroughfare, is sixty-five miles from Campobello. There was an Indian village there in the old times. Two young Indian girls had a strange habit of absenting themselves all day every Sunday. No one knew for a long time where they went or what they did. But this was how they passed their time. They would take a canoe and go six miles down the Grand Lake, where, at the north end, is a great ledge of rock and sixty feet of water. There they stayed. All day long they ran about naked or swam; they were wanton, witch-like girls, liking eccentric and forbidden ways.

They kept this up for a long time. Once, while they were in the water, an Indian who was hunting spied them. He came nearer and nearer, unseen. He saw them come out of the water and sit on the shore, and then go in again; but as he looked they grew longer and longer, until they became snakes.

He went home and told this. (But now they had been seen by a man they must keep the serpent form.) Men of the village, in four or five canoes, went to find them. They found the canoe and clothes of the girls; nothing more. A few days after, two men on Grand Lake saw the snake-girls on shore, showing their heads over the bushes. One began to sing.

"N'ktieh iében iut,
Qu'spen ma ké owse."

We are going to stay in this lake
A few days, and then go down the river.
Bid adieu to our friends for us;
We are going to the great salt water.

After singing this they sank into the water. They had very long hair.

NOTES

A picture of the man looking at the snake-girls was scraped for me by the Indian who told me this story. The pair were represented as snakes with female heads. When I first heard this tale, I promptly set it down as nothing else but the Melusina story derived from a Canadian French source. But I have since found that it is so widely spread, and is told in so many different forms, and is so deeply connected with tribal traditions and totems, that there is now no doubt in my mind that it is at least pre-Columbian.

Source:
Leland, Charles G. *The Algonquin Legends of New England; or, Myths and Folk Lore of the Micmac, Passamaquoddy, and Penobscot Tribes*. Boston: Houghton, Mifflin and Company, 1884.

143. Ne Hwas, the Mermaid

Passamaquoddy Tribe, United States

A LONG time ago there was an Indian, with his wife and two daughters. They lived by a great lake, or the sea, and the mother told her girls never to go into the water there, for that, if they did, something would happen to them.

They, however, deceived her repeatedly. When swimming is prohibited it becomes delightful. The shore of this lake sands away out or slopes to an island. One day they went to it, leaving their clothes on the beach. The parents missed them.

The father went to seek them. He saw them swimming far out, and called to them. The girls swam up to the sand, but could get no further. Their father asked them why they could not. They cried that they had grown to be so heavy that it was impossible. They were all slimy; they grew to be snakes from below the waist. After sinking a few times in this strange slime they became very handsome, with long black hair and large, bright black eyes, with silver bands on their neck and arms.

When their father went to get their clothes, they began to sing in the most exquisite tones:—

> "Leave them there!
> Do not touch them!

Leave them there!"

Hearing this, their mother began to weep, but the girls kept on:—

> "It is all our own fault,
> But do not blame us;
> It will be none the worse for you.
> When you go in your canoe,
> Then you need not paddle;
> We shall carry it along!"

And so it was: when their parents went in the canoe, the girls carried it safely on everywhere.

One day some Indians saw the girls' clothes on the beach, and so looked out for the wearers. They found them in the water, and pursued them, and tried to capture them, but they were so slimy that it was impossible to take them, till one, catching hold of a mermaid by her long black hair, cut it off.

Then the girl began to rock the canoe, and threatened to upset it unless her hair was given to her again. The fellow who had played the trick at first refused, but as the mermaids, or snake-maids, promised that they should all be drowned unless this was done, the locks were restored. And the next day they were heard singing and were seen, and on her who had lost her hair it was all growing as long as ever.

NOTES

We may very easily detect the hand of Lox, the Mischief Maker, in this last incident. It was the same trick which Loki played on Sif, the wife of Odin. That both Lox and Loki were compelled to replace the hair and make it grow again—the one on the snake-maid, the other on the goddess—is, if a coincidence, at least a very remarkable one. It is a rule with little exception that where we have to deal with myths which have passed into romances or tales, that which was originally one character becomes many, just as the king who has but one name and one appearance at court assumes a score when he descends to disguise of low degree and goes among the people. But when, in addition to characteristic traits, we have even a single anecdote or attribute in common, the identification is very far advanced. When not one, but many, of these coincidences occur, we are in all probability at the truth. Thus we find in the mythology of the Wabanaki, as in the Edda, the chief evil being indulging in mere wanton, comic mischief, to an extent not to be found in the devil of any other race whatever. Here, in a mythical tale, the same mischief maker steals a snake-girl's hair, and is compelled to replace it. In the Edda, the corresponding mischief maker steals the hair of a goddess, and is also forced to make restitution. Yet this is only one of many such resemblances in these tales. It will be observed that in both cases the hair of the loser is made to grow again. But while the incident has in the Edda a meaning, as appears from its context, it has none in the Indian tale. All that we can conclude from this is that the Wabanaki tale is subsequent to the Norse, or taken from it. The incidents of tales are often remembered when the plot is lost. It is certainly very remarkable that, wherever the mischief maker occurs in these Indian tales, he in every narrative does something in common with his Norse prototype.

Source:
Leland, Charles G. *The Algonquin Legends of New England; or, Myths and Folk Lore of the Micmac, Passamaquoddy, and Penobscot Tribes.* Boston: Houghton, Mifflin and Company, 1884.

144. Mermaid of the Teton Tribe

Teton Tribe, United States

THE Tetons have a legend of the mermaid. A young wife abandoned her infant to her younger brother's care, and plunged into a stream, which became her home henceforth. She did this because her husband had scolded her. Before going to her new home she told her little brother to bring her babe to the shore whenever it cried for food, and to call her by singing thus:—

Tan'-ke, mi-tun'-shka-la che'-ye lo' che'-ye lo'!

That is, "Sister, my sister's son cries indeed, cries indeed!"

The brother obeyed her, and on calling to his sister, she appeared, and nursed the infant. But the boy perceived that the mother had become a fish from the waist downward. The cruel husband learned at last what had happened, and he plotted to entice his wife ashore. Having succeeded in this, he cut off all the fishy part of her, and carried her to his lodge, with her brother's aid. But she did not long survive, and the husband lamented his cruelty for many days.

NOTES

Extracts from a paper read before the Anthropological Society of Washington, in November, 1888, entitled *Teton Folk-Lore*. Translated from the Teton MSS. of George Bushotter by J. Owen Dorsey. Part of this paper appeared in the *American Anthropologist*, vol. ii., No. 2, and another part in *Science*.

Source:
Dorsey, J. Owen. "Teton Folk-Lore Notes." *The Journal of American Folklore*. Vol. 2, No. 5 (Apr.-Jun. 1889). pp. 133-139.

145. The Takelma Mermaid

Takelma Tribe, United States

THERE is a class of imaginary, generally maleficent, beings that inhabit the woods or waters, and figure, as well as the animal "spirits," in the mythology. Such are the half-human hülüün wa-iwii, or mermaid, who, with other fabled denizens of the sea, taunts the unwary canoeman with jibes and insulting epithets, thus makes him lose his head, and, in his attempt to seek vengeance, causes him to sink beneath the water.

Source:
Sapir, Edward. "Religious Ideas of the Takelma Indians of Southwestern Oregon." *The Journal of American Folklore*. Vol. 20, No. 76 (Jan.-Mar. 1907). pp. 33-49.

146. The Pascagoula River Mermaid

Mississippi, United States

DURING that summer, Governor Périer, leaving New Orleans, visited the first settlements of the French at the Bay of St. Louis, at Biloxi, Pascagoula, and Mobile. While among the Pascagoulas, or bread-eaters, he was invited to go to the mouth of the river of that name, to listen to the mysterious music which floats on the waters, particularly on a calm, moonlit night, and which, to this day, excites the wonder of visitors. It seems to issue from caverns or grottoes in the bed of the river, and sometimes ascends from the water under the very keel of the boat which contains the inquisitive traveler, whose ear it strikes as the distant concert of a thousand æolian harps. On the banks of the river, close by the spot where the music is heard, tradition says that there existed a tribe different in color and in other peculiarities from the rest of the Indians. Their ancestors had originally emerged from the sea, where they were born, and were of light complexion. They were a gentle, gay, inoffensive race, living chiefly on oysters and fish, and they passed their time in festivals and rejoicings. They had a temple in which they adored a mermaid. Every night when the moon was visible, they gathered round the beautifully carved figure of the mermaid, and with instruments of strange shape, worshiped that idol with such soul-stirring music, as had never before blessed human ears.

One day, a short time after the destruction of Mauvila, or Mobile, in 1539, by Soto and his companions, there appeared among them a white man, with a long gray beard, flowing garments, and a large cross in his right hand. He drew from his bosom a book, which he kissed reverentially, and he began to explain to them what was contained in that sacred little casket. Tradition does not say how he came suddenly to acquire the language of those people, when he attempted to communicate to them the solemn truths of the gospel. It must have been by the operation of that faith which, we are authoritatively told, will remove mountains. Be it as it may, the holy man, in the course of a few months, was proceeding with much success in his pious undertaking, and the work of conversion was going on bravely, when his purposes were defeated by an awful prodigy.

One night, when the moon at her zenith poured on heaven and earth, with more profusion than usual, a flood of light angelic, at the solemn hour of twelve, when all in and was repose and silence, there came, on a sudden, a rushing on the surface of the river, as if the still air had been flapped into a whirlwind by myriads of invisible wings sweeping onward. The placid water was immediately convulsed; uttering a deep groan, it rolled several times from one bank to the other with rapid oscillations, and then gathered itself up into a towering column of foaming waves, on the top of which stood a mermaid, looking with magnetic eyes that could draw almost every thing to her, and singing with a voice which fascinated into madness. The Indians and the priest, their new guest, rushed to the bank of the river to contemplate this supernatural spectacle. When she saw them, the mermaid tuned her tones into still more bewitching melody, and kept chanting a sort of mystic song, with this often repeated ditty:—

> "Come to me, come to me, children of the sea,
> Neither bell, book, nor cross shall win ye from your queen."

The Indians listened with growing ecstasy, and one of them plunged into the river to rise no more. The rest, men, women, and children, followed in quick succession, moved, as it were, with the same irresistible impulse. When the last of the race disappeared, a wild laugh of exultation was heard; down returned the river to its bed with the roar of a cataract, and the whole scene seemed to have been but a dream. Ever since that time, is heard occasionally the distant music which has excited so much attention and investigation. The other Indian tribes of the neighborhood have always thought that it was their musical brethren, who still keep up their revels at the bottom of the river, in the palace of the mermaid. Tradition further relates that the poor priest died in an agony of grief, and that he attributed this awful event, and this victory of the powers of darkness, to his not having been in a perfect state of grace when he attempted the conversion of those infidels. It is believed also that he said on his death-bed, that those deluded pagan souls would be redeemed from their bondage and sent to the kingdom of heaven, if on a Christmas night, at twelve of the clock, when the moon shall happen to be at her meridian, a priest should dare to come alone to that musical spot, in a boat propelled by himself, and should drop a crucifix into the water. But, alas! if this be ever done, neither the holy man nor the boat are to be seen again by mortal eyes. So far, the attempt has not been made; skeptic minds have sneered, but no one has been found bold enough to try the experiment.

Source:
Gayarré, Charles. *History of Louisiana Second Series (Vol. I Part 2)*. New York: William J. Widdleton, 1867.

147. The Mermaid Child Ballad 289

Vermont, United States

1. THE first came up was the carpenter of the ship,
    And a hearty old fellow was he,
    Saying, "I have a wife in old England,
    And a widow I'm afraid she will be!"

    For the raging sea goes roar, roar, roar,
      And the stormy winds they do blow,
    While we poor sailors are drowning in the deep,
      And the pretty girls are standing on the shore.

2. The next came up was a little cabin boy,
   And a nice little fellow was he,
   Saying, "I'd give more for my daddy and my ma,
   Than I would for your wives all three!"

3. The next came up was a fair pretty maid,
   With a comb and a glass in her hand,
   Saying, ………………………………
   ………………………………

The rag-ing sea goes roar, roar, roar, And the storm-y winds they do blow, While we poor sail-ors are drown-ing in the deep, And the pret-ty girls are stand-ing on the shore.

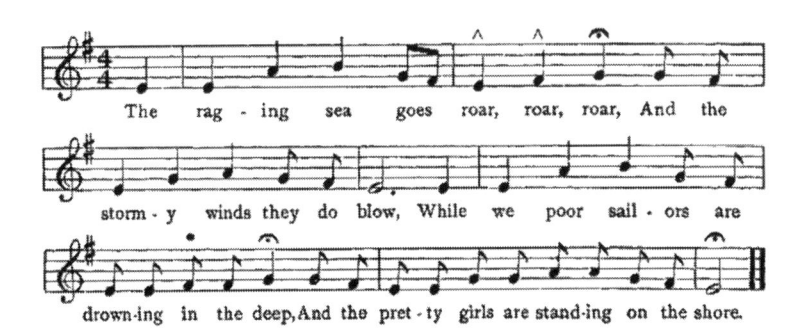

NOTES

Recorded by me October 11, 1904, from the singing of J. G. M., Newbury, Vt.

Source:
Barry, Phillips. "Traditional Ballads in New England. I." *The Journal of American Folklore*. Vol. 18, No. 69 (Apr.-Jun. 1905). pp. 123-138.

148. The Mermaid
Child Ballad 289

Massachusetts, United States

1. ONE night as I lay on my bed,
   A-taking of my ease,
   Thinking what a lodge the poor sailors have
   While they are on the seas.

2. Sailors they go through hot and cold,
   Through many a bitter blast,
   And oftentimes they are obliged
   To cut away the mast.

3. [Forgotten by the reciter.]

4. Up speaks up our captain so bold,
   And a clever old man was he:
   "I've got a wife in fair England,
   And a widow I'm afraid she will be."

5. Up speaks up our mate so bold,
   And a clever man was he:
   "I've got a wife in fair Ireland town,
   And a widow I'm afraid she will be."

6. Up speaks up our bos'n so bold,
   And a clever fellow was he:
   "I've got a wife in fair Scotland,
   And a widow I'm afraid she will be."

7. Up speaks up our little cabin-boy,
   And a smart little fellow was he:
   "I'm as sorry for my father and my mother too
   As you are for your wives all three."

8. ....
   ....
   This goodly ship she did split,
   And down to the bottom she did go.

NOTES

This fragmentary version of "The Mermaid" (Child, No. 289) I took down on January 4, 1878, from the recitation of Mrs. Sarah G. Lewis, who was born in Boston, Mass., in 1799, but lived most of her days in Sandwich and Barnstable. Mrs. Lewis thought she learned the song about 1808. The version is interesting because of its relation to Child's A in the first stanza. For a text from Missouri, contributed by Professor Belden, see this Journal, vol. xxv, pp. 176-177; for the tune (from Vermont) see Barry, this Journal, vol. xxii, p. 78. For broadside texts, see, for example, "Roxburghe Ballads" (ed. Ebsworth, viii, 446), Harvard College Library, 25242.4 (I, 207), 25242.17 (III, 36, 102, IV, 16, 147). The ballad is contained in "The Forget Me Not Songster" (New York, Nafis & Cornish), p. 79.

Source:
Kittredge, G. L. "Various Ballads." *The Journal of American Folklore.*
   Vol. 26, No. 100 (Apr.-Jun. 1913). pp. 174-182.

149. Shipwreck
Child Ballad 289

Missouri, United States

ONE Saturday night as we set sail,
Not being far from shore,
'Twas then that I spied a pretty fair maid
With a glass and a comb in her hand, her hand,
With a glass and a comb in her hand.

Chorus

    The stormy wind did blow,
    And the raging sea did roll,
    And we poor sailors came leaping to the top
    While the landsmen lay down below, below, below,
    While the landsmen lay down below.

Then up came a boy of our gallant ship,
And a noble-spoken boy was he;
Saying, "I've a mother in distant York town
This night is a-weeping for me."

Then up came a lad of our gallant ship,
And a beautiful lad was he,
Saying, "I've a sweetheart in distant York town
This night is a-looking for me."

Then up came the clerk of our gallant ship,
And a noble-spoken man was he,
Saying, "I've a wife in distant York town
This night a widow will be."

Then up came the captain of our gallant ship,
There is no braver man than he,
Saying, "For the want of a yawl-boat we'll be drowned

And we'll sink to the bottom of the sea."

Then three times round our gallant ship turned,
Three times round she turned;
Three times round our gallant ship turned,
Then she sank to the bottom of the sea.

NOTES

This was written down by Agnes Shibley of the Kirksville (Mo.) Normal School, who learned it from her mother. It was sent to Professor Belden by Miss Hamilton.

Source:
"Five Old-Country Ballads." *The Journal of American Folklore*. Vol. 25, No. 96 (Apr.-Jun. 1912). pp. 171-178.

150. The Mermaid
Child Ballad 289

United States

ONE Friday morning we set sail,
    And when not far from land,
We all espied a fair Mermaid,
    With a comb and glass in her hand

        The stormy winds they did blow
            And the raging seas they did roar,
        The sailors on the deck did go,
            And wished themselves on shore.

Then spoke a boy of our gallant ship,
    And a good lad was he,
My parents in fair Portsmouth town,
    This night will weep for me.

Then spoke a man of our good ship,
    No braver man than he,
I have a wife in fair London town,
    Who will a widow be.

Then spoke the captain of our ship.
  A valiant man was he,
We wan't a boat, we shall be drown'd,
  Shall founder in the sea.

The moon shone bright, the stars gave light,
  My mother looked for me,
She long may weep with watery eyes,
  And blame the ruthless sea.

Then three times round went our good ship.
  And sank immediately,
Left none to tell the sorrowing tale,
  Of our brave company.

Source:
"The Mermaid." *The Forget Me Not Songster*. Boston: G. W. Cottrell, n.d.

151. Little Girl, Mama Glau, and Humming-Bird

Trinidad

ONE time there was a little girl called Babé, and Babé was livin' at she nenine (godmother). One day Babé did want to see she muma and she pupa, so she asked she nenine to le' she go to see them. Now, on the way dere was a very deep river, an' this day dere was a big shower of rain an' the whole place was covered over with water. When Babé reached the river an' couldn' get over, she begin cryin'. Den a mama glau (mermaid) came up an' asked Babé what she was cryin' fo'. Babé tell she that she want to go over an' see she muma an' she pupa, but she couldn' get over de river. De mama glau tell she, "I will take you over de river, but you musn' let nobody know how you get over." So Mama Glau carry Babé over de river. Now you know Kilibwi (humming-bird) got very light ears. Mama Glau call Kilibwi and sen' him to listen to hear if Babé would tell anybody how she got over de river. Babé reached de house, an' everybody was surprise; an' dey wanted to fin' out how she got over, because dey all did know dat de river did wash away de whole place. Babé keep on tellin' dem dat she cross it she self. But dey wouldn' believe she. Den in a easy way she tell dem, "Mama Glau cross me."

Kilibwi was very far, but he hear Babé, an' he begin singin',—

> "Casa bilau bilau bil
> I Babé qui toyai Mama Glau."[1]

Kilibwi come right up to de house, singin',—

> "Casa bilau bilau bil
> I Babé qui toyai Mama Glau."

Now, when Babé was goin' back, she muma an' she pupa know dat if Kilibwi reach Mama Glau firs' an' tell she that Babé give out de secret, Mama Glau would kill Babé, so dey pick a lot of flowers an' scatter dem in de road. Kilibwi come down, singin',—

> "Casa bilau bilau bil
> I Babé qui toyai Mama Glau."

But he was so greedy, he had to stop to suck these flowers. So Babé reach de river before Kilibwi, an' she tell Mama Glau dat she didn' tell anybody how she get over. So Mama Glau cross she over again.
Now, Mr. Kilibwi come down, singin',—

> "Casa bilau bilau bil
> I Babé qui toyai Mama Glau."

So Mama Glau says to Kilibwi, "Get on me right shoulder an' sing dat song." He sing it on de right shoulder. She say, "Get on me left shoulder."

> "Casa bilau bilau bil
> I Babé qui toyai Mama Glau."

She say, "Get on me right ear."

> "Casa bilau bilau bil
> I Babé qui toyai Mama Glau."

She say, "Get on me left ear."

> "Casa bilau bilau bil
> I Babé qui toyai Mama Glau."

---

[1] "I Babé, who got Mama Glau into trouble."

Den she say, "Get in de palm of me lef' han'." An' after he get t'rough singin', Mama Glau hit him one slap an' grin' him up. An' de foam you see on de river whenever de rain fall is from Kilibwi. De people kill Mama Glau an' buil' a bridge over de river.

NOTES

The tale was told to me in New York City by Charles Penny of Trinidad. To him and to Grace Nail Johnson, who introduced him, editorial thanks are due.

Source:
P[arson], E[lsie] C[lews]. "Notes and Queries: A West-Indian Tale." *The Journal of American Folklore*. Vol. 32, No. 125 (Jul.-Sep. 1919). pp. 442-443.

152. The Boy and the Mermaid

Jamaica

ONCE a little boy went to the river to bathe. He was washed away to sea and his parents heard nothing about him, but he was told before going that if he went he would be drowned.

But he was a smart little boy. A mermaid came and took him and carried him to the bottom of the sea and asked him certain questions: If he ate fish? he said "No." If he ate beef? he said "No." If he ate mutton? he said "No." If he ate pork? he said "No." If he had said "Yes," the mermaid would have killed him, because its body was made of fish, beef, mutton and pork. So, as he didn't eat any of those things, the mermaid carried him to the shore, threw him out, and a sheep took him up. The master of the sheep asked him certain questions,—where he was from and what was his name. He told him and they carried him to his home. They were so glad to see him they went and invited friends to come and help them enjoy themselves and make merry.

NOTES

This fragment must belong to a story of a child promised before its birth to a water-spirit, as in Grimm 181 [The Nixie of the Mill-Pond] and Parsons, Sea Islands, 137.

Source:
Beckwith, Martha Warren. *Jamaica Anansi Stories.* New York: The American Folk-Lore Society, 1924.

153. Sea-Mahmy[1]

Jamaica

ONE day, height a hungry time, Blackbird have a feedin' tree in a sea. An' every day Blackbird go an' feed.

Annancy say unto Blackbird:—"Please, Bro'er Blackbird, please carry me over a you feedin' tree."

Blackbird say unto Annancy:—"Bro'er Annancy, you so cravin' you goin' to eat every bit from me."

He say:—"No, Bro'er Blackbird I won' do it."

Brother Blackbird say unto Annancy:—"A you no have no wing, how you a go?"

Well! Blackbird take out two of him tail feather, 'tick upon Annancy. He pick out two of him wing feather, 'tick upon Annancy. He take two feather out of him back again, 'tick upon Annancy; two feather out of him belly feather, 'tick upon Annancy.

Well! Blackbird an' Annancy fly in a the sea upon the feedin' tree.

Every feedin' Blackbird go fe pick, Annancy say that one a fe him.

Blackbird go upon the next limb, Annancy say a fe him.

Blackbird go upon the t'ird limb, Annancy say a fe him.

Till Annancy eat a good tummy-full.

Annancy drop asleep upon the tree.

Well! Blackbird take time, pick out all the feather back, an' Blackbird fly away.

When Annancy wake out of sleep he say:—"Make me fly."

He can't fly.

He broke a branch off a the tree, t'row in the sea. The branch swim.

Annancy say if the branch swim him will swim, an' he jump off a the tree, drop in the sea an' sink.

An' when he go down a sea bottom he meet Sea-mahmy.

He said to Sea-mahmy:—"Mumma, mother tell me me have a cousin down a sea bottom, ya."

Sea-mahmy say:—"I going to see if me and you are cousin."

---

[1] Mermaid.

Sea-mahmy put a pan of sand in the fire for well hot. When him get hot he take it off a the fire, give to Brother Annancy for drink it off.

Brother Annancy say:—"Cousin Sea-mahmy, it don' hot enough. Put it out a de sun fe make it hot more."

After him put it out a the sun then he say:—"Cousin Sea-mahmy, I think it hot now."

An' Sea-mahmy say:—"Well you must drink it off an' make I see if you an' me are cousin."

An' Annancy do drink it off.

Annancy spend t'ree day down a sea bottom.

Well! the next day Sea-mahmy said to him:—"Whé you going to come out."

Him said:—"Cousin Sea-mahmy, sen' one of you son fe carry me out a lan'."

Sea-mahmy give him one of him son, the name of that son call Trapong.

Well! Trapong an' Annancy travel, make middle in a sea.

Sea-mahmy call:—"Trapong, Trapong, fetch back 'tranger man, come back."

An' Trapong say:—"'Top, Brother Annancy, I think I hear my mother calling me back."

Annancy say:—"No, make way! War de 'pon sea!"

An' Trapong sail with Annancy on him back till they reach shore.

When they go to shore he say:—"Bro'er Trapong, take dis bag weigh me, see whé me weigh."

Trapong lift him up, say:—"Yes, Brother Annancy you heavy."

So Annancy come back out of the bag.

He say:—"Bro'er Trapong, you come in make I weigh you see."

Trapong went into the bag.

He tie Trapong, tie tight.

Trapong say:—"Brother Annancy you a tie me too 'trong."

He say:—"Me no a tie you fe see if you heavy?"

Trapong say to Brother Annancy:—"Me heavy?"

Annancy say:—"You heavy oh! You light oh! You heavy enough fe me wife pot." An' for all the bahl Trapong a bahl he gone back to him house an' Annancy eat him.

Jack Mantora me no choose none.

Source:

Jekyll, Walter, editor. *Jamaican Song and Story: Annancy Stories, Digging Sings, Ring Tunes, and Dancing Tunes*. London: David Nutt, 1907.

154. The Mermaid

Jamaica

ON ONE of the estates in Jamaica there is a large pond, sleeping under the shade of bamboos and jungle trees, which the negroes believe is haunted by a mermaid, who is to be seen occasionally combing her hair and polishing a golden table. It is not recorded whether the mermaid is black! They tell the tale of a former proprietor of the estate who wanted to drain the pond, and cut a deep trench for the purpose. The water gathered and hung over the trench, but refused to flow down it, presumably by the influence of the mermaid, who did not wish her stronghold to be disturbed.

Source:
"Jamaica." *Blackwood's Edinburgh Magazine.* Vol. 147, No. 896 (June 1890). pp. 778-790.

155. The Mermaid's Lake

Guyana

THERE was a captain of Indians who was also a Piai priest and doctor. He lived on this savanna. His little daughter went down to the river every day to bathe, and was frequently seen splashing, diving, and swimming with a companion of apparently her own age. Much notice was not taken of her doings, as she was a spoilt and wayward child, and allowed by her fond father to do, and to go, whatever and wherever she liked. But one day she was missing. Evening came, and the captain's daughter was not at home. Search was made for her in the river, but without success. At night the piaiman's wailing was heard supplicating the spirits of the river and savanna to inspire him with the knowledge of his daughter's fate. At the dawn of day he went down to the river and searched about the bank, rattling his goubi-shak-shak, or magic gourd, as it is indiscriminately called (but properly, as by themselves, eumaraca), and chanting in plaintive and sorrowful tones. At times he would place his ears to the ground and shake his eumaraca, and listen as if seeking to discover by sound a hollow space under ground—a passage from the river. Thus he went on, forming for himself an irregular path upward to the savanna, until he came to the lake. Here he sat down, and in sweetest tones implored for the restitution of his child. There was a motion in the water, and then appeared a mintje mama, mermaid, or merman, (Guiana legends tend to the belief of the hermaphrodite nature of these mysterious and fabulous creatures,) who laughed derisively and tauntingly while swimming about and lashing the water with his tail. Arrow after arrow, with unerring aim, sped from the captain's bow. The merman's head and breast were covered with them. He sank down into the lake. But his descent was for a moment only. He returned, and with him the captain's daughter swimming around and plucking out the arrows from the head and breast of her mysterious lover. The captain, tantalised and enraged beyond forbearance at this explicit sign of his daughter's unnatural affection, plunged into the pond with his uplifted cutlass, slashing right and left. A terrible commotion ensued, the water everywhere bubbled and foamed. But the captain has never been seen from that day.

In the bright moonlight nights an occasional Indian traveller passing by, and ignorant of the legend, has heard a woman's voice lamenting. It is the voice of the captain's daughter chanting the death song for her father's memory. In the dry season, when the lake is almost dry, they say that the merman and his Indian wife have retired to the river, and drawn the water after them.

One of these odd days or another, Mr. Leps will most certainly "catch a Tartar," as he persists against knowledge, and to the horror of the Hittia Indians, to dredge the "Mermaid's Lake " with his net, and to take out of it fish of delicious flavour.

I was one day repeating this story to a Dutch creole lady of the river, who in her younger days was an expert huntress with the gun and bow. She knew the story, and believed it. She had herself been troubled by a mischievous "merchild" (probably an otter or water-dog), who at one time went regularly to her fish pen and liberated the fishes entrapped. One day she caught him in the very act, and railed out at him; but he lashed his tail about and laughed heartily, as amused at her ill-temper.

Source:
Dance, Charles Daniel. *Chapters from a Guianese log-book; or, The Folk-Lore and Scenes of Sea-coast and River Life in British Guiana.* Georgetown: The Royal Gazette Establishment, 1881.

156. Water Mamma

Guyana

THE belief in the "Water Mamma," or "Mermaid," a being of supernatural power, is common to all people of a certain stage of mental development who live in the neighbourhood of the sea, lakes, or large rivers. But the formation of a society founded on a belief of its existence and superhuman intelligence, and for the purpose of its glorification by an obscene worship, is peculiar, as far as I know, to Africans and their descendants. .On the coast of British Guiana the offspring of the old African slaves still continue in its worship, although it must be admitted that it is fast disappearing under the potent influence of Christian civilisation; and yet it must be confessed, at the expense of some degree of shame, that several of the present members of the Water Mamma Society have a tolerable knowledge of the Holy Scriptures, and can read and write.

Endeavours have been made to trace the Water Spirit to the manatee (seacow, cuimure or quemoa); and although it very probably is the origin of the existence of the mythic creature in these waters, yet every one of the Indians and creoles, with whom I have spoken on the subject, denies that the two are identical. Whether it be a very degraded corruption, indeed, of "the wise old man of the sea," the Ægean Nereus who had the power of prophesying the future and of appearing to mortals in different shapes; or of one of the nymphs of the sea and of the fresh water, may not be an unreasonable conjecture.

The attachment of the Water Spirit to human beings is mostly sexual, and if there be not more than one of these mysterious creatures, it must be of an hermaphrodital nature. But there is abundant willing testimony to the fact that they are many—if not numerous—and of both sexes.

In the lower part of the rivers and on the coasts the Water Spirit attaches itself mostly to men, and, strange to say, evinces a peculiar penchant for married men.

A young married man is absent for a week or more from his young wife, whom he persuades to believe that he has received a mysterious mandate to go somewhere, which, on pain of death to him, her, and their child or children, he may not neglect: when the husband returns after his absence, he talks to his wife of heaps of money, for the Water Spirit is liberal with silver; but the wife sees none of it. The man's absence then becomes long and frequent. The young wife must bear her wrongs and her grief in silence, lest evil come on her and her husband and their little ones. She is henceforth a wife in nothing but in name.

A portion of the mystery of the Minje Mamma, Water Spirit, or Mermaid is cleared when we get to the knowledge of the society organised by its votaries. Men and women are admitted as members; and at their gatherings sensual dances excite the imagination until the dancers fall on the ground in ecstatic convulsions; and profligacy of the most atrocious kind seems to be their bond of union.

Source:
Dance, Charles Daniel. *Chapters from a Guianese log-book; or, The Folk-Lore and Scenes of Sea-coast and River Life in British Guiana.* Georgetown: The Royal Gazette Establishment, 1881.

157. Oiára, the Water-Maidens

Brazil

STORIES of water-maidens are common on the Lower Amazons. The Indians say that these maidens are exceedingly beautiful; they have long, black hair, in which they entwine the flowers of the morenú.[1] They entice the young men by their beauty, and by the sweetness of their songs; once in their embrace, they drag them down into the water, and nothing more is ever heard of them.

Although these tales are current among the Indians, I am inclined to think that they were introduced by the Portuguese. But there was, undoubtedly, an aboriginal myth which bore a considerable resemblance to the Old World stories, which have been tacked to it. The myth, as given by Dr. Couto de Magalhães, represents the Oiára (or Uauyará) as a male, not a female:

"The fate of the fishes was confided to Uauyará; the animal into which he transformed himself was the river-porpoise. No one of the supernatural beings of the Indians furnishes so many legends as this. There is not a settlement of the province of Pará where one may not hear a series of these stories, sometimes grotesque and extravagant, often melancholy and tender. The Uauyará is a great lover of our Indian women; many of them attribute their first child to this deity, who sometimes surprises them when they are bathing, sometimes transforms

---

[1] Pontederia. Dr. Barboza Rodriguez says that the oiára has the tail of a porpoise.

himself into the figure of a mortal to seduce them, sometimes drags them under the water, where they are forced to submit to him. On moonlight nights the lakes are often illuminated, and one hears the songs and the measured tread of the dances with which the Uauyará amuses himself."

Source:

Smith, Herbert H. *Brazil: The Amazons and the Coast.* New York: Charles Scribner's Sons, 1879.

158. Yara

Brazil

SHE was a water-witch who lured young men by her marvelous singing. After seeing her the youth would become melancholy and would haunt the river mouth day and night where he had first beheld her. His friends and people would remonstrate with and warn him of the enchantress "whose smile is death;" but the youth, be he chief or simple Indian would not listen; he would go to the river. There the beautiful being would appear and as he rushed to embrace her the waters would divide, and the two would disappear.

Source:

Chase, Eliza Brown. *Transcontinental Sketches: Legends, Lyrics and Romances Gleaned on Vacation Tours in Northeastern and Middle Canada and the Pacific States.* Philadelphia: John C. Winston, 1909. pp. 342-43.

159. The Story of the Yara

Brazil

DOWN in the south, where the sun shines so hotly that everything and everybody sleeps all day, and even the great forests seem silent, except early in the morning and late in the evening—down in this country there once lived a young man and a maiden. The girl had been born in the town, and had scarcely ever left it; but the young man was a native of another country, and had only come to the city near the great river because he could find no work to do where he was.

A few months after his arrival, when the days were cooler, and the people did not sleep so much as usual, a great feast was held a little way out of the town, and to this feast everyone flocked from thirty miles and more. Some walked and some rode, some came in beautiful golden coaches; but all had on splendid dresses of red or blue, while wreaths of flowers rested on their hair.

It was the first time that the youth had been present on such an occasion, and he stood silently aside watching the graceful dances and the pretty games played by the young people. And as he watched, he noticed one girl, dressed in white with scarlet pomegranates in her hair, who seemed to him lovelier than all the rest.

When the feast was over, and the young man returned home, his manner was so strange that it drew the attention of all his friends.

Through his work next day the youth continued to see the girl's face, throwing the ball to her companions, or threading her way between them as she danced. At night sleep fled from him, and after tossing for hours on his bed, he would get up and plunge into a deep pool that lay a little way in the forest.

This state of things went on for some weeks, then at last chance favoured him. One evening, as he was passing near the house where she lived, he saw her standing with her back to the wall, trying to beat off with her fan the attacks of a savage dog that was leaping at her throat. Alonzo, for such was his name, sprang forward, and with one blow of his fist stretched the creature dead upon the road. He then helped the frightened and half-fainting girl into the large cool verandah where her parents were sitting, and from that hour he was a welcome guest in the house, and it was not long before he was the promised husband of Julia.

Every day, when his work was done, he used to go up to the house, half hidden among flowering plants and brilliant creepers, where humming-birds darted from bush to bush, and parrots of all colours, red and green and grey, shrieked in chorus. There he would find the maiden waiting for him, and they would spend an hour or two under the stars, which looked so large and bright that you felt as if you could almost touch them.

"What did you do last night after you went home?" suddenly asked the girl one evening.

"Just the same as I always do," answered he. "It was too hot to sleep, so it was no use going to bed, and I walked straight off to the forest and bathed in one of those deep dark pools at the edge of the river. I have been there constantly for several months, but last night a strange thing happened. I was taking my last plunge, when I heard—sometimes from one side, and sometimes from another—the sound of a voice singing more sweetly than any nightingale, though I could not catch any words. I left the pool, and, dressing myself as fast as I could, I searched every bush and tree round the water, as I fancied that perhaps it was my friend who was playing a trick on me, but there was not a creature to be seen; and when I reached home I found my friend fast asleep."

As Julia listened her face grew deadly white, and her whole body shivered as if with cold. From her childhood she had heard stories of the terrible beings that lived in the forests and were hidden under the banks of the rivers, and could only be kept off by powerful charms. Could the voice which had bewitched Alonzo have come from one of these? Perhaps, who knows, it might be the voice of the dreaded Yara herself, who sought young men on the eve of their marriage as her prey.

For a moment the girl sat choked with fear, as these thoughts rushed through her; then she said: "Alonzo, will you promise something?"

"What is that?" asked he.

"It is something that has to do with our future happiness."

"Oh! it is serious, then? Well, of course I promise. Now tell me!"

"I want you to promise," she answered, lowering her voice to a whisper, "never to bathe in those pools again."

"But why not, queen of my soul; have I not gone there always, and nothing has harmed me, flower of my heart?"

"No; but perhaps something will. If you will not promise I shall go mad with fright. Promise me."

"Why, what is the matter? You look so pale! Tell me why you are so frightened?"

"Did you not hear the song?" she asked, trembling.

"Suppose I did, how could that hurt me? It was the loveliest song I ever heard!"

"Yes, and after the song will come the apparition; and after that—after that—"

"I don't understand. Well—after that?"

"After that—death."

Alonzo stared at her. Had she really gone mad? Such talk was very unlike Julia; but before he could collect his senses the girl spoke again:

"That is the reason why I implore you never to go there again; at any rate till after we are married."

"And what difference will our marriage make?"

"Oh, there will be no danger then; you can go to bathe as often as you like!"

"But tell me why you are so afraid?"

"Because the voice you heard—I know you will laugh, but it is quite true—it was the voice of the Yara."

At these words Alonzo burst into a shout of laughter; but it sounded so harsh and loud that Julia shrank away shuddering. It seemed as if he could not stop himself, and the more he laughed the paler the poor girl became, murmuring to herself as she watched him:

"Oh, heaven! you have seen her! you have seen her! what shall I do?"

Faint as was her whisper, it reached the ears of Alonzo, who, though he still could not speak for laughing, shook his head.

"You may not know it, but it is true. Nobody who has not seen the Yara laughs like that." And Julia flung herself on the ground weeping bitterly.

At this sight Alonzo became suddenly grave, and kneeling by her side, gently raised her up.

"Do not cry so, my angel," he said, "I will promise anything you please. Only let me see you smile again."

With a great effort Julia checked her sobs, and rose to her feet.

"Thank you," she answered. "My heart grows lighter as you say that! I know you will try to keep your word and to stay away from the forest. But—the power of the Yara is very strong, and the sound of her voice is apt to make men forget everything else in the world. Oh, I have seen it, and more than one betrothed maiden lives alone, broken-hearted. If ever you should return to the pool where you first heard the voice, promise me that you will at least take this with you." And opening a curiously carved box, she took out a sea-shell shot with many colours, and sang a song softly into it. "The moment you hear the Yara's voice," said she, "put this to your ear, and you will hear my song instead. Perhaps—I do not know for certain—but perhaps, I may be stronger than the Yara."

It was late that night when Alonzo returned home. The moon was shining on the distant river, which looked cool and inviting, and the trees of the forest seemed to stretch out their arms and beckon him near. But the young man steadily turned his face in the other direction, and went home to bed.

The struggle had been hard, but Alonzo had his reward next day in the joy and relief with which Julia greeted him. He assured her that having overcome the temptation once the danger was now over; but she, knowing better than he did the magic of the Yara's face and voice, did not fail to make him repeat his promise when he went away.

For three nights Alonzo kept his word, not because he believed in the Yara, for he thought that the tales about her were all nonsense, but because he could not bear the tears with which he knew that Julia would greet him, if he confessed that he had returned to the forest. But, in spite of this, the song rang in his ears, and daily grew louder.

On the fourth night the attraction of the forest grew so strong that neither the thought of Julia nor the promises he had made her could hold him back. At eleven o'clock he plunged into the cool darkness of the trees, and took the path that led straight to the river. Yet, for the first time, he found that Julia's warnings, though he had laughed at her at the moment, had remained in his memory, and he glanced at the bushes with a certain sense of fear which was quite new to him.

When he reached the river he paused and looked round for a moment to make sure that the strange feeling of some one watching him was fancy, and he was really alone. But the moon shone brightly on every tree, and nothing was to be seen but his own shadow; nothing was to be heard but the sound of the rippling stream.

He threw off his clothes, and was just about to dive in headlong, when something—he did not know what—suddenly caused him to look round. At the same instant the moon passed from behind a cloud, and its rays fell on a beautiful golden-haired woman standing half hidden by the ferns.

With one bound he caught up his mantle, and rushed headlong down the path he had come, fearing at each step to feel a hand laid on his shoulder. It was not till he had left the last trees behind him, and was standing in the open plain, that he dared to look round, and then he thought a figure in white was still standing there waving her arms to and fro. This was enough; he ran along the road harder than ever, and never paused till he was safe in his own room.

With the earliest rays of dawn he went back to the forest to see whether he could find any traces of the Yara, but though he searched every clump of bushes, and looked up every tree, everything was empty, and the only voices he heard were those of parrots, which are so ugly that they only drive people away.

"I think I must be mad," he said to himself, "and have dreamt all that folly"; and going back to the city he began his daily work. But either that was harder than usual, or he must be ill, for he could not fix his mind upon it, and everybody he came across during the day inquired if anything had happened to give him that white, frightened look.

"I must be feverish," he said to himself; "after all, it is rather dangerous to take a cold bath when one is feeling so hot." Yet he knew, while he said it, that he was counting the hours for night to come, that he might return to the forest.

In the evening he went as usual to the creeper-covered house. But he had better have stayed away, as his face was so pale and his manner so strange, that the poor girl saw that something terrible had occurred. Alonzo, however, refused to answer any of her questions, and all she could get was a promise to hear everything the next day.

On pretence of a violent headache, he left Julia much earlier than usual and hurried quickly home. Taking down a pistol, he loaded it and put it in his belt, and a little before midnight he stole out on the tips of his toes, so as to disturb nobody. Once outside he hastened down the road which led to the forest.

He did not stop till he had reached the river pool, when holding the pistol in his hand, he looked about him. At every little noise—the falling of a leaf, the rustle of an animal in the bushes, the cry of a night-bird—he sprang up and cocked his pistol in the direction of the sound. But though the moon still shone he saw nothing, and by and by a kind of dreamy state seemed to steal over him as he leant against a tree.

How long he remained in this condition he could not have told, but suddenly he awoke with a start, on hearing his name uttered softly.

"Who is that?" he cried, standing upright instantly; but only an echo answered him. Then his eyes grew fascinated with the dark waters of the pool close to his feet, and he looked at it as if he could never look away.

He gazed steadily into the depths for some minutes, when he became aware that down in the darkness was a bright spark, which got rapidly bigger and brighter. Again that feeling of awful fear took possession of him, and he tried to turn his eyes from the pool. But it was no use; something stronger than himself compelled him to keep them there.

At last the waters parted softly, and floating on the surface he saw the beautiful woman whom he had fled from only a few nights before. He turned to run, but his feet were glued to the spot.

She smiled at him and held out her arms, but as she did so there came over him the remembrance of Julia, as he had seen her a few hours earlier, and her warnings and fears for the very danger in which he now found himself.

Meanwhile the figure was always drawing nearer, nearer; but, with a violent effort, Alonzo shook off his stupor, and taking aim at her shoulder he pulled the trigger. The report awoke the sleeping echoes, and was repeated all through the forest, but the figure smiled still, and went on advancing. Again Alonzo fired, and a second time the bullet whistled through the air, and the figure advanced nearer. A moment more, and she would be at his side.

Then, his pistol being empty, he grasped the barrel with both hands, and stood ready to use it as a club should the Yara approach and closer. But now it seemed her turn to feel afraid, for she paused an instant while he pressed forward, still holding the pistol above his head, prepared to strike.

In his excitement he had forgotten the river, and it was not till the cold water touched his feet that he stood still by instinct. The Yara saw that he was wavering, and suffering herself to sway gently backwards and forwards on the surface of the river, she began to sing. The song floated through the trees, now far and now near; no one could tell whence it came, the whole air seemed full of it. Alonzo felt his senses going and his will failing. His arms dropped heavily to his side, but in falling struck against the sea shell, which, as he had promised Julia, he had always carried in his coat.

His dimmed mind was just clear enough to remember what she had said, and with trembling fingers, that were almost powerless to grasp, he drew it out. As he did so the song grew sweeter and more tender than before, but he shut his ears to it and bent his head over the shell. Out of its depths arose the voice of Julia singing to him as she had sung when she gave him the shell, and though the notes sounded faint at first, they swelled louder and louder till the mist which had gathered about him was blown away.

Then he raised his head, feeling that he had been through strange places, where he could never wander any more; and he held himself erect and strong, and looked about him. Nothing was to be seen but the shining of the river, and the dark shadows of the trees; nothing was to be heard but the hum of the insects, as they darted through the night.

Adapted from *Folklore Bresilien.*

Source:
Lang, Andrew, editor. *The Brown Fairy Book.* London and New York: Longmans, Green, and Company, 1904.

160. The Mermaid of the Gocta Cataracts

Peru

Jessie Kwak and her husband, Robert Kittilson, are travelers who visited Peru during a trip from September 2009 to February 2010. Kwak shared this tale in her travel blog, **Unpaved South America,** *and graciously provided permission for it to be reprinted here. The age of the tale is unknown.*

WHEN we hiked out to the Gocta Cataracts, our guide, Señora Teo, told us this story:

Not too long ago, there was a shaman named Gregorio. He and his wife lived by the river, and he would often go up to the base of the waterfall and speak with the mermaid that lived there. One day she said to him, "Gregorio, I would like to give you a gift. Ask me for anything, and it will be yours."

Now, Gregorio and his wife were very poor, so he thought for a moment and answered, "I would only ask for a good catch of fish to take home tonight."

The mermaid said to him again, "Gregorio, you may ask for anything you wish." But Gregorio answered that he would be content with just the fish. The mermaid granted his wish, and he took home the biggest catch he had ever gotten from the river.

While his wife dumped the fish out of the bag to clean them, however, a solid gold ring fell out, as well. She was surprised, and hid the ring away without saying a word.

The next time that Gregorio went to see the mermaid, she asked him the same question, and once again he replied that all his little family needed was a good catch of fish. The mermaid once again granted his wish, and that night, as Gregorio's wife was cleaning the fish, a solid gold bracelet fell out of the bag.

Now, Gregorio's wife became worried, and suspected that Gregorio was stealing. She said nothing to him, but resolved to follow him the next time he left the house.

The next day, when Gregorio left to see the mermaid, his wife followed behind. As they approached the base of the waterfall, she began to become scared, because she had always been warned to stay away from that place. But she continued following her husband.

When she arrived to the base of the waterfall she saw her husband speaking to a woman. The top half of the woman was pure silver, and her bottom half was the tail of a fish of pure gold. Gregorio's wife was stunned, and she let out a breath. The mermaid then saw her, and reached out for Gregorio, then dove into the water.

Gregorio's wife waited a moment, sure that her husband was playing a joke on her, but the minutes passed and he didn't surface. She ran to the base of the waterfall, calling out his name, but she found no one.

During holidays, Gregorio was always in charge of setting off the fireworks. When it rains, you can hear the boom, boom of the waterfall. The villagers say that this is Gregorio, forever trapped with the mystical mermaid.

Source:

Kwak, Jessie. "The mystical mermaid of the Gocta Cataracts." *Unpaved South America*. 1 Feb. 2010. <www.unpavedsouthamerica.com/2010/blog/the-mystical-mermaid-of-the-gocta-cataracts/>.

© 2010 Jessie Kwak. Reprinted by permission of Jessie Kwak.

Appendix

Bibliography of Sources

Abercromby, John. "Notes and Queries: Legends from Co. Meath." *The Folk-Lore Journal*. Vol. 7, No. 4 (1889). pp. 313-322.

Allan, Robert. "The Mermaid." *Beauties of the Scottish Poets; or, Harp of Renfrewshire: A Collection of Songs and Other Poetical Pieces*. William Motherwell, editor. Glasgow: William Turnbull, 1821.

Andersen, Hans Christian. *Hans Andersen's Fairy Tales*. Mrs. Henry H. B. Paull, translator. Wilhelm Petersen and Lorenz Frolich, illustrators. London: Frederick Warne & Co., [1872, 1883].

Árnason, Jón. *Icelandic Legends*. Geo. E. J. Powell and Eiríkur Magnússon, translators. London: Richard Bentley, 1864.

Arnold, Matthew. *Poems by Matthew Arnold*. G. C. Macauley, editor. London: Macmillan and Co., 1896.

Arnott, R. J. "Scottish Mermaids: 5th April 1907." *The Transactions and Journal of Proceedings of the Dumfries and Galloway Natural History and Antiquarian Society*. Volume 19. Dumfries: Standard Office, 1908. pp.142-157.

d'Aulnoy, [Marie Catherine Baronne]. *The Fairy Tales of Madame d'Aulnoy*. Miss Annie Macdonell and Miss Lee, translators. Clinton Peters, illustrator. London: Lawrence and Bullen, 1892.

Baring-Gould, S[abine]. *Curious Myths of the Middle Ages, Second Series*. London: Rivingtons, 1868. pp. 206-258.

Barry, Phillips. "Traditional Ballads in New England. I." *The Journal of American Folklore*. Vol. 18, No. 69 (Apr.-Jun. 1905). pp. 123-138.

Bassett, Fletcher S. *Legends and Superstitions of the Sea and of Sailors in All Lands and at All Times*. Chicago and New York: Belford, Clarke & Co., 1885.

Beckwith, Martha Warren. *Jamaica Anansi Stories*. New York: The American Folk-Lore Society, 1924.

Benedict, Laura Watson. *A Study of Bagobo Ceremonial, Magic and Myth*. New York: The New York Academy of Sciences, 1916.

Boas, Dr. Franz. "Cumberland Sound and Its Eskimos." *The Popular Science Monthly*. Apr 1885. pp. 768-779.

Borrow, George, translator. *The Mermaid's Prophecy and Other Songs Relating to Queen Dagmar*. London: Printed for Private Circulation, 1913.

Bottrell, William. *Traditions and Hearthside Stories of West Cornwall, Vol. 2*. Penzance: Beare and Son, 1873.

Buchanan, Robert. *Ballad Stories of the Affections: From the Scandinavian*. London: George Routledge & Sons, [1866].

———. *The Complete Poetical Works of Robert Buchanan, Volume II*. London: Chatto & Windus, 1901.

Burton, Sir Richard. *Lady Burton's Edition of Her Husband's Arabian Nights, Vol. 3.* Lady Isabel Burton and Justin Huntly McCarthy, editors. London: Waterlow & Sons, 1887.

———. *Lady Burton's Edition of Her Husband's Arabian Nights, Vol. 4.* Lady Isabel Burton and Justin Huntly McCarthy, editors. London: Waterlow & Sons, 1886.

———. *Lady Burton's Edition of Her Husband's Arabian Nights, Vol. 6.* Lady Isabel Burton and Justin Huntly McCarthy, editors. London: Waterlow & Sons, 1886.

Bushby, Mrs. *The Danes: Sketched by Themselves, A Series of Popular Stories by the Best Danish Authors.* Vol. 1. London: Richard Bentley, 1864.

Chambers, Robert, editor. *The Book of Days: A Miscellany of Popular Antiquities. Vol. 2.* Philadelphia: J. B. Lippincott & Co., 1879. pp. 612-613.

Chase, Eliza Brown. *Transcontinental Sketches: Legends, Lyrics and Romances Gleaned on Vacation Tours in Northeastern and Middle Canada and the Pacific States.* Philadelphia: John C. Winston, 1909. pp. 342-43.

Child, Francis James, editor. *English and Scottish Ballads, Volume 1.* London: Sampson Low, Son, & Co., 1861.

———. *The English and Scottish Popular Ballads, Part II.* Boston: Houghton, Mifflin and Company, 1884.

———. *The English and Scottish Popular Ballads, Part IX.* Boston: Houghton, Mifflin and Company, 1894.

———. *English and Scottish Popular Ballads: Student's Cambridge Edition.* Helen Child Sargent and George Lyman Kittredge, editors. Boston: Houghton, Mifflin and Company, 1904.

Craigie, William A. *Scandinavian Folk-Lore: Illustrations of the Traditional Beliefs of the Northern People.* London: Alexander Gardner, 1896.

Croker, Thomas Crofton. *Fairy Legends and Traditions of the South of Ireland.* London: John Murray, 1828.

Cross, Tom Peete. "An Irish Folk-Tale." *The Journal of American Folklore.* Vol. 23, No. 90 (Oct.-Dec. 1910). pp. 419-424.

Cunningham, Allan. *Poems and Songs.* London: John Murray, 1847.

Dance, Charles Daniel. *Chapters from a Guianese log-book; or, The Folk-Lore and Scenes of Sea-coast and River Life in British Guiana.* Georgetown: The Royal Gazette Establishment, 1881.

Dempster, Miss. "The Folk-Lore of Sutherland-Shire." *The Folk-Lore Journal.* Vol. 6, No. 3 (1888). pp. 149-189.

Dennys, N[icholas] B[elfield]. *The Folk-Lore of China.* London: Trübner and Co., 1876. pp. 114-115.

Dorsey, J. Owen. "Teton Folk-Lore Notes." *The Journal of American Folklore.* Vol. 2, No. 5 (Apr.-Jun. 1889). pp. 133-139.

"Five Old-Country Ballads." *The Journal of American Folklore*. Vol. 25, No. 96 (Apr.-Jun. 1912). pp. 171-178.

Garnett, Richard. *Poems*. London: Elkin Mathews & John Lane, 1893.

Gayarré, Charles. *History of Louisiana Second Series (Vol. I Part 2)*. New York: William J. Widdleton, 1867.

Giles, Herbert A., translator. *Strange Stories from a Chinese Studio, Volume 2*. London: Thos. De La Rue & Co., 1880.

Gliński, Antoni Józef. *Polish Fairy Tales*. Maude Ashurst Biggs, translator. London: John Lane, 1920.

Gregory, Lady. *A Book of Saints and Wonders*. London: John Murray, 1907.

Griffis, William Elliot. *Dutch Fairy Tales For Young Folks*. New York: Thomas Y. Crowell Co., 1919.

———. *Fairy Tales of Old Japan*. London: George G. Harrap & Co., 1911.

———. *The Mikado's Empire*. New York: Harper & Brothers, 1876, 1883.

Grimm, Jacob and Wilhelm. *Household Tales*. Margaret Hunt, translator. London: George Bell, 1884, 1892.

Hofberg, Herman. *Swedish Fairy Tales*. W. H. Myers, translator. Chicago: Belford-Clarke Company, 1890.

Hogg, James. *The Works of the Ettrick Shepherd: Poems and Ballads*. London: Blackie & Son, 1874.

Hood, Thomas. *Whims and Oddities: In Prose and Verse*. London: Lupton Relfe, 1826.

Hunt, Robert. *Popular Romances of the West of England: The Drolls, Traditions, and Superstitions of Old Cornwall*. 3rd edition. London: Chatto and Windus, 1903.

"Jamaica." *Blackwood's Edinburgh Magazine*. Vol. 147, No. 896 (June 1890). pp. 778-790.

Jamieson, Robert, editor. *Popular Ballads and Songs, Volume I*. Edinburgh: Archibald Constable and Co., 1806.

———. *Popular Ballads and Songs, Volume II*. Edinburgh: Archibald Constable and Co., 1806.

Jekyll, Walter, editor. *Jamaican Song and Story: Annancy Stories, Digging Sings, Ring Tunes, and Dancing Tunes*. London: David Nutt, 1907.

Joly, Henri L. *Legend in Japanese Art*. London: John Lane, The Bodley Head, 1908.

Jones, William. *Credulities Past and Present*. London: Chatto and Windus, 1880. pp 20-34.

Joyce, P. W. *Old Celtic Romances: Translated from the Gaelic*. London: C. Kegan Paul & Co., 1879.

Keightley, Thomas. *The Fairy Mythology: Illustrative of the Romance and Superstition of Various Countries*. London: George Bell & Sons, 1905.

Kirby, W. F. *The Hero of Esthonia: And Other Studies in the Romantic Literature of That Country, Volume 2*. London: John C. Nimmo, 1895.

Kittredge, G. L. "Various Ballads." *The Journal of American Folklore*. Vol. 26, No. 100 (Apr.-Jun. 1913). pp. 174-182.

Kwak, Jessie. "The mystical mermaid of the Gocta Cataracts." *Unpaved South America*. 1 Feb. 2010. <www.unpavedsouthamerica.com/2010/blog/the-mystical-mermaid-of-the-gocta-cataracts/>.

Lach-Szyrma, W. S. "Slavonic Folk-Lore." *The Folk-Lore Record*. Vol. 4 (1881). pp. 52-70.

Laing, Jeanie M. *Notes on Superstition and Folk Lore*. Edinburgh: John Menzies & Co., 1885. pp. 71-72, 78.

Landor, A[rnold] Henry Savage. *Across Widest Africa: An Account of the Country and People of Eastern, Central and Western Africa*. Vol. II. London: Hurst and Blackett Ltd., 1907. pp. 399-400.

Lang, Andrew, editor. *The Brown Fairy Book*. London: Longmans, Green, and Company, 1904.

———. *The Green Fairy Book*. London: Longmans, Green, and Company, 1892.

———. *The Grey Fairy Book*. London: Longmans, Green, and Co., 1900.

———. *The Pink Fairy Book*. London: Longmans, Green, and Co., 1897.

Lee, Henry. *Sea Fables Explained*. London: William Clowes and Sons, 1883.

Leland, Charles G. *The Algonquin Legends of New England; or, Myths and Folk Lore of the Micmac, Passamaquoddy, and Penobscot Tribes*. Boston: Houghton, Mifflin and Company, 1884.

Lewis, M[atthew] G[regory]. *Tales of Wonder, Volume I*. London: W. Bulmer and Co., 1801.

Leyden, John. *Poems and Ballads: With a Memoir of the Author by Sir Walter Scott*. Kelso: J. & J.H. Rutherford, 1858.

Low, Lieutenant Charles R. "A Chapter on Mermaids." *The United Service Magazine*. Volume 147 (July 1878). pp. 339-351.

MacCulloch, Sir Edgar. *Guernsey Folk Lore*. Edith F. Carey, editor. London: Elliot Stock, 1903.

MacMillian, Cyrus. *Canadian Wonder Tales*. London: John Lane, The Bodley Head, 1918.

MacPhail, Malcolm. "Folklore from the Hebrides. II." *Folklore*. Vol. 8, No. 4 (Dec. 1897). pp. 380-386.

"The Mermaid." *The Forget Me Not Songster*. Boston: G. W. Cottrell, n.d.

Milton, John. "Comus." *The Poetical Works of John Milton, Volume II*. Glasgow: Robert Malcolm, 1825.

Moore, A[rthur] W[illiam]. *The Folk-lore of the Isle of Man: Being an Account of Its Myths, Legends, Superstitions, Customs, & Proverbs.* London: D. Nutt, 1891.

Morrison, Sophia. *Manx Fairy Tales.* London: David Nutt, 1911.

Motherwell, William. *The Poetical Works of William Motherwell.* 2nd edition. Glasgow: David Robertson, 1847.

Motte-Fouqué, Friedrich de La. *Undine and Other Tales.* Fanny Elizabeth Bunnett, translator. London: Sampson Low, Son, and Marston, 1867.

Naaké, John Theophilus. *Slavonic Fairy Tales: Collected and Translated From the Russian, Polish, Servian, and Bohemian.* London: Henry S. King & Co., 1874.

Nakuina, Mrs. E. M. "The Shark-Man, Nanaue." *Hawaiian Folk Tales: A Collection of Native Legends.* Thos. G. Thrum, compiler. Chicago: The Lakeside Press, 1907.

Napier, James. "Old Ballad Folk-Lore." *The Folk-Lore Record.* Vol. 2 (1879). pp. 92-126.

Nisbet, R. *Cossack Fairy Tales and Folk Tales.* London: George G. Harrap & Co., 1916.

O'Hanlon, John. *Irish Folk Lore: Traditions and Superstitions of the Country.* Glasgow: Cameron & Ferguson, [1870].

Orczy, Baroness Emmuska. *Old Hungarian Fairy Tales.* London: Dean & Son, [1895].

Owen, Elias. *Welsh Folk-Lore: A Collection of the Folk-Tales and Legends of North Wales.* Oswestry & Wrexham:Woodall, Minshall and Co., 1887.

Pabke, Marie, and Margery Deane. *Wonder-World Stories.* New York: G. P. Putnam's Sons, 1877.

P[arson], E[lsie] C[lews]. "Notes and Queries: A West-Indian Tale." *The Journal of American Folklore.* Vol. 32, No. 125 (Jul.-Sep. 1919). pp. 442-443.

Quiller-Couch, Mabel. *Cornwall's Wonderland.* London & Toronto: J. M. Dent & Sons Ltd., n.d. [circa 1914].

Ralston, W. R. S. *The Songs of the Russian People.* 2nd edition. London: Ellis & Green, 1872.

Roby, John. *Traditions of Lancashire.* Vol. II. Fifth Edition. London: George Routledge and Sons, 1872.

Sapir, Edward. "Religious Ideas of the Takelma Indians of Southwestern Oregon." *The Journal of American Folklore.* Vol. 20, No. 76 (Jan.-Mar. 1907). pp. 33-49.

Sayce, A. H. "Cairene Folklore." *Folklore.* Vol. 11, No. 4 (Dec. 1900). pp. 354-395.

Schele de Vere, M[aximilian]. *Wonders of the Deep: A Companion to Stray Leaves from the Book of Nature.* New York: G.P. Putnam & Son, 1869.

Sinclair, A. T. "The Secret Language of Masons and Tinkers." *The Journal of American Folklore*. Vol. 22, No. 86 (Oct.-Dec. 1909). pp. 353-364.

Smith, Herbert H. *Brazil: The Amazons and the Coast*. New York: Charles Scribner's Sons, 1879.

Straparola, Giovanni Francesco. *The Facetious Nights by Straparola*. Volume 2 of 4. W. G. Waters, translator. London: Privately Printed for Members of the Society of Bibliophiles, 1901.

"Superstitions of the Passamaquoddies." *The Journal of American Folklore*. Vol. 2, No. 6 (Jul.-Sep. 1889). pp. 229-231.

Supplement to the Musical Library: March to December 1834. London: Charles Knight, 1834. pp. 15, 27.

Teit, J. A. "Water-Beings in Shetlandic Folk-Lore, as Remembered by Shetlanders in British Columbia." *The Journal of American Folklore*. Vol. 31, No. 120 (Apr.-Jun. 1918). pp. 180-201.

Tennyson, Lord Alfred. *The Complete Poetical Works of Alfred, Lord Tennyson, Poet Laureate*. New York: Harper & Brothers, 1884.

Theal, Georg McCall. *Kaffir Folk-Lore*. London: S. Sonnenschein, Le Bas & Lowrey, 1886.

Thorpe, Benjamin. *Yule-Tide Stories*. London: Henry G. Bohn, 1853.

Vinycomb, John. *Fictitious and Symbolic Creatures in Art with Special Reference to Their Use in British Heraldry*. London: Chapman and Hall, 1906. pp. 225-253.

Westropp, Thos. J. "A Folklore Survey of County Clare (Continued)." *Folklore*. Vol. 21, No. 3 (Sep. 1910). pp. 338-349.

———. "A Study of Folklore on the Coasts of Connacht, Ireland (Continued)." *Folklore*. Vol. 32, No. 2 (Jun. 30, 1921). pp. 101-123.

Wheatley, Henry B. "The Folklore of Shakespeare." *Folklore*. Vol. 27, No. 4 (Dec. 31, 1916). pp. 378-407.

Wilde, Oscar. *A House of Pomegranates*. London: James R. Osgood McIlvaine, 1891.

Wood-Martin, W[illiam] G[regory]. *Traces of the Elder Faiths of Ireland, Volume 2*. London: Longmans, Green, and Co., 1902.

Index

Bold page numbers indicate the beginning of a full article or tale.

A' Mhaideann-mhara, 217
Abdullah the Fisherman and Abdullah the Merman, 707
Aboo-dom-k'n and Lampeg-win-wuk, 774
Adventures of Bulukiya, The, 648
Ælian, 19, 64, 82-84, 103, 260
Africa, 15, 68, 88, 100, 102, 122, 136, 154, **727, 728**, 793
Agnes, 417
Agnete and the Merman, 411
Algonquin, 122, 775, 776
Allan, Robert, 229
Andersen, Hans Christian, 10, 130, **422**
Another Legend of the Mermaid, 218
Arabian Nights, 31, 106, 112, 121, **648, 669, 707**
Arnold, Matthew, 359, 363
Arnott, R. J., 190
Atargatis / Atergatis, 15, 79-80, *see also* Derceto
Aulnoy, Madame d', 614
Ayuh, the Nigerian Mermaid, 727

Baggesen, Jens, 411
banshee, 11-13, 120, 139, 147
Baring-Gould, Sabine, 4
Bassett, Fletcher S., 105
Bohemia (tales), 598
Bonnie Mermaid, The: (289E), 187
Book of Days, The, 54
Boy and the Mermaid, The, 788

Boy of Urashima, The, 751
Brazil (tales), 794, 795
Buchanan, Robert, 391

Cairene Mermaid, A, 727
Canada (tales), 768, 771, 772
Captured Mermaid, The, 289
Chambers, Robert, 54
Chapter on Mermaids, A, 41
Child Ballads
    Ballad 42A, 176
    Ballad 42B, 179
    Ballad 42C, 180
    Ballad 289, 781, 782, 784, 785
    Ballad 289A, 182
    Ballad 289B, 184
    Ballad 289C, 185
    Ballad 289D, 186
    Ballad 289E, 187
    Ballad 289F, 189
Children of the Mermaid, 243
China, 107, 121, 144, **735, 737**
Chinese Mermaids, 735
City under Sea, The, 297
Clark Colven, 176
Clerk Colvill, 179
Clerk Colvin, 180
cohuleen druith/druith, 18, 138, 232, 250-253, 255-256
Columbus, Christopher 33, 43, 68, 136
Comus, 301
Cossack, 515
Credulities Past and Present, 63
Cunningham, Allan, 219
Curious Myths of the Middle Ages, 4
Czech Republic, 598

Dagon, 13, 63, 76-79, 123, 138, 151
Denmark (tales), 399, 404, 408, 411, 417, 422, 437
Derceto, 15-16, 26, 80
  see also Atergatis
Donald and the Mermaid, 285
dugong, 33, 86, 100-104, 136, 148-149, 154
Duke Magnus and the Mermaid, 453
Dwellings under the Sea, 292

Egypt (tales), 727
enchanted cap, see cohuleen druith
England (tales), 300, 301, 304, 306, 319, 320, 322, 323, 325, 326, 329, 342, 344, 351, 352, 356, 357, 359, 363, 366, 391
Entangled Mermaid, The, 394
Estonia (tales), 496, 505, 507

Fables and Facts, 26
Faerie Queen, 125, 156, 157, 158, 165, 258,
  see also Spenser, Edmund
Faithless Fisherman, The, 507
Faroe Islands (tales), 398
Fictitious and Symbolic Creatures in Art, 150
Fictitious Creatures of the Sea, 150
Finland (tales), 485
Fintan, 138
Fisher and the Merman, The, 446
Fisherman and His Soul, The, 366
Fisherman Who Had Seven Sons, The, 244
Fisherman, The, 520
Flory Cantillon's Funeral, 257
Forsaken Merman, The, 359
Fortunio and the Siren, 629

France (tales), 614

Gamo-Gamo, The, 761
Garnett, Richard, 323
Germany (tales), 520, 521, 522, 524, 525, 526, 527, 528, 532, 538
Glaucus, 28, 151, 159, 303
Golden Mermaid, The, 532
Good Ferryman and the Water Nymphs, The, 601
Gould, Sabine Baring;
  see Baring-Gould
Greenland, 19, 64, 67, 127, **189**
Greenland, 189
Guernsey (tales), 392
Guyana (tales), 791, 793

halicore, see dugong
Hans, the Mermaid's Son, 437
Hawaii, 761
Haydn, Franz Joseph, 54, 351
Hebrides (tales), 217, 218
Hippocampus, 154
Hogg, James, 226
Hood, Thomas, 352
How the Jelly-Fish Lost His Shell, 754
How Two Girls Were Changed to Water-Snakes, and of Two Others That Became Mermaids, 775
Hudson, Henry 20, 43, 45, 65, 90, 136
Hungary (tales), 608
Hunter, Anne, 351

Iceland (tales), 168, 169, 170
Impossible Enchantment, An, 639
Inuit, **772**
Ireland (tales), 231, 234, 240, 241, 243, 244, 247, 249, 257, 261, 273, 277, 285, 287, 288

Isle of Man (tales), 289, 290, 291, 292, 294, 295, 297
Italy (tales), 629, 639

Jamaica (tales), 788, 789, 791
Japan (tales), 744, 745, 751, 754, 757
Jones, William, 63
Julnar the Sea-Born and her Son King Badr Basim of Persia, 669

kelpie, 42, 71, 109-111, 121, 126, 305, 404
King's Son and Messeria, The, 455
King's Son and the Princess Singorra, The, 466

Lady of Gollerus, The, 249
Lake-Dwellers, The, 505
Lapland (tales), 485
Lee, Henry, 74
Leyden, John, 203
Liban, the Sea Woman, 240
Lidushka and the Water Demon's Wife, 598
Little Girl, Mama Glau, and Humming-Bird, 786
Little Mermaid, The, 422
Lord Cuttle-Fish's Concert, 757
Lord of Dunkerron, The, 273
Low, Charles R., 41
Lutey and the Mermaid, 344

manatee, 33, 53, 100-104, 122, 148-149, 154, 710, 793
Marie Morgan, *see* Morgan
Massachusetts, 782
Melusina / Melusine, **4**, 125, 139, 147, 161-162, 776
Melusina (article), 4
Mermaid, The (289), 781, 782, 785
Mermaid, The (289C), 185
Mermaid, The (289D), 186

Mermaid, The (article), 74
Mermaid, The (Estonia), 496
Mermaid, The (Hogg), 226
Mermaid, The (Jamaica), 791
Mermaid, The (Leyden), 203
Mermaid, The (Tennyson), 357
Mermaid: A Ballad, The, 304
Mermaid (Windlass Song), The, 391
Mermaid and the Boy, The, 485
Mermaid Balladry, 58
Mermaid in Newfoundland, A, 771
Mermaid of Galloway, The, 219
Mermaid of Gob Ny Ooyl, The, 294
Mermaid of Lochinver, The, 216
Mermaid of Margate, The, 352
Mermaid of Martin Meer, The, 306
Mermaid of Padstow, The (ballad), 323
Mermaid of Padstow, The (tale), 322
Mermaid of Seaton, The, 325
Mermaid of the Gocta Cataracts, The, 801
Mermaid of the Magdalenes, The, 768
Mermaid of the Teton Tribe, 778
Mermaid of Zennor, The, 342
Mermaid Wife, The, 174
Mermaiden, The (Allan), 229
Mermaiden, The (Motherwell), 230
Mermaids (Guernsey), 392
Mermaids (article), 54
Mermaids and Mermen (article), 63
Mermaids and Mermen in Wales, 299
Mermaid's Courtship, The, 290
Mermaid's Lake, The, 791
Mermaid's Prophecy, The, 408

Mermaid's Revenge, The, 291
Mermaid's Rock, The, 325
Mermaid's Song, The, 351
Mermaid's Vengence, The, 329
Merman and Mermaid in Norway, The, 445
Merman and the Calf, The, 493
Merman and the Mermaid in the Faeröes, The, 398
Mer-man and Marstig's Daughter, The, 399
Merman, The, 356
Mermen and Mermaids in Iceland, 168
merrow, 18, 96, 123, 138, **231**, 248-249, **250, 261**, 320
Merrow-Maiden and Merrow-Man, The, 231
Merrymaids and Merrymen, 320
Milton, John, 301
Missouri, 784
Morgan, 18, 96, 123, 136, 255, 319
Morskoi (Tsar), 118, 512
Morva / Morvah / Morveth, 123, 343, 319
Morva or Morveth (Sea-Daughters), 319
Motherwell, William, 230
Motte Fouque, Friedrich de la, 538
Mr. Cuttlefish's Love Story, 608

naiads, 113, 148, 300
Napier, James, 58
Ne Hwas, the Mermaid, 776
Neck, 149, **447, 449**
Neckan, The, 363
Necks, Mermen and Mermaids, 447
Neptune, 28, 44, 69, 84, 112, 113, 123, 147, 151, 153-159, 302, 355, 512, 736
nereid, 29, 41, 83, 113, 123, 139, 147-148, 157, 300
Nereus, 28, 123, 147, 151, 300, 302, 453, 793
Netherlands, 394
Nick 29, 110, 111, 114, 126, 147, 148, 404
see also Nycke, Nycker
Nibelungen, 58, 124
Nigeria (tales), 727
Ningyo, 744
nissen, 148
nix, nixie, etc., 29, 34-35, 112, 113, 148, 163, 342, 365, **522, 526, 527, 528,** 532
Nix Labour, The, 526
Nixie of the Mill-Pond, The, 528
Noah, 16, 75-81
Norway (tales), 445, 446
Nycke, 404
see also Nick, Nycker
Nycker, 401
see also Nick, Nycke
nymph, 11, 15, 16, 18, 64, 70, 91, 94, 113-114, 121, 135, 142, 144, 147-148, 151, 176, 211, 213, 230, 232, **243,** 255, 276, 285, **300, 301**, 321, **484,** 596, **601, 614,** 793

Oannes, 13-14, 16, 63, 75-76, 78, 123, 147
Odyssey, The, 153, 164
Oehlenschläger, Adam Gottlob, 417
Oiára, the Water-Maidens, 794
Old Ballad Folk-Lore, 58
Old Man of Cury, The, 326
Orcadian Water Spirits, 215
Ottawa, 17-18, 122, 145
Overflowing of Lough Neagh and Liban the Mermaid, The, 234

Pascagoula River Mermaid, The, 779
Passamaquoddy, **774, 775, 776**

Peasant and the Waterman, The, 522
Peru, 17, 64, 122, **801**
Philippines (tales), 761
Poland (tales), 601
Poseidon, 28, 152, 155-158
Power of the Harp, The, 449
Princess of the Tung-T'ing Lake, The, 737
Proteus, 28, 147, 151, 159, 196, 301, 453

Rosmer Havmand, 33, 59-60, 115, 133, 255, 402-403, **404**, 421, 452
Rusalka, 117, 509-513
Russia (tales), 509, 515
Russian Water Spirits, 509

Sabrina Fair, 301
Scandinavia (tales), 493, 494, 495
Schele de Vere, Maximilian, 26
Scotland (tales), 190, 203, 215, 216, 217, 218, 219, 226, 229, 230, 391
Scottish Mermaids, 190
Sea Fables Explained, 74
Sea Nymph, The, 484
Sea-Mahmy, 789
Seamen's Distress, The (289A), 182
Sea-People, or Mermen and Mermaids in Shetland, 172
Sea-Sprite, The, 494
seal, 21, 25-26, 36, 38-41, 49, 65-66, 69, 82, 89, 91, 95, 97-104, 131-132, 136, 138-139, 148, 149, 154-155, 163, 168, **169, 172, 174**, 198-202, 242, 254-255, 261, 279, 283, 322, 323, 368, 393, 418, 515, 710, 727, **772**
Sedna, 772
selkie, 155, 174, 199-201

Shakespeare, William, 54-55, 96, 112, 135, 150, 165, 166, 271, **300**, 392, 403
Shark-Man, Nanaue; The, 761
Shepherd and the Sea-Folk, The, 495
Shetland Islands (tales), 172, 174
Shipwreck, 784
siren, 9, 16, 18, 22, 23, 24, 30-36, 44, 100, 104, 113, 114, 119, 123-127, 135, 139, 142, 144, 147, 151, 159, 160-166, 202-206, 299, 301, 303, 320, 325, 348, 352, 368, 393, 586, 629
see also syren
Slavonic Mermaids, 595
Slavonic Region (tales), 595
Soul Cages, The, 261
South Africa, 728
Spenser, Edmund 125, 150, 155, 157, 158, 165, 256,
see also Faerie Queen
sprite, 10, 11, 18, 35, 68, 71, 105-150, 176, 300, 401, **494**, 508, 513-14, 774
Stormy Winds Do Blow, The (289B), 184
Story of Tangalimlibo, The, 728
Story of the Yara, The, 795
Story of Tremsin, the Bird Zhar, and Nastasia, the Lovely Maid of the Sea, The, 515
Sweden (tales), 447, 449, 453, 455, 466, 484, 485
syren, 42, 47, 54, 63, 68, 190-191, 134, 232-33
see also siren

Takelma, 779
Takelma Mermaid, The, 779
Teeval, Princess of the Ocean, 295
Tennyson, Lord Alfred, 22, 191, **356, 357**

Teton Tribe, 778
Then Laughed the Merman, 169
Then the Merman Laughed, 170
Toda, the Archer, and the Queen of the World under the Sea, 745
Trinidad, 786
tritons, 16, 26, 29, 36, 63, 81-85, 123, 141, 145, 147, 151, 156, 158-159, 271, 300-301, 303, 367, 375, 389
Two Legends from County Meath, 288

Ukraine (tales), 515
Ulysses, 30, 42, 134, 151, 152, 163
Undine, 10, 17-18, 29, 117, 139, 248, **538**
United Kingdom (tales), 176, 179, 180, 182, 184, 185, 186, 187, 189
United States (tales), 761, 774, 775, 776, 778, 779, 781, 782, 784, 785

Venus, 16, 80-81, 564
Vermont, 781

Vinycomb, John, 150
Vishnu, 77-78
Vodyany, 68, 513-515

Wales (tales), 299
Water Mamma, 793
Water Nix, The, 527
Water Spirits and Mer Folk of Connacht, Ireland, 241
Water Spirits and Mer-folk of County Clare, 247
Water Spirits in Shakespeare, 300
water sprite, *see* sprite
Water Sprites and Mermaids, 105
Water-Smith, The, 524
Water-Woman, The, 521
White Cow, Red Cow, Black Cow, 287
Wilde, Oscar, 366
Wonderful Tune, The, 277
Wonders of the Deep, 26
Working Waterman, The, 525

Yara, 795
Yellow Dwarf, The, 614

Printed in Great Britain
by Amazon